Marcus David Gilman

The Bibliography of Vermont

or, a list of books and pamphlets relating in any way to the state, with biographical

and other notes

Marcus David Gilman

The Bibliography of Vermont
or, a list of books and pamphlets relating in any way to the state, with biographical and other notes

ISBN/EAN: 9783337015985

Printed in Europe, USA, Canada, Australia, Japan

Cover: Foto ©Raphael Reischuk / pixelio.de

More available books at **www.hansebooks.com**

THE

BIBLIOGRAPHY OF VERMONT

OR

A LIST OF BOOKS AND PAMPHLETS

RELATING IN ANY WAY

TO THE STATE.

WITH BIOGRAPHICAL AND OTHER NOTES.

PREPARED BY

M. D. GILMAN, Montpelier, Vt.
[WITH ADDITIONS BY OTHER HANDS.]

BURLINGTON :
PRINTED BY THE FREE PRESS ASSOCIATION.
1897.

INTRODUCTION.

By H. A. Huse, State Librarian.

This book is in remembrance of Marcus D. Gilman. Made by him as a memorial of others and their work, it now stands by the industry which he wrought in love of his State, by the gift of his children, and by an act of that State which did it as well as him honor, as a worthy and lasting memorial of himself.

How it came to have its being in its present shape is shown by the following letter from his daughter, Mrs. Cushman, and her husband, and the act of the Vermont legislature of 1894, authorizing the publication:

To the Librarian of the Vermont State Library, Montpelier, Vt.:

Dear Sir :—The "Bibliography of Vermont, or a List of Books and Pamphlets relating in any way to the State, with biographical and other notes; prepared by M. D. Gilman, Montpelier, Vt.," represents much thought and time and labor of its author.

The work was done by him during his years of retirement from active business and in love and loyalty to his native State.

We, his surviving children, as the only heirs of his beloved wife, Mrs. M. M. Gilman, have in our possession and ownership corrected slips of the whole work as published in 1879-80 in the *Argus and Patriot,* together with the author's additions made from time to time until his decease, January 5, 1889.

Feeling that this work is too important to remain inaccessible to those who are interested in the literary achievements of Vermonters, and furthermore desiring that the work should be preserved as a monument to our esteemed father, we hereby *present the entire work* to the Vermont State Library, in the assurance that it will be safely guarded there, and in the earnest hope that the State will be disposed, in the near future, to make the work more accessible by printing the same.

Respectfully yours,

HENRY IRVING CUSHMAN,

and

EMILY E. GILMAN CUSHMAN.

Montpelier, Vt., August 14, 1893.

At the legislative session next succeeding the presentation of the work to the State the following act was passed:

"AN ACT TO AUTHORIZE THE PUBLICATION OF THE GILMAN BIBLIOGRAPHY OF VERMONT.

It is hereby enacted by the General Assembly of the State of Vermont:

SECTION 1. The Printing Commissioners are authorized to procure the printing and binding of not to exceed eight hundred copies of the Gilman Bibliography of Vermont, at an expense to the state not exceeding two dollars and twenty-five cents a copy, to be disposed of as follows: one copy to each town and city clerk's office, one copy to each free public library in the state, fifty copies to the Vermont Historical Society, and the remainder to the State Library for sale or exchange under the direction of the trustees.

The Secretary of State shall procure copyright of the book for the State.

Approved November 24, 1894."

———

Charles Reed and Mr. Gilman had known each other as young men, and they had kept an acquaintance that was the more intimate as Mrs. Reed and Mrs. Gilman were sisters. At the time of Mr. Gilman's return to the East, Mr. Reed, who was State librarian and librarian of the Vermont Historical Society, was much interested in preparation for the then forthcoming publication of the Collections of the Vermont Historical Society. When Mr. Gilman retired from business in 1868 he could follow the bent of his mind and he soon became a student of New England history, his own inclination receiving added impetus from the zeal of his friend. He marked out his own line, however, and it was a new one; and on it he made his book.

With ample means at his command, as well as knowledge of books and love of them, he for many years took delight in gathering a library rich in local history, till, after the manner of many of those whose pleasure is in acquiring as well as having rare books, he sold a large part of his collection, but through life kept adding to the choice library which he retained.

In 1874, the year after Mr. Reed's death, Mr. Gilman became librarian of the Vermont Historical Society and continued in this position until he declined a re-election in 1881. It was while he was librarian of this society that he most zealously labored upon the matter presented in the following pages. It was a task involving infinite pains and work and was never ending. He began printing his Bibliography of Vermont in the *Argus and Patriot*, January 29, 1879, and the printing continued to June 9, 1880. He had meantime gathered much additional matter, which was published in the same paper in the issues immediately after, as a supplement to the Bibliography. The printing of the supplement was concluded in the issue for September 22, 1880. But to near the time of his death in 1889 Mr. Gilman sought and found new material and added it in manuscript to what he had printed in the two years named. The copy, in print and manuscript combined, became the property of his widow and at her decease, that of their daughter, the wife of Rev. Henry Irving Cushman, of Providence, R. I. The generous disposition made of it by them is set forth in their letter, and the act of 1894 made provision for this publication.

Hon. George Grenville Benedict, best qualified of all men for the task, was selected to edit the work. Mr. Thomas L. Wood, assistant state librarian, had collected many additional titles of Vermont books and these he freely placed at the disposal of the editor. Mr. Benedict himself has furnished 563 titles and 73 biographical sketches, and has made some hundreds of additions to the biographical notes and numerous additions to the list of newspapers given under the head of "Printing in Vermont." But, much as has been added, the addition and the work of making it only emphasize the research and labor of Mr. Gilman in creating the great body of the work, and his wisdom in planning the whole of it; for all additions have been upon the lines marked and followed by him. Mr. Benedict, with the knowledge brought to him by editing the book, pays tribute to "the vast amount of work and care which Mr. Gilman gave, for so many years, to the collection and annotation of the titles," and adds : "I have, as you know, spent many months of labor in preparing the Bibliography for publication. * * Perhaps in justice to myself (and to Mr. Gilman) I ought to have bracketed the more important additions I have made; but I have not done so. It is Mr. Gilman's Bibliography, simply edited by myself, with so much of care and labor as I could afford to give to it."

Mr. Gilman's work will commend itself; and best to those who know best and most concerning the men of whom he wrote and what they did. He would not want much said of it here or of himself, for he was a man of affairs and not of words unless they were words that recorded some historical fact.

In business he was a merchant, in politics a democrat, and in religion a spiritualist; and as to all his convictions he was decided and outspoken. He was a leader among his fellows and was prominent and energetic in all his undertakings. It should be noted that his election as representative of Montpelier to the House of Representatives in 1874, was as a democrat in a strongly republican town, and that he was prominent in the councils of his party wherever he resided. A happy family and social life were his, and they count most of all.

Marcus Davis Gilman was born in Calais, Vermont, January 28, 1820. He was a son of Dr. John Taylor Gilman, and a grand-son of Jonathan Gilman. Jonathan Gilman was born in Gilmanton, New Hampshire, May 31, 1763; married Susannah Dudley, November 9, 1783; moved to Vershire, Vermont, in 1796, remaining there until 1817, when he went to live with his son John in Calais, making his home there until his death, December 5, 1824.

Dr. John Taylor Gilman was born in Gilmanton, July 24, 1791 ; was a graduate of Dartmouth Medical College in the class of 1814, and began practice at East Calais in 1815, being the first physician resident in Calais. He married Ruth Curtis (who was the daughter of Col. Caleb Curtis and Polly Davis Curtis of Calais, and a grand-daughter of Rev. Caleb Curtis of Charlton, Mass.), and they had two children, Marcus Davis Gilman and John Melvin Gilman, the latter of whom studied law with Heaton & Reed in Montpelier, and now lives in St. Paul, Minnesota. Dr. Gilman died at East Calais, February 10, 1825. His widow married Nathaniel Eaton in 1829, and died in Middlesex, Vermont, July 28, 1866, at the home of her son, Mr. Gilman's half-brother, Caleb Curtis Eaton. Nathaniel Eaton, by his first wife, Ruth Bridgman, was the father of Dorman Bridgman Eaton (of Civil Service Reform fame) and Ruth Eaton ; and Marcus, until fifteen years old, lived at his step-father's on a farm in Calais.

He then came to Montpelier and entered the store of Baldwin & Scott as a clerk, remaining with them until he became of age, when he went to Northfield, Vermont, and began his mercantile career as a member of the firm of White, Gilman & Co. After two years in Northfield he returned to Montpelier, where he for two years was a member of the firm of Ellis, Wilder & Co. Mr. Gilman's school education was obtained in the common schools in Calais and at the Washington County Grammar School in Montpelier. He left the Washington County Grammar School to enter the store of Baldwin & Scott. He boarded in the home of the head of the firm, Daniel Baldwin, while working in Montpelier. Mr. Gilman married, at Montpelier, May 10, 1843, Maria Malleville Baldwin, a daughter of Daniel Baldwin and Emily Wheelock Baldwin and a grand-daughter of the first president of Dartmouth College. In 1845 Mr. and Mrs. Gilman moved to Chicago, where Mr. Gilman was for twenty-three years, the remainder of his business life, a merchant. While in Chicago he was a member of three successive firms, M. D. Gilman & Co., Gilman & Grannis, and Gilman, Grannis & Farwell. His business career was very successful. In 1855 he built on Michigan Avenue what was then characterized as the most costly and in many respects the most elegant residence in Chicago.

Mr. Gilman retired from business in 1868, and for the next three years he and his wife lived at Riverside in Newton, Massachusetts. They moved to Montpelier in the fall of 1871, where they converted the Daniel Baldwin homestead, now No. 1, Baldwin Street, into a new and costly residence. This was their home during the remainder of their lives.

Mr. Gilman died in Montpelier, January 5, 1889, and his widow died in Providence, Rhode Island, May 18, 1892. They are buried, with their children and three grand-children, in the Gilman–Cushman lot in Green Mount Cemetery, Montpelier.

The children of Mr. and Mrs. Gilman were :

(1)   John Baldwin Gilman, M. D., who was born in Chicago, July 5, 1847, and died in Montpelier, May 18, 1873.   He graduated at Harvard in 1868, and afterwards studied medicine in Germany and at the Boston Medical College.   In the Franco-German war, 1870-71, he served as assistant surgeon in the Prussian army, and at the close of his service received the decoration of the Iron Cross. After the close of that war he completed his studies in Boston, and in the fall of 1871 began practice in Topeka, Kansas.   Exposure and overwork in an epidemic brought upon him a severe sickness, which developed into quick consumption, and in April, 1873, he came to the family home in Montpelier, where he spent the last few weeks of his life.

(2)   Emily Eliza Gilman, born in Chicago, June 10, 1849; married in Chicago Rev. Henry Irving Cushman, April 13, 1868.   Their children were (1) Mary Alice, born in Boston, April 27, 1869; died in Providence, R. I., June 18, 1877. (2) Ruth Gilman, born in Newton, Mass., May 29, 1870; married 'William Gardner Anthony, February 17, 1896, at Providence, R. I.   (3) Robert, born in Boston, September 18, 1872.   (4) Marcus Gilman, born in Montpelier, July 25, 1875; died in Providence, R. I., July 18, 1877.   (5) Earl Baldwin, born in Providence, R. I., May 6, 1878; died in Providence, R. I., May 25, 1878.   (6) Albert Henry, born in Providence, R. I., September 26, 1880.   Mrs. Cushman died at Lamanda Park, Los Angeles County, California, March 14, 1895.

(3)   Sarah Alice Gilman, born in Chicago, March 21, 1851; died in Chicago, March 19, 1853.

(4)   Marcus Edward Gilman, born in Chicago, June 26, 1853; died in Chicago, November 9, 1853.

This introduction, however brief, should not conclude without a word of tribute to Mrs. Cushman, who made gift to the State of her father's work in its behalf.   In her early married life in Boston, while her husband was Dr. Miner's associate, and in Dr. Cushman's long pastorate in Providence, her lovely character was his most efficient help in pastoral work and influence.   Seeking a milder climate in hope of staying the progress of New England's most insidious disease she died in Southern California, March 14, 1895.   Her burial was in Green Mount Cemetery from the Gilman homestead in Montpelier.   It is right that those to whom she was unknown who read this book should here read what all who knew her knew that she was the exemplar of what is beautiful, good and pure—of true womanhood, wifehood and motherhood.

H. A. H.

Vermont State Library, Montpelier, Vt., August, 1897.

BIBLIOGRAPHY OF VERMONT.

Abbott, George N. *The Christologic Problem*; an Essay read before the Winooski Association, January 8, 1867. By George N. Abbott, South Newbury, Vt. Andover: Printed by Warren F. Draper. 1869. 8vo, pp. 20.

Abbott, Jacob. *Marco Paul's Voyages and Travels.* New York; n. d. 6 vols. 16mo.
Volume 4 consists of travels in Vermont.

Abbott, Simon C. *See Worcester, Record of Births, etc.*
Mr. Abbott was born in Thetford, Vt., May 28, 1826; where he resided until about 1846, when he went to Bradford, Vt., and learned the printer's trade in the office of the Bradford Gazette; and in 1849 he removed to Worcester with his father's family, where he resided until his death from consumption, January 3, 1857. He was a contributor to various newspapers.

Abbott, W. Scott. *The History of Darke County, Ohio, Past and Present.* Containing a History of the County, its Cities, Towns, etc.; General and Local Statistics; Portraits of Early Settlers and Prominent Men, an Outline History of Ohio and the Northwest Territory. By W. Scott Abbott. Illustrated. Chicago: W. H. Beers & Co. 1880. r'l 8vo, pp. 900.
Mr. Abbott was born in Barnard, Vt., January 19, 1830, and, besides his newspaper work in this State, at Braintree and Randolph, he has been a voluminous contributor to periodicals in other States, writing chiefly fiction and poetry. He went to Ohio in 1865, and in 1870 started and was one of the editorial staff of the Dayton Herald, and in 1876 started the "Bridgford Herald" in that State, moving the paper to the town of Greenville, calling it the "Greenville Herald," and selling it in 1877.

Abstracts of the Reports of the Benevolent Societies and Conference of Churches in Cheshire County, New Hampshire, for 1833. Bellows Falls, 1833. 8vo, pp. 16.

An Account of the Pelew Islands, situated in the Great South Sea. Composed from the Journals of Captain Henry Wilson and his Officers: Who, in August, 1783, Were there Shipwrecked in the Antelope Packet. Motto. Printed at Rutland, Vt., by Josiah Fay, for S. Williams & Co. MDCCXCVII. 12mo, pp. 96.

Adams, Andrew N. *A History of the Town of Fair Haven, Vermont.* In three Parts. By Andrew N. Adams. Fair Haven: Leonard & Phelps, Printers. 1870. 12mo, pp. 516.
See the above work, pp. 281–83, for biographical sketch of Mr. Adams.

Adams, Austin. *Classical Learning as an Element of Modern Scholarship.* An Address delivered before the Erosophian Society of Lombard University, on Tuesday, June 18th, 1867, by Austin Adams. Published by request. Dubuque: 1867. 8vo, pp. 26.
Mr. Adams was born in Andover, Vt., May 24, 1826; was graduated at Dartmouth, 1848; read law, and settled at Dubuque, Iowa, in 1854, where he practiced his profession; is now (1878) a Judge of the Supreme Court of Iowa.

Adams, C. B. *Fresh Water and Land Shells of Vermont.* 8vo, 19 pp. (No imprint.) Four Geological Reports. See Geology of Vermont.
Mr. Adams was born in Dorchester, Mass., January 11, 1814; and died at St. Thomas, January 19, 1853. He was for some time a Professor in Middlebury College; and was State Geologist to Vermont for several years. See Drake's Biog. Dic.

Adams, Charles K. *The Relations of Higher Education to National Prosperity.* An Oration delivered before the Phi Beta Kappa Society of the University of Vermont, June 27, 1876. By Charles Kendall Adams, Professor of History in the University of Michigan. Published by the Society. Burlington: Free Press Print. 1876. 8vo, pp. 27.
Charles K. Adams, L. L. D., was born in Derby, Vt., January 24, 1835; educated at the University of Michigan and in Europe; Professor of History University of Michigan, 1867–85; Professor of History Cornell University, 1881–5; President of Cornell, 1885–92; President of the University of Wisconsin, 1892; Author of Democracy and Monarchy in France, New York, 1872; German Version of the same, Stuttgart, 1873; British Orations. New York, 1884; Christopher Columbus, his Life and Work, New York, 1892; and of many papers, historical and educational, in various reviews and other periodicals; Editor-in-Chief of Johnson's Universal Cyclopædia, 1892.

Adams, D. *The Thorough Scholar:* or, The Nature of Language, with the Reasons, Principles and Rules of English Grammar. By Daniel Adams, M. B., Montpelier, Vt.: Published by Lucius Q. C. Bowles [Proprietor of the Copy Right.] January 1814. 12mo, pp. 103.

—*The Scholar's Arithmetic:* or Federal Accountant. By Daniel Adams, M. B. Seventh Edition. Montpelier, Vt. Printed by Wright & Sibley, For J— Prentiss. [Proprietor of the copyright.] 1812. 8vo, pp. 216.

Adams, Elmer B. *In the Circuit Court of St. Louis.* Opinion of Judge E. B. Adams in the three cases of Hammond Heirs vs. Lindell Heirs. St. Louis, Pierce Bros., Law Printers. 1879. 8vo, pp. 17.
Elmer B. Adams is a son of Jarvis Adams, and was born in Pomfret, Vt., October 27, 1842; he graduated at Yale in 1865, traveled in the South a year for the American Union Commission, which was organized in New York for aiding the Southern whites, writing letters for a magazine published by the commission and for newspapers, and then began the study of law at Woodstock, in this State. He was admitted to the bar at Rutland in 1868, and went to St. Louis to practice, where he has since remained. He did a successful private business until 1878, when he was elected Judge of the Circuit Court in that city for a term of six years.

—*The Thorough Scholar, etc.* English Grammar. 4th Edition. Published for Lucius Q. C. Bowles. Montpelier: 1817. 12mo, pp. 131.
Mr. E. P. Walton purchased the copyright of Adams' Grammar for Vermont in 1818, and published a new edition the same year.

Adams, F. W. *Theological Criticisms.* Or hints of the Philosophy of Man and Nature. In

Six Lectures. To which are appended two Poetical Scraps, and Dogmas of Infidelity. By F. W. Adams, M. D. Montpelier. Published by J. E. Thompson. 1843. 8vo, pp. 216, 32.

Dr. Adams was an eminent Physician in Vermont, and for many years a resident of Montpelier, where he died in December, 1858, aged 71. For a Sketch of Dr. Adams see Miss Hemenway's Vt. Hist. Gaz., Vol. 4, pp. 479–80.

Adams, Rev. Henry W. *A Discourse*, delivered before a Theological Association of Traveling and Local Preachers, in Danville District, N. H. Conference, in the M. E. Church, Newbury, Vt., March 24, 1843. By Rev. Henry W. Adams, B. A., Teacher of Ancient Languages and Mathematics in Newbury Seminary. Preached and Published by Request of the Association. Newbury: Printed by Hayes & Co. 1843. 8vo, pp. 43.

Mr. Adams was a native of Brookfield, Vt., born March 12, 1818. He published sermons, one or two books, and a poem on the Book of Job; was a graduate of Wesleyan University in the class of 1841, and was for a time a preacher in the New Hampshire Conference. Afterward he became an Episcopalian, and was a rector in Springfield. He died at Charlotte, N. C., October 21, 1881. He was a brother of Rev. Elisha Adams, who was born in Williamstown, Vt. in 1815, resided at Concord, N. H., and died suddenly at Concord, N. H., in August, 1880.

Adams, John Sullivan, *Can the Vermont Colleges be United?* Addressed to the Town Superintendents of Schools and to all thoughtful and liberal friends of a State Educational System. 1864. No imprint; 8vo, pp. 49.

J. S. Adams was born in Burlington in 1820; graduated at the University of Vermont in 1838; studied law with his father, Hon. Charles Adams; went to California in 1849; returned in 1851 to Burlington; clerk of Chittenden County Court 1854 to 1867; secretary of the State Board of Education 1856 to 1867; removed, 1867, to Jacksonville, Fla., where he held the offices of Postmaster, Commissioner of Immigration and Collector of Customs; established and edited the New South newspaper. Died at Jacksonville, April 23, 1876.

Adams, Warren P., A. M., [of Burlington.] *Quarterly Address*, to the Young Men's Lyceum of Troy Conference Academy, [Poultney.] February 25th, 1853. Burlington: Stacy & Jameson, Printers. 1853. 8vo, pp. 15.

Addison County. *Atlas of Addison County, Vermont.* From actual surveys by and under the direction of F. W. Beers, assisted by W. S. Peet and Others. Published by P. W. Beers & Co., 93 and 95 Maiden Lane, New York. 1871. Folio. pp. 48. Contains maps and historical sketches of each town.

—*List of Congregational Ministers, Churches, etc.* See Lamb, Dana.

—*History of*, See Swift, S.

—*Rules of Addison County Court, 1787–1805.* 18mo. pp. 4. No imprint.

—*Rules of Addison County Court*, adopted December Term, 1840. Printed by Eph. Maxham, Office of the People's Press, Middlebury. 12mo, pp. 8.

—*Vermont Patriot.* Extra. Correspondence of the Hon. Richard Rush and a number of citizens of Addison County, Vermont. Letter to Mr. Rush, Middlebury, Vt., April 25th, 1834. [And His Reply.] 8vo, pp. 16.

Is opposed to the re-charter of the U. S. Bank.

—*Gazetteer and Business Directory of Addison County, Vermont, 1882-3.* Compiled and published by Hamilton Child, Syracuse, N. Y., 1882. 8vo, pp. 551.

Address. *An Address to the Freemen of Vermont*, by their Delegation to the National Republican Convention, holden at Baltimore, Md., in December, 1831. H. H. Houghton, Printer, Middlebury, Vt. 8vo, pp. 16.

Signed by William Jarvis, Robert Temple, Phineas White, William A. Griswold, Dan. Carpenter and Thomas D. Hammond.

—*To Christian Parents of the Churches in Vermont.* E. W. Hooker, Amos Drury, and Hosea Beckley, Committee of the Convention. Rutland: W. Fay, Printer. 1833. 12mo, pp. 36.

—*Before the Reunion Society of Vermont Officers and the First Vermont Cavalry Society*, Nov. 4th and 5th, 1874. Burlington: Free Press Print. 1874. 8vo, pp. 34.

—*Before the Vermont State Agricultural Society*, at its Exhibition held at Rutland, September, 1852: Together with the Report of the Committee on Manufactured Goods. Published by the Society. Middlebury: Justus Cobb, Printer, Register Office. 1853. 8vo, pp. 63.

Continued.

—*Of Members of the House of Representatives* of the Congress of the United States, to their Constituents, on the Subject of the War with Great Britain. Middlebury. Printed by T. C. Strong. 1812. 12mo, pp. 32.

—*Another edition*, Bennington, Vt.: Printed by S. Williams & Co. 1812. The same, Windsor: Printed by Thomas M. Pomroy. 1812. 8vo, pp. 30.

A Federal address, in opposition to the war.

—*To the Freemen of Vermont*, by a Soldier of '77. n. d., n. p. [1808] 8vo, pp. 23.

A strong Federal pamphlet.

—*The Present State of Our Country Considered*, in an Address to the Freemen of Vermont, by a Farmer of Windham County. Motto. 12mo, p. 31, n. d. No imprint. [1808.]

—*To Heads of Families in General,* and to Professors in particular, upon the duty of Prayer, and the Education of those under their care. Selected from Late Eminent Authors. Windsor: Printed by A. Spooner, [For I. Newton, Norwich, Vt.] 1807. 12mo, pp. 60.

—*An Address to the People of the County of Franklin.* Middlebury, Vt.: Printed by Huntington & Fitch for the Publisher, March, 1806. 12 mo, pp. 10.

Gives an account of the short coming of County Clerk, 1798 to 1804.

Admonitions *Against Swearing, Sabbath-breaking, and Drunkenness.* Designed for the benefit of such as are guilty of one or more of these Vices. Motto. The Eleventh Edition. Windsor: Printed and sold by Alden Spooner. MDCCXCIV. 16mo, pp. 12.

The Adviser; *or Vermont Evangelical Magazine*, for the year 1809. Vol. I. The Profits of this Work are devoted to the use of the Vermont Missionary Society. The Editors appointed by the General Convention are the Rev. Messrs. Asa Burton, D. D., Gershom C. Lyman, Martin Tullar, Publius V. Booge, Heman Ball, John B. Preston, John Fitch, Leonard Worcester, Holland Weeks, Tilton Eastman, Bancroft Fowler, Thomas A. Merrill. Middlebury: Published by William C. Hooker, General Agent of the Editors, at whose store may be had complete sets of the Adviser. Price one dollar; bound $1.25. J. D. Huntington, Printer, 1809. 8vo.

Continued to January, 1816, 7 volumes in all, of about 400 pp. each. Published monthly; the later vols. printed by T. C. Strong.

AGRICULTURAL. *List of Premiums* given by the Washington County, Vt. Agricultural Society, Joshua Y. Vail, Secretary, 1822.

—*The Enfranchisement of Labor.* An Address delivered before the Vermont State Agricultural Society, at Brattleboro, Vt., Sept. 14th, 1854, by Charles Theodore Russell. Middlebury: Printed at the Register Book and Job Office. 1855. 8vo, pp. 21.

—*The Seventeenth Annual Fair* of the Addison County Agricultural Society at Middlebury, September 5th, 6th and 7th, 1860. Register Office Print. Middlebury: 12mo, pp. 16.

—*Premium List of the Fair of the New England and Vermont State Agricultural Societies,* held at Brattleboro, Vt., September, 1866. Rutland, Vt.: Tuttle, Gay & Co., Printers. 1866. 8vo, pp. 47.

—*Twenty-second Annual Fair* of the Vermont State Agricultural Society and Wool Growers' Association, to be held at St. Johnsbury, Tuesday, Wednesday, Thursday and Friday, September 10th, 11th, 12th and 13th, 1872. Rutland, Vt.: Tuttle & Co., Printers. 1872. 8vo, pp. 24.
Continued.

—*Thirty-first Annual Fair* of the Rutland County Agricultural Society, to be held at Rutland, Vt., Thursday and Friday, September 14th and 15th, 1876. Rutland, Vt.: Tuttle & Co., Printers. 1876. 8vo, pp. 20.
Continued.

—*Official Report* of the Special Committee of the Vermont State Agricultural Society, relating to the great State Trial of Mowing Machines and Hay Implements, held at Rutland, June 10th, 11th, 12th and 13th, 1872. Judges: George Hammond, Middlebury; Lawrence Brainerd, St. Albans; Henry Chase, Lyndon, Samuel Everts, Cornwall; James A. Shedd, Burlington. Rutland: Tuttle & Co., Printers. 1872. 8vo, pp. 12.

—*The Farmers' War*—Equal Taxation—Granges—Patrons of Husbandry. A Series of letters published in the Rutland daily Globe, from the pen of the Hon. S. M. Dorr, of Rutland, and now collected and published for general circulation, by order of the Rutland Grange of the Patrons of Husbandry. 1873. 8vo, pp. 8.

—*Officers, Regulations and Schedule of Premiums* of the Agricultural Society of White River Valley. 1874. Fair at Bethel, Vt., September 2d, 3d and 4th. Woodstock, Vt.: Luther O. Greene, Printer. 1874. 8vo, pp. 28.

—*The Same* for 1875. 8vo, pp. 32.

—*Officers, Regulations and Schedule of Premiums* of the Ascutney Agricultural Association. Second Annual Fair at Windsor, October 5th, 6th and 7th, 1875. Windsor, Vt.: Journal Company, Printers. 1875. 8vo, pp. 24.

—*Officers, Regulations and Schedule of Premiums* of the White River Agricultural Society.

Second Annual Fair to be held at Bethel, Vt., Tuesday, Wednesday and Thursday, September 16, 17 and 18, 1879. Montpelier, Vt.: Argus and Patriot Book and Job Printing House. 1879. 8vo, pp. 19.
Continued.

—*Windsor County Agricultural Society.* Annual Catalogue, containing list of Officers, Premiums, Rules and Regulations, for the year 1876. Thirty-first Fair to be held at Woodstock, Tuesday, Wednesday and Thursday, September 26, 27 and 28. Woodstock, Vt.: David P. Simpson, Printer, Standard Office. 1876. 8vo, pp. 32.
Continued.

—*Officers, Regulations and Schedule of Premiums* of the Union Agricultural Society, 1877. Fair at Tunbridge, Vt., October 2d, 3d and 4th. Montpelier, Vt.: Argus and Patriot Steam Book and Job Printing Establishment, Main Street, 1877. 8vo, pp. 7.

—*Fourteenth Annual Fair* of the Franklin County Agricultural and Mechanical Society to be held at Sheldon, Vt., September 10th, 11th, and 12th, 1879. St. Albans, Vt.: Albert Clarke's Power Presses. 1879. 12mo, pp. 40.

—*Premium List* of the Vermont State Agricultural Society and Wool Growers' Association, Twenty-ninth Annual Fair, to be held at Montpelier, Tuesday, Wednesday and Thursday, September 9th, 10th and 11th, 1879. Montpelier, Vt.: Argus and Patriot Book and Job Printing House, 1879. 8vo, pp. 4, 24, 4.

—*Washington County Agricultural Society.* List of Premiums and Officers for the year 1879. Fair to be held at Prospect Park, Montpelier, Vt., Wednesday and Thursday, September 24th and 25th. Montpelier, Vt.: Argus and Patriot Job Printing House. 1879. 16mo, pp. 16.

—*Rules and Premium List* of the Second Annual Exhibition of the Champlain Valley Poultry Association, to be held at Burlington, Vt., December 16th, 17th, 18th and 19th, 1879. Entries for Competition close December 16th, 12 M. Specimens must be delivered at City Hall before 12 M., December 16th, 1879. Burlington, Vt.: The Free Press Association. 1879. 8vo, pp. 30.

—*Rules and Premium List* of the First Annual Exhibition of the Wide-A-Wake Poultry Club, to be held at Town Hall, St. Johnsbury, Vt., December 30-31, 1879, and January 1, 1880. Entries close December 27th, 6 P. M. Specimens must be delivered at hall before 1 P. M., December 30, 1879. St. Johnsbury: C. M. Stone & Co., Printers. 1879. 8vo, pp. 24.

—*By-Laws* of Mountain Home Grange, P. of H., No. 138, Bondville. Vt. Manchester: Journal Newspaper and Job Office. 1880. 12mo, pp. 7.

—*Rules and Premium List* for the First Annual Exhibition of the Central Vermont Poultry Association, to be held at Village Hall, Montpelier, January 27th, 28th, 29th and 30th, 1880. Specimens must be delivered not later than 6 P. M., Monday, January 26th. Argus and Patriot Steam Printing House, Montpelier, Vt. 8vo, pp. 20.

—*Bulletins of the Vermont Agricultural Experiment Station*, Nos. 1 to 42, to July, 1894.
Continued.

—*Annual Reports of the Vermont Agricultural Experiment Station*, 1888 to 1895.
Continued.

—*Coos and Essex Counties Agricultural Society.* Tenth Annual Fair. To be holden at the Fair Ground and Riding Park, Lancaster, N. H., Tuesday, Wednesday and Thursday, September 16th, 17th and 18th, 1879. Lancaster: Printed at the Republican Office. 1879. 8vo, pp. 39, 1.

—*Hand Book of Vermont Fairs for 1881.* 8 vo., pp. 24.

See Jenison, S. H., Address, 1844; Ormsby, R. McK., Address, 1850; Fletcher, R., Address, 1848; Vermont State Grange; Vermont Horse Stock Company; Cutts, Hampden, Address 1850; Goodrich, Chauncey, "Northern Fruit Culturist;" King, W. S., Address, 1862; Marsh, Prof. L.; Needham, D., Address, 1862; Poultry Association; Barnum, A. M.; Collier, Peter, Addresses; Andrew, John A.; Vermont Merino Sheep Breeders' Association; Vermont Legislative Documents, 1872, and after, for State Board of Agriculture; Vermont Dairyman's Association; Lathrop, L. E; Perkins, George H., Report, 1877; Townsend, W. W., Dairyman's Manual, 1839; Address at Rutland, 1852.

Aiken, Charles A. *A Sermon on Temperance*, delivered in the First Congregational Church, Yarmouth, Sabbath evening, February 28, 1858. By Rev. Charles A. Aiken. Portland: Printed by David Tucker. 1858. 8vo, pp. 15.

—*Exercises connected with the Inauguration of Rev. Charles A. Aiken, D. D.*, as President of Union College, Schenectady, N. Y., Tuesday, June 28, 1870. Albany, N. Y.: Joel Munsell. 1870. 8vo, pp. 32.

—*Inauguration of the Rev. Charles Augustus Aiken, D. D.*, as Professor of Christian Ethics and Apologetics in Princeton Theological Seminary, November, 1871. New York.: Rogers & Sherwood, 94 and 96 Nassau Street. 1872. 8vo, pp. 31.

Dr. Aiken was born at Manchester, Vt., October 30, 1827; was graduated at Dartmouth College in 1846, and at Andover in 1853; was pastor of the Congregational Church at Yarmouth, Me., 1854-59; Professor of Latin at Dartmouth, 1859-66, and at New Jersey, 1866-69; President of Union College, Schenectady, N. Y., 1869-71; Professor of Christian Ethics and Apologetics at Princeton Theological Seminary, 1871-92. Died January 14, 1892. He translated and edited the Book of Proverbs, in the American edition of Lange's Commentaries; and wrote various articles for the Princeton Review and Bibliotheca Sacra.

Aiken, John F. *An Address* Delivered at the funeral of Mrs. Abel H. Denio, at the Congregational Church in Pawlet, Vt., Sunday, April 30th, 1876. By Rev. John F. Aiken. Published by request. Tuttle & Co., printers, Rutland, Vt.: 12mo, pp. 8.

See Dartmouth College Alumni, 1858.

Aiken, Samuel O. *The Chambers of Death.* A Sermon. By S. C. Aiken, Pastor of First Presbyterian Church, Utica, N. Y. New York: Published by J. N. Bolles, No. 136 Nassau Street. [1834.] 12mo, pp. 15.

—*Moral Reform.* A sermon delivered at Utica, on Sabbath evening, February 16, 1834, by S. C. Aiken, Pastor of the First Presbyterian Church, Utica. R. B. Shepard, Printer, 44 Genesee Street. 1834. 8vo, pp. 16.

Rev. Samuel C. Aiken, D. D., was born in Windham, Vt., September 21, 1791; graduated at Middlebury College, 1814; and at Andover Theological Seminary, 1817; was pastor of the First Presbyterian Church at Utica, N. Y., 1818-35; pastor of First Presbyterian Church, Cleveland, Ohio, 1835-61; pastor emeritus of the same church, residing in Cleveland until his death, January 1, 1879; Honorary D. D. from Middlebury College in 1842; delivered "An Address" in Utica, N. Y., before the Sunday School Societies in 1843.

Aiken, Rev. Silas, D. D.
Was born in Bradford, N. H., May 14, 1799. The family originated in the North of Ireland, and first settled in this country in Londonderry, N. H., in 1722. His father was Deacon in the Presbyterian church at Londonderry, and served in the Revolutionary war.

Silas fitted for college at Phillips Academy, Andover, Mass., and was graduated from Dartmouth, 1825, the valedictorian of his class; tutor at Dartmouth, 1825-28, and studied Theology meantime with President Tyler of the College; succeeded Nathan Lord, D. D., in the pastorate of the Congregational church at Amherst, N. H., 1829-37; pastor of Park street church, Boston, Mass., 1837-48; pastor of Congregational church, Rutland, Vt., 1849-63; resided in Rutland till his death, April 7, 1869. He received honorary D. D. from the University of Vermont in 1852. He was a corporate member of the A. B. C. F. M., and while in Boston a member of its Prudential Committee; a member of the Committee of Publication of the Massachusetts Sunday School Society; a Trustee of Dartmouth College, 1840-62; Preacher before the General Convention at Windsor, Vt., in 1853, and Moderator of the same body in 1853 and 1865.

Publications: "A Sermon," occasioned by the death of Judge Hubbard, of Boston, Mass. (Probably about 1848.) "Moses finding the Israelites worshiping the Molten Calf." (About 1848.) A Sermon preached at the Semi-Centennial of Park street church, Boston, in 1859. An exercise in a publication called "Worship in the School Room," by W. G. Wylie, was from his pen. "Essay on Infant Baptism," read before the General Convention of Congregational ministers and churches of Vermont, at Newbury, June, 1866, was published in the "Minutes" for that year.

Aiken, Rev. Solomon. *An Appeal to the Churches*, containing Animadversions on Three Ecclesiastical Councils; together with Observations on the Consociation of the Churches, and a Suit commenced and Charges Presented the Churches against their Representation forming the said Councils. [Dated Hardwick, Vt., 1821.] By Solomon Aiken, A. M. Montpelier, Vt. Printed by E. P. Walton. 1821. 8vo, pp. 120.

See Worcester, Leonard, "Appeal to the Conscience of Aiken."

Mr. Aiken was born in Hardwick, Mass., July 15, 1758; and died in Hardwick, Vt., June 1, 1833. He was grandfather of Miss F. C. Aiken, long on the Argus and Patriot staff, and now (1879) Mrs. M. E. Tucker of Montpelier. He resided in Hardwick from 1818 until his death. See Dartmouth College Alumni, 1784.

Aikens, Asa, Esq. *An Oration*, pronounced before the Republican Citizens of Windsor, on their Celebration of the Thirty-sixth Anniversary of American Independence. By A. Aikens, Esq. Printed at the office of the Vermont Republican. July, 1812. sm. 4to, pp. 8.

—*Practical Forms*, with Notes and References explanatory of the Law Governing the Cases to which they are applicable; being a convenient Manual for Attornies, Conveyancers, Men of Business, Judges and Registers of Probate, Executors and Administrators, Sheriffs, Town Officers, and Justices of the Peace. Second Edition: Carefully revised and corrected, with many additions. By Asa Aikens, of Windsor, Esquire. Windsor, Vt.: Published by Nathan C. Goddard, 1836. 12 mo, pp. 447, 1. First edition in 1828. Windsor. pp. 409, 1.

—*Tables of Interest and Discount*, also, Tables exhibiting the present worth at six per cent. Of all Annuities Certain, Pensions, Rents, Estates for years, and all Annual Incomes, (the duration of which is not contingent,) from one to eighteen years, inclusive ; Together with An Appendix Containing the Northampton Tables of the Expectation of Human Life, and corresponding Factors, with which to ascertain, by Multiplication, the Present Worth of Dower and other Estates and Incomes dependent on the continuance of a single life.   And a like set of Factors for determining, in the same manner, the Present Worth of all Fixed Annuities, etc., from one to one hundred years; Compiled from the Tables of Doctor Price : An Improved Time Table, and an Almanac for the residue of the Nineteenth Century : By Asa Aikens ; late a Judge of the Supreme Court of Vermont; Reporter of the Decisions of said Court; Author of Practical Forms, etc. Montreal: 1858. 4to, pp. (3) 22, (1) 29, (15.)

See Vermont Law Reports, 1827-28.   2 vols.

Mr. Aikens was from Barnard, Vt., and resided many years at Windsor, Vt.   See Pearson's Middlebury College Graduates, 1808.

Alden, Henry Mills. *God in His World :* An Interpretation. Harper & Brothers, New York: 1890. 8vo, 312 pp.

—*A Study of Death.* Harper & Brothers, New York: 1895. 8vo, 342 pp.

Mr. Alden was born in Mt. Tabor, Vt., Nov. 11, 1836; graduated at Williams College and Andover Theological Seminary; assisted in preparing Harper's Pictorial History of the Rebellion, 63-65; became managing editor of Harper's Weekly in 1864, and editor of Harper's Magazine in 1868.

Alexander, C. *A Grammatical System* of the English Language, Comprehending a plain and familiar scheme of Teaching Young Gentlemen and Ladies the Art of speaking and writing correctly their Native Tongue. By Caleb Alexander, A. M. Motto. Rutland, Vt.: Printed and published by Fay & Burt. 1819. 12mo, pp. 96.

See Drake's Biographical Dictionary : Sprague's Annals.

Allen, Charles A. *The Way of the Spirit.* A New Year's Sermon, preached in Montpelier, Jan. 6, 1866. By Rev. Charles A. Allen. 8vo, pp. 4.

Mr. Allen, a Unitarian, born in North Andover, Mass., founded the church of the Messiah, in Montpelier.

Allen, Charles L. *Medicine a Science.* An Address delivered before the Medical Class of the University of Vermont, Monday evening, June 9th, 1862.   By Charles L. Allen, M. D. Burlington: Times Book and Job Printing Establishment. 1862. 8vo, pp. 23.

Mr. Allen is a son of the late Dr. Jona. A. Allen, of Middlebury, Vt., and was born in Brattleboro, June 21, 1820. He was graduated at Middlebury College, 1842, and at Castleton Medical College in 1846; when he commenced the practice of his profession at Middlebury.

Allen, Ebenezer. *Short Biography of.*

See Barnes, Melvin.

Mr. Allen was second cousin to Ethan and Ira; for a sketch of the Allen family, see Governor and Council of Vermont, vol. 1, pp. 110-117; also Vermont Historical Magazine, vol. 1, pp. 560-574.

Allen, Miss Elisabeth. *The Silent Harp; or, Fugitive Poems ;* By Miss Elisabeth Allen. Motto. Burlington: Edward Smith, (Successor to Chauncey Goodrich). 12mo, pp. 120.

—*Sketches of Green Mountain Life: with Autobiography of the Author.* By Miss Elisabeth Allen. Motto. Lowell: Nathaniel L. Dayton. 1846. 12mo, pp. 160.

Miss Allen was born in Craftsbury, Vt., where she passed most of her time. At the age of sixteen an attack of fever wholly deprived her of hearing, and her chief amusement thereafter was composition in prose and poetry, upon which she was dependent for a livelihood.

ALLEN, ETHAN. *A Brief Narrative of the Proceedings of the Government of New York,* relative to their obtaining the Jurisdiction of that large District of Land, to the Westward from Connecticut River. Which, antecedent thereto, had been patented by his Majesty's Governor and Council of the Government of New Hampshire. And also, of the monopolizing Conduct of the Government of New York, in their subsequently patenting Part of the same Land, and oppressing the Grantees and Settlers under New Hampshire. Together with Arguments demonstrating that the Property of those Lands was conveyed from the Crown to the New Hampshire Grantees, by Virtue of their respective Charters. With Remarks on a Pamphlet entitled, "A State of the Right of the Colony of New York," &c., and on the Narrative of the Proceedings subsequent to the royal Adjudication, concerning the Lands to the Westward of the Connecticut River, lately usurp'd by New Hampshire. Intended as an Appendix to the General Assembly's State of the Right of the Colony of New York (with Respect to its Eastern Boundary   on Connecticut River, so far as concerns the late Encroachments under the Government of New Hampshire) published at their Session, 1773. By Ethan Allen. Bennington, 23d September, 1774.   Hartford : Printed by Eben Watson, near the Great Bridge. 8vo, pp. 211.

Referred to in Ira Allen's History of Vermont, p. 52 ; also in an official letter of Ethan Allen in Slade's Vt. State Papers, p. 93 ; and in Hiland Hall's Early Vermont, pp. 184, 185.

—*An Animadversory Address to the Inhabitants of the State of Vermont;* with Remarks on a Proclamation, under the hand of His Excellency George Clinton, Esq.; Governor of the State of New York. By Ethan Allen. Hartford : Printed by Watson & Goodwin, near the Great Bridge.   M.DCC.LXXVIII. 8vo, pp. 24.

Dated Bennington, August 9, 1778.

—*A Narrative of Col. Ethan Allen's Captivity,* From the Time of his being taken by the British, near Montreal, on the 25th day of September, in the Year 1775, to the Time of his Exchange on the 6th day of May, 1778, Containing His Voyages and Travels, With the most remarkable Occurrences respecting himself, and many other Continental Prisoners of different Ranks and Characters, which fell under his Observation, in the Course of the same ; particularly the Destruction of the Prisoners at New York, by General Sir William Howe, in the Years 1776 and 1777. Interspersed with some Political Observations. Written by Himself, and now Published for the Information of the Curious of all Nations.

"When God from chaos gave this world to be,
Man then he formed, and formed him to be free."
American Independence.   A Poem by Freneau.

Price Ten Paper Dollars. Philadelphia: Printed and Sold by Robert Bell, In Third Street. M.DCC.LXXIX. 8vo. Title, 1 leaf, pp. 46, in double columns.

Mr. Sabin says this is the first edition. A copy sold in March, 1866, for $56. It was reprinted with the same title, but in single columns. Philadelphia, Printed ; Boston, Reprinted by Draper & Folsom (1779). 8 vo., pp. 40. This is regarded as the second edition.

—*Third Edition;* same title. Philadelphia: Printed for and sold by William Mentz, in Cherry Alley, 1770. 12mo, pp. 64.

This is sometimes called the first edition.

—*Fourth Edition;* same title. Newbury: Printed by John Mycall, for Nathaniel Coverly of Boston, and Sold at his Shop, between Seven Star Lane and the Sign of the Lamb. 1780. 8vo, pp. 80.

—*Fifth Edition;* same title. Norwich: Printed by John Trumbull. 1780. 12mo., pp. 47.

It was also reprinted in Vol. II of the " Olive Branch " as an appendix. See Allen, Ira.

—*Sixth Edition;* same title, with the following addition : To which are now added a considerable number of explanatory and occasional notes, together with an index of reference to the most remarkable occurrences in the narrative. Walpole, N. H.: Thomas & Thomas. From the Press of Charter & Hale. 1807. 12 mo, pp. 158, Subscribers, 1 leaf.

—*Seventh Edition;* Albany: Published by Pratt & Clark, 1814. pp. 144. Printed by Moses Pratt, Jun., No. 162 Lion Street.

—*Eighth Edition;* A Narrative of Colonel Ethan Allen's Captivity. Written by Himself. Third Edition. With Notes. Burlington: H. Johnson & Co. 1838. 12 mo, pp. 144.

Mr. Goodrich calls this the " Third Edition."

—*Ninth Edition;* Allen's Captivity, being a Narrative of Colonel Ethan Allen, containing his Voyages, Travels, &c. Interspersed with Political Observations. Written by Himself. Boston: Oliver L. Perkins. 1845. 12mo, pp. 126. Preface by F. W. E.

This edition has a curious frontispiece, representing Allen in the act of demanding the surrender of the Fort at Ticonderoga.

—*Tenth Edition;* A Narrative of Col. Ethan Allen's Captivity. Written by Himself. Fourth Edition, With Notes. Burlington: Chauncey Goodrich. 1846. 12mo, pp. 120.

—*Eleventh Edition:* Ethan Allen's Narrative of the Capture of Ticonderoga, and of His Captivity and Treatment by the British. Written by Himself. Fifth Edition, with Notes. Burlington: C. Goodrich & S. B. Nichols. 1849. 8vo, pp. 50.

—*The same,* Burlington. Nichols and Warren, No. 4, Leavenworth Block. 1852, 8vo, pp 50.

—*Twelfth Edition;* A Narrative of the Captivity of Colonel Ethan Allen, from the time he was taken by the British, near Montreal, September 25th, 1775, to the time of his exchange, May 6th, 1778. 8vo, Dayton, 1849.

And there may be other editions of this work. It may be a question whether the edition called the third in this list should not be named the fourth, making thirteen in all, without the Olive Branch edition, which if counted, will make fourteen.

—*A Vindication of the Opposition of the Inhabitants of Vermont to the Government of New York,* and of their Right to form an Independent State, humbly submitted to the consideration of the Impartial World. By Ethan Allen. Printed by Alden Spooner, Printer to the State of Vermont. 1779. 8vo, pp. 172.

Reprinted in " Governor and Council " of Vermont, Vol. I, pp. 444-517.

—*The Present State of the Controversy between the States of New York and New Hampshire,* on the one part, And the State of Vermont on the other. Hartford: Printed by Hudson & Goodwin. M.DCC.LXXXII. 8vo, pp. 16.

This pamphlet is dated, " State of Vermont, January 17, 1782," and circumstances render it pretty certain that Col. Allen was the author. Reprinted, with notes, in " Governor and Council of Vermont," Vol. 2, pp. 355-363. See Vermont Historical Society Collections, Vol. 2, pp. 231-239, for a history of its origin, and a reprint of the original.

—*and Fay.* A Concise Refutation of the claims of New Hampshire and Massachusetts Bay to the Territory of Vermont ; with occasional Remarks on the long-disputed Claim of New York to the same. Written by Ethan Allen and Jonas Fay, Esq'rs. And published by order of the Governor and Council of Vermont. Bennington, the first day of January, 1780. Joseph Fay, Sec'ry. Hartford: Printed by Hudson & Goodwin. 8vo, pp. 20.

Reprinted, with notes, in " Governor and Council," Vol. 2, pp. 223-234.

—*Reason the only Oracle of Man, or a Compenduous System of Natural Religion.* Alternately Adorned with Confutations of a variety of Doctrines incompatible to it ; Deduced from the most exalted Ideas which we are able to form of the Divine and Human Characters, and from the Universe in General. By Ethan Allen, Esq. Bennington, State of Vermont: Printed by Haswell & Russell. M.DCC.LXXXIV. 8vo, pp. 477.

This singular book is the rarest of Allen's publications, and is remarkable as being the first work published in America in direct opposition to the Christian religion as has been alleged. An abridgement of it was published in New York in 1836, with the following title : "Reason, the only Oracle of Man ; or a Compendious System of Natural Religion. By Col. Ethan Allen. Published by G. W. and A. J. Matsell, 94 Chatham St., New York, 1836." 12 mo, pp. 106, including table of contents and index.

"The first edition of this work was printed by Mr. Haswell, of Bennington, Vt. Not long after its publication, a part of the edition, comprising the entire of several signatures, was accidentally consumed by fire; whether Mr. Haswell deemed this fire a judgment upon him for having printed the work or not, is unknown—but the fact is he soon after committed the remainder of the edition to the flames, and joined the Methodist connection; so that but few copies were circulated."—Introduction to Matsell's Edition, p. 1.—Sabin.

Mr. Matsell's story is a romance, so far as Mr. Haswell having committed any part of the edition to the flames is concerned; it is true that the entire edition, with the exception of about thirty copies, was destroyed by an accidental fire, said by one authority to have been caused by lightning, so that the work is now exceedingly scarce.

The liberal views contained in the Oracle of Reason, so generally censured and misunderstood at the time of publication, if put up in the dress of to-day, might become as popular as numerous publications universally accepted by the masses of readers. An hundred years have enlarged and greatly harmonized the religions of enlightened people.

Another edition, abbreviated, was published in 1854, viz: "Reason the only Oracle of Man; Or a compendious System of Natural Religion. By Col. Ethan Allen. Boston: J. P. Mendum, Cornhill. 1854." 12 mo, pp. 171.

Our attention was called to the following work of Ethan Allen by the Rev. Horace Edward Hayden, an Episcopal clergyman of Brownsville, Pa.

—*An Essay on the universal plentitude of Being,* and on the nature and immortality of the human soul, and its Agency. By Ethan Allen, Esq. Proposed as an appendix to a system of moral philosophy, lately published at Bennington, entitled Oracles of Reason. To which is subjoined a letter to Dr. Benj'n Gale in answer to one of his, on the subject of eternal Creation.

Printed in Mr. Henry B. Dawson's Historical Magazine, Morrisania, N. Y., vols. I, II, Third Series: 1873, where it occupies about twenty-three pages. We give in explanation the following extracts from the able note by Mr. Dawson prefaced to the work :

"Among those who have become distinguished in the United States, few have been more seriously misrepresented than Ethan Allen, * * misrepresentation has extended over his character and conduct, as a man and a citizen, * * and the opinions on religious subjects which he is known to have entertained and published to the world. Without noticing, in this place, other subjects concerning which Ethan Allen has been thus misrepresented, we may be allowed to refer to the opinions on religious subjects—opinions which have been very frequently represented as of the most obnoxious type of infidelity, etc. * * * The peculiar doctrines which Col. Allen published through the medium of the Oracle of Reason, as its author had reasonably supposed soon brought upon him the reproaches of many of those who read or professed to read them; and from that time to the present we imagine this work has served as the foundation on which have been constructed the greater number of the misrepresentations of his opinions on religious and other subjects." * * * * Soon after the publication of the Oracles, Col. Allen discovered, or supposed he discovered, one, at least, of those 'errors,' which he was evidently prepared to find therein; and agreeably to the promise he had publicly made in the preface to that volume, he promptly proceeded, as best he could, to 'rescind' that error, and present in its stead what he conceived to be a purer and better doctrine.

The 'error' to which we allude is found in Chapter II, Section VIII, page 94 of the Oracles, and concerns the 'essence of the Soul,' etc., * * and to correct the error into which he supposed he had fallen, Col. Allen prepared, with evidently great care, an Appendix to the Oracles, explanatory of his latest opinions on that subject.

The Appendix was intended to be published at a future day when it [would] not infringe on [its author's] fortune or present living; but so far as we can learn it was never published until the present time. It is a manuscript, evidently in the handwriting of its author, divided into an Introduction and four distinct Sections, extending over eighty pages of foolscap; but the letter to Doctor Gale, if it was ever attached to it, which is doubtful, has disappeared.

The subject of that Appendix, in itself, is scarcely such an one as would entitle it to admission into The Historical Magazine; but its author's position before the world, as one of the founders of the State of Vermont, and the purpose for which it was evidently written induced our lamented friend, Hon. George F. Houghton, of St. Albans, Vermont, to offer it to us, on condition that we would publish it in that work, and appropriate, from the anticipated profits arising from its publication, a designated sum toward the erection of a monument to the memory of the author of the Essay—promising at the same time, on his part, as an inducement for us to undertake what was not an agreeable duty, to prepare for it an appropriate prefatory note, in order that the publication of such a paper might be made as agreeable as possible to the readers of the Magazine and as remunerative as possible to ourself.

The death of our friend, soon after, deprived those who have survived him of the pleasure and instruction which the promised note from his pen would undoubtedly have secured to them, and the duty has devolved upon us to perform, for ourself, as best we may, the service which he undertook to do for us, and, in this brief and simple Note to introduce what will be welcomed, in many quarters, as a paper of unusual interest, while in others it will be regarded only as a literary or theological curiosity."

For a specimen of the early criticism of Allen's Oracle of Reason, see J. J. Henry's Journal of Arnold's campaign against Quebec, 1775, Munsell's ed. Note, pp. 120-127.

—*Ethan Allen and the Green Mountain Heroes of '76.* With a Sketch of the Early History of Vermont. By Henry W. De Puy. Buffalo: Phinney & Co., 1853. 12 mo, pp. 428.

—*De Puy's Ethan Allen and the Green Mountain Boys.* New York: J. C. Derby, 8 Park Place, 1854. 12mo, pp. 428.

—*Same.* Boston: 1853. 12mo, pp. 428.

—*The Mountain Hero and His Associates.* By Henry W. De Puy. Boston. Dayton & Wentworth, No. 86 Washington Street, 1855. 12mo, pp. 428.

Another edition of "Ethan Allen and the Green Mountain Boys."

—*The Life of Col. Ethan Allen*, by Jared Sparks, LL.D. Burlington: C. Goodrich & Company. 1858. 16mo, pp. 226.

—*Memoir of Col. Ethan Allen.* Containing the most interesting incidents connected with his private and public career. By Hugh Moore. Plattsburgh, N. Y: Published by O. R. Cook. 1834. 12mo, pp. 252.

—*Life of Ethan Allen.* By Jared Sparks. In Sparks' American Biography, Vol. I, first series. pp. 130.

Was also republished at Middlebury in 1848, in the same volume with Chipman's Memoir of Col. Seth Warner.

—*Report of the Committee under the act providing for the erection of a Monument over the grave of Ethan Allen.* Printed by order of the Senate, 1858. Montpelier: 8vo, pp. 7.

—*The Stephenson Statue of Ethan Allen.* Exercises attending the unveiling and presentation of a Statue of Gen. Ethan Allen at Burlington, Vt., July 4th, 1873, including an Oration by Hon. L. E. Chittenden. Burlington: Free Press Print. 1874. 8vo, pp. 66. Plate.

—*Ethan Allen; or, the King's Men.* An Historical Novel. By Melville. New York: 1836. 8vo.

—*Sketch of the Life of Ethan Allen*, by B. J. Lossing. Illustrated. In Harper's Monthly Magazine, November, 1858. 8vo, pp. 23.

A Statue of Ethan Allen, heroic size, in white marble, by Larkin G. Mead, was placed in the portico of the State Capitol at Montpelier, in 1861. It represents Allen in the act of demanding the surrender of Ticonderoga.

—*Ethan Allen, The Robin Hood of Vermont,* by Henry Hall. New York: D. Appleton & Co. 1892. 12mo, pp. viii, 207.

Compiled by Mrs. Henrietta Hall Boardman, a daughter of Mr. Hall, from notes and unpublished mss. left by Mr. Hall at his death in 1889.

—*Ancestry of Gen. Ethan Allen*, by O. P. Allen of Palmer, Mass.

See the Salem Press Historical and Genealogical Record for January, 1892.

Allen, Heman. *Allen's Exposition of the controversy subsisting between Silas Hathaway and himself.* Dated, Montpelier, October 15, 1822. 8vo, pp. 40. No imprint.

—*State of Vermont, Chittenden County, ss.* Heman Allen against Usal Pierson & Silas Hathaway. 8vo, pp. 24.

No imprint or dates, but probably 1822. Is a statement by the defendants, which includes Judge Brayton's Report of the Case, and all the evidence admitted.

—*Remarks of Mr. Allen's Counsel* upon the Petition of Silas Hathaway, Praying for a New Trial, etc. Dated, Montpelier, 16th October, 1822. No imprint. 8vo, pp. 40.

It is stated by Henry Stevens G. M. B., that this pamphlet was prepared by the Hon. Samuel Prentiss; it also includes the Opinion of the Hon. Daniel Webster upon the validity of the Act of the Legislature of Vermont, granting a new trial in the case in 1821.

This Heman Allen, of Colchester, was a nephew of General Ira and Col. Ethan Allen; and the three titles above are kindred to the famous Olive Branch case of General Ira Allen; and the contest was in relation to and a continuation of disputed land titles growing out of General Ira Allen's misfortune in consequence of the loss of the cargo of the Olive Branch.

See Allen, Ira. Olive Branch publications.

IRA ALLEN. *The Natural and Political History of the State of Vermont,* one of the United States of America. To which is added, an Appendix, containing answers to Sundry Queries addressed to the Author. By Ira Allen, Esquire, Major-General of the Militia in the State of Vermont. London: Printed by J. W. Myers, No. 2, Paternoster-Row, and sold by W. West, No. 1, Queens-Head Passage, Paternoster-Row. 1798. 8vo, pp. vii, 300.

Reprinted in Volume one, Collections of the Vermont Historical Society, pp. 319-499.

—*Twenty Thousand Muskets ! ! !* Particulars of the Capture of the Ship Olive Branch, in November, 1796, laden with Cannon, Muskets, etc., by His Majesty's Ship Audacious, in which the destination of the said Ship, and the use of the said Arms, etc., are discovered. London: 1797. 8vo, pp. 106.

Rich says this pamphlet was written by Mr. Allen. The date of publication indicates that it was Allen's first work in relation to the Olive Branch business.

—*Particulars of the Capture of the Ship Olive Branch,* laden with a Cargo of Arms, etc., the property of Major-General Ira Allen, destined for supplying the Militia of Vermont, and captured by His Brittannic Majesty's Ship of War, Audacious; together with the Proceedings and Evidence before the High Court of Admiralty of Great Britain. Vol. I. By Ira Allen, Esq.. of Vermont, in the United States of America, the Claimant in this Cause. London: Printed by J. W. Myers, No. 2, Paternoster Row, 1798. 8vo, pp. vi, 406.

Allen calls this Vol. 1; perhaps it may more properly be called the first edition.

—*Narrative of the Transactions* relative to the Capture of the American Ship, Olive Branch. 8vo, pp. 1, 368. [1804. Philadelphia.]

This is a part of what Allen calls Volume 2, and was hurried through the press without title page (and omitting many articles, for want of documents, which are included in the edition which follows), for distribution among the Citizens of Vermont prior to the meeting of the General Assembly of the State in October, 1804. This volume is made up largely of matter contained in the edition of 1798. See Allen's History of Vermont, pp. iii, iv.

—*Particulars of the Capture of the Ship Olive Branch,* laden with a Cargo of Cannon and Arms, the property of Major General Ira Allen, destined for supplying the Militia of Vermont, and captured by his Britannic Majesty's ship of war Audacious; together with the proceedings and evidence before the high Court of Admiralty and Appeal, in Great Britain, and an account of his imprisonment in France, and persecutions by a conspiracy of the two Hemispheres: with an Appendix, proposing a Ship Canal from Lake Champlain to the River St. Lawrence; the Evacuation of Ticonderoga, and Events of the War in 1777—Truce in 1780, to the end of the War—and a Narrative of Colonel Ethan Allen's Captivity, from 1775 to 1778. By Ira Allen of Vermont, the Claimant in this cause. Volume II. Philadelphia: Printed for the Author. 1805. (Copyright secured). 8vo, pp. xxx, 551.

This volume includes a resume of the first, with additions, including the Appendix.

In the latter part of 1802, about 160 pages of volume 2 of the Olive Branch was printed at Burlington, Vt.; but it is doubtful if many copies got into circulation. We quote from Mr. Allen's "Statements," 1807: "In the latter part of 1802 the Claimant resolved on publishing a second

volume of the Olive Branch, at Burlington, in Vermont; much pains was taken by a conspiracy against him to prevent the printing of it; but he proceeded to print about 160 pages, taken principally from the first volume, when the press was stopped until the author could gain time to write the other parts, which he accomplished in 1803, and delivered over the Manuscript to the printer, who after perusing it, gave the terms for which he would procure the paper and complete the printing; the Claimant furnished the whole of the money." Mr. Allen then took a long journey on horseback for his health, and returning in January, 1804, found that the printer had neglected to print any more of the book, and with difficulty he recovered the manuscript."

In a foot note Mr. Allen says: "It is to be observed, that in Vermont a powerful combination had formed against the Claimant, which was thought influenced the powers of the State. When Mr. Allen returned (to Burlington) he was furnished with four pistols and a loaded whip, well charged; these measures were said to make some consternation among the land thieves of Vermont, and while different measures were projecting to arrest and detain him, he packed up the papers necessary to compose the Olive Branch, and left Vermont."

Mr. Allen in the "Statements," gives an amusing account of the futile efforts to arrest and imprison him while attending the Legislature at Rutland, in 1804. Mr. Allen owned large tracts of lands about Burlington and in other parts of the State, but becoming involved pecuniarily through the loss of the Olive Branch and its cargo, the "land thieves of Vermont," as he calls them, during his long absence in Europe combined together and stripped him of his valuable possessions, and he was forced to leave the State, never to return. We do not think the great services rendered to Vermont by Mr. Allen have ever been fully appreciated, he appearing to have been overshadowed in history by the coarser career of his brother Ethan. We trust that some pen will yet do him justice. For a brief sketch of Mr. Allen see "Governor and Council" of Vermont, pp. 115-117, of Vol. 1. Mr. Walton thus closes the sketch: "his skill as statesman and diplomatist, his grand designs for the promotion of learning (he was the founder of the University of Vermont,) and the development of the material resources of the State, will forever stand, a monument more brilliant than brass and more lasting than marble." See also memoir of, by David Read, Vermont Historical Gazetteer, (Miss Hemenway's). Vol. 1, pp. 770-776, and by D. P. Thompson, Vermont Record, Vol. II., Nos. 5-20, 1864.

The following is the title to that part of Vol. 2 of the Olive Branch series printed at Burlington:

—*Extracts from the first volume of the Particulars of the Capture of the Ship Olive Branch,* laden with a cargo of arms, destined for the Militia of Vermont, and captured by His Brittanic Majesty's Ship of War, Audacious: with the evidence and proceedings in the High Court of Admiralty of Great Britain, and further proofs, recently taken by Commission. To which are added, the author's objects in going to Europe, the cause of his detention in England and France, with the principal effects they have produced on His property. By Ira Allen, the claimant in this cause. Burlington: Printed by John K. Barker. August, 1802. 8vo, pp. 160.

—*A Concise Summary of the Second volume of the Olive Branch.* A Book containing an account of Governor Chittenden's giving written instructions to General Ira Allen in 1795, to purchase Military Stores In Europe for the Militia of the State of Vermont; of his purchase of 24 Brass Field Pieces, 20,000 Muskets furnished with bayonets in France; of his being Captured by an English 74 Gun Ship, with consequences resulting therefrom. To which is Subjoined, General Allen's Circular Letter, on the subject of a Ship Canal of Commerce, and the advantage of British America in preserving peace between Great Britain and the United States. Philadelphia: Printed and sold by Thomas T. Styles, No. 84, South Front Street, & Solomon Wieatt No. 400, North Second-Street, at which places the second volume of the Olive Branch, is for sale. 8vo, pp. 15.

There is no date to this pamphlet, except near the end is a statement, signed by General Allen, dated Philadelphia, July 4th, 1806; and it was probably printed that year; as an enlarged edition followed in April 1807.

—*A Concise Summary of the Second Volume of the Olive Branch*, A Book containing an account of Governor Chittenden's giving written instructions to Gen. Ira Allen in 1795, to purchase Military Stores in Europe for the Militia of the State of Vermont, of his purchase of 24 Brass Field Pieces, 20,000 Muskets furnished with bayonets in France; of his being Captured by an English 74 Gun Ship, with consequences resulting therefrom. To which is Subjoined General Allen's Circular Letter, on the subject of a Ship Canal of Commerce, and the advantage of British America in preserving Peace between Great Britain and the United States. Including General Allen's Memorials to the Senate of the United States, of February, 1805, and December, 1806, and with other Documents and letters to Men of Great Respectability in Europe and America. Philadelphia: Printed for the Author. April, 1807. 8vo, pp. 24.

Mr. Sabin quotes an edition of the same, Philadelphia: 1804.

—*Statements applicable to the Cause of the Olive Branch*, which was a Cargo of Cannon and Arms, purchased by the Authority of the Governor of Vermont, to supply the Militia thereof, and Captured on its Passage from Ostend in France, to New York in the United States, by an English Man of War (In 1796,) which Statements are submitted for the Consideration of the Government and Ministers of Great Britain, the Government and Ministers of France, and the Government and People of the United States. By Ira Allen, Claimant of the Cargo of the Olive Branch. Philadelphia: Printed for the Author. July, 1807. 8vo, pp. 16.

It appears from page 10 of the above, that the first ten pages were printed in August, 1806, and copies "sent to Washington, London, and Vermont."

—*Ira Allen's Address to the Freemen of Vermont*, and Legislature Thereof, respecting a Cargo of Military Stores, captured by the British. Conduct of the Senators and Representatives of Vermont, and that of a Conspiracy. Philadelphia: Printed for the Author. August, 1808. 8vo, pp. 27.

—*Extracts From Volumes 5th, 1st & 4th* of select Speeches lately published in Philadelphia, which with remarks subjoined, are applicable to the cause of the Olive Branch, and consequences resulting therefrom. 12mo, pp. 6. n. p. n. d.

Was printed about June, 1809.

—*Copies of Letters to the Governor of Vermont*, an Address to the Legislature thereof, Respecting a Conspiracy against the Author ; and Respecting a Ship Canal From Lake Champlain to the River St. Lawrence : With Letters To the Allen Family on said subjects, and Compensation from the British Government, for the illegal Capture of the Cargo of the Olive Branch; with the Opinion of the Attorney General on the Case of the Olive Branch. By Ira Allen, Claimant of said Cargo. Philadelphia: Printed for the Author. January, 1810. 8vo, pp. 28.

—*Copies of Letters to the Governor of Vermont*, and address to the Legislature thereof, respecting a conspiracy against the author; and respecting a Ship Canal from Lake Champlain to the River St. Lawrence : with the Opinion of the Attorney General on the case of the Olive Branch. With letters to the Allen Family on said subjects, and compensation from the British Government. for the illegal Capture of the Cargo of the Olive Branch ; By Ira Allen, claimant of said cargo. Philadelphia: Printed by John Binns—For the Author. 8vo, pp. 61.

This title is without date, but the last document of the pamphlet is dated June 20, 1811, and the publication doubtless was in the summer of that year.

The contest over the cargo of the Olive Branch, after being in the English Courts for eight years, was decided in favor of Mr. Allen, but the expenses of the litigation far exceeded the value of the property involved, in addition to the loss of his estates in Vermont resulting primarily from the Olive Branch difficulties.

—*Some Miscellaneous Remarks*, and Short Arguments, on a Small Pamphlet, Dated in the Convention of the Representatives of the State of New York, October 2, 1776, and sent from said Convention to the County of Cumberland, and some Reasons given, why the District of the New Hampshire Grants had best be a State. By Ira Allen. Hartford, Conn.: printed by Ebenezer Watson, near the Great Bridge, M.DCC.LXXVII. 8vo, [May 1777.]

Reprinted in Vermont Historical Society Collections, Vol. 1, pp. 109–132. Also in Governor and Council, Vol. 1, pp. 376–389. See also, Hall's Bibliography of Vermont, Note.

—*Miscellaneous Remarks* on the Proceedings of the State of New York against the State of Vermont, &c. By Ira Allen. Hartford: Printed by Hannah Watson, near the Great Bridge. 8vo, Dated October 30th, 1777.

Reprinted in Collections of the Vermont Historical Society, Vol. 1, pp. 133–144.

—*Address* to the Inhabitants of the State of Vermont, by Ira Allen, dated at Dresden, November 27, 1778.

Gives the result of his official mission from Vermont to the Government of New Hampshire, in relation to the Union of Sixteen New Hampshire towns with Vermont.

Reprinted in Governor and Council of Vermont, Vol. 5, pp. 540–543.

—*A Vindication* of the Conduct of the General Assembly of the State of Vermont, Held at Windsor in October, 1778, against Allegations and Remarks of the Protesting Members ; with Observations on their Proceedings at a Convention held at Cornish, on the 9th Day of December, 1778. By Ira Allen. Arlington, 9th January, 1779. Dresden: Printed by Alden Spooner. 12mo, pp. 48.

—*Allen, Ira.* Founder of the University of Vermont. Oration on his Life and Public Services, delivered June 29, 1892, by J. E. Goodrich. Burlington: 1892, Free Press Print, 8vo, pp. 45.

Allen, John Johnson. *Post Prandial Poem*, written for the Reunion of the Sigma Phi Society at the Alpha Chapter, U. V. M., June 28, 1887. Burlington: 1887. pp. 19.

Allen, Jonathan A. *Address against Antimasonry in 1829.* See Masonic.

—*An Essay on Narcotic Substances*, embracing intoxicating liquids, tobacco, etc., by Jonathan A. Allen, M. D., Middlebury, Vt. Middlebury: American Office. 1835. 8vo, pp. 32.

Doctor Allen was a Physician in Middlebury, Vt.; he was born in Holliston, Mass., in 1787, and came to Vermont at an early day. See Swift's Hist. Middlebury, pp. 354–56.

Allen, J. Adams, M. D., LL. D. *Address* at the Public Exercises of the Chi Psi Fraternity at their Thirty-Sixth Annual Convention, with Alpha Mu Chapter, Middlebury College, Vt., June 8th, 1876. By J. Adams Allen, M. D., LL. D., Professor of the Principles and Practice of Medicine, Rush Medical College, Chicago, Ill. Chicago: Rand, McNally & Co., Printers and Engravers. 1876. 8vo, pp. 15.

—*Address* introductory to the Seventeenth Annual Course of Lectures in Rush Medical College, delivered November 1, 1859. By J. Adams Allen, Professor of Principles and Practice of Medicine. 8vo, pp. 16.

Mr. Allen, son of the late Dr. J. A. Allen, of Middlebury, Vt., was born in that town, January 16, 1826. See Pearson's Middlebury Graduates, 1845.

Allen, Joseph W. Allen, Joseph William, the fifth son of the late Hon. Heman Allen, was born in Milton, Vt., January 17, 1819; was graduated at the University of Vermont, 1839, read law, and practiced his profession at Burlington for several years, then at Milton and Richmond, where he died March 15, 1861. In the latter years of his life he edited and published two important legal works: "Fell on Guaranty," and "Reeves Domestic Relations." See Vermont Historical Gazetteer, Vol. 1, pp. 841–2.

Allen, Samuel. *Biography of,* See Barnes, Melvin.

Alling, Mrs. Martha (Sparhawk). *A sign to the Church.* A Sermon preached at the Washington St. Church, January 11, 1852, Occasioned by the death of Mrs. Martha Sparhawk Alling; By M. J. Hickok, Pastor of the Church. Rochester, N. Y. 1852. 8vo, pp. 18.

Mrs. Alling, daughter of Dea. Ebenezer Sparhawk, was born in Rochester, Vt., February 15, 1814.

Allis, Rev. O. D. *A Funeral Sermon on the Death of Charles M. Griswold,* who died in the Military Hospital at Galena, Ark., September 4, 1862. , Delivered in the Congregational Church at Randolph, September 21, 1862, By Rev. O. D. Allis. Montpelier: Printed at the Freeman Printing Establishment. 1863. 8vo, pp. 14.

Rev. O. D. Allis died in Dansville, N. Y., June 25, 1866, aged 41. He was ordained at Randolph, Vt., in 1860, and preached there and at West Randolph until 1865, when he was disabled by rheumatism from further labor.

ALMANAC. *Walton's Vermont Register and Almanac.* For the year of our Lord 1818. Being the second after Bissextile or Leap Year, and Forty second of Am. Independence. Montpelier, Vt.: Published by E. P. & G. S. Walton, at the Montpelier Bookstore. 18mo, pp. 132.

Continued :

In 1819 "k" was added to the word Almanac, and E. P. Walton's name appears as sole publisher until 1831. In 1820 the following addition was made to the title: "No. III. Calculated for the Meridian of Montpelier, Vt., in Latitude 44° 17m North, and Longitude 4° 38m East from Washington City ;" in 1823, "Astronomical Calculations by Zadock Thompson," and in 1824, "A. B." was appended to Mr. Thompson's name, and the longitude amended to read, "4° 25 m ;" in 1825 the letter "k" was dropped from the word "Almanack." In 1827, "A. M." appears in place of "A. B." as the appendage to Mr. Thompson's name ; and in 1831 the publishing firm was: "E. P. Walton & Co.;" in 1832–3, "Published by J. S. Walton, E. P. Walton, Printer ;" in 1834–5, "E. P. Walton" again appears as publisher ; 1836 to 1840, "Published by E. P. Walton & Son," and the words, "At the Montpelier Book Store" are omitted ; in 1837 a cut of the State House was placed upon the first page of the cover, for that year only, and at the bottom of the title page was added for that year only, "Price twenty cents single—

two dollars per dozen ;" in 1838, "Published Annually," follows the imprint, for that year only. In 1840 the title reads :

—*No. XXIII. Walton's Vermont Register and Farmers' Almanac for 1840:* Being Bissextile or Leap Year. Calculated for the Meridian of Montpelier, lat. 44° 17' north, long. 4° 25' east from the capitol at Washington. Astronomical calculations by Zadock Thompson, A. M. Montpelier: Published by E. P. Walton & Sons. 18 mo, pp. 144, 14.

A cut of the coat of arms of Vermont appears upon the first page of the cover of this number, and in 1841 the coat of arms gives place to a cut of the Winooski Falls in Marshfield, Vt., which in turn disappears the year following, to give place to a cut of a plow, which also retires in 1843. In 1849 an improved coat of arms appears on the cover for that year only ; in 1851, "Printed and published by E. P. Walton & Son ;" in 1853, "Published and printed by E. P. Walton & Son." pp 144, (2). In 1854, "Published and Printed by E. P. Walton, Jr."; and in 1856, with an enlarged coat of arms for that year ; in 1857, "Published by E. P. Walton. Walton's Steam Press." In 1858, Astronomical calculations are by Hosea Doton, A. M., and so continue.

From 1859 to 1868, "Published by S. M. Walton." In 1860 for the first time appears a map of the State, which is continued. In 1868, "E. P. Walton, Editor. Printed and sold by the Claremont Manuf'g Co." In 1871, "and Business Directory" is added after "Almanac ;" Claremont, N. H. Published by The Claremont Manufacturing Co., 1871 to 1880. S. I. Farman appears as publisher in 1881, and the White River Paper Co. from 1882 to 1891, inclusive. Since 1892 published by The Home Publishing Co., Burlington. After 1871 Mr. Walton's name does not appear as editor ; in 1872 the Longitude appears as 4° 27' East, etc.; in 1896 the number of pages is iv, 324, 30.

—*The Vermont Almanack* for the Year of Our Lord 1784 : Being Bissextile or Leap-Year and the Ninth Year of American Independence, containing the motions of the Sun and Moon, the Rising and Setting of the sun, and the Rising and Setting and Southing of the moon. Also, the Eclipses, Judgment of the Weather, length of days and nights ; Rising, Setting and Southing of the principal fixed stars ; Sun's declination, Moon's greatest north and south Latitude; Observable days of the church ; Tide, Interest and expence tables ; a list of Roads to most of the principal places on the continent. By Ned Foresight, Gent. Albany : Printed and Sold by S. Balentine at his printing office near the market House. Great allowance to those who buy to sell again. 12mo.

—*The Vermont Almanack* for the year of our Lord 1785. Being the first after Bissextile or Leap Year, and of our Independence the eighth. Containing everything necessary in an Almanack, and a great variety of instructive and interesting matter. Calculated for the Meridian of Bennington, Latitude 42 degrees, 45 minutes, North. By Eliakim Perry, Jr. Motto. Bennington: Printed by Haswell & Russell. 12 mo, pp. 24, not numbered.

—*An Astronomical Diary, or Almanack,* for the year of our Lord 1786. Of the Independence of the United States of America, the Tenth, and of the Sovereignty of the State of Vermont the Ninth. Being the second after Bissextile or Leap Year. Calculated for the Meridian of Bennington and latitude 43 deg., 4 min., North, from the Equator 2,584 miles, and from the Royal Observatory West longitude 72 degr., 48 min., which reduced to time makes nearly four hours and three-quarters, being about 4,320 miles, and from the angle of 51 degrees due South from London, 7 degrees, 56 minutes, or 546 miles horizontal zenith or perpendicular line of direction over Haswell's printing office. By Samuel Ellsworth, Esq., student in Astronomy. Bennington: Printed by Haswell & Russell. 12 mo, pp. 24.

—*The Universal Calender and North American Almanack,* for the year of our Lord 1790. And from the creation of the World, according to Sacred Writ, 5752. Being the second after Bissextile or Leap Year, and the fourteenth of the Independence of the State of Vermont and America. Calculated for the Latitude and Longitude of the State of Vermont. By Samuel Stearnes. Professor of the Mathematics, Natural Philosophy, and Physic. Printed at Bennington, Vt., by Haswell & Russell. 12 mo, pp. 24.

—*The same* for 1791. Printed at Bennington, by Anthony Haswell. Sold by him wholesale and retail.

—*An Almanac, and Register, for the State of Vermont,* for the year of our Lord 1794. Being the second after Leap Year and nineteenth of American Independence. Fitted to the Latitude and Longitude of Rutland. Printed at Walpole, N. H., by I. Thomas and D. Carlisle, Jr. For the Author. 18mo, 7 leaves of calendar, etc., 32 pp. of Register, and table of distances 4 pp.

—*Farmers' Useful and Entertaining Companion:* or New Hampshire, Massachusetts and Vermont Almanac, for the year of our Lord, 1795. Exeter: Stearns & Winslow. 12 mo, 12 leaves.

—*The Vermont Almanac and Register,* for the year of our Lord, 1795. Being the third after leap year, and the 19th of Independence of America. Fitted to the latitude and longitude of Rutland. Latitude 43° 21' north. Longitude 2° 9' east of Philadelphia. Vermont: Printed and sold wholesale and retail by Alden Spooner, at his printing office in Windsor.

12 mo, contains thirty leaves, no pagination. From the preface, this appears to be No. 2 of a series, of which No. 1, as per title, ante, was printed at Walpole 1794; they both purport to have been published in the "Nineteenth of American Independence."

—*Haswell's Calendar or Vermont Almanack* for the year of our Lord 1795; Being the third after Bissextile or leap year and the 19th of the Independence of America. Containing, etc., calculated for the meridian of Bennington, but will serve without sensible variation for the adjacent States. By Adam Astrologist. Bennington: Printed by A. Haswell and sold at his office in Bennington and by the different Post-riders.

—*Haswell's Federal and Vermont Register:* Together with an Almanac, for the year 1798. Bennington: 1798.

—*Haswell's Vermont and New York Almanack,* for the Year of our Lord 1800; Calculated for the Meridian of Bennington, etc. Bennington: Printed by Anthony Haswell. 12 mo, pp. 24.

—*An Astronomical Diary* or Almanac for the year of our Lord, 1802; Calculations by Joel Sanford. Bennington, Vt.: Printed by Goldier & Stockwell, and sold by the dozen, Thousand, or single. 12mo, pp. (24).

—*The Vermont Almanack,* for the year of our Lord 1803. By Isaac Rice. Bennington: Printed by A. Haswell.

—*Haswell's & Smead's Calender,* or the New england and New york Almanac, for the year of our Lord 1805. Bennington, Vt.: Printed by Haswell & Smead. 12mo, pp. (24).

—*Farmers' Calendar:* or the Vermont, Connecticut and New York Almanac, for the year of our Lord 1807. By Andrew Beers, Philom. Bennington: Printed by Anthony Haswell for Archibald Pritchard of Manchester, Vt.

—*Farmers' Calender:* or the Vermont, New York and Connecticut Almanac, for the year of our Lord, 1808. Bennington: Printed by A. Haswell, for the purchaser. 12 mo, pp. (40).

—*The Same* for 1811.

—*The Farmer's Calendar:* or the Vermont, New York and Connecticut Almanac for the year of our Lord 1810. By Andrew Beers, Philomath. No imprint. 12mo.

—*The Same,* 1813. Bennington, Vt.: Printed by William Haswell.

—*The Farmer's Calendar:* or the New York, Vermont and Connecticut Almanac, for the year of our Lord, 1812. By Andrew Beers, Philom. Bennington, Vt. Printed by William Haswell.

—*The Farmers' Calendar:* or the New York, Vermont and Connecticut Almanac for the year of our Lord 1815. By Andrew Beers, Philom. Bennington: Printed by Darius Clark & Co.

—*Beers's Calendar:* or Vermont Almanac, for the year of our Lord, 1804; And until the 4th of July, the 28th of the Independence of the United States of America. Manchester, Vt. Printed and sold by W. Stockwell, at his book store and printing office, by the gross, dozen or single. Great allowance made to those who purchase to retail. 12mo.

—*The Vermont Register and Almanac,* for the year of our Lord 1806, and the thirtieth of the Independence of the United States. Containing Much Useful Information. Middlebury: Printed and sold by Huntington & Fitch. 18 mo. pp. 144.

The first number was published 1802.

—*The Vermont Almanac,* for the year of our Lord 1807. Astronomical calculations by Eben W. Judd. Printed at Middlebury, Vt., by J. D. Huntington. 12mo.

—*Franklin's Legacy:* or the New York and Vermont Almanac, for the year of our Lord, 1801. Troy: Printed and sold by R. Moffit & Co. pp. 34.

—*Franklin's Legacy:* or the New York and Vermont Almanac, for the year of our Lord, 1806. By Andrew Beers, Philomath. Troy, N. Y. Printed and sold by Moffit & Lyon. 12 mo.

—*The Columbian Calendar:* or New York and Vermont Almanac, for the year of our Lord, 1819. By Andrew Beers, Philom. Troy: Printed and sold by Francis Adancourt. 12 mo.

—*The Ladies' and Gentlemen's Diary and Almanac,* for the year of our Lord, 1814. By Asa Houghton. Brattleborough, Vt.: Published by William Fessenden. Price 7 1-2 dolls., per gross, 75 Cts. per dozen, and 10 Cts. single. 12 mo.

—*The Ladies' and Gentlemen's Diary and Almanac,* with an Ephemeris, for the year of Creation according to sacred writ, 5782, and of the Christian Era, 1820. By Asa Houghton. Bellows Falls, Vt. Printed and Published by Bill Blake & Co. Price 9 dollars per gross, 87 1-2 cents per dozen, and 12 1-2 cents single. 12mo.

—*The Vermont Register and Almanac,* for the year of our Lord 1811, and the 35th of the Independence of the United States of America. Containing a great variety of useful information. Burlington, Vt. Printed by S. Mills. Sold wholesale and retail at his book store; by Swift & Chipman, Middlebury; Josiah Parks, Montpelier; Z. Lyon, Royalton; Farnsworth & Churchill, and Merrifield & Cochran, Windsor; Wm. Fay, Rutland; Wm. Fessenden, Brattleborough, and by the other booksellers and printers in Vermont. 18mo. pp. 102.
Continued, until 1824. This being number two.

—*The Vermont and New York Almanac,* for the year of our Lord Christ, 1812; Astronomical Calculations by Eben W. Judd. Burlington, Vt.: Printed by S. Mills. 12mo.

—*The New Hampshire and Vermont Almanack,* with an Ephemeris for the year of our Lord, 1805, * * * fitted to the latitude and longitude of the town of Windsor. * * * Printed at Windsor, Vt. By Nahum Mower.

—*Mower's New Hampshire and Vermont Almanac,* with an Ephemeris for the year of our Lord, 1806. Astronomical calculations by Amos Cole. Printed at Windsor, Vt., by Nahum Mower. 12mo.

—*The New Hampshire and Vermont Almanack for 1808.* Calculated by Amos Cole, Philom. Printed and sold at Windsor, by Alden Spooner.

—*The same* for 1809 bears the imprint H. H. Cunningham, and C. Spear. Windsor, Vt.

—*The same* for 1811. Windsor: Printed by Merrifield & Cochran.

—*The Complete New Hampshire and Vermont Almanac,* for the year of our Lord, 1812. * * * Calculations by Amos Cole, Philom. * * * Windsor, Vt. Published by Merrifield & Cochran.

—1813. do. Windsor, Vt. Published by P. Merrifield J. Cunningham, Printer.

—*The New England Farmers' Diary and Almanac,* for * * * 1816. * * * By Truman Abell. Windsor, Vt: Published by Jesse Cochran.

—*The New England Farmers Diary and Almanac,* from the year of the creation, according to the sacred writ, 5782, and of the Christian era 1820. Being Bissextile or leap year and the forty-fourth of American Independence, containing besides the usual astronomical calculations a great variety of needful and entertaining matter. Fitted to the Latitude and Longitude of Windsor, Vt., but will serve without sensible variation for the adjacent States. By Truman Abell. Philom. Motto. Windsor: Printed for the publisher Ebenezer Hutchinson, Hartford, by Ide & Aldrich.

—*Same.* 1834, by Ide & Goddard.
In 1841 Ide & Goddard, of Claremont, N. H., published it. 1846 and those after were published by the Claremont Manufacturing Company, which means Ide & Goddard, or Goddard & Ide.

—1821. The same.

—1822. The same (except that "Philom" is omitted.)

—1823. The same.

—1825. The same. Published by Newton & Tuft, Alstead, N. H., and Simeon Ide, Windsor, Vt.

—1826. The same.

—1827. The same.

—1828. The same.

—*The New England Farmers' Almanack,* by Truman Abell, 1819, and some years after. Printed at Windsor, by Simeon Ide, and Ide & Aldrich.

—*The New England Farmers' Diary and Almanac,* from the year of Creation, According to Sacred Writ, 5785; and of the Christian Era, 1823. By Truman Abell, Windsor, Vt. Printed for the Publisher, Ebenezer Hutchinson, Hartford, by Simeon Ide, and sold by them, and by the principal Booksellers in the Country. Price $9.00 per gross—$0.83 per dozen—and 12½ Cents single. 12mo.
Continued; the latest we have seen being No. XX, 1834, printed by Ide & Goddard.

—*The Youth's Almanac,* Astronomical Calculations by Truman H. Safford, Jr., of Royalton, Vt., a boy only nine years old. Bradford: Asa Low. 1845. 12mo, pp. 48.

—*The Same,* 1846. See Safford, T. H.

—*The Farmers' Almanack,* for the year of our Lord 1820. By Andrew Beers. Burlington, Vt: Printed by E. & T. Mills. 12mo, pp. 24.
Continued.

—*The same,* 1828 and 1829, by Zadock Thompson, A. M. Same imprint.

—*The Vermont Almanack,* for the year of our Lord 1820. By Andrew Beers, Philom. Burlington, Vt: Printed by E. and T. Mills. 12mo.
Continued.

—*The Christian and Farmers' Almanac, No. II,* for the year of our Lord 1824. Astronomical calculations by Andrew Beers. Burlington: Printed by E. & T. Mills. 12mo, pp. 48.
Continued after 1825 by Zadock Thompson, A. B., same imprint, No. xiii, 1835, by Zadock Thompson, A. M. Imprint the same.

—*The Vermont Directory and Commercial Almanac.* No. 2, 1856. With an Appendix. By W. W. Atwater. Burlington. Sold by merchants generally throughout the State. Geo. C. Rand & Avery, printers, Boston.
Continued with the imprints of Tuttle & Gay, and Tuttle, Gay & Co., Rutland, until 1868, when it was printed and sold by the Claremont Manufacturing Co. 18 ino, pp. 139, and Appendix, pp. 51.

—*The Vermont and New York Almanac,* for the year of our Lord 1808. Astronomical calculations by Eben W. Judd. Printed at Middlebury, Vt., by J. D. Huntington. 12mo.
Continued with the same imprint until 1812.

—*Swift's Vermont Register and Almanac,* for the year of our Lord 1812, and the thirty-sixth of the Independence of the United States. Middlebury: Published by Samuel Swift, at his Theological, Classical, and Law Book-Store. T. C. Strong, printer. 12mo, pp. 108.
Continued until 1818. 1811, by Swift & Chapman; 1816, by L. Fillmore & Sons.

—*The Vermont and New York Almanac,* for the year of our Lord 1813. Being the first after Bissextile or Leap Year, and the thirty-seventh of the Independence of the United States of America. Calculated for the Meridian of Middlebury, 44 deg. N. Lat. and 4 deg. E. Long. from Washington City. Astronomical calculations by Eben W. Judd. Middlebury, Vt.: Published by Samuel Swift, and sold at his book-store, also by the book-sellers, merchants, post-riders, etc., throughout the State. T. C. Strong, printer. 12mo, pp. 36.

—*Eaton's Anti-Masonic Almanac,* for 1833. Being the first after Bissextile or Leap Year, and the fifty-seventh of American Independence. Calculated for the Meridian of Montpelier, Vt., but will serve for the adjacent States.
View of Morgan, as confined in the dungeon at Fort Niagara.
Nor wife, nor children more shall he behold,
Nor friends—nor sacred home!
"In our boasted Republic, the blood of an American, who was taken from his home, bound, tortured, agonized, borne by the conspirators along the high roads with an impudent cavalcade of carriages and horsemen, cast into a fortress over which had floated the sovereign flag of the Union, and at last immolated, by harpies belonging to an organized and powerful institution who conceal their crime under the horrible delusion of their mystic tie."
Danville, Vt: Published and sold, wholesale and retail, by E. Eaton, Danville, and Capt. Ira White, Wells River, Vt. Price $9.50 per gross, 95 Cents per dozen, and 12½ cents single. 8vo, pp. 34.

—*The Anti-Masonic Almanac* for the year of our Lord, 1830; being Bissextile or leap year, and fifty-fourth of American Independence. Calculated for the meridian of Woodstock, containing besides the usual astronomical calculations, much interesting matter on the subject of Free-Masonry, a Narrative of the Abduction of William Morgan, etc., etc., with two cuts illustrating the Sublime Mysteries of Noodleism. Wood-cut. Woodstock: Printed by D. Watson. Price $5.00 per gross, 50 cents per dozen, 8 cents single.

—*The Vermont Anti-Masonic Almanac,* for the year of our Lord, 1831; being the third after Bissextile or leap year, and the fifty-fifth of American Independence. [Anti-Masonic Wood-cut.] Calculated for the Meridian of Montpelier, lat. 44 deg. 17 min. N. and lon. 4 deg. 25 min. E. from the Capitol of the United States at Washington. By Samuel Hemenway, Jr. Woodstock, Vt.: Hemenway & Holbrook, Printers.

—*No. II. The Gentleman's Almanack and Annual Register,* for the year of our Lord, 1820. By Zadock Thompson. Woodstock: Printed by David Watson.

—*The Farmers' Almanack,* for the year of our Lord, 1827. Calculations by Zadock Thompson. Printed, Woodstock, Vt., by David Watson.

—*The Complete New England Almanac,* Nos. I, II, III, by Marshall Conant for 1829, 1830 and 1831. Printed, Woodstock, Vt., by Rufus Colton, and R. & A. Colton.

—*R. & A. Colton's Vermont Miniature Register and Gentleman's Pocket Almanac,* for 1831. Astronomical Calculations by Marshall Conant. Woodstock, Vt., n. d. 24mo.

—*The Vermont Almanac, Pocket Memorandum and Statistical Register,* for the year 1843; being third after Bissextile or leap year. Astronomical Calculations by Hosea Doton. Vol. 1, No. 1. Woodstock, Vt.: Published by Haskell & Palmer. [Mercury Press.] 18mo. pp. 144.
Continued.

—*Lyon's Vermont Calendar or, A Planatory Diary,* For the year of our Lord, 1795. To which is annexed a Federal and State Register. Rutland, Vt.: James Lyon.

—*The Vermont Almanac and Register,* for the Year of Our Lord, 1796, Being Leap Year, and until July 4, the twentieth of the Independence of America. Fitted to the Latitude and Longitude of Rutland: Latitude 43° 21' North. Longitude 2° 9' East of Philadelphia. Vermont: Printed by James Kirkaldie, and sold wholesale and retail, at the Printing Office, Rutland: 16mo, pp. 54. (Interleaved.)

I have copies of the same, 1794, 1797, the former imperfect; how many numbers were published I am unable to say.

I give a few statistics from the Register for 1794, which are of interest at the present day. There were in 1793 two post roads established by Congress in Vermont, one in the east, and the other in the west part of the State, along Connecticut River, from Springfield, Mass., by Brattleborough, Charlestown, N. H., Windsor to Hanover, N. H. On the West side from New York, by Albany, Bennington, Manchester, Rutland, to Burlington.

Also a post road was established between Burlington and Montreal; and a British carrier arrived at Burlington every fortnight. The only post offices in the State given by the Register were Brattleborough, John W. Blake, Postmaster; Westminster, Reubin Atwater, Postmaster; Windsor, Alden Spooner, Postmaster; Bennington, David Russell, Postmaster; Manchester, Abel Allis, Postmaster; Rutland, Frederick Hill, Postmaster; Middlebury, Robert Huston, Postmaster; Vergennes, Alexander Brush, Postmaster; Burlington, John Fay, Postmaster. The rate of postage as given was, per single letter, 30 miles, 6 cents, 60 miles, 8 cents, 100 miles, 10 cents, 150 miles, 12½ cents, 200 miles, 15 cents, 250 miles, 17 cents, 350 miles, 20 cents, 450 miles, 22 cents, over 450 miles 25 cents. Double and triple letters, double and triple rates; one ounce, one dollar, and so in proportion.

The only custom house officer in the State was at Alburgh, Stephen Keyes, Collector. In 1793 there were five Masonic Lodges: Temple, at Bennington, North Star, at Manchester, Aurora, at Poultney, Dorchester, at Vergennes, Vermont, at Windsor. Of Ministers, Churches and Religious Assemblies, there were five Episcopalian, 36 Congregational, 13 Baptist, three Presbyterian. Of Literary Societies: University of Vermont, incorporated November 3, 1792; Clio Hall, (academy) at Bennington, incorporated October, 1780; Windham Hall, incorporated November 3, 1791; Cavendish Academy, incorporated October 26, 1792.

At the above date there was not a church organization, or a lawyer, within the present limits of Washington county; there were Justices of the Peace: Waterbury, then in Chittenden county, Richard Holden; Waitsfield, then in Chittenden, Benjamin Wait; Middlesex, then in Chittenden, Seth Putnam; Cabot, then in Orange county, Lyman Hitchcock; Montpelier, then in Orange, Jacob Davis, David Wing; Berlin, then in Orange, John Taplin; Wildersborough, now Barre, Benjamin Walker. The only Representatives from the present Washington county in the Legislature for the year 1793, were: Middlesex, Seth Putnam; Waterbury, Ebenezer Reed; Montpelier, Jacob Davis; Barre, Nathan Harrington; Cabot, James Morse; Berlin, John Taplin.

Deming does not give Waterbury a Representative in 1793, but gives correctly Jacob Bliss in 1792, as the first Representative from that town.

In a Middlebury Register for 1804, we find sixty Post towns in the State, with Timothy Hubbard postmaster at Montpelier; Ira Day at Barre, Bennet Beardsley at Cabot, and George Kennan, Jr., at Waterbury. Twenty-one Masonic Lodges; the only additional educational institution reported is Peacham Academy.

Of churches, etc., there were 39 Congregational, 20 Baptist, 3 Episcopalian, 3 Universalist, 2 Friends, and 1 Presbyterian,

—*Rutland County Almanac, 1861.* Astronomical Calculations for the meridian of Rutland, by W. W. Atwater. Issued by Pond & Morse, wholesale and retail dealers in drugs, medicines, chemicals, and patent medicines, opposite the depot, Rutland, Vt. George A. Tuttle and Company, printers. 12mo, pp. 56.

—*The same* for 1862.

—*Rutland Herald Almanac for 1876.* Illustrated. Published by the Herald Association, Rutland, Vt. Tuttle & Company, Book and Job Printers, Rutland, Vt. 8vo.
Continued for a year or two.

—*The Burlington Free Press Almanac.* Vol. 2. 1877. 12mo.
Continued.

Almon, J. *The Remembrancer;* or Impartial Repository of public events. 17 vols. London. 1775-1784.
Contains many papers relating to the War of the Revolution, and references to Vermont affairs and persons.

American Archives. *A Documentary History*, published by M. St. Clair and Peter Force. 4th series, 1774-1776, vols. i-vi: 5th series, 1776, vols. i-iii. Washington: 1837-1853. 9 vols. fol.
Interspersed throughout these volumes are many documents relating to the early history of Vermont.

American Cooking, or the Art of Dressing Viands, Fish, Poultry and Vegetables, etc., with cuts. * * * * * By an Orphan. 2d Edition, Improved. Woodstock, Vt.: Printed and Published for the Author. By A. Colton. 1831. 12mo, pp. 112.

The American Songster's Companion, a new selection of the most approved Songs. Danville. Published by Eaton & Baker. 1815. 24mo, pp. 84.

The American Taxation. *A Song of the Revolution.* 1776. W. W. Curtiss, printer, Bradford, Vt. 12mo, pp. 4. n. d. This song commences:
" While I relate my Story, Americans give ear,
Of Britain's fading glory you presently shall hear."

Anderson, Mr. *An Adventure in Vermont;* or the Story of Mr. Anderson. No. 62. Printed for the American Tract Society. 1825. 12mo, pp. 24.

Anderson, James. *Survey of the Congregational Churches* in the County of Bennington, Vt. From their Organization down to the present time. (1842.) Am. Quar. Register, Nov. 1842. Vol. 15.
Contains historical notes on each town in the county. Rev. Mr. Anderson was Pastor of the Congregational Church, Manchester, Vt., 1829-1858.

Andover. *Auditor's Report* for the Town of Andover, Vt., For the year ending January 28, 1871. 8 vo., pp. 8.
Continued.

Andrew, John A. *An Address* delivered at Brattleborough, Vt., by Invitation of the Agricultural Society of Vermont, at the Fair held by that Society and the Agricultural Society of New England, September 7, 1866. By John A. Andrew. Boston: Wright & Potter, printers, No. 4 Spring Lane. 1866. 8vo, pp. 44.

Angell, James Burrell. *The Fruitful Activity of the Life of Christian Faith.* A Discourse delivered before the Graduating Class of the University of Vermont and State Agricultural College, August 2, 1868, by James B. Angell, LL. D., President. Burlington: Free Press Steam Printing House. 1868. 8vo, pp. 20.
James B. Angell was born at Scituate, R. I., 1829; graduated Brown University, 1849; Professor of Modern Languages in that University, 1853-60; Editor Providence Journal, 1860-66; President of the University of Vermont, 1866-71; President of Michigan University after 1871; U. S. Minister to China, 1880-81; Member of the Canadian Fisheries Commission, 1887-8; Member of Deep Water Ways Commission, 1896.

An Answer to the Reverend Sylvanus Haynes' Piece Entitled, "A Brief and Scriptural Defence of Believers' Baptism by Immersion." By an Old Berean. Motto. Rutland: Printed A. D. 1801. 8vo, pp. 38, (1).

Anthony, James, *Trial of James Anthony for the Murder of Joseph Green;* before the Honorable Supreme Court of the State of Vermont, at their adjourned Term in the County of Rutland, February 28, A. D. 1814. Rutland: Published by Fay & Davison. 8vo, pp. 39.

Anti-Slavery. See *Slavery.*

Apocatastasis, *The,* See *Marsh, Leonard.*

Apsey, Rev. William S. *Causes for National Thanksgiving.* A Discourse delivered in the First Baptist Church, Bennington, Nov. 24, and repeated in the same place, Nov. 28, 1864. By Rev. Wm. S. Apsey, Pastor of the Church. Bennington: J. I. C. Cook & Son, Printers. 1864. 8vo, pp 14.

Archives of Science—and Transactions of the Orleans County Society of Natural Sciences. Editors: J. M. Currier, M. D., Newport, Vt. Geo. A. Hinman, M. D., West Charleston, Vt. Vol. I. October, 1870. No. I. (Seal) Published Quarterly. By J. M. Currier, M. D., Newport, Orleans County, Vt. Terms $2.50 per annum in advance. Single Numbers 75 cents. 9 Numbers, all published, ending July 1874. 8vo, pp. 256.

Arey, Harriet Ellen (Grannis.) *Household Songs and Other Poems.* New York: J. C. Derby, 1855. Boston: Phillips, Sampson & Co. Cincinnati: H. W. Derby. 12mo, pp. 254.
Mrs. Arey was born in Cavendish, Vt., April 14, 1819. Her father, John Grannis, was a member of the Canadian Parliament at the breaking out of the rebellion in 1837, and he afterward held offices of trust under the United States Government. Harriet Ellen was one of the earliest of that band of young women, now numerous, who pursued the course of study contended for by the claimants for a liberal education for her sex. She began her literary career in Cleveland, Ohio, as a contributor to the Daily Herald of that city, and for several years was a popular teacher there. In 1848 she married Oliver Arey, and soon after turned her attention from teaching to editing, and for several years conducted "The Youth's Casket," and "Home Monthly," published at Buffalo and Hartford, respectively. Mrs. Arey has contributed many articles to periodicals, educational, and others. Since about 1862 she has devoted herself almost entirely to the school

room, for several years at Whitewater, Wis., then at Yonkers, and at the present time (1878) she is teaching at Buffalo, N. Y. She writes us as follows: "I look upon myself as having done my best work in the school room, and am proud to write myself, by the grace of God, a teacher." Dated, Buffalo, Nov. 18, 1877. The Superintendent of Schools for Wisconsin, writes: "Mrs. Arey is a lady of rare attainments and accomplishments, beloved and admired by her pupils, and by all who know her in Wisconsin. It is not going too far to say that she was without a peer among the lady teachers of our normal and public schools."

Army of the Potomac. *The Society of the Army of the Potomac.* Report of the Eleventh Annual Reunion at Burlington, Vt., June 16, 1880. New York: 1880. 8vo, pp. 132.

Arnold Benedict. *Autograph letter* to the Committee of the Green Mountain Boys sitting at Charlestown, No. 4, defending himself from the charge of plundering the property of Major Skeene, at Skeenesborough, a day or two before the capture of Ticonderoga, May 10, 1775, with a copy of his orders to Capt. Herrick, May 8th, 1775, written at Castleton, Vt., to proceed immediately to Skeenesborough, etc.

See Stevens, Henry, a Catalogue of 5000 Books, etc., where these documents are printed in full, pp. 7-8.

Arnold, Josias Lyndon. *Poems.* By the late Josias Lyndon Arnold, Esq'r, of St. Johnsbury, Vt., formerly of Providence, and a Tutor in Rhode Island College. Printed at Providence, by Carter & Wilkinson, and sold at their bookstore opposite the market. M.DCC.XCVII. 12mo, pp. 141.

Mr. Arnold was a son of Dr. Jonathan Arnold, a prominent statesman of Rhode Island, and one of the first settlers and proprietors of St. Johnsbury, Vt. Josias Lyndon was born in Providence, R. I., April 22, 1768; and died at St. Johnsbury, June 7, 1796. He was graduated at Dartmouth College in 1788; was a teacher in the Academy at Plainfield, Conn., for a short time, studied law, but declined to practice, and accepted the position of tutor in Brown University. In the winter of 1791-2 he was called to St. Johnsbury by the sickness of his father, and decided to settle there; in March, 1795, he married Miss Perkins, of Plainfield, Conn., and they traveled on horseback to the wilderness home in Vermont. In the spring of 1796 he was attacked with a severe illness, which terminated his earthly career.

Arnold, Seth Shaler. *A Sermon preached at Alstead,* on the first Sabbath in January, 1826, with Historical Sketches of the Town. Alstead: Newton and Tufts. 1826. 8vo, pp. 48.

—*The Intellectual Housekeeper:* A Series of Practical Questions to his Daughters, by a Father; or Hints to Females on the Necessity of Thought in Connection with their Domestic Labors and Duties. Boston: Russell, Odiorne & Co. 1835. 12mo, pp. 47.

— *The Family Choir:* A collection of hymns set to music. 1837.

Mr. Arnold was born in Westminster, Vt., February 22, 1788. For a sketch of his life see Congregational Quarterly, January, 1869.

Arthur, T. S. *History of Vermont.* See Carpenter, W. H.

Articles *of the Chittenden County Conference of Churches,* with the Confession of Faith and Covenant, to be used in the admission of Members. Burlington: George J. Stacy, Printer. 1851. 12mo, pp. 15.

Asylum. See Vermont Asylum.

Atkinson, Rev. G. H., D. D. *Address,* delivered by Rev. G. H. Atkinson, D. D., before the Chamber of Commerce of the State of New York, upon the Possession, Settlement, Climate and Resources of Oregon and the Northwest Coast, including some remarks upon Alaska, Dec. 8, 1868. New York: John W. Amerman, Printer. No. 47 Cedar St. 1868. 8vo, pp. 17.

—*Centennial Sketch* of a remarkable Western man and head of a representative family of an American Pioneer—Rev. Wm. M. Stewart, of Semiahmoo, Whatcom Co., W. T. By Rev. G. H. Atkinson, D. D. 1876. No imprint. 8vo, pp. 4.

—*Centennial Paper.* The American Colonist in Oregon. An address delivered before the Pioneer Society of Oregon, at Astoria, Feb. 22, 1876. By Rev. George H. Atkinson, D. D. 8vo, pp. 8. No imprint.

—*History of the Congregational Church of Oregon City, Oregon.* 1844-1876. 8vo, pp. 4.

—*Reminiscences of Rev. E. Walker.* Funeral Discourse by Rev. G. H. Atkinson, D. D. Geo. H. Himes, Pr. Portland, (Or.) 1877. 8vo, pp. 8.

—*The Christian's Future Assured.* A discourse preached by Rev. G. H. Atkinson, D. D., in the Congregational church in Seattle, W. T., August 13, 1878, at the funeral of Mrs. M. F. Eells, one of the pioneer Missionaries of the A. B. C. F. M. to the Spokane Indians of Oregon, in 1838. Portland, Oregon: Publishing House of Himes the Printer. 1878. 8vo, pp. 6.

—*The Northwest Coast,* including Oregon, Washington and Idaho, a series of articles upon the N. P. R. R., in its relations to the Basins of the Columbia and of Puget's Sound. By Rev. G. H. Atkinson, D. D. Endorsed by the Portland Board of Trade. First published in the Oregonian. Portland, Oregon: A. G. Walling, Steam Printer and Bookbinder. 1878. 8vo, pp. 56.

—*The First Day Sabbath.* Its Law. By Rev. G. H. Atkinson, D. D. Portland, Oregon: D. H. Stearns & Co., Book and Newspaper Publishers. 1879. 8vo, pp. 15.

Mr. Atkinson was born in Newbury, Mass., May 10, 1819; in his early childhood the family moved to Newbury, Vt. He prepared for college at Newbury and Bradford, and was graduated at Dartmouth, 1843; and at Andover Theological Seminary, 1846; was licensed by the Orange Association, Vermont, 1846, and ordained at Newbury, 1847, and in October of that year sailed as a missionary to Oregon, where he was pastor of the Congregational church in Oregon City, 1848-1863, when he moved to Portland in the same State. He was Superintendent of the Am. Home Missionary Society for Oregon and Washington, from 1880 until his death. He died Feb. 25, 1889. He married October 8, 1846, Miss Nancy, daughter of Deacon Phineas, Bates of Springfield, Vt. See Tenney's Hist. Dartmouth Class, 1843, pp. 17-18.

He published two sermons, "Preaching Christ," at the ordination of Thomas Condon, in 1853; "Church Polity," before the Oregon Association, in 1859; he was a liberal contributor to the "Home Missionary," and to other periodicals on the Atlantic coast.

Atlas Maps. See Beers, F. W.; Addison, Bennington, Chittenden, Orange, Rutland, Washington, Windham and Windsor Counties.

Atwater, Jeremiah. *A Sermon,* preached before His Excellency, Isaac Tichenor, Esq., Governor, The Honorable, the Council, and House of Representatives of the State of Vermont at Burlington, on the Day of the Anniversary Election, Oct. 14, 1802. By Jeremiah Atwater, President of Middlebury College. Middlebury: Printed by Huntington & Fitch, for Anthony Haswell, Printer to the State. 1802. 8vo, pp. 39.

Mr. Atwater was a native of New Haven, Conn., and was graduated at Yale College, 1793; he was the first principal of Addison County Grammar School organized in 1797, and also the first President of Middlebury College, which position he held 1800-1809. He then removed to Pennsylvania, and thence, in 1815, to his native town, New Haven, Conn,, where he died in July, 1858, aged 84.

Atwater, Wilbur Olin. Report on Farm Experiments with Fertilizers. 1878. By Prof. W. O. Atwater. Motto. From the Report of the Connecticut Board of Agriculture for 1878. No imprint. 8vo, pp. 68.

Prof. W. O. Atwater is a son of W. W. Atwater, late publisher of the Vermont Directory and Commercial Almanac, (See Almanac, ante.) He entered the University of Vermont from Brandon, in 1861; graduated from Wesleyan University in 1865; pursued his studies in Chemistry in the Sheffield Scientific School (Yale) and in the Universities of Leipsic, Berlin and Munich; Professor of Chemistry University of East Tennessee, (Knoxville) 1871-3; Prof. of Chemistry Wesleyan University 1873-91; Director of U. S. Experiment Stations, U. S. Dept. of Agriculture, 1888 to date (1896); State Chemist of Connecticut, 1888 to date.

Author of "Materials of Plant Growth," 1879; "Chemical Plant Food," 1879; "The American Menhaden," New York, 1879; "Nutritive Qualities of Various Kinds of Fish," 1880; "Soil Supply of Nitrogen for Plants," 1881; "Fertilizers," U. S. Gov't Printing Office, 1882; "Pecuniary Economy of Foods," New York, 1888; "Foods and Beverages" 1888, and of numerous essays and papers on similar subjects contributed to scientific and agricultural journals in America, Germany and France. He is a recognized authority on such subjects on both sides of the Atlantic.

Atwill, Rev. E. R. *Sermon* on the death of Helen Leslie Underwood, (who died January 20th, 1873, aged 20 years and 7 months). By Rev. E. R. Atwill, Rector, at St. Paul's Church, Burlington, Vt., Sunday, January 26th, 1873. Burlington: Free Press Association. 8vo, pp. 20.

—*A Few Words to Children* of the Church about Confirmation, by E. R. Atwill, Rector of St. Paul's Church, Burlington, Vt. Burlington: Free Press Print. 1873. 8vo, pp. 8.

—*A Sermon* delivered in St. Paul's Church, Burlington, Vt., at a Service Celebrating the Fiftieth Anniversary of the Founding of the Parish, by the Rector, Rev. E. R. Atwill. Burlington: The Free Press Association. 1881. 8vo., pp. 20.

Preached June 12, 1881.

Austin, Rev. L. A. *Memorial* of Mary White Wicker, A Funeral Sermon delivered at Ticonderoga, N. Y., Aug. 26, 1865, by Rev. L. A. Austin, of Orwell, Vt. Printed by request, exclusively for private circulation. Andover: Printed by Warren F. Draper. 1865. 8vo, pp. 60.

Mr. Austin was born in Poultney, Vt., April 26, 1834; was graduated at Middlebury College in 1856; pastor of the Congregational church in Orwell, Vt., 1862-68; teacher in Manchester, Vt., 1869-72, and in Meriden, N. H., 1873-75; acting pastor at Plainfield, N. H., 1876 until 1880.

Austin, Samuel, of Tunbridge, Vt. *Reflections on Crimes and Punishments.* 12mo, pp. 12. n. p. n. d.

Mr. Austin was a member of the Legislature from Tunbridge in the years 1815,'16,'18,'19,'21,'22,'24, and 1825; he also held most of the town offices at various times.

Austin, Rev. Samuel. *Funeral Oration*, on Mr. David Ripley, of Windham, A Junior Sophister in Yale College, who died June 11, 1782, Ætat 22. Pronounced in the College Chapel, July 11, 1782. By Samuel Austin, a Classmate of the Deceased. New Haven: Printed by Thomas and Samuel Green. M.DCC.-LXXIII. sm. 4to, pp. 12.

The first publication of Samuel Austin.

—*The Evangelical Preacher*, a faithful, and an affectionate Preacher of Christ. A Sermon, delivered at the Ordination of the Rev. Leonard Worcester, to the Pastoral care of the Church in Peacham, Vt., October 30th, 1799. By Samuel Austin, A. M., Pastor of a Church in Worcester. Peacham, Vt.: Printed by Farley & Goss. 1800. 8vo, pp. 32.

The charge by the Rev. Noah Worcester, of Thornton, and the Right Hand of Fellowship by the Rev. Thomas Worcester, of Salisbury.

—*Masonic Oration in 1810.* See *Masonic.*

—*An Inaugural Address,* pronounced in Burlington, July 26, 1815, by Samuel Austin, D. D., President of the University of Vermont. Published by request of the Corporation. Burlington: Printed by Francis G. Fish. August, 1815. 8vo, pp. 18.

—*Religion The Glory of a Community.* A Sermon, Preached on the Day of General Election, at Montpelier, October 10, 1816, before the Honorable Legislature of Vermont. By Samuel Austin, D. D., President of the University of Vermont. Montpelier, Vt.: Printed by Walton and Goss, October, 1816. 8vo, pp. 27.

Rev. Samuel Austin was born at New Haven, Conn., October 7th, 1760; died at Glastenbury, Conn., December 4th, 1830; was graduated at Yale College, 1783; licensed to preach in 1784, settled at Fairhaven, Conn., in 1786, and in 1790 accepted a call to Worcester, Mass., where he became very popular, and continued his labors there until 1815, when he accepted a call to the Presidency of the University of Vermont; which position he resigned in 1821. On taking charge of the University he wrote: "Here I am, a solitary stranger, without my family; attempting to raise and render useful and respectable this institution. There are nine students at present; the number gradually increasing. I feel low." During the war of 1812 the University was necessarily closed for a considerable period.

Upon leaving Burlington, Mr. Austin was settled over a church at Newport, R. I., for four years, when increasing age and infirmities compelled him to resign active pastoral labors. See memoir in Am. Qr. Register. Vol. 9, pp. 201-220.

Avery, David. *A Sermon* preached at Greenwich, Ct., on the 18th of December, 1777, being A General Thanksgiving through the United American States. By David Avery, V. D. M., Chaplain to Col. Sherburne's Regiment. Motto. Norwich: (Conn.) Printed by Green & Spooner. 1778. 8vo.

See Jennings' "Memorials of A Century," Bennington, pp. 88-92; Bennington, "Meeting of the Church," etc.

—*Election Sermon,* 1780.

—*A Narrative* of the Rise and Progress of the Difficulties which have issued in a Separation between the Minister and People of Bennington, 1783, with a Valedictory Address. Bennington: Haswell and Russell, printers. 1783. 8vo, pp. 55.

Mr. Avery was the Congregational pastor at Bennington, May, 1780 to 1783.

Avery, W. W. and Davis, H. B. *Description of Vermont State Houses.* See *Vermont Capitol.*

Bailey, Mrs. Abigail. *Memoir of Mrs. Abigail Bailey.* By herself, with additions by her pastor. (Abigail Abbott, dau. of Dea. James Abbott of Newbury, b. 1746; d. 1815.) 207 p. p.

[Mr. F. P. Wells says: "This is rare, the only copy I know of has the title page torn out. It was written in Newbury.]

Bailey, B. F. *An Oration*, delivered at Burlington, Vt., on the Fourth of July, 1828, being the Fifty-Second Anniversary of American Independence. By B. F. Bailey, Esq. Burlington: Printed by E. & T. Mills. 1828. 8vo, pp. 18.

Mr. Bailey was born at Guildhall, Vt., in 1796, and died in Burlington, Vt., May 23, 1832. He was a lawyer and prominent citizen of Burlington. See Vt. Hist. Mag., Vol. I, pp. 646-7.

Bailey, Rev. Albert H., D. D. *Historical Sketch of the Protestant Episcopal Church in Vermont*, being a Sermon preached before the Special Convention, at Burlington, March 11th, 1868, on the occasion of the election of the second Bishop of Vermont.

Published pp. 7-23 of Journal of Convention of Protestant Episcopal Church of the Diocese of Vermont, 1868.

Bailey, Phinehas. *An Important System of Stenography*, containing Analagous Abbreviations, adapted to the convenience of Instructors and Practitioners. By Phinehas Bailey. Third Edition, enlarged and improved. Poultney, Vt.: Printed by Smith & Streeter. 1822. 18mo., pp. 44.

—*A Pronouncing Stenography*, containing a complete system of Short Hand Writing. Governed by the analogy of sounds, and Adapted to every language. By Phinehas Bailey. Second Edition. Burlington: Edward Smith. 1833. 16mo., pp. 32.

I am indebted to Mrs. P. L. Hopkins, of East Berkshire, Vt., a daughter of Mr. Bailey, for the following sketch of her father :

Mr. Bailey was born in Landaff, N. H., in 1787, was the youngest son of Major Asa Bailey, "a man of superior intellect, perseverance and energy," and Abigail Abbott, a woman of great moral strength and "devoted piety." She was a daughter of Dea. James Abbott, of Concord, N. H., a descendant of George Abbott, the venerable ancestor who emigrated from Yorkshire, England, 1640, and was one of the first settlers in Andover, Mass., 1643.

Sterling piety seems to have been the marked character of the Abbott family. It is said of one that "he was a puritan in faith and conduct." Of another, "he had ten sons and two daughters trained up in the covenant." Mrs. Bailey too, "through her unwearied faithfulness was enabled to see all of her children hopefully pious." To her faithful efforts and to his early consecration in baptism, Phinehas attributed his after course of life.

When Phinehas was four years old his mother was left with only six hundred dollars to provide for her younger children. When five years old he went to live with an older sister on a large farm; here he exercised his ingenuity in constructing little mill works in the brook, and odd little traps for mice.

As the boy bears the type of the man, so Phinehas in childhood often evinced the courage, bravery and ingenuity that characterized him afterwards; and his artless attractive ways "foreshowed a gentle heart." When a little boy he was sent with a little sister into the woods after the cow. He returned with the story that "a great black dog came close up to his sister in the woods and he took a big stick and drove him off." The next morning a few men went out and killed a large bear near the place where the children had seen him. Years after when telling the story to his own children, and being asked "why the bear did not eat him and his little sister up?" he replied, "my mother's *prayers* kept the bear from hurting us."

At one time going along the road alone, when a small boy, he was suddenly overcome with love and gratitude for one of his older sisters; and he knelt right down by the roadside and thanked the Lord for giving him such a *handsome* sister ! Later in life he was often as suddenly moved by the same sweet impulse—to kneel and thank the Lord for some good gift.

At fourteen years of age he was apprenticed to Mr. John Osgood, of Haverhill, N. H. At the expiration of his apprenticeship he settled in Chelsea, Vt., and formed a co-partnership with a man having the same trade as his own, who furnished the stock and tools, while Phinehas furnished the labor. While living in Chelsea Mr. Bailey united with the Congregational church, and also married there.

From the time of his conversion to the Christian religion, when about eighteen years of age, Mr. Bailey felt a strong desire to preach the gospel; but the want of proper education and means to obtain it, seemed fatal obstacles in the way. He found the barrier between him and the ministry growing more and more insurmountable every day.

Very early in his religious experience he formed the resolution that "always in public or private he would improve every opportunity to recommend the religion of Christ." In the large village of Haverhill he went from house to house and prayed and exhorted in nearly every family.

At one time he pressed into a bar-room and exhorted those who were swearing to desist. One of the men said "that was no place to preach !" another said "that Mr. Bailey had as good a right to preach there as they had to swear." Several swearers never used another profane word in his hearing.

Again in Franconia, N. H., he went into a store to repair a watch, but hearing a man in the store using very profane language, he gathered up his tools and went to a private house and asked for a table, saying, that a man in yonder store was so profane he could not stay there. Of course the remark was quickly carried back to the store. This village was chiefly owned by a manufacturing company. The agent was greatly concerned for the reputation of the place, and was unwilling to have it said that the inhabitants were so profane that a stranger could not stay in the place; and finally through the agent the profane man apologized. Mr. Bailey was soon solicited to help settle a difficulty between a Baptist brother and a deacon. The agent much interested collected witnesses for the trial while Mr. Bailey went to each party and made them agree to meet, and by the time the agent had got his witnesses and people together, there was no need of any trial; the brethren confessed to each other with penitence and tears; a prayer meeting followed, and the result of this incident was a revival of religion. Such were some of Mr. Bailey's efforts to serve his Redeemer while at work in his humble calling.

In 1818 there was a glorious revival in Chelsea, numbering about seventy converts besides many enlivened Christians. In the midst of this work of grace a ball was appointed; one of the managers being a young man who had been seriously impressed. Christians felt that such a gathering would hinder the Master's work, and assembled the same evening for the purpose of trying to *stop* the festivities by prayer. Just as the praying and dancing began, there came up a terrible thunder storm. The festive music and the thunder rose higher and higher, " but above and beyond all rose the low voice of prayer, reaching even to the throne of God." In a few minutes the dance was hushed and heard no more that night. The next day Mr. Bailey was accosted with, " Well, you got together last night to pray that we all might be struck with lightning, but you didn't make out to kill anybody!"

Again there was to be a grand county ball in Newbury, and again Christians determined to meet it with prayer; and again the ball was a complete failure. The hotel keeper complained bitterly to one of the praying brethren of the great loss *they* had caused him. Who would think of complaining of the *praying brethren*, for the failure of a ball in 1879 ! There are many accounts relating to his earnest "gospel work"—as we should call it now—which seem of great interest in these later drowsy times; we will mention but one more.

In one of the towns adjoining Chelsea the church was chiefly composed of old people. The younger seemed to think that religion was not made for them. Some of the live Christians of Chelsea sent word that they were going there to attend a meeting. They accordingly set out, a company of gospel workers, many of whom were young converts; one, a little girl only twelve years of age and very diffident. Some said "why not take some one who can talk?" On the way Mr. Bailey said to her, " If God gives you a message to those careless sinners, you will try and deliver it, will you?" She replied "I will try." The result of this gospel visit was a revival in that place.

From the time of that revival Mr. Bailey felt an ardent desire to preach the gospel. Night and day it was on his mind; but he saw no way of extricating himself from debt and supporting his family while studying to fit himself for so great a work. If this great desire of his heart, to be in the ministry, was indeed the call of God, what had he to do but to ask for the needed help and receive? He *did* ask that if it was his duty to become a minister he might be freed from debt and furnished the means of obtaining an education. About this time he accidentally found an old system of stenography, and according to his characteristic of searching out everything there was to be found out, he began to study the little pamphlet, never dreaming that in this would be found the answer to his prayers. He studied the book until he discovered the beauty of the idea of stenography, and enough to see the faults which suggested the thought of a system on an entirely original plan—to have *one sound for every letter and one letter for every sound*—and he worked unceasingly until he had got his work into type and print, which was first brought out in 1819 in Poultney, Vt., and afterwards it went through many editions. Some time previous to this Mr. Bailey had given up his trade, and depended upon teaching the higher branches, and after his system of short hand was published he easily earned from sixty to a hundred dollars per month; but he only looked upon it as the stepping stone to something higher. He gained access to different libraries and bought some books as he could, studying all of his leisure time. He went to Middlebury and was assisted by the college professors, though not as a regular student.

He studied Latin, Greek and Hebrew, logic, rhetoric, and nearly all of the studies that lie between the A, B, C and a finished education. Though he could never boast of a college education, he possessed a well stored mind; acquired by the most unaccountable energy and persistency. His acquisition of so much knowledge was partly owing to self-esteem, and a will to conquer everything! He would never for a moment admit that there was anything that he could not and would not grasp. In later years all of the difficult questions and problems that could be found were brought to him by his children, as puzzles; but he would never give up without mastering them. By teaching, his phonography principally, he was enabled to cancel his debts and buy more books.

Scott Brown in the "Phonographic Monthly," New York, says of his work: "Phinehas Bailey gives in his first edition published in 1819, as complete an analysis of the elements of our language as exists in the works of any Phonetician, and more complete than can be found in any lexicography. No consonant element, no fine shades of vowel sounds have been discovered and presented to the public, that Mr. Bailey had not discovered and presented in his little book fifty-seven years ago, away up among the green mountains of Old Vermont. There is not a recognized element of our language that Mr. Bailey has not furnished with a sign of its possessing positive value."

"We do not know that Isaac Pitman ever heard of Mr. Bailey or his Phonetic system, so that both men may deserve equal credit; but it is considerable for our people to be proud of, that in the practical application of Phonetics to the stenographic representation of our language, young America was ahead of Old England eighteen years. The people of New England, especially Vermont, will feel a just pride in this."

Dr. Julius Waldemar Zeibig, in his "History and Literature of Stenography," recently published, has given to Mr. Bailey the deserving place of priority in the invention of Phonography.

He studied theology under Rev. Calvin Noble, of Chelsea, Vt., and in 1823, was licensed to preach by the Orange Association in Thetford, Vt. He preached his first sermon in the town of Washington, and soon after, hearing of a vacant pulpit in Berkshire, started for that place; but on his way was detained by the people of Richmond and Waterbury and invited to preach alternately in the two places a year. He returned for his family; the morning arrived for the last good-bye to friends, and the last tears to fall, on the threshold of the little place that had been their home for thirteen years. A company of friends gathered around the door and sang a verse of the hymn, "Pilgrims, farewell." The venerable Mr. Noble grasped the young brother's hand and with his parting blessing said, "Until now you have had ministers and teachers to lead you in the way of life, but henceforth you are to lead others."

Mr. Bailey received a call from Waterbury and from Richmond to settle; but for some reason preferred to go to Berkshire. In September, 1824, he was ordained over the two churches of East and West Berkshire—the first settled minister in town.

Here he labored arduously, being his first charge; and he being the first pastor the church ever had, they were trusting and confiding in him. During his pastorate of ten years, sixty were added to the church. He owed his effectual labors greatly to his pastoral visits; going to every house in the course of the year for the purpose of talking with each individual about their spiritual welfare. His labors in this way were marked with many wonderful conversions, and a great revival in 1831.

His idea of authority was implicit obedience "to the powers that be"—to parents, teachers, or rulers. Sometimes he administered reproof to his family, or to his people with great severity; and sometimes with a little cunning and wit. At one time one of the deacons usually at his post, was absent at the prayer meeting,—it being a very rainy, windy night in the fall of the year, scarcely any one was present. After all the brethren who were there had "done their duty," the meeting was closed—not very late of course, and the few went home. Mr. Bailey took his tin lantern and walked a mile and a half up hill to the deacon's. The deacon tremblingly invited the minister to sit down, for now he expected a sharp reproof or the "first step of labor;" but to his surprise the minister seemed very happy, and sat down by the cheerful old fire-place and chatted about everything but the weather and the meeting. A dish of the deacon's good apples were eaten, a pleasant hour slipped by, and the minister took his leave. The deacon understood very well that if the minister could go there to call and not hurt him, *he* could go to prayer meeting; and his place was not vacant again for so trivial a cause as *rain* and *mud*.

After a while Mr. Bailey thought he better seek a new field; it might be better for the people and better for himself. There were a few immovable hearts that possibly might be impressed under other teachers, and they were a burden upon his mind; but when he came back years afterwards and found the same stationary souls, and the church scattered, he felt that he erred in leaving them when he did.

In 1833, he asked for a dimission, and was finally dismissed by a council. He then removed to Beekmantown, N. Y., preached four years, when he found himself disabled by the bronchitis. Now he thought was the time to commence an undertaking that appears to have been on his mind for some years. We find from an old letter written by his younger son from Burlington in 1834 that Mr. Bailey had been urging him to come home and print a Berean paper with him—the son was a printer by trade. The son says, "I hope you will not be grieved when I tell you that although I have no doubt your desire of having me print a Biblical paper is founded on the purest of motives for doing good, yet I view it beyond 'my power and limits to accomplish it; it is impossible! 'Count the cost,' is a good maxim, founded on reason and the Bible; therefore I hope you will not think of so extravagant an undertaking."

But he could not give up what he knew would be such a valuable acquisition in teaching the Bible. He removed to Essex, N. Y., and succeeded in getting the *promises* of a great many good people to support "A weekly paper devoted to the study of the Bible;" and some gave him money, expressing their fears at the same time. The oldest son was persuaded to undertake the work with him, and the paper was issued, "The Berean Guide," "A weekly paper devoted to the study of the Bible." The design was to have all Sabbath Schools and families pursuing the *same scripture* at *the same time.* This as far as we know, was the first advancement of this beautiful idea. The Prospectus says: "We hope to render assistance to Bible classes by furnishing them from time to time with interesting questions and profitable answers."

This grand conception was too early for those times. Mr. Bailey could not be made to believe two things; namely, that it cost a great deal of money to publish a paper for one object alone, like that; and that people would be *slow* to appreciate and support it.

In view of all the Sunday School *organs*—and some pretty weak ones—of different societies that find abundant support now, we sometimes wonder at the dealings of Providence that could not so order such an undertaking to prosper even forty-one years ago. (?) But it went down as hopeless, in a very short time.

Mr. Bailey then went to preaching again, first in Ticonderoga, then in Hebron, N. Y. and back to Berkshire again in 1845. We have passed hastily over the years—the history of his own family, the dark days of suffering and want, over the *deep* waters of affliction that God called him to pass through, as if to see how much human nature could endure, or to "show him how great things he must suffer for His sake;" he who was so anxious to take up Christ's work learned the same lesson that Paul did. Yet in those darkest days he could often rend the blackest cloud by prayer; during his life he received some of the most wonderful answers to prayer that have ever been recorded—prayer for house and home, food and raiment, as well as spiritual blessings. Prayer for daily bread was no vain petition upon his lips. He had unlimited faith in prayer.

He believed that in some cases when great favors are sought, the ear of heaven must be reached by fasting and prayer. Thus at such times he had in the seclusion of the fireside *family* fasts; and in times of coldness and declension in the church, he appointed *church* fasts.

At this time previous to Mr. Bailey's going to Berkshire, the family had such a fast. Mr. Bailey went to New York and on his way home he spent the Sabbath in Troy, with the pastor of the Free church, preaching for him half of the day. In the evening he went into conference meeting and asked for prayer—that he might be directed to a place of labor. The next morning he received a note from a lady, containing a small present and these words, "Go where God directs, do what He bids thee, and He will bear your expenses." It seemed like a heavenly message, and he resolved to obey it literally.

On his way home from Troy he fell in with an old friend who said to him, "I want you to go to Berkshire." Mr. Bailey replied "I will go." We think his trials and afflictions were never afterward as great as in the previous years. He remained in Berkshire until 1852, when he again left.

Mr. Bailey had a strong will and great force of character which necessarily must be the leader; this with his eccentricities gained for him some enemies. In his theology he was called "more Calvinistic than Calvin." He wrote 2,700 sermons, nor did he ever try to shy, or cover anything of those tougher doctrines of the Bible which ministers do not dare so much as read in the pulpit now. Yet under his administration he gathered more converts than they do under the smooth, galvanized, trumpery preaching of 1879. Many of his so-called eccentricities, his children can now look back upon with just pride.

From Berkshire he removed to Albany, Vt., and purchased a small farm. Here he spent his last days very happily; and here hidden away among the mountains of Vermont, in January, 1861, he laid down his cross for a glorious crown. He was carried back to his old home and buried among his first people. As we bowed very low over the frozen, waiting tomb, where terrors cringe and shiver with ice and cold, we could see and believe in the resurrection as never before—"The body sown in corruption, and raised in incorruption, sown in dishonor, and raised in glory." No wonder "the women turned from the sepulchre with great joy," when they found the grave had no power over the one they loved so well. Whether we choose for our precious dead some "dewy hill" mid sun and warmth and flowers, or some cave deep and dank with mould; and though a great stone be rolled against the door, it matters not; we know "they are not there, but have risen!"

> No more to feel life's rude winds blow,
> Or griefs that chill us as the snow,
> Or view our hopes go drifting by,
> Oh I never more to sigh or weep—
> He giveth His beloved sleep.

Bailey, Rufus William. *The Magnitude* of the Ministerial Office illustrated from the value of the soul. A sermon delivered July 4, 1821, at the ordination of Rev. Dana Clayes, to the pastoral care of the Church and Society in Meriden Parish, Plainfield, N. H. By Rufus William Bailey, A. M., Minister of Norwich, Vt. Hanover, N. H.: Printed by Ridley Bannister. 1821. 8vo, pp. 32.

—*An Address*, delivered at the close of the Sabbath School on Norwich Plain, November 9, 1819. By R. W. Bailey, Pastor of the South Church. Woodstock: Printed by David Watson. 1820. 8vo, pp. 12.

A Bake-Pan, *for Dough-Faces.* See Marsh, Leonard.

Baker, John C. *Sketches of an Excursion* through Vermont and among the White Mountains of New Hampshire, etc., etc., in 1864 and 1865. By John C. Baker. Montreal: 1869. 8vo, pp. 38.

Originally printed in the "Montreal Daily Witness," under the title of "A Buggy Ride among the Hills and Dales of New England.

Baker, Joseph. *Essays on the Civil Law.* By Joseph Baker. Montpelier: Printed at the Universalist Watchman Office. 1846. 12mo, pp. 44.

Bakersfield. *Exercises and Addresses* at the opening of Brigham Academy, Bakersfield, Vt., Thursday, August 14, 1879, with Appendix. Andover: Printed by Warren F. Draper. 1880. 8vo, pp. 56.

Balch, Rev. William S. *Lectures on Language*: As particularly connected with English Grammar. Designed for the use of Teachers and advanced Learners. By Wm. S. Balch. Motto. Providence: B. Cranston & Co., 1838. 12mo, pp. 252.

—*A Manual for Sunday Schools.* To which is added a Collection of Hymns. By Wm. S. Balch. Motto. Boston: A. Tompkins, 32 Cornhill. 1839. 16mo, pp. 144.

—*A Grammar of the English Language.* Explained according to the principles of Truth and common Sense, and adapted to the Capacities of all who think. Designed for the use of Schools, Academies and private Learners. By Wm. S. Balch. Second edition. Boston: B. B. Mussey, 29 Cornhill. 1840. 12mo.

First edition, 1839. Same imprint.

—*Ireland as I saw it.* The Character, Condition and Prospects of the People. By Wm. S. Balch. Motto. New York: Henry Lyon, 333 Broadway. Auburn: Vincent Kenyon, 96 Genessee St. Third edition. 1852. 12mo, pp. 432.

First edition by G. P. Putnam. N. Y. 1849.

—*A Brief Sketch of the Life of Christ.* Catechetically arranged, in the order of a Harmony of the Gospels. Designed for the use of small children in Sabbath Schools and private Families. By Rev. W. S. Balch. Motto. Fourth Edition. Boston: The Universalist Publishing House. No. 37 Cornhill. 16mo, pp. 56.

First published by Marsh and Capen, Boston, 1830, and many thousands sold.

—*The Constitution and By-Laws of the Young People's Institute.* Providence, R. I. Knowles, Vose & Co. 1837. pp. 8.

—*A Brief Account of the Last Moments of Rev. Aaron Leland Balch.* Published by Josiah Perkins. Fall River: 1840. pp. 12.

—*Circular to the Universalists of Rhode Island*, and Proceedings and Circular of the R. I. Convention of Universalists, (First Session). Held in Providence, April 11th and 12th, 1838. Providence: B. T. Albro. 1838. 12mo, pp. 16.

The same for April 16th and 17th, 1839, held at Cumberland; same for April 8th and 9th, 1840, at Woonsocket. pp. 12.

—*Individual Freedom the Foundation of a Democratic Government.* An Oration, Delivered in Pawtucket, Rhode Island, July 4th, 1839. By Wm. S. Balch. Pawtucket: Sherman & Kennicut. 1839. pp. 34.

—*Popular Liberty and Equal Rights.* An Oration, delivered before the Mass Convention of the R. I. Suffrage Association, held on Dexter Training Ground, in Providence, July Fifth, 1841. By Wm. S. Balch. Providence: B. F. Moore, Printer, 19 Market St. 1841. pp. 24.

—*The Constitution and By-Laws of the Western Mutual Improvement Association.* Organized in New York, April 3, 1844. New World Press. xxx Ann St. pp. 12.

—*Political and Social Equality.* A Sermon preached on Thanksgiving Day, Dec. 14, 1844, in the Bleeker Street Church. By Rev. Wm. S. Balch. New York: E. Winchester. New World Press, 24 Ann St. 1845. pp. 22.

—*Repentance:* Tract No. 3, pp. 4.

—*Punishment and Forgiveness :* Tract No. 4, pp. 4.

Being Nos. 34 and 36 as published by the "Woman's Centenary Association," of the Universalist Church.

—*Romanism and Republicanism Incompatible.* A Lecture, delivered in the Broadway Tabernacle, Monday Evening, April 5th, 1852, in review of "The Catholic Chapter in the History of the United States," as written by the Most Rev. John Hughes, D. D., Archbishop of New York. By Wm. S. Balch. New York : Dewitt & Davenport, Tribune Building, Nassau St. 1852. pp. 38.

—*A Class Book for Sunday Schools :* containing a correct system for keeping the entire records of each Sabbath, the name, age and residence of each scholar, and a blank form for making a Report at the end of each term : With directions for the management of schools. By Wm. S. Balch. Motto. New York : P. Price. 1845. pp. 24.

Now published by J. S. Cantwell, Cincinnati, Ohio.

—*Dangers of our Republic :* An Oration, delivered in Chester, Vt., July 4th, 1857. By Wm. S. Balch. New York : A. Taylor & Son, No. 40 Sixth Avenue. 1857. pp. 24.

—*Constitution and Rules of Order* of the General Convention of Universalists in the United States of America. Adopted 1855. New York : A. Taylor & Son. 1857. 16mo. pp. 16.

—*The Spirit Life.* A Discourse delivered in the Methodist Church at Richlands, North Carolina, November 15, 1868, at the Funeral service of John M. Frank. By Wm. S. Balch. Published by Request. Galesburg, Ill. 1868. 8vo, pp. 20.

—*Hard Times : The Cause and Cure.* A Lecture by Rev. W. S. Balch, delivered in Elgin, (Ill.) Dec. 28, 1873. pp. 8.

—*A Peculiar People ; or, Reality in Romance.* By William S. Balch. Second edition, Revised. Motto. Chicago : Henry A. Sumner & Co. 1882. 12mo, pp. 452.

[Letter from Rev. Mr. Balch, dated Dubuque, Iowa, March 1878.]

"In addition to the above I edited and published "*The Impartialist,*" a weekly paper in Claremont, N. H., in 1834-5; and for four years was joint editor and publisher of the "*Christian Messenger,*" a folio, and the "*Christian Ambassador*" R'l 8vo., both weekly papers in New York city.

I have delayed answering till now, as my books are in Elgin, where I went last week and copied the titles. I have not all of those books to spare, but will send a portion when I am there again ; I forgot that you desired copies or I should have sent them.

I add a brief notice of my early life, the most important portion, the foundation of any man's character and success. I hope you will not regard it as boastful on my part. I have tried to be modest. You will use it as shall seem to you best."

Fraternally,

WM. S. BALCH.

William Stevens Balch was born in Andover, Vt., April 13, 1806. He came up, like most sons of farmers in obscure towns, at hard work and a small chance for an education. He attended the district school three months in summer until eight years old, and three in winter till sixteen; when, having mastered all studies taught in such schools, his father permitted him to start on foot for Reading, to study with Rev. Mr. Loveland. Four miles from home he stopped to warm himself, and was induced to "take a school," at $7.50 a month and "board round." Eight weeks ended the engagement, when he was invited to an adjoining district to fill out the term of the "master,

turned out," at $8 a month ! The next summer his brother in New York city sent for him to assist in a private school —St. John's Academy; his father purchased him a vest for 83 cents, and gave him $8, all he could raise for the journey. He laid stone wall until 3 o'clock P. M., the day before leaving. A brother-in-law took him to the top of the Green Mountain in Peru, where he cut a cane and started into the world on foot, as far as Albany; there he engaged passage on a sloop at $3 for the city. He arrived there so shabby in his dress that his brother went next day to a second hand shop and rigged him for appearance in the streets. He remained but three months. The confinement injured his health ; and he despised what appeared to him the show and sham of city life. Without consulting his brother until fully resolved to return home he bought a passage on a sloop for Albany, leaving but 50 cents, and when there over 80 miles from home. At Lansingburg he bought a loaf of bread and half a pound of cheese, all he had to eat until reaching home. Tramps were not in fashion in those days. Two nights at a shilling, the usual price, left him 15 cents. This journey and the sight and air of his native hills cured him, and he at once engaged in the last school of the former winter. The day before it ended he was requested to fill an unexpired term in Chester, at $10 ! Such an offer he could not reject. His father did, on the ground it was a bad school, and he would lose what reputation he had gained. But he replied that he had agreed to go, and if he did his best he could not be blamed, as if he broke his contract by not trying. His father consented, and he succeeded to the full satisfaction of all. At 20 he was again invited to New York, where he taught a year. At 21 he engaged to continue, at $150. In less than a month a schoolmate came to the city seeking a place and offering to loan him $25 for three years, the first without interest. The offer was accepted, and satisfactory to all. With that sum he bought his first outfit, and started out as a lecturer on grammar, by the recommendation of Daniel H. Barnes, the founder of the high school system, and W. S. Cadell,, the author of a grammar. His first attempt was in Poughkeepsie, and very successful, realizing enough to take up his note and help him on his way, also a laudatory recommendation from the chief men of the place. In Hudson, Greenbush, Albany and Troy he met with good success. In Troy he had a large class, and gave private explanations to Mrs. Willard, of the Female Academy. Returning home, he entered the study of Rev. Mr. Loveland, to prepare for the ministry. In September an older preacher applied for fellowship and persuaded him to submit to an examination by the General Convention of Saratoga. A letter was given him. From that day to the present time his controlling thought and work have been devoted to the duties of his vocation ; not in the role of a sectarian, but as a teacher and helper of his fellowmen, on the broad principle of Universal Love, devoting himself to truth, right and humanity, but never to creed or sect, or rank, when they came into conflict. He has always preferred truth in another to error in himself. From sectarian and party schemes and plannings he has always kept aloof. When asked by his maternal grandfather, an Orthodox deacon, "Why he had decided to be a preacher?" " To help make the world better and happier," was his reply. The old man, then on his deathbed, laid his hands on his head, saying, "God bless you, my son, and guide and keep you in the path of duty."

From the outset he joined temperance and moral reforms with his preaching and wherever he has been his sympathy has been with the erring, the wronged and the suffering ; and tongue, pen and hands have been ready to help relieve. In all things he has been open, bold and generous, but never willing to act from policy at the dictate of another. While settled in Providence, he was among the first and most active to secure a "Republican Form of Government" for that State, which it did not enjoy living under the Royal Charter of Charles II. He was settled in New York before party power crushed the rights of the people. He has always been successful as a preacher, and highly esteemed as a man wherever he has lived. Twice he has sought the retirement of rural life, but nowhere has he been allowed to remain inactive, and at the age of 72 he is working as hard and successful as ever. Twice his friends have sought to honor him with two useless letters, D. D., but in both cases he has refused to accept them as not in accord with the humble spirit of the Master. While residing in Ludlow he was elected to represent that town in the Legislature, but without his knowledge or desire. In his second election he felt some interest, but said not a word to secure it. He was once offered, with every assurance of an overwhelming majority, the candidacy for Congress in one of the strongest Republican districts in Illinois. He refused all entreaties; saying he was not ordained to such a service, and, being thoroughly independent of party, he did not see how he could be of service in such a position. An obscure Democrat was elected by near 2,000, and all Democrats were ready to vote for him.

The labors of Mr. Balch have not been confined to his parishes. He has traveled and preached and lectured extensively in the Eastern, Middle and Western States, and has been several times into the Southern to preach and attend funerals, going one time 1,700 miles, and many times over 1,000. He has twice visited and traveled extensively in Europe; the last time extending his journey through Greece, Turkey, Syria, Palestine and Egypt, as far as Nubia, not curiously, but visiting most of the important places known to history. The early years of his ministry were darkened by ill-health, induced by over-study and ignorance of the laws of health, but for thirty years he has been vigorous, and capable of endurance as in his youth, and in nothing neglectful of his duties as a man and a minister.

Mr. Balch accepted a call to the pastorate of the Universalist Church at Dubuque, Iowa, in the spring of 1877, and at the end of the year desired to retire from active labor, but at the urgent request of the church and society continued as their pastor.

Mr. Balch died at Elgin, Ill., during the last days of December, 1887, or the first days of January, 1888.

Baldwin, Daniel. *A Memorial Service* held in the Church of the Messiah, Montpelier, Vt., August 7th, 1881. Printed for private distribution. 8vo, pp. 18.

See Miss Hemenway's Gazetteer of Vt., vol. IV, article Montpelier.

Baldwin, Frederick W. *Biography of the Bar of Orleans County,* Vermont, By Frederick W. Baldwin, Barton, Vt. Montpelier, Watchman Press, 1886. Royal 8vo, pp. 303.

Contains 175 biographical sketches and many portraits. "The aim of the author has been to give a more or less extended biography of every lawyer in regular standing ever in this County, also a few pioneers of the profession, who in the early days made the bar of Northeastern Vermont famous."

Baldwin, Thomas. *Open Communion Examined;* or, a brief Defence of the practice of Close Communionists. Windsor, Vt., 1789. 8vo.

Ball, Heman. *A Sermon* delivered before the Worshipful Master, the Wardens and Brethren of Union Lodge, at Middlebury, June 27th, 1797; being the festival of St. John the Baptist. By Heman Ball, A. M. Pastor of a church in Rutland, Vermont. Published at the request of the Lodge. Printed at Rutland, Vermont, by Josiah Fay, for S. Williams & Co., MDCCXCVII. 12mo, pp. 23.

—*Sermon* at Rutland, Vt., January 1, 1800, on the Death of George Washington. Rutland: 1800. 8vo.

—*The Faithful Minister.* A Sermon, delivered at Wallingford, November 10th, 1802, at the Installation of the Rev. Benjamin Osborn, to the Pastoral Care of the Congregational Church and Society in that town. By Heman Ball, A. M., Minister of the Gospel, Rutland, Vt. Rutland: Printed by Stephen Hodgman. M.DCCC II. 12mo, pp. 18.

—*A Sermon,* Preached before His Excellency, Isaac Tichenor, Esq., Governor; His Honor Paul Brigham, Esq., Lieutenant-Governor; The Honorable Council, and House of Representatives of the State of Vermont: At Rutland October 11, 1804. Being the day of General Election. By Heman Ball, A. M., Minister of the Gospel at Rutland. Printed by Haswell & Smead, Bennington: 1804. 8vo, pp. 31.

—*A Discourse,* delivered at Rutland, (East Parish,) before the Female Charitable Society,

January 15th, 1812. By Heman Ball, A. M., Minister of the Gospel, Rutland, Vt. Rutland: Printed by William Fay. 12mo. pp. 11.

Mr. Ball was born in Springfield, Ms., July 5, 1764; was graduated at Dartmouth College, 1791, and was pastor of the Cong'l Church, Rutland East Parish, 1797, until his death, Dec. 17, 1821. Mr. Ball was never married.

Ball, Miss Marietta. *Inquiry* as to the death of. See Smith, George G.

Ballard, C. R. *Vermont;* A Poem delivered before the Wheel-Barrow Society of Castleton Seminary, October 13, 1854, by Charles Rollin Ballard, A. B. Published by the Society. Rutland: Steam Press of George A. Tuttle & Co. 1854. 8vo, pp. 16.

Ballou, Daniel W.

A native of Richmond, Vt., where he was born July 23, 1824; died at Watertown, Wis., July 27, 1876.

When about five years of age his father moved to Lockport, N. Y., where young Ballou received a common school education and served a five years' apprenticeship in a printing office; he then attended three terms at Lima Seminary. He afterwards assisted Orsamus Turner in the preparation of his *History of the Holland Purchase of Western New York,* 1849-50; and conducted the Niagara *Democrat* for four years. In 1852 he became assistant editor of the Green Bay *Advocate,* while its editor was Secretary of State; and in 1854 established the Watertown *Democrat;* which he conducted until shortly before his death.

He was at one time President of the Wisconsin Editorial Association. He was one of the best writers in the State, never descending to the use of slang and personalities in the columns of his paper. He had long designed writing a *History of the Great Lakes of the West,* embracing their numerous historical associations.

Ballou, Eli. *Review of Rev. A. Royce's Sermons against Universalism:* In two Discourses, delivered in Williamstown, Vt., Oct. 10, 1838. By Eli Ballou, Pastor of the First Universalist Societies in Stowe and Morristown, Vt. Montpelier: Printed and published by F. A. McDowell, Universalist Watchman Office. 1838. 8vo, pp. 44. *See* Royce, A.

—*A Discourse,* delivered at the Funeral of Hon. Giles Harrington, at Alburgh Springs, Vermont, November 26, 1873, by Rev. Eli Ballou. Woodstock, Vt.: Luther O. Green, Printer.

BARNARD, VT., December 27, 1879.

Dear Sir :—I am not a Vermonter by birth. My native place is Jefferson county, New York, near the city of Watertown. I was born on the 1st day of December, 1808. My father, Chester Ballou, was a native of Massachusetts, descended from Maturin Ballou, of Providence, the progenitor of all the Ballous in this country. He was one of the persecuted Baptists who composed the Roger Williams colony, a Huguenot from France. My mother, Rachel Hayworth, was one of the Pennsylvania Friends or Quakers. In my childhood I enjoyed advantages for a common school education. When about twenty years of age I attended nearly two years the St. Lawrence Academy in Potsdam, N. Y., of which that celebrated teacher, Rev. Asa Brainerd, was then the Principal. I taught two terms of winter school in West Potsdam, and one in the town of Bangor, Franklin county, N. Y. As we had no Theological schools then, I studied for the ministry with Rev. Jonathan Wallace, of Potsdam, and entered the Universalist ministry in 1832, and was ordained at the St. Lawrence Association of Universalists at its session in June, 1832. Immediately after that I preached in Massena, Malone, Chateaugay, N. Y., and the village of Huntington, in the Province of Lower Canada.

In January, 1833, I moved with my wife to Swanton Falls, Vt., where I preached three years, half the time, and the other half in St. Albans, Fairfax and Berkshire. I also did some missionary work in Bakersfield, Enosburgh, Highgate, Sheldon and Alburgh; also in Canada, in the townships of Brome, St. Armand, Bedford, Stanbridge, the Sixth Concession, and other places. While in Swanton I taught the village school three terms, fifteen weeks each.

In 1836, I became the pastor of the societies n Stowe and Morrisville, where I remained four years.

In December, 1839, because of a bronchial difficulty I was obliged to suspend speaking in public, and in order to have some business that I could attend to and gain a living for myself and family, I purchased the "Universalist Watchman and Christian Repository." From Stowe I moved to Montpelier early in 1840, and continued to be the principal owner and editor of that paper for thirty years.

During my residence in Montpelier, I preached half the Sundays in East Montpelier for fourteen years; about two years in Barre; four or five years in Northfield and Marshfield; some in Calais, Duxbury, Williston, Richmond, East Randolph, Brookfield, Roxbury, and other places. I also attended a large number of funerals and weddings.

In November, 1839, in connection with Rev. H. Sampson and Rev. Jerome Harris, I engaged in an oral discussion of four days with Rev. Messrs. Grant and Marsh in the town of Danville, on the doctrines of endless punishment, and the final universal salvation. A few days after this I held an oral debate of four days, in St. Johnsbury, Vt., with a Methodist preacher by the name of Loveland. He affirmed that "Modern Universalism is a system of Infidelity," and I endeavored to defend our theological belief against this foul aspersion. Hon. Thomas Bartlett of Lyndon, presided as chairman.

I also engaged in an oral discussion with Rev. Miles Grant, the Adventist editor of "The World's Crisis," in Boston. This debate was held in Waterbury, and continued three days. I affirmed that the "Coming of Christ in his Kingdom" began during the generation living on the earth, when Jesus dwelt in the flesh, and Mr. Grant affirmed the end of the material world to be near at hand, and also the annihilation of all who die unconverted. These debates were never printed, excepting some accounts of them in the "Repository."

In 1857, I published a pamphlet of 84 pages, entitled "A Discussion on the Doctrine of Endless Punishment; Question, "Do the Scriptures teach that any part or portion of mankind will be endlessly punished for sins committed in this life?" Affirmative, Rev. Luther Lee; Negative, Rev. Eli Ballou. Ballou & Loveland, 1857. Montpelier.

In 1858, I preached the "Occasional Sermon" before the "General Convention," held in Boston, and also presided at two sessions of that Convention, one in Boston in 1860, and the other in the city of New York in the fall of 1861.

October 14, 1862, I gave a Biographical Sketch of the life and character of Rev. Hosea Ballou, 2d, D. D., before the Vermont Historical Society, at its annual session, delivered in the Representatives' Hall in the Capitol, at Montpelier. A copy of it was requested to be deposited in the archives of the Society; but I believe it has never been done.

In 1871 I made a visit to the State of Kansas, and acted as a missionary during three months. On my return I stopped at Maquoketa, Jackson county, Iowa, and preached all the time for a year to the society in that city. In the autumn of 1872 I returned to Vermont, and since then I have been pastor nearly seven years at South Woodstock.

I am now preaching every Sunday at Barnard Center in the forenoon, and at Bethel in the afternoon. I still regard Montpelier as my home, and live in the expectation that in a few years at most, when age closes my labors in the ministry, I shall return to the Capital to close my earthly life there, as I desire to have my mortal remains deposited in "Green Mountain Cemetery," by the side of those of my dear children.

I have thus given you a very succinct history of some of the events of my life. My health is still good, and I feel that, if nothing out of the ordinary course happens to me, I am still good for five years of active service, in the gospel field.

Fraternally yours,
ELI BALLOU.

Mr. Ballou died at Bethel, Vt., March 12, 1883.

Ballou, Hosea. *A Treatise on Atonement:* In which the Finite Nature of Sin is Argued, its Cause and Consequences as such; the Necessity and Nature of Atonement; and its Glorious Consequences, in the Final Reconciliation of All Men to Holiness and Happiness. By Hosea Ballou, of Barnard; Ordained Pastor of the United Societies of Barnard, Woodstock, Hartland, Bethel and Bridgewater, Author of a Pamphlet, Entitled "Notes on the Parables of the New Testament." (Texts.) Randolph,

(*Ver.*) Printed by Sereno Wright. 1805. 8vo. pp. xiii, 216.

—*Masonic Sermon* at Randolph, Vt., 1805.

—*Brotherly Love.* A Festival Sermon, before the Masonic Fraternity, delivered at Chester, Vt., June 24, A. L. 5806. 8vo, pp. 15. See Ferriss, W.

—*A Series of Letters* between the Rev. Joseph Buckminster, D. D., the Rev. John Walton, A. M., Pastors of Congregational Churches in Portsmouth, N. H., and the Rev. Hosea Ballou, Author of "Notes on Parables," "Treatise on Atonement," "A Candid Review," "The Child's Scripture Catechism," etc., Pastor of the Universalian Church and Society in said Portsmouth. Windsor: Printed by James G. Watts, for the Proprietor. Sold by Farnsworth & Churchill, and Merrifield & Cochran, Munroe & Francis, No. 4 Cornhill, Boston, (and others.) 1811. 18mo, pp. 154.

—*Hymns,* composed by different authors, by order of the General Convention of Universalists of the New England States and Others. Adapted to Public and Private Devotion. Copyright Secured. [Compiled by Hosea Ballou and Others, Committee.] Walpole, N. H. Printed for the Committee By George W. Nichols, 1808. 16mo, pp. 358 (2.)

—*A Candid Review of A Pamphlet entitled A Candid Reply.* The whole being a Doctrinal Controversy between the Hopkintonian and the Universalist. By Hosea Ballou. Portsmouth, N. H., W. Weeks, Printer. N. D. 16mo, pp. 207.

This Controversy commenced before Mr. Ballou left Vermont, and several Vermont Clergymen were connected with it: Dr. Burton, Rev. Mr. Tullar, Rev. Mr. Lyman, etc.

—*Oration Spoken before the Members of Vermont Lodge,* at the Celebration of St. John the Evangelist, 27th December, A. L. 5808. By Brother Hosea Ballou. Windsor, Vt., 1809. 8vo.

—*Biography of, by his son, Maturin M. Ballou;* Boston, 1859. 12mo. pp. 404. Also, Life of, by Rev. Thomas Whittemore, a larger work.

—*An Epistle to the Rev. Lemuel Haynes,* containing a brief Reply to his Sermon delivered at West Rutland, June, 1805, designed to refute the Doctrine of Universal Salvation. By Hosea Ballou, Preacher of that much despised Gospel. Barnard: April 22, 1806. 8vo, pp. 7.

Rev. Mr. Ballou was born in Richmond, N. H., April 30, 1771; and died in Boston, June 7, 1852. He began to preach at the age of about 21 years, and labored in various parts of New England. He was settled at Dana, Mass., in 1794, where he remained until 1800, when he accepted the invitation of the towns of Woodstock, Hartland, Bethel and Barnard, Vt., to preach for them, making the latter place his home; here he remained six years, not only doing his parish work, but in addition performing vast missionary labor in various parts of Vermont, the seed he then scattered taking root and producing an abundant harvest. It was in Barnard that his "Notes on the Parables," and also his greatest work, "Treatise on Atonement," (which latter was first printed at Randolph, Vt., in 1805,) were written.

In 1807, Mr. Ballou was settled over the Universalist Church in Portsmouth, N, H., where he continued until his removal to Boston, in 1817, when he became pastor of the School St. (2d Universalist) Church, where he remained until his decease.

Ballou, Hosea, 2d. *A Sermon,* delivered in the Universalist Meeting House in Roxbury on the evening of the third Sabbath in January, 1822. By Hosea Ballou, 2d, Pastor of the First Universalist Church and Society in Roxbury. Boston: Printed by Henry Bowen. 1822. 8vo, pp. 20.

—*Ancient History of Universalism,* from the time of the Apostles to the Fifth General Council, with an Appendix, Tracing the Doctrine to the Reformation. By Hosea Ballou, 2d., D. D. With Notes, by Rev. A. St. John Chambre, A. M., and T. J. Sawyer, D. D. Boston: Universalist Publishing House, 37 Cornhill. 1872. 12mo, pp. 313.
This work was first published in 1829, and a Second edition in 1842.

—*Letters* to Rev. Joel Hawes, D. D. In Reply to the Orthodox Tract, No. 224, entitled "Reasons for not embracing the doctrine of Universal Salvation." Boston: Printed by G. W. Bazin, Trumpet Office. 1833. 18mo, pp. 83.

—*The Twenty-Fourth and Twenty-Fifth Chapters of Saint Matthew's Gospel,* Illustrated with Notes, &c. By Hosea Ballou, 2d. Philadelphia: Gihon, Fairchild & Co. 1843. Royal 8vo, pp. 20. See Select Theological Library.
Dr. Ballou was born in Halifax, Vt., October 18, 1796; and died at Somerville, Mass., May 27, 1861. He was a grandson of Benjamin, elder brother of Rev. Hosea Ballou of Barnard, Vt., and Boston. He received his early education at Halifax, and about 1815 he was settled as pastor at Stafford, Conn., where he remained four or five years. July 29, 1821, he was installed pastor of the Church at Roxbury, Mass., and remained until June, 1838, when he was installed at Medford, Mass. The degree of D. D. was conferred upon him by Harvard University, in 1844; and in May, 1853, he was chosen first President of Tuft's College, Somerville, Mass., which he had been active in establishing, and after visiting Europe, and examining the Colleges there, on his return, August 22, 1855, entered upon his duties. In addition to the literary work of Dr. Ballou noticed already, in May, 1822, he became one of the editors of the *Universalist Magazine,* afterward the *Trumpet,* and in July, 1830, in connection with Hosea Ballou, Senior, he commenced the publication of the *Universalist Expositor,* which he edited many years under that title and the title of the *Universalist Quarterly.* In 1837 he published a collection of Psalms and Hymns for the use of Universalist Societies and Families. In 1833 he edited "Sismondi's History of the Crusades," published in Boston, 1833. 12mo, DRAKE.

Bancroft, Aaron. *A Discourse delivered at Windsor, Vt.,* on the 23d of June, MDCCXC, at the Ordination of the Rev. Samuel Shuttlesworth. Worcester: Printed by Isaiah Thomas, MDCCXC. 8vo, pp. 24.—Sabin.
A Distinguished Unitarian Minister, and Father of Hon. George Bancroft, the Historian. See Sprague's Annals.

Bangs, N. *An Examination of the Doctrine of Predestination,* as contained in a Sermon preached in Burlington, Vt., by Daniel Haskell, Minister of the Congregation. By Nathan Bangs, Minister of the Gospel. Motto. New York: 1817. 18mo, pp. 179.
A Distinguished Methodist Preacher and Author. See Drake's Biog. Dictionary.

Banks. *Report* of the Committee appointed by Act of the last Session of the Legislature, to Examine and Report the Situation of the Vermont State Bank. Montpelier, Vt. Published by order of the Legislature. Wright & Sibley, Printers. 1812. 8vo, pp. 40.
In same volume Report on the same subject, October 20, 1813. pp. 7.
See Records of the Governor and Council, Vol. 5, pp. 443-451.

—*By-Laws and Rules* of the Bank of Montpelier. E. P. Walton's Print. 1826. 12mo, pp. 8.

—*Suggestions of Counsel for Remonstrants* in the matter of the proposed Bank at Rutland, made to the Bank Committees, October Session, 1861. Montpelier: E. P. Walton, Printer. 1861. 8vo, pp. 8.

—*Report of the Committee on Banks,* relative to the St. Albans Bank, to the House of Representatives, October Session, 1858. Montpelier: E. P. Walton, Printer. 1858. 8vo, pp. 8.

—*Articles of Association* of the State Bank, Montpelier, Vt. Printed by S. S. Boyce. 1858. 8vo, pp. 28.

—*An Appeal to the Stockholders* of the Northfield Bank. April 15, 1862. 8vo, pp. 8.

—*Majority and Minority Reports* of the Committee on Banks, on Senate Bill, No. 3. Nov. 6, 1862. No imprint. 8vo, pp. 4.
See Vermont, Bank Commissioner's Reports.

BAPTISTS. *Proceedings of the Baptist Convention of the State of Vermont;* with the Reports of the Vermont Branch of the N. B. E. Society, and the Vermont Baptist Sabbath School Union, at their Annual Meetings, held in Waterbury, October, 1837. (Twelfth Anniversary.) Brandon: Vermont Telegraph Press. 1837. 8vo, pp. 26.
The "Vermont Baptist Convention" was founded in 1825, and incorporated in 1851. For 1848 the title reads:

—*Minutes of the Twenty-Third Anniversary of the Vermont Baptist State Convention,* Held with the Church in Whiting, October 11 & 12, 1848. Corresponding Secretary of the Board, C. A. Thomas, Brandon. Ludlow, Vt. Printed by W. O. Tower, Union Press. 1848. 8vo, pp. 27.
This form was followed until the following appears:

—*Minutes of the Vermont Baptist Anniversaries,* for the Year 1869. Montpelier, Vt.: Argus and Patriot Printing House. 1870. 8vo, pp. 87. Continued.

—*Shaftsbury Association.* (Formed in 1780.) *Minutes of the Shaftsbury Association* at their Annual Convention, held in Hillsdale, M.DCC.-LXXXIX. Printed by Haswell and Russell in Bennington (Vermont.) 1789. 12mo, pp. 12. Continued.

—*Minutes of the Fifty-Second Anniversary of the Vermont Baptist Association,* held at the Baptist Meeting House in Ira, on Wednesday and Thursday, October 4 and 5, 1837. Brandon: Vermont Telegraph Press. 1837. 8 vo, pp. 8.
Formed in 1785.
These two Associations were united in 1855 under the name of the "Vermont and Shaftsbury Association."

—*The Sixty-first Anniversary of the Woodstock Baptist Association,* held in the North Meeting House of the Baptist Church in Mount Holly, Sept. 15 and 16, 1845. Bellows Falls: Printed by S. M. Blake. 1845. 8vo, pp. 12.
Continued. Formed in 1786.

—*Minutes of the Barre Baptist Association* held with the Baptist Church at Braintree, Vt., September 12 & 13, 1860. Montpelier: Printed at the Freeman Printing Establishment. 1860. 8vo, pp. 8.
Continued. Formed in 1807.

—*Minutes of the Lamoille Baptist Association* (Formed 1809) held with Baptist Church of Hinesburgh, September 18th & 19th, 1850. Together with the Proceedings of the Lamoille Bible and Educational Societies. Brattleboro: J. B. Miner Printer. 1850. 8vo, pp. 16.
Continued.

—*Articles of Faith and Covenant,* of the Danville Baptist Association. To which is added A Familiar Dialogue on Close Communion. St. Johnsbury: Samuel Eaton, Printer. 1833. 18mo, pp. 36.

—*Minutes of the Fifty-Ninth Anniversary of the Danville Baptist Association,* (Formed in 1810) held with the Baptist Church at Barnston, P. Q., June 17 and 18, 1868. Newport, Vt.: Camp & Cummings, Book and Job Printers. 1868. 8vo, pp. 11.
Continued.

—*Minutes of the Fifteenth Anniversary of the Addison County Association,* (Formed in 1832) held with the Baptist Church in Charlotte, September 27 and 28, 1848. Middlebury: Printed by Justus Cobb. 1848. 8vo, pp. 12.
Continued.

—*Minutes of the Twenty-Third Anniversary of the Windham County Association,* (Founded in 1835) held with the Baptist Church in Brattleboro, Sept. 15th and 16th, 1858. Brattleboro: Printed by Geo. E. Selleck, opposite the Post Office. 1858. 8vo, pp. 14.
Continued.

—*Minutes of the Fairfield Baptist Association,* (name changed to Lamoille in 1847) held with the Church in N. Fairfield, Sept. 18 & 19, 1844. Middlebury, Vt. Maxham's Print. Observer Office. 1844. 12mo, pp. 12.

—*Minutes of the Onion River Baptist Association;* (merged in the Lamoille in 1847) held with the Church at Colchester, Vt., September 3 & 4, 1846. E. Poultney, Vt.: J. K. Seaver, Printer, Observer Office. 1846. 8vo, pp. 11.

—*Manual of the Baptist Church,* West Pawlet, Vt. Containing A Historical Sketch, Articles of Faith, Covenant and Rules of Order. Rutland: Tuttle & Company, Printers. 1874. 18mo, pp. 20.

—*History of the Shaftsbury Association.* See WRIGHT, STEPHEN.

—*A Summary of History and Declaration of Faith of the Baptist Church.* Published by order of the Church—Motto. Rutland: G. A. Tuttle & Co., Printers. 1861. 12mo, pp. 16.

—*A Vindication of Infant Baptism;* together with the Different Modes of Baptism, as Taught and Practiced by Christ and His Disciples. By a Paedobaptist. Vergennes: John E. Roberts. 1841. 12mo, pp. 23.

—*Twenty-Second Anniversary* of the Hudson River Baptist Association North of Independent Baptist Churches. Held in the Meeting House of the Baptist Church, Schenectady, June 11th and 12th, 1872. Next Session to be held with the Calvary Church, Albany, June 9th and 10th, 1873. Rutland: Tuttle & Company, Printers, 1872. 8vo, pp. 23.
Twenty-third Anniversary, same imprint.

—*The Practical Uses of Christian Baptism.* A Circular Letter from the Ministers and Messengers of the several Baptist Churches of the Northamptonshire Association, assembled at Northampton, June 15, 16, 1802, to the Churches in their Connexion. By Andrew Fuller, D. D., of Kittering. Montpelier: Printed by Wright & Sibley. 1814. 8vo, pp. 16.

—*Origin and Constitution* of the Society for Shaftsbury and vicinity, (Vt.) Auxiliary to the Baptist Board of Foreign Missions for the United States. Bennington, Vt. Printed by Darius Clark. 1816. 8vo, pp. 8.

—See ROWLEY, SAMUEL. Sermon at Rupert, Vt., 1813.

—See CONGREGATIONAL, Address to the Baptist Church, Middletown, Vt.; The Doings and Result of a Council, 1807.

Barber, E. D. An Address before the Anti-Masonic Convention of the County of Addison at Middlebury on the 12th of March, 1829. By E. D. Barber. Vergennes. Gamaliel Smith. 1829. 12mo, pp. 36.

—*Popular Excitements.* An Address delivered before the Anti-Masonic Convention holden at Middlebury, Vt., Feb. 26th, 1830. By E. D. Barber. Middlebury, MDCCCXXX. 8vo, pp. 19.

—*An Address,* delivered before the Rutland County Anti-Masonic Convention, holden at Rutland on the First day of June, 1831. By E. D. Barber. Published by Request of the Convention. Castleton: George Collingwood Smith, Printer. 1831. 8vo, pp. 14.

—*An Oration* delivered before the Addison County Anti-Slavery Society, on the Fourth of July, 1836. By Edward D. Barber. Middlebury: Knapp and Jewett, Printers, 1836. 8vo, pp. 16.

—*An Oration,* Delivered before the Democrats of Washington County, (Vt.) at Montpelier, on the 4th of July, 1839: By Edward D. Barber. Published by request of the Committee of arrangements. Printed at the Patriot office, 1839. 8vo, pp. 18.
Edward Downing Barber was born in Greenwich, N. Y., August 30, 1806; and died at Lake Dunmore Hotel, Vt., August 23, 1855. He was graduated at Middlebury College, 1829; and was widely known as a lawyer, editor, member of the Vt. Legislature, and an active leader of the Anti-masons; also a prominent member of the Free Soil portion of the Democratic party. Was member of the Vt. House of Representatives in 1832-34 and 1853, and Clerk of the same in 1834. Was Editor of the Middlebury *Anti-Masonic Republican and Free Press,* 1829 to 1836.

Barnard. Town of Barnard. Reports of the Selectmen and Auditors, For the Year ending March 6, 1860. 12mo, pp. 4.

—The same for 1873. 8vo, pp. 4.
Continued.

Barnard, D. D. A Discourse pronounced at Burlington before the Literary Societies of the University of Vermont, August 1st, 1838: On the day of their Annual Commencement. By Daniel D. Barnard. Albany: Printed by Hoffman & White. 1838. 8vo, pp. 56.
A New York State Politician and lawyer.

Barnes, J. The Green Mountain Traveler. By Josiah Barnes. New York: Derby & Jackson, 1861. 12mo, pp. 498.

Barnes, Melvin. *A few General and unmethodized Remarks* to a Medical Younger Friend, on Phrenology. By Melvin Barnes, M. D., of Grand Isle, Vt. Motto. Plattsburgh: J. M. Tuttle, Printer, August, 1853. 8vo, pp. 16.

—*A Circular*, or Short Biography of Col. Ebenezer Allen, known as Captain or Major, in the New Hampshire Grants, and its Rangers, A. D. 1777 and after. [n. p., 1851.] 8vo, pp. 16.

—*Reprint of a short Biography* of Colonel Ebenezer Allen, Also short Biographies of Lieutenant Samuel Allen and Dr. Jacob Roebeck. In addition, some Reminiscences of Lake Champlain, reprinted in part. Plattsburgh, J. W. Tuttle, Printer. 1852. 8vo, pp. 32, errata (1).

—*An Essay* on Animal Magnetism, the full title to which we are unable to give.

—*Sand-Bar Bridge Company.* An Address, At Annual Meeting, January 19th, 1854. By Dr. M. Barnes, of Grand Isle, Vt. The Company's President from October 8th, 1848 to 1854. 8vo, pp. 8. No imprint.

Dr. Barnes was born at South Hero, Vt., March 9, 1794; and died at Grand Isle, Vt., Dec. 8, 1860. He studied medicine with his Father, Melvin Barnes, Sen., and commenced the practice of his profession at Grand Isle in 1814, which he continued until about 1845, when failing health compelled him to relinquish practice. He represented the town in the Legislature in 1825-26; was Assistant Judge of the County Court, in 1828-9; a delegate to State Constitutional Conventions in 1828 and 1843; a County Senator in 1836. He devoted much time in the late years of his life to literary and scientific pursuits. Among his various prose and poetical publications the above are all that we are able to trace.

Barnet. *Church Controversy.* See MILLIGAN, JAMES.

—*The Manual* of the Congregational Church at Barnet, Vt. Woodsville: Wm. A. Pringle, Printer. 1878. 12mo, pp. 18.

Barnum, A. W. *Address* delivered to the Vergennes Agricultural Society, at their Annual Cattle Show and Fair, Held at Vergennes, Sept. 22, 1821. By Gen. A. W. Barnum, President of the Society. Middlebury: Printed by Copeland & Allen. 1821. 8vo, pp. 18.

Barre. *Facts for the People of Barre*, touching the Hostile attack of Rev. A. Royce, of this Town, upon the M. E. Church, in a Tract entitled, "Considerations for the People of Barre," &c. By the Official Board. Motto. Montpelier: Poland and Briggs, Printers. 1845. 8vo, pp. 51.

—*Report of the Superintendent* of Common Schools for the Town of Barre, for the year ending March 1, 1869. Montpelier: Freeman Steam Printing House and Bindery. 1869. 12mo, pp. 16.

Continued. See Educational, Barre Academy, and Goddard Seminary.

—*Annual Reports* of the Officers of the Town of Barre, for the year ending February 27, 1877. Montpelier: Freeman Steam Printing House and Bindery. 1877. 8vo, pp. 12.

Continued.

—*Catalogue of Books* of the Library of the Universalist Society, Barre, Vt. Montpelier, Vt.: Argus and Patriot Print. 1882. 18mo, pp. 16.

Barrett, James, LL. D. *Memorial Address* on the Life and Character of the Hon. Jacob Collamer. Read before the Vermont Historical Society, in the Representatives' Hall, October

20, 1868. By James Barrett, LL. D., Judge of the Supreme Court. Woodstock, Vt. 1868. 8vo, pp. 61.

—*Memorial Address* on the Life and Character of the Hon. Charles Marsh, LL. D. A paper read before the Vermont Historical Society, at Montpelier, October 11, 1870. By James Barrett, LL. D. 8vo, pp. 54.

—*State of Vermont.* Supreme Court, Special Term, July, 1877. Appeal in Chancery, Franklin County. Vermont and Canada Railroad Company vs. Vermont Central Rail Road Company—and others. Opinion of the Court by Barrett, Judge. 8vo, pp. 66.

—*Bill and Memorial* on the Advancement of the Science of Medicine and Surgery. [Drawn by Judge Barrett, Oct., 1853, at the request of the Doctors.] 8vo, pp. 15.

—*Report of the Committee* [Appointed by the Governor] Relating to Pleading and Practice. 8vo, pp. 20.

Drawn by Mr. Barrett, with the exception of about two pages by Mr. Royce. Stephen Royce, Lucius B. Peck, James Barrett, Committee.

Judge Barrett was born in Strafford, Vt., May 31, 1814. He read law, and located in Woodstock, Vt., in 1839, where he resided for forty years, removing thence to Rutland. He was a Judge of the Supreme Court of Vermont from 1857 to 1880. See *Dartmouth Alumni*, 1838.

Barrows, Samuel J. and Isabel C. *The Shaybacks in Camp.* Boston: Houghton, Mifflin & Co. 16mo. With Map of Lake Memphremagog.

Barruel, l'Abbe. *History of the Clergy* during the French Revolution. Burlington, Vt., 1794. 12mo.

Barstow, Z. S. *Remarks* on the "Preliminary History" of Two Discourses by the Rev. Aaron Bancroft, D.D. By Zedekiah S. Barstow. Bellows Falls. 1821. 8vo, pp. 24.

Mr. Barstow was a clergyman settled in Walpole, N. H.; several sermons by him were published at Keene, Boston, and elsewhere. See *Dartmouth Alumni*, 1839.

Bartholomew, Samuel. *Poems:* "Will Wittling, or the Spoiled Child." 12mo, pp. 80.

Probably printed at Middlebury, about 1800.

Mr. Bartholomew was from Watertown, Conn., in 1786, and settled in Cornwall, Vt., from whence he removed to Kentucky in 1812. See *Matthews' History of Cornwall*, pp 55-8.

Bartlett, J. R. *Methodism* in Williamstown, Vt. See Williamstown.

Bartlett, Robert. *A Sermon.* Delivered on the day of General Election, at Montpelier, October 13, 1825, before the Honorable Legislature of Vermont. By Robert Bartlett, Minister of the Universalist Church and Society in Hartland. Montpelier: Printed by E. P. Walton. 1825. 8vo, pp. 23.

Mr. Bartlett was a Universalist preacher, some time pastor of the church in Hartland, Vt.

Barton. *The Confession* of Faith and Covenant of the Congregational Church in Barton, Vt. With Scripture References. Adopted January, 1832. Windsor. Printed at the Chronicle Press. 1852, 16mo, pp. 8.

Barton, A. S. *Millerism Refuted by History*, in a Series of letters to a Friend. No. 1. Motto. Windsor, Vt. Published by Joseph Fairbanks. 1842. 12mo, pp. 24.

Mr. Barton was a native of Andover, Vt., and moved to Ludlow at the age of 16 years, where he died about 1872, aged about 70. He was an industrious writer for the newspapers against the Masonic Institution, also against Millerism. He wrote much on general politics, etc., his pseudonym being "Timothy Downing," and his publications were largely under the form of " Letters by Timothy Downing."

Barton, General William. *Biography of, etc.* By Mrs. Williams. Providence: 1839, 12mo, pp. 312.

> General Barton was a Hero of the Revolution, the captor of the British General Prescott, etc.
> He was one of the proprietors of the town of Barton, Vt., and from him the town took its name. He became involved in litigation in consequence of some unjust claims made against him growing out of his interest in the township, and for fourteen years he was confined within the jail limits of Caledonia County, and was released by his old companion in arms, General Lafayette, on his memorable visit to Vermont in June and July, 1825. See the above work, pp. 98–102. General Barton erected the first saw-mill in the township bearing his name.
> *See* NARRATIVE of the Capture of Gen. Prescott.

Batchelder, John P., M. D. *On the Causes which degrade the Profession of Physick:* An Oration delivered before the Western District of the N. H. Medical Society, at its Annual Meeting in May, 1818. By John P. Batchelder, M. D. Published by request of the Members. Bellows Falls, Vt. Printed by Bill Blake & Co. 1818. 8vo, pp. 10.

Bate, John. *The Truth Defended.* A Review of Rev. J. F. Walker's Sermon on "The Distinction between Salvation and Eternal Life." By Rev. John Bate. Republished from the Vermont Christian Messenger, by Request. [n. p. n. d.] 8vo, pp. 12.
> *See* WALKER, J. F.

Bates, Archibald L. *Trial of Archibald L. Bates* for the Murder of Mrs. Harriett Jane Bates, At Shaftsbury, on the evening of October 2d, 1838; to which is appended the sentence of Chief Justice Williams, and the Confession of the Murderer. 8vo, pp. 23.

Bates, Joshua. *Discourse* at Castleton on the organization of the Mount Vernon Institution. Middlebury, Vt. 1818. 8vo.

—*An Inaugural Oration.* Pronounced March 18, 1818. By Joshua Bates, A. M., President of Middlebury College. Published by request of the Corporation. Middlebury, (Vt.) Printed by J. W. Copeland. 1818. 8vo, pp. 26.

—*A Second Edition* of the same, Middlebury. 1818. 8vo, pp. 24.

—*Address:* What are the prominent Characteristics to be sought, by Education Societies, in young men applying for patronage? Middlebury College, Oct. 1, 1830. 8vo, pp. 8. See Register Am. Ed. Society, Vol. 3.

—*A Discourse*, on Honesty in Dealing; delivered at Middlebury, on the Annual Fast: April 15, 1818. By Joshua Bates, A. M., President of Middlebury College. Middlebury: Printed by J. W. Copeland. 1818. 8vo, pp. 23.

—*A Discourse*, delivered in Castleton, at the organization of the Vermont Juvenile Missionary Society, September 16, 1818. By Joshua Bates, D. D., President of Middlebury College. Middlebury, Vt.: Printed by Francis Burnap. 1818. 8vo, pp. 19.

—*A Sermon* preached on the Day of General Election, at Montpelier, October 11, 1821, before the Honorable Legislature of Vermont. By Joshua Bates, D. D., President of Middle-

bury College. Montpelier, Vt.; Printed by E. P. Walton, October, 1821. 8vo, pp. 31.

—*A Sermon*, preached at Pittsford on the First Anniversary of the Northwestern Branch of the American Education Society, February 7, 1821. By Joshua Bates, D. D., President of Middlebury College. Published by direction of the Society. Middlebury: Printed by Copeland and Allen. 1821. 8vo, pp. 46, (1).
> Contains the first report, and list of names, with donations.

—*The Scriptures our only Guide.* A Sermon, preached June 14, 1820, at the Ordination of the Rev. Ira Ingraham, as Pastor of a Church in Orwell. By Joshua Bates, D. D., President of Middlebury College. Middlebury: Printed by Copeland and Allen. 1821. 8vo, pp. 28.

—*Address in Castleton*, December 2, 1823, at the Commencement of the Vermont Academy of Medicine, connected with Middlebury College. [n. p.] 1824. 8vo, pp. 16.

—*Sermon at the Ordination* of Rev. Charles Y. Chase as Pastor of the Congregational Church at Corinth, Vt., 1821.

—*Influence of Christian Truth:* A Sermon, preached in Northampton, Mass., Sept. 21, 1825, at the Sixteenth Annual Meeting of the American Board of Commissioners for Foreign Missions. By Joshua Bates, D. D. President of Middlebury College. Boston: Printed by Crocker & Brewster. 1825. 8vo, pp. 24.

—*Lecture at Middlebury, Vt.*, on Moral Education. 1837.

—*The Ministry a Good Work.* A Sermon preached at the Induction of the Rev. Joseph Steele to the Pastoral Care of the Church in Castleton, Dec. 25, 1828. By Joshua Bates, President of Middlebury College. Castleton: Printed by Horace H. Houghton. 1829. 8vo, pp. 36.

—*Address of Rev. Joshua Bates, D. D.* at the Semi-Sentennial (*Sic*) Celebration of Middlebury College. 1850. [n. p., n. d.] 8vo. pp. 24.

—*A Sermon* delivered at Dudley, Mass., January 17, 1854, at the Funeral of the Rev. Joshua Bates, D. D. Minister of the Second Presbyterian Church in Albany. Published by request of the Bereaved Congregation. Albany: Charles Benthuysen Printer, No. 407 Broadway. 1854. 8vo, pp. 40.

—*Eulogy* on Rev. Joshua Bates, D. D. Former President of Middlebury College, Delivered on Commencement Day, August 9, 1854. By George Howe, D. D. Prof. of Biblical Literature, Theological Seminary, Columbia, S. C. Published at the request of the Alumni. Boston: Press of T. R. Marvin, 42 Congress street. 1855. 8vo, pp. 40.

> Rev. Dr. Bates was born in Cohasset, Mass., March 20, 1776; and died in Dudley, Mass., January 14, 1854. He was graduated at Harvard University, 1800; he was the son of a farmer of limited means, and toiled on a farm until he was seventeen years of age. On leaving Harvard he became an assistant teacher in Phillips Academy, pursuing a course of theological studies at the same time. Ordained pastor of the Congregational Church in Dedham, Mass., March 16, 1803, where he labored successfully until he accepted the Presidency of Middlebury College in 1818, which he filled with great ability and fidelity until his resignation, 1839. He was chaplain of the U. S. Senate the succeeding year, and was installed pastor of a church in Dudley, March 22, 1843, where he continued until his decease.

The publications of Dr. Bates are numerous, especially of sermons and addresses. We give a list of those only which in some way relate to Vermont.

Bates, Robert B. An Address delivered before the Washington Benevolent Society of the County of Addison in Bridport, at the Celebration of the birth of George Washington, on the 22 February, 1814. By Robert B. Bates, Esq. Middlebury: Printed by Timothy C. Strong. 1814.

A native of Connecticut and a prominent lawyer in Middlebury, Vt., 1813 to about 1833.

Bates, S. L. A sermon preached on the occasion of the death of Miss Mary Elizabeth Tenny, Former Principal of Montebello Institute. In the Congregational Church, Newbury, Vermont, February 15, 1880. By Rev. S. L. Bates, Pastor. Published by Request. Bradford, Vermont: Orange County Publishing Company, Printers. 1880. 8vo, pp. 13.

Battell, Joseph. *The Morgan Horse* and Register containing the History and Pedigree of Justin Morgan, founder of this remarkable American breed of Horses and of his best known Sons and Grandsons. Also Pedigree and History so far as known of most of the more prominent Stallions foaled before 1881 descended in male line from Justin Morgan, together with the Pedigrees of about one thousand animals registered in conformity with the Rules of the Morgan Register. Illustrated. By Joseph Battell. Vol. 1, Motto. Middlebury, Vt.: Register Printing Company. 1894. 8vo, pp. 1100.

—*Money and the Money Power.* Revised from Middlebury, (Vt.) Register. By Joseph Battell, Author of the Morgan Horse, The Horse, &c. Middlebury: 1896. Printed by the Register Company. pp. viii, 99.

Baxter, Gen. H. Henry. *Biographical Sketch of. Tributes and Funeral Services.* New York: Atlantic Publishing and Engraving Co. 1884. royal 8vo, pp. 63. With Portrait.

Gen. Horace Henry Baxter was born in Saxtons River, Rockingham, Vt., January 18, 1818. He was the railroad contractor who completed the Rutland & Burlington Railroad; was for a time President of the New York Central R. R. Co., and director in the Panama R. R. Co.; was owner of the Rutland Marble Quarry, and founder of the Baxter National Bank of Rutland. He was Adjutant-General of Vermont at the outbreak of the Civil War, and organized the first and second regiments of Vt. Vols. in the spring of 1861. He died at his residence in New York City, February 17, 1884.

Baxter, Jedediah Hyde. Statistics, Medical and Anthropological, of the Provost-Marshal-General's Bureau, derived from Records of the Examination for Military Service in the Armies of the United States during the late war of the Rebellion, of over a million recruits, drafted men, substitutes, and enrolled men. Compiled under direction of the Secretary of War by J. H. Baxter, A. M., M. D., Colonel and Chief Medical Purveyor, United States Army. Late Chief Medical officer of the Provost-Marshal-General's Bureau. In two volumes. Washington: Government Printing Office. 4to, pp. LXXXVII, 568; XXVIII 707. And many Plates. 1875.

Gen. J. H. Baxter, LL. D., was born in Strafford, Vt., May 11, 1837, being a son of Hon. Portus Baxter. He graduated from the University of Vermont in 1859, and from the Medical Department of the University in 1860; appointed Surgeon of the 12th regiment Massachusetts Volunteers in June, 1861; Surgeon of U. S. Vols. in April, 1862,

and placed in charge of the Campbell Hospital in Washington; subsequently Chief Medical Officer in the Bureau of the Provost-Marshal-General; brevetted Colonel March 30, 1865, for faithful service during the War; Lieutenant Colonel and Asst. Medical Purveyor U. S. A. July, 1867; Chief Medical Purveyor U. S. A. 1872; Colonel June, 1874; Surgeon General U. S. A. August, 1890. Died December 4, 1890. In 1876 he married Miss Florence Tryon of Boston, Massachusetts.

Baxter, Portus. *In Memoriam.* Hon. Portus Baxter. Eulogy, delivered March 8th, 1868, by Rev. Byron Sunderland, D. D. Also Resolutions of Condolence and extracts from the Press. Washington, D. C. Sam'l Polkinhorn, Printer. 1868. 8vo, pp. 23.

Memoir in Vt. Hist. Mag., Vol. 3, pp. 189-194

Baxter, Richard. *The Saint's Everlasting Rest;* or a Treatise of the blessed state of the saints in the enjoyment of God in Heaven. By Richard Baxter. Abridged by Benj. Fawcett. Boston: S. T. Armstrong. Middlebury: 1811: S. Swift. 12mo.

Another edition, 1814.

—*A Call to the Unconverted.* By Richard Baxter. Brattleborough, Vt. Printed by William Fessenden. 1813. 12mo, pp. 202.

Bayley, Kiah. *The Bible its own Interpreter.* An Essay on the Scriptural mode of Baptism, showing the true import of Scripture Language. By Rev. Kiah Bayley, Hardwick, Vt. (motto.) Windsor: Published by Bishop & Tracy. 1854. 8vo, pp. 24.

Rev. Kiah Bayley was born in Brookfield, Ms., March 11, 1770; and died at Hardwick, Vt., Aug. 17, 1857. He was graduated at Dartmouth College, 1793; and was ordained as a Congregational preacher, in 1797. He removed to Hardwick, Vt., in 1823, where he resided until his death, his occupation being farming, and preaching occasionally. He published many sermons and tracts, besides leaving a manuscript work on Baptism.

Baylies, Nicholas. *A Digested Index* to the Modern Reports of the Courts of Common Law in England and the United States: By Nicholas Baylies, Esq. In three volumes. Montpelier, Vt. Printed for the Proprietors, by Walton & Goss. 1814. 8vo, pp. xiv, 545. vii. 455. vii, 509.

—*An Essay* concerning the Free Agency of Man, or the Powers and Faculties of the Human Mind, the Decrees of God, Moral Obligation, Natural Law, and Morality. Montpelier, Vt. Printed by E. P. Walton, October, 1820. 16mo, pp. 215 (1).

Another edition, with the following title:

—*An Essay* on the Powers and Faculties of the Human Mind. Motto. Montpelier, Vt. Printed by E. P. Walton. 1829. 16mo, pp. 215 (1).

Judge Baylies was a native of Uxbridge, Ms., and died at Lyndon, Vt., Aug. 17, 1847, aged 75. He was a learned lawyer and judge; and resided in Montpelier, Vt., 1810—1835. See Memoir in *Vt. Hist. Mag.*, *Vol. 1*, p. 352, and *Dartmouth Alumni*, 1794.

Bayne, Thomas. *Scatter thou the People that delight in War.* A Sermon delivered in the Congregational Church, Irasburgh, April 12, 1863. On occasion of the Funeral of Henry Clay Flint, Captain Co. I, 1st Regiment Vt. Volunteer Cavalry. By Rev. Thomas Bayne. Printed for Private Distribution. Irasburgh, Vt. H. & G. H. Bradford, Printers. 1863. 8vo, pp. 20.

—*A Sermon* Delivered at the Congregational Church, Irasburgh, Vermont, May 2, 1866, on occasion of the Death of Hon. Ira Hayden Allen. By Rev. Thomas Bayne. Printed for private distribution. Montpelier: E. P. Walton, Printer. 1866. 8vo, pp. 34.

Mr. Bayne was "stated supply" to the Cong'l Church, Irasburgh, 3 or 4 years.

Beadle, W. A. *Narrative* of the Life of William Beadle, of Wethersfield, in the State of Connecticut. I. The Particulars of the "horrid massacre" of himself and Family. II. Extracts from the Rev. Mr. Marsh's Sermon at the Funeral of his Wife and Children. Hartford; Basil Webster, 1783. pp. 24.
Reprinted by Alden Spooner, Windsor, Vt. 1795. 12 mo.

Beall, Isaac. *A Funeral Discourse,* delivered before the Worshipful Master, Wardens and Bretheren of Center Lodge, at Rutland, on the 24th day of June, 1800, on the Solemnity of rearing a Marble Monument in memory of the Hon. Samuel Williams, Esq., Late Senior Warden of Center Lodge. By Isaac Beall, V. D. M. Published at the request of the Lodge. Vergennes: Printed by Chipman & Fessenden. 8vo, pp. 19.

—*A Sermon,* Delivered before His Excellency Jonas Galusha, Esquire, Governor, His Honor Paul Brigham, Esquire, Lieut. Governor, The Honorable Council, and House of Representatives, of the State of Vermont, at Montpelier, on the Day of General Election, Oct. 8, 1812. By Isaac Beall, Pastor of the Baptist Church of Christ in Pawlet. Published by order of the Legislature. Montpelier, Vt.: Printed by Wright and Sibley. 1812. 8vo, pp. 24.
Mr. Beall was Pastor of the First Baptist Church in Pawlet, Vt., 1800—1831; he died in Clarendon, Vt., in 1833, aged 82.

Beard, Kendall and Roxcinda, of Orange, Vt. *The Golden Wedding* of Kendall and Roxcinda (Richardson) Beard, December 4, 1878. A Poem, small 4to, pp. 8. No imprint.

Beaumont, W. *The Physiology of Digestion,* with experiments on the Gastric Juice. By William Beaumont, M. D. Surgeon in U. S. Army. Second Edition: Corrected by Samuel Beaumont, M. D. Burlington: Chauncey Goodrich. 1847. 12mo, pp. 303 (1).
See Drake's Biog. Dictionary.

Beckley, Hosea. *The History of Vermont;* with Descriptions, Physical and Topographical. By Rev. Hosea Beckley, A. M. Brattleboro: George H. Salsbury. 1846. 12mo, pp. 396.
See Tufts, James, for sketch of Rev. Mr. Whitcomb, by Mr. Beckley.
Rev. Mr. Beckley was born in Berlin, Ct., in 1780; and was graduated at Yale College, 1803, and was pastor of the Congregational church in Dummerston, Vt., 1808—1837; he died about 1844.

Beckwith, G. C. *A Sermon* on the Mode of Baptism. By G. C. Beckwith. Castleton: Printed by H. H. Houghton. 1831. 12mo, pp. 24.

Beecher, Lyman. *The Government of God Desirable.* A Sermon delivered at Newark, during the Session of the Synod of New York and New Jersey, October, 1808. By Lyman Beecher, A. M. Pastor of the Church of Christ. in East-Hampton, Long-Island. Published at the Request of many who heard it. Windsor: Re-printed by Alden Spooner. 1810. 8vo, pp. 20.

Beers, F. W. *Atlas Maps.* See Chittenden Addison, Washington, Windham, Windsor, Bennington, Rutland and Orange Counties.

Bell, Rev. Benjamin. *An Impartial History* of the Trial of Benjamin Bell for the pretended crime of Extortion, etc. Windsor (Vt.) 1797. 12mo, pp. 155.

—*A Discourse,* delivered at Cornish, N. H., 1792. Windsor, Vt. 1792. 8vo, pp. 51.

—*Sleepy Dead Sinners,* exhorted to awake out of their Sleep and to arise from the Dead. In a Discourse, on Ephesians v:14. By Benjamin Bell, A. M., Pastor of a Church in Windsor and Cornish. Printed by Alden Spooner, at his Printing Office in Windsor. 1793. 8vo, pp. 24.

—*The Character of a Virtuous Woman;* Delineated in a Discourse on Proverbs, xxxi:10, Delivered at Cornish, (N. H.) July 24th, 1794. By Benjamin Bell, A. M., Pastor of a Church of Christ in Windsor and Cornish. Published at the Request of those who heard it. Printed at Windsor, By Alden Spooner. 12mo, pp. 24.

—*The Nature and Importance of A Pure Peace Illustrated;* And the Means by which it may be obtained and cultivated, shown, and urged, In a Discourse on Romans, xiv:17. Delivered before several Members of both Houses of the Legislature of the State of Vermont, During their Session in Windsor, October, 1791. Published at their particular Desire. By Benjamin Bell, A. M., Pastor of a Church in Windsor and Cornish. Mottoes. Printed at Windsor by Alden Spooner. 8vo, pp. 19.
Not an official election sermon.

Bell, William. *Letters* Addressed to Rev. J. Clark, A Presiding Elder of the Methodist connexion, on the subject of a discourse delivered by him at the Methodist Chapel, St. Albans, Vt. From Psalms ix.27. By William Bell. Motto. Woodstock: 1831. 12mo, pp. 56.
Rev. Mr. Bell, a Universalist Minister of some note, was born in Windsor, Vt., June 16, 1791; died in Boston, Mass., April 20, 1871. See "Universalist Register," 1872.

Bellows, Henry W. *A Sermon* Preached at the Installation of Adams Ayer, as Associate Pastor of the Unitarian Society in Charlestown, N. H. June 7, 1855. By Henry W. Bellows, D. D., of the city of New York. With the Charge, Right Hand of Fellowship and Address to the People. Printed for private distribution. Brattleboro : O. H. Platt, Printer. 1855. 8vo, pp. 32.

—*Historical Sketch* of Col. Benjamin Bellows, Founder of Walpole. An address, on occasion of the gathering of his descendants to the consecration of his monument, at Walpole, N. H., Oct. 11, 1854. With an Appendix, containing an account of the family meeting. New York: John A. Gray, Printer. 1855. 8vo, pp. 125. Plates, and map.
Relates somewhat to Vermont.

Beman, Nathan S. S. *A Sermon* preached at Fairhaven, Vt. June 18, 1812, at the dedication of the new meeting house. By Nathan S. S. Beman, Pastor of the Third Congregational church in Portland, Me. Holiness becometh thine house, O Lord, forever. Ps. xciii:5. Middlebury. T. C. Strong. 1812.

—*An Oration,* pronounced at Middlebury, before the Associated Alumni of the College, on the Evening of Commencement, August 17th,

1825. Published by Request. By Nathan S. S.
Beman. Troy, Printed by Tuttle and Richards,
1825 8vo, pp. 40.

Rev. Dr. Nathan Sidney Smith Beman was born in New
Lebanon, N. Y., Nov. 26, 1785; and died in Carbondale,
Ill., August 6, 1871. He was graduated at Middlebury
College, 1807. Although never a permanent resident of
Vermont, he was in various ways intimately connected
therewith. He was pastor of the first Presbyterian
Church, Troy, N. Y., 1823–1863; he published many Ser-
mons, and compiled a "Church Psalmist."

Benedict, Benjamin Lincoln. *Rules of the
District Court* of the U. S for the Eastern District of New York, in effect July 1, 1893.
Compiled by B. L. Benedict, Clerk. Brooklyn.
1893. pp. 38.

Benedict, Charles Linnaeus. *Charge of Judge
Benedict* to the Grand Jury, delivered at the
October term, 1868, of the U. S. Circuit Court
for the Southern District of New York. pp. 7.

—*Charge to the Grand Jury* U. S. Circuit
Court, Southern District of New York, in reference to offences against the Customs and
Revenue Law of the United States, delivered
by his Honor Judge Benedict, May 10, 1860.
pp. 7. No imprint.

Judge Benedict was born in Newburg, N. Y., in 1824,
being the eldest son of Prof. George W. Benedict. He
graduated from the University of Vermont in 1844;
studied law in New York city and became a member of
the firm of Burr & Benedict; served in the Assembly in
1861 and 1862 and was appointed by President Lincoln, in
March, 1865, to be Judge of the Eastern District of New
York.

Benedict, George Grenville. *The Battle of
Gettysburgh,* and the Part taken therein by
Vermont Troops. By G. G. Benedict, Lieut.
and A. D. C. Burlington : Free Press Print.
1867. 8vo, pp. 24.

Read before the Vermont Historical Society, at a special meeting holden at Brandon, January 26, 1864.

—*Vermont at Gettysburgh.* [Another Edition.]
A Sketch of the Part taken by Vermont Troops,
in the Battle of Gettysburgh. By G. G. Bene-
dict, Lieut. and A. D. C. Burlington : The
Free Press Association. 1870. 8vo, pp. 27.
Appendix, IV.

—*Vermont in the Civil War.* A History of the
Part taken by the Vermont Soldiers and Sailors
in the War for the Union, 1861-5. By G. G.
Benedict, Burlington. Free Press Association,
Vol. I, 1886. 8vo, pp. xv. 620; Vol. II, 1888,
pp. VIII, 808, Maps and portraits.

—*Same,* Special Edition, limited to 150 copies,
2 large vols. 8vo. India proofs of portraits.
Same publishers, 1889.

—*Army Life in Virginia.* Letters from the
Twelfth Regiment Vermont Volunteers, and
Personal Experiences of Volunteer service in
the War for the Union, 1862-3. Burlington Free
Press Association, 1895. 8vo, pp. viii, 196.

G. G. Benedict was born in Burlington, December, 1826.
Second son of Geo. W. Benedict; Associate Editor of the
Burlington Free Press, 1853 to 1865, Editor in Chief 1865
to date; Lieut. 12th Vt. Vols.; State Senator, 1869-70;
State Military Historian, 1879-88; Secretary University of
Vermont, President Vermont Press Association, Presi-
dent Vermont Society Sons of the Revolution, United
States Collector of Customs for Vermont, 1889-93, etc., etc.

Benedict, George Wyllys. *An Oration,* de-
livered at Burlington, Vt., on the Fourth of
July, 1826. Being the Fiftieth Anniversary of
American Independence. By George W. Bene-
dict, A. M. Burlington, Printed by E. & T.
Mills. 1826. 12mo, pp. 26.

—*Report* on the subject of a Geological and
Topographical Survey of the State of Vermont.
Oct., 1837.

The above report occupies nine pages of the Report
and Correspondence on the above subject, printed by
order of the Vermont Senate.

—*New England Educational Institutions* in
relation to American Government. A Discourse delivered before the Phi Sigma Nu and
University Institute Societies of the University
of Vermont, at their Annual Celebration,
August 6, 1844. By George Wyllys Benedict.
Published by request of the Societies. Burlington : Chauncey Goodrich. 1844. 8vo, pp.
48.

—*History* of the University of Vermont.
See University of Vermont.

—*Joseph Torrey and George W. Benedict ;*
Memoir.

Professor George Wyllys Benedict was the son of
Rev. Joel T. Benedict, he was born at North Stam-
ford, Ct., Jany. 11, 1796; and died at Burlington, Vt.,
Sept. 24, 1871. He was graduated at Williams College in
1818; and was a Professor in the University of Vermont,
1825-47; Editor and Proprietor of the Burlington Free
Press, 1853-1865; State Senator, 1854-5; Treasurer Vt. and
Boston Telegraph Co. and builder of the lines of that
Company.
See Memoir, Joseph Torrey and G. W. Benedict; also
Annals of Williams College.

Benedict, Rev Joel Tyler. *A Sermon,* Delivered
at the Ordination of The Rev. Chandler Bates,
to the Pastoral care of the Congregational
Church in Newfane, July 4, 1821. By Joel T.
Benedict, Pastor of the Presbyterian Church,
Chatham, N. Y. [n. p. n. d.] 8vo, pp. 16.

Benedict, Robert Dewey. *Charter History of
the University of Vermont.* An Address delivered on the Centennial Anniversary of the
Granting of the first Charter of the University,
June 24, 1891. Burlington : Free Press Association, 1892. 8vo, pp. 46.

—*The Hereford Map and the Legend of St.
Brandan.* Delivered before the American
Geographical Society, March, 1892. Vol. XXIV,
No. 3. Bulletins of the Am. Geog. Soc. 1892,
pp. 46.

—*Remarks* at the Dinner given to the Delegates
to the International Marine Conference by members of the Admiralty Bar of New York, 1889.
Brooklyn, N. Y., 1889. 12 mo., pp. 15.

—*Two Hundred and Fifty Years Ago.* Address delivered before the New England Society
in the City of Brooklyn, N. Y., March 21, 1888.
In Ninth Annual Report of that Society, Brooklyn, N. Y., 1889.

—*Address* (on Ethan Allen's Literary Style and
use of Language) delivered at the Seventh Annual Dinner of the Vermont Association of Boston, January 31, 1893.

Printed in account of the dinner, pp. 29 to 43. Cambridge : The Riverside Press, 1893.

—*Reports of Cases* Argued and Determined in
the District Courts of the United States, within
the Second Circuit. By Robert D. Benedict.
Vols. I to X, for the years 1869 to 1882. New
York, Baker, Voorhees & Co.

In the issue of the last four volumes B. L. Benedict was
associated with R. D. Benedict.
R. D. Benedict was born in Burlington, October 3, 1828,
being the third son of Prof. G. W. Benedict. He graduated from the University of Vermont in 1848, went to New
York, studied law, was admitted to the New York Bar in

1851. Has been a leading Admiralty lawyer, in New York and Brooklyn, for many years.

Benjamin, Fannie Nichols. *The Sunny Side of Shadow.* Reveries of a Convalescent. Boston. Houghton, Mifflin & Co., 1887. 18mo. pp. 188.

Mrs. Benjamin is a native of Weathersfield, Vt., and the wife of Hon. S. G. W. Benjamin, the author and artist, U. S. Minister to Persia, etc.

Benjamin, L. N. *The St. Albans Raid;* or, Investigation into the charges against Lieut. Bennett H. Young and Command, for their Acts at St. Albans, Vt., On the 19th October, 1864. Being a Complete and Authentic Report of all the Proceedings on the Demand of the United States for their Extradition, under the Ashburton Treaty. Before Judge Coursol, J. S. P. and the Hon. Mr. Justice Smith, J. S. C. —By L. N. Benjamin, B. C. L. Montreal, 1865? 8 vo. pp. 480.

Some copies have the imprint, *Boston, A. Williams & Co.—1865.* SABIN. *See* SOWLES, E. A., Account of the Raid.

Bennett, Edmund Hatch. *The Law of Infancy and Coverture.* By Peregrine Bingham, A. Of the inner Temple. Second American from the last London Edition, with Notes and References to English and American Cases. By E. H. Bennett. Burlington. Chauncey Goodrich. 1849. 8vo. pp. vii, 396.

—*Fire Insurance Cases.* Embracing all the Reported Cases of Fire Insurance in England Ireland, Scotland, and America (including Canada and the British Provinces), from the Earliest Period to 1875. With Notes and References. By Edmund H. Bennett. Boston: Houghton, Mifflin & Co. 5 Vols., 8vo.

—*An Introduction to the Constitutional Law of the United States.* By John Norton Pomeroy. Especially designed for Students, general and professional. Fourth Edition, revised and enlarged by Edmund H. Bennett, Dean of the Boston University Law School. Boston: Houghton & Mifflin, 1868. pp. 709. 8vo, pp. xxxviii +709.

—*A Treatise on Easements.* By John Leybourn Goddard. First American from Second English Edition, enlarged by Edmund H. Bennett. Boston, Houghton, Mifflin & Co. 1880. 8vo, pp. 542.

Judge Edmund H. Bennett was born in Manchester, Vt., the son of Hon. Milo H. Bennett. He graduated from the University of Vermont in 1843; studied law at Harvard Law School; was admitted to the Bar in 1847; resided at Taunton, Mass., 1848-84; Judge of Probate and Insolvency for Bristol Co., Mass., 1858-83; lecturer in Harvard Law School 1870-72. Since 1876 Professor in and Dean of Boston University.

In addition to the above works Judge Bennett has edited and published Bingham on Infancy, Greenleaf's Reports, 9 vols.; English Law and Equity Reports, 3 vols.; Seven editions of Justice Story's Works; Massachusetts Digest of Decisions, 3 vols, Blackwell on Tax Titles; Indermaner's Principles of the Common Law; Benjamin on Sales; Story on Sales; Leading Cases in Criminal Law, etc.

Bennett, Rev. John. *Letters to a Young Lady* on a variety of useful and instructive subjects. Calculated to improve the Heart, to form the Manners and enlighten the Understanding. "That our Daughters may be as polished Corners of the Temple." By the Rev. John Bennett. Sixth American Edition. Two volumes complete in one. Brattleboro. Published by William Fessenden, 1811. 16 mo., pp. 318.

Bennett, Milo L. *The Vermont Justice,* being a Treatise on the Civil and Criminal Jurisdiction of Justices of the Peace, prepared primarily for the use of Justices of the Peace, and the junior members of the Bar in Vermont; Containing a succinct statement of the elementary and more common Principles of Law, whether derived from the Common Law, or Statutory Provisions, accompanied with a copious supply of Practical Forms; embracing also a summary of the Official Duties of Justices of the Peace, etc. By M. L. Bennett, Late Judge of the Supreme Court of Vermont. Burlington. 1864. 8vo. pp. iv, 802.

—*The Law of Railways,* including the Consolidation and other General Acts for regulating Railways in England and Ireland, with copious Notes of Decided Cases on their Construction, including the Rights and Liabilities of Shareholders, Allottees of Shares, and Provisional Committee Men; with Forms, etc. By Leonard Shelford, Esq., of the Middle Temple, Barrister at Law. First American from the third London Edition, with Copious Notes and References to Late English Cases and American Statutes and Decisions. By Milo L. Bennett, LL. D., one of the Judges of the Supreme Court of Vermont. In two volumes. Burlington: Chauncey Goodrich. 1855. Royal 8vo. pp. xxiii, xxxviii, 1236.

Judge Bennett was born in Sharon, Conn., May 28, 1789; and died in Taunton, Mass., July 7, 1868. He was graduated at Yale College, 1811; read Law, and practiced in Burlington, Vt. He was a Judge of the Supreme Court of Vermont, 1839-1859.

BENNINGTON. *At a Meeting* of those of the Church and Congregation of Bennington, who adhere to the Rev. Mr. Avery's Ministry The Honorable Jonas Fay and Moses Robinson, Esquires, were appointed a Committee, to acquaint Mr. Avery, that this meeting do approve of the Stating of the Facts, mentioned in his Narrative of the rise and progress of the Difficulties which have issued in a separation between him and his People, read to them this Day, and to request a Copy for the Press. Isaac Tichenor, Clerk. Bennington, Sept 25th, 1783. Bennington: Printed by Haswell & Russell. 8vo pp. 55.

The Church difficulty in this case arose from the fact that the Rev. Mr. Avery, who had been a Chaplain in the army, upon accepting a call to this Church, brought with his family a female slave, and insisted upon his right to retain her in that relation; hence the trouble.

—*First Census* of the Town of Bennington, Vermont, 1790. David Robinson, Assistant Marshal. Photo-lithographic facsimile by Julius Bien, New York. Folio, 5 sheets.

—*The Court House;* or 100 Days in Bennington. Terminating in the Spring of 1847. New York: 1847. 8vo. pp. 31.

—*Bennington and its Surroundings,* Plate. 1860. 8vo, pp. 16.

Issued by W. H. H. Nutting, Proprietor of the Mount Anthony House.

—*History of.* See JENNINGS, ISAAC.

—*Battle Monument Association.* A Statement By the Bennington Battle Monument Association. Horace Fairbanks, President. Chas. M. Bliss, Secretary. Mottos. A. S. Baker & Son, Printers. Bennington, Vt., 1877. 8vo, pp. 8.

—*Catalogue of the Free Library;* donated to the citizens of Bennington By Seth B. Hunt, Esq., and Trenor W. Park, Esq., June 23, A. D. 1865. Bennington: C. A. Pierce & Co., Printers. 1872. 8vo., pp. 120.

—*Reports of the Town Officers* of Bennington, for the Year ending March 3, 1873. Bennington, Vt.: The Vermont Gazette Power Print. 1873. 8vo, pp. 24.
Continued.
Report for 1872 printed by C. A. Pierce & Co.; 1877, by Cochran & Baker; 1878, by A. S. Baker & Son.

—*State of Vermont.* General Term, Nov., 1877. In Equity. The Town of Bennington vs. Henry F. Lothrop, Trenor W. Park, and Charles G. Lincoln. Opinion of the Court. New York. 1878. 8vo, pp. 29.

—*Report of the Advisory Committee of the Bennington Historical Society*, recommending a design for the Bennington Battle Monument. Bennington, July 9, 1885. pp. 8. No imprint.

—*Dedication of the Bennington Battle Monument*, and Celebration of the Admission of Vermont as a State, at Bennington, Aug. 19, 1891, with an Historic introduction and appendices. Published by authority of the Centennial Committee. Illustrated. Bennington: Banner Print. 1892. Large 8vo, pp. viii, 203.
Contains many portraits.

—*Official Programme* of the Vermont State Centennial and Dedication of the Bennington Battle Monument, at Bennington, Vt., August 19, 1891. Published for the State Centennial Commission. Bennington: Press of C. A. Pierce. 1891. pp. 40.

Bennington, Battle of. *Centennial Anniversary* of the Independence of Vermont and the Battle of Bennington, August 15 and 16, 1877. Westminster—Hubbardton—Windsor. Tuttle & Co., Rutland, Official Printers to the State of Vermont. 1870. 8vo, pp. 232. Numerous portraits and illustrations.
The above edition was suppressed, and the following substituted, with 3 additional portraits, and 20 pages of additional matter.

—*Same* title and imprint. 8vo, pp. 252.

—*The Battles.* 1777. Centennial Celebration, 1877. A Paper Read before The Worcester Society of Antiquity, at its Regular Monthly Meeting, December 4, 1877. By Rev. Albert Tyler. With Copious Notes. Worcester: Tyler and Seagrave, Printers. 1878. Rl. 8vo, pp. 23, (1).

—*Battle Centennial.*

—*Should be called* The Battle of Walloomsac, by Hon. S. D. Locke. 1892. 8vo, pp. 16.

—*The Battle of* with the part recently claimed as taken by New York Troops, fully explained by Henry D. Hall. Pittsfield, Mass. Sun Printing Co. 1894. 8vo, pp. 34.
A Reply to S. D. Locke's paper.
See Forbes, C. S.
See Hall, Hiland, Addresses, etc; Stark, Caleb, Memoir of Gen. John Stark; Keach, J. Address; Butler, J. D. Address before the Vt. Hist. Soc. 1848; Vt. Hist. Soc. Collections, addresses, etc; Address before the Vt. Hist. Soc. by Henry B. Dawson, at Burlington, Jan'y 23, 1861, printed in the Historical Magazine, Morrisania, N. Y., May 1870, and reprinted in the Argus and Patriot, Montpelier, Vt., June 27, July 4, 11, 1877. Coburn, F. W., Bennington Centennial, 1877; Chipman, D., Life of Seth Warner; Jennings, I., Hist. of Bennington; Battles of the

United States, by Sea and Land, By Henry B. Dawson, In two volumes. N. York: 1858, Vol. 1, pp. 255—266, for battle of Bennington, and same vol. pp. 224—236, is Mr. Dawson's account of the Evacuation of Ticonderoga, and the battle of Hubbardton, with official Reports, English and American, and citations of authorities; Battle of Plattsburgh and Lake Champlain, Vol. 2, pp. 378—389.
These two volumes are beautifully gotten up with fine illustrations.

Bennington County. *Atlas of Bennington County. Vermont.* From actual Surveys by and under the direction of F. W. Beers, assisted by Geo. P. Sanford & others. Published by F. W. Beers, A. D. Ellis & G. G. Soule, 95 Maiden Lane. New York. 1869. Folio, pp. 30, (8).

—*Survey of Congregational Churches in,*
See Anderson, James.

—*Gazetteer and Business Directory* of Bennington County, Vt., for 1880-1. Compiled and published by Hamilton Child. Syracuse, N. Y. 1882. 8vo, pp. 500.

Bennington Historical Society. A List of Officers of the Bennington Historical Society, a Statement of its Aims and Objects, and its Constitution. Bennington : C. A. Pierce & Co., Steam Job Printers. 1876. 8vo, pp. 16.
See Hall, Hiland.

Benson. A Narrative of the facts, connected with, as well preceding as subsequent to the Author's withdrawing from the Congregational Church, in Benson, Vt., April, 1838. Castleton, Vt. L. R. H. Robinson, Printer. 1841. 8vo, pp. 24.
Signed John Kellogg. Another church difficulty growing out of Burchardism.

Bent, Rev. J. A. *Thanksgiving,—A Feast Unto the Lord.* A Discourse Delivered in the Congregational Meeting-House of Stowe, Vermont, on the day of Public Thanksgiving, December 8, 1853. By Rev. J. A. Bent. Montpelier : E. P. Walton, Jr., Printer. 1854. 8vo, pp. 24.
Joseph Avery Bent was born in Middlebury, Vt., April 22, 1823; and was graduated at Middlebury College, 1845; was a teacher in Knox College, Ill., and elsewhere, 1845-1850. He became a Congregational preacher, and was one year at Stowe, Vt., and moved to the West.

Benton, J. H., Jr. *Points in Vermont History.* Address before the Boston Vermont Association, by J. H. Benton, Jr., January 27, 1892. Boston: Mudge & Son, Printers. 1891. 8vo, pp. 25.

—*Address by J. H. Benton, Jr.*, at the Dedication of the Bradford Public Library Building, Bradford, Vt., July 4, 1895. Boston: A. C. Getchell, printer. 1896. 8vo, pp. 62.

Benton, Reuben Clark. *The Distinction between Legislative and Judicial Functions*—a Paper read at the Meeting of the American Bar Association, at Saratoga, N. Y., August 20, 1885. by Reuben C. Benton. Reprinted from the Transactions of the Association. Philadelphia: Press of T. S. Dando & Co. 1885. pp. 18.

—*The Vermont Settlers* and the New York Land Speculators, by R. C. Benton. Minneapolis : Housekeeper Press. 1894. pp. 188.

Berlin. *Reports of the Town Officers* of Berlin, For the year Ending March 1, 1867. 8vo, pp. 4.
Continued.

Bethel. *Ye Greate Centennial* At Ye Publick Halle of Wilson's Taverne in Bethel Towne, on Wednesday ye 23d daye of ye 2d Monthe, A. D. 1876. Ye latch-stringe of ye Halle will be hunge out at earlye Candle Lighte. Ye entrance mite is ten cents or 1-10 of one Continental Dollar. Children under ten years of age, Free, Gratis, For Nothing. 8vo, pp. 4.

BIBLE. *The Holy Bible*. Containing the Old and New Testaments: Together with the Apocrypha: Translated out of the Original Tongues: And with the former translations diligently compared & revised: With Marginal Notes and References: To which are added an Index: An Alphabetical Table, Of all the Names in the Old and New Testaments, with their Significations: Tables of Scripture Weights, Measures & Coins: Brown's Concordance, &c. Embellished with Plates. Brattleborough: Printed for John Holbrook. 1816. Collins' Correct Stereotype Copy.

This is an engraved title, and the first page of the next leaf contains a typographical title as follows:

—*[Holbrook & Fessenden's Stereotype Hot-Press Edition.]* The Holy Bible: Containing the Old & New Testaments: Translated out of the Original Tongues, and with the former Translations diligently compared and revised, with Marginal Notes and References. Together with the Apocrypha. To which are added an Index: An Alphabetical Table of all the Names in the Old and New Testaments, with their Significations; Brown's Concordance. And, what has never before been added, An Account of the Lives and Martyrdom of the Apostles and Evangelists. With Plates. Holbrook & Fessenden. Brattleborough, (Vt.) 1821. Quarto: pp. 930 (2.)

The title page to the New Testament, is as follows:

—*The New Testament of our Lord and Savior, Jesus Christ*. Translated out of the Original Greek: And with the former Translation diligently compared and revised. To which are added, The Lives, Sufferings & Martyrdoms of The Apostles & Evangelists. Brattleborough: Printed for John Holbrook. 1816.

The title page to the Concordance is as follows:

—*[Stereotype Edition.]* A Brief Concordance to the Holy Scriptures of the Old and New Testaments: by which all, or most, of the principal Texts of Scripture may be easily found out. By John Brown, Late Minister of the Gospel at Haddington, in Scotland. Motto. Revised and Corrected. Stereotyped by B. and J. Collins. Brattleborough, (Vt.) Printed and sold by John Holbrook. pp. 56.

Then follows the following title, occupying a page:

—*Practical Observations on the Old and New Testaments*, Illustrating the Chapters, A very few excepted, In their Order; with Arguments to the Different Books. By the Rev. Mr. Ostervald, Professor of Divinity, and one of the Ministers of the Church at Neufchatel, in Switzerland. Brattleborough: Holbrook and Fessenden. 1820. pp. 124.

Total pp. in the Volume, 1112.

We have been thus particular in the description of this volume as we do not find it noticed in Dr. O'Callaghan's "List of Editions of the Holy Scriptures," &c.

—*The New Testament* of Our Lord and Saviour Jesus Christ. Brattleborough, Vt. Published by Holbrook & Fessenden. 1822. 18mo, pp. 336.

—*Holy Bible*. With Canne's Marginal References. Also An Index, A Table of Texts, and what has never before been added, An Account of The Lives and Martyrdom of the Apostles and Evangelists, with Plates. The Text corrected according to the Standard of the American Bible Society. Sterotyped by James Conner, New York. Brattleborough, Vt. Printed and Published by Holbrook and Fessenden. 1828. 4to.

Nine large woodcuts. This edition is noticed by Dr. O'Callaghan.

We have an edition of the Quarto Bible, in which all the title pages read, 1816, and on which are inscribed, "Second Edition," and Mr. Fessenden's name does not appear as one of the publishers; and in which "observations," etc., 124 pp. is omitted. J. Holbrook, Publisher. Brattleborough.

—*Bible*. *Brattleborough, Vt*. Printed by J. Holbrook. 1818.

Stereotype edition. 12mo.

—*Holbrook and Fessenden's Stereotype Edition*. The Holy Bible, containing the Old and New Testaments: Translated out of the Original Tongue; And with former Translations diligently compared and revised. Brattleborough, Vt. Printed and Published by Holbrook and Fessenden. 1872. 12mo.

A second edition of the same, published in 1828.

—*New Testament*: Brattleborough, Vt. Published by Holbrook & Fessenden. 1828. 24mo.

—*Holy Bible*. With Apocrypha, Canne's Marginal References, Index, &c. The Text corrected according to the standard of the American Bible Society. Stereotyped by James Connor, New York. Brattleboro, Vt. Published by Peck and Wood. 1833.

—*Brattleboro, Vt*. 1839. The Holy Bible. Published by the Brattleboro Bible Company. pp, 1003, 221.

Engraved Title.

—*Holy Bible*. Containing the Old and New Testaments: Together with the Apocrypha, Translated out of the Original Tongues, and with the former Translations diligently compared and revised, By the Special Command of his Majesty King James I. of England. With Marginal Notes and References. To which are added, An Index; An Alphabetical Table of all the Names in the Old and New Testaments, with their Significations; And Tables of Scripture Weights Measures, and Coins. Windsor: Published by Merrifield and Cochran. Sold Wholesale and Retail by them at the Sign of the Bible. Sold also by I. Thomas, Worcester; J. West & Co., Boston; I. Thomas & Co., Walpole, N. H., and S. Swift, Middlebury, Vt. John Cunningham, Printer. MDCCCXII. Quarto.

The separate title pages to the Old and New Testaments we omit. There are seven exceedingly coarse Engravings, six of which are by Isaac Eddy, of Weathersfield, Vt. This is the first edition of the Scriptures, published in Vermont, of which we have any knowledge.

Dr. O'Callahan collates this edition with great particularity, occupying a page and a quarter in his Octavo work, to which we are indebted for this and some other titles.

—*The Holy Bible Abridged*; or the History of the Old and New Testament. Illustrated with notes, for the use of children. Motto. Windsor: Printed and Published by Jesse Cochran, 1811. 24mo, pp. 180.

—*The Holy Bible abridged*; or the History of the Old and New Testament. For the use of Children. Adorned with cuts. Suffer Little Children, &c. Barnard, Vt. Published by

Joseph Dix, 1813. J. H. Carpenter, Printer. 24mo, pp. 124.

—*The New Testament of our Lord and Savior, Jesus Christ*, Translated out of the Original Greek; and with the former translations diligently Compared and Revised. Windsor, Vt. Printed by Jesse Cochran And sold wholesale and retail, at his Bookstore, and by the principal Booksellers in New England. 1816, 12mo. No pagination.

—*of Our Lord and Savior Jesus Christ*. Translated out of the Original Greek and with the former translations diligently compared and revised. Stereotyped by Hammond Wallis, New York. Windsor, (Vt.) Printed and sold by Simeon Ide. 1826. 12mo. pp. 372.

Another Edition of the same in 1828; also, 1832.

—*of Our Lord and Savior Jesus Christ:* Translated out of the Original Greek; and with the Former Translations Diligently Compared and Revised. Stereotyped by Hammond Wallis, New York. 12mo, pp. 372. Windsor, (Vt.) Ide and Goddard's Power Press.

No date, but printed in 1833, and is the same as the editions of 1826, 1828 and 1832.

—*Stereotyped Edition.* The New Testament of Our Lord and Savior Jesus Christ: Translated out of The Original Greek; and with the former translations diligently compared and revised. Stereotyped by T. H. & C. Carter, Boston. Newbury: Published by White & Read. 1825. David Watson, Printer. Woodstock: 12mo, pp. 283.

—Same title: Claremont, N. H. Published by Stevens & Blake. 1825. David Watson, Printer. Woodstock, 12mo. pp. 283.

Another Edition. Woodstock, Vt., Published by David Watson. 1825. 12mo. pp. 283.

—*The New Testament.* Woodstock, Vt. Rufus Colton. 1828. Small 8vo. pp. 201.

—Also an edition, Woodstock, 1827. Nahum Haskell, Printer.

—*Stereotype Edition.* The Holy Bible, Containing the Old and New Testaments; translated out of the Original Tongues; and with the former translations diligently compared and revised. Stereotyped by B. and J. Collins, New York. Woodstock, Vt. Published by Nahum Haskell and Timothy Bedlington. Boston: 1828. 12mo, pp. 790.

—*Holy Bible:* Woodstock, Vt. R. Colton & G. W. Seeley. 1830. 24mo.

—*The English Version* of the Polyglott Bible. With Marginal Readings and References. Woodstock, Vt. J. B. & S. L. Chase & Co. 1836. 16mo, pp. 867, and 267.

With Engravings.

—*The Polyglott New Testament,* With Marginal Readings and References. Woodstock, Vt. J. B. & S. L. Chase & Co. 1837. 16mo.

This is the New Testament of the edition of 1836, published separately.

—*Testament*, Bennington, Vt. By Darius Clark. 1824. 16mo.

Bigelow, Henry. *A Sermon* Delivered at Castleton, on the 22d of February, 1814, before the Washington Benevolent Society, of the County of Rutland, in commemoration of the birth of Washington. By Henry Bigelow, A. M.,

Pastor of the Congregational Church of Christ in Middletown, Vt. Published by request of the Society. Middlebury, Vt. Printed by Timothy C. Strong. 1814. 8vo, pp. 28.

Rev. Henry Bigelow was born in Marlboro, Ct., February 20, 1777; and died in Middletown, Vt., June 25, 1832. He was graduated at Yale College, 1802; and was pastor of the Church (Congregational) in Middletown, Vt., 1805, until his death.

Bigelow, Henry J. *Dr. Harlow's Case of Recovery* from the Passage of an Iron Bar through the Head. By Henry J. Bigelow, M. D., Professor of Surgery in Harvard University. With a plate. [Extracted from the American Journal of Medical Sciences for July, 1850.] Philadelphia: T. K. & P. G. Collins, Printers. 1850. 8vo, pp. 12.

[The accident treated of occurred at Cavendish, Vt., September 13, 1848, to Phineas P. Gage, during the construction of the Rutland and Burlington railroad.]

Bigelow, J. F. *The Hand of God in American History.* A Discourse delivered in the Baptist Church, Keeseville, N. Y., July 7, 1861; also before the United Literary Societies, Fairfax, Vt., July 15, 1861. By Rev. John F. Bigelow, Burlington: W. H. & C. A. Hoyt & Co., Printers. 1861. 8vo, pp. 42.

Bigelow, John M.

John M. Bigelow was born in Middlebury, Vt., June 23, 1804; and died near Detroit, Mich., July 18, 1878. At an early age he removed with his father's family to Granville, Licking County, Ohio. He read medicine at the Medical College at Cincinnati, and commenced practice in Lancaster, Ohio; he was Physician and Botanist to the Mexican Boundary Commission; he was also appointed Botanist to the Pacific Railway Surveys, and his report was published in Vol. IV of the Pacific Railway Reports. In 1860 he was appointed to take charge of the meteorological department of the survey of the great lakes, when he removed to Detroit; in 1866 he was appointed by President Johnson, Physician to the Marine Hospital at Detroit, but political pressure caused his removal by President Grant. He continued to live near Detroit, however, until his death. Dr. Bigelow was baptized into the Catholic Church at Cincinnati, in 1844 or 1845, by Bishop Purcell, D. D. While living at Lancaster, he wrote many editorials for the *Lancaster Gazette;* he also published in 1847 a "Catalogue of plants growing in Fairfield County, Ohio."

Bigelow, Lucius. *Oration* before the Reunion Society of Vermont Officers, October 31, 1878. By Sergeant Lucius Bigelow, 5th Vt. Volunteers. Montpelier, 1879. Printed by J. & J. M. Poland, 8vo, pp. 15.

Billings, F. *An Address* delivered at the Dedication of the School House in the Fifth District of San Francisco, September 23, 1854. By Frederick Billings, Esq. San Francisco, 1854. 8vo, pp. 20.

—*An Address* delivered at the Fifth Anniversary of the Orphan Asylum Society of San Francisco, at Musical Hall, Tuesday evening, February 5th, 1856. By Frederick Billings, Esq. San Francisco, Whitton, Towne & Co., Printers, Excelsior Job Office, No. 151 Clay Street, third door below Montgomery. 1856. 8vo, pp. 22.

—*Dedication* of the Bust of Frederick Billings, with sketch of his life, in Japanese, by Sho Nemoto. Tokio, Japan, 1895. 8vo, pp. 17.

¹ Frederick Billings was born in Royalton, Vt., September 27, 1823. He graduated from the University of Vermont in 1844; studied law and was admitted to the Bar of Windsor County in 1848; was Secretary of Civil and Military Affairs under Governor Eaton in 1846-48. He went to California in 1849, became a partner in the law firm of Halleck, Peachy, Billings & Park, and was Attorney

General for the State of California. In 1864 he returned to Vermont and to Woodstock, where he made a home which resembles one of the baronial estates of the Old World. He was president of the Woodstock R. R. Co., president of the Northern Pacific R. R. Co., the re-organization and success of which great enterprise was largely his work; a Director in the Nicaragua Canal Co., in the Delaware & Hudson Canal Co., and in various banking and other corporations. He gave the George P. Marsh Library and the Billings Library building to the University of Vermont. He died September 30, 1890.

Bingham, Caleb. *The American Preceptor*, being a new Selection of Lessons for Reading and Speaking, for the use of Schools. Second Vermont Edition. Middlebury, Vt. Timothy C. Strong, Printer. 1815. 12mo.

—*The Columbian Orator.* Containing a variety of Original and Selected Pieces; Together with Rules; Calculated to Improve Youth and Others in the Ornamental and Useful Art of Eloquence. By Caleb Bingham, A. M., Author of the American Preceptor, Young Lady's Accidence, etc. First Vermont Edition. Published according to Act of Congress. Middlebury: Printed and Published by William Slade, Jun. April, 1816. 12mo, pp. 300.

Bingham, Hiram. A Residence of Twenty-one years in the Sandwich Islands; or the Civil, Religious, and Political History of those Islands: Comprising A Particular view of the Missionary operations connected with the introduction and progress of Christianity and Civilization among the Hawaiian People. By Hiram Bingham, A. M., Member of the American Oriental Society, and late Missionary of the American Board. Hartford: Hezekiah Huntington. New York: Sherman Converse. 1847. 8vo, pp. 616.

—*Bartimeus* of the Sandwich Islands. New York: American Tract Society. pp. 58.

Mr. Bingham was born in Bennington, Vt., October 30, 1789; and died at New Haven, Ct., November 11, 1869. For a sketch of his life see *Congregational Quarterly*, No. 4, of Vol. 3, New Series, October, 1871.

Biographical Encyclopedia of Vermont of the Nineteenth Century. Boston: 1885. 4to. pp. 422.

Bishop, Abraham. Rod for the Fool's Back; or Abraham Bishop unmasked. By a Citizen of Connecticut. Reprinted, Bennington: 1800. 16mo. pp. 15.

Noah Webster was the author.

—*Oration* in Wallingford 11th March, 1801, before the Republicans of Connecticut, at their General Thanksgiving for the Election of Thomas Jefferson to the Presidency, and of Aaron Burr to the Vice Presidency. Bennington: Anthony Haswell. 1801. 8vo.

Bissell, Elihu. The Faithful Elder. A Funeral Sermon for the late Elder Elihu Bissell; Preached at Lancaster, Erie Co., N. Y., on Sunday Morning, Feb. 22, 1874. By William Waith, Pastor of the Church. Published by request of the Family. 8vo, pp. 15, (2).

Elder Bissell was born at Randolph, Vt., Sept. 2, 1802; and the family moved to Lancaster in 1807, where Elder Bissell ever after resided. Rev. William Waith has been pastor of the Presbyterian Church in Lancaster, N. Y., for over forty years. (1896).

Bittinger, J. Q. A sermon on the Life and Character of Dea. Elias Bates, of Hartland, Vt. Preached in the Congregational Church, April 27, 1872, by J. Q. Bittinger, Pastor. Claremont, N. H.: Printed by the Claremont Manufacturing Company. 1872. 8vo, pp. 16.

—*Address* at the Funeral of Benjamin Hinman Steele. n. p. n. d. pp. 35.

Mr. Bittinger was born in Berwick, Pa., March 20, 1831; was graduated at Dartmouth College in 1857, and at Andover in 1860; he preached at St. Albans, Vt., 1864–67, Hartland, Vt., 1869–73, and afterwards at Haverhill, N. H. Died 1894.

Blair, Hugh. Abridgement of Lectures on Rhetorick. Windsor, Vt. 1809. 12mo.

—The same. Brattleborough: Published by Holbrook and Fessenden. 1824. 12mo, pp. 202.

Blake, Edmund.

Mr. Edmund Blake, an old and respected citizen of Bellows Falls, Vt., died on Tuesday, August 8, aged 75 He was formerly a papermaker and later was connected with the canal and the lumber business. He published in 1847 a "Handbook for Farmers and Mechanics, Merchants, Lumber Dealers and Workmen," which has been extensively used in Vermont.

Blakely, Quincy. A Historical Discourse delivered at the Centennial Celebration of the Congregational Church in Campton, N. H., October 20, 1874, by Rev. Quincy Blakely, Pastor of the Church, and other papers read on the occasion, with an account of the proceedings at the celebration. Boston: Printed by Alfred Mudge & Son, 34 School Street. 1876. 8vo. pp. 78.

Mr. Blakely was born in Pawlet, Vt., September 17, 1824; was graduated at the University of Vermont in 1854, and at Union Theological Seminary in 1857; preached at Rodman, N. Y., 1858–62; at Campton, N. H., 1864; at Marlboro, N. H., 1888–90; Wakefield, N. H., 1891. Died Feb'y 25, 1892.

Blanchard, Rev. Amos.

Rev. Dr. Blanchard was born in Peacham, Vt., Sept. 8, 1800, and received an academical education at Peacham and Montpelier, graduating at Andover in 1828. He was at Cincinnati some three years as editor of the *Christian Journal*, but returned to Vermont in 1832, and was installed over the Congregational Church at Lyndon, Vt., Jan. 9, 1833; was dismissed in 1836, and subsequently was settled over different parishes in Mass., and N. H. Five of his sermons have been published: "The Nature and Extent of the Atonement;" on the "State of the Times;" 1837. On "Love of Home, its Influence on Religion and Character;" on "Christian Courtesy;" and a Sermon at the funeral of Rev. Benjamin Burge. He married, Aug. 2, 1829, Mary, daughter of Levi Bullock, of Barre, Vt. He died Jan'y 6, 1869.

Blanchard, Rev Jonathan. On the importance and Means of Cultivating the Social affections among Pupils. By J. Blanchard. Delivered before the Institute of Instruction at its Annual Meeting. Boston, August, 1835. 8vo, pp. 28.

—*Secret Societies*, a Discourse, delivered in the Sixth Presbyterian Church, Cincinnati, September 7th, 1845, by J. Blanchard, Pastor. Motto. Cincinnati: Printed by E. Clark, No. 7 West Fourth St., 1845. 8vo, pp. 14.

—*Secret Societies.* An argument before the State Congregational Association, at Rockford, Ill., afterwards delivered in two Discourses in the First Presbyterian Church, (Rev. Mr. Bascom's) in Galesburg, Ill., June 22, 1850, by J. Blanchard, President of Knox College. Text. Galesburg, Ill., Southwick Davis, Printer. 1850. 8vo, pp. 48.

—*A Funeral Sermon*, delivered on the Occasion of the Death of Mrs. Elizabeth S. Bascom, by Jonathan Blanchard, President of Knox College, Galesburg, Illinois, March 29, 1851. Eugene B. Hunt, Printer, Galesburg, Ill., 1851. 8vo, pp. 8.

—*The principles of Human Duty* and their Source. An Address before the Philadelphian Society of Middlebury College, August 19th,

1851. By Rev. Jonathan Blanchard, D. D., President of Knox College, Galesburg, Illinois. Published by the request of the Society. Middlebury : Justus Cobb, Printer, Register Office, 1851. 8vo, pp. 21.

—*Were the New Testament Churches* Slaveholding Churches? The Annual Sermon preached before the American Missionary Association, in the First Presbyterian Church, Cleveland, Ohio, September 24, 1851, by J. Blanchard, President of Knox College. pp. 16.
Printed with the report of the Association.

—*Annual Discourse* before the American Missionary Association, Oct. 21, 1863. pp. 10.

—*Christ purifying his Temple :* or, the Principle of the Puritans. A Sermon preached in the Mount Vernon Church of Christ (Rev. Dr. Kirk's) Boston, Massachusetts, Sabbath, Dec. 24, 1865, "Forefather's Day," by Rev. J. Blanchard, President Wheaton College, Wheaton, Illinois. Boston : Published by the Congregational Board of Education. 1866. 8vo, pp. 29.
Rev. Dr. Blanchard was born in Rockingham, Vt., January 19, 1811; and was graduated at Middlebury College, 1832. He read theology, and was pastor of a Presbyterian Church in Cincinnati, Ohio, 1838-45, when he was chosen President of Knox College, Galesburg, Ill., which position he held many years. His publications are a Debate on Slavery with Rev. N. L. Rice, D. D., and fifteen or twenty pamphlets.

Blanchard, V. W. *A New Mode* of Treating Disease by the application of Heat and Cold over the Ganglionic Centres of the sympathetic Nervous System. By Virgil W. Blanchard, M. D., Bridport, Vt. Boston : David Clapp, Printer. 1864. 8vo, pp. 18.

—*Lectures and Essays*, by Virgil W. Blanchard, M. D., Originator of the Food Cure System. New York : 1878. Published by the Blanchard Food Cure Company, 27 Union Square, N. Y. 8vo, pp. 72.

Blatchford, Samuel. *A Sermon*, delivered at the Ordination of the Reverend Absalom Peters, to the Pastoral Care of the Congregational Church in Bennington, July 5, 1820. By Samuel Blatchford, D. D., Pastor of the United Presbyterian Churches in Lansingburgh and Waterford. Bennington : Printed by Darius Clark. 1820. 8vo, pp. 27.

Bliss, F. S. *Steps in the Pathway* from Youth to Heaven. By Rev. F. S. Bliss. Motto. Montpelier : Eli Ballou, Book and Job Printer. 1868. 12mo, pp. 184.
See Marston, Moses.

Bliss, Henry C. See Dartmouth College, Class Day " Poem," 1868.

Bliss, James C., M. D. *The Beloved Physician.* A Tribute to the Memory of James C. Bliss, M. D. A Discourse on the combined influence of the Gospel and the Medical Profession in forming the Character. By Joel Parker, D. D., Pastor of the Fourth Avenue Presb. Church. Published by the Kappa Lambda Society. New York : 1856. 8vo, pp. 29.
Dr. Bliss was born in Bennington, Vt., January 3, 1791; he read medicine, and was graduated at the New York College of Physicians and Surgeons in 1815. He practiced his profession in New York city until his decease.

Bliss, J. I. *Sermon* preached at the funeral of Capt. Lucius H. Bostwick, in Calvary Church, Jericho, Vt., June 10, 1863. By Rev. J. Isham Bliss. Montpelier : Printed by E. P. Walton. 1863. 8vo, pp. 16.

Bliss, Zenas. *The Philosophy of Temperance:* An Address before the Temperance Society of the University of Vermont, October 18, 1842, By Rev. Zenas Bliss. Published by Request. Burlington : Chauncey Goodrich. 1842. 8vo, pp. 31.

—*The Idea* of the Spiritual Interpretation of Scripture. A discourse, delivered before the Society for Religious Enquiry. In the University of Vermont, at their Commencement Anniversary, July 31, 1843. By Rev. Zenas Bliss. Burlington : Printed by Stillman Fletcher. 1843. 8vo, pp. 72.
Mr. Bliss was born in Randolph, Vt., Nov. 24, 1808; and died in Amherst, Mass., Dec. 9, 1865. He was graduated at the University of Vt. in 1831; and preached in various places in Vermont until 1854, with the exception of about five years which he spent South for his health. At the latter date he retired from the ministry and settled upon a small farm in Amherst.

Blodgett, Constantine. *A Sermon*, preached before the Congregational Church, Pawtucket, Mass., on the late Fast, September 1st, 1837. By Constantine Blodgett, Pastor of the Church. Pawtucket, Mass. Robert Sherman, Printer. 1837. 8vo, pp. 20.

—*The Death of the Righteous.* A Sermon, preached at South Attleboro', February 27, 1841, at the Funeral of Rev. John B. M. Bailey, Pastor of the First Congregational Church. By Constantine Blodgett, Pastor of the Congregational Church, Pawtucket. Pawtucket : R. Sherman, Printer. 1851. 8vo, pp. 18.

—*The Ideal Pastor:* a Discourse Commemorative of Rev. Constantine Blodgett, D. D. delivered by Rev. Thatcher Thayer, D. D. at the Congregational Church, Pawtucket, R. I., January 1st, 1880. Providence : Sidney S. Rider. 1880. 8vo, pp. 28.
Dr. Blodgett was born in Randolph, Vt., Nov. 17, 1802; was graduated at Dartmouth College in 1826; taught in South Carolina, 1826-33; was pastor at Newmarket, N. H., 1834-36, and at Pawtucket, Mass., (now R. I.) 1836-71, and died there, December 29, 1879. See Dartmouth College Alumni.

Blodgett, Daniel E. *History of the Married Life* of Daniel E. Blodgett, of Baltimore, Vermont, who killed his wife at Laconia N. H., Saturday, January 31, 1874, as written by himself. Laconia, N. H.: Printed at the Democrat Office. 1874. 12mo, pp. 27.

Blood, Rev. Caleb. *Election Sermon, 1792.*
Mr. Blood was pastor of the third Baptist Church in Shaftsbury, Vt., 1789-1807. He died in Portland, Maine, 1814.

Boardman, E. J. *Immediate Abolition Vindicated.* An Address, delivered June 26, 1838, before the Randolph Female Anti-Slavery Society, at their Annual Meeting. By Elderkin J. Boardman, A. B., Pastor of the First Church in Randolph, Vt. Published by request. Montpelier, Vt. E. P. Walton & Son, Printers. 1838. 8vo, pp. 13, (2.)
Mr. Boardman was born in Norwich, Vt., June 1, 1791; and died in Marshalltown, Iowa, March 4, 1864. He was graduated at Dartmouth, 1815, and at Andover, 1820; was settled over various Congregational Churches in Vermont, 1822-1842; then a farmer until 1856; when he removed to Iowa, where he resided until his death.

Boardman, Rev. George N. *Baccalaureate Sermon* preached before the Senior Class of

Middlebury College, August 8th, 1858, By Rev. Geo. N. Boardman, Professor in the College. Published by Request of the Class. Middlebury: A. H. Copeland, Publisher. 1858. 8vo, pp. 22.

—*Repentance of Sin and Restoration from Calamity*. A Sermon preached in the Presbyterian Church, Binghamton, On the Day of the National Fast, September 26, 1861, by George N. Boardman. Binghamton: G. W. Reynolds. 1861. 8vo, pp. 18.

—*The Death of President Lincoln*. A Sermon, preached in the Presbyterian Church, Binghamton, Sabbath Morning, April 16, 1865, by George N. Boardman. Published by Request. 8vo, pp. 16. Binghamton, N. Y.: F. N. Chase. 1865.

—*The Value of Systematic Theology to the Preacher*. 8vo, pp. 19.

—*Female Education:* the Importance of Public Institutions for the Education of Young Women. An Address before the Officers and Students of Mount Holyoke Female Seminary, July 18, 1867. By Rev. George N. Boardman, D. D. New York: Charles Scribner & Co., 654 Broadway. 1867. 8vo, pp. 11.

Rev. George Nye Boardman was born in Pittsford, Vt., December 23, 1825, and was graduated at Middlebury College, in 1847, and remained there as tutor until 1849; he graduated at Andover Theological Seminary in 1852; was Professor in Middlebury College, 1853–59; Pastor of Presbyterian Church at Binghamton, N. Y., 1859-1871, and then Professor of Systematic Theology in Chicago Theological Seminary. Mr. Boardman has published other sermons, essays, etc; he writes:

                 Pittsford, Vt., July 1, 1878.

Yours of June 13, reached me a few days since in my vacation retreat. The information you have is correct, I think, so far as I am concerned. I have had published besides the sermons you notice, a sermon on the 50th anniversary of the organization of the First Presbyterian Church in Binghamton, N. Y., November, 1867. Also articles in the Bibliotheca Sacra, Toplady's Works, about 1856, Political Economy as a study for the minister, about 1864; Christian Fellowship about 1875. Also my Inaugural Address was published in 1871, October. I have not my papers here, and can not give you more reliable information—even the titles are given from a not very certain recollection. Wishing you success in your good work.   Yours truly,
            GEORGE N. BOARDMAN.

Boardman, S. W. *Memorial* of Deacon Samuel W. Boardman, born Nov. 27, 1789; Died May 13, 1870. By his son, Rev. S. W. Boardman, D. D. Prepared by request of the Advocate of Peace. Motto. Boston: 1870. 8vo. pp. 19.

Brother of Rev. G. N. Boardman. See Caverly's History of Pittsford, pp. 557-9.

Boorn. *Trial of Stephen and Jesse Boorn,* for the Murder of Russell Colvin, before an adjourned Term of the Supreme Court of Vermont, begun and holden at Manchester, in the County of Bennington, Oct. 26, A. D. 1819. To which is subjoined, the Particulars of the wonderful discovery thereafter, of the said Colvin's being alive, and his return to Manchester, where it was alleged the murder was committed; with some other interesting particulars, relating to this mysterious affair, disconnected with the trial. Rutland, Vt.: Printed and published by Fay and Burt, and by them offered for sale at their Book store, by the dozen, hundred, or thousand. [n. d.] 8vo, pp. 32.

This is one of the most remarkable murder trials on record; the prisoners were sentenced to be executed

January 28, 1820, and December 22 preceding, Colvin appeared in Manchester.

—*Trial of Stephen and Jesse Boorn,* for the Murder of Russell Colvin with the subsequent Wonderful Discovery of Colvin Alive, and an account of his return to Manchester, where the Murder was Alleged to have been committed; with other Interesting Particulars, relating to the Mysterious Affair in addition to the Trial. Second Edition. Rutland, Vt.: Printed and published by Fay and Burt, and for sale by them, at their Bookstore by the thousand, hundred, dozen or single. 8vo, pp. 36.

—*Mystery Developed:* or Russell Colvin, (supposed to be Murdered,) in Full Life; and Stephen and Jesse Boorn, (his convicted Murderers,) rescued from Ignominious Death by Wonderful Discoveries, Containing I. A Narrative of the Whole Transaction, by Rev. Lemuel Haynes, A. M. II. Rev. Mr. Haynes' Sermon, upon the Development of the Mystery. III. A Succinct Account of the Indictment, Trial and Conviction of Stephen and Jesse Boorn. Hartford: Published by William S. Marsh, R. Storrs, Printer. 1820. 8vo, pp. 48.

—*The Dead Alive*. By Wilkie Collins. Fully Illustrated. Boston: Shepard & Gill, publishers. 1874. 12mo, pp. 157.

A romance founded on the Boorn Trial.

—*Trial, Confessions and Conviction* of Jesse and Stephen Boorn, for the Murder of Russell Colvin, and the Return of the Man supposed to have been Murdered. By Hon. Leonard Sargeant, ex-Lieut. Governor of Vermont. Manchester Journal Office. 1873. pp. 48.

See Haynes, Lemuel; Sargeant, Leonard; Waldo, S. Putnam.

Booth Association. Report to the Booth Association, U. S. A. Made by Columbus Smith. Rutland: 1868. 8vo. pp. 64, 2.

—*The Same*, 1869. 8vo. p. 19.

Boston and Montreal Turnpike Company. The Act of Incorporation and the By-Laws. Peacham. Vermont. Printed by Samuel Goss. 1806. 8vo.

This Act was passed in 1805 by the Legislature of Vermont, and William Chamberlain, of Bradford, Samuel C. Crafts of Craftsbury, Stephen Royce, of Berkshire, and other prominent Vermonters were the Corporators.

Bostwick E. A Genealogical Register of the name of Bostwick, with the families of their respective Generations, Births, Marriages and Deaths, as far as obtained, from 1668 to 1850. By Erastus Bostwick. Burlington: Printed by Tuttle & Stacy. 1851. 12mo, pp. 50.

Botta, Mrs. Anne C. (Lynch). Hand-Book of Universal Literature. From the Best and Latest Authorities. By Anne C. L. Botta. 12mo.

—*Same*, New Edition, Revised. Boston: Houghton, Mifflin & Co. 1860. 8vo, pp. 575.

Mrs. Anne Charlotte (Lynch) Botta, was born in Bennington, Vt. Her father, a native of Ireland, at the age of sixteen, joined the United Irishmen of his native country, and for participating in the troubles of 1798, was imprisoned four years and then banished; he was offered a pardon and a commission in the British Army if he would swear allegiance to the Government, but he accepted imprisonment and banishment instead. He came to America, and married a daughter of an officer of our Revolutionary Army, and died soon after the birth of the subject of this sketch. Miss Lynch was educated at Albany, and then resided in Providence, R. I., a short time, where she published in 1841, the "Rhode Island Book,"

12mo. pp. viii, 352; she soon after removed to New York with her mother, where she has since resided. In 1848 an elegant 8vo. volume of her poems was published, illustrated by Durand, Huntington, Darley, and other leading American artists. Her contributions of poems, essays, tales, etc., to the Democratic Review, New York Mirror, and other periodicals and annuals are numerous. In 1855, she married Vincenzo Botta, a nephew of the American Historian.

Mr. Botta is a professor in the University of the City of New York. Mrs. Botta in her elegant retirement had constantly under her charge three or four young ladies whom she taught the accomplishments and elegancies of life, "brought them out" in society, and it may be inferred put them in the way of desirable marriages and settlements in life. She died in March, 1891.

Bottum, Roswell. *History of the Town of Orwell, Vt.*, from 1763 to 1851. By Hon. Roswell Bottum. 8vo. pp. 50. Rutland: Tuttle & Co., Printers. 1881.

Boutelle, Rev. A. *Sermon* occasioned by the Death of Newell Marsh, at Shasta City, California, November, 1852: delivered at Peacham, Vt., January, 1853, by Rev. A. Boutelle. Concord, N. H. 12vo. pp. 21.

Mr. Boutelle was born in Fitchburg, Mass., October, 1804, was graduated at Amherst College in 1828, and at Andover in 1831; preached at Peacham, Vt., 1851, until the time of his death, January 12, 1866.

Bowen, Benjamin. *A Narrative, or Youth's Mirror for the Dissembler,* containing the sufferings that followed from inconstant and false-hearted women, and the author's imprisonment and arraignment before Courts and Jurors. By Benjamin Bowen, of Swanton, Vt. Printed for the Author. 1847.

Boyce, Mrs. Laura Brigham.
Mrs. Boyce, the eldest daughter of Elisha Brigham, and sister of Dr. G. N. Brigham, formerly of Montpelier, Vt., was born in Fayston, February 27, 1840. Books and newspapers were the delight of her childhood, and her longing for knowledge was intense. At the age of ten she began to compose short poems, the first that her friends ever saw being a tribute presented to her teacher at the closing of school. Her first poem that was offered for publication was written at the age of 12 years, and appeared in the "Green Mountain Freeman," D. P. Thompson being at that time the editor. He gave her much encouragement that she remembers gratefully. She contributed to that paper many poems from time to time, and in later years articles in prose. Her early writings appeared under the pseudonym of "Minnie Moore," but after her marriage she usually appended her real signature. In the last ten years Mrs. Boyce has written many tales, essays, historical sketches, etc., etc., for different periodicals. Among the papers to which she has contributed are "The Vermont Watchman and Journal," "Argus and Patriot," "Green Mountain Freeman," "Vermont Farmer," published at St. Johnsbury, "The St. Albans Messenger," "The Vermont Record and Farmer," "The American Cultivator." "Zion's Herald," "Waverly Magazine," the three last Boston, Mass., papers, "The Saturday Evening Post," Philapelphia, Pa., and some others. She also wrote the history of Fayston for Miss Hemenway's Gazetteer. All her literary work has been done at a disadvantage, from a pure love of writing, in the rare leisure moments of a busy life, full of many cares. Mrs. Boyce continues (1880) to reside in Fayston.

Boyce, L. W.
See SMITH, MRS. D. T., (BOYCE.)

Boyce, Mrs. S. Minerva.
Mrs. Boyce is a native of Fayston, Vt., daughter of the late Hon. Ziba W. Boyce. She has written stories, poems, historical sketches, etc.; was a correspondent of the "Vermont Farmer," and a contributor to the "Boston Cultivator," "Argus and Patriot" and "Watchman and Journal." The early portion of her life was spent among the birds and flowers, the green hills and sparkling brooks, when not at school; she still loves the grand and glorious works of nature far better than all the magnificent works of art this wide world can afford. She still (1880) spends many leisure hours in the study of Geology, Ornithology and Botany, all of which afford her much pleasure.

Boyle, R. *Voyages and Adventures* of Captain Robert Boyle, in several parts of the World. Intermixed with the story of Miss Villars, an English lady, with whom he made his surprising escape from Barbary. Likewise including the History of an Italian Captive and the life of Don Pedro Aquilio, etc. Full of various and amazing turns of fortune. Montpelier, Vt. 1812. Printed by Wright & Sibley, for Isaiah Thomas and Company, Walpole, N. H. 12mo, pp. 262.

Boynton, Edward C. *History of West Point,* and its Military Importance during the American Revolution: And the Origin and Progress of the United States Military Academy. New York: D. Van Nostrand. London: Sampson Low, Son & Co. 1863. 8vo, pp. xvi, 408.

A native of Vermont, was graduated at West Point, 1846; served through the Mexican War, where he was severely wounded. He was a Professor at West Point, 1848-55; served in the Seminole War, 1855-6; was a Professor in the University at Mississippi, 1856-61; Capt. 11th U. S. Infantry, 1861; Adjutant and Quarter-Master at West Point until 1865; brevet Major U. S. A. 1865; resigned December, 1872. Author of a history of the United States Navy.

Boynton, N. *Original Prose and Poetry* embracing a variety of novel, moral and political subjects; by N. Boynton, of Derby, Vt. Published by N. Boynton. 1856. 16mo, pp. 253. See Vt. Hist. Gazetteer. Vol. 3, p. 194.

Bradford. *Manual* of the Congregational Church in Bradford, Vermont, with a catalogue of its Members: unanimously adopted June 3, 1859. Bradford: Butler & Fuller's Power Press Office. 1859. 16mo, pp. 32.

—*Report* of the Superintendent of Common Schools, for the town of Bradford, for the year ending March 31, A. D. 1862. By Rev. J. Britton. Published by vote of the town. G. C. Chamberlin, Printer, Bradford, Vt. 8vo, pp. 20.
Continued.

—*Financial Report* of the Town of Bradford, March 1, 1876. Bradford: Ben. F. Stanton, Book and Job Printer. 1876. 8vo, pp. 16.
Continued.

—*History of.* See MCKEEN, SILAS.

—*Catalogue* of Bradford Public Library, Bradford, Vt. Montpelier, Vt.: Argus and Patriot Steam Book and Job Printing Works. 1880. 16mo, pp. 39.

—*Bradford* Cook Book and Miscellaneous Recipes. To be sold for the benefit of the Organ Fund of the Congregational Church. Bradford, Vt.: Orange Co. Publishing Co., General Job Printers. 1881. 8vo, pp. 46.

Bradford, E. *Christ's Presence with His Ministers,* Illustrated. A Sermon, Delivered at the Ordination of the Reverend Daniel Gould, to the work of an Evangelist, At Fairlee—State of Vermont, Oct. 2, 1795. By Ebenezer Bradford, A. M. Pastor of the First Church in Rowley. Published by Desire. Newburyport: Printed by William Barrett, at his Printing Office, Market Square, 8vo, pp. 30.

—*The Qualifications,* Commission and Work of an Ambassador for Christ, Illustrated. A Sermon, delivered at the Ordination of the Rev. Nathaniel Lambert, to the pastoral care of the

Church of Christ in Newbury, in the State of Vermont, November 17th, MDCCXC. By Ebenezer Bradford, A. M., Pastor of the First Church in Rowly. Printed at Windsor, Vt., by Alden Spooner, MDCCXCI. 8vo, pp. 18.

Bradford, Oren. *The Old and New Earth; Millennial Day! and Day of Judgment.* By Oren Bradford. Motto. Rutland: Tuttle & Company, Printers. 1874. 12mo, pp. 32.

Bradley, Joshua, A. M. *An Improved Spelling Book,* or Youth's Literary Guide; containing an easy system of spelling and pronunciation, a short system of polite learning, and an English grammar: Being selected from the most approved authors on education, and arranged in such order as to render it a useful book for schools and private families throughout the American Government. By Joshua Bradley, A. M. Motto. Windsor: Printed by Oliver Farnsworth. 1815. 12mo, pp. 192.

—*A Spelling Book,* formed upon an Easy, Systematical Plan, and Designed for small Children and Beginners. By Joshua Bradley, A. M., Author of the "Youth's Literary Guide." Motto. Windsor: Printed by Oliver Farnsworth. 1815. Square 16mo, pp. 64.

—*Some of the Beauties of Free-Masonry ;* Being extracts from Publications, which have received the approbation of the Wise and Virtuous of the Fraternity: With Introductory Remarks, Designed to remove the Various Objections made against the order. By Joshua Bradley, A. M. Member of Newport Royal Arch Chapter No. 2.—Kt. R. C. K. M.—K. T.— and Grand Chaplain of Washington Encampment No. 2, of Newport, R. I. Rutland, Vt. Printed by Fay & Davison, 1816, 18mo, pp. VI., 818.

Mr. Bradley was pastor of the Baptist church at Windsor, 1814-15; he came from Newport, R. I.

Bradley, Stephen Row. *Vermont's Appeal to the Candid and Impartial World.* Containing a fair stating of the claims of Massachusetts-Bay, New-Hampshire, and New-York. The Right the State of Vermont has to Independence. With an Address to the Honorable American Congress, and the Inhabitants of the Thirteen United States. By Stephen R. Bradley, A. M. Hartford: Printed by Hudson & Goodwin. 8vo, pp. 51.

This pamphlet is without date, but was published early in 1780. It was also reprinted in the semi-weekly *Eagle,* Brattleboro, Nos. 57-62, 1851; also in Records of the *Governor and Council* of Vermont, pp. 200-222 of Vol. 2. An account of it may be found in *B. H. Hall's Eastern Vermont,* page 596. It is one of the ablest papers emanating from Vermont, during her twenty-five years' struggle for Independence.

Mr. Bradley was born in Cheshire, Conn., February 20, 1754; and died at Walpole, N. H., December 9, 1830. He was of "Round Head" ancestry, his grandfather having served under Cromwell; he settled in Connecticut about 1650. The subject of this sketch was graduated at Yale, 1775, entered the military service as Captain, 1776, where he continued as Adjutant, Commissary and Major until 1779. The first known of him in Vermont, was in May, 1779, at Westminster, where he was admitted as an Attorney at law, and appointed Clerk of the Supreme Court. He held most of the more prominent offices, and was one of the most able and foremost men in behalf of the independence of the State.

See *Hall's Eastern Vermont* page 593.

Bradley, Wm. Czar. *Oration* at Westminster, Vt. July 4, 1799. By Wm. C. Bradley. Wal-

pole: Printed by David Carlisle, for Thomas & Thomas. 1799. 4to, pp. 16.

—*Tribute* to the memory of, See Frothingham, F.; Willard, Mrs. S. B.

Mr. Bradley, son of Stephen Row, was born March 23, 1782, at Westminster, Vt.; and died there March 3, 1867. He entered Yale College, but was expelled for some alleged cause, and years after when he had become distinguished, the College authorities sent him a degree, saying that they had become convinced that he was not guilty of the wrong for which he was expelled; but Mr. Bradley declined to receive the degree. He was admitted to the Bar in 1802; was State's Attorney 1804-11; member of the Legislature, 1806-7, 1819 and 1852; Presidential Elector, 1856; Member of Congress, 1813-15, and again, 1823-27; Agent of the United States, under the treaty of Ghent; and member of the State Constitutional Convention in 1857. He was one of the most able men our State has produced; was the Democratic candidate for Governor for many years, as well as for most of the prominent offices in the State, but the party being in a minority, the State lost in a large degree the benefit of his services during the last forty years of his life. He received the degree of LL. D. from the University of Vermont in 1851.

Brainerd, Charles D. *Danville in the War of the Rebellion,* by Charles D. Brainerd. Printed by N. H. Eaton, Danville. 1878.

Mr. Brainerd served during the Civil War as a Captain in the 15th regiment, Vermont Vols., and Captain in the 17th Vt. Vols.

Brainerd, Ezra. *English Literature in Schools.* An Address delivered before the Vermont State Teachers' Association, at Rutland, January 31st, 1873. By Ezra Brainerd, Professor of Rhetoric, Middlebury College. Rutland: Tuttle & Co., Printers. 1873. 8vo, pp. 11.

—*The Geological Features* of the Marble Belt of Western New England. Proceedings of Middlebury Historical Society, pp. 7-21, vol. I., Part II. Middlebury. 1885.

—*The Original Chazy Rocks.* Reprinted from the American Geologist, Vol. II. Nov., 1888, pp. 7.

—*The Calciferous Formation* in the Champlain Valley. Bulletin of Am. Museum of Natural History, Vol. III, pp. 1-23. June, 1890.

—*The Chazy Formation* in the Champlain Valley. Bulletin of the Geological Society of America, Vol. II., pp. 293-300. March, 1891.

—*Life & Work* in Middlebury, Vt., of Emma Willard, by Ezra Brainerd, LL. D. 1893. 12mo., pp. 17.

Pres. Brainerd's Baccalaureate sermons have been printed yearly in the "Undergraduate" since 1887.

Ezra Brainerd, LL. D., was born at St. Albans, Vt., Dec. 17, 1844. His early life was spent in that town, where he received his preparation for college. He graduated from Middlebury College in 1864, receiving the first honor, and was immediately appointed tutor for the following year. After serving for two years as tutor he entered the Theological Seminary at Andover, Mass., where he graduated in 1868. He was at once appointed to the chair of Rhetoric and English Literature in Middlebury College, left vacant by the resignation of Professor Brainerd Kellogg. He filled this position until 1880, when he was made Professor of Physics and Applied Mathematics. In 1885, upon the resignation of the Rev. Dr. Cyrus Hamlin, he was appointed temporary president by the Board of Trustees, and on April 17, 1886, he was elected eighth president of the college. President Brainerd has given much study to several departments of Natural Science, and has made several important contributions to the Botany and Geology of Vermont. In 1887, he was one of the three commissioners appointed to revise the school laws of the State of Vermont. In 1888, he received the degree of LL. D. from Ripon College, Wisconsin, and also from the University of Vermont.

Braintree. *Auditors' Report* of the Claims against and in favor of the Town of Braintree,

For the year ending March 1, 1861. Montpelier : Printed at the Freeman Printing Establishment. 1861. 8vo, pp. 14.
Continued.

—Braintree Centennial. 1781–1881. 8vo, pp. 14.

—The History of Braintree, Vt., by H. Royce Boss, Rutland ; Tuttle & Co.,1883. 8vo, pp. 208.

Branch, & Co., H. D. *A Descriptive Catalogue* of Select Fruit and Ornamental Stock, cultivated and for sale at the Orwell Nurseries. H. D. Branch & Co., Proprietors. Orwell, Vermont. Rutland : Tuttle & Company, Printers. 1872. 8vo, pp. 11.

Brandon. *Evils of the Revolutionary War.* Brandon. 1842.
Title from E. P. Boon, New York.

—*Congregational Church.*
On first page of cover, "Brandon Congregational Church." On first page, "Cross," and below in red letters, "Brandon Congregational Church." On second page, "Franklin Tuxbury, Pastor. Installed May 25, 1865. E. D. Selden, Deacon and Clerk." 12mo, pp. 15.
Contains rules, etc., and a list of members in 1869. No imprint.

—*Congregational Church.* List of members, etc. May 25, 1872. 12mo, pp. 4.

—*Catalogue* of the Brandon Congregational S. S. Library, March, 1873. 12mo, pp. 11.

—*Catalogue* of Books in the Brandon Ladies' Book Club Library. March 1st, 1873. Rutland: Tuttle & Co., Printers. 1873. 12mo, pp. 12.

—*Catalogue* of books in the Brandon Baptist Sunday School Library. Revised Dec. 1877, Rutland: Tuttle & Co.,printers, 1877,12mo,pp.14.

—*Report of the Building Committee* of the Town Hall of the Town of Brandon. March 5th, 1861. H. Truss, Printer, Brandon, Vt. 1861. 8vo, pp. 9.

—*Report of the Minority* of The Building Committee Appointed by the Town of Brandon, to Superintend the Building of the Town Hall. Printed by order of Town, March 3, 1863. Rutland. Tuttle & Gay, Printers. 1863. 8vo, pp. 11.

—*Auditors' Report* for the Town of Brandon, March 4, 1862. And Report of Town Hall Committee. Rutland : Geo. A. Tuttle & Co., Printers. 1862. 8vo, pp. 19.

—*Annual Report* of the Board of Auditors for the Town of Brandon, February 25,1871. Rutland : Tuttle & Company Printers. 1871. 8vo, pp. 35.
Continued.

—*By-Laws of Neshobe Engine Co. No. 1.* Brandon, Vt. Adopted November 25, 1872. Organized October 28, 1872. " We strive to save !" Rutland : Tuttle & Co., Printers. 1872. 18mo, pp. 8.

—*Report of the Prudential Committee* of the Brandon Graded School District, 1877. Brandon : Mott Bros' Union Print, 1877. 8vo, pp. 8.
Continued.

—*Graded School Catalogue.*
See Educational.

—*By-Laws and Rules of Order* of the Sprague Guards of Brandon, Vt. Company C, First Reg't N. G. Vt. Adopted at a Meeting of the Company Nov. 16, 1878. Brandon : Stillman B. Ryder, Job Printer. 1879. 18mo, pp. 10, (2).

—*Catalogue* of the Farmers and Mechanic's Library, Brandon, Vermont. Brandon ; Mott Bros'. "Union" Print. 1877. 12mo, pp. 17.

Brattleboro. *A Description* of the Brattleboro Hydropathic Establishment, with a Report of 563 Cases treated there. [By Robert Wesselhoeft, the Proprietor.] Brattleboro : Printed by F. B. Miner. 1848. 8vo, pp. 32. View.

—*Also Report* of 392 cases treated in 1848. Brattleboro. 1849. 8vo, pp. 96.

—*Prospectus* of the Lawrence Water Cure, Brattleboro, Vt. Opened May 15, 1853. New York : Printed by Curran Dinsmore & Company. 1853. 8vo.

—*The Attractions of Brattleboro.* Glimpses of the Past and Present. By Henry M. Burt, Late Editor of the Northampton Free Press and Vermont Record. Brattleboro, Vt. D. B. Stedman Printer. 1866. 12mo, pp. 108. Plate.

—*The Eleventh Annual Report* of the Financial Condition of Brattleboro. February 1, 1867. Brattleboro : Press of D. B. Stedman, 1867. 8vo, pp. 12.
Continued.

—*Twentieth Annual Report* of the Financial Condition of the Town of Brattleboro for the Year ending February 7, 1876. Brattleboro : Printed by Geo. E. Selleck. 8vo, pp. 22.
Continued.

—*in the Vermont Historical Gazetteer*, Windham County. Vol. IV. Compiled and published by Miss Hemenway, Burlington, Vt. Price 50 Cents a Number. Brattleboro : D. Leonard, Steam Printer. 1879. 8vo, pp. 24.
This number was prepared by Henry Burnham.

—*Our Brattleboro Beaux.* By Goldthwaite Lyle. A Fifty dollar prize Story published in the Vermont Record, Nov. 16, 1865, et seq.

—*A Manual* for the use of the Centre Congregational Church of Brattleboro, Vt. 1859. Brattleboro: Printed by Geo. E. Selleck. 18mo, pp. 46.

—*Confession of Faith* and Covenant of the Congregational Church in Brattleboro' West. n. d. n. p. 16mo, pp. 4.

—*Catalogue* of the Brattleboro Village Library. E. J. Carpenter, Librarian. Brattleboro : J. H. Capen, Printer. 1860. 8vo, pp. 43.

—*Dedication* of the Baptist Meeting House.
See Foster, Joseph C.

—*C. E. Allen's Catalogue* of Greenhouse and Bedding Plant Department, for 1880. 64 Canal Street, Brattleboro, Vt. D. Leonard, Printer, Brattleboro. 8vo, pp, x. 88.

—*Brattleboro*, Windham County, Vermont. Early History, with Biographical Sketches of some of its Citizens. By Henry Burnham and edited by Abby Maria Hemenway, of the Vermont Historical Gazetteer. Brattleboro : Published by D. Leonard. 1880. 8vo, pp. 191. Portraits and Plates.

—*Brattleboro* in Verse and Prose, compiled by Cecil Hampden Howard, Brattleboro, 1885. Frank E. Housh, publisher. 12mo, pp. 59,

—*Proceedings* at the Dedication of the Brooks Library Building, Brattleboro, Vt., January 25, 1887. With address by Hon. Mellen Chamberlain, LL. D. Cambridge: John Wilson & Son. 1887. 8vo, pp. 52.

Bread Loaf Inn. *Ripton, Vt.* 1895. No imprint. pp. 43. Illustrations of Vt. Scenery.

Bridport.
See Smith Centennial Memorial.

Brierly, O. *The Religious Library.* A Collection of Select Literature. Edited by Rev. B. Brierly. Lowell: P. O'Niel, Printer. 1842. 8vo, pp. 588.

Briggs, F. J. *A Poem.* The Song of Moses and the Lamb. A Discourse By F. J. Briggs of New Haven, Vt. Middlebury: Printed by Knapp & Jewett for the Author. 1835. 12mo, pp. 20.

Briggs, William P. *An Oration* pronounced at Williston, July 4, 1829, by Wm. P. Briggs, Esq. Burlington: Printed at the office of the Free Press. 1829. 8vo, pp. 15.

Brigham, Gershom Nelson. *The Harvest Moon* and Other Poems. By G. Nelson Brigham. Cambridge: Printed at the Riverside Press. 1870. 12mo, pp. vi, (1) 180.

—*Second Edition,* same title, 1874. 12mo, pp. vi. (1), 212.

Dr. Brigham was born in Fayston, Vt., March 3, 1820, and died in Chicago, June 21, 1886. He was descended in the 6th generation from Thomas Brigham, who came from England in 1635, and settled in Cambridge, Mass., near the present University buildings; on the maternal side he was descended from Aquilla Chase, of New Hampshire. Dr. Brigham labored upon the farm until nearly twenty years old, and was educated in the District school, Washington County Grammar School, and similar institutions; read medicine, and was graduated at Woodstock, Vt., Medical College in 1845, and practiced Allopathy in Waitsfield and Warren, Vt., until 1854, when he adopted the Homœopathic system. Dr. Brigham moved to Montpelier, Vt., in 1854, and thence to Grand Rapids, Mich., in 1874. He was prominent in the formation of the Vermont Homœopathic Medical Society, of which he was for a long time President and Secretary. Dr. Brigham was a liberal contributor to the periodical and newspaper press, both in prose and verse; active in the lecture field, and delivered many addresses before medical and other organizations. He was a member of the Scientific Society of Michigan.

Brigham, Josiah Fay. *Memorial* to Josiah Fay Brigham, Esq., Of Bakersfield, Vt. Address at the Funeral (with Biography), by Rev. Geo. F. Wright, Friday, August 30. Sermon Preached by the Pastor, Sunday, September 1. Andover: Printed by Warren F. Draper, Main Street. 1878. 8vo, pp. 32

Brighton, (Vt.) *Annual Report* of the Selectmen, Treasurer, School District No. 5, and S. S. Committee of Brighton, for the year ending March 5, 1861. Portland: Ira Berry & Son, Printers. 1861. 8vo, pp. 8.
Continued.

Brockway, J. *The Resolution,* adopted by the State Temperance Convention, at Northfield, Vt., January 1858. Its Crudity and Absurdity, Or, the old theory of Government—"Protect the Good and Suppress the Evil," vs. The New To be rid of the Evil destroy the Good. Motto. By J. Brockway. Northfield. 1858. 8vo, pp. 26.

Bronson, A. *A Plain Exhibition* of Methodist Episcopacy. Burlington: 1844. 12mo, pp. 248.

Mr. Bronson was Rector at Arlington and Manchester, Vt., 1803-1833; and perhaps longer at the latter place.

Brookfield. Minutes of the proceedings of a Brigade Court Martial, Holden at Brookfield, on the Second Monday of February, A. D. 1822. Montpelier, Vt.: Printed by E. P. Walton. 1822. 8vo. pp. 54.
This was for the trial of Capt. John Orcutt, and other prisoners; Col. E. P. Walton, of the 5th Regiment, was President of the Court.

—*Report of the Financial Affairs* of the Town of Brookfield, including the Report of the Superintendent of Schools for the year ending March 1, 1881. 8vo, pp. 8.
Continued.

—*History of* See Wild, E. P.; Bushee, W. A.

Brookfield Town Library Report of the Centennial Proceedings, including an Address and Poem, with a list of the Founders. Montpelier 1891. pp. 27.

Brooks, Rev. Charles. An Essay on Terms of Communion at the Lord's Table. By Charles Brooks, Preacher of the Gospel. Windsor, Vt.: Printed for the Author, by Simeon Ide. 1822. 12mo., pp. 28.

—*A Reply* to the Rev. Elisha Andrews' Strictures on the Author's Essay in favor of Christian Communion: Also, (At the close) A further illustration of the Principle of Christian Communion. By Charles Brooks, Minister of the Gospel, and member of a church in the Baptist denomination. Windsor, Vt. Published for the Author. Simeon Ide, Printer. 1823. 8vo. pp. 59.

Brooks, Mrs. S. T. Chronicles of St. Johnsbury Academy in ye very olden time. By Mrs. S. T. Brooks. Published by many requests. Motto. Claremont, N. H.: The Claremont Manufacturing Company, Printers. 1877. 16mo, pp. 24.

Brown, A. Epistle to the Members of the Unitarian Congregational Church, Brattleborough, Vt. Brattleborough. 1836.

Brown, Adna. From Vermont to Damascus returning by way of Beyrout, Smyrna, Ephesus, Athens, Constantinople, Budapest, Vienna, Paris, Scotland, and England. By Adna Brown, with sixteen illustrations. Also instructions how to prepare for such a Journey. Boston: George H. Ellis, Printer, 1895. 12 mo, pp. 209.

Brown Association. Report to the Brown Association, U. S. A., made by C. M. Fisher, A. D. 1866. Published by order of the Brown Association. Middlebury: Printed at the Register Book and Job Office. 1866. 8vo, pp. 8.

Brown, Clark. The Moral and Benevolent Design of Christianity and Freemasonry Discussed: A Sermon Preached June 24th, A. L. 5808. At the Celebration of the Festival of St. John the Baptist, in Danville, (Vt.) By Clark Brown. A. M. A few years since Minister in Brimfield, Massachusetts. Danville: Printed by Ebenezer Eaton. 1808. 8vo, pp. 24.

—*The Utility of Moral and Religious Societies,* and of the Masonick in particular. A Sermon delivered in Putney, Vt., on the Anniversary of St. John the Baptist, June 24, 1814. Anno Lucis, 5814. Before the officers and members of Golden Rule, Mount Moriah, Blazing Star, and Columbian Lodges, of Free and Accepted Masons, in the County of Windham, Vt., joined by Jerusalem Lodge, from Westmoreland, N. H. To which is prefixed a prayer, comporting with the Sentiments of the Sermon. By Brother Clark Brown, A. M. Keene, N. H.: Printed by Brother John Prentiss, for the Lodges of Windham County, (Vt.) 1814. 8vo, pp. 24.

See Allen's Biog. Dic. pp. 148.

—*The Declaration of the* Independence of the United States, and the Constitution, with its several amendments. And the Constitution of Vermont. With an Extract from the Laws of the State, regulating Freeman's Meetings: To which is added the valledictory address of the Illustrious George Washington, on his retiring from the Presidency of the United States. Compiled by Clark Brown. Montpelier: Printed by Benjamin H. Wheeler, for Brown & Parks, 1807. 16mo. pp. 76.

Mr. Brown was the first stated Minister settled in Montpelier; he was hired in 1805, in accordance with a vote of the town, to preach one year, at five dollars per Sunday, in addition to what he could pick up in perquisites from marriages and extra sermons. But he only remained about six months in consequence of differences of opinion among the people on theological questions and in relation to Mr. Brown's real piety. The people appear to have become negligent in attending church, and Mr. Brown preached a pointed sermon in reference to it, which so offended them that they paid him for a full year's preaching and dismissed him.

Mr. Brown was a Unitarian, and the settlers of Montpelier having been in the habit of passing Sunday in horse racing and kindred sports, he probably felt that they ought to have a little brimstone in theirs.

Mr. Brown remained in Montpelier, and about the middle of November, 1806, started a weekly newspaper, the first published in town, called the Vermont Precursor, which he continued a few months, when he sold it to Samuel Goss, who a few months later re-christened it the Vermont Watchman, which is still continued. Mr. Brown afterwards went West, and died there. Mrs. Brown, after the death of her husband, pushed on further West, until she reached Oregon, where she established a school, out of which grew the Pacific University, of which Sidney H. Marsh was President, and his younger brother Joseph is Professor, both being natives of Burlington, Vt., sons of the late President James Marsh, of the University of Vermont; on the maternal side they are descended from Rev. Dr. Eleazar Wheelock, founder of Dartmouth College.

Brown, (Mrs. D. C.) Memoir of Rev. Samuel, and his son, Rev. A. L. Covell.

See Covell, Samuel.

[Brown, John] *The Elements of Medicine:* or, a translation of the Elementa Medicina Brunonis. With large Notes, Illustrations and Comments By the Author of the original work. The Sixth Edition. Fair Haven: Printed by James Lyon, at Voltaire's Head. M,DCC,XCVII. 12mo. pp. xiv, 404, (12).

Native of Berwickshire, England.
See Allibone's Dictionary, vol. I, page 258.

Brown, John. *A brief view of the Figures;* and explication of the Metaphors, Contained in Scripture. By John Brown, Minister of the Gospel at Haddington. First American Edition. Middlebury, Vt. Published by Samuel Swift. T. C. Strong, Printer. 1812. 12mo, pp. 480.

—*The Same Edition,* with a new title page pasted in. Middlebury: Published by A. Colton. 1832.

A Native of Carpow, Scotland.
See ALLIBONE, vol. I, page 257.

Brown Rev. J. Newton. *Fessenden & Co's Encyclopedia* of Religious Knowledge: or Dictionary of the Bible, Theology, Religious Biography, All Religions, Ecclesiastical History, and Missions; Containing Definitions of all Religious Terms; an Impartial Account of the Principal Christian Denominations that have existed in the world from the Birth of Christ to the Present Day, with their Doctrines, Religious Rites and Ceremonies, as well as those of the Jews and Mohammedans, and Heathen Nations, together with the Manners and Customs of the East, Illustrative of the Holy Scriptures, and a Description of the Quadrupeds, Birds, Fishes, Reptiles, Insects, Trees, Plants, and Minerals, Mentioned in the Bible; a Statement of the most Remarkable Transactions and Events in Ecclesiastical History; Biographical Notices of the Early Martyrs and Distinguished Religious Writers and Characters of all Ages. To which is added a Missionary Gazetteer, Containing Descriptions of the Various Missionary Stations throughout the Globe; by Rev. B. B. Edwards, Editor of Quarterly Observer. The whole Brought down to the Present Time, and embracing, under one Alphabet, the most Valuable Part of Camlet's and Brown's Dictionaries of the Bible; Buck's Theol. Dictionary; Abbott's Scripture Natural History; Well's Geography of the Bible; Jones' Biographical Dictionary; and numerous other Similar Works. Designed as a Complete Book of Reference on all Religious Subjects; and Companion to the Bible; Forming a Cheap and Compact Library of Religious Knowledge. Edited by Rev. J. Newton Brown. Illustrated by Wood-Cuts, Maps and Engravings on Copper and Steel. Brattleboro'; Published by Fessenpen & Co. 1836. Royal 8vo, pp. 1275.

—*Another edition;* Brattleboro', Vt.: Published by Joseph Steen & Co. Philadelphia: Lippincott, Grambo & Co. New York: Lewis Colby. 1854.

—*Other Editions.*

Mr. Brown was a Baptist clergyman and author, born in New London, Ct., June 29, 1803; died in Germantown, Pa., May 15, 1868. See *Drake's Dictionary of Biography.* The above work was re-published in England.

Brown, Samuel Gilman. *A Discourse* commemorative of the Hon. George Perkins Marsh. Delivered before the Faculty and Students of Dartmouth College, June 5, 1883, and before the Trustees, Faculty and Students of the University of Vermont, June 25, 1883, by Samuel Gilman Brown, D. D., LL. D. Published by request. Burlington: Free Press Print. 1883, pp. 37, (4).

See HANDOCK, C. B., Sermon on the death of.

Brown, S. R. *Views of the Campaigns* of the North-Western Army, &c. Sketches of the Campaigns of Generals Hull and Harrison—A minute and interesting account of the Naval Conflict on Lake Erie—Military anecdotes—Abuses in the Army—Plan of a Military Settlement—View of the Lake Coast from Sandusky to Detroit. By Samuel R. Brown. Motto. Burlington, Vt.: Printed by Samuel Mills. 1814. 12mo, pp. 156.

Browne, Francis Fisher. *The Every Day Life* of Abraham Lincoln. 1886.

Mr. Browne was born in South Halifax, Vt., Dec. 1, 1843; learned the printer's trade; served in the U. S. Army in the Civil War; founded "The Dial", a monthly literary Journal in Chicago, 1880, and edited several anthologies of poetry.

Brownson, John W. *The Vermont Disciplinarian, &c.*

See MILITARY.

Brownson, Orestes A. *A Discourse* on the Wants of the Times, delivered in Lyceum Hall, Hanover Street, Boston, Sunday, May 29, 1836. By Orestes A. Brownson. Boston: James Munroe and Company. 1836. 8vo, pp. 23.

—*Social Reform.* An Address before the Society of the Mystical Seven in the Wesleyan University, Middletown, Conn. August 7, 1844. By O. A. Brownson. Boston: Waite, Pierce & Company. 1844. 8vo, pp. 42.

—*Essays aud Reviews* Chiefly on Theology, Politics, and Socialism. By O. A. Brownson, LL. D. New York: 1852. 12mo, pp. XII, 521.

Republished from "Brownson's Quarterly Review."

—*Address on Temperance, at Walpole, N. H.* Keene, N. H. 1833. 8vo.

Among the many noted persons to whom Vermont has given birth, probably Mr. Brownson should occupy a place in the front rank. He was born in Stockbridge, Vt., September 16, 1803; in 1825 he became a Universalist Minister, preaching in Vermont and elsewhere, writing for and editing various periodicals of that denomination. In 1832 he joined the Unitarians, and in 1836 organized an Independent Society in Boston, to which he preached until about 1843, when he became a Roman Catholic, entering that communion in 1844, where he ever after continued.

Mr. Brownson has been a voluminous writer, and his works have attracted much attention, not only in this country, but in Europe. His first theological work was published in 1836, entitled "New Views of Christianity, Society, and the Church;" in 1840, he published "Charles Elwood, or the Infidel Converted," which is an autobiographic Sketch, and has passed through several editions in this country and England. "An Oration on the Scholar's Mission," *Burlington, Vt., V. Harrington.* 1843. 8vo, pp. 40. "The Spirit Rapper," in 1854, and "The Convert, or Leaves from My Experience," 1857; "The American Republic, its Constitution, Tendencies, and Destiny," *New York,* 1862, 8vo. The great labor of Mr. Brownson's life has been in connection with periodical literature; in 1838 he established the *Boston Quarterly Review,* of which five annual volumes were published, when in 1842 it was merged in the *United States Magazine and Democratic Review* of New York, to which Mr. Brownson became a stated contributor, and during the year and a half that he occupied this position he furnished many powerful articles, but some of his ideas not being in harmony with the time-honored principles of the Democratic party, with mutual respect and good feeling, he withdrew his connection from the *Democratic Review* about January 1, 1843. The articles by Mr. Brownson in the *Democratic Review* are a Review of Schmucker's Psychology;" "Brook Farm," a Socialist Association then at West Roxbury, Mass.; "Synthetic Philosophy;" "The Community System;" "Democracy and Liberty;" "Remarks on Universal History;" "The Present State of Society," being a review of Carlyle's "Past and Present;" "Origin and Ground of Government," in which advanced views of social and political equality are advocated; and at the close of the series, Mr. Brownson's connection with the *Democratic Review* ceased; his articles occupy about 250 pages. In 1844 he established in Boston "*Brownson's Quarterly Review,*" which he conducted almost single-handed, largely devoted to the interests of the Roman Catholic church, but also discussed questions of politics and literature. That this work is highly esteemed is evidenced by the fact that complete sets are valued at $200 each.

We give the following extract from a letter of a gentleman in Boston, under date of December 18, 1877, to whom we applied for information: "Mr. Brownson died about a year ago. I knew him well. He was a very able man, but the most obstinate one I ever knew; he went all through the changes in theology, and at last found rest in Mother Church. Through the efforts of Father Hecker, of New York, he was given an annuity of $1,200 a year, which made him comfortable the latter years of his life. His *Review* was, I think, merged into some other Catholic publication."

Mr. Brownson died in Detroit, Mich., April 17, 1876.

Buchanan, C. *The Works* of the Rev. Claudius Buchanan, LL.D. comprising his Christian Researches in Asia, with notices of the translation of the Scriptures into the Oriental Languages; together with the Star in the East, and his eras of Light, and Light of the World. To which is added the Healing Waters of Bethesda. Montpelier, Vt. Published by Lucius Q. C. Bowles. Walton & Goss, Printers. 1813. 12mo, pp. 369.

Buck, J. S. *An Historical Poem.* Milwaukee's Early Days. By James S. Buck. Read before the Old Settler's Club, January 5th, 1874. Milwaukee. 1874. 8vo, pp. 16.

—*The Chronicles* of the Land of Columbia, commonly called America. From the Landing of the Pilgrim Fathers, to the second reign of Ulysses the I, a period of two hundred and fifty-two years. In which is given a short account of the settlement of the country, the wars with the Amelakites that formerly occupied the land, the introduction of slavery, the formation of the different political parties in consequence of that, and the emigration to our shores, from the realms across the waters: the name of each chief ruler, and his Councilors, the War of the Revolution, of eighteen hundred and twelve, and the great rebellion; in ancient form. By the Prophet James. Book I— 1876. Published by F. W. Stearns, 114 Michigan St., Milwaukee, Wis. 8vo, pp. 112. Appendix pp 5., Contents pp 2.

—*Pioneer History of Milwaukee* from the first American settlement in 1833, to 1841, with a Topographical Description, as it appeared in a state of Nature. Illustrated with a Map. By James S. Buck. Milwaukee: Milwaukee News Company, Printers. 1876. 8vo, pp. viii, 292, (1.)

—*The Same.* Vol. 2, 1840 to 1846 inclusive. Milwaukee: Symes, Swain & Co., Book and Job Printers. 1881. 8vo, pp. 383.

—*The Address* with which Ichabod Explains his Post-Centennial Position. 8vo. pp. 8. A poem.

—*1877. Carrier's Greeting.* The Milwaukee News, with good wishes. 1877. Square 4to., pp. 8.

Mr. Buck was born in Lyme, N. H., November 9, 1812; he resided in Royalton, Barre, Norwich, Newbury and other towns in Vermont, until his removal to Milwaukee. Wis. He was a constant contributor of Historical sketches and poems to the Milwaukee newspapers. His father, Amasa Buck, formerly well known in New England, was principal of Norwich Military Academy, 1832-3; Middlebury College conferred upon him the honorary degree of A. M., in 1826. He died at Milwaukee, September 20, 1852.

Buckham, James. *Lora*, a Romance in Verse, by Paul Pastnor. Philadelphia: John E. Potter & Co. 1881. 8vo, pp. vi, 56.

James Buckham is a son of Pres. M. H. Buckham, a graduate of the University of Vermont, one of the editors of the Youth's Companion, and a frequent contributor in prose and verse to various periodicals.

Buckham, Matthew Henry. *Discourse* delivered at Westford, Vt., Aug. 16, 1863. Commemorative of Capt. John W. Woodward, 1st Vt. Cavalry, Who fell near Hagerstown, Md., July 6th, 1863. By Matthew H. Buckham, Professor in the University of Vermont. Burlington : Free Press Print. 1863. 8vo, pp. 22.

—*Discourse* Commemorative of Geo. Stanton Denison. Preached at Royalton, Vt., September 9, 1866, by Matthew H. Buckham, Professor in the University of Vermont. Burlington : Free Press Steam Job Printing Office. 1866. 8vo, pp. 30.

—*Inauguration* of Prof. M. H. Buckham, as President of the University of Vermont and State Agricultural College, August 2, 1871. Burlington : Free Press Association. 1871. 8vo, pp. 23.

Contains Inaugural Address, and action of the Trustees and Alumni in relation to the admission of women to the University.

—*Memorial Address* on the life and character of Rev. W. H. Lord.

See Vermont Historical Society Proceedings, October, 1878.

—*The Negro in the United States.* An Address delivered in Tremont Temple, before the American Missionary Association, May 29, 1878, by President M. H. Buckham, of the University of Vermont. Boston : Beacon Press : Thomas Todd, Printer, Corner Beacon and Somerset Streets. 8vo, pp. 8.

—*What Kind of an Education* shall we give to those of our children who are going to be farmers? By President M. H. Buckham. Burlington. 8vo, pp. 18. n. p. n. d. [1880.]

—*Another Edition.* pp. 12.

—*Medical Education.* An Address to the Medical Class in the University of Vermont at the opening of the session of 1881 by M. H. Buckham, President. Burlington : The Free Press Association. 1881. 8vo, pp. 16.

—*Remarks* at the Hearing on the Agricultural College Bill, October 30, 1890. 11 pp.

President Buckham was born in Hinckley, Leicestershire, England, July 4, 1832, the son of Rev. James Buckham; was graduated at the University of Vermont in 1851; was for a year Principal of an Academy in Lenox, Mass.; then studied at London University, England; in 1853 he was appointed tutor, in 1854, professor, and in 1871 was elected President of his *alma mater.* His published papers consist chiefly of addresses and essays on educational topics. Most of these were not published separately, but may be found in the Reports of the Vermont Board of Agriculture, the North American Review, and the files of the *Vermont Chronicle, Burlington Free Press,* etc., etc. He was also one of the authors of a 12mo. volume of about 200 pages, relating to Berkshire County, Mass., published in 1852 or 1853. He wrote a campaign life of William A. Wheeler, which was published anonymously in the same volume with Howells' life of R. B. Hayes.

Buel, A. W. *Speech* of Hon. Alex. W. Buel, in Defence of the Constitution and the Union. Delivered at a public dinner given to him by his Fellow-Citizens, at Detroit, November 19, 1850. Motto. Washington : Thomas Ritchie, Printer. 1851. 8vo, pp. 31.

—*An Address* before the New England Society of Detroit : Speeches, Reports, etc.

Mr. Buel was born in Poultney, Vt., December, 1813; and died at Detroit, Mich., April 17, 1868. He was graduated at Middlebury College, 1830, and was a teacher in Vermont and New York until 1834; read law in the mean time, when he removed to Detroit, where he practiced his profession until his death. He held various offices

of importance in Michigan; was a Member of Congress 1849-1851.

Buel, Rev. D. H. *Sermon* preached at the Funeral of Richard G. Cole, Esq., in St Paul's Church, Burlington, Vt., December 21st, 1864, by the Rev. D. H. Buel, Rector of St. Paul's Church. Printed by Request of the Vestry. Burlington : R. S. Styles, Printer. 1865. 8vo, pp. 16.

Buell, P. L. *A Phrenological Chart, etc.,* in seven degrees of Development ; Illustrated by Engravings. By P. L. Buell & N. Sizer, Phrenologists. First Edition. Woodstock, Vt.: Printed by Haskell and Palmer: Mercury Press. 1842. 12mo, pp. 84.

Bullard's *Oscillating Churn.* Manufactured and for sale by Bullard & Ellsworth, Barre, Mass., and Mosely & Stoddard, Poultney, Vt. Tuttle & Co., Printers, Rutland, Vt. 18mo, pp. 32.

Bullen, Joseph.

See Vermont Election Sermons, 1783.

Mr. Bullen was born in Sutton, Mass., and was settled over the Congregational Church at Westminster, Vt., 1774, where he also kept a store, and was a sharp trader. He removed to Athens, Vt., in 1785, formed a church, and remained until about 1800. He was then sent as a missionary to the Chickasaw Indians in Mississippi. He died in 1825.

Bunyan, J. *The Pilgrim's Progress* from this World to that which is to come. Delivered under the similitude of a Dream. By John Bunyan. Motto. Brattleborough, Vt. Published by John Holbrook. 1815. 12mo, pp. 311.

—*Heart's Ease in Heart Trouble, &c., &c.* Brattleborough : Published by William Fessenden. 1813. 18mo, pp. 179.

—*The Heavenly Footman* ; or a description of the Man that gets to Heaven. Together with the way he runs in, and the marks he goes by ; Also Directions how to run, so as to obtain. Montpelier, Vt. Printed by Walton & Goss, for Josiah Parks. February, 1811. 24mo, pp. 108.

BURCHARD, JEDEDIAH. *Sermons.*

See Eastman, C. G.

Burdick, C. F. "The Scholar for the Times." An Address delivered before the Bakersfield North Academy Lyceum. November 16, 1853. By Rev. C. F. Burdick. (Published by request.) Burlington : Stacy & Jameson, Printers. 1854. 8vo, pp. 16.

Burge, Rev. Caleb. *A Discourse* delivered November 14, 1811, at the ordination of the Rev. Samuel R. Hall, to the Pastoral Care of the Congregational Church and People in Rumford. By Caleb Burge, A. M., Pastor of the Church in Guildhall, (Ver.) Windsor, (Vt.) Printed by Alden Spooner. 1812. 8vo, pp. 36.

Mr. Burge was born in Tolland, Conn., May 25, 1782; was graduated at Middlebury College, 1806; studied theology with Rev. Abijah Wines of Newport, N. H.; was pastor of the Congregational Church in Guildhall, 1808-14; Brattleborough, 1814-19; Glastonbury, Conn., 1821-26; whence he went to Belleville, N. Y., and died at Warsaw, N. Y., August 31, 1838.

Burgoyne, Lt. Gen. John. *A State* of the Expedition from Canada, as laid before the House of Commons. By Lieutenant-General Burgoyne, and Verified by Evidence ; with a Collection of Authentic Documents, and an Addition of many Circumstances which were prevented from appearing before the House by the Prorogation of Parliament, Written and Collected by Himself, and dedicated to the Officers of the Army he Commanded. London: Printed for J. Almon. Opposite Burlington House, Piccadilly, MDCCLXXX. Quarto. pp. v. 140. LXII. Maps and plans.

—*Orderly Book* of Lieut. Gen. John Burgoyne, from his entry into the State of New York until his surrender at Saratoga, 16th Oct., 1777. From the original Manuscript Deposited at Washington's Head Quarters Newburgh, N. Y. Edited by E. B. O'Callagan, M. D., Albany, N. Y.: J. Munsell. MDCCC.-LX. Small 4to, pp. 221.

Burgoyne gives an account of the Battle of Hubbardton, and refers to the Battle of Bennington.

—*A Supplement* to " The State of the Expedition from Canada, containing General Burgoyne's Orders, respecting the principal movements, and operations of the army to the raising of the Siege of Ticonderoga. London: 1780. 4to, pp. 26.

Eighty copies reprinted in fac simile in 1865, by Joel Munsell, Albany, for F. S. Hoffman, Esq , of New York.

Burhans, Rev. Daniel. *The Scripture* Doctrine of the Election of Jacob, and Rejection of Esau, Considered. A Sermon Preached at Vergennes, in the State of Vermont, Sept. 12, 1810. Published at the request of the hearers. By the Rev. Daniel Burhans, A. M., Rector of Trinity Church, Newtown, (Conn.) Who is he that saith, and it cometh to pass, when the Lord commandeth it not? LAM. iii. 37. Horibile Decretum, fateor. *Calvin.* New Haven : Printed by Oliver Steele and Co. 1811. 8vo, pp. 16.

Burke, Edmund. *An Address* delivered before the Democratic Republican Citizens of Lempster, N. H., on the Eighth of January, 1839. By Edmund Burke, Esq., of Newport, N. H. Newport, N. H.: H. E. & S. C. Baldwin, Printers. 1839. 8vo, pp. 23.

—*The Protective System* considered in connexion with the Present Tariff, in a Series of Twelve Essays. Originally published in the Washington Union, over the Signature of "Bundelcund." Written by the Hon. Edmund Burke. Washington. 1846. 8vo, pp. 40.

—*Speech* delivered in the House of Representatives, Washington, June 13, 1840, on the Independent Treasury Bill. Washington: 1840. 8vo.

—*Speech* on the Tariff Bill, in the House of Representatives, Washington. July 8, 1842. Washington : 1842. 8vo.

Mr. Burke was born in Westminster, Vt., January 23, 1809. He died at Newport, N. H., January 25, 1882, aged 73. His father was a farmer in moderate circumstances, who greatly desired that Edmund should have a collegiate training, but was not in a condition to meet the necessary expenses. It was, however, decided that the son should become a member of one of the learned professions, and he began the study of Latin, with the purpose in view of reading law. Later he entered the office of Hon. William C. Bradley of Westminster. Young Burke pursued his studies for nearly five years and was then admitted to the Windham (Vt.) Bar. Soon afterward he became a member of the Cheshire (N. H.) Bar, and in April, 1830, he emigrated to Coos County. His first location in that section was at Colebrook, from which place he removed to Whitefield, where he remained in the practice of his profession until 1833, when he went to Claremont, N. H., to take charge of the *Argus* newspaper in that town. In 1834 Mr. Burke removed with his paper to Newport, which place was, with the exeeption of a five years' residence at Washington, D. C., afterward his home. A little later the *Argus* was united with the *New Hampshire Spectator,* then owned by Hon. Simon Brown, the new paper having the title of *Argus and Spectator* and being under the editorial control of Mr. Burke. So ably and successfully was the paper conducted that its manager acquired a national reputation and the result was that ex-President Polk and Felix M. Grundy, U. S. Senator from Tennessee, offered Mr. Burke the editorship of the *Union* of Nashville, the leading Democratic organ of that State. The position was accepted and a valedictory published in the *Argus and Spectator.* The many political friends of this young editor were so anxious for him to remain in New Hampshire that they pledged him a Democratic nomination for Congress. The unexpected compliment could hardly be declined, and permitting his name to be used, Mr. Burke received the nomination in 1838, and in March following was elected a Representative to the Twenty-sixth Congress of the United States, being then but thirty years of age. He was subsequently twice re-elected. Regarding his Congressional career, it is only justice to say that it was creditable to himself and honorable to his State. His speeches gained for him great popularity in his party. His addresses upon the independent treasury and upon the tariff showed great intellectual labor, and bore evidence of deep and critical research.

At the termination of his Congressional life, he was tendered by President Polk the office of Commissioner of Patents, which he accepted May 5, 1845. He performed the duties of that position until the accession of General Taylor to the Presidency. While in that office Mr. Burke wrote those famous papers on the tariff, originally published in the Washington *Union*, which were subsequently circulated in pamphlet form in every town in the Republic. After leaving the Patent Office Mr. Burke formed a connection with Thomas Ritchie, by which he became a joint editor of the Washington *Union*. In 1850, his connection with that paper having expired, he returned to Newport with his family, resuming the practice of his profession and engaging to a considerable extent in literary pursuits. He collected a miscellaneous library which was reported to be worth $20,000, while his collection of law books was estimated to be at least half as much more. In his latest years his greatest happiness was in the reading of literary works and in collecting rare volumes for his library. He was prominently connected with the Unitarian denomination. Mr. Burke married first Ann Watson, and second Mary Elizabeth Whitney, the latter and a daughter, Mrs. Col. George H. Dana, surviving. (1882.) The deceased left a property supposed to aggregate nearly if not quite $200,000.

BURLINGTON. *A Catalogue* of the Library of the Burlington Mechanics' Institute, with the Constitution of the Association, and a list of Members. Organized December, 1842. Burlington : Stilman Fletcher, Printer. 1845. 12mo, pp. 16.

—*Catalogue of Books* belonging to St. Paul's Parish Library, Burlington, Vt. Burlington : Chauncey Goodrich. 1847. 12mo. pp. 12.

—*A Catalogue of the Officers and Students* of the Burlington Union High School. For the Year 1851. Burlington : Printed by Chauncey Goodrich. 1851. 8vo, pp. 16.
Continued.

—*City Charter.* An Act to Incorporate the City of Burlington. With Explanations by Civis. Published for the voters. Burlington : Free Press Office. 1852. 8vo. pp. 35.

—*Reply of Veritas to Civis,* on the Village and City Charters, for Burlington. Published for the Voters. Burlington : Stacy & Jameson's Press. 1853. 8vo, pp. 26.

—*Report of the Selectmen* and other Officers to the Town of Burlington, March 6, 1860. Burlington : Free Press Print. 1860. 8vo. pp. 69.
Continued.

—*An Imperfect List* of the Names of Men, deceased, who were at some time Inhabitants of the Town of Burlington. Also Names, Date and Age of Men who have lived or died or lived and died in Burlington, in the State of Vermont. By William Noble. Burlington: No imprint. 1860. pp. 16.

—*Catalogue of the Library of the Young Men's Association* of Burlington, Vt. Burlington: R. S. Styles' Steam Job Printing House. 1872. 8vo, pp. 48.

—*Supplement to Catalogue* of the Young Men's Association of Burlington, Vt. May 1, 1873. 8vo, pp. 8.

—*Catalogue of Books* in the Teachers' Library, First Calv. Congregational Church, Burlington, Vt., April, 1873. Burlington: Free Press Steam Job Printing House. 1873. 12mo, pp. 15.

—*Programme of the Day*, July 4th, 1876, at Burlington, Vt. R. S. Styles, Steam Job Printer, Burlington, Vt. 12mo, pp. 4.

—*Catalogue of the Sunday School Library*, of the First Congregational Society, Burlington, Vt. Burlington: Stacy & Jameson, Book & Job Printers. 1854. 12mo, pp. 26.

—*Catalogue of the Sunday School Library* of St. Paul's Church, Burlington, Vt., October 10th, 1874. 12mo, pp. 12.

—*Catalogue of the S. S. Library* of the First Congregational Church, Winooski Avenue, Burlington, Vt. Burlington: Free Press Steam Printing House. 1875. 18mo, pp. 16.

—*Catalogue* of the First Baptist Sabbath School Library, Burlington, Vt. October 1st, 1878. Burlington: Free Press and Times Print. 1878. 8vo, pp. 20.

—*Manual* for the Communicants of the First Congregational Church in Burlington, Vt., from its Organization in 1805, to Sept. 1836. Burlington: Vernon Harrington. 1836. 18mo, pp. 40.

—*Manual* of the First Congregational Church, Burlington, Vt. No. II. 1867. Motto. Compiled by order of the Church. Burlington: Free Press Steam Print. 1867, 12mo, pp. 32.

—*Same.* No. III. Aug. 1885. pp. 35.

—*The By-Laws and Articles of Faith*, Covenant and Form of Reception, of the Third Congregational Church, in Burlington, Vermont, with the Roll of Members, 1867. Printed by order of the Church. Burlington: Free Press Print. 1867. 16mo, pp. 22.

—*By-Laws* and Articles of Faith, Third Cong'l Church. 12mo, pp. 34. 1879. Same imprint.

—*Manual* of the College Street Congregational Church, Burlington, Vt. 1889. Same imprint. pp. 17.

—*Jubilee:* 1817-1867. Services in celebration of the fiftieth anniversary of the Dedication of the First Congregational Church in Burlington, Vt., Wednesday, the ninth of January, 1867. Burlington: Times Press. 1867. 8vo, pp. 53.
Includes sermons by the Rev. E. E. Hale, and by the Pastor, Rev. L. G. Ware.

—*Manual* of the First Baptist Church, Burlington, Vt., containing Historical Sketch, Articles of Faith, etc. Burlington: The Free Press Association. 1880. 12mo, pp. 37.

—*City Directory* and Business Advertiser, from July 1869, to July 1870. Burlington, Vt.: The Free Press Association. 1869. 12mo, pp. 92.

—*City Directory* and Business Advertiser, for 1865-6. Published by Hiram S. Hart. Burlington: Free Press Steam Printing Establishment. 1865. 12mo, pp. 89.

—*City Directory* and Business Advertiser, July 1875, to July 1876. Burlington: Free Press Association. 1875. 12mo, pp. xxvi, 117.

—*City Directory* 1877-78. Published by the Free Press Association, College Street, Burlington, Vt. 12mo, pp. xxx, 160.
—The same, 1879-81. 12mo, pp. xix, (5), 127.
Same imprint. Continued.

—*American Telegraph Company.* Tariff of prices from Burlington, Vt. Feb. 3, 1859.
Broad sheet.

—*Cathedral of the Immaculate Conception.* Burlington, Vt. A Notice of Its Interior Decorations. R. S. Styles, Printer, Burlington, Vt. 8vo, pp. 15. n. d.

—*City Documents.* 1866. The Charter, and Ordinances, with the Address of Hon. A. L. Catlin, Mayor, June 7, 1865, and Annual Report of Officers and Committees of the City of Burlington, for the financial year ending Feb. 1, 1866. Burlington: Free Press Steam Job Printing Office, 1866. 8vo, pp. 142.
First report under the City Charter.

—*Report of the Committee* on Water Works, appointed by the City Council April 14, 1866, with the Analysis of Lake and River Waters by Prof. Henry M. Seeley, and the report of Wm. J. McAlpine, Hydraulic Engineer. Burlington: Times Book and Job Printing Office. 1866. 8vo, pp. 46.

—*Report* of D. C. Linsley, Engineer of Burlington City Water Works, to the City Council, made in compliance with a Resolution passed August 6, 1866. Burlington: R. S. Styles, Book and Job Printer. 1866. 8vo, pp. 44.

—*Reply* of Wm. J. McAlpine, to the Report of D. C. Linsley, Engineer of Burlington City Water Works, made to the City Council, October 7, 1866. 8vo. pp. 15.

—*Report of the Committee* on the supply of water for the City, and extracts from the Report of the Health Officer. Published by Order of the City Council. Burlington: Free Press Steam Job Printing House. 1866. 8vo, pp. 12.

—*The Question* of Water Supply for the City of Burlington. Letters of D. C. Linsley, Peter Collier and E. H. Phelps. Burlington: 1877.

—*The Water Supply* of Burlington, Vt. Report to Hon. Geo. F. Edmunds, by Wm. Pierson Judson, C. E. 1884, pp. 10.

—*Rules* of the Board of School Commissioners, and Regulations of the Public Schools of Burlington, Vt. Burlington: Free Press Steam Printing House, 1868. 12mo, pp. 14.

—*Annual Report* of the Superintendent of Public Schools, of Burlington, Vt. 1868-9. Burlington: R. S. Styles, Printer. 1869. 8vo, pp. 37.
Continued.

—*Annual Report* of the Health Officer of the City of Burlington, to the City Council, January 1, 1879. Burlington, Vt.: The Free Press Association, Printers and Binders, 1879. 8vo, pp. 27, (1).
Continued.

—*Terms* upon which the Public will be supplied with Gas by the Burlington Gas Light Company. 12mo, pp. 4, n. d. n. p.

—*Reports* of the Secretary and Treasurer of the Home for Destitute Children. For the year ending October 12, 1868. Burlington, Vt.: R. S. Styles, Steam Book and Job Printer. 1868. 8vo, pp. 41, (1).
Continued.

—*Constitution and By-Laws* of the Burlington Young Men's Association. Adopted February 4, 1864. Burlington: Times Book and Job Office. 1867. 18mo, pp. 14.

—*The By-Laws and Articles of Faith*, Covenant and Form of Reception, of the Third Congregational Church, in Burlington, Vt., with the Roll of Members, 1867. Printed by order of the Church. Burlington: Free Press Steam Print. 1867. 12mo, pp. 20.

—*City Directory and Business Advertiser.* July, 1873, to July, 1874. Burlington: Free Press Association. 1873. 12mo, pp. 132, (2).

—*By-Laws*, Rules of Order, List of Officers, and Roll of Members of Boxer Engine Company No. 3, of Burlington, Vt. Organized February 24, 1830. Burlington: Free Press Print. 1875. 18mo, pp. 38.

—*Constitution*, By-Laws, Sailing Regulations, &c., of the Lake Champlain Regatta Association. Burlington: Printed by Mark Thompson, Sentinel Office. 1876. 16mo, pp. 32, and table of Allowances.

—*Pocket Manual* of the First Congregational Church, Burlington, Vt.. 1878. Free Press Print. 24mo, pp. 11.

—*Amended Charter and Ordinances*, in force February 1, 1873, of the City of Burlington, Vt. Burlington: 1873. R. S. Styles, Printer. pp. 67 and index vii.

—*Annual Reports* of the Young Ladies Christian Association of Burlington, Vt, from 1867 to 1872. Burlington: Free Press Steam Printing House, 1872. 8vo, pp. 35.

—*Report* on the Moral and Religious Condition of the Community. Address upon a Union of Evangelical Churches in the City of Burlington, Vt., March 10, 1867, by Prof. Edward Hungerford. Burlington: Free Press Print, 1867. pp. 29.

—*Fletcher Free Library.* Catalogue of the Fletcher Free Library of Burlington. Burlington, Vt., 1877. Printed by Merrill & Crocker, Lawrence, Mass. pp. 661.
The Library, founded by Mrs. Mary L. Fletcher and Miss Mary M. Fletcher, was first opened to the public July 6, 1875. At the date of this catalogue, which was prepared by Miss H. M. Ames, it contained 10,600 volumes. In 1895 it contained upwards of 25,000 volumes.

—*St. Paul's Church*, Burlington, Vt. Sermon delivered on the Fiftieth Anniversary of the Founding of the Parish, by the Rector, Rev. E. R. Atwill. Burlington: Free Press Association. 1881. pp. 20.

—*Vermont Episcopal Institute.* Comprehensive Catalogue, and Retrospective Review of the past twenty-one years under the Administration of Rev. Theodore Austin Hopkins, Principal, now closing his labors, July 1, 1881. Burlington: Free Press Association. 1881. pp. 58.

—*Advice in Regard to Sanitary* Measures for the Prevention of Disease. Issued by the Health Department and Health Officer of the City of Burlington, Vt., May, 1885. pp. 8.

—*Sherman Military Band.* Catalogue of Art Loan Exhibition, held at the City Hall, Burlington, Vt., March 23rd to 28th, 1885. Burlington: Free Press Association 1885. pp. 62.

—*College Street Church*, Burlington, Vt. Remarks at the Re-opening of the Church, Dec. 5, 1886. Burlington: Free Press Association.

—*Statuta Diœcesis* Burlingtonensis Cum Facultatibus Sacerdotibus Ejusdem Diœcesis Concessis. Burlington: 1886.

—*Board of Trade. Charter, Constitution, By-Laws and Membership* of the Board of Trade, Burlington, Vt. Burlington: Free Press print. 1888. 16mo, pp. 20.

—*Manual* of the College Street Congregational Church, Burlington. [Formerly the Third Congregational Church of Burlington.] 1889. Free Press print. pp. 17.

—*Burlington and Thereabout. Guide to the Tourist.* C. H. Possons, publisher, Glens Falls, N. Y. 1889. 12mo, pp. 24.

—*Burlington, Vt. As a Manufacturing, Business and Commercial Center*, with sketches of its History, Attractions, Industries and Institutions. Illustrated. Published for the Board of Trade. 1889. Chas. H. Possons, Glens Falls, N. Y. pp. 152.

—*Charter and Revised* General Ordinances of the City of Burlington, Vt., with a Register of the City Government from its organization in 1865. Burlington: 1888. Free Press Association. pp. 165.

—*Home for Aged Women*, located at Burlington, Vt. Report of Trustees, with the By-Laws, Rules and Regulations. Burlington: Free Press Association. 1890. 12mo, pp. 16.

—*Religious Services* held in the First Calvinistic Congregational Church of Burlington, Vt., April 30, A. D., 1889, in Celebration of the Centennial Anniversary of the Inauguration of George Washington, as First President of the United States, April 30, A. D. 1789. Burlington: 1889. Free Press print. 4to, pp. 40.
Address by President M. H. Buckham.

—*Y. M. C. A. Address* of President W. J. Van Patten, with Resolutions and Statistical Report on the Occasion of the 26th Anniversary of the Young Men's Christian Association. Burlington: 1892. pp. 24.

—*Prospectus* of the Young Men's Christian Association, Burlington, Vt. 1892-93. Burlington: Free Press Association, Printers. pp. 36.

—*Illustrated. The Clipper Souvenir.* By Prof. J. E. Goodrich. 1893. 44 large pages.

—*Burlington, Vt., Statistics*, 1763 to 1893, Compiled by Charles E. Allen, City Clerk. For convenient reference. Burlington: Free Press Association. 1893. pp. 41.

Picturesque Burlington. A Hand-book of Burlington, Vt., and Lake Champlain, by Joseph Auld. Burlington: Free Press Association: Illustrated, 8vo. 1893. pp. XIV, 180.
—Second edition, 1894, pp. XIV, 190.

—*Larger Burlington.* To Advertise Burlington Industries. Illustrated. Free Press Association: 1895. pp. 64.

—*Inaugural Address* of the Mayor, W. J. Van Patten, April 1, 1895. Burlington: Free Press Association. 1895. pp. 26.

—*Permanent Street Improvements in the City of.* Reports of W. S. Bacot, C. E., and the Advisory Board, 1894. Burlington: Free Press Association. 1894. pp. 77.

—*Practical Burlington*, by N. C. Fowler, and Beautiful Burlington, by G. G. Benedict. [Published by the Burlington Board of Trade,] 1895. Burlington: Free Press Association. pp. 35. Illustrated.

—*Reports and Bulletins* of Additions to the Library, as issued annually.
—*History* of,
See Vermont Historical Gazetteer. Vol. I, pp. 487-733.

Burnap, Uzziah C. *Priestcraft Exposed.* A Lecture, delivered in Chester, April 9, 1830. Being the Annual Fast: Together with an Essay on the Clergy of the United States. By U. C. Burnap, A. M. Pastor of the Congregational Church in Chester, Vt. Windsor: Printed at the Chronicle Press, by John C. Allen. 1830. 8vo, pp. 28.

—*The Youth's Etherial Director*, or a Concise and Familiar Explanation of the Elements of Astronomy, together with Instructions and Tables for the Calculation and Delineation of Eclipses, designed, for the use of Schools and Academies and especially for such young ladies and gentlemen ;as;are unacquainted with the higher branches of the mathematics. By Uzziah C. Burnap, A. B. Middlebury:*Printed by J. W. Copeland. 1822. 8vo, pp. 96.

—*Bible Servitude.* A Sermon, delivered in the Appleton St. Church, Lowell, on the day of Annual Thanksgiving, November 30, 1843. By U. C. Burnap, A. M., Pastor of the Church. Lowell: A. E. Newton and A. O. Ordway. 1843. 8vo, pp. 20.

—*The Manifestations of God:* a Discourse, by U. C. Burnap, Pastor of Appleton Street Church, Lowell, Ms. Boston: T. R. Marvin, 24 Congress Street. New York: Mark H. Newman. 1845. 12mo, pp. 46.
He also published sermons on the Seventh Commandment, etc., Mr. Burnap was born in Windham, Vt., July 11, 1794; and was graduated at Middlebury College, 1821; read theology, and was pastor of a Congregational church in Chester, Vt., 1824-37; and then pastor in Lowell, Mass. See Pearson's Middlebury College Graduates.

Burnap, Wilder L. 'Address at Opening of the 34th Course of Lectures in the Medical Department of the University of Vermont, by W. L. Burnap, Professor of Medical Jurispru-

dence. Burlington: Free Press Association. 1887. pp. 15.

Burnham, Charles. *A Centennial Discourse*, delivered at Fayetteville, Vt., [Newfane] July 5, 1874. By Rev. Charles Burnham, Acting Pastor of the Congregational Church. Motto.
In History of Newfane, pp. 123-141.

Burnham, Henry. *History of Brattleboro.* See Brattleboro.

Burr and Burton Seminary. *Proceedings* of the Re-Union at the Burr and Burton Seminary, Manchester, Vt., June 27 and 28, 1871. New York: 1872. 8vo, pp. 40.
See Educational.

Burroughs, Eden. *Election Sermon*, 1778.
There were three Sessions of the Legislature in 1778; Windsor in March, Sermon by Mr. Powers; Bennington in June, and Windsor in October, and the Journals do not show that a sermon was preached at either of the two last sessions; but Mr. Burroughs' sermon was probably preached at Windsor.
Mr. Burroughs was a native of Connecticut, and was graduated at Yale College in 1757; he was settled over the church at Hanover, N. H., in 1775, where he remained thirty years or more, and then moved to Hartford, Vt., where he died May 22, 1813, aged 75. For forty years he was a trustee of Dartmouth College. Stephen Burroughs, of unsavory notoriety, was his son.

Burrows, Stephen. *A Sermon*, delivered in Rutland, on a Haymow. By Stephen Burrows, D. R. New England. Printed for the Purchaser, April 11, 1812. pp. 11.
See Drake's Dic. of Biography.

Burt, Henry M. *Burt's Illustrated Guide of the Connecticut Valley*, containing descriptions of Mount Holyoke, Mount Mansfield, Lake Memphremagog, Lake Willoughby, Montreal, Quebec. &c. By Henry M. Burt. Northampton: New England Publishing Company, 1867. 12mo, pp. 281.

Burton, Rev. Asa. *A Sermon* Preached at Windsor, before His Excellency Thomas Chittenden, Esq., Governor, His Hon. Paul Spooner. Esq., Deputy Governor, The Honorable Council, And the Honorable House of Representatives of the State of Vermont, On the Day of the Anniversary Election Oct. 13, 1785. By Asa Burton, A. M., Pastor of the Church in Thetford. Motto. Windsor: Printed by Hough and Spooner. M.DCC.LXXXVI. Small 4to, pp. 32.

—*A Discourse* delivered before His Excellency Thomas Chittenden, Esquire, Governor, The Honorable Council, and House of Representatives, of the State of Vermont; At Windsor, October 8th, 1795. Being the Day of General Election. By Asa Burton, A. M. Pastor of the Church of Christ in Thetford. Rutland: Printed by order of Legislature. M,DCC,XCV. 8vo, pp 33.

—*To be Greatest in Christ's Kingdom*, A necessary qualification in Gospel Ministers. A Sermon delivered at the installment of The Rev. Daniel Brock, A. M. To the Pastoral Care of the Church of Christ in Hartland, In the State of Vermont. November 11th, MD.CC-LXXX,IX. By Asa Burton, A. M. Pastor of the Church of Christ in Thetford. Published by Desire. Printed at Windsor, Vt., by Alden Spooner. M.DCCXCI. 8vo, pp. 22.

—*The True Sources of Comfort*, to the People of God under their Afflictions, Laid open to

View. In A Sermon, From Isaiah XL, 1. Occasioned By the Death of Lucy Thomson, Consort of the Reverend Lathrop Thomson. Delivered at Sharon, December 20th, 1792. By Asa Burton, A. M. Pastor of a Church in Thetford. Mottos. Windsor: Printed by Alden Spooner, for the Reverend Lathrop Thomson, M,DCC,XCIII. 8vo, pp. 15.

—*A Sermon* preached at the Funeral of Mrs. Joanna Shaw, Consort of Colonel Dan Shaw, of Lyme, N. H. November 24th, 1808. By Asa Burton A. M. Pastor of the Church of Christ in Thetford. [Published by Desire.] Hanover, N. H. Printed by Moses Davis. 104. 8vo, pp. 19.

—*Sermon* before the Phi Beta Kappa at Dartmouth College, Aug. 26, 1800. Hanover 1801. 8vo.

—*A Sermon* preached at the Ordination of the Rev. Caleb J. Tenney, to the Pastoral Care of the First Congregational Church of Christ in Newport, R. I., Sept. 12, 1804. Newport: Mercury Office. (1804). 8vo, pp. 24.

—*A Sermon* preached at the Ordination of the Rev. Timothy Clark, to the Pastoral Care of the Church of Christ in Greenfield, January 1, 1800. Windsor, Vt.: Printed by Alden Spooner. 1800. 8vo, pp. 24.
Newburyport, 1806. Reprinted.

—*A Sermon*, delivered at Montpelier, Vermont, at the Ordination of the Rev. Chester Wright, August 16, 1809. By the Rev. Asa Burton, D. D. Pastor of the Church in Thetford. Peacham, Vt,: From the Press of Samuel Goss. 1809. 8vo, pp. 24.

—*False Teachers Described*. A Sermon, delivered at Thetford, Lord's Day, December 24th, 1809. By Asa Burton, D. D. Pastor of the Church of Christ in Thetford. Printed by Particular Request. Motto. Montpelier, Vt.: Printed by Samuel Goss. 1810. 8vo, pp. 32.

—*The works of God an Important Study*. A Sermon, delivered June 26, 1811, at the ordination of the Rev. Benjamin White to the Pastoral Care of the Church of Christ in Wells, Maine. By Asa Burton, D. D. Pastor of the Church in Thetford, Vt. All Thy works praise Thee, O Lord—*David*. Kennebunk, Maine: J. K. Remich.

—*A Discourse* delivered at the funeral of Mrs. Lydia Hinckley, the wife of Col. Oramel Hinckley; who departed this life, Dec. 3, 1811, in the 44th year of her age. By Asa Burton, D. D. Pastor of the Church of Christ in Thetford. Montpelier: Wright and Sibley, 1811.

—*A Discourse* delivered Lord's Day, Oct. 13, 1811; at the funeral of Mrs. Maria Allen, consort of Dr. Joram Allen, and daughter of Col. Oramel Hinckley; who departed this life, Oct. 10, 1811, in the 22d year of her age. By Asa Burton, D. D. Pastor of the Church in Thetford. Montpelier: Wright and Sibley. 1811.

—*A Funeral Discourse*, occasioned by the death of Col. Oramel Hinckley, who departed this Life October 25, 1811, in the 45th year of his age; Delivered Lord's Day January 5, 1812, at his interment in Thetford. By Asa Burton, D. D. Pastor of the Church of Christ

in Thetford. Montpelier: Printed by Wright & Sibley. 1812. pp. 16, 12mo.

—*Sermon* at the Ordination of Rev. Thomas A. Merrill, at Middlebury, December 19, 1805.

—*Sermon* at the funeral of Mrs. Sophia Robinson, January 15, 1810.

—*National Fast Sermon*, January 12, 1815.

—*A Sermon* Delivered at the Installation of St. John's Lodge, Free and Accepted Masons, in Thetford, Vt., July 4, 1816. By Asa Burton, D. D. Pastor of the Church of Christ in Thetford. Published at the United request of the Masons assembled on the occasion. Concord: Printed by George Hough. 1816. 8vo, pp. 22.

—*Fellowship and Charity* Co-extensive with the Evils of Schism. Defended and Illustrated in a Discourse delivered in Thetford, Vt., in the Month of November, 1823. By Asa Burton, D. D. Pastor of the Church of Christ in that Place. Concord, N. H.: Printed by John W. Shepard. 1824. 12mo, pp. 30.

—*Essays* on some of the First Principles of Metaphysicks, Ethicks, and Theology. By Asa Burton, D. D. Pastor of the Church of Christ in Thetford, Vt. Portland: Printed by Arthur Shirley. 1824. 8vo, pp. 414.

Dr. Burton was born in Stonington, Conn., August 25, 1752; and died in Thetford, Vt., May 1, 1836. He was graduated at Dartmouth College in 1777; after which he and his classmate, Daniel Foster, continued at the College for the study of Divinity; in the fall of 1777 the Grafton Presbytery met at the house of President Wheelock, when the two young men were sent for, and after a brief examination, were licensed to preach.

His father and family removed to Norwich, Vt., in 1766, and young Burton was of those who "struck the first blows" where the College now stands; and as there were no suitable accommodations at Hanover, the Trustees met at his father's house in Norwich for two or three years.

Mr. Burton preached his first sermon at Norwich, soon after he was licensed; and then passed about one year with Rev. Dr. Hart, in his native town, in theological studies. In 1778 he preached about five months in Topsfield, Mass., but declined to settle there. He then preached several Sundays in Windsor, Vt., and next preached at Royalton, Vt., and also declined a settlement. He then preached a Sunday or two at Thetford, and finally accepted the unanimous call of the church and society to become their pastor, where he continued through life.

His first impressions of the people there were not favorable. He wrote: "They appeared to me to be very litigious, quarrelsome, intemperate, immoral, clownish and vulgar; and in view of towns around they stood lowest in public estimation. I felt as though I could not live among a people so degraded. But I was told the more degraded and immoral they were, the more room there was to do good; and if I pitched where Satan's camp was, there would be an opportunity for the display of courage, and to raise a degraded people to respectability." He was ordained at Thetford, January 19, 1779. His labors were arduous and remuneration small; there being no meeting-house, services were held in private houses in winter, and in barns in summer. His salary was never raised above $283.33. The town agreed to furnish him, in addition, 25 cords of wood annually; but the agreement was soon forgotten, or at least unperformed. Of course he and his wife were soon taught the most rigid economy, and when he became infirm with age, and a colleague was settled, he relinquished $133 of the pittance of a salary that he was receiving; which was, however, paid irregularly, and at the convenience of his people; yet his frugality and that of his wife was such that he accumulated about $1,000 during a ministry of more than fifty years, in addition to his real estate, which consisted of a wild lot assigned to him by the town at the time of his settlement. Here is a fine example for people who are constantly complaining of "hard times."

For an interesting Sketch of Dr. Burton, by Rev. Thomas Adams, from which these brief notes are mainly compiled, see *American Quarterly Register*, Vol. 10, pp. 321-341.

Burton, Asa Stevens. *Millerism Refuted by History*, in a series of Letters to a Friend. By A. S. Burton. Mottoes. Windsor, Vt. : Published by Joseph Fairbanks. 1842. 12mo, pp. 24.

Burton, H. N. *"Go Forward."* A Discourse Delivered at the Semi-centennial Anniversary of the Vermont Domestic Missionary Society, held at St. Johnsbury, Vt., June 17, 1868. By Rev. H. N. Burton. Printed by order of the Directors of the Society. Montpelier : Freeman Steam Printing and Bookbinding Establishment. 1868. 8vo, pp. 16.

Bush, Rev. George. Illustrations of the Holy Scriptures, derived principally from the Manners, Customs, Traditions, Forms of Speech, Antiquities, Climate, and Works of Art and Literature, of the Eastern Nations ; embodying all that is valuable in the works of Harmer, Burder, Paxton and Roberts, and the most celebrated Oriental Travellers ; embracing also the subject of the Fulfilment of Prophecy, as exhibited by Keith and others ; with descriptions of the Present State of Countries and Places mentioned in the sacred writings, illustrated by numerous landscape engravings, from sketches taken on the spot. Edited by Rev. George Bush, Professor of Hebrew and Oriental Literature in the New York City University. Published by the Brattleboro' Typographic Company. (Incorporated October 26, 1836.) Brattleboro', Vt. 1839. Entered, according to Act of Congress, in the year 1836, by John C. Holbrook, in the Clerk's Office of the District of Vermont. Stereotyped by Francis F. Ripley, New York. r'l 8vo, pp. 656.

—*The Bible Atlas*, or Sacred Geography Delineated in A Complete Series of Scriptural Maps, Drawn from the best Authorities, Ancient and Modern. By Richard Palmer. Revised and Compared with the most recent Authorities by Prof. George Bush, of the New York University. New York: Wm. M. Brownson. 1847. 8vo, pp. vii, (1,) 82, and 26 Maps.

Dr. Bush was an eminent biblical scholar and divine, born at Norwich, Vt., June 12, 1796 ; and died at Rochester, N. Y., September 19, 1859.

He was graduated at Dartmouth, 1818, and read theology at Princeton Theological Seminary ; he then made a brief missionary tour in Indiana, and was pastor of a Presbyterian church at Indianapolis, 1824-1829 ; in 1831 he became professor of Hebrew and Oriental literature in the University of the city of New York. In 1845 he adopted the views of Swedenborg, and finally became a Spiritualist. He published a valuable "Life of Mohammed," (Vol. x of Harper's Family Library,) 1832. In 1840 he commenced his "Commentaries" on some of the Books of the Old Testament, which were completed in 8 volumes, and have been highly commended. Prof. Bush published his very valuable "Illustrations of the Holy Scriptures," compiled from 46 British and foreign writers in 1836. "This work should be in the hands of every Biblical student."—*Allibone.*

In 1844 he published "Anastasis ; or the Doctrine of the Resurrection of the Body Rationally and Spiritually Considered," in which he opposed the doctrine of the physical construction of the body in another world, with arguments from reason and revelation. This book met with much opposition in some quarters, and the author replied in a work : "The Resurrection of Christ, in answer to the question whether He rose in a Spiritual and Celestial, or in a Material and Earthly Body ; (and) The Soul, an Inquiry into Scriptural Psychology." "Commentary on the Book of Psalms," *New York*, 1848. 8vo ; in 1855, a volume of "New Church Miscellanies, or, Essays, Ecclesiastical, Doctrinal, and Ethical," being a collection of articles he had written for the "New Church Repository"; in 1857 a work, "Priesthood and Clergy unknown to Christianity, or, the Church a Community of Co-equal Brethren, by Compaginator"; his latest

work, "An Exposition of the Four Gospels," etc., he did not live to complete. In 1860, Mr. W. M. Fernald edited and published in Boston, "Memoirs and Reminiscences of the late Prof. George Bush ; being for the most part voluntary contributions from different friends, etc."

Dr. Bush became pastor of the New Jerusalem church in New York city in 1845, also principal editor of the New Church Repository. Whatever the peculiarity of his views, Dr. Bush occupied a distinguished position as an intellectual and Biblical scholar.

See *Allibone; Drake; Griswold, R. W.; Duyckinck,* and supplement to same.

Bushee, Rev. W. A. *Sermon* preached to the 2d Con. Church and Society of Brookfield, December 21st, 1873, on the Twenty-Fifth Anniversary of the Dedication of their House of Worship. By Rev. W. A. Bushee. Montpelier, Vt.: Argus and Patriot Job Printing House. 1874. 8vo, pp. 16.

Bushnell, Jedediah. *A Farewell Sermon,* Preached to the Church and Society in Cornwall, May 29, 1836. By their late Pastor, Rev. Jedediah Bushnell. New Edition. Middlebury: Knapp and Jewett, Printers. 1836. 8vo, pp. 22.

Butler, F. *The Right Object of Life,* and its choice as affected by the School. An Address delivered in Bradford Academy, Bradford, Vt., at the close of the Fall Term, November 10, 1851. By Rev. Franklin Butler, Pastor of the Congregational church in Windsor, Vt. Published by the Executive Committee. Bradford, Vt.: Printed by A. B. F. Hildreth. 1852. 8vo, pp. 24.

Rev. Mr. Butler, brother of Dr. L. C. Butler, was born in Essex, Vt., October 3, 1814 ; died at Windsor, Vt., May 23, 1880. He was graduated at the University of Vermont, 1836, and at Andover, 1842 ; was pastor of a Congregational church at Windsor, Vt., 1842-1858 ; New England Agent for the American Colonization Society for a number of years, and was connected with the *Vermont Chronicle* and *Vermont Journal* as associate editor during the proprietorship of L. J. McIndoe, and at the decease of Mr. McIndoe became proprietor of the *Journal,* of which he was chief editor at his death. He married, first, the only daughter of ex-Gov. Carlos Coolidge, of Windsor, second, the widow of Mr. McIndoe.

For a full sketch, see *Argus and Patriot* of May 26, 1880.

Butler, James Davie. *Deficiencies in our History.* An Address delivered before the Vermont Historical and Antiquarian Society, at Montpelier, October 16, 1846. By James Davie Butler, Professor in Norwich University. Montpelier: Eastman & Danforth. 1846. 8vo, pp. 36.

Contains Whittier's song of the Vermonters.

—*Sermon* at Norwich, Vermont, February 22, 1848, during the Obsequies of Truman (B.) Ransom, Colonel of the Ninth Regiment. Hanover. 1848. 8vo.

—*and Houghton,* (G. F.) Addresses on the Battle of Bennington, and the Life and Services of Col. Seth Warner ; Delivered before the Legislature of Vermont, in Montpelier, October 20, 1848. By James Davie Butler and George Frederick Houghton. Published by order of the Legislature. Burlington : Free Press Office Print. 1849. 8vo, pp. 99.

—*Pre-Historic Wisconsin.* By Prof. James D. Butler, LL.D. Annual Address before the State Historical Society of Wisconsin, in the Assembly Chamber, February 18, 1876. 8vo, pp. 31, and 4 of plates.

—*Address* at the Rutland, Vt., Centennial Celebration, October 5, 1870. 8vo, pp. 8.

See RUTLAND, Centennial Celebration, pp. 46-70, and 89-93.

—*Incentives to Mental Culture* among Teachers. By James Davie Butler. Boston : Ticknor, Reed and Fields. MDCCCLIII. 12mo, pp. 37.

—*Nebraska*. Its Characteristics and Prospects, by Prof. James Davie Butler, LL.D. 12mo. pp. 36, (4). 1873.

—*The Naming of America*. A Paper read before The Wisconsin Academy of Sciences, Arts, and Letters. By Prof. J. D. Butler, LL.D. Madison, Wis.: Atwood & Culver, Printers and Stereotypers. 1874. 8vo, pp. 19.

—*A Farewell Discourse* delivered before the Second Congregational Church and Society in Danvers, Mass., July 18, 1852. By James Davie Butler. Salem : Printed at the Observer Office. 1852. 8vo, pp. 23.

—*Poematia*. "Blood Drops." Birthday Lines, and other verses of Society. Motto. Not Published. Madison, Wis.: M. J. Cantwell, Book and Job Printer, King St. 1874. 8vo, pp. 18.

—*How Dead Languages make Live Men*. A Defence of Classical Studies. A Paper read before the National Educational Association, at Detroit, August, 1874, by Prof. J. D. Butler, Madison, Wis. Worcester, Mass. 1874. 8vo, pp. 20.

—*Catalogue of Coins and Medals*, prepared by James D. Butler, LL.D., and D. S. Durrie, Esq., from the collection of James L. Hill, Esq., late mayor of the city and President of the late Bank of Madison. Madison, Wis. : 1874. 8vo, pp. 18.

—*A September Scamper*, by Prof. J. D. Butler, LL.D. 12mo, pp. 30. 1877.
Relates to Nebraska.

—*Governmental Patronage of Knowledge*. By Prof. James Davie Butler, LL. D. Madison, Wis. 8vo, pp. 50. 1877.

—*The American Flag*. "Flag of the Free Heart's Only Home." Prepared for the Wisconsin State Journal, by Prof. J. D. Butler, of the State University. Broadside. Being a brief history of the Flag.

—*Scenes in the Life of Christ*. Chicago. 1866.

—*Remarks at the Dinner* of the Semi-Centennial Celebration of Middlebury College. pp. 8.

—*American Pre-Revolutionary Bibliography*. By James Davie Butler, LL.D. From the Bibliotheca Sacra for January, 1879. Andover : 1879. 8vo, pp. 104.
Prof. Butler was born in Rutland, Vt., March 15, 1815. For a Sketch of his life, see *Vermont Historical Gazetteer*, Vol. III., pp. 1105-6.

Butler, L. C. *The Memorial Record of Essex*, Vermont. Prepared by L. C. Butler, M. D. Published by vote of the Town. Burlington : R. S. Styles, Book and Job Printer. 1866. 12mo, pp. 59, (2.)
Dr. Butler, of Essex, Vt., was a graduate of Woodstock, Vt., Medical College, 1843; Honorary M. D., Dartmouth Medical College, 1875; Secretary Vermont Medical Society, 1867-73; President 1873-5, inclusive; Assistant editor Medical and Surgical Reporter, Philadelphia, Pa., 1861-3, and contributor thereto since, and to the Boston Medical and Surgical Journal; author of Monographs on "The Properties and Therapeutic action of Veratrum Viride," 1865; "Decadence of the American race—the cause and remedy," 1867; "Cerebro Spinal Meningitis," 1868;

"New remedial agents," 1869; "Intoxication by Alcohol, Its medical, social and civil aspects—duty of Physicians in the premises," 1869; "Locality of Consumption in Vermont," 1872. Author of addresses on the "Prevention of disease," with reference to the duty of the State in relation thereto, 1874-78; on "Hygiene of the Farm," before the State Board of Agriculture, 1876; on "Man's six footed rivals in Reason and Intelligence," 1878; of the "Early History of Essex," in Miss Hemenway's Gazetteer, and of the Annual "Summary" for Vermont Registration Reports, for many years. In 1863 member of the editorial staff of Argus and Patriot, Montpelier, and weekly contributor to its editorial columns. Also "occasional correspondent" of sundry State and city journals. Dr. Butler died at Essex, Vt., May 25, 1888, aged 68 years.

Butterfield, Charles W. Spring Catalogue of Greenhouse Bedding Plants and Seeds, for 1878, Atkinson street, Bellows Falls, Vt. Montpelier, Vt. : Argus and Patriot Steam Book and Job Printing Works. 1878. 8vo, pp. 35.

By-Laws *of G Company*, Twenty fourth Regiment, National Guard, S. N. Y. Rutland : Tuttle & Co., Printers. 1872. 24mo, pp. 23.

Byington, Ezra Hoyt. *A Discourse* Commemorative of Ebenezer Carter Tracy, A. M., Late Senior Editor of the Vermont Chronicle. Delivered at his Funeral, May 18, 1862, in the Congregational Church at Windsor. By E. H. Byington, Pastor. Windsor, Vt.: Press of the Vermont Chronicle. 1862. 8vo, pp. 30.

—*The Trials of the Nation*—God's Method of Preparing it for a Higher Mission. A Discourse delivered on the Day of National Thanksgiving, August 6, 1863. In the Congregational Church at St. Albans, Vermont. By E. H. Byington. St. Albans, Vt.: Whiting and Davis. 1863. 8vo, pp. 23.

—*The Christian Directed*. A Practical Sermon preached in Windsor, Vt. By E. H. Byington, Pastor of the Congregational Church, April 4, 1869. Windsor : Vermont Chronicle Print. 8vo, pp. 14.

—*Review of Ministry in Windsor*. Farewell Sermon, preached in the Congregational Church, Windsor, Vt., Sabbath Morning, September 26, 1869, By Rev. E. H. Byington. Windsor : Vermont Chronicle Print. 1869. 8vo, pp. 16.

—*The Case of Rev. Robert Breck*, of Springfield, Mass. Worcester: 8vo. No imprint.

—*Biographical Sketch* of Rev. John Wheeler, D. D., President of the University of Vermont, 1833-48, by Rev. Ezra H. Byington, D. D. Cambridge, Mass.: Jno. Wilson & Sons. 8vo, pp. 20.

Cabot. *Selectmen's Report* for the Town of Cabot for the year ending March 7, 1876. Montpelier, Vt.: Argus and Patriot Steam Job Printing House. 1876. 8vo, pp. 4.
Continued.

Cahoon, Edward A. *"Eminent Americans"* ; "Life of George Washington."
These two little works were prepared for young people, and Sabbath schools, at the request of a publisher in New York.
Edward Augustus Cahoon was a native of Lyndon, Vt. He graduated from the University of Vermont in 1838; practiced law in Lyndon, and died in 1862. For sketch of the family, see "Vermont Historical Gazetteer," Vol. 1, pp. 341-56.

Calais. *Annual Reports* of the Officers of the Town of Calais, for the year ending March 2, 1876. 8vo, pp. 4.
Continued. See Waters, Reubin D.

Caldwell, James Stamford. *A Treatise* of the Law of Arbitration ; with an Appendix of Precedents. By James Stamford Caldwell. Second American from the last English Edition ; with Notes, and References to American and English Decisions, by Chauncey Smith. Burlington : Chauncey Goodrich. 1853. 8vo, pp. 539.

Caledonia County. *List of Congregational Churches* and ministers in,
See Worcester, Leonard.

—*Caledonia County Bible Society. Statement, and Remarks*, respecting the Caledonia County Bible Society. Published in conformity to a vote of the Society. Danville : Ebenezer Eaton, Printer. 1830. 8vo, pp. 15.

—*Atlas Map* of Caledonia County.
Same title and imprint as Chittenden County Atlas.

Cambridge. *Historical Sketch of,*
See Wheelock, E.

Camp, Hoel H. *Address* of Mr. H. H. Camp, Cashier of the First National Bank, Milwaukee, Wisconsin, on the History of Western Banking. Extracted from the official report of the Annual Convention of the American Bankers' Association at Saratoga, August 6th, 7th and 8th, 1879. New York : 1879. 8vo, pp. 13.

—*Coin Deposits* as Security for National Bank Notes. The Direct and Indirect Benefit to Arise Therefrom. By H. H. Camp, Milwaukee. [Read at Convention of American Bankers at Saratoga, August 12, 1880.] 4to, pp. (4.)
Mr. Camp was born in Derby, Vt., in January, 1822, being a son of the late Hon. David M. Camp, Lieutenant Governor of Vermont, 1836-1841. Mr. H.H. Camp received a mercantile business education in Montpelier, but settled at Milwaukee as a banker some forty years ago, where he continues. He is regarded as one of the most prominent and influential bankers in the western country.

Campbell, Edward R. *The Heroine of Scutari*, and other Poems. By Edward R. Campbell, Esq. New York : London : 1857. 12mo, pp. 334.
Mr. Campbell was born in Rockingham, Vt., August 27, 1787 ; and died at Windsor, Vt., May 4, 1857.

Campbell, George W. *Republicanism*. A Sermon, Delivered at the Dedication of the Congregational Meeting-house in Newbury, Vt., Nov. 13, 1840. By George W. Campbell. Published by the Congregational Society. Haverhill, N. H.: Published by John R. Reding. 1840. 8vo, pp. 18.

—*A Sermon*, Delivered at Newbury, Vt., Feb. 24, 1847, at the Ordination of the Rev. George H. Atkinson, as a Missionary to the Territory of Oregon, under the American Home Missionary Society. By Geo. W. Campbell, Pastor of the Congregational Society, Newbury, Vt. Newbury: Printed by L. J. McIndoe. 1847. 8vo, pp. 24.
See Atkinson, G. H.

Canfield, John Henry Hopkins. *In Memoriam* John Henry Hopkins Canfield. For Private Distribution. Burlington : Free Press Association. 1892. 8vo, pp. 39.

Canfield, Thomas Hawley. *Discovery, Navigation and Navigators* of Lake Champlain. 8vo, pp. 52, in Vt. Hist. Magazine, Vol. 1, pp. 656-707.

—*Northern Pacific Railroad*. Partial Report to the Board of Directors, of A portion of a Reconnoissance made in the summer of 1869, between Lake Superior and the Pacific Ocean, by Thos. H. Canfield, General Agent of the Company ; Accompanied with Notes on Puget Sound, by Samuel Wilkison, Esq., The Historian of the Expedition. For Private Circulation Only. May, 1870. [no imprint.] 8vo, pp. 96, 44. Maps.

—*Life of* ; His Early Efforts to open a route for the Transportation of the Products of the West to New England by way of the Great Lakes, St. Lawrence River and Vermont Railroads, and His Connection with the Early History of the Northern Pacific Railroad. With portrait. Burlington : 1889. 4to, pp. 48.

Cannon, LeGrand B. *Recollections* of the Iron-clads, Monitor and Merrimack, and Incidents of the Fights, by LeG. B. Cannon, late Col. and A. D. C., U. S. Army. Burlington : Free Press Steam Book and Job Printing House. 1875. 8vo, pp. 10.

—*Personal Reminiscences* of the Rebellion, 1861-1866, by LeGrand B. Cannon, Col. U. S. A. New York : 1895. 12mo, pp. 228.
"Printed for private distribution among my family and friends."

Carey, M. *The Olive Branch ;* or, Faults on Both Sides, Federal and Democratic. A Serious Appeal on the necessity of Mutual Forgiveness and Harmony. By M. Carey. Seventh Edition Enlarged. Middlebury, Vt. Printed and Published by William Slade, Jun. January, 1816. 12mo, pp. 468.

Carleton, Rev Hiram, D. D. *An Analysis* of the 24th Chapter of Matthew. By Rev. Hiram Carleton. Windsor : Printed at the Chronicle Press. 1851. 8vo, pp. 58.

—*Dr. Park's Sermon* on the Revelation of God in His Works. By the Rev. H. Carleton. Reprinted from the Theological and Literary Journal for Jan. 1858. 8vo, pp. 31.

—*Extemporary Preaching*. Reprinted from "The Theological and Literary Journal" for July, 1856. 8vo, pp. 28.

—*A Treatise* on the Meaning of the Derivatives of the Greek Root B A (‡). Boston, A. Williams and Co. 1875. 24mo, pp. 44.
Dr. Carleton was born in Barre, Vt., July 18, 1811 ; and was graduated at Middlebury College, 1833. He read theology at Andover Theological Seminary, and was settled as pastor of the Congregational Church at Stowe, Vt., in 1838. Became an Episcopal clergyman in 1867, and is Rector of a Church at Wood's Holl, Mass., (1895.)

Carpenter, Heman. *Family Re-Union* at the Celebration of the Sixtieth Birthday of Hon. Heman Carpenter, of Northfield, Vt., Monday the 10th day of July, 1871. Montpelier : Polands' Steam Printing Establishment. 1871. 8vo, pp. 18, (1).
For a biographical sketch, see "History of Northfield, Vt.," pp. 178-81.
Mr. Carpenter died at Northfield, January 16, 1884.

Carpenter, Matthew Hale. *War Power* Outside the Constitution. Matt. H. Carpenter's Review of Mr. Ryan's Address. Milwaukee, Wis.: Presses of Starr & Son. 1862. 8vo, pp. 16.

—*Argument* of Matt. H. Carpenter in the Supreme Court of the United States, March 3 and 4, 1868, in the matter of Ex Parte Wm. H. McCardle, Appellant. Reported by D. F.

Murphy. Washington: Government Printing Office. 1868. 8vo, pp. 83.

—*The Powers* of Congress. The Constitutionality of its Acts on Reconstruction. Alarming Tendency of the Seymour Democracy. Speech at Chicago, Ill.. August 12th, 1868. Washington, D. C. (1868.) 8vo, pp. 8.

—*State of Wisconsin*—Supreme Court. John Druecker vs. Edward Salomon. Immunity of the Executive from civil suit, for acts performed under color of office. Brief for Governor Salomon. Matt. H. Carpenter, Counsel. Milwaukee: F. H. Yewdale, printer. (n. d.) 8vo, pp. 28.

—*Sales of Arms* to French Agents. Speech of Hon. Matt. H. Carpenter, of Wisconsin, delivered in the Senate of the United States, February 29, 1872. Washington: 1872. 8vo, pp. 16.

—*Louisiana Affairs.* Speech in the Senate of the United States, January 29 and 30, 1874. Washington: John H. Cunningham, Printer. 1874. 8vo, pp. 48.

Mr. Carpenter was born in Moretown, Vt., in 1824; he became the adopted son of Paul Dillingham in his twelfth year; spent two years, 1853 and 1854, at the West Point Academy; studied law, and, on adopting the profession, removed to Wisconsin; was for several years District Attorney for the State, and practiced his profession before the Supreme Court of the United States; was elected a Senator in Congress from Wisconsin for the term commencing in 1869 and ending in 1875, serving on the Committees on the Judiciary, Patents, and Revision of the Laws. He also served as President *pro tem* of the Senate. Mr. Carpenter was again elected to the United States Senate from Wisconsin, for the term of six years from March 4, 1879. He died at Washington, D. C., February 24, 1881.

Carpenter, William. *A Poetical Paraphrase* on the Book of Job. By William Carpenter. Motto. Rutland: Printed for, and Sold by the the Author. M.DCC.XCVI. 8vo, pp. 55.
Not of Peacham.

Carpenter, W. H. and Arthur, T. S. *The History of Vermont,* from its Earliest Settlement to the Present Time. By W. H. Carpenter, and T. S. Arthur. Philadelphia: Lippincott, Grambo & Co. 1853. 12mo, pp. 200.
And advertisements, 36.

Carter, Rev. Charles F. *An Outlook on Religious Thought.* Sermon preached in the College St. Church, Burlington, Sept. 17, 1893. Burlington: Free Press Association. pp. 16.

Carter, Rev. N. F. *Tears for the Living, not the Sainted Dead.* Sermon in Memory of Joseph Clark Tolman. Preached at the First Congregational Church, Bellows Falls, Vt., Sept. 8, 1878, by Rev. N. F. Carter, Pastor. Bellows Falls: Printed at the Times Steam Printing Office. 1878. 8vo, pp. 13.
Mr. Carter was born in Henniker, N. H., January 6, 1830; was graduated at Dartmouth College, in 1853, and at Bangor in 1865; preached at Bellows Falls, Vt., 1874-1879, and later at Quechee, Vt.; is residing, 1895, at Concord, N. H.

Castanis, C. P. *The Greek Captive:* A Narrative of the Captivity and Escape of Christophorus Plato Castanis, during the Massacre on the Island of Scio By the Turks. Written by Himself. Worcester: 1845. 18mo, pp. 100.
Makes allusion to Col. J. P. Miller, of Montpelier, who conveyed supplies to the Greeks.

Castleton. *Report* of the Auditor and Other Officers of the Town of Castleton, 1866.

Rutland: Tuttle, Gay & Co., Printers. 1866. 8vo, pp. 12.
Continued.

—*Manual* of the Communicants of the First Congregational Church in Castleton, Vt., January, 1839. Motto. Rutland: Herald Office Print. 18mo, pp. 43.

—*Manual* for the Communicants of the First Congregational Church in Castleton, Vt. January 15, 1859. Motto. Rutland. G. A. Tuttle & Co., Printers. 1859. 12mo, pp. 36.

—*Ordination* of Mr. T. W. Ross, as Pastor of the First Liberal Christian Society, Castleton, Vt., 17th August, 1870. 8vo, pp. (4).

—*Report* of the Proceedings commemorating the One Hundredth Anniversary of the Organization of the Congregational Church in Castleton, Vt., Fairhaven: 1884. Frank W. Redfield, Printer. 8vo, pp. 52.
Contains Historical Address by Rev. Lewis Francis.

—*Epitaphs* of Castleton, Vt., Church Yard. pp. 48, (8.) No date.

—*Report* of the Proceedings commemorating the One Hundredth Anniversary of the Establishment of a Chartered School * * * in Castleton, Vt. 1787-1887. Rutland: Tuttle & Co. 1888. 8vo, pp. 104.

Castleton Medical College. *Fifty-Seventh Announcement* of Castleton Medical College, For the Fall Session, 1858. With A Catalogue of the Alumni, and of the Trustees and Faculty. Rutland: Tuttle & Co., Printers. 1858. 8vo, pp. 23, (1).
Continued. See Medical.

—*Castleton Seminary Memorial Anniversary,* Wednesday, June 29th, 1870. Rutland: Tuttle & Company, Printers. 1870. 8vo, pp. 47.
See Educational.

Catalogue, *Alphabetical and Analytical* of the Library of the University of Vermont, Burlington. Burlington: Free Press Office. 1854. 8vo. pp. iv. 163, (1).
See University of Vermont.

—*of Books* contained in the Chicopee Falls High School Library, together with the Regulations For the Government of the Same. Montpelier, Vt.: Argus and Patriot Steam Book and Job Printing Works. 1877. 12mo, pp. 14.

—*of the Library* of the St. Johnsbury Athenæum. St. Johnsbury, Vt. Cambridge: Printed at the Riverside Press. 1875. 8vo, pp. xviii, (6.) 390, (6.)

—*of the Vermont State Library* 1850. Arranged and prepared by the State Librarian, under the direction of the Governor, agreeably to an Act of the General Assembly. Montpelier: E. P. Walton & Son, Printers. 1850. 8vo, pp. 86.

—*of the Vermont State Library,* with a list of Duplicates for Exchanges, 1858. Montpelier: E. P. Walton, Printer. 1858. 8vo, pp. 63.

—*of the Vermont State Library,* September 1, 1872. Montpelier: J. & J. M. Poland, Printers. 1872. 8vo, pp. xiv, 200.

—*of the Fletcher Free Library.* See Burlington.

—*of the George P. Marsh Library.* See University of Vermont,

Cavendish. *Annual Report* of the School Superintendent for the town of Cavendish, Vt. March, 1865. Rutland: McLean, Job Printer, Opposite Depot, 1865. 8vo, pp. 12.
Continued.

—*Annual Report* of the Auditors and Selectmen for the town of Cavendish, Vt. for the Year ending February 15th, 1868. Ludlow: Black River Gazette Office. 1868. 8vo, pp. 16.
Continued.

Caverley, A. M. *History* of the Town of Pittsford, Vt., with Biographical Sketches and Family Records. By A. M. Caverly, M. D. Motto. Rutland: Tuttle & Co., Printers. 1872. 8vo, pp. VIII, 751.
Portraits and Map.

Cazier, Mathias. *Election Sermon, 1790.*
Mr. Cazier was a native of New Castle, Delaware; was graduated at Princeton, N. J., College, and was settled over the Congregational Church in Castleton, Vt., 1789-1792. He soon after removed to Massachusetts, and thence to Western New York, where he died in May, 1837, aged 77.

Chalmers, George. *Opinions of Eminent Lawyers* on various points of English Jurisprudence, Chiefly concerning the Colonies, Fisheries and Commerce of Great Britain: Collected and Digested, from the Originals in the Board of Trade, and other Depositories. By George Chalmers, Esq., F. R. S., S. A. Burlington: C. Goodrich and Company. 1858. Royal 8vo, pp. XXVIII, 787.

Chalmers, Rev. Thomas, D. D. *Discourses on the Christian Revelation.* Viewed in Connection with the Modern Astronomy. By the Rev. Thomas Chalmers, D. D., Minister of the Tron Church, Glasgow. Montpelier: Printed and Sold by E. P. Walton. 1819. 16mo, pp. 194.

—*The Evidence and Authority of the Christian Revelation.* By the Rev. Thomas Chalmers, one of the Ministers of Glasgow. Seventh Edition. Montpelier: Printed and sold by E. P. Walton. 1819. 12mo, pp. 194.
Bound in same volume with "Discourses."

Chamberlain, Jason. *Inaugural Oration.* Aug. 1, 1811.
See University of Vermont.

Chamberlain, Wm. Jr. *An Address* delivered at Windsor, Vt., before an Assembly of Citizens from the Counties of Windsor, Vt. and Cheshire, N. H. on the Fiftieth Anniversary of American Independence. By William Chamberlain, Jr. Published by Request. Windsor, Vt. Printed by Simeon Ide, 1826. 8vo, pp. 24.
Mr. Chamberlain was born in Peacham, Vt., May 24, 1797; and died at Hanover, N. H., July 11, 1830, from a sudden attack of pneumonia. His father was one of the early settlers of Peacham, and held the offices of Lieutenant Governor, Member of Congress, and many others. William, Jr., was graduated at Dartmouth College in 1818, and read law with Daniel Webster in Boston, and in 1820, at the age of twenty-three, he was called to the Professorship of Languages at Dartmouth, which position he held until his death. For a sketch of his life, see Smith's *History of Dartmouth College*, pp. 256-263, where it is stated that the above address was delivered at Hanover on the same day, which was not an impossibility, as the towns are only twenty miles apart.

Chamberlin, J. E. *Statement* of the Line of Descent, from the first comer in New England, of the branch of the Chamberlin Family in Newbury, Vermont. Represented in the seventh Generation by Abner Chamberlin. Prepared at Boston, 1824, by Joseph Edgar Chamberlin, Member of the New England Historic Genealogical Society. 8vo, pp. 11.

Champlain, Samuel De. *Discovery of Lake Champlain and Vermont.*
See Slafter, E. F.

Champlain Valley *Horticultural Society:* Proceedings of Convention. Burlington, Vt. 1851.
See Horticultural.

Chandler, Amariah. *The spirit of the gospel* essential to a happy result of our religious enquiries. An Address to the Society for Religious Inquiry in the University of Vermont. Burlington, August 7, 1827. By A. Chandler, Minister in Waitsfield, Alumnus of the Institution. Burlington: Printed at the Free Press Office. 1827. 8vo, pp. 16.

—*A Discourse,* delivered at Waitsfield, January 1, 1826. By Amariah Chandler, A. B., Pastor of the Congregational Society in Waitsfield. Montpelier: Printed by E. P. Walton. 1826. 8vo, pp. 15.

—*A Sermon,* Delivered on the day of General Election, at Montpelier, October 14, 1824. Before the Honorable Legislature of Vermont. By Amariah Chandler, A. B. Minister of the Gospel in Waitsfield. Montpelier, Vt.: Printed By E. P. Walton. 1824. 8vo, pp. 43.

—*The Reminiscences of Fifty Years.* A Discourse by the Rev. A. Chandler, D. D., delivered in the First Parish, Greenfield, Nov. 7, 1858, being the fiftieth anniversary of his license to preach the Gospel. Greenfield: 1858. 8vo, pp. 24.

—*Thoughts on Freemasonry.*
See Masonic. Mr. Chandler while residing in Vermont published several other sermons and pamphlets; he was born in Deerfield, Mass., October 27, 1782, and died in Greenfield, Mass., October 20, 1864; was graduated at the University of Vermont, 1807; settled over the Congregational church, Waitsfield, Vt., 1810 to 1830, then at Hardwick, Vt., two years, when he returned to Massachusetts, and was settled at Greenfield, over the Congregational church, 1832 until his death.

Channing, William E. *A Sermon,* preached at the Annual Election, May 26, 1830, before His Exc'y, Levi Lincoln, Governor, His Honor Thomas L. Winthrop, Lieutenant Governor, the Honorable Council, and the Legislature of Massachusetts. By William E. Channing. Montpelier: Re-printed by Geo. W. Hill. 1830. 8vo, pp. 33.

Chapin, Walter. *The Missionary Gazetteer,* Comprising A View of the Inhabitants, and a Geographical Description of the Countries and Places, where Protestant Missionaries have Labored; And a General History of Missions throughout the world; with an Appendix &c. By Walter Chapin, Pastor of the Church in Woodstock, Vt. Woodstock: Printed by David Watson. 1825. 12mo, pp. VI, 420.

—*Sermon* at Woodstock, Vt., Feb. 8, 1818. Sabbath before an Execution. Windsor: 1818. 8vo.
Rev. Mr. Chapin was born in West Springfield, Mass., in 1779; and died at Woodstock, Vt., July 27, 1827. He was graduated at Middlebury College, 1803, and was pastor of the Congregational church at Woodstock, 1810 till his death. He was editor of the "Evangelical Monitor," 1821-24.

Chapin, William A. *A Sermon*, delivered at the Funeral of Samuel P. Crafts, who died at Craftsbury, Nov. 17, 1824 ; in the 26th year of his age. By Wm. A. Chapin, A. M., Pastor of the Congregational Church in Craftsbury. Danville, Vt. Ebenezer Eaton, Printer. 1825. 8vo, pp. 23.

Chapman, G. T., D. D. *Sermons*, upon the Ministry, Worship, and Doctrines of the Protestant Episcopal Church. By G. T. Chapman, D. D. Late Rector of Christ Church, Lexington. Second Edition. Burlington : Chauncey Goodrich. 1832. 12mo, pp. 324.

Charleston. *History of.* 8vo, pp. (42.)
From Miss Hemenway's Gazetteer ; contains in addition portions of the history of Coventry and Westmore, and Orleans county items.

—*Historical Sketch*, Articles of Faith and Covenant, Rules and Catalogue of Members, Past and Present, of the Congregational Church in West Charleston, Vt. Boston : Press of Farrar & Barnard, 687½ Washington Street. 1869. 12mo, pp. 16.

Charlotte. *Articles of Faith*, Covenant and Form of Reception of the Congregational Church of Charlotte, Vt., with Principles and Rules and Catalogue of members to January, 1880. Printed by Order of the Church. Burlington : The Free Press Association. 1879. 12mo, pp. 23.

Chase, C. M. *The Editor's Run* in New Mexico and Colorado, etc., etc. By C. M. Chase, Editor of the "Vermont Union." Lyndon, Vt., Illustrated. [1882.] 8vo, pp. 223.
See Printing in Vermont—Lyndon.

Chase, F. *Gathered Sketches* from the Early History of New Hampshire and Vermont. Claremont, N. H.: 1856. pp. 215.

Chase, Irah. *Obligations* of the Baptized ; or, Baptism an Emblem of the Death and Resurrection of Christ, as connected with the State and Prospects of the Believer. A Sermon delivered before the Boston Baptist Association, Introductory to their Session at Cambridge, Mass., Sept. 17, 1828. By Irah Chase, Professor of Biblical Theology in the Newton Theological Institution. Boston: Printed by William R. Collier, No. 11, Merchant's Hall. 1828. 8vo, pp. 22.

—*A Discourse* on the Life and Character of, delivered before the Society of Inquiry, at Newton, June 27, 1865. By William Hayne, D. D. Boston : 1866. 8vo, pp. 46.

—*Tribute of Affection* to the Memory of, with an Appendix containing a genealogical record, and a list of his publications. Boston : Privately Printed. 1865. 8vo, pp. 100.
Mr. Chase was born in Stratton, Vt., October 5, 1793 ; and died at Newtonville, Mass., November 1, 1864. He was graduated at Middlebury College, 1814, and at Andover Theological Seminary, 1817 ; became a Baptist minister, and was a Professor in Columbia Theological School, Washington, D. C., and in Newton, Mass., Theological Seminary. He published "Life of John Bunyan," "Canons of the Holy Apostles," (a translation,) "The Design of Baptisms," "Infant Baptism an Invention of Man"; and was a contributor to Reviews on theological subjects.

Checkley, John. *A Short* and easy Method with the Deists : Wherein the certainty of the Christian Religion is Demonstrated, by Infalli-

ble Proof from four rules, which are Incompatible to any Imposture that ever yet has been, or that can possibly be. In a letter to a Friend. First American, from the Eighth London Edition. Windsor, Vt.: Printed by T. M. Pomroy. 1812. 16mo, pp. 168.
Beside the "Short and Easy Method," by Leslie, first printed in London, 1694, this volume contains : By J. Checkley, "A Discourse concerning Episcopacy," pp. 43-134 ; "The Epistle of St. Ignatius to the Trallians," pp 135-139 ; The Speech of Mr. John Checkley upon his Trial at Boston in New England, for publishing "The Short and easy method with the Deists;" "A Discourse concerning Episcopacy;" in defence of Christianity and the Church of England, against the Deists and Dissenters.—To which is added, the Jury's Verdict ; his Plea in arrest of Judgment ; and the Sentence of Court. Also by Checkley, "A specimen of a true dissenting Catechism, upon the right true-blue principles, with learned notes by way of explication." pp. 140-168.
The "Short and easy Method," to which was appended the "Discourse on Episcopacy," was first printed, London, by J. Applebee, and sold by John Checkley, at the Sign of the Crown and Blue Gate, over against the West End of the Town House in Boston, 1723. Mr. Checkley doubtless could not get it printed in Boston, on account of Puritan opposition. He was sentenced by the Court to pay £50 to the King. and give bonds for his good behavior ; and the next day he paid the money, including costs, into Court. The speech, trial, verdict, etc., was printed in London by Applebee, in 1728, a second edition in 1738 ; and this little volume, printed at Windsor, is the first American edition of the whole case. Nothing was ever published in New England, probably, on the Episcopal side of the question, so exasperating to the Calvinists or as they were sometimes called, Non-Conformists, and Dissenters, as this little work. The contest which followed the trial of Checkley was continued long after his decease, and did not finally subside until about 1770.
Mr. Checkley was born in Boston, of English parents, in 1680, and throughout his life was untiringly devoted to the interests of the English Church. He was well educated, finishing his studies at the University of Oxford; soon after his trial he went to England, and upon receiving Episcopal ordination returned, and was for many years rector of St. John's Church in Providence, Rhode Island being an asylum for those persecuted by the Puritans of the Massachusetts Bay. Mr. Checkley died February 15, 1753.
See Mr. Henry B. Dawson's edition of Checkley; Morrisania, N. Y., 1868, introduction by Rev E. H. Gillett, D. D.
Also Thomas' History of Printing, 2d ed. Vol. 2, pp. 219-221.

Cheever, George B. Discourse on James Marsh.
See Marsh, James.

Chelsea. Annual reports of the Officers of the Town of Chelsea, for the year ending Feb. 22, 1878. Chelsea : William H. Howard, Printer. 1878. 12mo, pp. (6).
Continued.

—*Manual* of the Congregational Church in Chelsea, Vermont ; Together with a catalogue of its Members to the present time. Adopted December 8th, 1859. Windsor : Vermont Chronicle Book and Job Office. 1860. 16mo, pp. 24.

—*Manual* of the Congregational Church, in Chelsea, Vermont, with Historical Sketch and Catalogue of Membership, from Organization to June, 1882. Burlington : Free Press Association. 1882. 8vo, pp. 63.

—*Proceedings* of the Centennial Celebration of the One Hundredth Anniversary of the Settlement of Chelsea, Vermont, together with the Orange County Veteran Soldiers' Reunion, Sept. 4, 1884. Keene, N. H.: 1884. Sentinel Print. pp. 120.
Contains Historical Address by Thomas Hale and Poem by Rev. E. E. Herrick.

Chemical Note-Cook, for the Country Class Room ; containing memoranda of principles to be illustrated by short courses of experiments in country villages. Interleaved for manuscript notes. Herald Office : (Rutland, Vt.) 1821. Price 25 cents. 8vo, pp. 24.

Cheney, Simeon Pease. The American Singing Book, contains more than 300 pages of a great variety of excellent Sacred and Secular Music, Old and New, for all purposes where such music is used. A valuable Feature in the Book is the Biographical Department, containing Biographies of Forty of the Leading Composers, Book-makers, etc., of Sacred Music in America, from William Billings to I. B. Woodbury, which alone is worth the price of the Book. The Publishers endorse this Book with great confidence, believing it to be the most Original, Important, and Interesting Singing Book Ever published in this Country, and in every sense worthy of its Grand Title. By Simeon Pease Cheney. Boston : Published by White, Smith & Company, 516 Washington Street. Copyrighted 1879, by White, Smith & Co. Gould, music printer, 18 P. O. Sq., Boston. pp. 320.

Mr. Cheney was born in Meredith, N. H., April, 1818. With his father's family he came to Derby, Vt., in 1824. He was a son of Elder Moses Cheney, and a brother of Prof. Moses E. Cheney, of Barnard, Vt. The two brothers have been teachers of vocal music, mainly in Vermont, for the past forty years. (1880.) See Vermont Historical Gazetteer, vol. i, pp. 419-423.

Chester. The Confession of Faith and the Covenant of the First Congregational Church, Chester, Vermont, with the names of the Pastors, Officers, and Members of the Church. Compiled from the Records by the Pastor, C. E. Lord, May, 1868. Ludlow : Black River Gazette Job Department. 1868. 16mo, pp. 32.

—*The Twenty-Fourth Annual Report* of the Town of Chester, for the year ending February 12, 1877. Auditors : S. H. Leonard, Wm. Kingsbury, T. H. Whitmore. Rutland : Tuttle & Company, Printers. 1877. 8vo, pp. 19.
Continued

Child, Gardner. An Oration delivered at Richmond, Vermont, on the Thirty First Anniversary of American Independence, July 4th, 1807. By Gardner Child. Motto. Bennington, Vt.: Printed by Anthony Haswell. 1807.

Child, Willard. *Sermon Preached* before The General Assembly of the State of Vermont : October 11, 1856, By Rev. Willard Child, D. D., of Castleton, Vt. Printed by order of the General Assembly. Montpelier : E. P. Walton, Printer. 1856. 8vo, pp. 23.

Dr. Child was a native of Woodstock, Ct., graduated at Yale and at Andover, and was pastor of Congregational churches in Benson and Pittsford, Vt., prior to 1842 ; he then left the State ; but returned to Castleton, Vt., in 1855, and continued there until 1864, when he removed to Crown Point. He died at Mooers, N. Y., November 13, 1877, aged 81 years, less 1 day.

Childs, A. P. *An Argument* by A. P. Childs of Bennington, Before the Committee of Ways and Means at Montpelier, December 10, 1880. 8vo, pp. 16.

Against the Taxation of Life Insurance Companies.

Childs, George T. *Address* by George T. Childs, Esq., of St. Albans, Vt., delivered before the Reunion Society of Vt. Officers in the Hall of the House of Representatives at Montpelier, Nov. 5, 1874. Burlington : Free Press Steam Job Printing House. 1874. 8vo, pp. 19.

Childs, Ward. *Five Sermons* on Sanctification. By Rev. Ward Childs, Pastor of the Church at Strykersville. Buffalo : Printed at the Spectator Office. 1837. 8vo, pp. 32.

Mr. Childs was born in Thetford, Vt., 1800 ; studied at Auburn Theological Seminary, 1825-27 ; preached in Onondaga Co., N. Y.; Morgan and Rome, O., 1830-33; Strykersville, N. Y., 1833-48; died at Chagrin Falls, O., Dec. 27, 1855.

Chipman, Daniel. *The Life* of Hon. Nathaniel Chipman, LL. D., formerly member of the United States Senate, and Chief Justice of the State of Vermont. With Selections from his Miscellaneous Papers. By his Brother, Daniel Chipman. Boston. Charles C. Little and James Brown. 1846. 8vo, pp. 12, 402.

—*The Life* of Col. Seth Warner with an Account of the Controversy between New York and Vermont, from 1763 to 1775. By Daniel Chipman, LL. D. Burlington : C. Goodrich & Company. 1858. 16mo, pp. 84.

—*Memoir* of Colonel Seth Warner. By Daniel Chipman, LL. D. To which is added, The Life of Colonel Ethan Allen, by Jared Sparks, LL. D. Middlebury : L. W. Clark. 1848. 16mo, pp. 226.

—*Speech* delivered at Montpelier, Jan. 6, 1836. Middlebury, 1837.

—*A Memoir* of Thomas Chittenden, the First Governor of Vermont ; with a History of the Constitution during his Administration. By Daniel Chipman, LL. D. Middlebury : Printed for the Author. 1849. 16mo, pp. 222.

—*An Essay* on the Law of Contracts, for the payment of Specific Articles. By Daniel Chipman. Middlebury : Published for the Author. J. W. Copeland, printer. 1822. 8vo, pp. XVI, 224.

—*An Essay* on the Law of Contracts, for the payment of Specific Articles. By Daniel Chipman. With a Supplement, By D. B. Eaton, of the New York Bar. Burlington : Chauncey Goodrich. 1852. 8vo, pp. 326.

—*Addresses.*

See Vermont Constitutional Conventions ; Young vs. Chipman; Vermont Law Reports, 1824.

Mr. Chipman was born at Salisbury, Conn., October 22, 1765; and died at Ripton, Vt., April 23, 1850. His father's family moved to Tinmouth, Vt., in 1775. He was graduated at Dartmouth College 1788; studied law with his brother Nathaniel, at Rutland, and commenced practice there, but in 1794 removed to Middlebury. He held many State offices; was member of Congress 1815-1817. He was distinguished in his profession, also in literature. He was the youngest of seven brothers, all highly distinguished men. For a more full sketch of his life, See Swift's *History of Middlebury*, pp. 262-268.

Chipman, Henry. *An Oration*, on the Study and Profession of the Law. Delivered at the Commencement of Middlebury College, on the 20th of Aug. 1806. By Henry Chipman, Candidate for the Degree of Master of Arts. Middlebury, Vt. Printed by J. D. Huntington, Nov. 1806. 12mo, pp. 19.

Chipman, Nathaniel. *Sketches of the Principles of Government ;* by Nathaniel Chipman, Judge of the Court of the United States, for the District of Vermont. Rutland : From the

Press of J. Lyon, Printed for the Author. June, 1793. 12mo, pp. 292.

—*Principles of Government:* A Treatise on Free Institutions. Including the Constitution of the United States. By Nathaniel Chipman, LL. D. Burlington: Edward Smith, (Successor to Chauncey Goodrich.) 1833. 8vo, pp. 8-330.

    Being a second edition, enlarged, of "Sketches," etc.

—*Law Reports, etc.,* 1793.

    See Vermont, Law Reports.

    Mr. Chipman was born in Salisbury, Conn., November 15, 1752; and died in Tinmouth, Vt., February 15, 1843. See Life of, by his brother, Daniel Chipman.

Champlain Valley Poultry Association. *Rules and Premium List* of the First Annual Exhibition of, to be held at Burlington, Vt., January 28, 29, 30 and 31, 1879. 8vo, pp. 16, (10.)

Chittenden. *Annual Report* of the Board of Officers for the Town of Chittenden, 1879. Rutland: Tuttle & Co. 1879. 8vo, pp. 16.

    See Olcott, Henry S., for Spiritual Manifestations by the Eddy family, at Chittenden.

Chittenden County. *By-Laws* of Chittenden County Grange. Adopted February 8th, 1876, at Essex, Vermont. Burlington: R. S. Styles & Son, Book and Job Printers. 1876. 18mo, pp. 8.

—*Atlas* of Chittenden Co. Vermont. From actual Surveys by and under the direction of F. W. Beers, assisted by Geo. P. Sanford & others. Published by F. W. Beers, A. D. Ellis & G. G. Soule, 95 Maiden Lane, New York. 1869. Folio, pp. 32, (8).

—*Articles* of the Chittenden County Conference of Churches, with the Confession of Faith and Covenant, to be used in the admission of Members. Burlington: George J. Stacy, Printer. 1851. 12mo, pp. 16.

—*Gazetteer* and Business Directory of Chittenden County, Vt., for 1882-3. Compiled and published by Hamilton Childs, Syracuse, N. Y. 1882. 8vo, pp. 584.

Chittenden, Lucius E. *The Law* of Baron and Femme, of Parent and Child, Guardian and Ward, Master and Servant, and of the Powers of Courts of Chancery; with an Essay on the terms Heir, Heirs, and Heirs of the Body. By Tapping Reeve. Second Edition, with Notes, and References to English and American Cases, by Lucius E. Chittenden. Burlington; Chauncey Goodrich. 1846. 8vo, pp. IV, (1), 493, (6).

—*A Report* of the Debates and Proceedings in the Secret Sessions of the Conference Convention, for proposing Amendments to the Constitution of the United States, held at Washington, D. C., in February, A. D. 1861. By L. E. Chittenden, one of the Delegates. New York: D. Appleton & Company. 1864. 8vo, pp. 626.

—*The Capture of Ticonderoga.* Annual Address before the Vermont Historical Society delivered at Montpelier, Vt., on Tuesday Evening, October 8, 1872. By Hon. Lucius E. Chittenden. Rutland: Tuttle & Company, Printers. 1872. 8vo, pp. 127.

    Also, Printed in Proceedings of the Vermont Historical Society, October 8, 1872. *Montpelier: Printed for the Society, 1872.*

—*Address* at the inauguration of the Stephenson Statue, at Burlington. See Allen, Ethan.

—*The Value of Instruction* in the Mechanic Arts. An Address before the American Institute of the City of New York, October Second, 1889, by L. E. Chittenden. Printed under the direction of the Board of Managers. New York. 1889. 8vo, pp. 28.

—*Recollections* of President Lincoln and his Administration. By L. E. Chittenden, his Register of the Treasury. New York: Harper Brothers. 1891. 8vo, pp. VIII, 470.

—*Personal Reminiscences,* 1840-1890, including some not hitherto published of Lincoln and the War. By L. E. Chittenden. New York: Richmond, Croscup & Co. 1893. 8vo, pp. 434.

—*The Unknown Heroine.* An Historical Episode of the War between the States, by L. E. Chittenden. New York: Richmond, Croscup & Co. 1893. 8vo, pp. 314.

    Lucius E. Chittenden was born in Williston, Vt., May 24, 1824, being the son of Giles' Chittenden, grandson of Truman Chittenden, and great grandson of Thomas Chittenden, the first governor of Vermont. He was educated at Williston Academy, studied law with his uncle, N. L. Whittemore of Swanton; was admitted to the Bar of Franklin County in September, 1843, removed to Burlington, 1844, and practiced law there until 1861, having as successive partners Wyllys Lyman, Edward J. Phelps and Daniel Roberts; was State Senator 1858 60; Delegate to the Peace Conference, February 1861; Register of the U. S. Treasury from March 1861 to March 1865; removed to New York City in 1865, and has practiced law there since that date.

Chittenden, Martin. *Mr. Niles's Resolution,* calling on the Governor for Evidence to Substantiate the Suggestion, in His Excellency's late Speech, relative to Impressment; together with His Excellency's Answer. Published by order of the House. Montpelier, Vt.; Printed by Walton & Goss, November, 1813. 8vo, pp. 8.

Chittenden, Thomas. *Remonstrance* of the Council of Vermont against the Resolve of Congress, 5 Dec., 1782. By Thomas Chittenden, of Bennington, Vt. Hartford: 1783. 12mo, pp. 20.

    The above title is from *Sabin's Bibliotheca Americana.* Probably the following is the origin and title of the work referred to:

    State of Vermont. In Council, Jan. 10th; 1783. On motion ordered that Col. Ira Allen & Thomas Tolman, Esq., prepare and Complete the draught of a Remonstrance or Letter to the President of the Hon'l. Congress, and lay the same before his Excellency the Governor for his approbation and signature.

    A Copy of a Remonstrance of the Council of the State of Vermont, Against the Resolutions of Congress of the 5th of December last, which interfere with their Internal Police. Hartford: Printed by Hudson & Goodwin. 1783. 12mo, pp. 20.

    See Record of the Governor and Council of Vt. pp. 254-262, vol. 3

Christ Church, Montpelier. *Easter* Statement and Appeal from the Vestry of Christ Church, Montpelier, Vt., to the Members of the Parish. Montpelier, Vermont: Argus and Patriot Job Printing House. 1872. 8vo, pp. 8.

The Christian Economy. *Translated* from the original Greek of an Old Manuscript, found in the island of Patmos, where St. John wrote his book of Revelations. Chelsea: William Hewes, Printer. 1841. 24mo, pp. 56.

The Christian Pilgrim. *Containing* An account of the Wonderful Adventures and miraculous escapes of a Christian, in his

Travels from the land of Destruction to the New Jerusalem. Montpelier: Published by E. P. Walton, 1819. 18mo, pp. 141, (2.)
With comical illustrations.

Christian Repository, *devoted* principally, to Doctrine, Morality, and Religious Intelligence. By Rev. Samuel C. Loveland. No. 1, Vol. I, July, 1820, David Watson, Printer. 12mo. —No. 5 of Vol. IX, February, 1829. 12mo, pp. 47.
A monthly magazine, devoted to the interests of the Universalist denomination, published at Woodstock, Vt. Subsequently it was published at Montpelier, Vt., under the name of the *Universalist Watchman*, by Ballou & Loveland, and Eli Ballou, and issued weekly in folio form; and was finally merged in the "Universalist" newspaper of Boston.
See Ballou, Eli.

Church Lands. A short History of late Ecclesiastical Oppressions in New England and Vermont. By a Citizen. In which is exhibited a Statement of the Violation of Religious Liberties, which are ratified by the Constitution of the United States. Richmond: Printed by James Lyon, at the Office of the National Magazine. 1799. 8vo, pp. 19.

Church of the Messiah. Library Catalogue of Sunday School of Church of the Messiah. Montpelier, Vt., Oct. 1877. 8vo, pp. 13.

Churches. See Baptists, Congregationalist, Methodist, Prot. Episcopal, Roman Catholic, Unitarian, Universalist, etc.

A Circular Letter to the Churches and Congregations of Vermont. (n. p. n. d.)

Churchill, Amos. History of Hubbardton, 1855.
Re-printed in Vermont Historical Gazetteer, with alterations, Vol. 3, pp. 746-778. See Hubbardton.

Circuit Court of the U. S. In Equity. To the Honorable the Judges of the Circuit Court of the United States for the District of Vermont. Dennis Lane, Perley P. Pitkin, and James W. Brock, citizens of Montpelier, Vt., bring this their bill of complaint against Luke Buzzel, a citizen of St. Johnsbury, in the County of Caledonia and State of Vermont. (1873.) No imprint. 8vo, pp. 160.

The Citizen Soldier. A Military Paper, Devoted to the Interests of the Militia. Major J. Swett, Jr., Editor. Vol. I. Windsor, Vt.: Published by Swett and Jackman. Stilman Fletcher, Printer. 1840–41. 4to, pp. 412.

Clarendon. Clarendon House. Clarendon Springs, Rutland County, Vt. 1874. In calling the attention of the public to Clarendon Springs as a place of resort, permit us to give a brief sketch of the place and Springs. Rutland: Tuttle & Co., Printers. 1874. 12mo, pp. 12.

—*The Same*, with same imprint, 1875 and 1876.

—*Report* of the Selectmen and Other Officers of the Town of Clarendon 1873. Rutland: Tuttle & Company, Printers. 1873. 8vo, pp. 12.
Continued.

—*Manual* of the Congregational Church, Clarendon, Vt., containing Historical Sketch, Articles of Faith and Covenant, with Standing Rules; together with List of Officers and Members. Clarendon, Vt. 1879. 12mo, pp. 15.

Clark, Ansel R. A Sermon delivered before the Auxiliary Education Society of Norfolk County, at their Annual Meeting in Walpole, June 13, 1832. By Rev. Ansel R. Clark, Secretary Western Reserve Branch, American Education Society, Hudson, Ohio. Boston: Printed by Perkins & Marvin. 1832. 8vo, pp. 24.
Mr. Clark was born at Lunenburg, Vt., June 27, 1800; was graduated at Dartmouth College, in 1826, and at Andover in 1829; was agent of the American Education Society, 1829-36; edited a paper, 1836-40; preached at Wellington, O., 1844-57, and at Huntington, O., 1858-73; and later at Collamer, O.

Clark Bros. Price List of Land Records, General Index Books, and Crown and Cap Deeds, manufactured by Clark Bros., (Successors to J. D. Clark & Son.) Journal Bindery, Moutpelier, Vt. Montpelier: J. & J. M. Poland, Printers. 18mo, pp. 8.

Clark, E. E. Clark's Revolving double thread family Sewing Machines. Montpelier: E. P. Walton, Printer. 1860. 18mo, pp. 7.

Clark, Henry. A Biographical Sketch of Edward Crafts Hopson. Read before the Vermont Historical Society, January 25, 1865. By Henry Clark, Esq., of Poultney. 8vo, pp. 6.

—*An Eulogy* on the Life and Services of President Lincoln, pronounced before the Citizens of Poultney and Vicinity, April 19th, 1865. By Henry Clark, Esq. Rutland: Tuttle, Gay & Company. 1865. 8vo, pp. 20.

—*An Historical Address*, delivered at Hubbardton, Vt., on the Eighty-Second Anniversary of the Battle of Hubbardton, July 7, 1859. By Henry Clark, with an Appendix Containing an Account of the Celebration. Rutland: George A. Tuttle & Co. 1859. 8vo, pp. 16.

—*Town Centennial Celebrations;* Their Historic Importance and Social advantages. An Essay prepared at the request of the Vermont Historical Society, and read at its Special Meeting holden at Burlington, January 22nd, 1862. By Henry Clark, Esq., of Poultney, Vt. 8vo, pp. 8.

—*Memorial Address* on the Life and Services of Rev. Pliny H. White. Pronounced before the Vermont Historical Society, at Montpelier, Oct. 19, 1869. By Henry Clark of Rutland. 8vo, pp. 16.

—*The Republic of Humanity.* An Address delivered before Killington Lodge, No. 29, I. O. of O. F. at Rutland, April 26, 1870. On the occasion of the fifty-first Anniversary of the Independent Order of Odd Fellows. By Henry Clark. Together with a Poem by Rev. Chas. Woodhouse. Rutland, Vt. 1870. 8vo, pp. [8.]

—*The School System of New England.* An Address delivered before the Otter Creek Valley Teachers' Association at Bennington, Vt., by Hon. Henry Clark of Rutland. 8vo, pp. 7.

—*Address*, Hist. Masonry in Rutland, 1870.
See Masonic.
Mr. Clark, son of Hon. Merritt Clark, was born in Middletown, Vt., February 18, 1828; he was educated in the common schools, Burr Seminary, at Manchester, and was two years in the University of Vermont, but left in 1846, on account of the failure of his health.
Mr. Clark entered political life as a Democrat, was a firm friend of Douglas, and a member of the Convention at Baltimore which nominated him for the Presidency. He was Postmaster at Poultney, 1852-1860; was Secretary

of the State Senate, 1861-1872. He has been an active member and officer of the Vermont Historical Society, and is connected with the Agricultural, Masonic, and other organizations in the State. He was connected with the Rutland *Herald*, *Globe*, and *Leader*, as editor for twelve years. He has delivered many addresses not included in the above list.

[Clark, Jonas.] *Mr. Sheriff Fay's "Expose" Unveiled.* Middlebury : Printed by Copeland and Allen. 1820. 8vo, pp. 19.
Relates to suits against Mr. Fay, Sheriff of Addison county, for alleged neglect of duty.

Clark, Nathanael George, D. D. LL. D. An Outline of the Elements of the English Language for the use of Students. By N. G. Clark, Professor of Rhetoric and English Literature in Union College. New York : Charles Scribner. 1863. pp. 220.

—*The Battle of the Orators,* or the Great Debate between Messrs. Webster and Hayne. With Introduction and Notes for the use of Students. Schenectady : Young & Graham. 1864. pp. 89.

—*Christian Trust and Hope.* A Sermon Preached at St. Albans, March 29, 1863. On the occasion of the death of Mr. Benjamin Fay Farrar. By Rev. N. G. Clark, Late Professor in the University of Vermont. (Printed by Request.) St. Albans: Whiting & Davis, Printers. 1863. pp. 13.

—*Universal Exposition*, Paris, 1867. Statistics of the American Board of Commissioners for Foreign Missions. 1866. pp. 8.
Prepared for the Massachusetts Exhibit at the Paris Exposition.

—*The American* Board of Commissioners for Foreign Missions. Brief Historical Sketch and Statistics, 1810–1876. Prepared for the Massachusetts Exhibit in the Department of Education and Science at the International Exhibition in Philadelphia, in 1876. Boston: Thomas Todd, Printer. 1876. pp. 12.

—*The Annual Address* and the Address to the Graduating Class, at the Fifty-first Anniversary of Mount Holyoke Seminary, June 21, 1888, Springfield, Mass. Springfield Printing and Binding Company. 1888. pp. 19.
Dr. Clark was also the author of articles on religious and literary subjects, and on Modern Missions, printed in the American Theological Review, the Boston Review, and the New Englander; and of reports and papers preserved in the reports of the American Board of Commissioners for Foreign Missions. One of these, an able paper on "India, its Need and Opportunity," read before the American Board in October, 1888, attracted much attention in England, and led to his election as a member of the Victoria Institute, of England, a distinguished honor.
Rev. N. G. Clark was born in Calais, Vt., January 18, 1825. He graduated at the University of Vermont in 1845, studied theology at Andover and Auburn, graduating from the latter in 1852. He was tutor in the University of Vermont, 1849-50 ; Professor of English literature and of Latin in the University, 1852-63. Professor of Rhetoric and English Literature in Union College, 1863-5. Foreign Secretary of the American Board of Commissioners for Foreign Missions, 1865-95. He died at his home in West Roxbury, Mass., January 3, 1896.

Clark, Nelson. *The Home-Charm of the Sanctuary.* A Sermon preached at the Re-opening of the House of Worship of the Evangelical Congregational Society in Quincy, January 9, 1853. By Nelson Clark, Pastor of the Church. Boston : Press of T. R. Marvin, 42 Congress St. 1853. 8vo, pp. 20.
Mr. Clark was born at Brookfield, Vt., in 1814; was graduated at Dartmouth College in 1838, and at Andover

in 1842 ; preached at Randolph, Vt., 1844-46, at Charlton, Mass., 1846-49; at Quincy, Mass., 1850-58, at Tiverton, R. I., 1858-66; at Somerset, Mass., 1866-68, and died at National, Iowa, March 16, 1880.

Clark, O. *An Address* delivered before the Cadets of Norwich University, at their Annual Commencement. Hanover: 1840. 8vo.

—*An Address* delivered before the Cadets of Norwich University, at their Annual Commencement, Aug. 18, 1842. By Maj. Gen. O. Clark of New York. Hanover: Printed by W. A. Patten. 1842. 8vo, pp. 17.

Clarke, Rev. Adam. *A Short History of the Israelites*, with an Account of their manners, etc. By Rev. Adam Clarke. Burlington, Vt.: 1813. Dennis Heartt, Printer. 1813. 12mo, pp. 300.

Clarke, Albert. *The Free Pass Abuse.* The Constitutional Power of the State to Regulate Railroads. Speech of Hon. Albert Clarke, of St. Albans, delivered in the Vermont Senate, Friday, November 13th, 1874. St. Albans, Vt.: Messenger Steam Printing House. 1874. 8vo, pp. 13.

—*St. Albans*, as A Summer Resort.
See St. Albans.

Clarke, Asahel. *Poem*, at Middlebury College, 1807.
See Middlebury College.

Clarke, Charles Cotesworth Pinckney. The True Method of Representation in large Constituencies. By C. C. P. Clarke, M. D., of Oswego, N. Y. Republished by Peter Cooper, with a Letter to his Fellow-Countrymen. 1872. 8vo, pp. 24.

—*The Commonwealth Reconstructed.* By Charles C. P. Clarke, M. D. New York : A. S. Barnes & Co., Chicago & New Orleans. 8vo, pp. 216.

—*Nova Instauratio Reipublicæ:* (The Commonwealth Reconstructed.) By C. C. P. Clarke. Oswego, N. Y.: Printed at the Daily Press Office. 1872. 8vo, pp. 32.
Mr. Clarke, a native of Tinmouth, Vt., was graduated at Middlebury, 1843, and at the College of Physicians and Surgeons in New York, 1847; practiced medicine at Middlebury, 1847-51, when he moved to Oswego, N. Y., where he still resides.

Clarke, Rev. Dorus. *A Sermon*, delivered at Chicopee Falls, March 24, 1839, on occasion of the Death of William L. Wyman, of Brookline, Vt., who was drowned in the Chicopee River. By Dorus Clarke, Pastor of the Fifth Congregational Church in Springfield. Springfield : Printed by Merriam, Wood & Co. 1839. 8vo, pp. 16.

Clarke, Mrs. D. W. C. *Lizzie Maitland*, Edited by O. A. Brownson. New York : 1857. 12mo, pp. 340.
Mrs. Clarke died at Burlington, Vt., May 23, 1866.
See Miss Hemenway's Vermont Historical Gazetteer, Vol. I, p. 938; and Hemenway, A. M., "Clarke Papers."

Clement, Jonathan. *Farewell Sermon* of Rev. Jonathan Clement, D. D., to the Congregational Church in Woodstock, Vermont. June 16, 1867. With an Historical Appendix. 1867. 8vo, pp. 27.
Hon. Frederick Billings asked the privilege of publishing this Discourse.
Dr. Clement was born in Danville, Vt., June 20, 1797. He graduated from Middlebury College in 1818. Instructor in Phillips Academy, Andover, 1820-30; preached in

Chester, N. H., Topsham, Me., and Woodstock, Vt. Resided after 1867 in Norwich. He received the degree of D. D. from Middlebury College, 1847. Died of old age and effect of a broken leg at Norwich, Sept. 6, 1881.

Six of Dr. Clement's sermons were published at different times.

Clinton, George. *George Clinton Papers.* Manuscripts. Vols. i–xxiii, 1763–1800.

These volumes, which are large folios, contain more than six thousand manuscript documents, and are in the New York State Library at Albany. In them are to be found abundant materials relative to the controversy respecting the New Hampshire Grants, and the troubles and skirmishes which grew out of it.

B. H. Hall's Bibliography of Vermont.

Closson, H. P. *Established 1852.* H. P. Closson's Descriptive Catalogue of choice Greenhouse and Bedding Plants, Seeds and Bulbs. Also Fruit and Ornamental Trees, small fruits, shrubs, etc., Cultivated and for sale at his Nursery and Green-houses, Thetford, Vermont. 1880. Claremont, N. H. 8vo, pp. 32.

Cobb, Enos. *An interesting publication!* An exposition of Dr. Cobb's art of discovering the Faculties of the Human Mind and bodily infirmities: To which is added an Auto-Biographical Sketch of the Author and a Poetic Description of several Cities, Towns and Villages which he has visited ; To which is added, a Guide for teaching his Art to others, explaining the use of his "Marked Strap," with a Blank Chart, in which a Description of any person may be inserted. An interesting Song on an eminent Lawyer! ! Montpelier: 1846. 12mo, pp. 32.

Cobb, L. *Cobb's Spelling Book.* Being a Standard for Pronouncing the English Language, &c. By Lyman Cobb. Revised Edition. Bennington: (Vt.) John C. Haswell. Stereotyped by J. S. Redfield, N. Y. 1835. 12mo, pp. 165.

Cobb, Rev. Lewis H., D. D. *The Old Paths.* A Historical Discourse, delivered at Springfield, Vt., on the Re-opening of the Congregational Church, May 30, 1869. By the Pastor. Claremont, N. H.: 1870. 8vo, pp. 18.

—*In Memory* of Deacon Oren Locke, Springfield, Vermont. Printed for his Family Friends. n. p. n. d. pp. 34.

Mr. Cobb was born in Cornish, N. H., June 30, 1827; was graduated at Dartmouth College in 1854, and at Andover in 1857; preached at Springfield, Vt., 1867–74, and later at Minneapolis, Minn; is now (1896) corresponding secretary of the Congregational Church Building Society, New York city.

Coburn, A. *The Scholar's Teacher*, being an Arrangement of Modern Geography on the Classification System. By A. Coburn. Montpelier, Vt. 1838. 12mo, pp. 13.

Coburn, Frank W. *The Centennial* History of the Battle of Bennington ; Compiled from the Most Reliable Sources and fully Illustrated with Original Documents and Entertaining Anecdotes. Col. Seth Warner's Identity in the First Action completely established. By Frank W. Coburn. Embelished with a Portrait of General Stark, a plan of the Battle Field, and other Engravings. Motto. Boston : George E. Littlefield, Antiquarian Bookstore, 67 Cornhill. 1877. 8vo, pp. 72.

Frank Warren Coburn, son of Lyman R. and Lucinda T. Coburn, was born at the foot of Fairlee Lake, in Thetford, Vt., June 3, 1853. His father served as a volunteer in the rebellion, 15th Regiment, Vermont volunteers, and shortly after his return from the army moved his family to Massachusetts, Frank finishing a limited education at Cambridge in that State. He was married December 25, 1878, to Hattie J. Marsh, of Somerville, Mass., and is associated with a brother in the stationery and printing business in Boston, Mass. The above is as yet the only production of his pen, with the exception of occasional newspaper articles. He is, however, collecting material for the history of his native State. (1880.)

See Gleig, George R.

Colburn, Warren. *Colburn's First Lessons* Intellectual Arithmetic, upon the Inductive Method of Instruction. By Warren Colburn, A. M. Stereotyped at the Boston Type and Stereotype Foundry. Bellows Falls: Published by Roswell S. Guild & Co. 1835. 16mo, pp. 178.

Colburn, Zerah. *A Memoir of*, written by Himself. Containing an account of the first discovery of his remarkable Powers ; His Travels in America and Residence in Europe ; A history of the various plans devised for his Patronage ; His return to this Country, and the Causes which led him to his present Profession ; with his peculiar Methods of Calculation. Springfield: Published by G. and C. Merriam. 1833. 12mo, pp. 204.

Mr. Colburn, a mathematical prodigy, was born in Cabot, Vt., September 1, 1804; and died at Norwich, Vt., March 2, 1839.

Colby, Geo J. *How to make money!* what is and what is not. Motto. By George Jewell Colby, Reading, Mich. Cincinnati: Colby Brothers. 1878. Landman, Pr., Cin. Price 5 cents. 16mo, pp. 32.

—*Price 5 Cents.* Just the Thing ! Greenback Songs, Poems, Facts & Figures. By Geo. J. Colby. Colby Brothers, Cincinnati, 1878. Attlesey Prtg wks. Cin. 16mo, pp. 40, (1).

These publications favor the Greenback Currency System. The author is a native of Richmond, Vt., or that vicinity, and was for many years connected with the Colby Wringer manufacturing concern at Waterbury, Vt., later in the same business in the State of Michigan, and now (1880) resides at Cincinnati.

Colby, John. *The Life*, Experience and Travels of John Colby, Preacher of the Gospel. Written by himself. Motto. Dover, N. H. 1854. 12mo, pp. 251, 66. Two volumes in one.

Elder Colby, a Baptist revival preacher, was born in Sandwich, N. H., December 9, 1787; and died at Norfolk, Va., November 28, 1817, whither he had gone in pursuit of health.

At the age of fifteen, with his father and family, he removed to Sutton, Vt., which ever after was his home. He labored upon his father's farm until he was 21, when with a limited education he began to preach, itinerating through New England, and as far south as Virginia.

Colby, Stoddard B. *Obituary notices of*, cut from newspapers, and pasted in book form. 8vo, pp. 7.

Mr. Colby was born in Derby, Vt. in February 1816; graduated at Dartmouth in 1836; studied law; in 1840 formed a law partnership at Montpelier with Lucius B. Peck; in 1864 was appointed Register of the U. S. Treasury; died in Haverhill, N. H., while on a visit, Saturday, September 21, 1867.

Colchester. *Sixteenth Annual Report* of the Select Men and other Officers of the Town of Colchester, Vt., for the year ending Friday, February 1st, 1879. Burlington, Vt.: The Free Press Association, Printers and Binders. 1879. 8vo, pp. 43.

Coleridge, S. T. *The Statesman's Manual;* or the Bible the Best Guide to Political Skill and Foresight : A Lay Sermon, addressed to the Higher Classes of Society. By S. T. Coleridge, Esq. Burlington : Chauncey Goodrich, 1832. 12mo, pp. 231.

COLLAMER, JACOB. *Oration* Delivered before the Phi Sigma Nu Society, of the University of Vermont, Burlington, August 6, 1828. By Jacob Collamer. Published by the Society. W. Spooner's print. Royalton: [n. d.] 8vo, pp. 19.

—*Speech* on Wool and Woolens. Delivered before the House, April 29, 1844. Washington: 8vo, pp. 16.

—*Speech* on the Constitutional Validity of the Act of Congress requiring the Election of Representatives to be by Districts. Washington : 1844. 8vo, pp. 13.

—*Speech* on the Annexation of Texas ; Jan. 23, 1845. Washington : 8vo, pp. 16.

—*Speech* in the House, June 26, 1846, on The Tariff. Washington : 1846. 8vo, pp. 16.

—*Speech* in the House of Representatives, on the Mexican War, February 1, 1848. Washington : 1848. 8vo, pp. 14.
In opposition to the War.

—*Speech* on the President's Message, United States Senate, December 9, 1856. 8vo, pp. 16.

—*Kansas Affairs in the Senate.* Minority Report of the Senate Committee on Territories. Made March 12, 1856, by Judge Collamer, of Vermont. Washington : 1856. 8vo, pp. 15.

—*Speech*, on Affairs in Kansas, in the Senate, April 3 and 4, 1856. Washington : 1856. 8vo, pp. 29.

—*Speech*, on The Tariff and Wool Interest ; in the Senate, February 26, 1857. 8vo, pp. 16.

—*In the Senate*, February 18, 1858, Mr. Collamer, from the Committee on Territories, submitted the Following as the views of the Minority On the Constitution of Kansas, adopted by the Convention which met at Lecompton, Sept. 4th, 1857. Washington : 1858. 8vo, pp. 7.

—*Speech*, on the Kansas Question ; in the Senate, March 1 and 2, 1858. 8vo, pp. 20.

—*Speech*, on the Report of the Kansas Conference Committee : delivered in the Senate of the United States, April 27, 1858. Washington : 1858. 8vo.

—*Speech* on the Acquisition of Cuba ; delivered in the Senate, February 21, 1859. Washington : 1859. 8vo, pp. 21.

—*Speech* on Slavery in the Territories. Delivered in the Senate, March 8, 1860. 8vo, pp. 24.

—*Speech* of Hon. Jacob Collamer, on presenting a Memorial from inhabitants of Swanton, Vt., proposing Amendments to the Constitution, delivered in the Senate of the United States, February 7, 1861. Washington, 1861. 8vo, pp, 8.

—*Speech* on the Treasury Note Bill, in the Senate, February 12, 1862, 8vo, pp. 15.

—*Speech* of Hon. J. Collamer, of Vermont, In the United States Senate, April 24, 1862, on the Bill to Confiscate the property and free the Slaves of Rebels. 8vo, pp. 16.

—*Speech*, on the Bill to Provide a National Currency ; in the Senate, February 11, 1863, 8vo, pp. 13.

—*Speech* on the Reconstruction of the Seceded States, made in the Senate, 6th of February, 1865. Washington : 1865. 8vo, pp. 8.

—*Addresses* on the death of Hon. Jacob Collamer, delivered in the Senate and House of Representatives, on Thursday, December 14, 1865. 1866. 8vo, pp. 85.

—*Memorial Address* on the Death of Judge Collamer, before the Vermont Historical Society, October 20, 1868.
See Barrett, James.

—*Statue of Jacob Collamer.* Addresses on the presentation of the Statue of Jacob Collamer of Vermont, by Hon. James M. Tyler of Vermont, Hon. George B. Loring of Massachusetts, Hon. Alexander H. Stevens of Georgia, delivered in the House of Representatives, Tuesday, February 15, 1881. Washington : 1881. 8vo, pp. 15.
Judge Collamer was born in Troy, N. Y., January 8, 1791. His father removed to Burlington and the son fitted for college there. He graduated from the University of Vermont in 1810. He read law in St. Albans with Hon. Benjamin Swift, and was admitted to the bar in 1813. In 1812 he served as Lieutenant of Artillery, on the frontier. In 1816 he removed to Royalton, and represented that town in the Legislature in 1821, 22, 27 and 28. He was States Attorney for Windsor County, 1822-24 ; Judge of the Supreme Court of Vermont 1833-41 ; Representative in Congress, 1843-49 ; appointed Postmaster General of the United States, by President Taylor in 1849, and held the portfolio till July, 1850, when he resigned in consequence of President Taylor's death, Judge of the Circuit Court of the Second Circuit of Vermont, 1850 to 1854 ; United States Senator from 1855 to 1865. He was the leading mind of the Senate on Constitutional questions and was the author of the Act of July 13, 1861, giving to the war for the Union Congressional sanction, and new powers to the President, which Mr. Sumner characterized as "a landmark in our history" and proper to be known as "The Collamer Statute." His statue, in marble, by Larkin G. Mead, was placed in the Capitol at Washington by the State of Vermont in 1872. He died in Woodstock, November 4, 1865.
For sketches of his life, see Barrett, J. Address before the Vermont Historical Society, 1868; Lanman's Biographical Annals ; Drake.

Collens, Daniel, A. M. *The Believers Triumph over Death.* Illustrated in a Sermon, Preached at Lanesborough, December 17, 1783, At the Funeral of Mrs. Huldah, Consort of Lieut. Andrew Squier. By Daniel Collens, A. M., Pastor of the Church in Lanesborough. Published at the Request of a number of the Hearers. Bennington : Printed by Haswell & Russell, M,DCC,LXXXIV. 8vo, pp. 29.

Collier, Peter. *Commercial Fertilizers.* A Paper prepared for the Report of the Vermont State Board of Agriculture, Manufactures and Mining, by Peter Collier, Secretary. Montpelier : J. & J. M. Poland's Print. 1872. 8vo, pp. 46.
See University of Vermont. Address, 1876.

—*Second Biennial Report* of the Vermont State Board of Agriculture, Manufactures and Mining, for the years 1873-74. By Peter Collier, Secretary of the Board. Montpelier : Freeman Steam Printing House and Bindery. 1874. 8vo, pp. 23.

—*Vienna International Exhibition.* Report on Commercial Fertilizers. By Peter Collier, Ph.D., Member of the Scientific Commission of the United States. Washington: Government Printing Office. 1875. 8vo, pp. 67.

See Vermont State Board of Agriculture, 1872 and after, for various papers by Professor Collier; he was some time Secretary of the Board, also a Professor in the University of Vermont. Subsequently was Chemist to the Agricultural Department at Washington, and later in charge of the New York State Agricultural Experiment Station, Syracuse, N. Y. He died at Ann Arbor, Mich., July, 1896.

Collins Family. *Report* to the Collins Association, U. S. A. By Columbus Smith. 1864. p. 1.

Colonial Wars. *Vt. Society of.*
See Vermont.

Colton, A. M. and G. Q. *In Memoriam* Dea. Walter Colton, Georgia, Vt. For the Family, by A. M. and G. Q. Colton. No imprint. 12mo, pp. 60.

Colton, Walter. *Land and Lee in the Bosphorus and Ægean;* or Views of Athens and Constantinople. By Rev. Walter Colton, Late of the United States Navy. Edited from the Notes and manuscripts of the Author, . By Rev. Henry T. Cheever. New York: Published by A. S. Barnes & Co., 1851. 12mo, pp. 366.

First edition in 1836, under the title, "A visit to Constantinople."

—*Deck and Port;* or Incidents of a Cruise in the United States Frigate Congress to California. With Sketches of Rio Janeiro, Valparaiso, Lima, Honolulu, and San Francisco. By Rev. Walter Colton, U. S. N. New York: A. S. Barnes & Co. 1850. 12mo, pp. 408.

Several editions were published; reprinted in London, 1851.

—*Three Years in California.* By Rev. Walter Colton, U. S. N. Late Alcalde of Monterey. New York: A. S. Barnes & Co. 1851. 12mo, pp. 451.

Several editions were published.

—*The Bible* in the Public Schools. A Reply to the Allegations and complaints contained in a Letter of Bishop Kenrick, to the Controllers of Public Schools. Philadelphia: 1844. 8vo, pp. 16.

—*The Sea and the Sailor.* Notes on France and Italy, and other Literary Remains of Rev. Walter Colton. With a Memoir by Rev. Henry T. Cheever. New York: Published by A. S. Barnes & Co. 1856. 12mo, pp. 437.

Mr. Colton was born in Rutland, Vt., May 9, 1797, and died in Philadelphia, January 22, 1851; he was graduated at Yale College, 1822; and at Andover Theological Seminary, 1825; and was soon after ordained as an Evangelist, and chosen a Professor and also Chaplain in Captain Alden Partridge's Military Academy, at Middletown, Conn., which positions he resigned in 1830 on account of ill health, and went to Washington, as assistant editor of a Missionary paper just started. While in Washington he supplied the pulpit for a short time where General Jackson attended church, and the General taking a fancy to Mr. Colton, he was often at the White House, and President Jackson, becoming aware of his infirm health, offered him a Chaplaincy in the Navy, or a Foreign Consulate. He chose the former, and was at once appointed, and sailed January 29, 1831, in the United States ship Vincennes for the West Indies; in 1832–5 he cruised in the "Constellation" to the Mediteranean, and in 1838 was assigned to Philadelphia, where in 1841–2, he was principal editor of the *North American.* In 1846 he was ordered to the Pacific Squadron, and was appointed Alcalde of Monterey, Cal., by Commodore Stockton, July 28, 1846. He established the first newspaper in California, entitled the *Californian,* which was afterwards transferred to San Francisco, and called the *Alta California.*

He built the first school-house in California, and, in letters to the Philadelphia *North American* and the New York Journal of Commerce, he was the first to make known the discovery of gold in California to the people of the Atlantic States. In 1849 he returned to Philadelphia. In addition to the works mentioned, Mr. Colton published "Ship and Shore," 1835; "Land and Sea," 1851; and while at Middletown, as Professor and Chaplain to the Cadets, several addresses before the Cadets and Students, and several articles of importance in the *Middletown Gazette:* "A Prize Essay on Duelling," "A Discussion of the Genius of Coleridge," "The Moral Power of the Poet, Painter, and Sculptor Contrasted," "Address to the Cadets of Captain Partridge's Academy on the death of Ex-Presidents Adams and Jefferson," "Address on the death of Cadet Ralph A. Wikoff," "A Plea for the Greeks," and others.

See Life by Rev. Henry T. Cheever; Duyckinck; Drake; Allibone; Vermont Historical Gazetteer, Vol. 3, pp. 1097-98.

Colver, Rev. Nathaniel. *The Prophecy* of Daniel, literally fulfilled: considered in three lectures. By Nathaniel Colver, Pastor of the First Baptist Free Church, Boston. Boston: William S. Damrell, No. 11 Cornhill. 16mo, pp. 61. 1843.

—*A Call* of God to the Christian Ministry, definite and imperative. A Sermon preached before the Boston Baptist Association, September 15, 1847. By Nathaniel Colver, Pastor of Tremont street Church, Boston. Boston: William D. Ticknor & Company. 1847. 8vo, pp. 23.

—*The Fugitive Slave Bill;* or God's Laws paramount to the Laws of Men. A Sermon, preached on Sunday, October 20, 1850, by Rev. Nathaniel Colver, Pastor of the Tremont St. Church. Boston: J. M. Hewes & Co., 81 Cornhill. 1850. 8vo, pp. 24.

—*and Davis, Rev. Jonathan.* Debate on Slavery. Report of a Discussion, on a resolution before the American Baptist Anti-Slavery Convention, held in the Tremont and Marlboro' Chapels, Boston, Wednesday, Thursday, and Friday, May 26, 27 and 28, 1841, between Elds. Nathaniel Colver, Pastor of the First Baptist Free Church, Boston, and Jonathan Davis, Pastor of the Bethel Baptist Church, Georgia. Vol. I, No. 8, of the Journal of the American Baptist Anti-Slavery Convention. Worcester, Mass.: July 1841. 12mo, pp. 108.

—*Memoir* of Rev. Nathaniel Colver, D. D., with Lectures, Plans of Sermons, etc. By Rev. J. A. Smith, D. D. Boston: Durkee and Foxcroft, Publishers, 151 Washington Street. 1873. 8vo, pp. 453.

A Baptist minister, born in Orwell, Vt., May, 1794, and died in Chicago, September, 25, 1870. His education was limited. He was a soldier in the war of 1812, and by trade a tanner. He began to preach in 1836 at Union Village, N. Y., and was settled successively in Boston, 1843, Detroit, Cincinnati, and then at Chicago in 1860; he was active as an anti-Mason and an Abolitionist. After the war he put in operation the "Colver Institute," at Richmond, for educating young men of color for the ministry. He published three lectures on Odd Fellowship in 1844.

A Companion to the Altar: Shewing the Nature and necessity of a Sacramental Preparation, in order to our worthy receiving the Holy Communion: wherein Those fears and scruples about eating and drinking unworthily, and of incurring our own damnation thereby, are proved groundless & unwarrantable. I will wash my hands in innocency, O, Lord, and so will I go to thine Altar. Psal. xxvi. 6. Burlington, Vt. Printed by S. Mills, For Ambrose Atwater. 1810. 8vo, pp. 31.

A Compendious View of the Gospel, and a few remarks on the Confession of Faith, of the Synod of Kentucky. By the Presbytery of Springfield. Windsor, (Vt.) Re-Printed by Alden Spooner. 1808. 12mo, pp. 72.

Comstock, John M. *First Annual Report* of the Secretaries of the Class of '77, Academical and Scientific Departments, Dartmouth College. Hanover, N. H., Jan. 1, 1878. 8vo, pp. 12.

—*The same*, Second Report, 8vo, pp. 12.

—*The same*, Third Report. Chelsea, Vt., Jan. 1, 1880. 8vo, pp. 20.

—*Necrology of Dartmouth Alumni* for 1876-7. 8vo, pp. 14.

—*The same*, 1877-8. 8vo, pp. 16.

—*The same*, 1878-9. 8vo, pp. 15.

—*The same*, 1879-80. 8vo, pp. 20.

—*Obituary Record* of the Graduates of Dartmouth College and the Associated Institutions for the year ending at Commencement, 1881. Hanover, N. H. 1881. 8vo, pp. 24.

Mr. Comstock, of Chelsea, Vt., prepared the above reports almost entirely. Since his graduation at Dartmouth in '77 he has been teaching at Chelsea, and doing some editorial work on the *Observer* at White River Junction in 1878-9. Later he was engaged in the preparation of Dartmouth Quinquennial Catalogue. He is Secretary of the Academical Class of 1877, and has been for several years the Corresponding Secretary of the General Convention of Congregational Ministers and Churches of Vermont. He is the son of David and Margaret (Laird) Comstock, was born in Williamstown, Vt., May 27, 1859, and fitted for college at Goddard Seminary, Barre.

Conant, Edward. *A Parsing and Drill Book* in the Elements of the English Language. By Edward Conant, A. M. Principal of the State Normal School, at Randolph, Vt. Rutland, Vt.: Published by Tuttle & Company. 1873. 12mo, pp. 156.

—*First Edition*, Montpelier, 1871.

—*Third edition*, Rutland, Vt.: Published by the Tuttle Company. 1887. 12mo, pp. 156.

—*Civil Government* of Vermont. Edward Conant, A. M. Rutland: 1890. 12mo, pp. 96.

—*Geography, History and Civil Government* of Vermont, by Edward Conant. Rutland. The Tuttle Co. 1890. 12mo, pp. 288.

Prepared as a text book for schools.

—*Revised Edition* of same, same publishers. 1895. pp. 292.

—*Vermont Primary Historical Reader and Lessons* on the Geography of Vermont, by E. Conant. Rutland: The Tuttle Company. 1895. 12mo, pp. 234.

Mr. Conant was born in Pomfret, Vt., May 10, 1829. He is a teacher by profession; and is the Principal of the State Normal School at Randolph. He was a member of the State Board of Education, 1866-7; member of the Constitutional Convention in 1870, and State Superintendent of Education 1874-80.

Conant, Marshall. 1836. *The Year Book:* an Astronomical and Philosophical Annual; in three parts, containing, Part I. Astronomy; an Exposition of its Principles, and the true Method of studying the Science. Part II. Extensive Astronomical Calculations, made for several different Meridians and Parallels, and fitted for General Use in all Parts of the United States. Part III. Miscellaneous Articles; including among other Matters useful and agree-able Notices of recent Inventions and Discoveries in the more practical Departments of Science and the Arts. By Marshall Conant. Boston: Monroe & Francis, 128 Washington Street. 1836. 12mo, pp. 110.

Mr. Conant published a series of Almanacs at Woodstock, about 1827 to 1833-4. See Almanacs.

Mr. Conant was born in Pomfret, Vt. January 5, 1801, and furnished a rare instance of a man educating himself in the face of great difficulties. He commenced teaching school in 1823, went to Boston, Mass., in 1834, and was engaged in teaching, being Principal of Bridgewater Normal School a large part of the time for several years, and mostly in Massachusetts, until his death, February 10, 1873.

Conant, Thomas Jefferson. *A General and Analytical* index to the American Cyclopædia. By the Rev. T. J. Conant, D. D., assisted by his daughter, Blandina Conant. New York: London: D. Appleton and Company. 1879. 8vo, pp. viii, 810.

He was born in Brandon, Vt., December 13, 1802, was graduated at Middlebury College in 1823, and was a Baptist minister, Orientalist, and Biblical scholar, and at different times connected with Columbian College, D. C., Waterville College, Me., Hamilton College, N. Y., and Rochester. In 1839 Mr. Conant published a translation of "Gesenius' Hebrew Grammar," which has passed through twenty editions or more; he has been engaged for more than twenty years upon a new translation of the Bible. His first elaborate production was an essay on the laws of translation, written while at Middlebury; his version of Job was published in 1857.

Mr. Conant's revision of "The Gospel of Matthew" was published in 1860; "The Book of Genesis," 1868; "The Book of Psalms," 1868; also an edition of the same, with additional notes, in the American edition of Lange's "Commentary," 1872; and "The Book of Proverbs," 1872.

Condie, Thomas. *Biographical Memoirs* of the Illustrious Gen. George Washington, late President of the United States of America, &c. Containing a History of the principal events of his life, with extracts from his Journals, Speeches to Congress, and Public Addresses. Also, A Sketch of his Private Life. Brattleborough: Published by William Fessenden. 1814. 12mo, pp. 287.

This edition is said to have been edited by the publisher.—*Sabin.*

CONGREGATIONAL. *Minutes of the First Fifteen Annual Meetings* of the General Convention of Ministers in the State of Vermont, From 1795 to 1810 inclusive. Montpelier: Poland's Steam Printing Establishment. 1877. 8vo, pp. 54.

These earlier reports were never printed separately in pamphlet form; since 1810 annual reports have been published. The "General Convention of Vermont" was organized August 27, 1795, "At a meeting of Delegates, convened by circular letters at the house of President John Wheelock, Hanover, N. H." This first convention was composed of the following persons: Rev. Messrs. Job Swift, Samuel Whiting, Lyman Potter, Asa Burton and Martin Tullar. Mr. Whiting was chosen Moderator, and Mr. Tullar Scribe.

The title-page of the report for 1818 is as follows: "Extracts from the Minutes of the General Convention of Congregational and Presbyterian Ministers in Vermont." 8vo, pp. 12.

In 1841 "Presbyterian" was dropped, and the title is as follows: "Extracts from the Minutes of the General Convention of Congregational Ministers and Churches in Vermont, at their Session at Woodstock, September, 1841. Windsor: Printed at the Chronicle Press. 1841." 8vo, pp. 19 (1). The Minutes are continued under this title, substantially, until 1862, when an arrangement was made to include the "Report of the Vermont Domestic Missionary Society," with the following title: "Minutes of the General Convention of Congregational Ministers and Churches in Vermont, at their Session at Norwich, June, 1862, with the Report of the Corresponding Secretary, and the Statistics of the Churches; Also the Annual Report of the Vermont Domestic Missionary Society. Windsor: Vermont Chronicle Book and Job Office. 1862." 8vo, pp. 48 and 47.

In 1866 the report of the Vermont Education Society was added, and the title reads: "Minutes of the Seventy-first Annual Meeting of the General Convention of Vermont, at Newbury, June, 1866: Forty-seventh Annual Report of the Vermont Domestic Missionary Society, and Forty-fifth Annual Report of the Vermont Education Society. Montpelier; Walton's Steam Printing Establishment. 1866." 8vo, pp. 92. Pagination continuous. Continued.

—*Articles of Consociation* Recommended to a number of Churches in the Western Districts of Vermont and parts adjacent, By Their Representatives met in Convention At Rutland, June 6, A. D. 1797. Fairhaven. Printed by J. P. Spooner. 1797. 8vo, pp. 13.

—*Articles of Consociation*, Revised, and with some additions, Recommended to a number of Churches in the Western Districts of Vermont, by their Representatives, met at Pawlet, June 7th, A D. 1798. Printed by J. D. Huntington, Middlebury, Vt. June, 1806. 12mo, pp. 16.

—*A Shorter Confession of Faith*, with Scripture proofs, and a Covenant, for the use of Christians, in receiving members to their Communion : to which is annexed Articles of Consociation, revised, and with some additions, recommended to a number of Churches in the Western District of Vermont, and parts adjacent, by their Representatives, met at Pawlet, June 7th, 1798. Middlebury : T. C. Strong. 1812.

—*Articles of Consociation*, adopted by the Congregational Churches in the Western Districts of Vermont, and Parts adjacent, A. D. 1798. To which is Annexed A Shorter Confession of Faith, with Scripture Proofs, and a Covenant for the use of the Churches in receiving Members to their Communion. The Second Edition ; Revised and published by Order of Consociation at Pittsford, June, 1817. Arlington, Vt. Printed by E. C. Storer. 1817. 12mo, pp. 22.

—*Articles of Consociation*, adopted A. D. 1798, by the Congregational Churches in the Western Districts of Vermont and parts adjacent ; and amended by the Churches, A. D. 1822. To which is annexed a Shorter Confession of Faith, with Scripture Proofs, and a Covenant for the use of the Churches, in receiving Members to their Communion. Poultney, Vt. Printed by Smith and Shute. 1822. 12mo, pp. 23.

—*A Narrative of the State of Religion*, Within the bounds of the General Assembly of the Presbyterian Church ; and of the General Associations of Connecticut and Massachusetts, and the General Convention of Vermont. [Philadelphia : William Bradford. 1822.] 8vo, pp. 8.

—*Fornication binds the criminal parties to marry*. The Decision of the Congregational Church in Rupert, Vt., relative to A Case of Discipline. The result of an Ecclesiastical Council, convened at that place August 31, 1814. A Dissertation delivered on the occasion by one of the Council. A Letter of Admonition addressed to the offender. And the form of Excommunication. With an Appendix containing strictures on fornication and divorcement. Bennington, Vt. Printed by Darius Clark : 1815. 8vo, pp. 40.

—*Constitution of the General Convention* of Congregational Ministers and Churches in Vermont. June, 1857. 8vo, pp. 8.

—*Constitution, By-Laws, etc.*, of Addison Co. Conference of Congregational Churches. Middlebury : Register Print. 1862. 12mo. pp. 12.

—*An Address* to the Baptist Church in Middletown, Vt. By a Late Member of the Same. In which the doctrine of Baptism as believed in and practiced by the Congregational Churches is Vindicated, both with respect to Subject and Mode. Rutland, Vt.: Printed by Stephen Hodgeman. For the Author. 8vo, pp. 76.

—*Report of* Committee on Pastoral Sustentation. To the General Convention of Congregational Churches and Ministers of Vermont. 8vo, pp. 8. n. d. n. p.
See Merrill, T. A., for History of General Convention of Vermont.

—*The Doings and Result* of an Ecclesiastical Council. of Enquiry, in relation to a Pamphlet published against the Baptist Church in Poultney by the Congregational Church in said town. Entitled Unscriptural Discipline Exposed and detected, in which the Baptist Church and Minister are implicated : Convened at the Baptist Meeting House in Poultney, November 26, 1806. Together with the address to the public by the Pastor of the Baptist Church, with the Statements, Defence, and a Supplement by said Church. Published by Request. Motto. Salem, N. Y.: Printed by Dodd and Rumsey. 1807. 8vo, pp. 84.

—*A Confession of Faith, and Covenant*, Recommended by the North Western Consociation, to the Churches Represented in this Body, to be used in the Admission of Members. Burlington, (Vt.) Printed by E. & T. Mills. 1818. 16mo, pp. 7.

—*The Constitution of Rutland Consociation:* Revised October, 1850. Windsor : Printed at the Chronicle Press. 1850. 12mo, pp. 16.

—*Systematic Beneficence*. An Essay read before the General Convention of Congregational Ministers and Churches of Vermont, at Bradford, June 20, 1877. Montpelier : J. & J. M. Poland, Steam Book and Job Printers. 1877. 8vo, pp. 16.

—*A Protest* addressed to the Congregational Churches and Ministers of Vermont. [Signed,] Geo. B. Safford, Lewis O. Brastow, J. E. Goodrich, Geo. E. Hall, S. P. Wilder, S. I. Briant, Chas. P. Watson, E. H. Higley, Chas. Van Norden, C. M. Winslow. [1879.] 8vo, pp. (12.)

—*The Bible and the Creeds*. An "Historical Consensus." [By J. E. Goodrich.] 8vo, pp. (4.)
Dated Burlington, Vt., July 15, 1879.
The two above titles relate to the action of the Congregational churches of Vermont, in relation to the "Creed," at the annual Convention in 1879.

—*A Review of the Protest* lately sent out by ten members of the General Convention of Congregational Ministers and Churches of Vermont. By Rev. Alfred Stevens, D. D., of Westminster West. Montpelier : Printed at the Vermont Chronicle Office. 1880. 8vo, pp. 11.

—*A Hundred Years of Congregationalism* in the Champlain Valley. Some Historical Facts presented in a Paper before the Congregational Club of Western Vermont at Middlebury Dec. 9, 1890, by Rev. A. W. Wild, and printed by the Club. Burlington: Free Press Association. 1891. 8vo, pp. 10.

—*An Historical Sketch of Home Missionary Work* in Vermont by the Congregational Churches. By Rev. C. S. Smith. Read at the Seventy-fifth Anniversary of the Vermont Domestic Missionary Society. Held at Montpelier, June 14, 1893. Montpelier: 1893. Watchman Publishing Co. 8vo, pp. 18.

—*Historical Discourse* at the One Hundredth Anniversary of the General Convention of Congregational Ministers and Churches of Vermont at Bennington, June 11, 1895, by Rev. A. W. Wild. Published by vote of the Convention. Burlington: Free Press Association, Printers and Binders. 1895. pp. 36.

See Vermont Missionary Society; Vermont Juvenile Missionary Society; Vermont Domestic Missionary Society Manuals and reports of Congregational Churches, and addresses on anniversary occasions in various towns.

Connecticut River. See Navigation of.

The Constitution *of the North-Western Branch* of the American Society for Educating Pious Youth for the Gospel Ministry: with instructions for Beneficiaries, Directions for Agents, and an Address to the Christian Publick. Middlebury: Printed by Copeland and Allen. 1820. 8vo, pp. 31.

—*Of the United States of America*, As agreed upon by their Delegates in the Convention, September 17th, 1787. Together with the Articles of Amendment, As adopted by the Congress of the said States, in the Year 1789. Windsor: Printed by Alden Spooner, 1790. 4to, pp. 28.

—*Of the State of New Hampshire*, and that of the United States; the Declaration of Independence, with President Washington's Farewell Address. Montpelier: Printed by Wright and Sibley, for Justin Hinds, Bookseller and Stationer, Hanover, N. H. 1811. 12mo, pp. 108.

—*Constitution and By-Laws* of the Vermont Veteran Association of Massachusetts. Adopted November 18, 1874. Fitchburg: 1874. 18mo, pp. 14.

—*Constitution and By-Laws* of the Vermont Numismatic Society. Adopted July 3d, 1877. Montpelier, Vt.: Argus and Patriot Job Printing House. 1877. 24mo, pp. 10, (1.)

Convention of Deaf Mutes. *Report of the Proceedings* of the Convention of Deaf Mutes, holden in Montpelier, Vt., February 18, 1852. To which is added an abstract of the Biography of Rev. Thomas H. Gallaudett, LL. D. Bradford, Vt.: Printed at the Family Gazette Office. 1852. 8vo, pp. 8.

Converse, James. *A Sermon*, delivered on the Day of General Election, at Montpelier, October 14, 1819, before the Honorable Legislature of Vermont. By James Converse, A. B. Pastor of the Congregational Church in Weathersfield. Published by Order of the Legislature.

Montpelier, Vt. Printed by E. P. Walton, October, 1819. 8vo, pp. 27.

Mr. Converse was graduated at Harvard College, 1799. He was pastor of the Congregational church in Weathersfield, Vt., 1802, until his death, January 7, 1839. Z. Thompson says, "He was eminently useful, and died universally loved and respected."

Converse, J. K. *The Relation* of Christianity, and of the several forms of Christianity, to the Republican Institutions of the United States: A Sermon preached before the Chittenden County Consociation, in Milton, June 24, 1833. By J. K. Converse, Pastor of the Calvinistic Cong. Church, Burlington, Vt. Burlington: Edward Smith. 1833. 8vo, pp. 32.

—*A Discourse* on the Moral, Legal, and Domestic Condition of our Colored Population, preached before the Vermont Colonization Society, at Montpelier, October 17, 1832. By J. K. Converse, Pastor of the First Congregational Church, Burlington, Vt. Burlington: Edward Smith. 1832. 8vo, pp. 32.

—*The Scripture* Doctrine of Atonement. A Sermon preached before the First Congregational Church and Society in Burlington, Vt., on Thanksgiving Day, Dec. 9, 1842. By J. K. Converse, Pastor. Published by Request. Burlington: Printed at the University Press, by S. Fletcher. 1843. 8vo, pp. 28.

—*The History of Slavery*, and the Means of elevating the African Race. A Discourse delivered before the Vermont Colonization Society, at Montpelier, Oct. 15, 1840. By J. K. Converse, Pastor of the First Congregational Church, Burlington, Vt. Burlington: Chauncey Goodrich. 1840. 8vo, pp. 24.

—*A Discourse:* "High Church Hostile to Republicanism." "Letters to Governor Paine on Capital Punishment."

—*In Memoriam* of the Rev. John Kendrick Converse, Former Pastor of the First Congregational Church, Principal of the Burlington Female Seminary, etc., etc. Extinctus Amabitur idem. Philadelphia, 1881. Printed by J. B. Lippincott & Co. large 12mo, pp. 99.

Prepared by his daughter, the late Miss Elizabeth S. Converse, with introduction by Rev. James Buckham.

Rev. Mr. Converse was born at Lyme, N. H., June 15, 1801; and was two years at Dartmouth College, 1823-4, but was graduated at Hampden-Sidney College, Virginia, in 1827; read theology at Princeton, N. J., and was pastor of the Calvinistic Congregational Church, Burlington, Vt., 1832-44; and was then Principal of the Burlington Seminary for young ladies, 1844-1870. For many years he was an active officer and worker in behalf of the objects of the Vermont Colonization Society. Mr. Converse died at Burlington, October 3, 1880.

Cook, Anson G. *The Furnace Man's Guide.* By Anson G. Cook. Revised and Enlarged, with a Cut of my New Cupola annexed, with Rules to Line and Operate it. Patented February 20, 1866. Burlington: Times Book and Job Office. 1866. 18mo, pp. 16, (2.)

Cook & Liscum. *Circular.* Cook & Liscum, Proprietors of Cook's Cupola. Patented February 20, 1866. All communications should be addressed to John Liscum, Burlington, Chittenden County, Vt. Burlington: R. S. Styles, Steam Book and Job Printer. 1871. 8vo, pp. 12.

Cook, Thomas. *Universal Letter Writer.* Montpelier. 1816. 12mo.

Cooke, Phinehas. *A Sermon* preached at Acworth, N. H., at the Dedication of the New Meeting-House in that Town, December 12, 1821: By Phinehas Cooke, Pastor of the Congregational Church in Acworth. Bellows Falls : Printed by Blake, Cutler & Co. 1822. 8vo, pp. 24.

—*A Discourse* Delivered at Acworth, before the Congregational Church in said Town, on Lord's Day, March 8, 1829. By Phinehas Cooke, Late Pastor of said Church. Published by request. Windsor: Printed at the Chronicle Press, by John C. Allen. 1858. 8vo, pp. 18.

—*Mis-application* and waste of Moral Power. A Sermon delivered at the Installation of Rev. Stephen Morse, over the Congregational Church in Sharon, Vt., March 9, 1836. By Phinehas Cooke, Pastor of the Church in Lebanon, N. H. Windsor: Printed at the Chronicle Press. 1836. 8vo, pp. 18.

Cooley, T. M. *Sketches* of the Life and Character of the Rev. Lemuel Haynes, A. M., For many years Pastor of a Church in Rutland, Vt., and late in Granville, N. Y. By Timothy Mather Cooley, D. D., Pastor of the First Church in Granville, Mass. With some introductory Remarks by William B. Sprague, D. D., of Albany, N. Y. New York: Harper & Brothers. 1837. 12mo, pp. 345.

Coolidge, A. J. and Mansfield, J. B. *A History and Description* of New England, General and Local. By A. J. Coolidge and J. B. Mansfield. Illustrated with numerous Engravings. In two Volumes. Vol. 1. Maine, New Hampshire, and Vermont. Boston : Austin J. Coolidge. 1859. Rl. 8vo, pp. xxv. 1023. Vol. 1 all issued.
Vermont occupies pp. 705 to 961.

—*History and Description* of New England. General and Local. By A. J. Coolidge and J. B. Mansfield. In Two volumes. Vol. 1, Maine, New Hampshire, and Vermont. Boston: Austin J. Coolidge, 1859. 8vo, pp. xxvii, 1023. 3 maps and 81 woodcuts. Second Edition. Boston. 1864.

Cooper, Jane. *Letters written* by Jane Cooper: To which is prefixed some Account of her Life and Death. Barnard : (Vt.) Published by Joseph Dix. I. H. Carpenter, Printer. 1812. 16mo, pp. 44.

Cornwall. *History of.*
See Matthews, L.

—*Constitution* of the Young Gentlemen's Society in Cornwall, with a Catalogue of their Library October 1829. Middlebury : Press of the American, 1830. 16mo, pp. 16.

—*Constitution and By-Laws* of the Lane Library Association, with a Catalogue of its Library. Middlebury : Printed at the Register Book and Job Office. 1860. 12mo, pp. 29.
This library was established by a legacy left by the late Gilbert C. Lane.

A Correspondence, *by Letters*, between Samuel C. Loveland, Preacher of the Doctrine of Universal Salvation, and Rev. Joseph Laberee, Pastor of the Congregational Church and Society in Jericho, Vt. Motto. Windsor, Vt. Printed for the Publisher. A. & W. Spooner, Printers. 1813. 12mo, pp. 67. (1.)

[Corry, John.] *Biographical Memoirs* of the Illustrious General George Washington, Late President of the United States of America, and Commander in Chief of their Armies, during the Revolutionary War. Dedicated to the Youth of America. Barnard, Vt.: Published by Joseph Dix. 1813. 24mo, pp. 160.
The first edition was printed in London, 1800.

Coulman, James. *The Sabbath Question* by a Searcher of the Scriptures. James Coulman. Rutland : Tuttle & Co. 1887. 32 pp, 8vo.

Coventry. *Manual of the Congregational Church*, in Coventry, Vt. Prepared by Pliny H. White, Acting Pastor. Montpelier : Freeman Steam Printing Establishment. 1868. 8vo, pp. 19.

—*History of.*
See White, P. H.

Covill, Rev. Samuel. *Memoirs* of Rev. Samuel Covill, including a History of the Origin and progress of Missionary Operations. To which is added a memoir of Alanson L. Covill. 2 vols. in one. Brandon : 1889. 12mo, pp. 174, 226.
Written by Mrs. D. C. Brown, a sister of Rev. Alanson L. Covill. Their father, Rev. Samuel Covill was a Missionary to the Tuscarora Indians; also to the Province of Upper Canada.

Coxe, A. Cleveland. *Practical Wisdom in the Planting of a Church.* A Sermon Preached at the Consecration of the Second Bishop of Vermont, Whitsun-Week, June 3, 1868, In Christ Church, Montpelier. By A. Cleveland Coxe, Bishop of Western New York. Published by request of the Diocesan Convention of Vermont. 1868. [n. p.] 8vo, pp. 34.

Crabb, George. *A History of English Law;* or an attempt to trace the Rise, Progress, and successive changes of the Common Law ; from the Earliest period to the present time. By George Crabb, Esq. (Of the Inner Temple,) Barrister at Law ; Author of English Synonymes Explained, Technological and Historical Dictionaries, &c., &c. First American Edition ; with definitions and translations of Law Terms and phrases, additional references, dates of successive Changes, explanation of abbreviations, &c. Burlington : Chauncey Goodrich. 1831. 8vo, pp. vii. 595.

Crafts, Samuel C. *Memorial of Samuel C. Crafts and Others*, Citizens of Vermont, praying for Further Protection to Domestic Industry, January 2, 1828. Washington : Printed by Gales & Seaton. 1828. 8vo, pp. 6. (20th Congress, 1st Sess., House Doc. 31.)

Cragin, A. H. *Loyal Supremacy.* All Rights to All Men ! Equality of White Men ! Speech of Hon. Aaron H. Cragin, of New Hampshire, in the Senate of the United States, January 30, 1868, on the Acts of Reconstruction. 8vo, pp. 12.

—*Execution of Laws in Utah.* Speech of Hon. A. H. Cragin, in the Senate, May 18, 1870. Washington. 1870. 8vo, pp. 23.
Mr. Cragin was born in Weston, Vt., February 3, 1821 ; he read law, and in 1847 moved to Lebanon, N. H., and practised his profession. He was a member of the New Hampshire Legislature, 1852-55; and a member of the

35th and 36th Congresses, and a Senator in Congress from New Hampshire, 1865 to 1877.

Crane, D. M. *The Good Man.* A Memorial Sermon of Rev. N. Cudworth. Delivered in the Baptist Church, North Springfield, Nov. 12, and repeated in the Baptist Church, Perkinsville, November 19, 1871. By Rev. D. M. Crane, A. M. Published by request. Rutland : Tuttle & Co., Printers. 1872. 8vo, pp. 22.

—*The Conscious State of the Dead.* A Lecture, Delivered in the Congregational Church, Springfield, Vt., January 22. 1871. By D. M. Crane, A. M. Published by Request. Rutland : Tuttle & Co., Printers. 1875. 8vo, pp. 26.

Mr. Crane was born in Brookline, Vt., February 29, 1812; he became a Baptist preacher and was pastor successively at Brookline, Grafton and North Springfield, Vt., Northampton, Boston and Dorchester, Mass.; Woonsocket, R. I.; Greenfield, Mass.; again at North Springfield; and Winthrop and again at Northampton, Mass. He died at West Acton, Mass., September 4, 1879.

Crevecoeur, Hector St. John. *Letters from an American Farmer :* Describing certain Provincial Situations, Manners, and Customs, not generally known ; and conveying some idea of the late and present Interior Circumstances of the British Colonies in North America. Written for the information of a Friend in England. By J. Hector St. John, a Farmer in Pennsylvania. A New Edition, with an accurate Index. London : Printed for Thomas Davies in Russell-Street, Convent Garden ; and Lockyer Davis, in Holburn. M.DCC.LXXXIII. 8vo, pp. (16), 326. First Edition: London, 1782.

An Edition Phila, 1794; and Paris, 1784, 1787.

He also published another work relating to the United States, in 3 volumes, Paris, 1801. Mr. St. John, as we call him, was born in Caen, France, in 1731; and died at Sarcelles, in November, 1813. He was sent to England to be educated, at the age of 16, and came to America in 1754, and settled on a farm near New York, and soon after married an American wife. He became acquainted with Ethan Allen, and expressed much interest in Vermont affairs, and applied to the Legislature through Col. Allen, that himself and his three sons might be made citizens of the State, which was done by Act of the Legislature in 1787; and the town of St. Johnsbury was named for him, and the towns of Danville and Vergennes were so named at his suggestion. Consult Vermont, Governor and Council, Vol. 3; Drake's Dictionary; Allibone; Duyckinck; Letters of St. John and Ethan Allen, in Vermont Historical Gazetteer, Vol. 1, pp. 388-9.

Crisis, The. *On the origin* and consequences of our political Dissentions. To which is annexed, the late Treaty between the United States and Great Britain. By A Citizen of Vermont. Albany : Printed by E. & E. Hosford. 1815. 8vo, pp. 96.

Crosby, A. B. *Memorial Address.* Prof. David S. Conant, M. D. Delivered to the Graduating Class, In the Medical Department of the University of Vermont, by A. B. Crosby, A. M., M. D., Professor of Surgery, with Remarks and Resolutions from other sources. Burlington : Times Book and Job Office. 1866. 8vo, pp. 30.

Crosman, Aaron. *A Funeral Sermon,* on the Death of the Hon. Joshua Stanton, Esq. late of Colchester, Vt., who died at Salisbury, Connecticut, on the twenty-eighth of October, 1806, Aged 38 years, While returning from a journey for the benefit of his health. By Aaron Crosman, A. M., Pastor of a Church in Salisbury. Burlington, Vt. Printed by Samuel Mills, Sept. 1807. 8vo, pp. 16.

Culver, J. W. *Loyal Mountaineers :* or the Guerilla's Doom. A War Drama, (In Three Acts) by J. W. Culver, Respectfully dedicated to the Grand Army of the Republic. Revised Edition. St. Albans, Vt.: E. A. Morton, Printer. 18mo, pp. 41. 1873.

Cumberland, R. *The Inquisition,* or Adventures of Nicolas Pedrosa ; By R. Cumberland. Windsor, Vt. Published by Pomroy & Hedge. 1816. 24mo, pp. 120.

Currier, John M. *Song of Hubbardton Raid,* delivered on The 50 (—I) the Anniversary of the Raid of the Citizens of Hubbardton, Vt., on Castleton Medical College, held at the residence of J. Sanford, M. D., Castleton, Vt., November 29, 1879. By John M. Currier, M. D. Three hundred copies printed for the members of the Castleton Medical and Surgical Clinic, for private distribution. Castleton, Vt. January, 1880. 12mo, pp. 36.

Dr. Currier is a native of Bath, N. H., where he was born August 4, 1832; he was graduated at Dartmouth Medical College, 1858, and settled at Newport, Vt., the same year, where he now resides. In addition to his profession, Dr. Currier gives much attention to archæological, scientific and historical matters, and has written much upon these subjects.

See Vermont Medical Journal; Archives of Science.

Curtis, Abel. *A Compend of English Grammar:* being an attempt to point out the Fundamental Principles of the English Language in a concise and intelligible manner, and to assist in writing and speaking the same, with accuracy and correctness. Written by Abel Curtis, A. B. Motto. Dresden (Dartmouth College.) Printed by J. P. & A. Spooner. 1779. 16mo, pp. 48.

The "finis," of probably one page, is missing.

Mr. Curtis was born at Lebanon, Conn., June 13, 1755, and died at Norwich, Vt., October 1, 1783. His father, Simeon, married Sarah Hutchinson, and the family was among the early settlers of Norwich, Vt. Abel was graduated at Dartmouth College in 1776; he married Miss Keziah Brown, of Norwich, May 12, 1779; she was born in Preston, Conn., April 4, 1764, and was therefore a little over fifteen at her marriage. They settled upon a farm at Norwich, and commenced housekeeping, as he says in his journal, November 22, 1779, and had two daughters, "Lucy, born February, 17th day of the moon, 1780; Salley, born December 6, 1782, about 6 o'clock p. m., and second day of the moon." The former married Thomas Emerson, (post), of Windsor, a merchant and banker widely known in his day. Mr. Curtis was a young man of brilliant promise, and although cut off at the early age of 28, he held many positions of trust and honor in the State. He was a member of the General Assembly, 1778, '81 and '82; with Elisha Payne, of Lebanon, N. H., (then considered a part of Vermont), Jonas Fay and Ira Allen, he was appointed January 10, 1782, an agent and delegate to Congress, it then being the expectation that Vermont would be immediately admitted into the Union; in March following he was appointed a member of the Board of War, and was also appointed by several towns on the Connecticut River, Commissioner to the Governor of New Hampshire, in relation to the union of certain New Hampshire towns with Vermont; in addition he was Town Clerk, Justice of the Peace and Judge of Windsor County Court at the time of his death. It is supposed that he wrote the first purely English grammar written and published in America. The private manuscript journal of Mr. Curtis has recently come into the possession of the Vermont Historical Society, through his grandson, Curtis Emerson, Esq., only surviving member of the family of Thomas Emerson. We are indebted to Rev. H. A. Hazen, of Billerica, Mass., for the title of Mr. Curtis' grammar, he possessing the only copy yet discovered.

Curtis, Rev. Harvey, D. D. *Address* before the Philadelphian Society of Middlebury College, at its Annual Meeting, Monday Evening, Aug. 13, 1838. By Rev. Harvey

Curtis. Middlebury: Office of the People's Press. 1838. 12mo, pp. 16.

Rev. Dr. Curtis was born in Adams, Jefferson County, N. Y., May 30, 1806; graduated at Middlebury College, 1831; studied theology nearly two years at Princeton Seminary; was pastor of the Congregational Church, Brandon, Vt., 1836-40; agent of A. B. C. F. M., 1840-43, residing at Cincinnati, O.; pastor of the First Presbyterian Church, Chicago, Ill., 1850-58; was President of Knox College, Galesburg, Ill., from 1858 until his death, which took place September 19, 1862. He published in addition:

A Sermon, "The Minister's Great Duty," Madison, Ind., 1843.

An address, before the United Literary Societies of South Hanover College, Ind., September 24, 1844, (published by the Societies.)

A sermon, before the Synod of Indiana, at Crawfordsville, on the subject of "African Slavery," October 14, 1848. Published by the Synod.

A sermon, preached in the First Presbyterian Church, Chicago, July 13, 1851, on "Secession considered as a means of purifying the Christian Church." Published by the church.

Inaugural Address at Galesburg, Ill., June 24, 1858, on assuming the Presidency of Knox College. Published by the Board of Trustees.

Cushing, Jacob. *A Sermon* at the Ordination of the Reverend Mr. Samuel Williams to the pastoral care of the First Church in Bradford, Preach'd November 20, 1765. By Jacob Cushing, A. M. Pastor of the Church in Waltham. Boston, New England: Printed by Richard and Samuel Draper, 1766. 8vo, pp. 39.

Samuel Williams was the Historian of Vermont, and was ordained at Bradford, Mass.

Cushing, Nathan. *Remarks* at the Funeral Services of Nathan Cushing, with Biographical Sketch. Woodstock, Vt.: Printed by Henry H. Woodbury. 1873. sm.4to, pp. (16).

Remarks by Hon. Frederick Billings, and Biographical Sketch by Henry Swan Dana, Esq. See Dana, H. S.

Cushman, Rufus Spalding. *An Historical* Enquiry into the Relations of the Federal Constitutions to African Slavery. By Rev. R. S. Cushman. Middlebury: 1860. 8vo, pp. 26.

—*Resolutions* and Discourse occasioned by the Death of Abraham Lincoln, at Manchester, Vermont, April 19, 1865. Middlebury: For the Committee. 1865. 8vo, pp. 20.

—*A Memorial* of Rufus Spalding Cushman, D. D., Late Pastor of the Congregational Church in Manchester, Vermont. Andover: 1877. 8vo, pp. 66.

Contains a Memoir and Sermon by Rev. C. B. Hulburt, President of Middlebury College, and the last sermon preached at Manchester, by Dr. Cushman, March 11, 1877.

Dr. Cushman was born at Fairhaven, Vt., August 30, 1815; and died at Manchester, Vt., May 15, 1877. He was descended from the Rev. Robert Cushman of Mayflower fame, and was graduated at Middlebury College, 1837; was a teacher in Alabama and Mississippi, 1838-40; read Theology at Lane, and Auburn Seminaries, 1840-43; was pastor of the Congregational church at Orwell, Vt., December, 1843 to 1862, and at Manchester, May, 1862, until his death.

Cutler, Calvin. *Doctrines the Means of Salvation.* A Sermon, preached at the Ordination of Rev. Milton Ward, to the Pastoral Care of the Church and Society in Hillsborough, N. H., July 23d, 1834. By Calvin Cutler, Pastor of the Presbyterian Church in Windham, N. H. R. Boylston, Printer, Amherst, N. H. 1835. 8vo, pp. 24.

—*Our Liberties in Danger.* A Sermon preached in Windham, New Hampshire, on the day of the Annual Thanksgiving, November 26, 1835. By Calvin Cutler, Pastor of the Presbyterian Church in Windham. Concord: Printed by Asa M'Farland, Opposite the Capitol. 1835. 8vo, pp. 19.

Mr. Cutler was born at Guildhall, Vt., October 10, 1791; was graduated at Dartmouth College in 1819, and at Andover in 1822; was pastor of the Congregational Church at Lebanon, N. H., 1823-27, and of the Presbyterian Church at Windham, N. H., 1828 until he died, February 17, 1844.

Cutting, H. A. *Report of the Geologist and Curator State Cabinet* for 1874 and 1875, with directions for Collecting Specimens and an Address on Parasitic Insects of Domestic Animals, given before a meeting of the State Board of Agriculture, Manufactures and Mining, at Westminster. By Hiram A. Cutting, A. M., M. D., State Geologist and Curator. Montpelier: Freeman Steam Printing House and Bindery. 1876. 8vo, pp. 24, 15.

—*The Same*, 1875-6. Rutland: Tuttle & Company, Book Printers. 1876. 8vo, pp. 26.

—*Meteorological Tables and Climatology of Vermont*, with map showing the Rainfall; also Suggestions and Directions about Foretelling Storms. By Hiram A. Cutting, A. M., M. D., State Geologist and Curator. Montpelier: J. & J. M. Poland, Official State Printers. 1877. 8vo, pp. 24.

—*Microscopic Revelations: Fungi*—Rust, Smut, Mildew and Mould. Animalcules—Water Mites, Sugar Mites, and Trichina Spiralis. An Address delivered at Albany, Vt., at a meeting of the Vermont Board of Agriculture. Also Report of condition of State Cabinet of Natural History for 1877 and 1878. By Hiram A. Cutting, A. M., M. D., State Geologist and Curator. Montpelier: J. & J. M. Poland, Steam Book and Job Printers. 1878. 8vo, pp. 32.

—*An Address upon Farm Pests*, including Insects, Fungi, and Animalcules, delivered at a meeting of the New Hampshire Board of Agriculture, by Hiram A. Cutting, A. M., M. D., State Geologist of Vermont. Manchester, N. H.: Printed by John B. Clarke. 1879. 8vo, pp. 75.

Mr. Cutting was a son of Stephen C. Cutting, of Concord, in which town he was born December 23, 1832. He was educated for a physician, receiving the degree of M. D. from Dartmouth College, N. H.; also the degree of A. M. from Norwich University. On account of ill health he did not enter a profession, but located at Lunenburg as a merchant in 1854, under the firm of J. G. Darling & Co. While he was successful as a merchant, he largely devoted his time to study; especially to the study of microscopic anatomy, geology and atmospheric phenomena. He is a member, either active or honorary, of some twenty scientific, historical and medical societies, among which are the "Vermont Medical Society," "Vermont Historical Society," "White Mountains Medical Society;" Fellow of the "American Association for Advancement of Science" and "Naturalist's Society of Rome", Italy, and member of the "Dartmouth Microscopical Club," "Boston Historical Society," "Geographical Society of Wisconsin," etc. In addition to the above list, he has published several pamphlets, and papers upon "Insects," "Ozone," "Geology," "Microscopy," "Revelations of the Microscope," and Natural History in general, also upon the "Atmosphere," and a work upon the "Climatology of Vermont." During the civil war he acted as a recruiting officer, enlisting about one hundred men. He has been postmaster at Lunenburg, examining Surgeon of the United States Pension Office, State Geologist and Curator, and Manager of the Vermont State Cabinet of Natural History. Was married in 1855 to M. E. Haskell, of Lennoxville, C. E., is a member of the Methodist church, and has been Superintendent of the Sunday school in Lunenburg for several years. He has a large library, and an extensive cabinet of minerals.

Cutting, H. P. *The Crisis. Slavery or Freedom. A Discourse.* Burlington. 1854. 8vo.

Cutting, Sewall S. *Influence of Christianity on Government and Slavery :* a Discourse, delivered in the Baptist Church in West Boylston, Mass., January 15, 1837. By Sewall S. Cutting, Pastor. Worcester : Printed by Henry J. Howland. 1837. 8vo, pp. 14.

—*Historical Vindications :* a Discourse on the Province and Uses of Baptist History ; delivered before the Backus Historical Society, at Newton, Massachusetts, June 23, 1857. By Sewall S. Cutting, Professor of Rhetoric and History in the University of Rochester. Boston : Gould & Lincoln. 1859.

—*Baptists and Religious Liberty.* Relations of Baptists to the Enunciation and Establishment of Religious Liberty. A Discourse delivered in the Warburton Avenue Baptist Church, Yonkers, N. Y., December 5, 1875, by Sewall S. Cutting, D. D. New York. A. D. F. Randolph & Co. 1876. 8vo, pp. 16.

—*Lake Champlain :* A Poem. Burlington, Vt. 1877. Small 4to, pp. 24.

Read before the Alumni of the University of Vermont, at Burlington, June 26, 1877.

Dr. Cutting was born at Windsor, Vt., Jan. 19, 1813; graduated at the University of Vermont, 1835; pastor of a Baptist Church in West Boylston, Ms., 1836-37, and at Southbridge, Ms., 1837-45: editor of the New York Recorder, 1845-'50, and '53-'55, and of the Christian Review, '50-'53; professor in the University of Rochester, 1855-68; secretary of the American Baptist Educational Commission, 1868; died at Brooklyn, N. Y., Feb. 7, 1882.

Cutts, Hampden. *Address* delivered before the Windsor County Agricultural Society, at their Annual Fair, held at Windsor, Vt., October 4th, 1849, By Hon. Hampden Cutts. Published by request. Woodstock : Printed at the Mercury Office. 1850. 8vo, pp. 16.

—*Readings of Shakspeare.* The undersigned is ready to make engagements for Shakspearean Readings with Lyceums and other Literary Associations. Address Hampden Cutts, North Hartland, Vt. Opinions of the Press. 4to, pp. 4. [1859]. No imprint.

—*Life and Public Services* of the Hon. William Jarvis. Published in the N. E. Hist. Gen. Register for July, 1866. 8vo, pp. 11.

Mr. Cutts has written a History of Hartland for the Vermont Historical Magazine, and a Sketch of the Gov. Spooner Family for the same; A Sketch of the Life of Major Charles Jarvis, being an Address before the Vermont Historical Society, Mr. Jarvis was a son of the Hon. William Jarvis, and fell in the civil war. Mr. Cutts was born in Portsmouth, N. H., August 3, 1802; and died in Brattleboro, Vt., April 28th, 1875. He was graduated at Harvard College, 1823; and read law with the distinguished Jeremiah Mason, of Portsmouth. In 1829 he married Mary Pepperrell Sparhawk, eldest daughter of Hon. William Jarvis, of Weathersfield, Vt., and in 1833 they removed to North Hartland, Vt., and in 1861, to Brattleboro.

Mr. Cutts represented Hartland in the Vermont Legislature in 1840-41-47, and 1858; and Windsor County in the State Senate, 1842-3; he was a Judge of the Windsor County Court, prominent in promoting the Agricultural interests of the State, and was an active member of the Vermont Historical Society; and at the time of his death, and for many years previously, he was the Vice-President for Vermont, of the "New England Historical and Genealogical Society."

Cutts, Mary. *The Autobiography of a Clock,* and other Poems. By Mary Cutts. Motto. Boston : Wm. Crosby and H. P. Nichols. New York : C. S. Francis & Co. 1852. 16mo, pp. 247.

—*Grondalla,* A Romance in Verse, by Idamore, Second edition. New York : Boston : Claremont. 1866. 12mo, pp. 310.

Miss Cutts is a sister of the late Hon. Hampden Cutts, of Hartland, Vt.

Cutts, Mary Pepperrell Sparhawk. *The Life and Times* of Hon. William Jarvis, of Weathersfield, Vt. By his Daughter, Mary Pepperrell Sparhawk Cutts. New York : Published by Hurd and Houghton. Cambridge : Riverside Press. 1869. 12mo, pp. xii, 451. Portrait.

Mrs. Cutts was the wife of Hon. Hampden Cutts. She dropped dead of heart disease as she stepped off the Ulster County express train at the Erie depot, Jersey City, on the morning of April 12, 1879. She was 68 years old, and had been on a visit to her daughter at Paterson, N. J. Mrs. Cutts was descended from the Pepperrell and Sparhawk families, distinguished in the early history of New England.

Daily Legislative Prayer Meeting *Session of 1870.* Montpelier : J. & J. M. Poland, Printers. 1870. 8vo, pp. 8.

Gives an account of the meetings during the Session.

Dallas, A. J. *An Exposition* of the Causes of the late War between the United States and Great Britain. Middlebury, (Vt.) Printed by William Slade, Jun. July 4, 1815. 8vo, pp. 59.

Damon, Sophia M. *Old New England Days.* A Story of True Life, By Sophie M. Damon. Boston. Cupples and Hurd, 94 Boylston St. 12mo, pp. vi, 434.

Mrs. Damon was born at Woodstock, Vt., July 13, 1836; she was a daughter of Doct. Isaiah Buckman, and Ruth Howe Davis, who was a daughter of Gen. Parley Davis, one of the first settlers of Montpelier. Mrs. Damon married W. L. Damon of Woodstock, March 16, 1851 : died at Woodstock, March 6, 1888. See Davis Genealogy.

Dana, A. G. *In Memoriam.* Cambridge : Printed for private distribution. 1863. 12mo, pp. 64.

Dana, Mrs. Eliza A. *Gathered Leaves.* (Poems). Cambridge : Private edition. 1864. 12mo, pp. 160.

Mrs. Dana, widow of the late Hon. A. G. Dana, M. D., LL. D., of Brandon, Vt., was a daughter of Roger Fuller, Esq., of Brandon. *See* Miss Hemenway's Vt. Hist. Gaz. vol. III, pp. 460-3.

Dana, H. S. *Biographical Sketch* of Nathan Cushing, Esq. Sm. 4to, pp. 7.

See Cushing, Nathan.

Henry Swan Dana, Esq., son of Charles and Mary (Gay) Dana, was born in Woodstock, Vt., October 17, 1823; fitted for college at Kimball Union Academy, and was graduated at Dartmouth, 1849; after graduating he went to Charleston, S. C., and was a teacher in the family of Dr. King until May, 1857, when he returned to Woodstock, where he has since resided. While in Charleston he read law with Hon. James L. Pettigru, but has never been admitted to the bar. At Woodstock he has been engaged in mercantile business, and largely in literary pursuits; since 1873 he has been Register of Probate for the District of Hartford.

Mr. Dana prepared the compendious history of the town of Woodstock, published in 1889; he has published many biographical and historical articles in the Woodstock newspapers, notably in the "Standard," in which he published in 1871 a five or six column original biographical sketch of the Rev. Aaron Hutchinson.

In 1860 he was employed by the Messrs. Merriam, of Springfield, Mass., in the preparation of a new edition of Webster's Dictionary. He was a member of the School Committee 1863-6, and was Superintendent of Schools in Woodstock about the same length of time.

Dana, Joshua M. *Incidents in the History of Vermont,* As sung by J. M. Dana before the Freemen of Calais, Vt., Sept. 1, 1840. Broadsheet.

Mr. Dana has written prose and poetry to some extent for newspapers, and was a frequent contributor to the columns of the Argus and Patriot. He was a native of

Calais, resided in Woodbury, Vt., many years, dying there in July, 1878.

Danby. *History of.*
See Williams, J. C.

Danville. *Caledonia County Teachers' Institute,* Danville, Vt., 1851. Catalogue. Danville. 1851.

—*Danville* in the late war.
See Brainerd, C. D.
A series of historical articles relating to Danville, by Henry Little, was printed in the North Star in 1876.

Dartmouth College. *Observations on Facts,* vindicating the Rights of Dartmouth College and Moors' Charity School to the Grant made by the Legislature of Vermont in June, 1785. Windsor : Vt. 1807. 8vo.
The Grant was the township of Wheelock.

—*Exercises of Class Day at Dartmouth College,* July 21, 1868. Claremont, N. H. 1868. 8vo, pp. 40.
Contains, "Poem" by Henry C. Bliss, of Hartford, Vt.; "Chronicles," by F. C. Hathaway, Hardwick, Vt.; "Address to the President," by John Ward Page, Montpelier, Vt.

Dascomb, A. B. *Memorial Record of Waitsfield, Vt.* Prepared by Rev. A. B. Dascomb. Published by vote of the Town. Montpelier : Printed at the Freeman Steam Printing Establishment. 1867. 12mo, pp. 30.

—*A Discourse* preached by Rev. A. B. Dascomb, to his people at Waitsfield, Vt., in Honor of our Late Chief Magistrate, on Sunday, April 23, 1865. Published by request. Montpelier : Walton's Steam Printing Establishment. 1865. 8vo, pp. 23.

Davenport, Charles N. *The Vermont Central Ring.* How the Road was plundered by its Managers. Bribery and Corruption. Argument of Charles N. Davenport, of Brattleboro. Delivered at St. Albans, Oct. 27-28, 1875, in the R R. Accounting, before Hons. Paul Dillingham, John L. Edwards and Dudley C. Denison, Special Masters in Chancery. St. Albans : Messenger Printing Establishment. 1875. 8vo, pp. 15.
Mr. Davenport, a distinguished lawyer of Vermont, died at his home in Brattleboro, April 12, 1882, at the age of 51.

Davis, D. D. *The Medical Expositor ;* or, A Critical Essay on the Alopathic, Homeopathic & Eclectic Theories and Practice of Medicine ; designed expressly for the Dissemination of a Thorough Knowledge of these Theories among the People. By Dr. D. D. Davis. West Randolph : Perkins & Cobb, Farmer Office, Printers. 1856. 12mo, pp. 80.

Davis, Gilbert A. *Centennial Celebration,* Together with an Historical Sketch of Reading, Windsor county, Vermont, and its inhabitants from the first settlement of the town to 1874. By Gilbert A. Davis. Bellows Falls : Steam Press of A. N. Swain. 1874. 8vo, pp. 160.

—*Historical Address* delivered at Windsor, Vt., July 9, 1877, at the Celebration of the One Hundredth Anniversary of the adoption of the Constitution of the State of Vermont. By Gilbert A. Davis of Reading. Rutland : Tuttle & Co., Book and Job Printers, 1879. 8vo, pp. 23.

—*Compilation* of School Laws.
See Vermont, Educational.
Mr. Davis is a native of Chester, Vt., where he was born December 18, 1835. He is a lawyer, and located in Reading in 1860; was a member of the Legislature, 1872-74, and of the State Senate, 1876-7; and Clerk of the House of Representatives, 1858, and again in 1861; was Register of the Probate Court, 1862-67.

Davis, Harriet M. *In memory of Mrs. Harriet M. Davis.* Born January 14, 1829. Died October 14, 1873. Cambridge : Printed at the Riverside Press. 1874. sm. 4to, pp. 47.
Mrs. Davis was from Burlington, Vt.

Davis, Henry. *An Inaugural Oration* delivered Feb. 21, 1810, by Henry Davis, A. M. President of Middlebury College. Published by request of the Corporation. Farrand Mallary & Co., Boston. Lyman Mallary & Co., Portland. 1810. 8vo, pp. 36.

—*A Sermon,* Delivered to the Candidates for the Baccalaureate in Middlebury College, August 12, 1810. By Henry Davis, D. D., President. Published by request. Middlebury, Vt. Published by Swift and Chipman. J. D. Huntington, Printer. 1810. 8vo, pp. 32.

—*A Sermon,* delivered on the Day of General Election, at Montpelier, October 12, 1815, before the Honorable Legislature of Vermont. By Henry Davis, D. D. President of Middlebury College. Montpelier, Vt.: Printed by Walton & Goss. 1815. 8vo, pp. 40.

—*A Sermon,* delivered before the American Board of Commissioners for Foreign Missions ; at their Seventh Annual Meeting, which was held at Hartford, (Con.) Sept. 18, 19, and 20, 1816. By Henry Davis, D. D., President of Middlebury College. Boston : printed by Samuel T. Armstrong, No. 50, Cornhill. 1816. 8vo, pp. 36.

—*A Narrative* of the embarrassments and decline of Hamilton College. By Henry Davis, D. D., President. (1833.) 8vo, pp. IX. 151. No imprint.
Relates somewhat to the affairs of Middlebury College, and other Vermont matters.
Rev. Henry Davis, D. D., was President of Middlebury College, 1810-1817; which covers the period of his residence in Vermont. He was a Professor in Yale and Union colleges, before coming to Vermont, and upon leaving the State he was chosen President of Hamilton College, Clinton, N. Y., and died there in 1852. He was graduated at Yale, 1796.

Davis, Miss Mary E. *Glenorie, and other Poems.* By Mary E. Davis. Montpelier, Vt.; Argus and Patriot Steam Book and Job Printing Works. 1877. 12mo, pp. 349.
Miss Davis is a native of East Montpelier, Vt.; being a daughter of Junius B. Davis, who was a son of Hezekiah Davis, Esq., one of the first settlers of the town. General Parley and Major Nathaniel Davis were brothers of Hezekiah, and the three were nephews of Col. Jacob Davis, the first settler in Montpelier. Miss Davis has published many poems in periodicals and newspapers, not included in the present volume.

Davis, Miss Minnie S. *The Harvest of Love.* A Story, for the Home Circle, By Minnie S. Davis, Author of Marion Lester. Boston : Published by A. Tompkins, 38 & 40 Cornhill. 1859. 12mo, pp. 256.
In addition, Miss Davis has published, "Clinton Forest," "Rosalie and Her two Homes," both stories for youth. She writes : "I have not the honor of being a native of Vermont, though my parents both were born in that State. While engaged in literary work I was residing in Bethel, Vt. My books can be obtained at the Universalist Publishing House, No. 37 Cornhill, Boston."

Davis, Phebe B. *Two Years and Three Months* in the New York Lunatic Asylum at Utica: Together with the Outlines of Twenty years' peregrinations in Syracuse. By Phebe B. Davis, formerly of Barnard, Vt. Syracuse: 1855. 12mo. pp. 87.

—*Reports on the Laws of New England*, by Mrs. Davis, Mrs. Dall, and others. Boston: 1855. 8vo.

Dawson, Henry B. *Ticonderoga and Hubbardton*, including references to authorities and, in full, the American and British official dispatches, in his Battles of the United States, by Sea and Land, I., 224-236.

—*Battle of Bennington*, also including references to authorities and, in full, the official despatches of both commanders, in his Battles of the United States, by Sea and Land, i., 255 —266.

—*The Battle of Bennington.* Written on the invitation of the Vermont Historical Society, and read before that body, at Burlington, January 23, 1861, and subsequently before the N. E. Historic, Genealogical Society, and the N. Y. Historical Society, in The Hist. Mag. of May, 1870, and The Argus and Patriot, of June 27, July 4, and 11, 1877.

—*Review of Vol. 1*, Vt. Hist. Soc. Coll., in The Hist. Mag., Jan'y, 1871.
See Hall, Hiland, Vindication, in reply to Mr. Dawson, also printed in Vol. ii, Coll. Vermont Historical Society.

—*Notes on Gov. Hall's Vindication*, with a Letter to that gentleman, in the Hist. Mag. for July, 1871.
Mr. Dawson has manifested a commendable interest in the marvelous and romantic history of Vermont during her early single handed struggle for thirty years before she was admitted into the Union. A friend at our elbow suggests the query whether Vermont would not have been better off not to have come into the Union at all. Mr. Dawson has published numerous articles relating to Vermont, which are scattered through the pages of *The Historical Magazine* for the past fifteen years or more, to many of which we refer in connection with the subjects treated. Mr. Dawson has a very large collection of valuable material relating to Vermont.
For biographical sketch, see *Drake's Biographical Dictionary; Duyckinck's Cyclopedia of American Literature;* and John Ward Dean, in *Historical Magazine* for December, 1878.

Day, Norris. *A Lecture* upon Bible Politics, by Rev. Norris Day. Montpelier: 1846.

Dean, Amos. *Lectures on Phrenology;* Delivered before the Young Men's Association for mutual improvement, of the city of Albany. by Amos Dean. Albany: Published by Oliver Steele, and Hoffman & White. 1834. Printed by Hoffman & White. 12mo, pp. 252.

—*Introductory Lecture* before the Franklin Library Association of the City of Hudson, Delivered January 7, 1840. By Amos Dean. Published by request of the Association. Hudson: Printed by P. Dean Carrique. 1840. 8vo, pp. 23.

—*Eulogy* on the Life and Character of the late Judge Jesse Buel, pronounced before the New York State Agricultural Society, at their Annual meeting, on the 5th February, 1840. By Amos Dean, Esq., of Albany. Albany: Printed by Charles Van Benthuysen. 18mo, pp. 29.

—*Address* delivered before the Young Men's State Association of the State of New York, at their First Annual meeting, at Geneva, Sept. 2, 1841. By Amos Dean, of Albany, President of the Association. Published by request of the Association. Albany: Printed by J. Munsell. 1841. 8vo, pp. 31, 3.

—*An Address* on Agricultural Education, delivered by Amos Dean, Esq., before the New York State Agricultural Society, at the Annual Fair at Albany, September, 1850. Published by request of the Society. Albany: Charles Van Benthuysen, Printer, 1851. 8vo, pp. 29.

—*Principles of Medical Jurisprudence:* designed for the Professions of Law and Medicine. By Amos Dean, Counsellor at Law, and Professor of Medical Jurisprudence in the Albany Medical College. Albany: Gould, Banks & Co., 475 Broadway. New York: Banks, Gould & Co., 144 Nassau Street. 1854. 8vo, pp. vi, (1), 664.

—*The History of Civilization*, by Amos Dean, LL. D. In Seven Volumes. Albany, N. Y.: Joel Munsell. 1868. 8vo, pp. xxiv, 695, 533, 508, 500, 517, 535 and 631.
Mr. Dean was born in Barnard, Vt., January 16, 1803; whither his father, Nathaniel Dean, had removed from Massachusetts, in early life. The family was subject to the usual hardships and deprivations of a new country, and Amos, manifesting an intense thirst for knowledge, found it difficult to procure books for its gratification. He continued on the farm until early manhood, when having procured a little money by teaching a district school, he entered Randolph Academy; in 1825 he entered the Senior class at Union College, Schnectady, graduating in 1826, when he commenced the study of the law with his uncle, Jabez D. Hammond, at Albany, N. Y. Mr. Dean was always foremost in all educational work; he and others, in 1833 organized the "Young Men's Association of Albany," the pioneer of those institutions for mental improvement; he was one of those who organized the "Albany Medical College," also the "Albany Law School," in the former of which he accepted the chair of Medical Jurisprudence, and of the latter he accepted the active management. In 1855 he was elected Chancellor and Professor of History in the University of Iowa, and after passing three summers there, he resigned and continued as the active manager of the Law School until his death. The works of Mr. Dean in addition to those mentioned, are the following:
"Manual of Law," 1838, "Philosophy of Human Life," 8vo, 1839. and numerous law treatises, all of which have been regarded as standard works.
His greatest work, "The History of Civilization," was commenced in 1833, and completed in 1863, thirty years after its inception, but was not published until after his decease, which occurred January 26, 1868. Mr. Dean ranked high as a lawyer, and continued in active practice until 1854, when he gave his whole time to the Law School and other duties. He was a lawyer, an educator, a scholar, and an author. See sketch of his life, prefixed to "The History of Civilization."

Dean, Cyrus B. *Trial of*, for murder.
See Trials.

Dean, James. *An Alphabetical Atlas*, or Gazetteer of Vermont; affording a summary description of the State, its several Counties, Towns, and Rivers. Calculated to supply, in some measure, the place of a Map. And designed for the use of Offices, Travellers, Men of Business, &c. By James Dean, A. M., Tutor in the University of Vermont. Motto. Montpelier: Printed by Samuel Goss, for the Author. January, 1808. 8vo, pp, 44.

—*An Oration on Curiosity*, pronounced in the University of Vermont, 24th April, 1810, on Induction into Office, By James Dean, A. M., Professor of Mathematics & Natural Philosophy. Published at the request of the students. (motto.) Burlington, Vt. Printed by Samuel Mills. May, 1810. 8vo, pp. 19.

Professor Dean was born at Windsor, Vt., and died at Burlington, Vt., January 20, 1849, aged 72. He was graduated at Dartmouth College, 1800; and was a tutor and Professor in the University of Vermont, and of Dartmouth College, 1807-1824. He was celebrated for his mathematical attainments.

For a Sketch of his life, see Miss Hemenway's *Historical Gazetteer of Vermont*, Vol. 1, pp. 599-601.

Dean, Lydia. *The Testimony* of Ferrisburg Monthly Meeting, concerning Lydia Dean, Deceased. New York: James Egbert, Printer. 1855. 12mo, pp. 8.

Dean, Paul. *A Discourse*, delivered before the First Universalist Society in Boston, on the Character and Death of the Rev. John Murray, their late senior pastor, Oct. 29, 1815. By Rev. Paul Dean, Pastor of said Church and Society. Motto. Boston: Printed by T. W. White. 1815. 8vo, pp. 16.

—*A Sermon*, preached before the Antient and Honorable Artillery Company, on the 177th Anniversary of their Election of Officers ; Boston, June 3, 1816. By Rev. Paul Dean. Second Edition : published by E. G. House. 1816. 8vo. pp. 32.

—*Masonic Address*, at Dedham, 1816. Attleborough: 1817.

—*Masonic Address* at Walpole, Mass., June 24, 1823. Boston : 1823. 8vo.

—*Eulogy* on the Character of Thomas Smith Webb. Boston: E. G. House. 1819. 8vo, pp. 16.

— *Discourse* before the African Society on the Abolition of the Slave Trade by the Government of the United States. July 14, 1819. By Paul Dean. Boston : Nathaniel Coverly. 1819. 8vo, pp. 16.

—*A Sermon* at the Instalation of the Rev. Hosea Ballou, 2d, Roxbury, July 26, 1821. Boston: 1821. 8vo, pp. 24.

—*Sermon* at the Instalation of the Rev. Robert Bartlett, over the Universalist Church and Society at Hartland, Vt. 1825.

—*An Address*, delivered before the most excellent Grand Royal Arch Chapter of Massachusetts, at the Consecration of Mount Lebanon Royal Arch Chapter, in the West Parish of Medway, June 24, A. L. 5825. By Paul Dean, G. H. P. Boston : Printed by Charles Crocker. 1825. 8vo, pp. 14.

Published with Jacob Ide's Discourse on the same occasion.

—*120 Reasons for being a Universalist*, or a Conversation between a believer in the Final Restoration, and a Sincere Inquirer after Truth. By Paul Dean, Pastor of the Central Universalist Church, Boston, Mass. Providence : R. I. Christian Telescope Office. John S. Greene, Printer. 1827. 18mo, pp. 36.

—*und Clarke, Samuel*, Addresses before the Massachusetts Grand Chapter, June 8, 1830. Boston : 1830. 8vo.

—*Election Sermon*. Massachusetts, 1831.

—*A Course of Lectures* in Defence of the Final Restoration. Delivered in the Bulfinch Street Church, Boston, in the Winter of Eighteen hundred and thirty-two. By Paul Dean. "I am

set for the Defence of the Gospel."—Paul. Boston : Published by Edwin M. Stone. 1832. 8vo, pp. 190.

—*Discourse* delivered at Bulfinch St. Church, on taking leave of the Society. Boston : 1840. 8vo.

Rev. Mr. Dean was born in Barnard, Vt., in 1789; and died in Framingham, Mass., October 1, 1860. He was pastor of the Universalist church in Barre, Vt., 1808 to 1811, and organized a church there in 1810, although a society was organized in Barre October 27, 1796, under the leadership of Rev. William Farwell, grandfather of John G. and A. D. Farwell, of Montpelier. Mr. Dean was installed over the Hanover street Church, Boston, in 1813, where he preached until 1823, and was then pastor of the Bulfinch street Church, May 17, 1823, to May 3, 1840. He was some time pastor of a Unitarian church at Easton, Mass. Mr. Dean was editor and associate editor of the "Independent Messenger," (Universalist) at Boston about 1833-36.

The Death of Abel, in five Books. The Death of Cain in five Books. The Life of Joseph, the Son of Israel, in eight Books. Two volumes in one. Sharon, Vt., Published by Z. J. & L. Burbank. Rufus Colton, Printer. Woodstock, 1829. 18mo, pp. 133, 58, 163.

Decalves, Alonzo. *Travels to the Westward*, or the unknown Parts of America : In the years 1786, and 1787. Containing an account of the Country to the westward of the river Mississippi, its Productions, Animals, Inhabitants, Curiosities, &c. &c. By Alonso Decalves. From the Herald—Office, Rutland. Printed by Josiah Fay. M.DCC.XCVII. 12mo, pp. 48.

De Costa, B. F. *Lake George ;* its scenes and Characteristics. With Sketches of Schroon Lake, the Lakes of the Adirondacks, and Lake Luzerne. By B. F. DeCosta. New York : Anson D. F. Randolph & Co., 770 Broadway. 1869. sm. 4to, pp. 186. Illustrations.

Relates to Lake Champlain, Ticonderoga, etc.

Deformity of Federalism ; or *Judicial Turpitude exposed*, being a Series of Numbers published in the North Star, addressed to the Judges of Essex County (Vt.) Court, By Investigator. To which is added the Reflections of a reformed Federalist, on the leading measures of his party since the Declaration of War, under the signature of Candor. Published August, 1815. 8vo, pp. 40.

DeGoesbriand. *See Goesbriand.*

Delano, Columbus. *Speech of Hon. Columbus Delano*, on the Mexican War, House of Representatives of the United States, Feb. 2, 1847. Washington, [1847]. 8vo, pp. 15.

—*Speech of Mr. Columbus Delano. of Ohio*, against the Bill declaring that "a State of War exists by the Act of the Republic of Mexico." Washington : 1846. 8vo, pp. 15.

—*Speech of Mr Delano, of Ohio*, on the Oregon Question. Delivered in the House of Representatives, Washington. Feb. 5, 1846. Washington : 1846. 8vo, pp. 15.

—*Speech of Hon. Columbus Delano*, delivered at Raleigh, North Carolina, July 24, 1872. 8vo, pp. 8.

Mr. Delano was born in Shoreham, Vt., in 1809, and removed to Mt. Vernon, Ohio in 1817, where he became a lawyer. He held many State offices, and was a member of Congress, 1845-7, and 1865-9; and was Secretary of the Department of the Interior, 1870-75.

Deming, Rev. A. T. *Sermon delivered at Bridport, Vt.*, July 10th, 1864, at the funeral of the late Chauncey M. Crane, Serg't in Co. F., 5th regiment Vt. Vols. By Rev. A. T. Deming. Rutland : Tuttle & Gay, Book and Job Printers. 1864. 8vo, pp. 24.

Deming, Calvin. *An Address*, delivered before the Chittenden Co. Medical Society, at Burlington, February 26, 1822. By Calvin Deming. Burlington : J. Spooner, Printer. 1822. 8vo, pp. 16.

Deming, Leonard. *The uncertainty of obtaining Justice by the Law.* Or a History of 292 Hen's Eggs, to which is added A short account of the new mode of hatching them, without the use of animal heat. By Leonard Deming. Motto. Published by the Author, of Middlebury, Vt., May, 1822. 8vo, pp. 10.

—*Read! Pause! Reflect!* Leonard Deming, Petitioner. vs. Wightman & Asa Chapman, Petitioners, October Session 1825. To the General Assembly now sitting : [n. p. n. d.] 12mo, pp. 12.
Relates to Deming's famous Egg Case.

—*A Collection of Useful, Interesting and Remarkable Events*, original and selected, from Ancient and Modern Authorities. By Leonard Deming. Motto. Middlebury : J. W. Copeland, Printer. 1825. 12mo, pp. 324. Plate.

—*Deming's Statistical View of the Legislature of Vermont.* 1850 : With a list of the principal officers of Vermont, &c. Montpelier : E. P. Walton & Son, Printers. 16mo, pp. (2), 33.

—*Catalogue of the Principal Officers of Vermont*, as connected with its Political History, from 1778 to 1851, with some Biographical Notices, &c. By Leonard Deming, Middlebury, Vt. Middlebury : Published by the Author. 1851. 8vo, pp. 208. Including the Appendix.

—*Appendix to Deming's Catalogue of Vermont Officers.* Middlebury : Printed by Justus Cobb. 1852. 8vo.
From pages 121 to 208 of the full Catalogue, the pagination being continuous. The Catalogue and Appendix are usually found bound in one volume.

—*Oblique Hints*, on the difficulties which often attend the instructions of Common Schools. Motto. Middlebury, Vt. Published by Leonard Deming. Boston : Edmond C. Deming. 1850. 16mo, pp. 36.

—*Trial of Cain, The First Murderer.* In Poetry, by rule of Court, in which a Predestinarian, Universalian, and an Armenian argue as Attorneys at the bar ; the Armenian as Attorney General, the others for the Prisoner.

—*Ambrose Gwinnet*, an innocent person, who was hung and gibbeted, and taken down alive. With an account of his various travels by sea and land.

—*Chequer Players' sure Guide.* By which any person who knows the alphabet and figures, can learn more of that scientific and diverting game in one week, than they can learn in any other way in six months.

—*Also, Songs and Ballads*, a large Assortment.
The following sketch of Mr. Deming was written by himself, and printed in "Deming's Statistical View of the Legislature of Vermont," 1850 :

In former sheets of this kind, some thought I ought to give them some of my own biography, no objections, gentlemen, you can have it.
Leonard Deming, whig, *without the aid of Treasury pap*, born in Canaan, Conn., September 5, 1787, removed to Middlebury village with my father and family, March 2, 1789, and have been, since the death of Judge Painter in May, 1819, the only person in that village who was there at the time my father moved there. In April, 1794, my father John Deming, moved to Salisbury, and lived there till 1807, and then returned to Middlebury. January 1, 1811, I was married to Miss Ruth Case, a daughter of Nathan Case, and she died February 23, 1823, leaving four children, two are living. My eldest son, Edmond C., keeps a barber shop at 56 Brattle street, Boston, where you will find a chip of the old block, should you call upon him. December 13, 1827, I was married to Miss Jerusha Benton, of Cornwall, who died December 23, 1829, leaving one little son who died when 3 years old. May 19, 1831, married Miss Dorothy Taylor, of Williston, who died June 17, 1835, leaving one son who is now a Freshman in Middlebury College. April 28, 1836, married Miss Ann Byington, of Hinesburgh, who is living, but in feeble health. In May, 1836, I had three fathers, four mothers, and one grand-mother living, and now but one father aged 88, and one mother aged 85, my second wife's parents.
Mr. Deming died August 20, 1853.

Deming, Philander. *Vermont Legislative Compendium* for 1864. Montpelier, Vt.: Published by P. Deming. Freeman Steam Printing Establishment. 1864. 16mo, pp. 24.
Mr. P. Deming was born in Carlisle, Schoharie Co., N. Y., Feb. 6, 1829. He graduated from the University of Vt. in 1861; was Assistant Editor of the Burlington Free Press, 1862-3; studied law at the Albany Law School, was subsequently Stenographic Court Reporter for the Third (N. Y.) Judicial District; resides in Albany. He is the author of "Adirondack stories" (1880,) of "Tompkins and Other Folks" (1885), and of various contributions to the Atlantic Monthly and other periodicals.

Denison, Charles. *Rocky Mountain Health Resorts.* An Analytical Study of High Altitudes in relation to the Arrest of Chronic Pulmonary Disease, by Charles Denison, A. M., M. D. Boston : Houghton, Osgood & Co. 1880. p. viii, 192.
Dr. Charles Denison was born in Royalton, Vt., graduated from Williams College 1867, and from the Medical Department of the University of Vermont, 1869. Since 1873, he has been a leading physician in Denver, Col. Author of "The Annual and Seasonal Climatic Maps of the United States," Chicago, 1886 ; "Moisture and Dryness," ibid ; The Preferable Climate for Pthisis, Report to the Ninth International Medical Congress, 1887 ; Reports on Climate and Consumption, made to the American Medical Association and International Medical Congress, 1876 ; and "Degenerative Heredity," reprinted from the New York Medical Journal, Dec. 1895.

Denison, Franklin. *The New Epic.* A Paper read before the Chicago Literary Club, December 3, 1877. Chicago : Legal News Co. Print. 1878. 12mo, pp. 32.
Franklin Denison, Esq., is a native of Royalton, Vt.. a graduate from the University of Vermont in 1864, and is a lawyer in Chicago, (1896.)

De Peyster, J. Watts. *Secession in Switzerland* and in the United States compared : Being the Annual Address, Delivered Oct. 20th, 1863, before the Vermont State Historical Society, in the Hall of Representatives, Capitol, Montpelier, By J. Watts De Peyster. Catskill, N. Y.: 1863. 8vo, pp. 72.

Devlin, B. *St. Albans Raid.* Speech of B. Devlin, Esquire, Counsel for the United States, in Support of their demand for the Extradition of Bennett H. Young, et al, charged with the robbery upon the 19th October last, of Samuel Breck, In the town of St. Albans. Montreal : 1865. 8vo, pp. 60.

Devol, Charles. *Pædobaptism.* A Sermon read before the Troy Annual Conference of the

Methodist Episcopal Church, Burlington, Vt., June 10, 1842. By Charles Devol, M. D. (mottoes.) Sandy-Hill, N. Y. Printed for the Author by G. & E. Howland. 1843. 12mo, pp. 16.

Dewey, C. C. *Woman Suffrage.* Speech of Hon. Chas. C. Dewey, delivered in the Council of Censors, Montpelier, August 4th, 1869. Journal Press, Montpelier, Vt.: 8vo, pp. 29.

Mr. Dewey was born in Randolph, Vt., in 1830; and died at Rutland, Vt., June 25, 1872. He read law, and practiced in Orange county, Vt., until 1859, when he removed to Rutland.

Dewey, S. *Account of a Hail Storm,* which fell on part of the Town of Lebanon, Bozrah, and Franklin, on the 15th of July, 1799 : Perhaps never equaled by any other ever known, not even in Egypt. By Sherman Dewey. [Copy Right secured.] Walpole, New Hampshire. Printed by Thomas & Thomas. 1799. 12mo, pp. 27.

Dewhurst, Rev. Frederick E. *The Higher and the Lower Wealth.* A Sermon by Rev. F. E. Dewhurst. Privately printed. Burlington, 1891.

—*The Mind of Christ ;* The Venture of Faith ; The Face of God. Three Sermons by Rev. F. E. Dewhurst. [Pastor of the Berean (Baptist) Church, Burlington, Vt.] Burlington : Free Press Association. 1892. pp. 63.

Dickens, Charles. *The Mystery of Edwin Drood.* Complete. By Charles Dickens. Brattleboro, Vt.: Published by T. P. James. 1873. 8vo, pp. XVI, 488.

At his death Mr. Dickens left this work in an unfinished state ; the last 284 pages are claimed to have been delivered by the spirit of Mr. Dickens, through a medium, Mr. Thomas P. James, of Brattleboro, Vt.

Dickinson, Rev. Pliny. *A Discourse* delivered at the Funeral of the Rev. Thomas Fessenden, Senior Pastor of the Church in Walpole, New Hampshire, by Pliny Dickinson. Brattleborough, (Vt.): printed by William Fessenden. 1813. 8vo, pp. 15.

Dickinson, Pliny, Jr. *A Sermon,* delivered January 6, 1808. At the Ordination of the Rev. Jason Chamberlain, to the Pastoral care of the Congregational Church and Society in Guilford, (Vt.) By Pliny Dickinson, Jr., A. M. Pastor of the Church in Walpole, N. H. Brattleborough : Printed by William Fessenden. 1808. 8vo, pp. 19.

Dike, Samuel W. *The Effect of Lax Divorce Legislation* upon the Stability of American Institutions. A Paper read before the American Social Science Association at Saratoga, Sept. 8, 1881. By Rev. Samuel W. Dike, of Royalton, Vt. Boston : Wright & Potter Printing Company, No. 18 Post Office Square. 1881. 8vo, pp. 14.

Diller, Jacob William. *Farewell Discourse :* Preached in St. Stephen's Church, Middlebury, Vt. By the Rev. Jacob William Diller, Rector of said Church. Published by request of the Vestry. Brooklyn : Printed by I. Van Anden, 39 Fulton Street. 1842. 8vo, pp. 16.

Dewey, John. *Psychology,* by John Dewey, Ph.D., Assistant Professor of Philosophy in Michigan University. New York : Harper & Brothers. 1887. 8vo, pp. xii, 427.

A second edition has been published.

—*Leibnitz's New Essays,* concerning the Human Understanding. A Critical Exposition. By John Dewey, Ph. D., Assistant Professor of Philosophy in the University of Michigan, and Professor-elect of Mental and Moral Philosophy in the University of Minnesota. Chicago : 1888. S. C. Driggs & Co. 12 mo, pp. xvii, 272.

—*The Study of Ethics.* A Syllabus. By John Dewey. Ann Arbor, Mich. 1894. Register Pub. Co. 8vo, pp. iv, 151.

—*Principles of Instrumental Logic.* By John Dewey, Professor of Philosophy in the University of Michigan. London : Swan, Sonnenschein & Co. 1894.

—*The Psychology of Number* and its Applications to Methods of Teaching Arithmetic. By Jas. A. McLellan and J. Dewey. Appletons, N. Y. 1895. 12mo, pp. xii, 309.

(International Ed. Series, No. 23.)

Professor Dewey was born in Burlington, Vt.; graduated from the University of Vermont, 1879; received degree of Ph.D. from John Hopkins University, 1884; Assistant Professor of Philosophy, University of Michigan, 1884-8; Professor of Mental and Moral Philosophy, University of Minnesota, 1888-9; Professor of Philosophy, University of Michigan, 1889 to date (1896).

Dillingham, Paul. *Speech* of Mr. Dillingham of Vermont, on the Right of the Members elected by General Ticket to Retain their Seats. Delivered in the House of Representatives, February 7, 1844. [n. p. n. d.] 8vo, pp. 8.

Mr. Dillingham was born in Shutesbury, Franklin county, Mass., August, 1800; removed to Waterbury, Vt., with his father, Paul senior, in 1805; adopted the profession of the law, and was admitted to practice in Washington county in 1824. He was Town Clerk and a Justice of the Peace in Waterbury for many years; was State's Attorney for Washington County, 1835 to 1838; member of the Constitutional Convention in 1836-37 ; Town Representative six years, and State Senator in 1841-2; Representative in Congress, 1843 to 1847, and Governor of Vermont in 1866-7; subsequently was Chairman of the Board of Trustees of the Vermont Reform School. Died at Waterbury, July 26, 1891.

Dimmick, Luther F. *Intemperance ;* a Sermon, delivered at the North Church in Newburyport. on the occasion of the Publick Fast, April 1, 1824. By Luther Fraseur Dimmick. Newburyport: Published by Charles Whipple, April, 1824. 8vo, pp. 30.

—*The Influence of Truth.* A Sermon delivered in Newburyport, March 20, 1827, at the Dedication of the New Brick Church in Titcomb Street. By L. F. Dimmick. Newburyport : Published by Charles Whipple, No. 4, State Street. 1827. 8vo, pp. 32.

—*The Duty of Progress in the Christian Calling :* a New Year's Sermon, delivered in the North Church, Newburyport, Jan. 2, 1831. By L. F. Dimmick. Newburyport, Mass.: Published by C. Whipple. 1831. 8vo, pp. 22.

—*A Memorial* of the Year Eighteen Hundred Thirty One: a Sermon delivered in Newburyport, Dec. 31, 1831, on occasion of a Public Thanksgiving of several of the Churches, for the Spiritual Mercies of the past Year. By L. F. Dimmick. Newburyport: Ephraim W. Allen & Co. 8vo, pp. 20.

—*A Call* to seek first the Kingdom of God: a Sermon, occasioned by the Death of Mr. Amos Pettingell, who departed this Life at New Haven, Conn., Nov. 30, 1831, aged Twenty Seven Years. Delivered in the Brick Church, Newburyport, also in the First Church, Newbury. Addressed particularly to the Young Men of his Acquaintance. By L. F. Dimmick. Newburyport: Published by Charles Whipple. 1832. 8vo, pp. 16.

—*The Position* of the American Republic with Reference to the rest of the World. A Discourse, delivered in the North Church, Newburyport, on the Annual Thanksgiving in the Commonwealth of Massachusetts, November 27th, 1834. Ry L. F. Dimmick, Pastor of the North Church and Society. Newburyport: Printed by Moss & Brewster. 1834. 8vo, pp. 24.

—*A Scriptural View* of the Honor due to Jesus Christ. Designed for Young Christians and others, who may wish to know what the Bible teaches on this Important Subject. By L. F. Dimmick, Pastor of the North Church, Newburyport. Newburyport: Charles Whipple. 1835. 16mo, pp. 96.

—*A Discourse* on the Moral Influence of Railroads. By L. F. Dimmick, Pastor of the North Church, Newburyport, Mass. Boston: Published by Tappan & Dennet. 1841. 16mo, pp. 125.

—*The End of the World not yet.* A Discourse, delivered in the North Church, Newburyport, on the last Evening of the Year 1841. By L. F. Dimmick, Pastor of the Church. Newburyport: Published by Charles Whipple. 1842. 12mo. pp. 48.

—*Memoir* of Mrs. Catherine M. Dimmick. By L. F. Dimmick, Pastor of the North Church, Newburyport. Boston: Published by T. R. Marvin. 1846. 12mo, pp. 214.

—*An Address*, delivered before the Musical Convention, at Newburyport, under the direction of Professor L. Mason, June 18th and 19th, 1851, by Rev. L. F. Dimmick, D. D., together with the Proceedings, and Names of all connected with the Convention. Newburyport: Huse & Nason, Printers. 1851. 8vo, pp. 38.

—*A Brief Memoir* of Rev. Paul Couch: an unusual Sufferer. By Rev. L. F. Dimmick, D. D., Pastor of the North Church, Newburyport. Newburyport: Moulton & Clark, 29 Market Square. 1858. 16mo, pp. 104.

—*Fortieth Anniversary*, A Discourse, Commemorative of Forty Years in the Christian Ministry. By L. F. Dimmick, D. D., Pastor of the North Church in Newburyport. Newburyport: William H. Huse & Co., Printers. 1860. 8vo, pp. 28.

—*Memorial* of Luther Fraseur Dimmick, D, D. Late Pastor of the North Congregational Church, Newburyport. By Rev. Leonard Withington, D. D. Boston: Press of T. R. Marvin & Co. 1860. 8vo, pp. 16.

Rev. Dr. Dimmick was born in Shaftsbury, Vt., November 15, 1790. In early youth he removed with his father's family to the State of New York; he was graduated at Hamilton College, 1816, and at Andover Theological Seminary, 1819; and was pastor at Newburyport, Mass., 1819, until his death, May 16, 1860.

Dix, John Ross. *A Hand Book* for Lake Memphremagog, with route list, by John Ross Dix, Author of "Pen and Ink Sketches," &c., &c., with Illustrations, by the Author. To be had at all Railroad Depots. Price 25 cents. Bos-

ton: Printed by Evans & Co. (1864.) sm. 4to, pp. 56.

Dobbins, P. (*Pseudon.*) *Furrago*, or a Miscellaneous Review of Politics in the United States. Brattleborough, Vt. 1807. 12mo.

Dolphin, James. *The Travels* of James Dolphin, with an Account of his being taken by the Indian Savages, and redeemed by a Spanish Lady, in the City of Mexico, who afterwards married him, and at her death left him her whole fortune. He was finally married to his former Lover, Polly Seamour. Montpelier: Published by Wright and Sibley. 1812. 18mo, pp. 72.

Doolittle, Eliakim.

Mr. Doolittle was of Pawlet, and uncle to Hon. J. R. Doolittle, late United States Senator, now of Chicago, Ill. Mr. Doolittle was a teacher of music, and about 1800 published a singing book. He is said to have been a child of song; and no mean composer; in his later years he became eccentric, wore tattered garments, long hair, etc.
See History of Pawlet, p. 71.

Doolittle, J. *J. Doolittle's Argument* in the Case of Jonathan Hagar *vs.* E. D. Woodbridge, et. al. Addison County Supreme Court, January Term. 1824. Middlebury: J. W. Copeland Printer. 8vo, pp. 38.

Mr. Doolittle was a distinguished lawyer of Middlebury, Vt. He was Judge of the Supreme Court, 1817–1825, and held other offices.
See Swift's History of Middlebury, pp. 278-9.

Dorr, Mrs. Julia C. R. "*Farmingdale.*" (a novel). By Mrs. Julia C. R. Dorr. New York: D. Appleton & Co. 1854. 12mo, pp. 392.

—"*Lanmere.*" (a novel). New York: Mason Brothers: 1856. 12mo, pp. 447.

—"*Sibyl Huntington,*" (a novel). Philadelphia: J. B. Lippincott & Co. 1870. 12mo, pp. 359.

—"*Expiation,*" (a novel). Philadelphia. J. B. Lippincott & Co. 1873. 12mo, pp. 323.

—"*Poems.*" Philadelphia: J. B. Lippincott & Co. 1872. 12mo, pp. 102.

—"*Bride and Bridegroom.* A Series of Letters.*" Cincinnati: Hitchcock & Walden. New York: Nelson & Phillips. 1873. 12mo, pp. 253.

—"*Vermont;*" A Poem. Written for the Vermont Centennial Celebration at Bennington, August 15th, 1877. Printed by Perry & Austin, Maplewood, Mass. 1877. 4to, pp. 12.

—*Friar Anselmo* and Other Poems, by Julia C. R. Dorr. New York: Charles Scribner's Sons. 1879. 12mo, pp. v, 178.

—*Afternoon Songs*, by Julia C. R. Dorr. New York: Charles Scribner's Sons. 1885. 12mo, pp. 184.

—*Bermuda.* An Idyl of the Summer Islands. By Julia C. R. Dorr. New York: Charles Scribner's Sons. 1884. 16mo, pp. 148.

—"*The Flower of England's Face.*" Sketches of English Travel by Julia C. R. Dorr, author of "Friar Anselmo," etc. New York and London: McMillan & Co. 1895. 16mo. pp. 259.

—*A Cathedral Pilgrimage*, by Julia C. R. Dorr. New York: The MacMillan Company, 1896. 16mo, pp. vii, 277.

—*The Fallow Field*, by Julia C. R. Dorr. With Illustrations in Charcoal by Zulma De Lacy

Steele. Boston : Lee & Shepard, Publishers. 1893. 4to, pp. 30.

Mrs. Steele is a daughter of Mrs. Dorr, and the illustrations are sketches of scenes in and about Rutland.

In addition to the above, Mrs. Dorr has written much for magazines at various periods. She is a native of South Carolina, but has resided in Rutland, Vt., for the past twenty-five years; she married Hon. S. M. Dorr, in 1847. For a biographical Sketch, see Miss Hemenway's *Historical Gazetteer of Vermont, Vol. III,* pp. 1101–4; *Cottage Hearth,* for January, 1876.

Dorr, Seneca M. *The Farmer's War*—Equal Taxation—Granges—Patrons of Husbandry. A Series of Letters published in the Rutland Daily Globe, from the pen of Hon. S. M. Dorr of Rutland, and now collected and published for general circulation, by order of the Rutland Grange of the Patrons of Husbandry. 1876. 8vo, pp. 8.

Hon. Seneca M. Dorr, for thirty years a resident of Rutland, Vt., died at his home in that town, Dec. 3, 1884, aged 64 years. Judge Dorr was born in Chatham Center, N. Y. He was a prominent free soiler in the days before the war, and became one of the founders of the Republican party. He was State Senator, 1865-6.

Doton, Hosea. *The Vermont Almanac,* pocket Memorandum, and Statistical Register, for the year 1843 : Being the third after Bissextile or Leap Year. Astronomical calculations by Hosea Doton. Vol. I. No. 1. Woodstock, Vt.: Published by Haskell and Palmer. Mercury Press. 18mo, pp. 144.

Hosea Doton of Woodstock was born in Pomfret, Vt., November 29, 1809. He began teaching in 1828, and for nearly 40 years was a large part of the time conducting schools in his native country. In 1845 Norwich University recognized his work by giving him the honorary degree of Master of Arts. Worthy of special mention is the private school conducted by him in Pomfret from 1850 to 1866. This gave the town the advantages of an efficient academy, and was specially successful in its original purpose of preparing young people for school work, as something over 150 of the pupils became practical teachers, including a large proportion who were more than ordinarily successful. Mr. Doton qualified himself as a civil engineer, was employed as such in the construction of the Northern Railroad of New Hampshire, and had charge of the building of the Woodstock railroad. His first published astronomical work was this Almanac, which was continued with the same publishers in similar form until 1856. His calculations for 1857 were not published, but the next year he began work for Walton's Vermont Register, and continued it without interruption for many years.

Mr. Doton died at Woodstock, Jan. 17, 1886.

Douglas, Malcolm.
See Norwich University.

DOUGLAS, STEPHEN ARNOLD. *Speech* in the House of Representatives, Washington, Jany. 7, 1844, on the bill to refund the Fine imposed on General Jackson at New Orleans. 8vo, pp. 18.

—*Speech* on the Annexation of Texas, in the House, Jany. 6, 1845. pp. 7.

—*Speech* on the Mexican War, in the House, May 13, 1846. pp. 16.

—*River and Harbor Improvements.* Letter to Governor Matteson, of Illinois. 1847. pp. 8.

—*Speech* on the Territorial Question, in the Senate, March 13 and 14, 1850. 8vo, pp. 31.

—*Speech* in reply to Mr. Soule, relative to the Public Lands in California. Delivered in the Senate, June 26th and 28th, 1850. pp. 14.

—*Speech* on the "Measures of Adjustment," Delivered in Chicago, Oct. 23, 1850. pp. 16.

—*Same Speech* revised and enlarged, and two other editions printed. Washington : 1851. pp. 32. New York : 1851. pp. 31.

—*Address at the Annual Fair* of the New York State Agricultural Society, held at Rochester, September, 1851. 8vo, pp. 41.

—*Oration,* on the Inauguration of the Jackson Statue, at the City of Washington, January 8, 1853. 8vo, pp. 16.

—*Speech in the Senate,* on the Munroe Doctrine, Feb. 14, 1853. pp. 16.

—*Speech, Senate,* in reply to Senators Clayton and Butler, on the Clayton-Bulwer Treaty on Central America, March 10, 17, 1853. pp. 39.

—*Letter* on the Nebraska and Kansas Territorial Bill. 1854. pp. 7.

—*Letter* in reply to the State Capital Reporter, Concord, N. H. 8vo, pp. 7.

—*Speech* in Support of an Amendment offered by him to the River and Harbor Bill, in the Senate of the United States. August 23, 1852. Washington: Printed by John T. and Lem. Towers. 1853. 8vo, pp. 15.

—*Letter of Senator Douglas,* Vindicating his Character and Position on the Nebraska Bill, Against the Assaults contained in the Proceedings in a Public Meeting composed of Twenty Five Clergymen of Chicago. April 6, 1854. pp. 14.

—*Execution of United States Laws.* Speech in the Senate, February 23, 1855, on the Bill to protect Officers and other Persons acting under the Authority of the United States. 8vo, pp. 8.

—*Remarks* on the Memorial of three thousand New England Clergymen; United States Senate, March 14, 1854.

—*Speech* on the Nebraska Territory, in Senate, January 30, 1854. pp. 15.

—*Speech* on Nebraska and Kansas, March 3, 1854. pp. 30.

—*Kansas Lecompton Convention.* Speech on the President's Message, in the Senate, December 9, 1857. pp. 15.

—*Kansas—Utah—Dred Scott Decision.* Speech Delivered at Springfield, Ill., June 12, 1857. pp. 14.

—*Report* of Senator Douglas of Illinois, on the Kansas-Lecompton Constitution. February 18, 1858. Printed by Lemuel Towers. 8vo, pp. 16.

—*Speech in the Senate,* Against the Admission of Kansas under the Lecompton Constitution : March 22, 1858. pp. 29.

—*Speech in the Senate* on the Pacific Rail Road Bill, April 17, 1858.

—*Non-Intervention — Popular Sovereignty.* Speech in the Senate, February 23, 1859, in Reply to Hon. A. G. Brown, of Mississippi, together with an Appendix. 8vo, pp. 32.

—*Non-Interference by Congress* with slavery in the Territories. Speech in the Senate, May 15 and 16, 1860. pp. 32.

—*Speeches* on the Occasions of his Public Receptions by the Citizens of New Orleans, Philadelphia, and Baltimore. 1859. pp. 16.

—*State of the Union.* Speech in the Senate, January 3, 1861. pp. 15.

—*Popular Sovereignty in the Territories.* Judge Douglas, in Reply to Judge Black. 8vo, pp. 24.

—*Popular Sovereignty the Dividing Line* between Federal and Local Authority. 1859. 8vo, pp. 65.

First printed in Harper's Magazine.

—*The Great Senatorial Campaign in Illinois* between Douglas and Lincoln, in 1858, in which each party made from twenty to twenty-five able Speeches to their Constituents.

This debate filled the newspapers of the day at the West, and a portion of the speeches were published in a pamphlet, as above, in 1860, which was gotten up as a partisan affair, and does not present the debate in an impartial manner, as to Mr. Douglas.

—*Popular Sovereignty in the Territories.* Rejoinder of Judge Douglas to Judge Black. In a letter dated Washington, November 16, 1859. 8vo, pp. 15.

—*Removal of Judge Douglas* by the Senate as Chairman of the Committee on Territories. Letter of Judge Douglas in reply to the Speech of Dr. Gwin at Grass Valley, Cal. Reprint from the Daily National, San Francisco, Sept. 16, 1859. 8vo, pp. 8.

—*Admission of Kansas* under the Wyandott Constitution. Speech in reply to Mr. Seward and Mr. Trumbull. In the Senate, February 29, 1860.

—*Remarks on Popular Sovereignty,* as maintained and denied respectively by Judge Douglas, and Attorney-General Black. By a Southern Citizen, [Hon. Reverdy Johnson.] Baltimore: 1859. 8vo, pp. 48.

—*Observations* on Senator Douglas' Views of Popular Sovereignty. Washington: 1859. pp. 16.

—*Brief Treatise* upon Constitutional and Party Questions, and the History of Political Parties, received orally from Judge Douglas, by J. Madison Cutts. New York. 1866. 8vo. pp. 221.

Judge Douglas delivered numerous other speeches and addresses, which appeared in the newspapers, but have not been gathered into pamphlet or book form.

—*Addresses* on the death of Hon. Stephen A. Douglas, delivered in the Senate and House of Representatives on Tuesday, July 9, 1861. Washington: Government Printing Office. 1861. 8vo, pp. 92.

—*Life of Stephen A. Douglas,* U. S. Senator from Illinois. Baltimore: 1860. 12mo, pp. 12.

—*The Life of Stephen A. Douglas.* By James W. Sheahan. New York: Harper & Brothers, Publishers. Franklin Square. 1860. 12mo, pp. 528. Portrait.

—*The Life of Stephen A. Douglas,* with Selections from his Speeches and Reports. By a member of the Western Bar. New York: Derby & Jackson. 1860. 8vo, pp. 264.

Second Edition in 12mo, New York, 1860. pp. 451.

—*Life of Stephen A. Douglas:* to which are added his Speeches and Reports. By H. M. Flint. New York. 1860. 12mo.

Second Edition, *John E. Potter, Philadelphia:* 1863. 12mo, pp. 408. Portrait.

—*Eulogy* upon the Hon. Stephen A. Douglas, delivered at the Smithsonian Institute. Washington, July 3, 1861. By John W. Forney. Philadelphia: Ringwalt & Brown. 1861. 8vo, pp. 28.

—*A Discourse* on the Life and Character of Hon. Stephen A. Douglas, By Rev. B. D. Ames: Delivered in the Methodist E. Church, at Brandon, (Vt.,) on Sunday, June 9th, 1861. [n. p. n. d.] 8vo, pp. 8.

—*A Voter's Version* of the Life and Character of Stephen A. Douglas. By Robert B. Warden. Columbus. (Ohio.) 1860. 12mo, pp. 131.

--*An Eulogy.* Delivered before the Chicago University, in Bryan Hall, July 3, 1861. By James W. Sheahan, of the Chicago Tribune. Fergus Printing Company, Chicago: 1881. 8vo, pp. 48.

—*Organization,* Constitution and By-Laws of the Douglas Monument Association; together with an Appeal to the Public. Chicago: Times Print. 1862. 8vo, pp. 19.

—*Address* at the laying of the Corner-Stone of the Douglas Monument at Chicago, September 6, 1866. By Major-General John A. Dix. New York: 1866. 8vo, pp. 35.

Mr. Douglas was born at Brandon, Vt., April 23, 1813; died at Chicago, Ill., June 3, 1860. His father having died while he was an infant, he and his sister were taken by their mother to a farm occupied by her brother, where young Douglas remained until 15 years of age, working upon the farm and attending the district school. At this period he apprenticed himself to a cabinet maker in Middlebury, where he remained two years, when he entered the academy at Brandon, and remained one year. In the meantime his mother and sister had married and settled in Canandaigua, N. Y., and young Douglas was persuaded to follow them to their new home, where he continued his studies at the Academy in that place for three years during a portion of which time he pursued a course of law studies. In 1833, when not quite 21 years of age, he located permanently in the state of Illinois, where he at once entered upon his great career as lawyer, judge, politician and statesman. Before leaving Vermont it is said he organized a band of "Jackson Boys," who proclaimed war upon the "Coffin hand-bills," they being a libel on General Jackson, and managed to destroy them as fast as they were placarded upon the walls and fences of the town. And thus he continued to battle against the enemies of the Democratic party during the entire period of his life. The above is a partial list of the works by and relating to Douglas.

Dow, Ann Eliza. *Life and Adventures* of Ann Eliza Dow, being a true narrative. Written by herself. Illustrated. Burlington: 1845. 8vo, pp. 24.

Dow, Peggy. *A Collection of Poetry.* Selected by Peggy Dow. Motto. Montpelier: Published by E. P. & G. S. Walton. 1818. 24mo, pp. 160.

Peggy was the wife of the itinerant preacher, Lorenzo Dow.

Draper, George Barnard, D. D. [Born in Brattleboro, Vt., in 1827.] Late Rector of St. Andrews Church, Harlem, N. Y. A Sermon in Memory of, preached by George F. Seymour, October 19, 1876. New York: 1876. 8vo, pp. 53.

Drury, Amos. A Sermon Preached in Rutland, June 18, 1828, before the Grand Royal Arch Chapter, of the State of Vermont. By Amos Drury, Pastor of the Congregational Church in

West Rutland. Published at the Request of the G. R. A. Chapter. Rutland: Printed by Edward C. Purdy. 1828. 8vo, pp. 16.

—*A Sermon*, preached at West Rutland, Vt., April 26, 1829; being the close of his Pastoral labors with the church and congregation in West Rutland; By Amos Drury, Pastor of the Congregational Church at Fairhaven, Vt. Motto. Rutland: Printed at the Herald Office, by E. C. Purdy. 1829. 8vo, pp. 16.

Also one or two additional addresses before the Masonic fraternity.

Mr. Drury was born in Pittsford, Vt., December 18, 1792; and died in Pittsford, August 18, 1841. He was settled over the Congregational church in West Rutland and Fairhaven, Vt., during his ministry, with the exception of about three years at Westhampton, Mass. See History Pittsford, p. 560.

Duane, James. *State of the Evidence* and Argument in Support of the Territorial Rights and Jurisdiction of New York against the Government of New Hampshire, and the Claiments under it, and against the Commonwealth of Massachusetts. By James Duane. One of the Commissioners appointed by the Legislature to manage those Controversies. Ms. folio, pp. 189.

This work is to be found in the Library of the New York Historical Society, and contains the legal argument upon which the State of New York rested its claims to the territory of Vermont. An account of the life of Duane is given in the Documentary History of New York. 8vo ed. vol. iv., pp. 1063-1084.

Duclos, Francis. *A Brief Sketch* of the Birth, Life & Sufferings, of Capt. Duclos, A Frenchman by Birth. Particularly During the American Revolution, together with a Statement of the Unfriendly and Cruel Treatment he has since received from the British Government in Canada. With some remarks, both in prose and verse, by the revisor of the work, on special and singular occurrences, that transpired from time to time, in and since the Revolution, By consent of the Author. St. Albans: Printed for the Author by J. Spooner. 1824. 8vo, pp. 20, 21.

Dudley, Daniel Bliss, of West Hartford, Vt., published an English Grammar about 1860.

Dudley, John. *Shall we save our Country,* or the Duty of Prayer for Rulers, as a means of Self-Preservation. A Sermon, delivered at Quechee Village, Thanksgiving Day, Nov. 27, 1845. By Rev. John Dudley. Woodstock, (Vt.): Printed at the Mercury Office. 1845. 8vo, pp. 12.

—*A Discourse on Means of a Revival.* Preached at Quechee, Vt. Windsor: Chronicle Press. 1849. 8vo, pp. 24.

—*A Half-Century Sermon*, preached at the Dedication of the New Congregational Meeting House of Danville, Vt., by Rev. John Dudley, December 20, 1851. Hanover: Printed at the Dartmouth Press. 1852. 8vo, pp. 23.

—*The Mexican War and American Slavery.* Sermon preached by Rev. John Dudley, of Quechee, Vt., on Fast Day, 1847. Hanover: Printed at the Dartmouth Press. 1847. 8vo, pp. 23.

—*Earnestness as a Principle of Reform.* Sermon preached at Danville, Vt., October 2, 1851.

Mr. Dudley was born in Richmond, Mass., November 3, 1807; was Missionary to Choctaw Indians for a time;

studied theology at New Haven, Conn.; was pastor of 4th Presbyterian church in Cincinnati, Ohio, 1836-1837; spent four years in Michigan; was pastor of Congregational church, Weathersfield, Vt., 1841-1845; stated supply of Congregational church, Quechee, Vt., 1845-50; stated supply of Congregational church, Danville, Vt., 1850-1855; and then engaged in a boarding and day school at New Haven, Conn.

Dudley, J. G. *Cotton*—A Paper on the Growth, Trade and Manufacture of Cotton. Prepared at the Request of the New York Historical Society. By J. G. Dudley. New York: G. P. Putnam & Co. 1853. 8vo, pp. 96.

Mr. Dudley was a native of Hartland, Vt., born in 1812; married Augusta, daughter of Hon. Asa Aikens, of Windsor, Vt. He was some time a merchant in Barre, Vt., and subsequently a wholesale dealer in domestic cotton goods in New York city where he died April 16, 1881.

Dudley, Myron S. *Addresses.* Congregational Church, Peacham, 1871.

See Peacham.

—*In Memoriam.* Martha Maria (Hale) Dudley. 12mo, pp. 4.

Mrs. Dudley was a native of Barnet. She was born April 7, 1837, and died July 20, 1876. She married Rev. M. S. Dudley, August 21, 1873.

—*History of Cornwall*, a Sketch by Rev. M. S. Dudley. Middletown: Constitution Office. 1880. 8vo, pp. 36.

Mr. Dudley was born at Peru, Vt., February 20, 1837; was graduated at Williams College in 1863; studied theology at Andover and at Union Seminary, N. Y.; preached at Otsego, N. Y, 1869-70; at Peacham, Vt., 1871-4, and at Cornwall, Conn., 1874-80; now (1895) pastor of the Congregational church in Nantucket, Mass.

Dunham, Josiah. *Masonic Oration* at Hanover, N. H. June 24, 1796. Hanover: 1796. 8vo.

—*Answer* to the "Vindication of the Official Conduct of the Trustees of Dartmouth College," in confirmation of the "Sketches," with Remarks on the Removal of President Wheelock. Hanover, N. H. 1816. 8vo, pp. 95.

—*An Oration*, in Commemoration of the Birth of our Illustrious Washington, pronounced at Windsor (Vt.) February 24, 1812, Before the Washington Benevolent Society. By Josiah Dunham. "We shall never see his like again." —*Shakespeare.* Published at the request of the Society. Windsor, Vt.: printed by Thomas M. Pomroy. 1812, 8vo, pp. 24.

—*An Oration at Windsor, Vt.,* Febr. 22, 1814, before the Washington Benevolent Society. Windsor: 1814. 8vo.

—*An Address* delivered at Hanover, N. H., in 1814. Hanover: 1814. 8vo, pp. 25, (3).

Mr. Dunham was a leading Federalist in Vermont during the administrations of Jefferson and Madison. He resided at Windsor, and there published the Washingtonian, a Federal newspaper, for several years. He was born at Columbia, Ct., April 7, 1769, and died at Lexington, Ky., May 10, 1844. He was graduated at Dartmouth College, 1789; was Secretary of State for Vermont, 1813-15. In the excited contest for the election of Governor by the General Assembly in 1813, there having been no election by the people, Mr. Dunham acted as Clerk, and the duty of counting the votes consequently devolved upon him. He was a gentleman of the old style, with ruffled shirt-front and long, full-ruffled wristbands, and the tradition is that in counting the votes his ruffled wristbands continually worked down over his hands, which made it necessary for him as continually to push them back with his fingers, and in so doing a ballot for Gov. Galusha, the republican candidate, is supposed somehow to have got entangled in the ruffles, thus electing the Federal candidate, Martin Chittenden, by one majority, he receiving 112 votes and Galusha 111; subsequently 112 members made affidavit that they voted for Galusha, but it was of no avail, as Chittenden had been "counted in." For a sketch of Mr. Dunham see Dartmouth Alumni, 1789;

Vermont, Reports of Committees, etc., in relation to the election of Governor in 1813.

Dunlap, John. *Sermon,* on Board of the Fleet at Whitehall, 1814. By John Dunlap. Bennington : 1823. 8vo.

Dunn, Rev. L. A. *A Semi-Centennial Discourse:* preached at the Fiftieth Anniversary of the Lamoille Baptist Association, holden at Colchester, Vermont, September 12th, 1862, by Rev. L. A. Dunn. Published by the Association : E. A. Fuller, Hon. J. M. Hotchkiss, Rev. N. P. Foster, Committee. 8vo, pp. 22.

Durkee, Charles. *Fugitive Slave Law as a "Finality."* Speech of Hon. C. Durkee in the House of Representatives, Washington, August 6, 1852. Washington : 1852. 8vo.

—*Minority Report* on the Reduction of Letter, Periodical and Pamphlet Postage. n. p. n. d. 8vo, pp. 8.

—*Speech of Charles Durkee,* of Wisconsin, on the California Question. Made in the House of Representatives, June 10, 1850. 8vo, pp. 15.

Mr. Durkee was born in Royalton, Vt., Dec. 5, 1807 ; and died at Omaha, January 14, 1870. He was a merchant, and removed to Wisconsin, and was in the Legislature in that State in 1837-8 ; and Representative in Congress from the same, 1848-50 ; United States Senator, 1855-1861 ; and in 1865 he was appointed Governor of Utah, by President Johnson.

Dutcher, L. L. *Historical Discourse,* on the Rise and Progress of the First Congregational Church, of St. Albans, Vt., By Dea. L. L. Dutcher. Prepared under the direction of the First Congregational Church and Society in St. Albans, and delivered at their Annual Meeting, Jan. 5th, 1860. St. Albans : Printed by E. B. Whiting. 1860. 8vo, pp. 12.

—*The History of St. Albans, Vt.,* Civil, Religious, Biographical and Statistical. By L. L. Dutcher, A. M. With valuable contributions from Hon. James Davis ; Rev. A. B. Swift ; Rev. J. H. Hopkins ; J. S. D. Taylor ; Mrs. B. H. Smalley, and others. With a fine portrait, engraved on steel, of Ex-Gov. J. Gregory Smith, President of the Northern Pacific and Vermont Central Railroads. And the History of Sheldon. Vt. By H. R. Whitney ; Rev. George B. Tolman and Rev. A. H. Bailey. St. Albans, Vt. Published from the Stereotypes of Miss Hemenway's Vermont Historical Gazetteer, Vol. II. By Stephen E. Royce. 1872. 8vo, pp. (94.)

Deacon Dutcher was born in St. Albans, Vt., July 31st, 1802 ; and died there September 18th, 1878. He was educated at the Franklin County Grammar School ; and read medicine, but, prefering pharmacy to medical practice, he commenced business at St. Albans in 1825, which he continued until near the close of his life. He held many local offices, and was an active member of the Congregational Church since 1826, and a Deacon since 1842. Deacon Dutcher contributed many articles to Miss Hemenway's Historical Gazetteer, to newspapers, and delivered addresses before the public, and the Vermont Historical Society, of which he was an officer and a liberal benefactor. The University of Vermont conferred upon him the honorary degree of Master of Arts, in 1868.

Dutton, Daniel Benedict.

A native, of Stowe, Vt., where he was born August 30, 1817. The family soon after moved to Norwich, Vt. He was at Dartmouth College one year ; read medicine and graduated at Willoughby Medical College, Ohio, 1845. He practiced his profession at Kirtland, Ohio, and at Greensburgh, Ind., but early abandoned the profession of medicine for that of music, and is the author of "A Collection of music arranged according to the figure system of Notation."

His system gained favor with the public rapidly, but unfortunately the manuscript for an enlarged edition was destroyed by fire in 1851. He went to Brookville, Ind., and soon after resumed the profession of medicine ; but on account of poor health taught school three years ; in 1863 he was Assistant Surgeon of the 123d Indiana Infantry, which marched with Sherman to "the sea." He married in 1847, and in 1870 was residing at Metamora, Ill., and had three children living. See Tenney, J. Dartmouth Class of 1843, pp. 136-7, and 161.

Dutton, George. *Life and Health :* or how to restore health and prolong Life : On rational principles. By Dr. Geo. Dutton, A. M. Rutland, Vt. Rutland : Warner & McLean, Job Printers. 1864. 18mo.

—*Hygienic Manual,* or How to Restore Health and Secure Longevity. On Rational Principles. By George Dutton. A. M., M. D. Author of "Life and Health," and Professor of Physiology. Rutland : McLean & Robbins, Printers. 1867. 18mo, pp. 84.

Dutton, Salmon. *An Examination of the Doctrine of Endless Misery,* as held by Calvinistic Theologians. Together with a Sketch of the Author's Life, to August, 1819. By Salmon Dutton, Esq. Cavendish, Vt. Boston : Henry Bowen, Printer, 8vo, pp. 62.

The title is partly surmised, as a portion of the title page is missing ; it was printed in 1819 or 1820. The work appears to be in defence of Universalism.

—*Thoughts on God,* Relative to His Moral Character, in comparison with the Character, which reputed Divines have given Him. To which is added a short supplement on the Doctrine of Free Agency ; Also a few observations on Prayer. By Salmon Dutton, Esq. Printed by Eddy and Patrick, Weathersfield, Vt. 1814. 18mo, pp. 102.

Mr. Dutton was an esteemed citizen of Cavendish, and held many offices of trust and honor.

Duty, Mark. *A Remarkable Dream,* or Vision which appeared to Mark Duty, Jr. At Pomfret, Vt., about four o'clock on the Morning of the 29th of November, A. D. 1807. Broadsheet.

Dwinell, Israel Edson. *Hope for our Country.* A Sermon, preached in the South Church Salem, October 19, 1862, by Israel E. Dwinell. Published by request. Salem : Printed by Charles W. Swasey, No. 27 Washington Street. 1862. 8vo, pp. 19.

—*Historical Sketch* of the Pacific Theological Seminary Association, with the Constitution and Board of Trustees. San Francisco : Printed by Town & Bacon. 1867. 8vo, pp. 28.

—*The Higher Reaches of the Great Continental Railway :* A High way for our God. A Sermon preached in the Congregational Church, Sacramento, May 9, 1869. By Rev. I. E. Dwinell, D. D., on the completion of the Overland Railway. Sacramento : H. S. Crocker & Co., Steam Printers. 1869. 8vo, pp. 13.

—*Service of the Suffering.* Sermon preached in the Congregational Church, Sacramento. April 23, 1871. By the Pastor, Rev. I. E. Dwinell. D. D, Printed for private distribution at the request and expense of a Parishioner. Sacramento : E. G. Jeffries, Printer, 1871. 8vo, pp. 13.

—*Memorial Sermon*, Delivered by the Rev. I. E. Dwinell, D. D., at the Congregational Church, Sacramento, California, on June 29, 1873. Sacramento: 1873.

—*Relation of Religion to Civilization*. By Rev. I. E. Dwinell, D. D. Reprinted from the Berkley Quarterly for October, 1881 San Francisco. A. L. Bancroft & Co., Printers. 1881. 12mo, pp. 16.

In addition to the above works, Dr. Dwinell has published many articles of importance in the "New Englander," "Bibliotheca Sacra," "Congregational Quarterly," "Christian World," besides numerous orations, addresses, etc., published in the newspapers.

Rev. I. E. Dwinell, D. D., son of Deacon Israel and Phila (Gilman) Dwinell, was born at East Calais, Vt., October 24, 1820, and died at Oakland, Cal., June 7, 1890. He was graduated at the University of Vermont in 1843, and at Union Theological Seminary, New York, in 1848. He was ordained Colleague Pastor with Rev. Dr. Emerson over the Third Congregational Church, Salem, Mass., November 22, 1849, where he continued until his removal to Sacramento, Cal., in July, 1863, to become pastor of the First Congregational Church of Christ in that city, where he preached for twenty years. From 1883 to his death he was Professor of pastoral theology in the Pacific Theological Seminary at Oakland, Cal.

Dwinell, Melvin. *Common Sense Views of Foreign Lands*. A Series of Letters from the East and from the West. By M. Dwinell. Rome, Ga. Printed at the office of the Courier. 1878. 12mo, pp. 402.

Mr. Dwinell was a brother of Rev. Dr. I. E. Dwinell, and was born at East Calais, Vt., July 9, 1825. He was graduated at the University of Vermont, in 1849, and in 1851 located at Rome, Georgia, and soon after became publisher, proprietor and editor of the Rome Courier, and so continued for many years.

During the civil war, Mr. Dwinell served his State on the side of the Confederacy with credit and honor to himself; he was wounded at the battle of Gettysburg, and went home to Georgia on a furlough; and being elected to the Legislature of his adopted State he did not return to the army. Mr. Dwinell died at Rome, Ga., Dec. 28, 1887.

The above work is a sketch of a four months' trip to southern Europe, Egypt, and the "Holy Land," in the spring and summer of 1876; and includes notes of a trip to California in August and September of that year.

Dwight, Rev. S. Edwards. *Description of the Eruption* of Long Lake and Mud Lake, in Vermont, in the summer of 1810, in a letter to the American Journal of Science. Boston: April 4, 1826. 8vo, pp. 18.

Being an account of Runaway Pond, so called.

Dwight, Timothy. *Travels;* in New England and New York: By Timothy Dwight, S. T. D. LL. D. Late President of Yale College; Author of Theology explained and Defined. In Four Volumes. 3 Maps. New Haven: Published by Timothy Dwight. S. Converse, Printer. 1821-2. 8vo, pp. 524, 527, 534, 527.

Volumes 2 and 4 contain much interesting matter relating to Vermont.

Dwight, Jasper, of Vermont. *A Letter to George Washington*, President of the United States; containing Strictures on his Address of the Seventeenth of September, 1796, notifying his Relinquishment of the Presidential Office. By Jasper Dwight of Vermont. Printed at Philadelphia for the Author. Dec. 1796. 8vo, pp. 48.—*Sabin.*

"Jasper Dwight, of Vermont," was the pseudonym in this instance of Col. Wm. Duane, of Philadelphia; and this slender thread alone connects this book with Vermont. It was Mr. Duane's first published work, and one of the most violent invectives against Washington, being far more abusive than the famous letter of Thomas Paine. A specimen: "Had you obtained promotion, as you expected, for the services rendered after Braddock's defeat, your sword would have been drawn against your country."

Mr. Duane was a warm friend of Jefferson, and a voluminous writer; he was born in the State of New York, near Lake Champlain. William J. Duane was his son.

See Drake's Biog. Dic.

[Dyer, Rev. Heman, D. D.] *The Voice of the Lord in the Waters.* Motto. New York. [1869.] 18mo, pp. 36, Portrait.

Is a narrative of the author's wonderful escape from death in a railroad accident near Hoosick Falls, N. Y., Oct. 4, 1869.

Rev. Heman Dyer was born in Shaftsbury, Vt., Sept. 10, 1810. At the age of six years he removed with his father's family to Manchester. At the age of 17 he was sent to the Academy in Arlington, where he fitted for college. In 1829 he went to Kenyon College, Ohio, an institution then recently founded and presided over by the Rt. Rev. Philander Chase, D. D. In this institution he remained as student or teacher for a little more than ten years. He was ordained as a Deacon in the Episcopal Church in 1834, by the Rt. Rev. C. P. McIlvaine, D. D., D. C. L., then Bishop of the Diocese of Ohio, and a year after he was ordained by the same Bishop as Presbyter.

In 1840 he moved to Pittsburg, Pa., where he had charge of a classical school, until he was elected a Professor in the Western University of Pennsylvania. A year later he was elected the Principal or President of the same. While there he received the degree of D. D. from Trinity College, Hartford, Ct. In 1849 he removed to Philadelphia where for a time he was connected with The American Sunday School Union. In 1852 he visited Europe. In 1854 he removed to New York and became the General Secretary and editor of the Protestant Episcopal Society for the Promotion of Evangelical Knowledge. He also acted as Corresponding Secretary of the Am. Ch. Mis. Society, as one of the managers of the American Bible Society, a member of the foreign committee of the Episcopal Church, a trustee of the Philadelphia Divinity School, of the General Theological Seminary, and a member of the New York Historical Society. In 1868 he made a second visit to Europe. He also visited Mexico in 1875.

He published while in Pittsburg "Sermon Commemorative of Prof. Daniel S. Stone." "An Address to his Bible Class," and while in New York, "The Voice of the Lord upon the Waters," besides numerous Reports upon the work of the Evangelical Knowledge Society and the American Church Missionary Society.

Dr. Dyer is at present (1881) Assistant Minister at the Church of the Ascension, New York City.

Earle, Jabez. *The Christian's Looking Glass,* or Sacramental Exercises: Third Edition. Montpelier, Vt. Published by Walton and Goss. 1817. 18mo, pp. 70.

Eastman, Charles Gamage. *Sermons, Addresses & Exhortations,* by Rev. Jedediah Burchard: with an Appendix, containing some account of proceedings during Protracted Meetings, Held under his direction, in Burlington, Williston, and Hinesburgh, Vt., December, 1835, and January, 1836. By C. G. Eastman. Burlington: Chauncey Goodrich. 1836. 12mo, pp. 119, (1.)

See Withington, Rev. Leonard.
Review of Burchard's Sermons by Eastman.

—*Poems.* By Charles G. Eastman. Montpelier; Eastman & Danforth. 1848. 12mo, pp. 208.

Exceedingly scarce.

—*Poems of Charles G. Eastman.* Montpelier, Vt.: T. C. Phinney, Publisher. 1880. Wright & Potter Printing Company 18 Post Office Square, Boston, Mass. 12mo, pp. xxi, 233.

Contains a fine steel engraved portrait and a biographical sketch of the author. This volume contains poems in the edition of 1848, as revised by the author, together with 23 new poems, among which are "The Old and New," and "Life's Mission," of over 500 lines each.

Charles G. Eastman was born at Fryeburg, Me., June 1, 1816; and died at Montpelier, September 16, 1860. He moved with his parents at an early age to Barnard, Vt.; he was educated at Royalton Academy, Windsor Academy, Kimball Academy, N. H., and at the University of Vermont; while in college he was associate editor of the

Burlington *Sentinel*, 1835-6. In the spring of 1838 he established the *Lamoille Express*, at Johnson, Vt., which he conducted two years, when he moved to Woodstock, and founded the *Spirit of the Age*, which he conducted with much ability until 1846, when he sold the establishment, and entered upon a wider field of labor by purchasing of J. T. Marston the *Vermont Patriot and State Gazette*, published at Montpelier, of which paper he was the editor and proprietor at the time of his death. Mr. Eastman was Postmaster at Woodstock and Montpelier for several years, and was State Senator from Washington county 1851-2. He published many poems in magazines, and his services as poet were in frequent demand at various college commencements. In 1846, Mr. Eastman married Mrs. Susan S. Haveus, daughter of Dr. John D. Powers, of Woodstock; they had one daughter and two sons, the daughter alone survives, and married a Mr. Hartshorn, they residing at Emmettsburg, Iowa, where Mrs. Eastman also resides a part of the time, her home, however, is at Montpelier. O (1880.)

Eastman, F. S. *A History of Vermont* from its First Settlement to the Present Time. With a Geographical Account of the Country, and a view of its Original Inhabitants. For the use of Schools. By F. S. Eastman. Brattleboro: Published by Holbrook and Fessenden. 1828. 16mo, pp. 110.

—*A History* of the State of New York. New York: H. A. White. 1828. pp. 455.

Mr. Eastman was a son of the Rev. Tilton and Experience (Smith) Eastman, and was born in Randolph, Vt., about 1800. He fitted for college at the Orange County Grammar School (Randolph), and was graduated at the University of Vermont in 1827. His life was spent principally in teaching, much of it at Roxbury, Mass. For some time he was employed in the Custom House, Boston. He died in Charlestown, Mass., in 1846, or 1847. *P. H. White.*

Eastman, Rev. Hubbard. *An Address* delivered before the Choir of Singers at an Exhibition of Sacred Music, at Cambridge Port, Vt., May 10, 1838. By Hubbard Eastman. To which is prefixed some Remarks on the Exercises, by Jesse Howard, Esq. Brattleboro: Geo. W. Nichols, Printer. 1838. 12mo, pp. 25.

—*Noyesism Unveiled*; a History of the Self-Styled Perfectionists; with a Summary View of their Leading Doctrines. By Rev. H. Eastman. Brattleboro: published by the Author. 1849. 12mo, pp. 432.

Eastman, Rev. Tilton. *A Sermon* preached in Sharon, Vermont, March 12, 1806, at the Ordination of the Rev. Samuel Bascom. By the Rev. Tilton Eastman, Pastor of the Congregational Church in Randolph, Ver. Hanover, N. H.: Printed by Moses Davis. 1806. 8vo, pp. 31.

—*A Sermon*, delivered at Montpelier, October 13, 1808; Before His Honor the Lieut. Governor, The Honorable Council, and House of Representatives of the State of Vermont. By Tilton Eastman, A. M. Pastor of a Church in Randolph. Published by order of the Legislature. Randolph, (Vermont) Printed by Sereno Wright, State Printer. 1808. 8vo, pp. 31.

Mr. Eastman was born in Amherst, Mass., graduated at Dartmouth College, 1796; and was pastor of the Congregational Church, Randolph, Vt., 1801-1830; and died there. July 8, 1842, aged 68.

East Montpelier. *Annual Reports* of the Officers of the Town of East Montpelier, for the Year Ending March 3, 1876. 8vo, pp. 4.
Continued.

East Smithfield, Pa. *Church Manual.*
See Poultney.

Eaton, Rev. Bennett. *An Essay on Death;* Its Author and Causes. By Rev. Bennett Eaton.

Middlebury: Register Book and Job Printing Establishment. 1866. 16mo, pp. 16.

Mr. Eaton was born in Enosburg, Vt., and died at Crescent, N. Y., March, 1872.

Eaton, Dorman Bridgman. *Supplement to* Chipman's Law of Contracts.
See Chipman, Daniel.

—*Circuit Court* of the United States, Northern District of New York. Ross Winans, against the New York and Erie Railroad Co. General Statement of Facts. N. York: 1856. 8vo, pp. 33.

—*Rail Road Tolls.* Argument of D. B. Eaton, Esq., before the Canal Committee of the New York House of Representatives, February 8, 1861. New York: 1861. 8vo, pp. 67.

—*Metropolitan Health Bill.* Remarks of D. B. Eaton, Esq., at a Joint meeting of the Committees of the Senate and Assembly, Albany, Feb. 2d, 1865, with An Appendix. Published by the Friends of the Bill. New York: 1865. 8vo, pp. 56.

—*Intellect and Education.* Oration before the Alumni of the University of Vermont, by Dorman Bridgman Eaton. August, 1867. [n.p. n.d.] 8vo, pp. 51.

—*Taxation* of the Panama Rail-Road Co. Argument of Mr. Eaton. 1868. New York: 1868. 8vo, pp. 26.

—*U. S. Supreme Court.* Christian E. Detmold against the Central Coal Mining and Manufacturing Company. Argument of Mr. Eaton. New York: 1869. 8vo, pp. 227.

—*The Public Health Association* of New York. A Paper read before the Association, Dec. 8, 1872. By D. B. Eaton, Esq. New York: 1872. 8vo, pp. 46.

—*Our Police Courts.* Speeches of D. B. Eaton, Esq. Before the Judiciary Committee of the General Assembly, Feb. 7th & 13th, 1873. New York; 1873. 8vo, pp. 40.

—*Report* of the Civil Service Commission to the President. April 15, 1874. Washington: Government Printing Office. 1874. 8vo, pp. 98.

—*Civil Service in Great Britain.* A History of abuses and reforms and their bearing upon American politics. By Dorman B. Eaton. Motto. New York: Harper Brothers, 1880. 8vo, pp. XII. (2), 469.

—*Publications* of the Civil Service Reform Association, No. 3. The "Spoils" System and Civil Service. Reform in the Custom-House and Post-Office at New York by Dorman B. Eaton. New York: Published for the Civil Service Reform Association by G. P. Putnam's Sons. 1881. 12mo, pp. viii, 123, (2).

—*Secret Sessions of the Senate.* Their Origin, their Motive, their Object, their Effect. By Dorman B. Eaton, New York: Henry Bessey. 1886, 8vo, pp. 80.

—*The Problem of Police Legislation* in New York City, by Dorman B. Eaton. New York: Geo. P. Putnam's Sons. 1895. 8vo, pp. 32.

Mr. Eaton was born in Hardwick, Vt., in June, 1822, was educated in the common schools, and graduated at University of Vermont in 1848. He read law at Harvard Law School and with the late Chancellor Kent, of New

York, where he began practice as a lawyer in 1850. In 1873 he succeeded George William Curtis as a member of the U. S. Civil Service Commission, and was its chairman till it was dissolved in 1875. In March, 1883, he was made a member of the New Civil Service Commission ; resigned 1885. He edited the Seventh edition of Kent's Commentaries ; drew up the law which created the Board of Health for New York City ; published in 1877 a large volume on the Civil Service of Great Britain of which a second edition was published ; and drafted the U. S. Civil Service law of January 16, 1883.

Eaton, Ebenezer. *Anti-Masonic Almanac* written and printed by Ebenezer Eaton, Danville, 1830–31–32–33–34.
Mr. Eaton was the founder of the *North Star*, which first appeared in 1806, and was in the Eaton family for seventy-five years.
See Almanac.

Eaton, Horace. *Various reports* as State Superintendent of Common Schools, and an Address before the Alumni of Castleton Medical College.
Dr. Eaton was born in Barnard, Vt., June 22, 1804, and was graduated at Middlebury College, 1825. He read medicine and practiced his profession, 1828-1848, at Enosburgh, Vt.; was a Professor in Middlebury College, and held many public offices, from Governor and Lieutenant-Governor of the State, down to Town Representative. Several temperance and other addresses by Dr. Eaton were published. He died July 4, 1855.
See Vermont Historical Magazine, vol. ii, pp. 152-3.

Eaton, Mrs. Marcia Jane (Hall). *Poems,* Printed, Not Published. Baltimore : Steam Press of Wm. K. Boyle & Sons, 1876. 12mo, pp. (6), 62.
A native of Orange county, Vermont. Married Rev. Sylvester Eaton, a Universalist clergyman, and now (1878) they reside in Brattleboro, Vt.

Eddy, Zachary, D. D. *Old Age. A Discourse* in Commemoration of Solomon Stoddard, Esq., of Northampton, Mass., who died October 16, 1860, in the ninetieth year of his age. By Zachary Eddy, D. D. Pastor of the First Church in Northampton. Boston : Press of T. R. Marvin & Son, 42 Congress St. 1860. 8vo, pp. 40.

—*A Discourse* delivered at the Funeral of Charles Augustus Dewey, LL. D., August 25, 1866. By Zachary Eddy, D. D., Pastor of the First Church in Northampton. Worcester : Printed by Edward R. Fiske. 1866. 8vo, pp. 42.

—*The Evangelization of our Country :* a Sermon in Behalf of the American Home Missionary Society, preached in the Broadway Tabernacle Church, New York, May 6, 1877. By Rev. Zachary Eddy, D. D. New York : The American Home Missionary Society. 1877. 8vo, pp. 26.

—*Immanuel ;* or, The Life of Jesus Christ our Lord from his Incarnation to his Ascension. With an Introduction by Rev. Dr. R. S. Storrs. Springfield, Mass : 1868. 8vo, pp. 752.
He was the principal compiler and editor of "Hymns of the Church," (Reformed) 1869, and was associated with Drs. Hitchcock and Schaff in preparing "Hymns and Songs of Praise," 1873. He also preached the sermon before the National Congregational Council in 1877, which was printed in the Minutes of that body. A dozen or more of his sermons and discourses were published. He received the degree of D. D. from Williams College. Dr. Eddy was born in Stockbridge, Vt., Dec. 19, 1815; was not a college graduate; was ordained in 1835; home missionary for several years in New York and Wisconsin; pastor of the Congregational Church, Warsaw, N. Y., 1850-55, Birmingham, Conn., '56-58, 1st Church, Northampton, Mass., '58-67, Ref. Ch., Brooklyn, N. Y., '67-71, Central Ch., Chelsea, Mass., '71-73, 1st Church, Detroit,

Mich, '73-84 ; Atlanta, Ga., 1884-7 ; died at Detroit, Nov. 15, 1891.

Edmunds, George Franklin. *The Life, Character and Services* of Solomon Foot. An Address before the Vermont Historical Society, at Montpelier, October 16, 1866. Montpelier : Walton's Steam Printing Establishment. 1866. 8vo, pp. 28.

—*Speech* of Hon. Geo. F. Edmunds, of Vermont, on the Admission of Nebraska ; Delivered in the Senate, December 19 and 20, 1866. 8vo, pp. 13.

—*Speech* of Hon. Geo. F. Edmunds, of Vermont, on the Joint Resolution Pledging the Faith of the United States to the payment of the Public Debt in Coin or its equivalent ; Delivered in the Senate of the United States, December 4 and 5, 1867. 8vo, pp. 20.

—*Argument* of Hon. Geo. F. Edmunds in the Supreme Court of the United States, February 10, 1871, in the case of Samuel Miller's Executors, Plaintiffs in Error, vs. the United States. Reported by D. F. Murphy. 8vo, pp. 39.

—*Impeachment of the President.* Opinion of Mr. Edmunds, of Vermont, In the Senate of the United States, May 11, 1868. 8vo, pp. 16.

—*Senator from Louisiana.* Speech of Hon. George F. Edmunds, of Vermont, in the United States Senate, March 16, 1875. 8vo, pp. 29.

—*Impeachment* of Wm. W. Belknap, Late Secretary of War. Opinion of Hon. George F. Edmunds, of Vermont, on the Question of Jurisdiction, in the Senate of the United States, May 16 and 17, 1876. 8vo, pp. 13.

—*Canadian Reciprocity Treaty.* Remarks of Hon. George F. Edmunds, of Vermont, in the Senate, January 22, 1875. 8vo, pp. 6.

—*Counting of the Electoral Votes.* Speech of Hon. George F. Edmunds, of Vermont, in the Senate, January 20, 1877. 8vo, pp. 19.

—*Mead's Statue of Ethan Allen.* Speeches of Hons. Justin S. Morrill and George F. Edmunds, of Vermont, in the Senate of the United States, June 10, 1876. 8vo, pp. 12.

—*Payment of Government Bonds.* Speech of Hon. George F. Edmunds, of Vermont, in the Senate of the United States, January 25, 1878. 8vo, pp. 31.

—*Speech* of Mr. Edmunds, of Vermont, in the Senate, on Military interference in Elections, May 9, 1879. Motto. Washington : 1879. 8vo, pp. 32.
See Vermont, Report on Statuary Hall, 1866.
Mr. Edmunds was born in Richmond, Vt., February 1, 1828; studied law, and was admitted to the bar in 1849. In 1851 he moved to Burlington, and was elected to the Legislature in 1854-5-7-8 and 1859, serving three years as Speaker, was in the State Senate in 1861-2, and its President pro tem. On the death of United States Senator Foot he was appointed to fill the vacancy, taking his seat in April, 1866. He had four successive elections as U. S. Senator, but resigned in April, 1891, on the expiration of twenty-five years of service in the Senate. He was a member of the Electoral Commission of 1866, and was elected President pro tem of the U. S. Senate, March 3, 1883. He was the author of the Edmunds law for the suppression of polygamy in Utah, and of many important public measures.

Edmunds—Olin. Spear—Bennet. *The Genealogical Record* of James Edmunds, corresponding Secretary of the American Bible Revision Association, who was born in Clarendon, Rutland County, Vermont, February 15, 1806, and died in Louisville, Kentucky, Feb. 9, 1861, and of his wife Cordelia Spear, who was born in Macedon, Wayne County, N. Y., and died in Hamilton, Madison County, New York, May 8, 1843. So far extended as to include first cousins. Louisville: Bradley & Gilbert, Printers. n. d. 8vo, pp. 88.

Edson, Jesse. *A Discourse,* delivered to the Young People of Halifax, October 17th, 1799, and made public at their request. By Jesse Edson, A. M. Pastor of the Congregational church in Halifax. Texts. Printed at Greenfield, Massachusetts, by Thomas Dickman. n. d. 8vo, pp. 23.

Mr. Edson was born in Buckland, Mass., in 1773; was graduated at Dartmouth College in 1794; studied divinity with Rev. John Emerson, of Conway, Mass.; was pastor of the Congregational Church in Halifax, Vt., 1796, till he died, December 14, 1805.

Edson, Ptolemy O'Meara. *Address* by P. O'Meara Edson, M. D., of Boston, Mass., delivered at the Second Annual Meeting of the First Vermont Cavalry Reunion Society at Montpelier, Nov. 4, 1874. Burlington : 1874. 8vo, pp. 15.

Dr. Edson is a native of Vermont ; he graduated from the University of Vt. in 1857, and from the Medical department of the University in 1860 ; practiced in Chester ; was Assistant Surgeon of the First Regiment, Vermont Cavalry, Nov. 5, 1861 to April 1, 1864 ; Surgeon Seventeenth Regiment Vermont Volunteers, April 1, '64 to February 27, '65. Removed to Roxbury, Mass., after the close of the Civil War, where he is still (1896) practicing his profession.

EDUCATIONAL.

The following educational titles are arranged alphabetically under the names of the institutions, as far as practicable.

We sent circulars to every institution in the State, of the classes here noticed, asking for information, to many of which no response was received. We are of the opinion that about one-third of the institutions in the State entitled to notice here are not represented.

—*Programme of Exhibition* At the close of the Winter Term of Mr. & Mrs. Ames' School. Charlotte, Vt. January, 20, 1860. 12mo, pp. (4.)

—*The Forty-Eighth Annual Meeting* of the American Institute of Instruction, will be held in Union School Hall, Montpelier, Vt.,; July 10th, 11th and 12th, 1877. Order of Exercises. 8vo, pp. 4.

—*Catalogue* of the Officers and Students of Bakersfield Academical Institution, for the year ending November, 1847. Burlington : Chauncey Goodrich. 1847. 12mo, pp. 23.
Continued.

—*Sixth Annual Catalogue* of Barre Academy, Barre, Vermont, for the year ending November, 1857. Montpelier: Printed at the Vermont Patriot Press. 8vo, pp. 19.
Continued.

—*The Origin* and Basis of Barre Academy, with an Address by the Prudential Committee. Windsor : Printed at the Vermont Chronicle Press. 1854. 12mo, pp. 12.

—*Announcement of Beeman Academy,* 1870-71. Catalogue of New Haven Academy. 1868-70 : and History, 1855-70. New Haven, Vermont. Burlington : R. S. Styles, Book and Job Printer. 1870. 8vo, pp. 22.
Continued.

—*Catalogue,* Rules, Regulations, and Course of Instruction of Bennington Graded School District. Bennington : Banner Steam Printing Establishment. 1877. 8vo, pp. 76.
Continued.

—*Catalogue* of the Officers and Students of Black River Academy, Ludlow, Vt. For the Academic Year 1849-50. Rutland : G. A. Tuttle. Printer. Herald Office. 1850. 8vo, pp, 16.
Continued.

—*Catalogue* of the Officers and Students of Bradford Academy, Bradford, Vt. Published November, 1865. Bradford, Vt. W. W. Curtis, Printer. 1865. 8vo, pp. 14.
Continued.
Founded in 1820.

—*Catalogue* of Books in the Merrill Library, Bradford Academy, January 1, 1878.. Bradford, Vt.: B. F. Stanton, Printer. 1878. 8vo, pp. 46.

—*Catalogue* of the Officers, Teachers and Pupils of the Brandon Graded School, at Brandon, Vt., For Two Years Ending June 16, 1876. Brandon : Mott Bros' Union Print. 1876. 8vo, pp. 30.
Continued.

—*Catalogue* of the Officers and Students of the Brandon Seminary, Brandon, Vt. Fall Term, 1859. Bellows Falls, Vt. Printed at the Phœnix Job Printing Office. 1859. 8vo, pp. 15.
Continued.

—*Catalogue* of the Officers and Students of Brattleboro Academy, West Brattleboro, Vt. 1874-5. Brattleboro: Printed by Geo. E. Selleck. 1875. 8vo, pp. 12.

Continued.
Was Chartered in 1801; Charter renewed in 1821.
For a few years its property was leased to "Glenwood Seminary."

—*Catalogue* of the Officers and Students of Bristol Academy, for the Academical year 1858-9. Burlington : Daily Times Book and Job Office. 1859. 8vo, pp. 16.
Continued.

—*A Catalogue* of the Officers and Students of the Burlington Union High School, For the year 1853. Burlington : Stacy & Jameson, Printers. 1853. 8vo, pp. 20.
Continued.

—*Twenty-Fourth Annual Catalogue* of the Trustees, Instructors and Students of Burr Seminary, Manchester, Vt. For the Year Ending July 9, 1856. Windsor : Printed at the Chronicle Press. 1856. 8vo, pp. 16.
Continued.

—*Proceedings* of the Re-Union at the Burr and Burton Seminary, Manchester, Vt., June 27 & 28, 1871. New York: 1872. 8vo, pp. 40.

—*History* of Burr Seminary. Am. Quar. Register, 1840, vol. xiii., pp. 34-7.

—*Catalogue* of the Officers and Students of Caledonia County Grammar School, Peacham, Vt. For the year Ending November, 1853. Windsor : Printed at the Vermont Chronicle Press. 1853. 8vo, pp. 16.
Continued.

—*Catalogue* of the officers and Students of Caledonia County Academy of Peacham, Vt. For the Academical year, 1870. Montpelier :

Poland's Steam Printing Establishment. 1870.
8vo, pp. 12.
Continued.

—*Catalogue* of the Corporation, Officers and
Students of Castleton Seminary, For the year
ending July 17, 1861. Rutland: Geo. A.
Tuttle & Co., Printers. 1861. 8vo, pp. 15.
Continued.

—*Castleton Seminary* Memorial Anniversary,
Wednesday, June 29th, 1870. Rutland: Tuttle
& Company, Printers. 1870. 8vo, pp. 47.
  Contains an address by Hon. Henry Clark, giving a
history of the institution, from its charter in 1787, under
the name of the Rutland County Grammar School, and
much other matter.

—*Catalogue* of the Trustees, Instructors, Stu-
dents and Patrons of Chester Academy. For the
Year Ending June 1st, 1872. Rutland: Tuttle
& Company, Printers. 1872. 8vo, pp. 15.
Continued.

—*Catalogue* of the Classical and English
Boarding School, Norwich, Vt., For the Year
Ending June 24, 1868. Montpelier: Printed at
Freeman Steam Printing Establishment. 1868.
8vo, pp. 17.
Continued.

—*Essex Classical Institute*, Essex, Vermont.
W. A. Deering, A. B. Principal, Geo. W.
Swain, Assistant. Miss Mary A. Powell,
Teacher of Music. L. C. Butler, M. D. Pres-
dent.
  Circular.
  June, 1877. 8vo, pp. 4.

—*Catalogue* of the Officers, Instructors and
Students of Essex Classical Institute, Essex,
Vt. 1877-8. Montpelier, Vt.: Argus and
Patriot Job Printing House. 1878. 8vo, pp.
(18).
Continued.

—*Catalogue* of the Teachers and Members of
the Essex County Teachers Institute, Holden
at Lunenburg, Vt., March, 1851. With Reports of Committees, Resolutions, &c. Published by a Committee of the Members. Newbury, Vt. L. J. McIndoe, Printer. 12mo, pp.
12.

—*Catalogue* of the Officers and Students of
the Georgia, (Vt.) Academy, For the year Ending November 17, 1852. St. Albans, Vt.
Printed at the Messenger Press. 1852. 8vo,
pp. 16.
Continued.

—*Historical Sketch and Catalogue* of Goddard
Seminary. Barre, Vt. 1872. Montpelier:
Poland's Steam Printing Establishment. 1872.
8vo, pp. 24.
  Chartered in 1863; building completed in 1869; first
graduations, 1870.
Continued.

—*Green Mountain Perkins Academy.* Semi-
Annual Exhibition, Wednesday Evening, De-
cember 17, 1875. At National Hall, South
Woodstock, Vt. Music: Woodstock Orches-
tra. 12mo, pp. (4).
Continued.

—*Twenty-Eighth Annual Catalogue* of the
Officers and Students of Green Mountain
Perkins Academy, South Woodstock, Vt., for
the year ending November 21, 1877. Woodstock, Vt.: Luther O. Greene. Printer. 1877.
8vo, pp. 19.
  Continued.

—*Second Annual Catalogue* of the Officers,
Instructors and Pupils of Glenwood Ladies'
Seminary, For the Year Ending July 17, 1862.
"The Gem cannot be polished without fric-
tion." West Brattleboro. Geo. A. Tuttle &
Co., Printers, Rutland. 1862. 8vo, pp. 24.
Continued.

—*Catalogue* of the Corporation, Teachers, and
Students, of Hinesburgh, (Vt.) Academy, For
the Year Ending November, 1849. Burlington: Sentinel Office Print. 1849. 8vo, pp.
10, (6).
Continued.

—*Catalogue* of the Officers and Students of
Lamoille County Grammar School, Johnson,
Vt. For the year Ending November, 1859.
Burlington: D. A. Danforth, Printer, 1859.
8vo, pp. 16.
  Merged into the State Normal School at the same place,
in 1866.

—*Catalogue* of the Officers and Students of
Leland Seminary, Townsend, Vt., for the
Academical year 1847-8. Hanover: Printed
at the Dartmouth Press, November, 1848 8vo,
pp. 16.
Continued.

— *Catalogue* of the officers and Students of
Lyndon Academy, for the quarter ending Nov.
21, 1834. Danville, Vt. Printed by E. Eaton,
1834. 16mo, pp. 8.
Continued.

—*First Annual Catalogue* of Marlborough
High School. Term commencing Aug. 19th,
1861; Ending Nov. 1st, 1861. Marlborough, Vt.
Brattleboro: Printed by George E. Selleck.
1861. 8vo, pp. 8.
Continued.

—*Catalogue* of the Officers and Students of
Middlebury Female Seminary. Middlebury:
Printed by Ovid Miner. 1830. 12mo, pp. 8.

—*Catalogue* of the Officers and Students of the
New Hampton Academical and Theological
Institution, year Ending October, 1847. Bos-
ton: Printed by Damrell & Moore. 1847.
12mo, and 8vo, pp. 24.
  Continued.
  Located at Fairfax, Vt.

—*17th Annual Catalogue* of Newbury
Seminary, and Female Collegiate Institute,
Newbury, Vt., 1850. L. J. M'Indoe, Printer.
1850. 8vo, pp. 24.
Continued.

—*First Triennial Catalogue* of the Newbury
Female Collegiate Institute, Issued by the
Esthetic Society, Newbury, Vt., Spring Term.
1853. L. J. M'Indoe, Printer, Newbury, Vt.
8vo, pp. 16.
Continued.

—*Circular* of the New Hampton Institution,
in Fairfax, Vt. 1853. Rutland: Tuttle &
Co. Printers. 8vo, pp. 8.

—*First Annual Catalogue* of the Officers, In-
structors & Students of North Bennington
Academy, For the year Ending Dec. 1, 1862.
North Bennington, Vt. Bennington: J. I. C.
Cook & Son, Printers. 1862. 8vo, pp. 16.
Continued.

—*Catalogue of the Officers and Students* of
Northfield Institution, from March to Novem-

ber, 1867. Northfield, Vt. Printed for the Institution, November, 1867. 8vo, pp. 16.
Continued.

—*North Western Branch* of the American Education Society. Constitution of. Middlebury, Vt. Printed by Francis Burnap. 1819. 16mo, pp. 9.

—*North Western Branch* of the American Educational Society.
See Peters, Absalom, Sermon and Report, 1824; Walker, Charles, Sermon and Report, 1826; Bates, Joshua, Sermon and first Report, 1821.

—*A Catalogue of the Officers and Students* of Orange County Grammar School, at Randolph, Vt. For the year ending December, 1844. Montpelier : J. T. Marston, Printer. 1844. 8vo, pp. 8.

—*Orange County Grammar School.* Edward Conant Principal. (Located at Randolph Center.) 1863. 8vo, pp. 8.
Was established in 1806 ; and continued until merged in the State Normal School at the same place in 1868.

—*Catalogue* of the Officers and Students of Orleans County Grammar School, for the year 1840. Concord, N. H. Printed by Asa McFarland. 1841. 12mo, pp. 12.
Continued.

—*Eleventh Annual Catalogue* of the Peoples Academy, For the Academical Year Ending November 18, 1857. Morrisville, Vt. Irasburgh : A. A. Earle, Printer. 1857. 8vo, pp. 23.
Continued.

—*Catalogue* of the Trustees, Officers and Students of Phillips Academy, Danville, Vt., for the year ending November 26, 1845. Danville : N. H. Eaton, Printer. 1845. 8vo, pp. 12.
Continued.

—*Catalogue* of the Trustees, Principal and Students of Randolph Academy. for the year ending August 14th, 1835. Montpelier : Knapp and Jewett, Printers. 1835. 12mo, pp. 12.

—*Report* of the Minority of the Committee on Education, on Senate Bill, No. 11, Entitled an Act in Amendment of Section Seventy One, Chapter Twenty, of the Compiled Statutes, Relating to Common Schools. O. G. Wheeler, For the Minority. Montpelier : Freeman Print. 1860. 8vo, pp. 8.

—*Catalogue* of the Royalton Academy, Royalton, Vt., For the Sixty-Fourth Year. October, 1871. Middlebury : Printed at the Register Job Office. 1871. 8vo, pp. 16.
Continued.

—*Catalogue* of the Officers and Students of the Rutland Graded School District for The Year 1872-3. Rutland : Tuttle & Co., Printers. 1873. 8vo, pp. 28.
Continued.

—*Catalogue* of the Officers and Students of the Rutland Union High School, for the year 1864-5. Rutland : Tuttle, Gay & Company. 1865. 8vo, pp. 24.
Continued.

—*Catalogue* of the Officers and Students of Saxton's River Seminary, Saxton's River, Vt. Nov., 1848. Bellows Falls, Vt.: Printed by John W. Moore. 1848. 12mo, pp. 15.
Continued.

—*Catalogue* of the Officers and Students of Shoreham Central High School, for the Academic Term Ending November 19th, 1875. Rutland : Tuttle & Co., Printers. 1875. 8vo, pp. 8.
Continued.

—*Catalogue* of St. Johnsbury Academy, St. Johnsbury, Vt., for the Academical year ending June, 1876. Montpelier : Printed by J. & J. M. Poland. 1876. 8vo, pp. 27, (4).
Continued.

—*A Catalogue* of the Officers and Students of Townsend Academy, Townsend, Vt. For the Academical Year 1843-4. Bellows Falls : Printed by S. M. Blake. 1844. 12mo, pp. 16.
Name changed to Leland Seminary in 1846.

—*A Quarterly Journal* Devoted to Female Education, Published by Ripley Female College, Poultney, Vt. Vol. II. January, 1867. No. 4. Rutland : Tuttle & Co., Printers. 1867. 8vo, pp. 32.
Continued.

—*The Claims of the Bible* to a Place in our Schools. An Address by Rev. J. E. Rankin, of St. Albans, Vt., Delivered before the Vermont Teachers' Association, at St. Johnsbury, Aug. 15, 1860 ; also read before the North-Western Association at Milton, Aug. 22, and published by request. St. Albans : Printed by E. B. Whiting, 1860. 8vo, pp. 19.

—*The School Journal* and Agriculturist. Volume Second. Windsor : Published by Bishop and Tracy 1848-9. Printed at the Chronicle Steam Press. rl 8vo, pp. 192.
Monthly Parts.

—*Catalogue* of the Instructors and Students of St. Johnsbury Academy, St. Johnsbury, Vt., 1844. Concord: McFarland's Press—Main Street. November, 1844. 8vo, pp. 11.
Continued.

—*Circular* of the Temple Grove Ladies' Seminary, Saratoga Springs, N. Y. containing a Brief Statement concerning the Buildings, Grounds, the General Plan of Education, Expenses, &c. Rutland : Tuttle & Co., Printers. 1868. 8vo, pp. 16.

—*The Teachers' Voice,* and Vermont Monthly Magazine. By Z. K. Pangborn. We Build School-Houses and Raise Men. Published with the Sanction of the Vermont Teachers' Association. Burlington : Chauncey Goodrich. January, 1853. No. 1, of Vol 1. 8vo, pp. 32.
And 10 pp. of Advertisements. No. 4 of Vol. 1 was printed at St. Albans, January, 1854.

—*Catalogue* of the Officers and Students of Thetford Academy and Boarding School, Thetford, Vt., for the Academical Year 1870. Hanover, N. H.: Printed at the Dartmouth Press. 1870. 8vo, pp. 15.
Continued.

—*Catalogue* of the Officers and Students of Underhill Academy, Underhill Flats, Vt., For the Year Ending 1860. Burlington : Daily Times Job Printing Establishment. 1860. 8vo, pp. 16.
Continued.

—*Fifteenth Circular and Catalogue* of the Academical Department of the Vermont Episcopal Institute, Burlington, Vermont. Burlington: Free Press Steam Job Print. 1874. 8vo, pp. 18.

—*Nineteenth Circular and Catalogue* of the Academical Department of the Vermont Episcopal Institute, for Boys, Burlington, Vt., Principal, The Rev. Theodore Austin Hopkins, A. M. Burlington: Free Press Steam Book and Job Printing House. 1878. 8vo, pp. 38.
Continued.

—*Vermont School Journal,* and Family Visitor: Devoted to the Educational Interests of Vermont. Montpelier: Published by a Committee appointed by the Vermont State Teachers' Association. Printed at the Freeman Office. Volume I. April 1859 to April 1860. 8vo, pp. 316, (2).
Published monthly, at one dollar per year, and continued until 1862, or after; vol. 3 bears the imprint West Brattleboro, Vt.

—*First Annual Catalogue* of the Vermont Conference Seminary and Female College, For the Academic Year, 1869. (Names of Students of five Terms.) Seminary Hill, Montpelier, Vermont. Montpelier: Freeman Steam Printing House and Bindery. 1869. 8vo, pp. 24.
Continued.

—*Catalogue* of the Vermont Methodist Seminary and Female College, 1876-'77. Seminary Hill, Montpelier, Vt. MDCCCLXXVI. 8vo, pp. 30, (1). No imprint.
Continued.

—*Thirty Second Annual Report* of the Directors of the Vermont Education Society, Auxiliary to the American Education Society. Presented at Windsor, June 22, 1853. Windsor: Printed at the Vermont Chronicle Press. 1853. 8vo, pp. 12.
Continued.

—*Vermont State Teachers Association.* Twenty Third Annual Meeting at Rutland, Thursday and Friday, Jan. 30, and 31, 1873. Journal Job Print, Manchester, Vt. 12mo, pp. (4).
Order of Exercises.
Continued.

—*Catalogue* of the Officers and Students of the Vermont State Normal School, at Johnson, for 1872-3. With full list of the Graduates. Burlington: Free Press Steam Book and Job Office. 1873. 8vo, pp 23.
Continued.

—*Catalogue* of the Officers and Students of the Vermont State Normal School, at Randolph Center, for 1869. Montpelier: Freeman Steam Printing House and Bindery. 1869. 8vo, pp. 16.
Continued.

—*Catalogue* of the State Normal School, at Castleton, Vermont. 1872-73. Rutland: Tuttle & Co., Printers. 1873. 8vo, pp. 15.
Continued.

—*English Literature in Schools.* An Address delivered before the Vermont State Teachers' Association, at Rutland, January 31st, 1873. By Ezra Brainerd, Professor of Rhetoric, Middlebury College. Rutland: Tuttle & Co., Printers. 1873. 8vo, pp. 11.

—*Ward's Seminary,* Saxton's River, Vt. Order of Exercises at the Annual Exhibition, Nov. 14th and 15th, 1853. 12mo, pp. (4).
Continued.

—*Catalogue* of the Trustees, Teachers and Students connected with the Washington County Grammar School, Montpelier, Vt., during the year ending July 25th, 1832. E. P. Walton, Printer, Montpelier, Vt. 12mo, pp. 8.

—*Catalogue* of the instructors and students of the Washington County Teachers' Institute, together with the Reports of Committees, Resolutions, etc. Holden at Berlin, April, 1847, Montpelier: E. P. Walton & Sons, Printers, 8vo, pp. 8.

—*Catalogue* of the Teachers and Students of Washington County Grammar School, Montpelier, Vt., For the Year Ending November, 1851. Printed for the Grammar School. Press of C. G. Eastman, State Street. 1851. 8vo, pp. 12.
Incorporated in 1800, and continued in successful operation until merged in the present Union School, etc., in 1858-9.

—*Annual Catalogue* of the Montpelier Union School, and Washington County Grammar School, for the year closing June 24. 1870. Montpelier, Vt.: Argus and Patriot Job Printing House. 1870. 8vo, pp. (16).
Continued.

—*Order of Exercises.* Washington County Grammar School, Montpelier, Vt. Friday, June 27, 1873, at 2 P. M. Music by the Union School. Levee at 8 o'clock in the evening. Music by House's Band. 12mo, pp. (4).

—*Catalogue* of the Washington County Grammar School Library, May 1, 1860. Montpelier: E. P. Walton, Printer. 1860. 8vo, pp. 15, (1),

—*Westminster Seminary.* Order of Exercises at the Semi-Annual Examination, May 14th, 15th and 16th, 1855. 12mo, pp. (4).
Continued.

—*Catalogue* of the Officers and Students of Westminster Seminary, for the First Three Terms of the Institution. November, 1850. Windsor: Printed at the Chronicle Press. 1850. 8vo, pp. 16.
Continued.

—*Catalogue* of the Teachers and Students of Wilmington High School, Wilmington, Vt. For the Fall Term, 1859. Brattleboro: J. H. Capen, Printer, 1859. 8vo, pp. 8.
Continued.

—*Catalogue* of the Officers and Students of West Randolph Academy, West Randolph, Vt., For the Academical Year, 1860. Montpelier: Printed at the Freeman Printing Establishment. 1860. 8vo, pp. 16.
Continued.

—*Biennial Catalogue* of the Officers, Teachers and Students of Williston Academy, at Williston, Vermont; November 1866. Free Press Steam Job Printing Office, 1866. 8vo, pp. 14, (6).
Continued.
See Vermont, Educational, Reports of State Superintendent, Secretary of the Board of Education, &c.; University of Vermont; Middlebury College; Norwich University; Hinman, C. T., Address, Newbury Seminary, 1841.

Edwards, Rev. John H. *Life given, not lost:* a Sermon, in Memory of Capt. Charles C. Morey, of the Second Vermont Regiment, preached in the Church, West Lebanon, N. H., May 14, 1865. By the Pastor, Rev. John H. Edwards. Hanover, N. H. Printed at the Dartmouth Press, 1865. 8vo, pp. 12.

Edwards, Peter. *Candid Reasons* for renouncing the Principles of Antipædobaptism, with an Appendix. 2d ed. Windsor, Vt. 1802. 12mo.

Egerton, Mrs. Emily. *Of Randolph, Vt.* Memoirs of.
See Nutting, R.

Elbridge, L. B. *The Torrent;* or an Account of a Deluge occasioned by an unparalleled rise of the New-Haven River, in which nineteen persons were swept away, five of whom only escaped, July 26th, 1830. By Lemuel B. Elbridge. Middlebury: Printed at the Office of the Free Press, by E. D. Barber. 1831. 12mo, pp. 61.

Elegant Poems. *Selected* from the writings of Goldsmith, Parnel, Pope, Watts, Blair, Cowper, &c. Bennington, Vt. Printed by Anthony Haswell. 1808. 18mo, pp. 115.

Elementary Law.
See Redfield, I. F.; Kinsman, J. B.; Smith, Chauncey; Roberts, William; Bennett, E. H.; Crabb, George; Dean, Amos; Bennett, Milo L.; Chalmers, George; Chittenden, L. E.

Elkins, Rev. Hervey. *A Discourse* on Modern Spiritualism, Delivered at Burlington, Vt., March 17, 1858. By Rev. Hervey Elkins, Universalist Minister at Williston, Vt. Burlington: George J. Stacy, Book and Job Printer. 1858. 8vo, pp. 32.

Elliot, James. *The Poetical* and Miscellaneous Works of James Elliot, Citizen of Guilford, Vt., and late a Non-Commissioned Officer in the Legion of the United States. In Four Books. Greenfield, Mass.: Printed for the Author. M,DCCXCVIII. 12mo, pp. 271, (5).
"Very rare. Only 300 copies printed. Contains a journal of his three years' services, from 1793 to 1796, and much other information."—*Sabin.*
Title from Sabin's Bibliography; the date given there, 1698, is evidently an error, and should read, 1798, as we give it.
Hon. James Elliot was born at Gloucester, Mass., August 18, 1775. His father died at sea, when he was an infant and his mother subsequently removed to New Salem, Mass., among her relatives. His early life was one of privation and toil. At the age of seven he went to work for Capt. Sanderson, a merchant and farmer at Petersham, Mass. Here he remained seven years and then went to Guilford, Vt., where he became clerk in a store. His spare moments were devoted to reading and study and he early developed an ardent patriotism, with strong proclivities for political discussion and writing. In his eighteenth year, he went to Springfield, Mass., and enlisted for the Indian war, July 12, 1793, as the first non-commissioned officer of a new company in the Second United States Sub-Legion, commanded by Capt. Cornelius Lyman. He served with honor throughout the war and returned to Guilford, August 23, 1796. Here he kept store and studied law, and about 1800 began to practice at the bar, occupying an office with his brother Samuel, in Brattleboro, Vt., which then became his home. He married Lucy Dow, daughter of General Dow, of New Hampshire, by whom he had two children, James Madison and Mary. The latter only survived him. He was Clerk of the Vermont House of Representatives in 1801 and 1802; Representative in Congress from 1803 to 1809; Representative to the State Legislature in in 1818 and 1819; Clerk of Windham County Court in 1819 and 1820, and continuously from 1826 to 1836 inclusive; Register of Probate from December 26, 1822 to November 30, 1834; State's Attorney in 1837 and 1838, and Justice of the Peace twenty-one successive years. He died November 10, 1839, in his 65th year.

Elliot, Rev. L. H. *Manly Strength.* A Sermon to Young Men, by Rev. L. H. Elliott, delivered in the Congregational Church of Bradford, Vt., Nov. 14th, 1875. Bradford, Vt.: Ben. F. Stanton, Book and Job Printer, and Stationer. 1876. 12mo, pp. 9.

—*A Sermon Commemorative* of the Life and Labors of Rev. Silas McKeen, D. D. Preached in Bradford, Vt., December 16th, 1877, by Rev. L. H. Elliot, Minister of the Congregational Church of Bradford. Published by request. Montpelier: J. & J. M. Poland, Steam Book and Job Printers. 1878. 8vo, pp. 19.

—*Pastoral Greeting* of Rev. L. H. Elliot, Bradford, Vt. 1876. 12mo, pp. 4.

—*The Same,* 1877. 12mo, pp. 4.

—*Pastoral Letter,* 1878. 12mo, pp. 4.

—*Memorial* of Mrs. M. P. S. Prichard, wife of Dea. G. W. Prichard. [Of Bradford, Vt.] Free Press Association. Burlington. 1879. Small 4to, pp. 24, (1).
Rev. Lester Hall Elliot was born in Croyden, N. H., August 1, 1835, and with his father's family moved to Jericho, Vt., in 1841. He was graduated at the University of Vermont in 1861, and at Union Theological Seminary, New York, in 1864. After preaching short periods in different places, he became pastor of the Congregational church at Bradford, Vt., in December, 1872, as successor of the Rev. Dr. McKeen, where he remained till 1880; subsequently removed to Waterbury, was appointed Corresponding Secretary of the Vermont Bible Society in 1885, which office he still (1896) holds.
We are indebted to Rev. Mr. Elliot for many favors in connection with the active interest he has manifested in this work.

Elliott, Samuel. *Oration* at West Springfield, (Mass.), July Fourth, Eighteen Hundred and Three. By Samuel Elliott, Esq. Bennington, Vt: Printed by A. Haswell & Co. 1803. 8vo, pp. 24.

—*An Oration,* Delivered at Brattleboro, Vt., February 22, 1812. At the Public Celebration of Washington's Birthday. By Samuel Elliot, Esq. Together with an Address, to the Washington Benevolent Society. By Jonathan Hunt, Jr., Esq. Brattleborough, Vt.: Printed by William Fessenden. 1812. 8vo, pp. 8.
Mr. Elliot dropped one t from his name, or the printer added one in the first title as above.

—*An Address* to the members of the Washington Benevolent Society, and Publick, delivered at the Semi-annual meeting of the county Society, of Windham County, Vt. at Newfane, June 11, 1812. By Samuel Elliot, Esq. Brattleborough: Wm. Fessenden. 1812.

—*Oration,* pronounced at Brattleborough, Vt., before the Washington Benevolent Societies, July 6, 1813, in Commemoration of American Independence. Brattleborough, Vt. 1813. 8vo.

—*A Voice* from the Green Mountains, on the Subject of Masonry and Antimasonry. By Samuel Elliot, Esq. Printed at Brattleboro', (Vermont,) by George W. Nichols. 1834. 8vo, pp. 32.

—*An Humble Tribute* to my Country: or Practical Essays, Political, Legal, and Miscellaneous, including a brief Account of the Life, Sufferings, and Memorable visit of General Lafayette. "'Tis all that I can give." By Samuel Elliot. Boston, Published by Otis, Broaders and Company, 1842. 18mo, pp. 240, v.
Judge Samuel Elliot, brother of James, was born in Gloucester, Mass., August 16, 1777. His father, who was a seaman, died at sea before his birth. His early years accustomed him to hardships, and his facilities for edu-

cation were meagre enough. As a young man he was clerk in a store at Guilford, Vt. About 1800, he opened a law office in Brattleboro, Vt., with his brother James, and soon became one of the more prominent of the earlier settlers of the town. He was a life-long public man in the best sense, with unblemished integrity, warm sympathies and ready versatility of talent. He served as postmaster during Jefferson's second term; was Register of Probate in 1807, 1808, 1813, 1814, 1838 and 1839; Representative in the Vermont Legislature in 1813, 1814, 1815, 1822, 1823, 1828 and 1829; State's Attorney in 1814, 1822, 1823, and 1824; Member of the Constitutional Convention in 1814; Judge of Probate in 1829 and 1830; Associate Judge of Windham County Court in 1844 and 1845, and Justice of the Peace for 27 successive years. He married Fanny Foster May 26th, 1805, and by her had one son. She died July 26, 1806, in her 23d year. November 24, 1808, he married widow Linda Hayes Pease, an aunt of President Rutherford B. Hayes, who bore him three sons and four daughters, and died January 5, 1833, 50 years and 11 months old. November 19, 1834, he married Sophia Flint, and by her had two daughters and two sons. She died December 27, 1845, in her 36th year. Samuel Elliot died in Brattleboro, Vt., December 10, 1845, leaving nine children living. His wife survived him but a few days.

Elliot, Rev. Samuel Hayes. *Rolling Ridge,* or the Book of Four and Twenty Chapters. Boston : Crocker and Brewster, 1838. 12mo, pp. 226.

—*The Sequel to Rolling Ridge,* by the Author of the latter, assisted by the worthy Mr. Fory. Boston : Crocker & Brewster, 1844. 12mo, pp. 248.

—*Emily Maria :* a True Narrative. By Rev. Samuel H. Elliot. New York : American Tract Society, 1846. 12mo, pp. 72.

—*The Parish Side.* By the author of some other books, and Clerk of the Parish of Edgefield. With illustrations. New York : Mason Brothers, 23 Park Row, 1854. 12mo, pp. 258.

—*Dreams and Realities* in the Life of a Pastor and Teacher. By the Author of "Rolling Ridge," "The Parish-Side," etc. New York : J. C. Derby, 119 Nassau St. Boston : Phillips, Sampson & Co. Cincinnati : H. W. Derby. 1856. 12mo, pp. 439.

—*New England's Chattels :* or, Life in the Northern Poor-House. New York : H. Dayton publisher, 107 Nassau St. 1858. 12mo, pp. 484.
A later edition of this book was published under the title "A Look at Home."

—*The Attractions* of New Haven, Conn. A Guide to the City, with Map and Illustrations. By S. H. Elliot, author of "Rolling Ridge," "Parish-Side," "Dreams and Realities," "New England's Chattels," etc. New York : N. Tibbals & Co. 1869. 12mo, pp. 141.
Samuel Hayes Elliot, son of Samuel Elliot, ante, was born at Brattleboro, Vt., October 23, 1809; graduated at Union College, Schenectady, N. Y., in 1841; studied Theology at New Haven, Conn.; was pastor of the Congregational church at Woodbridge, New Haven county, Conn., and subsequently at Westville, a suburb of New Haven, where he also started and conducted the West Rock Seminary until his health failed, in 1855, when he removed to New Haven. Through his remaining years of declining health he preserved a remarkable buoyancy of spirit, and busied himself in literary and mercantile pursuits until his death, which occurred September 11, 1869. He left a wife and four children.
Mr. J. H. Elliot, to whom we are indebted for most of our information in relation to the Brattleboro branch of the Elliot family, is a newspaper man ; he wrote us under date of Brattleboro, May 9, 1878: "I was one of the editors and proprietors of the Home Journal, New York, five years, and have been a newspaper writer all my life, but have never yet published in book form."
We believe Mr. Elliot has recently (1879,) resumed his position on the Home Journal. He was a son of Edwin Day Elliot, who was an elder brother of Rev. Samuel Hayes Elliot.

Ellis, Charles, Esq. *The Law of Fire and Life Insurance,* with Practical Observations. Part I. The Law of Fire Insurance. Part II. The Law of Life Insurance. By Charles Ellis, Esq., of Lincoln's Inn, Barrister at Law. Second American from the last English Edition, with Notes, Additions and References to American and late English Decisions, by William G. Shaw. Burlington : Chauncey Goodrich. 1854. 8vo, pp. 326.

Emerson, B. D. *First Class Reader:* A Selection for exercises in reading, from standard British and American Authors, in prose and verse. For the use of schools in the United States. By B. D. Emerson, Late Principal of the Adams Grammar School, Boston. Windsor, Vt.: Published by Ide and Goddard. 1834. 12mo, pp. 276.

Emerson, E. and Boyce, J. *Series of Letters* between Enoch Emerson and Joseph Boyce, relative to the Excommunication of said Emerson and others, from the Congregational Church, in Rochester, &c. Windsor, Vt. 1815. 8vo.

Emerson, Frederick. *Emerson's Second Part.* The North American Arithmetic. Part Second, uniting Oral and Written Exercises in Corresponding chapters. By Frederick Emerson, Late Principal in the Department of Arithmetic, Boylston School, Boston. Windsor: Nathan C. Goddard. 1841. 12mo, pp. 190, (2).

Emerson, John D. *In Memoriam.* Died at Underhill, Vt., Sept. 11, 1877, Miss Nellie Jane Holmes, aged 22 years, a native of Fairfax, Vt. 8vo, pp. 16.

Emerson, Lucy. *The New England Cookery,* or the Art of Dressing all kinds of Fish, Flesh, and Vegetables, and the Best Modes of Making Pastes, Puffs, Pies, Tarts, Puddings, Custards and Preserves, and all kinds of Cake, From the Imperial Plumb to Plain Cake. Particularly adapted to this part of our Country. Compiled by Lucy Emerson. Montpelier : Printed for Josiah Parks, Proprietor of the work. 1808. 18mo, pp. 81, (3.)
Mrs. Emerson was a sister of Thomas Reed, Esq., one of the early settlers of Montpelier; he was grandfather, through Thomas, Jr., of Charles A. Reed, Cashier of the Montpelier National Bank. Lucy was well educated, and married Cyrus Emerson, of Danville, Vt., and moved to Montpelier about 1804, where she resided until her death, September 18, 1855, aged 86. She taught school in Montpelier and elsewhere.
See History of the Reed family, page 203.

Emerson, Thomas. *A Pamphlet,* written by himself, wherein he gives an account of his trials, troubles and distress occasioned by the financial crash of 1837-8. n. d. n. p. 12mo, pp. 70.
Written while Mr. Emerson was in close jail, at Windsor, for debt.
Mr. Emerson resided at Windsor, Vt., and was one of the most prominent bankers and business men in the State prior to 1837; his trade in furs and peltries with the Indians and Indian traders at the west, especially in Michigan, was very extensive. There is a story that in trading with the Indians his foot was reckoned to weigh a certain number of pounds, and the Indians must pile furs enough into the opposite scale to balance it.
Mr. Emerson held a bond against one Thomas Palmer, a dealer in furs at Detroit, on which the interest was behind, and the following unique letter by Mr. Emerson to his attorney in Detroit relates somewhat to the matter:

WINDSOR, VT., August 1, 1834.

HENRY S. COLE, ESQ., Attorney-at-Law:

My Dear Hal:—I am rejoiced to say to you that the Lord hath been among us here in Windsor; that a day of Pentecost is here, and that there has been an outpouring of the Holy Ghost, and I have been snatched as a brand from the burning. I am now "laying up all my treasures in Heaven, where neither moth nor rust doth corrupt, and where thieves do not break through and steal." Oh, Hal! how I wish you and our old friend, Tom Palmer, might see the error of your ways. By the by, Mr. Palmer has not paid the interest on the bond for nearly two years; now I learn that the "pestilence is stalking at noon-day" among you, and we know not how soon you may go. Mr. Palmer ought to settle that bond. You, and he too, ought to prepare for death, and he ought certainly to settle that bond at once. Oh, Hal, if God would only open your eyes, and Mr. Palmer, surely he will pay the interest on that bond now. I pray nightly and daily for you and Mr. Palmer; and trust he will pay the interest on his bond. That the Lord will guard and keep you, dear Hal, and my friend Palmer, is our constant prayer; but do make him pay the interest on the bond. I will take furs, shingles, lumber, apples, fish, or anything he has. God bless and preserve you both; but please do not let Mr. Palmer forget to pay the interest on the bond.

Your devoted friend,

THOMAS EMERSON.

Harry Cole and Thomas Palmer both survived the cholera, and the bond was paid.

Emerson, William. *Sermon* preached at the Ordination of Rev. Robinson Smiley, Springfield, Vt., Sept. 23, 1801. Windsor, Vt.: 1801. 8vo, pp. 24.

—*A Sermon*, preached at the Ordination of Rev. Samuel Clark, to the Pastoral Care of the First Congregational Society of Christians in Burlington, April 19, 1810. By William Emerson, Pastor of the First Church in Boston. Burlington, Vt. Printed by Samuel Mills. 1810. 8vo, pp. 31.

Emmons, Ebenezer. *Geologist.* The Taconic System ; based on Observations in New York, Massachusetts, Maine, Vermont and Rhode Island. Albany : 1844. 8vo.

Emmons, George F. *The Navy* of the United States, from the Commencement, 1775, to 1853; with a Brief History of each Vessel's Service and Fate, as appears upon Record. To which is added a List of Private Armed Vessels, fitted out under the American Flag. Previous and Subsequent to the Revolutionary War; with their Services and Fate. Compiled by Lieut. George F. Emmons, U. S. N., under the Authority of the Navy Department. Washington : Gideon & Co. M.DCCCLIII. 4to, 31, pp. 208, (1).

Admiral Emmons was born in Vermont, August 23, 1811. He was appointed a Midshipman in 1828, and passed through all the grades of promotion, having reached that of Commodore, in 1868 and Rear Admiral in 1872. He took charge of the hydrographic office, 1870. He retired in 1873, and died July, 1884.

See Hammersly, Record of Naval officers.

Emmons, Nathaniel, D. D. *Discourse* at Wardsborough, Vt., Nov. 4, 1795, at the Ordination of James Tufts. Brattleborough. 1797. 12mo.

Englishman, The True-born. *A Satire*, by Daniel Defoe. Motto. Bellows Falls, Vt. Printed by Bill Blake & Co. For the Publisher, 1817. 12mo, pp. 36.

EPISCOPAL. *A Concise Statement* of the Principles of the only True Church. Bennington, Vt, 1790.

—*The Documentary History* of the Protestant Episcopal Church in the Diocese of Vermont, including the Journals of the Conventions From the year 1790 to 1832, inclusive. New York : and Claremont, N. H.: 1870. 8vo, pp. 418, (2.)

Prepared by a committee consisting of Rev. C. R. Bachelder, Rev. G. B. Mansur, D. D., and Rev. Albert H. Bailey, D. D.

—*Journal* of the Proceedings of the Fiftieth Annual Convention of the Protestant Episcopal Church in the Diocese of Vermont ; being the Eighth Annual Convention since the full Organization of the Diocese. Held in St. James' Church, Woodstock, on the 16th and 17th days of September, 1840. Burlington : Chauncey Goodrich. 1840. 8vo, pp. 35.

Continued,

Below we give the title for 1877.

—*Journal* of the Eighty-Seventh Annual Convention of the Protestant Episcopal Church, in the Diocese of Vermont, being the Forty-Fifth Annual Convention since the full organization of the Diocese. Held in Trinity Church, Rutland, on the 13th and 14th Days of June, 1877. Montpelier, Vt.: Argus and Patriot Job Printing House, 1877. 8vo, pp. 93.

Continued.

—*Constitution*, &c. of the Clerical Convention of the Diocese of Vermont; Together with the Form of Devotion used at the Quarterly Meetings. Burlington : D. A. Danforth, Book & Job Printer. 1858. 8vo, pp. 16.

—*Constitution and Canons* of the Protestant Episcopal Church in the Diocese of Vermont, as revised and unanimously Adopted In Convention, at St. James' Church, Woodstock, Wednesday, September 15, 1852. Burlington : Chauncey Goodrich. 1852. 8vo, pp. 22.

—*Constitution and Canons* of the Protestant Episcopal Church in the Diocese of Vermont, as revised and unanimously Adopted In Convention, at St. Paul's Church, Burlington, Wednesday, June 2, 1858. Bennington : Thomas J. Tiffany, Printer. 1858. 8vo, pp. 20.

—*Constitution and Canons* of the Church in the Diocese of Vermont. Montpelier: Argus and Patriot Job Printing House. 1871. 8vo, pp. 42.

—*A Serious Attack* upon the Rights of the Laity : being an Argument before the Right Rev. the Bishop of Vermont, upon a Hearing in the matter of the Excommunication of two Members of the Protestant Episcopal Church. n. p. n. d. [1874.] 8vo, pp. 31.

—*The Address* by the Bishop of Vermont to the Annual Convention of the Diocese, held in St. Paul's Church, Burlington, June 8th and 9th, A. D., 1881. Montpelier, Vt.: Argus and Patriot Job Printing House, 1881. 8vo, pp. 28.

—*Episcopal Register.* No. 2, of Volume 1. Middlebury, Vt. February, 1826. Published Monthly. 8vo, pp. 32.

No. 11 of volume 3 is the latest number I have met, and bears the imprint: Middlebury, Vt. Printed for the Proprietors, By J. W. Copeland, 1828. Price $1 a year. 8vo, pp 16. Was published about four years, commencing January, 1826.

See Graham, John A., Agent to the Protestant Episcopal Church of Vermont; Bailey, A. H. History of the Church of Vermont; Griswold, A. V., Addresses, 1816 and 1827 ; Hopkins, Rt. Rev. John Henry.

Erni, Henri. *Introductory Lecture*, delivered before the Medical Class of the University of

Vermont, May 12th, 1857. by Henri Erni, A. M., M. D., Professor of Natural Science in the Academical, and of Chemistry and Toxicology in the Medical Department of the University. Burlington: Printed by D. A. Danforth. 1857. 8vo, pp. 16.

Essay *on Christian Philosophy*, originally published in the Vermont Chronicle. Andover: Printed by William H. Wardwell. 1848. 8vo, pp. 42.

Essex. *Town of Essex.* Annual Report of the Town Officers for the year ending February 15, 1877. Burlington: Free Press Printing House. 1877. 8vo, pp. 18.
Continued.

—*Principles*, Articles of Faith, Covenant and By-Laws of the First Congregational Church, Essex Junction, Vt. 1880. Burlington: The Free Press Association. 1880. 18mo, pp. 12.

—*Memorial of*,
See Butler, L. C.

Essex County. *Complete List* of the Congregational Ministers and Churches in,
See Glines, J.

Evangelical Monitor. *No. 16, of Vol. 1.* Woodstock, Vt. Nov. 17, 1821. 8vo, pp. 8.
Was published every other Saturday, at Woodstock, Vt., by Walter Chapin, from April 14, 1821, to April 17, 1824, making three volumes.

Evans, John. *A Sketch* of the Denominations into which the Christian World is divided; Accompanied with A Persuasive Religious Moderation. To which is Prefixed a short account of Atheism, Deism, Judaism and Christianity. By John Evans, A. M. Motto. Bennington, Vt.: Printed by Darius Clark & Co. 1814. 8vo, pp. 158.
First published, London, 1794.
Mr. Evans was a Baptist minister. Settled in London, 1792-1827.

Evarts, Jeremiah. *Sermon* on the Death of, delivered in Andover, Mass., July 31, 1831. By Luman Woods. D. D., of Andover. Andover: 1831. 8vo, pp. 27.

—*Tribute to the Memory of*, By Gardner Spring, D. D.., of New York. Published by the Auxiliary Foreign Missionary Society of New York and Brooklyn. New York: 1831. 8vo, pp. 32.

—*Address* before the the American Education Society, at its 10th Annual meeting, (1827). 8vo, pp. 3.
See Quarterly Register, American Educational Society, Vol. 1.
Mr. Evarts was born in Sunderland, Vt., February 3, 1781; and died in Charleston, S. C., May 10, 1831. In a few years after his birth the family removed to Georgia, Vt.; he was graduated at Yale College in 1802, and for about two years was a teacher in Peacham academy; he then studied law in New Haven, Conn., and commenced practice in that city in 1806. In May, 1810, he removed to Charlestown, Mass., and became the editor of the Panoplist, a religious and literary monthly, which was succeeded in 1820 by the Missionary Herald, of which Mr. Evarts was the editor. He was Treasurer of the American Board from 1812 to 1822, and Corresponding Secretary from 1821 to the time of his decease. He wrote the ten annual reports of the American Board from 1821 to 1830; also, under the signature of William Penn, twenty-four Essays on the rights and claims of the Indians, which were published in 1829; he also wrote various other pieces on the same subject, one of which is an article in the North American Review; he also edited the volume of Speeches on the Indian Bill.
A memoir of his life was written by E. C. Tracy, and published in 1845, 8vo, pp. 448.

Hon. William Maxwell Evarts, born in Boston, February, 1818, is his son.

Everett, Horace. *Speech* of Horace Everett, in Committee of the whole on the Bill reported by the Committee of Ways and Means, to reduce and otherwise alter the duties on imports. Delivered in the House of Representatives, January 23, 1833. Washington: Printed by Gales and Seaton. 1833. 8vo, pp. 32.

—*Speech* of the Hon. Horace Everett, delivered before the Whig Convention of Windsor County, May 31, 1837. Published at the request of the Convention. Printed by J. B. & S. L. Chase & Co. Woodstock, Vt. 8vo, pp. 24.

—*Speech* of Mr. H. Everett, of Vermont, on the Case of Alexander McLoud. Delivered in the House of Representatives, Washington, September 3, 1844. 8vo, pp. 24.

—*Report on Indian Affairs;* Washington. 1834. 8vo, map.

—*Speech* in the House of Representatives. On the Indian Annuity Bill, June 3, 1836. Washington: 1836. 8vo, pp. 23.

—*Speech* of Hon. Horace Everett, of Vermont, in the House of Representatives, Washington, May 31, 1838, on the Cherokee Treaty. 8vo, pp. 47.

—*Address* to the Whigs of Vermont. July, 1848. Windsor: Bishop and Tracy's Steam Press. 1848. 8vo, pp. 32.
Mr. Everett was a native of Vermont, born 1780. Studied law, and settled in Windsor; served in the State Legislature in 1819, '20, '22, '23, '24, and 1843; was State's Attorney for Windsor County 1813 to 1817; member of the Constitutional Convention in 1827, and a member of the lower branch of Congress from 1829 to 1843. He died at Windsor, Vt., January 30th, 1851.

Faber, Rev. George Stanley. *A Sermon*, preached before the London Society for the Promotion of Christianity amongst the Jews, by the Rev. George Stanley Faber, B. A. Together with an appendix embracing the twenty-fourth anniversary of the American Society for Meliorating the Condition of the Jews. Middlebury: Justus Cobb, Printer. 1847. 8vo, pp. 36.

Fairbanks, Charles. *The American Conflict* as Seen from A European point of view. A Lecture, delivered at St. Johnsbury, Vt., June 4, 1863, By Charles Fairbanks. Boston: Press of Geo. C. Rand & Avery. 1863. 8vo, pp. 44.

Fairbanks, Rev. Edward T. *James K. Colby.* Memorial Address on, Delivered at the South Church of St. Johnsbury, Vt., Tuesday Evening, November 13, 1866. by Rev. E. T. Fairbanks. Riverside: 1867. 8vo, pp. 20.

Fairbanks, Erastus. *Executive Address* of His Excellency Erastus Fairbanks, Governor of the State of Vermont. Extra Session, April 23, 1861. Montpelier: E. P. Walton. 1861. 8vo, pp. 8.

—*The Valedictory Address* of Erastus Fairbanks, Governor of the State of Vermont, to the General Assembly, at their Annual Session; October, 1861. Montpelier: Freeman Printing Establishment. 1861. 8vo, pp. 24.

—*A Man in Christ.* Words said at his funeral, by Rev. E. C. Cummings. Cambridge: Riverside Press. 1865. 8vo, pp. 16.

Gov. Fairbanks was born in Brimfield, Mass., October 28, 1792; and died in St. Johnsbury, Vt., November 20, 1864.

Fairbanks Family of St. Johnsbury. (Fairbank in some early records and in some branches of the family.) sm. 4to, pp. 2.

Fairbanks, Joseph P. *Memorial of Joseph P. Fairbanks.* By Samuel H. Taylor. Riverside: 1865. 8vo, pp. 189.

Fairbanks, Rev. Henry. *The Fairbanks Family.* A genealogical sketch and Tables, by Prof. Henry Fairbanks. St. Johnsbury: 1888. 8vo, pp. 70.

—*Memorial of Horace Fairbanks.* With portrait; St. Johnsbury : Caledonian Print. 1888. 8vo, pp. 50.

Fairbanks, Rev. N. T. *Memorial* of John Simonds, Funeral Sermon delivered at Brandon, Vt., April 20th, 1869, By Rev. N. T. Fairbanks. Printed by Request exclusively for the relatives. Rutland : Tuttle & Co., Printers. 1869. 8vo, pp. 8.

Fair Haven. *Report* of the Trustees and Treasurer of the Village of Fair Haven, For the year 1872. To which is added a Statement of Disbursements and Receipts since 1868. Rutland : Tuttle & Co., Printers. 1872. 8vo, pp. 10.
Continued.

—*Business Directory* of Fair Haven, Poultney and Castleton, 1896-97. Compiled by R. S. Dillon. Rutland : The Tuttle Co. 1896. 8vo, pp. 160.

—*By-Laws* of Eureka Lodge, No. 73. Fair Haven, Vt. Rutland : Tuttle & Co., Printers. 1875. 24mo, pp. 8.

—*History of,*
See Adams, A. N.

Fairlee. *Annual Report* of the Superintendent of Common Schools for the Town of Fairlee. Submitted at the Annual Town Meeting, March 5, 1867. Fitchburg : Printed by Garfield & Stratton. 8vo, pp. 10.
Continued.

—*Financial Report* of the town of Fairlee, Vt., March 1st, 1879. Bradford, Vt.: Orange County Publishing Company, General Job Printers. 8vo, pp. 10.

Faith, *Explained* to the Understanding of Children. By the Author of "Repentance." Approved by the Vermont Sabbath School Union. Windsor, Vt.: Published by Richards and Tracy. 1838. 18mo, pp. 95.

Farley, Stephen. *Letters* addressed to the Rev. Noah Worcester, A. M. Containing Strictures on his theory of the natural filiation of our Lord Jesus Christ, and certain other opinions of that gentleman, advanced in his late publications, particularly his book entitled "Bible News." By Stephen Farley, A. M. Congregational Minister in Claremont, N. H. Windsor, [Vt.] Printed by Thomas M. Pomeroy. 1818. 12mo, pp. 67.

Farnham, Roswell. *Brief.*
See Vermont Copper Mining Co.

—*Oration* before the Reunion Society of Vermont Officers, at St. Johnsbury, Dec. 13th, 1877.

See Proceedings of the Reunion Society of Vermont Officers, pp. 271 to 283.

Hon. Roswell Farnham was born in Boston, Mass., July 23, 1827. In 1838 removed with his parents to Bradford, Vt., where he has since resided. He graduated from the University of Vt. in 1849; studied law ; was admitted to the bar of Orange county in 1857 ; was State's attorney 1859-61 ; Lieutenant of Co. D. First regt. Vt. vols. 1861 ; Lieutenant Colonel of the Twelfth regiment Vt. vols. 1862-3 ; State senator, 1868-9; Presidential elector 1876 ; and Governor of Vermont 1880-82.

Farnham, Thomas J. *Travels* in the Great Western Prairies, the Anahuac and Rocky Mountains, and in the Oregon Territory. By Thomas J. Farnham. Poughkeepsie : Killey and Lossing, Printers. New York and London : Wiley and Putnam. 1843. 12mo, pp. 197.
Another Edition, New York: Greeley & McElrath. 1843. 8vo, pp. 112.

—*Travels* in the Californias, and Scenes in the Pacific Ocean. By Thomas J. Farnham. New York: Saxton & Miles. 1844. 8vo, pp. 416.
The same work, with the following title :

—*Life and Adventures* in California, and Scenes in the Pacific Ocean. By Thomas J. Farnham. New York : Wm. H. Graham. 1846. 8vo, pp. 416.
Another edition in 1847.

—*History of Oregon Territory*, it being a Demonstration of the Title of the United States of America to the same. By Thomas J. Farnham, Esq. New York : J. Winchester. [1844.] 8vo, pp. 80.
Second Edition, 1845. 8vo, pp. 83.

—*Mexico :* Its Geography, its People, and its Institutions. By Thomas J. Farnham. New York : H. Long & Brother. [1846.] 8vo, pp. 64.
Another Edition, 8vo, pp. 80.

—*Life, Adventures, and Travels* in California. To which are added the Conquest of California, Travels in Oregon, and History of the Gold Regions. New York. 1849. 8vo, pp. 468.
The same, 1850; and 1853, 8vo, pp. 514.

—*Pictorial Edition!!* Life, Adventures, and Travels in California. By T. J. Farnham. To which are added Conquest of California and Travels in Oregon. New York: Sheldon. 1855. 8vo, pp. 468.

—*The Early Days of California;* Embracing what I saw and Heard there, with Scenes in the Pacific. By Col. T. J. Farnham. Philadelphia : J. E. Potter. 1860. 12mo, pp. VI, 314. 10 Plates.
Another edition, 1862.

Col. Farnham was born in Vermont in 1804; and died in California, September, 1848. He was a lawyer by profession, and removed early to Illinois, where, in 1836, he married the distinguished authoress and philanthropist, Eliza W. (Burhans) Farnham. In 1839 he organized and led a small expedition across the continent to Oregon and California, and in the latter place procured the release of a large number of American and English prisoners of the Mexican Government.

Farnsworth, J. H. and Dunn, L. A. *A Review* of the Fifth Annual Report of the Northern Educational Union. By J. H. Farnsworth and L. A. Dunn. Montpelier: 1858. 8vo, pp. 32.

Farrar, E. H., *The Half Day* Perpetual and Industrial Universal School. Poverty, Work and Want: Patrons and Agents for an ever growing enlightenment for every child, every day, everywhere. A Daily Paid Premium on Schooling. By E. H. Farrar, A. M., Fairfax, Vt. Burlington: Free Press Book Print. 1878. 8vo, pp. 20.

Fassett, A. *Election and Reprobation;* or the Decrees of God and the Accountability of Man Considered by Amos Fassett, Esquire. Printed in Bennington, Vermont, by Anthony Haswell. 1810. 24mo, pp. 75.

Fast Day Discourse. 8vo, pp. 24.
Title page missing, and no clew to the name of the Author, or to the exact date; but the internal evidence is that it was preached in Vermont, and during the War of 1812, as it favors a vigorous prosecution of the same.

The Fatal Effects of Seduction. *A Tragedy.* Written for the Use of the Students of Clio Hall, in Bennington, to be acted on their quarter day, April 28, 1789. Founded on the story of an unhappy young lady of Boston. By a Friend to Literature. Motto. Bennington: Printed by Haswell & Russell. 1789.

Faustus, Doctor. *The Devil* and Doctor Faustus. Containing the History of the Wicked life and horrid death of Doctor John Faustus, and showing how he sold himself to the Devil, to have power for twenty-four years to do what he pleased. Also the strange things done by him and Mephistophiles. With an account of how the Devil came to him at the end of the twenty-four years and tore him to pieces. Montpelier: Printed by C. C. Darling. 1807. pp. 12.

Fay, Rev. Cyrus H. *An Address* on "The Changes of a Century," delivered before the Members of Norwich University, Aug. 21, 1889. Newport, N. H. 1839. 8vo, pp. 31.

Fay, Heman A. *Collection of the Official Accounts,* in detail, of all the Battles fought by Sea and Land, between the Navy and Army of the United States, and the Navy and Army of Great Britain, During the years 1812, 13, 14, & 15. By H. A. Fay, late Captain in the Corps of U. S. Artillerists. New York: Printed by Conrad. 1817. 8vo, pp. 295.
Heman Allen Fay, son of Dr. Jonas Fay, was a twin brother of Ethan Allen Fay, and was born in Bennington, January 12, 1779; and died there August 20, 1865. He was graduated at West Point, 1808, appointed a Lieutenant in the Army, and served through the war of 1812, and soon after he was appointed military storekeeper at Albany, where he remained until a few years before his death.

Fay, Jonas. *A Concise Refutation* of the Claims of New Hampshire, &c.
See Allen, Ethan, and Fay.
For biographical sketch, see Hiland Hall's Early History of Vermont, pp. 463-4.

Felch, Rev. Cheever. *An Address,* Delivered on the Festival of the Nativity of St. John the Baptist, at Walpole, Mass., June 24, A. L. 5819. Before Adoniram R. A. Chapter, Montgomery, Constellation, Rising Star and St. Alban's Lodges, By Rev. Cheever Felch. Dedham: Printed by H. & W. H. Mann. 8vo, pp, 23.
Rev. Cheever Felch was of Rutland.

The Female American. *Or the Extraordinary Adventures* of Unca Eliza Winkfield. Compiled by Herself. Vergennes, Vt. Published by Jepthah Shedd and Co. Wright & Sibley, Printers. 1814. 18mo, pp. 270.

The Female Wanderer. *A very interesting Tale* Founded on Facts. Written by the Wanderer Herself. Brattleboro, Vt. Wm. E. Ryther, Printer. 1838. 24mo, pp. 43, (1.)

Fenian Raids *of 1866 and 1870.* Feb. 1, 1871. No imprint. 8vo, pp. 32.

Ferrin, Clark, Ela, D. D. *The Sermon,* Charge, Right Hand of Fellowship, and address to the People, at the Ordination of Mr. C. E. Ferrin, over the Congregational Church in Barton, Vt. December 10, 1851. Published by Request. Windsor: Chronicle Office. 1852. 8vo, pp. 40.
"The Ideal Excellence of the Christian Pastor." Sermon by Rev. O. T. Lanphear; Charge to the Pastor, by Rev. I. S. Clark; Right Hand of Fellowship, by Rev. L. H. Stone; Address to the People by Rev. Artemas Dean, Jr.

—*God the Judge* Doeth Right. A Sermon at the Funeral of Mrs. Lydia A. Duncan, Wife of Rev. L. H. Stone, at Glover, Vt. February 20th, 1852. By C. E. Ferrin, Pastor of the Congregational Church, Barton, Vt. Windsor: Printed at the Vermont Chronicle Press. 1852. 8vo, pp. 16.

—*The Evils of a Homeless Life in Pursuit of Gain.* A Sermon preached at the funeral of Mr. Timothy Mansfield, who died at San Francisco, Cal., December 14, 1852, and was buried at Barton, Vt., May 22, 1853. By C. E. Ferrin, Pastor of the Congregational Church, Barton, Vt. Windsor: Printed at the Vermont Chronicle Press. 1853. 8vo, pp. 19.

—"*Grateful Results* of the war against the Slaveholders Rebellion." A Sermon Preached at the Union Meeting of the Baptist, Methodist-Episcopal, and Congregational Societies, in Hinesburgh, Vt., on the Day of State and National Thanksgiving, December 7, 1865, by Rev. C. E. Ferrin, Pastor of the Congregational Church, Burlington: Free · Press Steam Printing Office. 1866. 8vo, pp. 21.

—*The Wine Texts of the Bible.* each arranged under the Hebrew or Greek word translated wine in that text; showing the different kinds of wine, their nature and uses, with a few Notes. Preface, Introduction, and Conclusion. By C. E. Ferrin. New York: 1877. 24mo, pp. 72.
One or two additional discourses by Mr. Ferrin have been published.
Rev. C. E. Ferrin, D. D., was born in Holland, Vt., July 20, 1818; graduated from the University of Vermont in 1845, and from Andover Theol. Sem. in 1850; pastor of the Congregational Church in Barton, Vt., 1851-54; Pastor of the Congl. Ch. in Hinesburgh, Vt., 1856-72; Pastor of the Congl. Ch. in Plainfield, Vt., 1878-81. Died at Plainfield June 27, 1881.
See sketch in Vt. Hist. Gaz., Vol. 4, p. 731.

Ferriss, W. *Five Sermons,* on the following Subjects, viz. I. The love of God to his Creatures. II. The Christian's evidence of his having passed from death unto life. III. The finite nature of things which are seen, and the eternal nature of things unseen. IV. God's Love to Zion. V. The Lamb of God which taketh away the sin of the world. By the late Rev. Walter Ferriss, Pastor of the Universalian Church in Charlotte and Monkton, Vt. "He, being dead, yet speaketh." To which is subjoined, A Festival Sermon. By Brother Hosea Ballou. Delivered at Chester, (Vt.) June 24. A. L. 5806. Randolph: (Ver.) Printed by Sereno Wright. 1807. 8vo, pp. 104.

[Fessenden, Thomas.] *Remarks* on the Doings of a Convention held at Cornish, N. H., Feb. 20, 1782, consisting of the Rev. Grafton Presbytery, Windsor Association, and others, etc. Westminster, [Vt.] Judah P. Spooner. 1782. 4to, pp. 34.
An early Vermont imprint.

—*A Theoretic Explanation* of the Science of Sanctity. According to Reason, Scripture, Common Sense, and the Analogy of Things : Containing an Idea of God : of his Creations, and kingdoms : of the Holy Scriptures : of the Christian Trinity, and of the Gospel System. By Thomas Fessenden, A. M. Pastor of the Church in Walpole, (New-Hampshire). Printed by William Fessenden for the Author. Brattleboro': 1804. 8vo, pp. 308.
The Father of Thomas Green Fessenden.

Fessenden, T. G. *Oration* at Rutland, Vt., July 4, 1798. Together with an Ode adapted to that occasion. Printed at Rutland, by Josiah Fay. 1798. pp. 31.

—*Democracy Unveiled;* or Tyrany Stripped of the Garb of Patriotism. By Christopher Caustic, L. L. D. &c. &c. &c. &c. &c. &c. &c. &c. &c. Motto. Boston : Printed by David Carlisle, For the Author. 1805. 12mo, pp. viii, 220.

—*The Modern Philosopher;* or Terrible Tractoration! In Four Cantos, most respectfully addressed to the Royal College of Physicians, London. By Christopher Caustick, M. D. A. S. S. Fellow of the Royal College of Physicians, Aberdeen, and Honorary Member of no less than Nineteen very Learned Societies. Second American Edition. Philadelphia : 1806. 8vo, pp. XXII, 271. Plate.

—*Democracy Unveiled;* or, Tyrany Stripped of the Garb of Patriotism. By Christopher Caustic, L. L. D. &c. &c. &c. &c. &c. &c. &c. &c. &c. Mottoes. In two volumes. Third Edition, with large Additions. New York : Printed for I Riley & Co. 1806. 8vo, pp. xxiv, 179, 238, (1).
"Terrible Tractoration" was first printed in London, 1803. The first American Edition was printed in New York, in 1804, with the following title :
Terrible Tractoration !! A Poetical Petition against Galvanising Trumpery, and the Perkinistic Institution. In four cantos. Most respectfully addressed to the Royal College of Physicians, by Christopher Caustic, M. D., L. L. D., Ass. Fellow of Royal College of Physicians, Aberdeen and Honorary Member of no less than nineteen very learned Societies. First American, from the Second Loudon edition, revised and corrected by the author, with additional notes. New York: Samuel Stansbury. 1804. 12mo, pp. xxv, (1). 192. 4 Plates.
Fourth edition, Boston, 1836. Fifth edition, with Caustic's Wooden Booksellers and Miseries of Authorship. Boston: 1837.

—*Original Poems.* By Thomas Green Fessenden, Esq. Philadelphia: 1806. 12mo, pp. XII, 203.
First printed, Loudon, 1804.

—*The American Clerks Companion,* and Attorney's Prompter : A collection of the most useful and approved Forms of Legal Instruments, Precedents in Pleading, &c By Thomas G. Fessenden, Attorney at Law. Brattleborough, Vt. Published by John Holbrook, 1815. 12mo, pp. 377.

—*The Ladies Monitor,* A Poem. By Thomas G. Fessenden. Motto. Bellows Falls, Vt.

Printed by Bill Blake & Co. 1818. 12mo, pp. 180.

—*The Husbandman and Housewife :* A Collection of valuable Receipts and Directions, relating to Agriculture and Domestic Economy. By Thomas G. Fessenden. Bellows Falls : Printed by Bill Blake & Co. 1820. 12mo, pp. 190.

—*The American Annual Register* of Public Events ; Fessenden & Co's Series, for the year 1831-32. Brattleboro', Vt., Fessenden, 1833.
This is vol. 7 of the set, which consists of eight volumes in all, and is rather scarce. Mr. Fessenden's name is connected with vol. 7 only.

—*The New American Gardner.* Boston : 1828. 12mo.

—*The Same,* Sixth Edition. Boston : 1832. 12mo, pp. 306, (1).

—*The Same,* Thirty Sixth Edition, New York: 1852.

—*Essay on the Law of Patents,* and New Inventions. Boston : 1810. 8vo.

—*The Same,* Second Edition. Boston : 1822. 8vo, pp. 425.
Mr. Fessenden commenced the publication of the New England Farmer's Almanac in 1828 ; Boston. Continued. He also published one or two addresses.
Mr. Fessenden was the son of the Rev. Thomas Fessenden, the minister at Walpole; and was born in Walpole, April 22, 1771; died in Boston, November 11. 1837. He was graduated at Dartmouth College in 1796, paying his expenses chiefly by his own exertions. In the autumn of 1796 he commenced the study of the law in Rutland, and after completing his preparatory studies he formed a law partnership with the Hon. Nathaniel Chipman, but was more inclined to literature than the law.
In 1801 he was employed as an agent for a company formed in Vermont for the purpose of securing in London a patent for some new invention, and while there it is said, being in want of money in consequence of the failure of his patent right and other enterprises, he produced "Terrible Tractoration," which was a success, and two or three editions were published in London.
Returning to this country, he settled at Boston in 1804; and in 1805 published "Democracy Unveiled," and other poems. He then published the Weekly Inspector in New York about one year. This was the first paper in the country to advocate the modern "Know nothing" doctrine, as to people of foreign birth ; and it lived from August 30, 1806 to August 22, 1807. In 1812 he returned to the law, opening an office at Bellows Falls ; and in 1815 removed to Brattleboro, where he published the Reporter, a political paper, about one year, and then edited the "Bellows Falls Intelligencer" from 1816 to 1822, from which time until his death he resided in Boston as the editor of the "New England Farmer," also of the "Horticultural Register," and the "Silk Manual," all published in Boston.
See Tyler, Royall ; consult Duyckinck, Buckingham's Reminiscences of Newspaper Literature, Drake, Allibone, etc.

[Fessenden, William.] *The Political Farrago,* or a Miscellaneous Review of the Politics of the United States. from the Administration of Washington, to that of Mr. Jefferson, in 1806. Including a Short History of "The Pittsburg Insurrection," Remarks on the "Louisiana Purchase," "Mammoth Cheese," Federalism and Republicanism, Atheism, and Deism, Illuminism and Witchcraftism, &c., &c., &c., &c. By Peter Dobbins, Esq. R. C. U. S. A. Motto. First Edition, with privilege of Copyright. Brattleboro: printed by William Fessenden for Himself. January, 1807. pp. 59. 12mo.

Field, Charles Kellogg. *A Genealogical History* of the family of the late General Martin Field, of Newfane, Vt., with a brief account of their English and American ancestors. By Chs.

Kellogg Field. Brattleboro : D. Leonard, Steam Job Printer. 1877. 8vo, pp. 33.

Mr. Field aided largely in the preparation of the history of Newfane, where he was born April 24, 1803, and was graduated at Middlebury College, 1822. He read law, and practiced his profession in Newfane, Wilmington and Brattleboro ; was repeatedly elected to the State Legislature from the towns of Wilmington and Newfane, and was a delegate to Constitutional Conventions in 1836 and 1870, and a member of the Council of Censors in 1869. Roswell M. Field, his brother, was born in Newfane, February 22, 1807, and died at St. Louis, Mo., July 12, 1869. Hon. Chs. K. Field died at Brattleboro, Sept. 16, 1880.

See the above Genealogy for full Biographical Sketch.

Field, Martin. *An Oration*, pronounced at Walpole, New Hampshire, before the Jerusalem, Golden Rule and Olive Branch Lodges, of Free and Accepted Masons, at their Celebration of the Festival of St. John the Baptist, June 24th, Anno Lucis 5,800. By Brother Martin Field, A. B. Motto. Putney : Printed by Cornelius Sturtevant. October. 1800. 4to, pp. 24.

Father of Hon. Charles K. Field, of Brattleboro, Vt. For Biographical Sketch, see Field, C. K., "Genealogy of the family of Martin Field ;" "History of Newfane," pp. 42-4.

Field, R. M.
See Trial for Libel, Torrey vs. Field.

Field, Timothy. A Sermon, delivered at Westminster, September 15, 1816. By Rev. Timothy Field, A. M. Pastor of the second Congregational Church in said Town. Printed in compliance with a vote of the Church. John Holbrook, Printer. 8vo, pp. 20.

—*Sermon*, at the Dedication of a New Meeting-House in Westminster, Vt., in 1829. By Timothy Field. Brattleborough : 1830. 8vo.

Fifield, B. F. Issued by the Vermont Republican State Committee. Remarks of Hon. B. F. Fifield before the Montpelier Garfield and Arthur Clubs. [At Montpelier, August 3, 1880.] 8vo, pp. 8.

Mr. Fifield was born in Orange, Vt., November 18, 1832 ; was graduated at the University of Vermont, 1855 ; he read law with Peck & Colby at Montpelier, and succeeded to their business after his admission to the bar in 1856, and continues to reside in Montpelier. He has been United States District Attorney for Vermont and is attorney for the Central Vermont and other railroads. In 1880 he was the Town Representative from Montpelier.

Fillmore, John. A *True Account* of the singular sufferings of John Fillmore, and others, on board of a noted Pirate ship, With an account of their daring Enterprise, and happy Escape from the tyrany of that desperate Crew, by Capturing their Vessel. Motto. To which is added a brief biography of Hon. Millard Fillmore, of Buffalo. Utica : Printed for Russell Potter. 1851. 12mo, pp. 21.

The original about John Fillmore was published by Anthony Haswell, Bennington: 1804. First printed Suffield, Conn., 1802.

Mr. Fillmore having a great desire for the sea, shipped on a merchant sloop for the West Indies, and was captured by Pirates. He was an early settler of Norwich, Conn., and was the great grandfather of Millard Fillmore, through Nathaniel and Nathaniel, Jr. The first settled at an early day at Bennington, where he died in 1814 ; Nathaniel, Jr., the father of Millard, was born in Bennington, in 1771, and early in life removed to Cayuga county, N. Y., where Millard Fillmore was born, January 7, 1800.

Finney, Darwin A. *Eulogies* of Hon. S. Newton Pettis and Hon. George W. Woodward, of Pennsylvania, on the Death of Hon. Darwin A. Finney, in the House of Representatives, Dec. 18, 1868. 8vo, pp. 4. n. p.

Mr. Finney was born in Shrewsbury, Vt., in 1814 ; and died in Europe, July 25, 1868. He removed to Pennsylvania when young, and was graduated at Meadville College ; he was a member of the Senate and Assembly of his adopted State, and in 1866 was elected to the Fortieth Congress.

FISH CULTURE. *Report*, Made under Authority of the Legislature of Vermont, on the Artificial Propagation of Fish. By George P. Marsh. Burlington : Free Press Print. 1857. 8vo, pp. 52, and Appendix, 62, (2).

—*Report of Commissioners* relative to the Restoration of Sea-Fish to the Connecticut River and its Tributaries. By Order of the Legislature of Vermont. Annual Session, 1866. Montpelier : Freeman Steam Printing Establishment. 1866. 8vo, pp. 35.

—*Report of the Fish Commissioners* of the State of Vermont. By Albert D. Hagar and Charles Barrett. For the Year 1867. Montpelier : Walton's Steam Printing Establishment. 1867. 8vo, pp. 25.

—*Report of the Fish Commissioners* of the State of Vermont, By Albert D. Hagar and Charles Barrett. For the Year 1869. Montpelier : Poland's Steam Printing Establishment, Journal Building. State Street, 1869. 8vo, pp. 16.

—*Report of the Fish Commissioners* of the State of Vermont by M. C. Edmunds and M. Goldsmith, For the Years 1871-2. Montpelier : J. & J. M. Poland's Steam Printing Establishment, 1872. 8vo, pp. 20.

—*An Address on Fish Culture*. Delivered before the Legislature of Vermont, On Tuesday Evening, November 12th, 1872. By Middleton Goldsmith, M. D. Rutland : Tuttle & Co., Printers. 1872. 8vo, pp. 16.

—*Report of the Fish Commissioners* of the State of Vermont by M. C. Edmunds and M. Goldsmith, for the Years 1873-4. Tuttle & Company, Printers. 1874. 8vo, pp. 80.

—*Report of the Fish Commissioners* of the State of Vermont, by M. C. Edmunds, For the Years 1875-6. Montpelier : Freeman Steam Printing House and Bindery. 1876. 8vo, pp. 14.

—*Report for 1877-78*. By M. Goldsmith and Charles Barrett. Rutland : Tuttle & Co. 1878. 8vo, pp. 24.

—*Charter and By-Laws* of the Vermont Association for the Protection of Fish and Game. Bennington : C. A. Pierce & Co., Steam Job Printers. 1876. 16mo, pp. 16.

—*Transactions* of the American Fish Culturists' Association, at its fifth Annual Meeting, February 8th, 1876. Rutland : Tuttle & Company, Printers. 1876. 8vo, pp. 20.

Fish and Game. A *Compilation* of the Laws of Vermont, relating to Fish and Game, in force January 1, A. D. 1877. Compiled by order of the Washington County Association for the Protection of Fish and Game, by the Counsel of said Association. Montpelier : Argus and Patriot Steam Job Printing House. 1877. 12mo, pp. 18.

See Laws of Vermont, 1878.

—*The Increase* and Preservation of Fish and Game. By Dr. Middleton Goldsmith, Fish Commissioner of Vermont. n. p. n. d. 8vo, pp. 6. .

—*Vermont Fish and Game League.* The Fish and Game Laws of Vermont, 1895-96. Montpelier: Argus and Patriot Press. 1895. 12mo, pp. 88.
This compilation embraces the Statutes of Vermont now in force (1896) relating to the preservation of Fish and Game, as revised by the Legislature of 1894. With constitution and officers of the Vermont Fish and Game League, roll of members, reports, etc., etc.

Fish, Henry C. *The School Question.* Romanism and the Common Schools. A Discourse, delivered on Thanksgiving Day, Nov. 24, 1853. By Henry C. Fish, Pastor of the First Baptist Church, Newark, New Jersey. New York: Holman, Gray & Co., Steam Printers, corner Center and White Sts. 1853. 8vo, pp. 20.

—*Freedom or Despotism.* The Voice of our Brother's Blood : its Source and its Summons. A Discourse occasioned by the Sumner and Kansas Outrages. Preached in Newark, June 8th and 15th, 1856. By Henry C. Fish, Pastor of the First Baptist Church. Newark, N. J., Douglass & Starbuck, Printers and Publishers, 123 Market Street. 1856. 8vo, pp. 24.

—*History and Repository* of Pulpit Eloquence, containing the Masterpieces of Edwards, Davies, John M. Mason, and others, with Historical Sketches of Preaching in the different countries represented, and Biographical and Critical Notices of the several Preachers and their Discourses, By the Rev. Henry C. Fish. New York: W. M. Dodd. 1856. 2 vols. 8vo, pp. 1244. Portrait.

—*Pulpit Eloquence* of the Nineteenth Century: being Supplementary to the History and Repository of Pulpit Eloquence, and containing Discourses of Eminent Living Ministers in Europe and America, with Sketches, Biographical and Descriptive, By the Rev. Henry C. Fish. New York: W. M. Dodd. 1857. 8vo, pp. x, 815.

—*A Semi-Centennial Sermon*, preached June 22d and 29th, 1851, upon the History of The First Baptist Church in Newark, N. J., for the First Half Century of its Ecclesiastical Existence, by the Pastor, Rev. Henry Clay Fish. New York: Lewis Colby. 1851. 18mo, pp. 108.

—*The Valley of Achor a Door of Hope;* or, the Grand Issues of the War. A discourse, delivered on Thanksgiving Day, Nov. 26, 1863. By Henry C. Fish, D. D. New York: Sheldon & Co. 1863. 8vo, pp. 24.

—*The Hour for Action.* Premium Essay. by Henry C. Fish, D. D., Pastor of the First Baptist Church, Newark, N. J. Philadelphia: American Baptist Publication Society, 530 Arch Street. 1866. 12mo, pp. 36.

—*The Great Inquiry*, and the Great Inquiry answered. By Henry C. Fish, D. D., Newark, New Jersey. Published by the American Tract Society, 150 Nassau-Street, New York. n. p. 12mo, pp. 46.
Mr. Fish also published: "Primitive Piety Revived; a Prize Essay," Boston. 1855. 12mo, of which twenty thousand copies were sold in two years. "Select Discourses from the German and French." 1858, 12mo. "The

Circular Letter of the East Jersey Baptist Association." 8vo, pp. 8. June, 1848.
Mr. Fish was born in Halifax, Vt., in 1820, and was pastor of the First Baptist Church in Newark, N. J., for many years.

Fisk, Rev. Joel.
He was born in Waitsfield, Vt., Oct. 26, 1796; was graduated at Middlebury College, 1835; read theology at Rutland, and his first settlement was over the Congregational Church at Monkton, 1826, for four years, then at New Haven, Vt., two years, Essex, N. Y., twelve years, then Canada several years; finally to Irasburgh, and thence to Plainfield, Vt., where after a year's labor at the latter place, he died, Dec. 16, 1856. His only published sermon, was, "Filial Respect, or the Way to make Family Blessings Perpetual," suggested by the death of his father.

Fisher, Joseph. *A Reunion* of the Descendants of Joseph Fisher, of Chester, Vt., held at the residence of A. Whitcomb, Grinnell, Iowa, Wednesday, August 28, 1878. Grinnell, Iowa: Herald Job Printing Office. 1878. 8vo, pp. 18.

Fisk, James Jr. *A Life* of James Fisk, Jr., being a full and accurate Narrative of all the Enterprizes in which he has been engaged. New York: 1871. 12mo, pp. 300. Plates.

—*The Life* of Col. James, Fisk, Jr. With sketches of Edward S. Stokes, his assassin, Miss Josephine Mansfield, his former Mistress, and various incidents in the checkered career of a Murdered Millionaire. New York: W. E. Hilton, Publisher, 128 Nassau St. [1872.] 8vo, pp. 58. Portraits.

—*The Fisk Murder.* A full, impartial, history of this dreadful Tragedy, and the principal persons concerned in it, from beginning to end ; together with all the true incidents and occurrences, and correct likenesses. This is the only account that can really be relied on. Issued from the Old Franklin Publishing House, Philadelphia. [1872.] 8vo, pp. 77.
Col. Fisk was a native of Pownal, Vt., he was born April 1, 1834. The English ancestors of Col. Fisk first settled in the colony of the Massachusetts Bay, but on account of intolerance and persecution they moved to Rhode Island, and settled at Smithfield, of which town Col. Fisk's father and grandfather were natives; James Fisk, Senior, having been born there March 19, 1813. When he was three years of age the family moved to Adams, Mass., and as soon as old enough, himself and two brothers and two sisters were placed in a cotton factory, which business Mr. Fisk followed until forty years of age, having reached the position of Superintendent of a mill at Pownal; in 1837 he moved to Bennington, and thence to Brattleboro in 1842; he commenced the peddling business in 1851.

Fisk, Rev. Perrin B. *Pastoral Letter* of Rev. P. B. Fisk, Lyndonville, Vt. 1870. 8vo, pp. 3.

—*The Same* in 1871 and 1872.
Mr. Fisk was born in Waitsfield, Vt., July 3, 1837; studied at Barre Academy, Vt.; did not take a college course; was graduated at Bangor Seminary in 1863; preached at West Dracut, Mass., 1863-5; at Peacham, Vt., 1866-70; at Lyndonville, Vt., 1870-4; at Springfield, Vt., 1874-7; and at Lake City, Minn., 1878, to the present time (1880). He has also published two sermons in the local newspaper.

Fisk, Theophilus. *Our Country*, its Dangers and Destiny. Oration, at Norwich, Vt., 1840.

FISK, WILBUR. *A Discourse* delivered before the Legislature of Vermont, on the day of General Election, at Montpelier, October 12, 1826. By Rev. Wilbur Fisk, A. M. Montpelier: Printed by Geo. W. Hill & Co. 1826. 8vo, pp. 40.

—*Objections* against the Doctrine of Universal Salvation : being the Substance of A Sermon Delivered in the Methodist Church in Springfield, Mass. By Rev. W. Fisk, A. M. Principal of Wesleyan Academy, Wilbraham, Mass. New York : J. Collard, Printer. 1829. 12mo, pp. 43.

—*The Curse of the Divine Law :* A Discourse delivered in the Methodist Church in Springfield, Mass., By Rev. W. Fisk, A. M., Principal of the Wesleyan Academy, Wilbraham, Mass. New York : J. Collard, Printer, 1829. 12mo, pp. 22.

—*A Sermon* delivered before his Excellency Levi Lincoln, Governor, his Honor Thomas L. Winthrop, Lieutenant Governor, the Hon. Council, the Senate, and House of Representatives of the Commonwealth of Massachusetts, on the Day of General Election, May 27, 1829. By Wilbur Fisk, A. M. Principal of the Wesleyan Academy, Wilbraham. Boston : True and Green, State Printers. 1829. 8vo, pp. 27.

—*Another Edition :* Montpelier : Published by George W. Hill. 1829. 8vo, pp. 28.

—*A Discourse* on Predestination and Election, preached on an especial occasion at Greenwich, Massachusetts. By W. Fisk, D. D. Brookfield : E. & G. Merriam, Printers. 1831. 8vo, pp. 32.

—*Science of Education :* Inaugural Address at Middletown, Conn. Sept. 21, 1831, as President of the Wesleyan University. New York : 1832. 8vo.

—*Address* to the Members of the Methodist Episcopal Church, on the Subject of Temperance. New York, Published for the Tract Society of the Methodist Episcopal Church, at the Conference Office, No. 200 Mulberry street. 1837. 12mo, pp. 16.

—*Travels in Europe, viz :* in England, Scotland, Ireland, France, Italy, Switzerland, Germany and the Netherlands. By Wilbur Fisk, D. D. President of Wesleyan University at Middletown, Conn., with engravings. Fourth Edition. New York : Harper and Brothers. 1838. 8vo, pp. 688.

—*Substance of an address* delivered before the Middletown Colonization Society, at their annual Meeting, July 4, 1835. By Wilbur Fisk, D. D. President of the Wesleyan University. Published by the Society. Middletown: Printed by G. F. Olmstead. 1835. 12mo, pp. 23.

—*An Appeal* to the citizens of Connecticut, in behalf of the Wesleyan University, by Wilbur Fisk, D. D. Middletown : William D. Starr Printer. 12mo, pp. 16.

—*True Greatness :* A Discourse on the Character of Rev. Wilbur Fisk, S. T. D., Late President of Wesleyan University, Delivered before the Faculty and Students of the University, in the Methodist Episcopal Church, Middletown, Conn., Wednesday afternoon, April 3d, 1839, And now published by their Request. By Rev. J. Holdich, A. M., Professor of Moral Philosophy and Belles Letters. Middletown : E. Hunt & Co. 1839. 8vo, pp. 36.

—*A Tribute* to the Memory of President Fisk. Delivered before the Young Men's Missionary and Bible Societies at the John-Street Methodist Episcopal Church, New York, May 17, 1839. By Rev. Professor Whedon, Of the Wesleyan University. Published by request of those Societies. New York : 1839. 8vo, pp. 23.

Mr. Fisk was born in Brattleboro, Vt., August 31, 1792; and died February 22, 1839. He was graduated at Brown University, 1815; studied law with Hon. Isaac Fletcher, Lyndon, Vt., but became a Methodist preacher and prominent in the denomination.

See Sprague's Annals, vol. 7, pp. 576-587; Life and Writings, by Joseph Holdich. New York. 1842.

Fitch, Rev. John. *A Sermon*, delivered at Danville, at the Request of Harmony Lodge, as a Tribute of Respect for the Memory of the late Gen. George Washington; February 26th, 1800. By John Fitch, A. B., Pastor of the Congregational Church in Danville. Peacham, Vermont. Printed by Farley & Goss, 1800. 8vo, pp. 24.

—*A Sermon*, delivered before His Excellency the Governor, the Lieutenant Governor, the Council, and House of Representatives, of Vermont, at Danville, November 10th, 1805 : Being the day of General Election. By John Fitch, A. B., Pastor of the Congregational Church in Danville. Peacham : Printed by Samuel Goss. 1805. 8vo, pp. 23.

November in the above should read October.

—*The Character* and work of a faithful Minister of the Gospel delineated. A Sermon, Delivered at the Ordination of the Rev. Nathaniel Rawson, to the Pastoral care of the Congregational Church in Hardwick, Vermont, Feb. 13, 1811. By John Fitch, Pastor of the Congregational Church in Danville. Danville : Printed by Ebenezer Eaton. 1811. pp. 22, 8vo.

—*The Excellence of the Bible.* A Sermon delivered before the Vermont Bible Society, at their Annual Meeting at Montpelier, October 19, 1814. By John Fitch, A. M., Pastor of the Congregational Church in Danville. Montpelier, Vt.: Printed by Walton and Goss, November, 1814. 8vo, pp. 16.

—*The Kingdom of Christ*, A Sermon delivered before the Vermont Missionary Society, at their Annual Meeting at Pawlet, Sept. 13th, 1813, by John Fitch, A. M. Pastor of the Congregational Church in Danville. Middlebury: T. C. Strong. Nov. 1813. 12mo, pp. 16.

Mr. Fitch was born in Hopkinton, Mass., in 1770, and was graduated at Brown University 1790; pastor of the Congregational Church, Danville, Vt., 1793-1816; when he retired from the ministry under a cloud. He was subsequently Preceptor of the Academy at Thetford, Vt., and lastly at Guildhall, Vt., where he died, December 18, 1827.

Flanders, Rev. A. B. Proceedings of Brooks Post, No. 25, Department of Vermont, G. A. R., Chester. Vt., upon the occasion of the Decoration of the Graves of their Fallen Comrades, May 30th, 1870. Mottoes. Brattleboro : Printed by Geo. E. Selleck. 1870. 8vo, pp. 14.

Flanders, G. T.

LETTER FROM MR. FLANDERS.

Lowell, March 8, 1879.

I send you today the sketch you were kind enough to solicit last September. Pardon my long and really needless delay. Yours truly,

G. T. FLANDERS.

My full name is George Truesdel Flanders; I was born in the town of Vershire, Vt., June, 28, 1820. Very early in my childhood my father moved to Orange, where he occupied a small farm; I am therefore son of a farmer, and my ancestry consists of farmers as far back as I can trace my descent. In Orange, which I usually speak of as my native place, for I know comparatively nothing of Vershire, I received a good common school education, and an academic education at the then famous Newbury Seminary. The degree of D. D. was conferred by Lombard University in 1871. I entered the Universalist ministry at the age of 19, and my chief pastorates have been Baltimore, Cincinnati, Chicago and New York. I have published several addresses and sermons, and in 1847 a book of 304 pages entitled: A Review of Alexander Hall's "Universalism against Itself," by G. T. Flanders, Zanesville, Ohio, 1847. In 1842 I edited and published one volume of a religious journal, entitled "The Genius of Truth."

Of late years, though actively engaged in the ministry, my attention has been chiefly given to Oriental studies, and I have written several articles, chiefly on India, its Religions and Philosophies, which have been published in the Universalist Quarterly Review. My life has been an active one, filled with preaching, debating, writing and study, and books have always been my dearest friends. I have accumulated a small library of 1,200 volumes, in which is one of the most valuable private collections of Oriental books in New England. I am now settled over one of the largest Universalist parishes in Massachusetts, at Lowell.

Such is the briefest outline of my life, and that I believe is all you want.

Rev. Dr. Flanders preached his farewell sermon at Lowell, Sunday, June 1, 1879, and on the 7th, sailed on a visit to Algeria, Africa.

Fletcher, Ebenezer. *Narrative* of the Captivity and sufferings of Ebenezer Fletcher, of New Ipswich, wounded at the Battle of Hubbardston, 1777; and taken prisoner, etc. Windsor, Vt. 1813. First edition.
Brinley Catalogue.

Fletcher Free Library. *Third Annual Report* of the Trustees. Burlington : R. S. Styles' Steam Job Printing House. 1877. 8vo, pp. 9.
Continued.

—*Catalogue* of the Fletcher Free Library of Burlington. Burlington, Vt. 1877. r'l 8vo, pp. (4), 661.

—*Bulletin No. 1* of the Fletcher Free Library of Burlington. Books Added from June 1, 1877, to Feb. 1, 1878. Burlington, Vt. 1878. 8vo, pp. 29.
Bulletins continued.

Fletcher, John. *Studies on Slavery*, in Easy Lessons. Compiled into eight studies, and subdivided into short Lessons for the convenience of Readers. By John Fletcher, of Louisiana. Fourth Thousand. Natchez—Charlestown—New Orleans—Philadelphia: 1852. 8vo, pp. 637.
An able defence of Slavery.
Mr. Fletcher was the son of William and Chloe Stebbens) Fletcher, and born at Williamstown, Vt.; was graduated at Dartmouth College, in 1815; studied law, and commenced practice at Concordia Parish, La., and after many years removed to Natchez, Miss., where he died in August, 1862, aged 71.

Fletcher, Richard. *The Service of a good Life.* A Discourse Commemorative of the Life and Character of Hon. Richard Fletcher, delivered at the request of Friends, in the Clarendon Street Baptist Church, Boston, July 11, 1869. By Rev. A. J. Gordon. Boston : Gould and Lincoln. 1869. 8vo, pp. 24.
Mr. Fletcher, son of Hon. Asaph Fletcher, was born in Cavendish, Vt., January 8, 1788. He was graduated at Dartmouth College, 1806, read law at Portsmouth with Hon. Daniel Webster, and soon settled at Boston, where he beame distinguished as a Jurist; he was a member of the Massachusetts Legislature, a member of Congress, 1837-39, and a Judge of the Supreme Court of Massachusetts. Mr. Fletcher bequeathed one hundred thousand dollars to Dartmouth College. He died in Boston, June 1, 1869.

Fletcher, Ryland. *Address* delivered at the Fair of the Windsor County (Vermont) Agricultural Society, By Ryland Fletcher, Esqr., October 5, 1848. Woodstock : Printed at the Age Office. 1848. 12mo, pp. 11.
Ryland Fletcher was born in Cavendish, February 1799, a son of Asaph Fletcher of that town, who was a member of the legislature, a member of the council, a presidential elector, and a prominent citizen. Ryland Fletcher was an ardent anti-slavery man and leading free soiler. He was Lieut. Governor of Vermont 1854-6, and Governor 1856-8. He represented Cavendish in the legislature 1861-2; presidential elector in 1864, and member of the constitutional convention of 1870; a colonel and brigadier general in the State militia. He was a leading member of the Baptist denomination. He married Mary Ann May, of Westminster, and was the father of Hon. Henry A. Fletcher, who was Lieut. Governor of Vermont 1890-92.

The Flying Roll; Or, The Miscellaneous Writings of Redemptio. Windsor, Vt. 1805. 12mo.

Foot, Solomon. *Speech* in the House, Washington, on the Oregon Question, Feb. 6, 1846. Washington : 1846. 8vo, pp. 16.

—*Speech* of Mr. Solomon Foot, of Vermont, on the Origin and Causes of the Mexican War. Delivered in the House of Representatives, Washington, July 16, 1846. Washington : Printed by J. & G. S. Gideon. 1846. 8vo, pp. 16.

—*Speech* on the Character and Objects of the Mexican War, Feb. 10, 1847. Washington : 8vo, pp. 16.

—*Proceedings* on the Death of Hon. Solomon Foot, including the Addresses delivered in the Senate and House of Representatives, on Thursday, April 12, 1866. Washington : Government Printing Office. 1866. 8vo, pp. 120.

—*Funeral Sermon.* Obituary Notices and Testimonials of Respect. By the Citizens of Rutland on the occasion of the Death of Hon. Solomon Foot, LL. D., Late United States Senator for the State of Vermont. Rutland : Tuttle, Gay & Company. 1866. 8vo, pp. 26.
See Edmunds, G. F., Life, etc., of Mr. Foot.
Born, Cornwall, Vt., November 19, 1802. Died, Washington, D. C., March 28, 1866. He was graduated at Middlebury College, 1826; was Principal of Castleton Academy one year, and for a time tutor in the University of Vermont, and also Professor of Natural Philosophy in the Vermont Academy of Medicine; studied law, and commenced practice at Rutland, in 1831, where he ever after continued to reside; was a member of the Vermont General Assembly in 1833, '36, '37, '38, and 1847; was Speaker of the House during the last three terms; was a member of the State Constitutional Convention in 1836, and State's Attorney for Rutland County, 1836 to 1842; was Representative in the lower House of Congress, 1843 to 1847, and was elected United States Senator from Vermont for the term commencing in 1851, and was continued in the Senate until his decease. He was President pro tem. of the Senate for several years.

Forbes, Charles S. 1856. 1876. *A Memento.* Sketch of the Ransom Guards of St. Albans, Vt., and their Centennial Excursion to Philadelphia, By C. S. F. St. Albans : 1876. 18mo, pp. 24 and Appendix.

—*The Second Battle of Bennington:* A History of Vermont's Centennial, and the one hundreth Anniversary of Bennington's Battle. A Civic and Military Review. By Charles S. Forbes. Illustrated. St. Albans, Vt.: Advertiser Printing Co. 1877. 12mo, pp. 96.
Mr. Forbes was born at Windsor, Vt., August, 1851; Academic Education; Removed to St. Albans in 1864; railroad clerk, 1870-78; Vestryman and Treasurer St. Luke's Episcopal church in 1876-77; Vermont Press correspondent, 1876-7; American Press representative for European tour of Gilmore's Band in 1878; May to October, corresponding for Boston Journal, and New York

Evening Express, and the American Register, Paris, on that tour. At present, General Agent and correspondent of the Boston Journal for Northern Vermont, New York and Canada; manager of Franklin Literary Club, St. Albans; a Washington correspondent during Electoral Count of 1876; special correspondent with Gen. Grant on his return to Galena and Chicago through the West from his tour of the world; Trustee of Public Library, St. Albans, 1875-6-7; Member of Wisconsin Historical Society. Has been connected with Burlington Free Press, St. Albans Messenger, and Advertiser; has been a delegate to and Secretary in several Republican Conventions of the State, and was one of the Boston Journal staff at the Chicago Convention in June, 1880; is editor and publisher of The Vermonter, (monthly) 1896.

Forbes, Darius. *Christian Union.* A Sermon, delivered at the dedication of the Union Meeting-House in Grafton, Vt. Jan 14, 1835. By Darius Forbes, pastor of the First Restorationist Church and Society in Chester, Vt. Motto. Published by request. Boston : Dill and Sanborn, Printers. 1835. 8vo, pp. 22.

—*The Mysteries of Providence,* A Sermon : preached at Ludlow, Vt., Saturday, December 18, 1847, at the Funeral of Rev. John A. Henry, Pastor of the First Universalist Society. By Darius Forbes, Minister in the Stone Chapel in Chester, Vt. Published by Request. Ludlow, Vt.: Mclean & Merrifield, Printers. 1848. 12mo, pp. 16.

Forbes, Robert. *A Narrative* of the Extraordinary Sufferings of Mr. Robert Forbes, his wife and five Children During an unfortunate Journey through the Wilderness from Canada to Kennebeck River in the year 1784. In which Three of their Children were starved to death. Taken partly from their own mouths, and partly from an imperfect Journal, and compiled at their request, By Arthur Bradman. Printed at Windsor, 1792, By Alden Spooner, and sold at his office. pp. 15.

Ford, Rev. William. *American Republicanism*—its Success, its perils, and the Duty of its present Supporters. Sermon delivered before the Citizens of Brandon, on the occasion of the National Fast, September 26, 1861. By Rev. William Ford. Rutland : George A. Tuttle & Co., Printers. 1861. 8vo, pp. 24.

—*Celestialism.* A Poem, delivered at the Town Hall, Brandon, February 11, 1862, on the occasion of a benefit given to Rev. B. D. Ames and Family. "I had a dream that was not all a dream." By Rev. William Ford. Brandon : Printed at Gazette Office. 1862. 12mo, pp. 11.

Mr. Ford was a Baptist preacher, a poet, and an editor. He was born in Glenville, N. Y., and the last 18 or 20 years of his life resided in Brandon, Vt. See Vermont Historical Magazine, Vol. 3, pp. 489—90.

Forestdale, (*Rutland.*) A Week at Forestdale, being a Summer Idyl.

Forsyth, William. *A Sermon,* Preached at Danville, before the Fraternity of Free and Accepted Masons, of Harmony Lodge, at the Celebration of the Festival of St. John the Baptist, June 25, 1798. By William Forsyth, A. M. "Love, Gratitude and Pity wept at once."—Thompson. Printed at Peacham, Vt., By Farley & Goss. 1798. 8vo, pp. 24.

—*A Sermon* preached at Windsor, October 10, 1799. Before His Excellency the Governor, the Lieutenant-Governor and Council, and the House of Representatives, of the State of Vermont. Printed for S. Williams, Printer to the State. M,DCC,XCIX. 8vo, pp. 19.

Fort Dummer. *Letter* of Gov. Shirley to the Board of Trade respecting. November 30, 1748. Mass. Hist. Soc. Coll., vol. iii, pp. 106-109.

—*Papers* relating to, 1744-45. New Hampshire Hist. Soc. Coll., Vol. 1, pp. 143, 147.

Foster, Rev. Amos. *Paul, a Model* for the Christian Minister. A Sermon delivered in Henniker, N. H., at the Ordination of Rev. Eden Burroughs Foster, August 18, 1841. By Rev. Amos Foster, Pastor of the Congregational Church in Putney, Vt. Concord : Printed by Asa McFarland, opposite the State House. 1841. 8vo, pp. 32.

Mr. Foster was born in Salisbury, N. H., March 30, 1797; was graduated at Dartmouth College, 1822; studied Theology with Rev. Roswell Shurtleff and Rev. Bennet Tyler, of Hanover, N. H.; was pastor of the Congregational church in Canaan, N. H., 1825-33; Putney, Vt., 1833-53; Ludlow, 1853-56; Acworth, N. H., 1857-66; was living at Putney in 1880.

Foster, Dan. *An Election Sermon;* Delivered before the Honorable Legislature of the State of Vermont; Convened at Westminster, October 8th, 1789. By Dan Foster, A. M. Printed in Windsor, by Alden Spooner, MDCCXC. Small 4to, pp. 26.

—*A Sermon,* delivered at Walpole, New Hampshire, before the Jerusalem, Golden Rule, and Olive Branch Lodges, of Free and Accepted Masons, at the Celebration of the Festival of St. John the Baptist, on the 24th June, A. L. 5800. By Dan Foster, A. M. Preacher of the Gospel in Charlestown, N. H. Putney: Printed by Cornelius Sturtevant. 1800. 4to, pp. 16.

—*Examination* of a late Publication, entitled the Doctrine of Eternal Misery, by Nathan Strong. Walpole, N. H. 1803. 8vo.

Foster, E. S., and Prouty, L. A. *The entire Correspondence* between Rev. E. S. Foster, [Universalist,] and Miss L. A. Prouty. [Orthodox.] Published by request. Chester, Vt. 1869. Rutland : Tuttle & Co., Printers. 1869. 8vo, pp. 86.

Being a discussion by letter—Universalism vs. Orthodoxy.

Foster, Rev. Festus, A. M. *An Oration* pronounced in the town of Northfield, Mass. July 5, 1813. Brattleborough : Printed by William Fessenden. 1813. 8vo, pp. 22.

Foster, Hosea B. (of Berlin, Vt.) *Poems:* Montpelier, Vt.: Printed by Ballou, Loveland & Co. 1860. 18mo, pp. 72.

Foster, John. *Essay on Decision of Character.* By John Foster. From the latest edition. Burlington : Chauncey Goodrich. 1830. 16mo, pp. 105.

Foster, Joseph C. *Providence illustrated.* A Historical Discourse, delivered at the Dedication of the Baptist Meeting-House, in Brattleboro, Vt., December 28, 1870. By Joseph C. Foster, Pastor of the First Baptist Church in Beverly, Mass. Boston : Press of Rockwell & Churchill, 122 Washington Street. 1871. 8vo, pp. 28.

Fowler, Bancroft. *A Discourse* delivered at Windsor, Vt., on the Fourth of July, 1811, in commemoration of the American Independence. By Bancroft Fowler, Minister of the Congregational Society in the East Parish of Windsor. Windsor, Vt.: Merrifield & Co.

Fowler, C. J. *Universalism* vs. The Truth. Sermon Preached in Union Hall, Bellows Falls, Vt., March 16, 1879, by C. J. Fowler, Evangelist. Published by the Committee. Bellows Falls: Times Steam Book and Job Office. 1879. 8vo, pp. 15.

Fowler, William C. *A Sermon*, preached at the Ordination of the Rev. Robert Southgate as Pastor over the First Congregational Church and Society in the North Parish of Woodstock, Vt. Jan. 4, 1832, by William C. Fowler. Woodstock: Printed by Rufus Colton. 1832. 8vo, pp. 23.

—*A Discourse*, delivered at Montpelier, October 17, 1834, before the Vermont Colonization Society. By William C. Fowler. Published by the Society. Middlebury: Knapp & Jewett, Printers. 1834. 8vo, pp. 32.

Prof. Fowler died at his home in Durham, Conn., Jan. 15, 1881, aged 87 years. He was a graduate of Yale in 1816, and was several years a tutor there; for several years he was professor of chemistry in Middlebury College, and afterward several years professor of rhetoric and oratory at Amherst college. He was a son in law of Noah Webster and editor of the University edition of Webster's dictionary in 1845; author of a treatise on the English language and several literary and historical works. He was a member of the Connecticut senate in 1864.

Fowler, William W. *Ten Years in Wall Street;* or, Revelations of inside life and experience on 'change: with illustrations and portraits. Hartford, Conn. Published by Dustin, Gilman & Co., 350 Asylum Street. 1870. 8vo.

—*Fighting Fires:* the great Fires of History: with illustrations. Hartford, Conn. Published by Dustin, Gilman & Co., 350 Asylum Street. 1873. 8vo.

—*Woman on the American Frontier:* with illustrations. Hartford, Conn. Published by S. S. Scranton & Co., 281 Asylum Street. 8vo.

Mr. Fowler was born in Middlebury, Vt., in 1832, his father being Prof. William C. Fowler of Middlebury College, and his mother a daughter of Noah Webster; graduated at Amherst College in 1854; studied law and practised for several years in New York; removed to Durham, Ct., where he died, Sept. 18, 1881, aged 49. (The above titles are copied from a catalogue.)

Francis, Lewis. *A Sabbath* at the Yosemite Valley. By Rev. Lewis Francis. Burlington: Free Press Association. 1871. 8vo, pp. 18

Being a Discourse in the Congregational church, Castleton, Vt., July 23, 1871.

—*Historical Discourse* on the 30th Anniversary of the Greenpoint Reform Church, Brooklyn, N. Y. By the Pastor, Rev. Lewis Francis. New York: McBride Bros. Printers. 1878.

Mr. Francis was a son of Gen. John Francis of Royalton, and a nephew of President John Wheeler; he graduated from the U. V. M. in 1856. He was pastor for some years at Castleton. See Castleton.

Franklin, Benjamin. *Pride breakfasted* with Plenty, dined with Poverty, and supped with Infamy. The Way to Wealth. By Dr. Franklin. Motto. Montpelier, Vt. Printed for Josiah Parks, At the Press of Walton & Goss. November, 1810. 18mo, pp. 31.

—*The Life of Dr. Benjamin Franklin.* Written by Himself. Montpelier: Printed by Samuel Goss, for Josiah Parks. 1809. 12mo, pp. 202.

—*The way to wealth* as clearly shown in the Preface of an old Pennsylvania Almanac. intitled Poor Richard Improved. Windsor, Vt. 1826. 18mo.

—*Works* of the Late Dr. Benjamin Franklin; Consisting of his Life, written by Himself. Together with Essays, Humorous, Moral, and Literary, chiefly in the manner of the Spectator. Printed and Sold by J. Lyon, Fair Haven, Vermont. 1798. 12mo, pp. 254.

—*The Life* and Essays of the late Doctor Benjamin Franklin. Written by himself. Brattleborough: Published by William Fessenden. 1814. 12mo, pp. 322.

Franklin County. *A Brief Survey* of the Congregational Churches in.
See Kingsley, P.

—*Statistics* Showing the Origin of Court Business of the County of Franklin, the Grand List and Population of the County, the location of its Banks, and the amount of Business done in St. Albans, exclusive of Butter and Cheese, and Business of Railroad Car Shops. Montpelier: J. &. J. M. Poland, Printers. 1872. 8vo, pp. 12.

—*Jury and Court Calendar* for Franklin County, September Term, 1865. St. Albans, Vt.: Vermont Transcript Printing Establishment. 1865. 12mo, pp. 16.

—*Atlas Map* of Franklin and Grand Isle counties.
Same title and imprint as Chittenden county Atlas.

Franklin County Grammar School, Vt. *Catalogue*, 1840, 1841. St. Albans: 8vo.

A Free Enquiry into the Causes, both Real and Pretended, for laying the Embargo. By a Citizen of Vermont. Windsor, (Vt.) Printed by Charles Spear. 1808. 8vo, pp. 28.

Freeman, Joseph. *The Proper Training* of Children. A Discourse on the proper training of Children. By Rev. Joseph Freeman, of Proctorsville, Vt. 1862. Published and sold for the benefit of the Baptist Church, at Bellows Falls, to aid them in paying for their place of worship. Ludlow: Warner's Book and Job Printing Office, 1862. 8vo, pp. 39.

Freeman, Russell. *A Father's Legacy to his Children.* Written in Prison, By Russell Freeman, Esq. A short time before he was murdered. Windsor, (Vt.) Re-Printed by A. Spooner. July, 1800. 12mo, pp. 12.

French, J. Clement. *Song of the Old Church* at Williamstown: A Poem, delivered before the Alumni of Williams College, at the Commencement, Tuesday afternoon, July 31, 1866. By Rev. J. Clement French, of Brooklyn, N. Y. Class of 1853. Chicago: Printed at the Tribune Company's Book and Job Office. 1866. 8vo, pp. 15.

—*God Worship and Man Worship.* Two Sermons in the Central Congregational Church of Brooklyn, N. Y., by J. Clement French, Pastor, June 9th, 1867. New York: Stone &

Barron, Printers, 42 Ann Street. 1867. 8vo, pp. 19.
Mr. French was born at Barre, Vt., May 3, 1832; was graduated at Williams College in 1853, and at the Union Theological Seminary in 1856; pastor of the Central Congl. Ch., Brooklyn, N. Y., 1857-70; of the Westminster Presb. Ch. Brooklyn, 1871-76, and of the Park Presb. Ch., Newark, N. J., 1879—He received the degree of D. D., from Williams College.

French War. *Reminiscences* of the French war; containing Rogers' Expedition with the New England Rangers under his command, as published in London in 1765; with Notes and Illustrations. To which is added an account of the Life and Military Services of Maj. Gen. John Stark; with Notices and Anecdotes of other Officers distinguished in the French and Revolutionary Wars. Concord, N. H.: Published by Luther Roby. 1831. 12mo, pp. 276.
Includes Rogers' disastrous expedition through Vermont in 1759. See account in Miss Hemenway's Vt. Hist. Gazetteer, vol. 1, pp. 263-5.

French, Warren C. *Biographical Sketch* of Hon. Andrew Tracy. By Hon. Warren C. French. Woodstock: Vermont Standard Print. 1884. 8vo, pp. 12.
Mr. French was born in Randolph, Vt., July 8, 1819; is a lawyer at Woodstock, was State Senator, 1858-9, and has held other prominent offices.

French, William. *Petition*, Report and Bill on the subject of a monument in honor of William French. In the House of Representatives November 9, 1852. Montpelier: E. P. Walton & Son. 1852. 8vo, pp. 16.
See Westminster Massacre.

Frenyear, Rev. C. P. *A Sermon*, Preached at the Funeral of William H. Carr, in Jamaica, Vt., October 7, 1869, by Rev. C. P. Frenyear; to which is prefaced an Obituary Notice by Hon. Hoyt H. Wheeler. Published by request. Montpelier, Vt.: Argus and Patriot Job Printing House. 1870. 8vo, pp. 16.
Mr. Frenyear was born of French parentage in Henryville, P. Q., July 4, 1836; he was brought up as a Roman Catholic, but joined a Baptist church at Fairfax, Vt., in 1856, and became a preacher of that faith; was pastor successively at Middletown, Ira, North Springfield, Jamaica and Townsend, Vt. He died May 13, 1876.

Frisbie, Barnes. *The History* of Middletown, Vt., in three Discourses, delivered before the Citizens of that Town. February 7 and 21, and March 30, 1867, by the Hon. Barnes Frisbie of Poultney, Vt. Published by request of the Citizens of Middletown. Rutland, Vt. Tuttle & Company, Printers. 1867. 8vo, pp. 130.
See Poultney.

Frost, Rev. D. S. *Funeral Sermon* of Lieut. A. L. Sanborn, 1st Reg't U. S. Colored Troops, Murdered at Norfolk, Va. By Dr. D. M. Wright, July 11, 1863. Preached at Thetford, Vt., Dec. 8, 1863, By Rev. D. S. Frost. [n. p. n. d.] 8vo, pp. 24.

Frost, John. *Oration, 1829.*
See Middlebury College.

Frothingham, Frederick. *On this Rock.* A Sermon delivered at the Dedication of the Church of the Messiah, in Montpelier, January 25, 1866. By Rev. Frederick Frothingham of Brattleboro. Montpelier: Published by Ballou, Loveland & Co. 1866. 8vo, pp. 11, (1.)

—*Tribute to the Memory* of William Czar Bradley of Westminster, Vt., who died March 3, 1867. By Fred'k Frothingham. Cambridge: John Wilson & Son. 1867. 8vo, pp. 15.

Fuller, Andrew. *Dialogues, Letters, and Essays, on Various* Subjects. To which is annexed an Essay on Truth; Containing an Inquiry into its Nature and Importance with the Causes of Error, and the Reasons for its being permitted. By Andrew Fuller. Second American Edition. Middlebury, Vt. Published by Samuel Swift. Printed by T. C. Strong, 1811. 12mo, pp. 256.

—*The Backslider*, or an inquiry into the nature, symptoms and effects of religious declention, with the means of recovery. By Andrew Fuller. Middlebury: Samuel Swift. 1812.

—*The Practical Uses of Christian Baptism.* A Circular Letter, From the Ministers and Messengers of the Several Baptist Churches of the Northamptonshire Association, Assembled at Northampton, June 15, 16, 1802, To the Churches of their Connexion. By Andrew Fuller, D. D. of Kettering. Montpelier: Printed by Wright & Sibley. 1814. 8vo, pp. 16.

—*The Same title*, with the imprint: Montpelier: Printed by Samuel Goss, 1807. 8vo, pp. 15.

Fuller, Abby Estey. *Prince Estey*, Story of a Pony; Born July 4, 1861; Died Nov. 19, 1879. 1881. No imprint. 8vo, pp. 18.
Mrs. Fuller is the daughter of the late Jacob Estey of Brattleboro, and wife of Ex-Governor L. K. Fuller.

Fuller, Levi Knight. *Address* on Uniform Musical Pitch, delivered, with Illustrations and Examples, at the Meeting of the Piano Manufacturers' Association of New York, Friday, Nov. 6, 1891. Pages 6 to 19 of Proceedings of a meeting of the above Association held to consider the Report of the Committee recommending "A 435" as a Standard International Pitch.
Levi K. Fuller was born in Westmoreland, N. H., February 24, 1841; removed to Brattleboro in 1854; engaged in the manufacture of the Estey organs; has been vice-president of the Estey Organ Co. for thirty years; State Senator, 1880-1; Commander of the Fuller Light Battery, Vermont National Guard, for many years; Lieutenant Governor of Vermont, 1886-7; Governor of Vermont, 1892-3. He is the author of seventeen circulars issued by the Committee of Piano Manufacturers on International Pitch; also of the Chapter on Inventions in "Men of Vermont;" and has written many articles for mechanical, scientific and other journals.

Fuller, Stephen. *A Sermon.* delivered at Orford, May 20, 1801, at the Ordination of the Rev. Sylvester Dana, to the Work of the Ministry in that Place. By Stephen Fuller, A. M. Pastor of a Church in Vershire. Printed at Hanover, N. H., by Moses Davis, 8vo, pp. 22.

—*A Sermon* delivered at the Ordination of the Rev. Jonathan Hovey, to the Pastoral care of the Church in Waterbury, Vt., Sept. 1, 1803. By Stephen Fuller, A. M., Pastor of a Church in Vershire. Randolph: Printed by Sereno Wright. 1804. 8vo, pp. 20.

—*A Sermon* delivered at the Ordination of the Rev. Joel Byington, to the work of the Gospel Ministry, in Chazy, N. Y. By Stephen Fuller, A. M., Pastor of a Church in Vershire, Vt. Middlebury: J. D. Huntington, 1809.

—*A Sermon* preached at Chelsea, Lord's Day, March 31, 1811. By Stephen Fuller, Pastor of a Church in Vershire. Danville: Ebenezer Eaton.

—*Four Sermons*, on the Nature and advantages of a Christian Connexion in Churches. By Stephen Fuller, A. M. Pastor of a Church in Vershire, Vt. Hanover, N. H. Printed by Moses Davis. 12mo, pp. 37, n. d. [About 1807.]

Mr. Fuller was pastor at Vershire 28 years, being his only settlement; he brought up and educated ten children, on a salary of about $400 per year.

See Vt. Hist. Gazetteer, for sketch of his life, pp. 1135–1136, of vol. 2.

Gage, Royal. *A Treatise* on Resistance and Non-Resistance: in which is included a Scriptural Distinction between the Church of Christ and the Civil Government of the World. Motto. By Royal Gage, Minister of the Gospel, Westminster, Vt. Brattleboro: Printed by J. B. Miner. 1848. 8vo, pp. 59.

Gallaudet, Susy Denison. *Charley*, A Village Story, by S. D. Gallaudet. G. P. Putnam's Sons. New York and London: 1893. 12mo, pp. 71.

Mrs. Gallaudet was born in Royalton, where the scene of the story of Charley is laid.

Gallup, Joseph A. *Sketches* of Epidemic Diseases in the State of Vermont; from its First Settlement to the Year 1815. With a Consideration of their Causes, Phenomena and Treatment. To which is added Remarks on Pulmonary Consumption. By Joseph A. Gallup, M. D. Boston: Printed by T. B. Wait & Sons. 1815. 8vo, pp. 419.

Re-published in England.

—*Pathological Reflections* on the Supertonic State of Disease. Read before the Vermont Medical Society, Convened at Montpelier, October 10, 1822. By Joseph A. Gallup, M. D. President of the Society; and of the Vermont Academy of Medicine, &c. Montpelier, Vt. Printed by E. P. Walton. 1822. 8vo, pp. 26.

—*Outlines* of an Arrangement of Medical Nosology. Founded on the Pathology of the diseased System. For the use of the Medical Class. Motto. By Joseph A. Gallup, M. D. Prof. Theo. and Practice of Med. &c. in the Vermont Acad. of Medicine. Woodstock: 1823. Printed by David Watson. 12mo, pp. 36, (1).

—*Second Improved Edition* of the same. Same imprint. 8vo, pp. 87, (4).

—*Observations* made during a visit to the Clarendon Springs, Vt., in relation to their Character and Properties, in a part of July and August, 1839. With an analysis of the Waters. By Joseph A. Gallup, M. D. Windsor: Printed by Tracy & Severance. 1840. 8vo, pp. 14.

—*Outlines* of the Institutes of Medicine: Founded on the Philosophy of the Human Economy, in Health, and in Disease. In three Parts. Motto. By Joseph A. Gallup, M. D. Author of Sketches of Epidemic Diseases in the State of Vermont: late President and Professor of Theory and Practice in the Vermont Academy of Medicine, and of the Clinical School of Medicine; Ex-President of the Vermont Medical Society; Corresponding Member of the National Institute; Hon. Member of the Medical Society of the State of New York, &c. Second Edition, Revised. (In two volumes.) New York: Collins, Brothers & Co. 1845. 8vo. pp. 416, 460. (First edition published in 1839.) Boston: Otis, Broaders, and Company, Portrait.

Dr. Gallup was born in Stonington, Conn., March 30, 1769; and died at Woodstock, Vt., October 12, 1849. He was graduated in medicine at Dartmouth College, 1798. He practiced in Hartland and Bethel, Vt., and removed to Woodstock in 1800. He first became known as a writer in the Vermont Gazette; from 1820 to 1823 was President of, and Professor in Castleton Medical College, and was for several years a lecturer in the Medical Department of the University of Vermont. He established at Woodstock, in 1827, the institution subsequently known as the "Vermont Medical College," which was incorporated in 1835.

Gannett, E. S. Sermon preached at the Funeral Obsequies of Hon. Charles Paine. By E. S. Gannett, D. D. Pastor of the First Unitarian Society, Boston, Mass. Together with Obituary Notices from other Sources. Northfield: Printed by Woodworth and Gould. 1853. 8vo, pp. 63.

Gaskill, Silas. *The American Botanist*, and Family Physician: In which The medical virtues of the Mineral, Animal and Vegetable productions of North America are exhibited; together with their uses in the practice of Physic and Surgery; Some of which are selected from Dr. Stearns, and other Authors, but mostly original. Comprehending A Treatise upon the principal disorders of the Climate; together with directions for preparing, compounding, and applying proper medicines for their cure. Likewise, A Large number of Indian discoveries in the Medical Art, never before published. By John Monroe. Compiled by Silas Gaskill. Wheelock, (Vt.) Published by Jonathan Morrison. 1824. Danville: Eben'r Eaton, Printer. 16mo, pp. 203.

Gathered Sketches from the Early History of New Hampshire and Vermont; Containing vivid and interesting Accounts of a great variety of the Adventures of our Forefathers, And of other Incidents of Olden Time. Original and Selected. Edited by Francis Chase, M. A. Claremont, N. H.: Tracy, Kenney & Co. 1856. 12mo, pp. 215.

Genealogy. *The Follett-Dewey*, Fassett-Safford Ancestry of Captain Martin Dewey Follett (1765-1831) and his wife, Persis Fassett (1767-1849), being a compilation of family records and extracts from various histories, official records and genealogical publications relating to the Folletts of Salem, Windham, Wyoming Valley, and Vermont, the Deweys, Fassetts, and Saffords, of Massachusetts, Connecticut and Vermont. Brief genealogical notice of the Hopkins, Robinson, Fay and other families of Vermont, together with accounts of the settlements of Wyoming Valley, and Vermont, the Wyoming Valley massacres, Bennington and other battles, and the diary of Capt. John Fassett, Jr., in the expedition of the Green Mountain Boys in 1775, by Henry P. Ward. Illustrated. 8vo. Columbus. 1896.

The Gentleman's Law Magazine: Containing A variety of the most useful Practical Forms of Writings, which occur in the course of business. By a Gentleman of the Bar. Middlebury, Vermont: Printed by Huntington and Fitch. 1804. Copy-Right secured. 12mo, pp. 348.

John Simmons, Esq., was the author.

A Geographical and Historical Poem of Vermont. By A Citizen of Washington County.

Northfield, Vt.: Published by Charles O. Kimball. 1852. With a map. 12mo, pp. 12.

GEOLOGY OF VERMONT. First Annual Report on the Geology of the State of Vermont. By C. B. Adams, State Geologist. Burlington: Chauncey Goodrich. 1845. 8vo, pp. 92.

—*Second Annual Report* on the Geology of the State of Vermont. By C. B. Adams, State Geologist, Prof. Chem, and Nat. Hist. in Middlebury College. Corres. member of the Bost. Soc. Nat. Hist.; of the Entom. Soc. of Pa.; member of the Assoc. Amer. Geologists, &c. &c. Burlington: Chauncey Goodrich. 1846. 8vo, pp. 267.

—*Third Annual Report* on the Geology of the State of Vermont, By C. B. Adams, State Geologist, &c. Burlington: Chauncey Goodrich. 1847. 8vo, pp. 32.

—*Fourth Annual Report* on the Geological Survey of the State of Vermont. By C. B. Adams, State Geologist, &c. Burlington: Chauncey Goodrich. 1848. 8vo, pp. 8.

—*Preliminary Report* on the Natural History of the State of Vermont. By Augustus Young, State Naturalist. Burlington: Chauncey Goodrich. 1856. 8vo, pp. 88.
Contains Obituary of Prof. Zadock Thompson.

—*Report on the Geological Survey* of the State of Vermont, by Edward Hitchcock, State Geologist. Burlington: Daily Times Office Print. 1858. 8vo, pp. 13.

—*Preliminary Report* on the Geology of Vermont by Edward Hitchcock, State Geologist. Printed by Order of the Senate. Montpelier: E. P. Walton, Printer. 1859. 8vo, pp. 16.

—*Report of the Committee* on so much of the Governor's Message as relates to the Geological Survey. Printed by Order of the Senate. 8vo, pp. 8. 1859. Montpelier: E. P. Walton, Printer.

—*Report on the Geology of Vermont*: Descriptive, Theoretical, Economical, and Scenographical; by Edward Hitchcock, LL. D., Edward Hitchcock, Jr., M. D., Professor of Hygiene and Physical Culture in Amherst College. Albert D. Hagar, A. M., Charles H. Hitchcock, A. M., Geologist to the State of Maine. In two volumes. Published Under the Authority of the State Legislature, By Albert D. Hagar, Proctorsville, Vt. Printed by the Claremont Manufacturing Company, Claremont, N. H. 1861. 4to, pp. 988, besides the plates.
Contains 38 Plates, some colored, and 365 wood cuts.

—*The Taconic and Lower Silurian Rocks* of Vermont and Canada. By Jules Marcou. From the Proceedings of the Boston Society of Natural History, November 6, 1861. Boston: 1862. 8vo, pp. 14.
See Hall, Frederick; Thompson, Z., Geography and Geology of Vermont; History of, Natural, Civil, &c.; also Address on the Natural History of Vermont; Report and Correspondence on the subject of a Genealogical Survey, 1838; Perry, John B.; Geology of Western Vermont; Article by Warren Upham, in American Journal of Science and Arts, December 1877; Emerson, E., The Taconic System; Perkins, George H., Geology and Natural History; Brainerd, Ezra.

George, N. J. T. *A Pocket* Geographical and Statistical Gazetteer, of the State of Vermont. Embellished with Diagrams. Multum in Parvo. To which is prefixed, a particular description of the City of Washington, and a large number of statistical Tables of the United States. Compiled from the most recent Authorities and Personal Observation. By N. J. T. George. Haverhill, N. H. Printed and Published by S. T. Goss. 1823. 18mo, pp. 264.

Gestrin, Prof. Charles E. H. *Vacation Labors.* By C. E. H. G. Sold by T. C. Phinney, Montpelier, Vt. Montpelier: Argus and Patriot Book and Job Printing House, 1879. 8vo, pp. 51.
Portrait of the late General Alonzo Jackman. Prof. Gestrin is a native of Sweden; was for some years Professor of Languages in Norwich University.

Gibson Association. *Report* to the Gibson Association of Vermont, U. S. A., made by Columbus Smith, A. D. 1867, containing the Gibson Constitution and information in his possession relative to Gibson property abroad ; likewise pedigree of different branches of the family, so far as he has been able to collect. Published by order of the Gibson Association. Middlebury: Register Book and Job Printing Establishment. 1867. 8vo, pp. 20. (Also, a supplementary report. 1869. 8vo, pp. 6.)

Gibson, William. *A Dialogue* concerning the Doctrine of Atonement, between a Calvinist and a Hopkinsian ; wherein a number of the Arguments on both sides of the question are endeavored to be candidly examined, that Truth may appear. Intended as an Answer to a late Publication of Mr. L. Worcester's on that and other subjects connected with it. Written by William Gibson, Minister of Ryegate. Text. Windsor: Printed by Alden Spooner. 1803. 8vo, pp. 78.

Giddings, F. C. *Full Report* of the Examination of F. C. Giddings charged with Wife Poisoning. Ludlow, Vt.: From the Transcript Office. 1866. 8vo, pp. 16.

Gilbert, G. N. Poem with valedictory Addresses, By G. N. Gilbert, Dartmouth, '78. Hanover. N. H. Published by Request. 8vo, pp. 8.
Mr. Gilbert was from Dorset, Vt., and read Theology at Leipsig, Germany.

Gilbert, Geo. H. *The Book of Job* as Poesy. A Dissertation presented to the Philosophical Faculty of the University of Leipsic by Geo. H. Gilbert. Rutland: The Tuttle Co. 1886. 8vo, pp. 75.

Gilbert, Lyman. *The Genius* of the Christian Religion. A Sermon, preached at the Dedication of the New-House of Worship erected by the Second Congregational Society in Newton, Ms., March 29, 1848. By Lyman Gilbert, A. M., Pastor of the Church. Boston: Press of T. R. Marvin, 24 Congress Street. 1848. 8vo, pp. 32.
Dr. Gilbert was born in Brandon, Vt., June 13, 1798; was graduated at Middlebury College in 1824, and at Andover in 1827; was Pastor of the Second Church in Newton, Mass., 1828-55, and in Malden, N. Y., 1859-63; in Government service, Brooklyn, N. Y., 1863-75; died 1885.

Gilbert, Margaret Ingersol. *Sacred Symbolism :* A Key to its interpretation. By Mrs. Margaret Ingersol Gilbert. Rutland: Tuttle & Company, Printers. 1878. 16mo, pp. 36.

Gilbert, Nathaniel Porter.
Was born in Pittsford, Vt., February 17, 1831, and died in Hubbardton, Vt., July 1, 1876. He was educated at Castleton Seminary, University of Vermont, where he was graduated in 1854, and was graduated at Andover Theological Seminary in 1859; Ordained at Rutland, Vt., July 18, 1860; Missionary of American and Foreign Christian Union in Chili, 1860–71; acting pastor of Congregational churches, Clarendon, Vt., 1874–5, Hubbardton, January, 1876, until his death. He published in Chili, "Devocionario para Todos Los Dias De La Sermana" (Book of Prayer for every day in the week.)
See Congregational Quarterly, July, 1877.

Gilman, J. F. *Instructions* in Pictorial Art, for Home Study ; with illustrations adapted to the requirements of the instructions. By J. F. Gilman, student in Nature's Academy of Design. Montpelier : Poland's Steam Printing Works. 1881. 8vo, pp. 8.
This work was suppressed by the author, and only a few copies got into circulation.
Mr. Gilman is a native of Massachusetts, but has (1880) resided in Montpelier several years, and is an excellent artist in portrait and landscape crayon work.

Gilt Edge Butter ; How to manufacture it successfully and profitably. Issued by the Vermont Farm Machine Company, Bellows Falls, Vt., U. S. A., 1877. 12mo, pp. 12.

Gleig, George Robert.
Mr. Gleig, a clergyman, was born in England, 1795, and received his education at Oxford. Having something of a military taste he joined the British army and served in the Peninsula war, and subsequently with the British army in the United States, in the campaign against Washington in the war of 1812. He was an eloquent and voluminous writer, and his military experience had a tendency to direct his pen toward a similar field in literature. Among his productions of this class may be mentioned a "Military History of Great Britain," a "Life of the Duke of Wellington," and many tales of the army, one series of which was published in 1829, under the title of the "Chelsea Pensioners" (See Allibone). "Saratoga" formed one of this collection, and has been republished in this country, in a volume entitled "Tales of Military Life, Second Series, Philadelphia, 1833." It is a narrative of the campaign of Gen. Burgoyne from the time that he took command of the British army at Montreal, until his surrender to Gen. Gates, and is assumed to have been related by one Capt. Macdirk to his companions. The worthy Captain is himself the hero of his own story, and fortunately for the hungry ears of his auditors he was continually placed in the most exciting positions, and where, too, he had ample opportunity to study the movements of his General. In the opening chapter he tells us that he joined a company of Provincials, composed mostly of Scotch emigrants, or descendants of old soldiers, who had settled along the St. Lawrence, and which was commanded by a gallant countryman of their own, one Fraser.
Until within a few years "Saratoga" has been considered as a very good specimen of historical fiction, and nothing more; but a liberal extract from it has been lifted to a higher dignity by Volume 1 of the "Collections of the Vermont Historical Society." The extract in question may be found in the latter volume, commencing on page 211 and ending on page 223, and headed "Account of the Battle of Bennington, by Glich, a German Officer who was in the Engagement, under Colonel Baum." This "account" comes, body and soul, right out of Rev. Mr. Cleig's story, and not the least singular part of it is, where the heading as above quoted sprung from. We have seen that Captain Macdirk is the hero, but who is Mr. Glich, the German officer? Rev. Isaac Jennings in his "Memorials of a Century," of Bennington, has quoted from the account, (although he spells the name *Glick*,) as also has Mr. F. W. Coburn in his "Centennial History of the Battle of Bennington." Some one has committed quite a mistake, and unless marked attention is called to it, it may assume alarming proportions in the years to come. A volume of such value as either of those of the "Collections of the Vermont Historical Society" is not allowed to slumber in the dust on a hidden shelf, but is often taken down, and its contents with pleasure read and noted by the historical student. Surely we have in history enough of that which is false without borrowing from the pages of romance.
                                                    F. W. C.
The above article has been kindly furnished by Mr. F. W. Coburn, of Boston, author of "Centennial History of

the Battle of Bennington," and in that work was, as he states, himself a victim of the "Glich Narrative Romance," as quoted by Rev. Mr. Jennings in "Memorials," and by the publishing committee in Vermont Historical Society Collections. The result of my investigations in relation to the subject is confirmatory of the correctness of the article by Mr. Coburn.
See Coburn, F. W.
I extract the following from Rev. Dr. Gleig's preface written in 1840 for an edition of the Chelsea Pensioners: "Of "Saratoga" I have nothing to say, except that I believe it to contain a tolerably accurate narrative of General Burgoyne's disastrous campaign; and that as it makes no pretention to more than this, it must be taken for what it is worth. The by-plot, if such it may be called, is by far too unimportant to deserve notice."

Gleiwitz, G. *The Realities* of Homeopathy, by G. Gleiwitz, M. D. Author of Letters on Physiology, etc., etc. Like is only discerned by like. Middlebury, Vt.: A. H. Copeland, Publisher. 1859. 8vo, pp. 52.

Glines, Jeremiah. *Complete List* of the Congregational Ministers and Churches in Essex County, Vt., from its first settlement to the present time, (1841). By Rev. Jeremiah Glines, of Lunenburg. Am. Quar. Register, vol. xiii., pp. 448–451.
With Historical notes of each Town.

—*Brief Thoughts* on religious belief and practice, by Rev. Jeremiah Glines, Lunenburg, July, 1873. From Emerson, Hartshorn & Co.'s Printing House, Main St., Lancaster, N. H. 12mo, pp. 15.

Glover. *Half Centennial Discourse* before the First Congregational Church. 1867.
See Perkins, S. K. B.

Goadby, John. *Remembrances* of Past Years; a Discourse Delivered at the Baptist Meeting House, Poultney, Vt., on the Fiftieth Anniversary of the Organization of the Church, April 8, 1852. By Rev. John Goadby. (motto.) Rutland : Tuttle's Book and Job Office. 1852. 8vo, pp. 16.

Going, Rev. Jonathan. *The Prospect of Death* an Incentive to Christian Constancy and Faithfulness. A Discourse delivered on Occasion of the Death of Rev. Jonathan Going, D. D., President of Granville College. With a Sketch of his Life. By Edmund Turney, Pastor of the First Baptist Church, Granville, Ohio. Published by request. Hartford: 1845. 8vo, pp. 32.
Dr. Going was born in Cavendish, Vt., March 7, 1786. He was graduated at Brown University, 1809; was pastor of the Baptist church in Cavendish, 1811-15, and of the Baptist church, Worcester, Mass., 1815-31. He was President of Granville college from 1837 until his death, November 9, 1844.

Goldsmith, Middleton. *A Report* on Hospital Gangrene, Erysipelas and Pyæmia, as observed in the Departments of the Ohio and the Cumberland, with cases Appended. By M. Goldsmith, Surgeon U. S. N. Published by Permission of the Surgeon General U. S. A. Louisville : Bradley & Gilbert, corner of Third and Green Streets. 1863. 8vo, pp. 95.
See Fish Culture.

Goldsmith, Oliver. *The Deserted Village*, Traveler, and Miscellaneous Poems. By Oliver Goldsmith, M. D. Middlebury, Vt. Published by H. Richardson, Jr. Francis Burnap, printer. 1819. 12mo, pp. 108.

—*Another edition. 1831.*

—*The Vicar of Wakefield, A Tale.* Motto.

Bellows, Vt. Published by James I. Cutler and Co. 1825. 18mo, pp. 143.

GOESBRIAND, LOUIS DE. *The Bishop* of Burlington regarding the Association of the Holy Family. pp. 14.

—*The Israelite* before the Ark of the Covenant and the Christian before the Altar, or, A History of the Worship of God. In two parts. Part I. The Worship of God among the Children of Israel before the days of Jesus Christ. Part II. The Worship of God since the days of Jesus Christ, or, the Rules, Ceremonies and Sacrifice of the Catholic church, by L. De Goesbriand, Bishop of Burlington, Vt. Free Press Association. 1890. 8vo. Part I, pp. viii, 214; Part II, pp. 167.

—*Sacerdotal Meditations.* Meditations for the Use of the Secular Clergy. Translated from the French of Father Chaignon, S. F. by L. De Goesbriand, Bishop of Burlington, Vt. 2 Vols. Santa Maria Intercede pro clero. Free Press Association. 1892. Vol. 1, pp. xiv, 792. Vol. II, pp. 598.

—*Fac simile* of St. Peter's Chains, kept in the church of St. Peter ad Vincula, Rome, and a Link of the Original Chain in Burlington, Vt. Edited by L. De Goesbriand, Bishop of Burlington, Vt. Free Press Association. 1893. pp. 16.

—*Christ on the Altar.* Instructions for the Sundays and Festivals of the Ecclesiastical Year. Explaining how the Life, Miracles and Teachings of Our Lord in the Holy Land are continued on the Altar of the Parish Church. By Right Rev. Louis de Goesbriand, D. D., Bishop of Burlington, Vt. With 2 chromo-lithographs, 63 full-page illustrations, 240 illustrations of the Holy Land and of Bible History, ornamental initials, tail-pieces, etc., etc. Benziger Brothers, New York, Cincinnati, Chicago. 4to, pp. 844.

—*Catholic Memoirs* of Vermont and New Hampshire. pp. 166.

—*History of Confession;* or, The Dogma of Confession Vindicated.

—*Jesus, the Good Shepherd.* Contains an account of St. Peter's relics in the Cathedral of Burlington, Vt. pp. 192.

—*The Labors of the Apostles.* Their Teaching of the Nations. pp. 212.

—*Manuel du Prêtre* aux États Unis, en Anglais et en Français. pp. 254.

—*A Relation* of the First Pilgrimage of the Diocese of Burlington to St. Anne de Beaupré. Burlington: 1882.

—*Devotion* to St. Anne in the Diocese of Burlington. Burlington: 1884.

—*Forty Hours' Devotion*—with Letter of the Bishop of Burlington, Vt.

—*St. Peter's Life.* The chains of St. Peter. St. Peter's Relics in the Cathedral of Burlington.

Right Rev. Louis de Goesbriand was born August 4, 1816, in the province of Brittany, France. After a course of three years in the Seminary of St. Sulpice, Paris, he was ordained priest by Bishop Rosate, July 13, 1840. In response to a call sent by the American Bishops to the Seminaries of Europe for volunteer priests, he came to the United States, and was assigned to the charge of Louisville, Ohio. He was subsequently Vicar General of the Diocese of Cleveland, Ohio, and Rector of the Cleveland Cathedral until 1853, when, upon the erection of the Diocese of Burlington, Vt., he was chosen its first Bishop. He was consecrated as Bishop in the Cathedral of New York, Oct. 3, 1853, by Mgr. Bedini, Archbishop Hughes of New York preaching the sermon. He was installed by Bishop Fitzpatrick, of Boston, Nov. 6th, 1853. He has made various journeys to France, Ireland, Rome and the Holy Land; has obtained large funds for his church; procured and superintended the erection of the stately Cathedral of the Immaculate Conception in Burlington; of St. Joseph's Church, Burlington; of the Providence Orphan Asylum, and of other churches and hospitals in his diocese. He has, by his Christian devotion and many virtues, won the respect and esteem of the people of Vermont of all denominations.

Good, Peter Peyto. *Exercises,* Designed to assist young persons to pronounce and spell correctly, also to practice writing and acquire punctuation with accuracy and effect. Upon an efficacious and approved principle. By Peter Peyto Good. Embellished with cuts. Stereotyped by D. Watson, Woodstock, Vt. 1830.

The exercises are all in a new system of spelling English words.

Goodell, Constans Liberty. *Oration,* delivered to the Citizens of Calais, Vt., July 4, 1849. Published by Request.

—*Thanksgiving Sermon,* preached at the Union Service of the First and South Congregational Churches, New Britain, Conn., November 26, 1863. By Rev. C. L. Goodell, pastor of the South Church. Hartford: Press of Case, Lockwood & Company. 1863. 8vo, pp. 15.

—*Sketch* of the Life of the late Governor Erastus Fairbanks, of Vermont, published in the "Congregational Quarterly" for January, 1865.

—*Life* of Rev. John Smalley, D. D., of Connecticut; in "Congregational Quarterly," July, 1873.

—*Life* of Mrs. Henry C. Stephens, of New York City. 1869.

—*Sermon,* Our Daughters as corner stones, polished after the similitude of a palace. By C. L. Goodell, D. D. Pastor Pilgrim Congregational Church, St. Louis, Mo. St. Louis: 1878. 8vo, pp. 14.

—*Sixth Anniversary Sermon,* Preached Nov. 24, 1878. By Rev. C. L. Goodell, D. D. Pastor Pilgrim Congregational Church, St. Louis. St. Louis: Davis & Freegard, Printers. 1878. 8vo, pp. 16.

—*One Million Dollars* a year for Home Missions. A Sermon in behalf of the American Home Missionary Society, preached in the Broadway Tabernacle Church, New York, May 8, 1881. By Rev. C. L. Goodell, D. D. New York: The American Home Missionary Society. 1881. 8vo, pp. 16.

The above titles are given as furnished by Mr. Goodell; Mr. Goodell's letter continues: "Of late years I presume some two hundred of my sermons and addresses "have been published in the daily press and in pamphlet "form. I have been abroad three times, visited Egypt, "Palestine, and the East in 1867; I have written a great "many articles, letters of travel, etc., for the press." Rev. Mr. Goodell was born in Calais, Vt., March 16, 1830; and was graduated at the University of Vermont in 1855, and at Andover Theological Seminary in 1858. He was Pastor of the Congregational Church in New Britain, Ct., 14 years, and of the Pilgrim Church in St. Louis, Mo., from 1873 till his death. In 1859 he married Miss Emily, daughter of Governor Erastus Fairbanks of St. Johnsbury, Vt.; they had two children.

Mr. Goodell died of apoplexy at St. Louis, the first week in February, 1886.

Goodhue, J. F. *The Church* of Christ one. A Sermon, Delivered at Williston, Vt., Sabbath, July 10, 1831. By Josiah F. Goodhue. Published by Request. Burlington : Printed by Foote & Stacy. 1831. 12mo, pp. 36, (8.)

—*A Sermon*, on the Character and Services of Rev. Thomas A. Merrill, D. D. Delivered before the Addison Association, at their meeting in Middlebury, June 6th, 1855. By Rev. Josiah F. Goodhue, Pastor of the Congregational Church, in Shoreham, Vt. Published at the Request of the Association. Middlebury : Printed at the Register Book and Job Office. 1856. 8vo, pp. 24.

—*Memoir* of Rev. Thomas A. Merrill. By Rev. J. F. Goodhue.
Same imprint as the above and pagination continuous. pp. 72 in both.

—*History* of the Town of Shoreham, Vt. From the date of its charter, October 8th, 1761, to the present time. By Rev. Josiah F. Goodhue. Published by the Town. Middlebury : A. H. Copeland. 1861. 8vo, pp. vi, (2),198.
Sometimes Swift's History of Addison County is found bound with the same.
Mr. Goodhue was born in Westminster, Vt., December 31, 1791, and died at Whitewater, Wis., in May, 1863. He was graduated at Middlebury College in 1821; studied theology, and was settled over a church in Williston, Vt., 1824 to 1834, when he accepted a call to the Congregational Church at Shoreham, Vt., where he remained 24 years.

Goodrich, Chauncey. The Northern Fruit Culturist, or Farmer's Guide to the Orchard and Fruit Garden. By Chauncey Goodrich. Second Edition, Corrected and Enlarged. Burlington: Chauncey Goodrich. 1850. 12mo, pp. 112.
Relates to the Fruits of Vermont, and their proper cultivation.
Mr. Goodrich was born in Hinsdale, Mass., and died in Burlington, Vt., September 11, 1858, aged 60. Mr. Goodrich was a bookseller and publisher, which business he followed in Hartford, Ct., six years; and moved to Castleton, Vt., in 1823, and thence to Burlington in 1827, where he conducted the publishing business through life. He also gave much attention to gardening and horticulture; in 1828 he was married to Arabella, a sister of President James Marsh.

Goodrich, C. A. A History of America, from the first discovery to the fourth of March, 1825. By Rev. Charles A. Goodrich, Fifth Edition. Bellows Falls, Vt.: 1825. 18mo, pp. 296, 20.

—*Ninth Edition.* Bellows Falls. James I. Cutler & Co. 1826. 12mo, pp. 296, 20. Twelfth Edition, Same Imprint. 1827.

—*Thirty-fifth Edition.* Same Imprint. 1833. 12mo, pp. 296, 20.

—*The Same.* Brattleborough, Vt. 1832. 12mo, pp. 296, 20.
Two hundred editions or more of this work have been printed; some of which read "A History of the United States, etc."

—*Outlines* of Modern Geography, on a new plan, carefully adapted to youth. With numerous engravings of Cities, Manners, Costumes, and Curiosities. Accompanied by an Atlas. By Rev. Charles A. Goodrich. Brattleborough, Vt.: Published by Holbrook and Fessenden. 1827. 12mo, pp. 252.

—*History* of the Church to the present time. Brattleboro: 1839. 8vo, pp. 504.

Title to first edition, 1829, "A View of all Religions," etc.

Goodrich, John Ellsworth. *The Bible* and the Creeds—an Historical Consensus. Burlington: 1879. pp. 4.

—*The Founder of the University of Vermont.* A Centennial Oration on the Life and Public Services of General Ira Allen, delivered Commencement Day, June 29, 1892, by Prof. J. E. Goodrich. Burlington : Free Press Print. 1892. 8vo, pp. 45.
Bound with the Oration of R. D. Benedict on the Charter History of the University.
Prof. Goodrich is also the author of an Address in memory of the Rev. Austin Hazen, delivered June 28, 1895, at Richmond, Vt.; and of a few other memorial addresses, privately printed. He edited the Obituary Record of the University of Vermont. No. I, 1895, containing sketches of Ira Allen, deceased Presidents of the University, and two hundred of the Alumni. He also wrote the article on Vermont for the 9th edition of the Encyclopædia Britannica; and Sketches of the Presidents of the University of Vermont for the National Cyclopædia of American Biography. He has been a frequent contributor to the Vermont Chronicle, the Burlington Free Press, and an Educational Monthly of N. Y. city. Mr. Goodrich was born in Hinsdale, Mass., Jan. 19, 1831; graduated from the University of Vermont, 1853; and from Andover Theol. Sem. 1860; Principal of academies in Hinsdale, Mass., and Montpelier, Vt., 1853-56; and in Meriden, N. H., 1871-72; Chaplain 1st Vermont Cavalry, 1864-5; acting pastor at Malone, N. Y., and Richmond, Vt., 1865-68; Supreintendent of City Schools, Burlington, Vt., 1869-71; Professor in the University of Vermont, of Rhetoric and Latin, 1872-77; of Latin and Greek, 1877-81; of Latin, 1881.—Librarian, 1873-86.

Goodwillie, Thomas. *A Sermon* preached at Montpelier, Before the Legislature of the State of Vermont, on the Day of the Anniversary Election, October 11, 1827. By Rev. Thomas Goodwillie, Pastor of the Presbyterian Church of Barnet, Vt. Montpelier : Printed by George W. Hill—Patriot Office. 1827. 8vo, pp. 35.
Was re-printed and had a large circulation. Mr Goodwillie was born in Barnet, Vt., September 27, 1800; and succeeded his father in 1825, as pastor of the "Associate Presbyterian Church" in Barnet. See Vermont Historical Magazine, vol. 1, pp. 284-299.

Goodwin, H. *A Vision*, of the Departed Spirit of Mr. Yeamans. By H. Goodwin. Brattleboro, Vt.: 1800. 12mo, pp. 11.
See A Vision.

Goodwin, Solomon, of Jamaica, Vt. The Spanish Court of Inquisition erected in Vermont, or, a Narrative of the Proceedings of several Baptist Elders and Churches. Brattleborough: Printed for the author. 1810. 8vo, pp. 48.

Governor and Council,
See Vermont.

Graham, John A. *A True Copy* of the Proceedings of John A. Graham, Esq., LL.D., Agent to the Protestant Episcopal Church of the State of Vermont, in North America, at the Court of London, A. D. 1795. Boston: 1795. 8vo, pp. 56.

—*The Correspondence* of John A. Graham, with His Grace of Canterbury, when on his mission as agent of the Church of Vermont, to the Ecclesiastical Courts of Canterbury and York, for the Consecration of Dr. Peters, Bishop elect of Vermont, 1794-5, etc. New York : J. Narine, Printer, Corner of Wall and Broad Streets. 1835. 8vo, pp. 26.

—*A Descriptive Sketch* of the present State of Vermont. One of the United States of America. By John A. Graham, LL. D. Late Lieutenant-Colonel in the service of the above State. London: Printed and sold, for the author, by Henry Fry, at the Cicero Office, Finsbury Place. 1797. 8vo, pp. vii. 186. Portrait and Plates.

—*An Address* to the Public; together with a Copy of a Letter to Stephen R. Bradley, Esq. Senator in Congress from Vermont. By John A. Graham. New York: 1805. 8vo.

—*Speeches* delivered at the City Hall of the City of New York, in the Courts of Oyer and Terminer, Common Pléas, and General Sessions of the Peace. By John A. Graham, LL. D., Counseller and Advocate in all the High Courts, and one of the Masters in Chancery for the State of New York. Second Edition, with Additions. New York: Printed and Published by George Forman. 1812. 8vo, pp. 140. Portrait.

Mr. Graham was born in Southbury, Ct., June 10, 1764; and died in New York, August 29, 1841. He removed to Rutland, Vt., in 1785, where he practiced law for several years. He was sent to England by the Diocese of Vermont to obtain the Consecration of Bishop Peters; but was unsuccessful. About 1805 Mr. Graham removed to New York, where he became distinguished in his profession.

Grafton. *The Report* of School Superintendent of the Town of Grafton, Vt., for the year ending March 31, 1871. Lewis B. Hibbard Superintendent. Ludlow: Gazette Job Printing Department. 1871. 8vo, pp. 16.
Continued.

—*The Financial Report* of the Auditors of the Town of Grafton, for the year Ending February 12, 1876. Rutland: Tuttle & Company Printers. 1876. 8vo, pp. 14.
Continued.

Grammar. *Inductive Grammar.* Designed for Beginners. By an Instructor. Windsor. Printed and published by S. Ide. 1829. 8vo, pp. 54.

Grand Army of the Republic. *By-Laws* of Post Brooks, G. A. R., (As Amended.) 16mo, pp. 8. No date, no imprint.

—*Proceedings* of Annual Encampment, Department of Vermont, held at Burlington, Vt.. January 12, 1872. With Reports of W. W. Henry, Dep't Commander, and the Officers of the Department Staff. Rutland: Tuttle & Co., Printers. 1872. 8vo, pp. 23.
The Same. Sixth Annual Encampment, at St. Albans, January 30th, 1873. Rutland, 1873. 8vo, pp. 24.

—*By-Laws*, Rules and Regulations of Johnson Post No. 23, G. A. R., Northfield, Vt. Montpelier: Printed by J. & J. M. Poland. 1876. 18mo, pp. 12.

—*Journal* of the Twenty-fifth Annual Encampment of the Department of Vt. G. A. R, Rutland: Tuttle & Co., Printers. 1892. 8vo, pp. 72.

—*Journal* of the Twenty-fifth National Encampment G. A. R. Rutland: Tuttle & Co., Printers. 1892. 8vo, pp. 412.

—*Journal* of the Seventh Annual Convention of the Woman's Relief Corps. Rutland: The Tuttle Co. 1891. 8vo, pp. 52.

—*Order of Exercises* of the Decoration of Soldiers' Graves in Montpelier, May 29, 1880. Poland, Printer. 8vo, pp. 4.

Continued.
Contains the names of 102 deceased soldiers whose graves are decorated.

Grand Isle County. *Atlas Map* of Grand Isle County.
See Franklin County.

Grandpre, L. De. *Voyage* to the Indian Ocean and Bengal in 1789-90. Translated from the French. Brattleborough, Vt. 1814. 12mo.

Grand Temple of Honor and Temperance. *Proceedings* of the fourth Annual Session of the Grand Temple of Honor and Temperance of the State of Vermont, held at St. Johnsbury, June 9th and 10, 1871. Montpelier: Argus and Patriot Job Printing House. 1871. 8vo, pp. 8.

Granville. East Granville Manufacturing and Transportation Co. Montpelier, Vt.: Argus and Patriot Steam Book and Job Printing Works. 1880. 12mo, pp. (8.)

Graves, Charles E. *A Serious Attack* on the Rights of the Laity: Being An Argument before the Right Rev. the Bishop of Vermont, upon a Hearing in the matter of the Excommunication of two members of the Protestant Episcopal church. n. p. n. d.

Graves, Hiram Atwell.
A native of Jericho, Vt., was graduated at Middlebury College, 1834. He read theology, and was pastor of a Baptist church in Springfield, Mass., 1837-40; in Lynn, Mass., 1840-42; and was sometime associate editor of the Christian Reflector, Boston, Mass. He went to the island of Jamaica for his health, but returned and died at Bristol, R. I., Nov. 3, 1850, aged 37. He published "The Attractions of Heaven," "The Family Circle," and probably other works.—*Pearson's Graduates of Middlebury College.*

Gray, Alonzo *An Address* before the Essex Agricultural Society, at Georgetown, Ms., September 30, 1841. Salem. 1842. 8vo, pp. 30.

—*Elements of Chemistry.* Andover, 1841. 12mo.

—*The Same*, newly revised and greatly enlarged, 40th edition. New York. 1853. 12mo.

—*Elements* of Scientific and Practical Agriculture. Andover. 1842. 12mo.

—*Elements* of Natural Philosophy. New York. 12mo. 1851.

—*Elements* of Geology. By Alonzo Gray, A. M., and C. B. Adams, A. M. New York. 1852. 8vo. The Same. New York. 1853. Harper & Brothers. 8vo, xv, 354.

—*The Smithsonian Institution.* 8vo, pp. 21.

—*Address* on Female Education. New York. 1854. 8vo.

Mr. Gray was born in Townsend, Vt., in 1808; died in Brooklyn, N. Y., March 10, 1860. He was graduated at Amherst College, 1834; was Professor of Chemistry and Natural Philosophy at Andover Academy, 1837-43; and subsequently Principal of Brooklyn Heights Female Seminary.

Gray, Edward. *Family Record* of Edward Gray and his wife, Mary Paddock, and their descendants. By Alonson Gray. Rutland: Tuttle & Co. 1889. 8vo, pp. 196.

Green, Beriah. *A Sermon*, preached in Poultney, June 29, 1826, at the First Annual Meeting of the Rutland County Foreign Missionary Society. By Beriah Green, Pastor of the Congregational Church in Brandon. Cas-

tleton, Vt. Published by Order of the Society. 1826. 8vo, pp. 40.
Includes First Report.

—*An Oration*, pronounced at Middlebury, before the Associated Alumni of the College, on the Evening of Commencement, Aug. 16th, 1826. By Beriah Green. Published by Request. Castleton: Printed by Ovid Miner. 1826. 8vo, pp. 39.

—*A Sermon*, preached at Brandon, Vt., Oct. 3, 1827, at the Ordination of the Rev. Messrs. Jonathan S. Green & Ephraim W. Clark, as Missionaries to the Sandwich Islands. By Beriah Green, Pastor of the Congregational Church in Brandon. Middlebury: Printed by J. W. Copeland. 1827. 8vo, pp. 28.
Mr. Green was born in Preston, Ct., in 1795; and was graduated at Middlebury College, 1819. He was pastor of the Congregational Church, Brandon, Vt., 1823–29; which appears to comprise his entire connection with Vermont. He died at Whitestown, N. Y., May 4, 1874.

Green, Horace, M. D., LL. D.
Dr. Green was born in Chittenden, Vt., December 24, 1802, and died at Greenmount, Sing Sing, N. Y., November 29, 1866. He read medicine in Rutland, Vt., and Paris, France; and practiced his profession in Rutland, altogether about twelve years; was Professor in Castleton Medical College 1840–43. In 1850 he assisted in founding the New York Medical College, of which he was President and a Professor until 1860. His published works are: "Treatise on the Diseases of the Air-Passages," which reached a third edition; New York: 1846. 8vo.; "Pathology and Treatment of the Croup," 1849. 12mo.; "On the Surgical Treatment of the Polypi of the Larynx, and the Edema of the Glottis;" "Report of 106 cases of Pulmonary Diseases, treated by Injections into the Bronchial Tubes with a Solution of Nitrate of Silver," 1856; "Selections from the favorite Prescriptions of Living American Physicians," 1858. He also contributed many papers to Medical and other journals in this country and in England.

Greene, Rev. R. A. *Sermon Preached* at the Funeral of Mrs. James Nichols, March 6, 1876, by Rev. R. A. Greene, Northfield, Vt. Montpelier, Vt.: Argus and Patriot Steam Book and Job Printing House. 1876. 8vo, pp. 12.

Greenleaf, Jeremiah. *Grammar Simplified;* or an Ocular Analysis of the English Language. By J. Greenleaf. Tenth edition. Corrected, Enlarged, and Improved by the Author. New York: Charles Starr. 1824. 8vo, pp. 50.

—*The Same*, Twentieth edition. New York, 1837. 8vo. pp. 50.
First edition was published about 1816.

—*The Labor Saving Grammar*, By the Author of Grammar Simplified. Copyright, 1843, by Jeremiah Greenleaf. Boston: Dexter S. King. 1843. sm. 4to, p. 32.
Mr. Greenleaf was a resident of Guilford, Vt. See History of Brattleboro, p. 116.

Greenleaf, Rev. Jonathan. *A Sketch* of the Settlement of the Town of Lyndon, in the County of Caledonia, and State of Vermont, collected from Authentic Records, and from Reliable Tradition, in March 1842, By Rev. Jonathan Greenleaf. Middlebury: Printed by Justus Cobb. 1852. 8vo, pp. 24.

Green Mountain Culturist. *Vol. 1, No. 3, 1852.* Monthly. Published by D. D. Bassett & Co., Middlebury Vt. 8vo, pp. 32.

Green Mountain Emporium, *and Literary*, Moral and Religious Record. By J. Milton Stearns. No. VIII. of Vol. I. Montpelier, Vt.

June, 1839. Allen & Poland, Printers. Monthly. rl. 8vo, pp. 15.
The Green Mountain Emporium was moved to Middlebury by Mr. Stearns in 1840 or '41.

The Green Mountain Gem; *A Monthly Journal* of Literature, Science and the Arts. A. B. F. Hildreth, Editor. Vols. 1 to 6. 4to, and 8vo, after vol. 1. Bradford, Vt.: Published by A. B. F. Hildreth. 1843–48.

Green Mountain Liberal Institute, *South Woodstock, Vt., Catalogues.*

Green Mountain Mining Company, *Vermont.* Boston: Morrill & Son, 1863. 8vo, pp. 18.

Green Mountain Poets. *A Collection of Poems* from the best talent in the Green Mountain State. Boston: Lee & Shepard. Claremont, N. H.: Claremont Stationery Co.; White River Junction, Vt.: White River Paper Co. [1881.] 12mo, pp. 522.
This is the A. J. Sanborn compilation, with the addition of a steel portrait of the late Charles G. Eastman for a frontispiece, and nine of his poems. See Sanborn, A. J.; Hemenway, Abby M.

The Green Mountain Repository. *Monthly* for the year 1832. All published. Edited by Z. Thompson, A. M. Burlington: Printed by Edward Smith. 1832. 12mo, pp. 284.

The Green Mountain Slate and Tile Company. Boston: Alfred Mudge & Son. 1865. 8vo, pp. 24.

Green Mountain Spring. *Devoted* to Discussions and Information Concerning the popular and Medical use of Water: to A Report of Water-cure Treatment; to the nurture and education of Children; to Diet and Health. Brattleboro, Vt. 1846. rl 8vo, pp. 500.
Title from Gowans.

Greensboro. *Soldiers* in the Civil War.
See Rollins, E. E.

—*History of,*
See Stone, J. P.

—*Manual* of the Congregational Church, in Greensboro, Vt. Published by vote of the Church, October, 1867. Montpelier: Printed at the Freeman Steam Printing Establishment. 1867. 8vo, pp. 16.

—*Annual Report* of the Officers of the Town of Greensboro, for the year ending February, 1881. Montpelier, Vt.: Argus and Patriot Steam Book and Job Printing House. 1881. 8vo, pp. 11.
Continued.

Gregg, W. P. and Pond, Benjamin. *The Railroad Laws* and Charters of the United States, now for the first time Collated. Arranged in Chronological Order, and published with a Synopsis and Explanatory Remarks. By W. P. Gregg and Benjamin Pond, of the Boston Bar. Vol. 1. Containing the Railroad laws and Charters of Maine, New Hampshire and Vermont. Vol. 2. Containing the Railroad laws and Charters of Massachusetts, Rhode Island and Connecticut. Boston: Charles C. Little and James Brown. 1851. 8vo, pp. XX. (2), 954. XX, 1193.
Contains the Laws and Charters of Vermont, 1831—1850.

Gregory, John. *"Everlasting Burnings."* A Discourse. By John Gregory, Pastor of the

Universalist Society, Burlington, Vt. "Prove all things, Hold fast that which is good." Burlington: E. & T. Mills, Printers. 1834. 8vo, pp. 16.

—*The Substance* of a Review of a Sermon, By Bishop Hopkins, Against Universalism; Preached before the Universalist Society, in Burlington, Vt., on Sunday Evening, March 29, 1835. By John Gregory. "The word is a Lamp unto my feet, and a Light unto my Path." David. Published by request of the Society. Montpelier: Wm. Clark. 1835. 8vo, pp. 12.

—*A Review* of a Sermon, by Bishop Hopkins, against Universalism; and preached before the Universalist Society, in Burlington, Vt., on Sunday Evening, March 29, 1835. By John Gregory, Pastor. Motto. [Published by request of the Society.] Burlington: Smith and Harrington. 1835. 8vo, pp. 24.

Contains the sermon in full; the first edition was abbreviated.

—*Anti-War*. Two Discourses delivered at Williston and Burlington, July, 1846. Likewise a Discourse, delivered at the Universalist State Convention, Montpelier, Aug. 26, 1846. By John Gregory. Motto. Burlington: Chester C. Briggs. Boston: Abel Tompkins. 1847. 12mo, pp. about 100.

—*The Cause of Rechab*: An Address delivered before the Green Mountain Tribe of Rechabites. Tents No. 1 and 4, Burlington and Williston, February, 1847. By John Gregory. Burlington: Chester C. Briggs. 1847. 8vo, pp. 28.

—*1776—1876*. Centennial Proceedings and Historical Incidents of the early settlers of Northfield, Vt., with Biographical Sketches of Prominent business men who have been and are now residents of the town. By Hon. John Gregory. Montpelier, Vermont: Argus and Patriot Book and Job Printing House. 1878. 8vo, pp. 319.

Many portraits and plates.

—*An Expose of Spiritualism*. By Rev. John Gregory. Montpelier: Poland's Steam Printing Establishment. 1872. 8vo, pp. 104.

—*Tipping His Tables*: Ramblings after a Rambler; Exposures of an Exposer. Elicited by "An Expose of Spiritualism by Rev. John Gregory, Northfield, Vt., 1872." By Allen Putnam. Boston: 1873. Wm. White & Co. 12mo, pp. 64.

The Hon. and Rev. John Gregory was born in Norwich, Conn., November 18, 1810; died at Northfield, Vt., of apoplexy, September 26, 1881. In early life he served as a fancy painter in New York and Albany. At the age of 21 he began to study for the Universalist ministry. He was ordained and settled, in 1832, at Salisbury, Herkimer county, N. Y. After two years, he removed to Burlington, Vt., and preached a year. Then to Woburn, Mass., where he preached two years. After another year in Vermont, he went to Charleston, S. C., where he edited the "Southern Evangelist," and supplied a pulpit. The climate not agreeing with him, he returned to Vermont, and preached in Montpelier, Berlin, Williamstown, and Northfield for a year. Next, he received a call to Quincy, Mass., where he preached three years, also representing that town in the Massachusetts General Court. Thence he went to Fall River for two years, and then back to Williston, where he preached three years. In 1850 he came to Northfield and settled on a farm at West Hill, now owned by J. E. Dole. For 25 years he was connected with the Vermont State Agricultural Society, claiming to

have been one of its originators, and as a Director and President two years. He was prominent in raising Morgan horses, French merino sheep, and fancy cattle. He helped establish, and for three years was President of the Dog River Valley Association. In 1850-1 he represented Northfield in the Vermont General Assembly, and was a State Senator in 1856-8. He was appointed an Assistant Inspector of Internal Revenue, by President Lincoln, and reappointed by President Johnson, serving ten and a half years. He was an earnest anti-slavery advocate, and frequently lectured on temperance.

For biographical sketch, see his history of Northfield, pp. 167-169.

Gridley, J. *History of Montpelier*; A Discourse delivered in the Brick Church, Montpelier, Vermont, on Thanksgiving Day, Dec. 8, 1842. By Rev. John Gridley, Pastor of said Church. Motto. Montpelier: E. P. Walton & Sons. 1843. 8vo, pp. 48.

—*The Young Man* Beguiled of His Strength. A Sermon Delivered in the Brick Church, Montpelier, Vt., on Sabbath Evening, the 29th March, 1846, By Rev. John Gridley, Pastor of the Church. Montpelier: Eastman & Danforth. 1846. 12mo, pp. 21.

Mr. Gridley was Pastor of the Congregational Church at Montpelier, December, 1841, to December, 1846, when he moved to Wisconsin. He died at Kenosha, Wis., (where he settled after leaving Montpelier), December 27, 1876, at the age of eighty years.

Gridley, Selah, M.D. "*The Mill of the Muses*," and other Poems. 12mo, pp. 267. (Published about 1830.)

Mr. Gridley was born in Farmington, Conn., in 1767, and died at Exeter, N. H., about 1826. He read medicine, and removed early in life to Castleton, Vt., where he practiced his profession until near the close of his life. He was the first President of the Medical School at Castleton, and was a Professor for many years in the institution. For a full sketch of his life see Miss Hemenway's Vermont Historical Gazetteer, Vol. III, pp. 534-6.

Grinnell, Josiah Busnell. *The Silver Wedding* Anniversary of Hon. J. B. Grinnell and Wife. Presentation Address: Poems and Responses. At Grinnell, Iowa, February 5, 1877. State Register Print. 8vo, pp. 20.

—*New Haven*, A Rural Historical Town of Vermont. Oration by Hon. J. B. Grinnell, and Addresses. Printed by request. Burlington: Free Press Association. 1887. 8vo, pp. 32.

—*Men and Events* of Forty Years. Autobiographical Reminiscences of an active career from 1850 to 1890, by the late Josiah Busnell Grinnell. With introduction by Prof. Henry W. Parker, D. D. Boston. D. Lothrop & Company. 1891. 8vo, pp. xvi, 426.

Mr. Grinnell was born in New Haven, Vt., in 1821; was graduated at Oberlin College in 1844, and at Auburn Seminary in 1847; preached at Union Village; New York City; Washington, D. C.; and at Grinnell, Iowa; State Senator 1856; was President of Grinnell University in 1860; member of Congress 1864-66; he held numerous presidencies of State Associations; was Receiver of the Central Railroad of Iowa; and held many minor offices. He died at Grinnell, Iowa, March 3, 1891.

Griswold, Rt. Rev. A. V. *Address* to the Diocesan Convention at Windsor, Vt., Sept 25, 1816. 12mo.

—*An Address* to the Twelfth Convention of the Protestant Episcopal Church in the Eastern Diocese, held at Claremont, N. H., September 26, 1827, By Rt. Rev. A. V. Griswold, Bishop of the Diocese. Middlebury, Vt.: Printed by J. W. Copeland. 1827. 8vo, pp. 16.

See Appleton's Cyclopedia, 1st edition, for biographical sketch.

Griswold, John. *The Triumph* of the Wicked, or Reign of Infidelity, illustrated in a sermon preached at Pawlet, on the Anniversary Thanksgiving of Vermont, December 6, 1804, from Revelations xi: 10. Containing some new thoughts respecting the two witnesses and the manner of their death. By John Griswold, A. M. Pastor of the Congregational Church in Pawlet. Bennington: Haswell & Smead, Printers. 12mo, pp. 60.

—*Funeral Sermon* delivered in Pawlet, Vt., January 12, 1813, on the occasion of the death of Ephraim Fitch, who was instantly killed in his mill. 1813. 8vo.

Mr. Griswold was born in Norwich, Conn., February 24, 1765; was graduated at Dartmouth, 1789, and Pastor of the Congregational Church in Pawlet, 1793-1830, and died there May 4, 1852.

GRISWOLD, RUFUS W. *The Biographical* Annual: containing Memoirs of Eminent Persons (Americans), Recently Deceased. Edited by Rufus W. Griswold. New York: Linen & Fennell. 1841. 12mo, pp. 307. 2 Portraits.

—*The Cyclopedia* of American Literature, by Evart A. Duyckinck and George L. Duyckinck. A Review. New York. 1856. 8vo, pp. 32.

Reprinted from the New York Herald of February 13, 1856. "A Malignant Review of a Useful Work."—*Sabin.*

—*The Female Poets* of America. By R. W. Griswold. Philadelphia. 1849. 8vo, pp. 400. Portraits.

Six or more editions have been published, the last revised and brought down to the present time, by R. H. Stoddard. New York, 1869. 8vo, pp. 487.

—*The Republican Court*, or American Society in the days of Washington. By Rufus Wilmot Griswold. With Twenty-one Portraits of Distinguished (American) Women, engraved from original Pictures by Woolaston, Copley, Gainsborough, Stuart, Trumbull, Pine, Malbone, and other Contemporary Painters. New York: D. Appleton and Company. M.DCCC.LV. rl 8vo, pp. IV, (4), 408.

An elegant and costly work. Four editions have been issued, revised and enlarged.

—*Gems* from American Female Poets, with Brief Biographical Notices. By Rufus W. Griswold. Philadelphia: H. Hooker. 1842. 32mo, pp. 192. Plate.

—*The Poets* and Poetry of America. With an Historical Introduction. By Rufus W. Griswold. Philadelphia: Carey and Hart. MDCCCXLII. 12mo, pp. xxiv, 468.

Eighteen or more revised and enlarged editions of this work have been published.

—*The Prose Writers* of America, By Rufus W. Griswold. Philadelphia: Carey & Hart. 1847. 8vo, pp. 552.

Seven editions or more have been published, the last in 1870, pp. 669, (1). Plates.

—*Sacred Poets* of England and America. from the Earliest to the Present Time. A New Improved Edition. D. Appleton & Co., New York. MDCCCXLIV. 8vo, pp. 552. Plates.

Many editions published; the last we have seen, 1866.

—*Statement* of the Relations of Rufus W. Griswold with Charlotte Meyers (called Charlotte Griswold), Elisabeth F. Ellet, Ann S. Stephens, Samuel J. Waring, Hamilton R. Searles, and Charles D. Lewis, with particular reference to their late unsuccessful attempt to have set aside the Decree granted in the Case of Griswold vs. Griswold. Philadelphia. 1856. 8vo, pp. 32.

"Contains some very curious particulars in relation to this scandalous affair."—*Sabin.*

—*Washington* and the Generals of the American Revolution. Philadelphia: Carey & Hart. 1847. 2 vols., 12mo, pp. 824; 330. 16 Portraits.

"Said to have been suppressed in consequence of a controversy concerning J. T. Headley's work with a similar title-page."—*Sabin.*

—*The Cypress Wreath*: a Book of Consolation for those who Mourn. Boston: Gould, Kendall & Lincoln. 1844. 32mo, pp. 128.

—*The Poets and Poetry* of England in the Nineteenth Century; 2d Edition in 1845, 8vo; 4th ed., in 1854.

—and *Lossing, Benson J.* Washington: A Biography: Personal, Military, and Political. New York: Virtue & Co. 1856-60. 3 vols., rl. 8vo, pp. vi, (1), 17, 768; 4, 740; (4), 652. Plates.

—*Catalogue* of the entire library of Rev. Rufus W. Griswold, D. D., LL. D. Sold at auction by Bangs, Merwin & Co., New York, May 23-28, inclusive, 1859. rl. 8vo, pp. 154, and contains 3280 lots.

Mr. Griswold was born in Benson, Vt., February 15, 1815; he died in New York city, August 27, 1857. Before he was 20 years of age he had visited the larger portion of his own country, and of Southern and Central Europe. He was at first a printer's apprentice, but studied divinity, and became a Baptist preacher. He soon, however, commenced a literary life, and was engaged as associate editor on many periodicals in Boston, New York and Philadelphia; and in addition to the list of his works already noticed, he published anonymously, in 1841, a volume of poems, also one of sermons. He also published "Christian Ballads, and other Poems," "Scenes in the Life of our Saviour" "Curiosities of American Literature," appended to Disraeli; "Napoleon and his Marshals," with H. B. Wallace, in 1847; the "Opal," a Gift for the Holidays. N. York, 1844. He edited the first American edition of the prose works of Milton, and was one of the editors of the works of Edgar A. Poe. Consult Allibone; Drake's Biographical Dictionary; Knickerbocker Magazine, vols. 36, p. 162, and 46, p. 398; Duyckinck; Appleton's Cyclopedia, 1st ed.

Mr. Griswold learned the printer's trade in Middlebury, and was a printer at Vergennes, 1833-39, as his imprints appear in this list. See Townsend, W. W.; Vergennes.

Gross, Thomas. *A Sermon*, delivered before His Excellency the Governor, the Lieutenant Governor, the Council, and the House of Representatives of Vermont, at Woodstock, October 8, 1807; Being the day of General Election. By Thomas Gross, A. M. Pastor of the Church in Hartford. Motto. Randolph: Printed by Sereno Wright. 1807. 8vo, pp. 23.

Mr. Gross was graduated at Dartmouth College, 1784, and was pastor of the Congregational church, Hartford, Vt., 1786-1808, when he removed to western New York, and died at Batavia, N. Y., March 18, 1843, aged 84.

Grout, Henry Martyn.

Brother to Rev. Lewis Grout; was born in Newfane, Vt., May 14, 1831; was graduated at Williams College, 1854, and was settled over different Congregational churches in Vermont and Massachusetts. He writes under date of January, 1878, that the following are the noteworthy publications by him: Sermon with appendix, "Commemorative of Hon. Edward Southworth," 1870; sketch of Hon. Edward Southworth, re-printed from *Congregational Quarterly*, 1871. "Trinitarian Congregationalism in Concord (Mass.)—A Historical Discourse," 1876. "The Gospel Invitation, sermons related to the Boston Revival of 1877;" a volume edited by Mr. Grout, contains a sermon by him: "The Door Opened, and Christ Within." His contributions to "Sermons by the Monday Club," are, to the first series, 1876: "David and Jonathan;" "Honest Industry;" "The Early Christian Church;" "Philip and the Ethiopian." To the second series, 1877; "Elijah on Carmel," "The Famine in Samaria," "Paul at Athens," "Paul at Jerusalem." To the third series, 1878: "Jehoshaphat Reproved," "Ahaz's Persistent Wickedness," "Jeremiah in Prison," "The Childhood and Youth of Jesus," "The Lord's Supper."

Two sermons "Victory over Death, or The Hope of the Resurrection," "The Childhood and Youth of Jesus." Re-printed from "Sermons by the Monday Club," for 1879. Mr. Grout furnished four additional sermons for the Club series for 1879: "The Keeping of the Sabbath," "The way of the Right- ous," "Queen Esther;" "Faith and Works," "Elijah on Carmel," and other sermons.

A portion of the above sermons have been published in a volume entitled "The Model Friendship."

Mr. Grout was honored with the degree of Doctor of Divinity, in 1878, by his *Alma Mater*, Williams College.

He died in Boston, Saturday, March 6, 1886.

GROUT, LEWIS. *The Isizulu.* A Grammar of the Zulu Language; accompanied with a Historical Introduction, Also With an Appendix. By Rev. Lewis Grout, Missionary of the American Board; and Corresponding Member of the American Oriental Society. Natal: Printed by James C. Buchanan, at Umsundusi: Published by May & Davis, Pietermaritzburg; J. Cullingworth, Durban. London: Trubner & Co., 60 Paternoster Row. 1859. 8vo, pp. lii, 432.

—*The Isizulu:* a revised Edition of a Grammar of the Zulu Language; with an Introduction and an Appendix. By Rev. Lewis Grout, late Missionary of the American Board among the Zulus; author of "Zulu-Land;" and a Corresponding Member of the American Oriental Society. Boston: American Board of Commissioners for Foreign Missions. 1893. London: Kegan Paul, Trench, Trubner & Co., Ltd. 8vo, pp. xxvi, 313.

—*History of the Zulu,* and other Tribes, in and around Natal: Printed by the Colonial Government, for the information of His Honor the Lieutenant Governor. Natal: 1853.

—*A Reply to Bishop Colenso's Remarks* on the proper Treatment of cases of Polygamy, as found Existing in Converts from Heathenism; by An American Missionary. Pietermaritzburg: 1855. 8vo, pp. 56.

—*An Answer to Dr. Colenso's "Letter" on Polygamy:* by an American Missionary. Pietermaritzburg: 1856. 8vo, pp. 103.

—*God's Delight in the Gates of Zion:* A Sermon Delivered at the Dedication of the House of Worship erected by the Congregational Church in Durban, Natal, Jan. 8, 1856, by the Rev. Lewis Grout, American Missionary. Pietermaritzburg: 1856. 8vo, pp. 24.

—*The Religion of Faith and that of Form.* A Discourse, (two in one.) Delivered in several different Places of Worship, Congregational, Presbyterian, and Wesleyan, at Durban. and Pietermaritzburg, during the autumn of 1857; by the Rev. Lewis Grout, American Missionary. Pietermaritzburg: 1857. 8vo, pp. 48.

—*The Primitive Polity of Christian Churches.* A Discourse Delivered at the Public Recognition of the Rev. George Y. Jeffreys, as Pastor of the Congregational Church in Durban, Natal, October 25th, 1857. By the Rev. Lewis Grout, American Missionary. Pietermaritzburg: 1857. 8vo, pp. 39.

—*The Christian Ministry;* Its Character, Duties and Claims. A Discourse, (two in one,)

Preached in the Congregational and Presbyterian Churches in Durban and Pietermaritzburg, by the Rev. Lewis Grout. American Missionary. Pietermaritzburg: 1858. 8vo, pp. 48.

—*Translations* of Psalms, Acts, and other portions of the Bible into the Zulu Language. printed and Published in Natal.

—*Zulu-Land;* or Life among the Zulu Kaffirs of Natal and Zulu-Land, South Africa; with map, and Illustrations, largely from original Photographs. By Rev. Lewis Grout, for fifteen years missionary of the American Board in South Africa; author of A Grammar of the Zulu Language, and Corresponding Member of the American Oriental Society. Philadelphia: 1864. pp. 351.

—*Reminiscences of Life* among the Zulu Kaffirs: Boston Review, November, 1865.

—*Colenso on the Doctrines;* A Review of his Notes on Romans: Congregational Review, September, 1869.

—*The Church-membership* of Baptized Children. Bib. Sacra, April, 1871.

—*An Essay* on the Zulu and other Dialects in South Africa: Journal of the American Oriental Society, 1849.

—*A Plan* for Effecting a Uniform Orthography of the South African Dialects: Jour. Am. Oriental Society, 1851.

—*An Essay* on the Phonology and Orthography of the Zulu and Kindred Dialects of South Africa: Jour. Am. Oriental Society, 1853.

—*Observations* on the Prepositions, Conjunctions, and other Particles, of the Isizulu and its Cognate Languages: Jour. Am. Oriental Society, 1859.

—*"In the Times of Old."* A Discourse on the Early History of the Congregational Church in West Brattleboro, Vt. Delivered December 31, 1876. By the Rev. Lewis Grout. "In treasuring up the memorials of the Fathers we best manifest our regard for posterity." Brattleboro: D. Leonard, Steam Job Printer. 8vo, pp. 32.

—*God's Delight in the Gates of Zion.* A second Discourse on the Early History of the Congregational Church and Society in West Brattleboro, Vt., covering two pastorates, 25 years, or from 1794 to 1819. By the Rev. Lewis Grout. New Haven: Tuttle, Morehouse & Taylor, Printers. 1894. 8vo, pp. 31.

—*The Place and Power* of each Family of African Language as Factors in the Development of Africa. An Essay at the Chicago Congress on Africa, August, 1893. By the Rev. Lewis Grout, Missionary among the Zulus, 1846 to 1862: Author of "A Grammar of the Zulu Language;" Author of "Zulu-Land;" and a Corresponding Member of the American Oriental Society. (No imprint.) 8vo, pp. 20.

The Funk and Wagnalls' Encyclopedia of Missions, published in 1891, contains a number of articles from Mr. Grout's pen, such as: A Sketch of most of the African Races; the Bantu-Zulu; the Berber, Negro, Nuba-Fulah, and Hottentot-Bushman; A Historical Sketch of the Soudan; A sketch of the several (10) American and

European Missions among the Zulus; and a Biographical Sketch of Rev. John T. Vanderkemp. Various addresses, sermons and papers by Mr. Grout have been published in the Missionary Herald, Vermont Chronicle and other periodicals.

Rev. Lewis Grout was born in Newfane, Vt., January 28, 1815. He was the son of Deacon John Grout and Azubah (Dunklee) Grout. His father was a native of Westminster, and his mother of Brattleboro, Vt. Lewis was the oldest of nine children, eight of whom were sons. They were accustomed to worship with the Congregational church in Marlboro until 1836, when they removed from Newfane to West Brattleboro. Lewis attended the Brattleboro Academy in 1834-5-6-7. He taught a district school in Marlboro in the winter 1835-6, in Putney 1836-7, and in East Guilford 1837-8. He attended Burr Seminary in 1838, entered Yale College the same year, and graduated thence in 1842. During a portion of the latter part of his collegiate course he was engaged in teaching in a military, classical and mathematical school at West Point, N. Y., where he also taught a year after graduating. He also studied Theology for two years at Yale Divinity College, 1844, and 1845, and one year at Andover Theological Seminary, where he graduated in 1846. In 1844 he paid his way by teaching a few hours a day in Miss Comstock's Ladies Seminary, and in 1845 by serving as Chaplain in the family of Gerard Halleck, Esq., editor of the "New York Journal of Commerce." October 8, 1846, he was ordained as a missionary, and married the same day to Miss Lydia Bates, in Springfield, Vt. He set sail from Boston, October 10, for South Africa, stopped a few weeks in Cape Town, and reached Natal, Africa, February 15, 1847. Here, among the Zulus, in the District of Natal, he labored as a missionary in the service of the American Board, for fifteen years, and at the end of that time, March 12, 1862, with impaired health, he set sail for his native land, and landed in Boston on the 7th of June. His mission life was one of much activity, labor and study of a pioneer character, full of solid reality, yet not a little diversified with what, in America, would be regarded as wild and romantic. Giving much time and attention to the study of African languages, especially the Zulu, of which it became his duty by appointment of the mission of which he was a member, to prepare a grammar; translating the Scriptures, and preparing other books in the Zulu tongue for the natives; having charge of the printing press for a time at his station; teaching, preaching and gathering a church; traveling and exploring; establishing a station where there was no trace of either Christianity or civilization, and so obliged to be, for himself and his people, architect and carpenter, brickmaker and mason, wheelwright and blacksmith, physician and dentist, farmer and magistrate; to say nothing of finding or building roads fording rivers, catching leopards; nothing of incidental studies in Natural History, of preparing a sketch of the native tribes, of having now and then a controversial tilt, as with the Colonial government (in behalf of the home or English government, the cause of humanity and Christian missions,) respecting the lands and rights of aborigines, or with Bishop Colenso on Biblical teaching and moral science, or the proper treatment of polygamy among a heathen people in their coming to embrace the Christian faith and enter the church,—the subject of this sketch found little time to be idle, or even to take the rest which a tropical clime made doubly important. Having returned to America, and been restored to a good measure of health, Mr. Grout preached a year for the Congregational church in Saxtons River, Vt., and then accepted a call to the church in Feeding Hills, Mass., where he was installed as pastor, and continued to labor till the first of October, 1865. He then received an appointment from the American Missionary Association as secretary and agent of that Society for New Hampshire and Vermont, and continued in the same till 1884; after which he served a year as financial agent of Atlanta University. In June, 1885, he entered upon pastoral work in charge of the church in Sudbury, Vt., and continued in this till September, 1888. Returning then to his home in West Brattleboro, he has been engaged in a variety of literary labors, of a historic, philological and missionary character.

Grout, William W. *An Oration* before the Reunion Society of Vermont Officers, November 4, 1869. By Gen. W. W. Grout. Rutland: Tuttle & Co. 1869. 8vo, pp. 29. The same reprinted: Barton: E. H. Webster, Printer, 1869. 8vo, pp. 34.

—*Geneva Award.* Speech of Hon. William W. Grout, of Vermont, in the House of Representatives, May 11, 1882. Motto. Washington: 1882. 8vo, pp. 18.

—*An Address* delivered by Hon. William W. Grout at the Sixteenth Annual Banquet of the Sons of Vermont in Illinois, Held at the Grand Pacific Hotel, Chicago, January 17, 1893. Chicago: 1893. 12mo, pp. 24.

—*Presentation* of the Statues of John Stark and Daniel Webster to Congress, for Statuary Hall. Remarks of Wm. W. Grout of Vermont in the House of Representatives, Dec. 20th, 1894. Washington: 1894. 8vo.

"Vermont congratulates New Hampshire and welcomes these her sons in commemorative marble to the Companionship of the Great, in marble and bronze, from other States."

General Grout was born in Compton, P. Q., May 24, 1836; he was graduated at Poughkeepsie Law School, 1857, and located at Barton, Vt., in 1858, where he had an extensive practice. He was Lieutenant Colonel of the 15th Reg't. Vt. Vols. in the late civil war, and represented Barton in the General Assembly in 1868, 69, 70 and 74; and Orleans County in the State Senate, 1876-7. He has held the office of State's Attorney, Town Agent, etc. He was elected to Congress in 1880, and again in 1884; and since then has served continuously in Congress to the present time, 1896.

Author of speeches on various public questions, delivered from time to time in the House of Representatives.

Guernsey, Alice M. 1492—1776. Five Centuries: A Centennial Drama. In five Acts. By Alice M. Guernsey. Boston, Mass.: The New England Publishing Company. 1876. 12mo, pp. 41.

Sometime teacher at Randolph, Vt.

Guild, J. H. *A Practical Treatise* on Spasmodic Asthma, with a full description of the only rational mode of cure. By J. H. Guild, M. D., Rupert, Vt. Rutland: Tuttle & Company, Printers. 1875. 8vo, pp. 51.

Dr. Guild was born in Pawlet, Vt., September 18, 1827; afterwards resided in Rupert; was a member of the House of Representatives from Rupert, 1872 74; and of the State Senate 1876.

Guilford. *Articles of Faith and Covenant* adopted by the First Congregational Church in Guilford, Vt., April 18, 1855. Boston: Press of T. R. Marvin & Son, 42 Congress St. 1858. 12mo, pp. 7.

Haddock, Charles B. *An Address* delivered before the Rail-Road Convention at Montpelier, Vt., January 8, 1844. By Charles B. Haddock, D. D. Professor &c, in Dartmouth College. Montpelier, Vt.: E. P. Walton & Sons, Printers. 1844. 8vo, pp. 24.

—*An Address*, delivered before the Vermont Medical College, at Woodstock, June 8, 1842. By Charles B. Haddock, Professor of Intellectual Philosophy, &c., in Dartmouth College. Published at the Request of the Faculty. Hanover: Printed by W. A. Patten. 1842. 8vo, pp. 24.

—*A Discourse* delivered at Hanover, N. H., May 7, 1841, on the occasion of the Death of William Henry Harrison, late President of the United States. By Charles B. Haddock, Professor of Intellectual Philosophy, &c. In Dart. Coll. Windsor, Vt.: Printed by Tracy and Severance. 1841. 8vo, pp. 24.

—*A Discourse*, Commemorative of Charles Brickett Haddock, D. D., Late Professor of Intellectual Philosophy and Political Economy. Delivered before the Faculty and Students of

Dartmouth College, April 19, 1861. By Samuel Gilman Brown, Professor in the College. Windsor, Vt.: Press of Bishop & Tracy. 1861. 8vo, pp. 30.

Charles Brickett Haddock, D. D., was born in Franklin, N. H., June 20, 1796; died in West Lebanon, N. H., January 15, 1861; was graduated at Dartmouth College, 1816, and at Andover Theological Seminary, 1819. His mother was a sister of Daniel Webster. Mr. Haddock was a Professor in Dartmouth College, 1819 to 1854; *charge d' affaires* from the United States to Portugal, 1851 to 1855; 4 years in the New Hampshire Legislature; and was father of the railroad system in New Hampshire. He has written with ability upon almost every subject; his sermons, orations, reports, and other writings are numerous, some of which have been collected and published in volumes.

Hager, Albert D. *Report* of Albert D. Hager, State Geologist of Vermont, on the Winooski Marble Quarries, at St. Albans, Vt. Boston: Alfred Mudge & Son, Printers, 34 School Street. 1866. 8vo, pp. 7.

—*The Marbles of Vermont.* An Address pronounced October 29, 1858, before the Vermont Historical Society, in the presence of the General Assembly of Vermont; By Albert D. Hager. Published by order of the General Assembly. Burlington: Times Job Office Print. 1858. 8vo, pp. 16.

—*Report* on the Economical Geology, Physical Geography and Scenery of Vermont: By Albert D. Hager, A. M., Proctorsville, Vt. Being a portion of the geological reports of the State made by Professor Hitchcock and his assistants; to which is added a description of some of the Lower Silurian Fossils found in Northern Vermont, By E. Billings, F. G. S. Printed by the Claremont Manufacturing Company. E. L. Goddard, Agent. 1862. 4to, pp. 252, with Map and 19 Plates.

—*Annual Report* of the State Geologist for the State of Missouri. (Coat of Arms.) Jefferson City: 1871. 8vo, pp. 23.

We give the following additional works of Mr. Hager, or with which he was connected :

He assisted Prof. Young in his "Preliminary Report on the Natural History of Vermont;" see Geology.

Belmont Coal Mining Co. Reports of Prof. George T. Chace, Prof. B. Silliman, Chas. T. Jackson, M. D., A. D. Hager, &c. Boston: 1863.—pp. 47. Bay State Coal Mine. Reports of Chas. T. Jackson, M. D., A. D. Hager, &c.—Boston. 1863. pp. 65. Report of the President and Directors of the Neguaket Mining Co., Lake Superior, with the Reports of Prof. J. S. Newbury, late U. S. Geologist, and A. D. Hager, Geologist of Vermont, &c. Boston: 1863. pp. 29. The Logan Copper Mining Co. Reports of A. D. Hager, A. M., and Charles Robb, Mining Engineer. Boston: 1864. pp. 16. Reports of the Stark Mining Co. By Charles T. Jackson, M. D., Prof. A. A. Hayes, M. D., and Albert D. Hager, A. M., State Geologist of Vt. 1864. pp. 22. Geological Surveys and Reports on the Property of the Tyson Iron Company, Plymouth, Vt. 1864. pp. 16. Norwegian Coal Company, Schuylkill Co., Pa. Reports of Prof. G. T. Chace of Brown Univ., R. I., Albert D. Hager Asst. State Geologist of Vt., &c. New York: 1864. pp. 32. Report on the Property of the Cornwall Copper Mining Co., by A. D. Hager, A. M., Chas. T. Jackson, M. D., Prof. A. A. Hayes, State Assayer, &c. Boston: 1864. pp. 20. Report on the Brandon Kaolin and Paint Co. By Albert D. Hager, A. M., State Geologist. 1864. Western Vermont Marble Co's. Quarries, Danby, Vt. Office 191 Broadway, N. Y. 1864. Report on the Richford Copper Mining Company, by Albert D. Hager, &c. Boston: 1864. The Green Mountain Slate and Tile Co. Reports of A. D. Hager, A. M., State Geologist of Vt., &c. Boston: 1865. pp. 24. Report on Copperas Hill Mining Co. 1864. pp. 15. Report on East Mt. Laffee Coal Mine, Schuylkill Co., Pa., by A. D. Hager, A. M., of Vt., and E. W. McGinnis, of Pottsville. New York: 1863. pp. 11. The Steam Stone Cutter Co., Rutland, Vt., 1865—pp. 12. The Kentucky National Petroleum and Mining Co. Principal office 35 W. 3d St., Cincinnati, O. 1865. pp. 24. Report on the American Variegated Marbles from Lake Champlain, Vermont. 164 Broadway, N. Y. pp. 8.

See Geology of Vermont; Fish Culture; Vermont, Report on Paris Exposition, 1867.

CHICAGO. June 19, 1879.

MR. GILMAN :—*Dear Sir* :—Your favor of the 16th is just at hand. I am too modest perhaps to write my own "sketch." I will give you the outlines, and you may fill the skeleton. Born in Chester, November 1, 1817. Didn't have first-rate chance at school. Folks were not rich. Started West in '36 peddling. Probably as green an 18-years-old as ever went out of Chester on a peddler's wagon. Sold lots of maps in 1836, but could not sell 'em in 1837. They were "getting down to specie payment and State banks" that year.

In 1839 went to Kentucky to work at my trade, carpenter and joiner, or keep school. Found folks there who did not know as much of books as I did, so I kept school till 1844 in the same village. Was good teacher. Went back to Vermont, worked at my trade summers, and kept school winters—successful teacher. Attended school teachers' conventions, etc., and folks thought I knew something about schools, so made me superintendent of schools in Reading and Cavendish. My reports were published for several years. Have not a copy myself, and don't know where there is one. No great loss I reckon. In the fall of 1856 was appointed by Judge Young Assistant State Naturalist, and put up the first cabinet in the old State House. The same fall was appointed first assistant State Geologist under Prof. E. Hitchcock. Worked four years in the survey of the State, and in 1861 published the result of our labors in two 4to vols. In 1859 furnished H. F. Walling a geological map of Vermont, and in 1860-61 published it and the State map got up by him and myself. My name as publisher, don't appear very conspicuous on the map, but I was the man.

In 1865, Gov. Dillingham sent me commission with request to report what I knew about re-stocking the Connecticut River with sea-fish. I didn't know anything, but at his request, "out of courtesy to the Legislature of New Hampshire," I kept the commission and next year Hon. Charles Barrett and I made report, and were appointed Fish Commissioners for five years. We reported in the years 1866, '67 and '69. During the war, after the Geological Report was out, I went as an expert to nearly every mine, quarry and oil-well in the United States and British Colonies. Made lots of reports which were published. I think I have a dozen or more at my residence —perhaps 20—may give the titles, etc., sometime. Was commissioned November 1, 1866, "to attend the Universal Exposition of 1867, Paris, France, in behalf of Vermont." Also February 20, 1867, was commissioned by the Grand Lodge of Vermont to "represent it in such grand and secular lodges in Great Britain and on the Continent of Europe as he may visit the ensuing year."

I was not particularly *smart* at anything, but in all things *was faithful*—did the best I could. Never had an investigation," so never was "white-washed," or "censured, as teacher or official. In 1870 made the great mistake of my life by leaving the good old State to accept the office of State Geologist of Missouri. Made one report which was published and maps of 29 counties on the scale of 4 miles to the inch, which was printed. My reports greatly offended some of the men who owned stock in the "Tin Mine" so-called. The State Senate voted unanimously to suppress my reports. I had said there was, to my mind, no evidence that tin ore was to be found in the State. I didn't know enough to know *tin*, and so Gratz Brown discharged me. No *tin* yet, however. I came here in 1873, April 1, and entered the Washingtonian Home as its Superintendent, remained there 18 months. There are lots of reformed men in this city of *my make* when there. Five have lived and died sober—so *that number* may be counted as *certainly* reformed. Out of 113 about 100 were reformed. The 10th Annual report of Washingtonian Home contains my report, pp. 40, Chicago, 1874 : Clark and Edwards, Printers.

I have also got up two reports of the Sons of Vermont, 1st and 2d.—or most of the 1st, and all the second. F. B. Williams was the Secretary, but I did that part of the work. So you see I have dabbled in several things before I came here. Have written considerable for newspapers, and some for magazines. I have two diplomas—one from Amherst, which conferred the honorable degree of A. M., and one from the Imperial Geological College of Vienna, of which I am corresponding member. Perhaps these last are not worth naming. I said to Prof. Hitchcock in letter of acceptance that it seemed hardly proper that I should have a diploma which I could not read. He said, "It was not because you could read Latin that we gave it, but because you had made such progress in science without a previous knowledge of Latin.

Yours truly,
A. D. HAGER.

Mr. Hager was subsequently Librarian of the Chicago Historical Society, for several years.

He died in Chicago, Sunday, July 29, 1888.

Hale, James. *Elements* of Geometry and Trigonometry, with an easy and concise system of Land Surveying. By James Hale. Bellows Falls, Vt. Published by James I. Cutler and Co., Printers. 1829. 12mo, pp. 115.

Hale, Robert Safford, *Thomas Hale* the Glover of Newbury, Mass., (1635) and his Descendants. By Robert S. Hale, LL. D. Boston : David Clapp & Son, Printers. 1877. 8vo, pp. 19.

Mr. Hale published in addition an important argument as counsel and a report as agent of the United States, before the British and American Mixed Commission, and possibly some speeches in Congress.

Mr. Hale, son of the late Hon. Harry Hale, of Chelsea, Vt., was born in that town September 24, 1822; graduated at the University of Vermont, 1842; read law and settled at Elizabethtown, Essex county, N. Y., for the practice of his profession; was Judge of Essex County Court, 1856-64; Regent of the University of New York, 1859; elected to the 39th and 43d Congresses.

On account of failing health Mr. Hale retired from the practice of his profession in May, 1880, and was succeeded by his son, Harry Hale. See Hale Genealogy; Lanman's Biographical Annals. Mr. Hale died at Elizabethtown, Dec. 14, 1881.

Hall, Arthur C. A. Right Rev. *The Virgin Mother.* Retreat Sermons on the life of the Blessed Virgin Mary, as told in the Gospels, by Rt. Rev. A. C. A. Hall, D. D., Bishop of Vermont. New York : Longmans, Green & Co., and London. 1894. 12mo, pp. 233.

—*The Church's Discipline* concerning Marriage and Divorce. First triennial charge by the Rt. Rev. A. C. A. Hall, D. D., Bishop of Vermont. New York : Longmans, Green & Co. 1896. 8vo, pp. 24.

Other works published by Rev. Mr. Hall before he became bishop are "Concerning Christ and His Church." Notes on Ephesians. James Pott & Co., N. Y. 1885. pp. 73. "The Gospel Woes." Lent Sermons by Rev. A. C. A. Hall, Mission Priest of St. John, the Evangelist. Same Publishers. 1891. pp. 96. "The Words from the Cross," Meditations for Holy Week. Same Publishers. 1892. pp. 78. "Reasonable Faith," four Sermons on the Gospels. Same Pubs. 1893. "The Example of the Passion, five Meditations." Same Pubs. 1893. pp. 78. "Meditations on the Lord's Prayer." Same Pubs. 1894. pp. v and 127.

Rt. Rev. Arthur Crawshay Alliston Hall was born in England in 1849 ; graduated at Oxford University ; studied theology, was admitted to holy orders, and entered the Society of John the Evangelist, at Cowley, near Oxford. After two years he was sent by his Superiors to Canada and the United States. He labored as a Missionary priest at Boston for 17 or 18 years, until 1891, when he was recalled to England by his Superiors. He was elected Bishop of the Episcopal Diocese of Vermont, August, 1893, Bishop Bissell, deceased : and was consecrated as Bishop February 2d, 1894.

Hall, Benjamin H. *A Collection* of College Words and Customs. Motto. Cambridge: Published by John Bartlett. 1851. 12mo, pp. 319.

—*A Collection of College Words and Customs.* By B. H. Hall. Revised and enlarged edition. Cambridge : Published by John Bartlett. 1856. 12mo, pp. 508.

—*History of Eastern Vermont,* from its earliest settlement to the Close of the Eighteenth Century, with a Biographical Chapter and Appendices. By Benjamin H.

Hall. New York : D. Appleton & Co., 348 Broadway. 1858. 8vo, pp. XII. (2), 799.

One of the best histories of Vermont yet published.

—*Second Edition :* Albany, N. Y.: J. Munsell, 1865. 2 Vols. rl. 8vo, pp. XII, (2), 799. Fifty copies on large paper.

The two editions are the same, as to the text,

—*Bibliography of Vermont ;* a Descriptive Catalogue of Books and Pamphlets relating to the History and Statistics of Vermont.

Which is included in Norton's "Literary Letter," new series. No. 2. 1860.

Contains about 300 titles.

Mr. Hall is a lawyer by profession, and a native and resident of Troy, N. Y. He is a graduate of Harvard College, and is at present editor of the *Troy Daily Whig* newspaper. He is grandson of Judge Lot Hall, prominent in the history of Vermont, of whom he has given a biography in his eastern Vermont, and son of Daniel Hall, who was a practicing lawyer in Troy from about 1810 to 1840,

Hall, Elias. *A Disclosure* of facts, in consequence of a decree for alimony by the Supreme Court. Addison county, Chancery Term, 1823, against Elias Hall, of Middlebury. Montpelier, Vt.: 8vo, pp. 62, and some wanting.

Hall, Fanny W. *Rambles in Europe :* or a Tour through France, Italy, Switzerland, Great Britain, and Ireland, in 1836. By Fanny W. Hall. In two volumes. New York : E. French, 146 Nassau St. 1839. 12mo, pp. XI, 228. VIII. 246.

The following letter from Gov. Hall is of interest in this connection:

NORTH BENNINGTON, December 20, 1878.

Dear Sir :—Fanny W. Hall, about whom you inquire, was born in Grafton, Vt., daughter of Rev. William Hall the first minister of that town. (See Thompson's Gazetteer.) She was sister of William Hall, Jr., who was a member of the State Council in 1815. (see Vermont Council Journal, Vol. vi, pp. 62-3 and index,) a member of the Assembly several years, and also a member of the Hartford Convention, the only stain, if it be one, on his patriotism and worth. She was also sister of Dr. Frederick Hall, Professor in Middlebury College and other institutions, etc., etc. (See Allen's and Drake's Biographical Dictionaries.) She also had a brother David A. Hall, a lawyer, who died in Washington City, many years ago. I was personally acquainted with Miss Hall, who was once at my house in Bennington. She was an intelligent, worthy and lady-like woman. Not many months ago I heard of her as living in the family of some relative in Buffalo, N. Y. She must, if living, be over eighty years old, and remains unmarried. She has been in the habit for many years of visiting in the family of the Hon. Charles Barrett, of Grafton, who if you desire it, can give you more particular information about her. The family of Halls to which she belongs is of another line than mine, and also from that of Benjamin H. Hall, whose ancestor, Judge Lot Hall, also resided in Windham county.

Very respectfully and truly yours,
HILAND HALL.

Hall, Frederick. *Eulogy :* On the late Solomon Metcalf Allen, Professor of Languages in Middlebury College, Pronounced according to appointment of the President and Fellows, March 17, 1818. By Frederick Hall, A.A.S. Professor of Math. and Nat. Philosophy. Published by request of the Corporation. Middlebury, Vt.: Printed by Francis Burnap. 1818. 8vo, pp. 16.

—*Statistical Account* of the Town of Middlebury, in the State of Vermont. Part First. By Frederick Hall. Boston : Printed by Sewell Phelps. 1821. 8vo, pp. 39.

It is also included in the "Mass. Hist. Society's Collections," 1822, Vol. xix. pp. 123-158.

—*Catalogue of Minerals* found in the State of Vermont, and in the adjacent States, together with their Localities; including a number of the most interesting Minerals which have been discovered in other parts of the United States; Arranged alphabetically. By Frederick Hall, Hartford: P. B. Goodsell, Printer. 1824. 8vo, pp. 44.

—*Letters from the East and from the West.* By Frederick Hall, M. D. Formerly Professor of Math. and Nat. Philosophy in Middlebury College, Vt., and late President of Mount Hope College, Maryland; Member of the Conn. Acad. Sci.; American Geol. Society; Acad. Arts and Sci. Mass.; Cor. Mem. Lyceum, N. Y., Columbian Institute, Washington, and of Several Foreign Societies; Cor. Sec. American Historical Society, Washington. Washington City: F. Taylor and William M. Morrison. [1840.] 8vo, pp. XI, 168.

Several of the letters were written from Bellows Falls, and Springfield, Vt., and relate somewhat to the Geology of that vicinity.

Dr. Hall was born at Grafton, Vt., in 1780 ; and died at Peru, Ill., July 27, 1843. He was the son of the Rev. William Hall, the first minister of Grafton. (See HALL, FANNY W.) Dr. Hall was graduated at Dartmouth College, 1803, and LL.D. there 1842. He was a tutor at Dartmouth, 1804-5, and at Middlebury College, 1805-6; Professor of Natural Philosophy and Mathematics there, 1806-1824; Professor of Chemistry and Mineralogy at Trinity College, Hartford; President of Mount Hope College, near Baltimore, and Professor at Columbia College, Washington, D. C., at the time of his death. He gave to Dartmouth College a Cabinet of Minerals and some thousands of dollars.

Hall, Henry. *Ethan Allen*, the Robin Hood of Vermont. By Henry Hall. New York: D. Appleton & Company. 1892. 12mo, pp. viii, 207.

Mr. Hall left the manuscript of this work in a fragmentary state, at his death, after which it was compiled and published by his daughter, Mrs. Henrietta Hall Boardman.

Mr. Hall was a native and resident of Rutland, where he was born September 14, 1814 ; he was at Middlebury College two years, but was graduated at Amherst, 1835. He taught in an Academy near Baltimore, Md., about two years; he then read law and was admitted to the Rutland County Bar in 1839; was Register of Probate 1839-1861, after which time he paid more attention to historical and literary study than to his profession.

Mr. Hall published, about 30 years ago, a series of 25 articles or more in the Rutland *Herald*, relating to the early history of Vermont; also articles in Miss Hemenway's Gazetteer; he delivered many lectures upon literary, religious, historical and scientific topics; and in 1876-7, wrote a series of 40 or 50 letters from Washington for the Rutland and other newspapers. He died in 1889.

See VERMONT HIST. SOCIETY. Addresses, 1862-3.

HALL, HILAND. *The Forty-sixth Anniversary of Bennington Battle.* An Oration Delivered in Pownal, August 16, 1823, Before a United Assembly of Citizens from Bennington and Berkshire Counties. By Hiland Hall, Esq. Motto. Bennington: Printed by Charles Doolittle. 1823. 8vo, pp. 12.

—*Remarks* of the Hon. Hiland Hall, made in the House of Representatives, May 5, 1834, on presenting a Memorial from Windham County, Vermont, on the subject of the Removal of the Public Deposits. Washington: Printed by Gales and Seaton. 1834. 8vo, pp. 8.

—*Speeches* of Mr. Hall, of Vermont, on The Virginia Bounty Land Claims. Delivered in the House of Representatives of the U. S., June 10 and 25, 1842. Washington: Printed at the National Intelligencer office. 1842. 8vo, pp. 23.

—*Speech* of Mr. Hall, of Vermont, on the Fortification Bill. Delivered in the House of

Representatives, May 24, 1836. 8vo, (n.p.) pp. 8.

—*Reports* on Revolutionary Claims. Washington: 1840-43.

—*Opinion of the Second Comptroller of the Treasury*, Hon. Hiland Hall, on a Claim of Alexis Coquillard, assignee of Joseph Bertrand, for a debt against the Potawattomie Indians, involving questions in regard to the Jurisdiction of the Accounting and other officers of the Government, in the adjustment of public accounts. Washington: Gideon & Co., Printers. 1851. 8vo, pp. 24.

—*Biographical Sketches* of the Late Governor John S. Robinson, and the Late Doct. Noadiah Swift. Read before the Vermont Historical Society, at its Special Meeting at Burlington, Jan. 24, 1861. 8vo, pp. 2.

—*The History of Vermont*, from its Discovery to its Admission into the Union in 1791. (Munsell's Monogram). Albany, N. Y.: Joel Munsell. 1868. 8vo, pp. xii, 521, (1). Map.

"An exhaustive work on that interesting portion of the History of Vermont, relating to the severe struggle which it carried on with the government of New York, for the maintenance of its title."—SABIN.

—*New York Land Grants in Vermont.*

See "Vermont Historical Society Collections," Vol. 1, pp. 147-160.

—*Vindication of Volume First* of the Collections of the Vermont Historical Society, from the Attacks of the New York Historical Magazine. Montpelier: 1871. 8vo, pp. 28.

Printed also in Vol. 2 of "Vermont Historical Society Collections," pp. VII,—XXV.

See DAWSON, H. B.

—*The Capture of Ticonderoga*, in 1775. A paper read before the Vermont Historical Society, at Montpelier, Tuesday, October 19th, 1869. By Hiland Hall. Montpelier: Poland's Steam Printing Establishment, Journal Building, State Street. 1869. 8vo, pp. 32.

Also printed in "Proceedings of the Vermont Historical Society," 1869.

—*Why the early Inhabitants* of Vermont disclaimed the jurisdiction of New York, and established an independent government. An Address delivered before the New York Historical Society, December 4th, 1860, by Hiland Hall. Bennington, Vt.: C. A. Pierce & Company, Printers. 1872. 8vo, pp. 16.

—*Letter* of Ex-Governor Hall to Senator Morrill, March, 1876, in relation to the claim of Rebecca Francis Bailey, daughter of Lieut. Edward Lloyd, a Revolutionary pensioner. 8vo, pp. 4.

Senate report, No. 187, 44th Congress, 1st session.

—*The Bennington* Battle Monument and Centennial Celebration. A Statement of the Bennington Historical Society in relation to these and kindred objects. To which is added An Account of the Battle of Bennington, by Ex-Gov. Hiland Hall, of Bennington, Vt. Milford, Mass. Cook and Sons, Steam Job Printers, Journal office, 1877. 8vo, pp. 20.

—*Letter* to the Members of the Bennington Battle Monument Association. June 1st, 1885. pp. 12.

In addition, Gov. Hall furnished the History of the town of Bennington, pp. 45, for Miss Hemenway's Historical Gazetteer of Vermont, and numerous other articles, historical and biographical for the same; and, as Chairman of the Committee on Revolutionary Claims in Congress, he wrote several able reports. In 1836, with Gov. Briggs, of Massachusetts, a Report on "Incendiary Publications;" he also furnished Historical papers for the New England Historical and Genealogical Register, Historical Magazine, and Lossing's Historical Record, Philadelphia.

He was President of the Vermont Historical Society for several years, and labored intelligently in its behalf, and was one of the principal editors of Volumes 1 and 2 in its Collections.

Gov. Hall was born at Bennington, Vt., July 20, 1795, where he still resides; he spent his boyhood on his father's farm, receiving a good English education; read law, and was admitted to the bar in 1819; and in 1827 he was elected to the State Legislature ; for several years was State's Attorney for Bennington County; member of the lower house of Congress, 1833 to 1843; Bank Commissioner for Vermont, 1843-1846; for four years a Judge of the Supreme Court. In 1850, Second Comptroller of the Treasury at Washington; from 1851 to 1854, Land Commissioner for California; Governor of Vermont, 1858 to 1860, and a delegate to the Peace Congress at Washington in 1861.

In 1859, Gov. Hall received the honorary degree of LL. D., from the University of Vermont. He was Vice-President for Vermont of the New England Historical and Genealogical Society of Boston.

We are under obligations to Gov. Hall for his ready aid counsel and encouragement in connection with this work.

Gov. Hall died at Springfield, Mass., Dec. 18, 1885.

Hall, John, D. D. *History* of the Presbyterian Church in Trenton, N. J. By John Hall, D. D. Member of the Presbyterian Historical Society, and of the Historical Societies of New Jersey, Pennsylvania and Wisconsin. New York : 1859. 12mo, pp. 453, VII.

The following reference to Vermont in the above work may be found on page 289, in the author's sketch of Rev. Dr. Elihu Spencer, some time pastor of the Presbyterian church at Trenton: "Dr. Spencer bequeathed to his five surviving daughters, and the children of a deceased one, three thousand acres of land in Saltash, [now Plymouth] Vermont, and to his son, John Eaton, one thousand acres in Woodstock, Vermont. There still remains in the possession of his descendants a lot of ground in the city of Trenton which has in the lapse of time become more valuable than all the Vermont acres." Perhaps so.

Hall, Rev. Nathaniel. *A Sermon* preached before the Evangelical Society, in Poultney, Vt., at its annual meeting Nov. 22, 1815.

Mr. Hall was born in Sutton, Mass, April 9, 1764; graduated at Dartmouth, 1790; was pastor of Congregational church, Granville, N. Y., Oct. 3, 1797, until his death, July 31, 1820.

Hall, S. R. *The Child's Assistant* to a knowledge of the Geography and History of Vermont. By S. R. Hall. Third Edition, with Plates. (Maps.) Montpelier, Vt.; Published by J. S. Walton. 1831. 12mo, pp. 75.

First edition in 1827, same imprint.

—*Lectures* on School-keeping. Boston. 1829. 12mo, pp. 136.

Several editions published. An enlarged and revised edition in 1852.

—*Lectures* to Female Teachers on School-keeping. 1832. 12mo, pp. 189.

—*The Child's Instructor*, or Lessons on Common Things. By S. R. Hall. Andover : Flagg & Gould, 1832. 12mo, pp. 140.

—*The Grammatical Assistant*, containing Definitions in Etymology, Rules of Syntax, and Selections for Parsing. 1833. 12mo, pp. 148.

—*A School History* of the United States, containing Maps, a Chronological Chart, and an outline of topics for a more extensive course of Study. 1833. 12mo, pp. 368.

Several editions.

—*The Arithmetical Manual*, containing exercises for Practice and Demonstrations of the Rules of Written Arithmetic. 1832. 12mo, pp. 288.

—*Practical Lectures* on Parental Responsibility and the Religious Education of Children. 1833. 12mo, pp. 176.

—"*The Alphabet of Geology.*" 1868.

—*The Geography* and History of Vermont, by S. R. Hall, LL. D. Also the Constitution of the United States, with Notes and Questions. Third Edition. Revised by Pliny H. White, Late Member of the Vermont Board of Education. Authorized by the Legislature of Vermont for use in the Schools of the State. Montpelier : Freeman Steam Printing House and Bindery. 1874. 12mo, pp. 280.

First edition published in 1864. Montpelier: C. W. Willard.

Mr. Hall was born in Croyden, N. H., October 27, 1795, and died in Brownington, Vt., June 24, 1877. After teaching several years, he studied theology with the Rev. Walter Chapin, of Woodstock, Vt., and his first settlement was at Concord, Vt., in 1822, and with the exception of about ten years that he was engaged in teaching in Andover, Mass., and Plymouth, N. H., he resided in Vermont until his death, preaching at Craftsbury and Brownington from 1840 until 1867, when age and infirmities compelled him to retire mainly from active service. He supplied at Granby and Victory about two years, in 1872-4. Besides those above mentioned Mr. Hall published several other small volumes, and contributed numerous articles to the Journal of Education, and other educational periodicals; he also rendered important assistance to Prof. Hitchcock in the Geological Survey of Vermont. While at Concord Mr. Hall established and taught a Normal School, which it is claimed was the first in the country ; at any rate he was the first teacher to introduce the black-board into the school room.

Hamlin, Mrs. Henrietta Anna Loraine,

Daughter of Rev. William Jackson, was born in Dorset, Vt., May 9, 1811 ; married to Rev. Cyrus Hamlin, September 3, 1838, and sailed for the mission at Constantinople, December 3, 1838, and died November 14, 1850. A biography of Mrs. Hamlin has been written by Mrs. Margaret Woods Lawrence; the book is a series of life pictures, and is prettily written. See Miss Hemenway's Vermont Historical Gazetteer, Vol. 1, pp. 192-195.

Hammond, Edwin. *In Memoriam*. Testimonial to the memory of Edwin Hammond by the Vermont State Agricultural Society and Wool Growers' Association, January 25, 1871. Tuttle & Co., Printers, Rutland, Vt. 8vo, pp. 4.

Hammond, George. *Register* of the Vermont Atwood Merino Sheep Club. Compiled by George Hammond. Rutland : The Tuttle Co., Printers. 1885. 8vo, pp. 1000.

Hammond, Jabez D.

See Lard, Rebecca H.

Hancock, John. *Governor* of Massachusetts. Proclamation for Neutrality, as to the Difficulties between New York and Vermont. March 26, 1784. Broadsheet. Boston, Printed.

Handbook for Farmers, Mechanics, etc. Containing a Lumber Dealer's Guide for timber measure : Scantling of timber measure : Board measure : wood table : etc. Bellows Falls, Vt., 1847. 12mo.

Hardwick. *To the Voters of Hardwick*. Statement by A. W. Davidson. Hardwick, Vt., February, 1877.

Relates to the accounts of the town liquor agent.

—*Annual Reports* of the Town of Hardwick, March 7, 1865. Montpelier : Walton's Steam Press. 1865. 8vo, pp. 8.

Continued.

—*Explanation* to the Candid Taxpayers of Hardwick. [By A. E. Judevine.] Feb. 1, 1882. 8vo, pp. 4.

Harlow, Rev. R. W. *A Masonic Address* and Review of the year, delivered at the Annual Festival & Meeting of Golden Rule Lodge, Free and Accepted Masons, Putney, Vt., December 23d, 1868. By Rev. R. W. Harlow. Printed by vote of the Lodge. Brattleboro: Frank D. Cobleigh, Printer. 1869. 8vo, pp. 11.

Harmon, D. W. *A Journal* of Voyages and Travels in the Interior of North America, between the 47th and 58th Degrees of North Latitude, extending from Montreal nearly to the Pacific Ocean, a distance of about 5,000 miles, including an account of the principal occurrences, during a residence of nineteen years in different parts of the Country. To which is added, A Concise description of the Face of the Country, its Inhabitants, their Manners, Customs, Laws, Religion, etc. By Daniel Williams Harmon, A Partner in the North West Company. Andover: Printed by Flagg & Gould. 1820. 8vo, pp. 432. Map and Portrait.
Edited by Rev. Daniel Haskel, of Burlington, Vt.
Mr. Harmon, son of Daniel and his wife Lucrecia (Dewey), was born in Bennington, Vt., Feb. 19, 1778; died in Montreal, March 26, 1845. He married at Burlington, Vt., in 1820, Elizabeth, a French and Indian half breed; he, however, commenced living with her in 1805, when she was 14 years of age; she died in Montreal, Feb. 12. 1861. They had eleven children.

Harmon, Henry A. *Tenth Anniversary* of the Class of 1867, at Williams College, Williamstown, Mass., July 3d, 1877. Rutland, Vt.: Tuttle & Co., Printers, 1877. 8vo, pp. 34.

Harmon, Joel, Jr. *The Columbian Minstrel,* a Singing Manual. 1809.
Mr. Harmon resided in Pawlet. This work contains 53 tunes and anthems, composed by Mr. Harmon, who taught music.
See History Pawlet, pp. 47-73.

Harmon Nathaniel. *Poetical Sketches* on various Solemn Subjects; Composed by Dea. Nathaniel Harmon, late of Bennington, of pious memory; written a short time before his death. Bennington: Printed by Anthony Haswell. 1796. 32mo.
Deacon Harmon was among the earliest citizens of Bennington, and was present at the battle in 1777.

Harpending, O. G. *The Peoples Companion,* including Children, or, the Principles which enter the Christian Life at its Beginning, illustrated by Six Parables of Our Savior, with Helps for Prayer, suitable to the subject. Motto. By O. G. Harpending. Bennington: Banner Steam Job Printing Establishment. 1881. 12mo, pp. 49.

Harrington, E. *Statistics* of the Manufactures and Commerce of Lake Memphremagog, By E. Harrington. Stanstead: 1864. L. R. Robinson. 8vo, pp. 8.

Harris, George. *Of Chester.* Price Fifty Dollars. The Arabian Farmer, and Horse Breaker. By George Harris. Seventh Edition. 1870. 18mo, pp. 101.
No Imprint.

Harris, Sullivan Dwight.
Mr. Harris was born in Middlebury, Vt., in 1812; married at twenty, and in 1836 moved to Ashtabula County, Ohio. In 1851 he became associate editor of the

Ohio Cultivator, and in 1855 sole proprietor. He was a writer of poetry from early youth, and more or less in manhood; and occupies a prominent place in the "Poets and Poetry of the West."

Harris, Wm. J. *The Church and the Bible.* A Sermon by the Rev. Wm. J. Harris, Rector of Trinity Church, Rutland, Vt. Rutland: Tuttle & Company, Printers. 1872. 18mo, pp. 21.

Harrison, William H. *A Biographical Sketch* of the Life and Services of Gen. William Henry Harrison, together with his Letter to Simon Bolivar. Printed at the Watchman Office, Montpelier, Vt., 1836. 12mo, pp. 30.

Hartford. *Auditors'* and Superintendent's Reports of the Town of Hartford, for the year ending February 16, 1881. Lebanon, N. H.: A. B. Freeman, Printer, Free Press Job Office. 1880. [?] 8vo, pp. 16.
Continued.

Hartford Convention. *The Proceedings* of a convention of delegates from the States of Massachusetts, Connecticut, and Rhode Island; the Counties of Cheshire and Grafton in the State of New Hampshire; and the County of Windham, in the State of Vermont; convened at Hartford, in the State of Connecticut, December 15th, 1814. Hanover: Printed by Charles Spear. 1815. 8vo, pp. 40.

—*Editions of Same:* Hartford, C. Hosmer, 1815; and Hartford, Andrus and Starr, 1815. 8vo, pp. 39 in each.

—*The Hartford Convention in an Uproar!* and the Wise Men of the East Confounded! Together with a short history of the Peter Washingtonians: Being the First Book of the Chronicles of the Children of Disobedience; otherwise falsely called "Washington Benevolents." By Hector Benevolus, Esq. Motto. Cartoon. Windsor, Vt. Printed for the Proprietor of the Copy-Right. 1818. 18mo, pp. 46.

—*An Edition of same:* Windsor, Vt. 1815.

Harvard College. *Fourth Report* of The Class of 1861 of Harvard College, Sept. 1871.—Jan. 7, 1878. Printed for the use of Class. James Edward Wright (Class Secretary.) Montpelier, Vt.: Freeman Steam Printing House and Bindery. 1878. 8vo, pp. 30.

—*Harvard College Class of 1887.* Report of the Class Secretary, [W. B. Howe,] No. 3. Burlington: Free Press Association. 1893. pp. 140.

Harvey, Peter. *Reminiscences* and Anecdotes of Daniel Webster, by Peter Harvey, Boston: Little, Brown and Company. 1877. 8vo, pp. x. (6), and 480.
Hon. Peter Harvey was born in Barnet, Vt., July 18, 1810; and died in Boston, Mass., June 27, 1877. He was the son of Alexander and Jennet (Brock) Harvey, who were born in Scotland, the former in 1747, and the latter in 1767; they settled in Barnet in 1775, and were married October 5, 1781, and had 16 children; three of whom died young, and eight sons and five daughters were married, most of whom resided in Barnet. Peter left home at the age of 15, and eventually formed a business connection in Boston, the firm being Emerson, Lamb & Harvey, then Harvey, Page & Co., next James Tufts & Co., and finally Nourse, Mason & Co. He was Treasurer of the Rutland railroad, and President of the Kilby Bank. He is best known as the firm friend of Daniel Webster. It was his fortune at an early age "to become intimately acquainted with the great Statesman, and to maintain

with him through life a more intimate friendship than was ever enjoyed by any other person." For a full account of Mr. Harvey and his family, consult "Vermont Historical Magazine," vol. 1, pp. 282-284: also "N. E. Historical Genealogical Register," January, 1877, page 108.

Hascall, Daniel.

Mr. Hascall was born February 24, 1782, probably at Bennington, Vt,, as his father and family moved from there to Pawlet, Vt., in 1787. He was graduated at Middlebury College, 1806, and became a Baptist preacher of much ability; was settled over the Baptist church in Hamilton, N. Y., 1813-1828, where he was mainly instrumental in establishing a Baptist Theological Seminary, of which he was Principal, 1828-36. After passing a few years at West Rutland, Vt., he returned to Hamilton, where he died June 28, 1852. His publications are, a "Work on Baptism;" "Elements of Theology;" "Analysis of Divine Revelation," and perhaps a few sermons.

Haskel, Daniel. *A Sermon*, delivered at the Ordination of the Rev. Hiram S. Johnson, as Pastor of the Church in Hopkinton, N. Y. November 4, 1814. By Daniel Haskel, Rector of a Church in Burlington, Vt. Burlington, Vt.: Printed by S. Mills, 1815. 8vo, pp. 28.

—*Remarks* on "Some Observations taken in Part from an Address, delivered in the New Meeting House in Brattleborough, July 7, 1816, by William Wells, Minister of the Congregation." By Daniel Haskel. Burlington, January 1, 1817. 8vo, pp. 16.

—*The Doctrine of* Predestination Maintained as Scriptural, Rational and Important. A Discourse, delivered to the Calvinistic Church and Society in Burlington, Vt., January 5th, 1817. By Daniel Haskel, Minister of the Congregation. Published by Request. Burlington: Printed by Samuel Mills. 8vo, pp. 24.

—*A Sermon* delivered in Randolph, at the Annual Meeting of the Vermont Juvenile Missionary Society, October 13, 1819. By Daniel Haskell, Pastor of a Church in Burlington. To which are added Reports, and Proceedings of the Society. Middlebury, Vt.: Printed by Francis Burnap. 1819. 8vo, pp. 40.
Contains Annual Proceedings.

—*A Sermon*, delivered at the Ordination of the Rev. Royal A. Avery, to the Pastoral Care of the Congregational Church in Cambridge, Vt., December 10th, 1823. By Daniel Haskell, A. M., President of the University of Vermont. Published by the Request of the Church and Society. St. Albans: Printed by J. Spooner. 1824. 8vo, pp. 36.
Mr. Haskel, or Haskell, was born in Preston, Conn., in June, 1784, and died in Brooklyn, N. Y., August 9, 1848. He was graduated at Yale College, 1802; read theology, and was Pastor of a Congregational Church at St. Albans, Vt., a short time, and of the Calvinistic Congregational Church at Burlington, 1810-1821; President of the University of Vermont, 1821-24, when his health failed, and he was incapacitated for steady labor. With J. C. Smith he published a Gazetteer of the United States, 1843, pp. 722; also, Chronology of the World, and assisted in the preparation of McCulloch's Geographical Dictionary.

Haskins, T. W. *Reasons for believing* the Advent of Our Lord Jesus Christ to be Pre-Millennial. A Discourse Delivered in St. Luke's Church, St. Albans, Vt., the Fourth Sunday after Trinity, July 14, 1878, and published by some members of the same. New York: E. P. Dutton & Company, 1878. 8vo, pp. 45.
Mr. Haskins was Rector of St. Luke's Church, but has since been transferred to the Diocese of Connecticut.

Haswell, Anthony. *Haswell's Mental Repast.* 12mo. pp. 384. (Bennington.) 1808.
Appears to have been published in monthly parts, consisting mainly of selections, commencing January 1, 1808, and discontinued at end of six months.

—*The Monthly Miscellany* or Vermont Magazine. 8vo, pp. 56.
Commenced in March, 1794, at Bennington.

—*Record* of the Family of Anthony Haswell, by Lydia, his deceased Consort, together with Several Elegiac Poems the tribute of Connubial Love to Unaffected Virtue. Printed by her Sons in June, 1799. Reprinted by her bereaved widower in June, 1815. 18mo, pp. 16.
The little pamphlet also contains a "record of the family of Anthony Haswell by Betsey, his second wife," who died April 26, 1815. His first wife died April 30, 1799—had 10 children; his second wife 7.

—*Songs* for the 4th of July, and 16th of August.
Broad sheet, printed on both sides, and contains thirteen songs, authorship as follows: Seven by Mr. A. Haswell, three by Mrs. A. Selden, of Vermont, one by Thomas Paine, one by Dr. Burne, and one, no signature, but said to be by Mr. T. Green Fessenden. n. d. n. p.

—*An Oration* delivered at Shaftsbury, on Sunday January 10, 1802, at the interment of Capt. Aaron Cole, in Masonic Order. By Anthony Haswell. Published by particular Request of the Lodges in the vicinity. Bennington: A. Haswell, Printer. 1802.

—*Memoirs* of Captain Phelps.
See Phelps, Matthew.
Mr. Haswell was born in England in 1756; died in Bennington, Vt., May 22, 1816. He came to this country at the age of 13, learned the printer's trade, and established the "*Gazette*," at Bennington, June 5, 1783.
Mr. Haswell was appointed Post-Master-General within and for the State of Vermont in 1784, Vermont at that time being a Free and Independent State. See sketch of Mr. Haswell in Vt. Hist. Gaz. Vol. 1, pp. 176-7.

Hathaway, F. C. *See* Dartmouth College, Class Day "Chronicles." 1868.

Hathaway, Silas. *Allen vs. Hathaway and Pierson,* See Allen, Heman.

Hatlinger, J. J. *Hungary.* An Address by J. J. Hatlinger, a Hungarian Exile and Brigadier General in the late federal army. Subject: Hungary. Brattleboro, Vt.: Printed by Geo. E. Selleck. 1867. 8vo, pp. 28.

Haven, K. *The book of Job* an Allegory: Briefly Illustrated in a Discourse, delivered before the Universalist Society in Bethel, Vt. Sept. 11, 1825. By Kittredge Haven. Motto. Woodstock: Printed by David Watson. 1825. 8vo, pp. 19.

—*An Address* delivered Before the Fraternity of Free and accepted Masons, Convened at Corinth, Vt., for the Consecration of Minerva Lodge, and the Installation of its officers, Sept. 20, 1827. By Companion Kittredge Haven. Motto. Royalton, Vt.: W. Spooner, Printer. 8vo, pp. 16.

—*The World Reprieved:* being a critical examination of William Miller's Theory, that the second coming of Christ and the destruction of the world will take place, About A. D. 1843. Compiled principally from articles originally written By Rev. Kittredge Haven. Motto. Woodstock, Vt.: Haskell & Palmer. 1839. 8vo, pp. 48.
Rev. Kittredge Haven was born in Framingham, Mass., February 24, 1793; and died at Shoreham, Vt., May 4, 1877. He read theology with Rev. Paul Dean at Boston, and preached his first sermon in July, 1819. He

was pastor of the Universalist Church at Barnard and Bethel, Vt., January 1, 1821 to January 1, 1828; and of the church in Shoreham, Vt., 1828—1865, after which the infirmity of age only permitted him to preach occasionally. A full biog. sketch was published in the Universalist, Boston, May 19, 1877. He was the maternal grandfather of Franklin Haven Bascom, of Montpelier.

Hawes, Rev. Edward, D. D. *Sermon* on Fifth Anniversary of his pastorate over First Church in Burlington, With various letters and a Parable. Compiled by E. L. Ripley. 1890. pp. 25.

Hawies, Rev. Thomas. *The Communicant's* Spiritual Companion : or an evangelical preparation for the Lord's Supper. In which are shown the nature of the ordinance, and the dispositions requisite for a profitable participation thereof : with meditations and helps for prayer, suitable to the subject. By the Rev. Thomas Hawies, D. D., Rector of Adwinekle, Northamptonshire, (Eng.) Middlebury : Samuel Swift. 1813. 16mo, pp. 142.

Hawker, Robert. *Zion's Pilgrim*, by Robert Hawker, D. D. 18mo. Middlebury : Samuel Swift. 1810.
Consisting of Dialogues, Essays, and Letters on various subjects.

—*Second* American Edition. Middlebury : Samuel Swift. 1811. 12mo.

Hawkins, Rush C. *Testimonial* to Col. Rush C. Hawkins, Ninth Regiment, N. Y. V., "Hawkins' Zouaves." New York : Latimer Brothers & Seymour. 1863. 8vo, pp. 9.

—*The United States* in Account with the Rebellion. n. d.
This tract was written by Col. Hawkins during President Johnson's administration, and the Union League Club of New York City printed and circulated 100,000 copies of it.

—*Statement* of Rush C. Hawkins, late a member of the Legislature of the State of New York, from the Eleventh Assembly District of New York City. New York : Union Printing Company. 1872. 8vo, pp. 20.

—*A Report* read by Col. Rush C. Haskins before the Union League Club, the evening of February 10, 1876, relating to the Cause of the Increase of the City Debt, and Recommending Measures for its more Economical Government in the Future. New York : John Polhemus, Printer. 1876. 8vo, pp. 28.

—*The First Books and Printers* of the Fifteenth Century. Titles of the First Books from the Earliest Presses, established in different Cities, Towns and Monasteries in Europe before the end of the Fifteenth Century, with brief notes upon their Printers. Illustrated with Reproductions of Early Types and first engravings of the Printing Press. By Rush C. Hawkins. New York : J. W. Bouton, 706 Broadway, London : B. Quaritch, 15 Piccadilly. 1884. Quarto, pp. xxx, 146.
The Introduction comprises a statement of the most important known facts bearing upon the Gutenberg-Koster controversy in relation to the invention of printing with movable metal types. The body of the work gives the titles, with notes, of two hundred and thirty-six publications, which it is believed were issued from a like number of presses, set up in the several European towns before the close of the fifteenth century. Illustrated with two reproductions of the earliest engravings of the printing presses and twenty-five reproductions in facsimile of pages of the books described. Only 300 copies were printed.

Of Gen. Hawkins's own collection, the List of Libraries of All Countries, Leipsic, 1895, says :
"As representing the early presses of Europe, this has no rival among the private collections of the world. There are 205 books representing 106 of the first printers of the fifteenth century, who set up presses in as many different places before the year 1501. Of these 53 are first books of first presses. There are about 300 other fifteenth century books of importance." Since this list was sent to the Leipsic publisher several valuable items have been added by Gen. Hawkins to his already unequalled collection. Of two volumes he possesses the only copies known to be in existence.

—*A Biographical Sketch* of General John Wolcott Phelps of Vermont, for the Association of Graduates of the United States Military Academy. East Saginaw, Mich.: 1885. 8vo, pp. 14.

—*Horrors in Architecture* and So-called Works of Art in the City of New York. (A satirical tirade.) New York : 1886. 4to, pp. 20.

—*Early Coast Operations* in North Carolina and Why Burnside did not renew the Attack at Fredericksburg. (For the Century War History.) New York : 1887. 8vo, pp. 32.

—*A Biographical Sketch* of the Rev. Aaron Hutchinson, A. M., of Pomfret, Vt. New York : 1888. 4to, pp. 35.

—*Report* on the Fine Arts at the Universal Exposition held at Paris in 1889. Illustrated. Washington : 1891. 8vo, pp. 111.
In addition to the above Gen. Hawkins has contributed many articles to Magazines, covering a wide range of subjects.
Rush Christopher Hawkins, A. M., Brevet Brigadier General, U. S. V., and officer of the Legion of Honor of France, was born at Pomfret, Vt., September 14th, 1831.
His father, Lorenzo Dow Hawkins, was a son of Dexter Hawkins, a soldier of the Revolution, who served in one of the Rhode Island regiments ; his mother was Louisa Maria Hutchinson, a great-granddaughter of Rev. Aaron Hutchinson, of Connecticut, who graduated at Yale College in 1747, moved to Vermont in 1776, and was the first settled Congregational minister in the central (eastern) section of that State. The Woodstock Society founded by him still exists. Before moving to Vermont he had charge of a congregation at Grafton in Massachusetts. He was one of the most accomplished classical scholars of his time. Young Hawkins left Vermont before he was fifteen years old, and until 1861 his time was divided for the most part between New York and the Western States ; and between the study of the law and business tours in the West.
At the breaking out of the War of the Rebellion he was at the head of an independent company of Zouaves in New York, organized for the purpose of attaining, as near as possible, to perfection in infantry drill. The evening after President Lincoln's first proclamation calling for troops, its members resolved to tender their services to the Goverument, and at half past seven o'clock the next morning Captain Hawkins was in the executive chamber of the Governor, being the first citizen of the State of New York to tender his services and those of his company for the suppression of the Rebellion.
Between the 17th and 26th days of April, 1861, he raised and organized the Ninth Regiment of New York Volunteer Infantry, which was afterward better known as "Hawkins' Zouaves." It participated in the movement against Big Bethel, the capture of Hatteras Inlet, the affair of Chicomocomico, the capture of Roanoke Island, the attack upon Winton, N. C., the battle of South Mills, where General Hawkins was wounded; South Mountain; Antietam, where the regiment lost more than sixty-three per cent of its numbers engaged; Fredericksburg and the siege of Suffolk, and was mustered out of the service in June, 1863. Gen Hawkins had charge of the perilous work of landing the Union troops through the surf at Hatteras Inlet, N. C., in August, 1861, and with the aid of the small tugboat Fanny, rescued from loss a hulk load of soldiers from his own regiment, which had been anchored and left in a most dangerous position among the breakers. In February, 1862, during the advance of an expedition up the Chowan River to Winton, Gen. Hawkins saved from capture the gunboat Delaware with two companies of troops on board and Vice-Admiral Rowau. This vessel was in the lead of the expedition, and during the ascent of the river Gen. Hawkins was on

the crosstrees of the foremast, from which position he discovered a large force of rebel infantry and artillery concealed among the trees and underbrush along the bank of the river in front of Winton, in time to prevent the vessel from going to the wharf, where she would have been easily captured. As a result of his discovery the Delaware sheered off, under a heavy fire of musketry and artillery, which opened as soon as the enemy saw that they were discovered. The gunboat escaped though struck by more than 150 bullets before she got out of range. Gen. Hawkins' escape from death was a narrow one, the ratlines being cut out of his hands by the bullets, while he was descending to the deck. The Union forces returned the next morning, bombarded, and captured the town and burned a part of it.

At Plymouth, on the Roanoke River, Gen. Hawkins organized the first body of loyal North Carolina troops, and created a nucleus around which was formed the First Regiment of North Carolina Volunteers. Twenty of these volunteers were hung by the rebel General Pickett, for the before unknown offence of constructive desertion—they having evaded the Confederate conscription.

Gen. Hawkins' brigade closed the fight after dark upon the disastrous field of Fredericksburg, December 13, 1862. In the evening orders having been given which indicated an intention to renew the battle the next morning, Gen. Hawkins proceeded to the headquarters of Gen. Wilcox, where he met some general officers and protested against the movement. The officers present requested Gen. Hawkins to proceed to headquarters and use the arguments with Gen. Burnside he had used with them for the purpose of inducing him to reconsider his declared intention to renew the battle. He accordingly rode, in darkness, and deep mud, to headquarters at the Philips House, where he had a protracted interview with Generals Sumner, Hooker, Franklin, Park and Colonel Hardie, during which Gen. Burnside entered the room and announced that he had arranged to renew the attack the next morning. The Ninth Corps was to lead, and turning to Gen. Hawkins, he said : "Your brigade shall be on the right and I will be with you." Gen. Sumner objected ; and a general discussion ensued. The conclusion was reached that the chances were very much against success; and Gen. Hawkins recrossed the Rappahanock with verbal orders countermanding the arrangements for a second attack.

After the Battle of Antietam, General Hawkins wrote to Simeon Draper, a confidential friend of the Secretary of War, a strong letter, describing the feeling among the volunteers about Gen. McClellan, and giving reasons why he should be removed from the command of the Army of the Potomac. The letter was read by Mr. Draper to Secretary Stanton, who read it to Pres Lincoln. When the reading was finished, the President said : "That is clear and to the point, and gives me a better idea of the feeling in the army than I have ever had from such a source before. I guess we must have a new commander." A change of commanders soon after took place.

In July, 1862, General Hawkins was placed under arrest by order of General Burnside, for denouncing General McClellan as a failure, but was released without charges having been preferred against him.

After the end of his term of service in the field, and until the end of the Rebellion, General Hawkins devoted his entire time to the promotion of the Union cause.

Since the close of his military career, General Hawkins has been an active participant in many movements connected with political reform, local, State, and federal. In May, 1864, he called to the attention of the Union League Club the necessity for a system of Civil Service, and was appointed with Dr. Francis Lieber and General Hayes, a committee to impress the importance of that subject upon the people, this being the first active movement in the United States in the interest of reforming a great national evil. In 1872 General Hawkins was a member of the New York Legislature; seven days after the adjournment, he resigned his seat and soon after published his "Statement" to his constituents, giving an account of the corrupt work of the session, his inability to stem the current of corruption, and the reasons for his resigning. In 1876 the Union League Club published his report relating to "The Cause of the Increase of the City Debt," which is the most complete account of the frauds of the "Tweed Ring" ever written. In 1884 he published his book upon the Titles of the earliest publications of the fifteenth century. His collection of books from the first fifteenth century presses is the most comprehensive one in the United States, and in certain respects stands sixth or seventh among the important collections of this class of books in the world. In it are many works illustrated with very early examples of the woodcutters' art. His library also comprises a large collection of books and

pamphlets relating to the history of the War of the Rebellion.

In 1889 General Hawkins was the United States Fine Arts Commissioner at the Universal Exposition held at Paris. His department achieved a notable success, and it was due to his well directed efforts that American wood engraving received that universal approval to which it is so justly entitled.

Since the close of the Civil War, General Hawkins has spent more than half his time in Europe, and has visited and studied the principal art collections and libraries, public and private, of all the European countries, except those of Russia and Spain. His knowledge of art, bibliography, and the early history of wood engraving has made him an acknowledged authority upon those subjects. Devotion to his high ideals of duty; fearless denunciation of wrong; and constant endeavor to secure high standards of political and social purity, have marked his life.

Hawley, Bostwick, D. D. *"Living and Dying* to others. Discourse Preached at the Funeral of Mr. Moses Jackman, November 13, 1863. By Bostwick Hawley, D. D., Castleton, Vt. Rutland : Tuttle & Gay, Printers. 1864. 8vo, pp. 11.

—*Truth and Righteousness* Triumphant. A Discourse Commemorative of the Death of President Lincoln : preached in the Washington Avenue M. E. Church, (Albany, N. Y.) April 20, 1865. By B. Hawley, D. D. Albany, N. Y.: J. Munsell. 1865. 8vo, pp. 20.

Hayes, Augustus Allen.
A distinguished chemist; born in Windsor, Vt., February 28, 1806; was graduated at Norwich, Vt., Military Academy, in 1823. After 1828 he resided in Boston and vicinity, as Consulting Chemist, State Assayer, etc. He contributed to the Proceedings of several Scientific Bodies, and to the "Journal of Science" and the "Annual Scientific Discovery." See Drake's Biographical Dictionary.
Mr. Hayes died in the latter part of June, 1882.

Haynes, Rev. Emory J. *Are these things so?* N. York: N. Tibbals & Sons. 1880. pp. 4, 296.

Haynes, E. M. *A History* of the Tenth Regiment, Vermont Volunteers, with Biographical Sketches of the Officers who fell in Battle. And a Complete Roster of all the officers and men connected with it, showing all changes of Promotion, Death or Resignation, during the Military Existence of the Regiment. By Chaplain E. M. Haynes. Published by the Tenth Vermont Regimental Association. 1870. 8vo, pp. 249.

Haynes, Lemuel. *A Sermon* delivered September, 1798. At the Annual Freemen's Meeting. By Lemuel Haynes, Pastor of a Church in Rutland. Printed at Rutland, Vt., by John Walker, Jun. M,DCC,XCVIII. 8vo, pp. 17.

—*The Nature and Importance* of true Republicanism ; with a few suggestions favorable to Independence. A Discourse, delivered at Rutland, (Vt.,) the Fourth of July, 1801. It being the 25th Anniversary of American Independence. By Lemuel Haynes, Pastor of a Church in Rutland. Made public at the request of the Audience. William Fay, Printer. 8vo, pp. 24.

—*Universal Salvation* a very Ancient Doctrine ; with some Account of the Life and Character of its Author. A Sermon Delivered at Rutland, West-Parish, in the year 1805. By Lemuel Haynes, A. M. Windsor : Re-printed by Alden Spooner. April 1806. 12mo, pp. 11.

Same. Seventh edition. New York : Printed for Cornelius Davis. 1810. 12mo, pp. 12.

More than twenty editions have been printed; See Loveland, S. C., Peck, John.

—*Divine Decrees* an Encouragement to the Use of Means. A Sermon, delivered at Granville, (N. Y.) June 25th, A. D. 1805, before the Evangelical Society, instituted for the purpose of aiding pious and needy young men in acquiring Education for the work of the Gospel Ministry. By Lemuel Haynes, A. M. Pastor of a Church in Rutland, Vt. Printed at the Herald Office, by W. Fay. 8vo, pp. 31.

—*A Letter* to Rev. Hosea Ballou, being a reply to his Epistle to the author : or, his attempt to vindicate the Old Universal Preacher. By Lemuel Haynes, Pastor of a Church in Rutland, (Vt.) Rutland : Printed by William Fay. 1807. pp. 17.

In Life of Haynes, by Cooley, pp. 105-121.

—*A Sermon Commemorative* of George Washington. Delivered before the Washington Benevolent Society, at Brandon, Vt., July 4, 1813, by Lemuel Haynes.

Title from Brinley catalogue, Part 2, p. 192.

—*Dissimulation Illustrated.* A Sermon delivered at Brandon, Vt., February 22, 1813, before the Washington Benevolent Society ; it being the Anniversary of Gen. Washington's Birthday. By Lemuel Haynes, A. M. Pastor of the Church in West-Rutland. Published at the request of the Society. Rutland : Printed by Fay & Davison, for the Society. 1814. 8vo, pp. 24.

—*The Sufferings*, support, and reward of faithful ministers illustrated ; being the substance of two sermons delivered at Rutland, and West Rutland, as Valedictory Discourses, May 24th, A. D. 1818, by Lemuel Haynes, A. M., late Pastor of the Church in that place. 12mo, pp. 34.

In Cooley's life of Haynes.

—*Mystery Developed ;* or, Russel Colvin, supposed to be murdered, in full life ; and Stephen and Jesse Boorn (his convicted murderers), rescued from ignominious death by Wonderful Discoveries. Containing, I. A narrative of the whole transaction, by Rev. Lemuel Haynes, A. M. II. Rev. Mr. H.'s Sermon upon the development of the Mystery. III. A succinct account of the endictment, trial, and conviction of Stephen and Jesse Boorn. 12mo, pp. 36.

See Cooley's life of Haynes.

—*The Prisoner Released.* A Sermon, delivered at Manchester, Vt., Lord's Day, Jan. 9th, 1820. On the Remarkable Interposition of Divine Providence, in the Deliverance of Stephen and Jesse Boorn, who had been under Sentence of Death, for the Supposed Murder of Russel Colvin. To which are added some particulars relating thereto. By Lemuel Haynes, A. M. Minister of the Gospel in Manchester. Hartford : 8vo, (pp. 22.)

—*Interesting Controversy* between Rev. Lemuel Haynes, and Hosea Ballou. Rutland. 1828.

—*Life of.*

See Cooley, T. M.

Mr. Haynes was a prominent character in Southwestern Vermont for 37 years. He was born, (out of wedlock) at West Hartford, Ct., July 18th, 1753; his father was an unmixed African negro, and his mother a white woman of "respectable ancestry in New England." He bore the name of neither his father nor mother, and tradition says that his mother, in a fit of displeasure with her host called her child by his name. He was abandoned by both his parents, and when five months old was carried to Granville, Mass., and bound out as a servant until he was twenty-one, to a pious family by the name of Rose, where he was well treated, and became pious. He "got his education in the chimney corner." He was a patriot in the Revolution; joined the "minute men" in 1774, and the regular army in 1775, and it is said was of the expedition against Ticonderoga, in 1776, which is the last we hear of him in the army. Mr. Haynes itinerated as a preacher for several years, 1776 to 1785, in Granville, Mass., and vicinity. Among the pious youth of Granville was a Miss Babbit, who was in deep religious anxiety. She was well educated and a school teacher; under the influence of Mr. Haynes she received spiritual light and the hope of salvation, and to compensate her deliverer she offered him her heart and hand for life, which were accepted. Mr. Haynes came to Vermont in 1785, and was settled at West Rutland until 1818, when he preached at Manchester one year, and removed to Granville, N. Y., in 1822, where he continued until his death, September 28th, 1833.

Haynes, Sylvanus. *A Sermon* delivered before His Excellency the Governor, His Honor the Lieut. Governor, the Honorable Council and House of Representatives of Vermont, at Montpelier, October 18, 1809. Being the Day of the General Election. By Sylvanus Haynes, Pastor of the Baptist Church of Christ in Middletown. Published by Order of the Legislature. Randolph (Vermont.) Printed by Sereno Wright, State Printer. 1809. 8vo, pp. 24.

—*A Sermon* Delivered by Special request, to the Military Department in Middletown, Vermont, on May 10, 1814. By Sylvanus Haynes, V. D. M. Pastor of the baptized church of Christ in Middletown. Rutland : Printed by Fay & Davison. 1814. 8vo, pp. 21.

—*An Answer* to the Rev. Sylvanus Haynes' Piece entitled, "A Brief and Scriptural defence of believers' Baptism by immersion." By an Old Berean. Motto. Rutland : Printed A. D. 1801. 8vo, pp. 39.

Mr. Haynes was from Massachusetts, and was settled over the Baptist Church in Middletown, Vt., 1790–1817, when he moved to Western New York.

Hayward, John. *The New England Gazetteer;* containing descriptions of all the States, Counties and Towns in New England ; Also of the principal Mountains, Rivers, Lakes, Fashionable Resorts, &c. Thirteenth Edition. Concord, N. H. Boston : By John Hayward. 1839. 8vo.

—*A Gazetteer of Vermont :* Containing Descriptions of all the Counties, Towns, and Districts in the State, and of its Principal Mountains, Rivers, Waterfalls, Harbors, Islands, and curious Places. To which is added, Statistical Accounts of its Agriculture, Commerce and Manufactures ; with a great variety of other useful information. By John Hayward, Author of the "New England Gazetteer," "Book of Religions," &c. Boston : 1849. 12mo, pp. 216.

Hazeltine, Samuel. *The Religious Experience* of Samuel Hazeltine. Written by himself. To which is prefixed some account of his life and death. Hanover, N. H. 1819. pp. 38.

Mr. Hazeltine was born in Newbury, Vt., 1798 ; died there 1819.

Hazeltine, S. W. *The Traveller's Dream* and

Other Poems. By Silas Wood Hazeltine. Boston : 1860. 12mo, pp. 150, (2).

A native of Vermont.

Hazen, Austin. *A Sermon;* on occasion of the Death of Rev. Austin Hazen, Pastor of the Congregational Church in Berlin, Vt. Preached At Berlin, December 27th, 1854. Windsor : Printed at the Vermont Chronicle Press. 1855, 8vo, pp. 16.

By Andrew Royce, pastor at Barre.

Hazen, Austin. *Address* delivered at Richmond, Vermont, June 28, 1895, in Memory of The Rev. Austin Hazen. Middletown, Conn. Felton & King, printers. 1895. 8vo, pp. 36.

Rev. Austin Hazen, of Richmond, Vt., was a son of Rev. Austin Hazen of Berlin. He graduated from the University of Vermont in 1855, and from Andover Theological Seminary in 1859. He was pastor of the Congregational churches at Jericho Centre and Richmond for forty years. He died and was buried at sea, on a voyage from New York to Genoa, Italy, May 22d, 1895.

Hazen, Azel W. *A Discourse* on the History of the First Church of Christ, in Middletown, Conn., for the Century ending July 4, 1876. Delivered July 9, 1876, by the Rev. A. W. Hazen, Pastor. Middletown, Conn. : Pelton & King, Steam Book and Job Printers. 1876. 8vo, pp. 15.

Mr. Hazen was born at Berlin, Vt., April 10, 1841; was graduated at Dartmouth College in 1863, and studied Theology at Hartford, Ct.; was ordained at Middletown, March 10, 1869, where he still remains. (1896.)

Hazen Family. *Four American Generations.* By Henry Allen Hazen, A. M., New Haven, Conn.

Re-printed from the N. E. Historical and Genealogical Register, for April, 1879. 8vo, pp. 7.

Appended to same : The Boundary Line of New Hampshire and Massachusetts. Journal of Richard Hazen, Surveyor, 1741. Communicated by the Rev. Henry A. Hazen, of Billerica, Mass. From N. E. Historical Genealogical Register, for July, 1879. 8vo, pp. 11.

Hazen, Hon. Frederick. *Proceedings* of the Court and Bar of Grand Isle County, on the Occasion of the Announcement of the Death of Hon. Frederick Hazen, of Alburgh, Vt., at the February Term, 1859. Died at Alburgh, Feb. 17th, Aged 58 years. St. Albans : Messenger Office Print. 1859. 8vo, pp. 8.

Hazen, H. A. *The Congregational* and Presbyterian Ministry and Churches of New Hampshire. Part I.—Towns, Churches and Pastors. Part II.—Alphabetical Catalogue of Ministers. By Henry A. Hazen. [Reprinted from the "Congregational Quarterly," Oct. 1875, and April, 1876.] Boston : Alfred Mudge & Son, Printers, 34 School Street. 1875. 8vo, pp. 72. (1.)

—*Historical Discourse* Commemorative of the Centennial Anniversary of the Congregational Church, Plymouth, N. H. Preached Dec. 24th and 31st, 1865. By Henry A. Hazen, Pastor. With Introduction and Notes relating to the Early History of the Town. Boston : Congregational Publishing Society, Congregational House. 1875. 8vo, pp. 38.

—*Manual* of the Congregational Church, Plymouth, N. H. 1867.

—*Vital Statistics.* From Congregational Year-Book, for 1879. 8vo, pp. 36-58.

—*The Same,* Three previous Series, 1876-7-8.

—*The Pastors* of New Hampshire, Congregational and Presbyterian. A Chronological

Table of the Beginning and Ending of their Pastorates. By Henry A. Hazen. A Supplement to the Annual Minutes. Published by request of the General Association. Bristol, N. H. Printed by R. W. Musgrove. 1878. 8vo, pp. 32, (2).

See Hazen Family.

—*Andover Theological Seminary.* Necrology, 1880-81. Prepared under the direction of the committee, by Henry A. Hazen, Secretary. Boston : Beacon Press, Thomas Todd, Printer, Corner Beacon and Somerset Sts. 1881. 8vo, pp. 12.

Henry Allen Hazen, son of Allen and Hannah Putnam (Dana) Hazen, was born in Hartford, Vt., December 27, 1832; Phillips Academy, Danville, Vt., 1847; Kimball Union Academy, Antrim, N. H., 1848-50; was graduated at Dartmouth College, 1854, and Andover Seminary, 1857. Ordained an Evangelist at St. Johnsbury, February 17, 1858; home Missionary at Bridgewater and Barnard, Vt., one year, and acting pastor at Hardwick one year, at Barton one year, and at West Randolph one year. 1861. Installed Plymouth, N. H., January 21, 1863, and remained until 1868, July 15. Installed at Lyme, N. H., September 2, 1868, for two years, and at Pittsfield, N. H., two years, until November 30, 1872, and installed at Billerica, Mass., May 21, 1874; dismissed May 4, 1879, and is now connected with the Congregational House, Boston, and resides in Newton. He is a Trustee of Kimball Union Academy, elected in 1870; also of the New Hampshire Missionary Society, 1872-4; Statistical Secretary and Treasurer of the General Association of New Hampshire, 1872-4; member of New Hampshire Historical Society, 1867; of Vermont Historical Society, 1876; of New England Historical Genealogical Society, 1875; and associate editor of the "Congregational Quarterly," 1875-78, when its publication was discontinued. Married July 9, 1863, Charlotte Eloise, daughter of Dr. George Barrett, and Mary Hatch (Jones) Green, of Windsor, Vt., and they have children; Mary, born November 23, 1864, died September 30, 1865; Emily, born August 5, 1866, and Charlotte, November 6, 1868.

It may not be improper to acknowledge in this place the many favors received from Mr. Hazen in the preparation of this work. (1880.)

Hazen, J. *The Primary Instructor*, An Improved Spelling Book. Being an easy System of Teaching the Rudiments of the English Language. By Jasper Hazen. Woodstock : Printed by David Watson. 1822. 12mo: pp. 84.

—Another Edition : Windsor, Vt. Printed and sold by Simeon Ide & Co. 1822. 12mo, pp. 84.

Rev. Mr. Hazen, the founder and for many years pastor of the Woodstock Baptists died in that village March 30, 1882, aged over 90 years. Mr. Hazen was widely known throughout the State, both as a preacher and a bee culturist, to which latter subject he had given much attention, and had written largely about for periodicals.

Hazen, Gen. Wm. B. *A Narrative of Military Service.* With Maps, Plans, Portraits, etc. Boston : Houghton, Mifflin & Co. 8vo.

Gen Hazen was descended from Edward, the immigrant ancestor, through Thomas 2d, Thomas 3d, and Thomas 4th; the latter moved to Hartford, Vt., in 1774.

William B. son of Stillman, was born in West Hartford, Vt., September 27, 1830; was graduated at West Point, 1855, and distinguished himself in the civil war, in which he held the rank of Major General of Volunteers, and commanded the Fifteenth Army Corps. He was the author of a work on the late Franco-Prussian war, published by Harper Brothers, New York, 1870, entitled, "School and Army of France and Germany;" also of "Barren Lands of the United States," 1874. December 15, 1880, he was promoted to be Brigadier General in the Regular Army, and was appointed Chief Signal Officer, at Washington, where he died January 10, 1887.

Gen. Moses Hazen of Revolutionary fame was descended from Edward the immigrant, through Richard 2d, Moses 3d; Gen. Moses was born in Haverhill, Mass., June 1, 1733, and died at Troy, N. Y., February 4, 1803.

After the Revolutionary war closed he settled in Vermont. The old Hazen road, so called, through Vermont to Canada, was constructed under his supervision for military purposes.

See Reid's Ohio in the war; Drake's Biographical Dictionary; N. E. Historical Genealogical Register, April, 1879, pp. 229-36.

Hebard, Ebenezer. *A Sermon*, delivered before the Worshipful Master, the Wardens and Bretheren of Central Lodge, At Rutland, October 8th, 1804. Being the Festival Dedication of Mason's Hall in that Place. By Ebenezer Hebard, Pastor of a Church in Brandon, Vt. [Published at the request of the Lodge.] William Fay, Printer. 12mo, pp. 21.

Mr. Hebard was pastor of the Congregational church, Brandon, 1799-1821.

Hebard, William. *Speech* of Mr. Hebard, of Vermont, on the President's Message, Communicating the Constitution of California. Delivered in the House of Representatives, U. S., in Committee of the Whole on the State of the Union, March 14, 1850. Washington : Gideon & Co., Printers. 1850. 8vo, pp. 8.

Judge Hebard was born in Windham, Conn., November 29, 1800, and died at Chelsea, Vt., October 22, 1875. When but a lad he removed with his father's family to Randolph, Vt., and was educated at Randolph Academy. He read law, and was admitted to the Orange County Bar about 1827, and opened an office at East Randolph, from whence he removed to Chelsea in 1845, where he resided until his death. He represented the town of Randolph in the General Assembly in 1835, '40, '41, and 1842; the town of Chelsea in 1858, '59, '64, '65, and 1872; was elected to the State Senate in 1836 and 1838; was States Attorney in 1832, '34, and 1836; Judge of Probate for Randolph District, 1838, '40, and 1841; delegate to the Constitutional Convention in 1857; member of the Council of Censors in 1834 and 1848; Judge of the Supreme Court, 1842-1844; member of Congress, 1849-1853. Judge Hebard left three sons and a married daughter. Mrs. Hebard died some years since.

Hemenway, Asa. *A Genealogical Record* of one branch of the Hemenway Family, from 1634 to 1880. Compiled by Rev. Asa Hemenway, of Manchester, Vt. Hartford, Conn. Press of the Case, Lockwood & Brainard Company. 1880. 8vo, pp. 92.

Mr. Hemenway was born in Shoreham, Vt., July 6, 1810; he graduated from Middlebury College, 1835, and from Andover, 1838; was a missionary to Siam, 1839-1850; afterwards preached in Cornwall, Ripton, Keeseville, N. Y., and W. Hartford, Vt. Died at Manchester, Vt., February 26, 1892.

Hemenway, Miss Abby Maria. *Poets* and *Poetry* of Vermont. Edited by Abby Maria Hemenway.

> Sweet are the pleasures that to verse belong,
> And doubly sweet a brotherhood in song.
> —*Keats.*

Rutland : George A. Tuttle & Company. 1858. 12mo, pp. XII, 400.

Contains interesting biographical notes.

—*A Second Revised Edition.* Boston. 1860. 12mo, pp. 514.

Some copies of second edition have the imprint, Brattleboro. 1860. *Sabin.*

—*Notes* by the Path of the Gazetteer. By Abby M. Hemenway. Vols. 1 and 2. 2 vols. small 4vo in parts. Chicago. 1886-89.

—*The Vermont* Historical Gazetteer : A Magazine, embracing a History of each Town, Civil, Ecclesiastical, Biographical and Military. Edited by Abby Maria Hemenway. In Three Volumes. Burlington, Vt.: Published by Miss A. M. Hemenway. 1867-90. 5 vols., 8vo, pp. XI, 1096 ; 1199 ; 1245 ; 1200 ; 1180. Portraits and Plates.

This work is a series of Town Histories, grouped in Counties, and was at first issued in numbers, quarterly, containing about 100 pages each, and was called the "Vermont Quarterly Gazetteer." ,Vol. V was nearly completed by Miss Hemenway, at the time of her death, and was published by her sister, Mrs. Carrie E. H. Page, of Brandon, Vt., in 1891. A sixth volume, comprising the towns of Windsor County, is in press, and will complete the work.

—*Rosa Mystica ;* or Mary of Nazareth, the Lily of the House of David. Motto. By Marie Josephine. New York : D. Appleton & Company. 1865. 12mo, pp. VIII, 290.

—*Rosa Immaculata*, or the Tower of Ivory, in the House of Anna and Joachim. Mottoes. By Marie Josephine. New York : P. O'Shea. 1867. 12mo, pp. XIV, 250.

—*The House of Gold* and the Saint of Nazareth. A Poetical Life of Saint Joseph. Mottoes. Rosa Mystica Series, Vol. III. By Marie Josephine. Baltimore : Kelly, Piet and Company, 174 W. Baltimore Street. 1873. 12mo, pp. XII, 296.

—*Songs of the War.* Motto. Albany : J. Munsell, 78 State Street. 1863. Part I. 12mo, pp. 96.

—*Clarke Papers.* Mrs. Meech and Her Family. Home Letters, Familiar Incidents and Narrations Linked for Preservation. By Miss Hemenway, Author of Rosa Mystica, etc. Limited Edition. Published by Miss Hemenway, Ed. Vt. Hist. Gaz. Burlington, Vt. [Free Press and Times Print. 1878,] Sqr. 4 to, pp. (4), 312.

—*Fanny Allen*, the First American Nun. A Drama, in five Acts. By Marie Josephine. Boston : Thomas B. Noonan and Company, 23 & 25 Boylston St. 12mo, pp. 60. n. d. [1878].

Miss Hemenway was born in Ludlow, Vt., October 7th, 1828, where she resided until 1865. It was here that she brought out her first work, the Poets and Poetry of Vermont; it was here also that she commenced the great work of her life, The Vermont Historical Gazetteer, and here the first six numbers were published, commencing in 1858. It was in Ludlow that she wrote the "Rosa Mystica," and compiled the "Songs of the War." From 1865 to 1885 she resided in Burlington. She then removed to Chicago, Ill., where she died suddenly of apoplexy, Feb. 24, 1890.

Henry, Luther, Esq. *Memorial* Proceedings in relation to his Death, by the Washington County Bar.

See Peck, Lucius B.

Henshaw, J. P. K. *An Oration* delivered before the Associated Alumni of Middlebury College, at the Public Commencement, on the 15th August, 1827. By J. P. K. Henshaw. Published by Request. Middlebury : Printed by J. W. Copeland. 1827. 8vo, pp. 48.

John Prentiss Kewley Henshaw, D. D., was born in Middletown, Ct., June 13, 1792; died at Frederick, Md., July 20, 1852. His father moved to Middlebury, Vt., in 1800; the son graduated at Middlebury College in 1808, and was ordained a Deacon at the age of 21, and was prominent in the Episcopal Church through life, was Presiding Bishop of Rhode Island, and published a number of Theological works.

Herder, James. *The Spirit of Hebrew Poetry.* By J. G. Herder. Translated from the German, By James Marsh. In Two Volumes. Burlington : Edward Smith, (Successor to Chauncey Goodrich.) 1833. 12mo, pp. 293, 320.

Herrick, George F.

Mr. Herrick was born in Milton, Vt., April 19, 1834; was graduated at the University of Vermont in 1856, and at Andover in 1859; became a missionary of the A. B. C. F. M., and went to Turkey, where he has remained with the exception of a visit to his native land. He has written for publication, "Notes on Matthew and Mark, in Turkish, Osmanli characters," pp. 400, 12mo, 1865; "First

Reading Book in Turkish, Osmanli characters," pp. 63, 16mo, 1866; "Belief and Worship of Protestant Christians, in Turkish, Osmanli characters," pp. 128, 16mo, 1868; "History of the Christian Religion and Church, in Turkish, Armenian characters," pp. 840, 8vo, 1871; "Notes on Acts, in Turkish, Armenian characters," pp. 200, 8vo, 1874. He has also written articles for reviews and public journals.

Hervey, James. *Meditations among the Tombs*, tending to reform the vices of the age and to promote Evangelical Holiness. By James Hervey, Late Rector of Weston-Favell in Northamptonshire. A new Edition. Montpelier: Printed by Samuel Goss for Josiah Parks. 1810. 12mo, pp. 144.

—*Meditations* and Contemplations, etc., etc. By James Hervey. Brattleborough: Published by William Fessenden. 1814. 12mo, pp. 336.
　See Meditations.

Hewes, R. *Rules and Regulations* for the Sword Exercise of the Cavalry. To which is added, the Review Exercise. The third American, from the London Edition. Revised and corrected by Robert Hewes, Teacher of the Sword Exercise for Cavalry. Middlebury, Vt.: Published by Swift & Fillmore. Printed by Timothy C. Strong. 1814. 12mo, pp. 76. (3.)

Hewett, D. *A Gazetteer* of the New England States. Concise and Comprehensive. By D. Hewett. New York : Charles S. Francis. 1829. 12mo, pp. 84.

Hibbard, John. *Letter* on the Subject of Baptism, to Comfort Seaver, Esq., of Royalton, Vt. Hanover, N. H.: 1795. 8vo.

Hibbard, Rev. Lewis B. *Garfield Memorial.* A Discourse delivered at Ludlow, [Vt.] September 26, 1881. By Lewis B. Hibbard. Published by the Citizens of the Town. Ludlow : Warner & Hyde, Printers. 1881. 8vo, pp. 12.

Hibernians. *Constitution* and By-Laws of the Ancient Order of Hibernians. Instituted March, 1852 ; Chartered March 16th, 1853 ; Adopted June 8th, 1857. Rutland, Vt.: Tuttle & Co. Printers, 1874.
　Second Edition, with same imprint, 1875.

Hickok, Laurens P. *The Idea of Humanity* in its Progress to its Consummation. An Address delivered before the Philomathean Society, in Middlebury College, at their Anniversary, July 29, 1847. By Rev. L. P. Hickok, D. D., Professor of Christian Theology, in Auburn Seminary, N. Y. New York : S. W. Benedict. 1847. 8vo, pp. 23.

Hickok, Rev. M. J. *National Changes*—Ruin and Safety. A Sermon delivered in the First Presbyterian Church, Scranton, Pa., July 5th, 1857. By Rev. M. J. Hickok, Pastor of the Church. New York : John F. Trow. 1857. 8vo, pp. 31.

—*The Mission of Calamity.* A Thanksgiving Sermon : Preached in the First Methodist Episcopal Church, Scranton, Pa., November 27, 1862. By M. J. Hickok, D. D., Pastor of the First Presbyterian Church in Scranton. Published by request. New York : John F. Trow. 1862. 8vo, pp. 28.
　Mr. Hickok was born in New Haven, Vt., August 22, 1809; graduated at Middlebury, 1835; was Assistant Professor of Languages, Delaware College, 1835-38; tutor at Middlebury College, 1841; pastor of a Presbyterian

church, Marietta, O., 1841-44, then pastor at Rochester, N. Y., and Scranton, Pa.

Hickox, John H. *An Historical Account* of American Coinage. By John H. Hickox, with Plates. Albany, N. Y.: Joel Munsell. 1858. imp. 8vo, pp. viii, 151. 5 Plates.
　Gives an account of Vermont coinage.
　Two hundred copies printed, of which five are on large paper.

Hicks, G. C. *Directory* and Legislators' Manual for 1855. Containing a full list of the State Officers and Members of both Houses, with their lodgings, residences, occupations, politics and birth places : and other information useful to persons connected with the Legislature. Published by G. C. Hicks. Rutland : Geo. A. Tuttle & Co's Steam Press, 1855. 24mo, pp. 24.

Higbee, Elnathan Elisha. *A Sermon*, preached at the Funeral of James F. Weston. By the Rev. E. E. Higbee. Published at the request of the Friends and associates of the deceased. Bethel, March 20, 1858. Windsor : Vermont Chronicle Book and Job Office. 1858. 8vo, pp. 20.
　Rev. E. E. Higbee, D. D. LL. D., was born April 27, 1830, in St. George, Vt., and died at Lancaster, Pa., Dec. 10, 1889. He graduated at the University of Vermont in 1849, and from the Theological Seminary of the Reformed church in Mercersburg, Pa., in 1853; Preached at Lancaster, Pa., Bethel, Vt., Emmettsburg, Md., Tiffin, O. and Pittsburg, Pa.; was Professor of Languages in Heidelburg College, Tiffin, O., Professor of Church History in Theological Seminary, Mercersburg, Pa., 1864-7; President Mercersburg College, 1867-81; State Superintendent of Public Instruction for Pennsylvania, 1981, to his death. For numerous tributes to his worth as a man and services as an educator, see Pennsylvania School Journal for February, 1890.

Hibbard, Homer Nash. *The Charter* and Ordinances of the City of Freeport, together with Acts of the General Assembly Relating to Towns and Cities, and other Miscellaneous Acts, with an Appendix. Compiled, Revised and Published by Order of the City Council by Homer N. Hibbard, City Attorney. Freeport, Illinois. Printed by Judson & McClure. pp. viii, 214. 1857.
　H. N. Hibbard is a native of Bethel, Vt. He graduated from the University of Vermont, 1850; studied law in Dane Law School, Harvard ; admitted to the bar in Burlington, 1853; practiced law in Freeport, Ill., and Chicago; was U. S. Register in Bankruptcy at Chicago, 1870, until expiration of the U. S. Bankrupt Law; Commissioner to revise Statutes of Illinois, and connected with various banking, insurance and manufacturing companies, and educational institutions.
　See Biographical Cyclopedia of Illinois.

Highgate. *The Champlain* Spring Water, its Character and use. Highgate, Vermont. E. B. Whiting & Co., Printers, St. Albans, Vt. 12mo, pp. 15.

Hill, Ira. *An Oration* delivered at St. Albans, July 4, 1809, in commemoration of American Independence. By Ira Hill. Burlington, Vt.: Printed by Samuel Mills. 1809. 8vo, pp. 23.

Hill, Howard F. *A Sermon* preached in Memory of General Alonzo Jackman, LL. D., in St. Mary's Church, Northfield, by Howard F. Hill, Rector of Christ Church, Montpelier, Vt., November 6, 1881. (For private circulation only.) Montpelier, Vermont : Argus and Patriot Book and Job Printing House. 1881. 8vo, pp. 19.
　Mr. Hill, son of Hon. John M. and grandson of the late Hon. Isaac Hill of New Hampshire, is a native of Concord and a graduate of Dartmouth.

Hincks, Rev. J. H. *The Mission* of a Child's Life. A Sermon preached in Bethany Church, Montpelier, Vermont, March 20, 1881, by the Pastor, Rev. John H. Hincks. Printed for Private Circulation. Montpelier: Joseph Poland, Printer. 1881. r'l. 8vo, pp. 26, (1).

Preached on occasion of the death of Mary, aged 7 years, daughter of Jas. W. Brock, Esq., and Clara, aged 13 years, daughter of J. Monroe Poland. Esq.

Hinesburgh. *Centennial* Celebration of the First Congregational Church of Christ in Hinesburgh, Vt., Sept. 10, 1890. Published by request. Burlington Free Press Association. 1890. r'l octavo, pp. 78.

Comprises Historical Address by Rev. E. H. Byington, D. D., reminiscences, letters, etc.;

Hinman, C. T. *An Address* delivered in the Methodist Church, Newbury, Vermont, November 17, 1841, before the Ladies' Literary Society of Newbury Seminary, on the Moral Power of Female Education. By Rev. C. T. Hinman, Teacher of Mathematics and the Greek Language. Published by request of the Society. Concord: Printed by Asa McFarland. 1842. 12mo, pp. 23.

Hinsdale, Ebenezer. *Letters* to and from Col. Hinsdale relative to Depredations by the Indians in 1755. New Hampshire Hist Soc. Coll. Vol. V., pp. 254–258.

History *of Little Henry.* Second American Edition. Middlebury, Vt.: Printed by Francis Burnap. 1817. 24mo, pp. 64.

Hitchcock, Calvin. *The Wisdom* of God in the Selection of his Ministers. A Sermon, delivered at Sharon, June 11, 1828, before the Norfolk County Education Society. By Rev. C. Hitchcock, of Randolph. Boston: Printed by Crocker and Brewster, No. 47, Washington Street. 1828. 8vo, pp. 32.

—*Needful* Constitution of Magistracy. A Discourse delivered before the Ancient and Honorable Artillery Company, June 7th, 1841, being the CCIIId Anniversary. By Calvin Hitchcock, of Randolph. Boston: Press of J. Howe, 39 Merchants Row. 1841. 8vo, pp. 21.

—*Historical* Notices of Congregationalism. A Discourse delivered before the Pastoral Association of Massachusetts, in Park Street Church, Boston, May 27, 1845. By Calvin Hitchcock. D. D., pastor of the First Church, Randolph. Boston: Press of T. R. Marvin, 24 Congress Street. 1845. 8vo, pp. 23.

—*A Sermon* preached at the Funeral of Mrs. Joanna Strong, Widow of the late Jonathan Strong, D. D., of Randolph, Mass., Dec. 26, 1845. By Rev. Calvin Hitchcock, D. D., Pastor of the First Congregational Church in Randolph. Gilmanton: Printed by Alfred Prescott. 1848. 8vo, pp. 15.

Dr. Hitchcock was born in Westminster West, Vt., October 25, 1787; was graduated at Middlebury in 1811, and Andover in 1814; was pastor of the Congregational church at Newport, R. I., 1815-20, and at Randolph, Mass., 1821-51, when he removed to Wrentham, living on a farm until his death, which occurred December 3, 1867. He received the degree of D. D. in 1841. For Biographical sketch, see Congregational Quarterly, Vol. 10, p. 289.

Hitchcock, Charles H.
See Geology of Vermont.

Hitchcock, Edward, *State Geologist of Vermont.*
See Geology of Vermont.

Hitchcock, Edward, Jr.
See Geology of Vermont.

Hitchcock, Ethan Allen.
Was born in Vergennes, Vt., May 18, 1798; and died at Hancock, Ga., August 5, 1870. His father was Samuel Hitchcock, one of the first settlers of Burlington, Vt., and his mother was a daughter of Ethan Allen. He graduated at West Point in 1817, and entered the Artillery Corps as 3d Lieutenant. He followed the regular army routine until 1855, when he resigned his commission and turned his attention to authorship. His publications are: "Alchemy and the Alchemists," 1857; "Swedenborg, a Hermetic Philosopher;" 1858; "Christ the Spirit," 2 vols., 1859; "Red Book of Appin," "Remarks on the Sonnets of Shakespeare," "Notes on the *Vita Nuova* of Dante," 1866; and a mystical interpretation of "Colin Clout."

See Appleton's Cyclopedia and Drake's Dic. for biog. sketches of Gen. Hitchcock.

Historical *and Descriptive Lessons,* embracing Sketches of the History, Character and Customs of all Nations. Brattleboro' [Vt.]: Holbrook & Fessenden. 1828. 12mo, pp. 336.

Historicus. [*Henry Croswell.*] Sham Patriot unmasked; or an Exposition of the fatally successful Arts of Demagogues, To exalt themselves, By Flattering and Swindling the People: In a variety of Pertinent Facts drawn from sacred and Profane History. By Historicus. Peacham: Printed by Samuel Goss. 1804.— 12mo, pp. 81.

Hobart, Alvah S. *Eighty-three years* a Servant. Or the Life of Rev. Alvah Sabin. By Alvah S. Hobart. Printed for the Author by the Review Printing Co., Cincinnati. O. 1885. 8vo, pp. 174.

Rev. Alvah Sabin was born in Georgia, Vt., October 23, 1793, and resided there until about 1876. He was for ten years a representative in the legislature; was Secretary of State in 1841, and was a representative in Congress from Vermont from December 5, 1853, to March 3, 1857. He died at Sycamore, Ill., January 28, 1885, and at his request, his grandson, Rev. Alvah Sabin Hobart, the author of the above volume, preached his funeral sermon.

Hobart, Rev. James. *A Confession* of Faith and Covenant adopted by the Church of Christ in Berlin. New Bedford : 1810. 8vo, pp. 8.

—*A Sermon,* delivered at Craftsbury, Vt., at the Dedication of the Congregational Meeting House, Thursday. Sept. 28th, A. D. 1820. Danville: Ebenezer Eaton, Printer. 8vo, pp. 14.

—*Sermon* on the death of Father Hobart. See Lord, W. H.

Father Hobart was in the ministry sixty-seven years, and his sermon and Confession of Faith are said to be the only articles from his pen that he ever gave to the press. Elder Hobart was born in Plymouth, N. H., August 2, 1766; and died in Berlin, Vt., July 16, 1862, aged 95 years, 11 months and 14 days. He was graduated at Dartmouth, 1794; studied theology with Dr. Burton, of Thetford, and was ordained over the Congregational church of three members in Berlin, November 7, 1798, and was dismissed in 1829. He continued to reside in Berlin, as an itinerant preacher in the towns in the vicinity, during the remainder of his life. He was a Calvinist, in the old-fashioned sense, though in the latter years of his life his views were greatly modified.

Hodges, Rev. C. W., A. M. *Sermons:* by the Rev. C. W. Hodges, A. M., Pastor of the Baptist Church in Bristol, Vt. Burlington : Published for the Author, by Chauncey Goodrich. 1850. 12mo, pp. 296.

The above volume contains 22 sermons. Mr. Hodges was born in Leicester, Vt., in 1872; and died at Bristol, Vt., in April, 1851. He was left an orphan at an early age, and without relatives to look after him; he found a home in the family of Sylvester Kenny, of Salisbury, where he was taught the Puritan doctrines, and joined the Congregational Church in Salisbury at the age of nineteen; not long after he became interested in the Baptist system, and joined a church of that persuasion in

Brandon, and soon after entered the field as a Baptist preacher. See "Weeks' History, Salisbury," pp. 310-12; Springfield, History of the Baptist Church.

Holbrook, Frederick. *The Address* of Frederick Holbrook, Governor of the State of Vermont, to the General Assembly, at their Annual Session, October, 1861. Montpelier: Printed at the Freeman Printing Establishment. 1861. 8vo, pp. 12.

Frederick Holbrook was born in East Windsor, Conn., Feb. 15, 1813, being the son of Dea. John Holbrook, who was for forty years a prominent citizen of Brattleboro. Educated in the schools and at Pittsfield, Mass. At 20 took a foreign tour. Returning in 1833 he settled in Brattleboro and devoted himself mainly to Agriculture. He was a contributor for many years to the Albany Cultivator; was one of the founders and President of the Vt. State Agricultural Society; and while a member of the State Senate in 1849-50 inaugurated a petition to Congress for a National Bureau of Agriculture, which led the way to the establishment of the Department of. Agriculture. In 1861 he was elected Governor of Vermont, and re-elected in 1862.; Under his administration twelve regiments of Vermont Volunteers, three batteries of Artillery, and three companies of Sharpshooters were enlisted for the War for the Union, and he commissioned more officers for the War than any of the other War Governors of Vermont. He was one of President Lincoln's most trusted supporters, and it was upon a document prepared by him and signed by other Governors of the loyal States, that a call for three hundred thousand men was issued August 4, 1862, after the Seven Days' Battles. After retiring from the Governorship Mr. Holbrook declined further public office. He has been chairman of the Board of Trustees of the Brattleboro Insane Asylum for about 40 years, and is still living in Brattleboro at the age of 83 years. He marled in 1830, Harriet, daughter of Joseph Goodhue of Brattleboro, and has three sons, Franklin F., William C., and John.

Holbrook, Rev. John C. *Sketch* of the Religious History of Dubuque, I. T., with Details relating to the Congregational Church. A Discourse by John C. Holbrook, Pastor of the Congregational Church of Dubuque. Dubuque: George Greene, Printer. 1846. 8vo, pp. 14.

—*A Discourse,* preached in the Congregational Church of Dubuque on the Lord's Day, February 27th, 1853, by Jno. C. Holbrook, Pastor of the Church. 8vo, pp. 11.

—*Our Country's Crisis:* a Discourse delivered in Dubuque, Iowa, on Sabbath Evening, July 6, 1856, by Rev. John C. Holbrook, Pastor of the Congregational Church. Text. Dubuque Republican Office, 19 Main Street. 8vo, pp. 12.

—*Discourses,* Dedicatory and Historical, by John C. Holbrook, Pastor of the Congregational Church, Dubuque, Iowa, Published by W. J. Gilbert. Printed at the Daily Times Book and Job Office, 56 Main Street, Dubuque: 1860. 8vo, pp. 16.

—*Sketch* of the History of the Congregational Church and Society in Homer, Cortland County, N. Y. By Rev. J. C. Holbrook, D. D. n. d. 8vo, pp. 9.

—*Difficulties of Infidelity.* A Sermon preached before the Cortland Co., N. Y., Bible Society at its Jubilee Meeting, being its Semi-centennial Anniversary at Homer. Dec. 18, 1866, by Rev. J. C. Holbrook, D. D., Pastor of the Congregational Church, Homer, N. Y. Homer: J. R. Dixon, Book and Job Printer, Republican Office. 1867. 8vo. pp. 23.

—*The Field and the Laborers.* A Sermon, delivered before the American Education Society, at the Anniversary Meeting in Boston, May 28, 1867. By Rev. John C. Holbrook, D. D. Homer, N. Y. Boston: Press of T. R. Marvin & Son, 42 Congress Street. 1867. 8vo, pp. 16.

—*Revivals of Religion.* By Rev. John C. Holbrook, D. D. Originally an Address delivered before the American Revival Association in Boston during anniversary week in May, 1868. From the Congregational Review for September, 1868. 8vo, pp. 14.

—*Cause for Rejoicing* in view of the recent Presidential Election, A Sermon, preached in the Congregational Church, Nov. 8th, and repeated, by request, Nov. 15, 1868, in the Baptist Church, Homer, N. Y. By Rev. J. C. Holbrook, D. D. Text. Homer, N. Y.: Jos. R. Dixon, Book and Job Printer, (Power Press.) 1867. 12mo, pp. 16.

—*Modern Evangelists.* By Rev. J. C. Holbrook, D. D. n. d. 12mo, pp. 12.

Dr. Holbrook was born in Brattleboro, Vt., January 7, 1808; was in business as a book-seller and publisher in Brattleboro and Boston till 1838, when he went to Iowa to engage in agricultural pursuits, but, having long desired to be a minister, he began to preach in 1841. He preached at Dubuque, Ia., 1842-53; at Chicago, Ill., acting also as editor, 1853-6; again at Dubuque, 1856-63; at Homer, N. Y., 1864-9; at Stockton, Cal., 1869-72, when he received a call to become the Secretary of the New York State Home Missionary Society, which office he has since filled, living at Syracuse. (1880.) Removed later to Stockton, Cal., where he is residing (1895.)

See Brattleboro, History of, pp. 159-60.

Holbrook, Wm. C. *A Narrative* of the Services of the Officers and enlisted men of the 7th Regiment of Vermont Volunteers (Veterans,) from 1862 to 1866. By Wm. C. Holbrook, Late Colonel 7th Vt. Veteran Volunteers. New York: American Bank Note Company. 1882. 8vo, pp. VIII, 219.

Note.—Col. Holbrook is the second son of Gov. Frederick Holbrook. He has been a lawyer in New York, and its Judge of the Court of that city.

Holland, J. G. *History* of Western Massachusetts. The Counties of Hampden, Hampshire, Franklin and Berkshire. Embracing an outline, or General History, of the Section, an account of its Scientific aspects and Leading Interests, and separate Histories of its one hundred Towns. By Josiah Gilbert Holland. In two volumes. Springfield: 1855. 12mo. pp. 520 and 619.

Relates somewhat to Vermont.

Hollister, Hiel. *Pawlet* for One hundred years. By Hiel Hollister. Albany: Printed by J. Munsell. 1867. 12mo, pp. 272.

Mr. Hollister thus writes of himself in the History of Pawlet, p. 208. "Pawlet has always been our home; our main occupation through life has been farming, though we kept district school seven winters, and was a merchant 1854-1861. Twice married, first in 1830; first wife died in 1832; have six children, all by second wife."

Holmes, James H. *A Manual* on Window Gardening. For Popular Use. By James H. Holmes. Montpelier, Vt.: James H. Holmes, Publisher. 1877. 12mo, pp. 184.

Holmes, Nellie Jane. *In Memoriam.* Died at Underhill, Vt., Sept. 11th, 1877, aged 22 years. 8vo, pp. 15.

Holton, Henry D., M. D. *Address* before the Vermont Medical Society, July 9, 1889. Reported from Transactions of the Society. Brattleboro. 1889. pp. 15.

Hooker, Edward Payson, D. D. *Memorial Discourse* at the Funeral of Rev. Joseph Steele, at Middlebury, May 2, 1872. By Rev. E. P. Hooker. Printed by Request of Friends. Middlebury: Printed at the Register Book and Job Office. 1872. 8vo, pp. 11.

—*Address* of Rev. E. P. Hooker at the Funeral of Miss Mary Ann Swift, daughter of Hon. Samuel Swift, at Middlebury, Vt., Oct. 4, 1870. Register Print, Middlebury. 8vo, pp. 7.

—*Memorial* of Deacon Ira Allen. By his Pastor, Rev. E. P. Hooker. Middlebury, Vt. 12mo, pp. 12. Hartford, Conn. 1874.

Mr. Hooker was born in Castleton, Vt.; was principal of Brattleboro Academy 1865-6; tutor in Middlebury College 1855-7; Professor in Fort Plain Institute, N.Y. 1857-8; graduated from Andover Theology Seminary, 1861; Pastor of Congregational Churches in Medford, Mass., Fair Haven, Vt., Middlebury, Lawrence, Mass. and Winter Park, Fla., President of Rollins College, Winter Park, 1885-95.

Hooker, E. W. *An Address* delivered before the Philadelphian Society in Middlebury College, August 18, 1834. By Edward W. Hooker. Windsor: Chronicle Press. 1834. 8vo, pp. 20.

—*Address* to Christian Parents of the Churches in Vermont. Rutland: W. Fay, Printer. 1834. 8vo, pp. 36.

This address was prepared under the direction of the "General Convention" of Vermont; the committee, consisting of Mr. Hooker, Amos Drury and Hosea Beckley. Mr. Hooker wrote the address.

—*Love as an element* in Christian Character. An Essay by the Rev. Edward W. Hooker, Bennington, Vt. pp. 13, in American Quarterly Register, Vol. XI.

—*Memoir* of Mrs. Sarah Lanman Smith, late of the Mission in Syria, under the direction of the American Board of Commissioners for Foreign Missions. By Edward W. Hooker, Pastor of the First Congregational Church, Bennington, Vt. Boston: Perkins & Marvin. 1839. 12mo. pp. 407.

—*The Divine Discipline* of the Ministry. An Address delivered before the Society of Inquiry, in the Theological Institute, East Windsor Hill, Ct., Aug. 5, 1839. By Edward W. Hooker, Pastor of the First Congregational Church, Bennington, Vt. Hartford, Ct.: B. Geer. 1839. 8vo, pp. 20.

—*An Address* Delivered before the Hastings and Mason Musical Association, at Pittsfield, December 25, 1837. By Edward W. Hooker, Pastor of the First Congregational Church in Bennington, Vt. Published by Request of the Association. Pittsfield: Printed by Phineas Allen and Son. April, 1838. 8vo, pp. 23.

—*An Address* delivered before the Society of Sacred Music, in the Theol. Seminary of East Windsor. Aug. 6, 1839. By Rev. Edward Hooker. New York: Printed by J. F. Trow, 36 Ann-Street, 1839. 8vo, pp. 23.

—*An Address* on Sacred Music, Delivered at Castleton, Sept. 28th, 1843: By Rev. Edward W. Hooker, D. D. Published by Request. Montpelier: E. P. Walton & Sons, Printers. 1843. 8vo, pp. 16.

—*Music*, as a part of Female Education. By Edward W. Hooker. Boston: Press of T. R. Marvin, 24 Congress St. 1843. 8vo, pp. 24.

—*Duties to the Aged.* A Sermon delivered at the Funeral of General David Robinson. Bennington, Vt. Dec. 14, 1843. By E. W. Hooker, D. D. Pastor of the First Congregational Church. Published by request. Bennington: Printed by Haswell and Bushnell. 1844. 8vo, pp. 16.

Appended are family records.

—*A Sermon*, occasioned by the Catastrophe on board the U. S. ship of War Princeton: Preached in the First Congregational Church, Bennington, Vt., March 17, 1844, by Edward W. Hooker. Published by request. Troy, N. Y.: From the Press of N. Tuttle. 1844. 8vo, pp. 24.

Mr. Hooker was born in Goshen, Ct., November 24, 1794; and died at Fort Atkinson, Wis., March 31, 1875. He was graduated at Middlebury, 1814, and at Andover, 1818. Was settled over the First Congregational Church in Bennington, Vt., 1832-1844; and at Fair Haven, Vt., 1856-62. The intermediate periods were passed outside the State.

See Congregational Minutes, Vermont, 1875, and Jennings' History of Bennington, pp. 112—115.

Hooker, Henry B. *Plea for the Heathen;* or Heathenism Ancient and Modern. Boston: Massachusetts Sabbath School Society. Depository, No. 24, Cornhill. 1832. 24mo, pp. 190.

—*Put off and Put on:* or the Vile and Beautiful Apparel. By Simon. Boston: Massachusetts Sabbath School Society, Depository, No. 13, Cornhill. 1836. 18vo, pp. 126.

—*A Memorial Sketch.* By A. C. Thompson. Boston: Congregational Publishing Society, Congregational House. 1881. 12mo, pp. 34.

Dr. Hooker was born in Rutland, Vt., August 21, 1802; was graduated at Middlebury College in 1821, and at Andover in 1825; preached in South Carolina, 1825-26; at Lanesboro, Mass., 1826-36; at Falmouth, Mass., 1837-57; was Secretary of the Massachusetts Home Missionary Society 1857-73, residing in Boston until his death, June 4, 1881; he left a widow and two daughters, one of the latter being Mrs. Capron, wife of a missionary to India, the other that of Mr. Arthur W. Tufts, of Boston. One of his sermons, entitled "The Funeral of the Soul," was published in the "National Preacher" for December, 1847, and "Conscience a Preacher," in July, 1859. Besides these he has written several tracts, and many articles for the newspapers.

Hooker, Herman F. *The Portion* of the Soul or Thoughts on its Attributes and Tendencies as Indications of its Destiny. Philadelphia: 1835. 32mo. Reprinted: London. 1836. 18mo.

—*Popular* Infidelity. Philadelphia: 1835. 12mo.

Later editions bear the title: "The Philosophy of Unbelief in Morals and Religion, as Discernable in the Faith and Character of men."

—*Family Book* of Devotion. 1836. 8vo.

—*The Uses of Adversity*, and the Provisions of Consolation. 1846. 18mo.

—*Thoughts* and Maxims. 1847. 16mo.

—*The Christian Life* a Fight of Faith. 1848. 18mo.

—*An Appeal* to the Christian Public, on the Evil and impolicy of the Church engaging in Merchandise, and evil-working of the Charity Publication Societies. Philadelphia: King & Baird, Printers. 1849. 8vo, pp. 24.

Mr. Hooker, son of James 2d, was born in Poultney, Vt., in 1806; and died in Philadelphia, July 25, 1865. He was graduated at Middlebury College in 1825, and studied divinity at Princeton Theological Seminary, and took orders in the Episcopal Church, but ill health compelled him to abstain from the use of his voice in the pul-plt, and he opened a book-store in Philadelphia, and became widely known and distinguished as an author. Union College conferred upon him the honor of D. D., in 1848.

Hopkins, Caspar Thomas. *Business versus Speculation.* A Lecture Delivered before the Students of the University of California, Sept. 1st, 1876, And Dedicated to the Youth of San Francisco, by C. T. Hopkins. Published by Request. San Francisco : Bacon & Company, 1876. 8vo, pp. 28. ·

—*Shall we educate* our Politicians? by Caspar T. Hopkins, Author of A Manual of American Ideas, etc., etc. Reprinted from the California Illustrated Magazine. San Francisco. 1892-8vo, pp. 19.

Mr. Hopkins was a son of the late Rt. Rev. Bishop of Vermont; born in Pittsburg, Pa., May, 1826; graduated from the University of Vermont, 1847; died at Pasadena Cal., Oct, 4. 1893.

Hopkins, Frederick W. *Eulogy*, at Norwich, Vt., February 22, 1848, During the obsequies of Truman B. Ransom, Colonel of the Ninth Regiment. By General Frederick W. Hopkins. Published by Request. Hanover : Printed at the Dartmouth Press. 8vo, pp. 32.

This is the first edition, and without the plate.

—*Eulogy*, at Norwich, Vt., February 22, 1848, during The Obsequies of Truman B. Ransom, Colonel of the Ninth Regiment. By Frederick W. Hopkins, Esqr., Adjutant-General of the State. Second edition, with a Plate representing the Storming of Chepultepec, Sept. 13, 1847, where Col. Ransom lost his Life. Troy, N. Y.: From the Press of Prescott and Wilson. 1849. 8vo, pp. 19.

—*A Manual* of the Rutland County Bar, containing the Rules of Practice in the Supreme Court of Judicature, the Court of Chancery, and of the Rutland County Court. Compiled by F. W. Hopkins, Clerk of the Courts. Rutland : McLean & Robbins, Printers. 1867.

Gen. Hopkins was born in Pittsford, Vt., September 15, 1807; and died at Rutland, Vt., January 21, 1874. He was graduated at Middlebury College, 1828; read law, and practiced that profession in Rutland through life. He held many of the local civil offices, and was prominent in Vermont military affairs.

HOPKINS, RT. REV. JOHN HENRY. *Address* delivered before the Young Men's Auxiliary Bible Society, Nov. 2, 1819. Pittsburgh : Butler & Lambdin. 1820. 8vo, pp. 21.

—*Defence of the Convention* of the Protestant Episcopal Church in the State of Massachusetts against the "Banner of the Church." Boston : 1832. 8vo, pp. 44.

—*Religion* the Only Safeguard of National Prosperity, A Thanksgiving Sermon Delivered at Boston, Dec. 1, 1831. Boston : 8vo, pp. 24.

—*The Pleasures* of Luxury Unfavorable to the Exercise of Christian Benevolence. A Sermon preached in the Old South Church, Boston, Jan. 18, 1832, before the Howard Benevolent Society. By Rev. John H. Hopkins, Professor of Systematic Divinity in the Massachusetts Theological School, and Assistant Minister of Trinity Church, Boston. Motto. Boston : Perkins & Marvin, 114 Washington St. 1832. 8vo, pp. 20,

—*Religious Education*, the safest means of Ministerial Increase. A Sermon, Preached by appointment, before the Connecticut Church Scholarship Society, in Christ Church, Hartford, September 26th, 1832. By Rev. John Henry Hopkins, D. D. Published by request of the Society. Boston : Stimpson & Clapp, 72 Washington Street. 1832. 8vo, pp. 32.

—*Christianity Vindicated*, in Seven Discourses on the External Evidences of the New Testament, with a concluding Dissertation. By John Henry Hopkins, D. D. Bishop of the Protestant Episcopal Church in the Diocese of Vermont. Burlington : Edward Smith. MDCCCXXXIII. 12mo, pp. xii, 174.

—*The Primitive Creed*, Examined and Explained ; In two Parts. The First Part Containing Sixteen Discourses on the Apostles' Creed ; designed for popular use. The Second Part containing a Dissertation on the testimony of the Early Councils, and the Fathers, from the Apostolic Age to the end of the fourth Century, with Observations on certain Theological Errors of the present day. By John Henry Hopkins, D. D. Bishop of the Protestant Episcopal Church in the Diocese of Vermont. Motto. Burlington : Edward Smith. 1834. 12mo, pp. XIV, 415.

—*The Primitive Church*, compared with the Protestant Episcopal Church of the present day : Being an examination of the ordinary objections against the Church in Doctrine, Worship and Government, designed for Popular use ; with a Dissertation on Sundry Points of Theology and Practice, connected with the subject of Episcopacy. By John Henry Hopkins, D. D., Bishop of the Protestant Episcopal Church in the Diocese of Vermont. Motto. Burlington : Smith & Harrington. 1835. 8vo, pp. 380. A second Edition of same.

See REID, JAMES.

—*The Importance* of Providing Religious Education for the Poor: connected with the True Principle of all Christian Charity. Two Discourses, preached by Request, in the Cathedral of Quebec, before the Quebec Diocesan Committee, of the Society for Promoting Christian Knowledge, on Sunday, the Twenty-fifth day of October, 1835. By John H. Hopkins, D.D., Bishop of the Protestant Episcopal Church, in the Diocese of Vermont. Published at the Request of the Gentlemen of the Vestry. Burlington: Smith and Harrington. 1835. 8vo, pp. 30.

—*Essay* on Gothic Architecture, with various Plans and Drawings for Churches: Designed chiefly for the use of the Clergy. By John Henry Hopkins, D. D., Bishop of the Protestant Episcopal Church in the Diocese of Vermont Burlington: Printed by Smith & Harrington. 1836. Quarto, pp. vi, and 46, also 13 pages of plates.

—*Letters* to John H. Hopkins, D. D., Bishop of the Protestant Episcopal Church for the Diocese of Vermont: Occasioned by his Lecture in Opposition to the Temperance Society. By an Episcopalian. Windsor: Printed at the Chronicle Press. 1836.

—*The Church* of Rome in her Primitive Purity, Compared with the Church of Rome, at the Present Day; Being a Candid Examination of her Claims to Universal Dominion. Addressed in the Spirit of Christian Kindness, to the Roman Hierarchy. By John Henry Hopkins, D. D., Bishop of the Protestant Episcopal Church, in the Diocese of Vermont. Burlington: Vernon Harrington. 1837. 12mo, pp. 406. Reprinted in London, 1839. pp. 396.

—*Statements* of the Studies, Terms and General Principles of the Vermont Episcopal Institute. Philadelphia: William Stavely. 1838. pp. 16.

—*Twelve Canzonets:* Sacred Songs; Words and Music; for the use of Christian families. London: and New York: 1839.

—*The Sacrifice of Atonement:* A Sermon preached by Request in St. Paul's Church, Burlington, on the Evening of Trinity Sunday, June 6, 1841. By John H. Hopkins, D. D., Rector, and Bishop of the Protestant Episcopal Church in the Diocese of Vermont. Published by Request: Burlington: Chauncey Goodrich. 1841. 8vo, pp. 23.

—*Scripture and Tradition.* A Sermon, preached at the Ordination of Ten Candidates for the Diaconate, in St. Paul's Chapel, New York, on the Third Sunday after Trinity, June 27th, 1841, By John H. Hopkins, D. D., Bishop of the Diocese of Vermont. Motto. Published by request. New York: Dean & Trevett, 121 Fulton Street. 1841: 8vo, pp. 24.

—*The Vermont Drawing Book* of Landscapes, Designed and Executed by John Henry Hopkins, D. D., Bishop of the Diocese of Vermont. No. 1. Ninth Edition. Burlington: Chauncey Goodrich. 1841. Quarto. 6 numbers in all. 7 to 9 leaves each.
Assisted by his sons in this work.

—*The Missionary Constitution,* the Oxford Tracts, and Nestorianism. A Charge delivered Wednesday, September 21st, 1842, in Trinity Church, Rutland, to the Clergy of the Diocese of Vermont, by John Henry Hopkins, D. D., Bishop of the Diocese. Burlington: Chauncey Goodrich. 1842. 8vo, pp. 40.

—*A Letter* to the Right Rev. Francis Patrick Kenrick, Roman Bishop of Arath, and Coadjutor of the Roman Bishop of Philadelphia, in answer to His Letter on Christian Union, Addressed to the Bishops of the Protestant Episcopal Church. By John Henry Hopkins, D. D., Bishop of the Diocese of Vermont. Burlington: Chauncey Goodrich. 1842. 8vo, pp. 10.

—*A Second Letter* to the Right Rev. Francis P. Kenrick, Roman Catholic Bishop of Philadelphia. By John Henry Hopkins, D. D., Bishop of the Diocese of Vermont. Second Edition. Burlington, Vt.: Published by C. Goodrich, S. Fletcher, Printer. 1843. 8vo, pp. 64.
Two editions.

—*Two Discourses* on the Second Advent of the Redeemer, with special reference to the year 1843. By John Henry Hopkins, D. D., Bishop of the Diocese of Vermont. Third Edition. Burlington: Published by C. Goodrich, S. Fletcher, Printer. 1843. 8vo, pp. 32.
Four editions.

—*The Novelties* which Disturb our Peace. A Letter addressed to the Bishops, Clergy, and Laity of the Protestant Episcopal Church, by John Henry Hopkins, D. D., Bishop of the Diocese of Vermont. Philadelphia: Herman Hooker. 1844. 12mo, pp. 71.

—*The Novelties* which Disturb our Peace. A Second Letter addressed to the Bishops, Clergy, and Laity of the Protestant Episcopal Church of the United States. By John Henry Hopkins, D. D. Bishop of the Diocese of Vermont. Philadelphia: Herman Hooker, 187 Chestnut Street. 1844. 12mo, pp. 80.

—*The Novelties, &c.* A Third Letter. 1844. pp. 84.

—*The Novelties* which Disturb our Peace. A Fourth Letter addressed to the Bishops, Clergy, and Laity, of the Protestant Episcopal Church in the United States. By John Henry Hopkins, D. D., Bishop of the Diocese of Vermont. Philadelphia: H. Hooker, 178 Chestnut Street, (Opposite Masonic Hall.) 1844. 12mo, pp. 71.
Another edition of these four letters was published by James M. Campbell & Co.

—*Sixteen Lectures* on the Causes, Principles, and Results of the British Reformation. By John Henry Hopkins, D. D. Bishop of the Protestant Episcopal Church, in the Diocese of Vermont. Philadelphia: James M. Campbell & Co. Saxton & Miles, New York. 1844. 12mo, pp. 387.

—*Episcopal Government.* A Sermon Preached at the Consecration of the Rev. Alonzo Potter, D. D., as Bishop of Pennsylvania. 1845. 8vo, pp. 24.

—*Letter* to the Rev. Samuel Seabury, D. D., Editor of the Churchman. 1846. 8vo, pp. 16.

—*A Pastoral Letter* addressed by the Bishop of the Protestant Episcopal Church in the State of Vermont, to the People of his Diocese, on the Subject of his Correspondence with the Rev. William Henry Hoit, Late Rector of Union Church, St. Albans. Burlington: Chauncey Goodrich. 1846. 8vo, pp. 47.

—*An Humble* but earnest Address to the Bishops, Clergy, and Laity of the Protestant Episcopal Church in the United States, on the Tolerating among our Ministry of the Doctrines of the Church of Rome. By John Henry Hopkins, Bishop of the Diocese of Vermont. New York: Harper & Brothers, Publishers, 82 Cliff Street. 1846. 8vo, pp. 23.

—*The Unity* of the Church consistent with Divisions of Party. Sermon before the General Convention of the Protestant Episcopal Church, assembled at St. John's Chapel, in the City of New York, on Wednesday, October 6th, 1847. By John H. Hopkins, D. D., Bishop of the Diocese of Vermont. New York: Daniel Dana, Jr. No. 20 John Street. 1847. 8vo, pp. 24.

—*Defect* of the Principle of Religious Authority in Modern Education. Address before the American Institute of Instruction, August 14, 1849. 8vo, pp. 26.

—*The Case* of the Rev. Mr. Gorham against the Bishop of Exeter, Considered. Address to the Clergy of the Diocese of Vermont, by John

H. Hopkins, D. D., Bishop of the Diocese, November, 1849. Burlington: Published by E. Smith & Co. 1849. 8vo, pp. 40.

—*Address* delivered by Request of the Selectmen of the town of St. Albans, Friday, August 2, 1850, on the Death of General Zachary Taylor, Late President of the United States, by John Henry Hopkins, D. D. Bishop of the Diocese of Vermont. St. Albans: Printed by E. B. Whiting. 1850. 8vo, pp. 26.

—*Fraternal Unity* in the Church of God. Triennial Sermon before the Bishops, Clergy and Laity Constituting the Board of Missions of the Protestant Episcopal Church in the United States of America. Preached in Christ Church, Cincinnati, Ohio, on Thursday evening, October 3, 1850, by the Rt. Rev. John Henry Hopkins, D. D., Bishop of Vermont. New York: Published for the Board of Missions, by Daniel Dana, Jr., No. 20 John Street. 1850. 8vo, pp. 15.

—*The History* and Results of the Confessional. 1850. New York: Harper & Brothers. 12mo, pp. 334.

—*The Divine Law* for the Support of the Ministry. A Sermon, in Grace Church, Boston, March, 1851. 8vo, pp. 20.

—*Hoffman* on American Canon Law. Article in the Church Review of January, 1851. pp. 26.

—*Address* at the First Annual Meeting of the P. E. Historical Society. June, 1851. 8vo, pp. 19.

—*Slavery*, its Religious Sanction, its Political Dangers, and the Best Mode of Doing it away. A Lecture delivered before the Young Men's Associations of the City of Buffalo and Lockport, on Friday, January 10, and Monday, January 13, 1851. By John H. Hopkins, D, D., Bishop of the Diocese of Vermont. Published by Request. Buffalo: Published by Phinney & Co. 1851. 8vo, pp. 32.

—*A Pastoral Letter*, Addressed to the several Parishes, by John Henry Hopkins, D. D., LL. D., Bishop of The Diocese of Vermont, at the request of The Convocation of The Clergy, September 16, 1852. Burlington: Stacy & Jameson, Printers. 1852. 8vo, pp. 15.

—*A Tract* for the Church in Jerusalem. The Right to make Proselytes from the Eastern Churches, on True Catholic Principle, Considered in a Letter of Friendly Remonstrance, to the Editors of the Church Journal. By John Henry Hopkins, D. D., LL. D. Bishop of the Diocese of Vermont. Burlington: Stacy & Jameson, Printers. 1854. 8vo, pp. 38.

—*The True Principles* of Restoration to the Episcopal Office. 1854. 8vo, pp. 39.

—*A Pastoral Letter*, on the Support of the Clergy. 1854. 8vo, pp. 8.

—*A Defence* of the Constitution of the Diocese of Vermont, in reply to the Strictures of the Episcopal Recorder. 1854. 8vo, pp. 26.

—*The Historical* Evidences of Christianity. XIVth Essay, pp. 363—383 in a volume. pp. 20.

—"*The End of Controversy*" Controverted. A Refutation of Milner's "End of Controversy," in a series of letters addressed to the Most Rev. Francis Patrick Kenrick, R. C. Archbishop of Baltimore. New York: Pudney & Russell. 1854. 2 volumes. 12mo, pp. 468, 398.
Three editions were printed.

—*Address* before the House of Convocation of Trinity College, Hartford, Ct., July 26, 1854. 8vo, pp. 30.

—*A Pastoral Letter* on the Subject of the Church Institute. 1855.

—"*To the Friends* of Sound Doctrine, Piety and Education," in behalf of the Vermont Episcopal Institute. October, 1855. pp. 4.

—*The Relations* of Science and Religion. A Discourse delivered at the Request of the Local Committee of the American Association for the Advancement of Science, in St. Paul's Church, Albany, on Sunday, the 14th after Trinity. August 24th, 1856. By John H. Hopkins, D. D., LL. D., Bishop of the Protestant Episcopal Church, in the Diocese of Vermont. Albany: Van Benthuysen, Printer, 407 Broadway. 1856. 8vo, pp. 30.

—*The American Citizen:* his Rights and Duties, according to the Spirit of the Constitution of the United States. By John Henry Hopkins, D. D. New York: Pudney & Russell. 1857. 12mo, pp. 459. Three editions.

—*Extract* from the American Citizen, his Rights and Duties in Reference to Slavery. By John Henry Hopkins. New York: Pudney & Russell. 1860. 12mo, pp. 121–144.

—*The Bible View of Slavery.* [1861.] 8vo, pp. 16.
This little tract brought a hornet's nest of replies about the Bishop's head from all sorts of people.
See LEA, H. C.

—*A Letter* to the Bishops and Delegates of the Protestant Episcopal Church now assembled at Montgomery. By the Right Reverend John H. Hopkins, D. D., LL. D., Bishop of Vermont. New York: 1861. 8vo, pp. 14.

—*Review* of a Letter from the Right Rev. John H. Hopkins, D. D., LL. D., Bishop of Vermont, on the Bible View of Slavery, by a Vermonter. Burlington: Free Press Print, 1861. 8vo, pp. 28.
See MARSH, LEONARD.

—*The Bishop* of Vermont's Protest, and Draft of a Pastoral Letter. n.p. n.d. 8vo, pp. 16. [Oct. 1862.]

—*Letter* to Rev. M. A. DeWolf Howe, D. D. 1863. n.p. n.d.

—*A Reply* to the Letter of Bishop Hopkins, addressed to Dr. Howe, in the Print called "The Age," of Dec. 8th, 1863. [By M. A. DeWolfe Howe.] Philadelphia: King & Baird, Printers. 1864, 8vo, pp. 18.

—*A Scriptural*, Ecclesiastical, and Historical View of Slavery, from the Days of the Patriarch Abraham, to the Nineteenth Century. Addressed to the Right Rev. Alonzo Potter, D. D., Bishop of the Protestant Episcopal Church, in the Diocese of Pennsylvania. By John Henry Hopkins, D. D., LL. D., Bishop of the Diocese of Vermont. New York: W.

I. Pooley & Co., Harper's Building, Franklin Square. 12mo, pp. vii, 376. No date, but was published in 1864.

—*Autobiography of*, in Verse. 1866. pp. 121. Privately printed.

—*The History* of the Church, In Verse, composed for the use of Bible-Classes, Schools, and Families, in the Protestant Episcopal Church in the United States. By John Henry Hopkins. D. D., LL.D., Bishop, etc. New York: 1867. 12mo, pp. 256.

—*The Law* of Ritualism, examined in its relation to the Word of God, to the Primitive Church, to the Church of England, and to the Protestant Episcopal Church in the United States. By the Rt. Rev. John Henry Hopkins, D. D., LL.D., Bishop of Vermont. Boston: Crown 8vo.; New York: 1867. Fourth Thousand; pp. 98. Four Editions; besides one in England, London: 1867. pp. 83.

—*A Candid Examination* of the question Whether the Pope of Rome is the Great Antichrist of Scripture. By the late Rev. John Henry Hopkins, D. D., LL.D., Bishop of Vermont. New York: Published by Hurd & Houghton. 1868. 12mo, pp. ix, 150.

—*Memorial* of The Right Reverend John Henry Hopkins, the first Bishop of Vermont, and the Seventh Presiding Bishop of the Church in the United States. New York: Pott and Amory, No. 5 Cooper Union. 1868. Square 4to, pp. (32).

—*Order* of Services at the Translation of the Remains of the Rt. Rev. John H. Hopkins, D. D. LL.D. June 10, 1873. pp. 8.

—*Description* of the Monument Erected to the memory of Bishop Hopkins. 8vo, pp. 4.

In addition Bishop Hopkins published many communications in the daily and weekly press. He left a large quantity of manuscripts, including a very great number of sermons.

The Rt. Rev. John Henry Hopkins, D. D., LL.D., D. C. L., Oxon, Bishop of Vermont, and Presiding Bishop of the Protestant Episcopal Church of the United States, was born in Dublin, Ireland January 30, 1792; and died at Burlington, Vt., January 9, 1868. He came to America in 1800; read and practiced law, but left the profession; read theology, and was ordained and elected Rector of Trinity Church, Pittsburgh, Pa., in May, 1824. In 1832 he was elected Bishop of Vermont, and at the same time accepted the Rectorship of St. Paul's Church, Burlington, which latter he resigned in 1856, that he might devote his time entirely to his Diocese and the building up of the Vermont Episcopal Institute. In 1863, by the death of Bishop Brownell, he became by seniority of Consecration, Presiding Bishop of the Protestant Episcopal Church in the United States.

See *Drake's Biog. Dictionary; Allibone;* and Hopkins, J. H. Jr., Life of the Bishop, a work of absorbing interest.

Hopkins, John Henry Jr., D. D. *Rich Trinity.* A Layman's Answer to "Poor Trinity." Examined by John H. Hopkins, Jr., M. A., Deacon. New York. 1859. 8vo, pp. 32.

—*Poor Trinity.* The Report of a Committee on the Condition of the Finances of Trinity Church, examined by John H. Hopkins, Jr., M. A., Deacon. New York. 1859. 8vo, pp. 29.

—*Liberty:* A Poem, Delivered before the Literary Societies of the University of Vermont, On Tuesday, August 3d, 1847. By John H. Hopkins, Jr., M. A. Published by Request. New York: D. Appleton & Co. 1847. 8vo, pp. 18.

—*The Faith* and Order of the Protestant Episcopal Church in the United States. New York: [n. d.] 12mo, pp. 14.

—*The Three Kings of Orient.* A Carol. By Rev. J. H. Hopkins, Jr. Illustrated, and printed in Colors. Boston: 8vo.

—*The Life* of the Right Reverend John Henry Hopkins, First Bishop of Vermont, and Seventh Presiding Bishop. By one of his sons. New York: F. J. Huntington & Co., 105 Duane street. 1873. 8vo, pp. 481. Portrait.

A Second edition in 1875.

—*Poems by the Wayside.* Written during more than forty years by John Henry Hopkins. James Pott, 12 Astor Place, New York. 1883. 12mo, pp. vii, 324.

—*A Champion of the Cross*; being the life of John Henry Hopkins, S. T. D., including extracts and selections from his writings, by Rev. Charles F. Sweet. New York. 1894. James Pott & Co. 8vo, pp. ix, 374.

Rev. John Henry Hopkins, Jr., was a son of the late Bishop Hopkins of Vermont. He was born in Pittsburg, Pa., 1820; graduated from the University of Vermont in 1839; was ordained as a deacon of the Episcopal Church in 1850, and as a priest in 1872; was rector of P. E. church in Plattsburgh, N. Y., and in Williamsport, Pa. Died at Hudson, N. J., Aug. 13, 1891. He founded the Church Journal and edited it for fifteen years. Besides the above he published Gregorian Canticles, 1866; Articles on Romanism, 1890, and a number of pamphlets, mostly controversial.

Hopkins, Josiah. *The Doctrine* of Decrees Essential to the Divine Character. A Sermon preached at New-Haven, Vt. Lord's Day, Feb. 23, 1812. By Josiah Hopkins, Pastor of the Congregational Church of Christ, in New-Haven. Published at the Request of the Hearers. Middlebury, Vt.: Printed by T. C. Strong. 1812. 8vo, pp. 19.

—*A Discourse*, delivered at Hinesburgh, Vermont, September 30, 1818, at the Ordination of Mr. Otto S. Hoyt, as pastor of the Church of Christ in that place. By Josiah Hopkins, A. M., Pastor of the Church of Christ in New-Haven, Vt: Motto. Middlebury, Vt.: Printed by Francis Burnap. 1818. 8vo, pp. 19.

—*The Christian Instructor.* Containing a Summary Explanation and Defence of the Doctrines and Duties of the Christian Religion. By Josiah Hopkins, A. M., Pastor of the Congregational Church in New-Haven, Vt. Middlebury: Printed by J. W. Copeland. 1825. 12mo, pp. 312.

—*Enquiry* whether we "ought to obey God, rather than Men," in a Review of a Sermon preached by the Rev. J. C. Lord, D. D., at Buffalo, N. Y., entitled "The Higher Law," its application to the "Fugitive Slave Bill," by Josiah Hopkins, D. D., Chagrin Falls, Ohio. Cleveland: Smead & Cowles' Steam Press 1851. 12mo, pp. 16.

See Levings, Noah; Parmelee, Ashbel, for funeral Sermon for Mrs. Lucy Parmelee, February 13, 1814.

Mr. Hopkins was born in Pittsford, April 18, 1786; began to preach in the Congregational church at New Haven, Vt., in 1809, and continued there until 1830, when he removed to Auburn, N. Y., thence to Ohio in 1848, and returned to Seneca Falls, N. Y., and died at Geneva, in 1862. He also published "Conference Hymns," "The Endless Punishment of the Wicked," and a work on "Congregationalism."

See Caverly's History of Pittsford, pp. 573-74.

Hopkins, Rev. Samuel. *The Evils of Gambling.* A Sermon, Preached in Montpelier, Vermont, April 19th, 1835. By Samuel Hopkins, Pastor of the First Congregational Church. Montpelier: E. P. Walton & Son, Printers. 1835. 8vo, pp. 18, (4).

—*The Puritans;* or the Church, Court, and Parliament of England, during the Reigns of Edward VI. and Queen Elizabeth. By Samuel Hopkins. Motto. In three volumes. Boston: Gould & Lincoln. New York: Cincinnati: 1860. 8vo, pp. xiv, 549, 539, 675.

Mr. Hopkins was born at Northampton, Mass., of an illustrious family, October 26, 1831; he succeeded the Rev. Chester Wright as pastor of the Congregational Church at Montpelier, in 1830, where he remained until the Burchard frenzy in 1835 drove this excellent man to calmer fields.

After leaving Montpelier, Rev. Mr. Hopkins was for many years pastor of a Congregational Church at Saco, Me. He subsequently published the above elaborate work and a volume of Sermons.

Mr. Hopkins died at Springfield, Mass., Feb. 10, 1887.

Hopkins, Rev. Samuel, A. M. *A new Edition* of two Discourses delivered by Samuel Hopkins, A. M. Minister of the Gospel, in Great Barrington. Sermon I. On the necessity of the knowledge of the Son of God, in order to the knowledge of Sin. Sermon II. A particular, and critical inquiry into the cause, nature and means of that CHANGE in which men are BORN OF GOD. From a copy revised and corrected by the Author, now Pastor of a Church in Newport, Rhode Island. Printed in Boston, A. D. 1768. Reprinted by Anthony Haswell, Bennington [Vermont] 1793. 12mo, pp. 120.

This Rev. Samuel Hopkins was the founder of the sect called "Hopkinsians;" he died at Newport, R. I., December 20, 1803, aged 82. See Allen's Biog. Dic.

Horr, R. G. *A plain talk* on what the Country needs. Speech of Hon. R. G. Horr, of Michigan, in the House of Representatives, Saturday, April 26, 1879. Washington, D. C.: R. O. Polkinhorn, Printer. 1879. 8vo, pp. 8.

Mr. Horr is a native of Waitsfield, Vt., and has been a member of Congress from Michigan.

Horticultural. *Proceedings* of the Horticultural Convention, held at Burlington, Vt., February 11, 1851, and organization of the Champlain Valley Horticultural Society; with an Appendix, containing a list of fruits, Reported by the Standing Fruit Committee. Keeseville, N. Y.: Printed at the Republican Office. 1851. 8vo, pp. 72.

Hosford, B. F. *Introductory Address* before the Young Men's Christian Association, of Haverhill. Delivered Sabbath Evening, Sept, 30, 1855. By Rev. B. F. Hosford. Haverhill: E. G. Frothingham, Printer. 1855. 8vo, pp. 16.

—*Paul,* and the Chief Cities of his Labors. By Rev. B. F. Hosford. Boston: Massachusetts Sabbath School Society. Depository No. 13 Cornhill. 1857. 12mo, pp. 257.

—*Discourse* at the Re-dedication of the Center Church, Haverhill, Mass., January 27, 1860. By B. F. Hosford, Pastor. Boston: Press of T. R. Marvin & Son, 42 Congress Street. 1860. 8vo, pp. 39.

Mr. Hosford was born at Thetford, Vt., November 11, 1817; was graduated at Dartmouth College in 1838, and at Andover in 1841; was pastor of the Center Congregational Church, of Haverhill, Mass., 1845-63, and died

there August 10, 1864. See Chapman's "Dartmouth Alumni."

Hoskins, Nathan. *A History* of the State of Vermont, from its discovery and settlement to the close of the year MDCCCXXX. By Nathan Hoskins. Motto. Vergennes: Published by J. Shedd. 1831. 12mo, pp. 316.

—*Strictures on Civil Liberty,* as it now exists in the North American Union: together with Propositions for Amending the Constitution of Vermont, additional to those of the Council of Censors, recommended to the Convention to be holden in January, 1850. By Nathan Hoskins. Bennington Vt.: Gazette Office, H. B. Knight, Printer. 1849. 12mo, pp. 36.

—*Notes* upon the Western Country, Contained within the States of Ohio, Indiana, Illinois, and the Territory of Michigan: Taken on a tour through that country in the summer of 1832. By Nathan Hoskins, Jr., Author of the History of Vermont. Greenfield: [Mass.] James P. Fogg. 1833. 12mo, pp. 108.

He was also the author of a pamphlet on the "Bennington Court Controversy." See Bennington.

Mr. Hoskins was born in Weathersfield, Vt., April 27, 1795. He was graduated at Dartmouth College in 1820, studied law, and practiced in Vergennes, 1823 to 1831; then moved to Bennington, and thence in 1859 to Williamstown, Mass., where he died April 21, 1869.

Hosmer, F. J. *A Glimpse* of Andersonville, and Other Writings, by Francis J. Hosmer, Springfield, Mass.: Press of Loring and Axtell. 1896. 8vo, pp. 90, 3.

Mr. Hosmer was a member of the Fourth Regiment, Vt. Vols.

Hosmer, Rev. Geo. W., D. D. *Report* of Delegates from the General Aid Society for the Army, at Buffalo, N. Y., to visit the Government Hospitals, and the Agencies of the U. S. Sanitary Commission. By Rev. George W. Hosmer, D. D. Montpelier, Vt.: Walton's Steam Printing Establishment. 1863. 8vo, pp. 16.

Hosmer, W. H. C. *The Prospects* of the Age. A Poem, delivered before the Literary Societies of the University of Vermont, at Burlington, August 3, 1841. By William H. C. Hosmer, A. M. Published by Request. Burlington: Chauncey Goodrich. MDCCCXLI. 8vo, pp. 19.

Hough, Rev. John. *A Sermon,* delivered April 10, 1810, at the Ordination of the Rev. Daniel Haskel, as Pastor of a Church in Burlington. By the Rev. John Hough, Pastor of the Church in Vergennes. Burlington, Vt. Printed by Samuel Mills, May, 1810.

—*A Sermon* preached at the Ordination of Rev. Beriah Green, over a Church in Brandon, Vt., April 16, 1823.

—*An Address* delivered before the Mechanical Association of Middlebury College, Commencement evening, Aug. 18, 1830, by John Hough, Professor of Languages. 8vo, pp. 8.

See "Register of Am. Ed. Society," vol. 3.

—*A Sermon* Delivered before the Vermont Colonization Society, at Montpelier, October 18, 1826. By John Hough, Professor of Languages in Middlebury College. Published by request of the Society. Montpelier: Printed by E. P. Walton—Watchman Office. 1826. 8vo, pp. 20.

Professor Hough was born in Stamford, Ct., August 17, 1783; and died at Fort Wayne, Ind., July 17, 1861. He graduated at Yale in 1802, studied theology, and came to Vermont as a missionary in 1806, and was settled at Vergennes in 1807. In 1812 he was appointed Professor of Greek and Latin in Middlebury College, with which he was connected in different professorships for twenty-seven years ; was a principal editor of the Adviser in 1814-15. In 1841 he removed to Ohio, and thence to Fort Wayne.

Hough, J. W. *Our Country's Mission*, or The Present Suffering of the Nation justified by its Future Glory. A Discourse preached at Williston, Vermont, On the day of the National Fast, August 4th, 1864. By Rev. J. W. Hough. Burlington: Free Press Print. 1864. 8vo, pp. 23.

Houghton Association. *Report* to the Houghton Association, U. S. A., made by Columbus Smith, A. D. 1869, containing information now collected, relative to Houghton property in England ; also several genealogies of different branches of this family. Published by order of the Houghton Association. Burlington, Vt.: Daily Free Press Book and Job Office. 1869. 8vo, pp. 60 and tables.

Houghton, George Frederick. *Address* on the Life and Services of Col. Seth Warner ; Delivered before the Legislature of Vermont, in Montpelier, October 20, 1848, By George Frederick Houghton. Published by order of the Legislature. Burlington : Free Press Print. 1849. 8vo, pp. 59.
See Butler, James Davie.
This address contains a valuable outline of facts relative to the Vermont and New York controversy.

—*A Memoir* of the Hon. George Tisdale Hodges. Written for the Annual Meeting at Montpelier, but read before the Special Meeting of the Vermont Historical Society, at Burlington, January 24, 1861. By George F. Houghton, Esq. 8vo, pp. 2.
Mr. Houghton was born in Guilford, Vt., May 31, 1820; and died at St. Albans, September 22, 1870. He was graduated at the University of Vermont in 1839 ; read law, and commenced practice at St. Albans in 1841. He held many offices of honor and trust in the State, and was one of the founders of the Vermont Historical Society, and through life one of its most constant and active supporters. He possessed a natural taste for historical, biographical and antiquarian matters, and his short Presidency of the Historical Society, 1868 until his death, increased its usefulness in a large degree ; he was indefatigable in the preparation of its two volumes of collections for publication; he also contributed many articles to the "New American Cyclopedia," to Miss Hemenway's "Vermont Historical Magazine," the "Dictionary of Congress," and other standard publications. He was for a time the editor and proprietor of the St. Albans *Transcript* and a contributor to other newspapers ; indeed, if his writings were collected together they would form volumes. In 1851 he married Miss Catherine Swift, daughter of Hon. Benjamin Swift, of St. Albans, who, with a son fifteen years of age, survived him at his decease.

Houghton, Henry Oscar. *Address* on Early Printing in America, delivered before the Vermont Historical Society, at Montpelier, Oct. 25, 1894, by Henry O. Houghton. [Printed in connection with an Address by Hon. Justin S. Morrill and Proceedings of the Vt. Historical Society, Oct. 16 and 25, 1894.] Montpelier : Watchman Pub. Co. 1894.
Mr. Houghton was born in Sutton, Vt., April 30, 1823. At the age of 13 he became an apprentice in the office of the Burlington Free Press, where he learned the "Art and Mystery of Printing." He graduated from the University of Vermont in 1846; went to Boston, was a reporter on the "Evening Traveller;" in 1849 with Mr.

Bolles he established a printing office in Cambridge, Mass., which later became famous under the name of The Riverside Press. He was successively a member of the firms of Hurd & Houghton, Houghton, Osgood & Co., and Houghton, Mifflin & Co., and known all over the world as one of the most eminent of American publishers. He died August, 1895, at East Andover, Mass., where he was temporarily sojourning.

House, A. H. *Conversation.* A Sermon : Delivered at Island Pond, Vt., February 14, 1858. By Rev. A. H. House, Pastor of Baptist Church, Passumpsic, Vt. Published by request. Montpelier : Printed by Ballou, Loveland & Co. 1858. 8vo, pp. 16.

How, Nehemiah. *A Narrative* of the Captivity of Nehemiah How, Who was taken by the Indians at the Great-Meadow-Fort above Fort Dummer, Oct. 11, 1745. Giving an Account of what he met with in his travelling to Canada, and while he was in Prison there. Together with an Account of Mr. How's Death at Canada. Boston : 1748. 16mo, pp. 22, (2.)
From Brinley Catalogue, Part 1, p. 59. Sold for $25 at that sale.
Great-Meadow-Fort was in the town of Putney, and Mr. How was cutting timber near the Fort at the time of his capture. The little garrison opened fire upon the Indians, and one was killed.

Howard, Carl Hampden Cutts.
See John W. Phelps.

Howard, Jacob M. *Speech* in the U. S. Senate, April 18, 1862, on the Confiscation of property. 8vo, pp. 16.

—*Speech* on the Joint Resolution for the Recognition and Readmission of Louisiana to the Union, delivered in the Senate of the U. S. Feb. 25, 1865. 8vo, pp. 15.

—*Speech* in the Senate, March 23 and 24, 1864, on Military Interference in Elections. 8vo, pp. 32.

—*Speech* in the Senate, January, 1864, on the Motion to expel Mr. Davis, of Kentucky, for offering a series of Resolutions in the Senate, tending to incite insurrection. 8vo, pp. 15.

—*Speech* in the Senate, April 16, 1869, on the San Juan Island Case. 8vo, pp. 13.

—*Speech* in the Senate, June 22 and 23, 1870, on the Memphis and El Paso Transcontinental Railroad. 8vo, pp. 26.

—*Secret Memoirs* of the Empress Josephine. Translated from the French. 1847.
Mr. Howard was born in Shaftsbury, Vt., July 10, 1805, and died in Detroit, Mich., April 2, 1871. He was graduated at Williams College, 1830, read law, and moved to Detroit in 1833, held many offices of honor and trust in Michigan, and was a member of Congress 1841-43, and of the U. S. Senate 1862-71. Lanman. Drake.

Howard, Rev. Leland. *A Sermon*, Delivered at Woodstock, February 18, 1818. At the Execution of Samuel E. Godfrey, for the Murder of Thomas Hewlet. By Rev. Leland Howard, Pastor of the First Baptist Society in Windsor. Windsor : Printed by A. & W. Spooner. 1818. 8vo, pp. 14.

—*Election Sermon.* 1831.
Mr. Howard was a pastor of the Baptist Church in the East Parish, Windsor, Vt., for some time.

Howard, William A. *Speech* delivered in the House of Representatives, Washington, March 23, 1858, on the Lecompton Constitution. 8vo, pp. 8.
Mr. Howard was born in Vermont, and was graduated at Middlebury College, 1839; he moved to Michigan, and

was a member of the 34th, 35th and 36th Congresses. In 1861 he was appointed Postmaster at Detroit; and in 1869 he was appointed Minister to China, but declined the position. Lanman.

Mr. Howard was at the head of the Michigan delegation to the National Convention of the Republican party at Cincinnati, in 1876, and it was his influence, it is said, that wheeled Michigan into line at the critical moment, and turned the scale in favor of Hayes. He died at Washington, D. C., April 10, 1880; at the time of his death he was Governor of Dakota; he had been in poor health for some time. He left a wife, two sons, and two married daughters. His remains were taken to Detroit, Mich., for interment.

Howe, George. D. D.
See Bates, Joshua, Eulogy on.

Howe, Timothy. *History* of the Medicinal Springs at Saratoga and Ballstown. By Timothy Howe. Brattleboro, Vt. 1804. 12mo.

Howes, Harvey. *Constitutional Address.*
See Vermont Constitutional Convention, 1870.
Mr. Howes died at Bennington, March 5, 1886, aged 79.

Howe Scales. January 1, 1879. Illustrated Price List of the improved Howe Scales, Manufactured by the Howe Scale Co., Rutland, Vt., U. S. A. Geo. A. Merrill, President; John B. Page, Treasurer; W. W. Reynolds, Superintendent. 16mo, pp. 35.

Hoyt, E. *Antiquarian* Researches; Comprising a History of the Indian Wars in the Country bordering Connecticut River and parts adjacent, and other interesting Events, from the first landing of the Pilgrims to the Conquest of Canada by the English, in 1760; with Notices of Indian Depredations in the neighboring Country, and of the first planting and progress of Settlements in New England, New York and Canada. By E. Hoyt, Esq. Greenfield, Mass : Printed by Ansel Phelps. Dec. 1824. 8vo, pp. (2), xii., 321.

—*Cavalry Discipline.* A Treatise on the Military Art. By Epaphras Hoyt. Brattleborough : 1793.
General Hoyt was born in Deerfield, Mass., December 31, 1765; and died there February 8, 1850. He gave much attention to historical researches, and also to military affairs.

Hoyt, Otto S., A. M. *A Sermon* preached at Poultney, (Vt.) on the Fifth Anniversary of the North-Western Branch of the American Education Society, January 12, 1825. By Otto S. Hoyt, A. M. Pastor of the Congregational Church in Hinesburgh. Published by the Society. Smith & Shute, Printers, Poultney. 1825. 8vo, pp. 28.
Rev. Otto Smith Hoyt was born in New Haven, Vt., May 22, 1793; and died there November 13, 1869. He was graduated at Middlebury College 1813, and was settled over the Congregational Church in Hinesburgh, Vt., September 30, 1818, to February 3, 1829, when on account of failing voice he was occupied 8 years in teaching, etc., and returned to Hinesburgh parish again February 28, 1838, and continued until April 14, 1854, when he retired from pulpit labor.

Hoyt, Ova P. *The Influence* of existing causes on our future History. An Address : delivered at the Presbyterian Meeting House, in Potsdam, July 4, 1826. By O. P. Hoyt, Pastor of the First Presbyterian Church in Potsdam. Printed by F. C. Powell, Potsdam, N. Y. 8vo, pp. 16.

—*A Sermon* delivered at the Dedication of the First Congregational Meeting House, Malone, N. Y. February 7, 1828. By the Rev. O. P. Hoyt, of Potsdam, N. Y. Fort Covington : Printed by Long and Hoard. 1828. 8vo, pp. 16.

Dr. Hoyt was born in New Haven, Vt., May 25, 1800; was graduated at Middlebury College in 1821, and at Andover in 1824; was Pastor of the Presbyterian Church in Potsdam, N. Y., 1825-30; preached in various places in New York and Michigan. He died at Kalamazoo, Mich., February 11, 1866.

Hubbard, A. O. *Five Discourses* on the Moral obligation and the Particular duties of the Sabbath. By A. O. Hubbard, A. M., Pastor of A Church in Hardwick, Vt. Hanover: Published by William A. Ruggles. W. A. Patten, Printer. 1843. 18mo, pp. 160.
Mr. Hubbard was a graduate of Yale and Princeton, and was pastor of the Congregational church at Hardwick, July 7, 1840, to May 1, 1843.

Hubbard, Rev. C. H. *The Support* of Government, and the Suppression of the Rebellion, Christian Duties. A Sermon Preached in the Second Congregational Church, Bennington, Sunday Afternoon, May 19, 1861. By Rev. C. H. Hubbard. Bennington, Vt.: J. I. Cook & Son, Printers and Publishers. 1861. 12mo, pp. 16.

Hubbard, John. *The Rudiments* of Geography; being a concise Description of various Kingdoms, States, Empires, Countries and Islands in the World, &c. &c. Barnard (Vt.): Published by Joseph Dix. J. H. Carpenter, Printer. 1814. 12mo, pp. 240.

—*The American Reader :* Containing a Selection of Narration, Harangues, Addresses, Orations, Dialogues, Odes, Hymns, Poems. &c. Designed for the Use of Schools, Together with a Short Introduction. By John Hubbard. First Bellows Falls Edition. Bellows Falls, Vt. Printed and published by Bill Blake & Co., and sold wholesale and retail at the Bellows Falls Bookstore, and by most of the principal booksellers in New England. 1817. 12mo. pp. 215.
John Hubbard, A. M., was born in Townsend, Mass., August 8, 1759, and was graduated at Dartmouth College in 1785; he was professor of Mathematics and Philosophy there, from 1804, until his death, August 14, 1810. He also published an " Essay on Musick."

Hubbard, John W.
Mr. Hubbard was son of Rev. Roswell Hubbard, and nephew and adopted son of Rev. Samuel Austin, many years pastor at Worcester, Mass., and President of the University of Vermont, 1815–1821. Mr. Hubbard was born in Brookfield, Vt., November 22, 1793; and died at Upton, Mass., September 17, 1825. He was graduated at Dartmouth College in 1814, and read law with Hon. C. P. Van Ness at Burlington, Vt.; commenced practice at Worcester, Mass., in 1817, and at his death was regarded as a young man of much promise and ability. He delivered the 4th of July oration at Worcester in 1811, on the occasion of the celebration by the young men of the town, between the ages of 16 and 21.

Hubbard, W. *A Narrative* of the Indian Wars in New England, From the first Planting thereof in the year 1607, to the year 1677: Containing A Relation to the Occasions, Rise and Progress of the War with the Indians, in the Southern, Western, Eastern and Northern parts of said Country. By William Hubbard, A. M. Minister of Ipswich. Motto. Brattleborough: Published by William Fessenden, 1814. 12mo, pp. 359.

Hubbardton. *Sketches* of the History of the Town of Hubbardton, Vt., with remarks on the Ancient Customs and Practices of the People and some Miscellaneous Articles. By an Old Man. Rutland: Steam Press of G. A. Tuttle & Co. 1855. 12mo, pp. (4), 64.
The advertisement is signed Amos Churchill.

Hubbardton Battle. *Act of Incorporation.* By-Laws and Officers of the Hubbardton Battle Monument Association. Rutland: George A. Tuttle & Company, Printers. 1857. 12mo, pp. 12.

Hubbell, Seth. *A Narrative* of the sufferings of Seth Hubbell & Family, in his beginning a settlement in the Town of Wolcott, in the State of Vermont. Danville, Vt.: E. & W. Eaton, Printers. 1829. 12mo, pp. 23.

Hudson, Charles. *A Reply* to Mr. Balfour's Essays, touching the State of the Dead, and a future Retribution. By Charles Hudson, Pastor of a Church in Westminster, Mass. Woodstock, Vt.: Printed by David Watson. 1829. 18mo, pp. 209.

—*A Series of Letters,* addressed to Rev. Hosea Ballou, of Boston; being a Vindication of the Doctrine of a Future Retribution, against the principal argmuents used by Him, Mr. Balfour and Others. By Charles Hudson, Pastor of a Church in Westminster, Mass. Woodstock, Vt.: Printed by David Watson. 1827. 12mo, pp. 307.

Hudson, Henry Norman. *Lectures* on Shakespeare. New York: 1848. 2 vols. 12mo.
A second edition was issued the same year. These lectures were favorably received by the leading reviewers of the country.

—*The Works* of William Shakespeare; The Text carefully restored according to the First Editions; with Introductions, Notes, Original and Selected, and a Life of the Poet. Boston: Munroe & Co. 1851-56. 11 volumes, 16mo.
As regards size and print, this edition is modeled upon the favorite one in England, known as the Chiswick Edition. It contains all the plays, poems and sonnets of Shakespeare, and has been highly commended both in this country and in England.

—*Shakespeare:* His Life, Art, and Characters, with an historical Sketch of the Origin and Growth of the Drama in England. By the Rev. H. N. Hudson. Two volumes. Boston: Published by Ginn Brothers. 1872. 12mo, pp. 474 and 495.

—*Classical English Reader.* By Rev. Henry N. Hudson. Boston: Ginn & Heath. 1878. 12mo, pp. xv, 452.

—*Classical English Reader.* Boston: Ginn and Heath, Publishers. 1880. 12mo, pp. xv, 452.
First edition, 1877.

—*English in Schools:* A Series of Essays by Henry N. Hudson. Boston: Ginn & Heath. 1881. 12mo, pp. (140.)
Contains an extract of nine pages from a personal sketch of Mr. Hudson, printed in the *Boston Sunday Herald*, Oct. 3, 1880.

—*Revised* and Enlarged edition of Hudson's School and Family Shakespeare, expurgated text. Boston: Ginn & Heath. 1881. 23 volumes, square 16mo.

—*Shakespeare's Complete Works.* Harvard Edition. By H. N. Hudson. In twenty volumes. Boston: Ginn & Heath. 1881. 12mo.

—*The Same* in ten volumes.
This Harvard Shakespeare is the most satisfactory and complete edition ever issued in this country, not only because it is remarkably tasteful and convenient, and embodies the results of the latest critical studies, but because it is suited to the tastes and wants of the average reader as well as students and scholars.
This is the edition by which Mr. Hudson is to be known in the coming time. Mr. Hudson is one of the three or four men in this country who are really competent either to edit or to annotate an edition of Shakespeare. Mr. Hudson began the Harvard Edition in 1873, after he had spent years of faithful toil and honest sense on both Shakespeare's text and Shakespeare's meaning. With excellent judgment he has given the textual notes in the appendix of each work, while the explanatory notes are given at the foot of each page. These notes are highly judicious, and specially commendable for their brevity.

—*Hudson's Text Book* of Prose. Boston: Ginn & Heath. 1881. 12mo, pp. xii, 636.
First edition, 1876.

—*Hudson's Text Book* of Poetry. Same imprint. 1880. 12mo, pp. 694.
First edition, 1875.
Mr. Hudson was born in Cornwall, Vt., January 28, 1814. He was brought up as a farmer, and in his youth apprenticed to a coach-maker in Middlebury; but overcoming all obstacles, he was graduated at Middlebury College in 1840. He taught school a year in Kentucky, and two years in Huntsville, Ala., where he wrote and delivered a course of lectures on Shakespeare, in 1843, which were delivered in the several following years in the principal cities of the United States; they were published in 1848. Mr. Hudson died at Cambridge, Mass., Jan. 16, 1886.
Mr. Hudson was ordained a clergyman of the Protestant Episcopal Church by Bishop Whittingham, in Trinity church, New York, in 1849. In 1850 he published a sermon entitled "Old Wine in Old Bottles." He has been a contributor to the *Church Review,* the *Democratic Review,* and the *American Whig Review,* and in 1857 he originated and edited the "American Church Monthly," published in New York. He was Rector of the Episcopal church in Litchfield, Ct., in 1859-60; and in the winter of 1860-61, delivered a new course of Shakespearian lectures in New York and other cities. On a Fast Day, appointed by President Buchanan, being January 4, 1861, Mr. Hudson delivered in New York a sermon entitled "Christian Patriotism," which was published. During the civil war he served as a chaplain in the army, and was some time stationed in South Carolina; he was subsequently with General Butler's army on the James, when, in consequence of the publication of a letter in the New York "Evening Post," reflecting on that officer, Mr. Hudson was placed under arrest; in 1865 he published "A Chaplain's Campaign with General Butler," which gives an account of his persecutions by that officer. New York: 1865. 8vo, pp. 66.
Mr. Hudson has published several school books; and in 1870 published his "School Shakespeare," in two volumes, containing a portion of the plays of the great bard, omitting such passages from the text as are not suitable for school purposes; this work is highly spoken of; published by Ginn Brothers & Co., Boston.

Hulbert, C. B. *Christian Service.* A Discourse delivered at the funeral of Wm. S. Southworth, Esq., September 8, 1875. By Rev. Calvin B. Hulbert, Pastor Second Congregational Church, Bennington, Vt. pp. 24.

—*The Mission of Calamity.* A Discourse delivered in the Second Congregational Church, Bennington, Vt., on the Sabbath following the Fatal Gasoline Explosion, January 25, 1874. By Calvin B. Hulbert, Pastor. With an Appendix containing full Notes of the Disaster, Obituary Notices of the Deceased, &c. Bennington: Banner Steam Job Printing House, 1874. 8vo, pp. 47.

—*The Vacant Sepulchre.* A Discourse, delivered at the Funeral of Alfred P. Roscoe, Esq., in the Congregational Church, New Haven, Vt., November 30, 1873. By Rev. Calvin B. Hulbert, with Remarks by Rev. S. Knowlton, Pastor. Published by Request. Bennington, Vt.: C. A. Pierce & Co., Printers. 1874. 8vo, pp. 17.

—*Conditions of Success.* Inauguration of Rev. Calvin B. Hulbert as President of Middlebury College, July 21, 1875. Andover: Warren F. Draper, Printer, Main Street. 1876. 8vo, pp. 28.

—*The Academy:* Demands for it, and the Conditions of its Success. An Address Delivered before the Associate Alumni of Barre Academy, at their Reunion, Barre, Vt., June, 1877, in Celebration of 25th Anniversary of the Principal's connexion with the Institution. By Calvin B. Hulbert, D. D., President of Middlebury College. Boston, Mass: New England Publishing Company. 1878. 8vo, pp. 29.

—*God not Altogether like Ourselves.* A Baccalaureate Discourse, delivered at Middlebury College, July 16, 1876. By Calvin B. Hulbert, President. Middlebury: Knapp & Bailey, Printers. 1876. 8vo, pp. 22.

—*What is Involved* in a Preparation for College. An Address delivered before the Literary Societies of Kimball Union Academy, Meriden, N. H., June 19, 1878, by Calvin B. Hulbert, D. D., President of Middlebury College.

—*Christ, the Harmony of the Doctrines* and the Unity of the Race. Baccalaureate Sermons delivered at Middlebury College, by Calvin B. Hulbert, D. D., President. New York: Collins & Brother, 414 Broadway. 1879. 8vo, pp. 46.

—*The Magnificence* of the Believer's Wealth. A Discourse delivered at Harwich, Mass., December 27, 1878, at the Funeral of Rev. Joseph R. Munsell, by Rev. Calvin B. Hulbert, D. D., President of Middlebury College. Also an Extract from a Commemorative Sermon Preached in Franklin, Vt., Jan. 19th, 1879, by Rev. Charles P. Watson, Pastor. 8vo, pp. 32.

No imprint. Mr. Munsell was a native of Swanton, Vt., where he was born October 6th, 1803.

—*The Sword Sheathed;* Or The Service of the Sanctuary the Security of the State. A Discourse delivered at the Centennial Celebration of the Adoption of the Name and Constitution of the State, Windsor, Vt., July 8, 1877. By Rev. Calvin Hulbert, D. D., President of Middlebury College. [Advanced sheets from the Vermont Centennial Volume.] Rutland, Vt.: Tuttle & Co., Official Printers and Stationers to the State. 8vo, pp. 24.

President Hulbert, son of Chauncey and Charlotte (Munsell) Hulbert, was born at East Sheldon, Vt., October 18, 1827. He was graduated at Dartmouth, 1853, and at Andover, 1859; he taught in the Academies at Swanton and St. Albans, 1854-6, and was pastor of the Congregational Churches in New Haven and Bennington, Vt., 1859-1875, when he was chosen President of Middlebury College, and so continued until July, 1880.

Hulburd, Oliver.

Mr. Hulburd was born in Rupert, Vt., in 1783; was graduated at Middlebury College, 1806; and was tutor and Professor there, 1808-1812; pastor of a Presbyterian church in Waynesborough, Ga., 1813, till his death, September 11, 1814. A volume of his sermons was published in 1818.

Hume, James N. *Address* on Temperance at Montpelier, 1840;

See Temperance.

Humphrey, Heman. *The Promised Land.* A Sermon, Delivered at Goshen, (Conn.) At the Ordination of the Rev. Messrs. Hiram Bingham & Asa Thurston, as Missionaries to the Sandwich Islands. Sept. 29, 1819. By Heman Humphrey, Pastor of the Congregational Church in Pittsfield, Mass. Boston: Published by Samuel T. Armstrong, no. 50 Cornhill. M. Crocker, Printer. 1819. 8vo, pp. 40, xvi.

See Bingham, Hiram.

Humphreys, David. *An Essay* on the Life of the Honorable Major-General Israel Putnam: Addressed to the State Society of the Cincinnati in Connecticut. By Col. David Humphreys. Brattleboro: Published by William Fessenden. 1812. 18mo, pp. 144.

Hungerford, Edward, Rev. *The Migration* of Fairies. A Story written for the Ladies' Fair, March 2, 1859. Burlington: 1859. 12mo, pp 23.

—*A Report* on the Moral and Religious Condition of the Community, being an Address before a Union of Evangelical Churches, in the City of Burlington, Vt., delivered in the White Street Congregational Church, March 10, 1867, by Prof. Edward Hungerford. Burlington: Free Press Print. 1867. 8vo, pp. 29.

—*The American Book* of Church Services, With Selections for responsive reading, and full Orders of Service, for the Celebration of Matrimony, for Funerals and other occasional Ministrations. Also an ample list of Selections of Sacred Music, with references for the guidance of Pastors and Choristers. Arranged by Edward Hungerford. Boston and New York: Houghton, Mifflin & Co. The Riverside Press, Cambridge, 1889. 12mo, pp. 374.

Second edition, 1891, same publishers, pp. xiv, 413.

—*Selections* for Responsive Reading. Arranged with proper reference to leadership and responsiveness between Minister and Congregation. By Rev. Edward Hungerford. Burlington: Free Press Association. 1893. pp. 178.

—*Selections* for Responsive Reading from the American Book of Church Services. Arranged by Edward Hungerford. Boston: Houghton, Mifflin & Co. 1890. pp. 413.

Hunt, Jonathan. *An Address* before the Washington Benevolent Society, at Brattleborough, Vt., February 22, 1812, Commemorative of George Washington.

Brinley Catalogue, Part 2, p. 192.

Hunt, William Morris. *Talks on Art.* Compiled by Helen M. Knowlton. First and Second Series. Boston: Houghton, Mifflin & Co. 1875, 1883. 8vo, pp. 75 ; 95.

The first series of these talks has passed through 20 editions and the second 10 editions.

William M. Hunt was born in Brattleboro, Vt., March 31, 1842; studied art at the Dusseldorf Academy, under Couture in Paris and with Millet, at Fontainebleau; returned to the United States in 1855. He died at the Isles of Shoals, Sept. 8, 1879. Some of his paintings are in the Boston Museum of Fine Arts and in the State Capitol at Albany, N. Y.

Hunting, George Field. *Vim:* A Poem Read before the Delta Psi Fraternity of the University of Vermont at their Twenty-fifth Anniversary, July 13th, 1875, by Rev. George Field Hunting. Printed for the Fraternity. Burlington: Free Press Printing House. 1875. 8vo, pp. 14.

Mr. Hunting is a native of Milton, Vt. He graduated from the University of Vermont in 1860; was appointed second lieutenant of the Third U. S. Artillery in February, '62; was promoted to first lieutenant, resigned September, '68; studied theology, became a Presbyterian clergyman and is President of Alma (Mich) College. (1896.)

Huntington, J. *The Divine Institution* and use of the Festival System of the Church. A Sermon preached in St. Stephen's Church, Middlebury, Vt., on Christmas Eve, 1842. By Rev. J. Huntington, Rector. Published by request of the Vestry. Middlebury : J. M. Stearns, Publisher. 1843. Vermont Observer Print. 8vo, pp. 20.

—*Poems.* By Rev. Jedediah Huntington, M. D. New. York : Wiley & Putnam. 1843. 8vo, pp. 217.

Mr. Huntington was Rector at Middlebury, 1842-3.

Hurd, Samuel.

Mr. Hurd was born in Corinth, Vt., January 3, 1804; and died at Troy, Miss., June 28, 1846. He was graduated at Dartmouth, 1822; read theology, and went to Mississippi, where he became President of North Mississippi College. He published, "A Dialogue on Baptism." Mr. Hurd was three times married, first to Miss Willis, of Hanover, N. H.; second, Miss Price, of Virginia, and third, Mrs. Mary Smith, of Mississippi. See Dartmouth Alumni.

Hutchinson, Aaron. *A well-tempered* Self-Love a Rule of Conduct towards others : A Sermon Preached at Windsor, July 2, 1777, before the Representatives of the Towns in the Counties of Charlotte, Cumberland and Gloucester, for the forming the State of Vermont. By Aaron Hutchinson, of Pomfret, A. M., Pastor of the Church in that and the two adjacent Towns, Hartford and Woodstock.

Also, Thou shalt not oppress a stranger : ye know the heart of a stranger, seeing ye were strangers in the land of Egypt, Exod. 23.9.

To loose the bands of wickedness, to undo the heavy burdens, and to let the oppressed go free, and that ye break every yoke:—and that thou hide not thyself from thine own flesh. Isa. 58.6, 8.

But he that doeth wrong, shall receive for the wrong which he hath done; and there is no respect of persons. Col. 3.25. So speak ye, and so do, as they that shall be judged by the law of liberty.—For he shall have judgment without mercy, that hath showed no mercy. James 2.12, 13.

Dresden : Printed by Judah Paddock & Alden Spooner. Small 4to, pp. 42.

Reprinted in Collections of the Vermont Historical Society, vol. 1, pp. 67-101.

Mr. Hutchinson was born in Hebron, Ct., in March, 1722; and died in Pomfret, Vt., September 27, 1800. He was graduated at Yale College, 1747; studied theology, and was settled over the Congregational church in Grafton, Mass., 1750-1773. In 1749 he married Miss Margary Carter, of Hebron, and they had ten children, all born in Grafton. About 1772-3 the new country at the north began to attract attention, and Mr. Hutchinson appears to have visited the valley of the Upper Connecticut in April, 1774; and he was hired by the respective towns of Hartford, Pomfret and Woodstock, to become the pastor of those towns for five years, his labors having already commenced. July 4, 1776, he moved his family from Grafton to the farm in Pomfret where he resided through his life, and continued preaching in the towns in the vicinity; the main support for his family being derived from the cultivation of his farm. He possessed a wonderful memory, and it was a saying that if the New Testament should be lost, he could repeat it entire. He gave out and recited the hymns without opening the hymn book; he fitted many young men for college, and his memory enabled him to dispense with books, and teach Latin and Greek while working in the field, his pupils following him as he followed the plow or swung the scythe. He had been invited to preach the sermon before the Windsor Convention to form the State, but the war cloud lowered ominously, and he thought the convention would not meet, made no preparations, and did not appear; accordingly a summons was sent him to appear before the convention and deliver his sermon; he

left the harvest field, and after a dusty ride from Pomfret to Windsor, delivered his discourse extempore, which the convention so highly approved that it was ordered to be written out and published. But he was slow in preparing it, and had to be spurred up to the work, which was finally sent to the Convention, then sitting at Bennington, in September following. It is said that while at Grafton, he fought many a battle for Calvinism, against the Arminian and other heretics.

We gather the above facts from a memoir by Henry Swan Dana, printed in the Woodstock Standard of August 17, 24, and 31, 1871.

—*A Biographical Sketch.*

See Hawkins, Rush C.

Hutchinson, K. M. *A Memoir* of Abijah Hutchinson, A soldier of the Revolution. By his Grandson, K. M. Hutchinson. Rochester : William Alling, Printer, 1843. 12mo, pp. 22.

Abijah Hutchinson was born in Lebanon, Conn., in 1756; he was a Connecticut privateer, lived half a century in Vermont, and moved in 1835 to Genesee, N. Y., where he died in 1843. His captivity among the Indians of Canada is detailed at length.

See Vt. Hist. Magazine, Vol. 2, p. 1131.

Hutchinson, Titus. *An Oration* delivered at the South Parish in Woodstock, Vermont, on the Fourth Day of July, A. D. 1806. By Titus Hutchinson. Randolph, Vermont : Sereno Wright. 1806. 8vo.

This oration is political and historical, with an appendix containing an ode on science and liberty, and an account of the celebration.—*Sabin.*

—*An oration* at Woodstock, July 4, 1809. Windsor, Oliver Farnesworth, Printer. 1809. small 4to, pp. 8.

—*Jurisdiction of Courts.* That of State Courts Original; that of United States Courts Derivative. The new Senate Law. By Titus Hutchinson, formerly Chief Justice of the State of Vermont. Montpelier : Printed at the Freeman Office. 1855. 8vo, pp. 15.

Titus Hutchinson, son, and youngest of ten children of Rev. Aaron Hutchinson, was born in Grafton, Mass., April 29, 1771; and died at Woodstock, Vt., August 24, 1857. He moved to Pomfret, Vt., with his father and family in 1776, worked on the farm, was fitted for college by his father, and graduated at Princeton, N. J., in 1793; studied law with his brother Aaron, Jr., at Lebanon, N. H., and in 1798 purchased a house in Woodstock, Vt., where he began practice, and resided all his life. He was Postmaster, State's Attorney, Town Representative 10 years; a Trustee of the University of Vermont; District Attorney, 1813-21; Judge of the Supreme Court of Vermont, 1825-1830, and Chief Justice, 1830-1833.

See Kendall, B. F.; Hutchinson, Aaron.

Hyde, James T. *A Tribute* to the Memory of Hon. Peter Starr, LL. D. of Middlebury, Vermont, preached at his Funeral, Sept. 5, 1860, by Rev. James T. Hyde, Pastor of the Congregational Church. Published by request of his Family. New York : Wm. C. Bryant & Co., Printers, 41 Nassau Street, cor. Liberty. 1860. 8vo, pp. 32.

Hymns. By the Rev. S. Medley, Minister of a Baptist Church in Liverpool, England. Together with an Appendix, approved of by the Rev. Caleb Blood, Baptist Minister of Shaftsbury, (Ver.). Price 25 cents. Bennington : Printed by A. Haswell. 1808.

—*A Choice Selection* of Hymns and Spiritual Songs; designed for Prayer, Conference and Camp Meetings. New Edition. Woodstock : Printed by David Watson. 1828. Small 16mo, pp. 460.

See Watts, Isaac.

—*Choice Collection* of Conference Hymns. Compiled from the writings of various Authors.

Motto. Montpelier, Vt. Printed by Walton & Goss. 18mo, p. 50, (2.) (Date of imprint wanting, probably 1810 or 1811.)

Ide, George B., D. D. *Pious Men* the Nation's Hope. By George B. Ide, D. D. Pastor of the First Baptist Church, Springfield, Mass. Boston: Gould and Lincoln, 59 Washington Street. 1863. 8vo, pp. 30.

Mr. Ide was born in Coventry, Vt., February 16, 1804; and was graduated at Middlebury College, 1830; he was pastor of a Baptist Church in Brandon, Vt., also in Derby, Vt.; then in Boston, Mass., and for many years in Philadelphia, and then in Springfield, Mass. He has published several works, the titles of which we have not obtained.

Independent Order of Odd Fellows. *Constitution*, By Laws and Rules of Order of Netis Lodge, No. 25, I. O. of O. F. Instituted December 1, 1852, at West Poultney, Vt. Rutland: Tuttle & Co., Printers. 1843. 12mo, pp. 23.

—*Constitution*, By-Laws and Rules of Lake Dunmore Lodge, No. 2, I. O. of O. F. instituted March 8, 1847, at Middlebury, Vt. Middlebury: Printed by Justus Cobb. 1850. 16mo, pp. 44.

See Woodhouse, Rev. Chas., Address at Rutland, 1870.

—*Constitution*, By-Laws and Rules of Order of Otter Creek Encampment of Patriarchs No. 7. Independent Order of Odd Fellows of Vermont. Instituted March 16th, 1871. Rutland: Tuttle & Co., Printers, 1872. 18mo, pp. 23.

—*Constitution*, By-Laws and Rules of Order, of Killington Lodge, No. 29, I. O. O. F. Organized September 11th, 1868. At Rutland, Vt. Rutland: Globe Paper Co. Printers. 1878. 18mo, pp. 29, (2).

—*Proceedings* of the R. W. Grand Encampment of the Independent Order of Odd Fellows, of the State of Vermont, at its Fifth Annual Session Held at Northfield, February 2, 1875. Montpelier, Vt.: Argus and Patriot Print. 1875. 8vo, pp. 18.

Continued.

—*Proceedings* of the Sixth Annual Session of the Right Worthy Grand Encampment of the Independent Order of Odd Fellows, of the State of Vermont, Held at Odd Fellows' Hall, Rutland, February 1, 1876. Rutland: Globe Paper Company, Printers. 1876. 8vo, pp. 35.

Continued.

—*Report* of the Proceedings of the Annual Session of the R. W. Grand Lodge of Vermont, Held at Montpelier, August 11, 1852. Friendship, Love and Truth. Woodstock: Printed by Haskell & Palmer. 1852. 8vo, pp. 44.

Continued.

The Same; Thirtieth Session, 1877. 8vo, pp. 149.

—*Proceedings* of the Eighth Annual Session of the R. W. Grand Encampment of the Independent Order of Odd Fellows, of the State of Vermont, Held at Odd Fellows Hall, Montpelier, February 5, 1878. St. Johnsbury: C. M. Stone & Co., Printers. 1878. 8vo, pp. 44.

—*Third Annual Report* of the Secretary of Odd Fellows' Mutual Relief Association of Vermont. 8vo, pp. (4). n. p. (1878).

—*Mysteries Revealed*, and Nothing Concealed. A New work on Odd Fellowship. Containing an exact expose of all the ceremonies, obligations, signs, pass-words and grips, according to the latest revision of the works of the Order, by the Grand Lodge of the Independent Order of Odd Fellows, in the United States. Together with a critical Review of the intrinsic Principles and Moral Influence of the Institution; and an unveiled Dissertation on the Uselessness and Dangers of Secret Societies. Compiled and published by E. B. Rollins, editor of the Green Mountain Eagle and Even Fellows Gazette. Motto. Wilmington, Vt.: Printed at the Eagle Office. 1850. 8vo, pp. 48.

—*Constitution*, By-Laws and Rules of Vermont Lodge, No. 2, of the Independent Order of Odd-Fellows. Montpelier, Vt. [Instituted May 15, 1845. Re-Instituted July 23, 1873.] Montpelier, Vt.: Argus and Patriot Steam Book and Job Printing Works. 1879. 18mo, pp. 43. (3).

—*Constitution*, By-Laws and Rules of Green Mountain Lodge, No. 1, I. O. of O. F., Instituted January 14, 1845, at Burlington, Vt. Burlington: The Free Press Association. 1880. 18mo, pp. 37, 4.

Indians, Iroquois. *Report* of the Commissioner Appointed by the Governor, on the Claim of the Iroquois Indians. Made to the Legislature, Nov. 3, 1855. Montpelier: E. P. Walton, Jr., Printer. 1855. 8vo, pp. 24. (James M. Hotchkiss, Commissioner.)

See Redfield, T. P., Report on the same, 1854.

Indian Narratives. *Containing* a correct and interesting History of the Indian Wars, from the Landing of our Pilgrim Fathers, 1620, to Gen. Wayne's Victory, 1794. To which is added A correct Account of the Capture and Sufferings of Mrs. Johnson, Zadock Steele, and others; and also a thrilling account of the Burning of Royalton. Motto. Claremont, N. H.: Tracy and Brothers. 1854. 12mo, pp. 276.

Industrial Reformers. *Constitution* and Rules of Order of the Industrial Reformers. Also the Constitution of the Insurance Department. The Order of the Industrial Reformers is purely a Mutual Benefit Society, without Secrets or Ritual. Our object is not Antagonism, but Unity of Purpose and Action for the Amelioration of the Laboring Masses. Organized February 1st, 1875. Rutland: Tuttle & Company, printers. 1875. 18mo. pp. 16.

Ingalls, Jeremiah. *The Christian Harmony.* A book of Church Music. Exeter, N. H.: 1805. Printed by Henry Ranlet. pp. 201.

Mr. Ingalls was born in Andover, Mass., 1764; lived at Newbury, Vt., 1787–1810; died at Rochester, Vt., 1838.

Ingersoll, Geo. G. *A Sermon*, Preached before the First Congregational Society in Burlington, Vt., April 12, 1826. By Geo. G. Ingersoll. Burlington: Printed by E. & T. Mills. 1826. 8vo, pp. 53.

—*A Discourse* delivered before the Legislature of Vermont on the day of General Election, October 14, 1830. Published at the request of the Legislature. Burlington; Chauncey Goodrich. 1830. 8vo, pp. 46.

—*A Sermon*, Preached before the First Congregational Society, on Thanksgiving Day. By Geo. G. Ingersoll. Published by request.

Burlington: 1831. Chauncey Goodrich, 8vo, pp. 24.

—*A Sermon* preached before the First Congregational Society in Burlington, Vermont. By Geo. G. Ingersoll. Printed by request. Burlington: Edward Smith. 1835. 12mo, pp. 24.

—*An Address* Delivered before the Literary Societies of the University of Vermont, August 2, 1837, By George G. Ingersoll, and Published by Request. Burlington: Hiram Johnson & Co. 1837. 8vo, pp. 46.

—*A Sermon*, preached before the First Congregational Society in Burlington, Vt. By their Minister, Geo. G. Ingersoll, and Published at their Request. Burlington: Chauncey Goodrich. 1841. 8vo, pp. 32.

—*The Death of Christ*. By Rev. Geo. G. Ingersoll. Printed for the American Unitarian Association. Boston: James Munroe & Co. 134 Washington Street. July, 1841. 12mo, pp. 36.

—*A Sermon* Preached on Fast Day before the First Congregational Society, in Burlington, Vermont, By their Minister, George G. Ingersoll, and Published at their request. University Press,—Burlington: Printed by Stilman Fletcher. 1843. 8vo, pp. 22.

—*A Farewell Address* to the First Congregational Society, in Burlington, Vt. Delivered June 2, 1844, By George G. Ingersoll. Printed for the Society, not Published. Burlington: Printed by Stilman Fletcher. 1844. 8vo, pp. 48.

—*Unitarianism* the Way of the Lord. A Sermon.

—*A Memorial* of Caroline Haskell Ingersoll, with Some Notes of her Family and of her Gifts to the City of Keene, and a Poem by Rev. Dr. George G. Ingersoll. Cambridge: John Wilson & Son. 1894. pp. 64.

Rev. Dr. Ingersoll was born in Boston, July 4, 1796; and was graduated at Harvard College, 1815; he was settled over the Unitarian church, Burlington, Vt., 1822—1844; was settled at East Cambridge, Mass., 1847; removed to Keene, N. H., 1849, and died there 1863.

Innis Association. *Report* to the Innis Association, U. S. A., Made by Columbus Smith, A. D. 1866. Containing the Innis Constitution and information in his possession relative to the Innis Property in Scotland. Published by order of the Innis Association. Middlebury: Printed at the Register Office. 1866. 8vo, pp. 17.

INSURANCE. *Help One Another*. Report of the Directors to the Company, for the Annual Meeting of the Vermont Mutual Fire Insurance Company, October 16, 1839.

Broadsheet. Continued.

—*A Circular*, By-Laws, and Act of Incorporation, of the Vermont Mutual Fire Insurance Company. Revised Oct. 1838. Montpelier: Wm. Clark, Printer. 1838. 12mo, pp. 31.

—*The Vermont Mutual Insurance Company* located at Montpelier, Vt. An explanation of the Plan with practical remarks on the subject. Montpelier: Power Press of Eastman and Danforth. 1850. 24mo, pp. 20.

—*Twenty-fifth Annual Report* of the Directors of the Vermont Mutual Fire Insurance Company, Montpelier, Vt., For the Annual Meeting, October 20, 1852, and an explanation of the Plan with practical Remarks on the Subject. Montpelier: Printed at the Patriot Office, James M. Stevens, Printer. 1852. 12mo, pp. 16.

Continued.

—*Circular*, By-Laws, and Acts of Incorporation of the Vermont Mutual Fire Insurance Company, Revised April, 1859. Montpelier: Printed by Ballou, Loveland & Company. 1859. 18mo, pp. 48.

—*Another Edition*, 1867.

—*The Same*. 1870. pp. 44, (4).

—*The Same*. 1873. pp. 44, (4).

Imprint the same for both.

—*Vindication* of the Vermont Mutual Fire Insurance Co., From Charges made by Agents of the Farmer's Ins. Company. 1872. 12mo, pp. 16.

—*Union Mutual Fire Insurance Company*, Montpelier, Vt. Abstract of By-Laws, Rates, and Instructions to Agents. Montpelier: Argus and Patriot Job Printing Works. 1875. 12mo, pp. 10.

—*First Annual Report* of the Union Mutual Fire Insurance Company, Montpelier, Vt., for the Year Ending August 1, 1876. Montpelier, Vt.: Argus and Patriot Book and Job Printing House. 1876. 12mo, pp. 4.

Continued.

—*By-Laws*, Act of Incorporation, and Instructions to Agents, of the Farmers' Mutual Fire Insurance Co. Revised, Oct. 21, 1852. Montpelier: Ballou & Burnham's Press. 1852. 18mo, pp. 32.

—*Fourteenth Annual Report* of the Farmers' Mutual Fire Insurance Company, August 1, 1864. Annual Meeting, October 19, 1864. Montpelier: Printed at the Freeman Printing Establishment. 1864. 12mo, pp. 8.

Continued.

—*Tariff of the Board of Underwriters*, of Montpelier, Vt., August 1, 1873. Montpelier: Poland's Steam Printing Establishment. 1873. 12mo, pp. 32.

—*Report* of the Directors of the Orange County Mutual Fire Insurance Company. January 9, 1851. Broadsheet.

Discontinued business.

—*Report* of the Windham County Mutual Fire Insurance Company, November 1, 1855. Broadsheet.

Discontinued business.

—*Fifteenth Annual Report* of the Rutland and Addison Mutual Fire Insurance Company, for the Annual Meeting, July 20, 1854. Rutland: George A. Tuttle & Co., Printers. 1854. 12mo, pp. 7.

Discontinued business.

—*Tariff* of the Association of Underwriters of Rutland, Vt., January 1, 1867. Rutland: Tuttle & Co., Printers. 1867. 12mo, pp. 30.

—*Tariff* of Rates of Fire Insurance, for the Towns of Bellows Falls, Cavendish, Chester, Ludlow, Proctorsville, Springfield and Vicinity. Rutland: Tuttle & Co., Printers. 1872. 12mo, pp. 32.

—*Tariff* Rates of Fire Insurance for the Town of Brandon, Vt. Rutland: Tuttle & Co., Printers. 1872. 12mo, pp. 12.

—*Tariff* of Rates of the Association of Underwriters, for Rutland County, Vermont. March 1st, 1875. Rutland: Tuttle & Co., Printers. 1875. 12mo, pp. 94.

—*The same* for the Towns of Middlebury, Cornwall, Weybridge, New Haven, Bristol, Addison, Bridport, Ripton and Lincoln. 12mo, pp. 24.

—*The same* for Fairhaven, Hydeville, West Castleton, West-Haven, Benson and Hubbardton. 12mo, pp. 16.

—*The Insurance* Law of the State of Vermont; being Chapter Eighty-Seven of the General Statutes of the State. Montpelier: Freeman Office. 1863. 12mo, pp. 13.

—*The National Life* Insurance Company of the United States. Office, Montpelier, Vt. Montpelier: Press of Eastman and Danforth. 1850. 16mo. pp. 36.
Incorporated November 13, 1848; organized November 8, 1849.

—*The National Life* Insurance Co., of the United States. Office, State Street, Montpelier, Vt. Motto. Officers. Doct. Julius Y. Dewey, President. Hon. Daniel Baldwin, Vice President. James T. Thurston, Secretary. Orren Smith, M. D., Medical Examiner. Fred W. Adams, M. D., Consulting Physician. Board of Finance, Homer W. Heaton, Albert L. Catlin, John A. Page.. Montpelier: Eastman & Danforth. 1851. 16mo, pp. 32.
Contains the first report, to March 1, 1851; reports continued annually.
—*For the use* of Agents and Medical Examiners only. To be carefully read, and as carefully preserved for reference. General and Special Instructions for the government of the Agents and Medical Examiners of the National Life Insurance Company of the United States. Montpelier, Vt. Whole Number of Policies 901 Cash Capital and accumulated fund, $112,000. Issued December 1st, 1852. Printed at the Patriot Office, by J. M. Stevens. 8vo, pp, 15.

—*Another Edition*. 1858. Montpelier: Printed at the Vermont Patriot Press. 1858. 16mo, pp. 29.

—*The National Life* Insurance Company. Montpelier, Vt. Ninth Annual Report. 1858. 22mo, pp, 64.
Continued.

—*Report* of the Directors of the National Life Insurance Company of the United States, Containing the result of the Quinquennial division of the Surplus made Feb. 1st, 1855. Office—State Street, Montpelier, Vt. Montpelier: Printed at the Patriot Office. 8vo pp. 8.

—*Surrender Value Tables*, Adapted to the Life Insurance Bond issued by the National Life Insurance Co., Montpelier. Vt. Computed by Elizur Wright. 16mo, pp. (4), 56.
—*The National Life* Insurance Company, Montpelier, Vt.. Montpelier: Freeman

Steam Printing House and Bindery. 1869. 16mo, pp. 39.
Contains 19th report.

—*Agent's Manual* 1875, National Life Insurance Company, Montpelier, Vt. Montpelier: Argus and Patriot Steam Printing Works. 1875. 16mo, pp. 17.

—*Report* of the Directors of the Champlain Mutual Fire Insurance Co., showing the condition of the company December 1st, 1878. R. S. Taft, President. No imprint. 12mo, pp. 9.
This company commenced business in 1873; and in 1878 levied assessments to the amount of 25 per cent. on its premium notes, and retired from business.

—*By-Laws*, Act of Incorporation and Instructions to Agents of the Husbandman's Fire Insurance Company, of Vermont, Montpelier, Vt.: Argus and Patriot Book and Job Printing Establishment. 1881. 16mo, pp. 26.
See Childs, A. P., Argument against taxing Life Insurance Companies.

Ira. *A Summary* of History of Declaration of Faith of the Baptist Church in Ira. Published by order of the Church. Motto. Rutland: G. A. Tuttle & Co., Printers. 1861. 12mo, pp. 16.

The Iris, *Advertiser and Intelligencer And Burlington Literary Gazette.* Worth & Foster, Proprietors. Zadock Thompson, Editor. Burlington: Published Semi-Monthly, for about sixteen months, in 1828-9. Large 8vo.
After the 6th number the title was simply the Iris.

Island Pond *Manufacturing Company.* Island Pond, Brighton, Vt. [n, p. n. d.] 8vo, pp. 16.

Jackman, A. *A Treatise* on the Doctrine of Numerical Series, both Ascending and Descending: Also the Binomial Theorem, with Integer and Fractional Exponents. Alonzo Jackman, M. A. Professor of Mathematics in Norwich (Vt.) University. Claremont, N. H. Published for the Author. 8vo, pp. 55.

—*The Circle Squared*, by Alonzo Jackman, LL. D., Professor of Mathematics and Natural Philosophy, in the Norwich University, Vt. Northfield, Vt.: Norwich University Press. 1876. 12mo. pp. 8.

—*In Memoriam*. Gen. Alonzo Jackman, LL. D.. Born March 20, 1809; Died February 24, 1879. A Sermon preached in St. Mary's Church, Northfield, Vt., June 1st, 1879, By F. W. Bartlett, Rector. 12mo, pp. 7, no imprint.
See Hill, Howard F., Memorial Sermon, 1881.
Professor Jackman was born at Thetford, Vt., March 20, 18·9; and died at Northfield, Vt., February 24, 1879. He was graduated at Norwich University, in 1836, and in 1837 was appointed a professor in the same, which position he occupied until his death, except intermissions of a few years. In 1840 he was associate editor of the Citizen Soldier, a paper published at Windsor in the interest of military education. An extended memoir of Professor Jackman was published in the Argus and Patriot, February 26, 1879.
Jackson, Daniel, Jr. *Alonzo and Melissa*, or the Unfeeling Father." An American Tale. By Daniel Jackson, Jr. Brattleboro: Published by Holbrook and Fessenden. 1824. 18mo, pp. 240.

Jackson, Mrs. Elizabeth. *The Honorable* and Pious Confession, of a true penitent, exemplified in the case of Mrs. Elizabeth Jackson Before the Congregational Church in Williamstown, Vermont; and the Baptist Church in said Town, June 3, 1805. "When I consider, I am afraid of Him." JOB. New London: Printed by Cady & Ells. 1805. 12mo, pp. 16.

Mr. and Mrs. Jackson had recently moved from Massachusetts to Williamstown, and the sin confessed, and repented of, was that she had been baptised into the Baptist Church by immersion, in Williamstown, when she had already received baptism in her infancy by sprinkling, and had joined a Congregational Church in Massachusetts. The difficulty appears to have arisen from the rivalry of the ministers of the two churches in Williamstown to "gather in" Mrs. Jackson."

Jackson, Samuel C. *A Sermon*, delivered in the West Parish of Andover, Dec. 30, 1827, being the last Sabbath in the year. By Samuel C. Jackson, Pastor of the Congregational Church and Society in said parish. Andover: Printed by Flagg and Gould. 1828. 8vo, pp. 30.

—*The Life and Death* of a Faithful Minister. A Discourse delivered May 10, 1839, at the Interment of Rev. Sylvester G. Pierce, Pastor of the First Congregational Church in Methuen: by Samuel C. Jackson, Pastor of the West Church in Andover. Methuen: Printed by S. Jameson Varney. 1839. 8vo, pp. 24.

—*Religious Principle*—a Source of Public Prosperity. A Sermon delivered before his Excellency John Davis, Governor, his Honor George Hall, Lieutenant Governor. the Honorable Council, and the Legislature of Massachusetts, at the Annual Election, on Saturday, January 7, 1843. By Samuel C. Jackson, Pastor of the West Church, Andover. Boston: Dutton and Wentworth, Printers to the State. 1843. 8vo, pp. 55.

—*Memorial* of Rev. Samuel C. Jackson, D. D. By Edward A. Park. Andover: Printed by Warren F. Draper. Main Street. 1878. 8vo, pp. 32.

Dr. Jackson was born in Dorset, Vt., March 13, 1802; was graduated at Middlebury College in 1821, and at Andover in 1826; was pastor of the West Church, Andover, Mass., 1827-49; Assistant Secretary of the Massachusetts Board of Education, 1849-76; died at Andover, July 26, 1878.

Jacob, Stephen. *A Poetical Essay* delivered at Bennington, on the Anniversary of the 16th August, 1777. By Stephen Jacob, A. B. 1778. Hartford: Printed by Watson and Goodwin, M,DCC,LXXIX. 8vo, pp. 8.

Reprinted in Vermont Historical Collections, vol. 1, pp. 263-270.

James, Edwin.

Mr. James was born in Weybridge, Vt., August 27, 1797. and died in 1862. He was graduated at Middlebury College in 1816, read medicine with his brother Daniel, at Albany, N. Y., botany with Prof. Torrey, and geology with Prof. Amos Eaton. He was attached to Maj. S. H. Long's first expedition to the Rocky Mountains. 1819-20, as Botanist and Geologist, and was occupied two years in preparing the Journal of the expedition for publication; and was then for more than twelve years surgeon and Indian Agent at the extreme outposts of the Government. After which he resided at Burlington, Iowa, as farmer, surveyor, and Indian Agent. He published "Expedition from Pittsburg to the Rocky Mountains." Philadelphia: 1823, 2 vols. 4to, and Atlas; London: 1823. 3 vols. 8vo. He also edited the life of John Tanner, and published five works in the Ojibwa language, among which is a translation of the entire Bible; also two or three other works, of which we have not the titles.

Jameson, John Alexander, LL. D. *Responsibilities* of American Merchants for the Conversion of the World to Christ. By John A. Jameson, Esq., Freeport, Ill. New York: I. W. Brinckerhoff, 150 Nassau Street. 1855. 16mo, pp. 47.

—*The Grounds* and Limits of Rightful Interference by Law with the Accumulation and use of Capital, including a View of the Law of Monopolies, by John A. Jameson, Judge of the Superior Court, Chicago, Ill. Springfield, Ill.: H. W. Rokker's Publishing House. 1882. 8vo, pp. 22.

—*The Constitutional Convention*; its History, Powers, and Modes of Proceeding. By John Alexander Jameson, Judge of the Superior Court of Chicago, and Professor of Constitutional Law, &c., in the Law Department of the Chicago University. Motto. New York: Charles Scribner and Company. Chicago: S. C. Griggs and Company. 1867. 8vo, pp. XIX, 561.

A second edition, 1869, and three subsequent editions.

Judge Jameson was born in Irasburgh, Vt., and was graduated at the University of Vermont in 1846. He read law, and commenced practice at Freeport, Ill., but soon removed to Chicago, where he became prominent as a lawyer and Judge. He was Judge of the Superior Court of Chicago, 1865-83; and Professor of Constitutional Law, University of Chicago, 1867-8. Author of various articles in the American Law Register.

He died at his home, Hyde Park, Chicago, June 16, 1890.

Jarvis, William. *Address* to the Whig Freemen of the County of Windsor. [June, 1838.] William Jarvis, George Johnson, Oliver Gleason, Committee.

Broad sheet.

—*Speech*; in Reply to the Speech of the Hon. C. P. Van Ness, delivered at Woodstock, in 1840, before the Democratic Convention. 18mo, pp. 24. 1840.

—*Speech* of Hon. William Jarvis, at the Whig Convention, at Windsor, July 4th, 1840. Woodstock, Vt.: Printed at the Mercury Press. 1840. 8vo, pp. 20.

—*The Life and Times* of Consul Jarvis. By Mary P. S. Cutts. 12mo, pp. XII, 451.

Mr. Jarvis published several addresses, and wrote much for the press.

See Cutts, Mary P. S.

Jefferds, Chester Daniel, Rev. *A Sermon* preached at the Funeral of Rev. Nathaniel S. Hazeltine, late Pastor of the Congregational Church in Springfield, Vt., January 24, 1860. 8vo, pp. 16.

Mr. Jefferds was born in Dixfield, Me., February 20, 1828, and died at Chester, Vt., November 22, 1862. He was settled over the Congregational church at Chester, October 20, 1858.

Jeffrey, W. H. *Richmond Prisons* in 1861-62. Compiled from the original documents kept by the Confederate Government. St. Johnsbury, Vt., 1893. pp. viii, 272.

Jenison, Silas H. *An Address* delivered at the Annual Fair of the Addison County Agricultural Society, October 1, 1844. By Silas H. Jenison, President of the Society. Published by Request. Middlebury: J. Cobb, Jr., Printer. 1845. 8vo, pp. 16.

Silas H. Jenison was born in Shoreham, Vt., May, 1791; was elected Lieutenant-Governor of Vermont, 1835; and became Governor by reason of no election of Governor by the people. He had five successive elections as Governor, 1836-41. He died in Shoreham in Sept. 1849.

Jenks, Benjamin. *Prayers* and Offices of Devotion: for Families, and for particular Persons, upon most Occasions. By Benjamin Jenks, late Rector in Shropshire, and Chaplain to the Rt. Hon. The Earl of Bradford. Motto.

Brattleborough: Printed by William Fessenden For John West & Co. Boston: 1811. 12mo, pp. xxiv, 372.

Jenks, Rev. William, D. D. *The Comprehension* Commentary of the Holy Bible; containing the Text according to the Authorized Version; Scott's Marginal References; Mathew Henry's Commentary, condensed, but retaining every useful Thought; The Practical Observations of Rev. Thomas Scott, D. D., with extensive Explanatory, Critical, and Philological Notes, selected from Scott, Doddridge, Gill, Adam Clarke, Patrick, Poole, Lowth, Burder, Harmer, Calmet, Stuart, Robinson, Bush, Rosenmueller, Bloomfield, and many other writers on the Scriptures. The whole designed to be A Digest and Combination of the advantages of the best Bible Commentaries, and embracing nearly all that is valuable in Henry, Scott, and Doddridge. Conveniently arranged for Family and private reading, and at the same time particularly adapted to the wants of Sabbath School Teachers, and Bible Classes; with numerous useful tables, and a neatly engraved Family Record. Edited by Rev. William Jenks, D. D., Pastor of Green Street Church, Boston; Member of the Amer. Antiq. and Mass. Histor. Societies; and formerly Professor of Oriental Languages, and of the English Language in Bowdoin Coll., Maine. Embellished with five Portraits, and other elegant Engravings, from Steel Plates; several Maps, and many Wood Cuts, Illustrative of Scripture Manners, Customs, Antiquities, etc. Brattleboro: Published by Fessenden and Co. 1835. r'l 8vo, in six volumes of 800 to 900 pages each.

Of this great work, Allibone says:

Now published (1860) by J. B. Lippincott & Co., Philadelphia. We consider it the best Family Commentary in the language, (and) still stands without a rival for the purpose for which it is intended.

Mr. Jenks was assisted by Rev. L. J. Hoadley and Mr. J. W. Jenks. The first edition was published at Brattleboro, in 1834. It is stated by Mr. F. S. Drake, that more than 120,000 volumes of the Brattleboro editions were sold.

—*A Companion to the Bible;* containing a new Concordance to the Holy Scriptures, with Authentic Illustrations on wood; a Guide to the Study of the Bible, embracing Evidences of Christianity, History of the Bible, Jewish Antiquities, Arts, Sciences, &c.; being Carpenter's Biblical Companion condensed, with the addition of Notes and many Illustrative Engravings; Biographical Notices of nearly every Author commonly quoted in English Commentaries, with a Select List of Biblical Helps, and Characteristic and Critical Remarks; an Index to the Bible; Wemyss's Symbol Dictionary; Chronological and other Tables; and a complete and full Gazateer of the Bible. Illustrated with a Map, Portraits, and numerous other Engravings. Edited under the supervision of Rev. William Jenks, D. D. Brattleboro: Published by the Brattleboro Typographic Company. (Incorporated October 26, 1836.) Stereotyped at the Boston Type and Stereotype Foundry.

—*A New Concordance* to the Holy Scriptures, in a Single Alphabet; being the most Comprehensive and Concise of any before published; in which not only any Word or Passage of Scripture may be easily found, but the Signification also is given of all Proper Names mentioned in the Sacred Writings. By the Rev. John Butterworth, Minister of the Gospel. A New Edition, with considerable Improvements, by Adam Clarke, LL.D. To which are added the Definitions of Cruden, and numerous illustrative Engravings, under the Superintendence of Rev. William Jenks, D. D. Brattleboro: Published by the Brattleboro Typographic Company, (Incorporated October 26, 1836.) Stereotyped at the Boston Type and Stereotype Foundry.

Jenne, Prince, Rev. *Governor Smith's Proclamation* for a Fast, Reviewed and Spiritualized. An Afternoon's Sermon, delivered at Plymouth in Vermont, April 13th, 1808, Being a Day set apart by Authority, as a season for Humiliation, Fasting, and Prayer. By the Rev. Prince Jenne, An Ordained Evangelist Preacher. Printed at Bennington, Vt., at the Press of Anthony Haswell. 1808. 12mo, pp. 23.

Jennings Association, *Report* to the Jennings Association, U. S. A. Made by Columbus Smith, C. M. Fisher, Agents. A. D. 1863. Containing information in their possession relative to the Jennings property in England; the Crest and Coat of Arms of the family; likewise several genealogies of different branches of the family in America and England. Published by order of the Jennings Association. Rutland: Tuttle & Gay, Printers. 1863. 8vo, pp. 29.

Jennings, Isaac. *Memorials* of A Century. Embracing A Record of Individuals and Events chiefly in the Early History of Bennington, Vt., and its First Church. By Isaac Jennings, Pastor of the Church. Boston: Gould and Lincoln, 59 Washington St. 1869. 12mo, pp. 408.

The Rev. Isaac Jennings, D. D., for thirty-three years pastor of the old First Church of Bennington Centre, Vt., died at Bennington, Aug. 25, 1887, aged 72. He was noted among New England Congregationalists. Mr. Jennings was a graduate of Yale College, class of 1837, among his classmates being Chief Justice Chase and Senator William M. Evarts. Mr. Jennings' last public act was pronouncing the benediction at the laying of the cornerstone of the Bennington Battle Monument.

Jericho. *Annual Report* of the Selectmen and other Officers of the Town of Jericho, to the Annual Town Meeting, March 4th, 1873. Burlington: Free Press Steam Job Printing House. 1873. 8vo, pp. 12.

—*The Soldiers' Record* of Jericho, Vt. Prepared by E. H. Lane. Published by vote of the town. Burlington: R. S. Styles, Book & Job Printer. 1868. pp. 47.

Jewett, Isaac Appleton. *Memorial* of Samuel Appleton of Ipswich, Mass.. with genealogical notices of some of his descendants; compiled by Isaac Appleton Jewett. Boston: MD,CCCL. 8vo, pp. 183.

—*Passages* in Foreign Travel. Boston: 1838. 2 vols.

Mr. Jewett was born in Burlington, Vt., Oct. 17, 1808. Memoir in Vt. Hist. Magazine, Vol. I, pp, 651-2.

Jewett, Luther, M. D. *A Discourse,* Delivered at St. Johnsbury, December 3, 1818. Being the day of the Annual Thanksgiving.

By Luther Jewett, M. D. Danville: Ebenezer Eaton, Printer. 1819. 8vo, pp. 15.

Relates to the early ecclesiastical history of the town.

Mr. Jewett was born in Canterbury, Conn., December 24, 1772; and died at St. Johnsbury, Vt., March 8, 1860. In childhood he removed with his parents to Putney, Vt., and graduated at Dartmouth in 1795. He was both a physician and a clergyman, and settled at St. Johnsbury as a physician in 1800; but soon commenced preaching and was settled for short periods in different places; was a member of Congress, 1815-1817, several years a member of the Legislature, and held many minor offices. In 1828 he commenced the publication of the Farmer's (weekly) Herald, at St. Johnsbury, the first newspaper published there, and continued it four years, during which time he also published two volumes of The Friend, a weekly paper devoted to the defence of Masonry from its political assailants.

Jewett, Milo Parker, LL. D.

Was born at St. Johnsbury, Vt., April 27, 1808. He graduated at Dartmouth College in 1828, and at Andover Theological Seminary in 1833; was a Professor in Marietta College, Ohio, 1835-38; and President of Judson Female College, Marion, Ala., and was ordained a Baptist minister there in 1842; was President of Vassar Female College at a subsequent period. Author of "Mode and Subjects of Baptism."

Died at Milwaukee, Wis., June 9, 1882.

Jillson, Clark. *Inklings of Song*: A Memento of my leisure hours. In two parts. By C. Jillson. Motto. Worcester: Frederick M. Stowell. 1851. 12mo, pp. 159.

—*Progress* Attributed to the laboring classes: A Poem delivered before the Worcester County Mechanics' Association, March 3d, 1853. By C. Jillson. Motto. Worcester: Printed by Edward R. Fisher. 1853. 12mo, pp. 36. Second edition 1877. 4to, pp. 34.

—*The Annual Address* Delivered before the Young Men's Rhetorical Society, of Worcester, Mass., Dec. 26, 1853. By Clark Jillson, President of the Society. Worcester; Press of Clark Jillson. 1877. 4to, pp. 8.

—*A Comprehensive Chapter* for the Tax Payers of Worcester. By a citizen. Motto. Worcester: 1861. 12mo, pp. 8.

—*The Inaugural Address* of Hon. Clark Jillson, Mayor of Worcester, to The City Council, January 6th, 1873. Worcester: Printed by Charles Hamilton, Palladium office. 1873. 8vo, pp. 29.

—*An Address* to the Graduating Class of the Worcester High School, June 30, 1873. By Clark Jillson, Mayor of Worcester. Worcester: Printed by Charles Hamilton, Palladium Office. 1873. 16mo, pp. 12.

—*Valedictory Address* of Hon. Clark Jillson, Mayor of Worcester, Delivered before the City Council, December 29th, 1873, With the veto messages. Worcester: Printed by Charles Hamilton, Palladium Office. 1874. 8vo, pp. 19.

—*First Reunion* of the Sons of Vermont at Worcester, Mass., February 10th, 1874. Address of Hon. Clark Jillson; together with Toasts, sentiments, speeches, Poetry and song. specially reported for publication. Worcester: Printed by Charles Hamilton, Palladium Office. 1874. 8vo, pp. 60.

—*The Inaugural Address* of Hon. Clark Jillson, Mayor of Worcester, to the City Council, January 4, 1875. Worcester: Printed by Charles Hamilton, Palladium Office. 1875. 8vo, pp. 19.

—*The Inaugural Address* of Hon. Clark Jillson, Mayor of Worcester to the City Council January ary 3d, 1876. Worcester: Printed by Charles Hamilton, Palladium Office. 1876. 8vo, pp. 21.

—*Valedictory Address* of Hon. Clark Jillson, Mayor of Worcester, Delivered before the City Council, December 29th, 1876. Worcester; Printed by Charles Hamilton, Central Exchange. 1876. 8vo, pp. 19.

—*A Sketch* of the Life of John Fairbanks Pond. By Clark Jillson. Worcester: Press of Charles Hamilton, Central Exchange. 1877. 8vo, pp. 11.

—*Report* of the Joint Committee of the City Council of Worcester, on rebuilding the Lynde Brook Dam. Together with a complete History of the Worcester Water Works, from 1722 to 1877. By Clark Jillson. Worcester: Press of Charles Hamilton, Central Exchange. 1878. 8vo, pp. 64.

—*A Poem*. Truth Forever Lives. Delivered Before the Alumni and School of Nichols Academy, at Dudley, Mass., June 21, 1878. By Clark Jillson, F. S. A. Worcester: Privately Printed. 1878. 8vo, pp. 8.

—*Sketch* of M'Donald Clarke. "The mad poet." "Men call me mad—'Tis a wonder I am not." Portrait. By Clark Jillson. Worcester: Privately Printed, fifty copies. 1878. 8vo, pp. 8.

—*Sketch* of Ransom Mills Gould. With an account of his death and the remarks at his funeral, by Col. William S. B. Hopkins, Rev. Thomas E. St. John, Hon. Clark Jillson, Gen. A. B. R. Sprague, Rev. G. W. Phillips, Dr. J. M. Rice, Chas. G. Reed, Esq., and Hon. G. F. Perry. By Clark Jillson. Worcester: Privately printed one hundred copies. 8vo, pp. 32.

Mr. Gould was a native of Newfane, Vt., where he resided until early manhood. He died at Worcester, Mass., May 25, 1878, from injuries received from being thrown from a carriage.

—*Family History*. Clark Jillson: His Ancestors and Descendants. By A Member of the Worcester Society of Antiquity. Worcester: Press of Clark Jillson. 1879. 8vo, pp. 28.

—*Annual Address* and Memorial Remarks before the Worcester Society of Antiquity. By Clark Jillson. Worcester: Press of Clark Jillson. 1880. 8vo, pp. 15, (1).

Mr. Jillson was born in Whitingham, Vt., April 11, 1825. He is descended from William Gillson (as the name used to be spelled) who came from Kent, England, and settled in Scituate, Mass., in 1633.

Mr. Jillson left the old home at Whitingham in 1843, to make his own way in the world; he was engaged in various occupations in different towns in Massachusetts and finally located permanently at Worcester as a machinist in 1745, where he has since resided with the exception of about one year and a half at Southbridge, Mass.

He has held many positions of trust and honor, and was Mayor of the city of Worcester in 1873, 1875 and 1876.

For an interesting sketch of Mr. Jillson see the above "Family History," pp. 13-28.

Johns, James. *A Brief Record* of the various fatal accidents which have happened in Huntington, from its early settlement to this day. By James Johns. Huntington, Vt. 1858. pp. 22.

—*Vermont* Autograph and Remarker. Huntington, Vt., April 27, 1864.

A periodical issued occasionally in pen print.

—*A Brief Sketch or Outline* of the History of Huntington. Containing a comprehensive account of its boundaries, original charter and present limits. First Settlement. First Organization, and Representation. Town Clerks. Constables. First Physician. Clergyman. Lawyers. First Militia Muster. First School, First Mechanics, and various other particulars that will be found under the several heads. By James Johns. Huntington, Vermont. 1861. 12mo, pp. 44.

These books by Mr. Johns are done entirely with the pen in fac simile of printing. I am not aware whether Mr. Johns prepared more than this one copy of the history of Huntington, which belongs to the Vermont Historical Society.

Mr. Johns was born in Huntington, September 26, 1797; died April 26, 1874. He was a farmer, and lived a bachelor all his life; he resided in Huntington until 1868, when he moved to Starksboro. He commenced pen printing at the age of 13, when his first article for the public appeared.

Johnson. *Annual Reports* of the Officers of the town of Johnson. For the Fiscal year ending March, 1877. Montpelier: Freeman Steam Printing House and Bindery. 1877. 8vo, pp. 8.

Continued.

—*Report* of the Committee appointed by the Town of Johnson, March 7, 1876, to investigate Certain Charges made by H. A. Waterman, against R. W. McFarland, together with other matters pertaining thereto. Montpelier, Vt.: Argus and Patriot Steam and Job Printing Works. 1876. 8vo, pp. 16.

Johnson, A. J.

Mr. Johnson, publisher of "Johnson's Atlas of the World," "Johnson's Universal Cyclopedia," and of other well known works, died in New York, on Tuesday, April 22, 1884. He was born in Vermont about 1827, and began active life as a teacher. At last he became enrolled in the guild of publishers, and found himself at the head of the greatest map publishing house in the world, and "Johnson's Atlas" became an authority. In 1877 he planned the greatest undertaking of his life, namely, his "Universal Cyclopedia of Useful Knowledge," which was first put upon the market complete in four large volumes. It was reissued 1894-6 in eight volumes. In the preparation of this work upward of $250,000 was paid to authors.

Johnson, Anna C. *Little Things.* By the author of Letters from a Sick Room. Boston : 1845. Published by the Mass. Sabbath School Society. 12mo, pp. 120.

—*Simple Sketches* and Plain Reflections. By the Author of Letters from a Sick Room. Boston : 1846. Published by the Mass. S. S. Society. 12mo, pp. 180.

—*Peasant Life* in Germany. By Anna C. Johnson, Author of "Iroquois" and "Myrtle Wreath." New York : 1859. Charles Scribner. 12mo, pp. 426. A second edition published in 1862.

—*Cottages of the Alps.* By the Author of Peasant Life in Germany. New York: 1860. Charles Scribner, publisher. pp. 401.

Author also of "The Myrtle Wreath," "Letters from a Sick Room," and "Iroquois—a narrative of personal experience among the Indians." Miss Johnson was born in Newbury, Vt., Sept. 20, 1818, and died in 1892. She wrote at times under the nom de plume of "Minnie Myrtle," and is called by that name by Allibone.

Johnson, Artemas N.

Mr. Johnson was born in Middlebury, Vt., in 1817, and is the author of the following works : "Instructions in Thorough Bass," 1844; "Choir Chorus Book," 1847; "Bay State Collection," 1849; "Melodia Sacra," 1852; "Handel Collection," 1854; "Instruction in Harmony upon the Pestalozzian System," 1854, &c. Editor of the Boston Musical Gazette, and Boston Musical Journal. *Allibone.*

Johnson, James, A. M. *A Sermon,* preached at the Anniversary Meeting of Free and Accepted Masons, at St. Albans, Vt. On the Festival of St. John, the Baptist, June 24, 1826. By Rev. James Johnson, A. M. "Every house is builded by some man; but he that built all things is God." Heb. III. 4. St. Albans: J. Spooner, Printer. 1826. 8vo, pp. 12.

Mr. Johnson was born in Massachusetts, and was graduated at Harvard, 1808; came to Vermont in 1817, and was settled over Congregational churches in Williston, St. Johnsbury, and Irasburg, and died at St. Johnsbury, October 31, 1856.

Johnson, J. G. *Integrity;* A Sermon by Rev. Jas. Gibson Johnson, Pastor of the Congregational Church, Rutland, Vt. Preached March 19, 1876. (No imprint.) 12mo, pp. 15.

—*History* of the Congregational Church, of Rutland, Vermont. A Discourse by the Pastor Rev. Jas. Gibson Johnson. Delivered February 4th, 1877. Prepared and Published by Request of the Church. (no imprint.) 8vo, pp. 28.

—*Unity* of the Christian Church. A Sermon preached in the Congregational Church in Rutland by Rev. Jas. Gibson Johnson, Pastor. April 20th, 1870. Published by the Young Men's Christian Union. 8vo, pp. 18.

Johnson, John. *A Mathematical Question,* Propounded by the Vicegerent of the World; Answered by the King of Glory. Enigmatically represented and Demonstratively opened. By John Johnson. The Fifth Edition, Corrected and Revised. Printed at Windsor, (Vermont). By Alden Spooner, and sold by him, Wholesale and Retail, at his Office. M. DCC. XCIV. 12mo, pp. 91.

—*A Mathematical Question,* propounded by the Vicegerent of the World; Answered by the King of Glory. Montpelier, Vt. Published by John Crosby. July, 1813. 18mo, pp. 143.

—*The Advantages* and Disadvantages of a Married State, as entered into with Religious or Irreligious Persons. Represented under the Similitude of a Dream. Windsor: Published by P. Merrifield. T. M. Pomroy, Printer. 1813. 12mo, pp. 23.

Johnson, Mrs. *A Narrative* of the Captivity of Mrs. Johnson. Containing an Account of her Sufferings, during Four Years with the Indians and French. Second Edition, corrected and enlarged. Windsor, (Vt.) Printed by Alden Spooner. 1807. 18mo, pp. 142.

This narrative was written by the Hon. John C. Chamberlain, one of the early settlers of Charlestown, N. H. See History of Charlestown, p. 304.

A Narrative of the Captivity of Mrs. Johnson, containing An Account of her Sufferings, during Four Years with the Indians and French. Together with an Appendix ; Containing the Sermons preached at her Funeral, and that of her Mother ; with sundry other interesting articles. Third Edition, corrected, and considerably enlarged. Windsor, Vt. Printed by Thomas M. Pomroy. 1814. 12mo, pp. 178.

Johnson, Oliver. "*Consider* this, ye that forget God." A Dissertation on the Subject of Future Punishment, delivered at Framingham, and other places. By Oliver Johnson, Editor of the

Christian Soldier. Boston : Published by Pierce and Parker, No. 9, Cornhill. 1832. 8vo, pp. 32.

—*An Address* delivered at Middlebury, by Request of the Vermont Anti-Slavery Society, Feb. 18, 1835. By Oliver Johnson. Montpelier : Knapp & Jewett Printers. 1835. 8vo, pp. 32.

—*Correspondence* between Oliver Johnson and George F. White. With an Appendix. New York : Oliver Johnson. 1841. 12mo, pp. 48.

Mr. Johnson published a "Life of William Lloyd Garrison and His Times," 8vo, Boston, 1881.

Mr. Johnson was born in Peacham, Vt., in 1809, and served an apprenticeship at the printer's trade in the office of the "Watchman," at Montpelier, Vt. He was an original abolitionist, having been connected editorially with the 'Liberator," New York "Tribune," "Anti-Slavery Standard," and "Christian Union." He died in Brooklyn, N. Y., Dec. 10, 1889.

Johnson, Samuel. *Rasselas*, Prince of Abissinia ; A Tale. By S. Johnson, LL. D. Second American Edition. Brattleborough : Published by William Fessenden. 1813. 16mo, pp. 177.

Bound in same volume, Dinarbas: A Tale. Same imprint. pp. 180.

Jones, Amanda. *Rules* and directions for cutting men's clothes, by the Square Rule : By which, in a few hours, A Person may acquire such a knowledge of the Art, as will enable them to cut to all Sizes and Fashions, with the greatest Accuracy. Improved Edition. Middlebury : Published by Amanda Jones. J. W. Copeland Printer. 1822, 12mo, pp. 23.

Jones, Charles E. *The Life* and Confessions of Charles E. Jones : Convicted of the Murder of Isaac Jackson, a Jew Peddler, at Springfield, Mass., December 7, 1857. Together with an Appendix, embracing his trial and the Speeches of Counsel. Written by Himself, in Prison. Montpelier, Vt.: Printed by Ballou, Loveland & Company. 1860. 12mo, pp. 168.

Mr. Jones was a native of Montpelier, son of the late Watson Jones, a famous stage driver in the early days. The sentence was commuted to imprisonment for life, and we believe Mr. Jones died in the prison at Charlestown a few years later.

Jones, Rev. Ezra. *The Source* and Design of Afflictions. A Sermon, delivered at Clarendon, Vt., June 3d, 1849, on the Occasion of the Death of Albert H. Wilson, at Panama, April 9, 1849. By Rev. Ezra Jones. Published by Request. Windsor : Printed at the Chronicle Press. 1849. 12mo, pp. 12.

Jones, J. *Manual for the use of Jones Multiplying* and Equalizing Hive. Containing also Hints useful for the management of Bees in all Sorts of Hives. By James Jones, Galway, Saratoga County, New York. Johnson, Vt.: Printed by W. B. Hyde. 1843. 12mo, pp. 8.

Jones, Henry. "*The Seven Churches in Asia,*" figurative ; and the Millenial Thousand years, so called, coming next after rather than before the End of the World : Vindicated in Four Lectures. By Henry Jones. Motto. Montpelier, Vt. Knapp & Jewett, Printers. 1834. 12mo, pp. 69, (1).

Mr. Jones was pastor of the Congregational church in Cabot, Vt., when this book was written.

—*Letters on Masonry.*

See Masonic.

See also "Proceedings of the Montpelier [Vt. Congregational] Association," in relation to Mr. Jones in connection with Masonry.

Jones, Rev. P. F. *Result of the Trial* of Rev. P. F. Jones, late Pastor of the Baptist Church, Fair Haven. Vt., July 13, 14, 15 and 16, 1869, before a Committe of Reference, on charges brought against him by Dea. A. Allen. 8vo, pp. 7.

—*Men, Brethren, Fathers!* Read my general Exposition and Defense. I have not exhausted the subject. I have no quarrel with my Spiritual Mother. I love her as a Son. I am defending myself against individuals only. Mottoes. State of Vermont, County of Rutland, Town of Fair Haven, Before a Committee of Reference: July 13, 14, 15 and 16, 1869. 1870. 8vo, pp. 20.

—*More Light.* Another Arraignment ! (Catskill, N. Y., October, 1877.) 8vo, pp. 11.

Jones, Sir William. *An Essay* on modern Bailments. By Sir William Jones, Knt. Late one at the Judges of the Supreme Court of Judicature of Bengal. From the last London Edition etc. Published by William Fessenden. Brattleboro, (Vt.) 1807. 12mo. pp. (II.) 141, xxi.

Another edition, 1813, same imprint.

Jones, Rev. Zebulon. *The Law and Act* of Baptism. By Rev. Z. Jones, East Hubbardton, Vt. (1876.) 8vo, pp. 3.

Josephus, Ben Gorion. *The Wonderful* and most Deplorable History of the Latter Times of the Jews: With the Destruction of the City of Jerusalem. Which History begins where the Holy Scriptures end. Whereunto is added A Brief of the Ten Captivities, with the Portrait of the Roman Rams, and Engines of Battery, etc. As also, of Jerusalem ; with the fearful and presaging Apparitions, that were seen in the air, before her ruin. Bellows Falls, Vt.: Printed by Bill Blake & Co. 1819. 12mo, pp. 209.

A Journal *of An Excursion*, made by the Corps of Cadets of the A. L. S. & M. Academy, Norwich, Vt. Under Command of Capt. A. Partridge, June, 1824. Windsor, Vt. Printed by Simeon Ide. 1824. 12mo, pp. 48.

See Partridge, A.; Norwich University.

Joyce, C. H. *Address* delivered before the Farmers' Club, at their Seventh Annual Fair, held at Brandon, September 9, 1870. By Col. C. H. Joyce, of Rutland. Published by request. Rutland : McLean & Robbins, Printers. 1870. 8vo, pp. 24.

—*Oration* delivered at Brattleboro, Vt., Memorial Day, May 30th, 1871. By Col. Charles H. Joyce, of Rutland. Rutland : John Cain, Steam Printer. 1871. 8vo, pp. 19.

—*Remarks* of Hon. Charles H. Joyce, of Vermont, in the House of Representatives on the Death of Vice-President Wilson, January 21, 1876. Washington: 1876. 8vo, pp. 6.

—*Early Resumption* of specie payments—Honest Money for the People—Every Promise must be Kept, Every Pledge Redeemed—Advance the Whole Line—No Step Backward. Speech of Hon. Charles H. Joyce, of Vermont, in the House of Representatives, April 8, 1876. Washington : 1876. 8vo, pp. 10.

—*Statue of Ethan Allen.* Remarks of Hon. C. H. Joyce, of Vermont, in the House of Representatives, May 18, 1876. Washington: 1876. 8vo, pp. 12.

—*The Recent Election* in Louisiana. Speech of Hon. Charles H. Joyce, of Vermont, In the House of Representatives, February 9, 1877.

—*The Electoral Vote* of Louisiana. Speech of Hon. Charles H. Joyce, of Vermont, in the House of Representatives, February 20, 1877.

—*Mexican War Pensions.* Speech of Hon. Charles H. Joyce, of Vermont, In the United States House of Representatives, Tuesday, February 26, 1878. Washington: R. O. Polkinhorn, Printer. 1878. 8vo, pp. 16.

—*Repeal of the Resumption Act* and the Remonetization of Silver. Speech of Hon. Charles H. Joyce, of Vermont, in the House of Representatives, January 26, 1878. Washington: 1878. 8vo, pp. 18.

Mr. Joyce was born in Hampshire County, England, January 30, 1830; he came to the United States with his parents in 1836, and settled in Waitsfield, Vt.; read law, and commenced practice at Northfield, Vt., in 1852; was State Librarian in 1855 and 1856; State's Attorney for Washington County 1856 and 1857; Major of Second Regiment, Vermont Vols., in 1861; and promoted to be Lieut. Colonel in 1862. After the war he resumed practice of the law at Rutland, Vt.; was a member of the Legislature in 1869, '70 and '71; and Speaker of the House during the latter term; member from the first District of Vermont, of the forty-fourth, forty-fifth, forty-sixth and forty-seventh Congresses, 1875-1883.

Keach, Rev. Israel. *An Address*, delivered on the Fifty-seventh Anniversary of the Bennington Battle, at Hoosick, on the Battle Ground, August 16, 1834. By Rev. Israel Keach. Troy: Office of the Troy Daily Whig. 1834. 8vo, pp. 16.

Copied largely from Governor Hall's address of 1823.

Keith, Reuel, D. D.

A Protestant Episcopal clergyman; was born in Pittsford, Vt., in 1793, and died at Sheldon, Vt., September 3, 1842. He was graduated at Middlebury College, in 1814, and was a tutor there, 1816-17; Rector of a church in Georgetown, D. C., for several years, where he acquired a high reputation; Professor of Humanity and History in William and Mary College, Va., 1822-26, and afterwards Professor of Pulpit Eloquence and Pastoral Theology in the P. E. Seminary of the Diocese of Virginia.

Among Dr. Keith's publications are his translation from the German of "Hengstenberg's Christology of the Old Testament," and a "Commentary on the Predictions of the Messiah by the Prophets." Alexandria, D. C. 1836. 3 volumes. An abridged edition published in London, 1847. For this work Dr. Keith received high commendations from Biblical students. See *Allibone.*

Keeler, Seth H. *The Apostolic Method* of Church Extension. A Sermon preached at Saco, June 22, 1853, before the Maine Missionary Society at its Forty-Sixth Anniversary. By S. H. Keeler, Pastor of the First Congregational Church in Calais. Augusta: William T. Johnson, Printer. 1853. 8vo, pp. 15.

—*A Brief Historical Sketch* of the Church in Mount Vernon, presented by the Acting Pastor, Rev. S. H. Keeler, D. D., at the Centennial of the Erection of the Congregational Meetinghouse, in Amherst, January 18, 1874. pp. 8.

Published with the Proceedings at Amherst, N. H.

Dr. Keeler was born in Brandon, Vt., September 24, 1800; was graduated at Middlebury College in 1826, and at Andover in 1829; was Pastor of the Congregational Church in South Berwick, Me., 1829-36, in Amesbury, Mass., 1836-9, in Calais, Me., 1839-67, in Mount Vernon, N. H., 1868-75. Died 1886 in Somerville, Mass.

Kellogg Family Record. 1878. 8vo, pp. 11.

Prepared by Mr. J. E. Kellogg, of Fitchburg, Mass. Includes the descendants of John Kellogg, whose son John settled at Benson, Vt., and was the ancestor of prominent persons of that name in the State; Hon. Loyal Case Kellogg and L. Howard Kellogg, were sons of John of Benson.

Kellogg, Henry. *Memorial* words on the Life and Character of the late Henry Kellogg. Motto. Troy, N. Y.: Printed for Private Circulation. 1878. 8vo, pp. 14.

Kellogg, John. *A Narrative* of the Facts connected with, as well preceding as subsequent to the Author's withdrawing from the Congregational Church, in Benson, Vt., April, 1838. Castleton, Vt.: L. R. H. Robinson, Printer. 1841. 12mo, pp. 24.

Kellogg, Loyal Case. *The Power of the President* to Grant a General Pardon or Amnesty for offences against the United States.

Occupies 31 pages in the American Law Register for September and October, 1869.

Mr. Kellogg was born in Benson, Vt., February 13, 1816, and died there November 26, 1872. He was graduated at Amherst College, 1836; read law at Rutland, and commenced practice at Benson in 1839. He was a member of the General Assembly of Vermont in 1847, 1850, 1851, 1859, and 1871; Judge of the Supreme Court, 1859-1868, and declined further service on account of failing health. He held many other positions of honor and trust in the State. The degree of Doctor of Laws was conferred at Amherst, in 1869. He wrote the excellent history of Benson for the Vermont Historical Magazine.

Kellogg, M. P. *The Student's Guide* and Teacher's Text Book. Being a Systematic arrangement of modern Geography, upon the classification system, adapted to the most approved Atlases now in use. By M. P. Kellogg, Teacher of Geography. St. Albans, Vt.: Printed by E. B. Whiting. 1842. 12mo, pp. 16.

Kellogg, William Pitt. The Louisiana Funding Bill. A Reply to the Protest of Certain New York Bond-holders, by Governor William P. Kellogg. New Orleans: 1874. 8vo, pp. 7.

—*Annual Message* of His Excellency Governor Wm. Pitt Kellogg to the General Assembly of Louisiana. Session of 1874. New Orleans. 1874. 8vo, pp. 31.

Mr. Kellogg, son of Rev. Sherman Kellogg, was born in Orwell, Vt., December 8, 1831, and has become somewhat notorious in Illinois and Louisiana.

Kelton, C. G. *The New England* Collection of Hymns and Spiritual Songs; adapted to Prayer, Conference and class meetings. Compiled by C. G. Kelton. Motto. Montpelier, Vt.: Published by G. W. Hill. 1829. 24mo, pp. 168.

Kelton, Dwight H. *Annals* of Fort Mackinac [Michigan.] By Dwight H. Kelton, Lieutenant U. S. Army. Chicago: Fergus Printing Company. 1882. Illustrated. 8vo, pp. 111.

Mr. Kelton is a native of East Montpelier, Vt., son of Judge Stillman S. Kelton.

Kenaston, Rev. T. H. *Memorial* of Rev. T. H. Kenaston. Compiled by Rev. L. C. Patridge, by order of Champlain Conference. Motto. Syracuse, N. Y. 1874. 12mo, pp. 96.

Mr. Kenaston was born in Sheffield, Vt., January 4, 1838, and died in the same town August 10, 1872.

[Kendall, B. F.] *The Doleful Tragedy* of the raising of Jo. Burnham, or the "Cat let out of the Bag." In five Acts, Illustrated with Engravings. By Timothy Tickle, Esq.

"I tell thee what, Mister, we Anties mean to turn up the Commonwealth and dress it, and set a new nap on't."
Woodstock, Vt.   Printed by William W. Prescott, 1832. 18mo, pp. 96.

With five wood cuts, probably by Benjamin Tuel, which are as difficult to match as is some of the dialogue as well as the poetry.

Mr. Prescott, the printer of the above work, came from Concord, N. H., and was a journeyman printer, and it is said was a very good Shakespearean scholar. It is claimed on very good authority that he rendered important assistance to Mr. Kendall in the above work.

The Key to this curious book is this. Joseph Burnham was a farmer in Pomfret, who was convicted of a rape and sent to the State Prison ; his son George Burnham, a resident of New York, and a man of some means, used to come occasionally to Woodstock, and from there go to Windsor to see his father. During one of these visits Jo. Burnham died, was carried to Woodstock, and buried.

Some months after, one Joshua Cobb went from Woodstock to New York, and while there wrote to friends in Woodstock that Jo. Burnham was alive in New York; he repeated the assertion in subsequent letters, and another person wrote to the same effect. This was at the time when anti-masonry was rampant in Vermont; and at length Jo. Burnham's case became involved in the anti-masonic excitement.

It became the general belief that Burnham had been permitted to escape from Prison, and that the corpse of another person had been buried in his stead. George Burnham was presumed to be a Mason, so was the Superintendent of the State Prison. It was supposed that by collusion between them Jo. was allowed to leave prison and depart the State. The excitement became so intense that it affected the Legislature which met soon after.

A committee consisting of Robert Pierpoint was sent to New York by the Legislature to ascertain if Burnham was still there. Citizens of Woodstock also went to New York to identify their man; he was found to be the exact counterpart of Jo. Burnham in every particular except the voice, and that alone enabled them to decide that he was another man. To make assurance doubly sure, the body which had been buried was disinterred, and though decay had done its work, some peculiarity of the teeth made it evident to those who had known him, that Jo. Burnham was indeed dead and buried. Timothy Tickle, Esq., the author of the "Doleful Tragedy of Jo. Burnham" was Benjamin F. Kendall, at that time editor of the newspaper "Henry Clay," at Woodstock. Some of the *dramatis personæ* were as follows :

Sir Richard Makefuss was R. Makepeace Ransom, of South Woodstock, one of the chief agitators in Anti-masonry, and a frequent member of the Legislature; Elder Lovely was Rev. Samuel C. Loveland, a Universalist minister, then of Reading; Parson Raw-limbs, was Rev. Mr. Rollins of Randolph, at one time editor of the Vermont Luminary ; Landlord Slate-stone, was James Slayton, of South Woodstock ; Squire Deal-He-Knows, was Jabez Delano, of West Windsor ; Farmer Dobbin was Amos Ralph ; Major Hard-Face, was Martin Flint, of Randolph; Master Slender was Joseph Hemenway, editor of the American Whig; Lord Mansfield was Hon. Titus Hutchinson ; General Hoax-Em, was Gen. Asaph Fletcher, Sheriff of Windsor County; Old Mordaceous was Jasper Luce, of Hartland ; Capt. Bang'em was Capt. Bingham, of Woodstock; Yardstick was Titus Hutchinson, Jr.; Deacon Piggin was Amariah Richmond ; Farmer Credulous was Daniel Lockwood ; Demurrer was Richard Hazen, a pettifogger of Woodstock ; Aunt Debby was Mrs. Daniel Lockwood ; Long Jaw, Lysander Raymond, of Woodstock ; Hawk Eye, Hawkins, of Reading ; Aunt Debby, Mrs. Shaw, of Woodstock ; Judy, Mrs. Delano.

An Amusing Episode of Anti-Masonic History in Vermont.

Somewhat more than half a century ago Vermont was convulsed with a "doleful tragedy" second only in its dark and mysterious incidents to the disappearance of Morgan. R. A. Perkins, formerly a resident of Woodstock, and now on the Springfield *Republican* staff, has recently gathered up the facts and written an account of this affair for the Bibliography of Vermont, edited by M. D. Gilman, Esq., of Montpelier. Mr. Perkins' narrative is as follows :

Kendall, B. F. *The Doleful* Tragedy of the Raising of Jo Burnham, or the "Cat Let Out of the Bag." In Five Acts. By Timothy Tickle, Esq. Woodstock, Vt.: Printed by William W. Prescott. 1838. Small 16mo, pp. 96.

The story of this little book involves a curious chapter in the political history of the state, which may be told thus: Joseph Burnham, a middle-aged Woodstock farmer, was convicted of rape on the person of a girl named Sarah Avery, of Pomfret, and sentenced to a term in the state prison. He was of Connecticut birth, and for a number of years before his conviction lived in Pomfret, where he had many relatives. Burnham's character was not the best, but neither was that of the girl, and the general belief in the vicinity was that he suffered unjustly. An effort was made to get him pardoned but before final action, on the 15th of October, 1826, he died in prison. The remains were given to his son George two days later, taken to Woodstock, and interred in the north burying ground in that town, by the easternmost Pomfret road. The story is simple and commonplace enough so far, but the remarkable part began soon after with the circulation of a rumor that a man named Lyman Mower, otherwise called Joshua Cobb, who once lived in Woodstock and knew Burnham there, had seen him in New York city alive and well, going by the name of Patrick Dolon. The matter attracted but little attention, however, until the rising of the masonic question in Vermont politics a few years later. The flood tide of excitement about this matter was nearly reached in 1829. The struggle between masons and anti-masons had become extremely bitter, and then this old Burnham rumor, coming up on the wave of feeling, assumed a degree of importance which, in view of the extremely slight evidence it rested upon, now seems almost incredible. The excitement caused by the Morgan abduction was at its height, and this Burnham affair took a place as a masonic outrage. The superintendent of the prison, the physician in charge and some of the other officers were masons. Burnham himself belonged to the order and so, it is said, did his son George, who lived in New York city and had been active in seeking for the release of his father by executive pardon. It was charged that Burnham had feigned death and been permitted to escape by the aid of the superintendent, the physicians and other masons, while the body of another man was buried by his friends as a blind ; and the charge came to have a belief so large as to be almost general, although warranted by no evidence except the story told by Mower, and he a man without reputation or standing. The newspapers took the matter up in the summer of the year last named ; charges and denials were made at every point, all that could be got in the semblance of evidence one way or the other was printed and hotly disputed about, and every day the excitement increased. Mower made an affidavit setting forth that he saw Burnham in New York in the fall of 1826, and that in January and February, 1828, he had for five or six weeks seen and talked with him almost daily, and that in company with A. P. Parsons he had at another time a "long, full and free conversation with him." Aaron B. Cutter, who had known Burnham when he once lived at West Cambridge, Mass., also made an affidavit setting forth that on the 16th of July, 1829, he saw the man in New York and had a talk with him. Cutter's character was such, however, that his evidence was thrown entirely aside when the formal investigation came. But these affidavits, with some whispers of impending developments about the prison, were at the time of their publication enough to give fury to the popular clamor, and in the latter part of October, 1829, the selectmen of Woodstock ordered the disinterment of the remains buried as Burnham's to settle the question by identification. The body was exhumed, but could not possibly be identified with certainty, and in a few days it was a second time disinterred in the presence of a great number of people, but with no better result. Some were positive that the body was Burnham's, others that it was not his, and the question was as far from settlement as ever. But at the same time, as the conduct of state officers was in question, the matter was taken to the legislature, and there the facts were at last established. The general assembly appointed R. Pierpoint, J. S. Pettibone and John Smith an investigating committee, which, on the 28th of October, made a report that was ordered printed in the newspapers. By this report it appears that after the committee had examined the officers of the prison, Mr. Pierpoint went to New York, found Mower, and offered him $500 if he would produce Burnham in Vermont within fifteen days, guaranteeing a pardon for the latter. Mower insisted that Burnham was living under the name of Dolon, but the man called Dolon being found by Pierpoint, Mower confessed that he was not Burnham and said he had been deceived as to the fact throughout. Mower made an affidavit by which he claimed to have been honestly mistaken in the affair, but the committee reported that Dolon had lived in New York for six or seven years and had worked for Mower on a building in the spring of the year 1826. The most obvious explanation of the whole matter is that some resemblance which Dolon bore to Burnham led Mower, alias Cobb, to make a thoughtless remark at first, and that as the excitement rose he and others lied deliberately from love of mischief and notoriety. The committee's report concluded : "We cannot hesitate to say that Jo Burnham died on the 15th of October, 1826, in the state prison, at Windsor." The story altogether reminds one irresistibly of the familiar tale of the three black crows.

The result was a sort of a victory for the masons, and of course they did not fail to celebrate it ; exultation was expressed upon every hand and sneering allusions to the "Jo Burnham farce" were heard constantly. Finally Dr. David Palmer wrote for the Woodstock *Courier*, then edited by B. F. Kendall, the prospectus of a book on the subject, to be published at the office of the paper. The announcement was intended merely as a sarcastic squib, but it was taken literally and people began to send in orders for the book, whereupon Mr. Kendall carried out the jest by writing and publishing this "Tragedy," which is worthy of a place in the "Curiosities of Literature. Benjamin Tuel, a jeweler's apprentice, made five engravings for it which are well calculated to keep in countenance Kendall's words. The characters were all taken from life and the book was given point by the fact that several of them—middle-aged, sober citizens, and one a minister—had traveled about the state giving dramatic representations of masonic ceremonies. Moreover, a strolling theatrical company happening along at Woodstock soon after the publication appeared, "Jo Burnham" was put on the boards and drew crowded houses for two weeks.

Characters in "Tragedy of Jo Burnham," differing from and in addition to those published above ; furnished by R. A. Perkins, Esq., Woodstock, Prof. J. M. Currier. Castleton, and Hosea Doten, Woodstock.

Major Hard-Face. Maj. Martin Flint, of Randolph, a leading anti-mason.—*H. Doten.*

Old Mordacious. Benjamin Sanderson, a farmer of South Woodstock.—*H. Doten.*

Baron Lucre. Hon. Elihu Luce, a farmer of Hartland. —*H. Doten.*

Deacon Piggin. Amariah Richmond, a cooper of Woodstock ; he was called "Piggin" Richmond, on account of his occupation, of making piggins.—*H. Doten.*

Demurrer, Oramel Hutchinson, a lawyer in Chester, son of Hon. Titus Hutchinson.—*H. Doten.*

Long-Jaw. Lysander Raymond, farmer in the west part of Woodstock.—*H. Doten.*

Hawk-Eye. Jared Rickard.—*J. M. Currier.*

Aunt Debby. Mrs. Sanderson, wife of Benjamin Sanderson.—*H. Doten.*

Judy. Mrs. Delano, wife of Jabez Delano.—*Doten.*

Judy. Mrs. D. Lockwood, according to *J. M. Currier.* The anti-masons appear to have pushed the "Outrage" business with as much vigor as is being used in our day.

—*The Ex-Chief Justice* and the Printer ; being a Report of A Trial for Libel, Titus Hutchinson vs. B. F. Kendall ; had before the Honorable County Court, for the County of Windsor, and State of Vermont, May Term, 1836 ; Including Plaintiff's Declaration, Pleadings, Testimony, Arguments, Charge, and Verdict ! ! ! With an Appendix, containing many interesting Reminiscences, Morceaus, and Incidents, with which the Public Life and Meandering Course of the late "Everlasting Candidate," are so profusely variegated.

Bassanio. Why dost thou whet thy knife, so earnestly ?

Shylock. To cut the forfeit from that bankrupt, there.
MERCHANT OF VENICE.

Oh, mighty Cæsar ! Dost thou lie so low?
Are all thy conquests, glories, triumphs, spoils,
Shrunk to this little measure? Fare thee well !
JULIUS CÆSAR.

By the Defendant. Woodstock, Vt. J. B. & S. L. Chase & Co. 1837. 8vo, pp. 72.

Being a history of tergiversation in politics for twenty-five years, culminating in a bitter personal quarrel.

Mr. Kendall was a native of South Woodstock, where he was born in October, 1799 ; he was for some time a merchant at Woodstock, then the editor and publisher of one or two newspapers there.

In 1836 he moved to Richmond, Va.. where for eight years he was book-keeper in the office of the then famous Richmond "Inquirer." In 1844 he moved to Union township in Northern Indiana, then a wild prairie, where he opened a farm, and resided until his death, March 7, 1854. He married Louisa Holton, who was born in Barre, Vt., in 1805 ; her mother being left a widow, married Dr. John D. Powers, of Woodstock, father of Dr. Thomas E. Powers. Mrs. Kendall resides in Woodstock, (1889) in a house owned by her half sister, Mrs. Charles G. Eastman, a half sister of the late Dr. Thomas E. Powers.

Kendall, B. J. & Co. *A Treatise* on The Horse and his diseases; containing valuable information. By Dr. B. J. Kendall & Co., Enosburgh Falls, Vt. Illustrated. Claremont, N. H.: 1879. 12mo, pp. 90.

Kendall, Edward Augustus. *Travels* through the Northern Parts of the United States, in the Years 1807 and 1808. By Edward Augustus Kendall, Esq. In Three Volumes. New York : Printed and published by I. Riley. 8vo. Vol. 1. pp. 330. Vol. 2. pp. 309, Vol. 3. pp. 312. All of Volume 3 commencing with p, 199 is devoted to Vermont.

Kendall, R. S. *Christ Preaching* to the Poor. A Sermon preached in the Congregational Church, Middlebury, Vt., on Sunday Morning, July 6, 1856. By R. S. Kendall. Published by Request. Boston. 8vo, pp. 20.

—*The Fearful Argument.* A Sermon preached in the Congregational Church, in Middlebury, Vt., January 1, 1854, by the Pastor [Rev. R. S. Kendall.] Middlebury : Justus Cobb, Printer. 12mo, pp. 16.

Kendrick, Elder Ariel. *A Brief Reply* to a Pamphlet lately published by S. Delanoe, (under the fictitious name of Candor) in favour of Universalism. Entitled, Miscellaneous Thoughts on the Doctrine of Limited Election and Reprobation, as it stands contrasted with Scripture and Reason. By Ariel Kendrick, Minister of the Gospel, Woodstock, Vt. Motto. Printed at Hanover, New Hampshire, by Benjamin True. 1798. 8vo, pp. 23.

—*A Funeral Sermon,* delivered at the Funeral of Capt. Samuel Comings, of Cornish, N. H., Jan. 8, 1826. By Elder Ariel Kendrick. Chronicle Press, Windsor, Vt. 1834. 12mo, pp. 16.

—*Sketches* of the Life and Times of Eld. Ariel Kendrick. Being A short account of his birth, Conversion, Call to the Ministry, and his labors as a Gospel Minister, with other incidents occurring under his notice. Written by himself. Ludlow, Vt.: Printed by Barton & Tower, "Genius" Office. 1847. 12mo, pp. 96.

—*Sketches* of the Life and Times of Eld. Ariel Kendrick. Written by Himself. Third Edition. Windsor, Vt.: Published by P. Merrifield. 1850. Chronicle Steam Press. 12mo, pp. 120.

Kendrick, Asahel Clark, D. D. *A Discourse* in Hamilton, New York, Aug. 14, 1850, at the funeral of the Reverend Abel Woods. By Asahel C. Kendrick, D. D. Boston: Ticknor, Reed and Fields. MDCCCL. 8vo, pp. 28.

—*We walk by Faith.* A Sermon delivered in the Baptist Church, at Saratoga Springs, N. Y., August 30, 1857, by Rev. Prof. A. C. Kendrick, of the University of Rochester. Cambridge : Printed at the Chronicle Office. 1858. 8vo, pp. 24.

—*The Life and Letters* of Mrs. Emily C. Judson. By A. C. Kendrick. New York: Sheldon & Company. 1860. 12mo, pp. 426. Portrait.

Prof. Kendrick, a Baptist Minister and scholar, son of Rev. Clark Kendrick, was born in Poultney, Vt., December 7, 1809; and was graduated at Hamilton College in 1831; he remained there as tutor and professor until 1837, when he became professor of Greek in Madison University; Professor of Greek in the University of Rochester 1851–85. He was a member of the American Committee for the Revision of the New Testament. Died at Rochester, N. Y., October 1895.

In addition to the above, Prof. Kendrick has published: "Child's Book in Greek," New York, 12mo; "Introduction to the Greek Language," 12mo; "Greek Ollendorf," 1852, 12 mo; "Echoes; or Leisure Hours with the German Poets," 1854, 16mo, pp. 148; "Life of Rev. Linus W. Peck." An American edition of Olshausen's Commentaries on the New Testament. 6 vols. rl, 8vo; besides numerous Sermons, and Contributions to Reviews and Magazines. See *Allibone: Drake.*

Kendrick, Clark. *A Sermon*, delivered in the Baptist Meeting House, at Poultney, Vt., on the thirty-fourth anniversary of American Independence, July 4, 1810. By Clark Kendrick, Pastor of the Baptist Church and congregation in said Town. Published by special request. Rutland: Printed by William Fay. 1810. 8vo, pp. 12.

—*A Sermon*, delivered September 14, 1814, in the Meeting-House in Rutland, (West-Parish) at a Thanksgiving to Almighty God, held by the inhabitants of said Parish, For the Fall of the British Fleet on Lake Champlain, and the defeat of their Army at Plattsburgh, on 11th inst. By Clark Kendrick, Pastor of the Baptist Church and Congregation in Poultney. Rutland: Printed by Fay & Davison. 8vo, pp. 16.

—*Plain Dealing* with the Pedo-Baptists, for their popular and unwearied Declamations in favor of their Open Communion, and against what they term The Close Communion of the Baptists. By Clark Kendrick, Pastor of the Baptist Church in Poultney, Vt. Rutland: Printed by Fay, Davison & Burt. 1818. 8vo, pp. 34.

—*A Sermon*, delivered on the day of General Election, at Montpelier, October 8, 1818. Before the Honorable Legislature of Vermont. By Clark Kendrick, Pastor of the Baptist Church and Congregation in Poultney. Published by order of the Legislature. Montpelier, Vt.: Printed by E. P. Walton, October, 1818. 8vo, pp. 58.

Elder Kendrick was pastor of the Baptist Church in Poultney, Vt., from its organization in 1802, until his death, February 29, 1824, in the 49th year of his age.

Kendrick, Nathaniel. *A Sermon* preached at Middlebury, before Union Lodge, No. 5, on the Festival of St. John the Baptist, June 24, 1812. By Nathaniel Kendrick, pastor of the Baptist Church in Middlebury. Ye are God's building—Paul. Middlebury: T. C. Strong. 1812.

—*The Trials* and encouragements of Christ's faithful Ministers. A Sermon delivered in the Chapel of the Baptist Literary & Theological Seminary, Hamilton, N. Y., March 19, 1824, Occasioned by the recent deaths of Rev. Obed Warren, of Covert, N. Y., and Rev. Clark Kendrick, of Poultney, Vt. By Nathaniel Kendrick, D. D., Professor of Theology in the Seminary, Hamilton: 1824. 8vo, pp. 31.

Kenfield, W. H. H. *Manual* of the Lamoile County Bar; containing the Rules of Practice in the Supreme Court and Court of Chancery. And of the Lamoille County Court. Compiled by W. H. H. Kenfield, Clerk of the Courts. Hyde Park, Vt.: The Lamoile News Print. 1878. 12mo, pp. 62.

Kent, Rev. Dan. *Electioneering* for office defended, with some directions as to the process: A discourse delivered before His Excellency Thomas Chittenden, Esq., Governor: the Honorable Council, and House of Representatives of the State of Vermont, at Rutland, Oct. 14, 1796; By Dan Kent, Pastor of the Church of Christ in Benson. Printed by order of the Legislature for Samuel Williams.

Mr. Kent was born in Suffield, Conn., April 10, 1758; and died in Benson, Vt., July 22, 1835. With his father, Cephas Kent, he removed to Dorset, Vt., about 1774; he began to preach about 1790, and supplied at Dorset for thirteen months, then in the winter of 1791–2, at Benson, Vt., where he was settled over the Congregational church from 1792–1828. It is said that nothing from him but his election sermon was published.

Kerlidou, Rev. J. *St. Anne* of Isle La Motte in Lake Champlain. Its History; Rules of Confraternity; Prayers, and Novena to St. Anne. By Rev. J. Kerlidou, Alburgh, Vt. Burlington: Free Press Association. 1895. 16mo, pp. 131.

Ketchum, Silas. *A Sermon* Preached to the Congregational Church and Society, and many other people, in Wardsboro, Vt., on Lord's Day, Sept. 24, 1865 ; the same being a Farewell Discourse. By Silas Ketchum, sometime Minister of the Church. Published by request. Brattleboro: Printed by D. B. Stedman. 1866. 12mo, pp. 12.

—*The Philomathic Club.* An outline History of its operations from its organization 19 Nov. 1859, to its transformation into the New Hampshire Antiquarian Society 19 Nov. 1873. Also A Catalogue of Curiosities in its possession at that time and Covering an incongruous Collection of Detached Facts concerning Persons and Places. The Whole hunted up, gotten together, Disarranged and Typographically composed by the Rev. Silas Ketchum, Secretary. Bristol: Fifty Copies privately printed by George Crowell Ketchum, 25 March, 1875. 8vo, pp. 270, 16.

This is an unique book, and of its interesting list of curiosities, a large portion were collected in Washington County, especially in the towns of East Montpelier, Calais and Barre.

—*Historic Masonry.* An Address: Delivered at the Installation of Officers of Union Lodge, No. 79, in the Town Hall, Bristol, N. H., Feb. 4, A. L. 5873. By Rev. Silas Ketchum, R. A.° Bristol: Printed by Geo. Crowell Ketchum. 5873. 8vo, pp. 12.

—*An Eulogy* on Henry Wilson, Vice-President of the United States, who was born in Farmington, N. H., Feb. 16, 1812. Died in the Capitol at Washington, Nov. 22, and was interred in Natick, Mass., Dec. 1, 1875. Pronounced at Salem Hall in Malden, Mass., Sunday Evening, Nov. 28, 1875. By Rev. Silas Ketchum, Pastor of the First Congregational Church, Maplewood. Malden: George Crowell Ketchum, Printer. 1875. 8vo, pp. 14.

—*The Original Sources* of Historical Knowledge. A Plea for their Preservation. By Rev.

Silas Ketchum, President of the New Hampshire Antiquarian Society; Member of the Historical Societies of New Hampshire and New York. Windsor, (Ct.): (125 Copies for private Circulation.) George Crowell Ketchum, Printer. 1879. 8vo, pp. 28.

—*Special Geography* of New Hampshire, published as a Supplement to Harper's High School Geography. N. York: 1877.

—*Installation* of Rev. Silas Ketchum, as Pastor of the Second Congregational Church of Windsor, Conn. In the Parish of Poquonock. Thursday, May 1, 1879. Windsor: (Twenty-five Copies for Personal Friends.) Geo. C. Ketchum, Printer. 1879. 8vo, pp. 20.

—*Paul on Mars Hill:* A Sermon. Preached to The Church in Freeman Place, Beacon Street, Boston. Lord's Day, Aug. 15, 1875. By Rev. Silas Ketchum, Pastor of the Congregational Church, Maplewood, Malden, Mass. Ancient Windsor: Printed by Mrs. Georgia C. Ketchum, A.M. MMMMMDCCCLXXX. 8vo, pp. 14.

Rev. Mr. Ketchum was born in Barre, Vt., December 4, 1835; he read theology at Bangor, Me., Theological Seminary, where he graduated in 1863. He was sometime a teacher, and was acting pastor of the Congregational Church, at Wardsboro, Vt., 1864-5; of the Congregational Church, Bristol, N. H., 1866-75; at Malden, Mass., 1875-6; and at Windsor, Conn. Mr. Ketchum was active in antiquarian and historical pursuits, and prominently connected with various Historical and Antiquarian Societies; also connected editorially with the *Vermont School Journal*, *Vermont Record*, and various other newspapers. He edited a Dictionary of New Hampshire Biography. The Vermont Historical Society has a full biographical sketch of Mr. Ketchum in manuscript.

He was descended through both his parents from the earliest settlers of Montpelier and Barre, his father Silas, senior, being a son of Roger W., who was a son of Justus, who removed from Massachusetts, and settled in Barre, in 1808, and in 1820, married Cynthia, daughter of Edmund Doty, who settled in Montpelier with his brother, Barnabas, Jr., in 1789.

The Dotys who settled in Montpelier are descendants in a direct line from Edward, who was a passenger on the Mayflower.

Mr. Ketchum died April 24, 1880, at the residence of Rev. Harlan P. Gage, at Dorchester, Mass.

Keyes, Elias. *An Address* to the Independent Freemen of Vermont. By Elias Keyes. Windsor: Printed for the Author. A. & W. Spooner, Printers. 1818. 12mo. pp. 12.

Relates to the election of members of Congress at that time.

—*To the Honorable* General Assembly of the State of Vermont, to be convened at Montpelier on the second Thursday of October next, your petitioner, Elias Keyes of Stockbridge in said State, petitioning, Humbly Showeth, &c. Dated, Stockbridge, September 18, 1823. 8vo. pp. 47. No imprint.

Mr. Keyes asks the General Assembly to authorize the Court to grant him a new trial in the case named.

Keyes Family. *Genealogy* Robert Keyes of Watertown, Mass., 1633. Solomon Keyes of Newbury and Chelmsford, Mass, 1653. And their Descendants: Also others of the name, by Asa Keyes. Brattleboro: Geo. E. Selleck, Printer. 1880. 8vo, pp. IV, (4,) 319. Portrait.

Judge Asa Keyes, author of the above work, was born in Putney, Vt., May 30, 1787; he has always resided in Vermont, and for the past 47 years at Brattleboro, where he died while the above work was in press. For biographical sketch see the above, pp. 175-6.

Keyes, Hon. Henry. *In Memoriam.* Testimonial by the Vermont State Agricultural Society to the Memory of Hon. Henry Keyes, its President. December 21, 1870. Tuttle & Co., Printers, Rutland, Vt. 8vo, pp. (4).

Mr. Keyes was an old and successful merchant of Newbury, and President of the Passumpsic railroad at the time of his death.

Kidder, K. P. *Kidder's Guide* to Apiarian Science, being a Practical Treatise, in every Department of Bee Culture, and Bee management, embracing the Natural History of the Bee, from the earliest period of the world, &c. By K. P. Kidder, Practical Apiarian. Burlington, Vt., Samuel B. Nichols, 146 Church Street. Chicago: Rufus Blanchard. 1858. 12mo, pp. 173, (2).

Kimball, Mrs. Anne L. N. *A Brief* Memorial of; By Rev. Silas McKeen. 8vo, pp. 4.

Mrs. Kimball was a daughter of Hon. Nathaniel Niles, and was born in West Fairlee, Vt., March 8, 1799, and died there September 10 1868

Kimball, Rev. Moses. *A Discourse* Commemorative of Major Charles Jarvis, of the Ninth Vermont Volunteers. Who was mortally wounded, Dec. 1, 1863, in an encounter with the enemy, near Cedar Point, N. C., delivered at his Funeral, in the Congregational Church at Weathersfield Bow, Vt., December 13, 1863. By Rev. M. Kimball. New York: 1864. 8vo, pp. 24.

Mr. Kimball was born in Hopkinton, N. H., July 24, 1799; died in Haverhill, Mass., September 17, 1868. He preached at Randolph, Vt., in 1832-33.

Kimball Union Academy. *Catalogue* of, for 1878-9. Montpelier, Vt.; J. & J. M. Poland, Printers. 1879. 8vo, pp. 20.

King, Mrs. Mary B. (Allen). *Looking Backward:* Memories of the Past. New York; 1870. 12mo, pp. 455.

Mrs. King was a native of Woodstock, Vt., and was for many years a teacher in Rochester, N. Y., where she died.

King, W. S. *Address* of W. S. King, Esq., at the Fair of the Vermont State Agricultural Society in Rutland. September 2, 1862. Middlebury, 1862.

Kingsbury, John Denison. *The Duty of Young Men.* A Sermon preached at Bradford, Mass., Feb. 24, 1867, by J. D. Kingsbury, Pastor. 8vo, pp. 11. Haverhill, (Mass.) 1867.

—*Sketch* of Rev. Silas Aiken, by Rev. John D. Kingsbury. Reprinted from the Congregational Quarterly for April, 1870. Cambridge: Welch, Bigelow and Company, Printers to the University. 1870. 8vo, pp. 22.

Mr. Kingsbury was from Underhill, Vt. He graduated from the University of Vermont, 1852; and from Andover Theological Seminary, 1856; was for some years settled in Brandon. Since 1866 has been pastor of the Congregational church in Bradford, Mass.

Kingsley, Phineas. *A Brief Survey* of the Congregational Churches and Ministers in the County of Franklin, Vt., from its first settlement to the present time. (1840.) By Rev. Phineas Kingsley, Sheldon, Vt.

American Quarterly Register, 1840, Vol. xii, pp. 352-357.

Kinsman, J. B. *The Vermont Townsman;* A Compilation of the Laws of Vermont in relation to the Powers, Duties, and Liabilities of Town Officers and Towns, with Forms, Directions, and Legal Decisions adapted to the Statutes of the State. By J. Burnham Kinsman Counsellor at law. Boston: Brown,

Taggart & Chase. Rutland: G. A. Tuttle & Co. Montpelier: C. G. Eastman; E. P. Walton. Burlington: E. A. Fuller; C. A. Goodrich. 1857. 8vo, pp. xxxiv, 425.

Kitchel, H. D. *The Indirect* and Secondary Influence of the Bible as an Elevating and Civilizing Power. An Address Before the Vermont Bible Society, at Montpelier, October 17, 1860. By Rev. H. D. Kitchel, D. D., President of Middlebury College. 8vo, pp. 13.

—*Addresses* at the Inauguration of Rev. H. D. Kitchel, D. D., President of Middlebury College. Middlebury: Register Book and Job Printing Establishment. 1866. 8vo, pp. 32.
Contains the addresses of the retiring and incoming Presidents.

—*Extracts* from an Appeal to the People for the Suppression of the Liquor Traffic. A Prize Essay. By Rev. H. D. Kitchel. 8vo, pp. 16.
Harvey Denison Kitchell graduated at Middlebury College, 1835; studied at Andover Theol. Sem., 1835-6; tutor Middlebury College, 1836-7; at New Haven Theol. Sem. 1837-8; Pastor Congregational Church, Thomaston, Conn., 1838-48; of First Congregational Church, Detroit, Mich., 1848-64; of Plymouth Church, Chicago, 1864-6; President of Middlebury College, 1866-73; resided subsequently at Liverpool, Ohio. Died 1896.

Kneeland, Abner. *The American* Definition Spelling Book. Abner Kneeland. Windsor, Vt. Printed by Nahum Mower. 1804. 12mo.

Labaree, Benjamin. *Moral Education.* Inaugural Address of the Rev. Benjamin Labaree, President of Middlebury College, delivered May 18, 1841. Published By request of the Corporation. Middlebury: Printed by Ephraim Maxham. 1841. 8vo, pp. 32.

—*A Sermon* on the death of General Harrison, delivered in Middlebury, Vt., on the day of the National Fast. By Rev. Benjamin Labaree, A. M. Middlebury: Printed by E. Maxham. 1841. 12mo, pp. 35.

—*Lecture.* The Education demanded by the Peculiar Character of our Civil Institutions. By Benjamin Labaree, D. D., President of Middlebury College, Vt. n. d. 12mo, pp. 32.

—*An Address* delivered at the Dedication of the Literary and Scientific Academy, Champlain, N. Y., on the 4th of July, 1842. By Rev. B. Labaree, D. D., President of Middlebury College. Middlebury: J. Cobb, Jr., Printer. 1842. 8vo, pp. 28.
See Middlebury College for Salutatory Address at Semi-Centennial, 1850; Baccalaurente Discourse, August 6, 1865.
Rev. Benjamin Larabee, D. D., LL. D., died in Walpole, N. H., Thursday, Nov. 15, 1883. He was born in Charlestown, N. H., June 3, 1801, and was graduated at Dartmouth College in 1828, and subsequently at Andover Theological Seminary. He was at one time president and professor of ancient languages in Jackson college, Tennessee, and secretary of the Education society, New York city. Afterwards he was president of Middlebury college 26 years. After his retirement from Middlebury college, he delivered lectures before the senior class. He received the honorary degree of D. D. from Burlington college, and of LL. D. from his alma mater. He left a widow and two sons.

Ladd, Jed P. *Centennial Oration,* Delivered at Alburgh Springs, July 4, 1876. By Hon. Jed P. Ladd. Furnished for Publication by request. St. Albans: Advertiser Printing House. 1876. 8vo, pp. 15.

Lake Champlain. *Reasons* Supported by Statistical information, against Bridging Lake Champlain, and in favor of the St. Lawrence and Champlain Canal. By a Vermonter. October, 1848, [n. p. n. d.] 8vo, pp. 24.

—*An Act* to Incorporate a Company for the Construction of a Ship Canal to connect the waters of Lake Champlain and the river St. Lawrence. 12 Victoriæ, Cap. 180. Montreal: Printed by Derbishire & Co. 1849. 8vo, pp. 60.

—*Proceedings* of the Convention Held at Saratoga Springs, August 21, 1849, relative to the St. Lawrence and Champlain Ship Canal; with the Separate Reports of the American and Canadian Committees. Saratoga Springs: 1849. 8vo, pp. 24.

—*A Descriptive* and Historical Guide to the Valley of Lake Champlain and the Adirondacks. Burlington Vt.: R. S. Styles' Steam Printing House. 1871. 12mo, pp. 144.

—*The First Battle* of Lake Champlain. Has History correctly located its Site. Read before the Albany Institute, Nov. 5, 1889, by George F. Bixby. Albany, 1893.

—*Lake Horicon,* (Lake George,) Montreal and Quebec. Map and Table of Distances. Burlington: C. Goodrich and Company. 1858. 18mo, pp. 48.

—*Lake George!* the Adirondacks, Lake Memphremagog, and Mount Mansfield! Burlington, Vt. R. S. Styles' Printing Establishment. 1867. 18mo, pp. 60, (2).
See Watson W. C., History of; Palmer, P. S., History of, and History of the battle of Valcour, on Lake Champlain, 1776; Canfield, Tho's H., History of; also, in Dawson's Battles by Sea and Land, Vol. i, pp. 167-175, account of battle of Valcour and others, with British and American Official Reports, and citations of authorities; Slafter, E. F., Voyages of Samuel De Champlain.

Lake Dunmore Hotel Company. Act of Incorporation and By-Laws, with a Short Description of Lake Dunmore and its Surroundings. Rutland: Tuttle and Co. Printers. 1853. 12mo, pp. 16.

Lake Memphremagog, the most attractive of Summer Resorts. The Passumpsic R. R. and its Connections. Description of Scenery. 1870. 24mo, pp. 35.

—*Wonders of,* by Burt. 1872.

—*Handbook of,*
See Dix, J. R.

—*Statistics of,*
See Harrington, E.

Lamb, Dana, and Merrill, Thomas A. *A Complete List* of the Congregational Ministers and Churches in Addison County, Vt., from the first settlement to the present time (1830.) By Rev. Dana Lamb and Rev. Thomas A. Merrill, D. D.
Gives nativity, birth and death; also a brief sketch of each town in the county.
See American Quarterly Register, 1839, vol. xii, pp. 52-63.

Lamb, Jonathan. *Spelling Book.* Burlington: 1829. 12mo, pp. 180.

Lamb, L. *The Militia's Guide;* Exhibiting a more comprehensive explanation, than before published, of the Posts and Duties of the several Officers of Review, from a General to a Sargeant. Designed For the Instruction of a Young and Undisciplined Militia. By

Larned Lamb, Esq., Lieutenant Colonel and Commander of the Third Regiment, in the Second Brigade, of the Fourth Division, of Militia in the State of Vermont. Montpelier: Printed by Samuel Goss, For the Author. 1807. 18mo, pp. 105, (3.)

Lambert, Nathaniel. *A Sermon* preached before His Excellency, Isaac Tichenor, Esq., Governor; His Honor, Paul Brigham, Esq., Lieutenant Governor; The Honorable Council; and the House of Representatives of the State of Vermont, October 8, 1801, at Newbury; it being General Election. By Rev. Nathaniel Lambert, A. M. Pastor of the Church in Newbury. Windsor: Printed by Alden Spooner, M.DCCC.I. 8vo, pp. 21.

Mr. Lambert was graduated at Brown University, 1787; and settled over the Congregational Church in Newbury, Vt., 1790-1820.

Lamoille County. *A Brief Survey* of the Congregational Churches and Ministers in.
See Robinson, S.

—*Manual* of Lamoille County Bar.
See Kenfield, W. H. H.

—*Atlas Map* of Lamoille and Orleans Counties.
Same title and imprint as Chittenden County Atlas.

Lane, Gilbert Cooke, A. M. *Poems by*, with a Biographical Sketch. Edited by Rev. Bernice D. Ames, A. M. Burlington: Printed by Danforth & Smalley. 1860. 12mo, pp. 31.

Mr. Lane was born in Weybridge, Vt., March 18, 1828; was graduated at Middlebury College in 1853, went South for his health, taught school there, returned home in 1855, and died November 10, 1858, aged 30 years.

Lane Manufacturing Company, *Montpelier, Vt.* Price List. 1876. Montpelier, Vt. Argus and Patriot Steam Job Printing works. 1876. 12mo, pp. 24.

Langdon, Chauncey. *An Oration* on the Virtues and Death of General George Washington, late President of the United States: delivered at Castleton, [Vt.], Feb. 22, 1800, agreeable to the recommendation of the President. By Chauncey Langdon. Rutland: Printed by W. Fay. 8vo, pp. 27.

—*An Oration* delivered in the Town of Poultney, (Vt.), on the Fourth of July, 1804. By Chauncey Langdon. Salem: Printed by Henry Dodd and David Rumsey, Jun. 1804. 8vo, pp. 30.

—*An Oration*, pronounced at Poultney, July 4, 1808. Being the Thirty-third Anniversary of American Independence. By Chauncey Langdon. Motto. Published by request of the hearers. Rutland, Vt.: Printed by Thomas M. Pomeroy. 1808. 8vo. pp. 32.

—*An Oration*, delivered in Castleton at Celebration of the Fourth of July, A. D. 1812. By Chauncey Langdon, A. M. Middlebury: Printed by T. C. Strong. 1812. 8vo, pp. 35.

Mr. Langdon was born in Farmington, Conn., in 1764; and died in Castleton, Vt., in July, 1830. He was graduated at Yale College, 1792, read law, and came immediately to Castleton, where he resided until his death. He was a member of Congress, 1815-16, and a member of the State Council a number of years, and held many county and town offices. See memoir in *Vt. Hist. Mag.* Vol. 3, p. 523.

Lanphear, Rev. O. T. *The Godly Man's Worth.* A Sermon at the Funeral of Orem Newcomb, on the Sabbath, October 15, 1854.

By O. T. Lanphear, Pastor of the Congregational Church, Derby, Vt. Published by request. Windsor: Printed at the Vermont Chronicle Press. 1855. 8vo, pp. 16.

—*"The ideal excellence* of the Christian pastor." A sermon preached at the Ordination of Mr. C. E. Ferrin over the Cong'l Church in Barton, Vt., Dec. 10, 1851, by Rev. O. T. Lanphear.
See Ferrin, C. E.

—*Peace by Power.* A discourse preached in the College Street Church, New Haven, (Ct.) Sabbath Evening, Oct. 9, 1864, by Rev. O. T. Lanphear, pastor of the church. New Haven: Printed by J. H. Burnham. 8vo, pp. 15.

—*A Discourse* in memory of Hon. Charles Sumner. Delivered in Dane Street Church, Beverly, Mass., March 15, 1874, by Rev. O. T. Lanphear, D. D., pastor. Published in the "Beverly Citizen," March 21, 1874.

—*Rev. George Trask.* A memorial discourse, by Rev. O. T. Lanphear, D. D., pastor of the Dane Street Church, Feb. 14, 1875. Published in the "Beverly Citizen," Extra.

Also author of "Thou shalt love thy Neighbor." Lowell, 1856; and "Account of the Celebration of the One Hundreth Anniversary of the Inauguration of Washington, held at Beverly, Mass." Beverly, 1889.

Rev. Orpheus Thomas Lanphear, D. D., was born in West Fairlee, Vt., January 26, 1820. He was a son of Sabin and Lucy (Lamb) Lanphear. He was graduated at the University of Vermont in 1845, and at Andover Theological Seminary in 1848. Among his college classmates were Revs. A. D. Barber, N. G. Clark, D. D., Ebenezer Cutler, D. D., C. E. Ferrin, and J. G. Hale. He preached one year at Milton; was then pastor of the Congregational church in Derby, October, 1849, to May, 1855; of the High street church, Lowell, Mass., September, 1855, to October, 1856; of the 2d Congregational church, Exeter, N. H., February, 1858, to February, 1864; of the College street church, New Haven, Conn., March, 1864, to February, 1867; and of the Dane street church, Beverly, Mass., 1867 to '87. He resides at Beverly. (1896.) He was a member of the Corporation of the University of Vermont, 1854 to 1857, and received the honorary degree of D. D. from the same in 1871.

Lard, Mrs. Rebecca (Hammond.) *Miscellaneous Poems* on Moral and Religious Subjects. By A Lady. Woodstock: Printed by David Watson. 1820. 18mo, pp. 143.

Mrs. Lard dedicated this work to her brother, the Hon. Jabez D. Hammond, late of Cherry Valley, New York; he was born at New Bedford, Mass., August 2, 1778; died at Cherry Valley, August 18, 1855. When about one year old, his father Jabez Hammond, and wife, with a family of seven children, moved to Woodstock, Vt. The subject of this sketch, with a limited education, taught school at the age of fifteen; he read medicine, and practiced sometime at Reading, Vt.; in 1805 he moved to Cherry Valley, where he read and practiced law. He was a member of Congress, 1815-17, and subsequently held many offices of honor and trust in the State of New York. He published "Political History of New York," to December, 1840; Albany, 1843. 2 vols. 8vo; also vol. 3, Syracuse, 8vo; "Julius Melbourn," 1851; and "Life and Times of Silas Wright." See *Allibone, Drake, Lanman.*

Mrs. Lard also published: The Banks of the Ohio. A Poem. Windsor, Vt.: Printed by Simeon Ide. 1823. 12mo, pp. 12.

Mrs. Lard, daughter of Jabez Hammond, was born at New Bedford, Mass., March 7, 1772; died at Paris, Ind., September 28, 1855. At the age of seven years Mrs. Lard, with her father's family, moved to Woodstock, Vt. With limited schooling, but great natural ability, by self-culture she fitted herself and began to teach school at the age of fourteen, which was her chief occupation in Vermont and Indiana for nearly half a century, and many of the best minds in Indiana received instruction from her. Her life struggle appears to have been a severe one, having a family of four children dependent upon her for support from their childhood, but bravely did she triumph over all obstacles. She moved from Vermont to Indiana in 1820, where she ever after resided, with the exception of about two years passed in Vermout. I am indebted to her niece, Mrs. Almira Sterling, of Woodstock, for the incidents of Mrs. Lard's life.

Lathrop, John. *Funeral Sermon* of Mrs. Lydia Whitney. Brattleborough : 1800. 12mo, pp. 13.

Lathrop, Joseph. *A Sermon* preached at Rutland, in the State of Vermont, February 1, 1797, at the Ordination of the Reverend Heman Ball, to the Work of the Gospel Ministry in that Place. By Joseph Lathrop, D. D. Pastor of the first Church in West Springfield, Mass. Rutland : Printed by Josiah Fay. M,DCC, XCVII, 8vo, pp. 34.

—*Sermon,* at Putney, Vt., June 25, 1807, at the Ordination of Elisha D. Andrews. Brattleborough : 1807. 8vo.

—*The Prophecy of Daniel* relating to the time of the end, opened, applied and improved, in two discourses delivered on a public Fast, April 11, 1811. By Joseph Lathrop, D. D. Pastor of the first Church in West Springfield. Springfield, Mass.: T. Dickman. Middlebury, Vt.: S. Swift.

Lathrop, Leonard E. *The Farmer's Library.* Or Essays Designed to encourage the pursuits, and promote the Science of Agriculture. By Leonard E. Lathrop, Esq. Motto. Second Edition Corrected and Enlarged. Windsor : Printed by Wyman Spooner. 1826. 12mo, pp. 300.

Lawrence, Edward A. *Misinterpretation of Providence ;* a Discourse delivered at Marblehead, December, 1846, on the Disasters at Sea, Sept. 19, 1846. By Edward A. Lawrence, Pastor of the First Church in Marblehead. With an Appendix, containing an Account of the Dedication of the Monument, and the Names of the Persons lost in the Terrible Gale. Marblehead ; Mercury Press, Washington Street, 1848. 8vo, pp. 19.

—*A Discourse,* on the Death of Hon. Daniel Webster, delivered Oct. 31, 1852, by Edward A. Lawrence, Pastor of the First Church, Marblehead. Boston : Press of T. R. Marvin, 42 Congress St. 1852. 8vo, pp. 29.

—*God in the Church* the Life of its History. An Inaugural Discourse, delivered July 20th, 1854, By Rev. Edward A. Lawrence, Professor in the Theological Institute, East Windsor Hill, Conn. Hartford : Press of Case, Tiffany and Company. 1854. 8vo, pp. 40.

—*The Mission of the Church ;* or, Systematic Beneficence. By Rev. Edward A. Lawrence, Marblehead, Mass. Published by the American Tract Society, 150 Nassau street, New York. n. d. 8vo, pp. 163.

—*A Discourse,* delivered at the Funeral of Rev. Leonard Woods, D. D., in the Chapel of the Theological Seminary, Andover, August 28, 1854. By Edward A. Lawrence, Professor in the Theological Seminary, East Windsor Hill, Connecticut. Boston : S. K. Whipple and Company, 100 Washington Street. 1854. 8vo, pp. 38.

—*The Progress of Peace Principles.* A Paper read before the Peace Congress at Geneva, Sept., 1874. By Edward A. Lawrence, D. D.,

Marblehead, Mass. Boston : J. E. Farwell, Printer, No. 34, Merchants Row. 1875. 8vo, pp. 23.

—*Does Everlasting Punishment* last forever? By Edward A. Lawrence, D. D. Boston : Beacon Press, Thomas Dodd, Printer, Corner Beacon and Somerset Streets. 1879. 8vo, pp. 15.

Dr. Lawrence was born at St. Johnsbury, Vt., October 7, 1808 ; was graduated at Dartmouth College in 1834, and at Andover in 1838 ; preached at Haverhill, Mass., 1839–44 ; and at Marblehead, Mass., 1845–54 : was Professor at the Theological Institute, at East Windsor, Conn., 1854–65 ; preached at Marblehead, 1868–73, where he still lives. (1880.)

See Chapman's "Dartmouth Album."

Lawrence, Byrem. *A Concise Description* of the Geological Formations and Mineral Localities of the Western States; Designed as a Key to the Geological Map of the Same. By Byrem Lawrence. Boston : Printed by Samuel N. Dickinson. 1843. 16mo, pp. 48.

Lawrence, M. *Address* of Hon. Myron Lawrence, with other proceedings of a meeting of Vermonters, Held in Boston, in behalf of Middlebury College. Boston : 1851. 8vo, pp. 16.

Mr. Lawrence was born in Middlebury, Vt., May 18, 1799 ; was graduated at Middlebury College, 1820, and practiced law in Belchertown, Mass., until his death, November 7, 1852.

Lawrence, Rev. Robert F. *A Sermon* preached at the Installation of Rev. J. Wood, in Townshend, Vt., January 10, 1850. By Robert F. Lawrence, Pastor of the Congregational Church in Claremont, N. H. Windsor : Printed at the Chronicle Press. 1850. 8vo, pp. 22.

Lea, Henry C. *Bible View* of Polygamy. To the Rev. John Henry Hopkins, Bishop of Vermont. Signed Mizpah. 8vo, pp. 4. n. p. n. d.

Leach, Beriah N., D. D.

Baptist Clergyman, son of Moses Leach. Born in Middletown, Vt., April 28, 1801 : Converted when 14 years old : Entered Hamilton University in 1820 : Tutor in 1823–4 : Married Priscilla Barber, of Middletown, Vt., in 1825 : Ordained Pastor in Cornwall, Vt., in October, 1826 : Pastor in Middlebury, Fredonia, Wyoming, Hamilton, N. Y., Middletown, Ct., and Brooklyn, N. Y. Once Principal of the Wyoming Academy : Five years Secretary of the Education Society of the State of New York, residing in Hamilton. He received the degree of D. D. from the University in 1859. A laborious and successful Pastor : He died of heart disease in Middletown, Ct., January 23, 1869, in the triumphs of Christian faith. He published several religious works, of which we have not the titles.

Leavenworth, E. W. *A Genealogy* of the Leavenworth Family in the United States, with Historical Introduction, Etc., By Elias Warner Leavenworth, LL.D., of Syracuse, N. Y. Being a revision and extension of the Genealogical Tree compiled by William and Elias W. Leavenworth, then of Great Barringtor, Mass., in 1827. Syracuse, N. Y.: S. G. Hitchcock & Co., 4 West Fayette Street, 1878. 8vo, pp. 375.

The family is largely represented in Vermont.

Leavitt, Rev. H. F. *A Funeral Sermon,* Preached April 5, 1845, At Vergennes, on the death of Mrs. Fanny Morgan, by Rev. H. F. Leavitt. Published by request. Vergennes : E. W. Blaisdell, Printer. 1845. 12mo, pp. 19.

Harvey Freegrace Leavitt was born in Hartford, Vt., December 1, 1796 ; and died at Grinnell, Iowa, November 11, 1874. He was graduated at Yale, 1816 ; and practiced law until 1829 ; began to preach in 1830, at Strafford, Vt.: and was pastor of the Congregational church there until

1836; then pastor at Vergennes, Vt., until 1860. He was four times married; the last time November 20, 1873. See *Vermont Congregational Minutes*, 1875.

Leavitt, Joshua. *Easy Lessons* in Reading; for the Use of the Younger Classes in Common Schools. By Joshua Leavitt. Stereotyped by F. H. Carter & Co., Boston. Keene, N. H. Published by J. Prentiss. 1835. 12mo, pp. 156.

Another edition, same imprint, 1837. Mr. Leavitt resided at Putney, Vt., when the book was first published.

Leavitt, Rev. William S. *God's Law* Unchangeable in its Claims. A Sermon preached in the Eliot Church, Newton, Ms.,on the Anniversary of the Landing of the Pilgrims, Dec. 22, 1850. By Rev. W. S. Leavitt, Pastor of the Church. Boston: Press of J. Howe, 39 Merchants Row. 1851. 8vo, pp. 24.

Mr. Leavitt was born in Putney, Vt., Jan. 26, 1822; graduated at Yale College in 1840; studied at Union Theological Seminary, '42-'44; was pastor of the Eliot Ch., Newton, Mass, '45-'53, Presb. Ch., Hudson, N. Y., '53-'67, 1st Ch., Northampton, Mass, '67-81.

Leclair, Peter. *Pedigree* and Particulars of Pure Bred Jersey Cattle, imported from the purest, choicest and oldest stocks in England by Peter Leclair, Winooski, (near Burlington) Vermont, Together with their Progeny. [1880.] 12mo, pp. 6.

Lee, C. *The American Accomptant;* being a plain, practical and systematic Compendium of Federal Arithmetic; &c &c. By Chauncey Lee, A. M. Lansingburgh: 1797. 12mo, pp. 207, (2.)

And 12 pages of Subscribers' names.

—*A Sermon* delivered before North Star Lodge of Masons at Manchester, Vt., June 24, 1814. By Chauncey Lee, A. M. Pastor of the Church of Christ in Sunderland, Vt. Bennington: Anthony Haswell. pp. 20.

—*The Duty* and Importance of Christian Watchfulness. A Sermon delivered at the funeral of Mr. William Bennett, of Manchester, Vt. (Who departed this life in the thirtieth year of his age.) Published at the request of the Free and accepted Masons of the North Star Lodge, of Manchester, of which the deceased was a Member. By Chauncey Lee, A. M., Pastor of the Church of Christ in Sunderland, Vt. Bennington: Printed by Anthony Haswell. M,DCC,XCIV.

Mr. Lee published in addition: "The Triumph of Virtue," a metrical version of the book of Job, 1807; Connecticut Election Sermon, 1813; Sermon on the death of Rev. A. R. Robbins, 1813; A Volume of Revival Sermons, 1824; "Letters from Aristarchus to Philemon," 1833.

Mr. Lee, son of Rev. Jonathan Lee, the first minister at Salisbury, Conn., was born at that place November 9, 1763. and died at Hartwick, N. Y., in December, 1842.

He was graduated at Yale, 1784; read, and practiced law; then read theology, and was pastor of the Congregational church at Sunderland, Vt., 1790-1797; then pastor of different churches in New York and Connecticut until his death.

He had a son, Rev. Chauncey Graham Lee, who was born in Sunderland, 1795. (Pearson says he was born in Colebrook, Conn., which is an error,) was graduated at Middlebury College. 1817, and was pastor at Mouroe, East Windsor, and Naugatuck, Conn., and died in 1871. See "Sprague's Annals," where it is stated that at the time of the settlement of Rev. Chauncey Lee at Sunderland, another minister was settled in the town on the same day, and the latter gained in a law-suit some land which had been given to the first settled minister, as he was settled two minutes first.

See Allen's Dictionary.

Lee, John S. *Nature and Art* in the Old World; or, Sketches of Travel in Europe and the Orient. By John S. Lee, Professor in St. Lawrence University, Canton, New York. Cincinnati: 1871. 12mo, pp. 441.

—*Sacred Cities:* Narrative, Descriptive, Historical. By John S. Lee, D. D. Professor of Ecclesiastical History in the Theological Department of St. Lawrence University, author of "Nature and Art in the Old World." Cincinnati: Williamson & Cantwell Publishing Co. 1878. 12mo, pp. 266.

—*Sketch* of Col. John Hawkes, of Deerfield, Mass., 1707-1784. By John Stebbins Lee, D. D. [1882.] 8vo, pp. 8.

Articles published in the "Universalist Quarterly," by Rev. Dr. Lee: "Inspiration of the Scriptures." October, 1848. 15 pp. "Qualifications of the Minister." April, 1850. 12 pp. "The Religion of Geology." October, 1851. 21 pp. "The Philosophy of Language." October, 1866. 18 pp. "Sources of Error in the use of Language." January, 1868. 20 pp. "The Province and uses of Ecclesiastical History," an Inaugural Address. October, 1869. 22 pp. "Religion in its Relation to Art." January, 1871. 22 pp. "Paul's Preaching at Athens." April, 1872. 17 pp. "Recent Explorations in Palestine." July, 1871. 16 pp. "The Natural and the Supernatural." April, 1874. 13 pp. "Antioch in Syria." January, 1875. 17 pp. "The Oriental Features of the Bible." January, 1877. 20 pp. "The Realistic Features of the Bible." July, 1879. 15 pp.

In addition Dr. Lee has published a dozen or more sermons and addresses, and more than sixty articles in publications of his denomination relating to various branches of theology.

John Stebbins Lee, son of Eli and Rebekah S. Lee, was born in Vernon, Vt., September 23, 1820. Was educated till 16 years of age in the common school, where he commenced the study of the Latin language. Then he attended the High School at Brattleboro, Vt., the Academy at Deerfield, Mass., Shelburne Falls Academy and West Brattleboro Academy, where he completed his preparation for College in June, 1841, and immediately entered Amherst College, from which he was graduated in August, 1845, among the first third of his class of 30. He commenced teaching at Swansey, N. H., the same month, taking charge of Mount Cæsar Seminary, of which he had charge for one year.

In July, 1846, he commenced his Theological studies with Rev. Dr. Hosea Ballou, 2d., afterwards first President of Tuft's College, Medford, Mass.

In April, 1847, he removed to West Brattleboro and took charge of Melrose Seminary, where he remained nearly two years. The Seminary was largely patronized under his charge.

In February, 1849, Mr. Lee removed to Lebanon, N. H., and took charge of the Universalist society there. He resigned his charge in February, 1851, and removed to Montpelier, Vt., where he assisted Rev. Dr. Eli Ballou in editing the *Christian Repository*, and preached there and in the surrounding towns.

In March, 1859, he accepted an invitation to take charge of the "Green Mountain Liberal Institute" in South Woodstock, Vt., where he remained for five years. He also preached in South Woodstock, Bridgewater and Woodstock, thus performing the labor of two men for most of the time. Wearied out by his labors, in 1864, he removed to Woodstock and took charge of the Universalist society for two years. He also performed the duty of Town Superintendent of schools.

In April, 1865, he resigned his charge at Woodstock, and accepted an invitation as Professor of Latin and Greek languages in St. Lawrence University, a new college established in Canton, N. Y. He also performed the duties of Principal of the Collegiate Department until July, 1868, when exhausted by his severe and unremitting labors he took a trip to Europe and Palestine.

His journey was rapid, but he gleaned rich fruits from it, by reason of the extensive preparation which he had previously made in the way of reading, especially in history and the classics. He lectured extensively on his travels in Northern New York and Vermont, among his old friends, and at their request he collected together the fruits of his tour, and published them in a volume, as noted above. The volume was issued in January, 1871, and in two months a second edition was called for, and large numbers of the work have been sold.

In April, 1869, on his return Mr. Lee took the chair of Professor of Ecclesiastical History and Biblical Archæology, in the Theological department of St. Lawrence University, which he has held ever since. His tour in the East was a special preparation for this position.

His lectures before his classes on the Bible Lands were partially collected and published in 1878, in a volume of 266 pages, as noted above. Mr. Lee has also in contemplation a volume on "Illustrations of the Bible." (1879.)

He was married to Miss Elmina Bennett, of Westmoreland, N. H., February 22, 1848, and their silver wedding was celebrated in Canton, N. Y., in 1873. Their children are five, three of whom graduated at St. Lawrence University. The eldest son, Leslie A., is instructor of Natural History in Bowdoin College. Mr. Lee received the honorary degree of D. D., from Buchtel College, Akron, O., in July, 1875.

Lee, Jonathan. *The labors* of a pastor defeated and his hopes disappointed. An address designed to be presented to a Mutual Council, called for the dismission of a pastor from his Charge. By Jonathan Lee, Late Pastor of the Congregational Church in Weybridge, Vt. Middlebury: Printed by Elam R. Jewett. 1837. 8vo, pp. 23.

He was a son of Milo, who was a son of Rev. Jonathan Lee, the first minister at Salisbury, Conn., and died in 1788, aged 70. The subject of our sketch was born at Salisbury, July 19, 1786, and died there in 1866. He was graduated at Yale, 1809, at Andover, 1812, and ordained over the Congregational church at Otis, Mass., June 28, 1815, where he remained until 1831; pastor at Weybridge, Vt., 1834-1837, when he returned to Salisbury, where he resided until his death. He published two sermons while at Otis, Mass. Rev. Chauncey Lee was his uncle.

Lee, Richard, *A short narrative* of the Life of Mr. Richard Lee. Containing a brief account of his nativity, Conviction, and Conversion, also, a hint of his trials respecting his gifts of Prayer, &c., in public. And his suffering by the enemies of Religion in a Christian land, as it is called; and also his trials by afflictive Providence. Second Edition. Burlington, Vt. Printed by Samuel Mills, for the Author. Feb. 1808. 12mo, pp. 18.

Leicester. *Auditors' Report.* To the Taxpayers of the Town of Leicester. 1871. 8vo, pp. 7.
Continued.

Leland, John. *The Blow at the Root.* Being a fashionable Fast Day Sermon Delivered in Cheshire, April 9, 1801. By John Leland. Motto. Bennington: A. Haswell, Printer. 1802.

—*Oration,* Delivered at Bennington, Vt., August 16, 1808. By John Leland. Bennington: Printed by Anthony Haswell. 1808. 8vo.

Mr. Leland resided at Cheshire, Mass.

Leonard, George. *A Sermon* delivered on the day of General Election, at Montpelier, October 12, A. D. 1820. Before the Honorable Legislature of Vermont. By George Leonard, A. M. Rector of St. Paul's Church, Windsor, Vt., and Trinity Church, Cornish, N. H. Published by Request of the General Assembly. Windsor, Vt.: Printed for the State, By Ide & Aldrich. October, 1820. 8vo, pp. 28.

—*A Discourse* Delivered at Trinity Church, Cornish, (N. H.) November 24, and at St. Paul's Church, Windsor, Vt., December 1, 1825: The days appointed in those States, respectively, by the Civil Authority, as Days of general Thanksgiving for the fruits of the earth, and other blessings of a merciful Providence. By George Leonard, A. M. Rector of St. Paul's Church, Windsor, (Vt.) and Trinity Church, Cornish, (N. H.) Published by request of said Societies.

Windsor: Printed by Simeon Ide. [n. d.] 12mo, pp. 8.

Mr. Leonard was born in Middleborough, Mass., April 6, 1783; was graduated at Dartmouth College, 1805, and settled over a Congregational Church in Connecticut; became an Episcopalian, and was Rector of St. Paul's Church, Windsor, Vt., 1818-1829; and died soon after the latter date.

Leonard, Samuel. *The Substance* of a Discourse, delivered at Poultney, Vt., in the New Meeting-House, on the Fourth of July, 1804. Being the Twenty-Eighth Anniversary of American Independence. By Samuel Leonard, Pastor of the Congregational Church in Poultney. Salem: Printed by Dodd & Rumsey. 1804. 16mo, pp. 33.

Leonard, Seth. *Spelling Book.* Rutland: 1816. 12mo, pp. 228.

A Letter *to the House of Representatives* in Congress Assembled, and to the Citizens of the United States, on the Nebraska Bill. (Signed A Citizen of Vermont.) Philadelphia: Printed. n. d. n. p. 8vo, pp. 16.

—*From a Blacksmith* to the Ministers and Elders of the Church of Scotland, in which the manner of public worship in that Church is considered; its inconveniences and defects pointed out; and methods for removing them humbly proposed. Motto. Burlington: Edward Smith. 1833. 18mo, pp. 108.

—*From an Elder* to a Younger Brother, on the Conduct to be pursued in Life. Middlebury, Vt.: Printed and Published by W. Slade, Jun. 1815. 24mo, pp. 119.

Leterz, *Moral, Political and Theological.* Jon. R. Forest, Editor and Publisher. Published Monthly, at 30 cents per year. Vol. I. No. 7. Winooski Falls, Vt., 1857. 8vo, pp. 8.

—*Moral, Political and Theological.* Jon. R. Forest, Editor and Publisher. Published Monthly, At 30 cents per year. Radical, Rational and Reasonable. Winooski Falls, Vt., 1858. Vol. 2. No. 5. 8vo, pp. 8.
Continued.

Levings, I. H. *Character of St. Paul* as a Preacher. An Address delivered before the Society for Religious Inquiry In the University of Vermont, August 2, 1857. By Rev. I. H. Levings. Burlington: Free Press Print. 1857. 8vo. pp. 31.

Levings, Noah. *The Christian Instructor Instructed.* Middlebury: 1827. 12mo, pp. 237.
See Hopkins, Josiah.

Lewis, M. G. *Abellino,* the Bravo of Venice. Translated from the German, by M. G. Lewis. Motto. Woodstock, Vt.: Published by Rufus Colton. 1832. 24mo, pp. 159.

Lewis, R. W. *Christian* Thanksgiving Perpetual. A Sermon preached by Rev. Robert W. Lewis, Sheldon, Vt., November 28th, 1861. Burlington: W. H. & C. A. Hoyt & Co., Printers. 1861. 8vo, pp. 14.

Lewis, Tayler. *Natural Religion* the Remains of Primitive Revelation. A Discourse, pronounced at Burlington before the Literary Societies of the University of Vermont, August 6th, 1839. By Tayler Lewis, Esq., Prof. of Greek and Latin, in the University of New York. Published at the request of the Societies. New York: Printed at the University Press, 36 Ann Street. 1839. 8vo, pp. 52.

Lighton, William Beebey. *Memoirs* of the Life of William Beebey Lighton : [Minister of the Gospel.] written by Himself. Motto. Wells River, Vt.: White & Clark, Printers. 1835. 16mo, pp. 244.

Lindsay, John W. *The English Language.* By Rev. J. W. Lindsay. From the Methodist Quarterly Review, April, 1861. 8vo, pp. 14.

Mr. Lindsay was born at Barre, Vt., Aug. 20, 1820; was graduated at Wesleyan University in 1840; studied theology at Union Seminary; preached at various Methodist churches in Mass., and N. Y.; was professor at Wesleyan University, 1848-60, and since 1868 has been connected with Boston University. (1880.)

Lindsey, Rev. John. *A Discourse,* Delivered before the Honorable Legislature of Vermont, on the Anniversary Election, October 10, 1822. By John Lindsey, Minister in the Methodist Episcopal Church. Montpelier, Vt.: Printed by E. P. Walton, 1822. 8vo, pp. 27.

Elder Lindsey was born in Lyme, Mass., July 18, 1788. He was converted at the age of eighteen years and became a Methodist preacher, and was Presiding Elder for the District of Vermont, 1818-1822. He died February 20, 1850. His biographer and descendants spell his name Lindsay; but in his Election Sermon it is printed as we give it.

See Sprague's Annals, Vol. 7 pp. 473-475.

Lincoln, B. *Hints* on the present State of Medical Education and the influence of Medical Schools in New England. With an appendix Containing a Review of a Letter by T. Woodward, M. D., addressed to Professor Lincoln and first published in the Vermont States-man of the 19th March, 1833. Motto. By Benjamin Lincoln. Burlington: Printed for the Author. 1833. 8vo, pp. 18, 9.

—*Dr. Lincoln's Appeal*, with Dr. Woodward's Letter to Professor Lincoln &c, reprinted in part from various Newspapers, in 1832-3. 8vo, pp. XVI, 76.

This paper war appears to have grown out of a rivalry between the Medical Department of the University of Vermont, and the Medical College at Castleton, Vt., primarily, on account of the admission of three Canadian Students to the former Institution.

—*An Exposition* of Certain Abuses, practiced by some of the Medical Schools in New England ; and particularly, of the Agent-Sending System, as practiced by Theodore Woodward, M. D. Addressed to Medical Gentlemen in the State of Vermont. By Benjamin Lincoln. Burlington : Printed for the Author. 1833. pp. 76.

Dr. Lincoln was professor of Anatomy and Surgery in the University of Vermont, 1829-34; he was born in Dennysville, Maine, in October, 1802, and died there, February 26th, 1835.

See Miss Hemenway's Historical Gazetteer of Vermont, Vol. 1, pp. 648-9, for sketch of his life.

Lincoln, R. W. *Lives of the Presidents* of the United States ; with Biographical Notices of the Signers of the Declaration of Independence; Sketches of the most remarkable Events in the History of the Country. By Robert W. Lincoln. Brattleboro, Vt.: Typographic Co. 1839. 8vo, pp. vi, 522. Plate.

—*Another Edition :* Brattleboro, Vt.: Published by G. H. Salisbury. 1850. 8vo, pp. vi, 445, 169.

Linsley, Daniel Chipman. *Morgan Horses :* A Premium Essay on the Origin, History, and Characteristics of this Remarkable American Breed of Horses. By D. C. Linsley, Middlebury, Vt. New York : C. M. Saxton and Company. 1857. 12mo, pp. (2), 340. Plates.

—*Linsley's Report* of his Survey of a Road from the Foot to the Summit of Mount Mansfield. Made October, 1865. Montpelier. 1866. 8vo, pp. 7.

Linsley, Rev. Joel H. *A Sermon* delivered at the Dedication of the Second or South Congregational Church, in Hartford, (Con.) April 11, 1827. By Joel H. Linsley, Pastor of said Church. Hartford : Published by D. F. Robinson & Co. P. Canfield, Printer. 1827. 8vo, pp. 32.

—*Lectures* on the Relations and Duties of the Middle Aged. By Joel Harvey Linsley, Pastor of the South Church in Hartford. Hartford : Published by D. F. Robinson & Co. Hudson and Skinner, Printers. 1828. 12mo, pp. 180.

—*The First Annual Address*, delivered before the Hartford Peace Society, at the Central Meeting House, March 18th, 1829. By Joel H. Linsley, with the First Annual Report of the Executive Committee, Treasurer's Account, and New Constitution. Published by the Hartford Peace Society. Hartford : Printed by Philemon Canfield. 1829. 8vo, pp. 24.

—*Address* delivered at the Annual Commencement of the Marietta College, Ohio, by Joel H. Linsley, D. D., on occasion of his Inauguration to the Presidency of that Institution, July 25, 1838. Published by order of the Trustees. Cincinnati : A. Pugh, P'r., Corner of Fifth and Main. 1838. 8vo, pp. 28.

—*A Commemorative Discourse*, delivered on the occasion of meeting for the last time in the Old House of Worship of the Second Congregational Church in Greenwich, December 5th, 1858. By Joel H. Linsley, D. D., Pastor of the Church. Together with complete lists of members from the organization of the church. New York: John A. Gray, Printer. 1860. 8 vo, pp. 51.

—*Judgment* tempered with Mercy. A Discourse preached in the Second Congregational Church, Greenwich, Conn., on the 27th day of November, 1862, appointed by the Governor of the State as the day of Annual Thanksgiving. By Rev. Joel H. Linsley, D. D., Pastor of the Church. New York : John F. Trow, Book and Job Printer. 1863. 8vo, pp. 18.

—*Exercises* at the Celebration of the 150th Anniversary of the Second Congregational Church, Greenwich, Conn., Wednesday, November 7th, 1866, including an Historical Discourse, by Rev. Joel H. Linsley, D. D., and Historical Sketches and Addresses from others. New York: Clark & Maynard, Publishers. 1867. pp. 108.

Rev. Dr. Linsley was born in Cornwall, Vt., July 16, 1790, and died in Greenwich, Conn., March 22, 1868. He was graduated at Middlebury, 1811; studied law at Vergennes with Mr. Edmond, and was a partner with Peter Starr, Middlebury, 1815-22. Studied theology, and was settled at Hartford, Conn., and Boston, until 1835; then President of Marietta College, Ohio, 1835-46; when he settled in Greenwich as pastor of the second Congregational society, where he remained until his death. He published in addition, a Master's Oration, 1814; an Oration on the Moral History of the United States, 1818; Address before the Connecticut Peace Society; two Reviews in the "Christian Spectator."

Linsley, Sarah W. *A Memorial* of Sarah W. Linsley, [first wife of Hon. Charles Linsley]. By Rev. Jacob W. Diller, Rector of St. Stephen's Church. Middlebury: Free Press Print. 1841. 8vo, pp. 14.

Literary and Philosophical Repertory.
See Middlebury.

Livermore, A. A. *A Sermon* at the Ordination of James Thurston. Windsor: Printed by Tracy and Severance. 1838. 8vo, pp. 16.

—*The Faith* once delivered to the Saints. A Discourse delivered at the Dedication of the Unitarian Meeting House in Windsor, Vt., Wednesday, December 9, 1846, By Rev. A. A. Livermore, Pastor of the Unitarian Church in Keene, N. H. Boston: Wm. Crosby and H. P. Nichols, 118 Washington Street. 1847. 8vo, pp. 28.

Livermore Association. *Report* to the Livermore Association, U. S. A., Made by Josiah Q. Hawkins, Agent, A. D. 1865, Containing Information already collected in America and England relative to the Livermore property in England; The Crest and Coat of Arms of the Family, likewise a Genealogy of the Livermore Family in England and America, so far collected. [Published by order of the Livermore Association.] Rutland: John Cain, Steam Job Printer. 1865. 8vo, pp. 38.

—*Report* to the Livermore Association, U. S. A., Made by Josiah Q. Hawkins, Agent, Brandon, Vt. Oct. 7. 1867. 12mo, pp. 8.

Locke, John. *An Essay* on the Human Understanding, with Selections from his other Writings, and a Life of the Author. Three volumes. Brattleborough: 1806. 12mo.

Locke, Putnam F. *Locke's Sermons.* Sermons written by Putnam F. Locke, of Ira, Vermont. In the Year of our Lord, 1804, A youth only thirteen years of age. Rutland: Printed for the Author. 12mo, pp. 24.

Loomis, Rev. Harmon.
Dr. Loomis was a native of Georgia, Vt., and died at Brooklyn, N. Y., January 26, 1880, aged 73. He was educated at the University of Vermont, and read theology at Andover and Princeton; for thirty years he was engaged in the work of the "American Seaman's Friend Society," and for the last twenty-five years of his life resided in Brooklyn.
Dr. Loomis published "Shadowing Wings," and some other books, of which we have not the titles. He spent several years in arranging the Bible in chronological order, which work was completed just before his death.

Lord, John K. *The Dangers* of the Scholar. An Address delivered before the Gamma Sigma Society of Dartmouth College, July 24, 1844. By the Rev. John K. Lord, of Hartford, Vt. Published at the request of the Society. Boston: James Monroe & Company. 1844. 8vo, pp. 32.

—*The Influence* exerted upon our Youth, and its effects. An Address delivered before the Senior Class of Kimball Union Academy Meriden, N. H., May 5, 1845. By the Rev. John K. Lord, of Hartford, Vt. Windsor, Vt.: Printed at the Chronicle Press. 1845. 8vo, pp. 24.
John King Lord, brother of the late William H., of Montpelier, was born in Amherst, N. H., March 22, 1819,

and died in Cincinnati, Ohio, July 13, 1849. He was graduated at Dartmouth College, 1836, and at Andover Theological Seminary 1841; was pastor of the Congregational Church, Hartford, Vt., 1841-1847, and of the Congregational Church in Cincinnati, 1847, until his death.

Lord, Nathan, D. D. *An Address* delivered at Hanover, October 29, 1828, at the Inauguration of the Author as President of Dartmouth College. By Nathan Lord, D. D. (Published by Request.) Windsor, Vt. 1828. Simeon Ide, Printer. 8vo, pp. 28.

—*The Resurrection.* A Sermon, preached April 3, 1859, on occasion of the death of Rev. John Richards, D. D., Pastor of the Church at Dartmouth College. By Nathan Lord, President. Concord: 1859. 8vo, pp. 26.

Lord, W. H. *A Sermon* on occasion of the Death of Hon. John McLean, Preached in Cabot, Vt., Feb. 7, 1855, By W. H. Lord, Montpelier, Vt. Montpelier: E. P. Walton, Jr., Printer. 1855. 8vo, pp. 30.

—*The Present* and the Future. A Sermon on Occasion of the Death of Mrs. Lucretia Prentiss, wife of Hon. Samuel Prentiss, Preached at Montpelier, Vt., June 17, 1855. By W. H. Lord, Montpelier, Vt. Montpelier: E. P. Walton, Jr., Printer. 1855. 8vo, pp. 24.

—*A Tract for the Times.* By Rev. W. H. Lord, Montpelier, Vt. National Hospitality. Montpelier: E. P. Walton, Jr., Publisher. Walton's Steam Press. 1855. 8vo, pp. 48.

—*The Remembrance* of the Righteous. A Sermon on occasion of the Death of Gen. Ezekiel P. Walton. Preached at Montpelier, Vt., November 29, 1855. By W. H. Lord, Montpelier, Vt. Montpelier: E. P. Walton, Printer. 1856. 8vo, pp. 24.

—*Life*, Death, Immortality. A Sermon on occasion of the death of Samuel Prentiss, LL.D. Preached in the Congregational Church, Montpelier, January 18, 1857. By Rev. Wm. H. Lord. Montpelier: E. P. Walton, Printer. 1857. 8vo, pp. 23.

—*A City* which Hath Foundations. A Sermon Preached on occasion of the Fiftieth Anniversary of the Organization of the First Congregational Church in Montpelier, Vermont, July 25, 1858. By W. H. Lord, Pastor. Montpelier: E. P. Walton, Printer. 1858. 8vo, pp. 32.

—*A Sermon* on occasion of the death of Hon. Ferrand F. Merrill, preached in the Congregational Church, Montpelier, May 8, 1859, By Rev. W. H. Lord. Montpelier: E. P. Walton, Printer. 1859. 8vo, pp. 24.

—*A Sermon* on the Causes and Remedy of the National Troubles. Preached at Montpelier, Vt., April 4th, 1861. By Rev. Wm. H. Lord. Published by Request. Montpelier: E. P. Walton, Printer. 1861. 8vo, pp. 22.

—*A Sermon* on occasion of the Death of Rev. James Hobart, preached in the Congregational Church, Berlin, Vt., July 18, 1862. By Rev. Wm. H. Lord. Montpelier: Walton's Steam Printing Establishment. 1862. 8vo, pp. 20.

—*In Memoriam.* Address at the Funeral of Mrs. James T. Thurston, Montpelier, Vt., April 3, 1865. 8vo, pp. 16. Also includes Obituary from Walton's Daily Journal, April 4, 1865.

—*The Uses* of the Material Temple. A Sermon Preached at the Dedication of Bethany Church, Montpelier, Vt., By Rev. W. H. Lord, Pastor, October 15, 1868. Montpelier: J. & J. Poland's Steam Printing Establishment. 1868. 8vo, pp. 30, (1).

—*Address* and Services at the Funeral of Dea. Constant W. Storrs, Montpelier, Vermont, March 26, 1872. Montpelier: J. & J. M. Poland, Printers. 1872. 8vo, pp. 19.

—*Woman's Mission* for Christ. A Sermon preached at the Funeral of Mrs. James R. Langdon, at Montpelier, Vermont, Aug. 3, 1873. By W. H. Lord. Montpelier: Printed by J. & J. M. Poland. 1873. 8vo, pp. 21, (3).

—*Sketch* of the Life of Hon. Samuel Prentiss, published in the U. S. Law Magazine.

—*Address* to the Princeton, (N. J.) Theological Students, 1876.
Rev. William Hayes Lord, D. D., was born in Amherst, N. H., March 11, 1824, and died at Montpelier, Vt., March 18, 1877. He was the fifth son of Rev. Nathan Lord, D. D., President of Dartmouth College, where he graduated in 1843, and at Andover Theological Seminary in 1846. Dr. Lord was pastor of the Congregational church at Montpelier from 1847 until his death. He was President of the Vermont Historical Society from 1870 to 1876, and was a liberal benefactor of the same. He wrote articles for the Princeton *Review*, and was for some time associate editor of the *Vermont Watchman*, and of the *Vermont Chronicle*. For sketch of his life see "Congregational Minutes" of Vermont, 1877.

Loveland, S. C. *The Wrestler*, who found an Evil Beast, contended with him, and threw him: Being an Answer to Mr. Peck's Poem: "Descant on the Universal Plan." Weathersfield, Vt.: Printed by Eddy and Patrick. 1814. pp. 32.
See Peck, John.

—*A Plain Answer* to 'A Sermon Delivered at Rutland West Parish in the year 1805; entitled, "Universal Salvation: A Very Ancient Doctrine: With Some Account of the Life, and Character of its Author. By Lemuel Haynes, A. M." In Prose and Poetry Composition. Weathersfield, Vt.: Printed by Eddy and Patrick. 1815. 8vo, pp. 27.

—*Greek Lexicon* of the New Testament. Woodstock, Vt.: 1828. 18mo.
See Christian Repository.

Luce, Samuel S. and Hannah G. *Poems.* By S. S. and H. G. Luce. Trempeleau: Chas. A. Leith, Publisher. 1876. 12mo, pp. 208.
Mr. Luce is from Stowe, and Mrs. Luce from Waterbury, born Dec. 28, 1824; they moved to Galesville, Wis., in 1857.
See Vt. Hist. Gaz. Vol. 4. pp. 855.

Ludlow. *Annual Reports* of the Selectmen and Auditors for the town of Ludlow, Vt., February 20th, 1856. Ludlow: Bacon and Warner, Printers, Blotter Office. 1856. 8vo, pp. 13.
Continued.

—*Annual Report* of the Auditors and Selectmen for the Town of Ludlow, for the year ending Feb. 18, 1871. Ludlow: Office of Black River Gazette. 1871. 8vo, pp. 10.
Continued.

—*Constitution and By-Laws* of Green Mountain Lodge, No. 1, I. O. of G. T., Ludlow, Vt. Ludlow: R. S. Warner, Book and Job Printer. 1860. 18mo, pp. 28, (1).

Lunenburg. *Manual* for the use of the Congregational Church, in Lunenburg, Vt. Windsor: Printed at the Vermont Chronicle Press. 1859. 18mo, pp. 24.

Lydius, John Henry.
See Some Reflections, under Vermont. For a Sketch of Lydius, see Vermont Historical Gazetteer, Vol. 3, p. 572, note.

Lyman, Charles. *Sermon* on the Occasion of the death of Charles Lyman, Esq. By Charles Wadsworth. November, 1848. Troy, N. Y.: J. C. Kneeland and Co.'s Steam Press. 1849. 8vo, pp. 36.
Mr. Lyman was born in Bennington, Vt., October 17, 1794. He was for many years a druggist in Troy, N. Y., where he died.

Lyman, Elijah. *A Sermon,* delivered on the day of General Election, At Montpelier, October 13, 1814, before the Honorable Legislature of Vermont. By Elijah Lyman, A. M. Pastor of the Congregational Church in Brookfield. Published at the request of the Legislature. Montpelier, Vt.: Printed by Walton and Goss, October, 1814. 8vo, pp. 28.

—*A Discourse,* delivered at the Ordination of the Rev. William Salisbury, to the Pastoral care of the Church in Waitsfield, October 7, 1801. By Elijah Lyman, A. M., Pastor of the Church in Brookfield. Printed at Randolph, Vt., by Wright & Denio. 1801. 8vo, pp. 20.

—*A Discourse* Commemorative of George Washington, delivered before the Washington Benevolent Society, at Chelsea, Vt., February 22, 1811.
Title from Brinley Catalogue, Part 2, p. 192.
Mr. Lyman was born in Lebanon, Ct., March, 1764; he was graduated at Dartmouth College, 1787, and was settled over the Congregational church in Brookfield, Vt., 1789, until his death, April 12, 1828.

Lyman, Gershom C. *A Sermon,* Preached at Manchester, Before His Excellency Thomas Chittenden, Esq., Governor; His Honor Paul Spooner, Esq., Lieut. Governor; The Honorable Council, and The Honorable House of Representatives of the State of Vermont, On the Day of the Anniversary Election, October 10, 1782. By Gershom C. Lyman, A. M. Pastor of the Church of Marlborough. God gives Wisdom to the wise, and Knowledge to those who know Understanding—Daniel ii, 21. The Price of Wisdom is above Rubies —Job xxviii, 18. Windsor: Printed by Hough and Spooner. M.DCC.LXXXIV. Small 4to, pp. 20.

—*A Sermon,* Preached at Wilmington, at the funeral of Jesse Cook, Esq. By Gershom C. Lyman, Pastor of the Church in Marlboro. Bennington: Printed by Haswell and Russell. 1790.

—*A Sermon* Preached to the Young People in Marlborough, at their request, May 31, 1809. By Gershom C. Lyman, A. M. Brattleborough: Wm. Fessenden. 1809.

—*A Sermon* preached at Marlborough, on the Public Fast, August 20th, 1812. By Gershom C. Lyman, D. D., Pastor of the Church in said Town. Brattleborough, (Vt.) Printed by William Fessenden. 1812. 12mo, pp. 23.
Mr. Lyman was born in Lebanon, Ct., in 1752; he was graduated at Yale College in 1773, and settled over the Congregational church in Marlboro, Vt., December 9, 1778, where he continued until his death, April 13, 1813.

Lyman, Joseph. *Sermon* at Halifax, Vt., Sept. 17, 1806, at the Installation of Thomas H. Wood. Northampton: 1807. 8vo.

Lynch, Anne C. See Botta.

Lynde, John. *A Key to English Grammar,* In which the most difficult Examples of Syntax are Illustrated. To abridge the labour of the Instructor, and facilitate the progress of the Learner. By John Lynde. Woodstock: Printed by D. Watson. 1821. 18mo, pp. 108.

Mr. Lynde was a native of Plymouth, Vt. Studied medicine in Woodstock, practiced in Plymouth, and in Maine, where he died,

Lyndon. *Sketch* of the History of.
See Greenleaf, Jonathan.

Lyne, Richard. *The Latin Primer, Part I.* Containing Rules of Construction, etc. By the Rev. Richard Lyne, Late master of the grammar school at Liskeard. Abridged for the use of Schools. Burlington, Vt. Printed by Samuel Mills. 1813. 12mo, pp. 18.

Lyon, Asa, A. M. *The Depravity* and Misery of Man. A Sermon delivered before the Vermont Missionary Society, at their Annual Meeting, at Woodstock, September 15, 1814. By Asa Lyon, A. M., Pastor of the Congregational Church in South Hero. Middlebury, Vt. Printed by Timothy C. Strong. 1815. ' 8vo, pp. 23.

Mr. Lyon was born in Pomfret, Ct., December 31, 1763; and died at South Hero, Vt., April 4, 1841. He was graduated at Dartmouth College, 1790; and was pastor of the Congregational church, at South Hero, 1802-1840. He was a member of Congress, 1815-17; 13 years in the Vermont Legislature, 9 years a Judge of Grand Isle County; and was regarded as one of the most talented men in the State. He published Sermons, Speeches, etc., a dozen or more. For a sketch of his life, see Dartmouth Alumni; Vermont Historical Gazetteer, Vol. 2, pp. 550-554.

Lyon, James *A Republican Magazine;* Or, Repository of Political Truths. By James Lyon, of Fairhaven, Vermont.

Nature has left this Tincture in the Blood,
That all Men would be Tyrants if they cou'd,
If they forbear their Neighbors to devour,
'Tis not for want of Will, but want of power.
    De Foe's Jure Divino.

Published at Fairhaven, (Vt.) M,DCC,XCVIII. 16mo, pp. 192.

This volume is composed of numbers 1 to 4 inclusive, bearing date from October 1, to December 15, 1798, under the following title: "The Scourge of Aristocracy, and Repository of Important Political Truths;" it relates almost entirely to the arrest, trial, conviction and imprisonment of Matthew Lyon, for an alleged violation of the odious alien and sedition laws passed under the administration of John Adams. James Lyon was a son of Matthew.
See White, P. H., Life of Matthew Lyon; also, Governor and Council of Vermont, Vol. 1, pp. 123-128; Adams' History of Fairhaven,

Lyon, Matthew. *Copy* of a Memorial of Matthew Lyon, forwarded to Congress by His Excellency, Governor Chittenden. Fairhaven, October 6, 1795. Broadsheet.

Protesting against the election of Mr. Israel Smith to Congress.
See Adams' History of Fairhaven; White, P. H., for sketches of the life of Lyon; also Governor and Council of Vermont, Vol. 1, pp 123-8.

—*Report of the Committee* on Privileges, to whom was referred on the sixteenth instant, a motion for the expulsion of Roger Griswold and Matthew Lyon, members of this House, for riotous and disorderly behavior, committed in the House, 20th February, 1798. Published by

order of the House of Representatives. Philadelphia, 1798. 8vo, pp, 24.

Mack, David. *Genealogical Records* of the Descendants of David Mack, to 1879, by Sophia Smith and Charles S. Smith. Rutland, Vt.: Tuttle & Company, Printers. 1879. 8vo, pp. 81.

Mack, Solomon.
(Title page wanting.)
Life of Solomon Mack, born in Connecticut in 1735, was a soldier in the French war, and spent the latter years of his life in Tunbridge, Vt.
12mo, 46 pages, including hymns composed and selected on different occasions.

Magill, S. W. *A Sermon,* preached at the funeral of Rev. Jedediah Bushnell, August 22, 1846, by Rev. Seagrove W. Magill, A. M., Pastor of the Congregational Church, Cornwall, Vt. Middlebury: Justus Cobb, Printer, 1847. 8vo, pp. 15.

—*An Address* delivered at the Temperance Tea-Party of the Young Men's Temperance Society, Middlebury, Wednesday evening, Feb. 26, 1845, By Rev. S. W. Magill, of Cornwall. Middlebury: J. Cobb, Printer. 8vo, pp. 16.

Mallary, Charles Daniel.
A brother of Rollin C. Mallary, and born in Poultney, Vt., January 23, 1801, was graduated at Middlebury College in 1821; he went South, and taught school several years: became a Baptist preacher, and was settled at Charleston and Columbia, S. C., for many years. He was the founder of Mercer University, and published the life of Elder Jesse Mercer, and several other works. He resided some time at Albany, Ga., and died in 1864.

Mallary, Rollin C. *An Oration* pronounced at the republican celebration of our National Independence, at Poultney, (Vt.) July 4, 1810. By Rollin C. Mallary, Esq. Published by request of the committee. Rutland: Printed by William Fay. 1810. 8vo, pp. 20.

—*An Oration* addressed to Republicans assembled at Poultney, Vt., July 4, 1814. By R. C. Mallary, Esq. Published by request of the auditors. Rutland: Printed by Fay & Davidson. 8vo, pp. 19.

—*Oration* at Whitehall, N. Y., July 4, 1817. 8vo. n. p. n. d.

—*An Address* delivered before the Association of the Alumni of Middlebury College, on the Evening of Commencement, August 18, 1824, By R. C. Mallary. Published by Request of the Association. Rutland: Printed by Wm. Fay. 1824. 8vo, pp. 27.

—*An Oration* pronounced at Rutland Fourth July, 1826; Being the Fiftieth Anniversary of American Independence, and the Year of Jubilee. By R. C. Mallary. [Published by Request of Committee of Arrangements.] Rutland: Published by William Fay. Brewster and Purdy, Printers. 8vo, pp. 24.

—*Speech* of Mr. Mallary, of Vermont. On the Tariff Bill. Delivered in the House of Representatives of the United States, March 3, 1828. Washington: Printed by Gales & Seaton. 1828. 8vo, pp. 34.

—*Speech* of Mr. Mallary, on the Tariff and Manufactures. January 13, 1831.

Mr. Mallary was born in Cheshire, Ct., May 7, 1784, and died in Baltimore, Md., in 1831, on his way from Congress. He was graduated at Middlebury College in 1805, and became a leading lawyer in Western Vermont, residing at Castleton, 1807-18, and at Poultney, 1818, until his death.

He held several local offices, and was a member of Congress, 1820, until his death.

Manchester. *Summary of Christian Doctrine, and Form of Covenant ;* adopted by the Congregational Church, in Manchester, Vt., October 14, 1829. Motto. Manchester : J. C. Osrum, Printer, 1838. 12mo, pp. 10.

—*Exercises* in Commemoration of the Fiftieth Anniversary of the Ordination of Rev. James Anderson As Pastor of the Congregational Church, Manchester, Vt., August 12, 1879. Manchester : D. K. Simonds, Printer. 1879. 8vo, pp. 52, (1.)
Contains an interesting history of the church.

—*Manchester and its Vicinity ;* A Guide Book for the use of the Guests of the Equinox House, Manchester, Vt. With Illustrations by W. H. Tyler and John Ross Dix. Boston : Geo. C. Rand & Avery. 1862. sm. 4to, pp. 11.

—*Manual* of the Congregational Church, in Manchester, Vt. Printed by order of the Church. Manchester : Printed by C. A. Pierce & Co. 1867. 18mo, pp. 82.

—*History of,*
See Munson, Loveland.

Manning, Samuel. *An attempt* to reconcile the doctrine of Election, Regeneration, and Salvation by Grace alone, with the Free Agency, Ability, Accountability and Criminality of Sinners : With remarks on the turpitude of Original Sin. Originally written in a letter to a Friend. By Samuel Manning. Motto. Windsor, Vt.: Printed by Alden Spooner. March, 1807. 16mo, pp. 70.

Mansfield, Mrs. Lucy (Langdon.) *Memorial* of Charles Finney Mansfield, Comprising extracts from his Diaries, Letters, and other Papers. New York : Baker & Goodwin, Printers. 1866. 8vo, 265, (2).
Mrs. Mansfield, daughter of James R. Langdon, of Montpelier, was born in Berlin, Vt., in 1841; and married the subject of this Memorial in 1861; he died in August, 1865. Mrs. Mansfield has since married again, and resides in the city of New York.

Maranville, R. E. *Catarrh and Rheumatism* can be cured. Proof. Facts for the Faithless and Unbelieving. By R. E. Maranville, Castleton, Vt. Rutland : Tuttle & Co., Printers. 1872. 12mo, pp. 16.
A Native of Poultney, was graduated at Middlebury College, and some time a teacher at Castleton Seminary.

Mansfield, John Brainerd.
Was born in Andover, Windsor Co., Vt., March 16, 1826, and died in Effingham, Kan., Oct. 29, 1886. He received an academic education, and was for several years engaged in canvassing for books and maps. He published with Austin J. Coolidge the first volume of a "History of the New England States," (Boston, 1860), but the civil war prevented the appearance of the second and remaining volume, which had been prepared for the press. After establishing a weekly paper called the "New England Meridian," he acted as war correspondent for that journal. In 1866 he published in Washington, D. C., "The American Loyalist," in which were printed biographies and speeches of members of the 39th congress. In 1867 he published a campaign paper in Baltimore, Md., after which he returned to Washington and was employed in the government printing office for several years. While in Washington he began the preparation of "A Sketch of the Political History of the United States of America," from the settlement of Jamestown to the present time, which he completed, but it still remains in manuscript.
See Coolidge, A. J., and Mansfield, J. B.

Manum, A. E. *A. E. Manum's Third Annual Circular* and Price List of Bee Hives, Section Boxes, Clamps, Comb Foundation, Crates, Italian Queens, etc. Bristol, Vermont. 1880. Herald Print, Bristol, Vt. 18mo, pp. 29.

Marble. *Report* of Albert D. Hager, State Geologist of Vermont, on the Winooski Marble Quarries, at St. Albans, Vt. Boston : 1866. 8vo, pp. 7, map.

—*The American* Marble Company, Incorporated by Special Act of the Legislature of Vermont. Capital Stock, $250,000, Shares $10. Not Subject to Assessment. Rutland, Vt. Tuttle & Company, Printers. 1867. 12mo, pp. 24.

—*The New American* Marble Company, Incorporated by Special Act of the Legislature of Vermont. Capital Stock $200,000. Shares, $100. Not subject to assessment. Rutland, Vt.: Tuttle & Company, Printers. 1871. 12mo, pp. 12.

—*Central Vermont Marble Co.*, Pittsford, Vermont. Charter, By-Laws and Reports of Prof. C. H. Hitchcock, Prof. J. S. Newbury, and others. New York : Town, Gildersleeve & Co., Printers. 78 Chambers St. 1873. 8vo, pp. 32.

Markoe, T. M., M. D. *An Introductory* Lecture, delivered in the Castleton Medical College, at the opening of the Spring session, 1847. By T. M. Markoe, M. D. Professor of Descriptive and Pathological Anatomy at the Castleton Medical College, and Lecturer on Pathological Anatomy at the N. Y. Hospital. Published by the Class. Troy, N. Y.: Steam Press of J. C. Kneeland and Co. 1847. 8vo, pp. 19.

Marlborough, Manuscript History of.
See Newton, Ephraim H.

Marsh, Rev. Abram. *The Importance* of the Sanctuary. A Sermon preached at the Dedication of the Congregational Church, in Tolland, Connecticut, October 25, 1838. By Abram Marsh, Pastor of the Congregational Church and Society in Tolland. Published by request. Hartford : Printed by John L. Boswell. 1839. 8vo, pp. 20.

—*A Discourse,* Reason for Law, with some special reference to the Traffic in Intoxicating Liquors, [delivered on Thanksgiving Day, Nov. 27th, 1845.] By Abram Marsh, [Published by request.] Pastor of the Congregational Church in Tolland, Conn. Hartford Courant Office Press. 1845. 8vo, pp. 15.

—*A Discourse* delivered on the Occasion of the death of Mrs. Presendia Benton, wife of Dea. Azariah Benton, who died April 23, 1851. By Rev. Abram Marsh. Pastor of the Congregational Church in Tolland, Ct. Published by request. Hartford : Printed by D. B. Moseley. 1851. 8vo, pp. 12.

—*The Liquor Traffic,* and Prohibitory Law. By Rev. Abram Marsh, Tolland, Conn. [1854.] 8vo, pp. 16.

—*A Discourse,* on occasion of the Death of Deacon William A. Sumner, of the Baptist Church, Tolland, Conn., who died Friday, August 21, 1868. By Rev. Abram Marsh, Pastor of the Congregational Church in Tolland. Printed by request of the Bereaved Family. Hartford : Printed by D. B. Moseley & Son. 1868. 8vo, pp. 13.

—*The Spirit of Christ* in His Ministers. A Sermon Preached at the Funeral of Rev. William D. Baldwin, July 13, 1872. Pastor of the Congregational Church, Willington, Conn. By Rev. Abram Marsh. Together with a brief Sketch of his life. Published by Request. Willimantic : Journal Steam Job Printing. 1872. 8vo, pp. 8.

Mr. Marsh was born in Hartford, Vt., June 15, 1802; and died in Tolland, Conn., September 2, 1877; he was educated at Thetford Academy, Dartmouth College, 1825, and Andover Theological Seminary, 1828. Ordained Evangelist at Reading, Vt., June 23, 1829, and preached there 1829-30; then installed at Tolland, Conn., where he continued as pastor, 1831-1869.

Marsh, Charles. *Essay :*
See Vermont Constitutional Convention, 1814.

—*A Vindication* of the Official Conduct of the Trustees of Dartmouth College, in Answer to "Sketches of the History of Dartmouth College," and "A candid analytical review of the Sketches," &c. Published by the Trustees. Concord : Printed by George Hough. September, 1815. 8vo, pp. 104.

Mr. Marsh was a distinguished lawyer of Woodstock, Vt. Born in Lebanon, Conn., July 10, 1765; and died in Woodstock, January 11, 1849. He came to Hartford, Vt., in 1774, and settled at Woodstock in 1779. He was the father of Hon. George P. Marsh.

See Barrett, J., for sketch of Mr. Marsh and his ancestry, in Memorial Address before the Vermont Historical Society, 1870; Governor and Council, Vol. I, pp. 235-38, for history of the Hartford branch of the Marsh family.

Marsh, Charles P. *Centennial Oration* delivered before the Citizens of Woodstock, Vt., and Vicinity, on the Fourth of July, 1876. By Charles P. Marsh. Beach, Barnard & Co., Printers, 98 Randolph Street, Chicago, Ills. 8vo, pp. 29.

Mr. Marsh has contributed many articles to newspapers, among others an able article on the famous lawyers of Windsor county, in the "Republican Observer," April 13, 1878.

Mr. Marsh was born at Weathersfield, Vt., January 7, 1816; graduated at the University of Vermont, 1839; read law with Hon. O. P. Chandler, Woodstock, and formed a law partnership with the late Gov. Washburn in 1870; member of the Constitutional Convention of 1870; representative in General Assembly, 1886-90; died January 13, 1893. He was twice married, in 1844 to Miss Mary Elizabeth Wright, who died in 1854; in 1859 to Miss Helen Amelia Brayton who, with a son, of his first marriage, survives him.

John Marsh, Esq., father of Charles P., was born in Claremont, N. H., in 1758; early in life he settled in Weathersfield, Vt., where he died aged 87.

Marsh, Daniel. *A Sermon*, delivered on the day of General Election, at Montpelier, October 14, 1813, before the Honorable Legislature of Vermont, by Daniel Marsh, A. M., Pastor of the Congregational Church in Bennington. Published at the request of the Legislature. Montpelier : Walton and Goss. October, 1813. 8vo, pp. 30.

—*A Sermon*, Delivered at Montpelier, before the Vermont Bible Society, at their Annual Meeting, October, 1813. By Daniel Marsh, A. M. Pastor of the Congregational Church in Bennington. Published at the Request of the Society. Montpelier, Vt. Printed by Walton & Goss. 1813. 8vo, pp. 16.

—*Dedication Sermon*, at Bennington, Jan'y 1, 1806.

Mr. Marsh was born in New Milford, Ct., May 10, 1762; he died at Jamesville, N. Y., December 13, 1843. He was settled over the Congregational church at Bennington, 1805-1820, and was settled at Rupert a short time, and thence to Jamesville. See sketch of his life in Jennings' History of Bennington; pp. 99-103.

He is not of the Hartford, Vt., family.

MARSH, GEORGE PERKINS. *Speech* of Mr. George P. Marsh, of Vermont, on the Tariff Bill. Delivered in the House of Representatives of the U. States, April 30, 1844. 8vo, pp. 16.

—*Speech* of Mr. G. P. Marsh, of Vermont, on the Mexican War, Delivered in the House of Representatives of the U. S., February 10, 1848. Washington : Printed by J. & G. S. Gideon. 1848. 8vo, pp. 16.

—*Speech* of Mr. George P. Marsh, of Vermont, on the Annexation of Texas. Delivered in the House of Representatives, U. S., in Committee of the Whole on the State of the Union, Jan. 20, 1845. 8vo, pp. 15.

—*Speech* of Mr. G. P. Marsh, of Vermont, on The Tariff Question, Delivered in the House of Representatives of the U. S., June 30th, 1846. 8vo, pp. 16.

—*Speech* of Mr. Marsh, of Vermont, on the Bill for establishing the Smithsonian Institution ; Delivered in the House of Representatives of the U. States, April 22, 1846. Washington : Printed by J. & G. S. Gideon. 1846. 8vo, pp. 15.

—*Address* before the American Institute, Oct. 25, 1855. 8vo.

—*Remarks* of Mr. George P. Marsh, on Slavery in the Territories of New Mexico, California and Oregon. August 3, 1848. 8vo, pp. 12.

—*Address* delivered before the New England Society of the City of New York, December 24, 1844. By George P. Marsh. New York : M. W. Dodd. 1845. 8vo, pp. 54.

—*Remarks* on an Address delivered before the New England Society of New York, December 23, 1844, by George P. Marsh. Boston : 1845. 12mo, pp. 23.

—*Address* before the Agricultural Society of Rutland County, Sept. 30, 1847. 8vo, pp. 24.— Rutland : 1848.

—*Address* delivered before the Burlington Mechanics' Institute, by George P. Marsh. April 5, 1843, and published at the request of the Institute. 8vo, pp. 26, Burlington : 1843.

—*The American Historical School :* A Discourse delivered before the Literary Societies of Union College, By George P. Marsh. Troy, N. Y.: 1847. 8vo, pp. 29.

—*An Apology* for the Study of English, delivered by George P. Marsh, on Monday, November 1, 1858, introductory to a series of Lectures in the Post-graduate Course of Columbia College, New York. (Published with an Address by Prof. Theodore W. Dwight.) New York : by authority of the Trustees. 1859. 8vo, pp. 37.

—*A Dictionary* of English Etymology. By Hensleigh Wedgwood, M. A., Late Fellow of Chr. Coll. Cam. Vol. I. (A—D.) With Notes and Additions, by George P. Marsh. New

York: Sheldon and Company, Publishers. Boston: Gould and Lincoln. 1862. r'l 8vo, pp. 247.

I am not aware that Mr. Marsh continued this work beyond the present volume.

The above work by Mr. Wedgwood is in high repute; complete in 3 vols. 8vo. London: 1867.

—*Lectures* on the English Language. By George P. Marsh. First Series. Motto. Fourth Edition. Revised and Enlarged. New York: Charles Scribner, Grand Street. London: Sampson Low, Son & Company. M,DCCC, LXI. r'l 8vo, pp. x, 715.

—*The Origin* and History of the English Language, and of the Early Literature it Embodies. By George P. Marsh, Author of "Lectures on the English Language," etc., etc. New York: Charles Scribner, Grand Street. London: Sampson Low, Son and Co. 1862. r'l 8vo, pp. xv, 574.

Several editions have appeared.

—*Man and Nature;* or, Physical Geography as Modified by Human Action. By George P. Marsh. Motto. New York: Charles Scribner & Co., No. 654 Broadway. 1871. r'l 8vo, pp. xix, 577.

—*Grammar* of the Old Northern or Icelandic Language. Burlington: 1838. 12mo, pp. 188.

—*The Earth* as Modified by Human Action. Being a new, revised and enlarged Edition of "Man and Nature." New York: Scribner, Armstrong & Co. 1877. 8vo, pp. 674.

"Man and Nature" was first published about 1864, and several editions have followed.

It first appeared under the present title in 1874.

—*Human Knowledge:* A Discourse delivered before the Phi Beta Kappa Society, at Cambridge, August 26, 1847. By George P. Marsh. Boston: Charles C. Little and James Brown. 1847. 8vo, pp. 42.

—*The Goths* in New England. A Discourse delivered at the Anniversary of the Philomathesian Society of Middlebury College, August 15, 1843. By George P. Marsh. Published by request of the Society. Middlebury: Printed by J. Cobb, Jr. 1843. 8vo, pp. 39.

—*Report* on Artificial Propagation of Fish.

See Fish Culture.

—*The Camel*, his Organization, Habits and Uses considered with reference to his Introduction into the United States. By George P. Marsh. Boston: Gould and Lincoln, 59 Washington Street. New York: Sheldon, Blakeman & Co. Cincinnati: George S. Blanchard. 1856. 12mo, pp. 224.

—*A Discourse* commemorative of the Hon. George Perkins Marsh, LL. D., Delivered before the Faculty and Students of Dartmouth College, June 5, 1883, And Repeated Before the Trustees, Faculty and Students of the University of Vermont, June 25, 1883, By Samuel Gilman Brown, D. D., LL. D. Published By Request. Burlington: Free Press Association. 1883. r'l 8vo, pp. 37, iv.

Printed at the expense of Hon. Frederick Billings of Woodstock.

—*Bibliography* of George Perkins Marsh, Compiled by H. L. Koopman. Burlington: The Free Press Association. 1892. 8vo, pp. 24.

This is a reprint of six and a half pages of the Catalogue of the Marsh Library, in the University of Vermont. It comprises 112 titles, together with titles of various works about Mr. Marsh, and list of titles of publications by Mrs. Marsh.

Mr. Marsh was born in Woodstock. Vt., March 15, 1801; was graduated at Dartmouth College in 1820. He subsequently removed to Burlington, Vt., where he studied law, was admitted to the bar, and came into an extensive practice, devoting, however, much time to politics. He was a member of the State Legislature in 1835, and a member of the Executive Council of the State of Vermont, 1835-6. In 1842 took his seat in the lower House of Congress, where he continued until he was appointed Minister to Turkey, in 1849. He was also charged with a special mission to Greece in 1852. In 1861 he was appointed Minister to Italy, in which position he was continued until his death at Vallombrosa, Italy, July 24, 1882.

He married in 1828, Miss Harriet Buell, of Burlington, who died in 1833. In 1839 he married Miss Caroline Crane, of Berkley, Mass., who survives him.

He is well known as an author and a scholar, but in this respect his works speak for themselves.

—*Life and Letters* of George Perkins Marsh, Compiled by Caroline Crane Marsh, In two volumes. Vol. I, New York: Charles Scribner's Sons. 1888. 8vo, pp. vi, 479.

The Second Volume of this work, owing to Mrs. Marsh's impaired health, has not appeared (1896.)

Marsh, Mrs. George P. *Wolfe of the Knoll*, And other Poems. By Mrs. George P. Marsh. New York: Charles Scribner, Grand Street. London: Sampson Low, Son & Company. 1860. 12mo, pp. 327.

Mrs. Marsh translated from the German The Hallig, or the Sheepfold in the Waters, published in Boston, 1856, pp. 298; two poems by her, A Lay of the Danube, and The Water of El Urbain, were printed in Harper's Magazine; and she prepared the articles on a number of Italian cities for Johnson's New Cyclopædia.

Marsh, James. *An Address* Delivered in Burlington, upon the Inauguration of the Author to the Office of President of the University of Vermont, Nov. 28, 1826. By James Marsh. Burlington, Printed by E. & T. Mills. 1826. 8vo, pp. 31.

—*Aids to Reflection*, in the Formation of a Manly Character, on the several grounds of Prudence, Morality, and Religion: Illustrated by select passages from our Elder Divines, especially from Archbishop Leighton. By S. T. Coleridge. First American, from the first London Edition; with an Appendix, and Illustrations from other works of the same Author; Together with a Preliminary Essay, and Additional Notes, By James Marsh, President of the University of Vermont. Burlington: Chauncey Goodrich. MDCCCXXIX. r'l 8vo, pp. lxi, 399.

—*Select Practical Works* of Rev. John Howe, and Dr. William Bates. Collected and Arranged, with Biographical sketches, by James Marsh, President of the University of Vermont. New York: G. & C. & H. Carvill. Burlington: Chauncey Goodrich. 1830. 8vo, pp. 550.

—*The Friend:* A Series of Essays, to aid in the formation of fixed Principles in Politics, Morals and Religion, with Literary Amusements Interspersed. By S. T. Coleridge, Esq. First American, from the Second London Edition, Complete in One Volume. (Edited by Prof. James Marsh, of the University of Vermont.) Burlington: (Vt.) Chauncey Goodrich. 1831. 8vo, pp. viii, 510.

—*The Spirit of Hebrew Poetry*, By J. G. Herder. Translated from the German, by James Marsh. In two Volumes. Burlington : Edward Smith, (Successor to Chauncey Goodrich.) 1833. pp. 293, and 320. 12mo.

—*Aids to Reflection*, by Samuel Taylor Coleridge, with a preliminary Essay, by James Marsh, D. D. From the Fourth London Edition, with the Author's last corrections, Edited by Henry Nelson Coleridge, Esq., M. A. Burlington : Chauncey Goodrich. 1840. 8vo, pp. 357.

—*Introduction* to Historical Chronology, By D. H. Hegewisch, Professor at Kiel, in Denmark. Translated from the German by James Marsh. Burlington : Chauncey Goodrich. 1837. 12mo, pp. 144.

—*Characteristics* of the Christian Philosopher : A Discourse commemorative of the Virtues and Attainments of Rev. James Marsh, D. D. Late President and Professor of Moral and Intellectual Philosophy in the University of Vermont. Delivered before the Alumni of the University, at their Annual Meeting, in August, 1843, and published at their request. By Rev. George B. Cheever, New York : Wiley and Putnam. 1843. 8vo, pp. 72.

—*The Remains* of the Rev. James Marsh, D.D., Late President and Professor of Moral and Intellectual Philosophy in the University of Vermont with a Memoir of his Life. Motto. Boston : Crocker and Brewster. 1843. 8vo, pp. viii, 642.
Compiled and Memoir written by Prof. Joseph Torrey.

—*The Remains* of the Rev. James Marsh, D. D. Late President, and Professor of Moral and Intellectual Philosophy in the University of Vermont ; with a Memoir of his Life. Motto. Third Edition. Burlington : Chauncey Goodrich. 1852. 8vo, pp. 642.
This volume contains of the additional works by President Marsh : "Letter to an Advanced Student ;" 8vo, pp, 24. "Remarks on Physiology :" 8vo, pp. 48. Remarks on Psychology :" 8vo, pp. 108. "On the Will :" 8vo, pp. 30. "On Conscience :" 8vo, pp. 23. "Discourse on Hypocrisy :" 8vo, pp. 15. "Three Discourses on the Ground and Origin of Sin :" 8vo, pp. 63. "Man's Need of Christ :" 8vo, pp. 53. "Discourse at the Dedication of the University Chapel," 1830 ; 8vo, pp. 25. "On Eloquence :" 8vo, pp. 19. "On Evangelism ; Read before an Association of Ministers, 1837 ;" 8vo, pp. 13.
President Marsh was born in Hartford, Vt., July 19, 1794 ; and died at Colchester, near Burlington, Vt., July 3, 1842. He fitted for College at Randolph Academy, and was graduated at Dartmouth, 1817, and at Andover, 1822. He was tutor at Dartmouth, and some time Professor at Hampden Sidney College, Virginia ; President of the University of Vermont, 1826 to 1833, and Professor of Moral and Intellectual Philosophy there until his death.
He married, first, Lucia, daughter of James Wheelock, of Hanover, October 14, 1824 ; second, Laura, sister of his first wife, January 7, 1835. He left three children, James, Sidney H., and Joseph W., the two former by his first and the latter by his second wife. James died at the Sandwich Islands 1859 ; Sidney H. and Joseph W. have been connected with the Pacific University of Oregon, the former as President, and the latter as a Professor.
Joseph W. Marsh and wife have children : James, aged 13 ; Willie and Laura, twins, 11 ; Sidney 9 ; David 7 ; and Frederick, nearly 3. (1879.)
See Brown, Clark, Note.

Marsh, Joel. *A Sermon* preached in Sharon, Vt., October 14, 1811. At the Funeral of Joel Marsh, Esq., Aged 65. By Rev. Isaiah Potter, of Lebanon, N. H. Hanover : Printed by Charles Spear. 1812. 8vo, pp. 16.
Mr. Marsh was one of the first settlers in Sharon.

Marsh, Leonard. *The Physiology* of Intemperance, an Address before the Temperance Society of the University of Vermont, June 29, 1841. By Leonard Marsh, M. D. 8vo, pp. 28. Burlington : Chauncey Goodrich. 1841.

—*A Bake-Pan* for the Dough-Faces. By one of them. Try it. Burlington, Vt.: Published by Chauncey Goodrich. 1854. 8vo, pp. 64. Plate.

—*The Apocatastasis ;* or Progress Backwards. A new "Tract for the Times." By the Author. Motto. Burlington : Chauncey Goodrich. 1854. 8vo, pp. 203.
Opposed to modern Spiritualism.

—*Review* of "A Letter from the Right Rev. John H. Hopkins, D. D., LL. D., Bishop of Vermont, on the Bible view of Slavery." By a Vermonter. Burlington : Free Press Print. 1861. 8vo, pp. 28.

—*The Higher Institutions* of Learning, and their Relations to the Community. [n. p. n. d.] 8vo, pp. 40.
Written at the suggestion of Rev. Dr. Wheeler.

—*The Shadow of Christianity*, or the Genesis of the Christian State. A Treatise for the Times, by the Author of the Apocatastasis. New York : Hurd & Houghton. 1866. 12mo, pp. 167.

—*On the Relations of Slavery* to the War ; and on the Treatment of it necessary to permanent Peace. A few Suggestions for Thoughtful and Patriotic Men. 8vo, pp. 8.

—*The Third Party* in the War. 8vo.

—*To the Hon. F. P. Blair* of Missouri. 8vo.
Professor Leonard Marsh was born in Hartford, Vt., June 29, 1800. He was graduated at Dartmouth College, 1827. Studied medicine, and began practice in Burlington, Vt., in 1840. He was Professor of Greek and Latin, also of Natural History and Physiology in the University of Vermont 1855 until his death, August 16, 1870. He was a brother of Rev. James Marsh, D. D., former President of the University of Vermont.

Marsh, Roswell. *Biography.* The Life of Charles Hammond, of Cincinnati, Ohio. By Roswell Marsh, of Steubenville, Ohio. Written in the year 1863. Printed at the Steubenville Herald office. 8vo, pp. 18.

—*A Comparison* of the Present with the former Doctrines of the General Government, on Slavery, the Territories, etc. By Roswell Marsh. Steubenville, Ohio. 1856. 8vo, pp. 23.

—*Important Correspondence.* Friendly Discussion of Party Politics in 1860-61. Letters of Hon. Roswell Marsh, and Hon. Charles Remelin. 8vo, pp. 51.

—*Proceedings* on the Retirement of Roswell Marsh, Esq., from the Practice of the Bar. Jefferson County, Ohio, Dec. 1, 1865. 8vo, pp. 8.
Hon. Roswell Marsh was born in Hartford, Vt., and died in Steubenville, Ohio, August 16, 1875, aged about 78. He was brother to President James, Professor Leonard, and Daniel Marsh, and settled at Steubenville when 28 years of age, which town was ever after his home. As a lawyer he was a leader at the Bar in Northern Ohio, and continued in active practice until 73 years of age. He wrote much for the public journals, upon political and other subjects. He was a liberal benefactor of the Vermont Historical Society, giving it his files of newspapers, a portion of his library, and a large quantity of his unpublished manuscripts, including a history of

the Administration of General Jackson, from the Whig standpoint, and a manuscript history of Egypt.

See Barrett, James. Memorial address before the Vermont Historical Society, 1870, on the life of Hon. Charles Marsh.

Marsh, Samuel. *Message* from God, etc. Montpelier : 1844. 8vo, pp. 16.

—*The Age of Prophecy* in which we Live. By Samuel Marsh, minister of the Gospel. Montpelier : Press of Eastman and Danforth. 1848. 16mo, pp. 16.

—*National Prosperity.* 16mo, pp. 16. 1849, no imprint.

Relates to slavery.

—*The Modern* Colporteur Revival System. Journal of the Experiment made during Six Months, A. D. 1830-1, in Montreal, L. C. Principally among the French Catholics. By Samuel Marsh, Minister of the Gospel. Montpelier : Press of Eastman-Danforth. 1849. 16mo, pp. 142.

—*"Hard Questions"* Answered, in two Parts. Part First. Fundamental Principles in the Philosophy of Religion. Part Second. Explanations of difficult and disputed points among Christians. By Samuel Marsh, Minister of the Gospel. Montpelier : Press of Eastman and Danforth. 1849. 16mo, pp. 72.

—*Universalism.* An attempt in Disguise, to make void the oath of the only true God. Montpelier : Press of Eli Ballou. 1850. 16mo, pp. 28.

—*A Discourse on Baptism.*

—*Reply* of Marsh to Ballou. Recommended by Clergymen : A. Royce, S. R. Hall, Joseph Underwood, A. Webster, John Dudley, of Danville, Homer T. Jones, of Plainfield, A. T. Bullard. Montpelier : 1850. 16mo, pp. 32.

—*Uncle Nathan ;* or, strict agreement with God in His word. Motto. Montpelier, Vt. : Printed by Ballou & Loveland. 1854. 16mo, pp. 218.

Rev. Samuel Marsh was born in Danville, Vt., July 3, 1796; and died at Underhill, Vt., April 1, 1874. He was graduated at Dartmouth in 1821, and Andover, 1824; and was pastor of Congregational churches in Vermont, at Derby Center, Danville, and Pomfret, until 1827, when he left the State, and returned in 1838, and preached in Hardwick, Walden, Marshfield, Plainfield, Wolcott, and Jericho, until 1857, when he retired to Underhill Flats.

Marsh, Sidney H. *An Inaugural Discourse,* By Sidney H. Marsh, President of Pacific University, Oregon. Burlington : Free Press Office. 1856. 8vo, pp. 20.

—*In Memoriam.* Rev. S. H. Marsh, D. D., First President of Pacific University. Born Aug. 29, 1825. Died February 2, 1879. Portland, Oregon : Job Printing and Publishing House of Himes, the Printer. 1881. 8vo, pp. 58.

President Sidney H. Marsh, of Pacific University, Oregon, was born at Hampden-Sidney College, Va., Aug. 29, 1825; graduated from the University of Vt. 1846; studied theology at Union Theological Seminary; went to Oregon as an evangelist 1853; elected President of Pacific University 1854; died February 2, 1879, at his residence in Forest Grove, in that State, aged 53. He leaves a widow, and five children living, viz: James Wheelock, age 16; Mary Henrietta, 14; George Haskell, 12; Lucia, about 10; and Winnifred, not quite 2. He has lost children, Anna, Leonard, and Emily, who came between Lucia and Winnifred. (1879.)

Marshall, A. V. *Obsequies* of Mrs. Ruth, wife of William C. Walker, at Mendon, Vt., August 3d, 1873. By Rev. A. V. Marshall, M. D. Assisted by Rev. H. H. Barnes. Rutland : Tuttle & Co., Printers. 1873. 8vo, pp. 15.

Marshall, E. F. *A Spelling Book* of the English Language ; or, the American Tutor's Assistant. Intended particularly for the use of 'Common Schools.' The Pronunciation being Adapted to the much Approved Principles of J. Walker. By Elihu F. Marshall. Stereotype Edition. Wells River, Vt. Printed and published by Ira White. 1830. 12mo, pp. 156.

—*Marshall's New Spelling Book,* and Elementary Principles of the English Language : Calculated to Teach spelling and reading by association, dictation, and the usual mode of exercising in Classes. Together with an abstract of Walker's Principles of Pronunciation. By Elihu F. Marshall, Author of a "Spelling Book of the English Language," &c. Montpelier, Vt.: Published by E. P. Walton and Son. 1838. 12mo, pp. 144.

Marshfield. *Manual* of the Congregational Church, Marshfield, Vt. Organized December 25, 1800. Reorganized May 18, 1826. Motto. Montpelier : Printed by J. & J. M. Poland. 1878. 18mo, pp. 8.

Marston, Moses. *Sermons* of Rev. Franklin S. Bliss ; together with A Sketch of his Life. By Moses Marston. Boston : Universalist Publishing House. 1878. 12mo, pp. VI, 240.

Mr. Bliss was pastor of the Universalist Church in Barre, Vt., 1857-1872; he was born in Cheshire, Mass., September 30, 1828; and died at Greensboro, N. C., March 23, 1873, where he was sojourning for his health.

We place on record the position of Mr. Bliss during the late civil war, as given by his biographer, p. 47; it is important, as being the only position a true and consistent Universalist can occupy in relation to the barbarous strife of war : "Early in his ministry Mr. Bliss became convinced that war was never under any circumstances justifiable, and that Christians should never engage in it or encourage it. He preached against war with as much zeal as against slavery and intemperance. All through the civil war he was a consistent Quaker. * * * He advocated the principles of peace, and continued to declare that the servants of Christ must not fight. He grieved at the terrible suffering the war produced ; but, most of all, at the wickedness of war itself, and at the low condition of Christian life which made war necessary or possible. He opposed war on principle, as antagonistic to both the letter and the spirit of the gospel of Christ."

Very large numbers of Universalists withdrew from that denomination during its era of political sectionalism, and the Episcopal Church has been greatly increased thereby.

Mr. Marston, son of Asa and Hannah (Davenport) Marston, was born in Williamstown, Vt., May 24, 1832. He was graduated at Middlebury College in 1856, obtaining his education mainly by his own exertions. He was a teacher in Green Mountain Institute at Woodstock, in 1856, and Principal of the same in 1857; but was compelled to leave on account of the failure of his health ; he began preaching in 1859, and was pastor of Universalist churches at Gaysville and Woodstock, Vt., and at Potsdam, N. Y.

From 1868 to 1873 he was Professor of Latin and Greek in St. Lawrence University, at Canton, N. Y., and since 1874 he has been Professor of English Literature in the University of Minnesota, at Minneapolis, where he still remains. (1879.)

Marston, W. A. *An Address* delivered before the St. Johnsbury and Lyndon (Vt.) Chapters of the '1001,' on Their Anniversary, January 1, 1845. By William Augustus Marston, B. G. of the Dartmouth Chapter. Boston : Samuel N. Dickinson, Printer. 1845. 8vo, pp. 27.

Martin, James L. *An Address* delivered by James L. Martin, Esq., at Londonderry, Vt.,

July 4, 1876. Rutland: Globe Paper Company, Printers. 1876. 8vo, pp. 8.
Mr. Martin was Speaker of the Vermont House of Representatives, 1878–80. See Biographical sketch in Legislative Directory.

Martin, Michael. *Confession* of Michael Martin, or Captain Lightfoot, who was hung at Cambridge, Massachusetts, in the year 1821, for the robbing of Major Bray. Also, An Account of Dr. John Wilson, who recently died at Brattleboro, Vt., believed by many to be the notorious Captain Thunderbolt. Brattleboro, Vt.: J. B. Miner, Publisher. 1847. 8vo, pp. 30, 12.
Thunderbolt was an associate of Lightfoot in his numerous crimes.

Martin, Rev. Solon. *On the Public* Worship of God. A Sermon, delivered at the Dedication of the Congregational Meeting-House in Corinth, Vt., October 23, 1845. By Rev. Solon Martin. Published by request. Bradford, Vt.: Printed by A. B. F. Hildrith. 12mo, pp. 16.

—*The Providence of God* a ground of encouragement in the day of trouble. A Sermon Delivered at Waits River, Vt., October 30th, 1864, at the Funeral of Josiah Clark, who was killed in the Battle of Occoquan, Sept. 19, 1864. By Rev. Solon Martin, Acting Pastor in the Congregational Church in Corinth. Published by request. Windsor: Printed at the Vermont Journal Office. 1865. 8vo, pp. 16.
Mr. Martin was born at Hanover, N. H., July 7, 1808; died at West Fairlee, Vt., November 9, 1878. He read theology, and was licensed as a Congregational preacher September 26, 1832, and preached at Concord, Vt., until 1838; Corinth, 1838–1855, at West Fairlee, 1855–1860, then at Corinth again until 1866, when he returned to West Fairlee, as acting pastor until near the close of 1872. He then made a trip to Colorado, intending to remain there with his children, but life in the new country was not congenial, and he returned to West Fairlee, where he preached until the close of his life. Mrs. Martin died the day following the death of her husband, and the funeral of both took place together.
See Vermont Congregational Minutes, 1879, pp. 40–41.

Mary Fletcher Hospital. *Regulations of.* 12mo, pp. 10. [1880.]
Established at Burlington by the lady whose name it bears; she was also one of the founders of the Fletcher Free Library at Burlington.

Mason, Mrs. Ellen H. Bullard. *Missionary Crumbs*, First Number. For the Woman's Union Missionary Society of America, for Heathen Lands. Motto. January. 1861. New York. 12mo, pp. 30, (2).

—*Tounghoo Women.* Ladies, will you approve or condemn? New York: Anson D. F. Randolph, Publisher, 683 Broadway. 1860. 8vo, pp. 50.

—*Great Expectations Realized*, or Civilizing Mountain Men. By Mrs. Ellen H. B. Mason, eighteen years connected with the Highland Clans of Burmah. Philadelphia. 1862. 12mo, pp. 480.
Mrs. Mason is a native of Brattleboro, Vt., where her father, Mr. Huntley, was a Baptist preacher. She married first Rev. Mr. Bullard, who was also a missionary. Rev. Edward Bullard, pastor of the Baptist church in Addison, Vt., is a son of this marriage.
Mrs. Mason is about sixty years of age and still resides in Rangoon, where she has acquired quite an estate. (1888.)

Mason, John. *A Treatise* on Self Knowledge; showing the Nature and Benefit of that Important Science, and the Way to attain it: intermixed with Various Reflections and Observations on Human Nature. By John Mason, A. M. Motto. Montpelier: Published by Lucius Q. C. Bowles. Wright & Sibley, Printers. 1813. 24mo, pp. 194.

—*A Treatise* on Self Knowledge; Showing the nature and benefit of that important Science, and the way to attain it: Intermixed with Various Reflections and Observations on Human Nature. By John Mason. Motto. Montpelier: Published by E. P. Walton. 1819. 18mo, pp. 177.

Mason, Thomas. *Sermon* on the Occasion of the Anniversary Thanksgiving, 1798. Printed at Rutland, by John Walker, Jr., for the subscribers. 1799.

MASONIC. By-laws of the Vermont Lodge, No. 1. [Published for the use of the Members.] Windsor, Vermont: Printed by Nahum Mower. Anno Lucis, 5803. 18mo, pp. 21, 8.

—*An Oration* Pronounced at Middletown, June 24, A. L. 5809, before Rainbow Lodge. By A Member of the Lodge. Rutland: Printed by William Fay. 1809. sm. 4to, pp. 8.

—*An Oration*, pronounced before George Washington Lodge, at Strafford, on the Anniversary of St. John the Baptist, June 25, A. L. 5810. By Brother Samuel Austin. Published at the Particular request of the Lodge. Randolph, (Vermont.) Printed by Br. Sereno Wright. 1810. 8vo, pp. 15.

—*The Law of God*, Against all Irreligious Associations; and for the Defence and Security of all those Formed for Charitable, Scientific and Religious Purposes. A Sermon preached in Windsor, (Vt.) October 8th, A. L. 5811: Before the Grand Lodge of the State. By Reverend Brother Jonathan Nye, A. M. Grand Chaplain to the Lodge. Published by the request and at the expence of the Lodge. Keene, N. H. Printed by Brother John Prentiss. December, 1811. 8vo, pp. 15.

—*Constitution* of the Grand Lodge of Vt. Windsor, Vt.: Printed by Alden Spooner. 1818. pp. 8.

—*Journals* of the Grand Lodge of Vermont, at their Annual Communications Holden at Montpelier, Oct. A. L. 5822 & 5823, with the Constitution, By-Laws and General Regulations of the same. Montpelier, Vt. Printed by E. P. Walton. 1824. 16mo, pp. 65, (4).

—*Appeal* to the people of Vermont, on the subject of the Anti-Masonic Excitement; by the Lodges of Freemasons in the County of Orange, and the Valley of White River. Chelsea: Printed at the Advocate Office. n. d. 16mo, pp. 23.

—*Letters on Masonry*, Addressed to the professed followers of Christ, now in connexion with the Institution of Freemasonry. By Henry Jones, Pastor of the Congregational Church in Cabot, Vt., a Royal Arch Mason. 1829. 8vo, pp. 48.
Mr. Jones was expelled from the Masonic Order, and these letters are full of venom.
See Jones, Henry.

—*The Constitution*, together with the By-laws and Ordinances of the Grand Lodge of

Vermont. Printed in Bennington, By Brother Anthony Haswell, A. L. 5796. pp. 8.

—*Regulations* of the Grand Chapter of Royal Arch Masons of Vt. 1805. William Fay, Printer, Rutland, January 14, A. L. 5805. pp. 12.
Continued.

—*Proceedings* of the Grand Lodge of Vermont at their Communication holden at Vergennes, in the County of Addison, October, A. L. 5806. Middlebury, Vermont: Printed by J. D. Huntington, 1806. pp. 12.
Continued.

—*Circular* by Joseph Winslow, Grand Secretary, Dated Windsor, March 24, 5814. Notifying the Lodges of Vermont of the fact that Antoni Lognoti and T. Knock, (who were successful in obtaining 300 dollars from the Grand Lodge of Pennsylvania to aid in ransoming 8 of their brethren from the Algerines, where they were held in captivity) were swindling the members of our fraternity and prostituting the Masonic institution to fraudulent purposes.

—*A Candid Appeal* by Masons of Waterford, Concord, Lyndon, St. Johnsbury, Peacham, Craftsbury and the Chapter at Danville. Montpelier: Printed by E. P. Walton. 1828.
Known as the "Danville Appeal."

—*Address* of the officers of the Grand Lodge to the people of Vt., Oct. 21, 1833.
Broadside on large sheet.

—*Appeal* to the inhabitants of Vermont by members of the Masonic Fraternity attending the Grand Lodge, October, 1829, signed by W. B. Haswell and Ninety-Nine others. Montpelier: Printed by G. W. Hill. Patriot Office. 1829. pp. 10.

—*The same*, signed by N. B. Haswell and 165 others, with their places of residence. Montpelier: Printed by G. W. Hill, Patriot Office. 1829. pp. 12.

—*Journal* of the Most Worshipful Grand Lodge of Vermont, at the Communication Holden at Montpelier, Oct. 7, A. L., 5828. Montpelier: Printed by G. W. Hill, Patriot Office. 1829. 18mo, pp. 17, (1).

—*Address*, Delivered before St. John's Lodge, No. 41, Thetford, Vt. At the opening of the New Masonic Hall, in that place, Feb'ry 18, 1829. By David Palmer, M. D., Master of the Lodge. Published by Order of the Brethren. Hanover: Printed by Thomas Mann, 1829. 8vo, pp. 16.

—*Proceedings* of the Anti-Masonick State Convention, Holden at Montpelier, August 5, 6, & 7: with Addresses to the People, on the Subject of Speculative Freemasonry. Published by Order of the Convention. East Randolph: Printed at the Vermont Luminary Office. 1829. 8vo, pp. 26, (1).

—*An Appeal*, to the Inhabitants of the State of Vermont, on the subject of the Anti-Masonic Excitement, by a Committee previously appointed for that purpose, made at a Public Convention, Holden at Middlebury, April 7th, 1829. And An Address, delivered before the Convention, by Jonathan A. Allen, M. D. Published by Order of the Meeting. Middle-

bury, Vt. Printed by Copeland & Steele, 1829. 8vo, pp. 36.

—*An Appeal* to the Inhabitants of Vermont by members of the Masonic Fraternity, present at Montpelier, at the Annual Communication of the Grand Lodge, October, 1829. Montpelier: Printed by G. W. Hill, Patriot Office. 1829. 18mo, pp. 12.

—*A Memorial* to the Legislature of Vermont, for the Repeal of Acts Incorporating the Grand Lodge and Grand Chapter of Vt. Presented Oct. 23, 1830. Signed, William Slade, E. D. Barber. Montpelier, October 22, 1830. 8vo, pp. 14.

—*Proceedings* of the Anti-Masonic State Convention, Holden at Montpelier, June 15 and 16, 1831, with Reports, Addresses, &c. Montpelier: Published by Order of the Convention. Gamaliel Small, printer. 1831. 8vo, pp. 23.

—*Evenings* by the Fireside, Or Thoughts on some of the principles of Speculative Freemasonry: By Amariah Chandler, Pastor of the Congregational Church in Waitsfield, Vt. Danville, Vt. E. & W. Eaton, Printers. 1829. 8vo, pp. 24.
Mr. Chandler was an active anti-Mason.

—*Proceedings* of the Anti-masonic State Convention, Holden at Montpelier, Vt., June 26 and 27, 1833; with Resolutions, Reports and Addresses. Montpelier: Knapp & Jewett, Printers. 1833. 8vo, pp. 32.

—*Masonic Oaths*, with Notes; to which are added practical Proofs of the character and tendency of Free-Masonry. Montpelier: Knapp & Jewett, Printers. 1834. 12mo, pp. 108.

—*Proceedings* of the Grand Council of Vt. 1854. Burlington, Printed by C. Goodrich. 1854. pp. 8.

—*The Same*. Second Edition, Burlington: Free Press Book and Job Printing House. 1873. pp. 8.
Organized at Rutland, June, 1822.
No Printed Records have been found prior to the reorganization, August 10, 1854.

—*Proceedings* of the Most Worshipful Grand Lodge of Vermont, at their Annual Communication in Burlington, on the Second Wednesday in January, A. L. 5856. Being the Ninth Day of Said Month. Burlington: Printed by P. P. Ripley. 1856. 8vo, pp. 118.
Continued.

—*The Same*, 1878, 8vo, pp. 134, 185.

—*Proceedings* of the Grand Royal Arch Chapter of the State of Vermont, at its Annual Session at Montpelier, August 13, 1857. Address of Grand Officers: Phillip C. Tucker, Vergennes, Vt., Grand High Priest. John B. Hollenbeck, Burlington, Vt., Grand Secretary. Burlington: Printed by D. A. Danforth, 1857. 8vo, pp. 50.
Continued.

—*Proceedings* of the Grand Encampment of the State of Vermont, A. D. 1858. Address: Daniel L. Potter, of Middlebury, Grand Master. John B. Hollenbeck, of Burlington, Grand Recorder. Burlington: Printed by D. A. Danforth, Sentinel Office. 1858. 8vo, pp. 72.
Continued.

—*By-Laws* of Union Lodge, No. 2, of Free and Accepted Masons, at Middlebury, Vt. Rutland: Geo. A. Tuttle & Co., Printers. 1858. 12mo, pp. 8.

—*The Same*, 1862, 8vo, pp. 24.

—*The Oaths* or Obligations of Freemasonry, with notes, together with Authenticated documents and Facts, illustrative of the Character and practical tendency of the Masonic System upon the Mind of Community. Irasburgh: A. A. Earle, Printer. 1859. 12mo, pp. 87.

—*By-Laws* of Killington Commandery, No. 6, of Knights Templar, Rutland, Vermont. Rutland: Herald Book and Job Office. 1867. 24mo, pp. 12.

—*By-Laws* of Davenport Chapter, No. 17, Rutland, Vt., together with the Officers and Members for 1869-70. Rutland: Tuttle & Co., Printers. 1870. 24mo, pp. 8.

—*By-Laws* of Wyoming Lodge, No. 80, of Free and Accepted Masons, Plainfield, Vt. Montpelier: Journal Printing Establishment. 1869. 18mo, pp. 16.

—*Another Edition.* 1871. Same imprint. 18mo, pp. 11.

—*By-Laws* of St. John's Lodge, No. 41, Ancient and Accepted Masons, Springfield, Vt. Revised July 25th, 1871. Charter Granted October 11, 1811. Reissued Jan. 15, 1857. Rutland: Tuttle & Co., Printers, 1871, 18mo, pp. 27.

—*By-Laws* of Rutland Lodge, No. 79, F. & A. M., Rutland, Vt. Rutland: Tuttle & Company, Printers, 1871. 18mo, pp. 7.

—*Proceedings* of the Grand Encampment of Vermont, from its organization, A. D. 1824, to 1852 inclusive. By W. H. S. Whitcomb, Assistant Grand Recorder. Burlington. Printed by Order of the Grand Commandery, 1870. pp. 22.
(Organized at Rutland, June 17, 1824.)

—*By-Laws* of Mount Moriah Lodge, No. 96. Together with the Constitution and By-Laws of the Grand Lodge of Vermont. Rutland: Tuttle & Company, Printers. 1871. 18mo, pp. 31. (East Wallingford.)

—*By-Laws* of Red Mountain Lodge, No. 63. Located at Arlington, Vt. Together with the Constitution and By-Laws of the Grand Lodge of Vermont. Adopted at Regular Communication held Oct. 27th, 1871. Rutland: Tuttle & Company, Printers. 1871. 18mo, pp. 31.

—*By-Laws* of Moose River Lodge, No. 82, F. A. and A. M. Concord, Vt. Together with the Constitution and By-Laws of the Grand Lodge of Vermont. Rutland: Tuttle & Company, Printers. 1871. 18mo, pp. 35.

—*By-Laws* of Poultney Chapter No. 10, Poultney, Vt. Together with the Constitution and By-Laws of the Grand Royal Arch Chapter of Vermont. Date of Charter, August 10th, 5854. Rutland: Tuttle & Co., Printers. 1872. 18mo, pp. 19.

—*By-Laws* of Webster Lodge, No. 61, Winooski Falls, Vt. Together with the Constitution and By-Laws of the Grand Lodge of Vermont. Chartered Jan. 15, 5863. Rutland: Tuttle & Co., Printers. 1872. 18mo, pp. 32.

—*By-Laws* of Lee Lodge No. 30, Free and Accepted Masons, Castleton, Vt. Chartered January 12th, 1854. Rutland: Tuttle & Co., Printers, 1872. 24mo, pp. 8.

—*By-Laws* of DeWitt Clinton Lodge, No. 15, Northfield, Vt. Montpelier: J. & J. M. Poland, Steam Printers. 1874. 18mo, pp. 26.

—*By-Laws* of Mystic Star Lodge, No. 97, Brookfield, Vt. Montpelier: J. & J. M. Poland. 1874. 18mo, pp. 32.

—*By-Laws* of Mount Zion Commandery, No. 9, Knights Templar, Northfield, Vt. Montpelier: J. & J. M. Poland, Printers. 1874. 18mo, pp. 10.

—*By-Laws* of Mad River Lodge, No. 77, Free and Accepted Masons, at Moretown, Vt. Montpelier: J. & J. M. Poland, Printers. 1875. 18mo, pp. 28.

—*By-Laws* of the United States Masonic Relief Association, of Factory Point, Vermont. Manchester. Journal Newspaper and Job Office. 1874. 24mo, pp. 8.

—*By-Laws* of Eureka Lodge, No. 75. Fair Haven, Vt. Rutland: Tuttle & Co., Printers. 1875. 24mo, pp. 8.

—*By-Laws* of the Lodge of the Temple, Lodge No. 94, of Free and Accepted Masons, Bellows Falls, Vt. Montpelier, Vt.: Argus and Patriot Job Printing House. 1881. 18mo, pp. 17.

—*Proceedings* of the Grand Council of Royal and Select Masons for the State of Vermont, held at Burlington, June 11th, A. D. 1874. A Dep. 2874. Edward S. Dana, Cornwall, M. I. Grand Master. W. H. S. Whitcomb, Burlington, Grand Recorder. Montpelier: J. & J. M. Poland's Steam Printing House. 1875. 8vo, pp. 56.

—*Proceedings* of the First Annual Council of Deliberation, A.·. A.·. Rite, for the District of Vermont, held at the city of Burlington, On the 20th day of the Hebrew month Shebat, A.·. M.·. 5635, answering to January 26, 1875, V.·. E.·. Printed by Order of the Council. 1875. 8vo, pp. 56.

—*The Same*, 1876, 8vo, pp. 35.
Continued.

—*Proceedings* of the M. W. Grand Lodge of Free and Accepted Masons of the State of Vermont, at its Annual Communication at Burlington, June 9 and 10, A. D. 1875, A. L. 5875. Rutland: Globe Paper Co., Printers, 1875. 8vo, pp. 312.
Continued.

—*Digest of Decisions* of the Grand Masters of Vermont. Prepared under the Supervision of a Committee of the Grand Lodge, together with the Constitution and By-Laws of the Grand Lodge. Rutland: Globe Paper Company, Printers. 1875. 8vo, pp. 24.

—*Proceedings* of the Council of Royal and Select Masons for the State of Vermont, held at Burlington, June 15, A. D. 1876, A. D. 2876. Albert C. Hubbell, Bennington, M. I. Grand Master, William H. S. Whitcomb, Burlington,

Grand Recorder. Burlington: Free Press Steam Job Printing House. 1876. 8vo, pp. 28, (4).
Continued.

—*The Same*, at Burlington, June 12th, A. D. 1873 ; A. Inv. 2873. Address of M. P. Grand Master : Edward S. Dana, Cornwall. And of Grand Recorder W. H. S. Whitcomb, Burlington. Same imprint. 8vo, pp. 48.

—*Proceedings* of the Grand Commandery of Knights Templar and the Appendant Orders, of the State of Vermont, June, A. D. 1874 ; A. O. 756. R. E. Sir Joseph L. Perkins, Grand Commander, St. Johnsbury. E. Sir J. Monroe Poland, Grand Recorder, Montpelier. 8vo, pp. 46.

—*By-Laws* of the Masonic Relief Association of Vermont. Home Office. Northfield, Vt. Montpelier : Press of J. & J. M. Poland. 1876. 12mo, pp. 12.

—*Records* of the Grand Chapter of the State of Vermont, 1804 to 1850 (inclusive). 1878. pp. 578.

—*Masonry in Rutland.* An Address given at the Dedication of Hiram Lodge No 101, at West Rutland, Vt. May 28, 1879. By Henry Clark. 1879. Mclean, Printer and Binder, Rutland. 8vo, pp. 28.

—*General Regulations* of the Grand Royal Arch Chapter of Vermont, as amended to June 15, 1879. Burlington, Vt.: Free Press Association. 1879. 8vo, pp. 7.

—*Records* of the Grand Lodge of Free and Accepted Masons of the State of Vermont, from 1794 to 1846 inclusive. Burlington, Vt.: The Free Press Association, Printers and Binders. 1879. 8vo, pp. 417, (8).

—*By-Laws* of Winooski Lodge, No. 49, Free and accepted Masons, Waterbury, Vt. Montpelier : Poland's Printing Establishment. 1860. 18mo, pp. 15.

—*Constitution* and By-Laws of the Grand Lodge of Vermont. pp. 16.

—*History* of Bird's Mountain Masonic Monument, 2,500 feet above the level of the sea, including a full report of laying the corner stone Aug. 27, 1886, by M. W. Marsh O. Perkins. Albany : Munsell, 1887. 8vo, pp. 82.
The writer believes it has caused many to read on the subject of Masonic antiquities who were not interested before.

—*Text Book* of the Ancient and Accepted Scottish rite of Freemasonry for Vt. Containing lessons taught in all the degrees from the Fourth to the 32d, inclusive. Compiled in a condensed form by Daniel Norris Nicholson, 32°, Com.-in-chief of Vt. Consistory. Free Press Association. 1893. pp. 190.
See Olcott, B. Sermon, 1781; Ball, Heman, Sermon, 1797; Beall, Isaac, Discourse, 1800; Bradley, Joshua, Beauties of Masonry, 1816; Ballou, Hosea, Sermons, 1805-6-7-8; Drury, Amos, Sermon, 1828; Dunham, Josiah, Oration, 1796; Elliot, Samuel, Essay, 1834; Forsyth, Wm., Sermon, 1798; Felch, Rev. C. Address, 1819; Fitch, John, Sermon, 1800; Harlow, Rev. R. W., Address, 1868; Haswell, A., Oration, 1802; Hebard, E. Sermon, 1804; Jewett, L.; Johnson, James, Sermon, 1826; Kendall, B. F., "Doleful Tragedy;" Kendall, N. Sermon, 1812; Nye, Jonathan, Sermon, 1811; Rollins, C. V. Masonic Text Book; Styles, E. Oration, 1781; Sheppard, John H. Address, 1850; Strong, E. Oration, 1782; Thompson, D. P. Timothy Peacock, Washburn, Reubin, Address, 1831;

Webb, T. S., Masonic Monitor; Williams, S. Discourse, 1812; Barber, E. D., Anti-masonic Addresses ; Dean, Paul, Addresses; Haven, K., Address, 1827; Kendrick, Nath'l, Sermon, 1812 ; Lee, C., Sermon, 1814; Sanders, D. C.; Slade, Wm.; Smith, A. C.; Brown, Clark, Sermons, 1808-1814; Parmelee, S., Sermon, 1825; Sias, S., Discourse, 1822; Palmer, David, Address, 1829.
The Grand Lodge of Vermont was formed, October 14, 1794, at a Convention called for that purpose. The First Chapter of Royal Arch Masons in America was organized in 1797, and the Knights Templar the same year at Philadelphia. The Grand Royal Arch Chapter for the six Northern States, was formed at Hartford, Conn., in January, 1798; the first Septennial meeting was held at Middletown, Conn., January 9, 1806. when the dispute between the Grand Chapters of New York and Vermont, relating to the independence of the latter and her right of admission, was settled by the admission of the Grand Chapter of Vermont into partnership with the Supreme Grand Chapter.
There are at present over 100 Lodges in the State of Vermont, with a membership of about nine thousand.
Vermont appears to be a favorite ground for all the isms that spring up; Vermont was at the front in anti-masonry, having cast her electoral vote in 1832, solitary and alone for William Wirt, an anti-masonic candidate 1or President of the United States; she was foremost for abolitionism, and is at the front in favor of political sectionalism; Mormonism also had its root in Vermont, Jo. Smith and Brigham Young, both being natives of the State.

Mather, Cotton. *Proposals* to Lawyers. From Essays to do Good. Barnard, Vt. 12mo.

Matthews, Rev. Lyman. *History* of the Town of Cornwall, Vermont, By Rev. Lyman Matthews. Middlebury : Mead and Fuller, Register Book and Job Office. 1862. 8vo, pp. 356.

—*Life* of Rev. Ebenezer Porter, D. D., 1837. Boston : 12mo, pp. 396.

—*Porter's Lectures* on Eloquence and Style ; Edited by Rev. Lyman Matthews.

—*A Sermon* before the Norfolk, Mass., Education Society. 1838.
Mr. Matthews was born in Middlebury, Vt., May 12, 1801; died in Cornwall, August 17, 1866. He was graduated at Middlebury in 1822, went south, and was a teacher in Georgia, Delaware and New Jersey about three years; and was graduated at Andover Theological Seminary, 1828; was settled over the Congregational Church, Braintree, Mass., in 1830, and left there in 1844 on account of failing health, retiring to a farm in Cornwall, where he remained until his death.

Mattocks, John. *An Address* delivered before "The Vermont Association of Chicago," January 17, 1877. Published by order of the Association. Chicago : Beach, Barnard & Co., Legal Printers. 1877. 8vo, pp. 23.

May, J. W. *Lascaris*, or The Greeks of the Fifteenth Century. By John W. May, Burlington. Chauncey Goodrich Printer. Burlington: 1846. 8vo, pp. 58.

McClintock, James. *Annual Lecture.* Introductory Lecture to the Course on Anatomy and Physiology, in the Vermont Academy of Medicine. Delivered April 7, 1841. By James McClintock, M. D., Professor, etc. Published by the Class. Castleton : Printed by L. R. H. Robinson. 1841. 12mo, pp. 12.

—*An Introductory Lecture* delivered in the Castleton Medical College, on the 10th April, 1843. By James McClintock, M. D., President of the College, Professor of Anatomy and Surgery, and Lecturer on Anatomy and Operative Surgery, in Philadelphia. Albany : Printed by C. Van Benthuysen and Co. 1843. 8vo, pp. 28.

McFarland, Asa. *A Sermon* Delivered at

Norwich, Vt., September 5, 1804, at the Installation of Rev. James Wheelock Woodward to the Pastoral care of the Church and Society in that place. By Asa McFarland, A. M., Pastor of the Church in Concord, N. H. Printed at Hanover, by Moses Davis. 1805. 12mo, pp. 30.

Contains the charge, by Rev. Isaiah Pattee, the Right Hand of Fellowship by Rev. Sylvester Dana.

McGowan, John. *The life of Joseph*, the Son of Israel. Chiefly designed to allure young minds to the love of the Sacred Scriptures. By John McGowan. In Eight Books. Brattleboro, Vt.: Printed by William Fessenden. 1813.

McIndoes Falls. *Manual* of the Congregational Church, McIndoes Falls, Vt. Montpelier: Press of Vermont Watchman. 1876. 12mo, pp. 8.

MacKeen, Joseph, LL. D.,

As he spells his name, own cousin to Rev. Silas McKeen, was born in 1792, in Vermont, probably in Orange County, as he was a school-mate of his cousin Silas, (see History of Bradford, page 415.) In 1818 he went to the city of New York, and for many years was engaged in the profession of teaching; 1848-1854 he performed the duties of Superintendent of city schools, and was then first assistant Superintendent until his death, 1856.

Mr. MacKeen edited for a year or two the Journal of Education, and as Superintendent of city schools wrote a number of valuable annual reports, the suggestions contained in which have greatly furthered the cause of public education in the State of New York. See Allibone.

McKeen, Miss Phebe F. *Thornton Hall*, or Old Questions in Young Lives. By Phebe F. McKeen. New York : Anson D. F. Randolph & Co. 1872. 8vo, pp. 325.

—*Theodora.* A Home Story. By Phebe F. McKeen. New York : Anson D. F. Randolph & Co. 1875. 8vo, pp. 480.

—*The Little Mother* and Her Christmas. By Phebe F. McKeen. Boston : D. Lothrop & Co. 1875. 8vo, pp. 55.

—*Memorials* of Phebe Fuller McKeen. By Annie Sawyer Downs and Henrietta Learoyd Sperry. Published for the Alumnae Association of Abbot Academy. Andover: Warren F. Draper. 1880. 8vo, pp. 20.

Miss McKeen was a native of Bradford, Vt., being a daughter of the late Rev. Silas McKeen, D. D. She was a teacher in Abbott Academy, Andover, Mass. She died June 1st or 2d, 1880, on the cars from New York to Boston, being on her return home from Baltimore, where she had passed the previous winter for her health. See McKeen's History of Bradford, Vt., pp. 434-5.

McKEEN, SILAS. *A Sermon*, delivered before the Vermont Colonization Society at Montpelier, October 15, 1828. By Silas McKeen, Pastor of the Congregational Church in Bradford. Montpelier: Printed by E. P. Walton, Watchman Office. 1828. 8vo, pp. 22.

—*The right Object* and use of religious investigation. An Address to the Society for Religious Inquiry in the University of Vermont, August 5, 1828. By Silas McKeen, an Honorary Member. Burlington: Printed at the Free Press Office. 1828. 8vo, pp. 11.

—*The Watchman's Report.* A Sermon delivered in Bradford, Vt. On Thanksgiving Day December 3, 1829. By Silas McKeen, Pastor of the Congregational Church in Bradford. January, 1830. Post Press, Haverhill, N. H. Henry F. Evans, Printer. 8vo, pp. 18.

—*The Triumphs of Christ's enemies* no cause of discouragement. A Sermon, delivered at Winthrop, June 21, 1830, on the evening previous to the meeting of the General Convention of Maine. By Silas McKeen, Pastor of the Congregational Church in Bradford, Vt. Published by Request. Portland : Printed by Shirley, Hyde & Co. 1830. 8vo, pp. 26.

—*A Farewell Sermon*, delivered January 20, 1833, to the Congregational Church and Society in Bradford, Vt. By Silas McKeen, their former Pastor. Printed by request of those concerned. Haverhill, N. H.: Printed by J. R. Reding. 1833. 8vo, pp. 16.

—*The Condition* and Prospects of our Country. A Discourse delivered in Belfast, Me., on Fast Day, April 20, 1837. By Silas McKeen, Pastor of the First Congregational Church in Belfast. 8vo, pp. 29.

—*A Scriptural Argument* in favor of Withdrawing Fellowship from Churches and Ecclesiastical Bodies tolerating Slaveholding among them. By Rev. Silas McKeen, of Bradford, Vt. New York : Published by the American and Foreign Anti-Slavery Society. William Harned, publishing Agent, 61 John Street. 1848. 12mo, pp. 38.

—*God's way in the Sea.* A Funeral Sermon, Preached at Bradford, Vt., April 25th, 1852 ; on the occasion of the Death of Eber D. Hovey, First Mate of the Steamship Independence, who, with several others, Perished in Matagorda Bay, Texas, March 26th, 1852. By Silas McKeen, Pastor of the Congregational Church in Bradford. Published by request. Bradford, Vt.: Printed by Simon C. Abbott. 1852. 8vo, pp. 14.

—*Rev. S. McKeen's Review* of "A Letter of Inquiry to Ministers of the Gospel of all Denominations, on Slavery. By A Northern Presbyter," (Rev. N. Lord, D. D., President of Dartmouth College.) Published by request of the Orange Association, New Hampshire. From the New Englander for August, 1855. 8vo, pp. 26.

—*"The Responsibilities of young Men."* A Sermon occasioned by the Death of Arthur H. Prichard, addressed to his friends, the Young Men of Bradford, Vt., March 30, 1856. By Silas McKeen, Pastor of the Congregational Church in that place. L. J. McIndoe, Printer. 1856. 8vo, pp. 17.

—*Civil Government* a Divine Institution. A Sermon Delivered before The General Assembly of the State of Vermont : October 9, 1857, By Rev. Silas McKeen, of Bradford, Vt. Montpelier : E. P. Walton, Printer. 1857. 8vo, pp. 34.

—*The Claims of Vermont.* A Sermon, delivered before the Congregational Convention of Vermont, Bennington, June 18, 1857. By Silas McKeen, Pastor of the Congregational Church, Bradford, Vt. Windsor : Printed at the Vermont Chronicle Office. 1857. 8vo, pp. 16.

—*Activity in Duty* urged from the Brevity of Life. A Sermon delivered in Bradford, Vt., March 25, 1858, at the funeral of Oliver J. Hardy, who died at Hayneville, Alabama, Feb. 26, 1858. By Rev. Silas McKeen, Pastor of the Congregational Church in Bradford. Bradford: L. J. McIndoe, Printer. 1858. 8vo, pp. 15.

—*The Duty* and proper manner of Family worship considered. A Sermon Delivered before Orange County Conference, at West Fairlee, Vt., September 28, 1858. By Rev. Silas McKeen, Pastor of the Congregational Church in Bradford. Published by Request of the Conference. E. A. Fuller's Book and Job office, Bradford, Vt. 8vo, pp. 18.

—*The Bible* the young Man's Perfect Guide. A Sermon delivered in Bradford, Vt., November 21, 1858, at the Funeral of Alfred Bliss King, who died in Fairlee, Vt., November 18th, 1858, at the age of 25 years, By Rev. Silas McKeen, Pastor of the Congregational Church in Bradford. Published by request of the Young Men's Christian Association. E. A. Fuller's Book and Job Office, Bradford, Vt. 8vo, pp. 20.

—*The Nature*, Duty and Benefits of a Pious Confidence in God. A Sermon delivered in Bradford, Vt., December 26, 1858; at the funeral of Mrs. Martha T. Peckett, wife of John B. Peckett, Esq. Who died suddenly Dec. 25, 1858; at the age of 66 years. By Rev. Silas McKeen, Pastor of the Congregational Church in Bradford. Published by request. E. A. Fuller's Book & Job Office, Bradford, Vt. 8vo, pp. 17.

—*Heroic Patriotism.* A Sermon, delivered at Bradford, Vt., Sabbath Afternoon, April 28, 1861, In the presence of the Bradford Guards, when under call to join the First Regiment of the Vermont Volunteers, and go forth in their Country's Service. By Rev. Silas McKeen. Published by request of the Company. Windsor, Vt.: Printed at the Chronicle Press. 1861. 8vo, pp. 16.
A list of names of members of the Company appended.

—*A Sermon* February 5, 1860, after the funeral of Mrs. Nancy B. Farnum. Windsor: 1860. 8vo, pp. 17.

—*A Memorial* of Col. George W. Prichard. By Rev. Silas McKeen, D. D. Bradford, Vt.: Cobb & Earle, Printers and Publishers. 1867. 8vo, pp. 11.

—*A History* of Bradford, Vt., Containing some Account of the place—of its First Settlement in 1765, and the principal Improvements made, and events which have occurred down to 1874. With Genealogical Records, and Biographical Sketches of Families and Individuals. By Rev. Silas McKeen, D. D. Written by Request of the Town. Montpelier, Vt.: J. D. Clark & Son, Publishers. 1875. 8vo, pp. 459. (3)
This book, although bearing the imprint of the Messrs. Clark, was printed at the office of the Argus and Patriot.

—*A Sermon*, in the National Preacher, 1832.

—*Funeral Sermon*, B. P. Baldwin, 1853.

—*Sermon* on Romanism, 1854.

—*Sermon* before the American Missionary Association, at West Meriden, Conn., 1854.

—*Friends of Good Order*, a discourse at Bradford, 1858.

—*Funeral Sermon* of Mrs. Bethia B. Albee, 1859.

—*Funeral* of H. H. Niles, 1864.

—*Memorial* of Rev. Increase S. Davis, 1865.

—*Funeral Sermon*, Mary A. Quimby, 1871.

—*A Tract*, no, 208, American Tract Society. "The worth of a Dollar."

—*Funeral Sermon* on the death of.
See Elliot, L. H.

—*Memorial* of Rev. Silas McKeen, D. D., of Bradford, Vt. (Printed by Alfred Mudge and son, 34 School St.) [Boston.] 8vo, pp. 49, (2), Portrait.
Prepared by Rev. William S. Palmer, of Norwich, Conn., and others; also contains funeral sermon by Rev. L. H. Elliot; remarks by Rev. J. K. Williams, of West Rutland, Vt., and vital statistics.
Rev. Dr. McKeen was born in Corinth, Vt., March 16, 1791; and died in Bradford, Vt., December 10, 1877. He began to preach in 1814, his first sermon at Vershire, Vt.; he then went immediately to Bradford, and preached a year as a candidate, and was formally settled over the Congregational church there October 28, 1815, where he continued through life, with the exception of about nine years that he was settled at Belfast, Maine—December, 1832, to May, 1842. Mr. McKeen published altogether about thirty discourses and essays. For a full sketch of the life of Mr. McKeen and his family and ancestry, consult his history of Bradford; also Congregational Quarterly, July, 1878.

McLeod, T. H. *Instrumental Calculation*, or a Treatise on the Sliding Rule. By T. H. McLeod. Middlebury: George Smith, Publisher. 1846. 12mo, pp. 192.

McQuill, Thursty. (*Pseudon ?*) The Connecticut by Daylight, from New York to White Mountains, Lake Memphremagog, Montreal and Quebec; via. New Haven, Hartford, Springfield, Northampton, Deerfield, Greenfield, Brattleboro, Bellows Falls, Windsor, White River Junction, Wells River, St. Johnsbury, Stowe, Burlington and St. Albans. By Thursty McQuill. The first descriptive Guide-Board ever published. Published by American News Company, New York. 1874. 12mo, pp. 108.

Meacham, James. *Nebraska and Kansas.* Speech of Mr. Meacham, of Vermont, in the House of Representatives, Feb. 15, 1854, Against the Nebraska and Kansas Territorial Bill, and in favor of maintaining the Government faith with the Indian Tribes. 8vo, pp. 7, n. p. n. d.

—*The California Question.* Speech of Hon. James Meacham, of Vermont, in the House of Representatives, May 14, 1850, In Committee of the Whole on the state of the Union, on Mr. McClernand's Bill relating to California. n. p. n. d. 8vo, pp. 8.

—*Speech* of Hon. James Meacham, of Vermont, in the House of Representatives, June 9 and 10, 1852, On the Modification of the Tariff. 8vo, pp. 7.

—*Defense of the Clergy.* Speech of Hon. James Meacham, of Vermont, in the House of Representatives, Washington, May 17, 1854. Washington: 8vo, pp. 8.

—*Speech* of Hon. James Meacham, of Vermont, on Kansas Affairs, delivered in the House of Representatives, April 30, 1856. Washington: 1856, 8vo, pp. 8.

—*Chaplains in Congress* and in the Army and Navy. 1854. 8vo, pp. 19.

—*Report* of Hon. James Meacham, of the

Special Committee of the Board of Regents of the Smithsonian Institution, on the Distribution of the Income of the Smithsonian Fund, &c. Washington : For the Smithsonian Institution. 1854. 8vo, pp. 63.

Mr. Meacham was born in Rutland, Vt., in 1810; died August 22, 1856. Was graduated at Middlebury College in 1832, and, a tutor there; studied Theology, and was settled in New Haven, Vt.; was called from his parish to the Professorship of Elocution and English Literature, in Middlebury College, when in 1849 he was elected a Representative in Congress, and was continued there until the time of his death.

Mead, Charles Marsh. *The Soul* Here and Hereafter : A Biblical Study, By Charles M. Mead, Professor in Andover Theological Seminary. Published by the Congregational Publishing Society, Boston : [1879.] 12mo, pp. xv, 462.

—*Exodus*, or the Second Book of Moses, By John Peter Lange, D. D., Professor of Theology in the University of Bonn. Translated by Charles M. Mead, Ph. D., Professor of the Hebrew Language and Literature in the Theological Seminary at Andover, Mass. New York : Scribner, Armstrong & Co. 1876. pp. 179.

Bound in a volume with a translation of Lange's Leviticus.

Mr. Mead has delivered various essays and lectures in Boston Courses, which have been published in their volumes. Also articles in periodicals : "A Glance at Prussian Politics," in Continental Monthly, N. Y., September and October, 1864; Eight important articles in the " Bibliotheca Sacra," 1863 to 1876; two or more in the " New Englander;" a Baccalaureate Sermon at Andover, 1877, together with numerous articles in newspapers.

Mr. Mead is a native of Cornwall, Vt., born January 28, 1837; was graduated at Middlebury College, 1856; was a teacher at Phillips Academy, Andover, Mass., 1856-8; Tutor at Middlebury College, 1859-60; graduated at Andover Theological Seminary 1862; he then passed about four years (1863-6) in Germany for study. Professor of Hebrew in Andover Theological Seminary, 1866-82; Lecturer at Princeton Theol. Sem., 1889.

Mead, Hiram. *Occasions* for Gratitude in the present National Crisis. A Sermon, preached in the Meeting-house of the First Congregational Church of South Hadley, on Thanksgiving Day, Nov. 21, 1861. Northampton: Printed by Trumbull & Gere. 1861. 8vo, pp. 21.

—*Farewell Words* to the Mount Holyoke Class of 1864. By Rev. H. Mead, Secretary of the Trustees. New York : John F. Trow, Printer, 50 Greene Street, 1864. 12mo, pp. 12.

—*Sermon* at the Installation of Rev. William E. Park, as Pastor of the Congregational Church of Gloversville, N. Y., July 21st, 1876. Gloversville, N. Y. pp. 17.

Printed with the other exercises at the installation.

Additional publications by Dr. Mead; Influence of the Masses on Literary Men, Address at Middlebury College 1867; History of Council Hall, 1874; Reading, an Address before a Teachers' Association, 1875; Rationalism in Modern Literature, Address before Evangelical Association, Detroit, 1877; A New Declaration of Faith, National Council, St. Louis, 1880; :The Manual of Praise for Sabbath and Social Worship, 1880. [Edited by Prof. Mead and F. B. Mead.]

Mr. Mead, brother of Charles M. Mead, was born in Cornwall, Vt., May 10, 1827; was graduated at Middlebury College, 1850; he was a teacher for two years at Flushing Institute, Long Island; Tutor at Middlebury College about three years and was graduated at Andover Theological Seminary 1857; Pastor of the First Congregational Church, South Hadley, Mass., 1858-67; Olive street church, Nashua, N. H., 1867-9. After which time until his death he was Professor of Sacred Rhetoric at Oberlin College, Ohio. Married, 1858, Aug. 5, Elizabeth S. Billings, of Andover. One son and one daughter. Died in Oberlin, May 18, 1881, aged 54 years and 8 days.

Middlebury College gave him the honorary D. D. in 1870.

Medical. *A copy* of the Petition of Doctors Hyde and Fitch, to the Hon. the General Assembly of Vermont. Praying for a Medical Lottery. Unto which are Annexed, the Recommendations of sundry Gentlemen ; and Dr. Duncan's Reasons why the Prayer of said Petitioners ought to be Granted. Printed in the Year 1800. 18mo, pp. 16.

The object was to publish a medical work by Dr. Stearns.

—*Catalogue* of the Officers and Students of the Clinical School of Medicine, at Woodstock, Vt. Connected with Waterville College. 1831. 12mo, pp. 10.

—*The Eastern Medical Reformer.* A Monthly Journal of Medical and Chirurgical Science. Motto. John B. Hibbard, M. D., Editor and Proprietor. Vol. 1. No. 2. Rutland, (Vt.) April, 1846. 12mo, pp. 32.

No. 2 of Vol. I, is all we have seen.

See Sylvester, W. E., Address, 1879.

—*Antisell, Thomas.* Address, Introductory to the Course of Lectures in the Chemical Department of the Vermont Medical College, delivered before the Class of Session 1854. By Thomas Antisell, M. D., Professor of Chemistry to the College, etc. Published by the Class of the College. Woodstock : Press of the Vermont Temperance Standard. 1854. 8vo, pp. 24.

See Castleton Medical College ; University of Vermont ; Vermont Medical Society ; Vermont Medical Journal ; Middlebury College ; Vermont Pharmaceutical Association ; Gallup, J. A , for Vermont Medical College at Woodstock ; Deming, Calvin. Chittenden County Medical Society ; Davis, D. D., Medical Expositor ; Dean, Amos, Medical Jusisprudence ; Goldsmith, M.; Gleiwitz, G.; McClintock, J., Addresses, 1841-3 ; Paine, Martyn ; Perkins, Joseph, Addresses, 1854, 1856 ; Gaskill, Silas ; Root, Erastus, address, 1817 ; Thayer, C. P., Vermont Medical Register, 1877 ; Thresher, L., Family Physician ; Thomson, S., Guide to Health ; Vermont Medical College ; Vermont Academy of Medicine ; Perkins, S. C., address, 1855; Markoe, T. M., Address, 1847 ; Thayer, W. H., Address, 1855. Holton, Address, 1889.

Meditations *among the Tombs ;* tending to reform the Vices of the Age, and to promote Evangelical Holiness. By James Hervey, Late Rector of Weston-Favell, in Northamptonshire. Second Edition. Windsor, Vt. Printed and Published by Jesse Cochran, and sold Wholesale and Retail at his Bookstore. 1814. 18mo, pp. 143.

See Hervey, James.

Meikle, James. *Solitude sweetened ;* or, Miscellaneous Meditations on various Religious Subjects, written in Distant Parts of the World. By James Meikle, late Surgeon at Cornwath. Texts. Fourth American Edition. Brattleborough : Published by William Fessenden. 1814. 12mo, pp. 324.

—*Another edition:* Brattleborough : Published by John Holbrook. 1817. 12mo, pp. 312.

Melvin, Eleazer *Journal* of Captain Eleazar Melvin, with eighteen men under his command, in the Wilderness towards Crown Point. 1748. N. H. Hist. Soc. Coll. Vol. v., pp. 207-211.

Mendon. *Annual Report* of the Officers of the Town of Mendon, for the Year Ending March 2nd, 1877. Rutland : Tuttle & Company, Printers. 1877. 8vo, pp. 12.

Continued.

Merrill, Arthur. *In Memoriam.* A Tribute to the Memory of Arthur Merrill, who died at Haverhill, N. H., November 27th, 1870, Aged 47 years. Tuttle & Co., Printers, Rutland, Vt. 8vo, pp. 4.

Merrill, Chester W. *Published* by Authority of the City Council. General Ordinances and Resolutions of the City of Cincinnati, in force July 1st, 1878, together with the Ordinances relating to Railroads and Street Railroads, and other Ordinances of General interest. Compiled under the direction of the City Solicitors. By Chester W. Merrill. Cincinnati Times Book and Job Printing Establishment. 1878. 8vo, pp. x, 676.

_{Chester Wright Merrill, son of the late Hon. Ferrand F Merrill, was born at Montpelier, Vt., April 23, 1846. Graduated at Dartmouth College in 1866. Studied law with Redfield and Gleason at Montpelier, Hoadly & Johnson, at Cincinnati, and at the law school of the Cincinnati College. Entered upon the practice of law at Cincinnati in 1871. He was for several years Librarian of the Public Library of Cincinnati. Married December 12, 1878, Mary Franklin, of Chillicothe, Ohio.}

Merrill, Daniel, A. M. *Balaam Disappointed.* A Thanksgiving Sermon Delivered at Nottingham West, April 13, 1815. A Day appointed by the National Government in which to rehearse God's Mighty Acts, and Praise his Name. By Daniel Merrill, A. M. Pastor of the Church of Christ in Nottingham West. Danville, Vt. Printed by Ebenezer Eaton.
_{See Dartmouth Alumni, for Biographical sketch, p. 51.}

Merrill, Rev. David.
_{Mr. Merrill was born in Peacham, Vt., September 8, 1798; and died there July 22, 1850. He was graduated at Dartmouth, in 1821, and at Andover, in 1825. and finally settled over a Presbyterian Church in Urbana, Ohio, in 1827, where he remained until 1841, when the difficulties between the "old and new schools" caused him to return to Peacham, where he became the colleague of Rev. Leonard Worcester, and succeeded him after his death in 1846. Mr. Merrill occupied a prominent and influential position among the clergy of Ohio, and was active in temperance work; in aid of this cause he wrote the famous "ox sermon," of 45 years ago, from Exodus XXI, 28-29, which had a circulation of more than two and a half million copies: which he followed in 1833 with "The Mate to the Ox," which had a large circulation at the west; it was from the text. I Timothy V: 22. He published an "Address before the Mechanics' Institute of Urbana," July 4, 1838. He was a prolific writer for the temperance, secular and religious press of Ohio, and left at his death over 650 manuscript sermons, besides an immense number of skeletons. A volume of his sermons, with a memoir by Thomas S. Pearson, was published: Windsor, Vt.: 1855. 12mo, pp. 288.}

Merrill, O. C. *An Oration* delivered at the Meeting-House in Bennington, on the 4th of July, 1806. By Orsamus C. Merrill. Bennington, Vt.: Benjamin Smead, Printer. 16 mo, pp. 56.
_{Biographical Sketch, See Jennings' History Bennington; Governor and Council. Vols. 6 and 7.}

Merrill, O. W. *A Farewell Sermon* delivered before the Congregational Church and Society at Corinth, Vt., Sunday morning, December 5th, 1858. By the Rev. O. W. Merrill. Published by request. E. A. Fuller's Book and Job Office, Bradford, Vt. 8vo, pp. 14.

Merrill, Samuel.
_{Brother of Rev. David, and born at Peacham, Vt., October 29, 1792, read law, and settled at Vevay, Ind., and in a few years moved to Indianapolis, where he continued to reside. He was State Treasurer, December 1822-1834, then President of the State Bank till 1844. He published "A Gazetteer of Indiana," etc., and in 1855 was in the book-selling and publishing business.}

Merrill, C. H. *The Father*, the Son, and the Holy Ghost. A Sermon preached in Brattleboro, Vt., February 11, 1883, by Rev. C. H. Merrill. Brattleboro: Printed by Selleck & Davis. 1883. 8vo, pp. 10.

Merrill, Thomas A. *A Sermon* preached in the Audience of His Excellency Isaac Tichenor, Esq, Governor: His Honor Paul Brigham Esq., Lieutenant Governor: The Honorable Council, and House of Representatives, of the State of Vermont, at Middlebury, on the Day of the Anniversary Election, October 9th, 1806. By Thomas A. Merrill, A. M. Pastor of the Church in Middlebury. Motto. Printed at Middlebury, Vermont, by A. Haswell; at the Press of J. D. Huntington. 1806. 8vo, pp. 30.

—*A Sermon* delivered before the Vermont Domestic Missionary Society, at their Annual Meeting, held in Royalton, Sept. 12, 1833. By Thomas A. Merrill, Pastor of the Congregational Church in Middlebury. [Published by request of the Directors.] Windsor: Printed at the Chronicle Press. 1834. 8vo, pp. 28.

—*History* of the General Convention of Congregational and Presbyterian Ministers in Vermont. Prepared by Rev. Thomas A. Merrill, D. D.
_{Am. Quar. Register, 1838, vol. xi., pp. 32-44.}

—*Semi-centennial* Sermons, Containing a History of Middlebury, Vermont, Delivered, Dec. 3, 1840, being the first Thanksgiving Day, after the expiration of half a Century from the organization of the Congregational Church, Sept. 5, 1790. By Thomas A. Merrill, D. D., Pastor of the Church. Motto. Middlebury: Printed by E. Maxham. 1841. 8vo, pp. 92.

—*The Fearful Argument.* A Sermon, preached in the Congregational Church, in Middlebury, Vt., January 1, 1854. By the Pastor. Middlebury: Justus Cobb, Printer, Register Office. 1854. 8vo, pp. 16.

—*An Essay* on the Study of the Latin Language in our Schools and Colleges, at the expense of writing and speaking English, especially extemporaneously. By Thomas A. Merrill, D. D., Late Pastor of the Congregational Church in Middlebury, Vt. New York: Published by Leavitt & Allen. 1860. 8vo, pp. 58.
_{Thomas Abbott Merrill, A. M., D. D., was born in Andover, Mass., January 18, 1780; and died at Middlebury, Vt., April 29, 1855. He was graduated at Dartmouth College, 1801, and was tutor there, and at Middlebury until 1805, when he was settled as Pastor over the Congregational Church at Middlebury, which office he held until his death. See Goodhue, J. F., for memoir.}

Merriman, T. M. *History* of Religion and Empire in Parallel from the Creation. Johnson, Vt., 1860. pp. viii, 520.

Merritt, Timothy. *A Discourse* on the War with England; Delivered in Hallowell, on Public Fast, April 7, 1814. By Timothy Merritt. Weathersfield, Vt. Printed by Eddy and Patrick. 1814. sm. 8vo, pp. 22.

METHODIST EPISCOPAL CHURCH. *The Experience* of several Eminent Methodist Preachers. With an Account of their call to, and success in the Ministry. In a series of Letters Written by Themselves, to John Wesley, A. M. Barnard, (Vt.) Published by Joseph

Dix. I. H. Carpenter, Printer. 1812. 12mo,
pp. 354, (2).
 Relates the experience of Methodist preachers in England.

—*Extracts* of Letters, Containing some Ac-
count of the work of God since the year 1800.
Written by the preachers and Members of the
Methodist Episcopal Church, to their Bishops.
Motto. Barnard, (Vt.) Published by Joseph
Dix, For the Purchaser. I. H. Carpenter,
Printer. March, 1812. 16mo, pp. 120.
 Relates wholly to the United States, and somewhat to
Vermont.

—*Minutes* of the Troy Conference of the Methodist Episcopal Church. Held at Albany, N. Y.,
June 2, 1841. (Being the Ninth Annual Session.) Albany: 1841. 12mo, pp. 16.
 Continued.

—*Fourth Annual Report* of the Troy Confer-
ence Missionary Society; Auxiliary to the
Missionary Society of the Methodist Episcopal
Church. 1854. Troy, N. Y. 1854. 12mo, pp.
66.
 Continued.

—*Troy Conference* Miscellany, Containing a
Historical Sketch of Methodism within the
bounds of the Troy Conference of the Metho-
dist Episcopal Church, with Reminiscences of
its deceased, and Contributions by its living
Ministers. With an Appendix. By Rev.
Stephen Parks. Albany: J. Lord, Philip
Street. Troy: W. H. Young. Burlington:
S. Huntington. 1854. 12mo, pp. 423.

—*Troy Conference* Directory, Session at Middlebury, Vt. 1858. Rutland: Geo. A. Tuttle
& Co. Printers. 12mo, pp. 8.

—*Minutes* of the Seventeenth Session of the
Vermont Annual Conference of the Methodist
Episcopal Church, Held at Barre, April 17-22,
1861. Published by Order of the Conference.
Montpelier: E. P. Walton, Printer. 1861.
8vo, pp. 40.
 Continued.

—*Minutes* of the Vermont Annual Conference
of the Methodist Episcopal Church, Held at
Chelsea, April 3-4-5-6, 1872. Twenty-Eighth
Session. Montpelier: Messenger Steam Printing House and Bindery. 1872. 8vo, pp. 74,
(1).

—*The Same*, Held at Barre, 1877. 8vo, pp. 58.
 Continued.

—*Troy Conference* of the Methodist Episcopal
Church. Programme and Directory of the
Forty-Third Annual Session, at the M. E.
Church, Glen's Falls, N. Y. Beginning April
21st, 1875. Bishop E. R. Ames, D. D., Presid-
ing. Glen's Falls, N. Y. 1875. 18mo, pp. 17.
 Continued.

—*Report* of the Vermont Conference Missionary Society. Auxiliary to the Missionary Society of the Methodist Episcopal Church, 1866.
Montpelier: Freeman Steam Printing Establishment. 1866. 12mo, pp. 35.
 Continued.

Middlebury Argus—*Extra*. Letter of the
Hon. Richard Rush, addressed to a Committee
appointed at a Public Meeting Held at Middlebury: April 1784? (Sic) [1834]. 12mo, pp.
16.
 In opposition to a re-charter of the United States Bank,
and in approval of the removal of the deposits by President Jackson.

Middlebury. *The Literary* and Philosophical
Repertory; embracing discoveries and improvements in the physical sciences, the liberal
and fine arts, essays, Moral and Religious, occasional notices, and review of new publications, and articles of miscellaneous intelligence.
Edited by a number of Gentlemen. Vol. I.
Middlebury, Vt.: Printed for S. Swift, by T.
C. Strong. 1813.
 This periodical was published occasionally, commencing in April, 1812, and terminating in May, 1817. 2 vols.
in all, pp. 476, 486. See Sanders, D. C.

—*A Manual* for the use of the Congregational
Church in Middlebury, Vt., Adopted and published by order of the Church, August 5, 1853.
Motto. Middlebury: Justus Cobb, Printer.
1853. 18mo, pp. 56.

—*Oration* by Prof. Brainard Kellogg, and
Poem by Mrs. J. C. R. Dorr, Delivered at the
Pioneer Centennial Celebration, Middlebury,
Vt., July 4th, 1866. Middlebury: Register
Book and Job Printing Establishment. 1866.
8vo, pp. 40.

—*A Manual* for the use of the Congregational
Church in Middlebury, Vt., adopted and published by order of the Church, August 5, 1853.
Middlebury: Justus Cobb, Printer. 18mo, pp.
56.

—*Catalogue* of the Officers, Teachers and Pupils
of Middlebury Graded School, 1871-2. Middlebury: Register Print. 12mo, pp. 32.

—*Manual* of the Congregational Church, Middlebury, Vt., December 16, A. D. 1875. Middlebury: Knapp & Bailey, Printers. 1876.
8vo, pp. 64.

—*Acts* of Incorporation of the Village of Middlebury, and By-Laws of the Corporation.
Middlebury: Justus Cobb, Printer. 1846.
12mo, pp. 16.

—*Act* of Incorporation of the Village of Middlebury, School Law, and By-Laws of the Village. Middlebury: Printed at the Journal
Office. 1877. 8vo, pp. 16.

—*19th Annual Report* of the Auditors, Selectmen, Treasurer, and Poormaster, of the town
of Middlebury, February 18, 1879. Middlebury:
Register Job Print. 1879. 8vo, pp. 23.
 Continued.

—*History of.*
 See Merrill, T. A.; Swift, S.; Hall, Frederick.

MIDDLEBURY COLLEGE. *The Laws* of
Middlebury College, in Middlebury, in Vermont; Enacted by the President and Fellows,
the 17th Day of August, 1803. Middlebury:
Printed by Huntington & Fitch. 1804. 8vo,
pp. 20.
 See Chipman, Henry; Oration, 1806.

—*Poem* spoken before the Philomathesian Society of Middlebury College, at the celebration
of the Anniversary of the Society, on the evening before the public Commencement, Aug. 18,
1807. By an Honorary Member of the Society.
Motto. Published by request of the Society.
Middlebury, Vt.: Printed by J. D. Huntington. 1807. 12mo. pp. 12.
 Hon. Asahel Clarke, of the class of 1806, was the author
of this poem. Mr. Clarke was a lawyer of note, and died
at Glen's Falls, N. Y., November 22, 1822, aged about
40; Hon. D. W. C. Clarke was his son.

See Davis Henry, Inaugural Oration, February 21, 1814; Baccalaureate, 1810; also Narrative in relation to Hamilton College, 1833.

See Proudfit, A. Sermon February 21, 1810.

—*Catalogue* of the Faculty and Students of Middlebury College, April, 1814. Rev. Henry Davis, S. T. D. President. Hon. David Chipman, A. M. Professor of Law. Frederick Hall, A. M. Prof. of Math. and Nat. Philosophy. Rev. John Hough, A. M. Prof. of Languages. Joel H. Linsley, A. B. Senior Tutor and Librarian. Samuel S. Davis, A. B. Junior Tutor.

Broadsheet.

See Hall, Frederick, Eulogy on the death of Prof. S. M. Allen, 1818.

—*Concise Account* of the Institution, Transactions and present Condition of Middlebury College Charitable Society. Middlebury, Vt. 1817. 8vo.

—*Statement* of Facts, relative to the appointment of the Author to the office of Professor of Chemistry, in Middlebury College, and the termination of his connexion with that College. By Gamaliel S. Olds, A. M. Greenfield: Printed by Denio and Phelps. 8vo, pp. 20. [1818.]

—*Eulogy* on the death of Dr. Bates by Rev. Geo. Howe, D. D. 1854.

See Bates, Joshua, Inaugural Address, March 18, 1818.

—*Laws* and Catalogue of Library of Middlebury College, 1811.

—*The Same*—1823. pp. 24.

—*Catalogue* of the Officers and Students of Middlebury College, and the Vermont Academy of Medicine, in connexion. November, 1827. Castleton: Press of the Vermont Statesman. 12mo, pp. 16.

Continued.

—*An Oration* delivered at Middlebury, before the Associated Alumni of the College, on the evening of the Commencement, August 19, 1829. Published by request. By John Frost, Utica, N. Y. 1829. 8vo, pp. 23.

Mr. Frost was from Sandgate, Vt., and of the Class of 1806. He died at Waterville, N. Y., March 1, 1842. See Pearson's Graduates of Middlebury College.

See Hough, Rev. John, Address, 1830.

—*The Philomathesian*, Vol. 1. No. 1. July, 1833. Monthly. Conducted by a Literary Association in Middlebury College. Middlebury: Printed by E. W. Blaisdell, at the Office of the Free Press. 8vo, pp. 40.

Continued.

See Hooker, E. W., Address, 1834.

—*Catalogue* of the Corporation, Faculty and Students of Middlebury College. October, 1836. Middlebury: Knapp and Jewett, Printers. 1836. 8vo, pp. 16.

Continued.

—*Character* and Characteristics of Middlebury College. By Auctor Incertus. Motto. Middlebury: 1837. 24mo, pp. 22.

—*Historical* Sketch of, by Rev. Professor Fowler. pp. 10. 1837.

See American Quarterly Register, Vol. 9, pp. 220–229.

See Curtis, Rev. Harvey; Address, 1838.

See Mallary, R. C. Address, August 18, 1824;

See Beeman, N. S. S. Oration, August 17, 1825;

See Green, Beriah, Oration, 1826; Southmayd, J. C., Address, 1826.

See Henshaw, J. P. K., Oration, 1827.

—*The Laws* of Middlebury College. Middlebury: Printed at the office of the People's Press. 1839. 8vo, pp. 24.

—*The Same.* Middlebury: Printed at the Register Office. 1862. pp. 19.

—*Catalogue* of the Corporation and Faculty of Middlebury College, with a Statement of the Terms of Admission, Course of Study, &c. Middlebury: J. Cobb, Jr. Printer. 1838. 8vo, pp. 16.

—*Catalogue* of the Library of the Philomathesian Society: Middlebury College. 1844. Middlebury, Vt. Printed by Ephraim Maxham. 1844. 8vo, pp. 27.

—*Catalogue* of Books in the Library of Middlebury College. 1833. 8vo, pp. 16.

—*Same*, 1833. pp. 29.

See Bates, Joshua, Address, 1824.

—*Catalogus* Senatus Academici, et eorum, qui munera et officia academica gesserunt, quique alicujus gradus laurea exornati fuerunt, in Collegio Medioburiensi 1802–1814. Medioburiae: Typis Timothei C. Strong. 1814. 8vo, pp. 8.

Continued.

—*Middlebury College* and Vermont Academy of Medicine. Catalogue of the Faculty and Students. 1821. Rutland: Wm. Fay's Print. 1821. 8vo, pp. 8.

Continued.

—*Address* delivered at the Inauguration of the Professors of Middlebury College, March 18, 1839. Published by request of the Corporation. Middlebury. 1839. 8vo, pp. 56.

See Labaree, Benjamin. Address, May 18, 1841;

See Marsh, George P. Address, the Goths in New England, 1843;

—*Address* by Rev. W. B. Sprague, July 30, 1844.

See Saxe, J. G. Progress, a Poem, 1846.

See Hickok, L. P. Address, 1847.

—*Addresses* and Proceedings at the Semi-Centennial Celebration of Middlebury, Vt., August 20, 21, and 22, 1850. Middlebury: Printed by Justus Cobb, Register Office. 1850. 8vo, pp. 179.

Addresses by President Labaree, Rev. Joshua Bates, D. D., and Rev. John Hough, D. D.; with a full account of the arrangements, proceedings at dinner, etc.

See Post, T. M., Address, 1850, and 1879.

Lawrence, Myron. Address and Proceedings in Boston, 1851;

Blanchard, Rev. J., Address, 1851.

—*Catalogue* of the Graduates of Middlebury College; embracing a Biographical Register and Directory. Prepared for the Press, under the direction of a committee of the Associated Alumni, by Thomas Scott Pearson, A. B. Windsor: Printed at the Vermont Chronicle Press. 1853. 8vo, pp. 144.

See Roberts, Daniel. Address, 1853.

Baccalaureate Address, 1853, by Professor Bittenger. J. Cobb, Printer. 12mo, pp. 20.

—*Junior Exhibition.* Middlebury College, April 26, 1853. 8vo, pp. (4).

See Boardman, Rev. G. N. Sermon, 1858.

—*First Report* of the Class of 1858. By "Old Rabbi," Class Secretary. Little Falls, N. Y. 12mo, pp. 8.

—*Catalogue* of the Library of Middlebury College. Middlebury: Printed at the Register Book and Job Office. 1859. 8vo, pp. 37.

—*Grand Rehearsal* of the Miracle of the Loquacious Ass. Unabridged History of the Class of '60. Middlebury College. Illustrated by Cruikshanks. Printed by Corn Cobb & Sarsaparilla Mead, Mud Bury, Vt.
A comical illustrated history of the Class of 1860; contains also order of exercises, Junior Exhibition, 1859.

—*Celebration* on the Sixtieth Anniversary of the Foundation of Middlebury College. Addresses and a Poem, on laying the corner stone of a new edifice. Published by the Students. Middlebury: Printed at the Register Book and Job Office. 1860. 8vo, pp. 35.
Addresses by President Labaree and Brainard Kellogg; Poem by E. H. Phelps.

—*Sixty-First Anniversary* of Middlebury College, August 13, 14 and 15, 1861. (Programme) 8vo, pp. (8).

—*Parkerian Prize Exhibition*, Middlebury College, Thursday Evening, August 13, 1861. Music by Doering's Band, of Troy, N. Y. 8vo, pp. (4).

—*Union of the Colleges.* 8vo, pp. 8. September, 1864. By A Trustee of Middlebury College.
Is opposed to a consolidation with the University of Vermont, under an act passed by the Legislature, granting the privilege.

—*A Baccalaureate Discourse*, delivered at Middlebury, Vt., August 6, 1865, By Benjamin Labaree, D. D., President of Middlebury College, on the Twenty-Fifth Anniversary of his Presidency. Published by request of the Trustees. Boston: Press of T. R. Marvin & Son. 1865. 8vo, pp. 28.

—*Sketch* of its condition, wants, etc. [1865]. 8vo, pp. 4.

—*Addresses* at the Inauguration of Rev. H. D. Kitchel, D. D., President of Middlebury College. Middlebury: Register Book and Job Printing Establishment. 1866. 8vo, pp. 32.

—*Special Advantages* of the Smaller Country Colleges. Address delivered before the Alumni of Middlebury College, July 1, 1879, at the Semi-Centennial Reunion of the Class of '29, by Rev. Truman M. Post, D. D. Boston: Mudge & Son, Printers. 1879.

—*Catalogue* of Subscriptions and Donations to a Fund of One Hundred Thousand Dollars for Middlebury College, Completed May 1st, 1869. Manchester: C. A. Pierce & Co., Job Printers. 1869. 8vo, pp. 8.

—*The Kaleidoscope*, 1875-76. Published by the Senior Class. Volume III. Rutland: Tuttle & Co., Printers. 1875. 8vo, pp. 48.
See Hulbert, C. B. Address, July 21, 1875; also Addresses, 1875.
See Allen, J. Adams. Address, 1876.

—*Catalogue* of the Officers and Students of Middlebury College, For the Academical Year, 1876-77. Published for the College. 1876. 8vo, pp. 27.
Continued.

—*Necrological* Report of the Associated Alumni of Middlebury College, for the year Preceding Commencement, for the years 1868 to 1876, in-clusive. Seven pamphlets; 8vo, pp. 8, 13, 16, 32, 15, 15, and 15.
See Tenney, Rev. H. M., Poem, 1879.

—*Inauguration* of Cyrus Hamlin, D. D., LL. D., as President of Middlebury College, Wednesday, July 6, 1881. Middlebury: Register Steam Book and Job Print. 1881. 8vo, pp. 19.

—*Catalogue* of the Officers and Alumni of Middlebury College, and all others who have received degrees, 1800 to 1889. Compiled by Thomas E. Boyce, A. M., Class of 1876, Professor of Mathematics. Middlebury: The Register Company, Printers. 1890. 8vo, pp 194.

The Middlebury *Selection of Hymns*, compiled principally from Cowper, Doddridge, Newton and Rippon. Middlebury: J. D. Huntington. 1809. 18mo, pp. 108.

—*Selection of Hymns*, Compiled from Various Authors. Second Edition enlarged. Middlebury: Printed by T. C. Strong for the Proprietor. 1814. 16mo, pp. 146.

Middlesex. *Annual Reports* of the Town of Middlesex, for the year ending March 1, 1864. Montpelier: Printed at the Freeman Printing Establishment. 1864. 8vo, pp. 8.
Continued.

Middletown. *History of.*
See Frisble, Barnes.

MILITARY. *An Act* for Regulating and Governing the Militia of the State of Vermont, and For Repealing all Laws heretofore passed for that purpose. Passed in October, One Thousand Seven Hundred and Ninety-Three. By Order of the Legislature. Windsor: Printed by Alden Spooner. M.DCC.XCIII. 12mo, pp. 20.

—*Militia Law.* An Act for Regulating and Governing the Militia of the State. Passed March 10th, A. D. 1797. 12mo, pp. 54.
Title-page and a few leaves at the end wanting.

—*The Vermont Disciplinarian;* Containing A System of Instructions in the Rudiments of Military Science; Designed To promote the Order and Discipline of the Militia of the State of Vermont. By John W. Brownson, Late an Officer in the Army of the United States. Bennington: Printed by Haswell & Smead. 1805. 12mo, pp. 104. Plates.

—*The Laws* of the State of Vermont, for Regulating and Governing the Militia. Bennington: Printed by Anthony Haswell, State Printer. 1809. 12mo, pp. 4, 41, and 5.

—*An Act* Regulating and Governing the Militia of Vermont. Passed November 10, 1818. Published by Order of the Legislature. Middlebury, Vt.: Printed by J. W. Copeland. 1819. 12mo, pp. 63.

—*Infantry Exercise* of the United States Army, Abridged for the use of the Militia of the United States. Third Edition—Corrected and improved. Montpelier, Vt.: Published by order of the Legislature. E. P. Walton, Printer. 1820. 12mo, pp. 107.
And 16 pages of plates.

—*An Act*, Relating to the Militia of the State of Vermont, passed the eleventh day of November, A. D. 1842, together with the Regulations of Uniform and the organization. Prepared and published for the use of the Militia, in conformity to the laws of the State, By Frederick W. Hopkins. Adjutant and Inspector General. Montpelier : E. P. Walton and Sons, Printers. 1843. 8vo, pp. 93.

—*An Act* Relating to the Militia of the State of Vermont, Part II, passed first day of November, A. D. 1843 : Together with the alterations of Organization since 1838. Prepared and published for the use of the Militia, in conformity to the laws of the State, By Frederick W. Hopkins, Adjutant and Inspector General. Montpelier : E. P. Walton and Sons, Printers. 1844. 8vo, pp. 32.

—*Report* of the (Senate) Committee on Military Affairs relative to the Militia of this State. Annual Session, 1862. H. E. Stoughton, for Committee. 8vo, pp. 21.

—*October Session*, 1862. Report of the (House) Committee on Military Affairs. A. B. Gardner, for Committee. 8vo, pp. 59.

—*An Act* for the Organization, Regulation and Government of the Militia of Vermont, passed by the General Assembly, at the Annual Session, 1862. Published by Authority. Montpelier : Printed at the Freeman Office. 1862. 8vo, pp. 22.

—*Muster Rolls* of the Vermont Regiments mustered into the service of the United States since the Commencement of the Rebellion. Carefully compiled from the Muster Rolls in the hands of the State Officers. Rutland : George A. Tuttle. 1862. 12mo, pp. (106).

—*Register* of Commissioned Officers of the Vermont Volunteers. In the Service of the United States. Adjutant & Inspector General's Office, Woodstock, Vt., June 1, 1863. Montpelier : Walton's Print, 8vo, pp. 37.

—*An Act Organizing* the Militia, Approved Nov. 22, 1864. Printed by Authority. Montpelier : Walton's Steam Press. 1864. 8vo. pp. 20.

—*General Order No. 1.* Regulations for Military Districts and Raising and Organizing Twelve Regiments of Militia. Montpelier : Walton's Steam Press. 1864. 8vo, pp. 18.

—*General Order No. 5.* Regulations for Completion of Organization of Companies of Militia, and for Draft. Montpelier : Walton's Steam Press. 1864. 8vo, pp. 15.

—*General Order No. 8.* Rules and Regulations for the Enrollment of the Militia and the Government of the Organized Militia. Montpelier : Walton's Steam Press. 1865. 8vo, pp. 73.

—*General Order No. 12.* Rules and Regulations for the Cavalry and Light Artillery of the Organized Militia. Montpelier : Walton's Steam Printing Establishment. 1865. 8vo, pp. 14.

—*General Order No. 2.* Regulations for raising and organizing Three Regiments of Active Militia. Montpelier : Printed at the Freeman Steam Printing Establishment. 1868. 8vo, pp. 98.

—*General Order No. 8.* Regulations for the Guidance of the Active Militia of the State of Vermont. Montpelier : Poland's Steam Printing Establishment. 1873. 8vo, pp. 36.

See Vermont, for Adjutant and Inspector General's Reports, Quartermaster General's Reports, Surgeon General's Reports, Legislative Documents; Hewes, R.; Lamb, L.; Rules and Articles of War ; Steuben, Baron de.

Miller, J. P. *The Condition of Greece*, in 1827 and 1828 ; Being an Exposition of the Poverty, Distress, and Misery, to which the Inhabitants have been reduced by the destruction of their Towns and Villages, and the Ravages of their country, by a Merciless Turkish Foe. By Col. Jonathan P. Miller, of Vermont. As contained in his Journal, Kept by order of the Executive Greek Committee of the City of New York ; Commencing with his departure from that place in the Ship Chancellor, March, 1827, and terminating with his return in May, 1828 ; during which time he visited Greece, and acted as Principal Agent in the distribution of the several cargoes of Clothing and Provisions sent from the United States to the old men, women, children, and non-combatants of Greece. Embellished with Plates. New York : Printed by J. & J. Harper. 1828. 8vo, pp. 300.

—*Letters from Greece.* [By J. P. Miller, George Jarvis, and a Greek Prince]. Boston : 1825. 8vo, pp. 20.

From Massachusetts Historical Society Catalogue. Col. Miller's first visit to Greece was in 1824. For a Sketch of the life of Col. Miller, see Thompson's History of Montpelier.

Miller, W *Evidences* from Scripture & History of the second coming of Christ about the year A. D. 1843, and of his Personal Reign of about 1,000 years. By Wm. Miller. Motto. Brandon : Vermont Telegraph Office. 1833. 8vo, pp. 64.

—**Miller, Rev W. A.** *Hints* against error and extravagance in Religion. A Sermon Delivered in substance, at a Camp-Meeting, near Sandy Hill, N. Y. Sept. 4, 1857, By W. A. Miller of the Troy Conference. Motto. Burlington : George J. Stacy, Book and Job Printer, Church Street. 1858. 8vo, pp. 11.

—*The Home of the Blessed.* A Sermon in Memory of Ruth Cooley, deceased, of Pittsford, Vt. Delivered at Pittsford, March 1st, 1874, By Rev. W. A. Miller, Text. Rutland : Globe Paper Company, Printers. 1874. 8vo, pp. 15.

—*Sermon* of Sorrow and Consolation and of Morality and Piety, by Wm. Abel Miller. Rutland ; Tuttle & Co., Printers. 1884. 8vo, pp. 194.

Milligan, James. *A Plea* for Infant Baptism, in seven parts. By James Milligan, Pastor of the Reformed Presbyterian Societies in Ryegate, Topsham, Barnet and Craftsbury. Motto. Danville : Printed by Ebenezer Eaton. 1818. 12mo, pp. 300.

—*A Narrative* of the Late Controversy between the Associate and Reformed Presbyterians of Ryegate and Barnet ; To which it is designed to add as an Appendix, A View of the Principles and Practice, which Christians ought to adopt and pursue in order to the Establishment of A Righteous, Permanent, and Universal Peace. By James Milligan. Motto. Danville ; Ebenezer Eaton, Printer— 1819. 8vo, pp. 136.

Mr. Milligan was of the Old School Presbyterian faith, and was settled over a church of that order in Ryegate, Vt., 1817-1839; when he left on account of a division in the church from its being infected with the ridiculous notion that a church member could not exercise the elective franchise, without being subject to the discipline of the church.

Milliken, D. L. *The Cottage Hearth,* a periodical for youth. Boston : 1874.
Continued.

—*An Oration* Delivered on the occasion of the Celebration of the 102d Anniversary of the Declaration of American Independence. At Maplewood, Mass., July 4, 1878. By D. L. Milliken. Printed by Wm. G. J. Perry, Maplewood Street. 12mo, pp. 19.
Mr. Milliken is a native of Springfield, Vt.; he was some time connected with the "Record," Brattleboro, and other newspapers in the State, as editor and publisher.

Milton. *Annual Report* of the Superintendent of Common Schools, for the Town of Milton. 1870. Burlington, Vt. R. S. Styles, Book and Job Printer. 1870. 8vo, pp. 6.

—*Annual Report* of the Selectmen & Auditors of the Town of Milton, Vt., February, 1876. Burlington : 1876. 8vo, pp. 11.

The Minister *Preaching* his own Funeral Sermon ; with an Account of the remarkable death of the Rev. Thomas Chamberlain. Montpelier : Published by Wright & Sibley. 1812. 24mo, pp. 96.

Minutes *of the Thirtieth Anniversary* of the Lake George Baptist Association ; Held with the Church at Minerva, N. Y., September 2 & 3, 1846. Alvin Barton, Cor. Secretary, Horicon, Warren Co., N. Y. East Poultney : Printed by J. K. Seaver, Vermont Observer Press. 1846. 8vo, pp. 8.

Minot, George R. *The History* of the Insurrections in Massachusetts, in the Year MDCCL XXXVI, and the Rebellion Consequent thereon. By George Richards Minot, A. M. Printed at Worcester, Massachusetts, by Isaiah Thomas. MDCCLXXXVIII. 8vo, pp. 192.
Known as the "Shay's Rebellion." Many of the first settlers in various sections of Vermont were refugees from the Shays party, and the authorities and people of Vermont being favorable to immigration, the Shays men who came within her borders with a view of settlement, were never seriously disturbed. Mr. Minot says : "Those decisive measures by the authorities of New York, obliged the malcontents to flee out of the State of New York, and to betake themselves to their last resort in Vermont." Governor Chittenden, however, in obedience to a bare majority of the General Assembly, but in opposition to his own views, issued a proclamation on the subject as a matter of courtesy perhaps to the Governor of Massachusetts ; for Vermont being an independent State, and not a member of the Confederation of States, was not bound by the articles of Confederation "binding themselves to assist each other against all force opposed to, or attacks upon them, or any of them," etc. And there was no extradition treaty existing between Vermont and any of the other States. See Tyler, Royall.

The Missisquoi *Spring Water* and its Wonderful Cures. New York : Anson Herrick & Sons. [1867.] 16mo, pp. 16.

Mitchell, W. *Address* before the Temperance Society, Middlebury, Vt. 1833.

—*Sorrow on the Sea.* A Sermon on the Wreck of the Home, October 9, 1837, Delivered in the Congregational Church, Rutland, November 5, 1837. By William Mitchell, Pastor of the

Church. Published by Request. Rutland : Herald Office Print. 1837. 8vo.

—*A Treatise* on the Relative Importance and Mode of Baptism ; comprising two discourses delivered in the Congregational Church, Rutland, March, 1838. By William Mitchell, Pastor of the Church. Motto. Windsor : Chronicle Press. No. 3, Pettes' Block. 1838. 8vo, pp. 48.

—*The Claims of Africa.* A Discourse delivered at Montpelier, at the Annual Meeting of the Vermont Colonization Society, October 19, 1843, by William Mitchell, Pastor of the Congregational Church, East Rutland. Burlington : Printed by Stilman Fletcher. 1843. 8vo, pp. 24.

—*Two Discourses* on Baptism. 1833.

—*Coleridge,* and the Moral Tendency of his Writings. By —— [Rev. William Mitchell, of Rutland, Vt.] * * New York : Leavitt, Trow & Co., 194 Broadway. 1844. 8vo, pp, 119.
Mr. Mitchell was born in Chester, Conn., in 1792, and died in Corpus Christi, Texas, 1867 ; was graduated at Yale, 1818, and at Andover, 1821. Preached in Rutland, Vt., 1833-46, and at Wallingford, Vt., 1847-52 ; then agent for the Vermont Colonization Society a few years, and removed to Texas about 1860.

Mix, Eldridge. *A Discourse* delivered in the Congregational Church, Bakersfield, Vt., January 16th, 1866, on occasion of the Installation of Rev. G. F. Wright, by Eldridge Mix. Printed by request of the Church. Burlington : Free Press Book and Job Printing House. 1866. 8vo, pp. 16.

—*A Discourse,* delivered Sabbath Evening, Nov. 4, 1866, before the Young Men's Christian Union of Burlington. By Rev. Eldridge Mix, Pastor of the First Congregational Church. Burlington, Vt.: R. S. Styles, Book and Job Printer. 1866. 8vo, pp. 23.

A Modern *Collection of Moral,* Religious and Interesting Stories ; designed for the service of American Youth. By a Lover of their Precious and Immortal Souls. Motto. Bennington : Printed by A. Haswell. 1802.

Monroe, John *The American Botanist,* and Family Physician; (with a very long title, most of which we omit.) By John Monroe. Compiled by Silas Gaskill. Wheelock, (Vt.) Published by Jonathan Morrison, 1824. Danville ; Eben'r Eaton, Printer. 12mo, pp. 203.
See Gaskill, Silas.

Monsigny, Mary. *Mythology;* or, A History of the Fabulous Deities of the Ancients. By Madame Monsigny. First American Edition. Randolph, (Vt.): Printed by Sereno Wright, for Thomas and Merrifield. 1809. 12mo, pp. 298.

MONTPELIER. *Something New,* or Memoirs of that truly Eccentric Character, the late Timothy Dexter, Esq., Together with his last Will and Testament. Montpelier : 1808. 8vo.
Sabin.

—*Records* of the Montpelier Lyceum, 1829 to 1836. pp. 353. 4to, Manuscript.
Belongs to the Vermont Historical Society.

—*Catalogue* of Books of the Montpelier Agricultural Library. Broadsheet. n. d. n. p.

—*Winooski Impetus.* Metropolis of Vermont. April 15, 1835, to March, 1836. 4to, Published monthly by a society of young men.

—*Confession of Faith*, Covenant, and rules of Church Government. Adopted by the First Congregational Church in Montpelier, March, 1832. E. P. Walton, Printer, 1832. 16mo, pp. 11.

—*Confession of Faith*, Covenants, and Rules of Church Government, adopted by the First Congregational Church in Montpelier, with a catalogue of resident members, June 2, 1839. Montpelier: E. P. Walton & Sons, Printers. 1839. 12mo. pp. 24.

—*Another edition*, 1842, same imprint. pp. 24.

—*Another edition*, 1876. Polands' Print. 18mo, pp. 32.

—*Catalogue* of the Bethany Church Sunday School Library, Montpelier, Vermont, January 1, 1871. Montpelier: Journal Print. 1871. 18mo, pp. 12.

—*Services* at the Dedication of Green Mount Cemetery, Montpelier, Vt., Sept. 15, 1855, with the Rules and Regulations. Published by order of the Commissioners. Montpelier: E. P. Walton, Jr., Printer. 1855. 8vo, pp. 40.

—*Child's Book.* Illustrated. Montpelier, Vt. E. P. Walton. 32mo, pp. 8.

—*Report* of Town Officers. 1844. Broadsheet.
The first printed Town Report. Continued.

—*Annual Reports of the* Officers of the Town of Montpelier, March 1, 1859. Walton's Steam Press. 8vo, pp. 8.
Continued.

—*Act* of Incorporation and By-Laws of the Village of Montpelier. 1848. pp. 12. Same 1855, pp. 12.

—*Third Edition*, with Amendments. 1864. 8vo, pp. 15

—*Fourth Edition.* 1875. Montpelier, Vt.: Argus and Patriot Steam Book and Job Printing House. 1875. 8vo, pp. 19.

—*Village Reports.* Annually.

—*Catalogue* of the Sabbath School Library of the First Congregational Church, (Brick church) Montpelier, Vt. Montpelier: Walton's Steam Printing Establishment. 1861. 12mo, pp. 18.

—*In Memoriam* of the Rt. Rev. John H. Hopkins, D. D., LL. D., D. C. L. Oxon, Bishop of Vermont. Historical Sketch of Christ Church Parish, Montpelier, Vermont. Description of the Church Building, Account of the Clerical Convocation, and of the Consecration of Rev. W. H. A. Bissell, D. D., Bishop-elect of Vermont, and the proceedings of the Diocesan Convention, etc., etc. Montpelier, Vermont: Printed at the Argus and Patriot Job Printing Office. 1868. 8vo, pp. 16.

—*Illustrated* Capital Advertiser! Issued by Farwell Brothers, Head of State Street, Hiram Atkins, Main Street, opposite Bethany Church, Montpelier, Vt. Printed at the Argus and Patriot Job Printing Office, Montpelier, Vt.: 1872. 12mo, pp. (8).

—*By-Laws* of Capitol Engine Co. No. 5, Montpelier, Vt. Revised May 21, 1872. Montpelier: Polands' Steam Press. 1872. 18mo, pp. 8.

—*Report* of the Committee on Water Supply for the Village of Montpelier, Nov. 20, 1873.

Montpelier: Poland's Printing Establishment. 1873. 8vo, pp. 20.

—*Lane's* Celebrated Patent Lever Set Circular Saw Mills, Manufactured by Lane, Pitkin & Brock, Montpelier, Vt. 1873. 8vo, pp. 58.

—*Illustrated Circular* of the Lane Mfg. Company, Montpelier, Vt. Organized May 19, 1873. Capital $120,000. Circular Saw-Mills, Turbine Waterwheels, Planing Machines, Matching Machines, Steam Engines, Mill Furnishings, &c. &c. Montpelier, Vt.: Argus and Patriot Steam Book and Job Printing House. 1875. 12mo, pp. 152.

—*History of.* See Gridley, J., and Thompson, D. P.

—*The History* of the Town of Montpelier, including that of the Town of East Montpelier, for the first one hundred and two years. [From Vol. IV, of the Vermont Historical Gazetteer, now in Press.] Montpelier, Vt. Published by Miss A. M. Hemenway. 1882. [Joseph Poland, Printer.] 8vo, pp. viii, 342, and 69. Portraits and engravings.

—*In God we Trust.* Constitution and By-Laws of the Hibernian Benevolent Society of Montpelier, Vt. Organized 1874. Montpelier, Vt.: Argus and Patriot Book and Job Printing Works, 1874. 18mo, pp. 16.

—*Exhibition* of the New Organ in Trinity Church, Montpelier, Friday Eve., Nov. 2, 1875. [n. p. n. d.] pp. 4.

—*Webb's Montpelier Directory*, 1875-6-7. W. S. Webb & Co., Publishers, New York. Motto, Truman C. Phinney, Bookseller and Stationer, Union Block, State Street, Montpelier, Vt. 8vo, pp. 50.

—*Montpelier Illustrated;* with a brief Sketch, by Hon. E. P. Walton.
See New York Daily Graphic, November 8, 1877.

—*Montpelier* Manufacturing Company's Children's Carriages and Boys Velocipedes, Montpelier, Vt. 1877. Twentieth Annual Catalogue. 8vo, pp. 32.

—*Pocket Directory* of the Village of Montpelier for 1877. Containing a List of Residents, Churches, Localities, Advertisements of Business Firms, and much other matter of Local Interest. Montpelier: Poland's Press. 1877. 18mo, pp. 90.

—*Church* of the Messiah, Montpelier, Vt. Covenant of Christian Fellowship. With list of names. 1877. 16mo, pp. 8.

—*By-Laws* of the Capitol Guards, Co. H. 1st Regt. N. G. of Vt. Montpelier, Vt.: Freeman Steam Printing House and Bindery. 1878. 16mo, pp. 6, (2).

—*Holiday Chimes.* Argus and Patriot, Montpelier, Vt., Job Printing of all kinds, neat, prompt, and reasonable prices. The best work done in Vermont. For Advertisement of Argus and Patriot Store see next page. [1879.] 8vo, pp. (20.)

—*Constitution* and By-Laws of the Saint John Baptist Benevolent Society of Montpelier, Vt. Incorporated November 23, 1872. Let us Love one another. Burlington: The Free Press Association. 1879. 18mo, pp. 20.

—*Representative* Business Houses of Montpelier. Montpelier, Vt. [1884.] No. 1. Vol. 1. 4to, pp. 8.

The **Montpelierian**. *Vol. 5.* No. 1. Seminary Hill, Montpelier, Vt., January 20, 1877. Published by the Literary Societies of the Montpelier Seminary and Female College. 4to, pp. 8, (4.)
Continued Monthly.

Montague, Erastus. *Trial* and Defence of. 1835. 12mo, pp. 60.
Relates to a Methodist church difficulty, in Bennington, 1834-5.

Moody, R. *An Address.* 1882.
See Temperance.

Moore, Augusta *Against* the Ministers of the New York and Brooklyn Ministerial Association. "They have made void Thy Law." By Augusta Moore. 1876: Printed at the Journal Office, Poultney, Vt. 8vo, pp. 60.
Miss Moore's pamphlet of 60 pages is very interesting reading; it treats of (Beecher's) Plymouth church, of which she is or was a member in regular standing, as certified by Thomas G. Shearman, October 3, 1874. She is well connected, being a niece of Mr. Stone, editor of the New York "Journal of Commerce." She appears to have been a firm friend to Beecher so long as she could stand it. In short the pamphlet is rich; full of typographical errors, to be sure; which in the copy I have, from the library of the late Chauncey K. Williams, of Rutland, have been corrected by a careful hand. This pamphlet could be further illustrated, but as it only came to my hand at the last moment I drop the subject.

Moore, Rev. John. *Memoir* of, by Rev. John G. Adams; with Selections from his Correspondence, and other writings. Boston: Published by A. Tompkins. 1856. 12mo, pp. 360. Portrait.
Mr. Moore was a Universalist Clergyman of considerable prominence, and well and favorably known in his day throughout New England. He was born in Strafford, Vt., February 5, 1797; and died in Concord, N. H., February 5, 1855.

Moore, H. L. B. *Poetical Precepts*; or a Collection of Original Hymns. By H. L. B. Moore. Irasburgh: H. & G. H. Bradford, Printers. 1863. 18mo, pp. 31.

Moore, John W. *Complete* Encyclopedia of Music, Elementary, Technical, Historical, Biographical, Vocal, and Instrumental. By John W. Moore. Boston: Published by Oliver Ditson & Co. 277 Washington Street. r'l 8vo, pp. 1002. n. d.
Copyright entered in the District Court of Vermont, 1852; and Preface dated Bellows, Falls, Vt., 1854. This work contains biographies of more than 4,000 musicians, and a dictionary of over 5,000 musical terms, and is the result of fifteen years' labor. Mr. Moore also published: "Vocal and Instrumental Self Instructor;" "Sacred Minstrel;" "Musician's Lexicon;" and in 1856 "The American Collection of Instrumental Music." 4to, pp. 125.
Mr. Moore was a son of Jacob Bailey Moore, M. D., (who also published several musical pieces) and born in Andover, N. H., 1807. He was for several years editorially connected with the Bellows Falls "Gazette," also in the same capacity with other papers. George H. Moore and Frank Moore, of New York, are his nephews. He now resides in Manchester, N. H. (1879.)
See Printing in Vermont.

Moore, Zephaniah Swift, A. M. *The Ministers* of Christ desire the Salvation of Sinners. A Sermon Preached October 6, 1813, at the Ordination of the Rev. Jacob Allen, to the Pastoral care of the Church in Tunbridge, Vt. By Zephaniah Swift Moore, A. M., Professor of Languages in Dartmouth College. Montpelier: Printed by Walton & Goss. March, 1814. 8vo, pp. 23.

Rev. Dr. Moore was born at Palmer, Mass., November 20, 1770; he died at Amherst, Mass., June 30, 1823. At the age of about eight years he removed with his father's family to Wilmington, Vt., where he labored on a farm till he was about eighteen. He prepared for College at Bennington Academy, and was graduated at Dartmouth College in 1793; he read Theology, and was settled over various Congregational churches until 1811, when he accepted the chair of Professor of Languages in Dartmouth College; in 1815 he was elected to the Presidency of Williams College, which position he held until the founding of Amherst College, when in 1821 he accepted the Presidency of the same, which he filled until his death. Dr. Moore also published several other sermons and addresses, none of which relate to Vermont.
See Durfee's History of Williams College; Sprague's Annals.

Morehouse, Mrs. Carrie Warner. *The Legend* of Psyche and other Verses, by Mrs. Carrie Warner Morehouse. St. Johnsbury: 1887 (?) Charles T. Walter, Publisher.

Morey, Capt. Charles C. *Sermon* in Memory of.
See Edwards, John H.

Morhouse, Abraham. *The Writings* of a Pretended Prophet. Rutland, Vt.: 1796. 12mo.

MORRILL, JUSTIN SMITH. *Admission of Kansas.* Speech of Hon. J. S. Morrill, of Vermont, on the admission of Kansas as a Free State into the Union. Delivered in the House of Representatives, June 28, 1856. 8vo, pp. 8.

—*Speech* of Hon. Justin S. Morrill, of Vermont, in the House of Representatives, February 6, 1857, on the Tariff. 8vo, pp. 8.

—*A Bill* donating public lands to the several States and Territories which may provide Colleges for the benefit of Agriculture and the Mechanic Arts. Introduced by Mr. Morrill of Vt. Dec. 14, 1857. 8vo, pp. 4.

—*Speech* of Hon. Justin S. Morrill, of Vermont, on the Bill Granting Lands for Agricultural Colleges; Delivered in the House of Representatives, April 20, 1858. 8vo, pp. 16.

—*Tariff.* Speech of Hon. Justin S. Morrill, of Vermont, in the House of Representatives, April 23, 1860. 8vo, pp. 8.

—*Speech* on the Utah Territory and its Laws—Polygamy and its License; in the House of Representatives, February 23, 1857. Washington: 1857. 8vo, pp. 14.

—*The Kansas Question.* The Minority Report of the Select Committee of fifteen. J. S. Morrill, and others, for Minority. Washington: 1858. 8vo, pp. 16.

—*Modern Democracy.* The Extension of Slavery in our own territory or by the Acquisition of Foreign territory wrong morally, politically, and economically. Speech of Hon. Justin S. Morrill, of Vermont. In the House of Representatives, June 6, 1860. 8vo, pp. 8.
Published by the Republican Congressional Committee.

—*State of the Union.* Speech of Hon. Justin S. Morrill, of Vermont, in the House of Representatives, February 18, 1861. 8vo, pp. 8.

—*Agricultural Colleges.* Speech of Hon. Justin S. Morrill, of Vermont, in the House of Representatives, June 6, 1862. 8vo, pp. 8.

—*The Tariff.* Speech of Hon. Justin S. Morrill, of Vermont, in the House of Representatives, June 28, 1866. 8vo, pp. 8.

—*Explanation* of the Internal Tax Bill. Speech of Hon. Justin S. Morrill, of Vermont, in the House of Representatives, March 12, 1862. 8vo, pp. 8.

—*The Impolicy* of making paper a Legal Tender. Speech of Hon. Justin S. Morrill, of Vermont, in the House of Representatives, February 4, 1862. 8vo, pp. 8.

—*Remarks* in reply to Mr. Voorhees, of Indiana, in the House, May 21, 1863. 8vo, pp. 8.

—*The Finances.* Speech of Hon. Justin S. Morrill, of Vermont, in the House of Representatives, January 13, 1863. 8vo, pp. 8.

—*Tax Bill.* Speech of Hon. Justin S. Morrill, of Vermont, in the House of Representatives, April 19, 1864. 8vo, pp. 7.

—*Speech* of Hon. Justin S. Morrill, of Vermont, on the Loan Bill ; in the House of Representatives, February 21, 1866. 8vo, pp. 8.

—*Speech* of Hon. Justin S. Morrill, of Vermont, on the Internal Revenue Bill ; in the House of Representatives, May 7, 1866. 8vo, pp. 8.

—*Speech* of Justin S. Morrill of Vt., in favor of Terminating the Reciprocity Treaty with Great Britain, Delivered in the House of Representatives, January 27, 1864. Washington, D. C.: 1864. 8vo, pp. 14.

—*Cabinet Officers* in Congress. Speech of Hon. Justin S. Morrill, of Vermont, Delivered in the House of Representatives, January 25, 1865. 8vo, pp. 8.
  See Vermont, Report on Statuary Hall, Washington, 1866.

—*Letter* on the Knit Goods Manufacture. Boston: 1866. 8vo.

—*The Currency.* Speech in the House of Representatives, December 11, 1867. 8vo, pp. 16.

—*An Exclusively* Paper Currency inconsistent with permanent prosperity. Speech in the House, January 24, 1867. 8vo, pp. 14.
  Regarded as an important speech.

—*The Funding Bill.* Speech of Hon. Justin S. Morrill, of Vermont, delivered in the Senate of the United States, March 3, 1868. 8vo, pp. 14.

—*Impeachment* of the President. Opinion of Justin S. Morrill, of Vermont, in the Senate of the United States, May, 1868. 8vo, pp. 14.

—*Eulogies* on Hon. Thaddeus Stevens, by Mr. Cameron, of Pa., and Mr. Morrill, of Vt., delivered in the Senate of the United States, December 18, 1868. 8vo, pp. 8.

—*Reciprocity Treaty.* Speech of Hon. Justin S. Morrill, of Vermont, delivered in the Senate, January 14, 1869. 8vo, pp. 14.

—*Public Debt* and Currency. Speech of Hon. Justin S. Morrill, of Vermont, delivered in the Senate of the United States, February 11, 1869. 8vo, pp. 7.

—*Eight-hour Law.* Speech of Hon. Justin S. Morrill, of Vermont ; In the Senate, Dec. 15, 1869. 8vo, pp. 16.

—*Funding Bill.* Speech of Hon. Justin S. Morrill, of Vermont, in the United States Senate, March 3, 1870. 8vo, pp. 8.

—*A Protective Tariff* or Free Trade. Speech of Hon. Justin S. Morrill, of Vermont, in the Senate, May 9, 1870. 8vo, pp. 20.

—*Annexation* of Santo Domingo. Speech of Hon. Justin S. Morrill, of Vermont, delivered in the Senate of the United States, April 8, 1871. 8vo, pp. 24.

—*The Tariff Bill.* Speech of Hon. Justin S. Morrill, of Vermont, delivered in the Senate of the United States, March 20, 1872. 8vo, pp. 8.

—*Senator from North Carolina.* Speech of Hon. Justin S. Morrill, of Vermont, in the Senate of the United States, April 12, 1872. 8vo, pp. 7.

—*National Colleges.* Speech of Hon. Justin S. Morrill, of Vermont, in the Senate, December 5, 1872. 8vo, pp. 15.

—*Reciprocity Treaty* with Canada. Speech of Hon. Justin S. Morrill, of Vermont, in the Senate of the United States, February 8, 1875. 8vo, pp. 22.

—*Hawaiian Reciprocity Treaty.* Speech in the Senate. Executive Session, March 18, 1875. 8vo, pp. 14.

—*Resumption* of Specie Payments. Speech in the Senate, January 6, 1876. 8vo, pp. 24.

—*Mead's Statue* of Ethan Allen. Speeches of Hon's Justin S. Morrill and George F. Edmunds, of Vermont, in the Senate of the United States, June 10, 1876. 8vo, pp. 12.

—*Education Fund.* Speech of Hon. Justin S. Morrill, of Vermont, in the Senate of the United States, April 26, 1876. 8vo, pp. 22.

—*Remonetization of Silver.* Speech of Hon. J. S. Morrill, of Vermont, in the United States Senate, January 28, 1878. 8vo, pp. 39.

—*The Library of Congress.* The Capitol and its Grounds. Speech of Hon. Justin S. Morrill, of Vermont, in the Senate of the United States, March 31, 1879. 8vo, pp. 12.

—*On Admission* of the Cabinet into Congress. Speech of Hon. Justin S. Morrill, of Vermont, in the Senate of the United States, April 28, 1879. 8vo, pp. 13.

—*Resumption* of Specie Payments. Speech of Hon. Justin S. Morrill, of Vermont, in the Senate of the United States, May 30, 1878. 8vo, pp. 16.

—*Republican* and Democratic Measures. Speech of Hon. Justin S. Morrill, of Vermont, in the U. S. Senate, June 11, 1879. 8vo, pp. 19.

—*Refunding* the National Debt. Speech of Hon. J. S. Morrill, of Vermont, in the Senate of the United States, January 15, 1880. Washington : 1880. 8vo, pp. 16.

—*Remarks* of Hon. Justin S. Morrill, of Vermont, against the reconstruction of the Capitol, and in favor of a Commission to select a site for a new Library, delivered in the Senate of the United States, May 18, 1880. Washington : 1880. 8vo, pp. 8.

—*The Tariff.* Speech of Hon. Justin S. Morrill, of Vermont, in the U. S. Senate, Dec. 8, 1881, on the Bill to appoint a Tariff Commission. Washington : 1881. 8vo, pp. 28.

—*Japanese Indemnity Fund.* Speech of Hon. Justin S. Morrill, of Vermont, in the Senate, Feb. 16, 1883. Washington : 1883. 8vo, pp. 21.

Other speeches by Morrill, in the U. S. Senate, are as follows :

—*Upon the Bill* proposing a reduction of Internal Taxes and of the Tariff, January 10, 1883.

—*Japanese* Indemnity Fund, February 16, 1883.

—*Coinage,* Silver Certificates and United States Notes, December 5, 1883.

—*Congressional* Library Building, February 7, 1884.

—*Democratic* Tariff Platforms reviewed, April 16, 1884.

—*Reciprocity Treaties,* so-called, including that with Mexico, unconstitutional, January 7, 1885.

—*Coinage* of Silver Dollars, February 4, 1885.

—*Impolicy* of an Excess of Silver Coinage, January 20, 1886.

—*Executive Sessions* with open doors, June 30, 1886.

—*A Tariff* Revision should leave our Industries and labor unharmed and prosperous, December 9, 1886.

—*Immigration* Abuses, Dec. 14, 1887.

—*The President's Message* hostile to Home Protection, Home Markets and Home Labor, April 11, 1888.

—*Land Grants* to Steam Railroads in the District of Columbia, July 2, 1888.

—*Protective Tariff* of 1888, January 22d, 1889.

—*Silver Coinage* in 1890, June 2d, 1890.

—*Colleges* for the Benefit of Agriculture and the Mechanic Arts, June 14, 1890.

—*Tariff* of 1890, July 30, 1890.

—*The Silver Policy* of 1891, January 6, 1891.

—*The Policy* of an eight hour day, February 6, 1891.

—*Unlimited Silver Coinage,* an Unlimited Disaster, January 6, 1892.

—*A few* more words on Silver, June 16, 1892.

—*McGarrahan Claim,* January 16, 1893.

—*On the Free Coinage* substitute for the House Bond Bill, February 1, 1896.

—*Sound Money* cheats nobody, August 21, 1893.

—*Some Marvellous* Senatorial Bills, and Quack Panaceas for Real and Imaginary Grievances, December 11, 1894.

All the above speeches were printed Washington, D. C.

—*Remarks* by Justin S. Morrill on the Presentation by him of a Library Building to the Town of Strafford, Saturday, September 22d, 1883. Published by request of the town. Burlington : The Free Press Association, 1883. 8vo, pp. 15.

—*State Aid* to the U. S. Land Grant Colleges. An Address in behalf of the University of Ver-

mont and State Agricultural College, delivered in the Hall of the House of Representatives at Montpelier, October 10, 1888. By Justin S. Morrill. Burlington : The Free Press Association. 1888. 8vo, pp. 28.

—*The Land Grant Colleges.* An Address delivered at the eighty-ninth Commencement of the University of Vermont and State Agricultural College, June 28, 1895, by Justin S. Morrill, LL. D. Burlington : 1893. Free Press Association. 8vo, pp. 28.

—*Remarks* in the United States Senate by Justin S. Morrill, of Vermont, upon the Tariff, Free Coinage, and Collateral Matter, June 2, 1896. Washington : 1896, 8vo, pp. 16.

—*Proceedings* at the Unveiling of the Portrait of the Honorable Justin S. Morrill, Senator of the United States from Vermont, at the Annual Commencement of Cornell University, June 20, 1883. Ithaca, N. Y., 1883. 8vo, pp. 15.

—*Address* of Justin S. Morrill on Presentation of his Portrait to the Vermont Historical Society, by Thomas W. Wood, Oct. 25, '94. (Printed together with the address of H. O. Houghton, on the same occasion.) Montpelier : Watchman Publishing Co. 1894.

—*Self Consciousness* of Noted Persons, Compiled in Leisure hours by J. S. M. Printed for Private Distribution. Cambridge : John Wilson & Son, University Press, 1882. Large 8vo, pp. iv, 81.

A Second edition was published by Ticknor & Co., 1887.

Mr. Morrill also delivered Speeches which we have not at hand : On the Currency, December 11, 1867 ; Franking Privilege, February 15, 1870; Free Banking and Specie Payments, December 4, 1873; Legal tender and silver coin, June 8, 1876; Pacific railroads, April 2, 1878; Remarks on the Reduction of the Tobacco Tax, February 17, 1879; together with several others not included in the above list.

Mr. Morrill was born in Strafford, Vt., April 14, 1810; was engaged in mercantile pursuits until 1848, when he turned his attention to agriculture. He was elected a Representative from Vermont to the lower House of the thirty-fourth Congress, (1855) and continuously re-elected to that branch, until in 1867 he took his seat as a Senator in Congress from Vermont, which position he still holds, (1896) being a longer term of continuous service in Congress than has been held by any other man since the organization of the Goverment.

On the 20th of October, 1896, he was re-elected for a sixth term in the U. S. Senate, receiving the unanimous vote of the Republicans in both branches of the legislature.

See Lanman's Biographical Annals of the United States Civil Government, ed. 1876; Poore's do. ed. 1878.

Morrisville. *Manual* of the Congregational Church in Morrisville, Vermont, adopted December, 1874. Prepared under the direction of the Pastor, V. M. Hardy. Montpelier, Vt. : Argus and Patriot Printing Works. 1875. 12mo, pp. 34.

Morse, Charles Fitch. *Future Punishment,* and Universalism. A Sermon by Rev. C. F. Morse, McIndoes Falls, Vt. Montpelier: Printed at the Vermont Chronicle Office. 1883. 8vo, pp. 12.

Mr. Morse is a native of Salem, Vt., born July 28, 1825 ; was graduated at Amherst College, 1853, and at Andover, 1856. He was appointed a missionary and sailed for Constantinople, January 5, 1857. His additional publications are : "The Pope and the Roman Catholic Church," a book of about eighty pages in the Bulgarian language ; he translated into Bulgarian "The Tract Primer," "Jones Catechism," and an "Epitome of the Gospels."

He also prepared a Bulgarian and English Dictionary, in two parts, of about 7500 words each. Mr. Morse married, August 10,1856, Eliza D. Winter, of West Boylston, Mass.

Morse, William. *A Sermon*, the substance of which was Delivered Before the Vermont Legislature, in the Congregational Meeting House, Montpelier, Sunday Afternoon, Oct. 16, 1825. By William Morse, Late Pastor of the Second Universalist Church, Philadelphia. Published by request. Woodstock: Printed by David Watson. 1825. 8vo, pp, 22.

Morton, D. O. *Christ displeased* with unfaithful Christians. A Sermon, Delivered in Middlebury, June 21, 1816, on a day appointed by the Congregational Church, for Fasting and Prayer. By Daniel O. Morton. A. M., Pastor of the Congregational Church in Shoreham. Watch ye—Stand fast in the faith—St. Paul. Middlebury, Vt. Published by William Slade, Jun. August, 1816. 8vo, pp. 21.

—*A Sermon* preached at Middle Granville, on the Third Anniversary of the Northwestern Branch of the American Education Society, February. 26, 1823. By Daniel O. Morton, A. M., Pastor of the Congregational Church in Shoreham. Poultney: Printed by Smith & Shute. 1823. 8vo, pp. 36.

—*A Sermon*, delivered in Shoreham, December 2, 1824, on the day of the State Thanksgiving. By Daniel O. Morton, A. M., Pastor of the Congregational Church. Poultney: Smith & Shute, Printers, 1825. 8vo, pp. 14.

—*A Narrative* of a Revival of Religion, in Springfield, Vermont. 1834. 12mo, pp. 16.

—*Memoir* of Rev. Levi Parsons, Late Missionary to Palestine, in three Parts. Compiled and prepared by Rev. Daniel O. Morton, A. M. Pastor of a Church in Shoreham, (Vt.) Published and Printed by Smith & Shute. Poultney (Vt.) 1824. 12mo, pp. 431.

—*Another edition:* Burlington: 1830.

—*A Sermon*, Delivered in Shoreham, January 31, 1827, at the Funeral of Deacon Stephen Cooper, who departed this Life on Monday, the 29th, Aet. 81 years. By Daniel O. Morton, A. M., Pastor of the Congregational Church. Castleton: Published by Request. Ovid Miner, Printer. 1827. 8vo, pp. 22.

—"*Wine is a mocker*, Strong drink is raging." A Discourse, delivered at Montpelier, October 16, 1828, on the formation of the Vermont Temperance Society. By Daniel O. Morton, Pastor of the Congregational Church in Shoreham. Montpelier: Printed by E. P. Walton, Watchman Office. 1828. 8vo, pp. 16.

Mr. Morton was born in Winthrop, Me., December 21, 1788; and was Minister to the Congregational church, Shoreham, Vt., 1814-1831; at Springfield, Vt., 1832-1837; then in Winchendon, Mass., five years; in Bristol, N. H., ten years, where he died November 25, 1852.

See Goodhue's History of Shoreham, pp. 115-119.

Mosely & Stoddard. *Facts for Dairymen*, relating to patents. Mosely's Cabinet Creamery. Statements by its manufacturers, Mosely & Stoddard, Poultney, Vt., regarding protection afforded them by letters patent; together with an Expose of counter claims and reports put forth by competing manufacturers. Rut-

land: Tuttle & Co., Book and Job Printers. 1880. 8vo, pp. 28.

The Mother's Book. *A Monthly Publication.* Edited by Mrs. Sophia A. Hewes. April, 1839. Vol. II, No. 4. Chelsea, Orange County, Vt.: Published by William Hewes. Hatch's Building, Main Street. 1839. 8vo, pp. 24.

Motte, M. J. *An Address* delivered at the Funeral of Mrs. Martha Freme, By Rev. M. J. Motte. Brattleboro: Printed by B. D. Harris & Co. 1849. 12mo, pp. 12.

Mount Mansfield *and its environs.* Views and Sketches. Concord, N. H. Published by H. P. Moore. 16mo, pp. 23. n. d.

Mount Mansfield Hotel, *Guide and Hand-Book.* Concord, N. H. 1879. 16mo, pp. 16.

Prepared under the direction of Hon. E. C. Bailey, proprietor and manager of the hotel.

Mowry, W. A. *Collections* of the New Hampshire Antiquarian Society. No. 1. Who invented the American Steamboat? A Statement of the evidence that the first American Steamboat, propelled by means of paddle wheels, was invented, constructed, and successfully operated on Connecticut River, about 1792, by Captain Samuel Morey, of Orford, N. H., and that Robert Fulton saw the Boat in operation. By Wm. A. Mowry, A. M. of Providence, R. I. Read before the New Hampshire Antiquarian Society at an adjourned meeting, October 22, 1874. Contoocook: Published by the Antiquarian Society. Bristol: George Crowell Ketchum, Printer. 1874. 8vo, pp. 28.

Moxley, John. *Every One* his own Tailor. The Improved Compass Rule, now called The Thirds, to Cut Garments. By John Moxley. Danville: E. Eaton, Printer. 1823. 16mo, pp. 16.

Mt. Holly. *Annual Report* of the Board of Auditors for the Town of Mt. Holly, 1872. Rutland: Tuttle & Co., Printers. 1872. 8vo, pp. 12. .

Continued.

Munger, Sendol Barns. "*Conquest* of India by the Church."

Mr. Munger was born in Fairhaven, Vt., October 5, 1802; died in Bombay, India, July 23, 1868. He was graduated at Middlebury College, 1828, and at Andover, 1833; he was a missionary to Bombay and Selna several years, and on account of the ill health of his wife returned to this country in 1842; he re-embarked for Bombay, January 3, 1846, and during the passage his wife died at sea, and was buried in the Indian Ocean. He was stationed at different points in India until his death. Mr. Munger was the author of several books and tracts, among which are: "A Memoir of Mrs. Mary E. Munger," his second wife; "The New Creature," several editions; "The Conquest of India by the Church."

He married, 1st, in 1834, Maria L. Andrews, of Bristol, Vt., she died March 12, 1846; 2d, in 1854, Mary E. Ely, of Chicago, Ill., she died June 3, 1856; 3d, September 9, 1862, Mrs. Sarah S. Paul, of Boston, who survived him.

Munsell, Rev. Joseph Rice.

Was born in Swanton, Vt., October 6, 1803; and died at Harwichport, Mass., December 24, 1878. He was graduated at Bangor Theological Seminary in 1831, and was pastor of various Congregational churches in Maine, 1831-1858, at Harwich, Mass., 1858-1868, when he returned to his native State, and was acting pastor at Franklin, Vt., 1868-1875, when he retired from active labor, and resided at Harwichport, until his death.

Mr. Munsell's entire ministerial life was of the nature of a Home Missionary, being spent in the service of feeble parishes.

In 1843 he published by request two Sermons: "The importance of searching the Scriptures," and "The Christian's hope in Death."

See Congregational Minutes, (Vt.) 1879, pp. 41-2.

Munson, Loveland. *The Early History* of Manchester. An Address delivered in Music Hall, Manchester, Vt., Monday Evening, December 27, 1875. By Loveland Munson of Manchester. Journal Print, Manchester, Vt. 1876. 8vo, pp. 63.

Munson, Myron A. *None more golden than Gold.* A Thanksgiving Discourse, preached at Moriah, N. Y., by Myron A. Munson, M. A., November 28, 1872. Cambridge : Printed at the Riverside Press. 1873. 8vo, pp. 24.

Mr. Munson was Pastor of the Congregational church Pittsford, 1865-1869.

—*God's Doing* and Man's Doing for Minnesota. A Thanksgiving Discourse, preached in Northfield, Min., by Myron A. Munson, M. A., November 24, 1870. Chicago: Lakeside Publishing and Printing Company, 1871. 8vo, pp. 24.

—*Duty* contemplated as Due-ty, that which is due. By Myron A. Munson, M. A. Boston: A. Williams & Co., 283 Washington Street, 1876, 8vo, pp. 16.

Murray, Lindley. *An English* Spelling Book with Reading Lessons, in three parts. First Burlington Edition, with Improvements, in which the principal objection to this valuable work is removed by a more modern and approved division of the syllables. Burlington, Vt. Samuel Mills. 1811. 12mo.

—*The English Reader,* or Selections in Prose and Poetry, &c. By Lindley Murray. Burlington, Vermont: Printed by F. G. Fish, for N. & N. Dunham, Milton. 1816. 12mo. pp. 288.

—*English Reader.* Bellows Falls: Printed by Bill Blake & Co. 1820. 12mo, pp. 290.

—*Another Edition :* Burlington, Vt. Printed by E. & T. Mills. 1824. 12mo, pp. 244.

—*Introduction* to the English Reader, or a Selection of Pieces in Prose and Poetry, etc. From the Seventh English Edition, improved by the Author. Burlington, Vt. 1817. Printed by Samuel Mills. 12mo.

—*The English Reader ;* or Pieces of Prose and Poetry, selected from the best Writers. Bennington: Printed and sold by Darius Clark. 1821. 12mo, pp. 264.

—*Sequel* to the English Reader; or, Elegant Selections in Prose and Poetry. By Lindley Murray, Author of an English Grammar, &c. Woodstock, (Vermont:) Printed by D. Watson. 1821. 12mo, pp. 299.

—*The English Reader ;* or Pieces in Prose and Poetry. Selected from the best writers. Designed to assist young Persons to read with propriety and effect, &c. By Lindley Murray, Author of an English Grammar, &c. Montpelier: Printed by E. P. Walton. 1823. 12mo, pp. 262.

—*English Reader* in Prose and Poetry, improved by the Addition of a Concordant and Vocabulary, the words pronounced according to John Walker, by Jeremiah Goodrich. Windsor, Vt.: Printed by Simeon Ide. 1833. 12mo.

—*English Grammar.* Adapted to the Different Classes of Learners. With an Appendix, Containing Rules and Observations for assisting the more advanced Students to write with Perspicuity and Accuracy. By Lindley Murray. Published by Samuel Swift, Middlebury, Vt. Also, by E. J. Backus, Albany; Tracy & Bliss, Lansingburg, N. Y.; Justin Hinds, Hanover; Isaiah Thomas & Co., Walpole, N, H.; 1812. Walton & Goss, Printers, Montpelier, Vt. 16mo, pp. 328.

—*Abridgement* of Murray's English Grammar, with Exercises in Orthography, etc., for the use of Schools, and the Younger Classes. From the 20th English Edition, Corrected by the Author. Burlington, Vt. Printed by E. & T. Mills. 1822. 16mo.

—*English Grammar,* adapted to the different Classes of Learners, with an Appendix Containing Rules and Observations for assisting more advanced Students to write with perspicuity. Windsor, Vt: Ide & Goddard. 1834. 12mo.

—*Another Edition :* Windsor, Vt. Published by N. C. Goddard. 1838. 12mo, pp. 238.

—*Abridgement* of Murray's English Grammar. With an Appendix, etc. Woodstock, Vt. Printed by David Watson. 1821. 16mo, pp. 108.

—*Abridgement* of Murray's English Grammar, with an appendix. From the 20th London edition. Bennington, Vt. Published by Darius Clark. C. Doolittle, Printer. 1824. 18mo, pp. 90.

Murray, W. H. H. *How Deacon Tubman* and Parson Whitney kept New Years. St. Johnsbury : 1886 (?) Charles T. Walter, Publisher.

Mussey, George L. *The Summons* and Trial of George L. Mussey, of Rutland, Vt., before the Congregational Church, of Rutland, Vt., October 30, 1863. Together with a bird's eye view of the witnesses used on trial : Also, his experience in getting a mutual and exparte Council and closing with something else. Reported by Moses Burbank, Reporter for the Public Press. Rutland : Courier Office Print. 1864. 8vo, pp. 48.

Mystery. 8vo, pp. 12.

This pamphlet was printed in Woodstock, in 1852, by Nahum Haskell, and is curious as being a record of some of the early "spiritual" doings in Vermont. It is filled chiefly with "communications," the first being from a no less distinguished spirit than Washington. Dr. Nathaniel Randall, of Woodstock, and his wife Marenda were the movers in the business, the medium being a young man brought from New Hampshire, and taken to their house where the "communications" were received, Mrs. Randall doing the writing and the Doctor paying the printer's bills. There was naturally some popular feeling against such operations at the time and some hints of violence, which being magnified by the actors, the "medium" was carried away in the night and this pamphlet published in rather secret fashion.

Mystery. *A. E. Simmons'* Communications, from His Father, Harrison, and Ballou, and, also, A Line from the Medium's Own Pen. November 10, 1852. Woodstock : Printed for the Medium. 1852. 8vo, pp. 16.

Mr. Simmons, of Woodstock, had some reputation among Spiritualists as a trance speaker.

The above two titles are from R. A. Perkins, Esq., Woodstock. See Simmons, A. E.

—**Narrative**. A Narrative of the State of Religion, etc.
See Congregational.

—*Narrative* of the Surprise and Capture of Major General Richard Prescott of the British Army, in his Head-Quarters, together with his Aid-de-Camp, Major Barrington, by a party of American Soldiers under Major General Barton, July 9, 1777. To which is added a statement of General Barton's Law-suit in Vermont, and his sufferings. Windsor, Vt. 1821. 8vo, pp. 20. Printed by W. Spooner.
See Barton, General William.

—*Of a Voyage*, taken by Capt. James Vanleason, from Amsterdam to China : And from thence to the Western Continent of North America, where he found a vast number of Indians, and one of the largest Rivers in the World. Also, an Account of Mr. Vandeleur's being left behind, and his marriage with the Sachem's Daughter, etc., etc. Written by his Own Hand, and sent to his Uncle at Philadelphia, in 1796. With some account of the Country. Printed for the Purchaser, Windsor, Vt. 1801. pp. 45.

—*A Very Surprising Narrative* of a young Woman discovered in a Rocky Cave ; after having been taken by the Savage Indians of the Wilderness, in the year 1777, And seeing no human being for the space of nine years. In a Letter from a Gentleman to his Friend. Putney, (Vt.): Printed for the Purchaser. M,DCC,XCVII. 12mo, pp. 12.

Naramore, Gay H. *Poems* and Letters to Don Brown, by Gay Humboldt, Alias Burr Lington, D. L. L. . Albany : E. H. Berder, Publisher. MDCCCLVII. 12mo, pp. 252.
Mr. Naramore is a native of Underhill, Vt.; he has published another volume of poems, and various prose articles, including the "History of Underhill" in Miss Hemenway's Gazetteer.

Navigation of Connecticut River. *Journal* of the proceedings of the Convention, Holden at Windsor, Vt., February 16, 1825 ; For the purpose of taking Preliminary Measures to effect an Improved Navigation on Connecticut River. Published by order of the Convention. Windsor, Vt.: W. Spooner, print. 8vo, pp. 12.

—*Report* of the President and Directors of the Connecticut River Company, with the Report of H. Hutchinson, Esq. Laid before the Stockholders, at their Annual Meeting, January 3d, 1826. Hartford, (Ct.) 8vo, pp. 54.
One proposition in this report was to make the Connecticut River navigable by locks as high up as Barnet, Vt., and run a canal from the later place to Lake Memphremagog.

—*Journal* of the Convention, holden at Windsor, Vt., Sept. 29th & 30th, 1830. For the purpose of taking into consideration subjects connected with the Improvement of the Navigation of Connecticut River. Published by order of the Convention. Windsor : Simeon Ide, printer. 1830. 8vo, pp. 19.
See Mowry, W. A., for steamboat on Connecticut River; Vermont, Governor and Council, Vol. 4, pp. 446–53; Vermont, Canals proposed; also, Governor and Council, Vol. 7, for Canals proposed, pp. 479–82.
See "Papers and Proceedings of Connecticut Valley Hist. Soc.", 1876–1881. Springfield, Mass., pp. 114–123, where it is stated that the Steamboat "Barnet," Captain Nutt, ascended the Connecticut River to the town of Barnet in 1829; the boat was a side-wheeler, high pressure, with two engines of twenty-two horse power each ; and could make about six miles per hour. The paper also contains a pretty full account of steam navigation on the upper Connecticut.

Needham, D. *Address* of Hon. Daniel Needham, of Hartford, Vt., delivered at the Wool Growers' Convention, at Rutland, September 9th, 1862. Printed at the request of the Convention by the Vermont State Agricultural Society. L. J. McIndoe, Printer, Windsor, Vt.: 8vo, pp. 18.

—*Oration* of Hon. Daniel Needham, at the Dedication of the Town House in Ayer, Mass., October 26th, 1876. Ayer, Mass.: 1876. 8vo, pp. 20.

Neilson, Charles. *An original*, Compiled and Corrected Account of Burgoyne's Campaign, and the Memorable Battles of Bemis's Heights, Sept. 19, and Oct. 7, 1777, from the most Authentic Sources of information ; including many interesting incidents connected with the same : and a Map of the Battle Ground. By Charles Neilson, Esq. Motto. Albany : Printed by J. Munsell, 1844. 12mo, pp. 291.

Newbury. *Annual Report* of the Superintendent of Common Schools, of the Town of Newbury, A. D. 1861-1862. By Rev. N. H. Burton. L. J. McIndoe, Printer, Windsor, Vt. 8vo, pp. 15.
Continued.

—*Manual* of the First Congregational Church in Newbury, Vt. Montpelier : Printed by J. & J. M. Poland. 1876. 12mo, pp. 24.

—*Selectmen and Auditors' Report* of the Financial Condition of the Town of Newbury, From March 1, 1875 to March 1, 1876. And Transactions of Town Officers, to February 11, 1876. Montpelier, Vt.: Argus and Patriot Steam Job Printing House. 1876. 8vo, pp. 13.
Continued.

—*Report* of the Committee Appointed to Investigate the Financial Books and Accounts, of the Town of Newbury, Vt., March 1, 1877. Montpelier, Vt.: Argus and Patriot Steam Job Printing House, 1877. 8vo, pp. 44.

Newbury Biblical Magazine. *Edited* by Prof. W. M. Willett. Motto. Newbury, Vt.: Printed by Hayes & Co. 1843. 8vo, pp. 48. Vol. 1, No. 1.

Newcomb, Rev. Harvey. *The Wyandot Chief :* or the History of Barnet, a converted Indian and his two Sons. By Harvey Newcomb, author of the "North American Indians." Written for the Massachusetts Sabbath School Society, and revised by the Committee of Publication. Second edition, revised. Boston : Massachusetts Sabbath School Society. 1839. 18mo, pp. 81.
First edition in 1835.

—*The Anabaptists :* being an Account of the Progress of the Reformation in Germany, from the Diet of Worms to the Death of Frederic, Elector of Saxony ; comprising the History of the Anabaptists, or Mennonites : with remarks on Fanaticism, Riots, War, Oaths, Baptism, the Sabbath, and other subjects. By Harvey Newcomb. Boston : Massachusetts Sabbath School Society. Depository, No. 13, Cornhill. 1836. 12mo, pp. 224.

—*The Young Lady's Guide* to the Harmonious Development of Christian Character. By Harvey Newcomb. Third Edition, revised and enlarged. Boston: James P. Dow, Publisher. 1841. 8vo, pp. 384.

—*The Four Pillars:* or the Truth of Christianity demonstrated, in Four Distinct and Independent Series of Proofs; together with an Explanation of the Types and Prophecies concerning the Messiah. By Harvey Newcomb. Boston: Seth Goldsmith, and Croker & Brewster. Sold at the Mass. Sabbath School Depository, 13 Cornhill. 1842. 12mo, pp. 298.

—*How to be a Man:* a Book for Boys, containing Useful Hints on the Formation of Character. By Harvey Newcomb, Author of the "Young Lady's Guide," etc. Boston: Gould, Kendall and Lincoln. 1847. 12mo, pp. 224.

—*A Cyclopedia* of Missions; containing a Comprehensive View of Missionary Operations throughout the world; with Geographical Descriptions, and accounts of the Social, Moral and Religious Condition of the People. By Rev. Harvey Newcomb. New York: Charles Scribner. 145 Nassau Street. 1854. 8vo, pp. 784.

—*The Harvest* and the Reapers; Home-work for all, and how to do it. By Rev. Harvey Newcomb, Author of "Cyclopedia of Missions," "How to be a man," "How to be a Lady," etc., etc. Motto. Boston: Gould & Lincoln, 59 Washington Street. New York: Sheldon, Blakeman & Co. Cincinnati: George S. Blanchard. 1858. 12mo, pp. 270.

Mr. Newcomb was born in Thetford, Vt., September 2, 1803, and died at Brooklyn, N. Y., August 30. 1863. He was the son of Simon and Hannah (Curtis) Newcomb, and in 1818 the family moved to Alfred, N. Y., then the far west. At 16 years of age he commenced teaching school, and continued in that occupation for about ten years; in 1826 he published a newspaper in Westfield, N. Y., for two years, and then edited the "Buffalo Patriot" nearly two years, in 1830 and 1831 he published the "Christian Herald," a paper for children, at Pittsburgh, Pa. From 1831 to 1840 he was engaged in writing children's and Sunday School books, of which more anon. He commenced to preach in 1841–2 at West Roxbury, Mass., and after preaching in various places until 1849 he returned to editorial life, as assistant editor of the "Daily Traveler," Boston, for about a year, and of the "New York Observer" two years. Several years were now devoted to book making, mission work, and preaching in the mission church, Brooklyn. In 1859 he became pastor of a Congregational church in Hancock, Pa., where he continued as long as his health allowed him to remain in active life. Mr. Newcomb wrote 178 volumes, mostly for children and Sunday schools; among them, fourteen volumes of Church history; "Manners and Customs of the North American Indians, 2 volumes, 18mo; "Pastor's Gift;" "The Faded Flower," 3d edition, 1850, Boston; "Memoir of Phebe Bartlett," of Northampton, Mass., Philadelphia, 1831? pp. 35. Many of his works had a very large circulation; of "Anecdotes for Boys," and "Anecdotes for Girls," 24,000 copies were sold; of "How to be a Man," and "How to be a Lady," 34,000 copies; of his question books for Sabbath schools, more than 300,000 copies. By a calculation made many years since, there had then, (1859) been circulated, of all his works, about sixty-five million pages. His largest work, and that for which he is most likely to be remembered, is the "Cyclopedia of Missions." He was a regular contributor to the "Boston Recorder" in 1837-42, and to the "Youth's Companion for a much longer period; he also contributed to the "Puritan Recorder, and the "New York Evangelist."

New County *from parts of Windham*, Windsor and Bennington Counties. Report of Committee. Feb. 18, 1867. Ludlow: Gazette Steam Job Printing Department. 1867. 12mo, pp. 7.

The **New England** *Economical Housekeeper*, and Family Receipt Book. Montpelier: Published by E. P. Walton & Sons. 1845.

New England Primer. *The Primer improved* or the Child's Companion; Embracing the usual variety contained in a Primer; Likewise a minor Catechism for Young Children, Dr. Watts' Catechism for Children, The Westminster Assembly's Shorter Catechism, and the highly excellent Hymns of Dr. Watts, entitled Divine Songs. Published by the Trustees of the Vermont Missionary Society. Sold by the Society's General Agent, Wm. G. Hooker, Middlebury, for 3 dollars a hundred.
—*Another Edition.* Middlebury, Vt. Printed by T. C. Strong. 1817.

Newfane. *1774—1874.* Centennial Proceedings and other Historical Facts and Incidents relating to Newfane, The County seat of Windham County, Vermont. Brattleboro: D. Leonard, Steam and Job Printer. 1877. 8vo, pp. 256. Portraits.

New Haven, Vt.
See Grinnell, J. B.

—**Newman, Rev. John.** *Eulogy,* Pronounced at the Funeral of the late Horace Clark, Esq., at West Poultney, Vt., on the 25th day of February, 1852. By Rev. John Newman. Rutland: Tuttle's Book and Job Office. 8vo, pp. 19.

Newport. *A Manual* for the use of the First Congregational Church of Newport, Vt. Prepared by George H. Bailey, Pastor. 1869. Newport: Camp & Cummings, Job Printers. 12mo, pp. 44.

—*The Same, 1881.* D. M. Camp & Co., Printers, Newport, Vt. 12mo, pp. 36.

Newspapers *in Vermont.* Brief notes on.
See Printing in Vermont.

Newton, Rev. Ephraim H. *The History* of the Town of Marlborough, Windham Co., Vt. By Rev. Ephraim H. Newton. Manuscript folio, about 300 pages.
Belongs to the Vermont Historical Society.
Mr. Newton was born at Newfane, Vt., June 13, 1787, and died at Cambridge, Washington County, New York, October 26, 1864. He was graduated at Middlebury College, 1810, and at Andover Theological Seminary, 1813; he was ordained at Marlborough, 1814, as successor to Gershom C. Lyman. D. D., and in the following year married Huldah, daughter of Major-General Timothy F. Chipman, of Shoreham, Vt. He continued at Marlborough until 1833, and was then settled over the Presbyterian church at Glen's Falls, N. Y., until 1837, when he accepted a call to the Presbyterian church at Cambridge, N. Y. Resigned in 1843, and was Principal of Cambridge Washington Academy, 1843 to 1848. In 1857, he gave his valuable mineralogical collection to Andover Theological Seminary, where he passed a few years in arranging it.
In 1863 he presented to Middlebury College his valuable Library, where it is arranged in an alcove bearing his name. He was an active laborer in the cause of education, a devotee to natural science, and earnest to win men to goodness.

Nichols, George. *Instructions* concerning the Registration of Births, Marriages and Deaths, in Vermont: Designed for Town Clerks, Physicians and Clergymen. By George Nichols, Secretary of State. Rutland: Tuttle & Co., Printers. 1868. 8vo, pp. 23.
See Vermont Legislative Directories, 1866-1880, Compiled by George Nichols.
See Vermont, Compilation of Grand-List Laws, by George Nichols. 1875.
Dr. Nichols was born in Northfield, Vt., April 17, 1827; read medicine at the Medical College, Woodstock. Vt.,

and has always resided in Northfield. He has held many local offices, and is chief manager of the republican party in Vermont. (1879.) See Northfield. History of, for a sketch of the Doctor. He was Secretary of State 1865 to 1884.

Nichols, Jonathan Bassett. *Godly and* Faithful. A Discourse in Memory of Deacon J. Bassett Nichols : preached in the Beneficent Congregational Church, Providence, December 6th, 1863, by Rev. A. Huntington Clapp. Providence : Knowles, Anthony & Co., Printers, 1864. 8vo, pp. 19.
Mr. Nichols was born in Middlebury, Vt., March 28, 1799, and died at Providence, R. I., Dec. 3, 1863.

Nichols, W. T. Esq. *Eulogy Pronounced* at the Funeral of the late Silas Bowen, M. D., at Clarendon, Vt., on the 20th day of May, 1858. By W. T. Nichols, Esq. Published by order of the Masonic Fraternity. Rutland : Geo. A. Tuttle & Co., Printers. 1858. 8vo, pp. 16.

Niles Nathaniel. *The Remembrance of Christ.* A Sermon, the Substance of which was delivered at Medway, West Parish, October 31, 1771. By Nathaniel Niles, A. M. Published at the Request of Hearers. Motto. Boston : Printed and sold by J. Kneeland, Milk St. M.DCCLXXIII. 12mo, pp. 42.

—*The Perfection* of God the Fountain of Good. Two Sermons, delivered at Torringford, in Connecticut, Lord's Day. December 21st, 1777, and published for a Number of the Hearers. By Nathaniel Niles, A. M. Norwich, Printed : Elizabeth Town : Re-printed by S. Kollock, 1791. 12mo, pp.40.

—*Another Edition.* 1820. Hallowell : Printed by E. Goodale. 8vo, pp. 32.

—*A Letter* to a Friend, who received his Theological education under the instruction of Dr. Emmons, concerning the Doctrine which teaches that impenitent Sinners have natural power to make themselves new Hearts. By Nathaniel Niles, A. M. Windsor : Printed by Alden Spooner. 1809. 8vo, pp. 40.

—*Two Discourses on Liberty ;* delivered at the North Church, in Newbury-Port, On Lord's Day June 5, 1774, and published at the general Desire of the Hearers. By Nathaniel Niles, M. A. Motto. Newbury-Port : Printed by I. Thomas and H. W. Tinges. MDCCLXXIV. 12mo, pp. 60.

—*Mr. Niles' Resolution,* calling on the Governor for Evidence relative to Impressment ; together with His Excellency's Answer. Montpelier : 1813. 8vo, pp. 8.
Judge Niles, statesman, clergyman, inventor, and politician, was born in South Kingston, R. I. April 3, 1741 ; and died at West Fairlee, Vt. October 31, 1828. He was one of the first settlers of West Fairlee, having located there in 1779. He held many State offices, and was a member of Congress from Vermont, 1791-5. He published many essays, addresses, and poems before coming to Vermont. Before coming to Fairlee, Judge Niles was engaged in the manufacture of wool cards, among other articles, in Connecticut, and the reason of his moving to Vermont was that he purchased for two dozen wool cards a large tract of land in the new town of Fairlee ; after making an examination of his land, he led a colony of his employees and others, and commenced a settlement in 1779. We have this incident from Rev. A. W. Wild of Peacham, whose grandfather was an associate and employee of Judge Niles, and came to Fairlee as one of the Judge's party.
For biographical sketches of Judge Niles see Sprague's Annals, Vermont Historical Magazine, vol. 2, pp. 910-12 ; History of Norwich, Ct., pp. 470-73.

Nimblet, D. *Life* of the Late Lucy Chaffee ; with an Historical account of her insanity and Trial, and the mysterious circumstances attending her last sickness, Death and burial. By Daniel Nimblet, Esq. Motto. Hinesburgh : Published by the Author. 1857. 8vo, pp. 89.

Noble, C. D. *Our Country—Its Glory and its* Shame. A Discourse, preached at Claremont, N. H. Nov. 30, 1843, on Thanksgiving Day. By Rev. C. D. Noble, Springfield, Vt. Claremont, N. H. Power Press Office, N. W. Goddard, Printer. 1844. 8vo, pp. 20.

Northern Tourist : *Or Guide* to Willoughby Lake House, Westmore, Vt. Bemis, Hall & Co., Proprietors. Boston : Press of Geo. C. Rand, 3 Cornhill. 1854. 16mo, pp. 15.

A Northern Tour : *being a Guide* to Saratoga, Lake George, Niagara, Canada, Boston, &c., &c. Through the States of Pennsylvania, New Jersey, New York, Vermont, Massachusetts, New Hampshire, &c. Philadelphia : H. C. Carey & I. Lea. 1825. 18mo, pp. v, 279.
Relates considerably to Vermont.

Northfield. *Act of Incorporation* and By-Laws of the Village of Northfield, Adopted January, 1856. Montpelier, Vt.: Argus and Patriot Printing House.

—*The Northfield Slate* Quarry Company. Boston : 1865. 8vo, pp. 15.

—*Auditors' Report* of the Financial Condition of the Town of Northfield, for the year ending March 1, 1866. Montpelier : Printed at the Freeman Steam Printing Establishment. 1866. 8vo, pp. 15.
Continued.

—*Savings Bank.* Act of Incorporation, By-Laws, &c. 1867. 12mo, pp. 12.

—*Manual* of the First Congregational Church in Northfield, Vt. July, 1876. Montpelier : Press of Vermont Watchman. 1876. 12mo, pp. 20.

—*Catalogue,* Constitution and By-Laws of the Northfield Library Association, Northfield, Vt. Organized, 1871. Montpelier : Freeman Steam Printing House and Bindery. 1877. 8vo, pp. 28.

—*Organization,* Act of Incorporation, with Amendments and By-Laws of Elmwood Cemetery, Northfield, Vt. Montpelier, Vt.: Argus and Patriot Job Printing House. 1871. 8vo, pp. 12.

—*History of,* see Gregory, John.

Norton, C. B. *Norton's Literary Letter.* New Series. No. 2. Small 4to. New York : 1860. pp. 41.
Contains a partial bibliography of Vermont.

Norton, Elijah. *Methodism Examined.* A Discourse, Preached upon John VI:47. In which the Doctrines of Faith and Final Perseverance of all Believers are illustrated and proven. In opposition to the Doctrine of Falling from Grace, and other Doctrines connected therewith. By Elijah Norton, of Woodstock. Printed at Windsor, Vt. By Alden Spooner. M.DCC.XCI. 8vo, pp. 24.

—*A Missionary Sermon,* in which the hidden Riches of Secret Places are discovered, and made to appear as Unrighteous Mammon, and ways devised to draw it out into God's Treasury for the Support of Missionary, Bible, and all other Religious and Benevolent Institutions. By Elijah Norton, Minister of the Gospel. The avails of this shall go into Missionary funds. Motto. Woodstock: Printed by David Watson. 1822. 18mo, pp. 34.

—*The Great Chain of Truth.* A Premium for Sabbath Schools. Designed for their Encouragement in Committing the Scriptures to memory: By which Little Children and All Others may Resist, Overpower, and Bind the Devil, in all his Temptations against them. By Elijah Norton. Woodstock: Printed by David Watson. 1820. 18mo, pp. 24.
Mr. Norton was a Congregational minister who lived in Woodstock.

Norton, Marcus P. *The Work,* Mission and Destiny of the Republican Party, briefly examined under the Administrations of President Lincoln and General Grant. Shall Official Party Treason and Republican Desertion go unpunished—The party purified and redeemed by the Exodus of the "Sore Headed," Disappointed" and "Office Seeking"—The coalition of Liberals and Democrats "Going West," or into the Valley of the Great "Salt River," in November, 1872. Rutland: Tuttle & Co., Printers. 1872. 8vo, pp. 17.

Norwich. *Manual* of the Congregational Church in Norwich, Vt., containing its Articles and Covenant, a Brief Sketch of its History, a List of its Officers, and a Complete List of its Members, alphabetically arranged, January, 1855. Dartmouth Press. Hanover: Jan. 1855. 8vo, pp. 21.

—*Report* of the Superintending School Committee of Norwich, Vt., for the School Year 1861-62. Hanover, N. H. Printed at the Dartmouth Press. 1862. 8vo, pp. 8.
Continued.

—*Report* of the Auditors and Superintendent of Schools, of the Town of Norwich, for the Year ending February 22, 1871. The Annual Town Meeting will be held at Union Hall, March 7, 1871, at 10 o'clock A. M. Montpelier, Vt.: Argus and Patriot Printing House. 1871. 8vo, pp. (12).
Continued.

—*Charter of,*
See Slafter, E. F.

Norwich University. *Catalogue* of the Officers and Cadets of the American Literary, Scientific and Military Academy, together with the Prospectus and internal regulations of the Institution, &c. &c. Norwich, Vt., November, 1822. Woodstock, Vt. David Watson, Printer. 1822. 8vo, pp. 8.
One hundred and thirty-five Cadets in attendance.

—*Another Catalogue,* Windsor, Vt. 1828. 8vo, pp. 20.

—*Catalogue* of the Corporation, Officers and Cadets of Norwich University, for the Academical Year, 1853-54. October 23, 1854. Montpelier: Printed at the Patriot office. 8vo, pp. 20.
Continued.

—*Regulations* for the Government of Norwich University. A Military College. Montpelier: Argus and Patriot Book and Job Printing House, 1874. 8vo, pp, 54, (4).

—*Rules* and Regulations for the Government of the Officers and Cadets of Norwich University, A Military College, Founded in 1834. Northfield, Vermont. Printed for the University. 1869. 12mo, pp. 16, (2).

—*Honor.* An Address to the Cadets of the Norwich University, at Northfield, Vermont, on the Commencement Day, July 18, 1871. By the Rev. Malcolm Douglas, D. D., Rector of St. Paul's Church, Windsor, Vermont. Montpelier, Vt.: Printed at Argus and Patriot Job Printing House. 1872. 8vo, pp. 39.

—*Circular* of the Norwich University Scientific and Military School, Northfield, Vt., 1877-8. Montpelier, Vt.: Argus and Patriot Steam Book and Job Printing Works. 1877. 8vo, pp. 16.

—*Circular* of the Norwich University Scientific and Military College, Northfield, Vermont. Montpelier, Vt.: Argus and Patriot Steam Book and Job Printing Works. 1879. 12mo, pp. 16.

—*Same,* 1876-7, Same imprint, pp. 11, (1).

—*Headquarters* Norwich University, Northfield, Vt., February 25, 1879. General Order No. 118. 8vo, pp. 8.
This institution was established at Norwich, Vt., in 1820, by Capt. Alden Partridge, under the name of the "American Literary, Scientific and Military Academy," and was incorporated as the "Norwich University" in 1834; it was removed to Northfield, Vt., in 1866.
See Journal of an Excursion; Partridge, Alden; Clark, O. Addresses, 1840 and 1842; History of Northfield, pp. 266-270.
Fay, C. H., Address, 1839; Jackman, A.
Memorial, etc., Commemorative of the late Alonzo Jackman, A. M.

Noyes, Daniel J. *Apostolic Test* of the Preaching which God has Ordained. A Sermon at the ordination of Mr. Henry Fairbanks and Mr. Henry A. Hazen, at St. Johnsbury, Vt., Feb. 17, 1858. By Daniel J. Noyes, Professor in Dartmouth College. Published by request. Boston: Press of T. R. Marvin & Son. 1858. 8vo, pp. 50.

Noyes, John. *An Oration* delivered in Brattleborough, July 4, 1811. By John Noyes, Esq. Brattleborough: W. Fessenden. 1811. 8vo, pp. 13.

—**Noyes, John H.** *"The Way of Holiness."* A Series of Papers formerly published in the Perfectionist, at New Haven. By John H. Noyes. Text. Printed by J. H. Noyes & Co. Putney, Vermont. 1838, 24mo, pp. 230.

—*The Witness.* Edited by J. H. & H. A. Noyes. Putney, Vt. Vol. 2. 1841. 4to, 26 nos. in a year.

—*The Resolutions* and Circular Address of the Convention of Perfectionists, held in New York and New Jersey, May 12, 1842. Putney, Vt. 8vo, n. d.
In 1843 Title changed to Perfectionist, edited by J. H. Noyes and J. L. Skinner, and with Vol. 4 the title reads "The Protectionist and Theocratic Watchman."
Mr. Noyes was born at Brattleborough, Vt., September 3, 1811; was graduated at Dartmouth College in 1830; studied at Andover one year; became a Perfectionist and Communist; lived in Putney, Vt., several years, and in 1848 founded the Oneida Community in New York State. Mr. Noyes died at Niagara Falls, Ont., April 13, 1886. See Eastman, Hubbard, "Noyesism Unveiled;" Chapman's "Dartmouth Alumni."

Nutting, Miss Mary Olivia. *Nellie Morris* and her cousin. New York: By Carlton &

Porter, of the Methodist Book Concern. 1861. 18mo, pp. 192.

—*Aunt Alice's Library.* New York: 1861. Carlton & Porter. 82mo.
Being a series of ten volumes for Sabbath schools.

—*Aunt Hatite's Stories* for the Little Folks at Home.
Another series of ten volumes, for Sabbath schools. Same imprint, 1862. 32mo. These two sets had a circulation of nearly twenty thousand copies.

—*Shooting at A Mark.* Same Imprint. 1864. 18mo, pp. 194.

—*Steps in the Upward Way.* A Story for Young Ladies. Written for the American Tract Society of Boston. 1867. 16mo, pp. 279.

—*Our Summer* at Hillside Farm. 1867. 16mo, pp. 256. Boston.

—*The Story* of William the Silent and the Netherland War. 12mo, pp. 480. Boston: 1869?

—*Historical Sketch* of Mount Holyoke Seminary. Founded at South Hadley, Mass., in 1837. Prepared at the request of the Department of the Interior. By Mary O. Nutting, Librarian. Washington: Government Printing Office. 1876. 12mo, pp. 24.
Miss Nutting was born in Randolph, Vt., and was graduated at Mount Holyoke Seminary, class of 1852. She now resides at South Hadley, Mass, (1877.)
Miss Nutting has for several years held the position of Librarian in Mount Holyoke Seminary, South Hadley. "Nellie Morris" and "Shooting at a Mark," were published without name; the others under the name of "Mary Barrett," being that of her maternal grandmother. Her middle name, "Olivia," was for Mrs. Dudley Chase, of Randolph, Vt.

Nutting, Rufus. *A Practical Grammar* of the English Language; Accompanied with Notes, Critical and Explanatory. By Rufus Nutting, A. M. Motto. Fourth Edition, Revised by the Author. Montpelier: Printed and Published by E. P. Walton, Proprietor of the Copy Right. 1828. 12mo, pp. 144.

—*Fifth Edition,* Same Title, 1829. pp. 144.

—*Nutting's New Grammar.* A Grammar of the English Language, in three Parts. Part I. Introduction to plain parsing; on the inductive plan. Part II. The Doctrines and precepts of English Grammar. Part III. Exercises on Part II. With an Appendix, Explanatory of many Logical and Rhetorical Terms. By Rufus Nutting, A. M., Professor of Languages in Western Reserve College. Motto. Montpelier, Vt.: E. P. Walton & Sons, Publishers. 1840. 12mo, pp. 184.

—*A Practical Grammar* of the English Language; accompanied with Notes, Critical and Explanatory. By Rufus Nutting, A. M. Third Edition, Revised and Enlarged. Montpelier: Printed and Published by E. P. Walton, Proprietor of the Copy Right. 1826. 12mo, pp. 144.

—*Memoirs* of Mrs. Emily Egerton. An Authentic Narrative. Prepared by Rufus Nutting, A. M., Professor of Languages in Western Reserve College. Boston: Printed by Perkins and Marvin. 1832. 18mo, pp. 180.
Mr. Nutting died at Detroit, Mich., July 12, 1878, aged 85. For an account of the Nutting family, see Miss Hemenway's Vermont Historical Gazetteer, vol. 2, pp. 1055-8, also Dartmouth Alumni.

Nutting, William. *An Address* to the Orange County Lyceum, at their First Meeting, June 23, 1831. By William Nutting. Published by the Lyceum. Chelsea: E. Avery, Printer. 1831. 16mo, pp. 14.

Nye, Jonathan. Masonic Sermon, 1811.
See Masonic.

Oakes, William. *Catalogue* of Vermont Plants. As published in Thompson's History of Vermont. By William Oakes. [Burlington. 1842.] 8vo. *Sabin.*

O'Callaghan, Rev. Jeremiah. *A Critical Review* of Mr. J. K. Converse's Calvinistic Sermon; also of the Erroneous Propositions of Two Inovators. By the Rev. Jeremiah O'Callaghan, R. C. Priest, Burlington, Vt. Burlington: Printed for the Author. 1834. 16mo, pp. 58.

—*Usury, Funds, and Banks;* also Forestalling Trafick, and Monopoly: likewise Pew Rent, and Grave Tax; together with Burking, and Dissecting; as well as the Gallican Liberties, are all Repugnant to the Divine and Ecclesiastical Laws, and Destructive to Civil Society. To which is prefixed A Narrative of the Author's Controversy with Bishop Coppinger, and of his Sufferings for Justice Sake. By the Rev. Jeremiah O'Callaghan, Roman Catholic Priest. Burlington: Printed for the Author. 1834. 8vo, pp. (4). 380.

—*Fifth Edition,* New York: 1866. 12mo.

—*The Creation* and Offspring of the Protestant Church; also the Vagaries and Heresies of John Henry Hopkins, Protestant Bishop; and of other False Teachers. To which is added a Treatise on the Holy Scriptures, Priesthood and Matrimony. By Jeremiah O'Callaghan, Roman Catholic Priest. Burlington: Printed for the Author. 1837. 12mo, pp. 328.

—*Exposure* of the Vermont Banking, By the Rev. Jeremiah O'Callaghan, Burlington, Vt., 1854. Burlington: Free Press Print. 8vo, pp. 32.

—*Atheism* of Brownson's Review.—Unity and Trinity of God. Divinity and Humanity of Christ Jesus.—Banks and Paper Money.—By the Rev. Jeremiah O'Callaghan, Catholic Priest. Burlington, Vt.: 1852. rl. 8vo, pp. 306, (2).

—*The Hedge* round about the Vineyard, Dressed up by the Rev. Jeremiah O'Callaghan, Roman Catholic Priest. Motto. Burlington: Printed for the Author. 1844. 12mo, pp. 360.
Father O'Callaghan was a native of Cork, Ireland, and was the first Roman Catholic Priest settled in Burlington, Vt., where he labored with much industry and success, 1830—1853. See Miss Hemenway's Vermont Historical Gazetteer, vol. 1. p p. 550-1; vol. 4, p. 422-3.

Odd Fellows.
See Independent Order of Odd Fellows.

The Oeconomy of Human Life. *In two parts.* Translated from an Indian Manuscript, written by an ancient Bramin. To which is prefixed an Account of the Manner in which the said Manuscript was discovered. In a letter from an English Gentleman, residing in China, to the Earl of —— Printed in Bennington, (Vt.). in the Year of our Lord 1788. 12mo, pp. 115.

Olcott, Bulkley. *Election Sermon ;* 1781.

—*Brotherly Love ;* A Sermon Preached before a Society of Free and Accepted Masons, in Charlestown, [N. H.] 27th of December, 1781. By Rev. Bulkley Olcott, A. M., Westminster, [Vt.] 1782. 4to, pp. 15.
Sabin.

—*Righteousness* and Peace, the Way to be acceptable to God, and approved of Men : A Sermon before a Society of the Most Ancient and Honorable Free and Accepted Masons, in Charlestown, [N. H.] December 27, 1782. Windsor, Vt.: Hough & Spooner. 1783. 4to, pp. 16.
Bulkley Olcott was born in Bolton, Ct., October 28, 1733 ; was graduated at Yale College in 1758, and in 1761 he was settled over the Congregational church at Charlestown, N. H., where he remained until his death, June 26, 1793. The Vermont Legislature held its annual October session in 1781, at Charlestown, on which occasion Mr. Olcott preached the sermon, and was also elected Chaplain for the session.
See Gov. and Council, vol. 2, p. 115.

Olcott, Henry S. *People* from the Other World. By Henry S. Olcott, Profusely Illustrated. Motto. Issued by Subscription only. Hartford, Conn.: American Publishing Company, 1875. 12mo, pp. 492.
Relates almost wholly to spiritual manifestations by the Eddy family in the town of Chittenden, Vt.

Olds, Gamaliel S. *Statement* of Facts, 1818.
See Middlebury College.

Olin, Stephen, D. D., LL. D. *Travels* in Egypt, Arabia, Petrea, and the Holy Land. By the Rev. Stephen Olin, D. D., President of the Wesleyan University, with Twelve Illustrations on Steel. In Two Volumes. New York : Harper & Brothers, Publishers, 329 & 331 Pearl Street, Franklin Square. 1854. 12mo, pp. xiv, 458, 478.
First edition in 1843.

—*Travels* in Greece and Turkey. New York : 1854. 12mo.

—*The Works* of Stephen Olin, D. D., LL. D., Late President of the Wesleyan University. Vol. 1, Sermons and Sketches ; Vol. 2, Lectures and Addresses. New York : Harper & Brothers. 1854. 12mo, pp. viii, 422, (2), 475.
First edition, 1852.

—*The Life* and Letters of Stephen Olin, D. D., LL. D., Late President of the Wesleyan University. In two volumes. New York : Harper & Brothers. 1854. 12mo, pp. vi. 361, (8), 486.
First edition, 1853.

—*College Life :* Its Theory and Practice. By Rev. Stephen Olin, D. D., LL. D., Late President of the Wesleyan University. New York : Harper & Brothers, Publishers. 1867. 12mo, pp. (2), 239.
The last literary work of Dr. Olin.

—*Early Piety.* New York : 1851. 18mo, pp. 75.

—*The Duty* of the Church to evangelize the World. An Address delivered in the Greene St. Church, on the Twenty-fourth Anniversary of the Missionary Society of the M. E. Church. By Rev. Stephen Olin, D. D. New York : Published for the Tract Society of the Methodist Episcopal Church, at the Conference

Office, 200 Mulberry-Street. n. d. 12mo, pp. 16.

—*An Address* at the opening of the Genesee Wesleyan Seminary, January 13, 1843. By Rev. Stephen Olin. Rochester. 1843. 8vo, pp. 24.
Rev. Dr. Olin was born in Leicester, Vt., March 2d, 1797 ; and died at Middletown, Conn., August 6th. 1851. He was a son of Judge Henry Olin, who was prominent in the Judicial and political history of Vermont, and the Doctor was one of the most eloquent Methodist preachers of his time in the denomination. For a full account of him see "Life and Letters," Sprague's Annals. Vol. 7, pp. 685-699 ; Allibone ; Duyckinck ; Drake.

Oliver, Daniel. *Address* before the Temperance Society, of the Medical Class in Dartmouth College, Oct. 31, 1832. Windsor, Vt.: 8vo, pp. 16.

—*On the relations* of Slavery to the War, and on the treatment of it necessary to permanent peace. A few suggestions for thoughtful and Patriotic Men. [n. p. n. d.] 8vo. pp. 8.

Oracles *of Reason,* As formed by the Deists are Husks for Deistical and Heathen Swine, etc. A Concise, but plain Answer to General Allen's Oracles of Reason. By Common Sense. Litchfield. n. d.

—*A Sermon* to Swine, by Common Sense. Litchfield. 1787.
See Allen, Ethan.

Orange County. *Atlas* of the County of Orange, Vt. Published by F. W. Beers & Co., 36 Vesey Street, New York. 1877. Folio, pp. 90.

—*Rules* Adopted by the County Court, for the County of Orange, December Term, 1845. Montpelier, Vt.: Eastman & Danforth. 1846. 18mo, pp. 8.

—*Rules* of the Supreme Court, and Court of Chancery, and of the Orange County Court. Arranged and published by S. M. Flint, Clerk of Orange County. April, 1851. L. I. McIndoe, Printer. Newbury, Vt.: 12mo, pp. 28.

—*To the Freemen* of Orange County, by the County Committee. Please read and circulate. Montpelier, Vt.: Scott & Thompson, Printers. 12mo, pp. 8.
Relates to the presidential campaign of 1848.

—*Atlas Map* of Orange County ;
Same title and imprint as Chittenden County Atlas.

Orcutt, Hiram. *Gleanings* from School-life experience ; or hints to Common School Teachers, Parents and Pupils. By Hiram Orcutt, A. M., Principal of North Granville Ladies' Seminary. Rutland : Geo. A. Tuttle & Co., Brown, Taggard & Chase, Boston. 1858. pp. 72, 12mo.

—*The Same,* Revised Edition. Same imprint. 1859. 12mo, pp. 144.

Order of the Eastern Star. *Transactions* of the Grand Chapter, Order of the Eastern Star, State of Vermont, held at Ludlow, June 3, 1874. Rutland : Globe Paper Company, Printers. 1874. 8vo, pp. 24.
This was the first session.

Ordronaux, John. *A Valedictory Address* delivered before the Medical Class of the University of Vermont, May 31st, 1865, by John Ordronaux, M. D., Professor of Physiology and Medical Jurisprudence. New York : Baker & Goodwin, Printers. 1865. 8vo, pp. 32.

Orleans County Natural & Civil History Society. *Constitution and By-Laws.* West Charleston Union Print. 1854. 18mo, pp. 12.

—*History* of Congregational Churches in.
See White, P. H.

—*History* of Newspapers in, by Pliny H. White. 1860. 8vo, pp. 4.

—*Awake*, Rebels in Vermont !
A Broadside called forth by the St. Albans Raid, so-called, in 1864. Barton, October 20, 1864.

—*1620–1870*. Pilgrim Memorial. Addresses at the celebration of the fifth Jubilee of Congregationalism, held at Barton, By the Congregational Churches of Orleans County, Vt., September 7, 1870. Published by the Orleans Conference. E. H. Webster, Printer. Barton: 8vo, pp. 36.

—*Atlas and Map* of Orleans County.
See Lamoille County.

Ormsby, R. McK. *Posthumous Works* of Kritz Lemberg, or The Wonders of Animal Magnetism: Containing A disclosure of the Mysteries of creation, and of the secrets of nature, together with a true historical account of the triumph of truth and justice over the blackest treachery. Motto. Boston: Published by B. B. Mussey. 1843. 12mo, pp. 117. A. B. F. Hildreth, Printer, Bradford, Vt.
It is a story founded on the mysteries of clairvoyance and animal magnetism, and I think was published originally in the "American Protector," a newspaper published at Bradford by A. B. F. Hildreth.

—*Reports* of the awarding committee, and Address by Robert McK. Ormsby, Esq., at the Fourth Annual Fair of the Orange Co., Agricultural Society, holden at Bradford, Vt. Printed by A. B. F. Hildreth. 1850, 8vo, pp. 23.

—*Intellectual Development.* Remarks before the Student's Lyceum, by Mr. Ormsby. Printed, Bradford, 1846?

—*A few Thoughts* on Common Schools, by "The Northern Inquirer." Bradford, Vt.: Northern Inquirer Office, A. C. Brown, printer. 1853. 16mo, pp. 80.

—*The American* definition Spelling Book, on an Improved Plan ; in which the spelling and pronunciation are generally upon the Principles of Noah Webster ; the Spelling Lessons arranged upon the inductive system. With Progressive Reading Lessons. Designed for The Use of Schools in the United State. By, R. M'K. Ormsby. Improved Editions. Bradford, Vt., Published by A. Low. 1844. 12mo, pp. 180.

—*Progressive* Lessons in the English Language. In two parts. A New System &c., By R. M'K. Ormsby, assisted by Rev. Charles W. Cushing, A. M., and R. Farnham, Jr., A. M. Bradford, Vt.: Published by R. Farnham, Jr., & Co. 1857. 12mo, pp. 168.

—*Vermont Speller ;* or Progressive Lessons in the English Language. In two parts. A New System of Teaching the Spelling, Pronunciation, Analysis, and Signification, of several Thousands of the words most generally in use in ordinary affairs, and in the Arts, Sciences, and Literature. By R. M'K. Ormsby. Carefully Revised. Electrotype Edition. Claremont,

N. H.: Claremont Manufacturing Company, E. L. Goddard, Agent. Bradford, Vt.: G. & E. Prichard, Agents. (1857.) 12mo, pp. 168.

—*A History* of the Whig Party, or some of its main features ; with an hurried glance at the formation of Parties in the United States, and the outlines of the History of the Parties in the Country to the present time, etc, etc. By R. McKinley Ormsby. Boston : Crosby, Nichols & Company. 1859. 12mo, pp. 377.

—*Another Edition.* 1860.

—*Darwin ;* or, God in Nature. Motto. By Robert McK. Ormsby. Second Edition. New York : Masonic Publishing Company. 729 Broadway, 1878. Small 4to, pp. 73.
Mr. Ormsby was born in Corinth, Vt., June 29, 1814 ; he was educated in the common schools, and at Bradford Academy. In 1833 he went west, and was at Massillon, Ohio, three years ; then at Louisville, Ky., six years, where he studied law and was admitted to the Bar. In 1842 he returned to Vermont, and in 1844 commenced the practice of his profession at Bradford, which he successfully continued there until 1866, when he removed to New York city, where he continued practice until his death at Mount Vernon, N. Y., February 20, 1881.

Orwell. Manual of the Congregational Church in Orwell, Vermont. Middlebury : Printed at the Register Book and Job Office. 1856. 18mo, pp. 34.

Osborn, Benjamin. *Truth Displayed ;* In a series of Elementary Principles, illustrated and enforced by Practical Observations. In Three Parts. I. On the Existence and Perfections of the Deity. II. On the Material and Visible Universe. III. On the Nature and Essence of the Finite Mind. By Benjamin Osborn. Motto. Rutland, Vt.: Printed by Fay & Davison. 1816. 8vo, pp. 626.

—*Conformity* to Truth, in Knowledge and Practice, essential to happiness. A Farewell Sermon at Tinmouth, Vt., Oct. 28, 1787. Bennington, Vt.: Printed by Haswell & Russell, 1788. 8vo, pp. 24.
Mr. Osborn was born in Litchfield, Ct., November 5, 1751 ; and died in Wallingford, Vt., July 7, 1818. He was the son of Benjamin, and was graduated at Dartmouth College, 1775 ; he was pastor of the Congregational church at Tinmouth, Vt., 1780–1787, and at Wallingford, 1802 until his death.

Osgood, Nathan. *An Oration,* delivered in Rutland, in the State of Vermont, on the Anniversary of American Independence, July 4th, 1799. By Nathan Osgood, Esq. Rutland : Printed by S. Williams. 1799. 8vo, pp. 16.

Pacific Coast Association of the Native Sons of Vermont.
See Sons of Vermont.

Page, John Ward. See Dartmouth College, Class Day Address to the President, 1868.
Son of Hon. John A. Page, State Treasurer, and resides in Montpelier. (1879).

Paine, Caroline. *Tent and Harem :* Notes of an Oriental Trip. By Caroline Paine. New York : D. Appleton and Company. M.DCCC. LIX. 12mo, pp. x, 300.
Mrs. Paine was a daughter of Hon. Elijah Paine, of Williamstown, Vt., where she was born.
She married her cousin, John Paine, of New York city, where she resides. (1879).

Paine, Charles.
Son of Hon. Elijah Paine : Governor of Vermont, 1841-3 ; Obituary and Funeral Obsequies of, See Gannett, E. S.
See History of Northfield, pp. 63-72.

Paine, Elijah. *A Collection* of Facts in Regard to Liberia, by Judge Paine, of Vermont: To which is added the Correspondence of the Rev. Benjamin Tappan, of Maine, and Francis S. Key, Esquire, of the District of Columbia. Woodstock, Vt.: Printed by Augustus Palmer. 1839. 8vo, pp. 36.

Judge Paine was born in Brooklyn, Ct., January 21, 1757; and died at Williamstown, Vt., April 28, 1842. He was graduated at Harvard College, 1781, and in 1782 pronounced the first Oration before the Phi Beta Kappa Society of the University, and was elected President of the Society in 1789. He read law, and was one of the first settlers in Williamstown, Vt., in 1784. He held many State offices, and was Judge of the Supreme Court, 1791-1795, United States Senator from Vermont, 1795-1801, and United States District Judge for Vermont, 1801-1842. For Biographical Sketch see Vermont Historical Gazetteer, vol. 2, pp. 1150-51, and American Cyclopedia.

Paine, Elijah.

Mr. Paine, son of Judge Elijah Paine, was born in Williamstown, Vt., April 10, 1796; and died in New York, October 6, 1853. He was graduated at Harvard College 1814; read law, and practiced in New York; was Judge of the Superior Court of New York, 1850, until his death. He published "Paine's United States Circuit Reports," and in connection with Judge Duer, "Practice in Civil Actions and Proceedings in the State of New York," 2 volumes, 1830. See Appleton's American Cyclopedia, Drake, Vermont Historical Gazetteer, vol. 2. p. 1152.

Paine, Martyn. A Defence of the Medical Profession of the United States; being a Valedictory Address to the Graduating Class at the Medical Commencement of the University of New York, Delivered, March 11, 1846, by Martyn Paine, A. M., M. D., Professor of the Institutes of Medicine and Materia Medica in the University of New York; Member of the Royal Verein für Heilkunde in Preussen; of the Medical Society of Leipsic; of the Montreal Natural History Society, and other Learned Associations. Fifth Edition. New York: Samuel S. & William Wood, no. 261 Pearl Street. Joseph H. Jennings, Printer, 111 Fulton Street. 1846, 8vo, pp. 24.

—*Letters* on the Cholera Asphyxia, as it has appeared in the City of New York: Addressed to John C. Warren, M. D., of Boston, and originally published in that City. Together with other Letters not before Published. By Martyn Paine, M. D. New York: Published by Collins & Hanney, Clayton & Van Norden, Printers. 1832. 8vo, pp. 160.

——*Medical* and Physiological Commentaries. By Martyn Paine, M. D., A. M. Motto. In two volumes. (Another Volume subsequently added, making three in all.) New York: Collins, Keese & Co. 254 Pearl Street. London: John Churchill. 1840. 8vo, pp. 716, 815.

Volume 3 contains 1st an examination of a Review, contained in the British and Foreign Medical Review, of the Medical and Physiological Commentaries, by the author, Martyn Paine, M. D. A. M., Professor of the Institutes of Medicine and Materia Medica in the University of New York. New York: Hopkins & Jennings, Printers, 111 Fulton Street. 1841. 8vo, pp. 8 and 96.

2d, Notice of Reviews by the British and Foreign Medical Review, and the Medico-Chirurgical Review, (April, 1841,) of the Medical and Physiological Commentaries, as contained in the Boston Medical and Surgical Journal of September 1841, by the author, Martyn Paine, M. D., A. M., Professor, etc. etc. Boston: D. Clapp, Jr., Printer. 1841. 8vo, pp. 8.

3d. Dr. Paine's answer to circular letters by Drs. Carpenter and Forbes. From the Boston Medical and Surgical Journal, Boston: D. Clapp, Jr., Printer. 1842. 8vo, pp. 8.

4th. A reply to an attack by Henry I. Bowditch, M. D., upon the essay on the principal writings of P. Ch. A. Louis, M. D., as contained in the Medical and Physiological Commentaries, by the author. Boston: Republished from the Medical and Surgical Journal. 1840. 8vo, pp. 56.

5th. Essays on the Philosophy of vitality as contradistinguished from Chemical and Mechanical Philosophy, and on the *modus operandi* of remedial agents. New York: Printed for the author, by Hopkins & Jennings. 1842. 8vo, pp. 70.

6th. A discourse introductory to a Course of Lectures on the Institutes of Medicine and Materia Medica, delivered before the Medical Class of the University of New York, at the session of 1841-42. Boston: D. Clapp, Jr., Printer. 1842. 8vo. pp. 33.

7th. A Lecture on the Improvement of Medical Education in the United States; introductory to a Course of Lectures in the University of New York, New York: Robert Craighead, Printer. 1843. 8vo, pp. 16.

8th. A defence of an Introductory lecture on the "Improvement of Medical Education in the United States," against an attack by the Medico-Chirurgical Review, Boston: D. Clapp, Jr., Printer. 1844. 8vo. pp. 6.

9th. A Lecture on the Physiology of Digestion, introductory to a Course of Lectures on the Institutes of Medicine and Materia Medica. Delivered before the Medical Class of the University of the City of New York, at the session of 1844-45. Fourth edition. New York: Printed for the Class, by Joseph H. Jennings. 1844-45. 8vo, pp. 24.

10th. A defence of the Medical Profession of the United States; being a Valedictory Address to the Graduating Class at the Medical Commencement of the University of New York, delivered March 11, 1846, Seventh Edition. New York: 1846. 8vo, pp. 24.

11th. Contributions in Physiology by Dr. Paine. The Circulation. (From the Boston Medical and Surgical Journal.) 1848. 8vo, pp. 8 and 4.

—*The Institutes* of Medicine. By Martyn Paine. A. M., M. D., Professor, &c., &c., &c. Motto. New York: Harper & Brothers, Publishers, 82 Cliff street. 1847. 8vo, pp. viii. 826.

—*The Same*, Eighth Edition, Revised. New York and London. 1867. 8vo, pp. xvi, 1145 and 9.

—*A Discourse* on the Soul and Instinct, Physiologically distinguished from Materialism, Introductory to the Course of Lectures on the Institutes of Medicine and Materia Medica, in the University of the City of New York. Delivered on the Evening of Nov. 2, 1848, by Martyn Paine, A. M., M. D., Professor, &c., &c. Motto. Published originally by the Medical Class. Enlarged Edition. New York. Republished by Edward H. Fletcher, 141 Nassau street. 1849. 12mo, pp. xi, 230.

—*Memoir* of Robert Troup Paine. By His Parents. Motto. Printed for private distribution, especially for the Classmates of the Youth. New York. John F. Trow, Printer, 49 Ann Street. 1852. 4to, pp. viii. 524, Portraits and plates.

Robert Troup, the only surviving child of Dr. Martyn and Mary Ann (Weeks) Paine, was born August 10, 1829, and died suddenly at Cambridge, in the spring of 1851, in his senior year at Harvard University.

Dr. Paine also published in 1856 an elaborate Treatise in the Protestant Episcopal Quarterly Review, on "Theoretical Geology," controverting the Geological interpretations of the Mosaic narrations of creation and the flood.

Dr. Paine was a son of the late eminent Judge and statesman, Hon. Elijah Paine, of Williamstown, Vt., and was born there, July 8, 1794; and was graduated at Harvard University, 1813. He studied medicine with Dr. John Warren, of Boston, Mass., and practiced in Montreal, P. Q., 1816-22, and then removed to New York, where he continued to reside until his decease, November 10, 1877. He acquired a large practice in New York, and became eminent and distinguished in his profession. He with others established the University Medical College of the City of New York, in 1841, and Dr. Paine for many years held the Chair of the Institutes of Medicine and Materia Medica, and subsequently that of Therapeutics and Materia Medica. In 1854 he was prominent in effecting a repeal of the law prohibiting dissections of the human body. See Appleton's American Cyclopedia, Drake, Allibone, Vermont Historical Gazetteer, Volume 2, p. 1151.

Paine, Thomas. *Rights of Man.* Bennington, Vt. 1791.

Painter, Abby V. *The Life and Death* of Miss Abby Victoria Painter, who died December 9, 1818, aged 22 years. Middlebury, Vt. Printed by J. W. Copeland. 1819. 8vo, pp. 16.
Miss Painter was a daughter of Hon. Gamaliel Painter, one of the first settlers of Middlebury.

Palmer, David. *Address* delivered before St. John's Lodge, No. 41, Thetford, Vt., at the opening of the new Masonic Hall in that place, Feb'ry 18th, 1829, by David Palmer, M. D., Master of the Lodge. Published by order of the Brethren. Hanover: Printed by Thomas Mann. 1829.

— *Anniversary* Address to the Graduates of the Vermont Medical College, 1839. By David Palmer, M. D. Woodstock: Printed by Augustus Palmer. 1839. 12vo, pp. 12.

Palmer, Edwin F. *The Second Brigade;* or, Camp Life. By a Volunteer. Motto. Montpelier: Printed for the Author By E. P. Walton. 1864. 12mo, pp. 224.
Relates to service by Vermont troops in the Civil War. Mr. Palmer is a native of Waitsfield, Vt., where he was born January 22, 1836. He was graduated at Dartmouth College 1862, was Second Lieutenant in the 13th Regiment of Vermont troops during the Civil War. He read law with ex-Gov. Dillingham, of Waterbury, and practices his profession. State Superintendent of Education 1889-92. He resides at Waterbury.

Palmer, John E. *Thoughts* Concerning the Unity of God and the distinct Personality and Sonship of Jesus Christ. In two Letters to A Friend. By John E. Palmer. Chelsea: S. S. Smith, Printer. 1835. 8 vo, pp. 16.

—*A Collection* of Valuables, consisting of pieces on doctrinal, practical and experimental subjects, written by Hosea Ballou, Pastor of the Second Universalist Society in Boston, and originally published in the Universalist Expositor and Universalist Magazine. Compiled by John E. Palmer. Motto. Montpelier. E. P. Walton & Son, Printers. 1836. 12mo, pp. 304, (2).
Mr. Palmer was a long time resident of Barre, Vt., having been settled over the Universalist society there in 1819, where he labored for 18 years, and, until his death, continued his work in the ministry in Northern Vermont and New Hampshire. He was born in Portsmouth, N. H., February 22, 1783, and died in Waterford, Vt., March 23, 1873. He removed to Danville, Vt., in 1806, and ever after resided in the State.

Palmer, Mary. *Miscellaneous* writings on Religious Subjects; Together with some extracts from a Diary. By Mary Palmer, late of Windham, Connecticut. Windsor, (Vermont,) Printed by Alden Spooner. 1807. 12mo, pp. 119.

Palmer, Peter S. *History* of Lake Champlain, from its First Exploration by the French in 1609 to the close of the year 1814. By Peter S. Palmer. Albany, N. Y.: J. Munsell, 78 State Street. 1866. 8vo, pp. 276.

—*Battle* of Valcour on Lake Champlain, October 11th, 1776. Plattsburgh, N. Y.: 1876. 8vo, pp. 24.

Palmer, T. H. *Address* on the Importance and necessity of the immediate establishment of a Normal School. Delivered before the Education Convention held at Brandon, January 5, 1841. By Thos. H. Palmer. Brandon: Published by request of the Convention. 1841. 12mo, pp. 23.

—*Palmer's Moral Instructor.* The Moral Instructor; or, Culture of the Heart, Affections, and Intellect while learning to read. Motto. By Thomas H. Palmer. Published by Thomas, Cowperthwait & Co., Philadelphia: A. V. Blake, New York; Durrie & Peck, New Haven; Brown & Packard, Hartford; Isaac H. Cordy, Providence; and John W. Foster, Portsmouth, N. H. 4 Parts. 12mo, pp. 72, 144, 144, 288.

—*Palmer's Arithmetic.* Arithmetic, Oral and Written, Practically Applied by means of Suggestive Questions. By Thomas H. Palmer. Motto. Boston: Published by Crocker & Brewster, No. 47 Washington Street. 1854, 12mo, pp. 348.
Mr. Palmer was born in Kelso, Scotland, December 27, 1782, and died in Pittsford, Vt., July 20, 1861. He learned the printer's trade, and immigrated to Philadelphia in 1801, where with his brother he carried on printing and bookselling until 1826, when with a competency he moved to Pittsford, which was ever after his home. In addition to the above, Mr. Palmer published a prize essay entitled the "Teachers' Manual," also two or three additional addresses relating to education. See Caverly's History of Pittsford.

Parish, Elijah. *A Sermon* preached at the Ordination of the Rev. Nathan Waldo, A. B. in Williamstown, Vermont, February 26, 1806. By Elijah Parish, A. M. Pastor of the Church in Byfield, Massachusetts. Motto. Hanover, N. H. Printed by Moses Davis. 1806. 8vo, pp. 15.

Park, Harrison G. *The Shortened Bed.* A Discourse on the Insufficiency of Ministerial Support, delivered by Harrison G. Park, Pastor of the First Church, Westminster, Vt. Texts. Bellows Falls, Vt.: Printed at the Argus Job Office. 1860. 8vo, pp. 14.

Park, Trenor W. *Arguments* of the Hon. Edward Stanley, of Counsel for the Receiver, and T. W. Park, Esq., of Counsel for Alvin Adams, with the charge of the Court, at the Trial of Alfred A. Cohen on a charge of Embezzlement, in the Case of Adams & Co., by H. M. Naglee, Receiver, *versus* Alfred A. Cohen, in the District Court of the Fourth Judicial District of the State of California, Hon. John S. Hager, Presiding, March, 1856. San Francisco: Whitton, Towne & Co., Printers, Excelsior Job Office, No. 151 Clay Street, Third door below Montgomery. 1856. 8vo, pp. 88.
Trenor William Park was born in Woodford, Vt., Dec. 8, 1823. He studied law with A. P. Lyman, of Bennington, and practiced his profession in that town till 1852, when he went to San Francisco, Cal., and became a member of the leading law firm of Halleck, Peachy, Billings and Park. He was the attorney of the famous Vigilance Committee; was associated with John C. Fremont in the Mariposa Mine, and accumulated a fortune. In 1864 he returned to Vermont; and among other enterprises purchased the Western Vermont R.R., and built the Bennington and Lebanon Springs railroad. He was managing director of the Pacific Mail Steamship Co., and President of the Panama railroad, (of which he held a controlling interest, till it was sold to the De Lesseps Canal Co.,) until his death. He died at sea on a voyage to Panama, Dec. 13, 1882. He married, in 1846, Laura V., daughter of Ex-Gov. Hiland Hall; she died in 1875 leaving two daughters and a son. In May, 1882, he married Ella F., daughter of A. C. Nichols, Esq., of San Francisco, who survived him.

Parker, B. C. C. *Introductory* Lecture before the Vermont Medical College, at Woodstock, Vt., on the second Tuesday of March, 1841. Mercury Office, 1841. 8vo, pp. 32.

Parker, Rev. C. C. *The Early History of Waterbury.* A Discourse Delivered February 10th, 1867. By Rev. C. C. Parker, Pastor of Congregational Church. Waterbury : Waterbury Job Printing Establishment. 1867. 8vo, pp. 28.

Mr. Parker was born at Underhill, Vt., Sept, 16, 1814. For biog. sketch see Vt. Hist. Magazine Vol. 4, p. 848-50. He died in Parsippany, N. J., February 15, 1880.

Parker, Rev. Daniel. *Church Privilege* and Obligation on Congregational Principles : A Discourse, Delivered in the First Congregational Church in Brookfield, Vt., March 9, 1845. By Rev. Daniel Parker, A. M. A member of the First Congregational Church in that town. Montpelier, Vt.: E. P. Walton & Sons, Printers. 1847. 8vo, pp. 19.

—*The Constitutional Instructor.* Published about 1849.

Parker, Rev. Hervey I. *The Origin* and Principles of Modern Rechabites ; An Address delivered in Burlington, Nov. 26, 1846, By Rev. Hervey I. Parker. Second Edition. Burlington : Bro. Samuel B. Nichols. 1846. 8vo, pp. 16.

Parker, Joel, D. D. *The Signs of the Times ;* a sermon, delivered in Rochester, December 4, 1828, being the day of Publick Thanksgiving. By Joel Parker, Pastor of the Third Presbyterian Church. Rochester, N. Y.: Printed by E. Peck & Co. 1829. 8vo, pp. 16.

—*Lectures on Universalism :* By Joel Parker, Pastor of the Third Presbyterian Church, Rochester. "Buy the truth and sell it not." (Copy-right secured.) Rochester, N. Y.: Printed by Elisha Loomis. 1830. 18mo, pp. 126.

—*A Morsel* for the Young Student for the Gospel Ministry ; or the First Epistle of Paul to Timothy, in the Original Greek, with a Literal Interlinear Translation on a plan of works recently published by the University Press in London. By Joel Parker, Pastor of the Free Presbyterian Church in New York. New York : Jonathan Leavitt, No. 182 Broadway. Boston : Crocker & Brewster. 1833. 32mo, pp. 70.

—*A Farewell* Discourse to the Free Presbyterian Churches : Delivered in the Chatham Street Chapel, on Sabbath Evening, October 27th. 1833. By Joel Parker, Pastor of the Free Presbyterian Church, Dey Street. New York : Published by W. T. Coolidge & Co., 55 Wall Street. 1834. 8vo. pp. 20.

—*Moral Tendencies* of our present Pecuniary Distress. A Discourse, delivered May 14, 1837. By Joel Parker, Pastor of the Presbyterian Congregation in New Orleans. New Orleans : Printed at the Observer Office, 42 Poydras St. 1837. 12mo, pp. 15.

—*Courtship and Marriage :* Moral Principles illustrated in their Application to Courtship and Marriage. By Joel Parker, D. D., Pastor of the Clinton Street Presbyterian Church, Philad. Philadelphia ; Perkins & Purves. 1845. 12mo, pp. 179.

—*Presbyterian.* A Discourse on the Scriptural and Liberal Character of the Government of the Presbyterian Church in the United States ; its unexclusive Spirit ; the Simplicity of its Worship, and the Character of its Teachings. By Joel Parker, D. D., Pastor of the Clinton Street Church, Philad'a. Published by request. 1849. 8vo, pp. 27.

—*Discussion* between Rev. Joel Parker, and Rev. A. Rood, on the Question, "What are the Evils inseparable from Slavery," which was referred to by Mrs. Stowe, in "Uncle Tom's Cabin." Reprinted from the Philadelphia Christian Observer of 1846. New York : S. W. Benedict, 16 Spruce St. 1852. 12mo, pp. 120.

—*Science and Religion.* A Discourse delivered before the Synod of New York and New Jersey, in Honesdale, Pa., on Wednesday Evening, October 18th, 1854. By the Rev. Joel Parker, D. D., Pastor of the Fourth Avenue Presbyterian Church, New York. New York : John A. Gray, Printer, 95 & 97 Cliff, Cor. Frankfort Street. 1854. 8vo, pp. 22.

—*The Duty* of the Present Generation of Christians to evangelize the World. A Sermon delivered before the Foreign Missionary Society of New York and Brooklyn, on Sabbath Evenings, October 31, and November 14. By Rev. Joel Parker, D. D., Pastor of the Fourth Avenue Presbyterian Church, N. Y. New York : Almon Merwin, Bible House, Astor Place. 1858. 8vo, pp. 31.

—*The Doctrine* of Divine Retribution. The Annual Discourse appointed to be delivered before the Synod of New York and New Jersey, at its sessions in Newark, in October, 1861. By Rev. Joel Parker, D. D. New York : John A. Gray, Printer, Stereotyper and Binder, Fireproof Buildings, Corner of Frankfort and Jacob Streets. 1862. 8vo, pp. 18.

Mr. Parker was a Presbyterian Minister, born at Bethel, Vt., August 27, 1799; and was graduated at Hamilton College in 1824. Pastor at Rochester, N. Y., 1826-30; Dey street church, N. Y., 1830-33; at New Orleans, 1833-38; of the Broadway Tabernacle, N. Y., 1838-40; President and Professor of Sacred Rhetoric in Union Theological Seminary, N. Y., 1840-2; Pastor of Clinton Street church, Philadelphia, Pa., 1842-52; of Bleeker Street church, N. Y., 1852-54; of 4th Avenue, N. Y., Presbyterian church, 1854, and after. His publications in addition to the above are; "Invitations to True Happiness," 1843. 18mo; "Reasonings of a Pastor with the Young of His Flock," 18mo; republished in London; "Notes on Twelve Psalms, with Questions," Philadelphia, 1849, 18mo; "Sermons on Various Subjects," 1852, 12mo; "Pastor's Initiatory Catechism," 1855, 32mo.
Dr. Parker has also edited various works, and contributed the article on the Presbyterian Church for Rupp's History of Religious Denominations.
Allibone, which see for further particulars.

Parker, R. F. *Investigation* by and Report of Hon. R. F. Parker, Railroad Commissioner of Vermont, and W. B. Gilbert, Esq., Civil Engineer, with Statement of Dr. M. Goldsmith and Dr. C. L. Allen, Attending Surgeons, Relating to the Accident upon the Rutland and Burlington Railroad, near the Summit in Mt. Holly, June 8, 1870. Rutland, Vt.: 1870. 8vo, pp. 8.

Parker, O. *A Sermon,* on Stealing Live Children and Returning Dead Ones. By Rev. O. Parker. Montpelier ; J. Poland, 1844. 8vo, pp. 12.

—*Revival Hymns*. A Collection of Hymns, selected from "The Christian Lyre," "Camp-meeting Hymn Book," and "Village Hymns." By O. Parker, Minister of the Gospel. Montpelier: E. P. Walton & Sons, Printers. 1842. 18mo, pp. 32.

Parker, Zechariah, Jun. *A Sketch* of the Arbitrary Proceedings of the Baptist Church, in Ludlow, Vt., relative to the Excommunication of Zechariah Parker, Jun., to which is added, Brief Remarks on Baptism and Close Communion. By Zechariah Parker, Jun. Text. Keene, N. H. Printed for the Author. 1832. 8vo, pp, 16.

Parmalee, S. N. *Analysis and Index to Laws*. Burlington. 1845.

Parmelee, Ashbel. *Two Sermons*. A Sermon delivered at the Interment of Miss Susan Winchester, (Daughter of Henry and Lois Winchester,) who died Dec. 28, 1814, in the 18th year of her age. By Ashbel Parmelee, Pastor of the Congregational Church, in Malone, N. Y. A Sermon delivered at the Funeral of Mrs. Lucy Parmelee: (Wife of the Rev. A. Parmelee and Daughter of H. and L. Winchester,) who died at Westford, Vt., Feb. 13, 1814. By Josiah Hopkins, A. M., Pastor of the Church of Christ, in New Haven, Vt. Middlebury, Vt. Printed by Timothy C. Strong. 1815. 8vo, pp. 27.

Mr. Parmelee was born in West Stockbridge, Mass., in 1785, and moved, with his father and family, to Pittsford, Vt., in 1787. He began to preach in 1809, and was settled at Malone, N. Y., in 1810, and preached there and in the vicinity until his death, in his 78th year.

Parmelee, Moses P. *Life Scenes* among the Mountains of Ararat. By Moses Payson Parmelee, Missionary of the American Board. Texts. Boston : Mass. Sabbath School Society, No. 13 Cornhill. 1868. 16mo, pp. 265.

Mr. Parmelee was born in Westford, Vt., May 4, 1834; was graduated at the University of Vermont in 1855; and at Union Seminary, N. Y., in 1861, having taught three years in the interval; was chaplain of the 3d Vermont Volunteers, 1861-3, when he was appointed a missionary of the A. B. C. F. M., for Turkey, where he still remains, (1896.)

Parmelee, Rev. Simeon, D. D. *Figurative* Instruction Ancient and Divine. A Sermon delivered at Lyndon, June 24, 1825, at the Installation of Unity Lodge of Free and Accepted Masons. By Simeon Parmelee. Pastor of a Church at Westford. Motto. Windsor : Printed by W. Spooner. 1825. 8vo, pp. 20.

—*In Memorial* of Rev. Simeon Parmelee, D.D., who was born at West Stockbridge, Mass., Jan. 16, 1782, spent the active days of his life in Vermont, and died at Oswego, N. Y., February 10, 1882, at the age of one hundred years and twenty five days. Text. Boston : (1882). Beacon Press, Thomas Todd, printer, No. 1, Somerset Street. 8vo, pp. 40.

Contains biographical sketch by Rev. A. F. Beard, D. D., of Syracuse, N. Y.; Commemorative discourse by Rev. J. A. Biddle, Oswego; Letters, notices, etc.

Simeon Parmelee was born in West Stockbridge, Mass. Jan. 16, 1782; studied Greek with Rev. J. Bushnell of Cornwall, Vt., and theology with Rev. Lemuel Haynes; ordained in Westford, Vt., 1808; pastor of Congregational Churches in Westford, 1808-37; Williston, 1837-43; Milton, 1852-4; Tinmouth, 1854-7; Underhill, 1857-63; Swanton, 1863-6. Resided subsequently at Oswego, N. Y.; except that he supplied the pulpit in Westford

1868-9. He married in 1806, Amira, daughter of Zebulon Mead of West Rutland, who died in January 1821, leaving two children ; married in Sept. 1821, Phebe, daughter of Lewis Chapin of Jericho. Twelve children were the fruits of these marriages. He died of old age at Oswego, Feb. 10, 1882. Beginning life as a wagon builder he spent a life of great length, usefulness and honor in the Christian Ministry; and the name of " Father Parmelee" was a household word in many Vermont homes.

Parmly, Eleazar. *Memorials* Written on Several Occasions during the Illness and after the decease of three little Boys. By those who loved them. Motto. New York. 1843. 8vo, pp. 52.

—*Thoughts* in Rhyme by Eleazar Parmly. New York : Printed by Thomas Holman, Corner of Centre and White streets. 1867. 8vo, pp. 600.

—*Address* delivered at the Eighth Annual Commencement of the Baltimore College of Dental Surgery, February, 1848. By Eleazer Parmly, M. D., D. D. S. Baltimore : John W. Woods, Printer. 1848. 8vo, pp. 21.

—*Also, a Temperance Address*, at Runsom, N. J. New York : 1844. 8vo.

Dr. Parmly assisted C. A. Harris, M. D., in editing the American Journal of Dental Science;" he also delivered in rhyme one or more addresses in New York, before Dental Societies.

Dr. Parmly was born in Braintree, Vt., March 13, 1797; died in New York city, December, 1874. He learned dentistry of his elder brother, completing his education as a surgeon-dentist in Paris. He then proceeded to London, and hung out his professional sign, where he practiced for several years with great success, especially among the nobility; he sold his business in London, and came to New York, where he invested a considerable part of his means in real estate.

Mr. Parmly continued to reside in New York until his death, in the practice of his profession, and dealing in real estate, always buying, but seldom selling. He also invested largely in real estate in Ohio, owning at one time a large part of the city of Painsville in that State. At his death he left an estate valued at five million dollars or more, to be divided between three heirs, a son and two daughters; Hon. Frederick Billings, of Woodstock, Vt., married one of the daughters.

Dr. Parmly was in his mature years punctilious in money matters; if any person owed him a cent, he wanted it; if he owed any person anything he wanted to pay it. An instance: Some years previous to the Doctor's death, Dr. O. P. Forbush, of Montpelier, passed a portion of his time yearly in the office of Dr. Parmly, and on one occasion Dr. Forbush was requested to go down town and collect a bank check. The Doctor replied that he did not know any one in the bank. Just then Dr. Parmly appeared and said he was going down town, and would identify Dr. Forbush, and they stepped into a Broadway stage. Directly Dr. Parmly examined his pockets, found he had no money, and said " Forbush you must pay my fare." The next day the son of Dr. Parmly handed Dr. Forbush a small envelope, saying, "Father left this for you." Upon opening it Dr. Forbush found six cents, the stage fare of the day before. Dr. Forbush said " it is nothing," and declined to receive it; the son said " Father will feel hurt if you don't take it," and the Doctor finally put it into his pocket.

Dr. Parmly was a near relative of Dr. Eleazar Wheelock, founder of Dartmouth College, and his name Eleazar was for the Rev. Doctor. Another of the family bore the name of Wheelock Parmly. There was also a Randolph Parmly, uncle to Dr. Eleazar; said to have been the first male child born in the town of Randolph, hence his name. I learn from Judge Barrett, of Woodstock, that Dr. Parmly always manifested great respect and veneration for the Wheelock family, and a few years before his death, upon visiting the cemetery at Hanover, N. H., where the remains of so many of that honored name rest, and finding that part of the cemetery in a somewhat dilapidated and uncared for condition, he caused to be put in complete order the grounds, monuments and stones which mark the resting places of the Wheelock family.

I am indebted to Dr. Forbush, of Montpelier, for many of the incidents in Mr. Parmly's life.

The following sketch of Dr. Parmly was furnished by his son, a resident of New York city. It does not cover the entire period of the doctor's life as clearly as desirable, but in connection with the above is valuable :

At an early age my father taught a district school in Vermont with marked success. The Trustees cautioned him not to mention his age, as many of his pupils were older than he. This was his first departure from farm labor. He then went to Montreal, and entered the printing office of a friend of his father, Maj. Levi Mower, but was not indentured, and the friendly relations of the Mower family always kept up. When learning the printer's art, he aspired to editorship, and soon set up his own articles. At this time his older brother, Levi Spear Parmly, had met with success in dentistry, having studied under the leading dentist of Boston, and he sought his brother in Montreal, and gave him such instruction as he could. Eleazar practiced in the Southern cities, chiefly in Lexington, Ky. Being dissatisfied with his knowledge of his profession, he went to Paris and put himself under the tuition of Dr. Maury, dentist to the King of France. From there he went to London, Eng., where he met with most flattering success, and would probably have remained there but for his strong attachment to home and kindred.

My father returned to New York in 1824 with but little means, as all he had saved up to that time and all savings for several years after were devoted to bettering the prospects of his family through education and establishing them in business. The Ohio investments were inconsiderable and unprofitable. He married in 1827, after which date he made investments in real estate. His extreme carefulness and promptness in meeting obligations gave him a reputation of having much greater means than he possessed. At his decease the estate was estimated at $2,000,000, but since then there has been a considerable shrinkage in its value. It was divided into four equal shares, and these shares distributed, according to the provisions of the will, among the heirs, who are a son, two daughters, and three children of a deceased daughter.   EHRICK PARMLY.

Parmly, Levi S. *On the Natural History* and management of the teeth. New York. 1820. 8vo.

—*A Practical Guide* to the management of the teeth. 1838. 12mo.

Mr. Parmly was also a dentist of high repute, being an elder brother of Eleazar Parmly above. Subsequently he was some time partner of Eleazar in New York. At an early age he was bound out to a man in Canada, where he went to live with an aunt, for seven years to learn the cooper's trade. Soon after his apprenticeship commenced, the late Dr. T. C. Taplin, for many years a prominent dentist and citizen of Montpelier, taught school in the Canadian town where young Parmly lived. Noticing that he was a bright and promising boy, he persuaded his master to allow him to attend school. At the close of the school, young Parmly expressed great repugnance to going back to the cooper's trade, but said he was bound to his master, and did not know how to get out of it. Mr. Taplin advised him to run away; but Parmly said he had no money or clothing, whereupon Mr. Taplin supplied him an outfit and a little money, and told him to get into Vermont as quickly as possible, and he would be safe.

Young Parmly followed instructions, and finally worked his way to New Orleans, where an uncle, who was a physician, resided. The uncle took an interest in the lad, and gave him protection and aid. He subsequently moved to New Orleans, where I am informed he died.

Parsons, Wm. Leonard, D. D. *A Sermon* on the death of Miss Marietta Ingham, one of the Founders of Ingham University : delivered at University Hall, Le Roy, June 6th, 1867. By Rev. Wm. L. Parsons, D. D. Rochester: E. Darrow & Kempshall, 65 Main Street. 1867. 4to, pp. 23.

Born at Fairhaven, Vt., in 1811; graduated at Oberlin, Ohio, 1838. He has published "Satan's Devices, and the Believer's Victory," Boston : 1864. 12mo. Contributor to Oberlin Quarterly Review, and Biblio. Sacra. In 1866 he was professor of Mental and Moral Science in Ingham Female University. Allibone.

Partridge, Alden. *Capt. Partridge's* Lecture on National Defence. At Windsor, Vt., June, 1821. n. p. n. d, 8vo, pp. 14.

—*Prospectus* of the American Literary, Scientific and Military Academy, Norwich, Vt. Windsor : 1820. 8vo.

—*Prospectus* and Internal Regulations of the American Literary, Scientifick, and Military Academy ; to be opened at Middletown, Connecticut, in August, 1825. 8vo, pp. 23.

—*Memorial* of Alden Partridge and Edward Burke, Appointed a Committee to memorialize Congress on the subject of the Militia : 25th Congress, 3d Session. Ho. of Reps. February 4, 1839. 8vo, pp. 19.

Capt. Partridge was born in Norwich, Vt., in 1785, and died there, January 16, 1854. He was graduated at West Point Military Academy in 1806, and was engaged there as a Professor, Engineer, and Superintendent, 1806-1818. He founded military schools at Norwich, Vt., Portsmouth, Va., Reading, Pa., Pembroke, N. H., Middletown, Conn., and at Brandywine Springs, Delaware. He lectured on military affairs in the large cities, and was a member of the Vermont Legislature in 1833-34, and 1839; Surveyor-General of Vermont in 1832. He published an "Excursion" in 1822; "Letters on Education, and on National Defence," "Journal of a Tour of Cadets," etc., in 1824; also 1827.

The Vermont Historical Society has in manuscript, Journals of Excursions of the "Norwich Cadets," under Capt. Partridge, in September and October, 1823, the first being a march to Manchester, Vt., via Woodstock, Chester, Andover, Londonderry, and Peru; returning via, Rutland, Sherburne, etc. At Manchester, Gov. Richard Skinner gave a reception, and, together with many of the citizens of the town, accompanied the cadets to the summit of Equinox Mountain. With the manuscript of this Excursion is a map neatly prepared, giving the elevation of each town and mountain peak on the entire route, as taken by Capt. Partridge. The second excursion was to Windsor, where the cadets were received with military and other honors from the citizens. The manuscript and map were prepared at the time by the late Hon. William G. Brooks, of Boston, and presented by him to the Vermont Historical Society in 1876. Mr. Brooks was graduated at Norwich under Capt. Partridge, and at the time of his recent decease was a distinguished member and officer of the Massachusetts Historical Society.

See Norwich University; Journal of an Excursion; Colton, Walter.

Pattison, Robert Everett, D. D.

Mr. Pattison was a clergyman and teacher. He was born in Benson, Vt., August 19, 1800; was graduated at Amherst College in 1826; ordained as a Baptist minister at Salem, Mass., in September, 1829. He was settled as pastor of the First Baptist church, Providence, R. I., in March, 1830; he was afterward Professor in Waterville College, Maine, and President of the same in 1836-40; then connected with various Baptist Institutions, and in 1871 president of the Chicago University.

His publications are: "Eulogy on Rev. Jeremiah Chaplin, D. D.," 1841; Address at the Western Baptist Theological Institution," Covington, Ky., 1847; "Comment on the Epistle to the Ephesians," Boston, 1859. 12mo. Also articles in the Baptist Review.

See Allibone ; Drake.

Patton, R. B. *Address*, delivered before the Philological Society of Middlebury College, on the evening of the 19th of August. By R. B. Patton, Professor of Languages, Middlebury : Printed by J. W. Copeland. 1823. 8vo, pp 16.

Paul, Hiland. *History of Wells*, Vermont, for the First Century after its Settlement ; By Hiland Paul, with Biographical Sketches by Robert Parks, Esq. Rutland : Tuttle & Co., Job Printers. 1869. 12mo, pp. 154.

Pawlet. *Constitution* and Catalogue of Pawlet Library. Bennington : Printed by Anthony Haswell. MDCCXCIX. 12mo, pp. 10.

History of, see Hollister, Hiel.

Peabody, A. P. *The Positive Philosophy*. An Oration delivered before the Phi Beta Kappa Society of Amherst College, July 9, 1867, and before the Phi Beta Kappa Society of the University of Vermont, August 6, 1867. By A. P. Peabody, D. D., LL. D., Preacher to the University, and Plummer Professor of Christian Morals in Harvard College. Boston : Gould and Lincoln. 1867. 8vo, pp. 28.

Peabody, William B. O., D. D. *A Sermon,* preached at the Ordination of the Rev. O. W. B. Peabody, as Pastor of the First Congregational Church and Society in Burlington, by William B. O. Peabody, D. D., Minister in Springfield, Ms. With the Remarks of Rev. John Cordner, on Giving the Fellowship of the Churches, Aug. 14th, 1845. Burlington : University Press, S. Fletcher, Printer. 1846. 8vo, pp. 24.

Peabody, Oliver W. B. *A Discourse,* delivered in the church of the First Congregational Society in Burlington, Sunday, December 21, 1845, the anniversary of the Sabbath which preceded the Landing of the Pilgrim Fathers at Plymouth. By Oliver W. B. Peabody. Burlington : University Press, S. Fletcher, Printer. 1846. 8vo, pp. 22.

Rev. Mr. Peabody was born in Exeter, N. H., July 9, 1799, and died at Burlington, Vt., July 5, 1848; he was pastor of the Unitarian church at Burlington, August, 4, 1845, until his death.

Peacham. *Catalogue* of the Officers and Students of the Caledonia County Grammar School, Peacham, Vt., 1834. Windsor : (1834) 16mo, pp. 16.

—*Confession* of Faith and Covenant, of the Congregational Church in Peacham, adopted January 21, A. D., 1813. St. Johnsbury: A. G. Chadwick. 1842. 12mo, pp. 8.

—*Addresses* delivered at the reopening of the Congregational Church in Peacham, Vermont, September 28, 1871. With an Appendix. Montpelier : Poland's Steam Printing Establishment. 1872. 8vo, pp. 66.

Compiled by Rev. M. S. Dudley, pastor of the church—1870-73, and Historical Discourse by him.

—*Report* of the Superintendent of Schools of the Town of Peacham, Vt., for the school year 1874-5. Montpelier. Poland's Print. 8vo, pp. 12.
Continued.

—*Catalogue* of the Library of the Juvenile Society. Organized at Peacham, Vt., August 9, 1810. Montpelier : Poland's Steam Printing Establishment. 1881. 8vo, pp. 24.

Peake, Rebecca. *Trial* of Mrs. Rebecca Peake, Indicted for the Murder of Ephraim Peake, Tried at Orange County Court, Dec. Term, 1835, Embracing the Evidence, Arguments of Counsel, Charge and Sentence. Montpelier : E. P. Walton & Son, Publishers, 1836. 12mo, pp. 88.

Pearse, James. *A Narrative* of the Life of, in two Parts. Part I. Containing a General Account of his early Life, his five years residence in Mississippi, Louisiana, &c. Part II. Containing an Account of his unfortunate imprisonment at Plattsburgh, &c. Written by Himself. Rutland : Printed by William Fay, for the Author. 1825. 12mo, pp. 144.

Pearson, Ora. *An Address* to Professing Heads of Families, on the Subject of Family Worship. Prepared and published by request of the Piscataqua Conference. 1831. 8vo, pp. 12.
Mr. Pearson was born in Chittenden, Vt. For Sketch of his life see Vermont Historical Gazetteer, Vol. 3, p. 87.

Pearson, Thomas Scott. *Sermons,* By the late Rev. David Merrill, Peacham, Vt. With a Sketch of his Life. Windsor, Vt. 1855. 12mo, pp. 288. Portrait.

—*Sketch* of the Life of the late Rev. David Merrill, prepared for Publication in a Volume of his Sermons. By Thomas Scott Pearson, A. M. Windsor, Vt. Printed at the Vermont Chronicle Press. 1855. 12mo, pp. 24.
See Middlebury College, for Catalogue of Graduates, etc.
Mr. Pearson was born in Kingston, N. H., September 14, 1828; and died at Indianapolis, Ind., November 10, 1856. For Memoir, See Vermont Historical Gazetteer, Vol. 1, pp. 370-71.

—**Pease, Rev. Allen Gaylord.** *Christ* the Resurrection and the Life. A Sermon preached at the Funeral of Harry S. Richards, Esq., in the Congregational Church in Norwich, Vt., Wednesday, November 16, 1853, By A. G. Pease. Published by Request. Albany : Joel Munsell, 78 State Street. 1853. 8vo, pp. 33.

—*Memoir* of Mrs. Mary Reynolds Page. Cambridge : Printed at the Riverside Press. 1873. 12mo, pp. VI, (4), 183.
Mrs. Page was the wife of the Hon. John B. Page, of Rutland, Vt.

—*Philosophy* of Trinitarian Doctrine ; A Contribution to Theological Progress and Reform. By Rev. A. G. Pease, Rutland, Vt. New York : G. P Putnam's Sons, Fourth Ave. and 23rd St. 1875. 12mo, pp. 183.
Aaron G. Pease was born in Canaan, Conn., February 22, 1811 ; and died in Rutland Vt., August 7, 1877. He was a brother of Rev Dr. Calvin Pease, and was graduated at the University of Vermont, 1837, and at Andover Seminary, 1841 ; he was pastor of the Congregational church at Pittsford, Vt., 1841-43, and at various places until 1847; then at Waterbury, Vt., until 1852 ; at Norwich, Vt., 1852-57, when his health failed. Member of the Vermont Legislature from Norwich, 1864-5 ; Superintendent Vermont Reform School, 1866-69; when he moved to Rutland.

—**Pease, Rev. Calvin, D. D.** *Import* and Value of the Popular Lecturing of the Day. A Discourse pronounced before the Literary Societies of the University of Vermont, August 3, 1842. By Calvin Pease. Published at the request of the Societies. University Press, Burlington: Chauncey Goodrich. 1842. 8vo, pp. 43.

—*Classical Studies.* By Calvin Pease, M. A., Professor in the University of Vermont. Bibliotheca Sacra for July, 1852, pp. 507-529.

—*The Distinctive* Idea of Preaching, By Calvin Pease, Professor in the University of Vermont. Bibliotheca Sacra for April, 1853, pp. 366-389.

—*Address* before the Graduating Class, in the Medical Department of the University of Vermont, June 4, 1856. By Calvin Pease. Burlington : 1856. 16mo, pp. 35.

—*Idea* of the New England College and its Power of Culture. An Address, delivered on the occasion of his Inauguration as President of the University of Vermont, August 5, 1856, by Rev. Calvin Pease. Burlington : Free Press Print. 1856. 8vo, pp. 52.

—*Sermon* preached before the Graduating Class, in the University of Vermont, August 2d, 1857, by Rev. Calvin Pease, D. D., President of the University. Burlington : Free Press Print. 1857. 8vo, pp. 40.

—*A Sermon;* preached in Burlington, November 17, 1858, at the Funeral of Noble Lovely, Esq., Who died Sunday evening, Nov. 14, 1858. By Rev. Calvin Pease, President of the University of Vermont. Printed for Private Distribution. Burlington : Daily Times Job Printing Establishment. 1858. 8vo, pp. 18.

—*Characteristics* of the Eloquence of the Pulpit. [Address before the Rhetorical Society in Auburn Theological Seminary, May 11, 1858, by the Rev. Calvin Pease, D. D., President of the University of Vermont.] Presbyterian Quarterly Review for October, 1858. pp. 177–220.

—*Sermon*, on Occasion of the Death of John G. Golland and Joshua V. R. Arthur. Members of the Senior Class, of the University of Vermont, by Calvin Pease, President of the University. November 13, 1859. Published for the Class. Burlington: E. A. Fuller, Bookseller and Stationer. Free Press Print. 8vo, pp. 25.

—*Sermon* Preached before the Graduating Class in the University of Vermont, July 31, 1859. By Rev. Calvin Pease, D. D., President of the University. Burlington: Free Press Print. 1859. 8vo, pp. 33.

—*Faith* and its Issue. A Sermon preached before the Graduating Class in the University of Vermont, July 29, 1860. By Calvin Pease, President. Printed for the Class. Burlington: E. A. Fuller, Bookseller and Stationer. Free Press Print. 1860. 8vo, pp. 36.

—*A Tribute* to the Memory of William C. Bloss, by Rev. Calvin Pease, D. D., Rochester, April 26, 1863. Rochester, N. Y.: 8vo, pp. 38.

—*A Tribute* To the Memory of Elisabeth Bloss Buell, from her Pastor, Rev. Calvin Pease, D. D., Rochester, March 8, 1863. Rochester, N. Y. 12mo, pp. 40.

—*In Memoriam.* Privately Printed. New Haven : Thomas H. Pease. 1865. 8vo, pp. 129.

Rev. Dr. Pease was born in Canaan, Conn., August 12, 1813; died at Burlington, Vt., September 17, 1863. His family removed to Charlotte, Vt., in 1826 and settled upon a farm; he was graduated at the University of Vermont, in 1838; and was Principal of the Academy at Montpelier, 1838-42; Professor in the University of Vermont, 1842-55; and President of the same until January 1862, when he became pastor of the First Presbyterian church, Rochester, N. Y., which position he held until his death. While at Montpelier, Dr. Pease became acquainted with the lady who afterward became his wife, Miss Martha, youngest daughter of the late Hon. Joseph Howes, of Montpelier, to whom he was married in May, 1843. They had five children, all daughters.

For biographical sketches, see Appleton's Annual Cyclopedia 1863, pp. 737-8 ; Vermont Historical Gazetteer, Vol. I, pp. 652-54; In Memoriam, Calvin Pease.

Peck, Miss Ellen O.

Daughter of Hon. Addison Peck of East Montpelier, Vt., of which town she is a native. Miss Peck commenced writing for magazines and newspapers at an early period in life, her first article, a poem, being sent to a Boston paper by her brother, without the knowledge of his sister, where it was printed; she was then fifteen years of age. Miss Peck has since become an industrious contributor to various periodicals, in prose and verse, her name appearing as a regular contributor to "The Cottage Hearth," Boston, "New England Journal of Education," and Mrs. Slade's magazine, "Good Times." Among her prose articles may be mentioned "The Early Home of Governor Peck," and of her poems, all of which are creditable, and notably her poetical address read before the Alumni of the Vermont Methodist Seminary, 1876. Miss Peck is

much interested in Education, teaching being one of her principal occupations. (1880).

See Peck, Ira B.; Peck, John.

Peck, Ira B. *A Genealogical History* of the Descendants of Joseph Peck, who emigrated with his family to this Country in 1638; and Records of his father's and grandfather's families in England; with the pedigree extending back from son to father for twenty generations, with their coat of arms and copies of wills. Also, an Appendix, giving an account of the Boston and Hingham Pecks, the descendants of John Peck, of Mendon, Mass.; Deacon Paul, of Hartford; Deacon William and Henry, of New Haven ; and Joseph, of Milford, Conn., with portraits of distinguished persons from steel engravings. By Ira B. Peck. Printed by Alfred Mudge & Son, Boston. 1868. 8vo, pp. 442.

The Peck families in Vermont are largely represented in the above work. It appears that a large proportion of them are descended from Joseph, brother of Rev. Robert Peck, the minister who immigrated from Hingham, England, in 1638. Information in relation to the Pecks in Washington county is not as full as it should have been, probably on account of a lack of interest and a general indifference in relation to the subject.

We give some additional facts in relation to Rev. Robert Peck, the "Minister of Hingham." As stated in the above work, he was Rector at Hingham, England, 1605-1638, but his sympathies being with the Puritans and opposed to the Church of England, he was prosecuted by Bishop Wren, which led him and a large part of his church to emigrate to America. Under his lead a party of 133 men, women and children embarked in the ship, "Diligent," of Ipswich, Captain John Martin, which left Gravesend, April 26, and arrived at Boston, Mass., August 10, 1638. The following are a few of the names composing this party : Robert Peck, wife, two children and two servants; Joseph Peck (brother of Robert, and ancestor of most of the Pecks in Vermont), wife, three sons, one daughter, two men and three maid servants; Edward Gilman, wife, three sons, two daughters and three servants. Edward Gilman was the ancestor of all the Gilmans in the United States, so far as known; he took the freeman's oath, together with Ralph Wheelock, ancestor of Rev. Eleazar Wheelock. Rev. Robert Peck, Joseph Peck, and many others, at Ipswich, Mass., March 13, 1639. To be admitted as a freeman at that time the person was required to be a respectable member of some Congregational (Calvinistic) church, and to subscribe the oath before the General Court, or the Quarterly Court of the county. Among other names, heads of families, who came in the ship "Diligent" were Foulsham, Chamberlain, Gates, Knights, Cooper, Cushing, Beale, a shoemaker, Sayer, James, Buck, Sutton, Lincoln, Smith, Allen, Hawk, etc. A complete list may be found in "Drake's Founders of New England," pp. 80, 81.

This colony appears to have been very well off, as many of the families brought with them from one to four servants each. They all settled at Hingham, Mass. Here also had previously settled, among others, four families of Hobarts, of whom was Rev. Peter, the first minister in the town. Rev. Father James Hobart, late of Berlin, Vt., was of this stock. The first meeting-house was erected in 1635, and at a town meeting, March, 1644-5, Edward Gilman and four other persons were empowered to build at the north end of the meeting-house one gallery for themselves, to remain their property, etc.

Rev. Robert Peck was ordained a "Teacher" in the church soon after his arrival, but it does not appear that he ever had a settlement, as he returned to his old Parish in England in 1641, the persecutions there having mainly ceased.

The following is a sketch of Rev. Mr. Peck by Rev. John Watson, who was the Rector of the same parish in England, 1683-1727 : "He was a man of very violent, schismatical spirit. He pulled down the rails, and leveled the altar and the whole chancel a foot below the church, as it remains to this day; but being prosecuted for it by Bishop Wren, he fled the kingdom and went over to New England with many of his parishioners. He promised never to desert them, but hearing that the Bishops were deposed, he left them and came back to Hingham and resumed his Rectory. He died in 1656."

Peck, Rev. J. Milton. *A Sermon ;* Preached in Trinity Church, Rutland ; before the Young

Men's Christian Association, in answer to their invitation, on the Evening of the Second Sunday after Christmas, the 5th of January, 1868, by the Rector, the Rev. J. Milton Peck. Claremont, N. H. The Claremont Manufacturing Company. 1868. 8vo, pp. 24.

Peck, John. *A Poem*, in opposition to the doctrine of Universal Salvation. Being a Descant on the Universal Plan. 1813. 18mo, pp. 18.

This poem consists of 131 stanzas, to which is appended the sermon by Rev. Lemuel Haynes, on the same subject, preached at Rutland, 1805.

—*An edition :* A Short Poem, containing a Descant on the Universal Plan. Also the Wrestler, who found an Evil Beast, contended with him, and threw him : being an answer to Mr. Peck's Poem. By Samuel C. Loveland. Weathersfield, Vt. Printed by Eddy & Patrick. 1814. pp. 32.

See Loveland S. C.

—*Another edition:* Descant on the Universal Plan. Corrected, with Rev. L. Haynes' Sermon. Rutland. 1823.

—*Also an edition :* A Descant on the Universal Plan, Corrected ; or, Universal Salvation Explained. By John Peck. With Rev. L. Haynes' Sermon. Boston : Printed for the Publisher, 1823. 12mo. pp. 24.

The title to Mr. Haynes' sermon appended is as follows : Universal Salvation a very Ancient Doctrine ; with some of the life and character of its author; A sermon deliv. ered at Rutland, West parish, in the year 1805. By Lemuel Haynes, A. M. Twentieth edition. pp. 25-35, pagination continuous.

Mr. Peck's Poem was reprinted at Boston in 1858, by Jonn P. Jewett & Co. The following stanza is a specimen :

> " Oh, charming news ! to live in sin,
> And die to reign with Paul !
> 'Tis so indeed—for Jesus bled
> To save the devil and all."

Mr. Peck was the ancestor of many of the families of that name in Washington county. He was born in Rehoboth, Mass., in 1734 or 35, and with his family moved to East Montpelier in 1806, and settled on a farm, where he died March 4, 1812. Several poems by him in manuscript are in possession of his grandson (through Nathaniel) Hon. Addison Peck, of East Montpelier. Mr. Peck, through his son, Squire, who settled on a farm in East Montpelier, was grandfather of the late Gov. Asahel Peck ; also through his son Gen. John Peck, who settled in Waterbury, he was grandfather of the late Hon. Lucius B. Peck, of Montpelier.

Peck, Lucius B.

—*Slavery in the Territories.* Speech of Hon. L. B. Peck, of Vermont, in the House of Representatives, Aug. 3, 1848. In Committee of the whole on the State of the Union, on the Army Appropriation Bill. 8vo, pp. 7.

—*Slavery in the Territories.* Speech of Hon. Lucius B. Peck, of Vermont, in the House of Representatives, April 23, 1850, In Committee of the whole on the state of the Union, on the President's Message transmitting the Constitution of California. 8vo, pp. 8.

—*Proceedings* of the Washington County Bar, in relation to the Deaths of Hon. Lucius B. Peck, and Luther Henry, Esq. At March Term, 1867. Published by vote of the Bar. Montpelier : Printed at the Freeman Steam Printing Establishment. 1867. 8vo, pp. 20.

Lucius B. Peck was born at Waterbury, Vt., Nov. 17, 1802; died in Lowell, Mass , December 27th, 1866.

He spent one year at West Point Academy, then studied law, and came to the Bar in Washington county in 1824; served in the State Legislature from Montpelier two years, and was a Democratic Representative in Congress from Vermont, 1847 to 1851; was United States District Attorney for Vermont, 1853 to 1857 and subsequently President of the Vermont and Canada railroad. Mr. Peck was regarded as one of the most eminent lawyers in the State.

Peck, Phinehas. *A Discourse*, delivered on the day of General Election, at Montpelier, October 9, 1817, before His Excellency Jonas Galusha, Esq., Governor ; His Honor Paul Brigham, Esq. Lieut. Governor ; the Honorable Council, and House of Representatives of the State of Vermont. By Phinehas Peck, Elder in the Methodist church, Lyndon. Jesse Cochran, State Printer. Windsor, Vt.: 1817. 8vo. pp. 23.

Elder Peck was of the Methodist persuasion, and the first settled minister in Lyndon, Vt., 1812-1819. He had preached there some years previous to his settlement. We have not ascertained where he came from, or what became of him.

Peck, Theodore S. *See Roster*, and Vermont Legislative Documents, containing Reports of the Adjutant and Inspector Generals.

Theodore Safford Peck was born in Burlington, March 22, 1843. He enlisted in the Army at the age of 18, and served throughout the War of the Rebellion, as member of the First Vermont Cavalry; Lieutenant Ninth Vermont Infantry; Aid-de-Camp, Brigade Quartermaster and Captain and Assistant Quartermaster of U. S. Volunteers, in the Army of the Potomac and Army of the James. In 1881 elected Adjutant and Inspector General of Vermont, and has held the office by successive elections to date, 1896.

Peck, Wallace. *The Story* of the Puritans ; a go-as-you-please History (part fact, part fiction,) from the First Leeway Voyage of the Mayflower down to the Close of the Doughnut Dynasty. By Wallace Peck. St. Johnsbury : 1889. Charles T. Walter, publisher. 8vo, pp. 90.

Peet, Lyman B. *Preparation for Death.* A Sermon preached at Bangkok, Siam, August 10th, 1845, at the Funeral of Mrs. E. R. Bradley, an Assistant Missionary of the American Board of Commissioners for Foreign Missions. By Rev. L. B. Peet. Bangkok : A. B. C. F. M. Press. 1845. 8vo, pp. 21.

—*Remarks* on the Best Term for God in Chinese ; also on the Proper Basis of Compromise on this Subject. Addressed to the Friends of Protestant Missions to the Chinese, by Rev. L. B. Peet, Missionary of the American Board of Commissioners for Foreign Missions at Fuhchau. Printed at Canton. 1852. 8vo, pp. 31.

Mr. Peet was born in Cornwall, Vt., March 1, 1809; was graduated at Middlebury College in 1834, and at Andover in 1837 ; sailed as a missionary of the A. B. C. F. M. for Siam in 1839, and was transferred to China in 1846; remained there until 1871 (with the exception of a three years visit to America,) when he went to West Haven, Ct., and died there January 11, 1878.

Peet, Stephen.

Born in Sandgate, Vt., in 1795; and died at Chicago, Ill., March 21, 1855. He was graduated at Yale College in 1823. He preached seven years in Euclid, O., and afterwards was a chaplain at Buffalo, N. Y., editing the Bethel Magazine and Buffalo Spectator ; then a missionary to Wisconsin, preaching at Green Bay in 1837. He was one of the founders of Beloit College, and helped to organize more than thirty churches in Wisconsin ; was some time minister at Milwaukee, afterwards took charge of an institute at Batavia, Ill., and was afterwards agent of an association to form a theological seminary in Michigan. He published " A History of the Presbyterian and Congregational Churches and Ministers of Wisconsin." 18mo, 1851.

Peirce, Bradford Kinney, D. D. *The Bible Scholar's Manual :* embracing a general account of the Books and Writers of the Old and

New Testaments, the Geography and History of Palestine, the History and Customs of the Jews, etc. For Bible classes and general reading. By Rev. B. K. Peirce. Edited by Daniel P. Kidder. New York : Published by Carlton & Phillips, 200 Mulberry Street. 1853. 24 mo, pp. 291, 51.

Dr. Pierce, philanthropist and author; born in Royalton, Vt., February 3, 1819; was graduated at Wesleyan University in 1841; for a few years he was a Methodist minister of the New England Conference, at different towns in Massachusetts; his health failing, he spent the next ten years in Roxbury, Mass., where he prepared a series of Sunday-School question books, " A Commentary on Acts," and " The Eminent Dead," which latter had a large sale. In 1850-55 he was agent for the New England Sunday-School Union; in 1856, Superintendent of Reform School for Girls at Lancaster, Mass.; Chaplain of the House of Refuge, Randall's Island, New York, 1863 to 1872, and since 1872, editor of Zion's Herald, Boston; received the degree of D.D. from W. U. in 1868. Also author of " Trials of an Inventor ; Life and Discoveries of Charles Goodyear." New York : 1867; " A Half Century with Juvenile Delinquents." New York : 1869; " Stories from Life," and " Sequel to Stories from Life," " Hymns for the Higher Life." Published by Thomas Y. Crowell : New York. 1867. sm. 4to. etc.

Peirce, Mrs. Melusina Fay. *Co-operative* Housekeeping; Romance in domestic economy. By Mrs. C. F. Peirce. Edinburgh : John Ross and Company. London : Sampson Low, Son & Marston. 1870. 12mo, pp. viii, 118.

Reprinted from the Atlantic Monthly for November and December, 1868, and January, February and March, 1869.

—*Report* of the Cambridge Co-operative Housekeeping Society. Cambridge : Press of John Wilson and Son. 1872. 8vo, pp. 10 (2.)

—*The Democratic Party.* A Political Study. By a Political Zero. Cambridge : Press of John Wilson and Son. 1875. 8vo, pp. 63.

—*Co-operation.* By Mrs. Melusina Fay Peirce, Cambridge, Mass. Read at Fourth Woman's Congress, Philadelphia, October 4, 1876. Todd Brothers, Printers, Washington, D. C. 8vo, pp. 15.

—*Municipal Suffrage.* Review of the Petition of Tax-paying women. Mrs. Melusina Fay Peirce's argument before the Committee on Woman Suffrage. [Delivered before a Committee of the Massachusetts Legislature, February, 1878.] 8vo, pp. 4.

Mrs. Peirce is a liberal contributor to magazines, etc. a few of her articles are as follows : " The Mediterranean Solar Eclipse," New York Galaxy, August, 1871; " Married, or Celibate Deaconesses," Churchman, Hartford, Conn., January 27 and February 3 and 10, 1872 ; "St. Paul on Celibacy," Church and State, New York, September 11, 1872; "The Externals of Washington," Atlantic Monthly, December, 1873 ; " Reckoning Day, A Story." Appleton's Journal, March 14, 1874 ; "Parish Organization," Church and State, October 7, 1874 ; "Educational Reviews," Atlantic Monthly, 1874-5-6-7-8 ; " George Elliot," Daily Advertiser, Boston, January 27, 1877. Mrs. Peirce was born in Burlington, Vt., February 24, 1836 ; she is a grand-daughter of the late Rt. Rev. Bishop Hopkins, of Vermont; her mother, Charlotte Emily Hopkins, married the Rev. Charles Fay, a native of Cambridge, Mass. (see Vermont Historical Gazetteer, Volume II, pp. 361-4) ; he was for many years Rector and an Educator at St. Albans, Vt.; Melusina, one of six daughters, married Professor C. F. Peirce, of Harvard University, and resides at Cambridge, Mass.

The People's *Circulating Library Association.* Located at Orfordville, N. H. 1860. "Telegraph" Print, Bradford, Vt. 8vo, pp. (8).

Perkins, Rev. F. T. *In Memoriam* Reverend Frederick Trenck Perkins, 1811-1893. Burlington, no imprint. 8vo, pp. 11.

Perkins, George H., Ph. D. *The Molluscan Fauna* of New Haven. By George H. Perkins, Ph. D. [From the Proceedings of the Boston Society of Natural History, Vol. XIII, October 6, November 3, 1869.] Boston : Press of A. A. Kingman. 1870. 8vo, pp. 110-163.

—*On an ancient Burial Ground* in Swanton, Vt., by Prof. George H. Perkins, Ph. D., of the University of Vermont. [From the Proceedings of the American Association for the Advancement of Science. Portland Meeting, August, 1873.] [Printed at the Salem Press, February, 1874.] 8vo. pp. 27.

—*Insects* Injurious to the Potato and Apple. By Geo. H. Perkins, Ph. D., Professor of Zoology in the University of Vermont and State Agricultural College. [From Third Report of State Board of Agriculture.] Rutland : Tuttle & Company, Printers. 1876. 8vo, pp. 559-606.

—On Some Fragments of Pottery from Vermont. By Geo. H. Perkins, of Burlington, Vt. [From the Proceedings of the American Association for the Advancement of Science, Buffalo Meeting, August, 1876.] 8vo, pp. 12.

—On Certain Injurious Insects. By Geo. H. Perkins, Ph. D., Professor of Zoology in the University of Vermont. [From Fourth Report of the Vermont Board of Agriculture.] Montpelier : J. & J. M. Poland, Official State Printers. 1877. 8vo, pp. 25.

—On Certain Internal Parasites of Domestic Animals. By Geo. H. Perkins, Ph. D., Professor of Zoology in the University of Vermont. [From the Fourth Report of the Vermont Board of Agriculture.] Montpelier : J. & J. M. Poland, Official State Printers. 1877. 8vo, pp. 10.

—On some of the Injurious Insects of Vermont. [From the Fifth Report of the Vermont Board of Agriculture.] Same imprint. 1878. 8vo, pp. 39.

—On the More Important Parasites of the Higher Animals. [From the Sixth Report of the Vermont Board of Agriculture.] By G. H. Perkins, Ph. D., Professor of Zoology in the University of Vermont. Montpelier, Vt.: Freeman Steam Printing House and Bindery. 1880. 8vo, pp. 40.

—*General Remarks* upon the Archæology of Vermont. By George H. Perkins, of Burlington, Vt. 8vo, pp. (4).

Being an Abstract, from Proceedings of the American Association for the Advancement of Science, Volume xxvii, St. Louis Meeting, August, 1878.

—*Archæology* of the Champlain Valley. 8vo, pp. (18).

In American Naturalist for December, 1879.

—*Catalogue* of the Flora of Vermont, including Phœnogamous and Vascular Cryptogamous Plants, growing without cultivation. [From the Tenth Report of the State Board of Agriculture.] By George H. Perkins, Ph. D., Professor of Natural History in the University of Vermont. Burlington : Free Press Asso. 1888. Large 8vo, pp. 74.

George Henry Perkins was born in Cambridge, Mass., Sept. 25, 1844; graduated at Yale College, 1867; took post-graduate course and received degree of Ph. D. from Yale, 1869; Professor of Zoology and Botany in the University of Vermont, 1869-81; Professor of Natural History in the same University 1881 to date. Married in 1870 Miss Mary J. Farnham, of Galesburg, Ill.

Perkins, Joseph. *Valedictory Address*, delivered to the Graduating Class, at the Fiftieth Commencement of Castleton Medical College. By Joseph Perkins, M. D. Professor of Materia Medica and Therapeutics. Rutland : Steam Press of George A. Tuttle and Co. 1854. 8vo, pp. 14.

—*An Address* delivered before the Medical Society of the State of Vermont, October 22, 1856. By Joseph Perkins, M. D., Published by order of the Society. Rutland : George A. Tuttle & Co., Printers. 1857. 8vo, pp. 14.

Perkins, Nathan, Jr., A. M. *A Discourse*, Delivered August 12, 1818 ; at the Ordination of Rev. Eli Moody, at Weybridge, Vermont. By Nathan Perkins, Jr., A. M. Published by request. Middlebury, Vt.: Printed by Francis Burnap. 1818. 8vo, pp. 23.

—*A Discourse* delivered November 24, 1819, at the Ordination of the Rev. Rufus William Bailey, to the Pastoral care of the South Congregational Church in Norwich, Vermont. By Nathan Perkins, Jun., A. M., Pastor of the 2d church in Amherst, Mass. Published by request. Woodstock : Printed by David Watson. 1820. 12mo, pp. 31.

Perkins, Norman C. *The June Training*, A Poem. Read at the Banquet of the Sons of Vermont in Chicago, January 17, 1878. 8vo, pp. 8.

—*The First Prize Speech* delivered in the Linonian and Brothers' Societies of Yale College, for the year 1854. New Haven : Published and for sale by L. W. Fitch. 1854. 8vo, pp. 65. Contains speeches of all the successful contestants, 12 in number.

—*Valedictory Poem* pronounced before the Senior Class in Yale College, Presentation Day, June 17, 1857. New Haven : Published by the Class. 1857. 8vo, pp. 18.

—*The Yale Literary Magazine*, for year ending July, 1857. New Haven : Published by Thomas H. Pease. Edited by five members chosen from the Senior class, of whom Mr. Perkins was one.

—*Vestigia Retrorsum* : Read at the Fourteenth Annual Dinner of the Chicago Yale Association, January 2, 1880, by Norman C. Perkins. Chicago: Jameson & Morse, Printers, 8vo, pp. 8.

—*A Rhyme* of the District School. Read at the Third Annual Banquet of the Sons of Vermont, Chicago, January 16, 1880, by Norman Carolan Perkins. Chicago : Printed by Jameson & Morse. 8vo, pp. 11. Mr. Perkins is a native of Pomfret, Vt., a graduate of Yale College ; he read law and moved to Chicago in 1857, and the following spring was admitted to the bar, and continues the practice of his profession in that city.

Perkins, Samuel E. Born at Brattleboro, Vt., in 1811 ; he read law and early in life settled at Richmond, Ind.; when quite a young man he was appointed a Judge of the Supreme Court of Indiana, where he was continued many years, and maintained a high position on the Bench. His publications are : "Digest of the Decisions of the Supreme Court of Indiana." Indianapolis : 1858. 8vo; "Pleadings and Practice under the code in the several Courts of Indiana." 1859. 8vo.

Perkins, S. G., M. D. *Valedictory Address* to the Graduating Class at the Fifty-Second Commencement of Castleton Medical College. By S. G. Perkins, M. D. Motto. Rutland : Geo. A. Tuttle & Co., Printers. 1855. 8vo, pp. 18.

Perkins, S. K. B. *Discourse* preached by Rev. S. K. B. Perkins, at the Semi-Centennial Celebration of the First Congregational Church of Glover, Vt., July 12th, 1867. Barton : A. A. Earle. 1867. 8vo, pp. 8.

Perkins, W. S. *A Discourse* preached before the Legislature of Vermont, on the Day of General Election, October 11, 1832. By William S. Perkins, Chaplain. Published at the request of the Legislature. Montpelier : Knapp & Jewett, Printers. 1832. 8vo, pp. 19. Mr. Perkins was minister of St. James's Church, Arlington, Vt., 1830-31. and Rector, 1832, and soon after appears to have left the State, as his name does not appear in the Journals of the Annual Conventions.

Perrin, Rev. Truman. *Dietetics*—Lecture Third. The Elements of Sound Health, Great Physical Vigor and Unusual Longevity. By Rev. Truman Perrin, A. M. Montpelier : Printed at the Freeman Steam Printing Establishment. 1861. 8vo. pp. 19. ✻ Mr. Perrin, a son of Zachariah and Mary (Talcott) Perrin, was born in Berlin. Vt., April 24, 1796. He was graduated at Dartmouth College, 1817; was pastor of Congregational churches at Braintree, Brandon and Derby in Vermont, and afterward at different places in New York, 1822–1827; he then went to Vincennes, Ind., preaching and teaching for several years; thence to various places in Alabama and Mississippi for several years; he married in Alabama in 1835; he some years since returned to Berlin, preaching in different places. He published several pamphlets on hygiene and scientific subjects, in addition to the above. Rev. William Perrin was his brother; and the wife of the late Hon. Daniel P. Thompson, of Montpelier was a sister. Mr. Perrin died at Washington, Mass., Nov. 19, 1869.

Perrin, Rev. William. *The Accident*, or Henry and Julia ; A Tale. With other Original Poems. By William Perrin. Montpelier : Printed by Walton and Goss. 1815. 12mo, pp. 63, (1).

—*Hebrew Canticles*, or a Poetical Commentary, or Paraphase, of the various songs of Scripture. Including Solomon's Song, Lamentations, &c. And a few miscellaneous Pieces. Philadelphia : 1820. 12mo, pp. 126.

—*Eloida*. A Poem. 1 vol. Mr. Perrin was born in in Berlin, Vt., April 25, 1792, and died there, in February, 1824. Was graduated at Middlebury College, 1812; studied theology, and preached in various places in Vermont, New York and Pennsylvania ; went to South Carolina for his health, and was pastor over a church there nearly three years ; he did not regain his health, and returned to Vermont. Pearson.

Perry, Capt. David. *Recollections* of an Old Soldier. The Life of Captain David Perry, a Soldier of the French and Revolutionary Wars. Containing many extraordinary Occurrences Relating to his own private History, and an Account of some Interesting Events in the History of the Times in which he lived. Nowhere else Recorded. Written by Himself. Windsor, Vt.: Printed and For Sale at the Republican & Yeoman Printing-office, directly opposite the Bank of Windsor. 1822. 16 mo, pp. 55.

Perry, John Bulkley. *The Natural History* of the Counties, Chittenden, Lamoille, Franklin, and Grand-Isle. By the Rev. John B. Perry. 8vo, pp. 67.

In Vt. Hist. Magazine, Vol. 2, pp. 21-88. A comprehensive and very interesting account of the Geology of North-Western Vermont.

—*Death* as the wages of Sin, and Faith in Christ as its Antidote. Discourses preached in Swanton, By John B. Perry, Second Pastor of the Congregational Church. Motto. Printed by request, and for the Author. Burlington : Free Press Print. 1861. 8vo, pp. 80.

Another edition as follows :

—*Life and Death*, or the Recompense of the Righteous and of the Wicked on Earth. Discourses preached at Swanton, (Vt.) by J. B. Perry, Second Pastor of the Congregational Church. Printed by request and for the Author. Burlington : Free Press Print. 1861. 8vo, pp. 80.

—*Queries* on the Red Sandstone of Vermont and its Relations to other Rocks. By the Rev. John B. Perry, of the Museum of Comp. Zoology, Harvard College, Cambridge. Extracts from the Proceedings of the Boston Society of Natural History, Dec. 18, 1867, Vol. XI. Boston: Press of Abner A. Kingman, Museum of Boston Society of Natural History, Berkeley Street. 1868. 8vo, pp. 16.

—*A Discussion* of Sundry Objections to Geology. By Rev. John B. Perry, of the Museum of Comparative Zoology, Harvard College, Cambridge. Cambridge : Welch, Bigelow and Company, Printers to the University. 1870. 8vo, pp. 32.

—*The "Eozoon" of Limestones* of Eastern Massachusetts. By John B. Perry, Palæontological Assistant in the Museum of Comp. Zoology, Harvard College, Cambridge. [From the Proceedings of the Boston Society of Natural History, April 19, 1871.]

—*A Review* of Sir Charles Lyell's Student's Elements of Geology. By John B. Perry. From the Bibliotheca Sacra, for July, 1872. Andover : Warren F. Draper, Publisher, Main Street. 1872. 8vo, pp. 480-510.

He also published 1857, "A Discourse on Rejoicing in Christ"; 1861, "Two Discourses on Justification before God by Faith in Christ"; 1864, "A Discourse on the Resurrection"; and various articles in different publications. See Vt. Hist. Gazetteer, Vol. 4, pp. 933-988.

Mr. Perry was born in Richmond, Mass., December 12, 1825; died in Cambridge, Mass , October 3, 1872. When six years of age he removed with his father and family to Burlington, Vt., and he continued a resident of the State until about 1868. He graduated from the University of Vermont in 1847. Mr. Perry was a preacher in the broadest sense ; he gave much attention to the Natural History of Vermont, and became an able and accomplished geologist of the School of Marcou, Barrande, Agassiz ; and of Dr. Emmons, of New York, in his later views of the geological formations in western Vermont. Professor Perry published several articles in relation to geology, especially upon the much debated question in the past relative to the geological formations in western Massachusetts and Vermont, and eastern New York ; his views being in accordance with those of the distinguished gentleman mentioned, and quite at variance with those of most, if not all, of our "State Geologists for Vermont." The theory of Professor Perry and those who coincided with him, and which Dr. Emmons formulated as a system under the name "Taconic," is now generally accepted by the most eminent geologists not only in this country but in Europe. For a sketch of the life and works of Professor Perry see "Congregational Quarterly" for April, 1873.

Peru. *Reunion Celebration.* Together with an Historical Sketch of Peru. Bennington County, Vermont, and its Inhabitants from the first settlement of the Town. By Ira K. Bachelder. Brattleboro: Phœnix Job Print. E. L. Hildreth & Co. 1891. 8vo, pp. vii, 144.

Peter The Great. *A New History* of the Life and Reign of the Czar, Peter the Great, Emperor of All Russia, and Father of his Country. Montpelier : Printed by Wright and Sibley, for P. Merrifield & Co., booksellers and stationers, Windsor, Vt. 1811. 12mo. pp. 316.

Peters, Absalom. *A Sermon*, Preached at Bennington, Vt.: on the Lord's Day, Sept. 29, 1822. By Absalom Peters, Pastor of the Congregational Church in that Town. Published by request of the Church. Bennington : Printed by T. Andrews. 1822. 8vo, pp. 21.

—*The Ministry* of the Word committed to Faithful and Able men. A Sermon preached at Middlebury, (Vt.) on the Fourth Anniversary of the Northwestern Branch of the American Education Society, January 14, 1824. By Absalom Peters, A. M., Pastor of the Congregational Church in Bennington. Published by the Society. Poultney, 1824. Smith & Shute, Printers. 8vo, pp. 40.

Contains the (Annual Report.)

—*The Duties*, Trials, and Rewards of the Gospel Ministry. A Sermon preached in Pittsfield, (Mass.) at the Installation of the Rev. Rufus William Bailey, as Pastor of the Congregational Church in that Town, April 15, 1824. By Absalom Peters, A. M., Pastor of the Church in Bennington, (Vt.) Pittsfield : Printed by Phinehas Allen. n. d. 8vo, pp, 24.

Dr. Peters was born in Wentworth, N. H., September 19, 1793; died in New York, May 18, 1869. He was descended from Hugh Peters and John Rogers, the martyr ; was settled over the Congregational Church, Bennington, 1820-1826, which was his only residence in Vermont. He married Harriet Hinckly Hatch, daughter of Reuben Hatch, of Norwich, Vt. See sketch of his life in Jennings' History of Bennington, pp. 104-106.

Pettengill, Amos. *The necessity* of regeneration in order to perform actions acceptable to God. A Sermon delivered at Champlain, N. Y., July 23, 1809. By Amos Pettengill, Pastor of the Church in that place. "The sacrifice of the wicked is an abomination ; how much more when he bringeth it with a wicked mind." Solomon. Burlington: S. Mills. 1810. 8vo, pp. 24.

—*A Call* to help the Lord. A Sermon Delivered at the Annual Meeting of the Moral Society in Dorset, Vermont, June 6, A. D. 1815. By Amos Pettengill, of Manchester, Vt. "He that is not with me is against me." Christ. "Who will rise up for me against evil doers? Who will stand up for me against the workers of iniquity ?" David. "The Lord hath need of him." Christ. Bennington, Vt. Printed by Darius Clark. 1815. 8vo, pp. 24.

—"*The Salvation* of men the grand object of a faithful preacher." A Sermon delivered at the Ordination of Mr. James Johnson to the Work of the Gospel Ministry in Potsdam, N. Y., March 11, 1812, by Amos Pettengill, of Champlain. Plattsburgh: Printed by A. C. Flagg.

—*Memoir* of the Life of. By Rev. Luther Hart. Boston : Massachusetts Sabbath School Society Depository, No. 24, Cornhill. 1834. 12mo, pp. 264.

Mr. Pettengill was born in Salem, N. H., August 9, 1780; was graduated at Harvard University, 1805; preached at Champlain, N. Y., 1807-12; at Manchester, Vt., 1813-15; at South Farms, Conn., 1816-22; and at Salem, Conn., 1822, until his death, August 20, 1830.

Pettengill, J. H.

Rev. John Hancock Pettengill, a champion of conditional immortality, whose writings had attracted attention in this country and in Europe, died in New Haven, Conn., March, 1877, in his seventy-third year, after a long and painful illness. He was a native of Manchester, Vt.

Pettengill, S. B. *The College Cavaliers.* A Sketch of the service of a Company of College Students in the Union Army in 1862, by S. B. Pettengill, a Member of the Company. Chicago: McAllaster & Co., Printers. 1883. 16mo, pp. 96.

A Record of the service of a Company of Dartmouth Students, who enlisted in the civil war, a third of whom were Vermonters.

Mr. Pettengill is a native of Grafton, Vt., was for a time Editor of the Rutland Herald, later a newspaper man in Oregon.

Phair, John P. *A Complete* History of Vermont's celebrated murder case, containing A Report of the Trial and conviction for the murder of Ann Freeze, at Rutland ; the hearing on Exceptions ; The Sentence ; "Dying Statement ;" Two Reprieves ; Legislative Proceedings ; Petitions for new trial, and final effort to stay execution. Compiled from the Stenographer's Report and Official Records, by E. C. Carrigan, correspondent of the Boston Journal." Boston : Published for the Author. 1879. 8vo, pp. 120.

Phair was hung at Windsor Prison, Thursday, April 10, 1879. He left a statement dated the day of his execution, declaring his innocence, which was published in the Boston Journal of April 14th.

Phelps, Mrs. Almira Hart Lincoln. *Geology* for Beginners. Brattleboro. 1832. 12mo.

Mrs. Phelps, sister of Mrs. Emma Willard, the distinguished educator of young ladies, married for her second husband Hon. John Phelps, of Guilford, Vt., in 1831, and resided in this State until 1837. While residing in Vermont Mrs. Phelps published "Botany for Beginners," 1832. 16mo. Of this work two hundred and seventy thousand copies had been sold up to 1867 ; "Lectures on Education; or the Female Student," Boston. 1833. 12 mo. Several editions, London, 1838, New York, 1842; "Caroline Westerley," 1833. 16mo, is No. 16 of Harper's Boy's and Girl's Library; "Chemistry for Beginners," 1834. 16mo; last edition, Philadelphia, 1865; with Mrs. Emma Willard, "Progressive Education"; translated from Madame Necker de Saussure; with Notes by Mrs. Phelps, and an Appendix; "A Mother's Journal of her Child's Last Year," Boston, 1835. 12mo; "Familiar Lectures on Natural Philosophy," New York : 1836, 12mo; "Familiar Lectures on Chemistry, for Schools, Families and Private Students," New York, 1836, last Edition. Philadelphia, 1865; "Natural Philosophy for Beginners," New York, 1837. 16mo, last edition, 1865, Philadelphia.

Mrs. Phelps published eight additional works, three before residing in Vermont, and five after leaving the State. She was born at Berlin, Conn., in 1793, and in 1856 she retired from teaching to her residence, Eutaw Place, Baltimore, where she was living as late as 1872.

"It is estimated that more than one million copies of her manuals have been sold."—Allibone.

"No woman in America, nor any in Europe, excepting Mrs. Marcet and Mrs. Somerville, has made such useful and numerous contributions to the stock of available scientific knowledge as Mrs. Phelps."—Mrs. Hale.

This work was mainly accomplished while she resided at Guilford. Mrs. Phelps was for some years the pupil of her sister Emma, in their native town, and after the marriage of the latter to Dr. Willard, in 1809, she passed two years with her in Middlebury.

Mrs. Phelps, after the death of her first husband, Mr. Lincoln, whom she married in 1817, and who died in 1823, was dependent upon her own efforts mainly for her support and that of her two children, and she at once entered the field of authorship and teaching. After her marriage to Mr. Phelps she gave up teaching, until in 1838 she took charge of a Seminary at Westchester, Pa., and afterward taught at Rahway, N. J., and in 1841,

with the assistance, guidance and advice of her husband, she took charge of Patapsco Female Institute, near Ellicott's Mills, Maryland, which, under her direction, became one of the most flourishing institutions in the country. Here she remained until her retirement in 1856.

Mr. Phelps, son of Timothy, who was a son of Hon. Charles Phelps, prominent on the New York side of the controversy between that State and Vermont, was born in Marlboro, Vt., November 18, 1777.

Mr. Phelps resided in Guilford, Vt., and was a prominent lawyer in Windham county; according to Deming he represented the town of Guilford in the Legislature, 1814 and 1818, and in the Constitutional Convention, 1814; was Register of Probate, 1809-10-11-12, and again in 1837, and a member of the Governor's Council, 1831; Allen's "Biographical Dictionary" calls him Judge Phelps, and says that "he drafted the Constitution of Vermont," which, interpreted, probably means that as a member of the Constitutional Convention in 1814 he may have drafted a proposed amendment. He died at Patapsco in 1848, according to Drake, and in 1849 according to Allibone, Mrs. Hale, and B. H. Hall.

Consult Allibone, Drake, and Mrs. Hale's "Woman's Record ;" and for the family history and genealogy of the Phelps family of Windham county see B. H. Hall's Eastern Vermont, pp. 679-94.

Phelps, Charles. *Lecture* delivered at Marlborough, Vt., July 4th, 1826. By Charles Phelps. Brattleboro : Printed for the author. 1826. 8vo, pp. 24.

Phelps, Charles. *Vermonters Unmasked;* or, some of their evil conduct made manifest, from facts too glaring to be denied, and many of them too criminal to be justified, as follows, viz. 1782. 8vo, pp. 12.

For a full account of Mr. Phelps, memoir, genealogy of his branch of the Phelps family, etc., consult B. H. Hall's Eastern Vermont; also Hiland Hall's Early Vermont.

Phelps, Charles E.

Mr. Phelps, son of Hon. John and his wife Almira, noticed above, was born in Guilford, Vt., May 1, 1833; with his parents he moved to Westchester, Pa., in 1838, and thence to Patapsco, near Ellicott's Mills, Maryland, in 1841. He was graduated at Princeton College in 1852, and at the Law School of Harvard University in 1853; began practice at the Maryland Bar in 1855; in 1858 he was elected a member of the American Association for the Advancement of Science. In 1859 he assisted in organizing the "Maryland Guards" for municipal purposes, and was chosen Captain, and afterwards Major, which latter commission he resigned April 19, 1861, rather than obey an order which he deemed treasonable. In 1860 he was a member of the City Council of Baltimore. In 1862 he was made Lieutenant-Colonel of the Seventh Maryland Regiment of Volunteers, promoted to the rank of Colonel in 1863, and honorably discharged on account of wounds in 1864, and was soon afterwards elected from Maryland to the 39th Congress, serving on the committee on Military and Naval Affairs. He was subsequently commissioned a Brigadier-General, for gallant conduct at the battle of Spottsylvania. Re-elected to the 40th Congress, he served on the Committees on Appropriations and on Expenses of the War Department. In 1864 he was one of a commission to revise the militia laws of Maryland. He was a member of the National Committee to conduct the remains of President Lincoln to Illinois.

See Lanman's Biographical Annals, edition 1876.

Phelps, Daniel Webster. *Eulogy* Pronounced at the Funeral of Daniel Webster Phelps, by the Rev. Byron Sunderland, D. D., May 30th, 1867. Motto. Washington, D. C. 1867. 8vo, pp. 12.

Mr. Phelps, son of Hon. S. S. Phelps, was born at Middlebury, Vt., in 1830; died at Washington, D. C., in 1867.

PHELPS, EDWARD JOHN. *A Sketch* of the Life and Character of Charles Linsley, read before the Vermont Historical Society. [At Brandon, Jan. 28, 1864.] By E. J. Phelps. Published by the Society. Albany, N. Y.: J. Munsell. 1866. 8vo, pp. 20.

—*Sketch* of the life of Isaac F. Redfield, Chief Justice of Vermont. Vermont Reports, vol. 49, appendix. 1877.

See Redfield, I. F.

—*Vermont Central Railroad.* Proposed Judicial Sale. Argument of Hon. E. J. Phelps, of Burlington, delivered before the Supreme Court of Vermont, at St. Albans, July 27, 1877, in behalf of certain First Mortgage Bondholders, in opposition to the Sale and against a Pretense that a Trust Debt, of the Nature disclosed by this Case, can be made a Lien prior to the Mortgages. Stenographically reported. Messenger Supplement, four Newspaper Pages.

—*Argument* in the case of Burdett vs. Esteys, involving the organ patent, delivered in the U. S. Circuit Court in New York, June, 1878. Stenographically reported. Evening Post, N. Y. pp. 60.

—*Brief* and Points of Argument in case Bean v. Beckwith, delivered in U. S. Sup. Court, 1874, on the subject of arbitrary arrests.

—*State of Vermont.* Supreme Court, General Term, 1879. James R. Langdon et als., vs. Vermont and Canada Railroad Co. et als. Mr. Phelps's Argument for the Vermont and Canada Railroad Co. Boston: 1879. 8vo, pp. 45.

The above are four of several hundred briefs of arguments in cases argued by Mr. Phelps *in banc*, printed for use in the same.

—*Chief Justice Marshall* and the Constitutional Law of his time. An Address before the American Bar Association at Saratoga, August 21, 1879, by E. J. Phelps. Reported by J. H. Simms, Stenographer. Philadelphia: E. C. Markley & Son. 1879. 8vo, pp. 22.

—*Lectures* on Topics connected with Medical Jurisprudence delivered before the Medical Department of the University of Vermont by E. J. Phelps. April, 1881. Burlington: The Free Press Association, 1881. 8vo, pp. 100.

—*Changes* in Statute Law. Annual Address before the American Bar Association, at Saratoga Springs, August, 1881, by Edward J. Phelps, of Vermont, President of the Association. Reprinted from the Proceedings of the Fourth Annual Meeting of the Am. Bar Association. Philadelphia, Markley & Son, Printers, 1881, 8vo, pp. 35.

—*Samuel Prentiss.* (Address before the Vermont Historical Society and the Legislature of Vermont, at Montpelier, Oct. 26, 1882.) Montpelier: pp. 24.

—*The Law of the Land.* Address delivered before the Edinburgh Philosophical Institution, at the opening of its session, Nov., 1886. Edinburgh, 1886, pp. 54; 2d ed., New York, 1886; 3d ed., London, 1887, pp. 64.

—*The Extradition Treaty* with Great Britain. (Letters to Mr. Bayard, Secretary of State, Nov. 23, 1885, and June 26, 1886, and Treaty as signed.) Foreign Relations U. S., for 1886, pt. II., pp. 1731—1744.

—*The Alaskan Boundary.* (Letter to Lord Salisbury, British Foreign Minister, Jan. 19, 1886, and Correspondence with Mr. Bayard, Secretary of State. Senate Exec. Doc., no. 148, 49th Cong., 1st sess. 1886.

—*Rights* of American Fishermen and construction of the Treaty with Great Britain of 1818. (Letter to Lord Rosebery, British Foreign Minister, June 2, 1886. Letter to Lord Iddesleigh, his successor in office, Sept. 11, 1886, and correspondence with Mr. Bayard, Secretary of State.) House Exec. Doc., no. 19, 49th Cong., 2d sess. 1887.

—*Ditto.* (Letter to Lord Iddesleigh, Dec. 2, 1886. Letter to Lord Salisbury, Jan. 26, 1887, and Correspondence with Mr. Bayard, Secretary of State.) Ibid., no. 153, 49th Congress, 2d sess. 1887. Reprinted, U. S. Foreign Relations for 1887, p. 454.

—*Proposed* Convention for protection of seals in Behring Sea. (Letters to Mr. Bayard, Secretary of State, Nov. 12, 1887, Feb. 18, 1888, Feb. 25, 1888.) Senate Exec. Doc., no. 106, 50th Cong., 2d sess. Reprinted: U. S. Foreign Relations, for 1888, pt. II., pp. 1827–1880.

—*Ditto*: (Letters to Mr. Bayard, Sep. 12, 1888.) Senate Exec. Doc., no. 55, 52d Cong., 1st sess.

—*The Dismissal* of Lord Sackville, British Minister at Washington. (Letters to Lord Salisbury and to Mr. Secretary Bayard.) U. S. Foreign Relations, for 1888, pt. II., pp. 1169–1718.

—*International Relations.* Address before the Phi Beta Kappa Society at Harvard University, June 29, 1889. Burlington: Free Press Asso., 1889, 8vo. pp. 31.

—*The Relation* of Law to Justice. (Address before the South Carolina Bar Association at Columbia, S. C., Dec., 1890.) Proc. Soc. for 1890. Also, pamphlet, 20 pp., Columbia, S. C., 1890.

—*The* United States Supreme Court and the sovereignty of the people. (Address at the Centennial Celebration of the Federal Judiciary, N. Y., Feb. 4, 1890.) New York: 1890, pp. 27. Also in Carson's History of the Supreme Court, Philadelphia, 1891.

—*Oration* at the Dedication of the Bennington Battle Monument; the Celebration of the Centennial of the admission of Vermont to the Union; and the Anniversary of the Battle, August 19, 1891, by E. J. Phelps. 1891. No imprint, 8vo, pp. 48.

—*Oral Argument* before the International Tribunal of Arbitration, at Paris in the Fur Seal Case, July, 1893. Stenographically reported and published by the U. S. Government in Official Report of Proceedings, Vol xv., Washington, 1895.

—*Same* reprinted from the official publication. Washington: Government Printing Office, 1895, 8vo, pp. 345.

—*The Monroe Doctrine.* An Address before the Brooklyn Institute of Arts and Sciences, March 30, 1896, by Edward J. Phelps, pages 73 to 100 of "America and Europe," in the Putnams' Series of "Questions of the Day." New York and London. G. P. Putnam's Sons, 1896.

—*United States* Circuit Court, District of New York. The United States vs. The Joint Traffic Association, the New York Central and Hudson River Railroad Company and others. Points of Mr. Phelps's argument for the Defendants. New York: 1896. Evening Post Printing office, pp. 28.

Mr. Phelps is also author of the following Magazine articles:

"The Constitution of the United States." Nineteenth Century, (London,) Feb. and Mar., 1888; "Bryce's American Commonwealth." Brit. Quart. Review, July, 1889; "The Age of Words," Scrib. Mag., Dec., 1889; "Divorce in the United States." Forum, Dec.,1889; "The Behring Sea controversy." Harper's Mag., Apr., 1891: "Irresponsible wealth." N. Amer. Rev., May, 1891; "The choice of Presidential electors." Forum, Feb., 1862.

Mr. Phelps has also written many poems, some of which have appeared in print; among which, "Essex Junction, or Lay of the Lost Traveler," and, "To My Cousin Jack," will not soon be forgotten.

Mr. Phelps is a son of the late Hon. Samuel S. Phelps; was born in Middlebury, Vt., 1822, and was graduated at Middlebury College, 1840. He was a teacher in Virginia, 1840-41 ; read law 1841-43, and practiced his profession in Middlebury about two years, and then in Burlington until 1851. Mr. Phelps was appointed second Comptroller of the United States Treasury in 1851, which position he held until the close of President Fillmore's administration, when he resumed practice in Burlington, which he has continued with marked success to the present time. (1896).

He was a member of the Vermont Constitutional Convention in 1870 ; became Kent Professor of Law in Yale College in 1881 and Lecturer on Constitutional Law in Boston University in 1882 ; was U. S. Minister to Great Britain, 1885-89 ; resumed the chair of Constitutional Law in Yale College 1889; was the leading counsel of the United States in the Behring Sea Tribunal of Arbitration in 1893.

Mr. Phelps is recognized as the most distinguished and brilliant lawyer in Vermont ; also as a statesman in the broadest sense.

Phelps, Egbert H. *Modern Benevolence*, a Satirical Poem, delivered before the Associated Alumni of Union College, July 25, 1860. By Egbert Phelps. New York: 8vo, pp. 37.

Son of Hon. S. S. Phelps.

Phelps, James H. *Collections* relating to the History and Inhabitants of the town of Townshend, Vermont. By James H. Phelps. Part I, Acton. Brattleboro : Printed by Geo. E. Selleck. 1877. 8vo, pp. 47.

The town of Acton was annexed to Townshend in 1840.

Phelps, John Wolcott. *The Cradle of Rebellions*. A History of the Secret Societies of France, By Lucien De La Hodde. [Translated by Gen'l John W. Phelps.] New York : Published by John Bradburn. 1864. 8vo, pp. 479.

First edition Lippincott & Co., Philadelphia, 1856.

—*Secret Societies*, Ancient and Modern. An Outline of their Rise, Progress and Character with respect to the Christian Religion and Republican Government. Edited by Gen'l J. W. Phelps. Motto. Second Edition. Chicago, Illinois: Ezra A. Cook & Co., Publishers. 1874. 12mo, pp. 240.

—*Life and Public Services* of General John Wolcott Phelps, by Carl Hampden Cutts Howard. Brattleboro : F. E. Housh & Co. 1887. 12mo, pp. viii, 58.

Allibone's Dictionary of Authors attributes the following to Gen. Phelps : "Sibyline Leaves, or Thoughts Upon Visiting a Heathen Temple. Brattleborough, Vt.: 1853. Anon.; * * * History of Madagascar. New York : 1884; Fables of Florian in English verse. Illus. New York : 1888. sq. 8vo.

The following letter from General Phelps refers to other works by him :

BRATTLEBORO, VT., August 30th, 1880.
MR. M. D. GILMAN,

Dear Sir :- In reply to your favor of the 28th inst., I send one of my works—The Cradle of Rebellions, a translation from the French.

I have also compiled a work, published in Brattleboro in 1876, called GOOD BEHAVIOR, designed for improving the manners of our public schools, and rendering them uniform throughout the Union. It was issued from the house of Messrs. Cheney & Clapp.

An address delivered by me before the Vermont Colonization Society, at Montpelier, in 1867, (I think) was published in Burlington, and may possibly be in the Collections of the Historical Society.

A report of my military services in the war of the rebellion was rendered by me some years ago, on a call for it, from the Adjutant General's office, U. S. Army. Whether yet printed or not, I do not know.

I have a map of Newport News, made by a young man under my command at that point, which is of sufficient interest to be framed and preserved somewhere. If you think that the Society rooms are a proper place for it, I will send it to you. [The map was received].

With regard to my descent, I am the son of John, who was the son of Timothy, who was the son of Charles Phelps, of Marlboro, who, as his epitaph reads (which I have lately seen) was an eminent jurist and theologian, born in 1717 and died in 1789. [See B. H. Hall's "Eastern Vermont."]

With respect to myself—since leaving the public service in which I assumed a position that was not sustained by Vermont, I have devoted my entire time to African Colonization, to the systematic inculcation of good behavior in public schools, and furthering the cause of Anti-masonry. My military services may be found in the report alluded to, and in "Cullum's Dictionary of West Point Graduates."

Very respectfully yours,
J. W. PHELPS.

Gen. Phelps was found dead in bed at his home in Guilford, Vt., Monday morning, Feb. 2, 1885, by one of his neighbors. He was alone in the house, his wife and child being on a visit to her parents in Northfield, and the house-keeper having gone to her home in the neighborhood for the night. He was last seen shoveling snow near his house Sunday afternoon, and in the evening a light was seen there until 9 o'clock. He evidently retired as usual and died without a struggle. Gen. Phelps was born in Guilford in May, 1813. He graduated 1836 at West Point, and was brevetted a second lieutenant. He served in the Florida and Mexican wars and was promoted to a captaincy for his gallantry in the latter, a position which he declined. He entered the war of the rebellion in 1861 as colonel of the first Vermont Volunteers, and was soon after brevetted brigadier general. Later he was with Gen. Butler in the department of the Gulf, and while stationed at Ship Island, he issued his famous emancipation proclamation to the negroes for which he was proclaimed an outlaw by the confederate government. His proclamation was also unfavorably received by the war department. An effort, on his part, to organize and arm some negro regiments at New Orleans, in June, 1862, led to his resignation, after which he resided in Brattleboro until 1884, when he went to Guilford. He was the anti-Masonic candidate for president in 1880, with Pomeroy as vice-president. He was a contributor to the Century and other magazines and newspapers, and was for some time president of a teachers's association in Vermont. He was first married in 1883 to Mrs. Davis of Northfield, who, together with a 9-months old child, survived him. He was a member of the Episcopal church of Guilford.

No more truthful estimate could be given of Gen. Phelps's character, than that contributed by General Rush C. Hawkins to the New York *Times*, on hearing of his death. It was as follows:

"General John W. Phelps of Vermont, whose death was announced in your paper this morning, was one of the most notable officers of the army. He was an accomplished soldier of the highest and best type, a patriotic citizen with an unblemished reputation, a scholar well versed in mathematics, science, history, theology, several of the dead and four or five of the living languages.

As a soldier, he was all that the best authorities demand, and even more, for it might be said of him, that he possessed an inner sense of duty which no written formula could prescribe. It was his faithful care, intelligence, and attention to his whole duty, as commanding officer, and above all his example of indefatigable industry, which made his command one of the best disciplined, best drilled and most efficent in the whole army.

He was not much of a believer in the extra-unofficial-off-duty-dress-parade business, which to many officers who were *poseurs*, seemed to be of so very much importance. Neither was he a martinet ; he had the rare good sense to accept the volunteer army for exactly what it was. He weighed its defects, and measured its virtues, and governed the performance of his duties accordingly. He knew he could trust its patriotic sense of duty and intelligence to imitate a good example, and its willingness to follow where it could not be driven ; and there never was a commanding officer more implicity obeyed, or more confidingly trusted.

It was my good fortune to have been ordered to his command at Newport News, Virginia, soon after the breaking out of the rebellion in 1861. When I reported to him with my regiment, I was given to understand that we were engaged in a most serious undertaking, involving as it did the national life, and that we could hope to overcome our foes only by taking advantage of all our resources, (he was the first to urge the organization of negro troops) and moulding our raw material into a well disciplined army; that the accomplishment of the latter was the immediate work at hand; and work he made of it, such as many of us had never dreamed of before; but we saw the necessity for labor, and the good sense involved in his orders and criticisms, and all worked with a will, officers and men, to reward the great industry of a commander who had won our affection, admiration, and deep respect.

We went to him as children go to school, and left him after three months' tuition, a thoroughly well disciplined regiment, of whose after record he was justly proud. To that kind hearted, quaint, honest old man, with his perfect sense of justice, the officers and men of my regiment owe a debt of gratitude, which can only be effaced from their memories, when the last survivor of that command shall have passed away.

This little statement, inadequate as it is, is the tribute I bring to the grave of an honored friend of a quarter of a century. I could not do less, I wish I could do more. Take him all in all, I have never known a man so free from the hypocricies, sins and vices which make humanity so despicable, as was John W. Phelps.

R. C. H.

New York, February 3, 1885.''

An extended sketch of General Phelps was printed in the Springfield (Mass.) *Republican* subsequent to his nomination for the Presidency, which was reprinted in the *Reformer*, Brattleboro, August 27, 1880.

Phelps, Matthew. *Memoirs and Adventures* of Captain Matthew Phelps; Formerly of Harwington in Connecticut, now residing in New Haven in Vermont. Particularly in two Voyages, From Connecticut to the River Mississippi, From December 1773 to October 1780. Compiled from the Original Journal and Minutes kept by Mr. Phelps, during his Voyages and Adventures, and revised and corrected according to his present recollection. By Anthony Haswell. From the press of Anthony Haswell, of Bennington, in Vermont. 1802. 12mo, pp. 210, and Appendix 63, (3), List of Subscribers, XII.

Mr. Phelps resided at New Haven, Vt., the last twenty five years of his life, and died there in 1817.

Phelps, Samuel Shethar. *Speech* of Mr. Phelps, of Vermont, on The War and the Public Finances, Delivered in the Senate of the United States, January 27th, 1848. 8vo, pp. 15.

—*Remarks* of Mr. Phelps, of Vermont, on The Oregon Bill, and also on the Compromise Bill: Delivered in the Senate of the United States, June 29 and July 24, 1848. 8vo, pp. 32.

—*Mr. Phelps' Appeal* to the People of Vermont, in Vindication of Himself, against the Charges made against him upon the occasion of his Re-Election to the Senate of the United States, in relation to his course as a Senator. Middlebury: Published by the Author. Nov., 1845. 8vo, pp. 43.

—*Mr. Phelps' Rejoinder* to Mr. Slade's ''Reply.'' Printed by J. & G. S. Gideon, Ninth Street, near Pennsylvania Avenue, Washington, D.C., [n. d.] 8vo, pp. 40.

—*Speech* in the Senate of the United States, on the Tariff Bill, Feb. 16, 19, 1844. pp. 35.

—He also wrote the Address of the Vermont Council of Censors in 1827.

—*Speech* of Mr. Phelps of Vermont, on the subject of Slavery, &c. In Senate, January 23, 1850. Gideon & Co. Printers. 8vo, pp. 16.

Judge Phelps was born in Litchfield, Conn., May 13, 1793; and died in Middlebury, Vt., March 25, 1855. He was graduated at Yale College, 1811; read law, and commenced practice in Middlebury, Vt.; was a member of the Council of Censors, 1827; member of the Governor's Council, 1831; Judge of the Supreme Court, 1831-38; United States Senator, 1839-51; and 1853-4 by appointment of the Governor. A Biographical Sketch may be found in the American ''Whig Review,'' Vol. 12, p. 93; and History of Middlebury, by S. Swift, pp. 291-93.

Phillips, Charles. *The Emerald Isle.* A Poem, by Charles Phillips, Esq., Barrister. Second American Edition. Middlebury: Published By William Slade, Jun. 1815. 16mo, pp. 202.

Phinney, T. C. *The Literary News*, A Monthly Journal of Current Literature. Published by T. C. Phinney, wholesale and retail Bookseller and Stationer, Periodicals, Fancy Goods, Pictures, etc. State Street, Montpelier, Vt. May, 1878. 8vo, pp. 8.
Continued.

Pierce, John, A. M. *A Discourse* delivered at the Dedication of the Brick Meeting-house, erected by the First Congregational Society, in Burlington, Vermont, on Thursday, 9 January, 1817. By John Pierce, A. M., Minister of Brookline, Massachusetts. Printed at Burlington, January 25, 1817. 12mo, pp. 20.

Pingree, Samuel E. *An Oration* before The Re-Union Society of Vermont Officers, in the Representatives' Hall, Montpelier, Vt., November 7th, 1872. By Col. Samuel E. Pingree, Hartford, Vt. Montpelier: Poland's Steam Printing Establishment. 1872. 8vo, pp. 18.

Pingry, William M. *A Genealogical Record* of the descendants of Moses Pengry, of Ipswich, Mass., so far as ascertained; Collected and arranged by William M. Pingry. Ludlow, Vt: Warner & Hyde, Book and Job Printers, 1881. 8vo, pp. 186.

For a sketch of Mr. Pingry see the above work, p. 46; he was born May 28, 1806, but he does not tell where, probably at Salisbury, N. H.

Piper, Rev. C. W. *Sermon* at the funeral of Mrs. Gardner Paige, of Bakersfield, Vt.: 1860. 8vo, pp. 15.

Pittsford. *The Confession* of Faith and Covenant of the Congregational Church in Pittsford, Vt. Windsor: Chronicle Press. 1834. 12mo, pp. 8.

—*Annual Report* of the Superintendent of Schools for the Town of Pittsford, Vt., for the year ending April 1st, 1872. Rutland: Tuttle & Co., Printers. 1872. 8vo, pp. 15.
Continued.

—*Annual Report* of the Selectmen and other Officers for the Town of Pittsford, for the year ending Feb. 16, 1875. Rutland: Globe Paper Co., Printers. 1875. 8vo, pp. 12.
Continued.

—*History of,*
See Caverly, A. M.

—*Manual* of the Congregational Church, Pittsford, Vt. Rutland: Tuttle & Co. 1896. 12mo, pp. 36.

Platt, James H., Jr. *Speech* of Hon. James H. Platt, Jr., in the House of Representatives, on the 14th Amendment, 1871. 8vo, pp. 14.

Hon. James H. Platt, Jr., was born in St. Johns, P. Q., of Vermont parents; removed with them to Burlington, Vt.; graduated from the Medical department of the University of Vermont in 1859, served as Captain in the Fourth Vermont, and on the staff of the Sixth Army Corps in the Civil War; settled in Petersburg, Va., 1865; elected to the 41st and 42d Congresses, from Virginia; during the later years of his life was extensively engaged in manufactures at Denver, Col. Died, 1895.

Plattsburgh, Battle of. *Mr. H. C. Dennison's Resolution*, calling on the Governor for copies of any correspondence he may have had with military officers, relative to detaching the Militia; together with His Excellency's Message, communicating the Correspondence. Published by order of the House. Montpelier, Vt.: Printed by Walton and Goss, October, 1814. 8vo, pp. 14.

Relates to Gov. M. Chittenden's recall of Vermont troops from Plattsburgh.

—*Republican,—Extra*. The Battle of Plattsburgh, 11th September, 1814. An Account of the Celebration of the Anniversary of the Battle of Plattsburgh, by the Citizens of Plattsburgh and the Clinton County Military Association, September 11, 1843. Plattsburgh: R. G. Stone, Republican Office. 1843. 16mo, pp. 12.

Poems. *Miscellaneous Poems* on Moral and Religious subjects, by a lady. Woodstock: 1820. 12mo, pp. 143.

Poland, Luke P. *Reconstruction.* Speech of Hon. Luke P. Poland, of Vermont, in the United States Senate, June 5, 1866. 8vo, pp. 8.

—*Address* delivered before the Vermont State Agricultural Society and Wool Growers' Association, at its Annual Fair, at Burlington, Thursday, Sept. 16th, 1869, by Hon. Luke P. Poland. Montpelier: Poland's Steam Printing Establishment, Journal Building, State Street. 1869. 8vo, pp. 23.

—*Report:* Mr. Poland, from the Select committee to investigate the alleged Credit Mobilier bribery, made the following Report: House of Representatives. 42d Congress, 3d Session. Report no. 77. February 18, 1873. 8vo, pp. 19.

—*The Geneva Award.* Remarks of Hon. Luke P. Poland, M. C., from Second District of Vermont, in the House of Representatives, June 9, 1874. 8vo, pp. 15.

—*Report No. 127.* 43d Congress. 2d Session, Condition of Affairs in the State of Arkansas. Report by Mr. Poland, from the Select Committee. February 6, 1875. 8vo, pp. 70. No imprint.

—*The Town of Ely.* Argument of the Hon. Luke P. Poland before the Special Committee of the Legislature upon the Subject, against the Bill to re-change the name of the town of Ely to Vershire; Dec. 8th, 1880. 8vo, pp. 24.

Additional Speeches and Reports in Congress by Mr. Poland:

—*Thirty-ninth Congress, First Session—Senate.*—Remarks on the death of Judge Collamer, December 14, 1865. Globe 56-57. Remarks on the death of Senator Foot. April 12, 1866. Globe 1908-9. Speech on Bill to pay for Army Supplies. July 6, 1866. Globe 3619-20. Speech on Post Office Appropriation Bill. May 7, 1866. Globe 2417 to 2419. Report on right of

D. T. Patterson to seat in Senate, July 27, 1866. Globe 4213-14. *Second Session — Senate.*—Speech on Bankrupt Law, January 19, 1867. 951-953 and 962. Speech on Salaries of District Judges, February 7, 1867. Globe 1067. Speech on authorizing special juries in District of Columbia, February 13, 1867. Globe 1240.

Fortieth Congress—House.—Speech on Colorado Election, March 20, 1867. Globe 227-8. Report on Contested Election Burch vs. Van Horn, Mo., December 18, 1867. Globe 257. Report on Contested Election, Switzler vs. Anderson, Mo., March 23, 1868. Globe 2071. Report on settlement of public accounts, March 23, 1868. House documents. Speech on case of Burch vs. Van Horn, January 8, 1868. Globe 389 to 391. Speech on election case of Smith vs. Brown, February 15, 1868. Globe 1198-1200. Speech on resolution to impeach Andrew Johnson, February 24, 1868. Globe 1394-5, also 1615. Report on Washburn-Donnelly case, June 1, 1868. Globe 2756-7. Speech on contested election, McKee vs. Young, Ky., June 22, 1868. Globe 3371-2. Speech on contested election, Switzler vs. Anderson, July 15, 1868. Globe 4084 to 4088.

Third Session—House.—Report on Letter of Secretary of War, February 17, 1869. House documents. Remarks on death of Thaddeus Stevens, December 17, 1868. Globe 131. Speech on case of Switzler vs. Anderson, January 21, 1869. Globe 516-518. Speech on the National Currency, February 17, 1869. Globe 1319-20. Speech on election case Menard vs. Hunt, La.

Forty-first Congress — Second Session—House.—Report on Letter of Secretary of the Treasury, February 23, 1870. Globe 1516. Report on Petition of ship builders, etc., for relief, August 6, 1870. Globe 2431. Report on resolution to expel W. Scott Smith from reporter's gallery, June 22, 1870. Globe 4602. Speech on contested election, Tucker vs. Booker, Va., February 1, 1870. Globe 948-9. Speech on contested election, Covode vs. Foster, Pa., February 9, 1870. Globe 1158-9. Speech on eligibility of Mr. Connor to a seat, March 31, 1870. Globe 2328. Speech on apportionment of Representatives in Congress, June 23, 1870. Globe 4748-9. Speech on election case of Barns vs. Adams, Ky., July 5, 1870. Globe 5191-2. Speech on Bill to enforce the 14th Amendment, April 19, 1871. Globe 804.

Forty-Second Congress, Second Session—House—Speech on Bill to increase Representatives in House, December 14, 1871. Globe 142. Speech personal and explanatory, January 17, 1872. Globe 446-7. Speech on submitting Ku-Klux report, February 19, 1871. Globe 1119 to 1122. Speech on case of Dr. John Emilio Howard, April 25, 1872. Globe 2789-90. Speech relating to muster in of officers, May 17, 1872. Globe 3167 68. Speech on Ku-Klux Outrages, May 30, 1872. App. Globe 492 to 495.

Third Session—House—Speech on Credit Mobilier subject, January 6, 1873. Globe 854 to 856. Speech on same subject, February 25, 1873. Globe 1717 to 1723. Speech on same subject, February 27, 1873. Globe App., 105 to 198. Remarks on the death of Garret Davis,

December 18, 1872. Globe 288-89. On Louisiana affairs, January 18, 1873. Globe 545.

Forty-Third Congress, First Session—House. —Speech on Revision of the Statutes, January 14, 1874. Globe 646-7. Speech on repeal of Bill increasing salaries of Members, December 11, 1873. Globe 150 to 152. Speech on Bill to repeal the Bankrupt Law, December 16, 1873. Globe 235-6. Speech on Bill to regulate Courts in Utah, June 2, 1874. Globe 4666 to 4674. Speech on revising laws of District of Columbia, May 14, 1874. Globe 3916-17. Speech on Bill for removal of causes to Supreme Court, March 27, 1874. Globe 4301 to 4303. Report on Bill for commission on liquor traffic. House documents. Report on relations between the general Government and District of Columbia. House documents.

Second Session—House—Speech on Bill for relief of Rollin White, December 11, 1874. 60 to 61. Speech on Impeachment of Judge Durell, January 7, 1875. Globe, 822-3. Speech on construction of laws imposing duties, January 22, 1875. Globe, 663 to 665. Speech on Force Bill, February 2, 1875. Globe, 1886. Speech on Arkansas Affairs, March 2, 1875. Globe, 2107 to 2110.

—*Address* before Windsor County Agricultural Society, Woodstock, September, 1873.

The following note from Mr. Poland is of interest:

I have made a hurried look through the "Globe" after my speeches and reports, and send you a list of such as I came upon. I took no minutes of a speech unless it occupied a column or more in the Globe. I made hundreds of little speeches in the current debates which cannot be dignified by the name of speeches. But what I send you makes a sufficiently long list. I happened to find a copy of my Credit Mobilier Report, and speech on the Geneva Award, which I send you. Yours truly, L. P. POLAND.

For biographical sketches of Mr. Poland, see Lanman's Biographical Annals, ed. 1876; Poore's Political Register and Congressional Directory, 1878; Vermont Legislative Directory, 1878, p. 123.

Luke Potter Poland was born in Westford, Nov. 1, 1815. He died at Waterville, Vt., July 2d, 1887.

His judicial opinions are contained in the Vermont Reports, volumes 21 to 38 inclusive. He made many political speeches and legal arguments, which were published in newspapers, and some in pamphlets.

Pomfret. *Proceedings* of the Citizens' Convention held at Pomfret, Vt., March 18, 1855: Also the speech of Hon. D. C. Littlejohn, before the New York Assemby, Feb. 15, 1855. Woodstock: Printed by Haskell & Palmer. 8vo, pp. 28.

In opposition to Know-nothingism.

—*Report* of the Town Superintendent of Common Schools, for the Town of Pomfret, for the Year ending March 18, 1853, Woodstock: Printed by Lewis Pratt. 1853. 8vo, pp. 16.

Pond's *New Phonographic Sphygmograph.* A Pocket Instrument Adapted to the Physician's Daily Use. Manufactured by Pond's Sphygmograph Co., Rutland, Vt. Rutland: Tuttle & Co., Printers. 8vo, pp. 20.

Pond, Sheldon. *Trial of Sheldon Pond* at the Addison County Court, June Term, 1855, for the murder of Decatur Cheney in Addison, Vt., Sept. 17, 1854. Middlebury: Published by L. W. Clark. 8vo, pp. 24.

Poor, John A. *The Trans-continental Railway.* Remarks at Rutland, Vermont, June 24, 1869. By John A. Poor. Printed by B. Thurston & Company. Portland; 1869. 8vo, pp. 76.

Pope, A. *An Essay on Man:* in four Epistles to H. St. John Bolingbroke. To which are added, the Universal Prayer, Messiah, and Elegy. By Alexander Pope, Esq. For the use of Schools. Windsor, Vt.: Published by J. Lowe. 1820. 18mo, pp. 72.

—*The same.* Windsor: Published by Pomeroy & Hedge. 1816. 12mo, pp. 61.

—*The same.* Windsor, Vt.: Printed by Farnsworth and Churchill, 1810. 12mo, pp. 70.

—*An Essay on Man:* In four Epistles, to H. St. John, Lord Bolingbroke. To which is added, the Universal Prayer, Messiah, &c. Brattleborough, (Vt.): Published by William Fessenden, Esq. 1814. 18mo, pp. 71.

—*An Essay on Man.* In Four Epistles. By Alexander Pope, Esq. Enlarged and Improved by the Author. Printed at Peacham, Vermont, By Farley & Goss, 1798. 8vo, pp. 44.

—*An Essay on Man, &c.* To which are added, Notes, Grammatical and Explanatory: Adapting it to the use of Schools. By Josiah Swett, M.A. Professor of Moral Philosophy in the Norwich University, and Author of a Grammar. Claremont, N. H.: 1852, 18mo, pp. 72.

The Portal to the Cabinet of Love, consisting of the Basia of Johannes Secundus, newly translated into English Verse with the Epithalamium. Also, Fragments—Being some poetical pieces on the kiss, &c. Weathersfield, Vt.: Printed and Published by Isaac Eddy. 1815. 16mo, pp. 98.

A work which would hardly meet public approval at the present day.

Port Henry. *Manual of the Board* of Education at the Union Free School and Academy, at Port Henry, N. Y. 1878. Rutland: Tuttle & Co., Printers. 1878. 8vo, pp. 24.

Porter, Mrs. Ann (Emerson.)

Mrs. Porter was a native of Newburyport, Mass., born in 1816; was married to Charles E. Porter, of Springfield, Vt.; has published, "Uncle Jerry's Letters to Young Mothers," Boston: 1854, 12mo. "The Lost Will," 1860. 18mo. Also two volumes for Sunday Schools, and articles in periodicals. See Hart's Female Prose Writers of America, ed. 1855, p. 387.

Porter, Charles W. *Statistical Information* relative to the Rates of Taxation in the several towns, cities and gores in Vermont, 1884 and 1885. Boston: 1886. pp. 42.

Porter, Ebenezer. *The fatal effects of Ardent Spirits.* A Sermon, by Ebenezer Porter, Pastor of the First Church in Washington, Conn. Motto. Middlebury, Vt.: Re-printed by T. C. Strong. 1812. 8vo, pp. 16.

Porter, Jane. *The Scottish Chiefs,* a Romance. Five volumes in Three. By Miss Jane Porter, Author of "Thaddeus of Warsaw," and "Remarks on Sidney's Aphorisms." Motto. Brattleborough: Published by John Holbrook. 1818. 3 vols. 12mo, pp. 285, 287, 289.

Porter, William T. *Life of William T. Porter,* By Francis Brinley. New York: D. Appleton and Company. 1860. 12mo, pp. vii, 273.

Mr. Porter was a native of Newbury, Vt.; born in 1806; he died in New York, July 19, 1858. He was at first a teacher, and subsequently became a printer and moved to New York about 1833, and for a while followed his trade as a printer in a book printing establishment; afterwards established the "Constellation," a weekly journal, which was merged into the "Spirit of the Times," a weekly paper, devoted to sporting news, live stock and kindred topics, which he conducted until 1856, when he sold his interest in the paper, and began with Mr. George Wilkes "Porter's Spirit of the Times," which he edited until his death. He was connected at various times with the "Farmer's Herald," "The Enquirer," "The New Vorker," and "The American Turf Register and Sporting Magazine." Mr. Porter edited Col. Hawker's "Instructions to Young Sportsmen," and T. B. Thorpe's "Big Bear of Arkansaw, and Other Stories," Philadelphia: 1835. 12mo; "A Quarter-Race in Kentucky, and Other Sketches," illustrative of character in the South and West, 1850, 12mo; "Major T. B. Thorpe's Scenes in Arkansaw, etc., with J. M. Field's Night in a Swamp, and other Stories;" in all more than sixty tales, originally published in "The Spirit of the Times." 1858. 12mo, pp. 402. Mr. Brinley, the biographer of Mr. Porter, was his brother-in-law, having married a sister of Mr. Porter. The latter was never married. See New York Historical Magazine, September, 1858, for obituary; also Bartlett's Americanisms, ed. 1859, preface, p. x.

Mr. Porter's brother, Dr. T. O. Porter, was an able teacher, and a successful writer; about 1844 he commenced, in connection with N. P. Willis, the publication in New York of the "Corsair," a weekly paper. George Porter, another brother, was also a well-known writer, and was connected with the "Spirit of the Times" for several years; he subsequently held a position on the "New Orleans Picayune," where he died in 1851. Frank, his youngest brother, was also a writer for the "Spirit," and succeeded George in the "Picayune;" his health failed, and a trip to Europe failed to restore him, and he returned to New Orleans and died. The sister, Mrs. Brinley, was a lady of superior mind, and an able writer. William T. was the last survivor of five brothers, known to the reading public; of these Benjamin alone left children. Mr. W. T. Porter was a free liver, and his excesses in this direction probably hastened his death.

Post, A. C. *Address* before the Castleton Medical College, 1843.

Post, Rev. Martin M. *A Thanksgiving Sermon*, delivered at Logansport, Ind., November 27, 1862, By Rev. M. M. Post. Logansport: Published by Dague & Rayhouser. 1862. 8vo, pp. 15.

Martin Mercillian Post was born in Cornwall, Vt., December 3, 1806; was graduated at Middlebury College, 1826, and at Andover, 1829; preached at Logansport, Ind., 1829, until he died, October 11, 1876.

Post, Rev. Truman Marcellus. *Heroism of the Democratic Ages;* an Address delivered before the Alumni Association of M'Kendree College, August 16th, 1844, by Rev. Prof. Post, of Illinois College. St. Louis: Missouri Reporter Office Print, 35 Locust Street. 1845. 8vo, pp. 20.

—*Genius.* An Address delivered before the Philomathesian Society, of Middlebury College, August 20, 1850. By Rev. Truman M. Post, of St. Louis, Missouri. Middlebury: Justus Cobb, 1850. 8vo, pp. 42.

—*The Mission of Congregationalism* at the West. An Address, delivered May 10, 1854, in Brooklyn, N. Y., before the American Congregational Union, by T. M. Post. New York: Clark, Austin & Smith. Boston: S. K. Whipple & Co. 1854. 8vo, pp. 45.

—*Religion and Education.* An Oration delivered at the Annual Commencement of Iowa College, Davenport, July 30th, 1856. By the Rev. Truman M. Post, D. D. of St. Louis. Davenport: A. P. Luse & Co., Printers, Bookbinders and Stationers. 1856. 8vo, pp. 27.

—*Our National Union;* A Thanksgiving Discourse, delivered in the First Trinitarian Congregational Church, November 29, 1860, by Truman M. Post, D. D. St. Louis: R. P. Studley and Co., Printers, Binders and Lithographers, Main and Olive Sts. 1860. 8vo, pp. 20.

—*Palingenesy.* National Regeneration. An Address by Rev. T. M. Post, D. D., delivered by invitation at the Washington University, November 4, 1864. St. Louis: George Knapp & Co., Printers and Binders. 1864. 8vo, pp. 17.

—*The Second Advent.* A Paper by Rev. T. M. Post, D. D. St. Louis: Davis and Freegard, Printers. 1878. 8vo, pp. 12.

—*Christian Union* consummated by no Infallible Authority in the Church, but by Consciousness of the Ever-present Christ. Sermon by Rev. T. M. Post, D. D. n. d. n. p. 8vo, pp. 19.

—*The Ministrant Church.* A Sermon before the American Board of Commissioners for Foreign Missions, at the Meeting in Salem, Mass., October 3, 1871, by Rev. Truman M. Post, D. D., of St. Louis, Missouri. Boston: Press of T. R. Marvin & Son, 131 Congress Street. 1871. 8vo, pp. 24.

—*Our Country* as a Factor in the Kingdom of Christ. A Sermon in behalf of the American Home Missionary Society, preached in the Broadway Tabernacle Church, New York, May 10th, 1874. By Rev. Truman M. Post, D. D. New York: 1874. 8vo, pp. 23.

—*Congregationalism;* the Life-story of one of its Eminent Divines. Address of Rev. T. M. Post, D. D., of St. Louis, before the General Association of Congregationalists of Missouri, Sunday Evening, October 28, 1877. Published by the Board of Deacons of the First Trinitarian Congregational Church of St. Louis. St. Louis: Davis & Freegard, Printers. 1878. 8vo, pp. 29.

—*Special Advantages* of the smaller country Colleges. An Address before the Alumni of Middlebury College, July 1, 1879, at the Semi-Centennial Re-union of the Class of '29. By Rev. Truman M. Post, D. D., St. Louis, Mo. Published at the Request of the Alumni and Corporation. Boston: Alfred Mudge and Son. 1879. 8vo, pp. 28.

—*A Biography* of,—Personal and Literary, by T. A. Post. Boston and Chicago.: Congregational Sunday School and Publishing Society. 1891. pp. xv, 507.

Truman Marcellus Post was born in Middlebury, June 3, 1810; and was graduated at Middlebury College, 1829; also at Andover. Tutor in Middlebury College, 1830-32; at Illinois College, 1833-34; and Professor there, 1834-48; pastor of Congregational church in Jacksonville, Ill., 1841-48; of a Presbyterian church in St. Louis, Mo., 1848-51, pastor of First (Trin.) Congregational church in St. Louis, 1851-82; Professor of History, Washington University, St. Louis. Died 1886.

The Postage Stamp Reporter. *An Illustrated paper* devoted to Stamp Collecting. Vol. 1. No. 1. Montpelier, Vt.: January, 1877. 8vo, pp. 8. Edited by C. F. Buswell. Continued Monthly.

Potter, Isaiah. *A Sermon* preached in Sharon, Vt., October 14, 1811. At the Funeral of Joel Marsh, Esq., aged 65. By Rev. Isaiah Potter of Lebanon, N. H. Motto. Hanover: Printed by Charles Spear. 1812. 8vo, pp. 16.

Potter, Lyman. *A Sermon* preached before the General Assembly of Vermont, on the day of their Anniversary Election, October 11, 1787, at Newbury. By Lyman Potter, A. M. Pastor of the Church in Norwich. Windsor, Vt.: Printed by Hough & Spooner, MDCC LXXXVIII. 8vo, pp. 23.

Poultney. *The Attractions* of Poultney, Fair Haven, Castleton, Hydeville, Middletown and Wells, Vt., and Granville, N. Y., for Business, Health and Pleasure. Poultney, Vt.: Geo. C. Newman, Printer. 1869. 12mo, pp. 28.

—*Poultney and Vicinity* as a place of Summer Resort, Price Ten Cents. Poultney, Vt.: A. J. Morris, Printer. 1858. 18mo, pp. 8.

—*A History* of the Town of Poultney, Vt., From its Settlement to the year 1875, with Family and Biographical Sketches and Incidents. Published by J. Joslin, B. Frisbie and F. Ruggles. Poultney: Journal Printing Office. 1875. 8vo, pp. 369.

—*The Manual* of the Congregational Church of East Smithfield, Penn'a. 1877. 24mo, pp. 16.

The Pedo-baptist Congregational Church of East Smithfield, Pa., was organized in Poultney, Vt., February 11, 1801, by Rev. Elijah Norton and Rev. Lemuel Haynes, the celebrated colored preacher. The church then consisted of Solomon Morse, Samuel Kellogg, Esq., and Nathan Fellows. Their Articles of Faith were penned by Mr. Haynes; and they immediately started for the "Far West," arriving the same month on the ground of what is now "East Smithfield." [Extract from Manual.]

Poultry Association. *Rules and Premium List* of the first Annual Exhibition of the Champlain Valley Poultry Association, to be held at Burlington, Vt., January 28,29, 30 and 31, 1879. Entries for Competition close Jan. 28, 12 m. Specimens must be delivered at City Hall before 12 m. 28th January, 1879. Burlington: Free Press and Times Steam Print. 1878. 8vo, pp. 16, (10).

Poultry Associations and Exhibitions.
See Agricultural.

Powars, Grant, A. B. *An Oration*, pronounced in the Meeting House at Thetford, Vt. upon the Thirty-sixth Anniversary of American Independence, July 4, 1812. By Grant Powars, A. B. Montpelier: Published at the Request of the Committee of Arrangements. Wright & Sibley, Printers. 1812. 8vo, pp. 16.

Powers, Rev. Grant. *The Kingdom of Christ.* A Sermon delivered at the Ordination of the Rev. Elderkin J. Boardman, to the Pastoral Care of the Church of Christ in Bakersfield, Vt., July 4, 1822. By Grant Powers, A. M. Pastor of the Church in Haverhill, South Parish, N. H. Haverhill, N. H.: Printed by Sylvester T. Goss. 1822. 8vo, pp. 31.

—*The Government of God Universal.* A Sermon, delivered at the installation of the Rev. Elderkin J. Boardman to the Pastoral care of the Church of Christ in Danville, Vt., Jan'y 3, 1827. By Grant Powers, A. M., Pastor of the Church in Haverhill, South Parish, N. H. Danville, Vt.: E. & W. Eaton, Printers. 1827. 8vo, pp. 22.

—*Historical Sketches* of the Discovery, Settlement, and Progress of events in the Coos Coun-

try and Vicinity, principally included between the years 1754 and 1785. By Rev. Grant Powers, A. M., C. H. S. Haverhill, N. H.: Published by J. F. C. Hayes. 1841. 12mo, pp. 240.

The four above titles were by the same man.

—*Another edition.* Haverhill, N. H.: Published by Henry Merrill. 1880. 12mo, pp. 240.

The Coos, *Cohos*, or *Cowas* Country was an undefined district of territory in the Northerly parts of New Hampshire and Vermont, embracing the "Rich Meadows" of the valley of the Connecticut, on both sides of the river.

Mr. Powers was a Congregational minister, and was born in Hollis, N. H., May 31, 1784; and died in Goshen, Conn., April 10, 1841. He was graduated at Dartmouth College, 1810; was minister at Haverhill, N. H., from 1815 to 1829, and at Goshen, Conn., from August 27, 1829, until his death. Several of his works in addition to the above were published.

Powers, Hiram. *Powers' Statue* of the Greek Slave. Boston: 1848. Eastburn's Press. 12mo, pp. 30.

—*Vindication* of Hiram Powers in the "Greek Slave" Controversy. Cincinnati: Printed at the office of the Great West. 1849. 8vo, pp. 16.

Mr. Powers was born in Woodstock, Vt., July 29, 1805; died in Florence, Italy, June 27, 1873.

In 1819 Mr. Powers with his father's family, moved to Ohio, and settled on a farm about four miles from Cincinnati. See Drake's Biographical Dictionary; Tuckerman's Book of the Artists, pp. 276-294.

Powers, Peter. *A Sermon* preached at Hollis, Feb. 27, 1765, at the Installation of the Rev. Peter Powers, A. M., for the towns of Newbury and Haverhill, at a place called Coos, in the Province of New Hampshire. By Myself. Published at the desire of many who heard it, to whom it is humbly dedicated by the unworthy Author. Motto. Portsmouth, in New Hampshire. Printed and sold by Daniel and Robert Fowle. 1765.

—*A Sermon* preached before the General Assembly of the State of Vermont on the day of their First General Election, March 12, 1778, at Windsor. Newburyport: Printed by John Mycall. 1778. 8vo, pp. 40.

Title from Brinley Catalogue. The first election sermon after the formation of the State in 1777.

—*Tyrany and Toryism Exposed.* Being the Substance of Two Sermons, Preached at Newbury, [Vt.] Lord's Day, September 10th, 1780. By Peter Powers, A. M., Pastor of the Church in said Newbury and Haverhill. Westminster: Printed by Spooner & Green. 1781.

Mr. Powers was born in Dunstable, N. H., November 29, 1728; and was graduated at Harvard, 1754. He was settled over the church at Newbury, Vt., and Haverhill, N. H., 1765-1784; there being no suitable accommodations for the installation ceremonies at Newbury, the committee voted that the services shall take place "down country where it is thought best;" and Hollis, N. H., was selected. Mr. Powers died in 1799 or 1800. See "History of the Coos Country," by Grant Powers; pp. 54-60.

Practical Forms. With Notes and References Explanatory of the Law Governing the Cases to which they are applicable, &c. Being a convenient Manual for Business Men, &c., &c. Windsor, Vt.: Printed and Published by Simeon Ide. 1823. 12mo, pp. 409.

Pratt, Rev. Allen. *A Sermon* Delivered at Pomfret, (Vermont) at the Ordination of the Rev. Ignatius Thomson, November 20th, 1805. By the Rev. Allen Pratt, Minister of the First Church of Christ in Westmoreland. (N. H.) "But speak thou the things that become sound doctrine." Randolph: Printed by Sereno Wright. 1806. 8vo, pp. 24.

Pratt, Miss L. J. *The Blind Girl's Offering,* or Stray Thoughts in Poetry and Prose. By L. J. Pratt. Swanton, Vermont. P. P. R. Ripley, Printer. 1853. 12mo, pp. 142.

—*The Unfortunate Mountain Girl.* A Collection of Miscellanies, in Prose and Verse. By Miss L. J. Pratt of West Berkshire, Vt. Boston: Damrell & Moore, 16 Devonshire St. 1856. 12mo, pp. 160.

Prentiss, Samuel. *An Oration* pronounced at Plainfield (Vt.) July 4, 1812, Before the Washington Benevolent Societies of Montpelier, Calais, Plainfield and Barre, being the thirty seventh Anniversary of American Independence. By Samuel Prentiss, Jun., Esq. Published at the request of the Societies. Montpelier, Vt.: Printed and for sale by Walton & Goss. 1812. 8vo, pp. 39.

—*Remarks* of Mr. Prentiss, of Vermont, in the Senate of the United States, March 1, 1836, on the Question of Reception of A Petition from the Society of Friends, Praying for the abolition of Slavery in the District of Columbia. Washington: Printed by Gales & Seaton. 1836. 8vo, pp. 14.

—*Speech* of the Hon. Samuel Prentiss, of Vermont, upon the question of the reception of the Vermont Resolutions, on the subject of the Admission of Texas, The Domestic Slave Trade, and Slavery in the District of Columbia. Delivered in the Senate, U. S., January 16, 1838. Washington: Printed by Gales & Seaton. 1838. 8vo, pp. 10.

—*Speeches* of the Hon. Samuel Prentiss, of Vermont, upon the Bill to Prohibit the Giving or Accepting Challenges to Duels in the District of Columbia, and for the Punishment thereof. Delivered in the United States Senate, March 2d and 30th, and April 6th, 1838. Washington: Printed by Gales and Seaton. 1838. 8vo, pp. 19.

—*Speech* of Mr. Prentiss, of Vermont, on the Bankrupt Bill. Delivered in the Senate of the United States, June 23, 1840. Washington: Printed by Gales & Seaton. 1840. 8vo, pp. 20.

—*Proceedings* on the occasion of the announcement of the death of the Hon. Samuel Prentiss, of Vermont, in the District Court, October Session, 1857. Windsor: Printed at the Vermont Chronicle Office. 1858. 8vo, pp. 16.

See Allen, Heman.
For sketch of the life of Judge Prentiss see Thompson's History of Montpelier, pp. 276-287, and for Genealogy, etc., History of Northfield, Mass., p 521; Lord, W. H., Life of Judge Prentiss; Governor and Council, Vol. 7, pp. 401-2.—Note; Phelps, E. J.

A Present for Children. Being a Compendium of Gospel Knowledge, useful to be learnt by heart, and treasured in the memory of Children. By a Friend of the Cause of Jesus. Motto. Bennington: Printed by A. Haswell. 1802.

Preston, Willard, D. D. *Farewell Sermon* at St. Albans, Vt., Sept. 10, 1815. Worcester: 1816. 8vo.

Mr. Preston was pastor of the Congregational church, St. Albans, Vt., January 8, 1812, to September, 1815; pastor at Burlington, 1822-24, and President of the University of Vermont, 1824-26, which comprised his residence in the State. Two volumes of his sermons were published after his death.

See Vermont Historical Gazetteer, vol. 1, p. 526-7, for biographical sketch.

Prindle, Cyrus. *Sinfulness of American Slavery.* A Discourse delivered in the Methodist Episcopal Church, Middlebury, Vermont, on Fast Day, April 9, 1841. By Rev. Cyrus Prindle, Pastor of the Church. Published by request. Motto. Middlebury: Printed by E. Maxham. 1841. 8vo, pp. 24.

—*Slavery Illegal.* A Sermon, on the occasion of the Annual Fast, April 12, 1850. Delivered in the Wesleyan Methodist Church, Shelburn, Vt. By Rev. C. Prindle, Pastor. Motto. Burlington: Tuttle & Stacy. 1850. 8vo, pp. 28.

PRINTING IN VERMONT.

The following brief outline of printing in Vermont may prove a starting point for some one to prepare an extended and particular history of newspapers, magazines, etc., of the State, together with biographical sketches of their publishers and editors.

We give the following extract from the address by Hon. E. P. Walton, before the Vermont Publisher's Association at Bennington, in August, 1877, the manuscript of which is in the archives of the Vermont Historical Society:

The first printing press in Vermont was probably brought by Samuel Gale, who was married in Brattleboro in 1773, a surveyor under New York in that year, and appointed Clerk of Cumberland [now Windham] County Court in 1774. He was an Englishman by birth, well educated, a gentleman in manners, and a Tory in politics. As Clerk of the Court, he of course fought on the Court side in the Westminster massacre of 1775, and for that he was arrested and imprisoned by the Whigs, and his property was confiscated by Vermont. In fact he was so long in prison under different authorities that he abandoned the country on his release by the Continental Congress, and took office in Canada, and subsequently a pension from the British government. The evidence that he brought the first printing press to Vermont is meagre, yet tolerably satisfactory. The "writing office," so runs the record, "of one *Pale,*" at Westminster, was confiscated to the use of the State by the Legislature in 1780. The name of *Pale* does not appear in Thomas' "History of Printing," neither does that of Samuel Gale; he not being a printer; but it is obvious that the P instead of a G is a natural clerical error. There is ample evidence that Gale was at Westminster in 1774-5, as Clerk of the Court; that he was a man of learning, ambitious of authorship, at Philadelphia in 1772, and actually an author subsequently in England. The most reasonable inference is that Gale brought printing materials with him to Vermont, with the intention of of using them, though by reason possibly of his short residence in the State, and a lack of printers, there is no evidence that these materials were ever used by him. For a sketch of Samuel Gale see B. H. Hall's History of Eastern Vermont, pp. 643-650.

The next press brought for the use of Vermont was established at Dresden, near Hanover, N. H., in 1778, by Timothy Green and Judah Paddock Spooner. In both Thomas' "History of Printing," and Zadock Thompson's Vermont, it is stated that they set up their press at Westminster in that year; but Thomas subsequently stated that they first went to Hanover, printed a newspaper for a short time, and afterwards removed to Westminster, and printed the first newspaper in Vermont. June 11, 1778. Dresden and Hanover, now one town, and several other New Hampshire towns, were annexed to Vermont; and in October, 1778, Dresden, Hanover, and nine other New Hampshire towns, were represented in the Vermont Legislature, and on the second day of the session it was "Voted, and Resolved, that Judah Paddock and Alden Spooner, be, and are hereby appointed Printers for the General Assembly of this State." A proclamation of Gov. Chittenden, dated June 3, 1779, was "Printed by Judah Paddock and Alden Spooner, Printers to the General Assembly of the State of Vermont." The first union of New Hampshire towns with Vermont was dissolved in February, 1779, and it is therefore probable that the brothers Spooner removed the office from Dresden to Westminster in that year, and that Timothy Green had taken the place of Alden Spooner. However that may be, it is certain that the first newspaper within the present limits of Vermont was issued at Westminster, February 12, 1781. I will describe it from a copy in the library of the Vermont Historical Society:

The sheet measures 17 by 12½ inches—Isaiah Thomas called it pot paper. Alas! how many printers and printing offices in Vermont have since "gone to pot !" the type to the smelter and refiner, to come out anew, brilliant as silver, to print the wisdom that is more precious than gold; and the poor printers, I would gladly hope with Benjamin Franklin, to "appear once more, in a new and more elegant edition, revised and corrected by the author." I read the title : "Vol. 1. Number 8. *The Vermont Gazette, or Green Mountain Post-Boy.* Monday, April 2, 1781. Pliant as Reeds, where Streams of Freedom glide ; firm as the Hills, to stem Oppression's Tide. Westminster. Printed by Judah Paddock Spooner and Timothy Green." So much for Mr. Walton.

[It is believed that the press used by Green and Spooner, which is now preserved in the rooms of the Vermont Historical Society at Montpelier, was the first printing press brought to New England, and the first press used in the English speaking colonies of North America, having been set up in 1639, in the house of Henry Dunster, the first president of Harvard College. It was used by Samuel Green, printer, of Cambridge, Mass., some of whose descendants were printers for a hundred years in Massachusetts and Connecticut. Timothy Green, printer of the Post Boy, was one of his descendants. Hon. H. O. Houghton, of Cambridge, Mass., in his valuable paper on "Early Printing in America," read before the Vermont Historical Society, Oct. 25, 1894, says: "That the press now here [in Montpelier] may be the press originally used by Samuel Green in Cambridge, and therefore one of the original presses sent over from Eugland, seems possible and perhaps probable. The press, so far as I can judge, answers pretty accurately to the description of the original press used by Dunster, or Daye. That it came afterward into the possession of Green, is beyond question. It is stated that when Green ceased to do business the presses reverted to the college. It is possible that they were then of very little value, and one of them might easily have passed from the college to Timothy Green, 3d, a descendant of Samuel Green, who established himself in Norwich, Conn. That Green afterwards formed a partnership with Judah P. and Alden Spooner of Vermont, is also a matter of record. They first established the press in Dresden, a part of Hanover, then incorporated within the boundary of Vermont, and afterwards removed it to Westminster. From that period to the present the different persons who have interested themselves in the matter have traced the press through various vicissitudes until it has reached its haven of rest in the care of the Historical Society of the State of Vermont. From all the evidence it seems to me that we can assume that there is a very reasonable probability that it is one of the two identical presses on which printing was first executed in this country."]

—Westminster.

Thompson's History of Vermont gives February, 1781, as the date when the publication of the first Vermont newspaper began at Westminster. This date has been accepted as correct and number eight of the newspaper (which was *The Vermont Gazette, or Green Mountain Post-Boy*) is dated April 2, 1781, as a copy in the possession of the Vermont Historical Society shows. This would bring the date of the first issue February 12, 1781, if it was a weekly publication. But a "find" of old almanacs made by Dr. Conland, representative from Brattleboro, shakes modern authority. In the Vermont Almanack of 1796, published at Rutland and now in Dr. Conland's possession, an article on printing has the following paragraph : "In Vermont the first piece that was printed was a newspaper at Westminster, by Judah P. Spooner and Timothy Green, entitled, *The Vermont Gazette and Green Mountain Post-Boy,* dated Thursday, December 14, 1780." Though the title given the paper in this article is slightly wrong, the date may very well be the proper one. The article appeared when Spooner was printing a newspaper at Fairhaven, and the 14th of December, 1780, was Thursday. Perhaps Spooner & Green published a tri-weekly, that is a paper they *tried* to get out once a week.

We now quote from the official Records of the General Assembly and Governor and Council :

March 16, 1780, the General Assembly "Resolved that the Governor and Council be and are hereby requested to obtain a printer to settle within this state for the purpose of printing the laws, etc., as soon as they shall judge it necessary."

June 12, following, the Council "Resolved that Joseph Fay, Esq., be and he is hereby appointed and requested to procure a printer in this State."

August 18, the same year the Council "Resolved that the agreement relative to a printer, between Stephen R. Bradley, Esq. in behalf of the State of Vermont and Mr. Timothy Green, printer at New London, Conn., be and hereby is ratified on condition that Mr. Green send his son to print for this State in lieu of Mr. Spooner."

"Resolved that Mr. Ezra Styles be and he is hereby appointed and impowered to repair as soon as may be to New London to inform Mr. Green of the ratification [of the agreement] made between Stephen R. Bradley, Esq., and Mr. Green aforesaid, and facilitate as much as possible the moving of the types and other apparatus for the purpose of printing, agreeable to said agreement."

October 14, 1780, the Council resolved : "Whereas it has been represented to this Council that there is a printing office in the town of Westminster within this State, the property of —— Pale [or Gale], formerly an inhabitant of that place, who has gone over to and joined the enemies of this and the United States of America, thereupon, Resolved that Ezra Stiles, Esq., be and he is hereby authorized and empowered to seize the same and take it into possession for the use of this State, and to retain the same until cause can be shown (by such as lay claim thereto), why it should not be adjudged forfeit and confiscated to the use of this State." It appears that at the above date Green and Spooner had not then moved from Dresden to Westminster.

It does not appear that the printing office referred to was ever put in operation at Westminster, by —— Pale [or Gale].

The next we hear of the matter is in Council, March 1, 1782. The General Assembly having appointed a committee for the purpose, the Council instructs the committee to examine into the cause why the printing office at Westminster has not answered the purposes expected, and to engage some suitable person to procure necessary material and operate the same, and if such a person cannot be secured, the committee, with the consent of the proprietors, are to move the material to Bennington, etc. It appears that the Westminster printers were dilatory in their work, but it does not appear that the office was moved to Bennington. See Assembly Journal, October 18, 1782; Governor and Council, Vol. 2, p. 12-13; Thompson's Vermont, Part 11, pp. 171-2.

The earliest Vermont imprint we have found, excepting the Proclamation noticed by Mr. Walton above, (which was undoubtedly printed at Dresden), is the acts and laws passed at the February Session at Windsor, 1781; with the imprint: "Westminster: Printed by Judah P. Spooner and Timothy Green, Printers to the State of Vermont." rl. 8vo, pp. 11. No date.

Probably the laws of the April Session, 1781, and perhaps others, were printed there, but the title pages are wanting.

We have in this list a Westminster imprint 1782; also, 1781. See Powers, Peter; Acts and Laws, under Vermont; Fessenden, Thomas.

—Bennington.

Mr. Anthony Haswell established a printing office at Bennington in 1783, and printed the first number of the *Vermont Gazette,* June 5th of that year, it being the second newspaper in the State. See Haswell, Anthony.

See Bennington, Meeting of the Church, etc., September, 1783, which is the earliest Bennington imprint we have met.

"The Vermont Gazette, or Freeman's Depository," Vol. 1, No. 1, June 5, 1783, Printed by Haswell & Russell. Size per page, 8x12 inches; No. 5, July 3, 1783, size 9¾ x 14, and No. 6, July 10, size increased to 11x15½, and June 5, 1786, further increased to 12x16½. June 12, 1786, Motto:

"With generous Freedom for our constant Guide,
We scorn control, and print for every Side,
Yet thus our liberal Motto we explain—
Freedom's our Life, Licentiousness our Bane."

November 1, 1790, Vol. VIII, No. 23, Mr. Russell retired, and the paper was continued by Anthony Haswell ; Motto:

"While decency and candor guide the Pen—
Our Press shall scorn the imperious frown of Men."

August 19, 1796, No. 13 of Vol. 14: "Printed at Bennington, by O. C. Merrill, for Anthony Haswell, until January 5, 1797, when the "Gazette" was superseded by "Tablet of the Times." No. 1, Vol. 1, January 5, 1797, by Merrill & Laugdon, until September 5, 1797, (Mr. Langdon retired May 18, 1797) when Mr. Haswell resumed the publication of the "Gazette," Vol. 1, No. 1, on which occasion in an editorial he said : "He removed from Massachusetts to Bennington and established the "Gazette," in company with Mr. David Russell, under the expectation of legislative patronage ; hope flattered them along until Mr. Russell, despairing of adequate recompense, quitted the business.* * * And in January, 1797, Mr. Haswell sold the Gazette, with one-half his printing apparatus, to Messrs. Orsamus C. Merrill and Reuben Langdon, who in their turn growing discouraged, quitted, one after the other, and left the press subject to removal or temporary stoppage. But having a large family to support, I have once more determined to strive against the stream, in hopes that the current will turn."

Mr. Haswell continued the paper until Thursday, March 6, 1800, when a new series was commenced, Vol. I, No. I, "Printed by Anthony Haswell for the Proprietors." This continued until March 30, 1801, when "Haswell's Vermont Gazette revived" appeared, printed by Anthony Haswell, Vol. I, No. I. April 19, 1802, the title, "Vermont Gazette" resumed, "By A. Haswell, Printer for the Western District of Vermont, and of the Laws of the Union." On this auspicious occasion Mr. Haswell, in an editorial, said: "he has commenced a new volume of said paper, flushed with hope, 'which springs eternal in the human breast,' that he shall reap from it, and business connected with it, a decent support for his family."

Prosperity continued until January 3, 1803, when the publication of the paper was suspended, as Mr. Haswell states in an editorial, "from the pressure of imperious necessity, arising from straightened circumstances," until April 6, 1803, when its publication was resumed by himself and sons, under the firm of Anthony Haswell & Co., by a new series, Vol. I, No. I. At the end of one year the sons retired, and Haswell continued until July 24, 1804, when financial difficulties necessitated a suspension of a week; then followed two numbers, August 7 and 14, 1804, in reduced size, "Printed for Anthony Haswell." September 4, 1804, the former size was resumed, "Printed by A. Haswell & B. Smead."

The paper was continued under this firm until January 6, 1806, when Mr. Haswell retired, and Mr. Benjamin Smead became the proprietor. Mr. Haswell in his valedictory said: "The subscriber who has performed the business of the editorship of the "Vermont Gazette" from the month of May, 1783, to the commencement of the year 1806, now finds himself under the necessity of relinquishing his business, at least for a time, * * * * after twenty-three years of unremitted attention to the type case and writing desk," etc.

The title to the paper under Mr. Smead was "The Vermont Gazette; An Epitome of The World." No. I, Monday, January 13, 1806. February 24, 1807, Vermont Gazette was dropped, and the name was "Epitome of the World," until October 26, 1807, when it is simply "The World," until April 10, 1809, when the name is again changed to "Green Mountain Farmer," Printed by Benjamin Smead, Vol. I, No. I. The next issue that we have is April 8, 1811, Printed by William Haswell; in 1813 Darius Clark & Co. took the place of Mr. Haswell, and October 24, 1814, Darius Clark alone was printer.

The "Farmer" of May 27, 1816, announces the death of Anthony Haswell, on the 22d instant, in the sixty-first year of his age, and gives a sketch of his life, occupying two columns.

In Vermont Historical Gazetteer the date of his death is given as the 26th, which is an error.

Soon after, Mr. Clark substituted the old name, "Vermont Gazette," in place of "Green Mountain Farmer," but the numbering of the Farmer is continued, Vol. VII, No. 47.

Mr. Clark continued the Gazette until September 2, 1823, when he retired for a time, and Charles Doolittle became publisher, of whom Mr. Clark said in his farewell editorial: "The paper will be continued by Charles Doolittle, a young man who has worked in the office the last three years." Mr. Clark continued as to himself: "It is about nine years since the editor commenced his employment as conductor of this paper, and it is necessary that he should have a vacation to arrange his pecuniary concerns."

Mr. Doolittle conducted the paper until the spring of of 1825, when Mr. Clark resumed control, it is to be hoped with his finances improved. But not so, for June 19, 1827, Mr. Clark's name disappeared as proprietor, and the paper was "Printed for the Proprietor." An editorial states: "The financial concerns of the 'Gazette' are placed under the superintendence of the proprietor's agent, with whom all matters of that character will be transacted."

This state of affairs continued until January 18, 1832, when John C. Haswell became publisher and proprietor, with the name of Andrew Jackson hoisted to the fore for President of the United States. Mr. Haswell in his salutatory says: "The present number of the Gazette commences the fiftieth year of its existence. The first editor of the 'Gazette,' the father of the present publisher, was fined and imprisoned, and his successors have been maligned and persecuted, by the Federalists," etc. Mr. Haswell announces his firm support of Gen. Jackson, etc.

June 18, 1833, Mr. Haswell enlarged the 'Gazette' to 16x26 inches per page; February 23, 1841, again enlarged to 17x28.

May 31, 1842, John C. and Zimri Haswell became pro-

prietors, the former as editor; September 20, 1842, Mr. John C. Haswell retired, and his place was supplied by Mr. J. Bushnell, and Zimri Haswell, and Mr. Bushnell conducted the Gazette until February 16, 1847.

At about the above date, through differences of opinion, and rivalries between the villages, two rival series of the "Gazette," each claiming to be continuation of the original Gazette, were commenced, one, published on Bennington Hill, the old line apparently, by Edwin Robinson; the other series, at the East Village, by J. C. Haswell, editor until March 28, 1849, when he was succeeded by H. B. Knight.

This series appears to have been an organ of the "Free Soil" element in politics.

Mr. Robinson was succeeded by the "Gazette Company," February 6, 1849, and the company was succeeded by Aikens & Lull, April 17, 1849, as publishers, Andrew J. Aikens, editor; May 16, 1850, Mr. Lull retired, and Mr. Aikens continued as publisher and editor.

The publication of the Gazette was suspended from 1853 to 1873. In the latter year it was revived by H. L. Stillson. In 1874-5 it was published by Childs Brothers, and from '76 to '80 by Baker & Cochran. It ceased publication in 1880.

According to Z. Thompson, the "Tablet of the Times" was established at Bennington, by Merrill & Langdon, January, 1797; and "The State Banner," by E. Davis in March, 1841, the latter being still published.

According to Gov. Hall, in Vermont Historical Gazetteer, vol. I, p. 176, Mr. A. Haswell commenced the publication of "The Monthly Miscellany or Vermont Magazine," in 8vo size, each number containing 56 pages, at Bennington, March, 1794; it was soon discontinued.

In January, 1808, Mr. Haswell commenced another monthly magazine, called "The Mental Repast," in 12mo. size, which was discontinued at the end of six months.

"Journal of The Times," Henry S. Hull Proprietor, William Lloyd Garrison, Editor, was published from Friday, October 3, 1828, until July, 1829, and perhaps after.

"The Battle-Ground," by Cady & Atkins, was commenced in August, 1853. After the issue of nine numbers, Mr. Atkins retired, and purchased "The Republican Standard," at Bellows falls, which he re-christened the "Bellows Falls Argus." (See Bellows Falls.) Mr. Cady continued "The Battle-Ground" about two months, when he transferred his subscription list to the "Bellows Falls Argus."

In 1871 "The Bennington Free Press" was established by C. M. Bliss, ceasing publication within a year.

"The Bennington State Banner" established in 1841, is still published (1896) by C. A. Pierce, by whom and by Pierce & Co., it has been published for 25 years or more.

"The Daily News," by Frank Pierce Armstrong, Vol. I, No. I, Monday, June 7, 1875. The latest we have seen is of September 26, 1875.

"The Vermont Centennial," by Childs Brothers, daily, June 16, to September 14, 1877.

In 1873 the "True Union," monthly, was published for a short time by the Union Company.

From 1881 to '83 the "Bennington County Reformer" was published by A. P. Childs. From 1891 on "The Reformer" was published by J. H. Livingston; continued, (1896.)

—Windsor.

Thomas in his history of printing says: "George Hough purchased the press and type of Green and Spooner, of Westminster, and removed them to Windsor, where, in company with Alden Spooner, he began printing in 1783."

Hough & Spooner commenced the publication of the third newspaper in the State at Windsor, August 7, 1783.

We give the title and a description of the paper:

"The Vermont Journal, and the Universal Advertiser." Vol. I. No. I. Thursday, August 7, 1783. Windsor: Printed by Hough and Spooner.

"From realms far distant, and from climes unknown,
 We make the knowledge of mankind your own."

The sheet measures, trimmed, 15½ by 12⅜ inches.

See Lyman, G. C. for Windsor imprint, 1784.

The "Journal" at Windsor has been continued to the present time, with the exception of a suspension of nine years, 1835 to 1844.

In March, 1801, Nahum Mower established the "Vermont Gazette," at Windsor, which was probably succeeded by "The Post Boy," also by Mower, which was published January, 1805 to January, 1808; its full name was "The Post Boy and Vermont and New Hampshire Federal Courier." It was a small affair, measuring 11x18¾, inches, trimmed.

"The Washingtonian," a staunch Federal paper, was commenced by Josiah Dunham, Thomas M. Pomroy, printer, Monday, July 23, 1810, and continued until Monday, July 12, 1813; size 21x26½ inches, trimmed.

See Dunham, Josiah.

"Vermont Republican," commenced at Windsor, January 1, 1808, published by Oliver Farnsworth, for the Proprietors; size 18x22 inches, trimmed; it was published until 1834.

"The Republican" was a Democratic paper, and the late General Sylvester Churchill, of the United States Army, was one of its founders and proprietors. General Churchill was born at Woodstock, Vt., August 2, 1783, and died at Washington, D. C., December 7, 1862. He was educated in the schools of his native town; he was a carpenter by trade, and appears to have followed that business mainly until he entered the army as Lieutenant of artillery in 1812; he worked at his trade in the erection of the first State House built in Montpelier, which was completed in the fall of 1808.

See Drake's Dictionary for additional biography.

"Windsor Statesman," by Tolford & Fletcher, published January, 1833–1840.

"The Spirit of Seventy-six," at Windsor, by Darius Jones, October, 1835–1837.

"Vermont Times," at Windsor, by C. H. Severance, June, 1839–May, 1841.

"Journal of Temperance," Vol. 1, No. 1, Windsor, March 30, 1832.

"Vermont Republican and Journal, Windham, Windsor and Orange County Advertiser," by Simeon Ide, November 13, 1830.

It appears that the "Republican" and "Journal" were merged into the above paper for a time.

"School Journal, and Agriculturalist," commenced 1847. See Educational.

—Newbury.

Nathan Coverly, Jr., had a printing office in Newbury, 1791-96, and published a newspaper there.

—Rutland.

Anthony Haswell established the first press at Rutland, where he printed the first number of the "Herald of Vermont; or Rutland Courier," June 25, 1792; in about three months it was discontinued in consequence of the destruction of the office by fire.

Monday, June 25, 1792. Vol. 1, No. 1, "The Herald of Vermont. Or, Rutland Courier." Printed in Rutland, at the southwest angle of the Court House Square, [every Monday morning] by Anthony Haswell. Motto:

"Let Sentiment flow free, and Candour guide—
We own no Party and espouse no side."

Size 10½x17 inches per page. Twelve numbers in all, the last September 10, 1792, when the paper was suspended on account of the destruction of the office by fire. This printing office was situated on the southwest corner of the common, between the present (1880) location of the Rutland Savings Bank and the house now occupied by William H. B. Owen, and was destroyed by fire either Sunday, September 16 or 23, 1792. On the 31st of October, 1792, the Legislature, then sitting in Rutland, passed an act granting a Lottery to Anthony Haswell, to raise Two Hundred (200) Pounds to repair the damages sustained by him on account of the destruction of his printing office by fire. The publication of the paper was never resumed.

In 1793, James, son of Matthew Lyon, of Fairhaven, established the "Farmer's Library," at Rutland, which he continued nearly two years, when he sold the establishment to Judge Samuel Williams, and Rev. Samuel Williams, LL.D., the historian of Vermont, when the name was changed to "Rutland Herald," the first number of which was published December 8, 1794; it is still published.

"The Farmer's Library; Or, Vermont Political & Historical Register." No. 1, of Vol. 1. Monday, April 1, 1793. A Political and Historical Paper, by J. Lyon; Published every Monday near the State House, Rutland. Motto: "The Freedom and Impartiality of the Press shall remain Inviolate." Size, 10x15½ inches per page.

In No. 1 of Vol. 2, April 9, 1794, Mr. Lyon substituted in place of "A Political & Historical Paper," etc., "A Republican Paper by James Lyon; Printed and Published every Wednesday, at the sign of the Bible, north of the State House in the Main Street, Rutland, Vermont."

The last number was issued Saturday, November 29, 1794, being No. 35, of Vol. 2, whole number 87, when as above stated the paper was sold to the Messrs. Williams, and the name changed as follows: "The Rutland Herald: Or, Vermont Mercury," Vol. 1, No. 1, Rutland, Vermont,—Monday, December 8, 1794. Size the same as the Farmers' Library. The paper was published by S. Williams & Co., In the Main street, a few rods north of the State House. Motto: "In the Knowledge and Virtue of the People, the Freedom, the Energy and Permanency of the American Government have their foundation." In the first number the proprietors say, "As we have

purchased of *Mr. Lyon*, Editor of the *Farmers' Library*, the Printing Office, Apparatus, and Privileges annexed by law to his Paper, it will for the future be carried on by the subscribers with the above title, under the direction of DR. WILLIAMS. * * * The price of the Herald will be *nine shillings per annum*, to those to whom we send the papers ourselves; *seven shillings and six pence* to those who call at the office and take them; and the lowest prices which are customary in Vermont to those of the posts who take them in considerable quantities.

Samuel Williams (at that time Chief Judge of the County Court), and Rev. Samuel Williams, LL. D., (who was the editor) Proprietors.

The Herald soon became an organ of the Federal party. With the issue of the second number. J. Kirkaldie's name appeared as printer, for S. Williams & Co. With No. 40, of Vol.2, October 3, 1796, the name of John S. Hutchins was substituted in place of Kirkaldie as printer; February 20, 1797, Josiah Fay became printer; and February 27, 1797. he was printer for Williams & Fay, until September 4; then, September 4 and 10, 1798, Fay & Walker, for S. Williams & Co., were printers; and then John Walker, Jun., who retired April 29, 1799, and the paper was then printed "for S. Williams." September 3, 1798, the name changed to "The Rutland Herald." January 20, 1800, William Fay became printer for Samuel Williams. Continued by Tuttle & Co., and now published by the Herald Association. (1896.)

1795, January,—"The Rural Magazine or Vermont Repository." A Monthly Magazine "Devoted to Literary, Moral, Historical and Political Improvement, Huc Undique, Gaza Congeritur." "Rutland: Printed by J. Kirkaldie for S. Williams & Co., A few rods North of the State House." Rev. Samuel Williams, LL. D.. Editor. Volume 1, fifty-six pages to a number, and Volume 2, fifty-two pages. Last number issued December, 1796. See Williams, S. & Co.

1802—"Vermont Mercury." The number for August 8th, 1803, Volume 2, No. 76, contains the following: "Rutland, Vt.; Published every Monday morning by Stephen Hodgman, A few rods North West of the Court House." Motto:

"Let Party Zealots rage and madly write,
And swear that White is Black and Black in White:
Ours be the nobler task to facts proclaim—
Candour our guide, and Truth our constant aim."

1808, July 25—"Vermont Courier" (Published on Mondays,) Rutland, (Vermont.) published by Thomas M. Pomeroy, a few rods North of the Court House." "Printing in general executed on short notice, and on moderate terms." Discontinued, May 30, 1810.

1846, March, "The Eastern Medical Reformer." A Monthly journal of Medical and Chirurgical Science. John B. Hibbard. M. D., editor and proprietor. Motto: "Magna est Veritas et Prevalebit." Was published monthly at Rutland, each number containing sixteen pages. The number for August, 1846, (Volume 1, Number 6) gives the names of "Asa Gates, of Bridgewater, and J. S. Tuttle, Clarendon Spa., Capt. J. M. Doyle, Pittsfield, Vt.," as "*Traveling Agents*" who are authorized to receive subscriptions; but does not give the "terms" of subscription. See Medical.

1848, August 29—"Rutland Republican." "Published every Tuesday Evening, Thrall's building, over Bell's store, Rutland, Vt., by Simeon Locke." Motto: "Free Soil, Free Speech, Free Labor and Free Men." After the first number it was published "every Thursday evening" instead of Tuesday. Only six numbers, I think, were issued.

1849, September—"The Vermont Union Whig." "A home newspaper for Vermont; Devoted in Politics to National Union, In Literature to a purer taste." "Published at Rutland and Brandon, every Wednesday. William C. Conant, Editor at Rutland; Samuel M. Conant, at Brandon." Motto:

"We shall exult if they who rule the land
Be men who hold its many blessings dear—
WISE, UPRIGHT, VALIANT, not a venial band
Who are to judge of danger which they fear,
And Honor which they do not understand.
WORDSWORTH."

(We believe that the first steam printing press ever used in Rutland County was in connection with this paper and that it was used for the first time in printing the first number of the paper issued in Rutland.)

1849, December 12—"The Vermont Star." Published every Thursday morning, by George A. Tuttle. "Publication Office at the Bookstore." "George A. Tuttle and H. Ladd Spencer, Editors." "Terms, $1.25, in advance." This was number 17 of volume 1, the former numbers having been published at Ludlow, in the county of Windsor. Tuesday, August 21st, 1849, the first number was issued at Ludlow. The publication day was afterwards changed to Wednesday, and remained so until its removal to Rutland. The paper seems to have been printed at Ludlow, but *published* from the above date at Rutland, down to and including number 32 of volume 1, March 28th, 1850, when the publishers announced that they shall issue no paper the next week, because of arrangements being made to have the paper thereafter printed at Rutland. At the close of volume 1 the publication of the paper ceased.

1855, January—"The Guard of American Liberty," edited and published by H. F. Potter. Devoted to "Know-Nothingism." Only a few numbers were ever issued.

1857, August 12—"The Rutland Courier." "Published every Friday morning by Cain & McLean." John Cain, Editor. "Terms—One Dollar per annum in advance." After a short time Mr. McLean retired, and Mr. Cain continued the "Courier" until 1873.

1858, July—"What's the News." "An original monthly paper, with original items, by William A. Bacon. For sale at the office of publication, the new bookstore in Merchants' Row, Rutland, Vt." *Terms*, fifty cents per year."

1861, April 29—"Rutland Daily Herald." "Published every morning in season for the morning trains leaving Rutland, at $6 per year, 50 cents per month, 2 cents per number." "Printed and published by George A. Tuttle & Co., who are also the proprietors, at Tuttle & Co.'s Printing Office on Washington street, first building west of the Town Hall." "Evening edition occasionally published on receipt of news of great interest." (When first issued it had no motto, but soon after it appeared with the following:)

"Let every American citizen, instead of crying Peace, Peace, when there is no Peace, rally upon the ramparts until Secession is silenced; until the roar of artillery has ceased."

Still published by the Herald Association, (1896.)

1866, July 21—"Rutland County Independent," "Published every Saturday morning in season for the mails to all parts of the county, by McLean & Robbins. Terms—$2 a year." (An introductory number was issued July 4, 1866, but the first regular number not until July 21.)

"The Rutland Leader," an eight page folio, commenced September 28, 1877; it was published a little over a year; edited by Hon. Henry Clark.

"Ragged Edge," A. A. Deming, Rutland, editor, publisher and "all hands." Issued at all seasons of the year, whenever the "boss" takes a notion.

"The Inquirer" was started as a Democratic organ in 1878, by A. V. Meyerhoffer; then published by J. D. Hanrahan for a year or two, ran but a short time, and was finally merged into the "Evening Review," a nondescript journal edited by H. W. Love, which was transferred from Burlington to Rutland.

Its title was "The Review and Inquirer," for a time, and then was "The Review;" printed by the Review Company, with editions for other towns. It ceased in 1886, and was followed by "The Rutland Telegram," published at first Daily and Weekly, and then with a Sunday edition added, by the Review Co. It ceased publication in 1891. The News, Daily and Sunday, was started in the same year by the News Company, but had only a brief existence; and from 1892 to 1895, The Herald was the only Rutland newspaper.

—Fairhaven.

At Fairhaven, after disposing of the "Farmer's Library" Col. Lyon appears to have started the "Fairhaven Gazette," published by his son, James Lyon, and Judah P. Spooner, which is believed to have been succeeded by "The Farmer's Library, or Fairhaven Telegraph"—by J. P. Spooner and W. Hennessy. The first number issued July 28, 1795.

See Lyon, James, "Scourge of Aristocracy," Also History of Fairhaven.

—Putney.

"The Argus," by C. Sturtevant & Co.., was started at Putney in 1797, as appears by a notice to that effect in the "Windsor Journal," of January 20, of that year.

—Burlington.

At Burlington, the first press, by Donnelly & Hill, 1797, and they published the "Burlington Mercury," until 1799.

The first number of the "Vermont Centinel" was published there by J. H. Baker, March 19, 1801; in 1810, named changed to "Northern Centinel"; in 1812, the word "Northern" was dropped, and the "Centinel" commenced; in 1814 it is "Northern Sentinel," and 1830 (with one interregnum) to 1844, "Burlington Sentinel." From 1845 to 1867 it was the "Sentinel and Democrat," In 1869 the Sentinel ceased publication. From 1848 to '52

a daily edition of the Sentinel was published by Geo. H. Paul.

"American Repertory and Advertiser," published at Burlington, Vt., by J. Spooner, 1821-2. Price two dollars per annum. Office over the Market, east side of Court House Square. I have No. 22 of Vol 1, Tuesday, February 26, 1822. Size of page 12x20 inches.

In 1871 a democratic paper was started under the title of "The Independent," by A. N. Merchant, and another "The Democrat," by H. C. Fay. In 1872, the Democrat was published by Mr. Merchant. In 1879 its title was "Democrat and Sentinel." In 1880 it ceased entirely.

Among the many editors who have graced the editorial chair of the Sentinel, have been Vermont's poet, John G. Saxe, and W. W. Waterman, a grand-son of Araunah Waterman, one of the first settlers of Montpelier.

A. N. Merchant, also published at St. Albans the "Home Visitor" for six years, and "Recorder," at North Hero, for the same length of time; he also published for a short time the "Sunday Sentinel," at Burlington and Rutland, and the "Souvenir" monthly at Burlington.

Mr. Merchant established in May, 1879, the "Rhode Island Democrat," at Providence, and being the only Democratic paper in that State, it attained substantial success.

The "Burlington Free Press," was established June 15, 1827, by Luman Foote. In February, 1828, H. B. Stacy became associated with Mr. Foote, and in January, 1833, Mr. Stacy became sole proprietor, until July, 1846, when D. W. C. Clarke, Esq., became its owner and editor; April 1, 1853, G. W. & G. G. Benedict became the proprietors, who were succeeded in 1866 by G. G. & B. L. Benedict. In 1868 the Free Press Association was organized by which the Free Press has since been published, G. G. Benedict remaining editor to the present time, (1896). After the Burlington Times was merged in the Free Press, in 1868, the title of the daily became "The Free Press and Times". The Press was published as a weekly until April, 1848, since which time it has been issued both daily and weekly. Previous to 1868, the daily was an evening paper. The morning edition was started in that year.

"Burlington Gazette," by Hinckley & Fish, September, 1814, to February, 1817.

The "Repertory," by Jeduthan Spooner, 1821-2.

"The Iris," semi-monthly, published by Worth & Foster; edited in 1829 by Zadock Thompson. A literary journal, born 1828, lasted 20 months.

"Green Mountain Repository," monthly, published by C. Goodrich, edited by Z. Thompson, 1832; lived one year.

"Green Mountain Boy," Richardson & Co., 1834-5.

"Free Soil Courier," started by E. A. Stansbury, 1848; published afterwards by Rev. Guy C. Samson, later by C. C. Briggs; ceased 1853.

"Burlington Times," daily and weekly, started by D. W. C. Clarke, in June, 1858; in 1860 passed to George H. Bigelow; in December, 1868, become merged in the "Free Press."

"Liberty Herald," 1846, published only a short time, and name changed to "Liberty Gazette," which continued a year or two.

"State Agriculturalist" commenced 1848. "Northern Register," monthly, commenced 1851. Both short lived.

"Rock Point Cadet." For private circulation. Published annually by the Pupils of the Vermont Episcopal Institute. Rock Point, Burlington, Vt. Nineteenth year." (1879). Rev. Theo. A. Hopkins, A, M., Principal.

"Vermont Musical Journal," a 16 page quarto, monthly, was commenced at Burlington by H. L. Storey, in October, 1866.

"Sunday Review," published by H. W. Love for a short time, being furnished to subscribers every Sunday morning by means of hand cars. This was continued until the proprietor "experienced" religion when the name was changed to "Saturday Review," and finally taken to Rutland, and merged with the "Inquirer."

For additional information. See Vermont Historical Gazetteer, Vol. 1, pp. 551-55; Walton's Registers, *passim.*

In 1896 the following papers are published in Burlington: "The Free Press and Times" daily, and "The Free Press" weekly; The "Clipper," weekly, by A. Armagnac; The "Earth," weekly, by Barrett & Johnson; The "Farmer's Advocate," weekly, by C. W. Scarff; The "News," evening, daily, by Joseph Auld; "The Sunday Sun," by the Burlington Publishing Co.; and the "University Cynic."

—Brattleboro.

The first printing press was set up at Brattleboro by Benjamin Smead in 1797, when he established the "Federal Galaxy," the first newspaper in the town, it being a 4 page sheet, 17x21 inches, and 4 columns to a page, subscription price $1.34 per annum; the "Galaxy" was continued until about 1802, when Mr. Smead removed to

Dansville, N. Y.; he subsequently returned to Bennington, Vt., where he published the "Gazette," January, 1806, to April, 1811.

The "Reporter" was started in February, 1803, by William Fessenden, a son of Rev. Thomas Fessenden, of Walpole, N. H., and was continued by him until his death in 1815, when the paper was continued by his father-in-law, Deacon John Holbrook, until about 1826, when it was merged into the "Messenger." Thomas Green Fessenden assisted his brother in the editorship of the "Reporter" about one year, 1814-15.

"The Independent Freeholder and Republican Journal," was started about 1808, by Peter Houghton, a printer; it was continued only a short time.

The "American Yeoman," by Simeon Ide, was established February 5, 1817, but not being remunerative, Mr. Ide, at the end of one year, moved the establishment to Windsor, Vt., and united it with the "Vermont Republican," in the office of which he had served his apprenticeship, having commenced in 1809.

The "Brattleboro Messenger" was established in 1822, by Alexander C. Putnam, a printer, and in 1826 he sold the paper to George W. Nichols, who continued the publication until 1834, when it was merged into the "Vermont Phœnix," with which Mr. Nichols continued about two years, when he soon purchased the "Windham County Democrat," which was established in 1836, by an association of democrats, with Joseph Steen editor for about one year, until Mr. Nichols came in; he continued the paper until the fall of 1853, when it was discontinued, and in the spring of 1855 Mr. Nichols moved to Kansas with his family, where he died the same year at the age of 73.

Mr. Nichols was born in Stowe, Vt., in 1782, and learned the printer's trade in the office of Isaiah Thomas, at Walpole, N. H.; he married, first, a daughter of Rev. Thomas Fessenden, of Walpole; second, a sister of Judge Howard, of Townsend, Vt.; the second Mrs. Nichols was for several years the editor of the "Windham County Democrat," and under her management the paper became one of the earliest champions of Woman's Rights in the country, and held a prominent position in the State.

"The Semi-Weekly Eagle" was established by B. D. Harris and William B. Hale, the first number printed August 10, 1847; it was an active Whig paper, and after about three years it was sold to an association of gentlemen, who placed Pliny H. White, then a young lawyer of West Wardsboro, in charge as editor and manager; he remained about one year, and subsequently became a Congregational clergyman, and prominent as a historical student and writer. Mr. Harris again took charge of the "Eagle," which he enlarged and changed to a weekly, which he continued until 1855, when it was united with the "Vermont Statesman."

The "Vermont Phœnix," the first number of which was published September 12, 1834, by George W. Nichols and William E. Ryther, arose from the ashes of the "Messenger," by Mr. Nichols, and the "Independent Inquirer," by Ryther. The "Inquirer," a liberal religious paper, was published about one year before uniting with the "Messenger" to form the Phœnix. Nichols & Ryther continued the Phœnix until 1836, September 30th, when they sold to G. C. Hall and J. C. Holbrook; the Phœnix was continued by various publishers, until 1855—Mr. Ryther being again in charge, 1849-51, and in 1852 the name changed to "Vermont Statesman" as above noted in union with the "Eagle," and the name of the combined paper was changed to "The Republican" January 1, 1855. February 3, 1855, the name "Phœnix" was resumed, and continued by various publishers to the present time, (1896.)

"The Flail," a Whig campaign paper, was published in 1840, Joseph Steen, editor.

"Vermont Record and Farmer." In July 1863, Daniel L. Milliken of the Brandon "Monitor" changed the name of his paper to "The Vermont Record;" he moved to Brattleboro, January 1, 1865, and for a time Mr. H. M. Burt, now of Springfield, Mass., was associated with him on the paper, the name being changed to "The Vermont Record and Farmer," being a 16 page quarto, 10¼ x 18½ inches per page, and continued by different hands to 1880.

"Asylum Journal," commenced in 1842, in connection with the Insane Asylum.

"The Water Cure World," by C. R. Blackall, M. D., an eight page quarto, monthly, commenced, April, 1860.

"The Household," a 20 page quarto devoted to domestic affairs, commenced in 1868, and had a large circulation, monthly. Discontinued, 1891.

"The Windham County Reformer," folio, weekly, by C. H. Davenport & Co., commenced in 1876, and has a circulation of 4300 copies, (1881).

See History of Brattleboro, pp. 180-185, Vol. V., Hemenway's Gazetteer, for a more extended account of Brattleboro newspapers, from which mainly we have condensed the above.

—Peacham.

At Peacham, Farley & Goss set up a press in 1798, and published the "Green Mountain Patriot," February, 1798, to March, 1807, when it was discontinued, and Mr. Goss moved to Montpelier, and purchased of Clark Brown the "Precursor," in September of that year, and rechristened it the "Vermont Watchman," which is continued. The numbering of the Watchman is consecutive from the commencement of the "Precursor."

For early Peacham imprints see Worcester, L.; Austin S.; Fitch, John; Forsyth, Wm.; Pope, A.

—Vergennes.

At Vergennes, Samuel Chipman set up a press, and commenced the publication of the "Vergennes Gazette," in August, 1798.

"Vergennes Vermonter," commenced January, 1838, by Rufus W. Griswold, and has been continued by others until the present time.

"Vergennes Citizen" commenced April, 1855, by Henry G. Judd; James Crane, Printer.

"Vermont Aurora," by Gamaliel Small, commenced at Vergennes, July 1, 1824, and in March, 1830, the office was destroyed by fire. After a suspension of about three months a new series was commenced, Vol. 1, No. 1, June 17, 1830, without any name of publisher or editor; its publication ceased March 31, 1831.

—Randolph.

In January, 1801, Sereno Wright opened a printing office, and commenced the publication of the "Weekly Wanderer," and continued it until 1811. In 1809, August 25, Mr. Wright in connection with Derrick Sibley, established the "Freemen's Press," a Democratic paper, at Montpelier.

"The Enterprise," commenced 1846, continued about one year.

"The Nonpareil," commenced 1847, published only a short time.

"Green Mountain Ægis," West Randolph, 1851.

"Vermont Luminary," at West Randolph, had an existence during the anti-Masonic fiasco.

"Orange County Eagle," by P. P. Ripley, at West Randolph, 1865.

The "Independent Statesman" was started at West Randolph in 1858, and continued two years, W. Scott Abbott being the editor, and appearing as one of the publishers. During the life of the "Statesman" there were issued from the same office five or six numbers of "The Ingleside," a literary paper also edited by Abbott, but the attempt to establish a periodical of that class failed.

For a Randolph imprint, 1801, see Smith, John.

—Middlebury.

The first printing office at Middlebury was established by Joseph D. Huntington and John Fitch, young men from Windham, Conn., in 1801; they commenced the publication of the "Middlebury Mercury," the first newspaper, December 16 of that year; terminated June 27, 1810.

"Columbian Patriot," Wednesday, June 7, 1815, Vol. II. No. 41. By William Slade, Jun.; size per page 12x19.

"National Standard," Vol. III, No. 37, May 8, 1816. By William Slade, Jun. Probably succeeded the Patriot.

"Anti-Masonic Republican," by E. D. Barber, commenced October, 1829; soon after succeeded by the "Middlebury Free Press," by Knapp & Jewett, Barber & Jewett, Editors.

"Middlebury People's Press, and Addison County Democrat," by Ephraim Maxham, Editor, commenced in the spring of 1836, subsequently H. Bell, Editor and Proprietor, Ephraim Maxham, printer; in 1842, Justus Cobb, Jr., succeeded Mr. Maxham as printer; September 27, 1843 is the latest we have seen; probably merged into "The Northern Galaxy, and Middlebury People's Press," H. Bell, Editor and Proprietor, published by J. Cobb, Jr.; we have No. 36, of Vol. VIII, January 10, 1844; soon after the title is simply "Northern Galaxy." The last we have seen, July 17, 1849, by J. H. Barrett & J. Cobb; soon after Barrett & Cobb became proprietors of the "Middlebury Register," as appears from No. 52, Vol. XV, issued April 23, 1851; the "Register" was subsequently published by Lyman E. Knapp & William J. Fuller, and so continued to 1875; after that by Knapp and Bailey; from 1879 to 1883 by R. M. Bailey; from that time to the present by the Register Company.

"American and Gazette," Vol. V, No. 28, issued May 25, 1836.

"Vermont Observer," B. Brierly, Editor and Publisher, E. Maxham, printer; Vol. 1, No. 26, issued May 2, 1843.

"Addison County Journal," started by the Journal Publishing Co., 1876; published later by Cobb and Fuller; discontinued.

"The Green Mountain Culturist," Devoted to Agriculture, Horticulture, Science, Education and the Mechanic Arts. Monthly. Vol I, No. 3. p. 32. By D. R. Bassett & Co.

See Swift's History of Middlebury, pp. 340–43, for additional facts. Also, Adviser.

—*Woodstock.*

The first Woodstock newspaper was the "Northern Memento," established by Isaiah H. Carpenter in 1805. The prospectus, issued in October of the preceding year, has perhaps enough interest to warrant its reproduction entire; it runs as follows :

Proposal of Isaiah H. Carpenter, for publishing in Woodstock, (Vermont,) A Weekly Newspaper, to be entitled THE NOTHERN MEMENTO.

Conditions. I. THE NORTHERN MEMENTO will be published every week on the day which will best accord with the arrival of the mail. II. It shall be printed with a handsome Type and good Paper, as large as either of the *Windsor* papers. III. THE price will be *One Dollar* and *Fifty Cents* per annum, delivered at the Office. IV. IF sufficient encouragement should be offered, the publication will commence some time in May next, of which previous information will be given.

To THE PUBLIC. Of all the numerous periodical publications daily sent out to the public newspapers are universally acknowledged to be the most useful. And when conducted with propriety, impartiality, and discretion, have the direct tendency to cultivate, improve, and enlarge the public mind. It is allowed, that newspapers are not and cannot be solely appropriated to, and employed in literary communications, and scientific researches; yet they are the medium through which every new improvement, or discovery in the arts and sciences are conveyed to the people at large; and that in the cheapest and most expeditious way possible. They are the *political* Salt of our country; and was the Freedom of the Press to be weakened or destroyed, and newspapers to lose their *Savour*, and the public patronage, our rights and liberties would fall with them. As well might you preserve your rights and privileges, your liberty and independence without the aid and assistance of the Press, as to save your bacon without salt. If then, the public welfare is so immediately connected with, and interested in, the circulation of well regulated and conducted newspapers, and the public are influenced in so great a degree by them; surely then, they are, and ought to be encouraged and supported by every honest, virtuous and independent American.

IN a Republican Government like ours, they are the necessary regimen to nourish and support social order. They are the constant sources of information, both Foreign and Domestic. And their efforts in all free governments are diffusive and lasting. And although Despots and Tyrants dread and fear them, as a mirror, in which may be seen their vices and deformity; yet to every true born son of Freedom, they are the Palladium of safety.

THE subscriber wishes that his abilities were equal to his zeal to serve the Public. And in conducting the paper for which he solicits the patronage of his Fellow Citizens; he pledges his utmost exertions to merit their favor and esteem. Viewing, as he does, the two great political parties, that now divide our common Country as both consisting of men who have fought and bled for her independence—Men possessing the greatest share of talents, and information; educated and brought up in habits of piety, virtue and morality—Men, whose honesty and integrity are unsuspected and unimpeached. Surely such men could never seriously mean to subvert and destroy the happiness and freedom of our Country.

UNINFLUENCED by the violence and spirit of party rage, the columns of THE NORTHERN MEMENTO, shall be free and open to the communications of all, when written with decency and decorum. Pieces calculated to amuse, inform and enlighten the mind, shall ever be received with pleasure, and the most grateful acknowledgments; whi e those aimed with the envenomed shaft of calumny and detraction against either private or public characters shall be rejected with merited contempt. Impressed with these ideas and views, and flattering himself with the hope of an extensive patronage and subscription; wishing the happiness and prosperity of his fellow citizens, he tenders them his service, and if encouraged will ever remain their Humble Servant.

OCTOBER, 1804.   ☛   ISAIAH H. CARPENTER.

This proposal was printed on sheets and circulated through Woodstock and neighboring towns for subscriptions, receiving 128 names as appears by the copies that have been preserved. The whole number of subscribers to the paper was doubtless somewhat larger than, that,

although quite small, and the prospect was such that Carpenter felt warranted in proceeding with the enterprise, and May 16, 1805, the first number of the Memento was issued. But it was not a success. Party spirit ran high at the time and the paper was Republican, notwithstanding the amusing suggestion of the prospectus that it would in politics stick tight to the fence; a sharp attack upon Benjamin Swan of Woodstock, state treasurer, who was a Federalist, occasioned the loss of some support, and after a troubled existence of nine months the Memento was discontinued in February, 1806. Carpenter's printing office was in his house, a wooden building yet in good condition, fronting south near the east end of the park.

The second newspaper published here was the "Woodstock Observer," started by David Watson in January, 1820, which had a fairly prosperous life. In the earlier years of this paper political parties hardly existed, but the Observer became National Republican upon the formation of that party during the administration of Adams, and so remained until the election of Jackson in 1828, when it became Jacksonian. At the beginning of its fourth year, in January, 1823, the paper was enlarged and given the additional title of "Windsor and Orange County Gazette," and in January, 1827, it was again enlarged. In November, 1823, it passed into the hands of Rufus Colton, who continued to publish it until 1833. In 1827, 1828, and perhaps in other years, Benjamin F. Kendall was the assistant editor, and in January, 1830, Colton announced that B. F. Fellows had taken the place; but under the masonic excitement of this time new papers sprang into existence which crowded the Observer into the background, and in 1833 its publication was finally suspended.

In 1820 a small Universalist quarterly magazine of 48 pages to the number was started by Rev. S. C. Loveland, called the "Christian Repository," Mr. Loveland appearing as editor and David Watson as printer. It was continued until 1827, when Mr. Loveland sold out to Rev. Robert Bartlett, who conducted it until 1829, when he sold to Rev. William Bell. Mr. Bell changed the form of the publication to that of a weekly newspaper which he called the "Universalist Watchman and Christian Repository," and published for about seven years, when he sold it to Rev. B. H. Fuller and Rev. J. M Austin, who moved it to Montpelier. Soon after being moved to that place Mr. Austin sold out to Rev. John Moore of Lebanon, N. H., and for a short time the paper was published at that place, but Rev. Joseph Wright finally become the sole owner and again took it to Montpelier, where he published it until July, 1840. It had absorbed several other papers and at this time had several titles—Universalist Watchman, Green Mountain Evangelist, Impartialist, and Christian Repository,—but coming then into the hands of Rev. Eli Ballou, all titles except the first one of Christian Repository were dropped, and the paper was continued by Mr. Ballou until May, 1870, when it was sold to the Universalist of Boston.

In February, 1830, was issued the first number of the "Domestic, Medical, and Dietetical Monitor, or Journal of Health," a monthly publication of 24 duodecimo pages, conducted by John Harding and printed by David Watson. The title indicates the character of this little periodical, which lived through only a few numbers.

"Bethlehem Star," Vol. 1, No. 5, 1824. Printed by David Watson. 12mo, p. 36.

In March, 1821, Rev. Walter Chapin of the Congregational church issued the prospectus of a small missionary paper to be published fortnightly at 50 cents per year and called the "Evangelical Monitor." The first number was printed April 14, 1821, and the publication was continued under the management of Mr. Chapin for two years, but it met with no great success and at the end of the second volume was discontinued. David Watson was the printer.

Another religious paper, also published fortnightly, was the "Gospel Banner," started by Rev. Jasper Hazen and Abner D. Jones of the Christian church in 1827, the first number being issued August 4th of that year; but it lived only a twelve-month. Rufus Colton printed it.

In the year 1828, David Watson started a paper called the "Vermont Inquirer," but it met with so little encouragement that but few numbers were printed.

"Universalist Watchman," by William Bell, commenced at Woodstock, 1829; moved to Montpelier, and name changed to "Christian Repository," which see.

The "American Whig" was established at about the beginning of the year 1830, by Hemenway & Sherwin. It absorbed the "Vermont Luminary" of Randolph and another paper called "Equal Rights," and appeared in March, 1830, Hemenway & Holbrook publishers, with the rather formidable title of "American Whig, Vermont Luminary and Equal Rights;" but the extra names were not long retained. The "Whig" was started under the direction of the anti-masonic county committee, Joseph Hemenway being the nominal editor, although much of the work was done by others, chief among whom was the Rev. S. C. Loveland. Holbrook remained but a short time, after which Hemenway published the paper alone until he sold out to Henry L. Anthony in 1835, who kept the "Whig" until it came to the end of its existence in 1836.

The first number of the "Henry Clay and Advocate of the American System," was issued September 4, 1830; B. F. Kendall, editor, David Watson, printer. After running a year the name was changed to "Vermont Courier and Farmers', Manufacturers', and Mechanics' Advocate." In 1834 the secondary title was dropped and a little later, the "Windsor Republican" having been united with it, the name was "Republican and Courier," until J. B. & S. L. Chase bought it in 1836, when it was again called the "Vermont Courier," and so remained until finally discontinued in 1838. Following Watson, William W. Prescott and C. K. Smith and Kendall under the firm name of C. K. Smith & Co., in turn were printers, but Kendall remained as editor until succeeded by the Chases.

These two papers, the "Whig" and the "Courier," united in opposing Jackson but were opposed to each other in the masonic war which raged so violently at the time, and fought with the utmost vigor and ferocity, their columns fairly bristling with capital letters and strong language. Kendall was what the opposition called a "Jackmason," that is, he acted with the masons but did not belong to the order. He was a better editor than the "Whig" ever had, and in fact the "Courier" under his management was considered the sharpest paper ever published in Vermont. While conducting the "Courier" Kendall was twice sued for libel, one of the parties, Titus Hutchinson, getting a small judgment. Mr. Kendall was born in Woodstock, in October, 1799, fitted for college but never entered, married Louisa Holton, of Woodstock, in 1828, went to Indiana and began farming in 1844, and died there March 7, 1854.

About the year 1830 Thomas E. Powers, John D. Powers, Thomas Russell, Nahum Haskell, Thaddeus Haskell, Benjamin Metcalf and a few other young men organized a club for free religious discussion which is remembered as the "infidel club," and for a year or more published a small monthly magazine called "Liberal Extracts," of infidel character. T. E. Powers was the active spirit in the club and in editing the magazine, and as both T. Haskell and Metcalf were practical printers, the work was all done in the family, so to speak. Metcalf invented two power printing presses at about this time, one of which printed both sides of the sheet at one operation, but neither proved successful. Of course these men mostly outgrew their infidel notions.

About the year 1831 an agricultural paper called the "Workingman's Gazette" was started here by William W. Prescott, but was short lived.

In the summer of 1833 Silas Estabrook published a small anti-Masonic campaign paper entitled the "Village Balance."

In 1836, the Whig being dead, an anti-Masonic campaign paper called "The Constitution" was published for a few weeks. Martin Flint of Randolph and Titus Hutchinson of Woodstock being the chief movers in the business, and Henry S. Hutchinson acting as editor. The opposition called it in derision, "Martin's Tupenny."

The same season another campaign paper called "The Hornet," a small sized affair, was published by "Timothy Tickle & Co.," with the purpose, as set forth in the prospectus, "to blow that musty concern, The Constitution, sky high." B. F. Kendall and T. E. Powers were the editors. Neither of these papers were issued more than five or six weeks.

Pretty much all Woodstock newspapers in these days were largely filled with personal abuse of political opponents, of such character as would have found little favor in the absence of extraordinary political excitement, and the little campaign papers were often fairly scurrilous.

In 1837 the "Vermont Mercury" was started by Nahum Haskell and Augustus Palmer, the first number being issued April 6, and had a tolerably long and prosperous life. In about ten years the name was changed to "Woodstock Mercury," and in 1853 the paper was given the additional title of "Windsor County Advertiser." The last number of the "Mercury" issued was at the close of its fourteenth yearly volume, March 8, 1855. It was always Whig in politics and was published throughout by Haskell and Palmer, and Mr. Haskell appeared as editor, but as he was a most industrious bookbinder and bookseller, much of the editorial work came to be done by other persons, chief among whom were Norman Williams and Thomas E. Powers. Pending the State election in 1842, a paper was published called the "Whig Advocate," with Charles P. Marsh, then a law student,

as editor, which was in fact a campaign edition of the "Mercury," and which had quite a large circulation.

The first number of the "Spirit of the Age" was issued May 8, 1840; Charles G. Eastman, editor and publisher. At the end of the third year the name was changed to "Woodstock Age" and so continued to November, 1845, when Eastman was succeeded by A. E. Kimball, and the old name resumed. Kimball was succeeded by E. M. Brown in May, 1847, and he by Wm. D. McMaster, who conducted it for thirty-four years. The "Age" was established as a Democratic paper and has always been such, except for a brief support of the Free Soilers when the old Democratic party split on the slavery question. In 1844 Eastman issued a campaign edition of the paper called the "Coon Hunter." The Age is now (1896) published by E. C. Dana.

"Henry Clay's Duels." [1844.] A campaign sheet from the "Age Office." 4pp. quarto.

The "Temperance Herald" was started in 1845, and continued about four years, with M. P. Parish as editor and publisher. The name indicates the purpose of this paper, which was established and supported by subscriptions from persons specially interested in the temperance subject.

In 1853 the sum of $500 was raised by subscription and the "Vermont Temperance Standard" was started, the first number being issued April 29 of that year; Thomas E. Powers, editor, Lewis Pratt, Jr., publisher. This paper met with great success, its circulation at the end of the first year being 3,000; the highest ever reached by a Woodstock newspaper. In January, 1855, Rev. Guy C. Sampson succeeded Powers as editor, and the circulation running down as the temperance excitement subsided, in January, 1857, Wilbur P. Davis and Luther O. Greene bought the paper, became editors and publishers, dropped the word "Temperance" from the title, and changed its character to that of a local newspaper. In August, 1860, Mr. Davis retired from the concern, after which Mr. Greene published it until his death in 1890. The "Standard" has been Republican in politics.

In the spring of 1855, an agricultural paper called the "Northern Farmer" was started by E. M. Brown and A. H. Crosby, which was in a few months sold to W. Scott Abbott, who moved it to West Randolph, where it died in 1856.

The first number of "The Otta Quechee Post" was issued September 15, 1871, the name was changed to "Woodstock Post" in August, 1872, and the last number was issued June 4, 1875. Robert A. Perkins, editor and publisher. The "Post" was Independent Republican in politics and supported Greeley in 1872.

All these Woodstock newspapers were issued weekly except as otherwise indicated.

"The Acorn," the first number of which was issued May 1, 1872, was an amateur paper, edited and printed by boys of about 16 years; was published monthly, had four three column pages, each form being 4¼ by 6 inches; subscription price 25 cents per year. John C. Dana, Wm N. Campbell, Harold S. Dana and Edward G. Bailey conducted it the first year, after which the two first named continued it alone. The "Acorn" had a prosperous existence for seventeen months, when its publication was abandoned, the last issue being the number for October, 1873. The "Acorn" was made up on the plan of larger papers, with its advertisements and several departments, was neatly printed in nonpareil type and was remarkably well edited; in fact, it was by all odds the brightest and best among several papers of its class then published in Vermont.

Among the newspaper editors of Woodstock there is one man who may be entitled to more than a passing notice in this place, although no great part of the work of his life was of a literary character. Thomas E. Powers, grandson of Dr. Stephen, and son of Dr. John D. Powers, was born in Woodstock, November 14, 1808. After leaving the village schools he attended Royalton Academy for a short time, and it being determined that he should study medicine, he attended lectures at the Castleton medical school in 1825, and at Hanover in 1826 and in 1827, when he graduated. He continued his studies in his father's office in Woodstock, and commenced practice there, but about the year 1831 married Mary E., daughter of Amos Warren, of Woodstock, and went to Hartland, with a view of establishing a practice in that place. The attempt was abandoned at the end of a year, however, and Dr. Powers returned to Woodstock, where he passed the remainder of his days. The professional work not being to his taste he gradually abandoned it for other pursuits, and for many years before his death did nothing whatever in medicine. In 1846 he was elected assistant secretary of the Vermont Senate, and was re-elected in the three years following. Here he got that knowledge of parliamentary law and of the ways of doing public business which afterwards did him such good service. Being elected representative by his native town, he was chosen speaker of the House in 1850, and in 1851 and 1852. He also represented the town in 1855 and 1856. In 1857 he was appointed superintendent of construction of the present State house, and carried the work through. He also superintended the building of the Woodstock court house in 1854, and was employed in some smaller work of the kind. In 1862 he was appointed U. S. Assessor for the second Congressional district of Vermont, and held the place for nine years. He died December 27, 1876, surviving his wife a little over two years. His only child, Ada A., married Charles D. Anderson, and died in 1862 at the age of 29.

"Tom" Powers was one of the most remarkable men the State of Vermont has produced. With natural strength and activity of mind, such as is rarely given to men, he was industrious and persistent in whatever he undertook, and it is easy to believe that with a slightly different disposition he would have made a great success in life. He was intensely pugnacious and domineering, and these qualities which with his splendid ability enabled him to readily become the acknowledged leader in whatever movement he joined, also led to the making of enemies upon every hand. By no means blind to the advantage of being on the side of the "strongest battalions" at the outset, upon once taking sides in a question he rode rough shod over all who disputed his way, conciliating none; and that course, however things might turn at the moment, was inevitably fatal to political success in the long run. Dr. Powers' best place was in public debate. Of commanding stature and presence and with a voice of remarkable power, he was able to crush most opponents by mere denunciation; and being able to reason clearly and rapidly, an adept at appealing to the prejudices of men, quick at retort and strong in sarcasm, he was an antagonist feared by all. Other men have accomplished more in Vermont legislation, but certainly no man ever approached him in effectiveness on the floor of the Vermont House. Espousing the cause of temperance he worked up the excitement by lecturing, organizing temperance conventions and in other ways, and finally fought the prohibitory law through the legislature and through the popular vote successfully. Echoes of his fierce denunciation of "rummies" are yet to be heard in the State. Other men have been more successful in politics in the State, but while on the summit of the temperance wave he had done so much to create, he probably had the strongest personal following ever known in Vermont. It was said that, single handed, he made Ryland Fletcher governor in 1856.

—Montpelier.

At Montpelier the first press was established by Clark Brown, in 1806, and he published the "Vermont Precursor," from about the middle of Nov. 1806, until the summer of 1807, when he sold out to Samuel Goss. I have a copy of the "Precursor" of July 24, 1807, vol. 1, No. 36, Samuel Goss, publisher. Mr. Goss changed the name to "The Watchman" about Dec. 1, 1807. The number of the "Precursor" I have measures 17x11 inches per page.

The Vermont Historical Society has a copy of "The Watchman" of Friday, Dec. 18, 1807, being Vol. 2, No. 57, which shows the numbering is consecutive from the commencement of the "Precursor."

Size of the "Watchman" 12x18 inches per page. Mr. Goss published "The Watchman" until 1810, when he sold to Ezekiel P. Walton and Mark Goss, who under the firm of Walton & Goss continued the business until 1816 or 1817, when Mr. Walton became sole proprietor, as appears from the issue of August 19, 1817; in 1822 size increased to 14x21; and after Mr. Hill established the "Vermont Patriot and State Gazette," in January, 1826, the size of "The Watchman" was increased to 15x22, and the name changed to "Vermont Watchman and State Gazette," which name was continued until, in 1836 or 7, upon the death of the anti-Masonic party in Vermont, an organ of that party, the "State Journal," was merged into "The Watchman," and the name again changed to "Vermont Watchman and State Journal," and is so continued at the present time. From 1817, "The Watchman" continued under the control of the Walton family until it passed into the possession of Messrs. J. & J M. Poland, in 1868. The elder Mr. Walton, in the early history of "The Watchman," like many other newspaper publishers, encountered financial storms which required all his energy and tact to overcome. On one occasion his establishment was attached for debts to the paper maker and others, when Gen. Walton bethought himself of a large lot of "Washington's Farewell Address," which he had recently printed, and which was packed away, and fortunately not discovered by the attaching officer; with a team Gen. Walton started through the country peddling the Address, and soon raised money

enough to relieve him of his embarrassment. In 1853 E. P. Walton, Jr., became sole proprietor and editor, and so continued until he sold out, in 1868.

"The Watchman" from its birth in 1807 to the present time has been an organ of most of the political parties, from the old Federal to the sectional Republican party of to-day, that have had an existence in opposition to the great historic National Democratic party. The paper has been enlarged from time to time, until it now measures 18x29 inches per page.

Mr. J. M. Poland having retired, January 1, 1880, the paper was conducted by Joseph Poland, until April, 1882, when he sold "The Watchman" to Mr. W. W. Prescott. Since 1893, the paper has been published by the Watchman Publishing Company.

The "Watchman" has been published daily at times, especially during the war, and for many years during sessions of the Legislature, under the title of the "Daily Journal." The "Argus and Patriot" has occasionally been published daily during sessions of the Legislature.

"The Freemen's Press, a democratic paper published at Montpelier, the first number of which was issued August 25th, 1809—not in 1812 or 1813, as is stated by Judge Thompson in his history of Montpelier. It was printed by Derrick Sibley, and subsequently by Wright & Sibley, for proprietors, who appear to have been the leading Democrats of Montpelier, and the neighboring towns.

The paper was devoted mainly to national politics, only a small space being given to local and State matters. This file begins with number three, and embraces a period of about two years and a half. In the issue of September 8th, the first in this file, there are but six lines of editorial, and those relate to the State election returns, which are published in part. There are five advertisements. Forbes & Langdon advertise for their customers to pay up, and also that they had "just received from Philadelphia a quantity of Scotch snuff of superior quality" Charles Huntoon—not mentioned by Thompson—general merchant, "offers for sale at his stores in Montpelier and Berlin a general assortment of English and India goods, etc., etc., which he will sell for salts of lye, ashes, butter, cheese, beef cattle, and all country produce." George B. R. Gove—also not mentioned by Thompson—being about to leave Montpelier, offers for sale "one House and Store, with five acres of land within 100 rods of the State House, pleasantly situated in the centre of business, and is one of the best stands for a merchant in the State." "Also an oil mill near Onion river bridge, also a gin distillery, new and complete, and a small farm in Berlin, and other lands." December 15, 1809, we learn that Silas Burbank had purchased the oil mill of Mr. Gove, and wanted flax seed, for which one gallon of oil, or one dollar in cash, would be given per bushel. October 13, 1809, Chester W. Houghton wanted a few thousand bushels of potatoes delivered at his distillery, for which he would give in exchange one quart of gin per bushel, or twenty cents in English goods. Josiah Parks, bookseller, publisher, and Justice of the Peace, was a persistent advertiser, continuing through the entire file of papers. So also were Justin and Elias Lyman, merchants, of Hartford, Vt. In the paper of May 2, 1811, was the marriage by Josiah Parks, Esq., of Ezekiel P. Walton, printer, and Miss Prussia Persons. November 5, 1809, James Peck opened a martial music school. December 2, 1809, Charles Bulkley, agent for the trustees of Montpelier Academy, politely said:

"The gentlemen and ladies of the vicinity are with pleasure informed that an additional room has been fitted up in the Academy, for the accommodation of a ladies' school. An instructor has been obtained, whose attainments are in every respect adequate, to instruct in the several branches of reading, grammar, geography, painting, embroidering, and the various kinds of needle work."

Sylvanus Baldwin, a stockholder in the paper, was also a liberal advertiser of houses and lands for sale, and to be let; and also of patent rights for sale. He was also interested in, and agent for, a cotton and woolen mill near "Paine's bridge." January, 1810, Thomas Reed continued the chair, cabinet, and painting business, at his old stand. July 4, 1810, the Democratic republican citizens of Montpelier, Calais, Marshfield and Plainfield, celebrated the 4th at Capt. Samuel Rich's, North Montpelier, and it would appear that the federals did not celebrate the 4th of July in those days. Col. Caleb Curtiss, of Calais, acted as Marshal, and Nahum Kelton, of Montpelier, as Assistant. "The Declaration of Independence was read, prefaced by some well-timed remarks by J. Y. Vail, Esq., a truly republican oration was delivered by Tim. Y. Merrill, Esq., which did honor to his head and heart!" A sumptuous dinner, in a grove, with regular and volunteer toasts followed, Josiah Parks being Chairman of Committee on toasts, which latter expressed the usual Democratic sentiments of the time.

September 2, 1810, a negro mob was published as having occurred in Boston at this time; the negroes seized a brother smoke, hurried him to the common, and cut off his ears. Were the Ku-Klux about in those days?

January 1, 1811, "Found near the Academy, last evening, a good bandanna handkerchief, which the owner may have by applying to D. Sibley." January 7, 1811, "good stock of hay at five dollars and fifty cents per ton, and cash, labor, pork, shingles, or grain, received in payment. I live on the West road in Calais, near Col. Curtis'," and signed William Thayer.

March 7, 1811, Amos Bugbee, who was a machinist, and connected with the cotton and woolen factory before mentioned, offered for sale Dutch plows. March 20, Josiah Fisk carried on the clothier's business, and blue dyeing at his shop in Montpelier.

May 30, 1811, the Press said "we notice in the last *Watchman* the following : 'our glorious federal triumph in New York; the Clinton interest is no more.' This is not the first time the patrons of this paper have been egregiously imposed upon in this way. De Witt Clinton is elected by over three thousand majority." In the same paper; "The 'large ox' noticed so conspicuously in the *Watchman* proved to be nothing more nor less than an *old stag*. He was much better off for hide than tallow, the former weighing 94 pounds more than the latter." Does the *Watchman* shoot as wide of the mark now-a-days?

November 11, 1811, brought the file near the war of 1812, and political feeling began to run high. The editor of the *Press*, usually so dignified, apologized to his readers for being compelled to denounce the statements of the *Watchman* as "willful lies." November 7, 1811, Wright & Sibley purchased the entire stock of the "Freemen's Press" establishment, and became sole proprietors; and about this time they removed "to the chamber of the White Store opposite Major Langdon's."

Morse's tavern, sometimes called "People's Rest," appears to have been the usual place for citizens' meetings, etc.

The "white store" was at that time occupied by Sylvanus Baldwin, then Postmaster, and afterward by Hon. Daniel Baldwin, his brother. The George B. R. Gove store stood where Cross & Son's extensive establishment now is, and was a one-story building, his gin distillery being up on the side hill in the vicinity where now is the tannery of Keith & Pecks. The "Morse Tavern," or "People's rest," stood where the "Church of the Messiah" now is, and was kept by the father of Moses Morse, a former well known citizen of Johnson.

We learn from Sylvanus Baldwin, Postmaster, that the mail facilities of Montpelier at that time were two mails per week each, from the South and West; and one mail per week each from the North and East. We notice that Washington news was from twenty to thirty days old when published in Montpelier.

How many persons are now living (1880) in Montpelier who were there in 1810? We at this moment think of but two—W. W. Cadwell, Esq., and Hon. Daniel Baldwin. Of course there may be others, but we do not happen to know them.

After the suspension of the Press there was no Democratic paper in Montpelier until 1826, when the Hon. Isaac Hill, of Concord, N. H., established the Vermont Patriot and State Gazette, the first number of which was issued January 17, 1826, it being 21x30 inches per page, remaining the same until April 10, 1841, when it was enlarged to 24x36 inches.

Immediately after the "Vermont Patriot and State Gazette" was established, the name of the "Watchman," the federal organ, was changed to "Vermont Watchman and State Gazette."

Mr. Hill placed his brother, George W. Hill, in charge of the Patriot as manager, under the firm of George W. Hill and Company, with Horace Steele as editor. The latter remained but a short time, and was succeeded by Hugh Moore, Esq., of Concord, N. H., who held the position a few years, he being an educated and accomplished gentleman, and in this connection it is proper to state that Mrs. George W. Hill, an educated and accomplished lady, rendered important service in the editorial department during the latter years of her husband's connection with the paper. Mr. Hill became sole publisher April 30, 1827, and so continued until 1834, when, the business not meeting his expectations, he sold the entire establishment to William Clark, a printer who had been some time foreman in the office. Mr. Hill was appointed Postmaster under General Jackson, and held the office until after the election of Van Buren. He soon after retired to a farm in Lowell, Vt., and about 1850 removed to Johnson, Vt., where he still resides, a hale old gentleman of the "olden time." (1880.)

At the time Mr. Clark purchased the paper he made an agreement with a young man from New Hampshire to do editorial work, proof reading, etc., for three hundred dollars per annum. This young man was Jeremiah T. Marston, who read law in Montpelier, and had just opened an office for the practice of his profession. This arrangement continued until April 1, 1838, when Mr. Clark sold out to Marston and George W. Barker, for the sum of $2,200, which was considered a large price. Mr. Clark had in the meantime married Fanny, daughter of Hon. Isaiah Silver, of Montpelier. After closing the sale of the paper he moved to New York city, and became connected with the great printing house of Trow & Company, where he continued until the failure of his eyesight, quite recently, when he retired from business, and now (1880) resides in Brooklyn, N. Y. Mr. Barker was Postmaster under Mr. Van Buren, and after the "Hard-cider-Log Cabin" Campaign of 1840 he retired from the newspaper business, to engage in building railroads, and died not long since in Sheboygan, Wis. At this time the political aspect was discouraging, but Mr. Marston, who was young and full of energy, determined to persevere, and became sole owner, manager and editor. He brought out the paper enlarged, as before stated, at an additional cost of twelve hundred dollars. Soon the prospect changed. President Harrison died. "Hard Cider" became stale, Marston pushed ahead with renewed vigor, and made the most sparkling, lively, wide-awake and best looking paper in the State, which he continued to do until January 1, 1846, when he sold the entire establishment to Charles G. Eastman and Joseph B. Danforth, who continued it under the firm of Eastman & Danforth, the former being editor and the latter business manager.

Mr. Marston accumulated during his connection with the paper fifteen to twenty thousand dollars, a handsome sum for those days, and soon after moved to Madison, Wis., where he engaged in commercial and farming business. He married a daughter of Jacob F. Dodge of Montpelier, and they have two daughters and one son, the former well married, we believe. Mrs. R. W. Hyde, of Montpelier, is a sister of Mrs. Marston.

In July, 1851, Mr. Eastman purchased the interest of Mr. Danforth, and remained owner, manager and editor of the "Vermont Patriot" until his death, September 16, 1860. Mr. Eastman was born in Fryeburg, Me., June 1, 1816, but in childhood his father and family moved to Barnard, Vt. He entered the University of Vermont at the age of eighteen, but remained there only two years, during which time he was associate editor of the Burlington *Sentinel*. In 1838 he established the *Spirit of the Age*, at Woodstock, which he published and edited until his removal to Montpelier. He was Postmaster at Woodstock and at Montpelier for several years, and a Senator for Washington county in 1851-52.

Mr. Eastman published a small volume of Burchard's Sermons in 1836; and in 1848 a volume of poems, 12mo, pp. 208. In addition he contributed many poems to reviews and magazines, and delivered poetical addresses at the University of Vermont, Dartmouth, and other colleges. In 1846 Mr. Eastman married Mrs. Susan S. Havens, daughter of Dr. John D. Powers, of Woodstock, and a sister of the late Dr. Thomas E. Powers. They had one daughter and two sons. The daughter married a Mr. Hartshorn, a native of Essex county, and they reside at Emmettsburgh, Palo Alto county, Iowa.

Mr. Danforth, after disposing of his interest in the Patriot, located at Rock Island, Ill., where he published the "Rock Island Argus," a Democratic paper with which he had been more or less connected since he left Vermont, and since then has published a "National" journal. He is a native of Barnard.

After the death of Major Eastman the paper was continued by the administrators of his estate until January 1, 1861, when it was sold to E. M. Brown, who had been publishing the "Age" at Woodstock, who continued its publication until the fall of that year, when financial embarrassments, existing before he came to Montpelier, and want of patronage because it was not a "live" newspaper, compelled Mr. Brown to relinquish its publication, which was then continued for a short time by the estate of C. G. Eastman. After a few weeks, the estate, not finding a purchaser, gave up the publication, and there was an interregnum in its issue, which lasted until February, 1863, when it was resumed by Hiram Atkins, who purchased the name and goodwill from the estate of Mr. Eastman.

When this purchase was made it brought the Bellows Falls Argus to Montpelier, with its subscription list of 1700 names, and united it with that of the Patriot, the combined list of the Argus and Patriot being three thousand copies per week, which has increased until it is over six thousand. At the outset Mr. Atkins and three men did all the work—mechanical, editorial, and keeping the books. Now (1880) twenty-three persons are directly connected with and employed in the office. Then there was not job printing enough done to keep one man busy; now teu to fifteen persons are employed continually in that department. This success was achieved despite the most virulent opposition until within a few years. When the consolidated papers began their issue at Montpelier it was in the midst of the great civil war. Many who intended to be good citizens, and to do no wrong to their neighbors, seemed to believe that if a man was a Democrat, voting the ticket of that party, he was a rebel and a traitor. Yet others, who knew better, but were actuated by business or political jealousy, charged the same thing. The Freeman said, "Now let us see who will dare patronize that paper," and all available social, business, and even religious influences were enlisted in the effort to "kill out" the Argus and Patriot. When the purchase was made from the Eastman estate, the Administrators signed the following card as part of the trade :

TO THE PUBLIC.

Hiram Atkins, having purchased of the estate of the late C. G. Eastman, the name, good will, etc., of the Vermont Patriot, and transferred the publication of the paper heretofore owned by him from Bellows Falls to Montpelier, we commend the Argus and Patriot to the support of the friends and patrons of Mr. Eastman, in the publication of the Patriot,

CHARLES REED,   } Adm'rs of the Estate of
JAMES T. THURSTON, }   C. G. Eastman.
Montpelier, February 10, 1863.

After that card had been published a few times, they requested that it might not appear, frankly admitting that it was his right to continue its publication, but declaring that the pressure on them because their names appeared appended to that card was greater than they could bear. Mr. Atkins took the card out of the paper, but he ever after that had his idea about the backbone of those men.

Another incident showing the animus of some otherwise worthy people toward the Argus and Patriot in its earlier days, is the fact that one gentleman, still living and an estimable man, occupying a good position in society and as a business man, went to an officer of Christ Church, and said, "You are not going to let Atkins have a seat in the church, are you?" The publisher of so disloyal a sheet was not even to be allowed to join in the public worship of God, nor to have the benefit of clergy. The mob spirit was invoked, too; one prominent Republican offered $500 to the man or men who would sack the office, and furthermore said he would pay all fines and penalties that might grow out of it. Brickbats and stones thrown through the windows of the office are still preserved, as mementos of those days. All that is a thing of the past. "Let the dead bury their dead "

The office of the Freemen's Press was located on the easterly side of Main street, south of and adjoining Bethany church, in a wooden building, yet standing, and now occupied by Fisher & Colton as a saddlery hardware store.

Mr. Hill located the Vermont Patriot on the westerly side of Main street, opposite Bethany church, in the wooden structure now owned by Thomas Moriarty, and occupied by William Miller as a grocery store. The printing office was in the second story, the rear part of the first story being occupied by a Mr. Watson, who subsequently went to Charleston, S. C., and died there, as a bookbindery, the front part of this lower floor being occupied by Mr. Hill as the post-office. A peculiar custom was in fashion in relation to mail delivery. The Southern and Western mails arrived by stage at about the same time, 10 to 11 o'clock A. M., when the little room would be crowded to excess by those waiting. After the mail was opened Postmaster Hill would read out in a loud voice the address of every letter received, upon the conclusion of which there would be a stampede of those for whom there were no letters.

The Patriot continued to be published in that building until it passed into the hands of Marston & Barker, when it was removed to State street, in the Ballou building, west of the bridge and opposite the First National Bank. Here the printing office was in the second story ; on the first floor in front, Mr. Marston had a bookstore, while in the rear a large reading room, well supplied with newspapers, was fitted up for the benefit of all who chose to use it. It was there that the friends of the editor of the Patriot of all parties gathered for political gossip and news; it was in this room that the election of James K. Polk to the Presidency was first announced in Montpelier, by a hurried scrawl from Hon. J. McM. Shafter, then Whig Secretary of State for Vermont, written at Burlington and forwarded by the stage driver to Col. E. P. Jewett, it reading as follows: "New York gone ; all gone ; we have got to take Polk, Texas and the devil." We also got by the election of Polk that vast and rich territory now comprising not only Texas, but New Mexico, Utah, Arizona, Nevada and California, to which

latter State Mr. Shafter moved some twenty-five years ago, becoming one of its wealthy and prominent men.

Upon the purchase of the Patriot by Eastman & Danforth the office and bookstore were removed across the bridge easterly, to a wooden building then standing on the southerly side of State street, opposite the westerly tenement of "Walton's Block," where it remained through the administration of Eastman, and also that of E. M. Brown.

When the Patriot was resuscitated and consolidated with the Argus, the Lyman & King store, on Main street, opposite the "old brick church," was leased for the office ; a year later the building was purchased for Mr. Atkins by Mr. E. F. Kimball, his father-in law. Since then a two story and attic extension have been put on in the rear, a French roof story added to its height, and a new front put in. The structure is now known as the "Argus and Patriot building."

"State Journal," by Knapp & Jewett. Vol. 1, No. 1, issued, Montpelier, Monday morning, October 31, 1831. An anti-masonic paper, and subsequently it became an appendage to the "Vermont Watchman," and so continues.

"The Voice of Freedom," E. A. Allen, publisher, C. L. Knapp, Editor, commenced in January, 1839, and was published some years; the "Freeman," at Montpelier, is its descendant.

"Botanic Advocate," monthly, commenced about 1837, continued about two years.

"Green Mountain Emporium, and Literary, Moral and Religious Record," by J. Milton Stearns, 8vo, monthly, 16 pages each, commenced November, 1838, continued only a short time, and moved to Middlebury.

[The Green Mountain Freeman was started in January, 1844, as the org n of the Liberty Party, by Joseph Poland. A little later C. C. Briggs became joint editor and publisher. In May, 1846, Mr. Briggs retired and H. D. Hopkins was associate editor till 1849. During seven years following the paper was owned successively by Jacob Scott, D. P. Thompson and S. S. Boyce. In 1861, the Freeman was purchased by Hon C. W. Willard, and was published and edited by him till 1869, when J. W. Wheelock purchased a half interest. In 1873 Mr. Wheelock became sole proprietor. After his death, in 1876, his son, Herbert R. Wheelock, became owner and editor, until 1885, when the paper ceased publication.]

"Vermont Family Visitor," commenced 1845, for about a year only.

"Vermont Temperance Star," 8 page quarto, monthly. By George B. Manser. Vol. 1, No. 6, is August, 1839.

"The Watchword," a temperance paper. Editorial Committee : Rev. J. C. W. Coxe, Rev. J. E. Wright, H. D. Hopkins, H. A. Huse. February 14, 1874. Only a few numbers issued.

"The Democratic Whig." E. P. Walton, Jr., Editor. No. 2. Published six months as a campaign paper, in support of Henry Clay and Theo. Frelinghuysen, May to November, 1844.

"The Harrisonian," by E. P. Walton & Sons, a Log Cabin Hard Cider Campaign paper, published May to November, 1840.

A Democratic campaign paper, by J. T. Marston, from the Patriot Office, Montpelier, May to November, 1840.

"Voice of the Soldier." Vol. 1, No. 9, is April 22, 1865. Sloan, U. S. A., General Hospital, Montpelier, Vt. Published and edited by the Soldiers in the Hospital, semi-monthly; size, 17x24 inches. Address 1st Sergt. Voss. The Hospital was situated on what is now known as "Seminary Hill." Mr. Will Sullivan was at that time a "soldier," and editor-in-chief of the "Voice."

"The Farmer," or "The Vermont Farmer," Vol. 1, No. 1, issued Friday, December 5, 1879; a weekly journal, by Lewis P. Thayer, late of the "News," Randolph, size 20x 26 inches per page.

"The Vermont News," Vol. 1, No. 4, Montpelier, Vt., Friday, July 9, 1880; a weekly political campaign sheet issued from the Farmer office, and of the same size as the Farmer; it was a Garfield paper, and suspended publication after the Presidential election in 1880.

"Vermont Temperance Banner," started in fall of 1879, under the auspices of W. W. Scott and J. P. Eddy. Published one number, and suspended for lack of patronage.

See MONTPELIER, for "Winooski Impetus," and "Montpelierian."

—St. Albans.

At St. Albans, Rufus Allen opened a printing office in 1807, and published for about one year, "The St. Albans Adviser;" The "Champlain Reporter," by Morton & Willard, was commenced in April, 1809, and continued until the spring of 1811; from this time until May, 1823, there was no newspaper published in Franklin county. At the latter date Jeduthan Spooner established "The Repository," which he continued until April, 1836.

"The Way of Holiness," a 4 page, quarto, religious

weekly, A. C. Rose, editor, A. A. Phelps, corresponding editor; commenced January 1, 1858. In 1860 its publication was transferred to Kinderhook, N. Y.

"Daily Telegraph," commenced Thursday, June 11, 1863; a 4 page quarto.

"Vermont Transcript," weekly, by Henry C. Cutler, commenced Monday, March 18, 1864. Mr. Cutler sold to Wilbur P. Davis, June 1, 1866.

"Vermont Daily Transcript," commenced May 14, 1868, by Wilbur P. Davis; W. P. Davis and A. Barnes, editors.

"Vermont Temperance Advocate." Vol. 1, No. 40, July 20, 1871. By Clarke & Taylor, weekly, eight pages, size per page, 16x22 inches.

See Vermont Historical Gazetteer, Vol. 2, pp. 330-331 for additional information.

From 1871 to 1874 the "Transcript" was published by A. N. Merchant. In 1875-6 C. S. Kinsley was publisher. In 1873 the "St. Albans Courier" was published by the St. Albans Paper Co. In 1874 the "Advertiser," semi-weekly, was started by the Advertiser Pub. Co. In 1878 it was transferred to E. H. Sears and a daily edition added. In 1880 it was merged in the "Messenger."

The "Vermont Sentry" was removed from Swanton to St. Albans in 1886 by C. R. Jameson, and was subsequently published by F. C. Smith till 1891, when it ceased publication.

The "Vermonter," monthly, was established by C. S. Forbes in August, 1895, and is a successful publication.

The "Franklin Journal" was started as an anti-masonic paper, May, 1833, Saml. N. Sweet, editor; afterward by Joseph H. Brainerd to Dec. 1837, when it was sold to E. B. Whiting, who changed the name to "St. Albans Messenger." Mr. Whiting commenced the daily edition in 1863. In 1871 Mr. Whiting sold to Clarke and Taylor, who purchased the Transcript and united the two papers under the title of "The Messenger and Transcript." In 1873 Albert Clarke became sole editor and proprietor until 1880, when the Messenger and Advertiser were consolidated under S. B. Pettingill as editor. From 1883 to 1886 A. J. Lang was the publisher. From '86 to '92 Warren Gibbs; since 1892 the paper has been published by the Messenger Company.

—Danville.

In Danville the first number of the "North Star" was published the first week in January, 1807, and is still (1880) continued by the descendants of its founder, Ebenezer Eaton, who established the first press in town, the manager being George E. Eaton, who represented that town in the Legislatures of 1876 and 1878. In 1882 the Star was published by Hoyt and Preston, and subsequently by A. B. Hoyt until 1891, when it ceased publication.

—Barnard.

At Barnard a printing press was in operation as early as 1812; we have not met with Barnard imprints of an earlier date.

The printing office at Barnard was exclusively a book and job office, as no newspaper was ever published there; nearly all the book imprints bear the names of "Joseph Dix, Publisher, and I. H. Carpenter, Printer." Mr. Dix was the owner of the establishment. We do not think this press was in operation at Barnard much over three years. Mr. A. C. Moore established a press and job office at Bethel about 1860, and in 1869 removed the office to Barnard, where he continued business for some years.

Mr. Dix was from Massachusetts; he resided some time at Worcester, and at one time was a merchant in Boston; he probably resided in Barnard three or four years, when it is said he moved to Rutland. He died in 1821.

Miss Dorothea L. Dix, the authoress and philanthropist, was a daughter of Joseph Dix, and was born in Worcester, Mass. Her schoolmates at Barnard remember her while there as a girl of twelve or fifteen years.

—Bellows Falls.

The following in relation to printing at Bellows Falls was principally furnished by John W. Moore, Esq., of Manchester, N. H.

The first newspaper published at Bellows Falls village, in Rockingham, Vt., was "The Bellows Falls Intelligencer," commenced in January, 1817; it was very neatly printed and of large size, by Blake, Cutler & Co., and was edited by Thomas Green Fessenden, a lawyer of the place. The Intelligencer was ably conducted, and was a zealous advocate of the doctrines of the old federal party. Mr. Fessenden continued to edit the paper until 1822, when he removed to Boston, Mass., and commenced there the "New England Farmer." He was born in Walpole, N. H., April 22, 1771; graduated at Dartmouth College in 1796, and died in Boston, Mass., November 11, 1837. The Intelligencer was edited for a time after Mr. Fessenden left it by William Masters, formerly employed in the

office of Jacob B. Moore, of Concord, N. H. Later the paper was edited by Cyrus Barton, by Edmund Burke, and yet later by John H. Wells. It was then sold to Mr. Samuel Taylor, who continued it until 1835, when it passed into the hands of Benjamin G. Cook, who changed its name to "Vermont Intelligencer." Mr. Cook sold the establishment to William Mack, and it was soon afterwards discontinued.

The "Vermont Chronicle" was commenced at Bellows Falls by Rev. E. C. Tracy, in April, 1826, and was removed to Windsor in October, 1828, and then to Montpelier in January, 1875, and is continued, being now (1896) published at St. Johnsbury.

The "Bellows Falls Gazette" was commenced by John W. Moore in 1838, and continued until 1851, when it was sold to O. H. Platt, and continued at Bellows Falls and Brattleboro for a short time, when Mr. Platt commenced a separate paper, "The Bellows Falls Times," which went into the hands of A. N. Swain, by whom it was published till 1888; then by Frank B. Brown; then by the Times Publishing Co.; then by Emerson and Co.; then (1896) by L. P. Thayer.

"The Republican Standard" was commenced by William F. Mack in 1850, and was discontinued in 1853, when it was purchased by Hiram Atkins, and merged into the "Bellows Falls Argus."

The "Bellows Falls Argus" was commenced December, 1853, by Hiram Atkins, and continued until February, 1864, when Mr. Atkins was persuaded to purchase the "Vermont Patriot," which he conducted with marked ability at Montpelier, as the Argus and Patriot. Since 1894 the paper has been published by the Argus & Patriot Publishing Co.

"The World of Music." By John W. Moore. An 8 page quarto, Vol. 1, No. 9, issued May 15, 1840.

—Arlington.

"The Register," Arlington, July 15, 1817. Published by E. G. Storer, at $2 per annum. Size, 12x19 per page.

—Poultney.

At Poultney about November, 1822, the first press was started by Sanford Smith and John K. Shute; Mr. Smith was a son of Rev. Ethan Smith; they published the "Poultney Gazette," which was commenced in November, 1822, the name being changed to that of "Northern Spectator" in January, 1825.

It was in the office of the "Spectator" that Horace Greeley learned the printer's trade, where he remained from the spring of 1826 until the publication of the paper was suspended in June, 1830.

See History of Poultney, pp. 89-93.

—Castleton.

At Castleton the first newspaper in town was "The Vermont Statesman," commenced in 1824 by Ovid Miner, Editor and Proprietor. Whig in politics.

Mr. Miner remained but a short time, but the paper was continued under different editors until 1855.

"The Green Mountain Eagle," was established about 1832 by Hon. Zimri Howe as principal proprietor, as an Anti-Masonic organ, and its existence terminated with that party.

See Vermont Historical Gazetteer, vol. 3, p. 516.

—St. Johnsbury.

At St. Johnsbury the first press was established by Luther Jewett, and he issued the first number of the "Farmer's Herald," July 8, 1828.

See JEWETT, L.; Vermont Historical Gazetteer, Vol. 1, pp. 402-3.

"The Friend," by Jewett & Porter. Volume 1, number 4, Wednesday, August 12, 1829. Size, 7x11 per page. Probably published about six months.

"The Weekly Messenger and Connecticut and Passumpsic River Valley Advertiser." By Samuel Eaton, Jr., Vol. 1, No. 1, weekly, commenced July 10, 1832; the latest we have seen is No. 52, vol. 1.

"The Caledonian," commenced in July, 1837, and still published.

The Vermont Farmer was started about 1870 by E. Hovey, of Waterford, ran through several hands, and finally was sold to American Cultivator, of Boston, Mass.

"The St. Johnsbury Index." Established in 1879 by A. B. Howe. Volume 1, number 2, issued Friday, December 12, 1879. A good looking weekly journal at $1.50 per year, with considerable local news, and not much politics.

The St. Johnsbury Republican, started by the Caledonia Co. Publishing Co., 1885. In 1892 a daily edition was started, which was discontinued in 1894. In 1895 the paper was purchased by L. P. Thayer.

—Chester.

"Freedom's Banner," weekly, by Prescott & Fellows. Volume 1, number 5, was issued June 25, 1828; the last we have seen is volume 2, number 5, June 24, 1829. With number 14, of volume 1, William W. Prescott became publisher, and he continued until number 30, of volume 1, when he was succeeded by B. F. Bellows. The "Banner" supported John Quincy Adams for the Presidency.

"Equal Rights, or Anti-Masonic Advocate," by J. Hemenway & E. J. W. Holbrook. Vol. 1, No. 4, is December 8, 1829.

"Freedom's Banner," commenced about 1823, and continued a year or two.

"Green Mountain Palladium," "World of Music," each published for a short time.

—Brandon.

At Brandon the "Vermont Telegraph," by Orson S. Murray, commenced 1829, and continued many years.

"The Brandon Post," by Patrick Welch, commenced 1849, and continued several years.

"North-eastern Christian Advocate," Rev. W. Ford, editor; a Baptist paper commenced January 1, 1857.

"Northern Visitor," by Rev. W. Ford; commenced Thursday, January 6, 1859, being a continuation of the Advocate; the last we have seen December 27, 1860.

"Brandon Gazette," H. Truss, editor, H. Tubbs, publisher. Commenced May, 1861.

"Brandon Monitor," D. L. Milliken editor and proprietor. Vol. 1, No. 1, Friday, July 4, 1862; at the end of six months the size was reduced one-third, and at the end of the year the paper suspended.

"Rutland and Addison County Whig." Published by the Brandon Whig Association. D. S. Murray editor. Vol. 1. No. 2, Brandon, March 12, 1840.

"Voice of Freedom," J. Holcomb editor and proprietor; commenced June, 1839, and the latest we have seen is No. 52, of vol. viii, June 17, 1847.

"The Otter Creek News," by D. C. Hackett; commenced in October, 1876; we have seen No. 6 of vol. 3.

The Brandon Union was started by A. N. Merchant in 1873, was published subsequently by H. M. Mott and Mott Brothers; then by Stillman B. Ryder; then by J. S. Tupper; now (1896) by the Brandon Publishing Co.

—Newfane.

"The Vermont Free Press." By Z. Eastman, editor and publisher; the first number printed June 7, 1834, at Fayetteville, and was continued about two years, when Mr. Eastman, considerably out of pocket, abandoned the enterprise, and moved to Chicago. See history of Newfane, pp. 113-16.

—Irasburgh.

"Yeoman's Record," commenced by E. Rawson, in 1845, stopped 1850.

"Orleans County Gazette," started by L. B. & J. L. Jameson, and continued five years, with several successive publishers; sold in 1855 to the "North Union" of West Charleston.

"Orleans Independent Standard," A. A. Earle, publisher. Commenced in 1856, and continued for ten years, when it was removed by Mr. Earle to Barton.

The "Green Mountain Express," started 1861 by H. & G. H. Bradford, and lived nearly a year.

—Springfield.

"Telegraph," 1853.

"Good Templars' Advocate and Fraternal Visitor." Vol. 1, No. 1, May, 1868, G. W. Foggett, publisher. 4 pages, monthly, size per page, 9x13 inches. No. 7 of Vol. 2, is 8 pages.

"The Enterprise." Vol. 1, No. 1, January, 1873, monthly. F. W. Stiles, publisher. 4 pp., size per page, 15x22 inches.

"The Springfield Bulletin." Vol. 1, No. 30, Saturday, September 9, 1876. Oliver A. Libby, editor and publisher. Weekly, 8 pages, size per page, 11x16 inches.

"The Independent." Vol. 1, No. 4, August 16, 1877. Charles F. Kelley, publisher. 4 pp., size per page, 12x16 inches.

"M. W. Newton's Monthly Journal." Vol. 1, No. 8, January 15, 1878. 4 pp., size per page, 6x9 inches.

"Vermont News." Vol. 1, No. 1, issued, Springfield, Vt., Saturday, November 15, 1879. 8 page folio, size per page, 13x21 inches. No name appears as editor or proprietor.

—Northfield.

"Star of Vermont," 1854.

"Northfield News," started 1879. George H. Richmond publisher. Present publisher (1896) F. N. Whitney.

"The Reveille." By Professor Charles Dole, of Norwich University; a quarto, 16 page monthly, Vol. XLI. New series, No. 9, is September, 1875. It was merged into a Boston paper about 1876.

—Royalton.

At Royalton, "Vermont Advocate and White River Advertiser," Wyman Spooner, editor and proprietor; commenced December, 1826, and continued at Royalton until February 2, 1830, when its publication was changed to Chelsea, Tuesday, July 20, and "White River Advertiser" dropped from the title; Tuesday, March 2, 1830, Dana Winslow, printer, until Tuesday, July 20, 1830. July 29, 1831, commenced Vol. 1, No. 1, new series, published by E. Avery, W. Spooner, editor, and name changed to "Vermont Advocate and State Paper." July 31, 1833, E. P. Walton, Jr., became publisher for the proprietor, in place of Mr. Avery, and so continued until August 28, 1833, which is the last date we have seen.

—Derby.

"The Northern Oziris." By J. M. Stevens, for the proprietors; Vol. 1, No. 1, weekly, commenced December 15, 1831; A. O. Houghton succeeded Mr. Stevens as publisher, after the issue of the second number. The latest we have seen is No. 15, Vol. 1.

Mr. Stevens was subsequently head printer on the "Vermont Patriot" at Montpelier, under J. T. Marston and C. G. Eastman.

—Johnson.

"Lamoille River Express," J. W. Remington, publisher, Charles G. Eastman, editor, commenced Friday, June 1, 1838; name changed to "Vermont State Paper and Lamoille and Orleans County Democrat," March 12, 1839, and continued until March 31, 1840, when Mr. Eastman made arrangements to establish the "Age" at Woodstock.

"The Scorpion," a campaign paper, by Charles G. Eastman, published weekly at Johnson, June 25, 1839, to August 30, 1839. Size 14x20 inches.

"Lamoille Standard," by Joseph Poland. Vol. 1, No. 44 is April 8, 1843, at Johnson; only published a short time.

"Family Visitor," established 1843, published only a short time.

"Lamoille Banner," commenced 1843.

—Sheldon.

"Republican," commenced about 1838, and continued not far from a year.

—Manchester.

"Bennington County Whig." 1838, for a year or two.

"Manchester Journal," commenced 1861. D. K. Simonds has been its publisher for many years.

—Chelsea.

"The Mother's Book," monthly, large 8vo., 24 pages, edited by Mrs. Sophia A. Hewes, January, 1838, to about 1840.

"Thursday News," commenced, 1838, and continued about two years.

"The Chelsa Post." Vol. 1, No. 44, Chelsea, Saturday, October 4, 1876. Published at West Randolph, by Lewis P. Thayer. Size 20x13 inches per page. Weekly. See Royalton.

—Swanton.

"North American," by H. J. Thomas. Vol. 1, No. 39, is January 8, 1840. Canadian politics.

"Swanton Herald," 1852. The Synchronist, 1859; lived but a short time.

"Swanton Courier," Vol. 3, No. 40, issued December 12, 1879; published every Saturday morning, office in Blake's block. T. H. Tobin, editor and proprietor to the present time (1896.) See "Vermont Historical Gazetteer." vol. 4, pp. 1100-2.

—Norwich.

"The Vermont Freeman," by St. Clair and Briggs. Vol. 1, No. 21, Norwich, Vt., April 22, 1843.

—Milton.

"Milton Herald," established in 1843, for only a short time.

—Waterbury.

"Free Mountaineer," 1849.

"Biblical Messenger," by A. A. Hoyt, monthly, published 1876-7.

"The Enterprise," by Mr. Hoyt, commenced January, 1875, and only a few numbers issued.

—Morrisville.

"American Citizen," 1851.

"The Vermont Citizen." A. A. Earle, editor. Vol. 7, No. 39, issued Thursday, December 18, 1879, suspended 1881.

"Lamoille News," 1881.

"News and Citizen," by Lewis & Fisk, 1883; published since 1885, by the Lamoille Publishing Co.

—Bradford.

"American Protector," A. B. F. Hildreth, editor. Vol. 1, No. 22, June 3, 1843, name changed to "Vermont Family Gazette," continued until about 1852, when the name was again changed to "White River Advertiser," and removed to White River Junction.

"The Northern Inquirer," by L. W. Bliss, publisher, and R. McK. Ormsby, editor, was commenced in 1851, changed to "Bradford Inquirer" about 1855, and the same year again changed to "Orange County Journal," and in 1857 merged into "Aurora of the Valley."

See Newbury newspapers.

"Green Mountain Farmer," semi-monthly, by L. R. Morris, commenced March, 1852, and published less than a year.

"Green Mountain Gem," by A. B. F. Hildreth, monthly, 8vo. pp. 24 each, 1843-48.

"Orange County Telegraph," by Chamberlain & Taylor, commenced in 1857; Mr. Taylor soon retired.

"National Opinion," A. A. Earle, editor, commenced in June, 1865; March 1, 1867, Mr. Earle retired, and D. W. Cobb became editor, and soon after proprietor. Mr. Cobb disposed of the paper to the "Bradford Publishing Co.," May 1, 1871. May 1, 1874, S. F. Stanton became editor and publisher, and June 6 of that year changed the name to "Bradford Opinion."

See McKeen's "History of Bradford," for additional, pp. 64-7.

"Bradford Opinion," Orange County Publishing Co., proprietors. D. W. Cobb, editor. No. 31, Vol. XIV, issued December 20, 1879.

From 1879 to '81 two "Bradford Opinions" were published, each claiming to be the "original Simon pure." In 1881, the two were united under the name of "The United Opinion," H. E. Parker, publisher, and so continues to date.

—Newbury.

"Christian Messenger," Methodist, commenced Friday, March 12, 1847; after a year or two it was moved to Montpelier, where it was published from about 1848 to 1853, then published at Northfield a number of years, when its publication was again transferred to Montpelier, where it is continued ; in January, 1849, the name was changed to "Vermont Christian Messenger."

"Aurora of the Valley," an 8 page quarto, semi-monthly, by L. J. McIndoe, commenced in April, 1848; subsequently enlarged to an 8 page folio, with D. B. Dudley, as associate editor for some time. In 1867 or 1868, the name was changed to "Vermont Cultivator," then to "Aurora and Cultivator."

"Northern Protestant and American Advocate," commenced in 1848.

—Ludlow.

At Ludlow, "Genius of Liberty," commenced in 1847, and only continued a short time.

"The Vermont Star," by George A. Tuttle. Vol. 1, No. 13, November 14, 1849.

"Voice Among the Mountains." Vol. 1, No. 1, Thursday, January 12, 1860; an 8 page weekly, size of page 9x12 inches; R. S. Warner, printer. No. 43, of Vol. 1, the size was increased about one third. In 1861 published in folio. September 12, 1861, is the last issue we have seen.

"The Blotter," Bacon & Warner, proprietors, W. A. Bacon, editor, R. S. Warner, publisher ; commenced in September, 1854, folio, size 17x24 inches, and in 1885, enlarged to 21x36 inches. The last number we have seen, December 20, 1855.

"Black River Gazette," Vol. 1, No. 1, commenced Wednesday, December 19, 1866, by Warner & Burbank; size 22x36, folio; enlarged to 22x38, April, 1867.

Mr. Burbank, one of the proprietors, died March 11, 1867; he was born in Campton, N. H., October 2, 1811; by profession a teacher; lived twelve years in Ludlow. Subsequent to the death of Mr. Burbank, Henry D. Foster appears as editor, and the paper published in quarto form, 8 pp, for a short time, but in July, 1872, is in enlarged folio. By Warner and Ryder, Stillman B. Ryder, editor.

"Black River Transcript." Vol. 1. No. 1, Tuesday, April 17, 1866, D. E. Johnson, editor and proprietor, the last number we have seen being No. 23, of Vol. 1.

—Braintree.

About 1865 Dan. Tarbell and his son-in-law, Estabrook, started "The World's Paper" at the Dan. Tarbell spiritual and free trade settlement, called Sandusky, which was devoted chiefly to Tarbell, and Tarbell philosophy. It lived two years or so, and went up. In 1857, Estabrook and W. Scott Abbott started "The Green Mountain Sibyl," devoted to spiritualism and literature. Dau. being at the bottom of it; but said bottom soon fell out, and the print-

ing office was taken to Randolph, and used in printing the "Statesman" and "Ingleside."

—Lyndon.

"The Vermont Union," established in 1865, C. M. Chase, proprietor.

LYNDON, VT., December 27, 1879.

Dear Sir:—I find under my papers on my table your letter of October 22 unanswered. Late now, but will reply:

1st, "Union" started February 1. 1865.

2nd, No such institution ever started in Vermont before or since.

3d, I graduated at Dartmouth, July, 1853. Taught music in the Cincinnati College in 1854-55-56; also at same time studied law with President Allen, of Farmers' College, College Hill, just out of the city. In 1856 went to Sycamore, Ill, continued law, and music teaching; admitted to the bar summer of 1857. Formed partnership with one Simonds, firm Simonds & Chase, also elected and served as police magistrate, or trial justice of the city till 1861 when I went into the army with a brass band, to kill the cussed rebels, of course, but none of them heard the music, and so not many "deceased" on my account. Was in Rolla, Mo., for three months and during that time somebody killed Lyon, which demoralized us somewhat. In 1863 went to Kansas; staid one year. First newspaper business, edited "DeKalb county, Ill., Sentinel," in 1858, and continued contributor for it several years, also corresponded with musical and other papers; was local editor on the "Leavenworth Times" in 1864; went to Congress in 1866 and 1868—no, no, come to think, I was *not* elected. Trained under M. D. Gilman, at St Louis in the summer of 1876, also helped *elect* Sam. Tilden. Ask something harder. Truly yours, C. M. CHASE.

—Sandusky.

"The World's Paper." Vol. 2, No. 16, June, 1866. By Daniel Tarbell. Size, 17x22 inches per page.

Devoted to Spiritualism. See Braintree.

— White River Junction.

"Republican Observer," started in 1878, by Thomas Hale, professing to represent the Daniel Webster and Henry Clay element in Vermont. We fear Mr. Hale falls short of the "mark of his high calling." Suspended in the spring of 1880.

—Wells River.

"The Riverside." By W. S. S. Buck. Vol. 1, No. 32, is August 16, 1879. Weekly, 8 page folio.

—Barre.

The first newspaper in Barre was "The Barre Times," monthly, by Stillman ; published during the year 1871.

"Barre Herald," by E. N. Hyzer, three numbers of which have been issued weekly ; to be continued.

The "Herald" died July 10, 1880, aged nine months.

"The Barre Enterprise," weekly, Dec. 11, 1880. to April, 1881. by L. P. Thayer; continued subsequently by W. F. Scott.

—Barton.

"Orleans County Monitor," George H. Blake, editor. Volume 8, number 51, issued December 22, 1879. Continued (1896) by same publisher.

—Richford.

"Richford Gazette," weekly, commenced Oct. 1, 1878, One dollar per annum. Continued.

For additional newspapers, etc., established in Vermont, and published for longer or shorter periods, see Walton's Vermont Registers; Thompson, Z., History of Vermont.

The above brief notes on printing and newspapers in Vermont are so meagre and fragmentary that I hesitated about printing them; but as they may be of slight service to the future historian of newspapers in the State, I decided to let them in.

AMATEUR PRINTING.

The first amateur paper in Vermont of which we have any record was the "Union World," of Burlington, in 1861; but it was not until 1872 that an amateur paper in every sense of the word appeared.

In the latter year five papers sprang into existence, two at Burlington, one at Rutland, one at Bennington, and one at Woodstock. They all had a fair run for about two years and after that slowly and surely went the way of all amateur papers, and "woodbined." Of these the "Acorn," of Woodstock, was the best in every respect. In 1873 the "Mustard Seed," of Bennington, was first issued, an offshoot of the "North Star," published at that place the year previous.

Between the early part of 1874 and the middle part of 1875, a few sheets dragged out a feeble existence, leaving behind them no records showing their age. One, the "Young American," however, was an exception. But it was only during the editor's attendance at school that it was published within the limits of the State.

In 1875 the "Model," of Rutland, was the only paper of any consequence in the State. It lived through fifteen numbers, and was followed by the "White Knight," afterwards the "Knight," of Morrisville. This paper was conducted until its seventh number, when it suspended. The "Postage Stamp Reporter," of Montpelier, took a high position in its particular branch of amateurdom, but suspended in September, 1877.

Several others, such as the "Young Folks Gazette," of St. Albans, "Buck's Monthly," of West Randolph, and the "Advance," of Brattleboro, especially the latter, have enjoyed a good reputation and extended circulation. The "Green Mountain Boy," was another live sheet. Besides these there have been nearly as many more that have struggled through a few months, and then died.

The first association of amateur journalists in Vermont was formed at Burlington, and called the Queen City A. P. A., Will H. Nichols being the first President. This association lasted a few months, and was then merged into a Green Mountain A. P. A. This latter association met for the first time at Burlington, January 17, 1874. The second convention was held at Montpelier in the fall of '75, and after that amateur affairs began to decline throughout the State.

NORTHFIELD.—"The Hatchet," started January, 1874, by George H. Richmond, now of the "Monthly." 4 pages, 8 columns; enlarged with April number to 12 columns. Fourteen numbers issued. Official organ G. M. A. P. A. Reached a circulation of over 1,000 copies.

"The Thunderbolt," started April, 1875, by E. E. Thompson. Monthly. 4 pages, 8 columns. Two numbers issued.

"The North Star," started April, 1878, by Fred L. Egerton. Monthly. Small four page paper. One copy issued.

"The Amateur Herald," started May, 1878, by E. E. Thompson and George D. Thomas. Monthly. Four pages, eight columns. Two numbers issued. Second number a double one.

BELLOWS FALLS.—"Coming Man," by Will H. Nichols. Jerry Leech, publisher, 1879.

UNDERHILL CENTER.—"Amateur Herald." George F. Terrill, editor; E. E. Thompson, publisher, June, 1879.

WEST RANDOLPH.—"Buck's Monthly," W. S. S. Buck, 1872, now publisher of "Riverside" at Wells River, ran some two years, enlarging to 16 pages at last days. Then merged into "Pen and Pencil," and edited by E. N. Hyzer, later of "Barre Herald."

"Golden Reaper," started April, 1879, by Tewksbury & DuBois. Yet alive (1880).

"Pen and Pencil," 1874, E. N. Hyzer, editor and publisher.

WINDSOR.—"Monthly Visitor," started 1878, by William Sargent.

BURLINGTON.—"Union World," started in 1861, S. W. Nichols, publisher. It suspended in about one year.

"Bee," was started in 1862, by Nichols and Stiles, publishers, who issued it six months, and then it suspended. Afterwards resumed by Stiles & Co., but suspended again in five months.

"Burlington Eagle," Burlington, 1872. Henry S. Kimball publisher. 25 cents per year. Four pages, 6½x4¼, two columns per page, and issued weekly. After its twelfth number the size was increased to 7¼x5½, and the price changed to $1. It was issued regularly till December, 1873.

"Union," Burlington, 1872. Sales & Nichols, publishers. Issued weekly. It started with four pages, 8½x6½, but enlarged to 9x7, with its ninth number, and after its fourteenth issue W. H. Nichols assumed the whole proprietorship and issued it in magazine form of 16 pages, monthly. It suspended in 1874.

WOODSTOCK.—"Acorn," in 1872. American Publishing Co., publishers. Four pages, 6x4½, three columns per page. With its 13th number the Acorn went into the hands of Campbell & Dana, who issued it for about one year.

RUTLAND.—"Amateur Monthly," 1872, McLean & Aiken, publishers. It had 16 pages, two columns per page, and was suspended after its fourth number.

"Rutland Times," Rutland, 1872, Frank M. McLean, publisher, until No. 25, Vol. 1, when it was published by McLean & Aiken. It had four pages, 4½x7, and was issued weekly. With No. 6, Vol. 2, it was changed to magazine form.

"Model," Rutland, 1876, C. E. Mailhoit, publisher. Four pages, 5½x6, and issued monthly. Suspended with No. 2, Vol. 2.

BENNINGTON.—"North Star," 1872, Park Valentine, publisher. Four pages, 7x5, and was issued monthly. Suspended with its fourth number.

"Mustard Seed," Bennington, 1873, Park Valentine, publisher. Four pages, 3x5, and printed monthly. Suspended with its 12th number.

MONTPELIER.—"The Vermonter," Fred H. Kimball, editor and publisher, July, 1879. Four pages, eight columns. "The representative amateur paper of Vermont."

The "Era," by Edward Clark, and the "Echo," by Charles F. Burnham, were started about 1875, while both editors were serving their apprenticeship in the "Argus and Patriot" office. Both journals proved very short lived, only one or two numbers being issued.

"Young American," Montpelier, 1874, William M. Kendall, Jr., printer and publisher. This was an eight paged paper, printed at Montpelier while its editor was attending school. After completing his education the paper was removed to its former place of publication, Lebanon, N. H., Mr. Kendall now being the editor and publisher of the "Dollar Weekly" at that place.

"Postage Stamp Reporter," Montpelier, 1877, C. F. Buswell, publisher. Eight pages, 7x5½, and was issued monthly. It was, as its name implies, devoted to stamp collecting. Discontinued on increase of postal regulation, with its September, 1877, number.

"Green Mountain Boys," Montpelier, 1877, Tuttle & Dewey, publishers. Eight pages, 6x8 and issued monthly.

"White Knight," Morrisville, 1876, "The order of the White Knights," publishers. Four pages, 7x10, and printed monthly. This paper was afterwards called the "Knight," and was conducted by George H. Sanborn. It was suspended with its 7th number.

"Advance," Brattleboro, C. D. Barrett, publisher, 1877. Four pages, 7x4½ and issued weekly. It was suspended in 1878.

"Vermonter," East Fairfield, 1877, D. R. Pomeroy, publisher. Four small pages with supplement. It did not live more than a few months.

"Young People's Gazette," St. Albans, 1877. Novelty Publishing Co., publishers. Printed in magazine form, 16 pages, and issued monthly.

The "Yankee Spice-Box." Vol. 1, No. 1, East Brookfield, Vt., March, 1876, at 25 cents per year, with quaint illustrations, pp. 4. Size per page, 6x9 inches. Monthly.

—Amateur Books.

"A Week of Sport," by Fred E. Darling, 1877. Leech and Darling, publishers, Bellows Falls.

"Ada, a Love Story." Anonymous, 1878. Charles D. Barrett, publisher, Brattleboro.

Several others have been published in the State, but we have been unable to gain any information in regard to them.

PROCEEDINGS, *of a Rutland County* Republican Convention, Holden at West Rutland, 30th July, 1813. Rutland: Printed by Fay & Davison. Broadside.

A war Convention.

—And Address of the Vermont Republican Convention Friendly to the election of Andrew Jackson to the next Presidency of the United States, Holden at Montpelier, June 27, 1828. Montpelier: Geo. W. Hill, Patriot office, 1828. 8vo, pp. 24.

—of the Convention, Holden at Windsor, Vt., January 20, 1836: for the purpose of taking preliminary measures for a Rail Road through the Valleys of the Connecticut and Passumpsic Rivers to the St. Lawrence. Published by the request of the Convention. Chronicle Press. Windsor, Vt. 8vo, pp. 24.

—of the Free Convention held at Rutland, Vt., July 25th, 26th and 27th, 1858. Motto. Boston: J. B. Yerrington and Son, 21 Cornhill. 1858. 8vo, pp. 185.

Relates to Progress, Free Thought, etc.

—of the Vermont Convention of Fruit Growers. [1848.] 8vo, pp. 8.

—and instructions Concerning the System of International, Literary and Scientific Exchanges, Established by Alexandre Vattemare.

Published by Order of the Legislature of Vermont. Burlington : Free Press Office. 1848. 8vo, pp. 80.

—*of the "Montpelier* [Vt. Congregational] Association," in reply to annexed statements of Henry Jones, one of that Body, in relation to the influence of Freemasonry in the Churches. Danville, Vt: E. Eaton, Printer. 1830. 12mo, pp. 22.
See Jones, Henry; Masonic; Letters on Masonry.

—*of the Annual Encampment*, Department of Vermont, Grand Army of the Republic, held at Burlington, Vt., January 12, 1872, with Reports of W. W. Henry, Dep't. Commander, and the Officers of the Department Staff. Rutland: Tuttle & Co. Printers, 1872. 8vo, pp. 23.
Continued.

—*of Brooks Post, No. 25*, Department of Vermont, G. A. R., Chester, Vt., upon the occasion of the Decoration of the graves of their fallen comrades. May 30, 1870. Motto. Brattleboro : Printed by George E. Selleck. 1870. 8vo, pp. 14.

—*of the Third Annual Convention* of the W. C. T. U. of Vermont, held at St. Albans, September 26th and 27th, 1877. St. Albans: Messenger Steam Printing Establishment. 1877. 8vo, pp. 32.

—*of the Vermont Juvenile Missionary Society*, at their Annual Meeting, in Vergennes, October 11, 1820. Middlebury : Printed by Copeland and Allen. 1821. 8vo, pp. 28.
See Vermont Juvenile Missionary Society.

—*And Revised Roster* of the Fifth New York Veteran Volunteer Cavalry Association. 1895. Published by the Sec'y, C. T. S. Pierce, Vergennes, Vt. Free Press Asso. 1895. pp. 41.

Proctor. *The Proctor Cook Book*, by the Ladies of the Union Church Society. Rutland : Tuttle & Co. 1895. 8vo, pp. 66.

Proctor, Redfield. *Message* of His Excellency Redfield Proctor, to the General Assembly of the State of Vermont, October Session, 1878. Montpelier : J. & J. M. Poland, Printers, 1878. 8vo, pp. 23.

—*Message* of Redfield Proctor, Retiring Governor, to the General Assembly of the State of Vermont, October Session, 1880. Rutland : Tuttle & Co., Printers. 1880. 8vo, pp. 35.
Redfield Proctor was born in Proctorsville, in the town of Cavendish, Vt., June 1, 1831. He graduated from Dartmouth College in 1851; studied law at the Albany, N. Y. Law School; and commenced practice in the office of his uncle, Judge Isaac F. Redfield. During the War of the Rebellion he was quartermaster of the Third Regiment, Vt. Vols., served on the staff of Gen. Wm. F. Smith; was major of the Fifth Vermont; and subsequently Colonel of the Fifteenth Vermont Regiment. After the close of the war he practised law at Rutland, till he became interested in some of the Rutland marble quarries, and in time was made President of the Vermont Marble Company, the heaviest marble company in the world. He was a member of the Vermont House of Representatives in 1867, '68 and '88; was State Senator, 1874-5; Lieutenant-Governor, 1876-8; Governor of Vermont, 1878-80; Secretary of War under Pres. Harrison, 1889 to 1891, when he resigned to accept an appointment to the U. S Senate, to fill the vacancy caused by the resignation of Senator Geo. F. Edmunds. He was elected U. S. Senator in 1892 for the unexpired portion of the term and also for the full term, beginning March 4, 1893. He married Miss Emily J. Dutton of Cavendish, and they have had five children, of whom two sons and two daughters are living.

The Progressive Reader or Juvenile Monitor. Carefully selected from the most approved writers, Designed for the Younger Classes of Children in Primary Schools. Motto. Stereotyped by Fisk & Chase, Concord, N. H. Montpelier, Vt.: Published by George W. Hill. 1833. 18mo, pp. 216.

Prompter, The. *The Prompter*, or a commentary on common sayings and subjects which are full of common sense—the best sense in the world. Motto. Windsor, Vt.: Published by Simeon Ide. 1827. 18mo, pp. 96.

Proudfit, A. *Ministerial Labor and Support:* A Sermon preached at Middlebury, Feb. 21, 1810, at the Ordination of Mr. Henry Davis, and his induction as President of Middlebury College. By Alexander Proudfit, Pastor of the first Presbyterian Church in Salem, N. Y. Salem, N. Y.: Dodd & Rumsey.

—*A Sermon* preached August 19, 1817, before "The Middlebury College Charitable Society for educating indigent youth for the Gospel Ministry." By Alexander Proudfit, D. D. Motto. Middlebury, (Vt.): Printed by Frederick P. Allen, October, 1817. 8vo, pp. 32.

Prouty, Miss L. A. *Discussion;* Universalism vs. Orthodoxy.
See Foster, E. S.

Psalms, *Carefully* suited to the Christian Worship in the United States of America. Being an Improvement of the old Version of the Psalms of David. Motto. Rutland, Vt.: Printed by Fay & Davison. 1844. 24mo, pp. 299.
In same volume, Hymns and Spiritual Songs, in three Books. By I. Watts, D. D. Same imprint. pp. 268.
—*And Hymns.* Choice Selection of Psalms, Hymns, and Spiritual Songs, for the use of Christians. By John Mackenzie, John Rand, Benjamin Putnam, Christopher Martin and Jasper Hazen. Motto. Woodstock : Printed by David Watson. Price 68 cents. 1819. 18mo, pp 600.
The first book printed in Woodstock. Two or more editions printed.
—*Carefully* suited to the Christian Worship in the United States of America. Rutland, Vt.: 1814. 24mo.

Publishers, Editors & Printers. *Convention* of Vermont Publishers, Editors and Printers, Held at Montpelier, November 8, 1867, and Records of the Association. 1868 and 1869. Montpelier : Printed by J. & J. M. Poland. 1870. 8vo, pp. 23.
Continued.

Putnam, Allen. *Tipping his Tables.* See Gregory, John.

Putnam, B. *A Sketch* of the life of Elder Benj. Putnam, embracing his Christian Experience, call to the Ministry, together with an account of the Religious Changes Through which he has passed, especially those of recent date, with some of the most prominent reasons for his present views of Divine Truth. Written by Himself. Woodstock : Printed by David Watson. 1821. 12mo, pp. 216.

Putnam, Rev. N. F. *A Sermon* preached in St. Andrew's Church, St. Johnsbury, Vt., Nov. 17, A. D. 1878, by Rev. N. F. Putnam. Printed for St. Andrew's Church Guild, by Royal Cummings, St. Johnsbury. 1878.

Quechee. *The Manual* of the Congregational Church in Quechee, Vt., 1881. Times Steam Book and Job Print. Bellows Falls, Vt.: 12mo, pp. 33.

The Quicksilver Mining Company. *Annual Report* (with Tables and Tabular Statements.) Submitted at the Annual Meeting of the Stockholders, Held in New York, June, 1896. Burlington: Free Press Association, 1896. 8vo, pp. 44.

Quarterly Journal, *devoted* to Female Education. Published by Ripley Female College, Poultney, Vt. January, 1866. (Vol. I, No. 4.) Fair Haven, Vt.: D. Leonard, Printer. (n. d.) 8vo, pp. 36, and cover. Plate.

Quincy, and Others. *An Address* of Members of the House of Representatives of the Congress of the United States, to their Constituents, on the subject of the War with Great Britain. Bennington, (Vt.): S. Williams & Co. 1812. 8vo.

RAILROADS.

VERMONT CENTRAL AND VERMONT AND CANADA.

—*An Act to Incorporate* the Vermont Central Railroad Company. Passed by the Legislature of Vermont, at their October Session, 1843. Charlestown: 1845. 8vo, pp. 12.

—*Another Edition,* including by-laws. Montpelier, Vt.: E. P. Walton & Son, Printers. 1850. 12mo, pp. 16.

—*Report of the Engineer* on the Route surveyed (via. Northfield) for the Vermont Central Railroad, from Connecticut River at Hartford, Vt. to Lake Champlain, at Burlington. Boston: S. N. Dickinson, Printer. 1845. 8vo, pp. 12.

—*Report of the Survey* of the Gulf Route from Berlin via. Montpelier to Royalton. Boston: Lathrop & Bense, Printers. 1845. 8vo, pp. 12. Map.

—*First Annual Report* of the Directors of the Vermont Central Railroad Company, to the Stockholders. Submitted July 15, 1846. Montpelier: E. P. Walton & Sons, Printers. 1846. 8vo, pp. 24.

—*Second Annual Reports* of the Directors and Treasurer of the Vermont Central Railroad Company: Submitted to the Stockholders, June 4, 1847. Montpelier: E. P. Walton & Sons, Printers. 1847. 8vo, pp. 14.

—*Third, Fourth, Fifth and Sixth* Annual Reports, imprint the same.
Continued.

—*Rules and Regulations* of the Vermont Central Railroad. Montpelier: E. P. Walton & Sons, Printers. (1849). 12mo, pp. 23.

—*Proceedings* of the Convention of the Northern Lines of Railway, Held at Boston, in December, 1850, and January, 1851. Boston: 1851. 8vo, pp. 128.
Relates largely to the Vermont Central.

—*Report* of the Trustees of the Vermont Central Railroad Company, appointed to report upon the condition of the Company, and the issue of mortgage Bonds. Presented to the Directors, November 14, 1851. Boston: Printed by W. S. Drummond. 1851. 8vo, pp. 16.

—*Letter* to the Shareholders of the Vermont Central Railroad from Josiah Quincy, Jr. March, 1852. Boston: 1852. 8vo, pp. 26.

—*Reply* of the Directors to the Letter of Josiah Quincy, Jr., to the Stockholders of the Vermont Central Railroad. Published by Order of the Corporation. Montpelier: E. P. Walton & Son. 1852. 8vo, pp. 45.

—*Statement* to the Stockholders of the Vermont Central Railroad Company, as read at Cochituate Hall, Boston, April 20, 1852, by John W. Seymour. Boston: 1852. 8vo, pp. 22.

—*Proceedings* of the Stockholders of the Vermont Central Railroad, at a Special meeting Holden at Northfield, Vermont, May 4, 5, 1852: Printed by Order of the Corporation. Montpelier: E. P. Walton & Son. 1852. 8vo, pp. 16.

—*Report* of the Investigating Committee of the Vermont Central Railroad Co. to the Stockholders, July 1, 1853. Boston: Press of George C. Rand, No. 3 Cornhill. 1853. 8vo, pp. 348.

—*Report* of the Committee on Consolidation. Vermont Central Railroad Co., and Vermont & Canada Railroad Co. Boston: 1856. 8vo, pp. 26.

—*Henry B. Stacy* vs. Vermont Central Rail Road Co. Chittenden County, Supreme Court, January Term, 1859. Plaintiff's Brief. Wm. Weston, For Plaintiff. 8vo, pp. 15. Appendix, pp. 6.

—*Constitution* of the Vermont Central Railroad Library Association, and Catalogue of Books. Northfield, Vt., 1859. Montpelier: E. P. Walton, Printer. 1859. 8vo, pp. 26.
Another edition, St. Albans, 1874. 8vo, pp. (58).

—*Constitution* of the Vermont Central Railroad Library Association, and Catalogue of Books. St. Albans, Vermont: 1874. 8vo, pp. 51 (and 4.)

—*Statement of Facts and Points,* arising under the Suit of the First Mortgage Bondholders of the Vermont Central Railroad Company, for the Removal of the Trustees of Said Bondholders, Pending in the United States Circuit Court for the District of Vermont. Boston: Press of George C. Rand & Avery. 1862. 4to, pp. 31.

—*The Vermont* and Canada Rail Road Co. v. The Vermont Central Rail Road Co. et als. Supreme Court of Vermont, Franklin County, January Term, 1861. Opinion of the Court. Rutland: Printed by Geo. A. Tuttle & Co. 1862. 8vo, pp. 28.

—*New York to Montreal,* The Harlem, Harlem Extension, Rutland and Burlington, and Vermont Central Railroads. Illustrated Map and Time table. Price 20 cts. For sale at News Offices and on boats and cars. New York: 1870. sqr 12mo, pp. 40.

—*Report* of the Special Committee Appointed by the Legislature, at its Biennial Session in 1872, to Investigate Charges Against Certain Railroad Companies. Montpelier: Nov., 1874. 8vo, pp. 23.

—*In Chancery.* Franklin County. Vt. & Canada Railroad Company vs. Vt. Central

Railroad Company and others. C. W. Willard, Solicitor, 8vo, pp. 8. Dec. 16, 1875.

—*State of Vermont.* Franklin County. In Chancery. Vt. & Canada Railroad Company vs. Vt. Central Railroad Company and others. C. W. Willard Solicitor of the Vermont & Canada Railroad Company. 8vo, pp. 18. March 3d, 1876.

—*In Chancery.* Franklin County, September Term, 1876. Vt. & Canada Railroad Company vs. Vt. Central Railroad Company and others. The Answer of the Vermont & Canada Railroad Company to the Petition filed Dec. 26, 1876, by the Central Vermont Railroad Company and Others. C. W. Willard, Solicitor for the Vermont & Canada Railroad Co, rl. 8vo, pp. 27.

—*In Chancery.* Franklin County. Vt. & Canada Railroad Company vs. Vt. Central Railroad Company and Others. Accounting. Hon. Paul Dillingham, Hon. D. C. Denison, and John L. Edwards, Special Masters. Orator's request for Special findings. C. W. Willard, Solicitor for Orator. 1877. rl 8vo, pp. 86.

—*Charters and Mortgages* of the Vermont Central Line. Railway Laws of Vermont to 1857. Rutland and Burlington Charter. Table of Contents ; Vt. Central R. R. Co., Charter ; Vt. & Canada Charter ; Vt. & Canada, Amendments to Charter ; Vermont & Canada Lease ; Vermont Central R. R. Co., First Mortgage, also Second Mortgage ; Private Corporations ; General Railroad Law ; Acts Relating to Railroad, 1851, to 1856. Charter of Champlain & Connecticut River R. R. Co. Six different Amendments to the same. Burlington : Printed by M. D. L. Thompson & Co. 1857. 8vo, pp. 141.

—*Vt. Central et al.* Charters of the Vermont Central, Vermont and Canada, and Central Vermont Railroads. The first and second Mortgages and Deeds of Surrender of the Vermont Central Railroad Company. Orders and Decrees in the cause Vermont and Canada R. R. Co. vs. Vermont Central R. R. Co., et al. St. Albans : Advertiser Steam Printing House. 1875. 8vo, pp. 427, viii.
Contains a history of the various and intricate operations of the Managers of the Vermont Central railroad.

—*Hearing* before the Special Masters to adjust the Accounts of the Receivers and Managers of the Vermont Central and Vt. and Canada R. R's. Testimony of John Gregory Smith, from the Official Minutes. St. Albans : Advertiser Printing office. 1875. 8vo, pp. 188.

—*Reports* of the Committee and Trustees of the Vermont Central Railroad First Mortgage Bondholders, for the year ending February 8, 1865. Boston : 1865. 8vo, pp. 28.

—*The same* for 1866. 8vo, pp. 22.

—*The same* for 1867. 8vo, pp. 14.

—*Annual* Report of the President and Directors to the Stockholders of the Vermont and Canada Railroad Company, November 1, 1860. St. Albans : Whiting & Davis, Printers. 1860. 8vo, pp. 24.
Continued.
See Davenport, C. N., Argument, in 1875.

—*A Review* of Proceedings in the Legislature of Vermont, October Session, 1847, on the Bill Granting to the Vermont and Canada Railroad Company the Right to Bridge Lake Champlain, Opposite Rouses Point. From the Vermont Watchman & State Journal. Montpelier : E. P. Walton & Sons, Printers. 1847. 8vo, pp. 29.

—*Circular* of Trustees and Managers of Vt. Central and Vt. & Canada R. R's. May, 1867, St. Albans, Vt.: Printed by E. B. Whiting & Co. 1867. 8vo, pp. 10.

—*Report* of the Trustees and Managers of the Vermont Central Railroad to the First and Second Mortgage Bondholders and Stockholders of the Vermont and Canada Railroad Company. For the year ending May 31, 1868. Boston: 1868. 8vo, pp. 11.

—*The same* for 1869. 8vo, pp. 11.

—*The same* for 1870. 8vo, pp. 12.

—*The same* for eighteen months ending November 30, 1871. Boston: 1872. 8vo, pp. 16.

—*The Vermont Central* and Vermont and Canada Railroads. Report of the Trustees and Managers, and Action of the Stock and Bondholders, at Horticultural Hall, Boston, Oct. 2, 1872. Boston : Printed by Rand, Avery & Co. 1872. 8vo, pp. 89.

—*Report* of the Joint Special Committee to Investigate the Vt. Central Railroad Management. Ordered by Joint Resolution adopted at the Biennial Session, 1872. St. Albans : Messenger Printing Establishment. 1873. 8vo, pp. 470, 56, 4, 21.

—*In Chancery.* Rutland Railroad Co. vs. Central Vermont R. R. Co. Et Al. Answer of Defendants. J. Gregory Smith and Worthington C. Smith. Filed September 24, 1875. 8vo, pp. 19.

—*The same,* Answer of Defendant, Central Vermont R. R. Co. Filed Sept. 24, 1875. 8vo, pp. 6.

—*In Chancery.* Franklin County, September Term, 1876. Vermont & Canada R. R. Co. vs. Vermont Central R. R. Co., et als. Petition of the Central Vermont R. R. Co., Receivers, &c., for leave to sell the Vt. Central & Vermont & Canada Railroads. B. F. Fifield, Solicitor. 8vo, pp. 15.

—*Answer* to the Petition, by the various parties in interest. 8vo, pp. 129.

—*Amendment* to the Petition, filed May 16, 1877. 8vo, pp. 36.

—*Testimony* in the Case, on the Petition to Sell, 8vo, pp. 74.

—*Petitioners' Brief* in the Case. B. F. Fifield, L. P. Poland, Asahel Peck, for Petitioners. 8vo, pp. 30.

—*Brief* for Vt. & Canada Railroad Company opposing the Petition. By C. W. Willard and Aldace F. Walker. 8vo, pp. 83.

—*Brief* of 1st and 2d Mortgage Bondholders, in opposition to the Petition. pp. 11.

—*Brief* of the Rutland Railroad Co., in opposition, By J. Prout, Solicitor. 8vo, pp. 19.

—*Brief* in behalf of 2d Mortgage Bondholders, opposed to the Petition for leave to sell. By F. A. Brooks, for himself and others. 8vo, pp. 18.

—*Points* in behalf of certain First Mortgage Bondholders in opposition to the Petition. By E. J. Phelps, July, 1877; Special Term. 8vo, pp. 23.

—*Report* of the Special Masters, in the case of Vermont and Canada R. R. Co. vs. Vermont Central R. R. Co., And Others. Filed April 24, 1877. St. Albans, Vt.: Advertiser Print. 1877. 8vo, pp. 175.
Paul Dillingham, Dudley C. Denison, and John L. Edwards, Masters. Purports to give a pretty full history of the management of the Vermont Central from 1861 to 1873.

—*Supreme Court.* Franklin County. Special Term, July, 1877. Vermont & Canada R. R. Co. vs. Vt. Central R. R. Co. Points in behalf of Certain First Mortgage Bondholders, of the Vt. Central R. R. Co.
See Phelps, Edward J.

—*Vermont & Canada* Railroad Company, vs. Vermont Central Railroad Company and others. Supreme Court, July Term, 1877. Opinion of the Court. 8vo. pp. 66.
Petition denied. See Barrett, James.

—*The Summer Excursionist* of the Central Vermont Railroad Co. For the Season of 1877. St. Albans, Vt. Frank Wood, Railroad Printer, 352 Washington st., Boston. 16mo, pp. 176.

—*James R. Langdon,* et al., vs. Vermont & Canada Railroad Co., et al. Franklin County. In Chancery, April Term, 1878. 8vo, pp. 33, 35, 9, 64, 52, and 22.
Contains a pretty full history of the case.

—*State of Vermont.* Supreme Court, General Term, 1879. James R. Langdon, et als., vs. Vermont & Canada Railroad Co., et als. Opinion of Hon. James Barrett, (Late First Associate Justice of the Supreme Court) as filed by him in Court, January 12, 1881. 8vo, pp. 16.

—*U.S. Circuit Court,* District of Vermont, February Term, 1881. Judith W. Andrews et als. vs. J. Gregory Smith et als. Opinion of Hon. Hoyt H. Wheeler, Overruling Defendants' plea to Jurisdiction. 8vo, pp. 15.

—*United States Circuit Court,* District of Vermont. October Term, 1881. Jonathan Dwight et als. vs. Central Vermont Railroad et als. Mr. Phelps' Argument for Plaintiffs on Jurisdictional Questions Raised by the Pleas of Defendants. Boston: 1881. 8vo, pp. 36.
See Vermont Railroad Commissioner's Reports.

RUTLAND AND BURLINGTON.

—*Report* of the Directors of the Rutland and Burlington Rail Road Company, at their Annual Meeting, at Rutland. Held 12th January, 1848. Burlington: Free Press Office. 1848. 8vo, pp. 13.
Report for 1849, pp. 22; for 1850, pp. 15; for 1851, pp. 18; for 1852, pp. 7; report for 1853, Broadside; report for 1854, pp. 12; report for 1855, pp. 16; report for 1856, pp. 12, 1857, pp. 14; 1858, pp. 13; 1859, pp. 12; 1860, pp. 13; 1861, pp. 12; 1862, pp. 12. Continued.

—*The Opinion* of the Chancellor, in the Case of Byron Stevens vs. The Rutland and Burlington Railroad Company and Others. Burlington: Chauncey Goodrich, 1851. 8vo, pp. 38.

—*Paris Fletcher* et als. vs. Rutland and Burlington R. R. Co. et als. In Chancery, Rutland County, March Term, 1858. Opinion of Bennett, Chancellor. Burlington: Daily Times Print, 154 Church Street. 1858, 8vo, pp. 20, (1).

—*In Chancery.* Windham County Term, 1863, Cheever & Hart, Trustees, et al. v. The Rutland and Burlington R. R. Co. Birchard & Stewart, Trustees, et. al. Opinion of Chancellor Barrett, upon the Motion of Orators For Injunction or Receiver. Rutland: Printed by Tuttle & Gay. 1863. 8vo, pp. 22.

—*Copy of a memorial* to the Legislature, of the Managers and Trustees of the Rutland & Burlington Rail Road. Rutland: Tuttle, Gay & Co., Printers, 1865. 8vo, pp. 13.

—*Cheever and Hart,* Trustees, et als., Versus The Rutland & Burlington R. R. Co., et als. Depositions and Exhibits on the Part of the Defendants Page, Birchard and Eldridge. Rutland, Vt.: Tuttle & Company, Printers. 1867. rl 8vo, pp. 802.

—*The Same Case,* Testimony of the Orators. Bellows Falls, Vt.: Printed at the Times Book and Job Office. 1865. rl 8vo, pp. 561.

—*Shall Rutland be Mortgaged?* January 1st, 1869. 8vo. pp. 8.
Written by the late C. C. Dewey, of Rutland.

—*Investigation by and Report* of Hon. R. F. Parker, Railroad Commissioner of Vermont, and W. B. Gilbert, Esq., Civil Engineer, with statement of Dr. M. Goldsmith and Dr. C. L. Allen, Attending Surgeons, Relating to the Accident upon the Rutland & Burlington Railroad, near the Summit in Mt. Holly, June 8th, 1870. Rutland, Vt.: 1870. 8vo, pp. 8.

—*Supreme Court of Vermont,* General Term, November 1869. James Cheever and William T. Hart, Trustees, et al., vs. The Rutland and Burlington Railroad Co. et al. Opinion of the Court Delivered at Rutland, Feb. 5, 1870, By Hon. Benj. H. Steele, one of the Justices. Boston: 1870. 8vo.

—*Reports* of the Managers of the Rutland Railroad Co. To the Stockholders; with the official proceedings of the Meeting at Rutland, January 30th and 31st, 1872; with an Appendix containing the Charter and By-Laws, the Contract and Leases to the Managers of the Vermont Central and Vermont and Canada Railroads, together with the Papers laid before the Stockholders by the President. Rutland: Tuttle & Co., Printers. 1872. 8vo, pp. 62. Appendix 62. (6.)

—*Mortgages* of the Rutland Rail Road Company, with the votes of Stockholders Relating thereto. Rutland: Tuttle & Company, Printers. 1873. 8vo, pp. 27.

—*Annual Report* of the Rutland Railroad Co., to the Stockholders, for the year ending January 30th, 1873. Rutland: Tuttle & Company, Printers. 1873. 8vo, pp. 15. map. The same for the years 1874 and 1875.
Continued.

—*Mortgage* of the Rutland Railroad Co., with the votes of Stockholders and Directors relating thereto. Rutland: Tuttle & Co., Book and Job Printers. 1878. 8vo, pp. 8.

—*Modification* of Contract of Rutland Railroad Company, with Central Vermont Railroad Company, (Trustees and Managers,) February

25, 1876. Rutland : Tuttle & Company, Printers. 1876. 8vo, pp. 8.

—*A Letter* to the Directors of the Rutland Railroad Company, concerning an alteration of their Records. By George B. Chase, Director of the Company, 1867-1873. Boston : Franklin Press: Rand, Avery & Company. 1879. 8vo, pp. 61.

—*Report of the Special Auditor* upon the Financial Condition of the Rutland Railroad Company and an Extract from the Records of the Company concerning the Action of the Directors in Reply to a Letter addressed to them by George B. Chase, November, 1879. Rutland : Tuttle & Co., Book and Job Printers. 1870. 8vo, pp. 21.

MISCELLANEOUS.

—*Proceedings of the Convention*, Holden at Windsor, Vt., January 20, 1836 : For the purpose of taking preliminary Measures for a Rail Road through the Valleys of the Connecticut and Passumpsic Rivers to the St. Lawrence. [Published by request of the Convention.] Chronicle Press. Windsor, Vt.

—*Report of the Engineer* on the Survey of the Valley Rail Road, in Vermont. Montpelier : William Clark. 1837. 8vo, pp. 40.
The Passumpsic Route.

—*Letters* on the Vermont and Massachusetts Railroad, Addressed to Hon. Thomas H. Perkins, By Charles Hudson. First published in the Boston Courier. Boston : 1844. 8vo, pp. 21.
Treats largely of Vermont products and trade.

—*First Annual Report* of the Directors of the Vermont and Massachusetts Railroad Company, made to the Stockholders, February, 1845. Boston : White, Lewis & Potter, Printers. 1845. 8vo, pp. 11.
Continued annually.

—*Harlem Extension Rail Road Company.* Local Freight Tariff, to take Effect May 1st, 1872. Joseph Child, General Agent, General Offices, New Lebanon, N. Y. Rutland : Tuttle & Co., Printers. 1872. 8vo, pp. 12. (30).

—*Address* to the Stockholders of the Vermont and Massachusetts Rail Road Company, adopted by the Convention held at Greenfield, Oct. 25, 1845. Greenfield : Steam Press of Merriam & Mirick. 1845. 8vo, pp. 16.

—*Act of Incorporation* and By-laws of the Connecticut and Passumpsic Rivers Railroad Corporation. Boston : 1846. 12mo, pp. 23.

—*Circular* to the Stockholders in the Connecticut and Passumpsic Rivers Railroad, Dec., 1851. 8vo, pp. 8.

—*Copy* of An Agreement, between the Connecticut and Passumpsic Rivers Railroad Company, and the Connecting Roads, for the Extension of the Passumpsic Railroad to the Canada Line. Boston: 1855. 8vo, pp. 8.

—*Report of Committee* to locate the Connecticut and Passumpsic Rivers Railroad, from Barton to Canada Line. Boston : 1857. 8vo, pp. 8.

—*Connecticut* and Passumpsic Rivers Railroad Company vs. William W. Baxter. Windsor County Court, May Term, 1858. 8vo, pp. 12.

—*First Annual Report* of the Directors of the Connecticut and Passumpsic Rivers Railroad Company, October 6, 1846. Newbury, Vt., Printed by L. J. McIndoe. 1846. 12mo. pp. 11.
Continued.

—*2d Annual Report* of Passumpsic Railroad. 1847. 12mo. pp. 12.

—*3d Report*, 1848. 12mo, pp. 8.

—*4th Report*, 1849. 8vo, pp. 13.

—*5th Report*, 1850. 8vo, pp. 8.

—*6th Report*, 1851. 8vo, pp. 12.

—*7th Report*, 1852. 8vo, pp. 16.

—*8th Report*, 1853. 8vo, pp. 12.

—*9th Report*, 1854. 8vo, pp. 10.

—*10th Report*, 1855. 8vo, pp. 13.
Continued.

—*Connecticut* and Passumpsic Rivers Railroad. 1847. Printed by L. J. McIndoe, Newbury, Vt. 8vo, pp. 8, and Map of the Route.
A description of the route, account of productions, etc.

—*Circular* to the Stockholders in the Connecticut and Passumpsic Rivers Railroad, Dec. 1851. 8vo, pp. 8.

—*W. R. Gilbert's* Missisquoi Railroad Report, Received January 15th, 1852. 8vo, pp. 8.

—*Proposed Railroad Routes*, between Rutland and Woodstock. Reasons why Rutland should not be mortgaged. (1860.) 8vo, pp. 20. No imprint.

—*Brief Statement of Facts* relative to the Proposed Railroad from Fitchburg to Brattleborough, under Charters lately obtained for the same in the States of Massachusetts and Vermont. Boston: 1844. 8vo, pp. 24.

—*State of Vermont.* Supreme Court, General Term, at Burlington, July, 1858. Jonathan Sturges and Thomas Douglas, Against Shepherd Knapp and George Briggs, and the Troy and Boston Railroad Company. Opinion of the Court, by Isaac F. Redfield, Chief Justice. Troy, N. Y.: 1859. 8vo, pp. 24.

—*Woodstock Railroad Company.* The Directors of the Woodstock Railroad Company to the people of the Town of Woodstock and adjoining towns: n. d. n. p. Probably 1867. 8vo. pp. 16.

—*Woodstock Railroad Company.* (First) Annual Report of the Directors, for the year ending December 31, 1867. 8vo, pp. 8. No imprint.

—*Second Annual Report*, Dec. 31, 1868. 8vo, pp. 18.
Continued.

—*Engineer's Report.* To Peter T. Washburn, President of the Woodstock Railroad Company. [1869.] 8vo, pp. 8.

—*The Trans-Continental Railway.* Remarks at Rutland, Vermont, June 24, 1869. By John A. Poor. Portland: 1869. 8vo, pp. 76, (1).

—*Across the Continent.* Atlantic & Pacific Railway, Portland & Rutland Railroad, official record of the corporators, April 30, 1868. Portland: Printed by Thurston & Company. 1868. 8vo, pp. 59.

—*First Annual Report* of Directors of the Portland, Rutland, Oswego & Chicago Railway Company. Submitted July 26, 1871. Portland: Printed by B. Thurston & Co. 1871. 8vo, pp. 58.

—*Portland and Ogdensburg Railroad.* Reprint of Letters of J. C. Woodman, May 1868, to the citizens of Portland, originally printed in the "Eastern Argus" newspaper. 8vo, pp. 32.

—*Circular.* To the Voters of Vermont, on the Management of Railroads. March, 1871. 12mo, pp. 4.

—*Vermont Division* of the Portland and Ogdensburg Trunk Railroad Line. Comprising the Lamoille Valley, Montpelier and St. Johnsbury and Essex County Railroads. A Statement showing the Security, Safety, and Value of the First mortgage six per cent gold bonds of the Vermont Division. St. Johnsbury Vermont, June, 1871. Published by the Executive Committee. 8vo, pp. 16.

—*20-year gold bonds* issued by the Vermont Division of the Portland and Ogdensburg Trunk Railroad. Interest payable in gold, in Boston, May 1st and Nov. 1st, free of Government tax. Being a first and only mortgage upon the entire Property. Trustees for the Bondholders, A. T. Lowe, Boston ; Luke P. Poland, St. Johnsbury. Financial Agents : E. & T. Fairbanks & Co., St. Johnsbury, Vt., Fairbanks & Co., New York, Fairbanks, Brown & Co., Boston, Fairbanks & Ewing, Philadelphia. June, 1871. 8vo, pp. 24.

—*Portland* and *Ogdensburg* Railroad Line. The Grand Avenue for through business, also its assurances for local and Tourist business, and its financial Condition. New Extensions and connections, with a map. Published by the Executive Committee of the Vermont Division. New York : 1872. 8vo, pp. 8.
Dated, St. Johnsbury, Vt., September 1872.

—*Joint Mortgage* of the Lamoille Valley Railroad Co., Montpelier & St. Johnsbury R. R. Co., and the Essex County R. R. Co., composing the Vermont Division of the Portland & Ogdensburg Trunk Railroad Line, to Abraham T. Lowe, Esq., Pres't 1st National Bank, Boston, and Hon. Luke P. Poland, St. Johnsbury, Vermont, Trustees for the Bond-holders. Published by the Executive Committee of Joint Companies. n. p. 1871. 8vo, pp. 36.

—*Northern Pacific Railroad.* Partial Report to the Board of Directors, of a Reconnoissance made in the summer of 1869, between Lake Superior and the Pacific Ocean, by Thos. H. Canfield, General Agent of the Company ; accompanied with Notes on Puget Sound. By Samuel Wilkeson, Esq., The Historian of the Expedition. For Private Circulation Only. May, 1870. No imprint. 8vo, pp. 96, 44, and maps.

—*Opinion and Order* of the Court of Chancery of Caledonia County, in the Petition of A. B. Jewett and A. W. Hastings, Receivers of the Lamoille Valley, Montpelier and St. Johnsbury and Essex County Railroad Companies, comprising the Portland & Ogdensburg Railroad, Vermont Division. By Jonathan Ross, Chancellor. St. Johnsbury : C. M. Stone & Co., Book and Job Printers. 1879. 8vo, pp. 24.

—*Montpelier* & Wells River Railroad Report. January 7, 1873, Roderick Richardson, Prest. 8vo, pp. 8.

—*The Free Pass Abuse.*
See Clarke, Albert, Speech on.

—*Financial Statement* of the Montpelier and Wells River R. R. Report made by the Special Committee to the Stockholders, October 13, 1874. Montpelier : Freeman Steam Printing House and Bindery. 1874. 12mo, pp. 11.

—*Charter and Amendments*, of the Northern Pacific Rail Road Company, Approved July 2d, 1864. Burlington, Vt.: R. S. Styles, Book & Job Printer. 1870. 8vo, pp. 61.

—*The Lake Champlain* and St. Lawrence Junction Railway, of Canada. Prospectus, Map, Reports of Engineers, etc. [1877.] 8vo, pp. 9, xi, 3.
See "Governor and Council," Vol. 7, pp. 482–87, for early railroad projects. See also Haddock, C. B., Phelps, E. J., Willard, C. W.

Rand, Festus G. Autobiography of Festus G. Rand. A Tale of Intemperance. With a preface by Rev. T. B. Taylor, A. M., and a recommendation by John B. Gough. Price, twenty-five cents. Montpelier : J. &. J. M. Poland, Printers. 1868. 8vo, pp. 32.

Rand John. A Letter to Elder Elias Smith : Containing an Examination of his Thirteen Reasons for believing the Salvation of All Men. By John Rand, Elder in the Church of Christ. Published for the benefit of the Public. Motto. Danville : Ebenezer Eaton, Printer. 1818. 8vo, pp. 16.

Randall, Rev. E. H. An Address on the Occasion of the Funeral Obsequies of the late President Lincoln, delivered before the Citizens of Randolph, Vt., April 19, 1865. By Rev. E. H. Randall. Montpelier : Walton's Steam Printing Establishment. 1865. 8vo, pp. 12.

—*A Discourse Commemorative* of the 50th Anniversary of the Consecration of St. Paul's Church, Pawtucket, R. I. Delivered on Sunday, October 20, 1867, by Edward H. Randall, associate Rector. Also a collection of items relative to the history of the Sunday School. Pawtucket : R. Sherman & Co. 1868. 8vo, pp. 28.
Rev. Mr. Randall is a native of Northfield, Vt.; born in 1837; he is a brother of G. P., J. J. R., and Col. F. V. Randall.
Mr. Randall is at present Rector at Poultney, Vt. (1896.)

Randall, Guerdon P. *Hand Book of Designs*, containing plans in perspective of Court Houses, Universities, Academies, School Houses, Dwellings, &c. Chicago : 8vo.
G. P. Randall was a native of Northfield, Vt., and for many years resided in Chicago as a successful architect. He paid much attention to the Philosophy of Light, and its wonderful phenomena, and was noted as a lecturer upon this subject in the North-west. He died at Northfield, Vt., Sept. 20, 1884, aged 63 years. He was a brother of J. J. R. Randall, of Rutland, and of Col. F. V. Randall.

Randall, Phineas. *A Book of Acrostics*, with two short Poems. Middlebury : N. Drury, Printer. 1836. 12mo, pp. 16.

Randolph. *Annual Report* of the town of Randolph, for the year ending March 1, 1877. Thayer & Upham, Printers. Herald Office, West Randolph, Vermont. 8vo, pp. 13, (1).
Continued.

—*Manual* of the Congregational Church of West Randolph, Vt. Adopted by vote of the Church, December, 1880. West Randolph : Herald and News Print. 1881. 16mo, pp. 33.

—*The Semi-Centennial* of the Congregational Church of West Randolph, Vt., October 21st, 1881. West Randolph, Vt.: The Herald and News. 1881. 8vo, pp. 27.

—*The Confession of Faith* and the Covenant of the First Congregational Church in Randolph, Vermont. Adopted August 26, 1858. 18mo, pp. 4. No imprint.

Random Shot, The. Designed to Kill Wild Game, and Clear the Air from Noxious Exhalations. Windsor, (Vermont): A. Spooner, 1805. 8vo, pp. 15.

Rankin, Rev. A. *Discourse* on the Duty and Blessings of Christian Union, Love and Peace, by Rev. A. Rankin, A. M. Essex, Vt. Published by Request. St. Albans: Messenger Print, 1858. 8vo, pp. 38, (1).

Rankin, Rev. J. E., D. D. *A Spurious Fear* of God. A Discourse delivered in St. Albans, Vt., on the National Fast Day, January 4th, 1861, by Rev. J. E. Rankin. St. Albans : Whiting & Davis, Printers. 1861. 8vo, pp. 16.

—*Consolation* at the Death of Believers. A Discourse preached in St. Albans, March 23, 1862, at the funeral of Mrs. Lydia Brigham. By Rev. J. E. Rankin, Pastor First Congregational Church, St. Albans, Vt. St. Albans: Whiting and Davis, Printers. 1862. 8vo, pp. 15.

—*The Loss of a Wife.* A Discourse delivered at the Funeral of Mrs. Marshall Mason. By Rev. J. E. Rankin. St. Albans, Vt.: Henry A. Cutler, Printer. 1862. 8vo, pp. 12.

—*Moses and Joshua.* A Discourse on the Death of Abraham Lincoln, preached in the Winthrop Church, Charlestown, (Mass.) Wednesday Noon, April 19, 1865. By J. E. Rankin, Pastor. 8vo, pp. 16. Boston: Dakin & Metcalf. n. d.

—*The Sources* of New England Civilization. An Address before the Vermont Historical Society, delivered at Montpelier, October 16, 1866. Montpelier: Walton's Press. 1866. 8vo, pp. 24.

—*The Claims of the Bible* to a Place in our Schools. An Address.
See Educational.

—*The Divinity of the Ballot.* A Discourse by Rev. J. E. Rankin, D. D., pastor of Cong'l Church, Washington, D. C.
Published in 1887. Has already reached a circulation of 130,000 copies.
Dr. Jeremiah Eames Rankin was born in Thornton, N. H., January 2, 1828 ; graduated at Middlebury College, 1848; read theology at Andover, and was pastor of the First Congregational Church at St. Albans, Vt. 1857-1863, subsequently pastor of Churches in Lowell, Mass., Boston, Washington, D. C. and Orange, N. J; has been chaplain of the U. S. House of Representatives; Professor of Pastoral Theology, Howard University, Washington, D. C. and President of Howard University, since 1889.

Ranney, D. H. *The Evangelical Church ;* or true Grounds for the Union of the Saints. By Darwin H. Ranney, A. M. Woodstock, Vt.: Mercury Press. 1840. 12mo, pp. 144.

—*Also,* "Christian Alliance at Home."

Mr. Ranney was born in Chester, Vt., November 13, 1812, and was graduated at Middlebury College, 1835. He has been pastor of Baptist churches in Westport, N. Y., Ludlow, Vt., Claremont, N. H., and of a Unionist church in Dover, Vt., 1844-49, and subsequently in Wilmington, Vt. He died in West Brattleboro, September 27, 1870.

Ranney, Waitstill R., M. D. *Reminiscences* of the late Waitstill R. Ranney, M. D., of Townshend, Vt. New York: 1855. 12mo, pp. 171.

—*Transactions* at the Eighth Family Reunion of the Descendants of Waitstill Ranney and Jeremiah Atwood, Chester, Vt., 1866. New York : 1866. 8vo.

Ransom Guards. 1856. 1876. *A Memento.* Sketch of the Ransom Guards of St. Albans, Vt., and their Centennial Excursion to Philadelphia. By C. S. F. St. Albans: Messenger Steam Print. 1876. 16mo, pp. 23, (2).

Rawson, Nathaniel. *A Discourse* addressed to the Congregational Church and Society in Hardwick, Vermont. By Nathaniel Rawson, Pastor of the Church. Delivered the Sabbath next succeeding the Ordination, Feb. 17, 1811. Montpelier, Vermont: Printed at the office of Walton & Goss. June, 1811.

Rawson, Rev. Thos. R.
Mr. Rawson was born in Townsend, Vt., July 10, 1803, and died at Albany, N. Y., May 20, 1877. He was graduated at Amherst College, 1830, read theology, and was settled over the Congregational church at Peru, Mass., 1834-1836; removed to Albany, where he remained until his death, except the years 1831-2, when he was settled at Malta, N. Y.
He published "Dominie and Patrick ; or, The Bible vs. the Papacy." See "Congregational Quarterly," July, 1878, page 451.

Raymond, Henry J. *The Relations* of the American Scholar to his Country and his Times. An Address delivered before the Associate Alumni of the University of Vermont, at Burlington, Vt., August 6, 1850. By Henry J. Raymond. Published at the request of the Association. New York: Baker and Scribner, 145 Nassau Street. 1850. 8vo, pp. 58.
Henry Jarvis Raymond, founder of the New York Times, graduated at the University of Vermont in 1840. He married Juliet, daughter of the late J. W. Weaver of Colchester, Vt. He died in New York, June 18, 1869.

Read, David. *The Best* Way to Remove the Curse of Intemperate Drinking, Considered in reference to the Views of Temperance Men, Moderate Drinkers, Drunkards and Rumsellers. By David Read. Burlington: Chauncey Goodrich. 1849. 8vo, pp. 20.

—*Nathan Reed;* His Invention of the Multi-Tubular Boiler and Portable High-Pressure Engine, and Discovery of the true mode of Applying Steam Power to Navigation and Railways. A Contribution to the Early History of the Steamboat and Locomotive Engine. By his Friend and Nephew, David Read. New York: Published by Hurd and Houghton. Cambridge: Riverside Press. 1870. 12mo, pp. 201.

Hon. David Read was born in Warren, Mass., July 24, 1799; died Oct. 1, 1881; he was admitted to the bar in Vermont in 1823, and began to practice in St. Albans. He removed to Burlington in 1838, and the following year became Treasurer of the Vermont University, holding the position three years. Afterwards he lived several years in Colchester, where he built a handsome residence. In 1843-4 Mr. Read was a member of the State Senate. Returning to Burlington he was elected Recorder in 1865, '66 and '67. He was interested in the marble quarries near

Mallett's Bay, and was one of the originators of the Winooski Marble Company, an unsuccessful enterprise. Mr. Read was much interested in historical matters, and was the author of the valuable Chittenden County Chapter, and of the history of Colchester, in Miss Hemenway's Gazetteer. He was the author of various well-written newspaper and magazine articles. He was a man of great intelligence, of integrity, of independent judgment and strong will. He was twice married, and left three children by his second wife, namely, Mrs. M. M. Colburn of Burlington, Capt. Ogden B. Read, Eleventh U. S. Infantry, and Mr. Edward M. Read of St. Louis. His second wife was a sister of the late President and Prof. James Marsh of the University of Vermont.

Read, Rev. Hollis. *The Christian Brahman ;* or Memoirs of the Life, Writings and Character of the Converted Brahman, Babajee, Including illustrations of the domestic habits, manners, customs, and superstitions of the Hindoos ; a sketch of the Deckan and notices of India in general, and an account of the American Mission at Ahmednugger. By the Rev. Hollis Read, American Missionary to India. In Two Volumes. New York : Leavitt, Lord & Co., 180 Broadway. Boston : Crocker & Brewster. 1836. 12mo, pp. 264, 275.

Mr. Read was born in Newfane, Vt., August 26, 1802; was graduated at Williams College, 1826; read Theology at Princeton, N. J.; married Miss Caroline Hubbell, of Bennington, Vt., June 21, 1830, and August 2, the same year, they sailed for Calcutta; he was in the employ of the A. B. C. F. M. seven years, five of which were in India 1830-1835, when he returned home on account of the failure of the health of Mrs. Read. He was for 27 years pastor of various churches in Connecticut and New York; after 1865 was on the "Honorable Retired Ministerial Roll," residing at Elizabeth, N. J. His published works, in addition, are, "Read and Ramsey's Journal in India," 12mo, pp. 367. Philadelphia ; 1836; "God in History, or Divine Providence historically illustrated," two volumes, 12mo, pp. 432, 408; "Memoirs and Sermons of W. J. Armstrong, D. D., late Secretary of the A. B. C. F. M.," 12mo, pp. 400; "India and its People, Ancient, Modern, Moral, Civil and Religious Condition." "The Sepoy Mutiny," 8vo, pp. 384, illustrated; "Palace of the Great King, or The Power, Wisdom, and Goodness of God illustrated in the Multiplicity and Variety of His Works" (God in Natural History); "Commerce and Christianity; A Prize Essay; Subject, The Moral Power of the Sea, or The Relation of Commerce to the Spread of the Gospel," 18mo, pp. 200; "The Coming Crisis of the World, or the Great Battle, and the Golden Age," 12mo, pp. 345; "The Negro Problem Solved, or Africa as she was, as she is, and as she shall be," 12mo, pp. 417; "The Footprints of Satan, or the Devil in History."

Reading
History of the town of. See Davis, G. A.

A Real Treasure for the Pious Mind, Selected from the Collections and Writings of the Countess of Huntington, Mrs. Rowe, Miss Harvey, Dr. Watts, Mr. Perrin, Mr. Smith, &c. Tenth Edition. Bennington : Printed by Anthony Haswell. 1807. 18mo, pp. 104.

Rechabites. *Constitution* of the Tribe of Rechabites. Printed at The Gazette Office, Bennington, Vt. 1846. 12mo, pp. 8.

REDFIELD, ISAAC FLETCHER. *Sketch* of the Hon. Isaac Fletcher, late a Representative in Congress, from the fifth district in Vermont. By Isaac F. Redfield. Burlington : Printed by Stilman Fletcher. 1843. 12mo, pp. 28.

—*Charge to the Grand Jury* in Washington County, November Term, 1842. By Isaac F. Redfield, one of the Judges of the Supreme Court. Published by Request of the Grand Jury and the Members of the Bar. Burlington : Chauncey Goodrich. 1842. 8vo, pp. 16.

—*A Brief Biographical Notice* of the Hon Charles K. Williams, LL. D. Prepared in 1852. See Williams, Charles K.

—*Opinion* in regard to the Power of the Legislature to modify the Charter of Trinity Church, New York. Boston: 1858. 8vo, pp. 24.

—*Opinion* in regard to the Constitutional Right of the States to tax shares in domestic corporations held by non-residents ; showing the grounds upon which the Statute of Vermont imposing a Special tax upon the Railway Stock of non-residents must be regarded as invalid. By Isaac F. Redfield. Cambridge : Printed by H. O. Houghton. 1862. 8vo, pp. 24.

—*Argument* on behalf of the American Tract Society, New York, in the matter of the Legacies of Luman Pease and Elnathan Jones. 1868. 8vo, pp. 108.

—*Commentaries* on Equity Pleadings, and the incidents thereof, according to the Practice of the Courts of Equity of England and America. By Joseph Story, LL. D., one of the Justices of the Supreme Court of the United States, and Dane Professor of Law in Harvard University. Motto. Seventh Edition, carefully revised, with large additions. By Isaac F. Redfield, LL. D. Boston : Little, Brown and Company. 1865. 8vo, pp. XXXIII, (1), 802.

—*Commentaries* on the Conflict of Laws, Foreign and Domestic, in regard to Contracts, Rights and Remedies, and especially in regard to Marriages, Divorces, Wills, Successions, and Judgments. By Joseph Story, LL. D., &c. Motto. Sixth Edition, carefully revised and considerably enlarged. By Isaac F. Redfield, LL. D. Boston : Little, Brown, and Company. 1865. 8vo, pp. XXXIV, 868.

—*A Treatise* on the Law of Evidence. By Simon Greenleaf, LL. D., Emeritus Professor of Law in Harvard University. Motto. Twelfth Edition, carefully revised, with large additions. By Isaac F. Redfield, LL. D. Boston : Little, Brown, and Company. MDCCCLXVIII. rl. 8vo, 3 volumes, pp. LXXI, 675 ; LXXIII, 637 ; XXXVII, 518.

—*Judge Redfield's Letter* to Senator Foot upon the points settled by the war ; the Status of the States attempting Secession; What benefits we have derived from the war ; the true Policy of restoring the Government Under the Constitution. New York : Published by Hurd & Houghton. Boston : E. P. Dutton and Company. 1865. 12mo, pp. 30.

—*Commentaries* on Equity Jurisprudence, as administered in England and America. By Joseph Story, LL. D., &c. Motto. Ninth Edition. Carefully Revised, with Extensive Additions, By Isaac F. Redfield, LL. D. In two Volumes. Boston : Little, Brown, and Company. 1866. 8vo, pp. LXXXIV, 767 ; V, 853.

—*A Practical Treatise* upon The Law of Railways. By Isaac F. Redfield, LL. D. Chief Justice of Vermont. Second Edition. Boston : Little, Brown, and Company. M.DCCC.LVIII. 8vo, pp. lxxxvii, 823.

—*Leading American Railway Cases,* on most of the important questions involved in the law of Railways, arranged according to subjects. With Notes and Opinions by Isaac F. Redfield, LL. D. Being a Supplement to the Author's work on Railways. Boston : Little, Brown, and Company. 1870. 8vo, pp. xliii, 656.

—*The same,* Second Edition. 2 Vols. 1872 Same imprint. 8vo, pp. xlvi. 682 ; li, 721.

—*The Law of Railways;* embracing Corporations, Eminent Domain, Contracts, Common Carriers of goods and passengers, Telegraph Companies, Constitutional Law, Investments, &c., &c. By Isaac F. Redfield, LL. D., Chief Justice of Vermont. Fourth Edition, Greatly Enlarged. Two volumes. Boston : Little, Brown, and Company. 1869. 8vo, pp. 693, lxx (1) 748.

A Fifth Edition, with additions, published in 1873.

—*The Law of Wills,* embracing also, the Jurisprudence of Insanity ; the Effect of extrinsic evidence ; the Creation and Construction of Trusts, so far as applicable to Wills; with Forms and instructions for preparing Wills. By Isaac F. Redfield, LL. D. Boston : Little, Brown, and Company. 1864. 8vo, pp. Lxxvi, 796.

—*Part II. of same.* Same imprint: 1866. 8vo, pp. cxviii. and 955. A Fourth Edition in three volumes, published in 1876. 8vo, pp. lxxvii, 738. xcvi. 668. lxxxvi, 706.

The preface to the third volume was written about ten days before the death of Judge Redfield, and was probably the last work of his life.

—*The Law of Carriers* of Goods and Passengers, private and public, inland and foreign, by Railway, Steamboat, and other modes of transportation ; also the construction, responsibility, and duty of Telegraph Companies, the responsibility and duty of Innkeepers, and the Law of Bailments of every class, embracing Remedies. By Isaac F. Redfield, LL. D. Cambridge, Mass.: Published by H. O. Houghton and Company. New York : Hurd and Houghton. 1869. 8vo, pp. lvii, 599.

—*Leading and Select American Cases* in the Law of Bills of Exchange, Promissory Notes and Checks : Arranged according to subjects. With Notes and References. By Isaac F. Redfield and Melville M. Bigelow. Boston : Little, Brown, and Company. 1871. 8vo, pp. lxii, 760.

Judge Redfield's judicial opinions, so far as reported, may be found in Vermont Reports, vol. 8 to vol. 33, covering the period of 25 years that he sat upon the Bench of the Supreme Court of Vermont. He was leading editor of the Law Register for many years, and, in addition, published various articles upon law topics, as well as biographical sketches of eminent men.

Judge Redfield was born in Weathersfield, Vt., April 10, 1804; and died in Charlestown, Mass., March 23, 1876. See Memoir, by Hon. E. J. Phelps, in vol. 49 of Vermont Law Reports, pp. 519–528; also Resolutions and Remarks by Hon I. D. Peck, upon his retirement from the Bench, in Vermont reports, vol. 36, page 762. See also Veazey, W. G., Memorial Address, 1880; and biographical sketch published in the Argus and Patriot, March 30, 1876.

Redfield, T. P. *Report* on the Claim of the Iroquois Indians upon the State of Vermont, for their "Hunting Ground." By Timothy P. Redfield, Esq. Printed by Order of the House of Rep's. Montpelier : E. P. Walton, Jr., Printer. 1854. 8vo, pp. 40.

Timothy Parker Redfield, a brother of Isaac F., was born in Coventry, Vt., November 3, 1811. He was graduated at Dartmouth College, 1836; read law and commenced practice at Irasburgh, Vt.; was a member of the Legislature in 1839, and a State Senator in 1848, and removed to Montpelier the same year, where he became prominent in his profession. He was a Delegate to the Democratic National Convention held at Chicago in 1864, being one of the Committee on Resolutions in that body, and the Democratic candidate for Governor that year, and again in 1865. He was elected a Judge of the Supreme Court in 1870, which position he held until 1884, when he declined further service on account of ill health. He died at Chicago, March 27, 1888.

Redington, L. W. *Address* of L. W. Redington, delivered at the annual meeting of the Waddington Agricultural Society at Waddington, N. Y., September 10, 1874. Ogdensburg : Republican and Journal Print. 1874. 8vo, pp. 13.

—*Vermont Liquor Law*—The Nuisance Act. Argument of Lyman W. Redington, in the Supreme Court of Vermont, Rutland County, January Term, 1880, in the Matter of State vs. John Haley, With extracts from the Brief where necessary to explain the Argument. Rutland : Tuttle & Co., Printers. 1880. 8vo, pp. 20.

He also published a pamphlet, "Plain Talk on the Tariff."

Mr. Redington is a native of Waddington, St. Lawrence county, N. Y., born March 14, 1849. He read law, and practiced at Rutland, Vt., which town he represented in the Legislature, 1878–9. See Legislative Directory of that year, p. 137.

Reed, George B. *Sketch of the Early History* of Banking in Vermont. 8vo, pp. 28.

Read before the Vermont Historical Society at its annual meeting at Montpelier, Tuesday afternoon, October 14, 1862.

—*Sketch of the Life* of the Honorable John Read, of Boston, 1722-49. By George B. Reed. Boston : Privately Printed. 1879. 8vo, pp. 18, iv.

Mr. Geo. B. Reed is a native of Montpelier, where he was born July 28, 1829; son of the late Thomas Reed, Esq., an early and prominent citizen of the town. He has been for many years a law bookseller and publisher in Boston. He is well versed in the history of Vermont, and has been a liberal donor to the Vermont Historical Society. (1880.)

Reed, John, D. D. *Extracts* from a work entitled an Apology for the Rite of Infant Baptism, By John Reed, D. D. Barnard, Vt.: Published by Joseph Dix. J. H. Carpenter, Printer. pp. 24.

Reese, D. M. *Address* before the Castleton Medical College, 1842.

Registers and Almanacs,
See Almanac.

Reid, Rev. James. *Remarks on the Lecture* of the Rt. Rev. Bishop Hopkins, against the Temperance Society, Published in his late Work, entitled "The Primitive Church compared with the Protestant Episcopal Church of the Present day." By the Rev. James Reid, Rector of Trinity Church, St. Armand, Lower Canada. Frelighsburg, L. C.: Standard Office, 1836. 12mo, pp. 31.

The Religious Courtship: *Being Historical discourses* On the Necessity of Marying Religious Husbands and Wives only ; as also of Husbands and Wives being of the same Opinions in Religion. With an Appendix, Of the Necessity of taking none but Religious Servants ; and a Proposal for the better managing of Servants. Third American, from the twenty-third London Edition. Montpelier, Vt.: Printed by Derick Sibley, for Josiah Parks. 1810. 12mo, pp. 348.

It is hardly necessary to say that the author was Daniel De Foe.

Religious Tracts. From the Press of Thomas M. Pomroy, Rutland. Printed for the Vermont Religious Tract Society, and deposited for sale, by the hundred at first cost, at the store of Doct. Wm. G. Hooker, Middlebury, General Tract Agent, to whom all communications on the subject of Tracts are to be made. Price 2½ cents; or 2¼ cents stitched in blue. 1809.

In a 12mo volume containing the following, bound together: Tracts Nos. 1, 2, 3, 5, 6, 7, 28, and a Sermon by Rev. Lemuel Haynes, entitled, "Universal Salvation a very ancient Doctrine."
See Haynes, L.; Vermont Religious Tract Society.

—*No. IX.* From the Press of Alden Spooner, Windsor. Printed for the Vermont Tract Society, and deposited for sale by the hundred, at first cost, at the store of Wm. G. Hooker, Middlebury, General Tract Agent. A Sermon Delivered at Newark, during the Session of the Synod of New-York and New-Jersey, October, 1808. By Lyman Beecher, A. M. Pastor of the Church of Christ, in East Hampton, Long Island. 8vo, pp. 20.

—*No. X.* From the Press of J. D. Huntington, Middlebury. Printed for the Vermont Religious Tract Society, and deposited for sale, by the hundred, at first cost, at the store of William G. Hooker, General Tract Agent, to whom all communications on the Subject of Tracts are to be made. Price 5 cents, stitched. 1810. General Religion the best friend of the people; or, the Influences of the Gospel, when known, believed and experienced, upon the manners and happiness of the People. 12mo, pp. 24.

Remmele, John. *The Design and Nature of Atonement.* Three Sermons. Windsor: Printed by Hough and Spooner. 1786. 4to, pp. 42.
Brinley Catalogue.

Report of the Proceedings of the Convention of Deaf Mutes, Holden at Montpelier, Vt., February 18, 1852. To which is added an abstract of the Biography of Rev. Thomas H. Gallaudet, LL. D. Bradford, Vt.: Printed at the Family Gazette Office. 1852. 8vo, pp. 8.

Resolutions in Congress, June 30, 1777, in opposition to the Recognition of the State of Vermont. Broadside. Philadelphia, Printed.

Reunion Society of Vermont Officers. *Proceedings* of the Reunion Society of Vermont Officers, 1864–1884, with Addresses delivered at its Meetings by W. G. Veazey, L. O. Brastow, P. T. Washburn, W. W. Grout, E. M. Haynes, Geo. F. Edmunds, S. E. Pingree, John C. Tyler, George T. Childs, C. H. Joyce, Redfield Proctor, Roswell Farnham, Lucius Bigelow, John R. Lewis, M. T. McMahon, Albert Clarke, G. G. Benedict, W. C. Holbrook, and Aldace F. Walker, And a Roster of the Society. Burlington: Free Press Association. 1885. 8vo, pp. viii, 487.

Re-unions of Vermont Soldiers. *Second Reunion* of Eighth Regiment Vermont Volunteers at White River Junction, September 2, 1873. Report of the Meeting. Poem by Geo. N. Carpenter. 1874: Kenosha Union Print. 8vo, pp. 18.

—*Report* of the Sixth Annual Re-union of the 13th Vt. Volunteer Asso. Addresses, also roster of regiment. Burlington: Free Press Asso. 1803. pp. 64.

—*Sixteenth Regiment,* Vermont Volunteers. Reunions and Roster. Montpelier: Argus and Patriot Printing House. 1889. 8vo, pp. 27.

Revolutionary War. *Archives of New York* State in the Revolutionary War, prepared under the direction of the Regents of the University of the State of N. Y., by Berthold Fernow. Albany: 1887. 4to, pp. 646.

Contains names of about 40,000 officers and privates, State Troops, Militia, Minute men, Rangers, Green Mountain Boys, Vermont Militia, and list of the killed, wounded and prisoners, etc., with index.

Reynolds, Rev. John. *A Voice from Prison;* or An Appeal to Christians, in behalf of State Prisoners. A Sermon. By Rev. John Reynolds, to which is added an Account of a Revival among the State Prisoners in Vermont. Boston: Printed by A. Wright. 1833. 12mo, pp. 36.

—*Recollections of Windsor Prison;* Containing Sketches of its History and Discipline; with Appropriate Strictures, and Moral and Religious Reflections. By John Reynolds. Third Edition. Boston: Published by A. Wright. 1839. 12mo, pp. 252.

The Author was for some years a convict in the Windsor Prison.

Rhea, Mrs. Martha Ann (Harris). *Looking unto Jesus.* A Sermon occasioned by the death of Mrs. Martha Ann Rhea, preached at Oroomiah, Persia, October 11, 1857, by Rev. Austin H. Wright, M. D. Missionary of the Am. Board of Com. for For. Missions. Published by Request. Boston: Press of T. R. Marvin & Son, 1858. 8vo, pp. 37.

Mrs. Rhea, daughter of James and Eunice Harris, was born in Westminster, Vt., April 4, 1828. When she was quite young the family removed to Homer, N. Y. In 1851 she went as a Missionary to Persia, and in 1854 she was married to Rev. Samuel A. Rhea, of the Persian Mission.

Rice, Roswell, Jr. *Mental Vision,* on the Ruins of the Fall; the Atonement by Christ; the general Resurrection, and final Judgement: with the addition of some poetry on religious subjects. First Edition. Composed and edited by Roswell Rice, Jr. Bennington: Printed for the Proprietor. 1828. 12mo, pp. 249, (3).

Rice, William. *An Account* of the Life and Death of Deacon William Rice, who Departed this Life A. D. 1833. Written by his Sister, Louis Graves; For the benefit of Sabbath Schools. [n. p. n. d.] 12mo, pp. 8.

Rich, Charles. *An Oration* delivered at Orwell, at the Request of sundry of the inhabitants of that and the adjacent towns, on the Fourth of July, A. D. 1804. By Charles Rich of Shoreham. Bennington: Printed by Haswell & Smead. 1804. 8vo, pp. 36.

—*Speech* of Mr. Charles Rich in Congress, accompanying his Resolutions on Prohibitions. Middlebury: 1821. 8vo.

Mr. Rich was born in Hampshire Co., Mass. in 1871, and was a Representative in Congress from Vermont, 1811 to 1812, and again 1817 to 1824. He died at Shoreham, Vt., Oct. 15, 1824.
See Goodhue's History of Shoreham, pp. 28, 49, 63, 67, 127, 132, 142.

Richards, Cyrus S.
Was born at Hartford, Vt., March 11, 1808; was graduated at Dartmouth, 1835, and became Principal of Kim-

ball Union Academy at Meriden, N. H., the same year, and continued as such as late as 1868.

He published: "Latin Lessons and Tables," Boston: 1859. 8vo; several editions. Also "Latin Synopses."

Richards, John. *Eulogy* pronounced before the Citizens of Windsor, Vt., on William Henry Harrison, late President of the United States; At the National Fast, May 14, 1841. By John Richards. Windsor: Published by N. C. Goddard. 1841. 8vo, pp. 20.

—*A Discourse* at the Ordination of Rev. Franklin Butler, Pastor of the Congregational Church in the East Parish of Windsor, Vt., Jan. 18, 1843. By Rev. John Richards, Pastor of the Church at Dartmouth College. [Published by Request.] Windsor: Printed at the Chronicle Press. 1843. 8vo, pp. 24.

Richards, S. *Sketches of Farmington, Conn.*, from its first Settlement to the present time. By An Inhabitant. Windsor, Vt.: Chronicle Press. 1832. sm. 8vo, pp. 16.

Richardson, I. P. *An Oration* Delivered in Bennington, July 4, 1807. By I. P. Richardson, Esq. Bennington; Haswell & Smead, Printers. 1807.

Richmond, Thomas. *God Dealing with Slavery.* God's Instrumentalities in emancipating the African Slave in America. Spirit Messages from Franklin, Lincoln, Adams, Jackson, Webster, Penn, and others. To the Author, Thomas Richmond. Motto. Chicago: Religio-Philosophical Publishing House, S. S. Jones, Proprietor. 1870. 12mo, pp. 236.

Mr. Richmond was born in Barnard, Vt., Dec. 8, 1796; he was brought up on a farm, and received a common school education; at the age of nineteen he left home and located at Syracuse, N. Y., where he was engaged in the manufacture of salt and as a merchant until 1832 when he moved to Richmond, Ohio, where he engaged in the forwarding and commission business; in 1840 he moved to Cleveland, Ohio, where he continued the same business on an extended scale until 1847 when he moved to Chicago and continued the business on a still larger scale until the great fire of 1871. Mr. Richmond was a member of the Ohio legislature in 1837-8; also a member of the Illinois legislature in 1854-5. Mr. Richmond was brought up a Congregational Calvinist; he became a Spiritualist in 1854. After 1871 Mr. Richmond gathered up the fragments from the wreck of his life accumulations and retired to his native town near Woodstock, Vt., where he still resides in the enjoyment of good health and a green old age. (1880.)

Rider, Darwin. *History* of the Trotting Stallion Grey Norman. Rutland: Tuttle & Co., Printers. 1870. 24mo, pp. 8.

Riggs, Rev. Herman C. *The Supremacy of man.* A Thanksgiving Day Sermon delivered Thursday, Nov. 18, 1869, by Rev. Herman C. Riggs, pastor of the Cong'l Church, St. Albans, Vt. St. Albans: E. B. & W. H. Whiting, Printers. 1870. pp. 26.

Ripley and Thomas. *Catalogue* of Thoroughbred Short-Horn Stock. The property of Messrs. Ripley & Thomas, near Fort Lyon, Bent County, Colorado Territory. Rutland: Tuttle & Co., Printers. 1871. sm. 4to, pp. 15.

Ripley, Wm. Y. W. *Vermont Riflemen* in the war for the Union, 1861 to 1865. A History of Company F, First United States Sharp Shooters. By Wm. Y. W. Ripley, Lt. Col. Rutland: Tuttle & Co., Printers. 1883. 12mo, pp. 204.

Rix, William. of Royalton, Vt.] Incidents of Life in a Southern City During the War. A series of Sketches written for the Rutland Herald by a Vermont Gentleman, who was for many years a prominent Merchant in Mobile. Printed for private Distribution. n. p. n. d. 8vo, pp. (31).

Robbins, Rev. Ammi R. *Journal* of the Rev. Ammi R. Robbins, a Chaplain in the American Army, in the Northern Campaign of 1776. New Haven: Printed by B. L. Hamlen, Printer to Yale College. 1850. 8vo, pp. 48.

Contains an account of his journey through Rupert, Pawlet, Dorset, Manchester, Arlington, Bennington, etc.

Robbins, R. D. C. *Egypt and the Books of Moses*, &c., translated from the German of E. W. Hengstenberg. Andover: 1843. 8vo.

—*Xenophon's Memorabilia* of Socrates, with Notes, and Introduction. New York: 1853. 12mo.

Mr. Robbins assisted in the preparation of Andrews' Latin English Lexicon, 1851, 8vo; and edited Stuart's Commentary on the epistle to the Hebrews, 3d and 4th American editions, 1854-60; Commentary on the Epistle to the Romans, 3d and 4th American editions, 1854, 1859; and Commentary on Ecclesiastes, edited and revised, 1862; he has also contributed to Bibliotheca Sacra, &c.

Mr. Robbins was born in Wardsboro, Vt., 1812, was graduated at Middlebury College, 1835; at Andover Theological Seminary, 1841; and was Abbot Resident at the latter Institution until 1848, when he became Professor of Languages at Middlebury College, where he remained until 1872, when he resigned and moved to Newton Highlands, Mass.

Roberson, Lewis. *Select and Original Dialogues*, Orations and Single Pieces, designed for the use of Schools. By Lewis Roberson. Motto. Weathersfield, Vt.: Published by the Author. Isaac Eddy, Printer. 1816. 16mo, pp. 180.

Roberts, Daniel. *An Address* before the Alumni of Middlebury College, at Commencement, August 10, 1853. By Daniel Roberts. Published by Request. Brandon: Printed at the office of the Post. 1853. 8vo, pp. 11.

—*Vermont Centennial Address.* Bennington, August 15th, 1877. By Daniel Roberts. 8vo, pp. 8.

—*A Digest* of all the reported Decisions of the Supreme Court of the State of Vermont; also of all the Decisions of the Courts of the United States for the District of Vermont, which are found in the Vermont Reports, by Daniel Roberts. Burlington: (Free Press Print). 1878. 8vo, pp. xxv, 866.

Mr. Roberts has also published several other addresses, 4th of July, etc., besides historical and biographical articles of importance in Miss Hemenway's Vermont Historical Gazetteer.

Mr. Roberts is a native of Wallingford, Vt., born May 25, 1811; he was graduated at Middlebury College, 1829, read law with Hon. Harvey Button at Wallingford, and was admitted to the Rutland County Bar, at the September term, 1832; traveled in the Western States about one year, and then located at Jacksonville, Ill., in the office of the late Hon. Murry McConnell, where he practiced his profession 1833-35, and returning to Vermont on a visit, he was prevailed upon to remain and open a law office in his native town, and after about one year at Wallingford, he moved to Manchester, Vt., where he continued his profession 1836-56; Mr. Roberts then moved to Burlington, Vt., where he has continued in active practice to the present time (1896).

It is not going too far to state that Mr. Roberts is regarded by the profession as one of the most able lawyers in the State.

Roberts, Lemuel. *Memoirs of Capt. Lemuel Roberts;* containing Adventures in Youth, Vicissitudes experienced as a Continental Soldier, Sufferings as Prisoner, Escapes from Captivity, (etc). Written by Himself. Bennington, Vt.: A. Haswell. 1809. 8vo, pp. 96.

Roberts, William. *A Treatise* on the Construction of the Statutes 13 Eliz. C. 5, and 27 Eliz. C. 4, relating to Voluntary and Fraudulent Conveyances, and of the Nature and Force of different considerations to support Deeds and other Legal Instruments in the Courts of Law and Equity, by William Roberts, of Lincoln's Inn, Author of A Treatise on the Statute of Frauds, and a Treatise on the Law of Wills and Codicils. Third American, from the last English Edition, With additional Notes, and references to American and later English Decisions. Burlington: Chauncey Goodrich. 1845. 8vo, pp. viii, (6), 675.

Robinson, Rev. Charles S. *Songs for the Sanctuary:* or, Hymns and Tunes for Christian Worship. New York and Chicago : A. S. Barnes and Company. 1865. 8vo, pp. 456.
Many editions of this work have been published.

—*The Martyred President :* A Sermon Preached in the First Presbyterian Church, Brooklyn, N. Y., by the Pastor, Rev. Charles S. Robinson, on the Morning of April 16th, 1865. New York : John F. Trow. 1865. 8vo, pp. 31.

—*The Memorial Pulpit.* Sermons preached in the Presbyterian Memorial Church, Madison Ave., corner of Fifty-third Street, New York City, by the Pastor, Chas. S. Robinson, D. D., 1873. Published each week by A. S. Barnes & Co., 111 William St., New York. 12mo.

—*A Selection of Spiritual Songs* with Music for the Church and the Choir. Selected and arranged by Rev. Charles S. Robinson, D. D. New York : Scribner & Co. 1878. 8vo, pp. 441.

—*A Selection of Spiritual Songs* with Music for use in Social Meetings. Selected and arranged by Rev. Charles S. Robinson, D. D. New York : Scribner & Co. 1878. 8vo, pp. 237.
Author of "Studies of Neglected Texts," 1883 ; "Sermons in Songs," 1885 ; Sabbath Evening Sermons, 1886 ; "Simon Peter ; Early Life and Times," 1887 : the "Pharaohs of the Bondage and Exodus," 1887 ; "Studies in Mark's Gospel," 1888 ; "From Samuel to Solomon," 1889 ; "Studies in Luke's Gospel," 2 vols., 1889 ; "Simon Peter, Later Life and Labors," 1894 ; besides many collections of sacred songs.
Dr. Robinson was born in Bennington, Vt., March 31, 1829 ; was graduated at Williams College, 1849 ; at Princeton Theological Seminary, 1855 ; Pastor at Troy, N. Y., 1855–60 ; Brooklyn, N. Y., 1860–8 ; American Chapel, Paris, France, 1868–70 ; Madison Avenue, Thirteenth Street and New York Presbyterian Churches, New York City, 1870–.

Robinson, Rowland E. *Forest and Stream Folks.* New York : Forest and Stream Publishing Co. 1886. 8vo, pp. 24.

—*Uncle Lisha's Shop.* Life in a Corner of Yankeeland, by Rowland E. Robinson. New York : Forest and Stream Publishing Co. 1887. 12mo, pp. 187.

—*Sam Lovel's Camps.* Uncle Lisha's Friends under bark and canvas. A sequel to Uncle Lisha's Shop, by Rowland E. Robinson. New York : Forest and Stream Publishing Co. 1889. 12mo, pp. 253.

—*Vermont.* A study of Independence. By Rowland E. Robinson. Boston and New York : Houghton, Mifflin and Company. The River-

side Press, Cambridge. 1892. 16mo, pp. vi, 370.
One of the series of American Commonwealths.

—*Danvis Folks.* By Rowland E. Robinson. Boston and New York : Houghton, Mifflin & Co. 1894. 16mo, pp. 349.

—*In New England Fields* and Woods. By Rowland E. Robinson. Boston and New York : Houghton, Mifflin & Company. The Riverside Press, Cambridge. 1896. 16mo, pp. viii, 287.
Mr. Robinson has supplied the following biographical sketch :
"My parents were Rowland T. and Rachel Robinson. I am the youngest of their four children and was born in Ferrisburgh, Vt., May 14, 1833. I am a farmer, and with the exception of a few years spent in New York as a designer on wood, have lived on the farm to which my grandfather came in 1797, from Vergennes, where he came with his wife from Newport, R. I. in 1792. He was the great-grandson of Rowland Robinson, who came from England to Newport in 1675. For many generations my ancestors, on both sides, were Quakers, with the exception of my mother's grandfather, George Gilpin, who was a Colonel in the Revolutionary Army, a member of Washington's staff, and a pallbearer at his funeral. My life has been very uneventful. In 1870 I was married to Anna Stevens of East Montpelier, and we have three children. For more than two years I have been entirely blind, and for a longer time quite dependent on my wife for the revision and copying of my manuscripts."
Ferrisburgh, March 7, 1896.

Robinson, Sarah. *Genealogical History* of the Families of Robinsons, Saffords, Harwoods and Clarks. By Sarah Robinson. Bennington, Vt : 1837. 12mo, pp. 96.
Mrs. Sarah (Harwood) Robinson was the wife of Samuel Robinson, Esq., the first Justice of the Peace appointed in the State under the authority of Vermont.
See Vermont Historical Gazetteer, Vol. 1, p. 168.

Robinson, Rev. S.
—*A Brief Survey* of the Congregational Ministers and Churches in Lamoille County, Vt., from its first settlement to the present time. Compiled by Rev. S. Robinson, Morristown. Am. Quar. Register. 1841. Vol. XIV, pp. 129, 132.
With historical notes of each town.

Rochester. *Articles of Faith and Covenant* of the Congregational Church, Rochester. Adopted, February, 1842. Windsor: Chronicle Press. 12mo, pp. 8.

—*History* of the Town of Rochester, Vt. Published by order of the Town. Montpelier, Vt.: Eli Ballou, Book & Job Printer. 1869. 12mo, pp. iv, 92.

—*Annual Catalogue* of the Rochester High and Graded School for 1896-97. Incorporated in 1886. Organized in 1892. Burlington : Free Press Print. n. d. 12mo, pp. 16.

Rockwell, Rev. J. E. *Sketches* of the Presbyterian Church, containing a brief Summary of arguments in favour of its primitive and apostolic character and a view of its principles, order and history, designed especially for the youth of the church. By the Rev. J. E. Rockwell. Philadelphia : Presbyterian Board of Publication, No. 265 Chestnut Street. 1854. 16mo, pp. 282.

—*Seed Thoughts,* or selections from Caryl's Exposition of Job. With an introduction, by the Rev. J. E. Rockwell, D. D. Philadelphia : Presbyterian Board of Publication, No. 821 Chestnut Street. 1869. 12mo, pp. 180.

Mr. Rockwell was a Presbyterian, born at Salisbury, Vt., 1816, and graduated at Amherst College, 1837. He published in addition: "Visitors' Questions," 1857. 16mo; "Young Christian Warned," 1857. 16mo; "Scenes and Impressions Abroad." New York: 1859; "My Sheet Anchor." Philadelphia: 1864. 32mo. Also sermons, addresses, reports, and contributions to periodicals.

Roe, Mrs. Marion H. (Marion P. Hooker, of Poultney.) Home Scenes and Heart-tints : A Memorial of Mrs. Marion H. Roe. Motto. New York : John F. Trow & Co., Printers, 50 Green Street. 1865. 12mo, pp. 208.
By Alva D. Rowe.

Roebeck, Jacob.
Biography of, see Barnes, Melvin.

Rogers, Ammi. *Memoirs* of the Rev. Ammi Rogers, A. M. A Clergyman of the Episcopal Church. Educated at Yale College in Connecticut, Ordained in Trinity Church in the City of New York,—Persecuted in the State of Connecticut, on account of Religion and Politics, for almost twenty years : and finally, Falsely Accused and Imprisoned in Norwich Jail, for two years, on the charge of Crimes said to have been committed in the town of Griswold, in the County of New London, when he was not within about one hundred miles of the place, And of which he was absolutely as innocent as the Judge who pronounced the sentence, or as any other person in the world. Also, an Index to the Holy Bible ; And a concise view of the Authority, Doctrine, and Worship, in the Protestant Episcopal Church. Composed, compiled and written by the said Ammi Rogers, Late Rector of St. Peter's Church in Hebron, Tolland Co., Conn., &c. Motto. Third Edition : With additions, omissions and alterations. Middlebury, Vt.: Printed by J. W. Copeland. 1830. 12mo, pp. 268.

Rogers, Robert.
See French War.

Rollins, C. V. *The Masonic Text Book*, containing the Monitorial Work of the First Three Degrees of Masonry, with a Digest of Masonic Law, Compiled from the decisions of the different Grand Masters of the Grand Lodge of Vermont, together with Rules for Masonic Trials, and Forms for Installation Ceremonies, &c. Also, a Uniform Funeral Service, With the date of Charter, number, name and number of members of each Lodge under the Jurisdiction of the Grand Lodge of Vermont, with date of their regular communications, Carefully Compiled and arranged by C. V. Rollins. Also an Historical Sketch of the Reorganization of the Grand Lodge after the Morgan Excitement ceased. Rutland : Tuttle and Company, Printers. 1870. 18mo, pp. 109.

—*Rollins' Masonic Text Book*, containing the Monitorial Work of the first Three Degrees of Masonry, together with Ceremonies of Installation, Consecration, Dedication, laying Foundation Stones, and Burial Service, Digest of Masonic Law, Rules for Masonic Trials, Forms for Masonic Documents, Etc. Revised and Enlarged &c. By C. V. Rollins. Rutland : Tuttle & Company, Printers. 1872. 12mo, pp. 280.

Rollins, Rev. Edward B. *Antimasonic Tract, No. 3.* Containing the Renunciation of Freemasonry. By the Rev. Edward B. Rollins, of Strafford, Vermont. Boston : Published by William R. Collier, at the Office of the Anti-Masonic Press. 1829. 12mo, pp. 12.

—*Mysteries Revealed.*
See Independent Order of Oddfellows.

Rollins, E. E. *The Memorial Record* of the Soldiers who enlisted from Greensboro, Vermont, to aid in subduing the great Rebellion of 1861–5, Accompanied by a brief History of each Regiment that left the State. Prepared by E. E. Rollins. Montpelier : Printed at the Freeman Printing House. 1868. 12mo, pp. 77.

Roman Catholic. *The Constitution and By-laws* of the St. Mary's R. Catholic Benevolent Society ; Established in 1860. Burlington : Times Book and Job Office Print. 1860. 18mo, pp. 13, (2).

—*Specification* of the Material to be Provided, and the Labor to be performed in the Erection of a new Cathedral, to be located upon the land Cor. St. Paul and Cherry Streets, Burlington, Vt., According to the Plans, Elevations and Sections furnished by the Architect, P. C. Keely. Burlington : Printed by Danforth & Smalley. 1861. 8vo, pp. 35.
See De Goesbriand.

Rood, Anson.
A Series of articles on Slavery, written in reply to Rev. Dr. Joel Parker, and published in book form. Mr. Rood was born in Jericho, Vt., and was graduated at Middlebury College, 1825 ; read Theology, and was pastor of a Congregational church in Danbury, Ct., then removed to Philadelphia, as pastor of a Presbyterian church. Assistant editor Philadelphia North American, 1849–51. Died 1887.

Rood, H. *A Sermon* delivered at the funeral of Caleb Webster, of North Haverhill, N. H. By Rev. H. Rood. November 18, 1847. Newbury, Vt.: L. J. McIndoe, Printer. 1848. 8vo, pp. 12.

Root, Erastus, A. B. *An Inaugural Dissertation* on the Chemical and Medicinal Properties of the Mineral Spring in Guilford. Read before the Second Medical Society of the State of Vermont, on the 8th day of January, 1817. By Erastus Root, A. B. Brattleborough : Simeon Ide, Printer. 1817. 8vo, pp. 15.

Roots, Benajah. *Election Sermon*, 1779.

—*Installation Sermon*, at Rutland, Vt. 1773.
Mr. Roots was born in Woodbury, Ct., in 1726, and was graduated at Princeton College, N. J., in 1754. He was settled over the Congregational church in Rutland, 1773, until his death, March 15, 1787.

Rossiter, E. W. *Trial* of Rev. E. W. Rossiter, at North Granville, Vt. (1823 ?) 8vo.
See Sabin's Dict. vol. 18, p. 21.

Roster. *Revised Roster* of Vermont Volunteers, and Lists of Vermonters who served in the Army and Navy of the United States, during the War of the Rebellion, 1861-66. Compiled by authority of the General Assembly under direction of Theodore S. Peck, Adjutant General. Montpelier, Vt.: Press of the Watchman Publishing Co., 1892. 4to, pp. vi, 863.

Rowley, Samuel. *The Ministerial Work, &* Call, & Ordination, Illustrated in A Sermon Delivered in Rupert, (Vt.) October 28, A. D. 1813. At the Ordination of Mr. P. W. Reynolds, By Samuel Rowley, V. D. M., Pastor of the Baptist Church in Granville, N. Y. To which are added the Ceremonies of Ordination. Salem N. Y.: J. P. Reynolds, Printer. 1814. 8vo, pp. 32.

Rowley, Thomas.
The early poet of the "Green Mountain Boys," was a native of Hebron, Ct., and settled in Danby, Vt., in 1768, where he resided mainly, and held many town offices until about the close of the Revolutionary War, when he moved to Shoreham, Vt., where he resided until near the time of his death, which occurred at the home of his son Nathan, in Benson, Vt., about 1803. Mr. Rowley, though lacking the advantages of education, was a wit, and possessed the true spirit of a poet, and many of his pieces were very popular and universally sung by the "Green Mountain Boys" during the War of the Revolution; many of his poems were published in the *Rural Magazine*, edited by the Rev. Samuel Williams at Rutland, and in the *Bennington Gazette*; a pamphlet of 23 pages was published in 1802, entitled "Selections and Miscellaneous Works of Thomas Rowley." For Sketch of his life and selections from his poetical works see "History of Shoreham," by Rev. J. F. Goodhue, pp. 162-179; "History of Danby," Vt.

Rowson, Susanna. *Charlotte Temple.* A Tale of Truth. By Mrs. Rowson, Author of Victoria, The Inquisitor, &c. Windsor: Published by Preston Merrifield. 1815. 18mo, pp. 168.

Roxbury. *Annual Reports* of the Town of Roxbury, March 1, 1866. 8vo, pp. 4.
Continued.

Royalton. *Annual Report* of the Auditors of the Town of Royalton, for the Year Ending February 29, 1876. Montpelier, Vt.: Argus and Patriot Steam Job Printing House. 1876. 8vo, pp. 7.
Continued.

—*Commemorative Exercises* at the One Hundredth Anniversary of the Organization of the Congregational Church, Royalton, Vermont. And the Fortieth Anniversary of the Ordination of the Pastor, Cyrus B. Drake, D. D., October 10th, 1877. Motto. 1777-1837-1877. small 4to, pp. 41. No imprint.
Contains a Historical Sermon by Dr. Drake, Addresses by Rev. A. C. Washburn, Hon. Frederick Billings, and others. Rev. Dr. Drake died April 21, 1878.

Royce, Andrew. *Universalism:* A Modern Invention; and not according to Godliness. Two Discourses. By A. Royce, acting Pastor of the Cong. Church, Williamstown, Vt. Windsor: Printed at the Chronicle Press. 1838. 8vo, pp. 56.

—*Universalism:* A Modern Invention, and not according to Godliness. By Andrew Royce, Acting Pastor of the Cong. Church, Williamstown, Vt. Second Edition, With an Examination of Certain Reviews. Windsor: Printed at the Chronicle Press. 1839. 16mo, pp. 207.

—*Considerations* for the people of Barre (Vt.) respecting the Hostility of the Methodists, of this Town, towards the Congregationalists. Montpelier: Printed by E. P. Walton and Sons. 1844. 8vo, pp. 18.
See Barre.
See Ballou, Eli, in reply.

—*Funeral Sermon.*
See Hazen, Austin.
Rev. Andrew Royce was born in Marlow, N. H., in June, 1805, but came to Vermont in childhood, residing in Barre, and Sharon, Vt. He read law, and practiced some four years, when he was converted by the Rev. Sherman Kellogg, who was the father of William Pitt, the Louisiana *Statesman* / and began to preach in 1834, and was settled over Congregational churches in Williamstown, Vt., five years, Barre, Vt., sixteen years; and was then agent for the Bible Society, etc. He died in Waterbury, Vt., October 15, 1864.

Royce, Homer E. *Acquisition of Cuba.* Speech of the Hon. Homer E. Royce, of Vermont, in the House of Representatives, February 15, 1859. 8vo, pp. 7.
Judge Royce was a native of Berkshire, Vt., where he was born in 1819; he practiced law at Berkshire, 1844 to 1869, and at St. Albans, 1869 to 1870; Representative in the Legislature, 1846-7 and 1861, State Senator, 1849, '50 and '51; Member of Congress 1857 to 1862; Assistant Justice of the Supreme Court of Vermont, 1870-82; Chief Justice, 1882 till his death in 1890.

Royce, M. S. *A Series* of Brief Historical Sketches of the Church of England, and of the Protestant Episcopal Church in the United States. By M. S. Royce, Rector of St. Paul's Church, Franklin, Tennessee. New York: General Protestant Episcopal Sunday School Union and Church Book Society, 762 Broadway. 1860. 16mo. pp. 198.
Mr. Royce was born in Rutland, Vt.

Rublee, Horace,
A native of Vermont, born about 1830; at the age of ten years removed to Wisconsin, and in 1860 was State Librarian, and Editor of the "State Journal," at Madison. He was also a poet, and is assigned a place in the "Poets and Poetry of the West."

Rules and Articles of War; with the Different Acts of Congress on Military affairs: Also, the late acts for raising 20,000 &c., &c., &c. With a List of the General Staff, War Department, And the Several Districts as they are numbered. Also, new Rules and Regulations. In short, everything as it regards the Officer or Soldier. To which is added, a complete List of all the Officers in the Army and Navy: With an Index. Burlington, Vermont: Samuel Mills, printer. 1813. 8vo, pp. 151.

Rules *of the Federal Courts* of the United States of America, within the Vermont District; A Roll of the Practising Attornies; and the names of the Commissioners appointed by the Circuit Court in said District, to take depositions and acknowledgements of bail and affidavits, conformably to the laws of the United States. Rutland: Printed by Fay & Davison. 18mo, pp. 23. (About 1818).
Contains list of attorneys, 1792 to 1818.

Rules *of the Supreme Court* and Court of Chancery for the State of Vermont. Rutland: Printed by Fay, Davison & Burt. [1817]. 12mo, pp. 12.

—*The same.* Middlebury: Printed by Copeland and Allen. 1821. 12mo, pp. 6.

—*The same.* Burlington: J. Spooner, Printer. 1821. 12mo, pp. 15.

Runnels, M. T. *Addresses* and Proceedings at the Centennial Anniversary of the Congregational Church, in Sanbornton, N. H., November 12 and 13, 1871. Compiled by order of the Church, by M. T. Runnells, Pastor. Hartford, Conn: Press of Case, Lockwood & Brainard. 1872. 8vo, pp. 82.

—*A Genealogy* of the Runnels and Reynolds Families in America; with Records and Brief Memorials of the Earliest Ancestors, so far as known, and of many of their Descendants, bearing the same and other Names. In Three Parts, with an Appendix. By Rev. M. T. Runnels, A. M., Pastor of the Congregational Church in Sanbornton N. H. Motto. Boston: Alfred Mudge & Son, Printers, 34 School Street. 1873. 8vo, pp. 855.

—*A Memorial* of Miss Martha A. Piper. Compiled at the request of her mother, by Rev. Moses T. Runnels, Pastor of the Congregational Church in Sanbornton, N. H. Boston: Alfred Mudge & Son, Printers, 34 School Street. 1875. 8vo, pp. 66.

Mr. Runnells was born at Cambridge, Vt., January 23, 1830; was graduated at Dartmouth College in 1853, and at East Windsor, Ct., in 1856; was employed by the American Sunday School Union, 1856-59; preached at Orford, N. H., 1860-65, and Sanbornton, 1868-80, subsequently at Charlestown, N. H., and at Newport, N. H.

Rupert. Vermont. *Fornication* binds the criminal parties to marry. The Decision of the Congregational Church in Rupert, Vt., relative to a Case of Discipline. With the Result of a Council. Bennington: 1815. 8vo, pp. 40.

Rural Magazine, Rutland.

See Williams, S. & Co.

Rush, Benjamin. *Religious Tracts.* No XV. From the Press of T. C. Strong, Middlebury. 1812. Printed for the Vermont Religious Tract Society. An Inquiry into the effects of Ardent Spirits upon the Human Body and Mind, with an Account of the Means of preventing, and of the Remedies for Curing them. By Benjamin Rush, M. D.

Rush, Richards.

See Addison County.

Russell, Charles Theo. *The Enfranchisement of Labor.* An Address delivered before the Vermont State Agricultural Society, at Brattleboro, Vermont. September 14, 1854. By Charles Theo. Russell. Middlebury: Printed at the Register Book and Job Office. 1855, 8vo, pp. 21.

Russell, John, Jun. *A History* of the Vermont State Prison, from the passing of the Law for its Erection in 1807, to July, 1812. Containing a minute Description of the Prison Buildings, the Manufactures, Number of Prisoners, their Crimes, when committed, their Term of Commitment, &c., &c. Together with the Rules, Regulations, Laws, &c., of Said Prison, and a list of the officers who have been concerned in its Management. To which is added, some Remarks on the Utility of the Institution. By John Russell, Jun., Windsor, Vt.: Published by Preston Merrifield, for the proprietor of the Copyright. Wright & Sibley, Printers, 1812. 12mo, pp. 91.

Contains a view of the Prison, which was engraved by Isaac Eddy, of Weathersfield, Vt.

—*The History* of the War between the United States and Great Britain, Chiefly Compiled from Public Documents, with an Appendix, Containing Correspondence, Treaty of Peace, list of Vessels Captured, &c. Compiled by J. Russell, Jr. Second Edition. Hartford: 1815. 8vo, pp. 402.

Mr. Russell, son of John and Lucretia (Preston) Russell, was born in Cavendish, Vt., July 31, 1793; died at Bluffdale, Green county, Ill., January 21, 1863; he was graduated at Middlebury College, 1818, the profits of his two works, "History of Vermont State Prison," and "History of the War of 1812," mainly supporting him while in college. Immediately after his graduation Mr. Russell went to McIntosh Co., Georgia, where he taught a short time, when he moved to White Water, Ind., where, on the 25th of October, 1818, he married Laura Ann, daughter of Capt. Gideon Spencer, of Vergennes, Vt., who was then on his way west. In 1819 Mr. Russell moved to Bonhommie, St. Louis Co., Mo., where he was tutor in a private family five years; while at this place he wrote his famous temperance Tale, "The Venomous Worm," or the "Worm of the Still," which gave him great celebrity, and was printed in many languages in Europe, and found a place in American and British school books of the time. "The Venomous Worm" was first printed in the "Missourian," a local newspaper at St. Charles, Mo. Mr. Russell moved to Vandalia, Ill., in 1825, where he taught in a high school, and was assistant editor of the "Illinois Magazine," by James Hall. In 1828 Mr. Russell purchased a farm at Bluffdale, which was ever after his home.

Mr. Russell joined the Baptist church at Vergennes, Vt., in 1816; he was licensed as a preacher Feb. 9, 1833, but it does not appear that he ever assumed the duties of the ministerial profession. He was editor of the "Advertiser," Louisville, Ky., 1841-2, and principal of Spring Hill Academy, at Louisiana, Mo., 1843-50.

The additional publications by Dr. Russell are: "The Serpent Uncoiled, or a full length View of Universalism." 1841, 8vo, pp. 127; "The Momoners," 8vo, pp. 250; also, "Little Granite," "Allin Wade," "Lame Isaac," "Going to Mill," "Ellenwood, the Outlaw," "Piasa," and the "Spectre Hunter."

Gov. Ford in his history of Illinois speaks of Mr. Russell as "a man of genius and a fine writer;" Gov. John Reynolds of Illinois in his "My Own Times," devotes pp. 436 to 440 to Mr. Russell.

Dr. Russell received the honorary LL. D. from the University of Chicago, 1862; he was a liberal contributor to the Chicago Historical Society, and his name appears frequently in its proceedings, and at his death a liberal portion of his books and papers were deposited with that Society. He held a distinguished rank in Illinois in educational and literary circles; he was the first president of Shurtleff College, at Alton, Ill., for one year, 1831-2; at the organization of "Illinois College" at Jacksonville in 1832, Professor Russell was prevailed upon to deliver the inaugural address in Latin.

Mr. Russell was sometime editor of the "Backwoodsman," a newspaper at Grafton, Ill.; most of his later publications, whether in book form or in magazines and newspapers, were published anonymously.

Rev. Dr. J. M. Peck of Illinois, on a visit to New York, procured the publication of a small volume for Prof. Russell, which was stereotyped and had a large circulation, but the publishers never knew the name of the author.

Prof. Russell's "Piasa," written for an Eastern Magazine, ran rapidly through the American press, and about three years later it appeared in a French periodical, bearing the name of a Frenchman who had traveled in this county, as the author—Rev. Dr. Peck exposed the fraud.

For an elaborate sketch of Dr. Russell, see "Life of Richard Yates, War Governor of Illinois," by Prof. U. V. Reavis.

Ruter, Martin, D. D. *An Easy* entrance into the Sacred Language; being a concise Hebrew Grammar, without points. Compiled for the use and encouragement of learners, and adapted to such as have not the aid of a teacher. By Martin Ruter, D. D. Cincinnati: Published by Martin Ruter, for the Methodist Episcopal Church. Morgan and Lodge, Printers. 1824. 12mo, pp. 96.

Rev. Dr. Ruter was born in Sutton, Mass., in April, 1785; and died in Texas, May 16, 1838. His father, who was by trade a blacksmith, removed to Bradford, Vt., with his family, in 1793, where, and in the adjoining town of Corinth, the family resided. Young Ruter was converted to Methodism at the age of 15 years, and when about 18 years of age he became an assistant circuit preacher, being some time located in Montreal, P. Q. After a few years he went to Ohio, and was subsequently President of Augusta College, Kentucky, also of Allegheny College, Pa., and having resigned the last position, he went as a Missionary to Texas where he remained until his death. For a more full account of him, see "History of Bradford," pp. 166-9.

RUTLAND. *A Letter* to the First Congregational Pedo-Baptist Church, at Rutland in Vermont: With a Collection of Hymns, Letters, &c., from the works of Emmons, Wesley, and others. Also, Dr. Robbins' account of the late revival in Plymouth, Mass. By Peter Philanthropos Roots. Motto. Hartford: Printed and sold by Hudson & Goodwin. 12mo, pp. 156.

No date, but about 1795.

—*Articles of Faith,* adopted by the Rutland Consociation, September, 1831. 16mo, pp. 7.

—*Act of Incorporation* and By-Laws of the Rutland Savings Bank, in Rutland, Vermont. Incorporated November, 1850. Rutland : Printed at Tuttle's Book and Job Office. 1852. 12mo, pp. 16.

—*Reports* of the Town Superintendents of Common Schools, to the Freemen of Rutland, at the Annual Town Meeting, holden March 29, 1852. Rutland : Tuttle's Book and Job Office. 1852. 8vo, pp. 8.
Continued.

—*The Articles*, Profession of Faith, and other Standards of the Congregational Church, in East Rutland, Vermont, with a List of the Members. Rutland : George A. Tuttle & Co., Printers. 1856. 12mo, pp. 23.

—*Selectmen's Report* to the Town of Rutland, March 3, 1857. Rutland : George A. Tuttle & Company, Printers. 1857. 8vo, pp. 15.
Continued.

—*Catalogue* of the Rutland High School Library. 1857. Rutland : George A. Tuttle & Co., Printers. 1857. 12mo, pp. 15.

—*Auditors' Report* of Accounts of Village Trustees, for Year ending May 28, 1861. And Water Commissioners' Accounts, Year ending July 1, 1861. Rutland : John Cain, Steam Printer. 1861. 8vo, pp. 12.

—*Same for 1862*. Same imprint, pp. 8.
Continued.

—*Services* at the Dedication of Evergreen Cemetery, Rutland, Vt., October 16th, 1861. Published by order of the Trustees. Rutland : Printed by Geo. A. Tuttle & Co. 1861. 8vo, pp. 20.

—*Preserve this for Reference*. Amended Act of Incorporation and Ordinances of the Village of Rutland. 1866. Rutland : Printed by Tuttle, Gay & Co. 1866. 8vo, pp. 28.

—*A Manual and Directory* of the Corporate Village of Rutland, and Business Advertiser. Compiled by Frederick W. Hopkins, Clerk of County Court. Rutland : Tuttle & Co., Publishers. 1867. 12mo, pp. 54.

—*Report* of the Trustees and other Officers of the Village of Rutland, April 20, 1867. Rutland : Tuttle & Company, Printers. 1867. 8vo, pp. 16.
Continued annually, since 1867, with varying titles, imprints and number of pages.

—*Tariff and Revised Tariff* of the Association of Underwriters of Rutland, Vt. Rutland : 1867. 12mo.

—*Articles*, Profession of Faith, and other Standards of the Congregational Church, in East Rutland, Vermont, With a list of the members. Rutland : Tuttle & Company, Printers. 1868. 12mo, pp. 28.

—*Twelfth Report* of Registry and Returns of Births, Marriages and Deaths, in Rutland. Dec. 31, 1868. Rutland : 1870. 8vo.

—*Missionary Association*, Annual Report of, with a Catalogue of Annual Subscribers. 1868. Rutland : Tuttle & Co., Printers. 1868. 12mo, pp. 15.

—*Shall Rutland be Mortgaged?* 8 vo, pp. 8.
An address to the tax payers of Rutland, January 1, 1869, against bonding the town in aid of the Rutland and Woodstock Railroad.

—*1770. 1870. Centennial Celebration* of the Settlement of Rutland, Vt., October 2d, 3d, 4th, and 5th, 1870, including the Addresses, Historical Papers, Poems, Responses at their dinner table, etc. Compiled by Chauncy K. Williams, Rutland : Tuttle & Co., Printers. 1870. 8vo, pp. VIII, 122.

—*Preserve this for Reference*. Amended Act of Incorporation and Ordinances of the Village of Rutland, 1871. Rutland : Tuttle & Co., Printers. 1871. 8vo, pp. 36.

—*The Rutland Baptist Church Manual*, containing the Declaration of Faith, Covenant, History of the Church, List of Officers, Members, etc. Rutland : Tuttle & Company, Printers. 1871. 24mo, pp. 51.

—*History of the Rutland Baptist Church*, by Rev. E. Mills. n. d. n. p. 18mo, pp. 51. [1871.]

—*Directory of the Village of Rutland*, and Business Directory of Whitehall, Fort Edward, West Rutland, Castleton. Compiled by Fitzgerald & Dillon, Albany, N. Y. Rutland : Tuttle & Co., Publishers, 1872. 12mo, pp. 108.

—*By-Laws of Vermont Lodge*, No. 1, Knights Pythias. Rutland, Vt. Rutland : Tuttle & Co., Printers. 1872. 16mo. pp. 11, (1).

—*Annual Report of the Trustees* and Other Officers of the Village of Rutland. 1873. Rutland : Tuttle & Co., Printers. 1873. 8vo, pp. 28.
Continued.

—*History of Rutland newspapers*.
See Williams, C. K.

—*Organized* February 8, 1864. By-Laws of Union Hook & Ladder Co. Of Rutland. Rutland : Globe Paper Co., Printers. 1873. 18mo, pp. 8

—*Constitution*, By-Laws, and Rules of Order of Rutland Typographical Union. No. 165. Organized, May, 1873. Rutland, Vt.: Globe Paper Co., Printers, 1874. 18mo, pp. 18.

—*Constitution and By-Laws* of the Ancient Order of Hibernians. Instituted March, 1852 ; Chartered March 16th, 1853 ; Adopted June 8th, 1857. Rutland, Vt.: Tuttle & Co., Printers. 1874. 16mo, pp. 16.

—*An Edition* of the same, 1875, same imprint. 16mo, pp. 16.

—*Rutland Directory*, embracing the Village of Rutland, Center Rutland and West Rutland. Also, a Business Directory, 1874–75. Compiled by Fitzgerald & Dillon. Albany. N. Y. Price $1.50. Rutland : Tuttle & Co, Publishers. 1874-5. 12mo, pp. 107.

—*Rules* of the St. Patrick's Roman Catholic Benevolent Society, West Rutland, Vt. Rutland : Tuttle & Co., Printers. 1875. 12mo, pp. 7.

—*Rutland Directory*, embracing the residents of the Village of Rutland, Center Rutland and West Rutland, also a Business Directory, and a Street Directory for 1876-7. Compiled by R. S. Dillon & Co., Albany, N. Y. Price $1.50. Rutland : Tuttle & Co., Publishers. 1876. 8vo, pp. 100.

—*The Constitution and By-Laws* of Rutland and Bennington Conference of Congregational Churches. 1859. Rutland : Geo. A. Tuttle & Co's Steam Presses. 1859. 16mo, pp. 15.

—*Manual* for the use of the Congregational Church in West Rutland, Vt. Adopted and Published by Order of the Church. Windsor : Printed at the Vermont Chronicle Office. 1858. 12mo, pp. 28.

—*Manual* of the Congregational Church in Rutland, Vermont, 1877. Published by the Church. (No imprint.) 8vo, pp. 39.
Contains list of members from its organization in 1788.

—*Manual of the First Congregational Church*, West Rutland, Vt., Organization and Early History. Rutland : Globe Paper Co., Printers. 1877. 12mo, pp. 28.

—*Another edition*, 1877, same imprint, 8vo, pp. 8.

—*Report* of the Committee on Water Supply. April, 1878. Rutland : Tuttle & Co., Printers. 1878. 8vo, pp. 30.

—*Annual Report* of the Board of Trustees and other Officers of the Rutland Graded School District, for the year ending March 19, 1878. Rutland : Tuttle & Co., Printers. 1878. 8vo, pp. 12.
Continued.

—*Catalogue* of the Rutland Graded Schools and of the High School Library, for the school year ending June 21, 1878, with the Manual of Rules and Regulations. Published by Order of the Board of Education. Rutland : Tuttle & Co., Printers. 1878. 8vo, pp. 45.
Continued.

—*Official Military and Naval Records* of Rutland, Vt., in the War of the Rebellion, 1861-66. Compiled by J. H. Goulding. Rutland : Tuttle & Co., Printers. 1891. 8vo, pp. 100.

—*Constitution*, Rules and By-Laws of Court Rutland No. 7, Foresters of America. Rutland : Tuttle & Co., Printers. 1896. 16mo. pp. 66.

—*Young Ladies' Cook Book*, by the Young Ladies' Mission Circle of the Methodist Church, Rutland, Vt. Rutland : Tuttle & Co., Printers. 1896. 12mo, pp. 52.

—*Knights of Honor.* A Statement of the Objects and Benefits of the Order. By-laws of Rutland Lodge No. 1281, K. of H., located at Rutland, Vt. Rutland : F. M. McLean, Printers 5 Grove St. 1881. 18mo, p. 12.

Rutland County (*Republican*) *Convention.* Held at West Rutland, July 30, 1813. Rutland : Printed by Fay & Davison. Broadsheet.
This was a war convention, of which Hon. James Witherell was President, and Robert Temple, Esq., Secretary.
Hon. Jonas Galusha and Hon. Paul Brigham were recommended for Governor and Lieutenant Governor.

—*Complete list* of Cong'l Ministers and Churches, in.
See Steele, Joseph.

—*Statistics of the Bar of.*
See Williams, C. L.

—*Minutes* of the First Annual Meeting of the Rutland County S. S. Union, held at East Poultney, Vt., January 18th and 19th, 1865, together with the Report of the Secretary.

Published by Order of the Society. Rutland : Tuttle, Gay & Co., Printers. 1865. 12mo, pp. 12.

—*Rutland County Almanac*, 1862. Issued by Pond & Morse Geo. A. Tuttle & Co. Printers, Rutland: 1861. sm. 8vo, pp. 40.

—*Rules* of Rutland County Court. Adopted April Term, 1840. 8vo, pp. 11.

—*Atlas* of Rutland County, Vermont. From actual Surveys by and under the direction of F. W. Beers, assisted by F. S. Fulmer & Others. Published by F. W. Beers, A. D. Ellis & G. G. Soule, 95 Maiden Lane, New York. 1869. Folio. pp. 37. (10).

—*Foreign* Missionary Society.
See Green, Beriah, sermon and first report, 1826.

—*Gazetteer* and Business Directory of Rutland County, Vt., for 1881-82. Compiled and published by Hamilton Child. Syracuse, N. Y. 1882. 8vo, pp. 643.

—*1781, Rutland County, 1881.* Centennial Celebration of the Organization of Rutland County, Vt., Held under the auspices of the Rutland County Historical Society, at the Town Hall, Rutland, Vt., March 4, 1881. Including the addresses, etc., and Proceedings of the Rutland Co. Hist. Society. Compiled by Lyman Williams Redington, of Rutland. Montpelier : Argus and Patriot Book Print. 1882. 8vo, pp. 194.

Ryegate. *Church Controversy.*
See Milligan, James.

Sabbath Schools. *First* Annual Report of the Vermont Sabbath School Union : Presented at Castleton, September 13, 1826. Published by order of the Society. Rutland : Printed by William Fay. 1826. 12mo, pp. 16.
Continued. Was organized and Constitution adopted, September 14, 1825.

—*The Sabbath School Guide.* By Rev. J. J. Shipherd. No. 1. Burlington : Published by C. Goodrich. 1828. 12mo, pp. 60.
Semi-annually.

—*Youth's Herald*, and Sabbath School Magazine, Vol. II. February, 1830. No. 2. Middlebury : By the Vermont Sabbath School Union. Ovid Miner, Printer. 1830. 18mo, pp. 32.

—*Sabbath School Reporter.* No. 1. of Vol. 2. Castleton, March 1, 1834. Monthly. 12mo, pp. 16.

—*Proceedings* of the First Annual Meeting of the Franklin County Sunday School Union, Held at Swanton Falls, On Tuesday, June 14th, 1864. St. Albans : Vermont Transcript Print, 1864. 8vo, pp. 8.

—*A Report* of the Organization of the Rutland County Sabbath School Union. Together with the Constitution and the Instructions of the Board of Managers to the Town Committees. Compiled and Published by Order of the Board by J. Henry Giles, Secretary. March 14, 1864. Rutland : Tuttle & Gay, Printers. 1864. 12mo, pp. 8.

—*Report* of the Sixth Annual Convention of the Vermont Sunday School Association, Held at Bradford, October 13th, 14th and 15th, A. D. 1874. Published for the Association by A. M. Butler, State Secretary, Essex. Montpelier,

Vt.: Argus and Patriot Steam Printing Establishment. 1875. 8vo, pp. 56.

Sabine, James. *The Demise* of the President improved in a Sermon, delivered on Fast Day, May 14, 1841, as recommended by government. By James Sabine, Rector of Christ Church, Bethel, Vermont. Bethel: From the Log Cabin Press. 1841. 12mo, pp. 30.

Safford, Truman H.
Mr. Safford was born in Royalton, Vt., Feb. 19, 1810; died at Belmont, Mass., Nov. 7, 1880. Bred a farmer, without the advantages of a liberal education, he developed decided literary tastes, and was an earnest student in search of knowledge. Intrusted in early life with the confidence of his townsmen, he filled various positions of trust in their gift, and as a member of the Legislature was the author and advocate of the law giving fugitive slaves the right of trial by jury. He was the author of many beautiful sketches under the title of the "Distinguished Dead of Mt. Auburn." At one time he projected and edited a little sheet, "The Mt. Auburn Memorial."

Safford, Truman Henry, Jr. *The Youth's* Almanac, for the year 1846. Being second year after Bissextile or Leap Year. Astronomical Calculations. By Truman H. Safford, Jr. Calculated for the vicinity of Bradford, Vt.: Bradford, Vt.: Published by A. Low. A. B. F. Hildreth, Printer. 12mo, pp. 46.
Mr. Safford, Mathematician and Astronomer, was born in Royalton, Vt., January 6, 1836; graduated at Harvard University, 1854. His youthful precocity was remarkable; in his 9th year he could multiply four figures by four figures with wonderful rapidity; his first almanac was prepared in 1845, when he was but nine and a half years old. At the age of 14 he astonished the world by the production of the elliptic elements of the first comet of 1849. Answers to the longest and most difficult questions, read to him but once, were usually given without effort or fatigue. He was connected with the Cambridge Observatory from March, 1863, to December 28, 1865, when he was appointed Director of the Chicago Observatory, which position he still holds (1880.) After the death of Professor G. P. Bond, in February, 1865, the incomplete report of his valuable discoveries was written out in full by Mr. Safford, constituting the 5th volume of the "Annals of the Observatory," *Drake's Dictionary.* See "Ladies' Repository," Cincinnati, 1849, for account of the different examinations of young Safford, and notice of his life.

Sage, Sylvester. *A Sermon,* Delivered before His Excellency The Governor, The Honorable Council and House of Representatives of the State of Vermont, at Westminister, on the Day of the Anniversary Election, October 13th, 1803. By Sylvester Sage, A. M., Pastor of the first Church in Westminster. Windsor: Printed by Alden Spooner. 1803. 8vo, pp. 31.

—*A Sermon,* Delivered at the Installation of Rev. Jesse Townsend, A. M., to the Pastoral care of Christ's Church in Durham, State of New York, June 20, 1798. By Sylvester Sage, A. M., Pastor of Christ's Church, in Westminster, State of Vermont. Catskill: Printed by M. Croswell. 8vo, pp. 24.

—*A Sermon,* delivered at the Installation of the Rev. Reuben Emerson, A. M., over the First Church of Christ in Reading, Massachusetts, October 17, 1804. By Sylvester Sage, A. M., Pastor of the First Church of Christ in Westminster, Vermont. Salem: Printed by Joshua Cushing. 1805. 8vo, pp. 28.
Mr. Sage was born in Berlin, Conn., January 24, 1765; was graduated at Yale, 1787, and was settled over the Congregational church in Westminster, Vt., 1790-1807; then in Braintree, Mass., two years, when he returned to Westminster, and continued there until his death, January 21, 1841. Two other sermons by Mr. Sage were pub-

lished, but they do not relate to Vermont. See "Deming's Catalogue," p. 196.

Salem. *Annals of.*
See White, P. H.

Salisbury. *History of.*
See Weeks, John M.

Sanborn, A. J. *Green Mountain Poets.* Edited by A. J. Sanborn, A. M., Principal of Middlebury High School. Claremont, N. H.: 1872. 12mo, pp. 511.
A compilation of selections from Vermont poets.

Sanborn, Edwin D. *An Oration* delivered at St. Johnsbury, Vt., July Fourth, 1851. By Edwin D. Sanborn, Prof. &c. in Dart. College, Hanover, N. H. Published by Request. Hanover: Printed at the Dartmouth Press. July, 1851. 8vo, pp. 23.

—*An Address,* in commemoration of the completion of the First Free Bridge l across Connecticut River, by Prof. E. D. Sanborn. Together with Report of Proceedings, and remarks by others. July 1st, 1859. Hanover, N. H.: 8vo, pp. 40.

Sanborn, Rev. R. S. *Eulogy,* on the Intellectuality of Daniel Webster, delivered in Northfield, Vt. By Rev. R. S. Sanborn. West Randolph: Printed at the Ægis Office. 1852. 8vo, pp. 12.

SANDERS, DANIEL CLARKE. *A History* of the Indian Wars with the first settlers of the United States, particularly in New England. Written in Vermont. (Motto.) Montpelier, Vt.: Published by Wright and Sibley. 1812. Wright and Sibley, Printers. 18mo, pp. 319.
This is one of the best written Indian histories of its period, and is exceedingly scarce, on account of a bitter and unjust criticism, which caused the author to suppress and destroy the work as far as possible, only a few copies apparently getting into circulation.
The late Samuel G. Drake, of Boston, said to the writer, "This book of Dr. Sanders' is infinitely superior, not only in a literary point of view, but in the accuracy of its historical facts, to Mr. Henry Trumbull's work upon the same subject, and issued the same year."
The criticism referred to appeared in the "Literary and Philosophical Repertory," No. 5, 1814, a periodical published at Middlebury, Vt., by "An Association of Gentlemen." (See Middlebury.) We quote a few passages from the criticisms of these "Gentlemen:" "To exhibit all that is incorrect, and groveling and affected in style, and erroneous and puerile and paltry in sentiment, would require an inordinate portion of our work." * * "The opinion expressed respecting the time when Christianity may successfully be disseminated among the Indians, is the opinion of the modern school of infidelity." * * "But our most serious ground for censure against this work is the deadly hostility which it manifests against the religious principles of the fathers of New England." * * "Not more rancorous was the hatred of Voltaire, of Hume and of Gibbon to the Gospel of Christ, than that which our author displays toward correct principles of religion," etc. * * "Our author has adopted the cant of every licentious advocate of infidelity and irreligion, and of every unprincipled and daring propagator of error, and impiety and guilt." * * "But the rancour of his heart is not satisfied." * * "What is actually the intention of the author of this book, whether to aid the cause of infidelity and open irreligion, or simply to aim a blow at orthodoxy, it is impossible for us to determine." * * "That parent we cannot but declare lost to his duty who allows the "History of the Indian Wars" to be within the reach of his children, to corrupt their principles and poison their minds, and to lay the foundation of their irreligion and guilt, of their misery and perdition. We give a few of the passages in Dr. Sanders' book quoted by this critic, and which appear to him so objectionable:
"Even the *good* Christians of New England, with all their faith in the doctrine of disinterested benevolence, sold those Indians whom they took in war as slaves to the West Indies."—Page 204.

"Rhode Island, not being deemed sufficiently orthodox on tenets much agitated in those days, was not usually invited to join the holy bands in the wars against the savages; Connecticut raised her quota of 190 men, placed under the conduct of Capt. Mason; about 60 Mohegans and 200 Narragansetts were permitted without any religious scruples, to join on the way in these holy crusades. The troops from Massachusetts did not arrive in season for the main action, having been detained by disputes and discussions concerning the covenant of grace and works, a controversy introduced by the celebrated Mrs. Anne Hutchinson, a zealous antinomian of Boston, who was banished for her opinions by the meek and benevolent Christians and Clergy of that colony, and sent near New Haven among the Indians, who soon murdered both her and her numerous family."—Page 43-44.

"Though we call the savages cruel, yet their cruelties are tender mercies compared with the atrocities of the very founders of New England, when in 1676 they tried and executed by English laws, the Indians who had surrendered with views of being safe, at least in their persons."

"The English troops were very orthodox, no doubt; but their wild excesses are to be deeply regretted; and it must be allowed by all that their barbarities were sometimes such as to make them differ very little in character from that of the savages themselves; and if christians could conduct as these did, what more could infidels do? Orthodox creeds do not always sanctify the heart and conduct."—Page 50.

Possibly the sentiments advanced by Dr. Sanders were some fifty years in advance of his time, but we surmise that the savage attacks upon him by the "Gentlemen" of Middlebury were instigated by envy and jealousy towards the University of Vermont, of which Dr. Sanders was President.

The "Indian Wars" of Dr. Sanders' was surreptitiously reprinted by an enterprising printer at Rochester, N. Y., in 1828, omitting chapter 27, 12 pages, which treats of the morality, virtues and vices of the Indians, and with the addition of accounts of the battles of General Jackson, with the following title:

"A history of the Indian wars with the first settlers of the United States to the commencement of the late war. Together with an appendix not before added to this history, containing interesting accounts of battles fought by Gen. Andrew Jackson, with two plates." *Rochester, N. Y. Printed by Edwin Scrantum.* 1828. pp. 180.

We select from Dr. Sanders' other publications those relating to Vermont:

—*The Pleasures* and Advantages of Friendly Society. A Sermon preached at Vergennes, State of Vermont, On St. John's Festival, June 26th, A. D. 1792, before the Free and Accepted Masons of Dorchester Lodge, No. XII. And Published at their Request. By Daniel Clarke Sanders, A. M., A Candidate for the Gospel Ministry. Printed at Windsor, State of Vermont, By James Reed Hutchins, For the Masonic Fraternity of Vergennes. MDCCXCII. Square 4to, small. pp. 16.

—*A Sermon* on the Death of the wife of Dr. Hoyt, New Haven, Vt., 1795.

—*A Sermon*, on occasion of the Death of Mr. Martin Harmon, A. B., who died in the City of Vergennes, July 25, 1798. Æt. 24. Published by desire of the hearers. By Daniel Clarke Sanders, A. M. Minister of the Congregation in Vergennes. Vergennes: Printed by G. and R. Waite. 1798. 8vo, pp. 22.

—*A Discourse* in commemoration of General George Washington. By Rev. Daniel Clarke Sanders, D. D. Burlington, Vt.: 1800. small 4to, pp. 20.

A Discourse addressed to Washington Lodge, No. 7, on the Festival of St. John, Dec. 27, 1800. By Daniel Clarke Sanders. Burlington, Vermont: Printed for Washington Lodge, By John K. Baker. A. L. 5801. (1801.) 8vo, pp. 16.

—*A Discourse*, on the occasion of the Death of Mr. Eldridge Packer, of Shelburne. By Daniel Clarke Sanders, A. M., President of the University of Vermont, at Burlington. Burlington, Vermont: Printed by John K. Baker. 1802. 8vo, pp. 16.

—*A Sermon*, preached before His Excellency Isaac Tichenor, Esq., Governor; His Honor Paul Brigham, Esq., Lieutenant Governor; the Honorable Council and House of Representatives of the State of Vermont, October 11, 1798, In the City of Vergennes, on Occasion of General Election. By Daniel Clarke Sanders, A. M., Minister of the Congregation in Vergennes. Printed by Order of the Legislative Assembly. Vergennes: Printed by G. and R. Waite. 1798. 8vo, pp. 22.

—*A Discourse on Slander*, delivered at Burlington, on the Lord's Day, December 27, 1801. By Daniel Clarke Sanders, A. M., President of the University of Vermont. Burlington, Vermont: Printed by John K. Baker. 1802. 8vo, pp. 16.

—*A Discourse*, on Occasion of the Death of William Coit, Esquire, Who died, February 15th, 1802, Aetatis 46. By Daniel Clarke Sanders, A. M., President of the University of Vermont, at Burlington. Burlington, Vermont: Printed by John K. Baker. 1802. 8vo, pp. 16.

—*A Sermon* on the Death of Mr. Henry Lyman, Merchant, of Montreal. 1809.

—*A Discourse*, on the decease of Mrs. Martha Russell, who died, at Burlington, January 23d—Interred on the 26th—1805, after a mental derangement during the preceding seven years. Aged 50. The Consort of David Russell, Esquire. By Daniel C. Sanders, A. M., President of the University of Vermont, in Burlington. Bennington: Printed by Haswell & Smead. 1805. 8vo, pp. 24.

—*A Charge to the Graduates in The University of Vermont*, at Burlington, at the public Commencement, September 9th, 1807. By Daniel C. Sanders, A. M., President. Burlington: Printed by Samuel Mills. 1807. 8vo, pp. 16.

—*An Address to the Students* in The University of Vermont, May sixth, 1807; on occasion of the Death of William Homer Coit, member of the Sophomore Class, who died, December 23, 1806, Aged 18, being the first instance of mortality among the members, since the organization of the Institution. By Daniel C. Sanders, A. M., President of the College. (Motto.) Burlington: Printed by Samuel Mills. August, 1807. 8vo, pp. 16.

—*A Discourse* at the Funeral of Mrs. Emily Jewett, aged 27, who died of a Consumption, 4th June, 1809, the Consort of Mr. Moses Jewett, in Burlington. By Daniel C. Sanders, D. D., President of the University of Vermont. Burlington, Vt.: Printed by Samuel Mills. 1809. 8vo, pp. 24.

—*A Discourse*, Preached in Burlington before Washington Lodge, No. 7, on the Festival of St. John the Baptist, 24th June, 1811, by Daniel Clarke Sanders, D. D., President of the University of Vermont. Burlington, Vt.: Printed by Samuel Mills. 1811. 8vo, pp. 32.

—*A Charge to the Graduates* in the University of Vermont, in Burlington, at the Public Commencement, 29th July, 1812. By Daniel C. Sanders, D. D., President. Burlington, Vt.: Printed by Samuel Mills. 1812. 8vo, pp. 14.

—*A Discourse*, pronounced in the chapel of the University of Vermont, 29th April, 1813. Occasioned by the death of Doct. Cassius F. Pomeroy, A. M., and Ebenezer Gilbert, Member of the Sophomore Class. Published at the request of the Students. By Daniel Clarke Sanders, D. D., President. Burlington: Printed by Samuel Mills. 1813. 8vo, pp. 24.

Dr. Sanders was born in Sturbridge, Mass., May 3, 1768; died in Medfield, Mass., October 18, 1850; was graduated at Harvard College in 1788, and received his D. D. from the same institution in 1799. He was preceptor of Cambridge Grammar School; studied theology; was ordained, and settled at Vergennes, Vt., June 12, 1794; and in 1799 he removed to Burlington, and in 1800 was chosen President of the University of Vermont, he being the first President of the Institution, which position he held until 1814. During the first six years of his presidency he gave all the instruction given in the College, except during a single term. After leaving the University he was settled over the church in Medfield, from 1815 to 1829. His last public discourse was delivered at Sherburne and was an eulogy on John Quincy Adams, April 30, 1848. More than thirty of his discourses have been published.

Sandham, Miss. *The Twin Sisters*, or the advantages of Religion. By Miss Sandham. Second American Edition. Motto. Middlebury: Printed and Published by William Slade, Jun. 1815. 16mo, pp. 215.

Sargeant, Leonard. *The Trial*, Confession and Conviction of Jesse and Stephen Boorn, for the murder of Russell Colvin, and the return of the man supposed to have been murdered. By Hon. Leonard Sargeant, Ex-Lieut. Governor of Vermont. Manchester, Vt.: Journal Book and Job Office. 1873. 8vo, pp. 48.

Hon. Leonard Sargeant, late of Manchester, died at the residence of his daughter, in Johnstown, Pennsylvania, on the 18th of June, 1880, in the eighty-seventh year of his age. His remains were brought to his life-long home for interment. Mr. Sargeant was long a prominent member of the bar in his native county of Bennington, and at different times was honored by his fellow-citizens with almost every civil office from justice of the peace to lieutenant-governor of the state, filling them all with credit to himself and usefulness to the community. Not long after his admission to the bar he was employed as associate counsel with Governor Skinner in the Boorn trial, and was the last survivor of the principal actors in that famous case.

Sargent, (L. M.) *Letters* to John H. Hopkins, D. D., occasioned by his lecture in opposition to the Temperance Society. By an Episcopalian. Windsor: Printed at the Chronicle Press. 1836. 24mo, pp. 168.

Savage, R. A. *The* Memorial Record of the Soldiers from Stowe, Vermont, who fought for our Government during the Rebellion of 1861-5. Prepared by R. A. Savage. Montpelier: Printed at the Freeman Steam Printing Establishment, 1867. 12mo, pp. 104.

Sawyer, Harriet N. W. *Reminiscences* of a Deceased Sister. A Brief Memoir of Mrs. Harriet N. W. Sawyer, who died at Huntington, Indiana, June 16, 1841. Newbury, Vt.: Published by Hayes & Company. 1843. 18mo, pp. 123, (3).

Sawyer, Joseph W. *A Sermon* Delivered on the day of General Election, at Montpelier, October 9, 1823, Before the Honorable Legislature of Vermont. By Joseph W. Sawyer, A. M., Pastor of the Church and Congregation in Whiting. Montpelier, Vt.: Printed by E. P. Walton. 1823. 8vo, pp. 45.

Mr. Sawyer was a Baptist, and, says his biographer "he was hopefully converted at the age of five years," and began to preach in Fairfield, Vt., at the age of 19; then at Hubbardton in 1816, and in Whiting in 1822. He was then in various places, mostly out of the State, until he returned to Whiting, about 1854. He was born in Monkton, Vt., May 6, 1794; and died in Whiting, June 26, 1859.

Sawyer, Rev. Thomas Jefferson, D. D.
—*Thoughts* on the Divine Goodness, relative to the Government of Moral Agents, Particularly Displayed in Future Rewards and Punishments. "God will have all men to be saved, and to come unto the knowledge of the truth." 2 Tim. ii.: 4. Translated from the French of Ferdinand Olivier Petitpierre, formerly Minister of Chaux-de-fond. Philadelphia: Gihon, Fairchild & Co. 1843. rl. 8vo, pp. 56. Edited by Dr. Sawyer.

—*Endless Punishment.* In the Very Words of Its Advocates. By Thomas J. Sawyer, S. T. D. Contents: Introduction; Universalism; Orthodoxy; General Description of Hell; Some Accounts of Hell Fire and the Torments; Some Peculiar Properties of Hell-Fire; Fire and Frost; Other Means of Torture; Some Accessory Torments; Quite another Class of Sufferings; Sufferings of Loss; The Pains of Memory; Pains of an Upbraiding Conscience; Torments from Malignant Passions; Sufferings occasioned by Fear; The Damned suffer Unfriended and Unpitied; The Saints rejoice in the Miseries of the Damned; All these Multiplied and Dreadful Torments absolutely without End; The Eternity of Hell-Torments banishes all Hope, and produces Despair; The Damned wish and pray to Die; Endless Torment in Hell-Fire is the Just Punishment of Sin; All Mankind, without Exception, deserve Endless Damnation; All are born totally Depraved, yet are required to keep a Holy Law; The Destiny of all Souls irrevocably fixed at Death; Far the Greater Part of Mankind will finally be damned; The General Judgment; Conclusion; Appendix; Words quoted in the Volume. Price $1, postage paid. Boston. 1879.

The following auto-biographical sketch was furnished by Dr. Sawyer, under date of March 25, 1878:

I was born in the town of Reading, Windsor county, Vt., on the 9th of January, 1804. My father, Benjamin Sawyer, was a respectable farmer, of moderate means, to whom my mother, Sally York, bore twelve children, nine of whom grew up to adult age, and of whom five are still living, and among whom, at the age of seventy-four years, I now occupy the middle point, two boys older and two younger. My father was one of the earliest settlers of the town, having removed with his father's family from Pomfret, Conn., in company with Deacon John Weld. Our school district and neighborhood was known as the Sawyer neighborhood, as originally four brothers and two sisters settled in it.

I enjoyed very good advantages for acquiring a common school education, as we always had six months school in the district every year. At the age of eighteen years I had acquired such a mastery of the branches then taught in such schools as to become a teacher myself. After I began to teach I also began to take a few weeks tuition at Chester Academy, in the autumn, after the harvest was over. I entered Middlebury College in the autumn of 1825, and graduated in 1829, having completed my preparation after I was twenty-one.

As we had no theological schools then, I went to study with Rev. William S. Balch, in Winchester, N. H., preaching occasionally, reading the Iliad of Homer, and studying such theology as I had opportunity to find.

In April, 1830, I went to New York, and took pastoral charge of a very small society there. With this I continued till the autumn of 1845, when I removed with my family to Clinton, Oneida county, N. Y., and took charge of the Clinton Liberal Institute. I succeeded in converting this into a Universalist school, and opened in connection with it a primitive theological school, from which I sent out about five and twenty students, more than twenty of whom are still in our ministry, among whom I beg to name Prof. Leonard, Rev. C. A. Skinner, Rev. B. F. Bowles, Clark R. Moor, George H. Deere, Richard Eddy, etc.

At the close of 1852 I returned to New York, and, having preached for what was formerly called the Dry Dock Society a year, I returned to my old parish, and continued with it till the spring of 1861, when I resigned, and returned to Clinton, where I remained, preaching for the parish there till January 1, 1863, when I again returned to New York, and took editorial charge of the "Christian Ambassador." This paper was founded by Philo Price in 1831, under the name of "Christian Messenger," and I was the theological editor of it for several years. Indeed, I was more or less connected with it till I left New York in 1845, and wrote for it as I had opportunity afterwards. It passed under several names, as "Christian Messenger," "Universalist Union," "Christian Ambassador," and is now published at Utica, N. Y., as the "Christian Leader," (since moved to Boston, Mass.) I continued to edit this paper through 1863 and 1864, and was associate editor through 1865.

In the autumn of 1865 I moved my family to Star Landing, N. J., and took possession of a farm which I had purchased. Here I remained, working on my farm and preaching occasionally in the neighborhood, till the autumn of 1869, when I came to College Hill, Mass., and assumed the duties of Professor of Systematic Theology in this school, to which I had been elected.

I called at my own motion the educational convention which was held in New York in the spring of 1847, which resulted in the establishment of Tuft's College, of which I was one of the original Trustees. I was also chiefly instrumental in calling the first meeting in New York city to consider the necessity of establishing a theological school, which resulted in the founding of the "Canton Theological School," and the "St. Lawrence University," of which I was also one of the original Trustees, and for several years President of the Board. I received the Honorary Degree of S. T. D. at Cambridge, in 1850.

The books which I have written, and which have been published, are as far as I can now recollect, as follows:

Letters addressed to Rev. W. C. Brownlee, in reply to a course of Lectures by him against Universalism. By Rev. Thomas J. Sawyer. New York: 1833. Printed and published by Philo Price. 18mo, pp. 176.

A Statement of Facts relative to the Attack made on Universalism by Dr. Brownlee; and the late editorial conduct of the *Christian Intelligencer*, addressed to the members of the Reformed Dutch Church. By Rev. Thomas J. Sawyer. New York: 1834. P. Price. 18mo, pp. 22.

Letters to Rev. Stephen Remington, in Review of his Lectures on Universalism. By Rev. T. J. Sawyer. New York: 1839. P. Price. 16mo.

A Sermon delivered in the Orchard street Church, May 3, 1840, occasioned by the death of Miss Elizabeth W. Trombley. By Rev. T. J. Sawyer. New York: 1840. P. Price.

The Occasional Sermon, delivered before the Universalist General Convention at its session in the city of New York, September, 1841. Together with thirteen other sermons delivered on the same occasion. New York: 1841. P. Price, 130 Fulton St.

Endless Punishment. Its Origin and Grounds examined; with other Discourses. By T. J. Sawyer, Minister of the Orchard street (Universalist) Church, New York. New York: C. L. Stickney, 140 Fulton St., Second Floor, 1845. 16mo, pp. 252.

Review of E. F. Hatfield's "Universalism as it Is." By T. J. Sawyer. New York: 1841, P. Price. 16mo, pp. 320.

A Discussion on the Doctrine of Eternal Salvation: Question: "Do the Holy Scriptures teach the doctrine of Endless Punishment?" Affirmative, Rev. Isaac Westcolt. Negative, Rev. Thomas J. Sawyer, D. D. New York: 1854. Bunce Brothers, Publishers, 134 Nassau St. 12mo, pp 188.

A Discussion of the Doctrine of Universal Salvation. Question: "Do the Scriptures teach the final salvation of all men?" Affirmative, Rev. Thomas J. Sawyer, D. D. Negative, Rev. Isaac Westcolt April, 1854. New York. Henry Lyon, Auburn N. Y.: A. V. Kenyon. 12mo.

Who is our God? The Son of the Father? A Review of Rev. Henry Ward Beecher. By Thomas J. Sawyer,

D. D. New York: 1859. Thatcher & Hutchinson. 12mo, pp. 40.

Besides these works I have published various articles in our *Quarterly*. I have also written several tracts, which are now, I believe, among the tracts published by the "Women's Centenary Association," one of which is called, "What is Universalism?" and another, "Will you think of It?"

Besides the occasional sermon mentioned above, I have preached two more before the United States Convention, one in Middletown, Conn., and the other at Rochester, N. Y., in 1876.

Lately I wrote an article for the *North American Review*, one of a series of articles on the subject of "Endless Punishment" found in the March and April numbers of the present year, 1878. Thomas J. Sawyer

It is not out of place to state that Caroline M., the wife of Rev. T. J. Sawyer, is a lady of fine intellectual power and culture, and of wide reputation as an authoress, our only regret being that she is not a native of Vermont. The late Mrs. McEntee, wife of the artist, was a daughter of Mr. and Mrs. Sawyer.

Saxe, John Godfrey. *Progress:* A Satire, by John G. Saxe. Second Edition. New York: John Allen. Boston: Jordan and Wiley. MDCCCXLVII. 8vo, pp. 82.

Read at Middlebury College Commencement, 1846.

—*Poems.* Eleventh Edition. Boston: Ticknor and Fields. MDCCCLIX. 12mo, pp. 192. Portrait.

—*The Fly-ing Dutchman;* or The Wrath of Herr Vonstopplenose. By John G. Saxe, with Sixteen comic Illustrations. Motto. New York: Carlton, Publisher, 413 Broadway. (Late Rudd & Carlton.) MDCCCLXII. 12mo. 83 leaves.

—*The Poems of John Godfrey Saxe.* Complete in one Volume. Highgate Edition. Boston: James R. Osgood and Company, Late Ticknor & Fields, and Fields, Osgood & Co. 1873. 12mo, pp. xii., 491.

This is the thirty-eighth edition.

—*The Money-King* and Other Poems. With Portrait. Boston: 16mo.

—*Poems.* Blue and Gold Edition, Portrait. 32mo. Boston.

—*The same*, Cabinet Edition, Portrait. Boston: 16mo.

—*The same*, Uniform with Farringford Tennyson, with Portrait. Boston: 16mo.

—*The same*, Diamond Edition. Boston: 18mo.

—*The same*, Red-Line Edition. Boston: small 4to.

—*The same*, Household Edition with Illustrations. 12mo.

—*Clever Stories* of Many Nations, rendered in Rhyme. Illustrated. Boston: small 4to.

—*The Masquerade*, and Other Poems. Boston: 16mo.

—*Fables and Legends* of Many Countries, rendered in Rhyme. Boston: 16mo.

—*The Proud Miss MacBride.* Illustrated by Augustus Hopping. Boston: small 4to.

—*Leisure-Day Rhymes.* Boston: 16mo.

Mr. Saxe was born in Highgate, Vt., June 2, 1816; was graduated at Middlebury College, 1839; studied law, and practiced in his native State from 1843 to about 1850, when he removed to Burlington, where for five years he conducted the *Sentinel*, a Democratic newspaper. In 1851 he was chosen State's Attorney for Chittenden county, and subsequently was the Democratic candidate for Governor of Vermont. He subsequently devoted himself almost entirely to literature and lecturing, residing in Brooklyn, N. Y. For a time he was editor of the "Argus," Albany.

His first volume of poems was published in 1849, to which he makes allusion in a letter to his friend and brother poet, Major Charles G. Eastman, dated Highgate, December 21, 1849: "I too have made a book, and I drop you this line to say that the very special copy which I intend for you, one of the few extra bound for the author, has not yet come to hand. When it does, I shall take the first opportunity to get it into your hands," etc. Major Eastman had published a volume of his poems in 1848. In another of Mr. Saxe's letters to Major Eastman, dated Burlington, May 31, 1859, he says: "When you come to the State Convention, I want you to come directly to my house, and stop with me. If you bring your wife, so much the better. Like Dogberry, I have two gowns, one for you, and everything comfortable about me, and you shan't suffer in my *hospitium.* Moreover, you shall be 'well let alone'—come and go as you like, and put your feet on things in the best room in the house. Remember what I say, and come down—it *is* down—the day before," etc.

More than forty editions of Mr. Saxe's Collected Poems have been issued in America and England.

Mr. Saxe died at Albany, N. Y., March 31, 1887.

Scott, M. L. *Homeopathy,* or Nature's Healing Law, contrasted with Allopathic or Empirical mode of Practice, by M. L. Scott, M. D., Homeopathic Physician and Surgeon. Bradford, Vt. : G. C. Chamberlin, Printer. 8vo, pp. 19. n. d.

Scott, Rev. Orange. *An Appeal* to the Methodist Episcopal Church. Boston: 1838. 8vo.

—*Autobiography:* Also Life of, by Rev. L. C. Matlack. New York : 1847. 12mo.

Rev. Mr. Scott was born in Brookfield, Vt., February 13, 1800; died at Newark, N. J., July 31, 1847. His father was from Willington, Conn., and his mother, Lucy Wheeler, from Halifax, Vt. Shortly after his birth the family moved to Berlin, Vt., and in 1806 they were living in Stanstead, L. C., and after about six years returned to the States. In September, 1820, while living in Barre, Vt., Mr. Scott was converted at a camp meeting, and in about six months began to hold meetings himself, and in another six months he was licensed to exhort in the Methodist Episcopal church. He finally became one of the most eminent and distinguished men in that church; second only to Rev. Wilbur Fisk. He was for some time Editor of the "True Wesleyan." See "Sprague's Annals," vol. 7, pp. 667-71.

Scott, O. W. Mrs. "*The Gilead Guards,*" A Tale of the Civil War. New York : Hunt and Eaton. 1891. 16mo, pp. 300.

The characters in this novel are taken from Orleans County, Vt.

Scott, Thomas. *The Force of Truth.* An Authentic Narrative. By Thomas Scott, D. D. Author of a Commentary on the Bible, &c. Brattleborough : Published by John Holbrook. 1819. 24mo, pp. 164.

—*Commentaries.* Brattleboro: 1834. Fessenden & Co. 6 vols. rl. 8vo. About 800 pp. each.

Scott, Walter. *The Lady of the Lake.* A Poem in six Cantos, By Walter Scott, Esq. Montpelier, Vt. : Published by Lucius Q. C. Bowles. 1813. Wright and Sibley, Printers. 18mo, pp. 320.

Scott, William. *Lessons in Elocution,* or a Selection of Pieces in prose and verse, for the improvement of Youth in Reading and Speaking. By William Scott. To which is prefixed Elements of Gesture, illustrated by four Plates ; and rules for expressing, with propriety, the various passions of the mind. Also an Appendix containing lessons on a new plan. Montpelier, Vt. : Published by E. P. & G. S. Walton. 1818. 12mo, pp. 383.

—*Another* edition, by E. P. Walton. 1820. pp. 407.

Scudder, Rev. Evarts. *Address* given at the Funeral of the Rev. E. C. Hooker, Stockbridge, Dec. 8, 1873, By Rev. Evarts Scudder, of Great Barrington. Published by request, for private distribution. 12mo, pp. 19.

Mr. Hooker was a son of Rev. Edward W. Hooker; was born in Bennington, Vt., July 9, 1832; was graduated at Williams College in 1857. and at Princeton in 1860; was pastor at Newburyport, Mass., 1860-64; at Nashua, N. H., 1865-68; at Stockbridge, Mass., 1870, until he died, December 5, 1873.

Seabury, Edwin. *A Discourse* Delivered at Westminster, Vermont, on the day of the Annual Thanksgiving, December 6, 1855, By Rev. Edwin Seabury. Bellows Falls : Printed at the Phenix Job Office. 1855. 8vo, pp. 16.

Seaver, Miss Emily. *Poems,* By Emily Seaver. Motto. Boston : A. Williams & Co. 1878. 16mo, pp. 120.

Miss Seaver, daughter of Norman and Anna Maria (Lawrence) Seaver, who are natives of Groton, Mass., was born in Charlestown, Mass., in 1835, and lived in Boston and vicinity till 1860, when she moved to Rutland, Vt., where she still resides, (1880.) Her brother, Rev. N. Seaver, was Pastor of the Congregational church at Rutland several years.

Seaver, Norman. *The Hand* of God as seen in the fall of Richmond. A Discourse Delivered in the Congregational Church in Rutland, Vermont, on Sunday, 9th of April A. D. 1865, by Rev. Norman Seaver, Pastor. Rutland : Tuttle, Gay & Company. 1865. 8vo, pp. 16.

—*A Discourse* delivered at the funeral of Hon. Solomon Foot, in the Congregational Church, Rutland, Vt., April 3, 1866, by Rev. Norman Seaver, Pastor of the Church. Rutland : Tuttle, Gay & Company. 1866. 8vo, pp. 26.

Secker, Thomas. *Five Sermons* against Popery. By Thomas Secker, L. L. D. Late Lord Archbishop of Canterbury. Windsor, Vt. : Printed by Simeon Ide. 1827. 24mo, pp. 118.

—*Secondary Lessons,* or the Improved Reader ; Intended as a Sequel to the Franklin Primer, by a Friend of Youth. Third Edition. Bellows Falls : Published by James I. Cutler & Co. 1829. small 16mo, pp. 214.

Seeley, Henry M. *Death :* Its Economy and Beneficence. An Address delivered before the Medical Class of the University of Vermont, Tuesday Evening, June 9th, 1863. By Henry M. Seeley, M. D. Burlington : Times Book and Job Printing Establishment. 1863. 8vo, pp. 26.

Segur, Seth Willard.

Mr. Segur was born in Chittenden, Vt., December 24, 1831; and died in Tallmadge, Ohio, September 24, 1875. Mr. Segur was graduated at Middlebury College, 1859, Auburn Theological Seminary, 1862, and was pastor of Congregational churches, Tallmadge, 1862-71; Gloucester, Mass., 1871-3; West Medway, Mass., 1873, until his death, while on a visit to his old parish in Ohio. His publications are : "The Relation and Responsibilities of Pastor and People;" and Sermons on "The True Manhood;" "The Nation's Hope;" and "National Blessings and Duties."

Selden, Almira. *Effusions of the Heart,* contained in a number of Original Poetical pieces, on various subjects. By Almira Selden. Motto. Bennington : Printed by Darius Clark, 1820. 12mo, pp. 152.

A native of Bennington, Vt.

Select Reading. Vol. 1. No. 1. Montpelier, Vt. : June, 1877. 8vo, pp. 8.

Issued by Vermont Methodist Seminary and Female College.

Select Sentences, from some of the First Reformers, on several Important Religious Subjects. Intended to show what were the Sentiments of those Eminent writers Respecting the Leading Truths of the Gospel. Montpelier: Printed for John Crosby, August, 1813. 18mo, pp. 36.

Senter, Oramel Stevens. *The Health and Pleasure-Seeker's Guide;* or, where to go and what to see. Containing a description of the country from Philadelphia to Clifton Springs, etc. By O. S. Senter. Philadelphia : 1874. 12mo, pp. 126. Illustrated.

Mr. Senter was born in Thetford, Vt., March 11, 1823; graduated at Dartmouth, 1848; read law with P. T. Washburn, at Woodstock, and practiced at Springfield, Mass., 1851-53; then read divinity at East Windsor, Ct.; preached in Vermont one year, 1855-6; taught school in Orange, Ct., 1856-7; missionary in Minnesota, 1857-9; then resident at Thetford, Vt., preaching, lecturing, and assistant editor of Vermont Chronicle; next ordained as an evangelist at Berlin Corner, Vt., May 8, 1862. He was residing at Philadelphia in 1877; returned to Vermont in 1879.

Sermons. *Sixteen Short Sermons,* Making a solemn Appeal to the Consciences of Men. Printed by William Slade, Jun. Middlebury, Vt.: Sept., 1816. 12mo, pp. 16, 8.

Sessions, John. *Address,* delivered before the Board of Common School Visitors of Chenango Co., N. Y., at their Semi-annual Meeting, held at the Court-house, Norwich, June 8, 1840. By John Sessions, Pastor of the Presbyterian Church in Norwich. R. Northway, Printer, Utica: 1840. 8vo, pp. 22.

Dr. Sessions was born at Putney, Vt., September 29, 1795; was graduated at Dartmouth College in 1822; studied divinity at Princeton; preached to several Presbyterian Churches in New York, 1825-48; since then has been a teacher, and is now living at Oakland, Cal. (1880.)

—*The Seven Wonders of the World;* Magnificent Buildings, &c. with an account of the present state of Palmyra, or Tadmor of the Dessert. Danville, Vt.: E. & W. Eaton, Printers. 1826. 12mo, pp. 54. Quaint illustrations.

Sex, *The Philosophy of,* by H. Edwin Lewis, author of "Lights and Other Poems." Burlington. The Vermont Medical Publishing Company. 1896. 16mo, pp. 51.

Seymour, T. H. *Oration* at Norwich University, on Education, 1831.

Seymour, W. P. *Address* before the Castleton Medical College, 1858.

Shafter, O. L. *An Address* before the Putney, (Vt.) Temperance Society, delivered July 3, 1835. By Oscar L. Shafter. Fayetteville: Edwin C. Church, Printer. 1835. 8vo, pp. 24.

—*Human Progress:* its relations to the Reason, acting in Right Method. An oration delivered by Hon. O. L. Shafter before the Associated Alumni of the Pacific Slope, at the College Hall of the College of California, on Wednesday, June 7, 1866. Oakland: Printed by the Evening Tribune Publishing Co. 8vo, pp. 22.

—*Memorial of Oscar Lovell Shafter,* Being words spoken at his Burial by Rev. Dr. Stebbins, a Sermon Preached on the following Sunday by Rev. L. Hamilton, a Sketch of his Life and Character, given before the Supreme Court of California, by Hon. John W. Dwinelle, And lines to his memory from the New

York Evening Post. San Francisco: 1874. 8vo, pp. 25.

Oscar Lovell Shafter, LL. D., was born in Athens, Vt., Oct. 19, 1812, and died in Florence, Italy, January 23, 1873. He fitted for college at Wilbraham Academy, in Massachusetts, and graduated at Wesleyan University in Connecticut, in 1834. He studied law at Harvard University, and entered upon the practice of his profession in Wilmington, Vt., in 1837. He was a candidate of the "Liberty Party," then in its infancy, for governor and for the United States Senate. He removed to California in 1854, where he practiced law for ten years, when in 1864, he was elevated to a seat on the bench of the Supreme Court of that state, which he held till 1867, when he resigned on account of declining health. He was endowed with superior ability, was a sound lawyer and an able judge.

His brother, Hon. James McM. Shafter, Secretary of State for Vermont, 1842-49, resides at San Francisco, Cal. See "Shafter Memorial," pp. 133-5.

Sharon. *Annual Reports* of the Selectmen and Auditors of the Town of Sharon. Tuesday, March 1, 1870. Woodstock: Printed at the Vermont Standard Office. 8vo, pp. 8.
Continued.

Shaw, Benjamin *The Fatal Looking-Glass,* or Universalism Looked in the Face. By Benjamin Shaw. Woodstock. Published by the Author. 1828. David Watson, Printer. 8vo, pp. 54.

—*Two Hundred and Thirteen Questions* asked by Rev. Abel C. Thomas, a Universalist, and answered by Rev. Benjamin Shaw, a Methodist. Woodstock, Vt.: 1873. 8vo, pp. 18.
Mr. Shaw lived in Bridgewater, Vt,

—*A Journal* of Benjamin Shaw's Life, from 10 years old to 84. Woodstock, Vt.: 1873. 8vo, pp. 16.

Shaw, Elijah. *The Hero* of four Wars ! ! Elijah Shaw's Narrative of his 21 years services in the American Navy, and some of the Brilliant Exploits of American Seamen during the War with France in 1798 ; war with Tripoli—1802 to 1805 ; war with England—1812 to 1815 ; war with Algiers—1815 to 1816 ; and the Suppression of the Pirates—1822-27. Third Edition. Rochester, N. Y. 1845. 16mo, pp. 63.
Mr. Shaw was a native of Vermont, born January 22, 1771.

Shaw, George B.
See Vermont. Law Reports, Vols. 9 and 10; Governor and Council Vol. 7, p. 301.

Shaw, William G. *The Law* of Fire and Life Insurance, with Practical Observations. Part I.—The Law of Fire Insurance. Part II.—The Law of Life Insurance. By Charles Ellis, Esq., of Lincoln's Inn, Barrister at Law. Second American from the Last English Edition with Notes, Additions and References to American and late English Decisions, by William G. Shaw. Burlington: Chauncey Goodrich. 1854. 8vo, pp. 326.
See Vermont: Law Reports, Vols. 30-35, 1859-64.

Shay's Rebellion.
See Tyler, Royal.

Shedd & Van Sicklen. *Catalogue* of Pure-Bred Short Horns, The Property of Shedd & Van Sicklen, Burlington, Vt. Burlington : R. S. Styles' Steam Book & Job Printing House. 1870. 8vo, pp. 23.

Shedd, Rev William. *The Influence of Temperance* upon Intellectual Discipline. A Discourse delivered before the Temperance Society of the University of Vermont, April 30, 1844, by Rev,

William Shedd. Burlington : University Press. 1844. 8vo, pp. 31.

Shedd, Rev. William G. T. *A Sermon,* Preached at the Installation of Rev. Francis B. Wheeler, in Brandon, Vt., May 29, 1850. By Rev. William G. T. Shedd, Professor of English Literature in the University of Vermont. Published by request of the Church and Society. Printed at the Chronicle Press, Windsor. 1850. 8vo, pp. 22.

—*Method and Influence of Theological Studies.* A Discourse, pronounced at Burlington, before the literary Societies of the University of Vermont, August 5th, 1845, By Rev. William G. T. Shedd. Published by the Societies. Burlington : University Press. S. Fletcher, Printer, 1845. 8vo, pp. 52.

—*The True Nature of the Beautiful,* and its Influence upon Culture. A Discourse delivered before the Literary Societies of Amherst College, August 13, 1851. By Rev. William G. T. Shedd. Professor of English Literature in the University of Vermont. Published by the Societies. Northampton : Hopkins, Bridgman & Co. 1851. 8vo, pp. 31.

—*The Guilt of the Pagan.* A Sermon: By William G. T. Shedd, D. D. [preached May 3, 1863, before the Board of Foreign Missions of the Presb. Church.] Boston : 1864. 12mo, pp. 24.

—*The Nature and Influence of the Historic Spirit.* An Inaugural Discourse, by William G. T. Shedd, Brown Professor in Andover Theological Seminary. [From the Bibliotheca Sacra for April, 1854.] Andover : Press of W. F. Draper & Brother. 1854. 8vo, pp. 52.

Professor Shedd was born in Acton, Mass., in 1820; removed with his father to Burlington about 1835; graduated at the University of Vermont in 1839; and from Andover in 1843; Pastor at Brandon, Vt., 1843-45; Professor in the University of Vermont 1845-52, when he left Vermont for wider fields, in which he became distinguished. Professor of Sacred Rhetoric and Pastoral Theology, Auburn Theological Seminary 1852-3; Professor of Ecclesiastical History, Andover Theol. Seminary 1853-62; Pastor of the Brick (Presb.) Church, New York 1862-3; Professor of Biblical Literature, Union Theol. Seminary 1863-4; Professor of Systematic Theology Union Theol. Seminary 1864-90 Died in New York Nov. 17, 1894: Edited the Works of Coleridge (7 Vols.) 1853; Augustine's Confessions 1860; Published Lectures on the Philosophy of History 1856; History of Christian Doctrine, 2 vols., 1863; Homiletics and Pastoral Theology, 1867; Theological Essays 1877; Literary Essays 1878. "Endless Punishment," 1886; Proposed Revison of the Westminster Standards, 1890 and other Theological Works. His most important work was his System of Dogmatic Theology, the third and concluding volume of which was published in 1894.

Shelburne. *Catalogue* of the Free Library of Shelburne, Vt. 1896. n.p.n.d. 8vo, pp. 16.

Sheldon. *History of.*
See Dutcher, L. L.

Shelton, F. W. *Lectures* before the Huntington Literary Association. By the Rev. F. W. Shelton, Minister of St. John's Church, Huntington. New York : Printed by J. P. Prall, 9 Spruce Street. 1850. 8vo, pp. 36.

—*An Address* delivered at the Funeral of Mrs. Upham, in Christ Church, Montpelier, on Whit-Sunday, May 11th, 1856. By Rev. F. W. Shelton. Montpelier : E. P. Walton, Printer. 1856. 8vo, pp. 15, (1)

Mr. Shelton published in addition : "The Trolloplad; or, Traveling Gentlemen in America; a Satirical Poem." New York : 1837. 12mo. "The Gold Mania; a Lecture."

1850. 8vo. "The Use and Abuse of Reason ; a Lecture." 1850. 8vo. "Salander and the Dragon; a Romance of New York." 1851. 18mo. "The Rector of St. Bardolph's; or Superannuated." 1853. 12mo; a new edition, 1856. "Up the River." (Hudson.) 1853. 12mo. "Chrystelline; or, The Heiress of Fall-Down Castle ; a Romance." 1854. 12mo. "Peeps from the Belfry; or, The Parish Sketch Book." 1855. 12mo ; new edition, 1856. "The Tinnecum Papers." 1848. Besides other articles in the Knickerbocker Magazine. Several of the above works were published while Mr. Shelton resided in Montpelier.

Frederick William Shelton was born at Jamaica, Long Island, in 1814; he was graduated at the College of New Jersey, in 1834 ; was ordained a minister of the Protestant Episcopal Church in 1847, and was assistant of Rev. George B. Manser, Rector of Christ Church, Montpelier, a short time in 1847-8, and was Rector of the same, 1854-66; resided at Carthage Landing on the Hudson at the time of his death, June 20, 1881.
See Duyckinck; Allibone.

Shepard, Sylvanus. *The Phœnix Chronicle.* The word Phœnix signifies arising out of its own ashes. The Bonfire, in which 450 Books were burnt : A View of Montpelier, and all the Country Villages in the State, &c. &c. By Sylvanus Shepard. Printed for the Author. 1825. 8vo, pp. 18.

Mr. Shepard is remembered by the old citizens of Montpelier as an odd character, about town in early days. His brother William Shepard was one of the early settlers of East Montpelier, and became an opulent farmer; more than fifty years ago he erected the two story brick dwelling near the line of East Montpelier and Plainfield, on the main road, which has since been a landmark, and is still occupied by his descendants. (1880.)

Sheppard, John H. *A Plea for Freemasonry.* An Address delivered at Burlington, Vt., on the Festival of St. John the Baptist, June, A. L. 5850. Before Washington Lodge, and Visiting Fraternities. By R. W. John H. Sheppard. Motto. Burlington: Printed by Chauncey Goodrich. 1850. 8vo, pp. 37.

Sherburne. *Annual Report* of the Selectmen, Auditors, and Overseer of the Poor. For the Town of Sherburne, Feb. 27th, 1857. 8vo, pp. 4.
Continued.

Shipherd, J. J. *The Sabbath School Guide:* or, a selection of interesting and profitable Scripture lessons, illustrated and applied, by questions and answers. Designed as a permanent System of Sabbath School instruction. By John J. Shipherd, Minister of the Gospel. [To be published in Semi-annual Numbers.] No. III. Motto. Middlebury : Vermont Sabbath School Union. Ovid Miner, Printer. 1829. 24mo, pp. 64. No. II. Same Title, 1828.

—*The Bible Class Book;* designed for Youth and Adults, in Sabbath Schools and Bible Classes. By John J. Shipherd, Minister of the Gospel. Motto. Middlebury : Published by Vt. S. S. Union. O. and J. Miner, Printers. MDCCCXXX. 24mo, pp. 24.

Shoreham. *Catalogue* of the Officers and Students of Shoreham Central High School, for the Academic Term Ending November 10th, 1875. Rutland : Tuttle & Co., Printers. 1875. 8vo, pp. 8.

—*History of,*
See Goodhue, J. F.

A Short Expose *of the Management* of the Finances of the State of Vermont, Addressed to the Freemen and Tax-Payers, by a member of the late Legislature. Patriot Office, Montpelier, Vt. 1844. 8vo, pp. 8.

Shrewsbury. *Annual Report* of the Board of Auditors for the Town of Shrewsbury, 1871.

Rutland: Tuttle and Company, Printers. 1871. 8vo, pp. 23. Continued.

Shuttlesworth, Samuel. *A Discourse Delivered* in presence of His Excellency, Thomas Chittenden, Esq., Governor; His Honor Peter Olcott, Esq., Lieutenant-Governor, The Honorable Council, and House of Representatives of the State of Vermont; at Windsor, October 13, 1791. Being the Day of General Election. By Samuel Shuttlesworth, A. M., Pastor of a Church in Windsor. Printed at Windsor, State of Vermont, By James Reed Hutchins, For and by Order of the General Assembly. MDCCXCII. 8vo, pp. 16.

Mr. Shuttlesworth was a native of Dedham, Mass.; ordained pastor of the Congregational church in Windsor, Vt., June 23, 1790; was subsequently dismissed, and died in October, 1834, aged 84 years.
See Sprague's Annals; Bancroft, Aaron.

Sias, Solomon. *A Discourse*, delivered at St. Johnsbury, before Harmony Lodge of Free and Accepted Masons, at the Anniversary of St. John the Baptist, June 24, Anno Lucis. 5822. By the Rev. Solomon Sias, Past Most Eminent Grand Commander of the Maine Encampment of Knights Templars and appendant Orders. Danville, Vt.: E. Eaton, Printer, 1822. 8vo, pp. 15.

Sill, Rev. Elijah. *Election Sermon.* 1788.

Mr. Sill came from New Fairfield, Ct., to Dorset, Vt., and was settled over the Congregational church there 1784-1791; which is all we learn of him in connection with Vermont. He was graduated at Yale College, 1748.

Silloway, T. W.
See Vermont Capitol.

Simmons, A. E. *Spiritual Communications.*
See Mystery.

—*Spiritualism.* A. E. Simmons' Communications, from Daniel Webster [and others. November 22, 1852. Woodstock, Vt.: Printed for the Medium. 1852. 8vo, pp. 24.

Simmons, James. *The Early Settler.* A Poem, delivered by James Simmons, Esq., before the Old Settler's Society of Walworth County, Wisconsin, at their Annual Meeting, held at Walker's Hall, Geneva, Wis., June 10th, 1874. Geneva Lake Herald, Print. 8vo, pp. 16.

—*The History of Geneva, Wisconsin.* An Authentic Account of the First Discovery and Settlement of the Village and Town of Geneva, their Development and Progress to the Present Time, and their Present Condition and Resources; with Sketches of the Lives of Prominent Early Settlers. By James Simmons. Published at the Office of the Geneva Lake Herald. 1875. 8vo, pp. 101.

Mr. Simmons was born in Middlebury, 1821, and was graduated at the College there in 1841, read law, and commenced practice in Geneva, Wis., and in 1851 commenced the mercantile business at Greenwood, Ill.

Simons, Rev. Volney M. *Infant Salvation.* A Discourse Preached in the M. E. Church, St. Albans, Vt., Sept. 29, 1859. On the death of Frank Hamilton Woodward, Son of R. C. M. Woodward, M. D., of St. Albans, Vt., By Rev. Volney M. Simons. Published by request. Second Edition. St. Albans: E. B. Whiting, Printer. 1860. 8vo, pp. 27.

Sinbad the Sailor. *The Seven Voyages* of Sinbad the Sailor; to which is added The Story of Little Hunchback. Woodstock: Printed by David Watson. 1826.

Illustrated with wood cuts. small 12mo.

Singing Book. *Carmina Sacra*; or Northern Collection of Church Music. Fairhaven, (Vt.) Published by Colton Warren and Sproat. Printed by Smith & Shute, Poultney, (Vt.) 1823. pp. 308, (4.)

See Warren. C. J.; Cheney, S. P.

Sizer, N. *Phrenological Chart.*
See Buell, P. L.

Skeel, Rev. Thomas. *A Sermon* preached in the audience of His Excellency, Jonas Galusha, Esq., Governor, His Honor, Paul Brigham, Esq., Lieut. Governor, The Honorable Council and House of Representatives of the State of Vermont, at Montpelier on the day of election October 10, 1811. By the Rev. Thomas Skeel. Rutland: Printed by William Fay, Printer to the State. 8vo, pp. 15.

—*A Discourse* on the Nature, Properties, and Conversion of the Soul. By Rev. Thomas Skeel. "I speak as to wise men, judge ye what I say." St. Paul. Bennington, Vermont: Printed by William Haswell. 1811. 12mo, pp. 36.

Sketches of the War, between the United States and the British Isles: Intended as a faithful History of all the material events from the time of its Declaration in 1812, to and including the Treaty of Peace in 1815: Interspersed with Geographical Descriptions of Places, and Biographical Notices of distinguished Military and Naval Commanders. Volumes I and II. Rutland, Vt.: Published by Fay and Davison. 1815. 8vo, pp. IV, 496.

Published in eight numbers, and is a very good history of the war of 1812.

Skinner, Dolphus. *A Lecture Sermon* on the Spring Season of the Gospel, before the First Universalist Society in Langdon, (N. H.) May, 1823. By Dolphus Skinner. Bellows Falls: Printed by Blake, Cutler and Co. 1823. 8vo, pp. 23.

—*A Masonic Discourse*, delivered before Mount Vernon Lodge in Washington, (N. H.) at the Festival of St. John the Baptist, on the twenty-fourth of June, A. L. 5824. By Comp. Dolphus Skinner, Chaplain of St. Paul's Lodge at Alstead, and Pastor of a Church in Langdon. Bellows Falls: Printed by Blake, Cutler & Co. 1824. 8vo, pp. 24.

Skinner, J. O. *A Discourse* delivered at the Funeral of Gen. Horace Wadsworth, of South Hero, Vt., April 7, 1864. By Rev. J. O. Skinner, pastor of the Universalist Church, St. Albans, Vt.

Skinner, O. A. *A Sermon* delivered in the Universalist Meeting House in Woburn, Mass., Wednesday evening, January 13, 1830. In Reply to Dr. Beecher's Sermon against Universalism, delivered in the Congregational Meeting House in said Town, Thursday evening, January 7, 1830. By O. A. Skinner, Pastor of the First Universalist Church in Woburn, Mass. Published by request. Boston: Printed at the Trumpet Office, 40 Cornhill. 1830. 8vo, pp. 22.

—*A Sermon* delivered before the First Universalist Society in Woburn, Mass., on the First

Sabbath in April, 1829. By O. A. Skinner. Motto. Boston: Marsh and Capen. 1829. 8vo, pp. 18.

—*The Claims of the Militia.* Artillery Election Sermon, 1839. Boston: 1839. 8vo, pp. 24.

—*The Child's Catechism.* By Otis A. Skinner. Boston: pp. 36.

—*Easy Lessons for Small Children* in Sabbath Schools. By Otis A. Skinner. Boston: pp. 18.

—*Letters* on the Moral and Religious Duties of Parents. By A Clergyman. Boston: 18mo.

—*A Series of Sermons* in Defense of the Doctrine of Universal Salvation. By Rev. O. A. Skinner, D. D. Boston: 18mo.

—*Letters to Rev. B. Stow, R. H. Neale, and R. W. Cushman, on Modern Revivals.* By Otis A. Skinner. Boston: Abel Tompkins. 1842. 12mo, pp. 144.

—*A Duty to Government and to God.* A Sermon preached in the Warren Street Church, Boston, on Thanksgiving-Day, November 29, 1850, and repeated by request in the same Church, December 15, 1850. By Otis A. Skinner. Boston: A. Tompkins, Cornhill. 1851. 8vo, pp. 24.

—*Family Worship;* Containing Reflections and Prayers for Domestic Devotion. By Otis A. Skinner. Fourth Edition. Boston: Published by A. Tompkins & B. B. Mussey. 1849. 18mo, pp. 216.

—*The Death of Daniel Webster:* A Sermon, delivered in the Warren Street Church, Sunday, November 14, 1852. By Otis A. Skinner. Boston: Published by A. Tompkins, 38 Cornhill. 1852. 8vo, pp. 40.

—*"The Christian Lawyer."* A Sermon delivered in the Fifth Universalist Church in Boston, February 18, 1855, at the Funeral of John C. Danforth, who died February 14, 1855. By Rev. Otis A. Skinner. Boston: 1855. 8vo, pp. 32.

—*The Life,* Labors and Character of Rev. Otis A. Skinner, D. D., A Discourse delivered in the Warren Street Universalist Church, on Sunday, October 6th, 1861. By Rev. Thomas B. Thayer, Pastor of the Society. Boston: Abel Tompkins, 25 Cornhill. 1861. 8vo, pp. 22, (2).

Rev. Otis Ainsworth Skinner was a distinguished Universalist clergyman, born in Royalton, Vt., July 3, 1807, died at Naperville, Ill., September 18, 1861. He commenced preaching at the age of 19, in the towns in Vermont and New Hampshire, in the vicinity of his birthplace; in 1829-31 was pastor of the church in Woburn, Mass., pastor at Baltimore 1831-36, and then about a year at Haverhill, Mass., when he took the charge of and built up the Fifth Universalist Society in Boston, Mass., where he ministered 1837-46; he then took charge of the Orchard Street Church in New York, for three years, when he returned to his old position in Boston in 1849, where he continued until 1857; when at the urgent solicitation of his brother Samuel, a distinguished minister of the same denomination in Chicago, he moved to Elgin, Ill., and was called to the Presidency of Lombard University, at Galesburg, Ill., and entered upon the duties of the position in August, 1857.

Dr. Skinner was largely instrumental in the establishment of Tuft's College, having in its infancy, by his personal efforts raised by subscription the sum of one hundred thousand dollars. His life was an active one; at Baltimore he established a religious paper, "The Southern Pioneer;" and at Haverhill, he commenced another paper, "The Gospel Sun," and in 1843, he began in Boston the publication of the "Universalist Miscellany," of which he was associate editor six years. In addition to the publications mentioned, Dr. Skinner published a volume, "Universalism Illustrated and Defended;" a volume, "Letters on the Knapp excitement;" also Sabbath School Books, and several other occasional sermons. Rev. Dr. T. B. Thayer of Boston, published a life of Dr. Skinner in an 8vo, volume. Boston: 1861.

Skinner, Warren. *Four Sermons* Delivered at Cavendish, Vt., on the Doctrine of Endless Misery, by Warren Skinner. Woodstock, Vt.: Printed by E. Avery, September, 1830. 12mo, pp. 96.

—*Capital Punishment.* A lecture Delivered before the Hon. Legislature of Vermont, and citizens of Montpelier, Sunday evening, Oct. 26, 1834, by Rev. Warren Skinner. Published by request. Montpelier: George W. Hill, 1834. 8vo, pp. 19.

—*Christ's Kingdom in the Earth.* A Sermon, Delivered before the Honorable Legislature of the State of Vermont, at Montpelier, October 9, 1834, by Rev. Warren Skinner. Montpelier: Printed by George W. Hill, 1834. 8vo, pp. 28.

—*The Christian Ministry.* A Sermon, Delivered before the Vermont Universalist Convention, convened at Montpelier, Jan., 7, 1833, at the ordination of Rev. John M. Austin, by Warren Skinner. Montpelier, Vt.: George W. Hill, 1833. 8vo, pp. 25.

Rev. Warren Skinner was a distinguished clergyman of the Universalist denomination in Vermont. He died at Cavendish, Vt., October 7, 1874, aged 84. He was born in Brookfield, Mass., June 2, 1791, but resided nearly all his life at Proctorsville, Vt. Several other sermons by him were published. See sketch of his life in "Universalist Register," for 1875.

Slade, James M. *An Address* Explanatory of the Principles and Objects of the United Brothers of Temperance, delivered on the Third of July, 1847, at Shoreham, Vt., by James M. Slade. Published at the Request of the State Assembly. Vergennes: E. W. Blaisdell, Jr., 1848. 8vo, pp. 17.

James M. Slade was born at Middlebury, September 8, 1812, a son of Hon. William and Abigail (Foote) Slade. He received a common school education, and established himself as a merchant at Middlebury; was a leading spirit in the organization of the American party, 1855; was elected Clerk of the House of Representatives in 1853, and again in 1854 and 1855; was elected Lieut. Governor in 1856, and again in 1857. In 1867 and '68 he was one of the Assistant Judges of Addison County; from 1870 to '74 he was one of the trustees of the Reform School; Town Representative in 1870. He held the usual town offices. Mr. Slade died at Middlebury, April 10, 1875.

J. M. Slade, a son of Hon. J. M. Slade, above, was born in Middlebury, June 27, 1844; graduated at Middlebury College in 1867; studied law and was admitted to the bar December, 1868. He was Secretary of Civil and Military affairs in 1870 and '71; was Town Representative of Middlebury in 1874 and '75; was elected State's Attorney for Addison County in 1878; subsequently Judge of Probate for the Addison District, which office he now holds, 1896. He has held the usual town offices.

Slade, William. *An Oration,* pronounced at Middlebury, Vt., on the Anniversary of American Independence, July 4, 1814, by William Slade, Jr. Esq. Middlebury: Printed by Slade & Ferguson. 8vo, pp. 40.

—*Vermont State Papers;* being a collection of Records and Documents, connected with the Assumption and Establishment of Government by the People of Vermont; Together with the Journal of the Council of Safety, the First Constitution, the early Journals of the General Assembly, and the Laws from the year 1779 to 1786, inclusive, to which are added the proceedings of the first and second Council of Censors. Compiled and published by William Slade, Jr., Secretary of State. Middlebury: J. W. Copeland, Printer. 1823. 8vo, pp. xx, 567, (1).

—*An Oration*, pronounced at Bridport, July 4, 1829, by William Slade, Esq. Published by request. Middlebury, Vt.: Printed by Ovid Miner. MDCCCXXIX. 8vo, pp. 32.

—*Masonic Penalties.* H. H. Houghton, Printer. Castleton, Vt.: Middlebury, July 15, 1830. 8vo, pp. 52.

See Masonic, Memorial to the Legislature, etc., October, 1830.

—*Speech of* Mr. Slade of Vermont, on the Apportionment Bill, delivered in the House of Representatives, U. S., January 31, 1832. 8vo, pp. 6.

His first speech in Congress.

—*Speech* of Mr. Slade, of Vermont, on the Resolution relative to the Collector of Wiscasset. Delivered in the House of Representatives, May, 1832. Washington: Printed at the office of Jonathan Elliott, Penn. Avenue. 1832. 8vo, pp. 52.

—*Letters* of Mr. Slade to Mr. (B. F.) Hallett, Editor of the Boston Advocate. February, 1836. 8vo, pp. 16,29. No. imprint.

An effort to show that the Anti-Masons ought not to vote for Mr. Van Buren, in 1836.

—*Speech* of Mr. Slade, of Vermont, on the Tariff Bill, Delivered in the House of Representatives, January 29, 1833. 8vo, pp. 24.

—*Speech* on the subject of the Abolition of Slavery and the slave trade within the District of Columbia. Delivered in the House of Representatives, December 28, 1835. 8vo, pp. 11.

—*Speech* on the same subject in the House, December 20, 1837. To which is added the intended conclusion of the speech. Suppressed by Resolution of the House. 8vo, pp. 24.

—*Pledges Broken and Power Abused.* Speech of Mr. Slade, of Vermont, on the Bill making appropriations for the Civil and Diplomatic Expenses of the Government for the year 1839. Delivered in the House of Representatives, February 22, 1839. 8vo, pp. 16.

—*Speech* of Mr. Slade, of Vermont, in the Case of the New Jersey Election: Delivered in the House of Representatives, December 10, 1839. 8vo, pp. 8.

—*Speech* on the Question of appointing Chaplains to Congress; in the House of Representatives, Dec. 27, 1839. 8vo, pp. 8.

—*Speech* on the Right of Petition, Slavery in the District of Columbia, &c.; in the House of Representatives, 18th and 20th of January, 1840. Washington: 1840. 8vo, pp. 45.

Another edition: pp. 46.

—*Speech* of Mr. Slade, of Vermont, in favor of a Protection Tariff, Delivered in the House of Representatives, December 20, 1841. 8vo, pp. 24.

—*Speech* of Mr. Slade of Vermont on the Tariff Bill, delivered in committee of the whole on the State of the Union, July 11 and 12, 1842. 8vo, pp. 16.

—*Address* delivered before the Young Men's Temperance Society of Middlebury, Vt., November 23, 1842, on the Occasion of the Death of F. A. M. Ferre, A Member of the Society, by William Slade. Washington: Printed by Gales and Seaton. 1843. 8vo, pp. 15.

—*Gov. Slade's Reply* to Senator Phelps' Appeal. Burlington: Chauncey Goodrich. 1846. 8vo, pp. 32.

—*To the People of Vermont.* Being Gov. Slade's Reply to Senator Phelps' Rejoinder. 8vo, pp. 40, 4. Oct. 10, 1846.

—*Letters* of Hon. William Slade, upon Free Soil and the Presidency. 1848. [n. p.] 8vo, pp. 16.

While Secretary and Agent of the National Board of Popular Education, Mr. Slade published eleven annual Reports—1848–1858—inclusive, of 30 to 40 pages each.

See Vermont, Law Reports, 1844; Vermont, Compiled Laws, 1825.

Hon. William Slade was born in Cornwall, Vt., May 9, 1786. He was graduated at Middlebury College, 1807: read and practiced law, and was an editor, publisher and bookseller. He held many minor offices, and was a member of Congress, 1831-43; Governor of the State of Vermont, 1844-46. He was subsequently Secretary and agent of National Board of Popular Education, having for its object the furnishing of the West, (if anybody knows where that is) with teachers. In this occupation he continued until about the time of his death, at Middlebury, January 18, 1859. See History of Middlebury; History of Cornwall; also Poore's and Lanman's Dictionaries of Congress.

Slafter, Edmund F. *A Discourse* Delivered in St. John's Church, Jamaica Plain, Roxbury, on Sunday, July 28, 1850, on the occasion of the death of Gen. Zachary Taylor, late President of the United States. By the Rev. Edmund F. Slafter, Rector. Published by request of the Wardens and Vestry. Boston: Charles Simpson, 106 Washington Street. 1850. 8vo, pp. 12.

—*A Sermon* on the planting and growth of the Protestant Episcopal Church in the United States, preached in the University Hall, St. Andrew's Parish, Norwich, Vt., July 18, 1863. By the Rev. Edmund F. Slafter, of Boston. 8vo, pp. 14.

—*The Charter of Norwich, Vt.*, and names of the original Proprietors: with brief Historical Notes. By the Rev. Edmund F. Slafter, A. M. Cor. Sec'y N. E. Hist. Gen. Society. Reprinted from the New England Historical and Genealogical Register for Jan., 1869. Boston: David Clapp & Son, Printers. 1869. 8vo, pp. 8.

—*The Assassination Plot* in New York in 1776. A Letter of Dr. William Eustis, Surgeon in the revolutionary army and late Governor of Massachusetts. With notes by the Rev. Edmund F. Slafter, A. M. Corresponding Secretary of the New England Historical Genealogical Society. Reprinted from the New England Historical and Genealogical Register for April, 1869. Boston: Printed by David Clapp & Son. 1868. 8vo, pp. 6.

—*Memorial of John Slafter*, with Genealogical Account of his Descendants, including Eight Generations. By the Rev. Edmund F. Slafter, A. M. Privately Printed for the Family. Boston: Press of Henry W. Dutton & Son. 90 & 92 Washington Street. 1868. 8vo, pp. x, 155.

Plate and Portraits.

—*The Vermont Coinage.* By the Rev. Edmund F. Slafter, A. M., Member of the Boston Numismatic Society; Corresponding Member of the Vermont Historical Society, etc. Reprinted from the First Volume of the Collections of the Vermont Historical Society. Fifty Copies only printed. Montpelier, Vt.: Vermont Historical Society. M,DCCC,LXX. rl. 8vo, pp. 30, and 2 of plates.

—*Discourse delivered* before the New England Historic, Genealogical Society, Boston, March 18, 1870, on the occasion of the Twenty-Fifth Anniversary of its Incorporation. By the Rev. Edmund F. Slafter, A. M., Corresponding Secretary of the Society. With proceedings and appendix. Boston: New England Historic, Genealogical Society. 1870. rl 8vo, pp. 59.

—*The Copper Coinage* of the Earl of Sterling. 1632. By the Rev. Edmund F. Slafter, A. M. Member of the Boston Numismatic Society, etc. Boston: Privately Printed. 1874. small 4to, pp. 14.

—*Sir William Alexander* and American Colonization, including three Royal Charters: A Tract on Colonization: a Patent of the County of Canada and of Long Island; and the Roll of Knights Baronets of New Scotland: with annotations and a Memoir, by the Rev. Edmund F. Slafter, A. M. Boston: Published by the Prince Society. 1873. small 4to, pp. IX+283.
Portrait of Sir William Alexander.

—*Voyages of the Northmen to America.* Including extracts from Icelandic Sagas relating to Western voyages by the Northmen in the tenth and elventh centuries in an English translation by North Ludlow Beamish: with a synopsis of the historical evidence and the opinion of Professor Rafn as to the places visited by the Scandinavians on the Coast of America. Edited with an Introduction by the Rev. Edmund F. Slafter, A. M. Boston: Printed for the Prince Society. 1877. 2 maps. 4to, pp. 162.

—*Voyages of Samuel De Champlain.* Translated from the French by Charles Pomeroy Otis, Ph. D. With Historical Illustrations, and a Memoir by the Rev. Edmund F. Slafter, A. M. Vol. I. 1567-1635. Five Illustrations. Boston: Published by the Prince Society. 1880. small 4to, pp. viii, (2), 340.

—*Voyages of Samuel De Champlain.* Translated from the French by Charles Pomeroy Otis, Ph. D. With Historical Illustrations, and a Memoir By the Rev. Edmund F. Slafter, A. M. Vol. II. 1604-1610. Heliotype Copies of twenty local maps. Boston: Published by the Prince Society. 1878. small 4to, pp. xiv, (2), 273.
Vol. III, to complete the work, not quite ready. Vol. II contains the account of Champlain's discovery of the lake which bears his name, and the adjoining territory of Vermont and New York.

—*Pre-Historic Copper Implements.* An open letter to the Historical Society of Wisconsin. By the Rev. Edmund F. Slafter, A. M. Corresponding Member of the Wisconsin Historical Society; Corresponding Secretary of the New England Historic Genealogical Society;

Honorary Member of the Royal Historical Society of Great Britian, &c., &c. Boston: Privately Printed. 1879. 8vo, pp. 15.
Re-printed from the "New England Historical and Genealogical Register," for January, 1879.

—*The Knox Manuscripts:* Being the Substance of a Report made at the Annual Meeting of the New England Historic Genealogical Society, January 5, 1881, on the arrangement and binding of the manuscripts presented to the Society by the late Rear Admiral Henry K. Thatcher, with practical observations on the proper disposition of old manuscript letters and other documents. By the Rev. Edmund F. Slafter, A. M., Corresponding Secretary of the Society, etc., etc. Boston: The Society's House, 18 Somerset street. M,DCCC,LXXXI. 8vo, pp. 12.

—*History and Causes* of the Incorrect Latitudes as recorded in the Journals of the Early Writers, Navigators and Explorers relating to the Atlantic Coast of North America. 1535-1740. By the Rev. Edmund F. Slafter, A. M., etc., etc. Boston: Privately Printed. 1882. 8vo, pp. 20.
Rev. Mr. Slafter was born in Norwich, Vt., May 30, 1816; he fitted for college at Thetford Academy, and was graduated at Dartmouth College, 1840, and at Andover Theological Seminary in 1844. He was ordained in Trinity church, Boston, Mass., in 1844, and was Rector of St. Peter's church, Cambridge, and St. John's church, Jamaica Plain, till 1853, when his health failed. He was Financial Superintendent of the American Bible Society for the Protestant Episcopal Church for twenty years.
Mr. Slafter was an acknowledged authority in historical matters, and an active and valuable member and officer of the New England Historic Genealogical Society.

Slavery and Anti-slavery. *Address* of the Starksborough and Lincoln Anti-Slavery Society, to the Public, Presented 11th Month, 8th, 1834. Middlebury: Knapp and Jewett, Printers. 1835. 8vo, pp. 36.

—*An Appeal* to the Females of the North, on the subject of Slavery, by a Female of Vermont. Printed at Philadelphia, Pa. 1838. pp. 12.

—*Address* of the Baptist Anti-Slavery Convention held at Waterbury (Vt.), on the 29th and 30th of September, 1841. (n. p. 1841.) Folio, pp. 2.

—*Address* of the Starksborough and Lincoln Anti-Slavery Society to the Public. Middlebury: Knapp and Jewett, Printers. 1835. 8vo, pp. 36.

—*Slavery in Vermont*, and in other parts of the United States. Woodstock, Vt.: Davis & Greene, Printers. (n. d.) 8vo, pp. 16.

—*Reports and Resolutions* on Slavery, and the Repeal of the Missouri Compromise. Printed by Order of the House of Rep's. Montpelier: E. P. Walton, Jr., Printer. 1854. 8vo, pp. 20.

—*Reports* and Resolutions on Slavery, &c., By the Select Committee of the Senate. Montpelier: E. P. Walton, Jr., Printer. 1855. 8vo, pp. 8.

—*General Assembly* of the State of Vermont. Session of 1856. Reports of Select Committees of the Senate on Slavery and the Condition of Kansas. And on the Outrage on the Freedom of Debate in Congress. Burlington: Free Press Print. 1856. 8vo, pp. 22.

—State of Vermont. In House of Representatives. Report of the Select Committee on Slavery, The Dred Scott Decision, and the Action of the Federal Government. Submitted Thursday, Nov. 18, 1858. Montpelier : E. P. Walton, Printer. 1858. 8vo, pp. 82.

See Boardman, E. J. Address 1838; Barber, E. D., orations, etc.; Converse, J. K.; Vermont Colonization Society; Cutting, H. P., Discourse, 1854; Fletcher, John, Studies on Slavery; Hopkins, Rt. Rev. J. H., View of Slavery; Johnson, Oliver, Address, 1835; Rood, Ansen, in reply to Rev. Dr. Joel Parker; Prindle, Cyrus, Discourse, 1841.

Slayton, Henry K. *Genealogical and Biographical Sketch* of the Slayton Family of Calais, Vermont. 1879. 24mo, pp. 12.

Hon. Henry K. Slayton was born in Calais, August 29, 1825 ; married Eliza A. Mitchell, of Manchester, N. H., in 1850, by whom be had one son, Edward M.; he was educated in the common schools of Calais and the Montpelier Academy. He taught school two winters, then went to Boston at the age of 18, and served as a clerk three years, when he returned to Calais and opened a country store, in which business he continued until 1863, when he moved to Manchester, N. H., where he established a wholesale produce and provision business in 1864, in which he was succeeded by his son in the spring of 1873.

Mr. Slayton has given much attention to politics; formerly a Democrat in the nearly unanimous Democratic town of Calais until the "free soil" invasion in 1848, he was a delegate to the first republican National Convention in 1856 at Philadelphia, and an alternate to the Chicago Convention in 1860; was Town Representative from Calais in 1858-9, and a Representative in the New Hampshire Legislature from Ward 3, Manchester, in 1871-2; in the State Senate from Manchester, 1877-78, and a member of the Constitutional Convention in 1876.

He made a trip to Cuba in 1863, and thence to New Orleans, where he wholesaled dry goods. In 1873 he made an extended trip to England, Scotland, and the Continent of Europe, attending the World's Fair at Vienna, on his route.

Mr. Slayton published many able articles in newspapers in advocacy of a specie basis, and was the author of the "hard money" resolutions which passed the New Hampshire and Vermont Legislatures in 1878, and of the resolution in relation to the "Bland Silver bill" which was passed by the Vermont Legislature in the same year.

See the above Genealogical sketch.

Smalley, Mrs. B. H. *The Young Converts;* or memoirs of the Three Sisters, Debbie, Helen and Anna Barlow. Compiled by A Lady. Edited by Rev. J. T. Hecker. New York : 1861. 12mo, pp. 263.

—Another Edition; The Young Converts; or memoirs of the Three Sisters, Debbie, Helen and Anna Barlow. Compiled by Mrs. Julia C. Smalley. Edited by Very Rev. Z. Druon, of St. Albans, Vt. Claremont, N. H.: 1868. 12mo, pp. 181.

We do not think the work is improved by the omissions in the second edition.

See Miss Hemenway's Vermont Historical Gazetteer, pp. 365-7, of Vol. II.

Smalley, David Allen.

See United States Circuit Court, his Decisions, etc. Judge Smalley was born in Middlebury, Vt., April 8, 1809; died at Burlington, March 10, 1877. He received an academical education, read law with his uncle B. H. Smalley at St. Albans, was admitted to the Franklin County Bar in 1831, and soon after commenced practice at Jericho; in 1836 he removed to Burlington where he ever after resided. He was a leading Democrat in Vermont, was many years Chairman of the State Committee, and one term chairman of the National Committee; he was Chairman of the Vermont delegations to National Conventions in 1852 and 1856; was a State Senator from Chittenden County in 1842; appointed by President Pierce Collector of Customs for Vermont in 1853, and on the death of Judge Prentiss, in February, 1857, he was appointed United States District Judge by President Pierce, which office he held until his death. Judge Smalley married May 22, 1833, Laura, daughter of the late Colonel Bradley Barlow, of Fairfield, Vt., and sister of Hon. Bradley

Barlow, of St. Albans; she died at Burlington, August 9, 1879, at the age of 70; three sons survive, Col. Henry A. Smalley, of New York, Bradley B. Smalley, Esq., and Mr. Eugene Smalloy, both of Burlington.

Many of Judge Smalley's decisions and opinions were published in various forms; he also wrote several biographical and historical articles for Miss Hemenway's Vermont Historical Gazetteer.

Smart, Rev. W. S., D. D. *Lessons from the War.* By Rev. W. S. Smart, Pastor of the Congregational Church, Benson, Vt. Rutland: Printed by Geo. A. Tuttle & Co. 1862. 8vo, pp. 27.

—A Discourse delivered in the Congregational Church, on the occasion of the Funeral of Mr. Philo Wilcox, Esq., of Benson, Vermont. On Monday, August 28th, A. D. 1865, By W. S. Smart, Pastor. Printed for private circulation. Rutland : Tuttle & Co., Printers. 1865. 8vo, pp. 15.

Dr. Smart was chaplain of the Fourteenth Regiment, Vt. Vols. during its term of service. He is pastor of the Congregational church in Brandon.

Smith, Albert. *An Inaugural Address* delivered at Mercersburg, Pa., at the Annual Commencement of Marshall College, September 26th, 1838. By Albert Smith, Professor of Ancient Languages in the Institution. Chambersburg: Henry Ruby, Printer. 1835. 8vo, pp. 28.

—Benevolence above Righteousness. A Sermon preached at the Funeral of the Hon. Nathaniel O. Kellogg, at Vernon, Conn., May 15, 1854. By Albert Smith, Pastor of the Church in Vernon. Hartford : Press of Case, Tiffany and Company. 1854. 8vo, pp. 34.

—Rest of the Pious Dead in Christ. A Sermon preached at the Funeral of Mr. Kimball W. Gould, by Rev. A. Smith, Pastor of the Congregational Church, Northfield, Vt., Sabbath, July 4, 1852. Concord : Steam Power Press of McFarland & Jenks. 8vo, pp. 14.

Dr. Smith died April 24, 1863.
See biography in Presbyterian Historical Almanac, 1864.

Smith, A. C. *The Ancient Landmark* and Masonic Digest. Respectfully dedicated to the M. W. Grand Lodge of Michigan. Edited and Published, by A. C. Smith. Devoted to Masonry, Literature, the fine arts and general Intelligence. Mt. Clemens, Michigan. 5851-5.

Volumes 1 and 2, fortnightly in 4to, of about 200 pp. each; volumes 3-4, 8vo, monthly, nearly 400 pp. each.

—Installation Address to St. Paul Lodge No. 3, by Brother A. C. Smith, P. M. Delivered on the evening of Dec. 22, 1857, the 237th Anniversary of the Landing of the Pilgrims. Printed by order of the Lodge. St. Paul : Pioneer and Democrat Office. 8vo, pp. 10.

—A Random Historical Sketch of Meeker County, Minnesota. From its first settlement, to July 4. 1876. By A. C. Smith, President of the Bar, and Old Settlers Associations for said county. With an accurate map by Henry L. Smith. Litchfield, Minn. Belfoy & Joubert, Publishers. 1877. sqr. 12mo, pp. 160, (2).

—In Memoriam. Hon. A. C. Smith who Fell Asleep Sept. 20th, 1880, aged 66 years. Litchfield, Minn. : Litchfield News Ledger Print. 1880. 12mo, pp. 16.

Hon. Abner Comstock Smith was born in Brookfield, Vt., February 14, 1814. His father, John Smith, a native of Rockingham, Vt., was one of the pioneer settlers of Brookfield, where he died in 1863, in his 83d year. The subject of this sketch was educated at the common schools, and at the academy in Randolph; he read law at Woodstock, with Marsh & Swan, and one year in Washington, D. C., with Hon. W. L. Brent. He was a clerk in the Treasury Department at Washington under Hon. Levi Woodbury, 1836-39, when he settled in Mount Clemens, Mich., where he resided until 1855. During his residence in Michigan he published the "Macomb County Gazette" four years, and also "The Ancient Landmark," a Masonic paper, about the same length of time; he was a member of the Michigan State Senate, 1845-6, and a District Judge, 1851-4. In 1855 Judge Smith moved to St. Paul, Minn., where he published the daily "Free Press" six months. He was Register of the Land Office at Minneapolis and Forest City, 1857-8. Mr. Smith married, May 1, 1839, Elisabeth D., eldest daughter of Hon. D. Azro A. Buck, formerly a member of Congress from Vermont; they had four children, three of whom are living; Carrie L. is the wife of Edwin S. Fitch, of Hastings, Minn; Ella B. married Laban B. Dixon, and resides in Chicago; Henry L. is an architect in Chicago, (1880). Mr. Smith was one of the pioneer settlers of Litchfield, Meeker county, where resided until his death, September 20, 1880, in the practice of his profession. See United States Biographical Dictionary for a full sketch of his life.

Smith, Asa D., D. D. *An Address,* delivered at a Reunion of the Sons of Weston, (Vt.) July 4, 1853. By Rev. Asa D. Smith, D. D., with A Sketch of the Accompanying Exercises. Boston : 1853. 8vo, pp. 45.

Smith, Rev. Bezaleel.
Mr. Smith was born in Randolph, Vt., April 2, 1797, and died there May 15, 1879. He fitted for college at the Orange County Grammar School, and was graduated at Dartmouth, 1825; read theology, and preached to various Congregational churches in New Hampshire, 1827-70, when he returned to Vermont, and was acting pastor at West Hartford, 1871-77, when he retired to the place of his birth. In 1860 he published a New Year's Sermon, "The Setting up of the Tabernacle," Ex. 40 :2, which was printed in the Congregational Journal. See Vermont Congregational Minutes, 1879, pp. 42-3.

Smith, Rev. Benjamin. *Thoughts on Revivals;* By Rev. B. B. Smith, Rector of St. Steven's Church, Middlebury, Vt. Middlebury : Printed by J. W. Copeland, 1828. 12mo, pp. 23.

Smith *Centennial Memorial.* Rutland : Tuttle & Co., Printers. 1872. 8vo, pp. 56.
Being a gathering of the descendants of Samuel Smith and his wife Hannah, who settled in Bridport, Vt., September 8, 1770.

Smith, Chauncey. *A Treatise* on the Law of Arbitration ; with an Appendix of Precedents. By James Stamford Caldwell. Second American from the last London Edition, with Notes, and References to American and English Decisions, by Chauncey Smith. Burlington : Chauncey Goodrich. 1853. 8vo, pp. xii. 539.

Smith, Columbus. *Report* of a Search made in England for a property reported to belong to the Gibb's in U. S. A., in the years 1847-48, by Columbus Smith, Esq., Agent for the Acting Gibbs Association of Vermont. Containing a short History of the Gibb's in England ; likewise several Genealogies of the different branches of the Gibb's Family. (Published by order of the Directors of the Acting Gibbs Association of Vermont.) Middlebury : Justus Cobb, Printer. 1848. 8vo, pp. 28.

—*Report* of the Follansbee Association, U. S. A. Made by Columbus Smith, A. D. 1865. Containing information now in his possession, and in the possession of the different branches of the Follansbee Family in America, relative to the Follansbee Property in England ; likewise several Genealogies of different branches of the family. Published by order of the Follansbee Association. Middlebury : Print-

ed at the Register Job Office. 1865. 8vo, pp. 28. (Also a supplementary report. 1869. 8vo, pp. 6.)

—*Index for persons* in America claiming properties abroad, either as next of kin, Heirs at law, legatees or otherwise. Compiled by Columbus Smith, of West Salisbury, Vermont, A. D. 1868. Burlington : Free Press Steam Book and Job Printing House. 1868. 12mo, pp. 22.

—*Report of the Booth Association* of the United States, by Columbus Smith, A. D. 1868, Containing the organization, the Booth Constitution, and information relative to Booth property in England ; also Pedigrees of the different branches of the Booth family in America and England. Burlington : Free Press Steam Printing House. 1868. 8vo, pp. 64.

—*Report to the Brown Association, U. S. A.,* made by Columbus Smith, A. D. 1868. Published by order of the Brown Association. Burlington : Free Press Steam Book and Job Printing House. 1868. 8vo, pp. 126.
See Gibson Association; Houghton Association; Booth Association; Innis Association; Willoughby Association; Jennings Association; Brown Association.

Smith, Rev. Charles Strong. *Systematic Beneficence.* An Essay Read before the General Convention of Congregational Ministers and Churches of Vermont, at Bradford, June 20, 1877. Montpelier: J. & J. M. Poland, Steam Book and Job Printers. 1877. 8vo, pp. 16.
Mr. Smith was born in Hardwick, Vt., July 24, 1824; graduated at the University of Vermont in 1848, and at the East Windsor Theological Institute, Connecticut, in 1853. He preached in New Preston, Conn., for the next two years, and the two years following at North Walton, N. Y. He represented the town of Hardwick in the General Assembly of Vermont in 1863, and in December of the same year accepted the Secretaryship of the Vermont Domestic Missionary Society. In 1875-76 he was associate editor of the *Vermont Chronicle,* and subsequently editor of the same. Mr. Smith resides in Montpelier.

Smith, Daniel. *Report of a Missionary Tour* through that part of the United States which lies west of the Allegany Mountains ; performed under the direction of the Massachusetts Missionary Society. By Samuel J. Mills, and Daniel Smith. Andover : Printed by Flagg and Gould. 1815. 8vo, pp. 64.
The report contains interesting accounts of Indiana, Illinois, Missouri, Kentucky, Mississippi, Tennessee and Louisiana ; the missionaries having visited the latter State just after the battle of New Orleans.
Mr. Smith was born in Bennington, Vt., in 1789, and died at Louisville, Ky., in 1822. He was stationed at Natchez, Miss., as a missionary, 1816-20. He was a son of Hon. Noah Smith, of Bennington. Sprague; Drake; Allibone.

Smith, Mrs. D. T. (BOYCE).
Mrs. Smith, daughter of Hon. Z. W. Boyce, is a native of Fayston, Vt. She now resides at Dubuque, Iowa. Under the pseudonym "Maud Meredith," she commenced literary work in 1876; her first contribution being to the Argus and Patriot in that year ; in addition, she has furnished stories, sketches and poems to the Watchman, Montpelier ; Phœnix, and Household, Brattleboro ; Commonwealth, Boston; Independent, New York; Tribune, Chicago; Peterson's Magazine, and various newspapers in Missouri and Iowa. Mrs. Smith is at present passing through the press a volume of her poems.
Mr. Boyce, father of Mrs. Smith, was a native of North Fayston, born October 1, 1812. Since 1852 he has been a liberal contributor of historical, biographical and poetical articles to the Freeman, and Argus and Patriot at

Montpelier. Mr. Boyce held town offices for the last forty years of his life, and was a member of the Legislature in 1862-3. He died in Fayston, June 27, 1877.

Smith, Eli B. *Ministers, Examples to Believers* A sermon preached before the graduating class of the New Hampton Theological Institution, August 15, 1847. By Eli B. Smith, Professor of Sacred Theology and Pastoral Duties. Boston : Printed by Damrell and Moore, 52 Washington Street. 1847. 8vo, pp. 23.

Mr. Smith was born in Shoreham, Vt., April 15, 1803; was graduated at Middlebury College in 1823; studied theology at Andover and Newton; preached to a Baptist church in Buffalo, N. Y., 1826-29, and in Poultney, Vt., 1829-33; was President of the New Hampton Theological Institution, 1833, and died at Colchester, Vt., January 5, 1861.

Smith, Elihu. *A Sermon* delivered at Castleton, Vt., at the interment of Deacon Eber Gridley, who departed this life in the forty-fifth year of his age ; Lord's Day, March 4, 1821 : It being the stated Communion of the Church. By Elihu Smith, A. M., Pastor of the Church. Published by request. Motto. Rutland : Printed by William Fay, 1821. 8vo, pp. 16.

Smith, Ethan. *A Farewell Sermon*, delivered at Haverhill, N. H., June 30, 1799. By Ethan Smith. Peacham, Vt.: 1800. 8vo, pp. 27.

—*Two Sermons* on one subject, delivered at Washington. N. H., on Lord's Day, November 4, 1804, by Ethan Smith, Pastor of the Church in Hopkinton. Texts. Printed at Windsor, Vermont, by Nahum Mower, 1805. 8vo, pp 39.

—*Memoirs of Abigail Bailey*, (wife of Major Asa Bailey of Landaff, N. H.) with sundry original biographical sketches, by Rev. Ethan Smith, 1815. 12mo, pp. 275.

—*Ministers of Christ*, made Instruments of Man's Salvation. A sermon delivered at Tinmouth, Vermont, at the Installation of Rev. Stephen Martindale, to the Pastoral charge of the Church of Christ in that place, January 7, 1819. By Ethan Smith, Pastor of a Presbyterian church in Hebron, N. Y. Texts. Rutland : Printed by Fay and Burt. 1819. 8vo, pp. 26.

—*The Blessing* of Abraham come on the Gentiles. A lecture on Infant Baptism, delivered at Bolton, N. Y., August 3, 1818. Published at the request of the hearers. Second edition. By Ethan Smith, Pastor of the Congregational church in Poultney, Vt. "They are the seed of the blessed of the Lord, and their offspring with them." Poultney : Smith & Shute, Printers. 1824. 12mo, pp. 95. (4 Lectures.)

—*View of the Hebrews*; Exhibiting the Destruction of Jerusalem ; the certain Restoration of Judah and Israel; and an address of the Prophet Isaiah, relative to their Restoration. By Ethan Smith, Pastor of a church in Poultney, Vt. Motto. Poultney : Printed and Published by Smith & Shute. 1823. 12mo, pp. 187.

Another edition enlarged 1825. pp. 285. Same imprint.

—*View of the Trinity*. A Treatise on the Character of Jesus Christ, and on the Trinity in Unity of the Godhead ; with Quotations from the primitive Fathers. Second edition. By Ethan Smith, Pastor of a church in Poultney, Vt. Poultney : Published and Printed by Smith & Shute. 1824. 12mo, pp. 202. (2.)

—*Sermon at the* Ordination of Harvey Smith as Pastor of the Congregational church at Weybridge, Vt., March 8, 1825.

Rev. Ethan Smith was born in Belchertown, Mass., December 9, 1762; and died at Boylston, Mass., August 29, 1849. He was graduated at Dartmouth college 1790; read theology with Drs. Burroughs, of Hanover, and Burton of Thetford, Vt. He was Pastor of various Congregational churches in New Hampshire, New York and Massachusetts, and at Poultney, Vt., 1821 to 1827, which constituted his only residence in Vermont.

Smith, Mrs. Eva Munson.

was born July 12, 1843, at Monkton, Vt. Her parents were William Chandler Munson, one of the best musicians and educators of his day, and Hannah Bailey-Munson. She inherited her father's musical and literary talents, began composing for publication at the age of 14 years, and when 16 years of age her literary productions found place in the Home Journal, published at Winchester, Tenn., whither her parents had moved some years before, and in other publications, under the nom de plume of "Ruth Chester." She was educated at the Mary Sharp College in Winchester, and the collegiate department of Rockford, Ill., Seminary, graduating therefrom in 1864. While in charge of the music department of Otoc University in Nebraska, she married George Clinton Smith of Nebraska City in 1869. They removed to Springfield, Ill., where she was for a number of years associate editor of the Saturday Mirror and a contributor to the Illinois State Journal.

Her Missionary drama entitled "The Field is the World," has been given in nearly every State of the Union, in Canada, Sandwich Islands, England and other countries of Europe, and she compiled "Woman in Sacred Song;" twenty-five or thirty of its poems and songs being her own. This work of a thousand pages, quarto, she edited, having collected material from 830 hymnologists and song writers of all ages, beginning with the Magnificat of Mary; and also the data for biographical sketches, and the music by fifty different women, set to 140 of the 3000 poems.

In 1893 she delivered an address in Assembly Hall of the Woman's Building at the World's Exposition upon "Woman in Sacred Song," which elicited great praise.

Smith, Ezra P. *Poisoned ?* or, Deacon Smith's Dead Wife ! Being a full, detailed account of Mrs. Smith's death by Poison ! Given to her—alleged--by her husband, Ezra Smith, the well-known Baptist Deacon. All about Mrs. Champlin, the Deacon's Particular friend. How many a happy Home has been destroyed by a bad woman ! Philadelphia, Pa. : Issued by Old Franklin Publishing House. 8vo, pp. 30.

Smith, Rev. Henry. *The truly Christian Pulpit* our Strongest National Defence. A Discourse in Behalf of the American Home Missionary Society, preached in the Cities of New York and Brooklyn, May, 1854. By Rev. Henry Smith, D. D., President of Marietta College, Ohio. New York : Published by the American Home Missionary Society, Bible House, Astor Place. 1854. 8vo, pp. 32.

—*The True Missionary Spirit* in the Church the Measure of her Christian Principle. A Sermon, before the American Board of Commissioners for Foreign Missions, at their Meeting in Springfield, Mass., October 7, 1862. By Henry Smith, D. D., Pastor of the North Presbyterian Church, Buffalo, N. Y. Boston : Press of T. R. Marvin & Son, 42 Congress Street. 1862. 8vo, pp. 27.

—*God in the War :* A Discourse preached in Behalf of the U. S. Christian Commission on the day of the National Thanksgiving, August 6th, 1863, by Rev. Henry Smith, D. D., Pastor of the North Presbyterian Church, Buffalo, N. Y. Buffalo : Printing House of Wheeler, Matthews & Warren, Office of the Commercial Advertiser. 1863. 8vo, pp. 34.

—*The Religious Sentiments* proper for our National Crisis. A Sermon delivered on Sabbath Evening, April 23, 1865. By Henry Smith, D.

D., Pastor of the North Presbyterian Church, Buffalo, N. Y. Buffalo: Printing House of Matthews & Warren, Office of the Buffalo Commercial Advertiser. 1865. 8vo, pp. 32.

Mr. Smith was pastor of the North Presbyterian Church, Buffalo, N. Y., 1862-65.

—*Memorial* of the Rev. Henry Smith, D. D., LL. D., Professor of Sacred Rhetoric and Pastoral Theology in Lane Theological Seminary, May 8th, 1879, Together with Commemorative Resolutions. Published by order of the Board of Trustees. Cincinnati: Elm Street Printing Company, Nos. 176 and 178 Elm Street. 8vo, pp. 40.

The additional publications of Dr. Smith are: "The Abuse of Analogy in Theological Investigation," being his graduation theme at Andover, September 11, 1837; "Farewell Hymn," sung by his class on the same occasion; "Isle aux Noix," an article published about the time of his graduation; "Fears of the Wicked Reasonable," 1835; "Inaugural Address," as President of Marietta College, 1846; "The Mission of Women," 1846; "Translation of Crusius' Homeric Lexicon," 1846; "Address before Western College Society," 1850; "The Christian Pulpit," 1854; "The Christian Sabbath," 1858; "Our National Crisis," 1865; "An Essay on Marietta College and Lane Seminary," 1868; "The Dynasty of the Maccabees," 1870; "Memorial Discourse on the Rev. Dr. D. H. Allen," 1871; "His Buffalo Ministry," 1873; "The First Christian Sermon Analyzed;" "Translation of Tischendorf's Paper on the Sinaitic Manuscript." Also numerous poems in newspapers, and a series of letters from Europe in the Marietta "Register," and Cincinnati "Gazette," which include letters in reference to the fifty-two battle fields in Switzerland which he visited.

Dr. Smith was born at Milton, Vermont, December 16, 1805; died at Cincinnati, Ohio, in January, 1879; was graduated at Middlebury College, 1827; taught one year at Castleton, two years tutor at Middlebury, taught a high school at Marietta, Ohio, 1832-3, and was graduated at Andover Theological Seminary, 1837, was professor of Languages Marietta College, 1837-46, and President of the same 1846-55, when he accepted a Professorship in Lane Theological Seminary, Cincinnati, which he retained until his death.

Dr. Smith's father, Harry Smith, was born in Bennington, Vt., May 2, 1783, and married Phœbe Henderson, April 24, 1803; she was born at Bennington, January 19, 1784; he died at Milton, in 1812; his widow then took charge for a time of a Young Ladies' Seminary at Middlebury, and subsequently married Rev. Dr. Joel H. Linsley, *ante*, and lived to see two of her sons become eminent. Dr. Smith married Hannah, daughter of Rev. Joshua Bates, President of Middlebury College, September 16, 1837. Dr. Smith's grandfather, Noah Smith, was a brother of Governor Israel Smith, of Vermont, and was born at Canaan, Conn., January 29, 1755, and died at Milton, Vt., in 1812; he married Chloe Burrill in 1779. See Vermont Historical Society Collections, vol. 1, pp. 253-4; Governor and Council, vol, 4, pp. 168-9.

Albert Smith, elder brother of Rev. Dr. Henry, was graduated at Middlebury, 1831, and at Andover, 1835; Pastor at Williamstown, Mass., 1836-38, Professor in Marshall College, Pa., 1838-40, and Professor of Rhetoric, etc., at Middlebury College, 1840-44, when he returned to pastoral work, and died at Monticello, Ill., in 1862.

"Pearson's Graduates of Middlebury College," states that Albert and Henry Smith were from Hartford, Conn., which is an error.

Smith, H. O. *Report* to the Wilson Association, which see.

Smith, John, A. M. *A Sermon* preached in Randolph, June 3, 1801, at the Ordination of the Rev. Mr. Tilton Eastman. By John Smith, A. M., Professor of the Learned Languages, at Dartmouth College. Printed at Randolph, (Vermont) By S. Wright & J. Denio. MDCCCI. 8vo. pp. 26.

This pamphlet has an invitation card attached to it which reads as follows: "Ordination Ball. The company of Miss Lydia Edgerton is requested at Mr. J. Warner's Hall, in Randolph, on Thursday, the 4th inst., at one of the clock p. m. B. Edgerton, W. Arnold, A. Edgerton, J. Edson, Managers. Randolph, June 3, 1801."

Smith, Hon. John. *Speech in the House of Representatives,* Washington, in defence of the Independent treasury bill.

Mr. Smith, the father of Gov. John Gregory Smith, of St. Albans, was a Democratic member of Congress from Vermont, 1839-1341; of the above speech, his biographer says: "It was of ability, and, judged in the light of subsequent events, would be considered eminently wise and just. The political storm that swept the country in 1840, carried Mr. Smith away with it, and his congressional career was terminated." He was subsequently one of the Trustees and President of the Vermont and Canada Railroad. See Vermont Historical Gazetteer, vol. 2, pp. 316-317.

Smith, George Gregory. *Court of Inquiry,* July 20 and 21, 1875, As to the cause of the death of Miss Marietta N. Ball, July 24, 1874, before Justice Farnsworth. Report of proceedings had on investigation of rumors implicating George Gregory Smith, with comments of the Press. St. Albans: Advertiser Steam Printing House. 1875. 8vo, pp. 51.

Smith, Mrs. J. Gregory. *From Dawn to Sunrise:* A Review, Historical and Philosophical, of the Religious Ideas of Mankind. Motto. By Mrs. J. Gregory Smith. Rouses Point, N. Y.: Lovell Printing and Publishing Co. 1876. 12mo, pp. 406.

—*Seola.* A Novel. Boston: Lee & Shepard, Publishers. New York: Charles T. Dillingham. 1878. 12mo, pp. 251.

—*The Iceberg's Story.* sm. 4to, pp. 10. A Poem inspired by passing an iceberg July 28, 1881, in mid-Atlantic between Liverpool and Quebec.

—*Selma.* By Mrs. J. Gregory Smith. New York: John W. Lovell Company. 1880. 16mo, pp. 251.

—*Atla.* By Mrs. J. Gregory Smith. New York: Harper & Brothers. 1886. 12mo, pp. 284. Also published in London by Ward & Downey. 1886.

—*Poems.* Original and compiled. By Mrs. J. Gregory Smith. St. Albans: Messenger Co. 1889. 12mo, pp. 185.

—*Notes of Travel.* By Mrs. J. Gregory Smith. St. Albans Messenger Co. 1886. 12mo, pp. 123.

Mrs. Smith is a native of St. Albans, Vt., being a daughter of the late Hon. Lawrence Brainard; she married Ex-Governor J. Gregory Smith, who is a son of the late Hon. John Smith, noticed above, and well known throughout the country in connection with his successful management of large railroad interests in Vermont. Mrs. Smith is a lady of almost marvelous industry and perseverance, not only in connection with general literature, and the pre-historic condition of the earth and its inhabitants, for she has said that she knows comparatively little this side of the flood; but her active influence pervades all the affairs of life, and she is pre-eminent in her household as wife and mother.

In 1864 Mrs. Smith addressed circulars to Vermonters, asking aid for a National Fair at Washington, D. C., for the purpose of stimulating enlistment in the District of Columbia for the Civil War. Her appeal was successful, and her method and form were adopted in the other States. As a member of the "Women's Centennial Executive Committee," and "Manager for Vermont," she issued in 1876 three stirring circulars addressed to the ladies of Vermont in the interest of the "Women's Department" of the Centennial Exposition at Philadelphia, through which means about twenty-five hundred dollars was raised.

In 1864 Mrs. Smith achieved distinction in connection with the famous "St. Albans Raid," and through the late Adjutant General and Ex-Gov. P. T. Washburn she holds a Lieut. Colonel's commission for gallant conduct on that occasion.

Smith, Joshua, or Joseph? *Trial of the Persons* indicted in the Hancock Circuit Court, for the murder of Joseph Smith, At the Carthage Jail, on the 27th day of June, 1844. 12mo, pp. 44. n. p. n. d.

Verdict, not guilty.

The Mormon, Joe Smith, was born in Sharon, Vt., December 23, 1805, and was treacherously murdered in jail by a mob at Carthage, Hancock County, Ill., June 27, 1844, in defiance of promised protection by Governor Thomas Ford. The parents of Joe Smith were obscure and poor, and when he was ten years of age, the family, consisting of the parents and nine children, moved to Palmyra, N. Y., where Mormonism was developed. Of the Book of Mormon we have gathered the following facts from various sources, but largely from information communicated by J. H. Gilbert, published in the "Detroit Post and Tribune" of December 2, 1877. Mr. Gilbert is a printer, and was formerly proprietor of the "Sentinel" at Palmyra; he set the type and printed the first edition of the "Mormon Bible," and preserved for himself a copy in sheets, which is still in his possession. The book is a quarto of 580 pages, the contents divided into chapters, broken into frequent paragraphs, but the verses were not numbered, as in the later editions. Upon the title page appears the name of "Joshua Smith" as "Author and Proprietor." In subsequent editions he appears simply as "Translator, or Author." This change was rendered necessary to carry out the theory afterward adopted, that Smith dug up the plates containing hieroglyphics, and translated them by means of a pair of supernatural spectacles. Mr. Gilbert's narrative continues : "One pleasant day in the summer of 1829, Hiram Smith, Joe's Brother, came to the office to negotiate for the printing of a book; the arrangements were completed; five thousand copies were to be printed for $3,000, a well-to-do farmer named Martin Harris, living in the neighborhood, becoming security, by giving a mortgage upon his farm, through which in the end he was financially ruined." The work was at once commenced, occupying about eight months, Mr. Gilbert setting all the type, except 30 or 40 pages, and doing all the press work on a hand press. "The copy was brought to the office by Hiram Smith, written on foolscap paper, in a good, clear hand. The handwriting was Oliver Cowdery's, and not a punctuation mark in the entire manuscript. The sentences were run in without capitals or other marks to designate where one left off or another began, and it was no easy task to straighten out the stuff." Mr. Gilbert, discovering that large portions were stolen from the Bible, verbatim, used to have a copy of the same on his case to aid him in deciphering and punctuating the work. At first Smith brought to the office every day just enough copy for that day, but finally, for the greater convenience of the printer, was, after much urging, induced to bring a quire at a time, the copy being taken away by Smith as fast as the printer was through with it. Mr. Gilbert speaks of Joe Smith as a lazy, good-for-nothing lout, chiefly noted for his capacity to hang around a corner grocery, and punish poor whiskey. He was a "water witch," and had a magic stone, through which he pretended to discover hidden treasure, and half the boys in Palmyra were digging pits after pots of gold, some of which pits are still pointed out to visitors. By the magic powers of this stone he discovered the Mormon plates, and translated them by means of magic or supernatural spectacles; he dictated the book concealed behind a curtain, and it was written down by Cowdery. This course seemed necessary by the fact that Smith could not write.

It is now pretty well established that the "Book of Mormon" was written in 1809 to 1812 by Solomon Spalding, a Presbyterian preacher, as a popular religious romance. He sent it to Pittsburgh, where it lay in a printing office several years, he not being able to raise the money to secure the printing of it, and after his death it was returned to his widow, about 1824.

By some means, not known, it fell into the hands of Sidney Rigdon, who with Joe Smith concocted the scheme by which it was subsequently brought out as the work of Smith, the dealings with the outside world being manipulated by Hiram, an elder brother of Joe Smith.

For a full history of Smith and Mormonism in its early period, consult "Autobiography of Joseph Smith," J. B. Turner's "Life of Joseph Smith," Ford's History of Illinois, and "My Own Times," by Governor John Reynolds, of Illinois; also Frisbie's History of Middletown, Vt., pp. 43-64; Rev. Dr. Kidder's History of Mormonism, etc.; History of Wells, Vt.

As the Rev. Solomon Spalding's connection with the Mormon Bible is of interest, we condense an account of him from the "Dartmouth Alumni," p. 39; Mr. Spalding was born in Ashford, Conn., in 1761, and died at Amity, Washington Co, Pa., in 1816. He was graduated at Dartmouth in 1785, read theology, and preached in Connecti-

cut eight or ten years, when poor health compelled him to retire from the ministry. In 1795 he was married, and soon after went into business with his brother Josiah, in Cherry Valley, N. Y., and in 1799 the firm moved to Richfield, N. Y., and purchased large tracts of land in Pennsylvania and Ohio, to superintend which Solomon moved to Salem, Ohio, but the war of 1812 deranged their plans, and caused great losses. Josiah, then visiting his brother, found him in poor health and low spirits, writing a work of fiction, suggested by the opening of a mound in which were discovered some human bones, and some relics indicative of a former civilization. He entitled his work a "Manuscript Found," and in it imagined the fortunes of the extinct people. Josiah left him thus employed. Not long after, probably in 1814, Solomon went to Pittsburgh, Penn., where he was followed by Sidney Rigdon, then a printer, and afterwards a noted Mormon.

Rigdon told his employer of Spalding's novel, who borrowed the manuscript, and offered to print it, which was refused, and the author wandered to Amity, the place of his death. His widow returned to New York with the manuscript, and while absent from home a stranger called upon her and desired to examine it, that he might confirm or refute a current report in the West that it had become the Mormon Bible. She permitted him to visit her house, and obtain it from a certain chest; he went, and reported that he could not find it, and Mrs. Spalding never saw it afterwards. The supposition is that Rigdon copied the work at Pittsburg, and that the stranger purloined the original to avoid a future exposure.

The story in the "Dartmouth Alumni" was embodied from a letter written by the brother, Josiah Spalding, in January, 1855, and although his account differs in some minor particulars from that of Mr. Gilbert, yet the two strengthed each other as to the main facts.

Smith, Matthew. *Genealogy* of Descendants of Matthew Smith of East Haddam, Conn., By Mrs. Sophia (Smith) Martin. Rutland : Tuttle Co. 1890. 8vo, pp. 270.

Smith, Nathan R. *A Physiological Essay* on Digestion. By Nathan R. Smith, M. D., Professor of Anatomy and Physiology, in the University of Vermont. Motto. New York : Published by E. Bliss and E. White, No. 128 Broadway. 1825. 8vo, pp. 93.

Smith, Noah. *A speech* delivered at Bennington on the (first) Anniversary of the 16th of August, 1777. By Noah Smith, A. B. Hartford: Printed by Watson & Goodwin. MDCCLXXIX.

Re-printed in Vermont Historical Society collections, Vol. 1, pp. 255-261. Mr. Smith was a brother of Governor Israel Smith. For biographical sketch see "Collections, Vermont Historical Society," Vol. 1, pp. 253-4; Smith, Rev. Henry, note.

Smith, Oliver. *An Oration*, pronounced at Johnson, July 4th, 1826, being the 50th Anniversary of the independence of the United States. By Oliver Smith, A. M., Counsellor at Law. Burlington : Printed by E. & T. Mills. 1826. 8vo, pp. 31.

Smith, P. H. *Green Mountain Boys*, or Vermont and the N. Y. Land Jobbers. Pawling : 16mo, clo. 1885.

Smith, Reuben. *Africa Given to Christ :* A Sermon Preached before the Vermont Colonization Society at Montpelier, Oct. 20, 1830. By Reuben Smith, Pastor of the Calvinistic Congregational Church, Burlington, Vt. Published by the Board of Directors. Burlington : Chauncey Goodrich. 1830. 8vo, pp. 24, 3 plates.

—*The Pastoral Office :* Embracing Experiences and Observations from a Pastorate of forty years. Philadelphia : 18mo.

Mr. Smith was pastor of the "First Calvinistic Congregational Society" in Burlington, 1826-32.

Smith, Ruth R. *The Pension Case* of the late Capt. James T. Smith; or, perjury exposed.

By Ruth R. Smith, [of Newbury, Vt.] Motto. Montpelier: Poland's Print. 1879. 8vo, pp. 32.

Smith, Gen. William Farrar. *From Chattanooga to Petersburg,* under Generals Grant and Butler. A contribution to the History of the War, and a Personal Vindication by William Farrar Smith, Bvt. Major-General U. S. Army and late Major-General of Volunteers. Boston and New York: Houghton, Mifflin & Company. 1893. crown 8vo, pp. vi, 201. With Maps and Plans.

—*The Reopening* of the Tennessee River near Chattanooga, Oct. 1863, as Related by Major-General George H. Thomas, and the Official Record compiled and annotated by Bvt. Major-General Wm. Farrar Smith. Washington, D.C.: Press of Mercantile Printing Co. 8vo, n. d. pp. 40.

Gen. Wm. F. Smith was born in St. Albans, Feb. 17, 1824; graduated from U. S. Military Academy 1845; was Colonel of the Third Regt. Vermont Volunteers; served with high distinction through the civil war, in command of a division in the Army of the Potomac as commander of the Sixth and Eighteenth Army Corps; Chief Engineer of the Department of the Cumberland; and in other important positions. Placed by act of Congress on the retired list of the U. S. Army, with rank of Major, March 1, 1889. See Vol. II Hemmenway's Gazetteer for additional particulars.

—*The Relief of the Army* of the Cumberland, and the opening of the Short Line of Communication, Between Chattanooga, Tennessee and Bridgeport, Ala., in October, 1863, by Wm. Farrar Smith, Bvt. Major-General U. S. Army. Wilmington, Del.: C. F. Thomas & Co., Printers. 1891. pp. 60, with maps.

Gen. Smith was also the author of three articles in the Magazine of American History, published in October, November and December, 1885, entitled: "The Campaign of 1861-1862 in Kentucky;" of an article in the same Magazine for January, 1886, entitled: "Operations before Fort Donelson;" of three articles in the same Magazine published in March, April and May, 1886, entitled: "Shiloh;" and of an article entitled: "The Genius of Battle," published in the North American Review.

Gen. Wm. F. Smith was born in St. Albans, Feb. 17, 1824; graduated at West Point, July 1, 1845; was Asst. Professor of Mathematics at West Point and served on light-house construction duty before the civil war. In July, 1861, was appointed Colonel of the Third Vermont, was commissioned Brigadier General of Volunteers, August, '61; served in the Defence of Washington and in the Peninsular Campaign of 1862; promoted Major-General of Volunteers, July 4, 1862; commanded a division in the Maryland Campaign, at South Mountain and Antietam; in Nov., 1862, was assigned to the command of the Sixth Army Corps, and engaged at Fredericksburg; transferred to command of the Ninth Army Corps, 1863; later in that year was Chief Engineer of the Department of the Cumberland; distinguished himself by the famous reopening of the Tennessee River near Chattanooga, and Relief of the Army of the Cumberland in Oct., '63. In March, 1864, assigned to command of the Eighteenth Corps, engaged at Cold Harbor and Petersburg; on special duty, 1865. In Nov., 1865, resigned as Major-General of Volunteers and in March, 1867, resigned as Major of Engineers in the regular Army; President of the International Telegraph Co., 1864-73; Police Commissioner New York city, 1875-81; Civil Engineer in service of the U. S. since 1881; reappointed Major U. S. A., Feb., '89, and retired Mar. 1, 1889. Gen. Smith resides at Wilmington, Del.

Smith, William L. G. *Fifty Years of Public Life:* The Life and Times of Lewis Cass. By W. L. G. Smith. New York: 1856. 8vo.

Mr. Smith was born at West Haven, Vt., March 16, 1814, and was graduated at Middlebury, College. 1833. He read law, and commenced practice at Buffalo, N. Y., in 1836; was United States Consul at Shanghai, for several years. Others of his publications are: "Uncle Tom's Cabin as it is; or, Life in the South." Published at Richmond: Philadelphia: and Buffalo: 1852. 12mo.

"Fifteen thousand copies of this work were sold in 15 days.

—*Observations on China* and the Chinese. N. York: 1863. 12mo.

Smith, Worthington. *Duties and Responsibility* of the Christian Ministry, A Sermon, preached in Enosburgh, Vermont, March 5, 1829, at the Ordination of Rev. John Scott. By Worthington Smith, Pastor of the Congregational Church in St. Albans. Published at the Request of the Church and Society in Enosburgh. St. Albans: J. Spooner, Pr. 1829. 8vo, pp. 18.

—*Address* on the subject of petitioning the General Assembly to abolish the traffic in ardent spirits. Delivered in St. Albans, on the day of the State Fast, April 10th, 1833. By Rev. Worthington Smith. St. Albans: J. Spooner, Pr. 1833. 8vo, pp. 12.

—*A Discourse,* Delivered in St. Albans, at the Funeral of Dea. Horace Janes, March 16th, 1834. By Rev. Worthington Smith. St. Albans: J. Spooner, Pr. 1834. 8vo. pp. 15.

—*A Sermon* delivered at the Dedication of the Washington Street Church, in Beverly, March 29, 1847. By Worthington Smith, Pastor of the Congregational Church in St. Albans. Salem: Palfray and Chapman, Printers. 1837. 8vo, pp. 20.

—*A Discourse* delivered Feb. 23, 1840, on the occasion of the death of Rev. Benjamin Wooster. By Worthington Smith, D. D., Pastor of the Congregational Church in St. Albans, Middlebury: Justus Cobb, Printer. 1847. 8vo. pp. 20.

—*Popular Instruction,* and its Relation to the Higher Institutions of Learning. A Discourse delivered on Thanksgiving Day, November 26th, 1846. By Worthington Smith, D. D., Pastor of the First Congregational Church in St. Albans, Vt. St. Albans, Vt.: Printed by E. B. Whiting. 1846. 8vo, pp. 16.

—*A Discourse,* delivered November 17, 1847, at the interment of the Hon. Benjamin Swift, Late U. S. Senator from the State of Vermont; By Worthington Smith, D. D., Pastor of the First Congregational Church in St. Albans, Vermont. Published by request. St. Albans, Vt.: Printed by E. B. Whiting. 1848. 8vo, pp. 20.

—*An Inaugural Address* Delivered July 31st, 1849. By Worthington Smith, D. D., President of the University of Vermont. Published by the Corporation. Burlington: University Press. 1849. 8vo, pp. 26.

Dr. Smith was born in Hadley, Mass., October 11, 1795, and died at St. Albans, Vt., Feb. 13, 1856. He was graduated at Williams' College, 1816, and at Andover, 1819; became pastor of the Congregational Church at St. Albans, in 1823, where he resided until his death; his salary at first was $500, and never exceeded $700 per year. In 1849 he was chosen President of the University of Vermont, which office he held until 1855. See interesting memoir of Dr. Smith by Prof. Joseph Torrey.

—*Sermons,* with a memoir. 8vo, pp. 368.

See Torrey, Joseph.

Smith, W. C. *Proposition for the Funding* of a portion of the Public Debt at a Reduced Rate of Interest, for increasing the National Currency, and preparing the way for a Restoration of the Paper Currency to a sound specie basis. Speech of Hon. Worthington C.

Smith, of Vermont, delivered in the House of Representatives, January, 1869. Washington: F. & J. Rives & Geo. A. Bailey. 1869. 8vo, pp. 14.

—*Increase of Banking Facilities.* Speech of Hon. Worthington C. Smith, of Vermont, in the House of Representatives, June 7, 1870. 8vo, pp. 8.

A resident of St. Albans, Vt., and a brother of ex-Gov. J. Gregory Smith.

Worthington Curtis Smith was born in St. Albans, April 19, 1823, the son of John and Maria (Curtis) Smith. He graduated from the University of Vermont in 1843. From 1845 to 1860 was engaged in the manufacture of carwheels and railroad supplies in extensive iron foundries in St. Albans and Plattsburg; was a director and president of the Vermont & Canada R. R.; trustee and vice-president of the Vermont Central R. R., and president of the Missisquoi Valley R. R. He was elected to the Fortieth Congress in 1866, and was re-elected to the Forty-first and Forty-second Congresses. He died at St. Albans, January 2, 1894.

Snow, Simeon. *Observations on Remarks* made by Ebenezer Newcomb, on a Pamphlet entitled Free Communion of all Christians at the Lord's Table, etc. By Simeon Snow, Pastor of the Church in Wardsborough. Brattleboro: Printed for the Author. 1806. 18mo, pp. 12.

—*Free Communion,* of all Christians, at the Lord's Table; illustrated and defended in a Discourse. To which is added, a short specimen of the proceedings of the Baptist Church and Council, in their labors with, and withdrawing fellowship from the author. By Elder Simeon Snow. Texts. Newburyport: Reprinted. From the Press of E. W. Allen. March. 1807. 12mo, pp. 48.

The church referred to was in Guilford, Vt.

Society of the Army of the Potomac. *Report* of the Eleventh Annual Re-Union, at Burlington, Vermont, June 16, 1880. New York: Macgowan & Slipper, Printers, 30 Beekman Street. 1880. 8vo, pp. 132.

—*Report* of the Twenty-Seventh Reunion, at Burlington, Vt., Sept. 16 and 17th, 1896. Same Printers. 1896. 8vo, pp. 123.

Song of the Vermonters. *"Ho, all to the borders!"*

See Whittier, John G.

Songs. *A Collection of Familiar Songs.* Mark Thompson, Printer. [Sentinel Office, Burlington]. 8vo, pp. 28.

Sons of Vermont. *First Re-union* of the Sons of Vermont, at Worcester, Mass., February 10th, 1874. Address by Hon. Clark Jillson; Together with Toasts, Sentiments, Speeches, Poetry and Song. Specially Reported for publication. Worcester: 1874. 8vo, pp. 60.

—*Proceedings* of the Illinois Association Sons of Vermont. Constitution, By-Laws, &c. Chicago: Beach, Barnard & Co., Legal Printers, 104 Randolph Street. 1877. 8vo, pp. 58.

—*Second Annual Report* of the Illinois Association of the Sons of Vermont, Chicago, for the year 1877-78. Chicago: Jameson & Morse, Printers. 1878. 8vo, pp. 64.

See Mattocks, John. Address, January, 1877.

—*Third and Fourth Annual Reports* of the Illinois Association of the Sons of Vermont

for the year 1878-9 and 1879-80. Chicago: Jameson & Morse, Printers. 1880. 8vo, pp. 56.

—*Third and Fourth Annual Reports* of the Sons of Vermont, Chicago, For the Years 1878-79 and 1879-80. Chicago; Jameson & Morse, Printers. 1880. 8vo, pp. 56.

—*Pacific Coast Association* of the Native Sons of Vermont, San Francisco, Cal. Report for the years 1879-80 and 1880-81. San Francisco: H. S. Crocker & Co., Printers. 1881. 8vo, pp. 53, (6).

—*Green Mountain Echo.* Representing the Pacific Coast Association, Native Sons of Vermont. San Francisco, Cal.: May, 1882. Vol. 1, No. 1, 4to, pp. (4).

Edited by Geo. W. Hopkins. Monthly.
Continued.

—*The Brooklyn Society of Vermonters.* Record of the Organization and Dinner, March 4, 1891; Together with its Constitution, Officers, Members and Addresses. Brooklyn, N. Y.: 1891. 8vo, pp. 56.

—*The Vermont Association of Boston:* An Account of the Seventh Annual Dinner, January 31, 1893, with a List of Members. Cambridge: Riverside Press. 1893. 8vo, pp. 58.

Southmayd, Daniel S. *The True Advancement of Gospel Truth;* A Sermon, preached on the day of the Annual Thanksgiving, November 26, 1829, by Daniel Southmayd, Pastor of the Calvinistic Church in Concord, Mass. Boston: Printed by Pierce and Williams. 1830. 8vo, pp. 24.

Mr. Southmayd was born in Castleton, Vt., February 11, 1802; was graduated at Middlebury College in 1822; studied theology at Andover; was pastor of the Congregational church in Concord, Mass., 1827-32; was an editor in Lowell, Mass., and in New York city, and died at Fort Bend, Texas, January 13, 1837.

Southmayd, Jonathan C. *Address,* delivered before the Philological Society of Middlebury College, on the Evening of the 15th of August. Montpelier: Printed by E. P. Walton. 1826. 8vo, pp. 15.

—*A Discourse on the Duty of Christians* with regard to the Use of Distilled Spirits. Preached at Montpelier, March 16th, 1828. By Jonathan C. Southmayd, Preceptor of Washington County Grammar School. Published by Request. Montpelier: Printed by E. P. Walton. 1829. 8vo, pp. 16.

Mr. Southmayd was a native of Castleton, Vt., and was graduated at Middlebury College in 1817; read theology, but was principally occupied in teaching; was Preceptor of the Washington County Grammar School at Montpelier from about 1822 to 1835 and subsequently of the Academy in Burlington; he died at Sutherland Falls, Vt., in October, 1838, aged 45 years. He was an excellent teacher, and of the highest integrity and purity of character.

Sowles, Edward A. *History of the St. Albans Raid.* Annual Address before the Vermont Historical Society delivered at Montpelier, Vt., on Tuesday Evening, October 17, 1876. St. Albans: Messenger Printing Works. 1876. 8vo, pp. 48.

See Benjamin, L. N., for History of the Raid; Devlin, B., speech at the trial.

—*Free Government.* Its Principles and its Development. The Oration of the Hon. Edward A. Sowles, at Swanton, on the Fourth of July, 1879. 8vo, pp. 7.

—*Address at the Bankers Convention* holden at Saratoga, August 6th, 7th and 8th, 1879. Subject, "Money, what it is, and how to provide it."

Mr. Sowles is a native of Alburgh, Vt., born October 23, 1831. He was graduated at the University of Vermont in 1857; read law, and settled at St. Albans in 1868, where he has been engaged in the practice of his profession, and banking.

Mr. Sowles has given much attention to historical matters relating to Vermont, and has prepared and delivered several historical addresses which have not been printed.

Spafford, H. G. *Some Cursory Observations* on the ordinary construction of Wheel-Carriages; with an attempt to point out their defects, and to show how they may be improved; with engravings. By Horatio Gates Spafford, A. M. Albany: 1815. 8vo, pp. 12.

Born in Tinmouth, Vt., February 18, 1778; died of cholera at Lansingburg, N. Y., August 7, 1832. His father, John Spafford (or Spofford) was a native of Connecticut, and one of the first settlers of Tinmouth; at the head of a company of militia he was with Allen and Arnold at the Capture of Ticonderoga; joined Col. Warner in his expedition against Crown Point, and, reaching there before Warner, received himself the sword of the acting commandant, which remained in his family at the time of his death. He died at Lowville, N. Y., where he was a pioneer settler, March 24, 1823, aged 71. Spafford's Landing, at Lowville, was so named for him. Mr. Spafford was a member of the Legislature of Vermont 1791, and the same year a member of the Convention that adopted the constitution of the United States.

The publications of Mr. H. G. Spafford are: "A General Geography," etc. Hudson: 1809, 12mo. "A Gazetteer of New York." Albany: 1813. 8vo; a second edition, 1824. This was the first Gazetteer of the State. "Pocket Guide for Canals of New York." 1824. 18mo; second edition, Troy: 1825, 12mo. "New York Pocket Book." 1825, 8vo.

Spalding, Ephraim. *Reasons for Baptizing My Infant Child:* A Sermon preached at Ludlow, Vt., August 25, 1839. By Ephraim Spalding, late Missionary to the Sandwich Islands. Windsor: Printed at the Chronicle Press. 1839. 8vo, pp. 20.

Spalding, Geo. B. *The Presence* and Purpose of God in the War, A Thanksgiving Sermon preached at Vergennes, Vt., November 26th, 1863, By Rev. Geo. B. Spalding. Published by request. Burlington: Free Press Print. 1863. 8vo, pp. 21.

—*A Discourse* Commemorative of General Samuel P. Strong, preached in the Congregational church, Vergennes, Vermont, Sunday, February 28th, 1864, by Rev. George B. Spalding. Published by request. Burlington: Free Press Print. 1864. 8vo, pp. 22.

—*A Discourse* delivered in the First Church of Dover, May 18, 1873, on the Two Hundred and Fiftieth Anniversary of the Settlement of Dover, N. H. By George B. Spalding, Pastor of the First Church. Published by request. Dover, N. H.: Freewill Baptist Printing Establishment. 1873. 8vo, pp. 29.

—*A Discourse* Commemorative of the Character and Career of Hon. John Parker Hale. Delivered in the First Parish Church, Dover, N. H., on Thanksgiving Day, Nov. 27, 1873. By Rev. George B. Spalding. Concord, N. H.: Printed by the Republican Press Association. 1874. 8vo, pp. 19.

—*The Relation* of the Church to Children. An address delivered at Haverhill, N. H., before the New Hampshire Sunday School Convention,

Nov. 6, 1873. Bristol, N. H.: R. W. Musgrove. 8vo, pp. 12.

—*The Dover Pulpit* During the Revolutionary War. A Discourse Commemorative of the Distinguished Service Rendered by Rev. Jeremy Belknap, D. D., to the Cause of American Independence, preached by Rev. George B. Spalding, July 9, 1876. [Published by request.] Dover, N. H.: Morning Star, Steam Job Printing House. 1876. 8vo, pp. 31.

—*A Semi-Centennial Discourse.* delivered at Laconia, N. H., June 18, 1878, on the Fiftieth Anniversary of the Organization of the Conference of Churches of Strafford County, By George B. Spalding, D. D. Published by Request. Dover, N. H.: Freewill Baptist Printing Establishment. 1878. 8vo, pp. 20.

—*The Idea* and Necessity of Normal School Training. An Address by Rev. George B. Spalding, D. D., of Dover, N. H. Delivered at the Dedication of the Normal School Building at Gorham, Maine, Dec. 26, 1878. Published at Request. Portland: Daily Press Job Printing House. 1879. 8vo, pp. 12.

—*Annual Report* of the Board of Trustees of the State Normal School, to the New Hampshire Legislature. June Session, 1879. Manchester: John B. Clarke, State Printer. 1879. 8vo, pp. 12.

Report prepared by Mr. Spalding, President of the Board of Trustees.

—*The Relation* of the Church to Children. An Address by Rev. George B. Spalding, D. D., Dover, N. H., delivered before the New Hampshire Sunday School Convention, at Haverhill, November 6, 1879. [Published by Request.] Bristol, N. H.: R. W. Musgrove, Printer. 1879. 8vo, pp. 8.

—*Discourse* on the Death of President Garfield, preached in the First Church, Dover, N. H., September 25, 1881, by Rev. George B. Spalding, D. D. Dover, N. H.: 1881. 8vo, pp. 24.

Mr. Spalding published in 1868 a political tract, entitled "Scriptural Policy," Hartford, Conn. He was a regular correspondent of the "New York Courier and Enquirer," previous to 1859, while his brother, James Reed Spalding, was one of the principal editors; when his brother founded the "New York World," in 1859, George B. did regular editorial work on the same; he subsequently wrote for the "New York Times," and later, for five years was principal editor of the "Watchman and Reflector."

George Burley Spalding, the seventh of nine children, was born in Montpelier, Vt., August 11, 1835, son of Dr. James and Eliza (Reed) Spalding. Dr. James Spalding was the son and third of twelve children of Deacon Reuben Spalding, one of the early settlers of Vermont. George Burley was graduated at the University of Vermont in 1856; he read law in Vermont one year, and in Tallahassee, Florida, about the same length of time, when he became connected with newspapers as above related. He abandoned the law, and read theology at Union and Andover Theological Seminaries, graduating at the latter in 1861; was pastor of Congregational Churches, at Vergennes, Vt., October 5, 1861, to August, 1864; then at Hartford, Conn., until March 23, 1869, when he was installed over the First Church in Dover, N. H.; subsequently pastor of Presbyterian Church in Syracuse, N. Y.

Mr. Spalding was a member of the New Hampshire Legislature from Dover, 1878, and received the honorary degree of D. D. from Dartmouth College.

See "Granite Monthly," vol. 1, pp. 197-9, for biographical sketch.

Spalding, James R. *The True Idea of Female Education.* An Address delivered at Pittsfield, Mass., before the Young Ladies Institute, at its

Annual Commencement, August 22, 1855. By James R. Spalding. Published by Request. New York: John F. Trow, Printer, 53 Ann Street. 1855. 8vo, pp. 28.

—*Our Lesson and Our Work* or Spiritual Philosophy and Material Politics. An Oration at the Semi-Centennial Anniversary of the University of Vermont, August, 1854. 8vo, pp. 33.

See University of Vermont, Semi-Centennial anniversary.

James Reed Spalding was born in Montpelier, Vt., November 15, 1821; died at the residence of his brother, Dover, N. H., October 10, 1872. He prepared for college at the Washington County Grammar School; was graduated at the University of Vermont in 1840; read and practiced law in Montpelier; went to Europe, and while there acted as correspondent of the "New York Courier and Enquirer," over the signature of "Sigma," his letters attracting much attention; upon his return he became associate editor of that paper; in 1859 he mainly established the "New York World," disposing of his interest therein in 1862; he soon after became connected with the "New York Times," where he continued until failing health compelled him to abstain from labor. An appropriate tribute to Mr. Spalding's worth was published in the "New York World," October 12, 1872, written by Richard Grant White.

Spalding, Joshua. *The Gospel Minister's Farewell.* A Sermon preached at the Tabernacle, in Salem, (Mass.) April Twenty-fifth, A. D. 1802. By Joshua Spalding, late Pastor in that Church. Bennington: Printed by Anthony Haswell & Co. n. d. 8vo, pp. 18.

Spelling Book. Exercises, designed to assist young persons to pronounce and spell correctly, also to practise writing and acquire punctuation, with accuracy and effect, upon an efficatious and approved principle, etc. To which is added an Index, etc. By Peter Peyto Good. Embellished with cuts. Stereotyped by D. Watson, Woodstock, Vt.: 1830. Price 25 cents single, $1.00 for five, or $2.25 per dozen. 12mo, pp. 120.

Spear, J. A. (of Braintree, Vt.) *A Fable.* The Convention of Beelzebub and his near friends and his speech to the Convention. [n. p. n. d.] 8vo, pp. 8.

—*The Farmer's Orchardist;* By J. A. Spear: In which Inoculating and Ingrafting, together with the Cultivation of Fruit Trees, and a few Garden Vegetables, are taught in a very plain yet simple manner. A description is also given of a very choice though not large selection of Fruit, recommended for extensive cultivation. Brandon: Vermont Telegraph Press. 1842. 12mo, pp. 28, (1).

Spencer, G. D. *A Poem* on the Hubbardton Raid, read in the Congregational Church, Hubbardton, May 12, 1880. By G. D. Spencer. In reply to Poem of J. M. Currier, M. D. Rutland, Vt.: Tuttle & Co., Book and Job Printers. 1880. 18mo, pp. 34.

See Currier, J. M.

Spencer, H. A. *To the Ministers* and Members of the Methodist Episcopal Church of the Springfield District, Vermont Conference. Windsor, Vt.: Sept. 1st, 1879. 8vo, pp. (4.)

Mr. Spencer is well known as an active and leading Methodist divine in Vermont; he has been settled at Montpelier, St. Albans, Windsor and elsewhere.

Spencer, H. Ladd. (A native of Castleton, Vt.) *Poem* by H. Ladd Spencer. Boston: 1850. 8vo, pp. 95.

Spencer, Ichabod S. *Comparative Claims* of Home and Foreign Missions: a Sermon, preached in the Second Presbyterian Church in Brooklyn, on the day of the Annual Contribution for Home Missions, April 2d, 1843. By Ichabod S. Spencer, D. D. Brooklyn: A. M. Wilder, 51 Fulton Street. 1843. 8vo, pp. 30.

—*A Pastor's Sketches;* or, Conversations with Anxious Inquirers respecting the Way of Salvation. By Ichabod S. Spencer, D. D., Pastor of Second Presbyterian Church, Brooklyn, N. Y. New York: Published by M. W. Dodd, Brick Church Chapel, City Hall Square, opposite the City Hall. 1840. 12mo, pp. 414.

—*Second Series.* 1853. 12mo, pp. 430.

—*Fugitive Slave Law.* The Religious Duty of Obedience to Law, a Sermon preached in the Second Presbyterian Church in Brooklyn, Nov. 24, 1850. By Ichabod S. Spencer, D. D. New York: Published by M. W. Dodd, Brick Church Chapel, City Hall Square, opposite the City Hall. 1850. 8vo, pp. 31.

—*Triumph in Suffering.* A Discourse delivered at the Funeral of the Rev. I. S. Spencer, D. D., Pastor of the Second Presb. Church in Brooklyn, L. I. By Gardner Spring, D. D., LL. D., Pastor of the Brick Presb. Church in the City of New York. New York: M. W. Dodd, Publisher. 1855. 8vo, pp. 29.

—*Sermons* of Rev. Ichabod S. Spencer, D. D., late Pastor of the Second Presbyterian Church, Brooklyn, L. I. Author of "A Pastor's Sketches." With a Sketch of his life, by Rev. J. M. Sherwood. In two volumes. New York: Published by M. W. Dodd, Corner of Spruce St. and City Hall Square. 1855. 12mo, pp. 473, 479.

—*Evidences of Divine Revelation.* In a Letter to a Judge. By Ichabod S. Spencer, D. D. Boston: The American Tract Society. Depositories, 28 Cornhill, Boston; and 13 Bible House, Astor Place, N. Y. 1865. 16mo, pp. 120.

Rev. Dr. Spencer was born in Rupert, Vt., February 23, 1798; died in Brooklyn, N. Y., November 23, 1854. He was graduated at Union College, 1822; read theology and was pastor of a Congregational church in Northampton, Mass., 1828-32; and of a Presbyterian church at Brooklyn, N. Y., 1832 until his death.

He published: A Discourse occasioned by the great fire in New York, 1835. A Discourse on the claims of seamen, 1836. A Sermon on the Day of the National Fast, observed on account of the death of the President of the United States, 1841. A Sermon in the National Preacher, on Living and Walking in the Spirit, 1841. A Sermon in the National Preacher, entitled "Solomon's Experience and Observation—Hatred of Life, 1849." A Sermon on the necessity of the Sufferings of Christ. "Discourses on Sacramental Occasions; with an Introduction by Gardner Spring, D. D." New York: 1861. 12mo; also re-published in London. "Evidences of Divine Revelation." Boston: 1865. 18mo.

Several editions of "A Pastor's Sketches" were published in this country and in England; and it was also published in French in France.

A Biographical Notice of Dr. Spencer may be found in "Sprague's Annals," Vol. 4, pp. 710-722.

Spencer, J. G. *Cosmopolitania;* A Poem by J. G. Spencer. Rutland: The Tuttle Co. 1889. 12mo, pp. 120.

Sperry, L. *The Botanic Family Physician,* or, the secret of Curing diseases with vegetable proportions. Also containing divers Formulas or Recipes, etc. By Doctor L. Sperry. Cornwall, Vt.: Published by the Author. 1843. 12mo, pp. 60.

Spicer, Tobias. *Religion* the only Source of National Prosperity. A Sermon, delivered before the Honorable Legislature of the State of Vermont, Met at Montpelier, October 10, 1833. By Rev. Tobias Spicer, A. M. Montpelier: Printed by Geo. W. Hill. 1833. 8vo, pp. 26.

—*An Attempt* to explain some part of the Seventh Chapter of St. Paul's Epistle to the Romans. By Tobias Spicer, Minister of the Gospel. Text. Vergennes: Printed by Gamaliel Small. 1830. 8vo, pp. 24.

—*A Vindication* of the Character of the Apostle Paul. By Tobias Spicer, Minister of the Gospel. Texts. Vergennes: Printed by Gamaliel Small. 1830. 8vo, pp. 24.
Elder Spicer was one of the early Presiding Elders of the Methodist Church in Vermont.

Spiritualism.
See Mystery; Richmond, Thomas; Olcott, Henry S. for Eddy manifestations at Chittenden; Simmons, A. E.; Sprague, Achsa; Gregory, John; Marsh, L., The Apocatastasis.

Spooner, Shearjashub. *An Inaugural Dissertation* on the Physiology and Diseases of the Teeth. Submitted to the Examination of John Augustine Smith, M. D., President, And the Trustees and Professors of the College of Physicians and Surgeons of the University of the State of New York; and publicly defended, for the Degree of Doctor of Medicine, April 6th, 1835. By Shearjashub Spooner, Member of the Montreal Medical Society. Motto. New York: J. & W. Sandford, Printers, 17 Ann Street. 1835. 8vo, pp. 32.
Mr. Spooner was born at Brandon, Vt., in 1809; His father, Paul Spooner, who early in life settled in Brandon, was a nephew of Lieut.-Gov. Paul Spooner, who settled early in Hartland, Vt., where he died September 5, 1789; he was prominent in the early history of Vermont. His son Paul settled in Hardwick, Vt., and was Representative, etc.
The historians of Vermont, down to and including Mr. Walton in Vol. 1. of the Governor and Council, have treated Lieut.-Gov. Paul and his son Paul as one and the same person; the appearance of the "Spooner Memorial" in 1871, set the matter right, and Mr. Walton made the proper correction in Vol. 2, p. 498, of the Governor and Council.
Dr. Shearjashub Spooner received his crooked name from his grandfather of the same name, who lived and died in Petersham, Mass.; born August 14, 1735, died April 25, 1785; he was the fourth child of Deacon Daniel and Elizabeth (Ruggles) Spooner, and Lieut.-Gov. Paul Spooner was the tenth and last child of the same, having been born March 30, 1746. Deacon Daniel was twice married subsequent to his first marriage, viz., in 1767 and 1780.
This branch of the Spooner family was prolific; eight of Deacon Daniel's ten children had sixty-two children in the aggregate, while of the other two one died young, and the other was married but had no children.
The subject of our sketch, Dr. Shearjashub Spooner, was a dentist of distinction, graduated an M. D. from the College of Physicians and Surgeons of New York, 1835; Allibone says he was graduated at Middlebury College, 1830, but his name does not appear in Pearson's list of graduates. He practiced dentistry with great success in New York until 1858, when he retired to Plainfield, N. J., where he died in 1859.
He was an author of distinction and published: "Dissertatio, Medical Inauguration," etc., New York: 1836. "Guide to Sound Teeth," 1836, 12mo; 2d edition, 1839. "Essay on the Art of Manufacturing Mineral Teeth," 1837, 8vo. "Practical Treatise on Surgical and Mechanical Dentistry," 1838, 8vo. "Anecdotes of Painters, Engravers, Sculptors and Architects, from Ancient to Modern Times; with the Monograms, Ciphers and Marks used by Distinguished Artists to certify their works," 1853, rl. 8vo, pp. 1,300. In 1865, a new edition in two vols. imp. 8vo, price $10. Also an edition of 100 copies 4to, with 100 photographs inserted, $40; advanced to $75; and copies extended to six volumes, 4to, by the insertion of over 1,000 engraved portraits, price, $1,000. This valuable work contains 12,000 biographical notices of artists, lists of their best works, a glossary of terms, tables, etc.
Dr. Spooner purchased and restored the plates of, and reissued, "Boydell's Shakespeare Gallery," at $100 for the 100 plates; and purchased with the object of restoring and engraving from, the plates of the "Musée Francaise," which in consequence of the refusal of the Government to remit the import duty, were returned to France—the Doctor losing the purchase money. He contributed professional and other articles to periodicals.
Four of Dr. Spooner's brothers became eminent as physicians.
See Allibone; Spooner Memorial.

Spooner, Thomas. *Memorial of* William Spooner, 1637, And of his Descendants to the Third Generation; of his Great-Grandson, Elnathan Spooner, and of his Descendants to 1871. By Thomas Spooner. [Private edition.] Cincinnati: Robert Clarke & Co. 1871. 8vo, pp. 242.
The Spooner family was prominent in Vermont.

Sprague, Miss Achsa. *The Poet* and other Poems. By Achsa Sprague. Boston: William White & Co. 1864. 12mo, pp. 304.
These poems are said to have been inspirational, and partake somewhat of the Spiritual phenomena.

—*Achsa W. Sprague* and Mary Clarke's experiences in the First ten Spheres of Spirit Life. Medium, Athaldine Smith, Oswego, N. Y. Springfield, Mass.: 1881. 12mo, pp. 36.
Miss Sprague was chiefly known as a trance lecturer under what she claimed to be spirit influence,— a pioneer advocate of the "Spiritual" philosophy in New England. She was born in Vermont. Her youth was one long struggle with poverty. Remarkable from her earliest years for an eager thirst for knowledge, the circumstances of her father's family forbade any save the most limited gratification to her ruling desire. Achsa was the sixth child of a large family. She attended the public school until she was twelve years of age, when she began teaching. At twenty she was prostrated by a sickness which lasted seven years, and was restored, as claimed, by spirit aid. By the advice of spirit friends she began public lecturing at South Reading, Vt., in 1854, and continued in the field of reform as a trance lecturer till she passed on at Plymouth, Vt., July 6, 1862.
She was a rapid writer of poetry, usually under "Spirit inspiration," sometimes writing five hundred lines at a single effort. They contain many beautiful thoughts of the future life. Her public addresses were characterized by intense earnestness and vivid word painting. Wherever she went she made hosts of friends.

Sprague, Rev. I. N. *President Lincoln's Death.* A Discourse delivered in the Presbyterian Church in Caldwell, N. J., on the day of National Mourning, June 1st, 1865. By Rev. I. N. Sprague, Pastor. Published by Request. 8vo, pp. 20. Newark, N. J.: Advertiser Office. 1865.
Mr. Sprague was a native of Poultney.

Sprague, W. B. *The Annual Sermon*, preached before the American Society for Meliorating the Condition of the Jews, on May 9, 1847, in the Presbyterian Church, Mercer St., New York. By the Rev. William B. Sprague, D. D., of Albany, N. Y. Middlebury: Justus Cobb, Printer. 1847. 8vo, pp. 36.

—*A Discourse*; delivered at Montpelier, on the evening of October 20, 1852, the Fortieth Anniversary of the Vermont Bible Society. By William B. Sprague, D. D., Minister of the Presbyterian Church, Albany. Together with the Society's Annual Report, etc. Albany: E. H. Pease & Co., Publishers. 1852. 8vo, pp. 56.

—*Discourse* before the Vermont Classical Seminary, Castleton, Vt., 1830.

Spring, Gardner. *Something Must be Done:* A New Year's Sermon, preached on the last day of the old year, by Gardner Spring, A. M.

Pastor of the Brick Presbyterian Church in the city of New York. Fourth Edition. Middlebury, Vt.: Published by Wm. Slade, Jun. July, 1816. 8vo, pp. 34.

Spring, Samuel. *The Exemplary Pastor.* A Sermon Preached at the Ordination of the Rev. Azel Washburn, in Royalton, September 3, M. DCC.LXXX.IX. By Samuel Spring, A. M. Pastor of the North Church of Newbury-Port. Published by Desire. Printed at Windsor, Vermont: By Alden Spooner. M. DCC.XC.I. 8vo, pp. 40.

Springfield. *Historical Manual* of the Congregational Church in Springfield, Vt. July, 1869. Text. Claremont, N. H.: Printed by the Claremont Manufacturing Co. 1869. 8vo, pp. 50.

—*Catalogue* of Springfield Town Library. Springfield, Vt.: G. W. Foggett, Printer. [1879.] 8vo, pp. 46.
Established 1871.

—*Annual Report* of the Superintendent of Public Schools, of the Town of Springfield, For the year ending March 31, 1873. Springfield, Vt.: E. D. Wright, Printer. 1873. 8vo, pp. 16.

—*Auditors' Report* for the Town of Springfield, with the Report of Superintendent of Schools, for the year ending February 9, 1878. Springfield, Vt.: E. D. Wright, Printer. 1878. 8vo, pp. 15.
Continued.

—*Rules and Regulations* of School District No. 7, Springfield, Vt. Springfield: Vermont Record Job Office. 1867. 24mo, pp. 8.

—*History* of the Town of Springfield, Vermont, with a Genealogical Record, by C. Horace Hubbard and Justus Dartt. 1752–1895. Boston: George H. Walker & Co., 160 Tremont St. 1895. 8vo, pp. xi, 617.

Squier, Miles P. *The Province* of the American Scholar; an Inaugural Address. By Rev. Miles P. Squier, A. M., Professor of Intellectual and Moral Science in the Beloit College. Delivered July 9th, 1851, at the first commencement anniversary of the institution. New York: John F. Trow, Printer, 40 Ann Street. 1851. 8vo, pp. 37.

The Problem solved; or, Sin not of God. By Miles P. Squier, D.D., Professor of Intellectual and Moral Philosophy, Beloit College. New York; Published by M. W. Dodd, Corner of Spruce St. and City Hall Square. 1855. 12mo, pp. 255.

—*Reason and the Bible*, or, the Truth of Religion. By Miles P. Squier, D. D., Prof. of Intellectual and Moral Philosophy, Beloit College. New York; Charles Scribner, 124 Grand Street. 1860. 12mo, pp. 340.

—*The Miscellaneous Writings* of Miles P. Squier, D. D., late Professor of Intellectual and Moral Philosophy, Beloit College, Wisconsin. With an Autobiography, edited and supplemented by Rev. James R. Boyd. Geneva, N. Y.: From the Press of R. L. Adams & Son. n. d. 12mo, pp. 408.
Dr. Squier was born in Cornwall, Vt., May 4, 1792; was graduated in Middlebury in 1811, and at Andover in 1814; preached at Vergennes, Vt., 1814-15; was pastor of the

First Presbyterian Church, Buffalo, N. Y., 1816-24; Secretary of the Geneva Agency of the American Home Missionary Society, 1826-34; Professor of Intellectual and Moral Philosophy in Beloit College, Wis., 1849-63, resided at Geneva, N. Y., where he died June 22, 1866. For biographical sketch, see Presbyterian Historical Almanac for 1867.

Stacy, John Baldwin. *In Memoriam.* John Baldwin Stacy, a Member of the Senior Class in Dartmouth College, Died May 9th, 1880. Discourse at the Funeral at Vershire, Vt., May 9th, 1880. By Prof. H. E. Parker. Published by the Class. 8vo, pp. 8.

St. Albans. *The Franklin County Bank*, St. Albans, Vermont; or, a New, Novel, and Interesting System of Banking, introduced by Oscar A. Burton. 1861. 8vo, pp. 29.

—*Manual* of the First Congregational Church, of St. Albans, Vt.; Compiled by vote of the church, March, 1869. St. Albans, Vt.: E. B. and W. H. Whiting, Printers. 1869. 12mo, pp. 27.

—*History* of; reprinted from Miss Hemenway's Vermont Gazetteer. St. Albans, Vt.: By Stephen E. Royce. 1872. 8vo, pp. 94.
See Dutcher, L. L.

—*And Vicinity* as a Summer Resort. By Albert Clarke. St. Albans: Messenger Job Printing House. 1872. 8vo, pp. 40.

—*Annual Report* of the Board of Officers of the Village of Saint Albans, March, 1875. St. Albans: Messenger Steam Printing Establishment. 1875. 8vo.
Continued.

—*Annual Report* of the Officers of the Town of St. Albans for the Fiscal year Ending Feb'y 25, 1876. Printed by Authority. St. Albans: Advertiser Steam Printing House. 1876. 8vo, pp. 32.
Continued.

—*Pocket Directory* of the Village of St. Albans for 1877 and 1878. Containing a list of Residents, Churches, Societies, Advertisements of Business Firms, and much other matter of local interest. St. Albans: Messenger Steam Print. 1877. 12mo, pp. 72.

—*Manuscript Copy* of the Charter of, in Archives of Vermont Historical Society.

—*A Centennial History* of St. Albans, Vt. Organized July 28, 1788. By Henry K. Adams. St. Albans: Wallace Printing Company. 1889. 12mo, pp. 149.

St. Albans Raid. *The St. Albans Raid*, Investigation by the Police Committee of the City Council of Montreal, into the charges preferred by Counsellor B. Devlin against G. Lamothe, Esq., Chief of Police; and the Proceedings of Council in reference thereto. Montreal: 1864. 8vo, pp. 78.
See Benjamin, L. N.; Sowles, E. A.; Devlin, B.

Stanley, Ruth. *The Religious Experience* and Counsels of Mrs. Ruth Stanley, late of Shaftsbury, deceased. Dedicated to her children. Bennington: Printed by A. Haswell. 1802.

Stark, Caleb. *Memoir and Official Correspondence* of Gen. John Stark, with notices of several other officers of the Revolution. Also, a Biography of Capt. Phineas Stevens, and of Col. Robert Rogers, with an Account of his

Services in America during the "Seven Years' War." By Caleb Stark. Concord: Published by G. Parker Lyon. 1860. 8vo, pp. 495.

Stark, John. *Life of, Etc.*
See Stark, Caleb. Also consult "Farmer and Moore's Collections," volume 1, pp. 92–116; Life of, "Sparks' Am. Biography," volume 1. See French War.

Starr, Peter. *Tribute to the Memory of.*
See Hyde, J. T.

A Statement of Facts in relation to the New Hampton Institution, by Prof. M. A. Cummings, A. M., in A Letter to Hon. A. J. Rowell, North Troy. Fairfax, Vt. 1859. Montpelier: E. P. Walton, Printer. 1859. 8vo, pp. 20.

State Prison. *Biennial Report* of the Officers of the Vermont State Prison, for the two years ending July 31, 1876. Rutland: Tuttle & Company, Book and Job Printers. 1876. 8vo, pp. 31.
Continued.

—*History of.*
See Reynolds, John; Russell, John, Jun.

Steam Stone Cutter. *The Steam Stone Cutter* Will do the Work of More than Thirty Men; Has Sixteen Drills arranged in two Gangs; Strikes with the force of One Thousand Pounds; Equivalent to Twelve Hundred Strokes of a Single Drill per minute; Will cut Stone Smooth and Straight enough for Building or Masonry at any Angle; Can be applied to any kind of stone. The Company will lease the Machines. Pamphlets containing full particulars sent free; Communications relating to the Machine should be addressed to the Steam Stone Cutter Co., Rutland, Vt. Office in New York City, at No. 18 Wall street, with W. O. Ruggles. New York: Slote & Janes, 93 Fulton street. 1865. 8vo, pp. 27.

Stearns, J. M. *The Rights of Man* the true basis of Reconstruction. An Address delivered at North Springfield, Vt., July the Fourth, 1866. By John M. Stearns, Counsellor at Law, Williamsburgh, N. Y. Williamsburgh, N. Y.: Printed by L. Darbee & Son. 1866. 8vo, pp. 16.

—*The Bible in Harmony* with Nature. Atheism abnormal and monstrous. Spirit life and Material Entities. By John M. Stearns, A. M., Counsellor at Law. Brooklyn: Published by D. S. Holmes. 12mo, pp. 87.
Mr. Stearns was born in Reading, Vt., December 13, 1810; he was connected with newspapers in Vermont for several years, and now (1880) resides in Brooklyn, N. Y.

Stearns, Samuel, LL.D. *The American Oracle.* Being an account of recent discoveries in the arts and sciences, with a variety of religious, political, physical and philosophical subjects, &c., by Samuel Stearns. London: 1791. 8vo, pp. 627, xviii.
Dr. Stearns was born at Lancaster, Mass., in 1747 and became a prominent man during the Revolutionary war, but having tory proclivities he was compelled to fly to England, where he remained until after the end of the war. While there he received the degree of LL.D. and F. R. S., and after his return taught astronomy and other higher branches of mathematics; the late Asa Houghton, of Putney, Vt., who published so many almanacs, was one of his pupils. In the latter part of his life for a while he was incarcerated in Newfane, Vt., jail for debt. While there, he wrote a poem entitled "The Widower in Jail Exposed to Sale," dated July 15, 1786. He was much soured by his many rebuffs of fortune. He was a gentleman worthy of kind regards, and although he now sleeps in a humble grave, his memory is cherished by

the few relatives and appreciative friends who still survive. A tombstone marks his grave in the cemetery at Brattleboro, Vt. Dr. Stearns prepared the first Nautical Almanac that was published in this country. In 1772 he designed publishing an American Dispensatory, and to make the work as complete and useful as possible, he traveled in nine of the American States and in England, Scotland, Ireland and France. In a journal which he kept he claims that he traveled 11,607 miles by land and 11,578 miles by water. He intended to publish his Dispensatory in two large volumes by subscription, but failed to obtain a sufficient number of subscribers, although George Washington, Benj. Rush and other eminent men were subscribers. He made an ineffectual effort to induce the legislatures of Massachusetts and Vermont to grant him a lottery whereby he might realize sufficient means to enable him to publish his great work. Failing in all his efforts to secure the publication of his great work, he abbreviated the same and got up the *American Herbal*, which was printed at Walpole. N. H., in 1801, and entitled the *American Herbal* or *Materia Medica*. While practising medicine in the town of Dummerston, Vt., he wrote a dissertation upon the practice of medicine, but it was never printed. The manuscript was in possession of the late Dr. J. A. Allen, when he resided in Brattleboro; it indicated more than ordinary ability.
See Medical, Petition to the Legislature of Vt., for a lottery to aid Dr. Stearns.

Stebbins, Rufus P. *A Sermon* delivered at the Ordination of Charles A. Allen, as Minister of the Church of the Messiah, in Montpelier, March 1, 1865. By Rufus P. Stebbins, D. D., of Cambridge, Mass. Reprinted from the Monthly Journal. Montpelier: Ballou, Loveland & Co. 12mo, pp. 27.

Steele, George M. *Infant Baptism.* A Sermon preached on Sunday, May 29, 1859, in the M. E. church, Watertown, Mass. By George M. Steele, preacher in charge. Boston: Geo. C. Rand & Avery, City Printers, No. 3, Cornhill. 1859. 8vo, pp. 16.
Dr. Steele was born in Strafford, Vt., April 13, 1823; graduated at Wesleyan University in 1850; stationed at various places in Massachusetts; President of Lawrence University, Wisconsin, since 1865; received the degree of D. D. from Northwestern University in 1866; has contributed to various periodicals.

Steele, Joseph. *Complete List* of Congregational Ministers and Churches in Rutland County, Vt., from the first settlement to the present time. By Rev. Joseph Steele, of Castleton.
See American Quarterly Register, 1841, volume xiv, pp. 34–42, with historical notes of each town.

Steele, Zadock. *The Indian Captive;* or a Narrative of the Captivity and Sufferings of Zadock Steele. Related by Himself. To which is prefixed an Account of the Burning of Royalton. Motto. Montpelier, Vt.: Published by the Author. E. P. Walton, Printer. 1818. 12mo, pp. 142. (2.)

Steuben, Baron De. *Regulations for the Order* and Discipline of the Troops of the United States. By Baron De Steuben, Late Major-General and Inspector-General in the Army of the United States. Windsor: Printed by Alden Spooner. M.DCC.XCII. 12mo, pp. 91.

—*Regulations for the Order* and Discipline of the Troops of the United States. By Baron De Steuben, Late Major-General and Inspector-General of the American Army. To which is added the Manual Exercise and Evolutions of the Cavalry, as practiced in the Late American Army. Printed pursuant to order of State, Bennington, Vt.: By Anthony Haswell, State Printer. 1809. 18mo, pp. 105, (1,)

Stevens, Alfred. *A Review* of the Protest lately sent out by ten members of the General

Convention of Congregational Ministers and Churches of Vermont. By Rev. Alfred Stevens, D. D., of Westminster West. Montpelier: Printed at the Vermont Chronicle Office. 1880. 8vo, pp. 11.
See Congregational.

Stevens, Benjamin Franklin. *B. F. Stevens's Facsimiles of Manuscripts* in European archives Relating to America, 1775-1783, with Descriptions, Editorial Notes, Collations, References and Translations. Issued only to Subscribers, at 4 Trafalgar Square, Charing Cross, London. Vol. I, folio, November, 1889.

Volume 1 contains 130 documents. Of this series of transcripts of important documents, 24 volumes had been issued up to 1895. Vol. xxiv, dated November, 1895, contains documents 2024 to 2107. The following extract from the Introduction to Vol. I gives some idea of the nature of these documents:

"My first group of five volumes is made from unpublished documents in private Archives not examined by the Royal Commission on Historical Manuscripts, and this material is now for the first time placed at the disposal of historical students. They open two important subjects—(a) Secret Intelligence, and (b) Conciliatory Bills.

The confidential and private correspondence of the British Government with its political agents and spies, includes secret and intercepted intelligence from the time of the receipt in England of the news of the signing of the Declaration of Independence, until the signing of the Paris Treaty of Peace in 1783. Similar secret intelligence obtained by France, Holland and Spain through their respective agents or spies is also intended to be given. This correspondence is absolutely essential to a clear understanding of the diplomatic, political and military phases of the Peace Negotiations, and will very considerably modify, and sometimes conflict with, current opinions of persons and of events.

Of equal importance are the papers on the peculiarly interesting conception and preparation of Lord North's two Conciliatory Bills introduced into Parliament in February, 1778.

Only two hundred copies are being made and the photographic negatives are destroyed as the work progresses. I believe no facsimile work of this kind and of this magnitude has ever before been undertaken either by private or public enterprise for enabling students to practically transfer a great mass of important historical material to their own libraries for examination and comparison at their leisure."

—*Christopher Columbus.* His own Book of Privileges, 1502. Photographic Facsimile of the manuscript in the Archives of the Foreign Office in Paris, now for the first time published with expanded text, translation into English and an Historical Introduction. The Transliteration and Translation by George P. Barwick, B. A., of the British Museum. The Introduction by Henry Barisse. The whole compiled and edited with preface by Benjamin Franklin Stevens. London: 4 Trafalgar Square, Charing Cross. B. F. Stevens. 1893. Folio, pp. lxvi, 283.

Elaborately and elegantly printed, with illuminations and illustrations; in antique binding of wood with pigskin back, and anchor clasps. Only 300 copies printed.

B. F. Stevens was born in Barnet, Vt., being a son of Henry Stevens, the antiquarian. He spent three years in the University of Vermont, in the class of 1857; but left college before taking a degree. He went to England in 1860 to join his elder brother, Henry Stevens, and has been an eminent bibliographer in London to date (1896). He has been U. S. Despatch Agent in London from 1866 to date. He edited "The Campaign in Virginia, 1781—Reprint of pamphlets in the Clinton-Cornwallis Controversy, etc." London: 2 vols; "Gen. Sir William Howe's Orderly Book at Charlestown, Boston and Halifax," "The Manuscripts of the Earl of Dartmouth, Vol. II., American Papers," published by the Historical Manuscripts Commission of England. London: 1865, with introduction by Mr. Stevens, 8vo, pp. xxi, 673.

He married Miss Whittingham, daughter of Charles Whittingham, of the celebrated Chiswick Press, of London.

Stevens, Beriah. *System of Arithmetic.* Saratoga, N. Y.: 1822. 8vo, pp. 423.

Stevens, Enos. *Rudiments of Astronomy*; containing a Description of the Globes of the Solar System, and a Table of the Longitude of the Planets and Moon, on every Day of the year 1849, etc. By Enos Stevens. Boston: 16 Devonshire Street, Damrell & Moore, Printers. 1849. 12mo, pp. 60.

Mr. Stevens was born in Barnet, Vt., 1816; was graduated at Middlebury College in 1838. See Pearson's Graduates of Middlebury College.

STEVENS, HENRY. *An Account* of the Proceedings at the Dinner given by Mr. George Peabody to the Americans connected with the Great Exhibition, at the London Coffee House, Ludgate Hill, on the 27th October, 1851. London: William Pickering. MDCCCLI. 8vo, pp. 114, (1).

—*American Bibliographer.* Parts I and II. (All published.) rl. 8vo, pp. vii, 96. Chiswick Press, 1854.

Only 100 copies printed. Withdrawn from sale in favor of the Nuggets.

—*Historical Nuggets.* Bibliotheca Americana or a Descriptive Account of my Collection of Rare Books relating to America. Henry Stevens G. M. B., F. S. A. 2 vols., fcp 8vo, pp. XII. 436; (2), 437. London: Printed by Whittingham and Wilkins. MDCCCLXII.

A few copies were issued in 1858, with a different title.

This work, printed in the best style of the Chiswick Press, comprises 3,000 titles alphabetically arranged, of rare books relating to America, most carefully given in full, with the collation and price of each work. It is intended, as far as it goes, to be a Manual for Collectors of this expensive class of books.

—*Bibliotheca Americana.* A Catalogue of Books relating to the History and Literature of America. Sold by Auction, by Puttick and Simpson. London: M. DCCC.LXI. 8vo, pp. VI. 273.

This catalogue contains 2,415 lots with collations, etc. "It is one of the most carefully prepared auction catalogues ever issued."—J. Sabin's Bibliog. of Bibliog.

This work served as the model of the Maisonneuve elaborate Bibliotheque Americane."

—*Catalogue of My English Library* collected and described by Henry Stevens. London: Printed by C. Whitingham, Nov., 1853. For Private Distribution. rl. 8vo, pp. xi, 107.

This little Manual was prepared in 1853, and printed for private distribution. It contains a list of about 5,700 volumes of standard English books, and was designed to aid collectors in the choice of their English books and editions. The contents are given of the principal collected works, together with the dates of birth and death of most of the deceased authors.

—*An Analytical Index* to the Colonial Documents of New Jersey, in the State Paper Offices of England. Edited with notes and references to printed works and manuscripts in other depositories, by William A. Whitehead. New York: D. Appleton & Co. 1858. 8vo, pp. xxxii, 504.

—*Schedule* of two thousand American Historical Nuggets Taken from the Stevens Diggins in September, 1870, and set down in Chronological Order of Printing from 1490 to 1800. Described and Recommended as a Supplement to my Printed Bibliotheca Americana. By Henry Stevens, G. M. B., F. S. A., etc. Privately Printed. London: Stevens' Bibliographical Nuggetory, Oct. 1, 1870. 4to, pp. (4) 20.

Describing above 1,350 works on America. Blue cloth extra, on thick or thin hand-made paper.

—*Gorton, Samuel.* A Copie of an Answer sent to Nathaniel Morton of New Plymouth, concerning some part of his Booke intituled New Englands Memorial. Edited by Henry Stevens, and carefully printed from the original autograph manuscript in his possession. London: Chiswick Press. 1862. 4to.

Privately printed, in a very limited number, on hand-made paper, in the best style of the Chiswick Press.

—*Franklin, Benjamin.* Dissertation on Liberty and Necessity, Pleasure and Pain. London, 1725. With an Introduction by Henry Stevens. Carefully reprinted in Fac-simile by Charles Whittingham, Chiswick Press, London: 1857. Privately Printed, only 25 copies, 8vo.

Franklin, while in London, working as a compositor, at the age of eighteen years, wrote and printed himself 100 copies of this tract. Soon after, becoming convinced of his error in printing so free a work, he informs us that, having given away a very few copies, he destroyed the rest, and wrote another tract refuting this. The present is a reprint of one of the two copies of the original edition known to exist, viz. that in the posession of Mr. Henry Stevens. It was reprinted in Dublin, in 1733, in sixteen instead of thirty-two pages, but only a single copy of the Irish edition is known, belonging to Mr. Stevens' Franklin collection.

—*Memorial* de Don Diego Colon, Uirrey y Almirante de las yndias a S. C. C. Mag^d el Rey don Carlos sobre la conversion e consvacio de las gentes de las yndias, en q ofrece con su psona y hazienda de ayudar pa q aya efecto, cierta negociacio q olant de S. M. se avia puesto por pte del clerigo Casas pa el remedio de la trra firme. Año de Mdxx, Impressa por Carlos Whittingham en la Ciudad de Londres a costa de Enrique Estevans, de Vermont, 24 junio, 1854. 12 pages, black letter. 4to.

Edited with Epistle Dedicatory of two pages to Dr. Reinhold Pauli, from the original manuscript of the Second Admiral of the Indies, then in possession of Henry Stevens, and printed at the Chiswick Press. The young King of Spain, Charles, had asked Columbus respecting the benevolent scheme of Las Casas for civilizing and christianizing the Indians of Terra Firma, urging the Admiral's co-operation. This is Don Diego Columbus' favorable reply. This and the next five lots form an interesting series of Spanish historical tracts, printed uniformly in black letter, similar to that of the Las Casas tracts of 1552, and of the same sized page. The six volumes are all bound neatly in paste-grained roan of six different colors, with different side gold ornaments, and different fancy end papers. Only 100 copies of each were printed, and sold in sets only, at £3, 3s. net.

—*Carta* del señor don frey Bartolome de las Casas al Illustre y Muy Magnifico señor don Mercurino Arborio de Gattinara Chanceller de S. Mag. el rey don Carlos en q suplica a s. s. q se le conceda la provincia del çenu q se cuente entre la trra q se le señalare pa poner remedio a los agravios de los yndios en la trre fime. Año de mdxx. Impressa en Londres: en casa de Carlos Whittingham a costa de Enrique Estevans. 24 junio 1854. 11 pages in black letter, 4to.

Las Casas, who had taken great interest in the welfare and christianizing of the Indians, had been promised an extensive grant of land on the coast of Terra Firma, between Darien and Trinidad, for the purpose of founding a colony for improving and civilizing the natives. In this important long autograph letter he repeats his request to Charles the Fifth, through his Chancellor, and urges his benevolent scheme. It was printed in 1854 from the original autograph manuscript then in the possession of Mr. Stevens.

In the epistle dedicatory to Arthur Helps, Esq., a full account of the subject of the letter is given in English.

—*Carta de* amonestacio del obpo de Chiapa don fray Bartolome de las Casas a los Muy M. Señores presidôte y oydores de la real audiencia q residen en la ciudad de Grãs-a-dios, tocante a la libertad y jurisdiçion ecclica y execucion dlla y a la libertad y remedios dlas injusticias y agravios d los yndios de su obpado. Año de Mdxlv. Fue impressa en la Ciudad de Londres: en casa de Carlos Whittingham a costa do Enrique Estevans de Vermont. 24 junio, 1854. 10 pp. black letter, 4to.

This important letter, printed from the original autograph manuscript in the possession of Mr. Henry Stevens, never before printed, is dated the 22d of October, 1545. In the long epistle dedicatory to Peter Force, of Washington, a full abstract of the letter is given in English.

—*Carta de* don frey Bartolöe de las Casas Obispo de Chiapa a los Muy Rev. y Charissimos Padres del capitulo provincial de Guatimala, y del de Chiapa, mostrando su parecer sobre de p no se vendiesen los repartimientos o encomiendas de los yndios. Año de Mdliv. Impressa en la Ciudad de Londres : en casa de Carlos Whittingham a costa de Enrique Estevans de Vermont, 24 Setembre, 1854. Black letter, 21 pages, 4to.

Edited by Henry Stevens, of Vermont, in 1854, and beautifully printed at the Chiswick Press in black letter, uniform with Las Casas' tracts of 1552, from the original unpublished manuscript then in his possession. The MS is not dated, but was probably written in 1554. Dedicated to Sir Frederick Madden.

—*Carta de* Hernando Cortes, Marques del Vallo a S. C. C. Mag^d el rey don Carlos Quinto Mosstrandole su paresçer acerca de los repartimientos de los yndios, sobre si conviene al seruj del rey q los naturales de la nueba Spaña esten todos en su cabeça, o algunos en los Spañoles pobladores della. Año de Mdxlii. Impresso en Londres por Carlos Whittingham a costa de Enrique Estevans, 20 Oct. 1854. 12 pages, black letter, 4to.

First privately printed from the original manuscript in 1854, then in the possession of Mr. Stevens. It is not dated, but was manifestly written in 1541 or 1542, when the Emperor and Las Casas were getting up the famous *New Laws of the Indies*, printed in 1543. The Emperor had asked Cortes' advice respecting the encomiendas and the treatment of the Indians in Mexico. This is the conqueror's sensible reply. The volume is dedicated in a long epistle in English to Leopold von Ranke, the historian, in which is given an abstract of the important historical document.

—*Parescer* o Determinaciö de los señores theologos de Salamanca sobre de que no deben ser baptizados los yndios sin examinaciö estrecha de su voluntad y concepto del dho sacramento. Año de Mdxli. [In Latin.] Impressum Londini apud Carolum Whittingham, impensis Henrici Stevens. 1854. 14 pp. 4to, black letter.

This important manuscript was edited by Henry Stevens, and privately printed for him at the Chiswick Press in 1854, from the original, then in his possession. It is dated the first of July, 1541. Las Casas and others had complained much of the ill-treatment and slavery of the Indians by the Spaniards in America, until finally Charles V referred the grand question to the faculty of the University of Salamanca, whether Indians who had been baptized could be made slaves? This curious document is the official answer, signed by the Dean and all the Faculty. The volume has a long explanatory dedication in English, to Sir Thomas Phillips.

—*The Declaration of Independence;* or, Notes on Lord Mahon's History of the American Declaration of Independence. By Peter Force, Esq., Author of the Documentary History of the United States. Collected, edited, and reprinted, with Biographical and Bibliographical Memoir of Col. Force, by Henry Stevens, F. S. A. The second issue, of only 50 copies. With a Portrait. Privately printed by C. Whittingham, Chiswick Press. London. 1879. 8vo.

—*Historical* and Geographical Notes on the Earliest Discoveries in America 1453-1530. With comments on the Earliest Charts and Maps ; the mistakes of the early Navigators and the Blunders of the Geographers ; the Asiatic Origin of the Atlantic Coast Line of North America ; how it crept in and how it crept out of the Maps. The whole World Illustrated by the Tehuantepec Railway Company's Map of the World on Mercator's Projection and Photo-Lithographic Fac-Similes of many of the earliest Maps and Charts of America By Henry Stevens G M B M A etc Sometime Student at Yale College in Connecticut Now resident in London. New Haven: Office of the American Journal of Science. London : Henry Stevens, 4 Trafalgar Square. 1869. 8vo, pp. 54. Maps.

One of a few copies printed for presents. See Stevens, Simon.

Another edition : New York : 1869. Only 40 copies printed. 8vo, pp. 40.

—*Sebastian Cabot*—John Cabot Endeavored by Henry Stevens G M B etc Corresponding member of the American Oriental Society and of the New England Historic Genealogical Society etc. Boston: Office of the Daily Advertizer London: Office of the Author 4 Trafalgar Square March 1870. sm. 4to, pp. 32.

—*Colton Mather and Witchcraft.* Two Notices of Mr. Upham His Reply. Boston: T. R. Marvin & Son, 131 Congress street. London : Henry Stevens, 4 Trafalgar Square. May 1870, sm. 4to, pp. 30.

—*American Books* with tails to 'em. A private pocket list of the incomplete or unfinished American periodicals transactions memoirs judicial reports laws journals legislative documents and other continuations and works in progress supplied to the British Museum and other libraries By Henry Stevens G M B F S A etc Sometime Student in Yale College in America now of London. I will buy with you sell with you Shakespeare Privately Printed London: At Stevens's Bibliographical Nuggetory No 4 Trafalgar Square IV July 1873 small 4to, pp. (40).

—*Bibliotheca Historica* Or A Catalogue of 5000 Volumes of books and manuscripts relating to the history and literature of North and South America among which is included the larger proportion of the extraordinary library of the late Henry Stevens Senior of Barnet Vt Founder and first President of the Vermont Historical & Antiquarian Society. The whole comprising such a collection of ancient and modern books rich and rare useful and common as seldom occurs for sale in any country including many titles never before recorded in an American catalogue Edited with introduction and notes by Henry Stevens G M B F S A etc Sometime Student in Yale College Now residing in London at 4 Trafalgar Square To be sold by auction by Messrs Leonard & Co at their Library Sales

Room No 50 Bromfield Street in Boston on Tuesday the 5th Wednesday the 6th Thursday the 7th Friday the 8th day of April 1870 Sale each day to commence at 10 in the forenoon and 2 o'clock in the afternoon. Boston: H. O. Houghton and Company. Cambridge: Riverside Press. 1870. 8vo, pp. xv (1), 234.

Valuable for the introduction and historical notes it contains.

"Beautifully printed and profusely annotated. One of the few bibliographical works which combine amusement with profit and instruction."—J. Sabin, *in his Bibliography of Bibliography.*

—*Catalogue* of the Percival Library, the property of the late Mrs. George Atkinson, of No. 2 Highbury Park, Islington. Described and dispersed by Henry Stevens of Vermont F S A, etc. C. Whittingham, Chiswick Press, London, 1879, post 8vo, cloth, uncut. A few copies on very fine and large hand-made paper, cloth, uncut.

This is intended as a model of a printed catalogue of a small, choice, private library. It is carefully made, with notes and descriptions. The collection is of about 3,000 volumes, many of the volumes specially and extensively illustrated, and is described in 1,273 lots, filling 248 pages. The prices are given, and the books have been sold.

—*The Humboldt Library.* A Catalogue of the Library of Alexander von Humboldt with a Bibliographical and Biographical Memoir by Henry Stevens. London : Henry Stevens. 1863. 8vo, pp. xii, 791.

Another edition. Large paper. 1878.

This remarkable collection of scientific books in all languages, including an extraordinary number of privately printed works and presentation copies, fills 891 pages, in 11,139 lots, comprising above 17,000 volumes. The collection was burned at Sotheby's, in July, 1865. Nearly the whole of the catalogue was destroyed, being at the time of the fire unfinished. A few of the large paper copies have now (1878) been completed, and are offered for sale. Twelve copies were taken off on very fine and thick hand-made paper, imp. 8vo, price in cloth, uncut 42s net.

—*The Bibles* in the Caxton Exhibition MDCCCLXXVII Or a bibliographical description of nearly one thousand representative Bibles in various languages chronologically arranged from the first Bible printed by Gutenberg in 1450-1456 to the last Bible printed at the Oxford University Press the 30th June 1877 With an Introduction on the History of Printing as illustrated by the printed Bible from 1450 to 1877 in which is told for the first time the true history and mystery of the Coverdale Bible of 1535 Together with bibliographical notes and collations of many rare Bibles in various languages and divers versions printed during the last four centuries Special edition revised and carefully corrected with additions Flavoured with a Squeeze of the Saturday Review's homily on Bibles by Henry Stevens G M B F S A M A Etc Sometime Student in Yale College in Connecticut in New England Now residing in London Bibliographer Lover of Books Fellow of the Royal George & Zoological Societies of London Foreign Member of the Amer Antiq Society Corresp Member of the Historical Societies of the States of Massachusetts New York Connecticut Maine Vermont New Jersey Maryland Pennsylvania & Wisconsin and Secretary of State and American Minister near Noviomagus Blk Bld Athm Club London and Patriarch of Skull and Bones at Yale University London Henry Stevens IV Trafalgar Square Scribner

Welord & Armstrong New York Messrs Simpkin Marshall & Co Stationers Hall Court London MDcccLxxviii

An enlarged edition, 1878, same title. 8vo, pp. (8), 151, (1).

—*Bibliotheca Geographica & Historica* or A Catalogue of a Nine Days Sale of rare and valuable ancient and modern books maps charts manuscripts autograph letters etcetera illustrative of historical geography and geographical history general and local annals biography genealogy statistics ecclesiastical history poetry prose and miscellaneous books very many relating to North and South America and others to Europe Asia Africa Australia Oceanica Collected used and described With an introduction on the progress of geography and notes and annotatiuncule on sundry subjects together with an essay upon the Stevens system of photobibliography By Henry Stevens G M B F S A M A of Yale Etc Fellow of the Royal Geog & Zoological Societies of London and Citizen of Noviomagus Foreign Member of American Antiquarian Society of Worcester and Fellow of the American Geographical Society of New York Corresponding Member of the American Oriental Society and of the Historical Societies of Massachusetts New York Maine Wisconsin Pennsylvania Connecticut New Jersey and Vermont and Blk Bld Athm Club London Ptolemy's world by Mercator 1578 Part I. To be dispersed by auction by Messrs Puttick & Simpson 47 Leicester Square London the 19th to 20th November 1872 London Henry Stevens at the Nuggetory 4 Trafalgar Square July 25 1872 8vo, pp. IV, 14, 301.

We give this title in full, and verbatim, as a matter of curiosity.

The same on fine paper, interleaved and illustrated with about 400 photographs of the titles, neatly mounted, and bound in half blue morocco, gilt tops, £5, 5s. Only ten copies so done up.

—*Laws of the Indies.* Leyes y ordenanças nueuamête hechas | por su Magestad, pa la gouernacion de las Indias y buen trata | miento y conceruacion de los Indios, *etc.* The New Laws and Ordinances of his Majesty the Emperor Charles, the Fifth King of Spain, for the Government of the Indies and for the good treatment and preservation of the Indians, which are to be observed both in the Council and in the Royal Audiencias resident in the Indies as well as by all other governors, judges and private persons therein. Done into English out of the original Spanish by Henry Stevens, G M B, F S A, etc. [Colophon. Imprinted by Command of the Council of the Indies in the town of Alcala de Henares, in the house of Joan de Brocar, July 8, 1543.] Privately printed at the Chiswick Press, London : H. Stevens, 4 Trafalgar Square. 1876. Folio.

This beautiful volume, a masterpiece of printing from the Chiswick Press, comprises—1st, a collective title, dedication, and historico-bibliographical introduction by Henry Stevens, 10 pages; 2d, a lithographic fac-simile, carefully traced by John Harris, of the Leyes, in large black letter, from the unique copy, printed on vellum, in the Grenville Library, British Museum, 26 pages; and 3d, a translation into English, 32 pages. In all 68 pages. Only a very limited number of copies taken off. On large best hand-made paper, £4 4s. neatly bound. On purest English vellum, made expressly for the work, £17 17s., bound in morocco extra by F. Bedford.

—*British Museum Catalogues*, by Henry Stevens, of Vermont, viz : 1. A Catalogue of American Books in the Library of the British Museum, Christmas, 1856. pp. 650. 2. A Catalogue of Mexican and other Spanish American and West India Books in the Library of the British Museum, Christmas. 1856. pp.64. 3. A Catalogue of Canadian and other British North American books in the Library of the British Museum, Christmas, 1856. pp. 10. 4. A Catalogue of American Maps in the Library of the British Museum, Christmas, 1856. pp. 14. London : 1862. Printed by Charles Whittingham, Chiswick Press. Cloth, 8vo.

These four Catalogues, bound in one volume, comprising about 750 large 8vo pages in double columns, uniform with the "Bibliotheca Grenvilliana," describing about 20,000 volumes, are printed by Whittingham on fine toned paper, in the best style of the Chiswick Press. At the beginning are inserted the rules for Cataloguing Books, Maps, Music, etc., adopted in the British Museum, first printed in 1842, but now revised, with additions, alterations and amendments to 1862. There is also added a detailed description of the classification of books on the shelves in the British Museum. These Catalogues contain all the American Books that had drifted into the British Museum Library to the beginning of 1857. The four volumes in one, cloth 25s.

—*Photo-Bibliography*, or a word on Printed Card Catalogues of old rare beautiful and costly books and how to make them on a cooperative system ; And two words on the establishment of a Central Bibliographical Bureau or Clearing-House for Librarians. By Henry Stevens of Vermont. Privately printed for the Author by C. Whittingham, Chiswick Press. 1878. Neatly bound in roan, square 16mo.

Dedicated to the Librarian of the Future, whose bibliography is to be as exact as his spelling. Extensively illustrated with reduced fac-simile titles, and six sample Cards.

—*The History* of the Oxford Caxton Memorial Bible. Printed in Oxford and bound in London in twelve consecutive hours, June 30th, 1877. By Henry Stevens. London : Privately printed at the Elzevir Press for the Author, March 25th, 1878. 32 pp. on best hand-made paper, illustrated, morocco, square 16mo.

Copies on very thin fine paper, and bound in silk or thin morocco, to be inserted within the cover of the Bible, at the same price.

At the end is given a complete list of all the 100 copies of the Memorial Bible that had been allotted as presents up to Easter, 1878.

—*The Universal Postal Union* and International Copy-Right A paper read before the Library Association at Oxford October 3d 1878 by Henry Stevens of Vermont F S A etc. Sometime Student at Yale College in Connecticut now residing near the British Museum in London, with a Bibliographical appendage. London : Published by the Author at IV Trafalgar Square, and sent to any part of the Universal Postal Union on the receipt of Half-a-Crown. MdcccLxxix. 8vo, pp. 4, 66.

This little book on the Postal Union is designedly made a stocking-horse to carry off some of the Author's stock of his own bibliographical and historical publications; as well as to carry a catalogue of a small portion of the valuable collection he has accumulated of the materials of American history and literature herein offered for sale. The Postal Union 54 pp.; Author's own publications, No. 1 to xxviii, pp. 55 to 66 ; Catalogue of Author's Collection of Books on America, for sale, pp. 67 to 128.

—*Benjamin Franklin's Life and Writings.* A Bibliographical Essay on the Stevens Franklin Collection of Books and Manuscripts, Containing a History of the Franklin Papers, and List of 200 printed Books of and relating to

Franklin. Privately printed. Five steel portraits and facsimile of Franklin's celebrated letter to Strahan. London : 1880. imp. 8vo, pp. 36.

—*Stevens' Historical Collections.* Catalogue of the first portion of the extensive and varied collections of rare Books and Manuscripts relating chiefly to the History and Literature of America, Comprising the great Collections of Voyages and Travels of De Bry (in Latin and German) Hulsius Thevenot Purchas and Hakluyt with early separate Voyages of the Dutch English and French Navigators ; Early American History and Literature ; Burns' Autograph Poems ; black-letter and other early English and American Ballads ; Chaucer's Works 1532 ; highly important Collections of Manuscripts relating to Sir Francis Drake, the colony of Georgia, New England and Virginia, including 18 of the earliest Autograph Letters of Washington and Henry Stevens' Franklin Collection Bibliography which will be sold by Auction, by Messrs. Sotheby, Wilkinson & Hodge, Auctioneers, at their House, Strand, London, 11th July, 1881, and four following Days, at one o'clock precisely. London: Dryden Press. rl. 8vo, pp. (4), v, (1), 229, (1).

—*Who Spoils our New English Books ?* Asked and Answered by Henry Stevens of Vermont Bibliographer and lover of books Fellow of the Society of Antiquaries of Old England &c., &c. * * * as well as Citizen of Noviomagus et cetera. London : Henry Newton Stevens 115 St. Martin's Lane over Against the Church of St. Martin in the Fields, Christmas, MDCCC LXXXIV. 16mo, pp. 38. No pagination.

This little typographical gem from the Chiswick press, is inscribed by Mr. Stevens to the memory of his friends, Charles Whittingham and William Pickering, Printer and Publisher " whose beautiful books are their epitaphs and whose epitaphs embalm their memories."

—*Recollections of Mr. James Lenox,* of New York, and the Formation of his Library, by Henry Stevens, of Vermont, Bibliographer, &c., &c., &c. London : Henry Stevens and Son, 115 St. Martin's Lane over Against the the Church of St. Martin in the Fields, MDCC LXXXVI. 16mo, pp. x, 24.

—*The Dawn of British Trade* to the East Indies, as recorded in the Minutes of the East India Company, 1599-1603. Containing an account of the Formation of the Company, the first adventure and Waymouth's Voyage in search of the N. W. passage. Now first printed from the original MSS., with an introduction by Sir George Birdwood. London : Henry Stevens & Son, 115 St. Martin's Lane, over Against the Church of St. Martin in the Fields. 1886. royal 8vo.

Henry Stevens was born at Barnet, Vt., August 24, 1819, son of Henry Stevens the Antiquary; entered Middlebury College, 1838; graduated at Yale College 1843; and at Cambridge Law School 1844; established himself in London, 1845, as agent for the British Museum in the purchase of American works; was also purchasing agent for the Library of Congress, the Smithsonian, and other public and private libraries; died at London Feb. 28, 1886. The letters "G. M. B." attached to his name in many of the titles of his books, stand for Green Mountain Boy. "Noviomagus" of which he called himself a citizen, was the ancient name of a town of the Regni, in England, now Bromley, near London.

Stevens, Phineas. *Journal* of Capt. Phineas Stevens to and from Canada—1749. "New

Hampshire Hist. Soc. Coll." Vol. v. pp. 199-205.

Stevens, Simon. *The Tehuantepec Railway.* Its Location, Features and Advantages Under the La Sere Grant of 1869. New York : D. Appleton & Co., 1869. 8vo, pp. xxiii, 73, 88. And Historical and Geographical Notes 1453-1869, By Henry Stevens, G. M. B. F. S. A., etc. Fellow of the Royal Geog. Soc. of London Cor. Member Amer. Antiq. Soc. and of the Hist. Socs. of Mass., Conn., Maine, Vt., N. J., Penn., and Wiscon. and Blk. Bld. Athm. Clb. London: pp. 40.

Simon Stevens is a brother of Henry Stevens above.

Stevens, Thaddeus. *An Address* delivered on the Fourth of July, 1835, at an Anti-Masonic Celebration. Pittsburgh : 8vo, pp. 8. n. d.

—*Speech* of Hon. Thaddeus Stevens, of Pennsylvania, on the Presidential Question, and the Slavery Issue, delivered in the House of Representatives, August 12, 1852. Washington : 1852. 8vo, pp. 8.

—*The Tax Bill.* Speech of Hon. Thaddeus Stevens, of Pennsylvania, in the House of Representatives, April 1862. Washington, D. C.: 1862. 8vo, pp. 4.

—*Reconstruction.* Speech of Hon. Thaddeus Stevens, of Pennsylvania. Delivered in the House of Representatives of the United States, Dec. 18, 1865. Washington, D. C.: 8vo, pp. 8.

—*Basis of Representation.* Speech of Hon. Thaddeus Stevens, of Pennsylvania, delivered in the House of Representatives, January 31, 1866. Washington, D. C.: McGill & Witherow, Printers and stereotypers. 1866. 8vo, pp. 7.

—*Speech* of Hon. T. Stevens, of Pennsylvania, delivered in the House of Representatives, March 19, 1867, on the Bill (H. R. No. 20), Relative to Damages to loyal men, and for other purposes. 8vo, pp. 8.

—*Eulogies* on Hon. Thaddeus Stevens, by Mr. Cameron, of Pa., and Mr. Morrill, of Vt., in the Senate of the United States, December 18, 1868. Washington: 1869. 8vo, pp. 8.

—*Memorial Addresses* on the Death of Hon. Thaddeus Stevens, in the U. S. House of Representatives. Washington : 1869.

Mr. Stevens was born in Danville, Vt., April 4, 1792, and died in Washington, D. C., August 11, 1868. He was graduated at Dartmouth College, 1814, read law with Hon. John Mattocks, at Peacham, and at York, Pa. He held many offices in Pennsylvania, and was in Congress 1848-1853, and from 1859 until his death. His speeches are scattered through the Congressional Globe. For Sketches of his life, see Drake's Biog. Dic., Dartmouth Alumni, and Lauman's Biog. Annals. Also, for more extended notices, see Harris' "Review of the Political Conflict in America; " "Biographical History of Lancaster County, Pa." also by Harris.

Stewart, Dugald. *Elements of the Philosophy* of the Human Mind. By Dugald Stewart, F. R. S., Edin. Professor of Moral Philosophy in the University of Edinburgh. Published by William Fessenden, Bookseller, Brattleborough, Vermont : 1808. 8vo, pp. 496.

Stewart, John W. *Message of the Governor* to the General Assembly of the State of Vermont, October, 1870. Burlington : Free Press Steam Book and Job Office, 1870. 8vo, pp. 12.

Among Mr. Stewart's published speeches and addresses are Speech on the Inter-State Commerce Bill in the 48th Congress; Speech on the Tariff in the 51st Congress; Oration at the laying of the Corner Stone of the Bennington Battle Monument, August 16, 1887 and Address at the Dedication of the Monument to Gov. Thomas Chittenden, in Williston, August 19, 1896. John Wolcott Stewart was born in Middlebury, Nov. 14, 1825; graduated from Middlebury College in 1846; was admitted to the bar of Addison County, 1850; represented Middlebury in the legislature 1856, '57, '64, '65, '66, '67 and 1876; Speaker of the House 1865, '66, '67 and 1876; State Senator 1861-62; Governor of Vermont, 1870–72; member of the 48th, 49th and 50th Congresses, 1883-89.

Stiles, R. Cresson, M. D. *An Introductory Lecture* to the Course of Instruction in the Medical Department of the University of Vermont, by R. Cresson Stiles, M. D., Professor of Physiology and Pathology. February, 1858. Burlington: Free Press Print. 1858. 8vo, pp. 22.

—*A Valedictory Address,* delivered before the Medical Class of the University of Vermont, June 1st, 1860, by Prof. R. Cresson Stiles, M. D. Burlington: Danforth & Smalley, Printers. 1860. 8vo, pp. 19.

St. Johnsbury. *Chronicles* of St. Johnsbury Academy.
See Brooks, Mrs. S. F.

—*Atheneum.* Regulations for the use of the St. Johnsbury Atheneum. Boston: Printed by Arthur W. Locke & Co. 1871. 8vo, pp. 8.

—*Catalogue* of the Library of.
See Catalogues.

—*Confession of Faith,* Covenant and Catalogue of the First Church in St. Johnsbury. With Historical Sketches, &c. Boston: Printed by Damrell & Moore, 16 Devonshire Street. 1850. 12mo, pp. 18.

—*The Second Congregational Church* in St. Johnsbury, Vermont. Published by request of the Church. Concord, N. H.: Printed by Asa McFarland. May, 1841. 12mo, pp. 24.

—*Historical Sketch,* Articles of Faith and Covenant of the Second Congregational Church, St. Johnsbury, Vt. Concord, N. H.: 1864. 12mo, pp. 11.

—*Articles of Faith* and Covenant of the South Congregational Church, St. Johnsbury, Vt. Concord, N. H.: 1864. 12mo, pp. 17.

—*St. Johnsbury Atheneum.* Bulletin of Books added from 1890-1895. Caledonian Print. 16mo. pp. 40.

—*Report* of the Semi-Centennial of St. Johnsbury Academy, 1892. Caledonian Print. 8vo, pp. 68.

—*Semi-Centennial Souvenir* St. Johnsbury Academy. St. Johnsbury: 1892. Caledonian Press. 8vo, pp. 110.

—*General Catalogue* of St. Johnsbury Academy. Containing the names of all the students since the foundation of the school. St. Johnsbury: 1892. Caledonian Press. 8vo, pp. 96.

—*St. Johnsbury Illustrated.* A Review of the Town's Business, Social, Literary and Educational Facilities. With Glimpses of Picturesque Surroundings. Compiled by Arthur F. Stone. Containing nearly 300 illustrations. St. Johnsbury: 1891. Caledonian Press. C. M. Stone & Co. folio, pp. 100.

Stockbridge. *Manual* of the Congregational Church, Stockbridge, Vt. Windsor: Printed at the Vermont Chronicle Office. 1858. 18mo, pp. 15.

Stone, Benjamin P. *The Christian Ministry* a Divine Institution; a Sermon preached at Compton, N. H., March 24, 1842, at the Ordination of Rev. Charles Shedd, as Pastor of the Congregational Church; also, at Bristol, June 8, 1842, at the Installation of Rev. Daniel O. Morton. By Benjamin P. Stone, Secretary of the New Hampshire Missionary Society. Concord: Printed at the Congregational Journal Office. August, 1842. 8vo, pp. 21.

—*The Peculiar Presence of God* with the Good Man. A Sermon delivered on the Death of the Rev. Joseph Lane, late Secretary and Agent of the New Hampshire Bible Society, at Pembroke, Oct. 13, 1850, by the Rev. Benjamin P. Stone, Secretary of the New Hampshire Missionary Society. Concord: Printed by McFarland and Jenks, Main Street. 8vo, pp. 16.

Mr. Stone was born in Reading, Vt., February 11, 1801. He was graduated at Middlebury College, 1828; read theology and was pastor of different Congregational Churches in New Hampshire; Agent of the New Hampshire Missionary Society 17 years; editor of Congregational Journal, Concord, N. H.; he published several sermons and 22 annual reports of the New Hampshire Missionary Society. He died November 26, 1870. See Vermont Historical Magazine, Vol. 2, pp. 153-4.

Stone, C. M. *A Memorial* of C. M. Stone. With portrait. St. Johnsbury: Caledonian Press. 1890. 8vo, pp. 40.

Stone, Mason S. *Course of Studies* for the Schools of Vermont, compiled by Mason S. Stone. Rutland: The Tuttle Co. 1895. 8vo, pp. 32.

Stone, J. P. *A History of Greensboro,* and the Congregational Church, delivered November 24, 1854. By Rev. James P. Stone. Published by request of the Church. Montpelier: E. P. Walton, Printer. 8vo, pp. 40.

Storey, Wilbur F. *The Suppression* of the Chicago Times. 8vo, pp. 32.

This is a history of one of the most indefensible outrages upon the freedom of the Press, and the rights of the people, ever perpetrated in this country. It took place about four o'clock A. M., June 3, 1863, at which hour a military mob surrounded the office of the "Times," broke down the doors, and stopped the press when about half the morning edition of the paper had been printed. The mob in military uniforms of the United States seized the printed sheets, carried them into the street, tore them to pieces and trampled them under their feet. As stated by Mr. J. F. Joy, in his argument at the hearing before Judges David Davis and Thomas Drummond, both of the United States Court, the former having been appointed by President Lincoln in 1861: "In a state where the Courts are all open, the people all quiet, within the limits of which there is profound peace, where no semblance of martial law or the occasion for any exists, a man is found dressed with the brief authority of a Major General, who a short time since was a clerk in one of the offices of this city, (Chicago) never distinguished for any great wisdom or soundness of mind, who now resolves by a military order to assume the censorship of the press—to try, condemn and execute its conductors without the intervention of Court and jury, and without a hearing even —to suspend the power of the Constitution and the laws. If General Burnside may suppress The Chicago Times, he may equally suppress every other paper in the country." The order of General A. E. Burnside suppressing the Times was revoked by order of President Lincoln, June 4, before the conclusion of the hearing in Court on the injunction granted by Judge Drummond against the order of Burnside, which ended the case not only of the Times, but ended military interference with the freedom of the press thereafter during the civil war. And yet the extra session of Congress in 1873 was occupied almost wholly with the question, whether almost any obscure employe of whatever kind of an administration of the

General Government might happen to be in power, should have authority to order the military of the United States to take possession of the polls at elections, and thus virtually destroy that dearest boon of freedom, the power of a free ballot.

Mr. Storey was born in Salisbury, Vt., December 19, 1819. His family is a collateral branch of the Story family of which the well known jurist was a member. The first ten years of Mr. Storey's life were passed upon the farm of his parents. At this time the family moved to Middlebury, and at the age of eleven years Mr. Storey went into the office of the "Middlebury Free Press," to learn the printing business, where he remained until seventeen years of age, with the exception of a single winter, when he attended the village school, which, with the small school privileges at Salisbury, were all the school advantages he ever enjoyed.

At the close of his apprenticeship Mr. Storey had saved $17, to which his mother added $10, and with this capital he commenced life for himself. Proceeding to New York city, he secured a situation as compositor on the "Journal of Commerce," where he worked at the case a year and a half, when, in the spring of 1838, he determined to "Go West," and he reached Laporte, Ind., with $250, being his savings while in New York. Learning that the Democrats of Laporte were about to establish a newspaper, he made an arrangement whereby he was to run the mechanical part of the paper, while E. A. Hannegan, subsequently United States Senator, was a volunteer editor. Soon after, when Mr. Storey was not quite nineteen, the entire control of the paper fell into his hands, but the times were unfavorable and the enterprise failed, and in the ruins was buried the capital saved in New York. He then purchased a drug store, which venture was also a failure. The Democrats of Mishawaka about this time started the "Tocsin," and Mr. Storey went over, edited the paper a year and a half, when he removed to Jackson, Mich, where he read law two years, and then started the "Jackson Patriot," which soon absorbed the other Democratic paper published there. At the end of a year and a half he was appointed Postmaster by Polk. He sold the Patriot on becoming Postmaster, and after losing the post office he again opened a drug store, adding books and stationery.

While in Jackson he was elected to the Constitutional Convention in 1850; he also acted as Inspector of the State Prison; but editorial aspirations haunted him, and when an opportunity offered to secure a sixth interest in the "Detroit Free Press" he availed himself of it and moved to Detroit in 1853. At this time the "Free Press" was at a low ebb, not paying expenses, but Mr. Story infused such energy and tact into the business that he soon became sole proprietor. In eight years he not only paid for the entire concern, but accumulated $30,000 from its earnings; for nearly all this period he performed the entire editorial labor of the daily and other editions. He was the first man at the office in the morning, and he never left until the next morning, when the forms were locked ready for the press. It was not uncommon for him to lie down upon his table at four o'clock in the morning, and three or four hours later be ready to resume the labors of the day. He knew every detail of the business management and ordered the disposition of every handful of "matter" as it went into the "forms." Having made the "Free Press" all that could be made of a newspaper in Detroit, he sighed for more worlds to conquer, and in 1861, purchased the "Chicago Times," which was in a similar condition of poverty to that of the "Free Press" at the time he purchased it.

For several years his labors and life in Chicago were a close repetition of what they had been in Detroit. Before he brought the "Times" up to his standard, and made it a paying concern, he had sunk the forty thousand dollars brought from Detroit, and another thirty thousand dollars provided by friends; but finally he made the "Times" a great success financially, its value being estimated at two millions of dollars.

Although Mr. Storey is not quite sixty years old (1878) the vast labor he has performed has produced its effect; his abundant hair, black as jet when he went to Chicago, is now white as snow, and his once robust constitution is somewhat exhausted. He has been three times married; no children.

Mr. Storey died at Chicago, Oct. 27, 1884.

Stowe. *Report of* the Selectmen and Other Officers to the Town of Stowe, February 15th, 1861. Montpelier: 8vo, pp. 8.
Continued.

—*Memorial Record* of the Soldiers from Stowe, in the Civil War, 1861-5.
See Savage, R. A.

—*(Reminiscences of)*—Swallows on the Wing. 1866.

Streeter, Russell. *An Interesting* Controversy between Rev. Clark Brown, Clergyman of the Standing Order, in Swanzey, (N. H.) and Russell Streeter, Professional Servant of Jesus Christ. Consisting, I. Of an Anonymous Piece published in the New Hampshire Sentinel, in which the writer misrepresented the sentiments and preaching of the Itinerant Universalists, in the Vicinity of Keene, etc. II. A Letter to Mr. Brown, (having learned he was the "Writer" of the above Mentioned Publication) in answer to his misrepresentations. III. Mr. Brown's Reply to that Letter. IV. A Plain Answer to Mr. Brown's Reply. The Whole Submitted to the Perusal of Christians of every Denomination, Particularly those of Swanzey, and its Vicinity. By Russell Streeter. Windsor, (Vt.): Printed by Jesse Cochran. 1814. 12mo, pp. 14.

—*A Sermon,* delivered at the Installation of Rev. Sebastian Streeter, as Pastor of the First Universalist Church and Society, in the City of Boston, May 13, 1824. By Russell Streeter, Minister of the Universalist Society in Portland. Boston: Printed by Henry Bowen, No. 4 Province-House Row. 1824. 8vo, pp. 31.

—*A Christmas Sermon,* delivered in the Universalist Meeting House, in Watertown. Mass. December 25, A. D. 1827. By Russell Streeter, Pastor. Published by request. Boston: Henry Bowen. 1828. 8vo, pp. 16.

—*The New Hymn Book,* designed for Universalist Societies. Compiled from approved Authors, with variations and additions. By Sebastian and Russell Streeter. Boston: Marsh and Capen. 1829. 12mo, pp. 408.

- *A Sermon,* delivered at the funeral of Miss Abigail Reed, of Westford, Mass., aged twenty years; who departed this life on the tenth of September, 1831, the victim of modern revivals. By Russell Streeter. Published by request. Worcester: Spooner & Church, Printers. 1831. 8vo, pp. 20.

—*Visitor.* Conversation on the Subject of Infant Damnation, between a Professed Calvinist and a Universalist. By Russell Streeter. Press of the Universalist Watchman, W. W. Prescott, Printer. 1831. 8vo, pp. 12.

—*The crafty designs* of the Orthodox Clergy exposed, through the carelessness of one of their Agents. Together with A Solemn Appeal to all lovers of Civil and Religious Liberty. Motto. Woodstock, Vt.: E. Avery, Printer. 1830. 8vo, pp. 16.

—*Sermon* at Shirley, Mass. 1833. 8vo, pp. 8.

—*Familiar Conversations,* in which the Salvation of all Mankind is clearly exhibited and Illustrated; and the most important objections which are now brought against the Doctrine are fairly stated and fully answered. By Russell Streeter. Motto. Second edition. Woodstock: Published by Nahum Haskell. 1835. 12mo, pp. 288.

—*Mirror of Calvinistic,* Fanatical Revivals, or Jedediah Burchard & Co. During a protracted meeting of twenty-six days, in Woodstock, Vt. To which is added the "Preamble and

Resolutions" of the town, declaring said Burchard a Nuisance to Society. By Russell Streeter. Motto. Woodstock, Vt.: Published by the Author. Power Press, C. K. Smith & Co. 1835. 8vo, pp. 120.
Another Edition.

—*Mirror of Calvinistic Fanaticism*, or J. Burchard & Co., during a protracted Meeting of twenty-six days in Woodstock, Vt. By Russell Streeter. Woodstock: N. Haskell. 1835. 16mo, pp. 168.

Father Streeter was connected with most of the newspapers and periodicals of his denomination as editor or contributor; he also published a little volume: "Latest News from Three Worlds, Heaven, Earth and Hell." Fifty or sixty of his sermons have been published. Father Streeter was born at Chesterfield, N. H., April 15, 1791; he began to preach in 1810, as an itinerant in Vermont, and thereafter resided in the State with the exception of a few years at Portland, Me., and Shirley, Mass.; his permanent residence being at Woodstock, after 1834, where he passed the evening of his days with two of his married daughters. He died at Woodstock, February 15, 1880.

Rev. Sebastian Streeter was his elder brother. For a full sketch of the life, labor and works of Father Streeter, see the "Universalist," first number in January, 1873.

Strong, Cyprian. *A Sermon* preached at Hartford, before the Board of Trustees of the Missionary Society, in Connecticut, At Ordination of the Rev. Jedediah Bushnell, as a Missionary to the New Settlements ; January 15th, A. D. 1800. By Cyprian Strong, A. M. Pastor of the First Church in Chatham. Hartford : Printed by Hudson & Goodwin. 1800. 8vo, pp. 16.

Mr. Strong was mixed up in the "Trial for Libel Case," Torrey *vs*. Field.

Strong, Maj.-Gen. George C. *Cadet Life at West Point.* By an Officer of the United States Army. Boston : 1862. 12mo.

Gen. Strong was born in Stockbridge, Vt., in 1832; and was graduated at West Point in 1857, where he served as Captain of Cadets three years. He was on Gen. McDowell's staff at Bull Run, and next served on Gen. McClellan's staff. He was detailed as ordnance officer by Gen. Butler to the department of the Gulf, and was on the General's staff at New Orleans. He led the assault on Fort Wagner, July 18, 1863, and died from wounds then received.

See Drake; Allibone; Parton's "Butler in New Orleans," 4th to 16th ed. pp. 188.

Strong, James. *An Address* on the necessity of Education and the Arts in a Republican Government. Delivered before the Phi Sigma Nu Society of the University of Vermont, at Burlington, August 7th, A. D. 1827. By James Strong. Printed for the Society, Burlington : Printed at the Free Press Office. 1827. 8vo, pp. 24.

—*Freedom of Thought*, the True Mean. An Address delivered before the Philomathean Society of Troy Conference Academy, West Poultney, Vt., on the Evening of July 15, 1851. By James Strong, A. M., Formerly Teacher of Languages in that Institution. New York : John F. Trow, Printer, 49 Ann St. 1851. 8vo, pp. 31.

Strong, Jonathan. *A Discourse*, delivered in the North Meeting House in Bridgewater, at the funeral of Doctor Ziba Bass, September 25, 1804. By Jonathan Strong, A. M., Pastor of the church in Randolph, Mass. Randolph (Vt.) : Printed by Sereno Wright. 1805. 8vo, pp. 16.

Strong, Latham Cornell. *Poke O'Moonshine.* By Latham Cornell Strong, Author of Castle Windows. New York : G. P. Putnam's Sons. 1878. 12mo, pp. 117.

This book is dedicated to the people of the Lamoille Valley, and tells the story in poems of some of the French and Indian legends extant in that valley at the present day, connected with the French and Indian wars of 1755-61, during a part of which period Emil La Moille, who was banished from France, and his daughter Clemence, resided in the valley bearing his name. A young French noble, Francois Du Bois, the accepted lover of Clemence in France, came over about 1755, and joined his regiment under Dieskau. Du Bois discovered accidentally the cabin of La Moille and Clemence; after Dieskau's final defeat near Lake George, Du Bois deserted and through an Indian guide. Clemence secreted him in a cave in Poke o' Moonshine Mountain. The poems contain the story in full.

Col. Strong, Troy's Poet Laureate, was born in that city, June 12, 1845; died at Tarrytown, N. Y., Dec. 17, 1879; he was a young man of fine talents and highly educated; he published in addition to the above, "Castle Windows," 1876, 12mo, pp. 229; "Midsummer Dreams," 1879, 12mo, pp. 174, besides numerous sketches and poems in Troy and New York newspapers; he was a member of Gov. Tilden's staff in 1874-5.

Mr. Julian Scott, author of the painting of the Battle of Cedar Creek in the State House at Montpelier, accompanied Mr. Strong through the Lamoille Valley in gathering the threads for the "Poke O'Moonshine."

Stuart, Carlos D. *Ianthe and other Poems.*
Title page wanting.

Mr. Stuart was born in Berlin, Vt., in 1820; died at Northampton, Mass., January 23, 1862, and "left a volume of poems ready for the press, [since published] which will be published with his other literary productions in a series of volumes. He was co-editor of the New York *Sun*, 1843-53, and subsequently was co-editor of the *Evening Mirror*."—Allibone.

Sturdevant, James M., M. D. *Memorial of.* New York.: 1873. 8vo, pp. 44. Portrait.

Mr. Sturdevant was born in Tinmouth, Vt., March 11, 1800: moved with his father's family to Ellisburg, N. Y., in 1813; read medicine and practiced his profession in various towns in New York, and died at Rome, August 10, 1873.

Styles, E. *Oration* at Charlestown, N. H., Dec. 27, 1781, before the Vermont Lodge of Freemasons. Westminster : 1782. 4to, pp. 8.

This is one of the early Vermont imprints; title from the catalogue of the Massachusetts Historical Society.

Sullivan, Thomas R. *Sermon* preached at Chester, Vt., at the Dedication of the Union Meeting-House. Chester, Vt.: 1829. 8vo.

Sumner, Samuel. *History* of the Missisco Valley. By Samuel Sumner, M. A. With an introductory notice of Orleans County, By Rev. S. R. Hall. Published under the auspices of the Orleans County Historical Society. Irasburgh : A. A. Earle, Book Printer. 1860. 8vo, pp. 76.

Sunderland, Byron. *A Discourse* on the Polity of the Presbyterian Church ; by B. Sunderland, delivered in the First Presbyterian Church, Washington, D. C., Sunday Evening, November 13th, 1853. Washington : Henry Polkinhorn, Printer. 1853. 8vo, pp. 21.

—*A Discourse* on "The Eastern Question," or the Present European War, by Rev. B. Sunderland, Pastor of First Presbyterian Church, Washington, D. C., July 29, 1854. Washington : Printed by Robert A. Waters. 1854. 8vo, pp. 21.

—*The Crisis of the Times* ; a Sermon preached in the First Congregational Church, Washington, D. C., on the evening of the National Fast, Thursday, April 30, 1863, by Rev. Byron Sunderland, D. D. Text. Washington: National Banner Press. 1863. 12mo, pp. 36.

—*"Who is my Neighbor?"* A Sermon by Rev. Byron Sunderland, D. D., delivered in Washington, D. C., Feb. 25, 1866. Boston: Press of John Wilson and Sons. 1866. 8vo, pp. 20.

Dr. Sunderland was born in Shoreham, Vt., November 22, 1819; was graduated at Middlebury College in 1838; studied theology at Union Theological Seminary; preached in various places in New York State, 1843-52; has been pastor of the First Presbyterian Church, Washington, D. C., since 1853. (1896.)

A Surprising Account of the Captivity and Escape of Philip M'Donald & Alex M'Cloud, of Virginia, from the Chickkemogga Indians, and of the Great Discoveries in the Western World, From June 1779, to January 1786, when they returned in health to their friends, after an absence of six years and a half. Written by themselves. Printed at Rutland, Vermont, by Josiah Fay, for S. Williams & Co. MDCCXCVII. 8vo, pp. 14.

Sutherland, David. *Christian Benevolence.* A Sermon, delivered at Newbury, Vt., before the Washington Benevolent Society, at the Celebration of the Anniversary of the National Independence, July 4, 1812. By David Sutherland, Minister of the Gospel, Bath, N. H. Windsor: Printed by Thomas M. Pomroy. 1812. 8vo, pp. 15.

Swanton. *The History* of the Town of Swanton, By Perry and Barney. Early Indian History and French Settlement by Rev. John B. Perry. Civil, Religious, Military and Biographical from the First English Settlement, by George Barney. Published in unison with the same in Vol. IV, Vermont Historical Gazetteer, Miss Homenway, Editor and Publisher. Swanton, Vt.: By order of George Barney. 1882. 8vo.

Pages 933 to 1147 of Vol. IV of the Gazetteer.

Sweetser, William. *A Dissertation on Intemperance,* to which was awarded the Premium offered by the Massachusetts Medical Society. By William Sweetser, M. D. Professor of the Theory and Practice of Physic in the University of Vermont. Boston: Hillard, Gray and Company. 1829. 8vo, pp. 98.

—*An Address,* delivered March 24, 1830, before a meeting of the young men of Burlington; assembled for the purpose of Forming a Temperance Society. By William Sweetser, M. D. Published by Request of the Society. Burlington: Chauncey Goodrich. 1830. 16mo, pp. 12.

—*An Address,* delivered before the Chittenden County Temperance Society, August 26, 1830. By William Sweetser, M. D. Published by Request of the Society. Burlington: Printed by Chauncey Goodrich. 1830. 16mo, pp. 10.

—*Address* before the Castleton Medical College, 1847.

A native of Boston, 1797; Professor of the Theory and Practice of Medicine in the University of Vermont, 1825-32; died 1875.

Swett, Charles F. *A Champion* of the Cross, being the Life of John Henry Hopkins, S. T. D., including Extracts and Selections from his writings, by Rev. Charles F. Swett. New York: James Potts Co., Publishers. 1894. 12mo, pp. ix, 379.

Swett, J., Jr. *Swett's Murray.* An English Grammar; comprehending the Principles and Rules of the Language; Illustrated by appropriate Exercises; on the basis of Murray. By J. Swett, Jr., A. M. Teacher of Moral Science and English Literature, and Lecturer on Geology, in the New England Seminary, Windsor, Vt. Windsor, Vt.: Published by Josiah Swett, Jr. 1843. 12mo, pp. 180.

Swett, Josiah. *A Sermon* preached in the Union Meeting House, West Randolph, Vt., Sunday, Nov. 23, 1851, at the Funeral of the late Mrs. Sarah E. Weston: By the Rev. Josiah Swett, M. A., Rector of Christ Church, Bethel, Vt. Motto. Montpelier: E. P. Walton & Son. 1852. 8vo, pp. 24.

—*A Sermon* preached in Christ Church, Bethel, Vt., Saturday, October 15, 1853, At the Funeral of the late Mrs. Nancy C. Tarbox (who was instantly killed on being thrown from a carriage, October 12, 1853.) By Rev. Josiah Swett, M. A. Motto. Windsor: Chronicle Print. 1853. 8vo, pp. 24.

—*Forms of Prayer* to be used in Families, as set forth in the Prayer-Book; To which are added occasional Prayers and Thanksgivings, with Hymns for Family Devotion, chiefly from the same source. Claremont, N. H.: 1861. 12mo, pp. 32.

—*The Firmament in the Midst of the Waters;* Being an Exegesis of Gen. I. 6, 7, 8. Read before the convocation of the Protestant Episcopal Church in the Diocese of Vermont, at their meeting in March, 1862. By the Rev. Josiah Swett, M. A., Rector of Christ Church, Bethel, and St. Paul's Church, Royalton. (Greek Motto). Claremont, N. H. : Claremont Manufacturing Company. E. L. Goddard, G. G. and L. Ide. 1862. 8vo, pp. 32.

Mr. Swett edited "Thomson's Seasons," 1844; "Pope's Essay on Man," 1844; and was a contributor to "The True Catholic;" also co-editor of the "Citizen Soldier," Windsor, Vt. Born in Claremont, N. H., 1814, and was some time connected with Norwich University.

Swift, Eliphalet Y. *Reminiscences* of the Life and Character of Mrs. Sophia Woodbridge Dwight, by Rev. E. Y. Swift, with additions by Rev. B. W. Dwight. January 1, 1862. New York: John F. Trow, Printer, 50 Green Street. 1862. 8vo, pp. 33.

Published with Reminiscences of Benjamin Woolsey Dwight, M. D.

Mr. Swift was born in Fairfax, Vt., January 16, 1815; was graduated at Middlebury College in 1839, and at Andover in 1842; has preached in Chillicothe, Ohio, Northampton and South Hadley, Mass., and Clinton, New York, and since 1868 at Denmark, Iowa.

Swift, Rev Job. *Discourses* on Religious Subjects by the late Rev. Job Swift, D. D. To which are prefixed Sketches of his life and character, and a Sermon preached at West Rutland, on the occasion of his death, by the Rev. Lemuel Haynes. Motto. Middlebury, Vermont: Printed by Huntington and Fitch. Nov. 1805. 12mo, pp. 300.

—*Vermont Election Sermon.* 1784.

Dr. Swift was born in Sandwich, Mass., June 17, 1743; he was graduated at Yale in 1765, and began to preach soon after; came to Vermont in 1784, and was settled over the Congregational church at Manchester two years, at Bennington sixteen years, and then at Addison until his death, October 20, 1804. Hon. Samuel Swift of Middlebury, Hon. Benjamin Swift, and Dr. Noadiah Swift, all distinguished men, were his sons. For Sketch of his life see Jennings' History of Bennington, pp. 92-99.

Swift, Samuel. *History of* the Town of Middlebury, in the County of Addison, Vermont: To which is Prefixed a Statistical and Historical Account of the County, written at the request of the Historical Society of Middlebury. By Samuel Swift. Middlebury: A. H. Copeland, 1859. 8vo, pp. 444.
Portraits and Plates.

—*An Oration* delivered in Middlebury, at the Celebration of the Fourth of July, A. D. 1809. By Samuel Swift, Esq., A. M. Middlebury: J. D. Huntington. 1809.

—*Statistical and* Historical account of the County of Addison, Vermont, Written at the Request of the Historical Society of Middlebury. By Samuel Swift. Middlebury: A. H. Copeland. 1859. 8vo, pp. 132.
Illustrations.
Hon. Samuel Swift, A. M., L L. D., son of Rev. Job Swift and his wife, Mary Ann Sedgwick, sister of Hon. Theodore Sedgwick, was born in Armenia, N. Y., August 3, 1782; died in Middlebury, Vt., July 7, 1875. He removed to Bennington, Vt., with his father in 1786; and was graduated at Dartmouth College in 1800. He settled at Middlebury, Vt., in 1801, as a tutor in the college there one year; then studied law which he practiced until 1812 when he quit the profession from conscientious scruples. He was County Clerk 1814–46; Judge of Probate 1816–41; Secretary of State several years; member of Constitutional Conventions 1828 and 1835; State Senator 1838–9, and Town Representative 1816–17, '29, '41 and '46. He married Mary Bridgman, daughter of Captain Jonathan Young, and they had ten children, three of whom survive, Hon. George S. and Edward of Detroit, and Samuel, who resides near Salem, Oregon. (1880.)

Sylvester, Wm. E., M. D. *An Historical* Sketch of Epidemic Yellow Fever in the United States. An Essay prepared for the Annual Meeting of the Vermont State Medical Society, at Montpelier, October 8, 1879. By William E. Sylvester, M. D., New York. Montpelier, Vt.: Argus and Patriot Job Printing House. 1879. 8vo, pp. 11.
Mr. Sylvester was from Bethel, Vt., and was graduated at Dartmouth Medical College, and is now assistant Physician in the New York City Insane Asylum on Ward's Island. (1880.)

—*Synopsis of* the Vermont Liquor Law. [n. p. n. d.] 1874. 12mo, pp. 4.

—*Synopsis of* the Laws of Vermont relating to the Traffic in Intoxicating Liquors. Brattleboro: 1880. pp. 11.

Taber, Charles. *A Testimony* of the Monthly Meeting, Concerning the Death of Charles Taber, deceased. New York: 1855. 12mo, pp. 8.
Mr. Taber was a Quaker preacher, born in Massachusetts March 27th, 1783; and with his father and family removed to Montpelier, Vt., about 1795, where he resided about eight years. He resided in Starksboro, Vt., 15 years.

Taft Family Gathering. *Proceedings at* the Meeting of the Taft Family at Uxbridge, Mass., August 12, 1874. Uxbridge: 1874. 8vo, pp. 103.
The branches of the family in Vermont were largely represented.

Taggart, Samuel. *Christ Jesus* the Lord, the Great Subject of Gospel Preaching: A Sermon preached in Brattleboro East Society, January 13, 1819, at the Ordination of the Rev. Jonathan M'Gee to the Pastoral care of the Church and Congregation in that place. By Samuel Taggart, A. M., Pastor of the Presbyterian Church in Coleraine. Brattleboro: Printed by John Holbrook. 1819. 8vo, pp. 21.
Mr. Taggart was a Presbyterian clergyman, native of New Hampshire. See Sprague's Annals. Vol. 3, pp. 377–81.

Taylor, Charles F., M. D. *The Treatment* of Lateral Curvature of the Spine, by Specific exercises. By Charles F. Taylor, M. D. New York: Printed by Henry Ludwig, No. 39 Centre Street. 1859. 8vo, pp. 16.

—*Theory and Practice* of the Movement Cure: or, the Treatment of Lateral Curvature of the Spine; Paralysis; Indigestion; Constipation; Consumption; Angular Curvatures and Other Deformities; Diseases Incident to Women; Derangements of the Nervous System; and Other Chronic Affections, by the Swedish System of Localized Movements. By Charles Fayette Taylor, M. D. With Illustrations. Philadelphia: Lindsay & Blackiston. 1861. 12mo, pp. 295.
Dr. Taylor was born in Williston, Vt., 1827; graduated in the Medical Department of the University of Vermont, 1856; appointed Resident Surgeon in the New York Orthopedic Dispensary. His publications in addition are: "The Mechanical Treatment of Angular Curvature, or Pott's Disease of the Spine;" New York: 1864, 16mo. "Spinal Irritation, or the Causes of Backache Among American Women;" 1864, 8vo. "Infantile Paralysis and its Attendant Deformities," Phila.: 1867, 12mo; also medical pamphlets, and papers in various medical journals. See Allibone.

Taylor, George H., M. D. *An Exposition* of the Swedish Movement Cure. Embracing the History and Philosophy of this System of Medical Treatment, with Examples of Single Movements, and Directions for their use in Various Forms of Chronic Disease, forming a Complete Manual of Exercises; together with a Summary of the Principles of General Hygiene. By George H. Taylor, A. M., M. D., Principal Physician to the Remedial Hygienic Institute of New York City. New York: Fowler & Wells, publishers, No. 308 Broadway. 1860. 12mo, pp. 408.

—*An Illustrated Sketch* of the Movement Cure; its Principles, Methods and Effects. By Geo. H. Taylor, M. D. Author of "Exposition of the Movement Cure," and Physician of the Institute. New York: Published at the Institute, 67 West 38th Street. 1866. 12mo, pp. 60.
Born in Williston, Vt., in 1821; graduated at the New York Medical College, 1852. Has published in addition "The Movement Cure in every Chronic Disease." 1862, 12mo, 4 editions the same year. See Allibone.

Taylor, Henry B. *Some Account* of the ancestors, Relatives and Family of Henry Boardman Taylor, with a memoir written by himself, and a supplement By Rev. B. S. Taylor, Brought down to October, 1802. Burlington: Free Press Asso. 8vo, pp. 72.

Taylor, Hesekiah. *A Funeral Sermon* preached at Newfane; Occasioned by the death of Mr. Henry Sawtell, his wife and five children, who were all consumed by the flames of his house, which took fire on the 2d of February, 1782. By the late Rev. Hesekiah Taylor, formerly pastor of the Church in that place.
In history of Newfane, pp. 177–185. Account of the fire in same. p. 24–5.
Mr. Taylor was pastor of the Congregational Church, Newfane, from its organization, 1774, until 1811.

Taylor, J. *The Lives of the Holy Evangelists* and Apostles, with their martyrdoms, for preaching the Gospel of our Lord Jesus Christ. By J. Taylor, B. D. Barnard, Vt.: Published by Joseph Dix. I. H. Carpenter, printer. 1813. 18mo, pp. 120.

Taylor, Matthew. *Matthew Taylor's Proclamation* for the Millennium ; with the addition of five pieces on different subjects. First. On the fulfillment of the Prophecies, being in the present time. Second. On foreknowledge, with man's free Agency. Third. On God's decrees with foreordination. Fourth. On Regeneration. Fifth. On the doctrine of Universal Salvation. Second year of the Millennium, 36th of our Independence—the year of our Lord, A. D. 1812. Rutland : Printed for the Author. 8vo, pp. 14.

Taylor, Samuel H. *Memorial* of Joseph P. Fairbanks. By Samuel H. Taylor. Riverside: 1865. 8vo, pp. 189.

TEMPERANCE. *The Fatal Effects of Ardent Spirits.* A Sermon by Ebenezer Porter, Pastor of the First Church in Washington, Conn. Middlebury, Vt.: Reprinted by T. C. Strong. 1812. 8vo, pp. 16.

—*An Address* to the Inhabitants of the State of Vermont on the use of Ardent Spirits ; by a Committee of the Legislature appointed for that purpose. Oct., 1817. [Paul Brigham, Chairman.] Montpelier : Printed by E. P. Walton. 1817. 8vo.

—*An Address,* delivered before the Williston Temperance Society, March 8, 1832. By Dr. Robert Moody, of Burlington. Published by Request. Burlington : Chauncey Goodrich. 1832. 8vo, pp. 24.

—*An Appeal* to the People of Washington County, upon the subject of Temperance. By a committee of the Washington County Temperance Society. January 2, 1832. 8vo, pp. 8.

—*Annual Report* of the Vermont Temperance Society, Communicated at their Meeting, Held at Montpelier, October 14, 1834. Montpelier : E. P. Walton's Print, Watchman Office. 1834. 8vo, pp. 16.

—*The Same,* 1837. Same imprint. pp. 18.

—*Constitution and By-Laws* of Middlebury Association No. 1, of the United Brethren of Temperance of the State of Vermont, January, 1847. Middlebury : Justus Cobb, Printer. 16mo, pp. 19.

—*Constitution and By-Laws* of Mount Nebo Division No. 9, Sons of Temperance, Middlebury, Vt., Oct. 12, 1848. Middlebury: Printed by Justus Cobb. 1850. 16mo, pp. 48.

—*Proceedings at the Annual Meeting* of the Vermont State Temperance Society, Held at Windsor, Jan. 16, and 17, 1850. Windsor : Printed at the Chronicle Press. 1850. 12mo, pp. 16.

—*Proceedings of the Grand Division* of the Sons of Temperance of the State of Vermont, embracing the three quarterly Sessions and the regular annual Session, October, 1851. Motto. Middlebury : Justus Cobb, Printer. 1852. 8vo, pp. 154.
  Continued.

—*Remarks on the Lecture* of the Rt. Rev. Bishop Hopkins, against the Temperance Society, published in his late work entitled "The Primitive Church compared with the Protestant Episcopal Church of the present day." By the Rev. James Reid, Rector of Trinity Church, St. Armand, Lower Canada. Frelighsburg, L. C.: Standard Office. 1836. 8vo, pp. 82.

—*Report of the Select Committee of the House,* on the Temperance Memorials. Montpelier : E. P. Walton & Son. 1837. 8vo, pp. 12.

—*Versus Intemperance :* An Address, or concise Treatise on the Nature and Effects of Alcohol. Delivered in the Brick Church, Montpelier, Vt., before the Temperance Society of that place, on the day of Simultaneous Meetings throughout the World, February 25th, 1840. By the Rev. James Nelson Hume. Boston : 1840. 12mo, pp. 26 and 24.

—*The Philosophy of Temperance :* An Address before the Temperance Society of the University of Vermont, October 18, 1842, by Rev. Zonas Bliss. Published by request. Burlington : Chauncey Goodrich. 1842. 8vo, pp. 31.

—*Rechabite Songster and Tee-Total Minstrel.* Burlington: 1848. pp. 48.

—*Constitution* and By-Laws and Rules of Order, of Washington Division, Number Twenty-seven, of the Sons of Temperance, of the State of Vermont. Instituted in Barre, March 7th, 1849. Montpelier : Press of Eastman & Danforth. 12mo, pp. 32.

—*Constitution* and By-Laws of Green Mountain Division, No. 5, Sons of Temperance, Montpelier, State of Vermont. Instituted April 12, 1848. Montpelier : Press of Eastman & Danforth. 1849. 12mo, pp. 31.

—*Constitution,* By-Laws and Rules of Order of Eureka Division, No. 81, of the Sons of Temperance of the State of Vermont, instituted at East Middlebury, May 4, 1849. Middlebury : Printed by Justus Cobb. 1852. 16mo, pp. 52.

—*The Vermont Liquor Law Sustained.* Opinion of Judge Bennett. Circuit Session, September Term. 1855. 8vo, pp. 27.

—*Constitution,* By-Laws and Rules of Order of Capital Division, No. 84, of the Sons of Temperance, of the State of Vermont. Instituted at Montpelier, 1859. Montpelier : Printed by Ballou, Loveland & Co. 1859. 12mo, pp. 31, (1).

—*Report of the Executive Committee* of the Vermont State Temperance Society. Rutland: December 6, 1861. 8vo, pp. 4.

—*Autobiography* of Festus G. Rand. A Tale of Intemperance. With a Preface by Rev. T. B. Taylor, A. M., and a Recommendation by John B. Gough. Price 25 cents. Montpelier : J. & J. M. Poland, Printers. 1868. 8vo, pp. 32.

—*Another Edition.* St. Albans, Vt.: M. F. Wilson, Printer. 1871. 8vo, pp. 63.

—*Address* of the Vermont State Temperance Convention, adopted January 17, 1894. Burlington, Vt.: Courier office. 1849. 8vo, pp. 7.
  See Brockway J.; Woman's Christian Temperance Union. Kitchel, H. D., Morton, D. O., Sermon, 1828; Porter, Ebenezer; Read, David, Essay, 1849; Hopkins, Rt. Rev. J. H., Lecture, 1836; Rush, Benj.; Slade, Wm., Addresses; Southmayd, J. C., Discourse, 1828; Shedd, W., Address, 1844; Slade, James M., Address, 1848; Sweetser, W., Addresses, 1830 ; Synopsis of Vermont Liquor Law, 1874; Smith, Worthington, Address, 1833 ; Ferrin, C. E., "Wine Tests"; Marsh, L.; Magill, S. W., Address, 1845; I. O. of G. T.

Tenny, Erdix, D. D. *A Sermon*, preached at Thetford, Vermont, September 13, 1848, at the interment of Rev. Elisha G. Babcock, late pastor of the Congregational Church in that place. By Erdix Tenny, Pastor of the Congregational Church in Lyme. Hanover: Printed at the Dartmouth Press. 1848. 8vo, pp. 15.

—*A Sermon*, preached on occasion of the Annual Thanksgiving, in Lyme, New Hampshire, Nov. 30, 1854. By Erdix Tenny, Pastor of the Congregational Church in Lyme. Hanover: Printed at the Dartmouth Press. January 8, 1855. 8vo, pp. 19.

—*A Sermon*, preached at Lyme, New Hampshire, on occasion of the Annual Fast, April 5, 1855. By Erdix Tenny, Pastor of the Congregational Church in Lyme. Hanover: Printed at the Dartmouth Press. 1855. 8vo, pp. 18.

—*American Slavery* not Sanctioned by the Bible. A Sermon, preached at Lyme, New Hampshire, at the Annual Thanksgiving, November 27, 1856. By Erdix Tenny, Pastor of the Congregational Church in Lyme. Hanover: Printed at the Dartmouth Press. 1857. 8vo, pp. 24.

—*A Sermon*, preached in Lyme, New Hampshire, September 8, 1866, at the close of a Ministry of 37 years. By Erdix Tenny. Hanover: Printed at the Dartmouth Press, by Chapin & Whitcomb. 1866. 8vo, pp. 16.

Mr. Tenny was born in Corinth, Vt., June 11, 1801. He was graduated at Middlebury College in 1826; read theology at Andover Seminary, and was settled over the Congregational church, at Lyme, N. H., in 1831, where he continued until 1868, when he retired from active service on account of ill health. He resided in Westboro, Mass., from his departure from Lyme, to May, 1880, when he removed to Norwich, Conn., where he died November 14, 1882, leaving a widow and three out of his ten children.

Tenney, Horace A. *Genealogy* of the Tenney Family, more particularly of the family of Daniel Tenney, and Sylvia (Kent) Tenney, his wife, late of Laporte, Lorain County, Ohio. Compiled by Horace A. Tenney. Madison, Wis.: M. J. Cantwell, Book and Job Printer, King street. 1875. 8vo, pp. 76.

Mr. H. A. Tenney was born in South Hero, Grand Isle County, Vt., February 22, 1820. He is a printer, news paper publisher and lawyer, and now resides in Chicago Ill. (1880).

See Tenney Genealogy for a sketch of his life, and a history of his branch of the Tenney family, which is largely represented in Vermont.

Tenney, Rev. H. M. *The Ministry of Nature.* A Poem before the Alumni of Middlebury College, July 1, 1879. Middlebury: Register Print. 18mo, pp. 8.

Tenney, Jonathan. *Memorial of the Class* Graduated at Dartmouth College, July 27, 1843, with notes of its Septenary Meetings; also, Sketches and Tables, Biographical and Statistical, for the first twenty-five years of the Class History of all who ever were members of the Class. Prepared at the Request, and for the use of the Class, By Jonathan Tenney, Permanent Secretary. Albany, N. Y.: J. Munsell, State Street. 1869. 8vo, pp. 164.

Mr. Tenney was born in Corinth, Vt., September 14, 1817 and was graduated at Dartmouth College in 1843. By profession a teacher, but devoted much time to literary pursuits. Besides numerous contributions to newspapers and magazines, and as editor of various newspapers, he published the following works: A dozen or more school reports of the towns of Manchester, Boscawen, N. H.; several State and County educational reports; "Watch Re-

pairers' Handbook," 1868; various college and academical catalogues, reports, circulars, etc.; "Genealogical and Historical Memoirs of the Tenney Family," a work of about 500 pages. Died at Albany, N. Y., January or February, 1888.

See "Memorial of Class of 1843" for sketch of his life, pp. 108-112.

Tenney, Jesse E. *Address*, delivered before the Calhoun County Agricultural Society Fair, held at Marshall, Michigan, October 7th and 8th, 1856, by Prof. J. E. Tenney. Marshall: Seth Lewis, Printer. 1857.

J. E. Tenney was born in Orwell, Vt. He graduated from Middlebury College, 1838, and lived some time in Franklin, Vt., where he practised law and taught school. He is now (1880) a lawyer in Lansing, Mich., and has been mayor of that city. His wife is State Librarian of Michigan.

Thayer, Charles P. *The Vermont Medical Register*, for the year 1877, Containing a complete list of the Regular Physicians, Dentists and Druggists in the State, with their residences, Post Office Address, dates and source of Degrees, Laws of the State affecting these Professions, and a mass of other useful information concerning them. Edited by Charles P. Thayer, M. D. Burlington: Free Press Printing House. 1877. 12mo, pp. 120.

Thayer, Samuel White. *The Beloved Physician.* Sermon preached in the First Congregational Church, Burlington, November 19, 1882, by Rev. L. G. Ware. Burlington: F. P. Asso. 1882.

Thayer, Wm. Henry. *An Address* before the Vermont Medical College, Introductory to the Lectures of 1855, by Wm. Henry Thayer, M. D., Professor of the Principles and Practice of Medicine. Published by the Class. Woodstock, Vt.: Printed by Haskell & Palmer. 1855. 8vo, pp. 17, (3).

The Devil let loose, or a Wonderful Instance of the Goodness of God. Being the substance of a letter from a gentleman in South Carolina, to his friend in Annapolis, in Maryland. "Though the wicked join hand in hand, yet they shall not go unpunished." Proverbs xvi, 5. Printed in New York, and reprinted in Bennington, Vermont, by Anthony Haswell. 1800. 12mo, pp. 24.

The letter is signed Spectator.

The Infant School Primer. By Mrs. Teachem. Montpelier, Vt.: Published by J. S. Walton. E. P. Walton, Printer. 12mo, pp. 24. n. d. but about 1832.

Thetford. *Confession of Faith and Covenant* of the First Congregational Church in Thetford, Vt. Adopted April 4, 1831. Text. Thomas Mann. 1840. 12mo, pp. 45.

Thomas, A. C. *Analysis and Confutation* of Miller's Theory of the End of the World in 1843. By Abel C. Thomas. Montpelier, Vt.: Printed and Published by Eli Ballou. 1843. 8vo, pp. 30.

Mr. Thomas is a distinguished clergyman of the Universalist denomination, and resides in Philadelphia. (1880).

Thomas, C. A. *A Sermon* Delivered before The General Assembly of the State of Vermont. By C. A. Thomas, D. D., of Brandon, Vt. Published by order of the General Assembly. Montpelier: E. P. Walton, Printer. 1858. 8vo, pp. 15.

Mr. Thomas was ordained and settled over the Baptist church in Brandon, Vt., in 1835, and was occupying the same position as late as 1872.

Thompson, Charles M. *The Nimble Dollar*, with other stories. By Charles Miner Thompson. Contents: "The Nimble Dollar," "A Tangled Web," "A Victim of Twins," "The Reward of Heroes," "The 'Story' of Leon," "Prince Joe," "Wolcott's Mistake." Boston and New York: Houghton Mifflin & Co. 1895. 12mo, pp. 224.

Charles M. Thompson is a grandson of D. P. Thompson, the novelist.

Thompson, Daniel G. *A First Latin Book*, introductory to Caesar's Commentaries on the Gallic war. For use with Harkness', Andrews and Stoddard's, Bullion and Morris', and Allen's Grammars. By Daniel G. Thompson, Teacher in the Springfield (Mass.) High School. Chicago: S. C. Griggs and Company. 1872. 12mo, pp. vii, (2), 215.

—*The Problem of Evil.* An introduction to the Practical Sciences. By Daniel Greenleaf Thompson, author of "A System of Psychology." London: Longmans, Green and Co. 1887. 8vo, pp. viii, 281.

—*The Religious Sentiments* of the Human Mind. By Daniel Greenleaf Thompson. Author, &c. London: Longmans, Green & Co. And New York: 15 East 16th St. 1888. 8vo, pp. viii, 176.

Mr. Thompson was born in Montpelier, Vt., and now (1880) resides in New York city, in the practice of law. He is a son of the late Hon. Daniel Pierce Thompson, Vermont's distinguished novelist. Mr Thompson has written more or less for periodicals; he published articles on "Intuition and Inference," in the "Mind, A Quarterly Review of Psychology and Philosophy," published in London; his Articles occupy twenty-one pages in the July and October numbers, 1878.

THOMPSON, DANIEL P. *The Adventures* of Timothy Peacock, Esquire, or Freemasonry Practically Illustrated. Comprising A Practical History of Masonry, exhibited in a Series of amusing Adventures of a Masonic Quixote. By a Member of the Vermont Bar. Middlebury: Knapp and Jewett, Printers. 1835. 12mo, pp. 218.

This book was published anonymously, in the height of the anti-masonic excitement, apparently in ridicule of the institution of Masonry.

—*May Martin*, or the Money Diggers.

A Prize Tale, first published in the "New England Galaxy," and in book form, Montpelier: 1835. Passed through many editions. This was the first of the many popular stories by Mr. Thompson.

—*Revised Statutes*, of Vermont, 1 Vol. 1835.

See Vermont, Revised Statutes, etc.

—*The Green Mountain Boys.* A Historical Tale of the Early Settlement of Vermont. Montpelier: 1840. 12mo, pp. 364.

Numerous editions have been published in Boston and elsewhere. This work and "May Martin" were republished in England.

—*Locke Amsden*, or the Schoolmaster. Boston: 1847. 12mo, pp. 231.

—*An Address* pronounced in the Representatives' Hall, Montpelier, 24th October, 1850, before the Vermont Historical Society; By Daniel P. Thompson. Published by order of the Legislature. Burlington: Free Press Print. 1850. 8vo, pp. 22.

—*The Rangers*, or the Tory's Daughter. Boston: 1851. 12mo, pp. 329.

—*Tales* of the Green Mountains, etc. Including May Martin. Boston: 1852. 12mo pp. 380.

—*Gaut Gurley*, or the Trappers of Umbagog. Boston: 1857. 12mo, pp. 360.

—*The Shaker Lovers*, and other Tales. Burlington: 1848. 8vo.

—*The Doomed Chief*, or Two Hundred years ago. Philadelphia: 1860. 12mo, pp. 473.

—*History* of the Town of Montpelier, from the time it was first Chartered in 1781 to the year 1860. Together with Biographical Sketches of its most Noted deceased Citizens. Written in accordance with a vote of the Town in March Meeting, 1859. By D. P. Thompson. Montpelier: E. P. Walton, Printer. 1860. 8vo, pp. 312. Portrait.

—*Centeola*; And Other Tales. New York: 1864. 12mo, pp. 312.

In addition, Mr. Thompson wrote extensively for newspapers and periodicals, historical sketches, etc., which have not appeared in book form.

The latest editions of Mr. Thompson's works now in print are as follows: "May Martin," "Guardian and Ghost," "The Shaker Lovers," "Ethan Allen and the Lost Children," "The Young Sea Captain," "The Old Soldier's Story," "A New Way to Collect a Bad Debt," and an "Indian's Revenge," in one volume, pp. 380. "Locke Amsden, or the Schoolmaster," pp. 231. "The Rangers, or the Tory's Daughter," illustrating the Revolutionary History of Vermont, and the "Northern Campaign" of 1777, 2 vols. in 1. pp. 174, 155. "Green Mountain Boys," pp. 364. The above four volumes bear the imprint Nichols & Hall, Boston: 1876. 12mo.

Daniel Pierce Thompson was born at the foot of Bunker Hill, October 1, 1795; died in Montpelier, Vt., June 6, 1868. When a child he moved to Berlin, Vt., with his father and family, and settled upon a farm. He was graduated at Middlebury College, 1820; read law and, commenced practice at Montpelier, Vt., where he ever after resided. Judge Thompson held many offices of honor and trust, although devoting a large portion of his time to literary pursuits. For biographical notices see "Duyckinck's Cyclopedia of American Literature," for the best sketch of Mr. Thompson; "Drake's biographical Dictionary;" "Pearson's Graduates of Middlebury College;" "Green Mountain Freeman," at Montpelier, July 1, 1868; "Watchman," at Montpelier, June 10, 1868.

Thompson, George. *Address* of George Thompson, (M. P.) of England, to the Legislature and Citizens of Vermont, Delivered in Representatives' Hall, October 22, 1864. Montpelier: Published by P. Deming, Printed at the Freeman Steam Printing Establishment. 1864. 8vo, pp. 18.

Thompson, John C. *An Oration*, pronounced at Burlington, Vermont, July 4, 1828. By John C. Thompson. Burlington: Printed at the Free Press Office. 1828. 8vo, pp. 32.

Thompson, Oliver Dana. *A Report* of the trial of, for the murder of his wife, in Cornwall, Vt., Feb. 16, 1837. Addison County Court, June Term 1838. Middlebury: Printed at the office of the Green Mountain Argus. 1839. 8vo, pp. 24.

THOMPSON, ZADOCK. *A Gazetteer* of the State of Vermont; containing a Brief General View of the State, A Historical and Topographical Description of all the Counties, Towns, Rivers, &c. Together with a Map and several other Engravings. By Zadock Thompson, A. B. Montpelier: Published by E. P. Walton and the Author. E. P. Walton, Printer. 1824. 12mo, pp. 310, (2.)

—*History* of the State of Vermont, from its earliest settlement to the close of the year 1832. By Zadock Thompson, A. M., Author of the Gazetteer of Vermont. Burlington: Edward Smith. 1833. 18mo, pp. 252.

Another Edition; Burlington; Smith & Harrington. 1836. 18mo, pp. 253.

—*History of* Vermont, Natural, Civil and Statistical, In Three parts, with a new Map of the State, and 200 Engravings. By Zadock Thompson. Burlington : Published for the Author by Chauncey Goodrich. 1842. 8vo, pp. (4.) 224, 224, 200, (4.)

In later editions the Appendix is usually found bound with this work.

—*Appendix to* the History of Vermont, Natural, Civil and Statistical. 1853. By Zadock Thompson. Burlington : Published by the Author. Stacy & Jameson, Printers. 1853. 8vo, pp. 63, (1,) map.

—*Natural History* of Vermont. An Address Delivered at Boston, before the Boston Society of Natural History, June, 1850. By Zadock Thompson. Burlington : Published by Chauncey Goodrich. 1850. 8vo, pp. 32.

—*History of* the State of Vermont ; for the use of Families and Schools. By Zadock Thompson, Author of Gazetteer of Vermont, Geography of Vermont for Children, &c., &c. Burlington : Smith & Company. 1858. 12mo, pp. 252.

—*Geography and Geology* of Vermont, with State and County Outline Maps. For the use of Schools and Families. By Zadock Thompson. Burlington : Published by the Author. Chauncey Goodrich, Printer. 1848. 12mo, pp. 218, (1.)

—*The Youth's* Assistant in Practical Arithmetick. Designed for the use of Schools in the United States. By Zadock Thompson, A. B. Author of the Gazetteer of the State of Vermont. Woodstock : Printed by David Watson. 1825. 8vo, pp. 160.

First Edition.

—*The Youth's* Assistant in Theoretick and Practical Arithmetick. Designed for the use of Schools in the United States. By Zadock Thompson, A. M. Author of the Gazetteer of the State of Vermont. Second Edition with Corrections and Additions. Woodstock, Vt.: Printed and sold by David Watson.

Another edition. Burlington, Vt. Printed by E. & T. Mills. 1828. 12mo, pp. 58.

—*Thompson's New* Arithmetic. Improved Edition. Woodstock, Vt.: Printed by David Watson. 1828. 12mo, pp. 216.

—*Thompson's New* Arithmetic. The Youth's Assistant in Theoretic and Practical Arithmetic. Designed for the use of schools in the United States. By Zadock Thompson, A. M. Author of the Gazetteer of Vermont. Improved Edition. Woodstock, Vt.: Printed by David Watson. 1829. 12mo, pp. 216.

—*The Youth's* Assistant in Theoretic and Practical Arithmetic ; Designed for the use of Schools in the United States. By Zadock Thompson. A. M. Author &c. Tenth Edition. Burlington : Vernon Harrington. 1837. 12mo, pp. 168.

—*Geography and History* of Lower Canada. Designed for the use of Schools. By Zadock Thompson, A. M. Late Preceptor of Charleston Academy. Stanstead and Sherbrooke, L. C. : Published by Walton & Gaylord. 1835. 12mo, pp. 110. Map.

—*First Book* of Geography, for Vermont Children. By Zadock Thompson. Burlington : C. Goodrich, Printer. 1849. 18mo, pp. 74.

—*Journal of* a Trip to London, Paris, and the Great Exhibition, in 1851. By Zadock Thompson. Burlington : Published by Nichols & Warren. George J. Stacy, Printer. 1852. 12mo, pp. 144.

—*Guide to* Lake George, Lake Champlain, Montreal and Quebec, with Maps, Tables of Distances and Routes from Albany, Burlington, Montreal, &c. Burlington : 1845. 24mo, pp. 48. Price 40 cts.

Title from Gowans.

—*Northern Guide.* Lake George, Lake Champlain, Montreal and Quebec, Green and White Mountains, and Willoughby Lake, with Maps and Tables of Distances. By Zadock Thompson, Author of History and Gazetteer of Vermont. Published by S. B. Nichols. Burlington : Stacy and Jameson. 1854. 18mo, pp. 56.

—*Northern Guide.* Lake George, Lake Champlain, Montreal and Quebec, Green and White Mountains, and Willoughby Lake, with Maps and Tables of Distances. By Z. Thompson. Author of History and Gazetteer of Vermont. Burlington : Published by S. B. Nichols. 1857. 18mo, pp. 45.

See Almanacs, Green Mountain Repository; and Iris. Mr. Thompson was connected with Walton's Register and other Almanacs, 1823, until his death.

Mr. Thompson was born in Bridgewater, Vt., May 29, 1796, and died at Burlington, January 19, 1856. For sketches of his life, see Drake's Biographical Dictionary; Geology, Preliminary Report, by Augustus Young, 1856, Obituary of Prof. Thompson, pp. 37-47.

Mr. Thompson devoted the entire period of his life to the interests and welfare of his native State, and his labors are more gratefully appreciated as time passes. The best monument to his memory is his works. The people of Vermont have not publicly manifested that gratitude to the memory of Mr. Thompson which his labors merit ; even in the history of Burlington, in which town Mr. Thompson passed the larger part of his life, as published in Miss Hemenway's Gazetteer, less than one page is devoted to him.

We publish at the expense of the State glowing eulogies upon our ephemeral politicians, such as Members of Congress, etc., and upon our military heroes, as we call them, and yet the services of such men as Mr. Thompson will endure in the grateful memory of succeeding generations long after the other classes named shall have passed into oblivion, and be remembered no more.

Thomson, Andrew. *Sermons on Infidelity.* By Andrew Thomson, D. D., Minister of St. George's, Edinburgh. First American Edition, with a preliminary Essay. Windsor, Vt.: Richards and Tracy. New York : Jonathan Leavitt. 1833. 16mo, pp. 213.

Thomson, Ignatius. *The Patriot's Monitor,* for Vermont : Designed to impress and perpetuate the first principles of the Revolution on the minds of Youth ; Together with some Pieces Important and Interesting, Adapted for the use of Schools. By Ignatius Thomson. Motto. · Randolph, Ver.: Printed by Sereno Wright. 1810. 12mo, pp. 227, (1.)

—*Monitor* for New Hampshire. Same Imprint, and date.

—*An Oration,* delivered at Pomfret, July 4th, 1809 ; Commemorating the Day that gave our Nation Birth. By Ignatius Thomson. Windsor : Printed by Farnsworth & Churchill. 8vo, pp. 22.

Mr. Thomson was pastor of a Congregational church in Pomfret, Vt., from 1805 to 1811.

Thomson, James Bates, LL. D.

Mr. Thomson was a native of Springfield, Vt.; graduated at Yale College, 1834; has published: "School Algebra and Key," New Haven, Ct.: 1843, 12mo; "Key to Legendre's Geometry," 1844, 12mo; "Practical Arithmetic," New York: 1845, 12mo, and Key; "Mental Arithmetic," 1846, 16mo; "Higher Arithmetic and Key," 1847, 12mo; "Table Book," 1848, 16mo; "Rudiments of Arithmetic," 1852, 12mo; "Arithmetical Analysis," 1854, 12mo; "Practical Surveying," 8vo. Allibone.

Trübner's Guide to American Literature, ed. 1859. lxxxvi., lxxxix., says of Mr. Thomson's works: "Ivison and Phinney, of New York, in the first six months of 1855 sold 38,500 of Mr. Thomson's books, and were paying him $10,000 per annum, as his share of the profits arising from his Arithmetical Books." * * "They circulated 100,000 copies of his Arithmetical works yearly."

Thomson, S. *New Guide to Health ;* or Botanic Family Physician. Containing A Complete System of Practice, upon a plan entirely new, with a description of the vegetables made use of, and directions for preparing and administering them to cure disease. To which is added A Description of Several Cases of Disease attended by the Author, with the mode of Treatment and Cure. By Samuel Thomson. Montpelier : Printed for the Publisher. 1851. 12mo, pp. 122.

Several editions,—the first, Boston, 1822.

Mr. Thomson was the founder of the Thomsonian system of medical practice.

Thorn, Leonard C. *Our Mountain Vale,* a Poem, delivered before the Vergennes Lyceum. By Leonard C. Thorn. Burlington : 1854. 8vo, pp. 24.

Thoughts on the Divine Goodness, Relative to the Government of Moral Agents, particularly displayed in future Rewards and Punishments. Translated from the French of Ferdinand Oliver Petitpierre, formerly Minister of Chau-defond. Montpelier : Printed by Geo. W. Hill, Patriot Office. 1828. 12mo, pp. 148.

Thrall, Samuel R. *A Sermon,* preached at Wells River, Vt., March 28, 1847, being a valedictory address, by Samuel R. Thrall, upon resigning his pastoral relation to the people. Newbury, Vt.: Printed by L. J. McIndoe. 1847. 8vo, pp. 16.

Dr. Thrall was a native of Rutland.

Thresher, Leonard. *The Family Physician,* Nurse's Guide, and Farmer's Horse and Cattle Doctor, in Three Parts. By Dr. Leonard Thresher. Part First Gives the Causes, Symptoms and Treatment of all diseases incident to Mankind. Part Second Gives the Causes, Symptoms and Treatment of all diseases of the Horse, Neat Cattle and Sheep, and the Management of Hens, Turkeys, Ducks, Geese and Bees. Part Third. Materia Medica and the Preparation of Medicines. Montpelier : Argus and Patriot Job Printing House. 1781. 8vo, pp. 406.

—*The Ladies'* Private Medical Guide : With an Appendix of Recipes, etc. By Leonard Thresher. Montpelier: Journal Steam Printing Establishment. 1875. 12mo, pp. 104.

—*A Thrilling Tale.* Running a Time Table. A Brakeman's Story. Published by Henry & Johnson, Burlington, Vermont. 1873. 8vo, pp. 16.

Filled out with patent medicine advertisements.

Ticknor, Luther, M. D. *Annual Address* before the Medical Institute, Yale College, 1841. 8vo.

Brother of Caleb Ticknor, M. D., and a native of Jericho, Vt.; died at Salisbury, Conn., in 1846, aged 55. Obituary in "New York Journal of Medicine," May, 1846.

TODD, JOHN. *Religious Teachers Tested :* A Sermon Delivered at the Dedication of the Union Meeting House, in Groton, Massachusetts, January 4, 1827. By John Todd. Published by the Union Church. Cambridge : Published by Hilliard & Brown. 1827. 8vo, pp. 46.

—*An Address,* Delivered in the Chapel of Amherst College before the Alexandrian Society, the Tuesday preceding Commencement, August 26, 1828. By John Todd, A. M., Pastor of the Union Church in Groton, Mass. Amherst: J. S. & C. Adams, Printers. 1828. 8vo, pp. 31.

—*An Address* Delivered in the Chapel of Amherst College, Sabbath Evening, Aug. 25, 1833. Delivered and Published at the Request of the Society of Inquiry. By Rev. John Todd, Pastor of the Edwards Church, Northampton. Amherst : J. S. & C. Adams, Printers. 1833. 8vo, pp. 22.

—*The Pulpit*—Its Influence upon Society. A Sermon Delivered at the Dedication of the Edwards Church, in Northampton, Mass., December 25, 1833. By Rev. John Todd, Pastor of the Edwards Church. Northampton : J. H. Butler. 1834. 12mo. pp. 72.

—*Principles and* Results of Congregationalism. A Sermon Delivered at the Dedication of the House of Worship Erected by the First Congregational Church in Philadelphia, November 11, 1837. By Rev. John Todd, Pastor of the First Congregational Church. Philadelphia : William Marshall & Co. 1837. 8vo, pp. 64.

—*New England :* Her Character and Destiny. An Address, Delivered before the Societies of Religious Inquiry in Amherst College and the University of Vermont, at their Anniversaries, 1841. By Rev. John Todd. Published by the Societies. Northampton : J. H. Butler. 1841. 8vo, pp. 39.

—*History of* the Medium of Preserving and Communicating Knowledge. A Lecture Delivered before the Young Men's Society of Pittsfield, September 13, 1842. By John Todd. Pittsfield : E. P. Little. 1842. 8vo, pp. 32.

—*The Pulpit Tested.* A Sermon Delivered at the Centennial Anniversary of the Congregational Church in Great Barrington, Dec. 23, 1843. By John Todd. Pittsfield : E. P. Little. 1844. 16mo, pp. 67.

—*We Know Not* What We Shall Be. A Sermon Delivered at Lenox, January 9, 1846, on the occasion of the funeral of Samuel Shepard, D. D. By John Todd. Pittsfield, Mass. : Published by E. Warden. 1846. 8vo, pp. 29.

—*Colleges Essential* to the Church of God. Plain Letters addressed to a Parishioner in behalf of the Society for the Promotion of Collegiate and Theological Education at the West. By John Todd, D. D. New York : Printed by Leavitt, Trow & Company, 33 Ann Street. 1848. 8vo, pp. 32.

—*A Great Man Fallen :* A Sermon delivered at the funeral of Lemuel Pomeroy, Esq., in Pittsfield, August 28, 1849, by John Todd, D. D.

(Printed, not published, for the family of the deceased.) Pittsfield: Axtel, Bull and Marsh, Printers. 1850. 8vo, pp. 33.

—*Tendencies of Intellectual Preaching.* A Sermon, delivered in the Brattle Street Church, Boston, May 26, 1853, before the General Convention of Congregational Ministers of Massachusetts. By John Todd, D. D., Pastor of the First Congregational Church in Pittsfield. Northampton: Press of Hopkins, Bridgman & Co. 1853. 8vo, pp. 33.

The Good never die: A Sermon, delivered at Pittsfield, April 8, 1861, at the Funeral of Rev. Heman Humphrey, D. D., by John Todd. Pittsfield: Henry Chickering, Printer. 1861. 8vo, pp. 26.

—*Missions* Created and Sustained by Prophecy. A Sermon before the American Board of Commissioners for Foreign Missions, at their meeting in Pittsburgh, Penn., Oct. 5, 1869. By Rev. John Todd, D. D., Pastor of the First Church, Pittsfield, Mass. Boston: Press of T. R. Marvin & Son, 131 Congress Street. 1869. 8vo, pp. 26.

—*John Todd.* The Story of his Life told by himself. Compiled and edited by John E. Todd, Pastor of the Church of the Redeemer, New Haven, Conn. New York: Harper and Brothers, Publishers, Franklin Square. 1876. 8vo, pp. 529.

Rev. Dr. Todd was born in Rutland, Vt., October 9, 1809; died at Pittsfield, Mass, August 23, 1873. He was graduated at Yale College, 1822, and at Andover Seminary 1826; was pastor of a Congregational church at Groton, Mass., 1827-1833; at Northampton 1833-36; at Philadelphia 1836-42; and at Pittsfield, Mass., 1842, until near the time of his death. He was a principal founder of Mt. Holyoke Seminary, but his fame rests largely upon his popularity as an author. It is said that his works have had a larger circulation than those of any other American author upon kindred subjects. The following is a list of his works, as we find it in Allibone; "Lectures to Children," Northampton,1834.16mo; was translated into French, German and Greek; many American and English editions were printed, of which over one hundred thousand copies were sold previous to 1859; "A Second Series of the Same," Northampton: 1858. Many English and American editions. "Student's Manual;" Northampton: 1835. 12mo; sale to 1864, United States, 20,000, and in England 120,000 copies, and many editions have been sold since that date. "Index Rerum;" Northampton: 1836. 4to; to September, 1864, 33 editions in the United States, and many in England had been published. "Sabbath School Teacher;" Northampton: 1836. 12mo; many editions, both in England and the United States. "Truth Made Simple;" Northampton: 1819. 16mo; many editions in the United States and England. "Great Cities:" Northampton: 1841. 18mo; several editions in the United States, and also in England. "Lost Sister of Wyoming; Northampton; 1841. 18mo; several editions in England and the United States. "Young Man;" Northampton: 1843. 18mo; many editions in both countries. "Simple Sketches;" Pittsfield: 1843. 2 vols. Three editions in England prior to 1856. "Stories Illustrating the Shorter Catechism;" Northampton: 1850-51. 2 vols. 18mo. "Summer Gleanings," 1852. 18mo; London: 1853. 12mo. "Daughter at School;" Northampton: 1853. 12mo; several editions in the United States and England. "Questions on the Lives of the Patriarchs; Northampton: 1855. 18mo; fifteen editions the first year in the United States, and several in England. "Questions on the Life of Moses;" Northampton; 18mo; new edition, Pittsfield: 1864. "Questions on the Books of Joshua and Judges;" 1863. "The Angel of the Iceberg and other Stories;" 1859. 18mo; several editions in the United States and England. "The Bible Companion;" Philadelphia: 18mo, Boston: 18mo. "Future Punishment;" New York; 1863. 12mo. "Mountain Gems;" Boston; 1864. 4 vols. 16mo, containing his contributions to the Sunday School Times for 1863. "The Water Dove, and other Gems;" Edinburgh: 1868. 18mo. "Sketches and Incidents, or Summer Gleanings;" 1866.

12mo. "Nuts for Boys to Crack;" New York: 1866. sqr. 12mo. "Polished Diamonds;" Boston: 1866. 16mo. "Hints and Thoughts for Christians;" New York: 1867. sqr. 12 mo. "Serpents in the Dove's Nest;" Boston: 1867. 18mo, pp. 28. "Woman's Rights;" 1867. 18mo, pp. 27. This elicited "Woman's Wrongs; a Counter-Irritant," By Gail Hamilton, (Abigail Dodge) 1868. "Mountain Flowers;" Northampton; 1869. 16mo. "The Sunset Land; or the Great Pacific Slope." Boston: 1869. 16mo. London: 1870. 12mo. Collective and complete editions, socalled, of Dr. Todd's works were published in England in 1841, '44, '50, '53, '58, '61, '63, '64 and 1868.

Dr. Todd was also a contributor to Sartain's and Graham's magazines and other periodicals. He published "The Life of Thomas Scott, The Biblical Commentator, written for the Young." Northampton: 1865. 18mo; and he edited in 1850 "Field's Scripture Illustrated, by Interesting Facts." Dr. Todd published orations, sermons and addresses in addition to the above list.

Todd, Timothy. *An Oration* Delivered at East Guilford, in Connecticut, the Fourth of July, 1801. On the Anniversary of American Independence. By Timothy Todd. Published at the request of a numerous and respectable circle of acquaintance, in Connecticut and Vermont, Rutland: Herald Office. Printed by William Fay. 12mo, pp. 8.

Topsham. *Annual Report* of the Town of Topsham, for the year ending March 1, 1882. Montpelier: Argus and Patriot print. 1882. 8vo, pp. 8.

Torrey, Rev. Henry Augustus Pearson. *The Philosophy* of Descartes, in extracts from his writings, selected and translated by Henry A. P. Torrey, A. M., Marsh Professor of Philosophy in the University of Vermont. New York: Henry Holt & Co. 1892. 16mo, pp. xii. 351.

The above is one of the Holt series of modern philosophers.

Torrey, Joseph. *A Discourse* on the importance to young men to Mental Cultivation. By Joseph Torrey, Professor of Languages in the University of Vermont. Salem: Printed by Warwick Palfray, Jun. 1833. 8vo, pp. 20.

—*Remains of the Rev. James Marsh, D. D.,* Containing his Metaphysical and Theological writings, with Life. By Professor Joseph Torrey. Boston: 1843. Second Edition. Burlington: 1845. 8vo, pp. 642.

—*The Discovery* and Occupation of Lake Champlain. A paper read before the Vermont Historical Society, at its 21st Annual Session, at Montpelier, October 16th, 1860, by Rev. Joseph Torrey, D. D. 8vo, pp. 14.

—*Select Sermons* of the Rev. Worthington Smith, D. D., late President of the University of Vermont. With a Memoir of his Life, by Rev. Joseph Torrey, D. D., Professor of Intellectual and Moral Philosophy. Andover: Warren F. Draper. Boston: Gould and Lincoln; Crosby, Nichols, Lee & Co. New York: John Wiley. Philadelphia: Smith, English & Co. 1861. 8vo, pp. 368.

—*A Theory of Fine Art.* By Joseph Torrey, late Professor of Moral and Intellectual Philosophy in the University of Vermont. New York: Scribner, Armstrong & Co. 1874. 12mo, pp. 290.

Published after the author's death.

—*Services in Remembrance* of Rev. Joseph Torrey, D. D., and of George Wyllys Benedict, LL. D., Professors in the University of Vermont. [n. p. n. d.] 8vo, pp. 66.

—*General History* of the Christian Religion and Church, from the German of Dr. Augustus Neander. Translated from the second and improved edition by Joseph Torrey, Professor of Moral and Intellectual Philosophy in the University of Vermont. Volume I, comprising the first great division of the History. Boston: Crocker & Brewster. London: Wiley & Putnam. 1847. 8vo, pp. xxiii. 740. Vol. II, 1848, pp. xxxix, 768. Vol. III, 1850, pp. xxx, 626. Vol. IV, 1851, pp. xxviii, 651. Vol. V, 1854.

A revised edition of Prof. Torrey's translation of this great work, in 5 vols. was brought out in 1871, which has had many American editions.

Torrey, Mary C. *America.* A Dramatic Poem. New York: Anson D. F. Randolph. 1863. 12mo, pp. 110.

Published anonymously.

—*Index* to Neander's General History of the Christian Religion and Church. Boston: Houghton, Mifflin & Co. 1881. 8vo, pp. 239.

Miss Torrey is a daughter of Prof. Joseph Torrey.

Professor Torrey was born in Rowley, Mass., February 2, 1797, and died in Burlington, Vt., November 26, 1867. He was graduated at Dartmouth College, 1816; at Andover, 1819; was pastor of the Congregational church in Royalton, Vt., 1824-1827; Professor in the University of Vermont, 1827, until his decease, and President of the same, 1863-1865.

Torrey, Susanna.

See Trial for Libel, Torrey *vs.* Field.

The Touchstone, or A Humble, modest inquiry into the nature of Religious Intolerance. Whether it ever existed? Whether those who practice it are conscious of it? Whether it is found in these regions? And the way to detect it in ourselves. By A Member of the Berean Society. Motto. Brattleborough, Vt.: Published by Simeon Ide. 1817. 16mo, pp 36, and some wanting at the end.

Townsend, W. W. *The Dairyman's Manual;* Containing some of the most important processes from the best sources for making Butter and Cheese. With an Essay on Mechanical Powers, as applied to domestic uses. By William W. Townsend. Illustrated by wood engravings. Vergennes: Rufus W. Griswold, Printer. 1830. 24mo, pp. 116, (6.)

Townshend. *History of.*

See Phelps, James H.

—*Articles of Faith,* and form of Covenant, adopted by the Congregational Church of Christ, in Townshend, Vt., April 25, 1828. With Scripture Proofs and Illustrations, to which is added Resolutions of President Edwards. Bellows Falls: Printed by James I. Cutler & Co. 1828. 12mo, pp. 12.

Tracy, Andrew. *Biographical Sketch of.*

See French, Warren C.

Tracy, E. C. *Memoir* of the Life of Jeremiah Evarts, Esq., late Corresponding Secretary of the American Board of Commissioners for Foreign Missions. By E. C. Tracy. Boston: Published by Crocker and Brewster. 1845. 8vo, pp. 448.

See Evarts, J.

Rev. Ebenezer Carter Tracy was born in Hartford, Vt., June 10, 1796, and died at Windsor, Vt., May 15, 1862. He was graduated at Dartmouth College, 1819; at Andover Seminary, 1822; was tutor at Dartmouth College, 1823-5; edited the "Vermont Chronicle" from 1826 to 1828, and from 1834 to his decease. He was for short periods editorially connected with the "New York Journal of Commerce," "Journal of Humanity," and the "Boston Recorder."

Tracy, Ira.

Mr. Tracy was born in Hartford, Vt., January 15, 1806; died at Bloomington, Wis., November 10, 1875. He was graduated at Dartmouth, 1829 and at Andover, 1832; he was a missionary to China and India, 1834-41; then preached in Ohio, Wisconsin and Minnesota, 1846-61, when he retired to a farm at Bloomington, where he resided until his death. He published "Duty to the Heathen," "Errors of Swedenborg," "The Mode of Baptism," and "The Christian's Inheritance." See "Congregational Quarterly," Vol. 18, p. 434, for sketch of his life.

Tracy, Joseph, D. D. *Christian Liberty.* A Sermon at the Ordination of the Rev. Daniel Wild, as Pastor of the Congregational Church in Brookfield, Vt., July 1, 1830. By Rev. Joseph Tracy. Published by Request of the Church and Society, and of the Ordaining Council. Windsor: Printed at the Chronicle Press, by John C. Allen. 1830. 8vo, pp. 16.

—*Idolatry Misrepresents* the Deity. A Sermon; Delivered at the Ordination of Rev. Ira Tracy, at Hartford, Vt., Oct. 28, 1832. By Joseph Tracy. Published by Request. Windsor, Vt.: Richards and Tracy, Publishers. 1833. 8vo, pp. 16.

—*Natural Equality.* A Sermon before the Vermont Colonization Society, at Montpelier, October 17, 1833. By Joseph Tracy. Windsor, Vt.: Chronicle Press. MDCCCXXXIII. 8vo, pp. 24.

—*An Address* before the Society for Religious Inquiry in the University of Vermont, August 6, 1839. By Rev. Joseph Tracy. Boston: Published by Crocker & Brewster. 1839. 8vo, pp. 28.

—*Three Last Things;* Resurrection, Judgment, and Final Retribution. Boston: 1839. 18mo, pp. 104.

—*The Great Awakening.* A History of the Revival of Religion in the time of Edwards and Whitefield. By Joseph Tracy. Sixth Edition. Boston: Congregational Board of Publication. 1857. 12mo, pp. xx, 483.

The first edition was published in 1841.

—*History* of the American Board of Commissioners for Foreign Missions. 1842. Royal 8vo; another edition was published the same year.

—*Refutation of Charges* against the Sandwich Island Missionaries. Boston. 1844.

—*Essay on Christian Philosophy,* Originally Published in the Vermont Chronicle. Andover: Printed by William H. Wardwell. 1848. 8vo, pp. 42, (1).

—*Discourse Commemorative* of Rev. John Wheeler.

See University of Vermont, 1864.

—*A Memorial* of the Semi-Centennial Anniversary of the American Colonization Society, Celebrated at Washington, January 15, 1867.

Edited by Mr. Tracy.

Contributor to Memorial Volume A. B. C. F. M., 1862. Co-editor, with the Rev. Doctor H. B. Smith, of the American Theological Review, started in 1859.

Mr. Tracy was born in Hartford, Vt., November 3, 1794; was graduated at Dartmouth College, 1814, and was pastor of Congregational churches in Thetford and West Fairlee, Vt., June 26, 1821, to 1829. He edited the Vermont Chronicle five years, the Boston Recorder one year, and afterwards became Secretary of the Colonization Society at Boston. He died at Beverly, Mass., March 24, 1874. Rev. E. C. and Ira Tracy were his brothers.

Treaties. *The Several Treaties* which have been negotiated and signed between the United States of America and Great Britain, since the year 1782. Windsor, Vt.: Printed by Alden Spooner. 1815. 8vo, pp. 91.

Treatises. *A Treatise on Diseases*, with a collection of valuable Receipts for Dyeing, &c. This Pamphlet will be found to contain much valuable information and should be laid up for future reference in cases of emergency. Enosburgh Falls, Vermont: Published by B. J. Kendall, M. D. 12mo, pp. 82.

—*A Treatise* on Christian Baptism and open Communion. Entered according to act of Congress, in the year 1831, by Phineas Randall, in the Clerk's office of the District Court of Vermont. Preface dated August, 1831. 12mo, pp. 12.

—*A Treatise* on the Law and the Gospel. Written by a Farmer. Hanover, N. H.: Printed by Moses Davis. For the Author. 1807. pp. 25.
The author's name is not given, but at the close of the paper he signs himself D——S, B——d, Vermont, April 10, 1807.

TRIALS, OPINIONS, &c.
Trial for Libel. Susanna Torrey, Plaintiff, R. M. Field, Defendant. E. C. Church, Printer. n. p. n. d. 8vo, pp. 38.
This cause came on for trial by jury at Woodstock, on Friday the 28th day of November, 1835, before Judges Collamer, Porter and Briggs. The Plaintiff demanded ten thousand dollars damages, (and the jury gave her one dollar) for a libel on her character, published in the Bellows Falls Intelligencer, on the 17th and 24th days of May, 1834.
A scandal case in which a large number of very good people were mixed up, and created much excitement in its day.

—*The Trial of Cyrus B. Dean,* for the murder of Jonathan Ormsby and Asa Marsh, before the Supreme Court of Judicature of the State of Vermont, at their Special Sessions, begun and holden at Burlington, Chittenden County, on the 23d of August, A. D. 1808. Revised and corrected from the minutes of the Judges. Copyright secured. Burlington: Printed by Samuel Mills. Sold at his Bookstore; by Mills and White, Middlebury, and by the principal Booksellers in the United States. 1808. 8vo, pp. 48.
The prisoner was convicted, and sentenced to be executed on the 28th day of October, 1808, which sentence was carried into execution.
See Tyler, Royall.

—*Trial and Defense of Erastus Montague.* 1835. 12mo, pp. 60.
Relates to a Methodist church difficulty in Bennington in 1834-5.

—*Argument of Matt. H. Carpenter* in the McCardle Case, Washington, D. C.
See Carpenter, M. H.

—*Opinion of the Judges* of the Supreme Court of Vermont, on the Constitutionality of "An Act Providing for Soldiers Voting." St. Albans: Whiting and Davis, Steam Printers. 8vo, pp. 26.

—*State of Vermont.* Supreme Court. Caledonia, Vt., 1846. Smith, Treasurer of the Associate Congregation of Ryegate vs. John Nelson, Adm'r de bonis non, with the will annexed, of William Nelson, deceased. Williams, Chief Justice, delivered the Opinion of the Court. 12mo, pp. 46.

—*In Chancery.* General Term of Supreme Court. October, 1872. From Washington County. Moses Holden, Adm'r of Jesse Johnson, vs. Charles Reed, Adm'r of Ruth Johnson. Brief for Defendant. Heaton and Reed, Randall and Durant, Solicitors. 8vo, pp. 4.

—*In Chancery.* Vermont Copper Mining Co. vs. Henry Barnard. Orange County Court, January Term, 1866. R. Farnham, L. B. Peck, Solicitors. Montpelier: Printed at the Freeman Steam Printing Establishment. 1865. 8vo, pp. 22.

—*Kentucky Jurisprudence.* A History of the Trial of Miss Delia A. Webster. At Lexington, Kentucky, Dec'r 17-21, 1844, before the Hon. Richard Buckner, On a charge of aiding slaves to escape from that Commonwealth, with Miscellaneous Remarks, including her views on American Slavery. Written by Herself. Motto. Vergennes: E. W. Blaisdell, Printer. 1845. 12mo, pp. 84.
Miss Webster was a native of Vergennes.

—*Trial and Execution* of John Ward, for the murder of Mrs. Griswold. Burlington: 1868. 12mo, pp. 138.

—*A Defence of a Suit now Pending* between Ebenezer Smith, Plaintiff, and Peabody Utley, Defendant; Together with affidavits and witnesses. (Copyright Secured.) Printed in the year of our Lord, 1819.
A Case in Windham County.

—*Supreme Court.* General Term, 1859. Hart, Leslie & Warren, Against The Farmers and Mechanics Bank, Lane, Corning, and Heirs of Cook and John Peck. Defendants' Points. Roberts & Chittenden, G. F. Edmunds, Counsel for Defendants. Burlington: Daily Times Book and Job Printing Establishment. 1859. 8vo, pp. 14.

—*In the Supreme Court* of the State of California. July Term, 1857. Robert McMillan, appellant, vs. Thomas G. Richards, et. als., Respondents. Brief for Appellant, by Solomon Heydenfeldt, and Shafter, Park & Shafter, Attorneys. Sterett, printer, 145 Clay Street. 8vo, pp. 9.

—*The same,* same party vs. John G. Hyatt, Garrett N. Vischer, et als. Brief of same Attorneys. Imprint the same. 8vo, pp. 4.

See Bates, A. L., Trial for Murder in 1838; Bell, Rev. B., Ecclesiastical trial, 1797; Brookfield, Court Martial, 1822; Boorn, Stephen and Jesse, Trial for Murder; Giddings, F. C.; Allen, Heman; Peake, Rebecca, Trial for Murder, 1835; Anthony, James, Trial for the murder of Joseph Greene, 1814; Phair, John P.; Young vs. Chipman; Murray, G. L., Church trial; Thompson, O. D., for murder. Pond, S., for murder.

Truair, John. *A Sermon,* delivered at Montpelier, Lord's day Evening, March 7, 1813, by Rev. John Truair, Pastor of the Congregational Church in Cambridge. Montpelier, Vt.: Walton & Goss. 1813. 8vo, pp. 20.

—*The Alarm Trumpet.* A Discourse, delivered at Berkshire, (Vt.) Sept. 9, 1813, the day of the National Fast, appointed by the President, on account of the War. By John Truair, late Pastor of the Church in Cambridge, Vt. Montpelier, Vt.: Walton & Goss. 1813. 8vo, pp. 27.

Trumbull, James Hammond. *Origin of the Expedition Against Ticonderoga.* 1869. 8vo, pp. 15.

Tufts, James. *A Sermon,* delivered at Townshend, (Vt.) February 4, 1821. On the occasion of the Death of the Rev. Luke Whitcomb, late Pastor of the Church in that place, who died in Savannah, (Geo.) January 2, 1821. By James Tufts, Pastor of the Church in Wardsborough, Vt. Motto. Brattleborough : Printed by Holbrook & Fessenden. 1821. 8vo, pp. 59.

Contains a biographical sketch of Mr. Whitcomb, by Rev. Hosea Beckley, pastor at Dummerston, Vt.

Tunbridge. *Statement* of the Accounts of the Town of Tunbridge, Feb. 20, 1866. Windsor : Printed at the Vermont Journal Office. 1866. 12mo, pp. 8.

Continued.

—*By-Laws* of Tunbridge Light Infantry. Northfield : A. Hoffman, Printer. 1859. 18mo, pp. 12.

Tupper, Frederick, Jr. *Anglo-Saxon Daeg Mael.* Dissertation presented to the Board of University Studies of the Johns Hopkins University for the Degree of Doctor of Philosophy, by Frederick Tupper, Jr., Professor of Rhetoric and English Literature in the University of Vermont. Baltimore : The Modern Languages Association of America. 1895. 8vo, pp. VII, 132.

Turner, Edward. *Faith and Reason.* A Discourse, Delivered in the First Congregational Church, Burlington, Vt., Sunday, July 18, 1847, By Edward Turner. Published by request. Burlington : S. Fletcher, Printer. 1847. 8vo, pp. 15.

Tutherly, Herbert Everett. *Notes upon Military Science and Tactics,* by H. E. Tutherly, Captain First U. S. Cavalry, Professor of Military Science in the University of Vermont, and on duty with the Vermont National Guard. Copyright reserved. Burlington: 1896. 8vo, pp. 16.

—*Elementary Treatise* on Military Science and the Art of War. By Herbert E. Tutherly, Captain 1st U. S. Cavalry, Professor of Military Science and Tactics at the University of Vermont, and on duty with the Vermont National Guard. Part I. Burlington: Free Press Association, 1897, large 8vo, pp. 160 (3).

Tuttle, Calvin. *Family Record* of Calvin Tuttle and his Wife, Ruth Ann Miner, their Ancestors and Descendants. Collected and compiled by Emmett George Tuttle, East Dorset, Vt., 1871. Rutland : Tuttle & Co., Printers. 1871. 8vo, pp. 26.

Tuttle, George F. *The Descendants* of William and Elizabeth Tuttle, with numerous biographical notes and sketches, by George F. Tuttle. Rutland : Tuttle & Co. 1883. 8vo, pp. 754.

Tyler, Edward Royall. *Holiness Preferable to Sin* : A Sermon. By Edward R. Tyler, Pastor of the South Church, Middletown, Conn. New Haven : Printed by Baldwin & Treadway. 1829. 8vo, pp. 37.

—*Lectures on* Future Punishment. By Edward R. Tyler, Pastor of the South Church, Middletown, Conn. Texts. Middletown, Conn.: Printed by Parmalee & Greenfield. 1829. 12mo, pp. 180.

—*The Doctrine* of Election. A Sermon. By Edward R. Tyler, Pastor of the South Church, Middletown, Conn. Middletown : Published by Edwin Hunt. New Haven : Baldwin and Treadway, Printers. 1831. 8vo, pp. 28.

—*The Congregational Catechism,* containing a General Survey of the Organization, Government and Discipline of Christian Churches. New Haven : Published by A. H. Maltby. 1844. 12mo, pp. 137.

He was a son of Judge Royall Tyler, born in Guilford, Vt., August 3, 1800; died September 28, 1848; was graduated at Yale, 1825; at New Haven Theological Seminary 1827; was settled over the Congregational church in Middletown, Ct., the same year, where he continued until 1832 ; then at Colbrook, Ct., two years, when he engaged in anti-slavery work; then edited the Congregational Observer, and finally established the "New Englander," which he edited until his death.

Also a Sermon, "Slavery a Sin, *per se.*"

See Obituary in "New Englander," vol. vi, p. 603, by Rev. L. Bacon.

Tyler, George P. *The Successful Life.* A Discourse on the Death of President Lincoln, delivered April 19, 1865, at the Center Church, Brattleboro, by the Pastor, Rev. G. P. Tyler. Published by request. Brattleboro : Printed at the Vermont Record Office. 1865. 8vo, pp. 12.

Rev. Mr. Tyler was a Congregational minister, born in Brattleboro, Dec. 10, 1809, and was for some time a pastor at Brattleboro, and later resided in Lausingburgh, N. Y., where he died in 1895. He was a son of Judge Royall Tyler. While residing at Brattleboro he edited a revised edition of the "Encyclopedia of Religious Knowledge," Brattleboro : 1858 ; another edition 1863. See Brown, J. Newton.

Tyler, James M. *Address on* the Presentation of a Statue of Jacob Collamer. See Collamer, Jacob.

Mr. Tyler was born in Wilmington, Vt., April 27, 1835 ; member of Congress from Vermont, 1879-83; Justice of the Supreme Court from 1887 to date (1896).

For biog. sketch see Vt. Legislative Directory. 1880. p. 103.

Tyler, Mrs. Mary. *The Maternal Physician ;* A Treatise on the Nurture and Management of Infants, from the birth until two years old. Being the result of sixteen years' experience in the Nursery. Illustrated by extracts from the most approved Medical Authors. By an American Matron. Motto. New York : Published by Isaac Riley. 1811. 12mo, pp. 291.

Mary, wife of Chief Justice Royall Tyler, was a woman of singular beauty and richness of character and one of the ablest among the many educated and refined women who adorned the earlier history of our State. She was born in Watertown, Mass., in 1775. Her father, Joseph Pearce Palmer, a graduate of Harvard, was Quartermaster-General of the army besieging the British forces in Boston, until its re-organization under Washington, who offered him the same position in the Continental army, but as he promoted Gen. Mifflin, of South Carolina, over him, Gen. Palmer felt obliged by military etiquette to resign. As a child in Cambridge she sat at the table with Gen. Joseph Warren on the very day he crossed to Bunker Hill to meet his death.

Mrs. Tyler was eighteen years younger than her husband. They were married in 1794. In the winter of '96 he brought his wife and infant son to Guilford, where and in Brattleboro they resided until his death, in 1826; all but one of their nine sons and two daughters were then living. She survived her husband forty years, dying in 1866, having completed her ninety-first year.

At the time of the publication of "The Maternal Physician," sixteen years of married life had fitted her to advise her country-women as to the management of children. The work was very favorably received by the medical faculty. Dr. James Thatcher, author of the American New Dispensary, whose diary as surgeon of the American Army during the Revolutionary War has recently been published, twice refers to the book in terms of eulogy, speaking of it (p. 220) as "the work of a fascinating American writer," and again, (p. 635) quotes in support of his own opinion that "of a late sensible writer, the author of the Maternal Physician, a production replete with interesting matter, and worthy the attention of every nursing family." The advice is that of an experienced matron to a young mother, not merely or mainly as to the physicking but the management of children, conveyed not in a dry but entertaining style and containing many passages of marked literary merit.

TYLER, ROYALL. *The Contrast, A Comedy*; in five acts; Written by a Citizen of the United States; Performed with applause at the theatres in New York, Philadelphia and Maryland; And Published (under an Assignment of the Copy-Right) By Thomas Wignell. Motto. Philadelphia: From the Press of Prichard & Hall, in Market Street, Between Second and Front Streets. M,DCC,XC. 12mo, pp. viii, (10). 79.

Contains sixteen pages of names of subscribers for 557 copies of the work, embracing the most distinguished names, official, and others, in the country.

This was the first play in which the Yankee dialect and story telling, since so common, were introduced; it was also the first American play ever acted upon a regular stage by an established company. Duyckinck, in his "Cyclopedia of American Literature," says the "Contrast" was first put upon the stage "at the old John Street Theatre in New York, under the management of Hallam and Henry, April 16, 1786," and that the author gave the copyright to the principal actor in the piece, Mr. Wignell, who published it by subscription. Duyckinck appears to have obtained his information, in part at least, from "Dunlap's History of the American stage," pp. 72-3. J. T. Buckingham in his "Reminiscences," is in accord with Duyckinck and Dunlap.

On the other hand, the Rev. Thomas P. Tyler, D. D., in a sketch of his father, Judge Tyler, printed in the Argus and Patriot, November 5, 1879, states that the "Contrast" was written in the winter of 1788-9, in three week's time, as is stated in the preface; that it was brought out at the Park Street Theatre, New York. etc.

In reply to a letter of inquiry, Rev. Dr. Tyler wrote us under date of December 11, 1879; "Duyckinck, Dunlap and Buckingham are mistaken. It should be April 16, 1789, and was probably so intended. No other edition of the Contrast than the one I send you was ever printed."

—*The Algerine Captive*; or the Adventures of Doctor Updyke Underhill, Six years a Prisoner among the Algerines. Two volumes in one. Hartford: Printed by Peter B. Gleason & Co. 1816. 18mo, pp. 252.

The first edition in two volumes was printed, Walpole: 1797. 12mo, pp. 428.

Another edition in two volumes. London: 1802. 12mo, pp. xxiv, 190, xi, 228.

—*Reports of* Cases in the Supreme Court of Vermont. Two volumes. 1800-10. New York.

—*The Yankee* in London, being the first part of A Series of Letters Written by an American Youth, during nine months residence in the city of London; addressed to his friends in and near Boston, Massachusetts. Vol. 1. [All published.] Motto. New York: Printed and published by Isaac Riley. 1809. 12mo, pp. ix, 180.

It is proper to state that Judge Tyler never crossed the Atlantic, his description of scenes in London being entirely imaginary.

—*May Day*, or New York in an uproar. 1787. A Comedy.

—*The Georgia Spec*. or Land in the Moon, 1797.

A three act Comedy performed at the Boston Theatre with success.

—*A Fourth of July Ode*, and a Convivial Song, for the Celebration at Windsor, Vt., in 1799.

—*The Original of Evil*. 4to, 1793.

Mr. Tyler gained great reputation by his contributions to the "Farmer's Weekly Museum," published at Walpole, N. H., by Joseph Dennie, Mr. Tyler furnishing those agreeable and humorous articles purporting to be "From the Shop of Messrs. Colon & Spondee." From J. T. Buckingham's "Reminiscences," who was at that time "Printer's Devil" in the office of the "Museum," we gather many interesting anecdotes of the times of Tyler and Fessenden:

"Colon & Spondee" came out almost every week, with new varieties of their small wares; T. G. Fessenden produced his political lampoons, under the signature of "Simon Spunkey;" Dennie wrote with great rapidity, and generally postponed his task until he was called upon for "copy," which was often given out a paragraph at a time, sometimes being written in the composing room while the compositor was waiting to put it in type. One of the best of his "Lay Sermons" was written at the village tavern, directly opposite the printing office, in a chamber where he and his friends were amusing themselves with cards. If he happened to be engaged in a game when I applied for copy, he would ask some one to play his hand for him while he could give the "devil" his due. When I called for the closing paragraph he said, "call again in five minutes." "No," said Tyler, "I will write the improvement for you." He accordingly wrote a concluding paragraph, and Dennie never saw it until it was in print. Tyler's contributions to the Museum were numerous, and would form several volumes if collected together; he could vary his style from "grave to gay, from lively to severe," as easily as he could draw on his glove.

Mr. Tyler was born in Boston, July 18, 1757; the son of Royall Tyler, a distinguished citizen of Boston in colonial times, and died in Brattleboro, August 16, 1826; he was christened William C. Tyler, but had the name changed to Royall by act of the general court after the death of his father. He was graduated at Harvard, 1776; studied law, it is said, in the office of John Adams, and for a time was aid to General Sullivan in 1778, also to General Lincoln during the Shays' rebellion in 1786-7. He was sent by General Lincoln to the Governments of New York and Vermont to make arrangements for the delivery of Shays and his adherents to the authorities of Massachusetts, should they escape to those States. The result of his mission to Vermont was not entirely satisfactory, as appears from Minot's history, which says: "With respect to that Government, [Vermont] the Legislature had been officially informed, that on the 13th of February, [1787], General Lincoln dispatched Royall Tyler, Esq., one of his Aids de Camp, to request their assistance in apprehending the rebel ring-leaders: That, upon his communicating his instructions and request in writing, the subject of them was put in Committee, [See Governor and Council of Vermont, Vol. 3, pp. 119, 125 and 126] and a report made for requesting the Governor [Thomas Chittenden], to issue his proclamation, enjoining it upon their citizens not to harbor the leaders or abettors of the rebels: That this report was accepted by their lower House, and sent up to their Council, where there also appeared eight or nine assistants, [Councillors] in favor of it: That it would of course have passed there, but for the Governor's objections, which were at first founded upon his not having given the subject a proper consideration, but were afterwards bottomed upon more serious principles: These were said to have been raised, from the impolicy of issuing a proclamation which might impede the emigration of subjects from other States into that; and the imprudence of opposing the sense of their people, who began to assemble in arms in a neighboring town, [probably refers to Windsor or Rutland] and who might create an insurrection, and surround the Legislature, unless the report were dismissed: There being no prospect of Mr. Tyler's effecting the object of his request, he departed [from Vermont] with strong apprehensions, that the bulk of the people in that State were for affording protection to the rebels, and that no immediate or effectual aid would be granted."

Mr. Tyler removed to Guilford, Vt., in 1790, where he commenced the practice of his profession. In 1800 he was elected a Judge of the Supreme Court, and remained upon the bench until 1813, the last six years as Chief Justice.

He was, in addition to his literary work already mentioned, a prolific contributor to various journals, the Portfolio of Philadelphia, established by Dennie on his removal there in 1800; the New England Galaxy, Polyanthos, by Buckingham, in Boston, and others. A volume of his articles in the Museum, etc., was collected and published in 1801.

Mr. Tyler's elevation to the Supreme Bench did not apparently lessen his literary ardor, as he contributed his " Author's Evenings " to Dennie's Portfolio, from 1800 to 1812. "He was a wit, a poet, and a Chief Justice."

The following is copied from a paper in the handwriting of Judge Tyler, found in a package of manuscripts relating to the Shays Rebellion, recently presented to the Vermont Historical Society by the Rev. Dr. Tyler, of Brattleboro. This paper appears to be a copy of a report to the Governor of Massachusetts, or to General Lincoln, by Judge Tyler, while on his mission to the Legislature of Vermont at Bennington, in February, 1787:

"The Governor [Thomas Chittenden] in my presence said that whenever people were oppressed they will mob and that the people who fought the Bennington action are now under guard, giving his opinion plumply against our cause, and that it would not do for this State to have any concern with Massachusetts quarrels. In the company of last evening I heard numbers of respectable men, to appearance, requesting him not to have anything to do with those just persons who have fled into this State for shelter, and further the Governor said he did not conceive the nature of their offense to be such that it was the duty of this State to be aiding in sending them away to the halter. General Ethan Allen in my presence said that those who hold the reins of the government in Massachusetts were a pack of damned rascals, and that there was no virtue among them, and that he did not think it worth anybody's while to try to prevent them who had fled into this State for shelter from cutting down our maple trees; and the common people flocked around him as though he had a sight to show. The commonality aver that they will shelter anybody who applies to any of their houses for shelter, and it is generally said that our quarrel will be ten thousand pounds advantage to this State."

The feeling in Vermont was so intense against giving up to the authorities of Massachusetts any of the Shays men, that Judge Tyler felt some fears for his own safety, as shown by the following extract from a letter of February 21, 1787, written at Pittsfield, Mass., by Gen. Benjamin Lincoln to Judge Tyler: "As soon as you find your person in danger, or that your services cannot avail, pray return; you have done a great deal; we cannot command success; to deserve it has the same merit."

Another incident in the Shays rebellion should be noticed; that the military of Massachusetts fillibustered into the independent State of Vermont, and took therefrom several persons. Mr. Minot tells the story as follows:

"On the 16th of February, 1787, General Shepard detached a party of horse from Northfield, Mass., under the command of Captain Samuel Buffington, for the purpose of apprehending certain insurgents, who had fled to Vermont. Upon their arrival within that Government, although they had procured a warrant from a Magistrate to apprehend the objects of their search, yet the people assembled in such numbers and evinced such a hostile disposition towards them, that they were obliged to relinquish their pursuit, and return to Massachusetts. They, however, in the evening, sent a small number from their body, among whom was Mr. Jacob Walker, to secure one Jason Parmenter, who had acted as a Captain with the insurgents. Unfortunately for Walker, they soon overtook the person whom they were sent after, accompanied in his flight by several others. The sleighs of the opposite parties unexpectedly ran upon each other; and on Parmenter's hailing and receiving no answer he ordered his men to fire; but mischief was prevented by their guns not going off. Parmenter and Walker then raised their pieces together and fired. The latter was shot through the body, and died in half an hour. The survivor and his associates escaped by the help of the woods and the deep snow, into Vermont, where, however, they were all taken next day, by a body of infantry, detached from the militia by Captain Buffington; Parmenter was afterwards tried and convicted of treason."

The sequel as to Parmenter and another under sentence of death is this, as told by Mr. Minot: The insurgents on May 21, 1787, captured Joseph Metcalf and Medad Pomeroy, prominent persons in Warwick, Mass., and vicinity; notice was given that these persons would be held as hostages to secure the lives of Jason Parmenter and Henry M'Cullock. The hostages were conveyed to a place of safety without the State of Massachusetts; it is not stated whether they were taken to Vermont or Rhode Island, the latter State having positively refused to comply with the request of Massachusetts to surrender refugees fleeing within her borders. Rhode Island had not forgotten the persecutions endured by her first settlers, under Roger Williams, in being barbarously driven and banished from Massachusetts.

Parmenter and M'Cullock were not executed. There seems to be a little confusion in Mr. Minot's history as to whether the "warrant from a Magistrate," to Captain Buffington, was issued by a Magistrate of Massachusetts or Vermont; the balance of evidence is that whatever "warrant" he had, was from the former State, for no Magistrate in Vermont at that time was authorized to issue any such warrant; therefore I use the word, "fillibustered."

We print the following letter from the Rev. Thomas P. Tyler, D. D., a son of Judge Royall Tyler, although it was not written with a view to publication:

Brattleboro, Nov. 30, 1877.

For some time past I have been engaged in writing a memoir of my father, Hon. Royall Tyler, Chief Justice of Vermont in the early years of this century. He was one of the distinguished men of his day, not only as a Jurist, but as a polished writer, standing prominent in the circle of wits who first gave character to the lighter literature of New England. He was the author of the first American work of fiction re-published in London, and of the first comedy successfully brought out on the stage. Having retired from professional life at three score, I undertook this work on the instigation of my eldest brother, since deceased, and of Mr. Chittenden, of New York, whom I do not know personally, but presume to be a descendant of our grand old Governor. My design then was to publish, but change of pecuniary circumstances renders this impossible now, but I have continued it as a labor of love, intending to make a large and firmly bound manuscript volume which I propose ultimately to commit to the care and keeping of the Vermont Historical Society. I have also my father's published books, "The Algerine Captive," "The Yankee in London," "The Contrast," (a comedy.) If lost, these probably could not be replaced, having been these sixty years out of print. These also, I design to have firmly re-bound, and placed in your archives—all this, of course, dependent on your willingness to take charge of them, and on your favorable judgment as to the advisability of such a disposition of them. Among Judge Tyler's papers I find a package marked "Shays Rebellion." He was an aid to General Lincoln, and was sent to meet the Governor and Legislature of Vermont at Bennington. These papers are various: Letters from Gen. Lincoln; minutes of conferences with our officers; accounts of expeditions in pursuit of the rebels; one scrawl from Shays himself declining to walk into a trap baited for him. These are at your service, if you think best to take them. My brother, Royall Tyler, Judge of Probate, and my sister, reside here now, but in a very few years there will not be a descendant of the Chief Justice left in the State. Hence my anxiety to leave such mementoes as I can of one whom I naturally regard as one of the brightest ornaments of the judicial and literary history of Vermont.

In all this you will not see any sufficient reason for my troubling you about the matter now, but I trust what I have to add will suffice for an apology. Fifty years have elapsed since my father's death. His contemporaries have long since passed away. The materials for biography are of course mainly letters and other manuscript, or printed documents. It is singular, but true, that the department wherein information is most important to be obtained (that of the law) is just where it is most meagre and unsatisfactory. There were, as you are aware, several trials during his session on the Supreme bench, in which the violence, heat and animosities of politics, the virulence of which passes all our experience, arrayed the people as partisans on either side. Such was especially the case in the Embargo war times. In the Blacksnake affair there were several trials, some of which I learn from father's letters were prepared by himself for publication, but my most diligent efforts have failed to find one of them. I do find from the letters of Senator Robinson and other of his friends, that in their judgment his charges to the juries, and other official acts in the conduct of the trials, contributed much to allay partisan feeling and bring the people back to sentiments of justice and patriotism. You will conceive what an "hiatus valde deflendus" is the utter want of any report of the trials.

The distinguished and Honorable Hiland Hall, who has interested himself and aided me in this matter, advised me to communicate with you, thinking that if copies of the trials were in the Historical or State Libraries, you might be able to procure me the loan of them.

My brother, Rev. George P. Tyler, D. D., formerly pastor of the Congregational Society in this village, presented to the Vermont Historical Society a manuscript report of one of these Trials. He thinks you would let me take it for the purpose of this Biography, to be carefully preserved and returned. I am well aware that you may be restrained by rules prohibiting the removal of pamphlets or manuscripts from your care, but, as my object is to reduce to definite form the materials of history these manuscripts or pamphlets contain, I hope that no by-laws, however wholesome, may stand in the way of your sending me by express, any manuscript or other document that may aid me in this work.

My brother, Rev. George P. Tyler, D. D., formerly an active member of the Vermont Historical Society, now resides in Lansingburgh, N. Y. He thinks you will return the manuscript he gave you, for a temporary use by me. The Rev. Dr. Hull of Montpelier, an old and esteemed friend of mine, will, I think, assure you that you may safely intrust anything of the kind to my care.

Very respectfully,
THOMAS P. TYLER.

The Black Snake affair alluded to by Rev. Dr. Tyler, grew out of the capture of a smuggling boat, called the "Black Snake," which under the embargo act of 1808 did a large smuggling business on Lake Champlain, and in her capture that year, several lives were lost, and the crew of the boat were tried for murder, and several convicted, Cyrus B. Dean, however, being the only one finally executed.

See Trials, C. B. Dean. For a full history of the affair see Dea. L. L. Dutcher's account in Vermont Historical Gazetteer. Vol. 2, pp. 342-347.

For a most interesting sketch of Judge Tyler, prepared by his son, Rev. Thomas P. Tyler, D. D., of Brattleboro, and read before the Vermont Bar Association at Montpelier, October 28, 1879, see Argus and Patriot, of November 5, 1879; also History of Brattleboro, for a full history of the Tyler family.

Consult Duyckinck; Buckingham's Newspaper Reminiscences, and Personal Memoirs; Minot, G. R., Governor and Council, Vol. 3, pp. 357-380.

Tyler, Royall. *A Book of Forms*, with occasional Notes. By Royall Tyler, Esq., Attorney at Law. Brattleboro, Vt.: Published by Joseph Steen. 1845. 12mo, pp. 96.

Royall Tyler, the younger, was the son of Judge Royall Tyler. He was born in Brattleboro April 19, 1812, and died in that town Oct. 27, 1896, being the last survivor of a family of 11 children. He graduated from Harvard Law school in 1834, studied in the office of Charles C. Loring of Boston, and was admitted to the Bar in 1837, but discontinued the practice of law when he was elected county clerk in 1851. He held the office of judge of probate for fifty years, from 1846 till his death, being probably the oldest probate judge in service in New England. He had also represented Brattleboro in the Legislature and had been State's attorney.

He was a member of the Episcopal church. His wife, who was a daughter of Judge Asa Keyes, survives him, with one daughter.

Ullery, Jacob G. *Men of Vermont.* Brattleboro, Vt.: Transcript Publishing Company. 1894. rl. 8vo, pp. 825.

Union Agricultural Society. *Officers, Regulations*, and Schedule of premiums, of the Union Agricultural Society, 1877. Fair at Tunbridge, Vt., Oct. 2, 3, and 4. Montpelier, Vt.: Argus and Patriot Print. 1877. 8vo, pp. 7.

United States. *Acts passed* at the Third session of the Fifth Congress of the United States. State of Vermont. Rutland: Printed by Samuel Williams. M,DCC,XCIX. 8vo, pp. 202, (2).

—*The Same*, First session of the Sixth Congress. Same imprint. M.DCCC. 8vo, pp. 223. vii.

—*Rules and Regulations* in Bankruptcy, adopted by the Circuit and District Courts of the United States, for the District of Vermont. Rutland, Vt.: White & Guernsey. 1842. 8vo, pp. 24.

See Rules.

—*Circuit Court.* Vermont District. In Equity. Riley Burdett vs. Jacob Estey and Others. Argument of E. W. Stoughton, for Complainant. New York: 1876. 8vo, pp. 143.

—*Circuit Court* for the District of Vermont. Charles M. Pond, et als., survivors of Wm. P. Burrill, deceased, vs. the Vermont Valley Railroad, et als. E. W. Stoughton, Esq., Counsel for Compl'ts. Hon. George F. Edmunds,

Counsel for Def'ts. Woodruff, Circuit J. n. d. n. p. [1871.] 8vo, pp. 32.

—*Supreme Court* of the United States. December Term, 1850.—No. 137. Wyllys Lyman, George P. Marsh, John Peck, and John H. Peck, Plaintiffs in Error, vs. The Bank of the United States. In Error to the Circuit Court, United States, for the District of Vermont. [Gideon Print.] 8vo, pp. 112.

—*Circuit Court*, for the District of Vermont. At Rutland, October Term, 1862. In the matter ex parte Anson Field. Application for Habeas Corpus, And order on Marshal Baldwin to show Cause. Decision of His Honor, Judge Smalley, Adjudging the Marshal guilty of contempt ; and that he pay a fine therefor, and be not permitted within the Court to act as one of its officers, until he purges himself of said contempt by compliance with the order. Burlington ,Vt.: W. H. & C. A. Hoyt & Co., Printers. 1862. 8vo, pp. 27.

—*Regulations for* the Subsistence Department of the Army of the United States. Rutland, Vt.: Geo. A. Tuttle & Co., Printers. 1861. 12mo, pp. 40.

—*Southern District of New York.* Orlando B. Potter, Nathaniel Wheeler, "Grover and Baker Sewing Machine Company " et " Wheeler and Wilson Manufacturing Company" vs. Abraham Fuller, agent for the sale of "Williams & Orvis " Sewing Machines in the City of New York. Application for injunction to restrain defendant from further infringement of complainants' patents. Decision of His Honor Judge Smalley, Decreeing the Injunction. Phonographically reported by Andrew J. Graham, No. 274 Canal Street, New York. New York: L. W. Payne, Printer, No. 37 Park Row. 1862. 8vo, pp. 17.

—*United States Circuit Court, Vermont.* Riley Burdett v. Jacob Estey & Co. Testimony before Hon. John W. Stewart, Master. For Complainant, E. J. Phelps, J. M. Tyler, C. B. Stoughton, K. Haskins. For Defendants, Dickerson, Beaman & Dickerson. Jay Read Pember, Law Stenographer. 1879. sm. folio, pp. 446.

UNIVERSALISM. *Form* for Constitution and by-laws for the use of Universalist and other liberal churches. Montpelier: Ballou & Burnham's Press. 1851. 12mo, pp. 16.

—*A Discussion* on the Doctrine of Endless Punishment: Question: Do the Scriptures teach that any part or portion of Mankind will be Endlessly Punished for Sins Committed in this Life? Affirmative, Rev. Luther Lee ; Negative, Rev. Eli Ballou. Montpelier: Published for W. Hosea Ballou, By Ballou and Loveland. 1857. 12mo, pp. 84.

See Christian Repository: Ballou; Balch ; Lee, J.S.; Marston, M.; Streeter, R.; Dean, Paul ; Haven, K.; Sawyer, T. J.

UNIVERSITY OF VERMONT.

Under the classifications in this work, some duplicate titles may be found under the names of authors.

I am indebted to Professor J. E. Goodrich, Librarian at the University of Vermont, not only for active assistance in the preparation of the list of works relating to the University, but also for his ready and constant aid in behalf of this bibliography from its incipient state to the present time, (1880.)

CHILD, GARDNER. *An Oration* on Eloquence, delivered at Burlington, May 12th, 1806, on the Anniversary of the Phi Sigma Nu Society at Burlington College. By Gardner Child, Member of the Senior Class. Burlington, Vermont : Printed by Greenleaf & Mills, July, 1806. 12mo, pp. 26.

SANDERS, DANIEL C. *An Address* to the Students iu the University of Vermont, May Sixth, 1807; ou Occasion of the Death of William Homer Coit, Member of the Sophomore Class, Who died December 23, 1806, Aged 18, being the First Instance of Mortality among the Members, since the Organization of the Institution. By Daniel C. Sanders, A. M., President of the College. Burlington: Printed by Samuel Mills. August, 1807. 8vo, pp. 16.

—*A Charge* to the Graduates in the University of Vermont, at Burlington, at the Public Commencement, September 9th, 1807. By Daniel C. Sanders, A. M., President. Burlington: Printed by Samuel Mills. 1807. 8vo, pp. 16.

—*The Laws of.* Burlington, Vt.: Printed by Samuel Mills. 1809. 8vo, pp. 28.

DEAN, JAMES. *An Oration* on Curiosity, pronounced in the University of Vermont, 24th April, 1810, on Induction into Office. By James Dean, A. M., Professor of Mathematics & Natural Philosophy. Published at the Request of the Students, Burlington, Vt. Printed by Samuel Mills. May, 1810. 8vo, pp. 19.

CHAMBERLAIN, JASON. *An Inaugural Oration*, delivered at Burlington, August 1, 1811. By Jason Chamberlain, A. M., Professor of the Learned Languages in the University of Vermont. Published by Order of the Corporation, and at the Request of the Students. Second Edition. Burlington, Vt. Printed by Samuel Mills. 1811. 8vo, pp. 21.

Mr. Chamberlain was born in Hollister, Mass., February 9, 1783, and was graduated at Brown University, 1804; was settled over the Congregational church at Guilford, Vt., 1808; was Professor in the University of Vermont, 1811-14 ; then went to Jackson, Mo., and practiced law, and was drowned while going the circuit of the courts, in Arkansas, in 1820.

SANDERS, DANIEL C. *A Charge* to the Graduates in the University of Vermont, in Burlington, at the Public Commencement, 29th July, 1812. By Daniel C. Sanders, D. D., President. Burlington, Vt.: Printed by Samuel Mills. 1812. 8vo, pp. 14.

—*A Discourse*, pronounced in the Chapel of the University of Vermont, 29th April, 1813. Occasioned by the Death of Doct. Cassius F. Pomeroy, A. M., and Mr. Ebenezer Gilbert, Member of the Sophomore Class. Published at the Request of the Students. By Daniel Clarke Sanders, D D., President. Burlington, Printed by Samuel Mills. 1813. 8vo, pp. 24.

AUSTIN, SAMUEL. *An Inaugural Address*, pronounced in Burlington, July 26, 1815, by Samuel Austin, D. D., President of the University of Vermont. Published by Request of the Corporation. Burlington: Printed by Francis G. Fish, August, 1815. 8vo, pp. 18.

GROSS, EZRA C. *An Oration* delivered before the Phi Sigma Nu Society of the University of Vermont, at their Anniversary Celebration, August 13, 1823. By the Hon. Ezra C. Gross.

Burlington, Vt.: Printed by E. & T. Mills. 1823. 8vo, pp. 16.

MARSH, JAMES. *An Address* delivered in Burlington, upon the Inauguration of the Author to the Office of President of the University of Vermont, Nov. 28, 1826. By James Marsh. Burlington: Printed by E. & T. Mills. 1826. 8vo, pp. 31.

YALE, CALVIN. *Some Rules* for the Investigation of Religious Truth ; and Some Specimens of Argumentation in its Support. An Address delivered before the Society for Religious Inquiry in the University of Vermont, at Burlington, August 8, 1826. By Rev. Calvin Yale, of Charlotte, an Honorary Member. Published by Request. Montpelier : Printed by E. P. Walton, Watchman Office. 1826. 8vo, pp. 15.

—*Constitution and By-Laws* of the College of Natural History of the University of Vermont, Adopted on the Fourteenth day of October, 1826. Burlington: Printed by E. & T. Mills. 1826. 16mo, pp. 11.

—*Laws of the University of Vermont.* Burlington: Printed by E. & T. Mills. 1827. 8vo, pp. 22.

Also, Editions of 1842, 1851, 1860, 1874 and later dates,

CHANDLER, A. *The Spirit of the Gospel* Essential to a Happy Result of our Religious Inquiries. An Address to the Society for Religious Inquiry in the University of Vermont. Burlington, August 7, 1827. By A. Chandler, Minister in Waitsfield. Alumnus of the Institution. Burlington: Printed at the Free Press Office. 1827. 8vo, pp. 16.

STRONG, JAMES. *An Address* on the Necessity of Education and the Arts in a Republican Government, Delivered before the Phi Sigma Nu Society of the University of Vermont, at Burlington, August 7th, A. D. 1827, By James Strong. Printed for the Society. Burlington. Printed at the Free Press Office. 1827. 8vo, pp. 24.

McKEEN, SILAS. *The right Object* and Use of Religious Investigation. An Address to the Society for Religious Inquiry in the University of Vermont, August 5, 1828. By Silas McKeen, an Honorary Member. Burlington: Printed at the Free Press Office. 1828. 12mo, pp. 11.

COLLAMER, JACOB. *An Oration* delivered before the Phi Sigma Nu Society of the University of Vermont, Burlington, August 6, 1828. By Jacob Collamer. Published by the Society. Royalton: W. Spooner's Print, 8vo, pp. 19.

—*An Exposition* of the System of Instruction and Discipline pursued in the University of Vermont. By the Faculty. Second Edition. Burlington : Chauncey Goodrich. 1831. 8vo, pp. 32.

—*Lincoln, Benjamin.* An Exposition of Certain Abuses, Practiced by Some of the Medical Schools in New England : and Particularly, of the Agent-sending System, as Practiced by Theodore Woodward, M. D. Addressed to Medical Gentlemen in the State of Vermont. By Benjamin Lincoln. Burlington: Printed for the Author. 1833. 8vo, pp. 76.

—*Hints* on the Present State of Medical Education and the Influence of Medical Schools in

New England. With an Appendix Containing a Review of a Letter by T. Woodward, M. D., addressed to Professor Lincoln and first Published in the Vermont Statesman of the 19th March, 1833. By Benjamin Lincoln. Burlington : Printed for the Author. 1833. 8vo, pp. 76.

HENRY, C. S. *The Importance* of Exalting the Intellectual Spirit of the Nation ; and Need of a Learned Class. A Discourse pronounced before the Phi Sigma Nu Society of the University of Vermont, August 3, 1836. By the Rev. C. S. Henry, Professor of Intellectual and Moral Philosophy, Bristol College, Pennsylvania. Burlington, New Jersey: J. L. Powell. 1836. 8vo, pp. 44.

—*Catalogue of the Books* belonging to the Library of the University of Vermont. Burlington : Vernon Harrington. 1836. 8vo, pp. 03. (1).

—*Another* edition, 1843, pp. 93, (1), 24, (1).

INGERSOLL, GEO. G. *An Address* delivered before the Literary Societies of the University of Vermont, August 2, 1837, by George G. Ingersoll, and published at their request. Burlington : Hiram Johnson & Co. 1837. 8vo, pp. 46.

BARNARD, DANIEL D. *A Discourse* pronounced at Burlington before the Literary Societies of the University of Vermont, August 1st, 1838 ; on the Day of the Annual Commencement. By Daniel D. Barnard. Albany : Printed by Hoffman & White. 1838. 8vo, pp. 56.

LEWIS, TAYLER. *Natural Religion* the Remains of Primitive Revelation. A Discourse, pronounced at Burlington, before the Literary Societies of the University of Vermont, August 6th, 1839. By Tayler Lewis, Esq., Professor of Greek and Latin in the University of New York. Published at the Request of the Societies. New York : Printed at the Office of the University Press, 36 Ann Street. 1839. 8vo, pp. 52.

TRACY, JOSEPH. *An Address* before the Society for Religious Inquiry in the University of Vermont, August 6, 1839. By Rev. Joseph Tracy. Boston : Published by Crocker & Brewster, 47 Washington Street. 1839. 8vo, pp. 28.

BENEDICT, G. W. *History of the University*, by Professor George Wyllys Benedict.
American Quarterly Register, Vol. xiii, pp. 391-402. 1841.

MARSH, LEONARD. *The Physiology of Intemperance*, an Address before the Temperance Society of the University of Vermont, June 29, 1841. By Leonard Marsh, M. D. Burlington : Chauncey Goodrich. 1841. 8vo, pp. 28.

TODD, JOHN. *New England:*—Her Character and Destiny. An Address, delivered before the Societies of Religious Inquiry, in Amherst College and the University of Vermont, at their Anniversaries. 1841. By Rev. John Todd. Published by the Societies. Northampton. J. H. Butler. 1841. 8vo, pp. 39.

HOSMER, WILLIAM H. C. *The Prospects of the Age.* A Poem, delivered before the Literary Societies of the University of Vermont, at Burlington, August 3, 1841. By William H. C. Hosmer, A. M. Published by Request. Burlington : Chauncey Goodrich. 1841. 8vo, pp. 19.

WHEELER, JOHN. *A Discourse*, delivered July 6, 1842, at the Funeral of James Marsh, D. D., Late Professor of Moral and Intellectual Philosophy in the University of Vermont. By John Wheeler, D. D., President of the University. Burlington: Chauncey Goodrich. 1842. 8vo, pp. 29.

PEASE, CALVIN. *Import and Value* of the Popular Lecturing of the Day. A Discourse pronounced before the Literary Societies of the University of Vermont, August 3, 1842. By Calvin Pease. Published at the request of the Societies. Burlington : University Press. Chauncey Goodrich. 1842. 8vo, pp. 43.

BLISS, ZENAS. *The Philosophy* of Temperance: an Address before the Temperance Society of the University of Vermont, October 18, 1842, by Rev. Zenas Bliss. Published by Request. Burlington : Chauncey Goodrich. 1842. 8vo, pp. 31.

—*Catalogus Senatus Academici*, et eorum qui Munera et Officia gesserunt, quive alicujus Gradus Laurea donati sunt, in Universitate Viridimontana. Burlingtoniae : Typis S. Fletcher, Academiae Typographi; MDCCCXLIII Rerumpublicarum Foederat. Americanarum summae Potestatis Anno LXVIII. 8vo, pp. 29.

BLISS, ZENAS. *The Idea* of the Spiritual Interpretation of Scripture. A Discourse, delivered before the Society for Religious Inquiry, in the University of Vermont, at their Commencement Anniversary, July 31, 1843. By Rev. Zenas Bliss. Burlington: Printed by Stilman Fletcher. 1843. 8vo, pp. 72.

BROWNSON, O. A. *An Oration* on the Scholar's Mission, by O. A. Brownson. Burlington, Vt.: V. Harrington. 1843. 8vo, pp. 40.

CHEEVER, GEORGE B. *Characteristics* of the Christian Philosopher: A Discourse Commemorative of the Virtues and Attainments of Rev. James Marsh, D. D., Late President, and Professor of Moral and Intellectual Philosophy in the University of Vermont. Delivered before the Alumni of the University, at their Annual Meeting, in August, 1843, and published at their request. By Rev. George B. Cheever. New York : Wiley & Putnam. 1843. 8vo, pp. 72.

SHEDD, WILLIAM. *The Influence* of Temperance upon Intellectual Discipline. A Discourse delivered before the Temperance Society of the University of Vermont, April 30, 1844, by Rev. William Shedd. Published by Request. Burlington : University Press. Printed by Stilman Fletcher, 1844. 8vo, pp. 31.

BENEDICT, GEORGE WYLLYS. *New England* Educational Institutions in Relation to American Government. A Discourse delivered before the Phi Sigma Nu and University Institute Societies of the University of Vermont, at their Annual Celebration, August 6, 1844. By George Wyllys Benedict. Published by Request of the Societies. Burlington : Chauncey Goodrich. 1844. 8vo, pp. 48.

—*Report of the Commissioners* to Examine the University of Vermont. In, House of Representatives, Oct. 11, 1844. 8vo, pp. 8.

SHEDD, WILLIAM G. T. *The Method* and Influence of Theological Studies. A Discourse, pronounced at Burlington, before the Literary Societies of the University of Vermont, August 5th, 1845, by Rev. William G. T. Shedd. Published by the Societies. Burlington: University Press. S. Fletcher, Printer. 1845. 8vo, pp. 52.

HEADLEY, J. T. *The One Progressive Principle.* By J. T. Headley. Delivered before the Literary Societies of the University of Vermont, August, 1846. New York: Published by John S. Taylor. MDCCCXLVI. 8vo, pp. 32.

—*A Catalogue of Books* in the Library of the Phi Sigma Nu Society, of the University of Vermont. Burlington: University Press. 1846. 8vo, pp. 40.

HOPKINS, JOHN H., Jr., *Liberty:* a Poem, delivered before the Literary Societies of the University of Vermont, on Tuesday, August 3rd, 1847. By John H. Hopkins, Jr., M. A. Published by Request. New York: D. Appleton & Co., 200 Broadway. 1847. 8vo, pp. 18.

SMITH, WORTHINGTON, D. D. *An Inaugural Address* delivered July 31st, 1849. By Worthington Smith, D. D., President of the University of Vermont. Published by the Corporation. Burlington: University Press. 1849. 8vo, pp. 26.

WITHINGTON, OLIVER W. *A Poem,* delivered before the Associate Alumni of the University of Vermont; at the Annual Commencement, August, 1849. By Oliver Wendell Withington. Burlington: Free Press Office Print. 1849. 8vo, pp. 21.

WILKES, HENRY. *The Age* and Theology. An Address delivered before the Society for Religious Inquiry of the University of Vermont, at Burlington, August 5, 1850. By Henry Wilkes, D. D. Pastor First Congregational Church, Montreal. Published at the request of the Society. Burlington: Tuttle & Stacy. 1850. 8vo, pp. 27.

RAYMOND, HENRY J. *The Relations* of the American Scholar to his Country and his Times. An address delivered before the Associate Alumni of the University of Vermont, at Burlington, Vt., August 6, 1850. By Henry J. Raymond. Published at the Request of the Association. New York: Baker & Scribner, 145 Nassau Street. 1850. 8vo, pp. 58.

WASHBURN, E. A. *The Issue* of Modern Philosophic Thought. An Oration delivered before the Literary Societies of the University of Vermont, at Burlington, Vt., August 6, 1850. By the Rev. E. A. Washburn. Published by the Societies. Boston: Phillips, Sampson & Company, 110 Washington Street. 1850. 8vo, pp. 32.

—*A Catalogue* of Books belonging to the University Institute Society of the University of Vermont. Burlington: Printed by Chauncey Goodrich. 1851. 8vo, pp. 26, (1).

—*Alphabetical and* Analytical Catalogue of the Library of the University of Vermont, Burlington. Burlington: Free Press Print. 1854. 8vo, pp. iv, 163, (1).

WHEELER, JOHN. *A Historical* Discourse, by Rev. John Wheeler, D. D., an Address, by James R. Spalding, Esq., and a Poem, by Rev. O. G. Wheeler, delivered on the Occasion of the Semi-centennial Anniversary of the University of Vermont, with an Account of the Proceedings at the Celebration. Burlington: Free Press Print. 1854. 8vo, pp. 149.

SPALDING, JAMES R. *Our Lesson* and Our Work, or Spiritual Philosophy and Material Politics. An Oration by James R. Spalding. See Wheeler, John, etc., above, pp. 47-79.

WHEELER, O. G. *A Poem.* See Wheeler, John, above, pp. 83-108.

PEASE, CALVIN. *Address,* delivered before the Graduating Class, in the Medical Department of the University of Vermont, June 4, 1856, by Calvin Pease, President of the University. Burlington: Free Press Print. 1856. 18mo, pp. 35.

—*Sermon,* preached before the Graduating Class, in the University of Vermont, August 3, 1856. By Calvin Pease, President of the University. Burlington: George J. Stacy, Printer. 1856. 8vo, pp. 35.

—*Idea of* the New England College and its Power of Culture. An Address, delivered on the Occasion of his Inauguration as President of the University of Vermont, August 5, 1856. By Calvin Pease. Burlington: Free Press Print. 1856. 8vo, pp. 52.

—*Sermon,* preached before the Graduating Class in the University of Vermont, August 2d, 1857. By Calvin Pease, D. D., President of the University. Burlington: Free Press Print. 1857. 8vo, pp. 40.

ERNI, HENRI. *Medical Address.* May 12, 1857.

LEVINGS, I. H. *Character of St. Paul* as a Preacher. An Address delivered before the Society for Religious Inquiry, in the University of Vermont, August 2, 1857. By Rev. I. H. Levings. Published by the Society. Burlington: Free Press Print. 1857. 8vo, pp. 31.

STILES, R. C. *Medical Address.* 1858; also, 1860.

WHEELER, JOHN. *Influence of* the Professions on Civilization. A Valedictory Address, delivered before the Medical Class of the University of Vermont, June 8th, 1859. By John Wheeler, D. D. Burlington: Free Press Print. 1859. 8vo, pp. 20.

PEASE, CALVIN. *Sermon,* on Occasion of the Death of John G. Golland and Joshua V. R. Arthur, Members of the Senior Class of the University of Vermont, by Calvin Pease, President of the University, November 13, 1859. Published for the Class. Burlington: Free Press Print. 8vo. pp. 25.

—*Sermon,* preached before the Graduating Class in the University of Vermont, July 31, 1859. By Rev. Calvin Pease, D. D., President of the University. Burlington: Free Press Print. 1859. 8vo, pp. 33.

—*Faith and its Issue.* A Sermon preached before the Graduating Class in the University of Vermont, July 29, 1860. By Calvin Pease, President. Printed for the Class. Burlington: E. A. Fuller, Bookseller and Stationer. Free Press Print. 1860. 8vo. pp. 36.

—*Catalogue of the Lambda Iota Society.* Founded 1836. Motto. New York: John F.

Trow, Printer, 377 & 379 Broadway, Corner of White Street. 1860. 8vo, pp. 24.
Continued.

ALLEN, CHARLES L. *Medical Address.* June 9, 1862.

SEELEY, HENRY M. *Medical Address.* June 9, 1863.

TRACY, JOSEPH. *A Discourse* Commemorative of Rev. John Wheeler, D. D., Late President of the University of Vermont. Delivered at Burlington, August 2, 1864, by Joseph Tracy, D. D. Cambridge: Printed at the Riverside Press. 1865. 8vo, pp. 31.

—*Report of the Trustees* of the Vermont Agricultural College. October 19, 1865. Montpelier: Walton's Steam Printing Establishment. 1865. 8vo, pp. 21. (Senate Document.)

ORDRONEAUX, JOHN. *A Valedictory Address* delivered before the Medical Class of the University of Vermont, May 31st, 1865, by John Ordroneaux, M. D., Professor of Physiology and Medical Jurisprudence. New York: Baker & Godwin, Printers, Printing-House Square, Opp. City Hall. 1865. 8vo, pp. 32.

—*The First Annual Report* of the University of Vermont & State Agricultural College: October 23, 1866. Montpelier: Walton's Steam Printing Establishment. 1866. 8vo, pp. 14.
Continued annually till 1871, then biennially.

CROSBY, A. B., *Memorial Address.* Prof. David S. Conant, M. D. Delivered to the Graduating Class in the Medical Department of the University of Vermont, by A. B. Crosby, A. M., M. D., Professor of Surgery. With Remarks and Resolutions from other Sources. Burlington: Times Book and Job Office. 1866. 8vo, pp. 30.

PEABODY, A. P. *The Positive Philosophy.* An Oration delivered before the Phi Beta Kappa Society of Amherst College, July 9, 1867, and before the Phi Beta Kappa Society of the University of Vermont, August 6, 1867. By A. P. Peabody, D. D., LL. D., Preacher to the University, and Plummer Professor of Christian Morals in Harvard College. Boston: Gould and Lincoln, 59 Washington Street. 1867. 8vo, pp. 28.

—*A Catalogue* of the Officers and Students of the University of Vermont and State Agricultural College, with a Statement of the Several Courses of Instruction. 1867–8. Burlington: Times Book and Job Office. 1867. 8vo, pp. 39.
Continued.

ANGELL, JAMES B. *The Fruitful Activity* of the Life of Christian Faith. A Discourse delivered before the Graduating Class of the University of Vermont and State Agricultural College, August 2, 1868, by James B. Angell, LL. D., President. Burlington: Free Press Steam Printing House. 1868. 8vo, pp. 20.

DUNSTER, EDWARD S. *The Relations* of the Medical Profession to Modern Education. An Address delivered at the Commencement of the University of Vermont, June 16, 1869. By Edward S. Dunster, M. D., Professor of Obstetrics and Diseases of Women and Children. [Reprinted from the N. Y. Medical Journal, December, 1870.] New York: D. Apple-

ton and Company, 90, 92 & 94 Grand Street. 1870. 8vo, pp. 25.

—*Inauguration* of Prof. M. H. Buckham, as President of the University of Vermont and State Agricultural College, August 2, 1871. Burlington: Free Press Association. 1871. 8vo, pp. 23.

KING, A. F. A. *An Introductory Lecture* on Obstetrics, by A. F. A. King, M. D., (Professor of Obstetrics and Diseases of Women and Children) delivered before the Medical Department of the University of Vermont, at Burlington, Vermont, May 6th, 1872. 8vo, pp. 15.

—*Services* in Remembrance of Rev. Joseph Torrey, D. D., and of Geo. Wyllys Benedict, LL. D., Professors in the University of Vermont. Free Press Steam Book and Job Office. Burlington: 1874. 8vo, pp. 66.

—*Catalogue* of the Officers of Government and Instruction, the Alumni and other Graduates of the University of Vermont and State Agricultural College, Burlington, Vt., 1791–1875. Burlington: Free Press Steam Book and Job Printing House. 1875. 8vo, pp. 110.
Triennials issued also in 1846, 1851, 1854, 1858, 1867; General Catalogues 1875 and 1890.

—*Report* of the Joint Special Committee appointed to inquire into the expenditure of the Fund paid by State to the University of Vermont and State Agricultural College; Made to the General Assembly of Vermont, November 18, 1874. Montpelier: Freeman Steam Printing House and Bindery. 1875. 8vo, pp. 8.

—*Roll of Alumni* and Students of the University of Vermont who served in the Army and Navy of the United States during the Rebellion of 1861–65. Burlington: 1875. 8vo, pp. 10.
See General Catalogue of 1875, pp. 111–120.

HUNTING, GEORGE F. *Vim: a Poem* read before the Delta Psi Fraternity of the University of Vermont at their Twenty-fifth Anniversary, July 13, 1875, by Rev. George Field Hunting. Printed for the Fraternity. Burlington: Free Press Printing House. 1875. 8vo, pp. 14.

COLLIER, PETER. *Opening Address* delivered before the Medical Class of the University of Vermont, Thursday, March 9th, 1876, by Prof. Collier. Burlington: R. S. Styles & Son, Book and Job Printers. 1876. 8vo, pp. 15.

HENRY, M. H. *Specialists* and Specialties in Medicine. Address delivered before the Alumni Association of the Medical Department of the University of Vermont, Burlington, June 27, 1876. By M. H. Henry, M. A., M. D., Surgeon-in-chief to the State emigrant Hospitals, Ward's Island, New York; President of the Alumni Association of the University of Vermont; Fellow of the New York Academy of Medicine; Member of the Medical Society of the County of New York; &c., &c. New York: Wm. Wood & Co., 27 Great Jones Street. 1875. 12mo, pp. 22.

ADAMS, CHARLES K. *The Relations* of Higher Education to National Prosperity. An Oration delivered before the Phi Beta Kappa Society of the University of Vermont, June 27, 1876. By Charles Kendall Adams, Professor of History in the University of Michigan. Published by the Society. Burlington: Free Press Print. 1876. 8vo, pp. 27.

—*Fourth Annual Exhibition* of the Park Gallery, University of Vermont. Burlington: Free Press Print. 1877. 8vo. pp. 16.
Continued.

CUTTING, SEWALL S. *Lake Champlain;* a Poem. By Sewall S. Cutting, D. D. Burlington, Vt.. 1877. 12mo, pp. 24.

MORSE, EDGAR T. *Valedictory Address* delivered at the Twenty-Fourth Annual Commencement of the Medical Department of the University of Vermont. June 26, 1877. By Edgar T. Morse. Published by the Class Committee. Burlington: Free Press Print. 1877. 8vo, pp. 23.

CRESSY, N. *Reports* of A Course of Lectures on Veterinary Science, delivered at the University of Vermont and State Agricultural College, by Noah Cressy, M. D., March, 1877. 8vo, pp. 22.

—*Medical Department* of the University of Vermont. Twenty-fifth Annual Commencement, at the City Hall, Thursday, June 27th, 1878, at 8 o'clock, P. M. 12mo, pp. 4.

—*1879.* Delta Psi Fraternity. U. V. M. 18mo, pp. 21.

GRINNELL, A. P. *History* of the Medical Department of the University of Vermont. An Introductory Address delivered before the Medical Class, March 4, 1880. By A. P. Grinnell, M. D., Professor of Physiology and Microscopic Anatomy. Burlington: The Free Press Asso. 1880. 8vo, pp. 16.

ROOSA, D. B. ST. J. *Universities* in the United States. An Address delivered at the Commencement of the Medical Department of the University of Vermont, June 27, 1881, by Daniel B. St. John Roosa, M. D. Published at the Request of the Medical Faculty. Burlington: Free Press Asso. 1881. 8vo. pp. 15.

MORRILL, JUSTIN S. *State Aid* to Land Grant Colleges. An Address in behalf of the University of Vermont and State Agricultural College, delivered in the Hall of the House of Representatives at Montpelier, Oct. 10, 1888, by Justin S. Morrill. Burlington: Free Press Asso. 1888. 8vo, pp. 28.

BURNAP, W. L. *Introductory Address* at the opening of the Thirty-fourth Course of Lectures in the Medical Department of the University of Vermont. By Wilder L. Burnap, Professor of Medical Jurisprudence. Printed by Request of the Medical Class. Burlington: Free Press Asso. 1887. 8vo, pp. 15.

—*Ariel.* A Sophomore Annual, Published at the University of Vermont. February, 1886, E. N. W. Robbins, Printer, Malone, N. Y. pp. 121 (8.)

—*The Ariel.* Published by the Junior Class of the University of Vermont. 1889. 8vo, pp. 116,16.
Printed at the Rome, (N. Y.) Sentinel Printing House.

—*Same,* '90, 8vo, pp. 128 (28.)

—*Same,* Vol. IV. 1891, pp. 188 (30.)

—*Same,* '92, pp. 172, xxvi.
Printed by Charles H. Possons, Glens Falls, N. Y.

—*Same,* '93, motto. pp. 184, xxxix.

—*Same,* '94, pp. 190, xxxx.

—*Same,* '95, pp. 205, xxxix.

—*Same,* '96, pp. 233, xlv.

—*Same,* '97, pp. 240, lxiii.

—*Same,* '98. Volume xi, (Printed by the Free Press Association) pp. 299, lviii.

—*The Agricultural College Bill.* Hearing before the Committee on Education, Thursday, Nov. 6, 1890. Remarks by A. Messer, of Rochester, Master of the State Grange. 8vo, pp. 12.

—*Acts of Congress* and Acts and Resolves of the General Assembly of the State of Vermont relating to the University of Vermont and State Agricultural College. n. d. [1890.] 8vo, pp. 15.

—*Remarks* of President M. H. Buckham at the hearing on the Agricultural College Bill, Oct. 30, 1890. n. d. pp. 11.

—*The Agricultural College.* The Proposition of the State Agricultural Society. Remarks of Mr. C. M. Winslow, at the hearing before the Educational Committee Nov. 5, 1890. pp. 3.

—*University of Vermont.* Description of the Courses of Instruction in the Classical, Engineering and Chemical Departments. 1890-91. 8vo, pp. 21.

—*A History* of the Class of 1833-37, of the University of Vermont, with an Album of Photographs of members of it, and of the Faculty at that time so far as obtainable. Presented to the Library of the University by James W. Hickok, one of the younger members of the class. Burlington: Free Press Association. 1891. 8vo, pp. 28.

—*Thirty-eighth Annual* Announcement of the Medical Department (organized in 1823) of the University of Vermont for the year 1891. Burlington: The Free Press Association. 1890. 8vo, pp. 31.
Continued.

—*Charter History* of the University.
See Benedict, Robert D.

—*The Founder* of the University of Vermont.
See Goodrich, J. E.

—*The Land-Grant Colleges.* An Address delivered at the Eighty-ninth Commencement of the University of Vermont and State Agricultural College, June 28, 1893. By Justin S. Morrill, LL. D. Burlington: The Free Press Association. 1893. 8vo, pp. 28.

—*Thirteenth Annual* Field Day, University of Vermont, May 29, 1896. Score-Card. Burlington: Free Press Print. n. d. 12mo, pp. 8.

—*Roster* of the Corps of Cadets of the University of Vermont, Oct. 1893. Burlington, Vt.: Free Press Print.

—*Obituary Record,* University of Vermont, compiled by a Committee of the Associate Alumni. No. 1. Burlington: 1895. 8vo, pp. 147.

—*The Situation* in Cuba. 1897. A descriptive address delivered by Captain Guy Howard, U. S. Army, before the Phi Beta Kappa

Society of the University of Vermont, January 15, 1807. Burlington: Hobart J. Shanley & Co. 8vo, pp. 33.

Upham, Don A. J.
A native of Weathersfield, Vt., born May 31, 1809; died at Milwaukee, Wis., July 19, 1877. He was graduated at Union College, 1830; Professor of Mathematics at Newark, Del., for three years; in 1834, settled at Wilmington, in that State, as an attorney-at-law, and served as City Attorney; he was for three years editor and proprietor of the Delaware Gazette. In 1837 he moved to Milwaukee, Wis., and was a member of the Territorial Legislature, 1840-41-42; County Attorney 1843, and in 1846 President of the first Constitutional Convention of Wisconsin. In 1851 he was elected Governor of the State, but was "counted out," and his whig opponent, L. J. Farwell, was "counted in." From 1857 to 1861 Mr. Upham was United States District Attorney for Wisconsin.

Upham, James, D. D. *An Address* Delivered May 25, 1859, before the Ladies' Literary and Missionary Association, connected with the New-Hampton Institution, Fairfax, Vt., on occasion of the death of Mrs. Eliza Smith, wife of Pres. Eli B. Smith, D. D., By James Upham, Professor of Sacred Literature and Eccl. History. Published by the Society. Burlington: Free Press Print. 1859. 8vo, pp. 39.

—*The Victor Vanquished.* A Discourse delivered at the funeral of Eli Burnham Smith, D. D., Late President of the New Hampton Institution, Fairfax, Vt., January 9th, 1861, By James Upham, D. D., Professor of Sacred Literature and Ecclesiastical History, Fairfax, Vt. Bellows Falls, Vt.: Printed at the Phenix Job Printing Office. 1861. 8vo, pp. 34.

Upham, William. *Speech* of Mr. Upham of Vermont, on the Three Million Bill. Delivered in the Senate of the United States, Monday, March 1, 1847. Washington: Printed at the Congressional Globe Office. 1847. 8vo, pp. 8.

—*Speech of* Mr. Upham, of Vermont, on the Ten Regiment Bill, and the Mexican War. Delivered in the Senate of the United States, February 15, 1848. 8vo, pp. 19.

—*Speech of* Hon. W. Upham, of Vermont, in the Senate of the United States, July 26, 1848. On the Compromise Bill, to establish Territorial Governments in Oregon, New Mexico and California. 8vo, pp. 7.
Mr. Upham made a report on Revolutionary Claims, February 9, 1849. 8vo, pp. 3.

—*Speech of* Hon. William Upham, of Vermont, on the Compromise Bill. In Senate, July 1 and 2, 1850. 8vo, pp. 16.

—*Obituary Addresses* on the occasion of the Death of The Hon. William Upham, a Senator of the United States, from the State of Vermont, Delivered in the Senate and House of Representatives, January 15, 1853. 8vo, pp. 8.
Mr. Upham was born in Leicester, Mass., in August, 1792; died at Washington City, January 14, 1853. He removed to Vermont with his father in 1802, and settled in Montpelier. Spent some time in the University of Vermont, studied law, and became one of the most distinguished jury lawyers in the State. Was a member of the General Assembly of Vermont in 1827-28 and 1830, and State's Attorney for Washington County in 1829. He was a Senator in Congress from 1843 to the time of his death.
For biographical sketches of Senator Upham, see History of Montpelier, pp. 263-8; Lanman's Biographical Annals; Poore's Political Register and Congressional Directory, ed. 1878.

Upham, Samuel C. *Notes of* A Voyage to California, via Cape Horn, in the years 1849-50. By Samuel C. Upham. 45 Illustrations. Philadelphia: Published by the Author. 1878. 8vo, pp. 594.

—*Notes from Sunland,* on the Manatee River, Gulf Coast of South Florida, its Climate, Soil and Productions. By Samuel C. Upham. Second Edition. Braidentown, Fla.: Philadelphia: 1881. 12mo, pp. 83, (8).

—*Florida:* Past and Present, with Notes from Sunland on the Gulf Coast of South Florida. By Samuel C. Upham. Illustrated. Jacksonville, Fla.: 1883. 18mo, pp. 115.
Mr. S. C. Upham was born at Montpelier, Vermont February 2, 1819, his father being an elder brother of the late Senator William Upham. He "emigrated early," and after traveling through the Southern States, made a trip to the Mediterranean on a U. S. vessel. In 1849 he went to California, and in 1850 was one of the founders of the Sacramento Transcript, the fifth newspaper published on the Pacific Coast, and the first daily outside of San Francisco. After a few months' connection with this paper, he returned to Philadelphia, and in '51 commenced the publication of the Sunday Mercury. He was its publisher for five years, when he sold the paper and for twenty-four years afterwards he was a manufacturer of and dealer in perfumery and stationery in Philadelphia. In 1879 he went to Florida and engaged in orange culture. He died in Philadelphia, June 29, 1885.

Upham, William Keyes. *Supreme Court of Ohio.* December Term, A. D. 1853. Nathan Harris vs. The Columbiana County Mutual Ins. Co. Argument for Defendants, By W. K. Upham. 8vo, pp. 11.
Mr. Upham, son of Hon. William Upham, was a native of Montpelier, born April 3, 1817; he was one of the most talented and brilliant young men ever raised in Montpelier. He read law, and was admitted to the bar in his native town; about 1844, he moved to Salem, Ohio, thence to New Lisbon, and finally to Canton in the same State; he became one of the most prominent lawyers in Ohio, ranking with Chase, Stanton, Corwin, Vinton, John A. Bingham and others of that class. He died at Canton, March 22, 1865.

Useful Essays and Instructive Stories, selected for the improvement of the Minds, and the Forming of the Manners, of the Youth of the United States. By a Friend of Science. Motto. Press of Anthony Haswell in Bennington, Vermont, 1807. 24mo, pp. 112.

Vail, Henry H. *The Metrical System of Weights and Measures.* Designed to Accompany Ray's Series. Cincinnati: Sargent, Wilson & Hinkle. n. d. [1866.] 12mo, pp. 23.
Henry H. Vail, son of Joshua Vail, was born in Pomfret, May 27, 1839, graduated at Middlebury in 1860, and, after some experience in teaching school in Vermont and Ohio, entered the employ of the above named school book publishing concern at Cincinnati in 1866. He became a partner in the firm (which is now Van Antwerp, Bragg & Co.) in 1875, and still remains with it (1895). Mr. Vail has charge of the Editorial Department of the business and the work of his hand of course appears in a multitude of books.

Vail, Jackson A. *Rockwell Castle;* or a thirty days trip from Highgate Springs to Boston, including ten days Confinement in Brattleboro Prison, or the Vermont Insane Asylum, and Adventures on the way. 8vo, pp. 16.
Mr. Vail, son of J. Y. Vail, Esq., one of the first settlers in the town, was born and died in Montpelier; he was a lawyer of much prominence, and represented the town of Montpelier in the Legislature, 1848-9.

Van Ness, C. P. *Oration* at Jericho, Vt., July 4, 1809. Rutland: 1809. 8vo, pp. 24.

—*An Oration* delivered at Williston, July 4th, 1812, to a general and very numerous meeting of the Republicans of Chittenden County. By Cornelius P. Van Ness, Esq. Published at the request of the committee of Arrangements. Burlington, Vt.: Printed by Samuel Mills. 1812. 8vo, pp. 48.

—*To the Publick.*—Burlington: March 15, 1827. 8vo, pp. 15.

Relates to the controversy in relation to the election of a United States Senator from Vermont, in which Governor Van Ness was a defeated candidate.

—*Speech* of the Hon. C. P. Van Ness, delivered at the late Democratic Convention at Woodstock, Vermont, And published by the request of the State Committee. Burlington : Printed at the Sentinel Office. 1840. 8vo, pp. 16.

—*To the Public.* Washington, February 15th, 1848. 8vo, pp. 7.

This is a paper in favor of the election of Zachary Taylor to the Presidency.

Governor Van Ness was born at Kinderhook, N. Y., January 26, 1782; and died in Philadelphia, December 15, 1852. He resided in Vermont 1806–1841. He was U. S. District Attorney, Collector of Customs, Commissioner to settle the Northern Boundary of the United States under the Treaty of Ghent ; Chief Justice of the Supreme Court of Vermont; Governor of Vermont; U. S. Minister to Spain, and Collector of the Port of New York.

For a sketch of Governor Van Ness, by Hon. David A. Smalley, see Miss Hemenway's Historical Gazetteer of Vermont, Vol: 1, pp. 608–614.

Veazey, W. G. *An Oration* before the Reunion Society of Vermont Officers, in the Representatives Hall, Montpelier, Vt., October 25th, 1866. By Col. W. G. Veazey, Rutland, Vt. Rutland : Tuttle, Gay & Co., Printers, 1866. 8vo, pp. 26.

—*Address* in memory of Hon. Isaac Fletcher Redfield, LL. D., Late Chief Justice of the State of Vermont, pronounced before the Alumni Association of Dartmouth College, June 23, 1880, by Wheelock G. Veazey. Concord : Printed by the Republican Press Association. 1881. 8vo, pp. 19.

For biographical sketch of Judge Veazey, see Vermont Legislative Manual, 1888, p. 343. In 1889 Judge Veazey resigned as Assistant Justice of the Supreme Court of Vermont to accept an appointment as U. S. Interstate Commerce Commissioner, which office he resigned in 1896.

Vergennes. *Acts and Laws* for Incorporating and Regulating the City of Vergennes and the Bye Laws of said City, from its first organization to the end of the Year 1800. Published by order of the Corporation. Vergennes : Printed by Chipman & Fessenden. 1801.

—*The Laws of Vergennes :* Being an Act to amend and reduce into one Several Acts relating to the Corporation of the City of Vergennes, and the By-Laws of said city. Vergennes : Printed by R. W. Griswold, for the Corporation. 1833. 12mo, pp. 30.

See Griswold, R. W.

—*Manual of the Congregational Church* in Vergennes, Vt., 1879. Organized, September 17th, 1793. With Historical Sketch, &c. 12mo, pp. 35.

Vershire, *Manual of the Congregational Church* Vershire, Vermont, 1863. Motto. Windsor : Printed at the Vermont Chronicle Press. 1863. 12mo. pp. 16.

Vilas, C. H. *A Genealogy* of the Descendants of Peter Vilas. Compiled and edited by (467) C. H. Vilas. Madison, Wis.: Published by the Editor. 1875. 8vo, pp. 221.

The more prominent members of the Vilas Family are Vermonters.

A Vision; Showing the sudden and surprising Appearance, the Celestial Mien, and Heavenly Conversation of the departed Spirit of Mr. Yeamans, Late Student at Yale College, to, and with Mr. H. Goodwin, his Friend and Class-Mate. Printed in the year 1775. Reprinted at Windsor, (Vermont), 1795. 12mo, pp. 8.

See Goodwin, H.

—**VERMONT.** *Some Reflections* on the Disputes between New York, New Hampshire, and Col. John Henry Lydius of Albany. To these Reflections are added Some Rules of Law—fit to be observed in purchasing land, etc. New Haven : Printed and sold by Jonn Mecom. 1764. 12mo, pp. 21. (2).

Advocates the Lydius claim. Mr. Lydius claimed a large tract of land within the present limits of Vermont, under an Indian title. See H. Hall's Early Vermont, pp. 169, 175; and for memoir of Lydius, pp. 494–497. A copy of the above sold for $28 at the Brinley sale in New York in March, 1879.

—*A Petition* to His Majesty, King George the Third. To the King's Most Excellent Majesty. The Humble Petition of the several Subscribers hereto, your Majesty's Most Loyal Subjects, Etc. Dated in New England, November, 1766. And in the Seventh Year of His Majesty's Reign. 1766. sm. 4to, pp. 5.

This is one of nineteen petitions which contain autograph signatures of 624 Green Mountain Boys who had settled on lands in what is now Vermont, asking relief from the claims of New York. For a full account of the same see a reprint, including the names of the signers, in vol. 1. Vermont Historical Society's Collections. A copy of the above pamphlet sold for $26 at the Brinley sale, March, 1879.

—*The Memorial* of Peter Livius, Esq., one of His Majesty's Council for the Province of New Hampshire in New England, to the Lords Commissioners for Trade and Plantations; with the Governor's Answer and the Memorialist's Reply, printed Article by Article, also their Lordship's Report thereon to His Majesty, and the Opinion of the Attorney and Solicitor General in 1752, referred to by the Governor. n. p. 1773. 8vo, pp. 50.

Relates to the controversy respecting the New Hampshire Grants. Excessively rare. Sold at the Brinley sale for $26.

—*Two Reports* on the Matter of Complaint of Mr. Livius against Governor Wentworth. London : 1773. 4to, pp. 15.

—*(1.) A State of the Right* of the Colony of New York, with respect to it's Eastern Boundary on Connecticut River, so far as concerns the late Encroachments under the Government of New Hampshire. And also a State of the Rights of the Colony of New York, so far as concerns the Grants formerly made by the French Government of Canada, of Lands on Lake Champlain, and at and to the southward of Crown Point. Agreed to and published by the General Assembly of the Colony of New York, at their session in M.DCC. LXXIII. New York : Printed by H. Gaine, Printer, Bookseller and Stationer, at the Bible and Crown, Hanover Square. 1773. Folio, pp. 28.

See Allen, Ethan, "A Brief Narrative," Etc., in reply to the above.

—*(2.) A Narrative* of the Proceedings subsequent to the Royal Adjudication concerning the Lands to the Westward of Connecticut

River, lately usurped by New Hampshire, with Remarks on the Claim, Behavior, and Misrepresentations of the Intruders under that Government. Intended as an appendix to the General Assembly's State of the Right of the Colony of New York (with respect to its Eastern Boundary on Connecticut River, so far as concerns the late Encroachments under the Government of New Hampshire.) Published at their session 1773. New York: Printed by John Holt, near the Coffee House. M.DCC. LXXIII. Folio, pp. 28, and appendix 34 leaves.

Reprinted in the Brattleboro Semi-Weekly Eagle, in January and February, 1851.

See Allen, Ethan, "A Brief Narrative of the Proceedings," Etc., in reply to the above.

—*(3.) Appendix*, containing Grants, Acts of Government, and other Proofs concerning the Encroachments of the Colony of New Hampshire, and the Conduct, Claims, and Misrepresentations of its Grantees, referred to in the preceding "State of the Right of the Colony of New York, with respect to its Eastern Boundary on Connecticut River, so far as concerns the Encroachments under the Government of New Hampshire," and also in the "Narrative of Proceedings Subsequent to the Royal Adjudication concerning the Lands to the Westward of Connecticut River, lately occupied by New Hampshire." Folio, pp. 66.

Doubtless printed in 1773.

The three titles above are from B. H. Hall's Bibliography of Vermont; they are connected together, and relate to the same subject; for reply see Allen, Ethan.

Allen's "A Brief Narrative," etc., brought $65 at the Brinley sale; and his "A Vindication," etc., brought $105.

Mr. Henry B. Dawson of Morrisania, N. Y., has (1879) copies of the works covered by the above three titles, with manuscript notes on the margin, being the same copies sent by the Assembly of New York to "Edmund Burke, Esq., Agent for the Colony of New York at the Court of Great Britain," for his use in arguing the case before the King in council.

—*An Address*, of the Inhabitants of the Towns of Plainfield, Lebanon, Enfield, (alias Relhan) Canaan, Cardigan, Hanover, Lime, Orford, Haverhill, Bath, and Landaff to the Inhabitants of the several Towns in the Colony of New Hampshire. Norwich: Printed by John Trumbull, M.DCC.LXXVI. 12mo, pp. 16.

Signed in behalf of the inhabitants of the towns before mentioned, by order of their Committees. Nehemiah Esterbrook, Chairman, Bezaleel Woodward, Clerk. Hanover, July 31, A. D., 1776.

This address appears to have been one of the first steps towards a union of several New Hampshire towns with Vermont.

Reprinted in Governor and Council, Vol. 5, 507-13.

—*Journals* of the Provincial Congress, Provincial Convention, Committee of Safety, and Council of Safety of the State of New York, 1775-1777. Albany: 1842. 2 vols. folio.

Contain many documents and records, relating to the people of New York and Vermont during the first three years of the Revolution.

—*The Documentary History* of New York; arranged under the direction of the Hon. Christopher Morgan, Secretary of State. By E. B. O'Callaghan, M. D. Albany: 1849-50. 4 vols. 4to and 8vo.

Volume IV. from pp. 331 to 623 of the 4to. edition, and from pp. 531 to 1034 8vo edition, contains a series of papers relating to the Vermont Controversy with New York, and forms perhaps the most complete collection of printed documents upon the subject, covering the period from 1749 to the settlement of the controversy in 1790.

—*Vermont.*—New Connecticut.

See "Papers and proceedings of Connecticut Valley Hist. Society 1876-1881," Springfield, Mass., Article,

"Dartmouth College and the State of New Connecticut," pp. 152-206.

—*Observations* on the Right of Jurisdiction claimed by the States of New York and New Hampshire over the New Hampshire Grants (so called), lying on both sides of the Connecticut River, in a Letter to the Inhabitants of those Grants. Danvers: Printed by E. Russell, at his Printing Office, MDCCLXXVIII. 12mo, pp. 15.

Signed, Republican, January 6, 1778. Reprinted in Governor and Council, vol. 5, pp. 513-521.

—*A Public Defence* of the Right of the New Hampshire Grants (so called) on both Sides Connecticut-River, to associate together, and form themselves into an Independent State. Containing Remarks on Sundry Paragraphs of Letters from the President of the Council of New Hampshire to his Excellency Governor Chittenden, and the New Hampshire Delegates at Congress. Dresden: Printed by Alden Spooner. 1779. 12mo, pp. 56, 4.

Reprinted in Governor and Council, Vol. 5, pp. 525-539.

A copy of the above sold for $100 at the Brinley sale in New York, March, 1879.

At a three day's sale in Boston by Sullivan Bros. & Libbie, September 23-5, 1879, of books from the library of W. Elliot Woodward, Esq., of Roxbury, Mass., a copy of "A Public Defence," etc., in fine condition, No. 1434, star, on the catalogue, sold for fifteen dollars.

As the auctioneer, Sullivan, remarked, (the sales being mostly on orders held by the auction house), the audience was "small, but select," numbering not more than a dozen persons, of whom four or five were librarians representing prominent institutions in Boston, and one Vermonter.

After the sale of a rare book, at whatever price it may fetch, it is usual for the auctioneer to rest a moment, that the audience may "catch their breath." During the rest of perhaps twenty seconds after the above book was sold the following pleasant episode occurred:

Vermonter.—(To auctioneer.) "Mr. Sullivan, Vermont books are selling pretty well."

Boston librarian (under a salary of four thousand dollars, or more): "It is a New Hampshire book."

Vermonter: New Hampshire Grants is Vermont."

Bostonian; "The town [Dresden imprint] is in New Hampshire."

Vermonter: "It was at date of imprint a part of Vermont."

A smile all around, and another Boston librarian posted in history, but receiving a salary of perhaps seven or eight hundred dollars, said: "Mr. Vermonter you are right." And the sale proceeded.

—*An Address* to the Inhabitants of the New Hampshire Grants (so called) lying westward of Connecticut River. [By Hon. Timothy Walker, Concord, N. H.]

Dated July 18, 1778, and signed Pacificus; it is in reply to "Observations on the Right of Jurisdiction," etc. Reprinted in Governor and Council, vol. 5, pp. 521-525.

—*A Collection* of Evidence in Vindication of the Territorial Rights and Jurisdiction of the State of New York against the Claims of the Commonwealth of Massachusetts and New Hampshire, and the People of the Grants, who are commonly called Vermonters. Mss. folio, pp. 363.

This work is to be found in the library of the New York Historical Society, and was compared with the original by Jonathan Morin Scott, who signed a statement to that effect at Philadelphia, November 13th, 1780.

See Hall's Bibliography of Vermont.

—*Report of* the Committee on the part of the General Assembly of New York, as to the boundaries of New York. Mss. folio, pp. 25. [Title conjectural.]

The work intended to be referred to is preserved in the library of the New York Historical Society.

See Hall's Bibliography of Vermont.

—*A Copy* of a Remonstrance of the Council of the State of Vermont, Against the Resolutions of Congress of the 5th of December last, which interfere with their internal Police. Hartford: Printed by Hudson & Goodwin. M.DCC. LXXXIII. 12mo, pp. 20.

See Chittenden, Thomas.
Reprinted in the Governor and Council of Vermont, Vol 3, pp. 254-262.
A copy of the above little pamphlet brought $40 at the Brinley sale.

—*Abstract of* an Act to provide for the valuation of Lands and Dwelling-Houses, and the enumeration of Slaves within the United States. To which are added, Instructions and Regulations for the Principal and Assistant Assessors, Made in Pursuance of Said Acts; and the Instructions of the Secretary of the Treasury of the United States. Published by Order of the Board of Commissioners. Vergennes: Printed by G. and R. Waite. 1798. 8vo, pp. 35.

—*The Colony* of New York, and Vermont, in 1772-3. By Hon. Hiland Hall.

See (Dawson's) Historical Magazine. Vol. III, second series, pp. 22-3

—*The New York* Dellius Patent. By Hon. Hiland Hall.

See (Dawson's) Historical Magazine. Vol. III, 2d series, pp. 74-6, and 251.

—*First Fast Day*; June 18, 1777.

See (Dawson's) Historical Magazine. Vol. III, 2d series, pp. 110.

—*Gov. Martin Chittenden* and the War of 1812.

See (Dawson's) Historical Magazine. Vol III, 2d series, pp. 83-85.
See Journals of the Continental and Confederate Congress, 1774 to 1788, 2d edition, 13 vols. Philadelphia: 1800-1801. And Secret Journals, etc., from the first Meeting to the close of the Confederation, and the adoption of the Constitution, 1788. 4 vols. Boston: 1821. These volumes contain all the proceedings in Congress relating to the Vermont controversy with New York.
See Collection of original Historical Papers relating to Vermont in "Rural Magazine; or Vermont Repository," vol. I, 1795. By Samuel Williams & Co.; Hiland Hall's Early History of Vermont, which is exhaustive of the Vermont side especially of the controversy with New York; the "Governor and Council of Vermont," edited by Hon. E. P. Walton, in eight volumes, contains a large amount of matter relating to the New York controversy; The Collections of the Vermont Historical Society, vols. 1 and 2 contain many documents in relation to the subject, including the "Haldimand Papers," in Vol. 2; History of Charlestown, No. 4, by Rev Henry H. Saunderson, pp. 53, 206, contains much information relating to Vermont from 1757 to 1783; Capture of Ticonderoga in 1775—see "Connecticut Historical Society Collections," Vol. 1, pp. 163-188; Clinton, George; Chittenden, Thomas; Duane, James; Dawson's Historical Magazine, 2d and 3d series, for numerous historical papers, relating to Vermont; New Hampshire Provincial and State Papers, etc., 10 vols. 1867-1878; Hall, B. H., "History of Eastern Vermont."

—*Records of* the Council of Safety and Governor and Council of the State of Vermont, to which are prefixed the Records of the General Conventions, from July, 1775 to December, 1777. Edited and Published by Authority of the State by E. P. Walton. Montpelier: Steam Press of J. and J. M. Poland. 1873 to 1880. 8 volumes, 8vo, vol. 1, pp. viii, 556; vol. 2, pp. viii, 528; vol. 3, pp. viii, 540; vol. 4, pp. iv, 554; vol 5, pp. iv. 569; vol. 6, pp. iv, 574; vol. 7, pp. iv, 527; vol. 8, pp. iv. 517.

Illustrated with plates and portraits.
Contents: Vol. 1. General Conventions in the New Hampshire Grants, 1775-77; the first Constitution of Vermont; Council of Safety, 1777-78; Record of the Governor and Council, 1778-79. Appendices: Proceedings of the Congress and Committee of Safety for Cumberland County, 1774-77; Gloucester County Committee of Safety; Some Miscellaneous remarks, etc., by Ira Allen, 1777; Manifesto of the Westminster Convention, 1776; Dr. Thomas Young to the Inhabitants of Vermont, 1777; Remarks on Article Three of the Declaration of Rights, by Hon. Daniel Chipman; the name "Vermont"; first Union of New Hampshire towns with Vermont, 1778-79; Proclamation of Pardon by Governor Chittenden, 1779; Vindication of the Opposition of the Inhabitants of Vermont, to the Government of New York, by Ethan Allen, 1779; Enforcement of Authority in Cumberland County, 1779; Additions and Corrections.

Vol. 2. Record of the Governor and Council, 1779-82; Records of the Board of War. Appendices: The first Vermont Council Chamber, by Hiland Hall; Resolutions of Congress, 1779, and action of Vermont thereon; the Claim of Massachusetts to a part of Vermont; Vermont's Appeal to the candid and impartial World, by S. R. Bradley; a Concise Refutation of the Claims of New Hampshire and Massachusetts Bay to Vermont, by Ethan Allen and Jonas Fay; Mission of Ira Allen to the Middle States, 1780; action of Congress on Vermont, 1780; second Union of New Hampshire Towns and part of New York with Vermont, 1781; the Haldimand Correspondence, 1779-83; Protest of Adherents to New York, against Vermont, 1779, and Origin of the Charlestown Convention, January, 1781; Additions and Corrections.

Vol. 3. Record of the Governor and Council, 1782-91. Appendices: Resolutions of Congress, hostile to Vermont, 1782; Renewed Application of Vermont for Admission into the Union; Insurrection in Windham County, 1783-84; Obstacles in Congress to the Admission of new States, 1785-6; Conflicting Titles to Land in Vermont; Vermont at the period of Shays' Rebellion, 1784-87; Vermont Acts of Sovereignty; Settlement of the Controversy with New York; the Vermont Convention of 1791; Admission of Vermont into the Union; Papers of Charles Phelps, Esq., 1770-77; Additions and Corrections.

Vol. 4. Record of the Governor and Council, 1791-1804. Appendices: Vermont in 1791, as viewed by a Virginian; Amendments to the Federal Constitution; Letters of Public officers of Vermont, 1791-1802; Internal Improvements; Champlain Canal and Navigation of Connecticut River; Surveillance of the Northern Frontier by British Troops, 1783-96; Extradition of Fugitives from Justice, 1796-99; Addresses of the General Assembly to Presidents of the United States, and replies; Obituary Notices of Governor Chittenden and Jonathan Arnold; Governor's Speeches to the Assembly, and Replies, 1797-1803; the Kentucky and Virginia Resolutions of 1798, and Answers of Vermont; last Speech of Governor Chittenden; Additions and Corrections.

Vol. 5. Record of the Governor and Council, 1804-13. Appendices: Governor's Speeches to the General Assembly, and Replies, 1804-12; Amendments to the Federal Constitution; State Capitals, and State Houses; the Vermont State Bank, 1806-12; Northern Boundary Line of Vermont; Addresses of the General Assembly to the Presidents of the United States, and Replies, 1806-1812; the State Prison; British Intrigue in New England, 1809; Domestic Manufactures in Vermont, 1809; Correspondence between Governor Tichenor, of Vermont, and Governor Craig, of Canada, in 1809, on the Suppression of Counterfeiting in Canada; Origin and Causes of the Union of New Hampshire Towns with Vermont, 1778 and 1781.

Vol. 6. Record of the Governor and Council, 1813-22. Appendices: Governor's Speeches to the General Assembly and Replies, 1813-21; Boundary Line between New York and Vermont; Proposed Amendments to the Federal Constitution; Vermont opposed to the Hartford Convention; Vermont in the War of 1812; Vermont on Slavery and the Missouri Question, 1819-20; Rights of the respective States to the Public Lands of the United States; Additions and Corrections.

Vol. 7. Record of the Governor and Council, 1822-31; Appendices: Governor's Speeches to the General Assembly, 1822-30, inclusive; Proposed Amendments to the Federal Constitution, etc.; Internal Improvements in Vermont, 1823-45; Visit of Lafayette to Vermont in 1825; Additions and Corrections.

Vol. 8. Record of the Governor and Council, 1832-36. Appendices: Governor's Speeches to the General Assembly; Boundary Line between Vermont and New Hampshire; Tenure of the Executive office; Resolutions on topics of National Policy; the Second State House; Judges of the Supreme Court Arraigned, and Vindicated; Biographical and Historical; Claim of the Cognawaga Indians to Vermont; Additional Historical Documents; Some old maps touching Vermont; Tour of President Monroe in Vermont; Lists of some officers; Chronological Index to the 8 volumes; List of portraits and engravings; Acknowledgements; Additions and Corrections. This volume closes the series, the Council having been superseded by a State Senate in 1836.

These volumes are of great value to the student of Vermont history, the appendices especially containing a vast amount of historical material, copiously illustrated with notes, biographical and other, by Mr. Walton, not elsewhere readily accessible.

See "Stevens' Papers," some 30 volumes; see "Allen Papers," 4 volumes, both in manuscript in the Secretary of State's office at Montpelier.

—*Vermont State Papers.*
See Slade, William.

CONSTITUTION AND CONSTITUTIONAL CONVENTIONS.

—*The Constitution* of the State of Vermont, as established by the General Convention elected for that purpose, and held at Windsor, July 2d, 1777, and Continued by Adjournment to December 25, 1777. Hartford: Printed by Watson and Goodwin. 8vo, pp. 24.
The first Constitution of the State.

—*The Constitution* of the State of Vermont. As Revised by the Council of Censors. And Recommended for the Consideration of the People. Windsor: Printed by Hough and Spooner. Printers to the State of Vermont, M, DCC,LXXXV. 4to, pp. 44.

—*The Constitution* of Vermont. As established by Convention in the Year 1778, and Revised by Convention in June, 1786. Windsor: Printed by Hough and Spooner. M,DCC,LXXXVI. 4to.

—*The Constitution* of Vermont, as Revised and Amended by the Council of Censors, at their Session holden in Rutland, October, 1792. Printed by order of the Council. By Anthony Haswell, Printer for the State in the Western District, at the Rutland Press.

—*The Constitution of Vermont.* As Adopted by the Convention Holden at Windsor, July Fourth, One Thousand, seven hundred and ninety-three. Windsor: Printed by Alden Spooner. M,DCC,XCIII. 4to, pp. 29.

—*Journal of the Convention of Vermont,* at their Session, begun and holden at Montpelier, in the County of Jefferson, on Thursday, the Seventh day of July, A. D. 1914. Published by Order of Convention. Danville: Printed by Ebenezer Eaton. 1814. 8vo, pp. 23.

—*An Essay on the Amendments* Proposed to the Constitution of the State of Vermont, by the Council of Censors. Delivered at the Celebration of Washington's Birth Day, at Norwich, on the 22d of February, 1814. By Charles Marsh, Esquire. Hanover, N. H.: Printed by Charles Spear. 8vo, pp. 24.

—*Journal of the Convention of Vermont,* Assembled at the State House, at Montpelier, On the 21st day of February, and dissolved on the 23d day of February, 1822. Published by Order of the Convention. Burlington: J. Spooner, Printer. 1822. 8vo, pp. 39.

—*Journal of the Convention of Vermont,* Convened at the State House at Montpelier, June 26, A. D. 1828. Published by order of the Convention. Royalton: Printed by Wyman Spooner. 8vo, pp. 22.

—*Journal of the Convention* Holden at Montpelier, on the 6th day of January, A. D. 1836,

agreeable to the Ordinance of the Council of Censors, made on the 16th day of January, 1835, together with the Amendments of the Constitution, as Adopted by the Convention. St. Albans: J. Spooner, Printer 1836. 8vo, pp. 124.

—*Speech* of Hon. Daniel Chipman, delivered in the Convention Holden at Montpelier, on the Sixth day of January, 1836. While in Committee of the whole on the proposed Articles of Amendment to the Constitution, Constituting a Senate. Motto. Middlebury: Printed by E. R. Jewett. 1837. 8vo, pp. 25.

—*Journal of the Convention,* Holden at Montpelier, on the fourth day of January, A. D. 1843, agreeable to the Ordinance of the Council of Censors, Made on the Fourteenth day of February, 1842, to consider certain Amendments proposed to the Constitution of the State of Vermont. Published by Order of the Convention. Montpelier: J. T. Marston. 1843. 8vo, pp. 34, (1).

—*Journal of the Constitutional Convention,* Holden at Montpelier, on the Second day of January, A. D. 1850, Agreeable to the Ordinance of the Council of Censors : Made on the twenty-eighth day of February, 1849, to consider certain amendments proposed to the Constitution of the State of Vermont. Published by order of the Convention. Burlington: Sentinel Office Print. 1850. 8vo, pp. 115.

—*Constitution of The State of Vermont :* Adopted by Conventions held in the Years 1786, 1793, 1828, 1836 and 1850. Published by Order of the General Assembly. Montpelier: E. P. Walton & Son. 1852. 8vo, pp. 56. (1).

—*Journal of the Proceedings* of the Constitutional Convention, assembled at Montpelier, on the First Wednesday of January, 1857. Burlington : George J. Stacy, Book and Job Printer. 1857. 8vo, pp. 39.

—*Journal of the Proceedings* of the Constitutional Convention of the State of Vermont, begun and held at the State House in Montpelier, on the 8th of June, 1870. Printed by Authority. Burlington : Free Press Print. 1870. 8vo, pp. 75, iii.

—*A Last Resort.* Published for Gratuitous Distribution. To all Civilized Men and Women this small pamphlet is respectfully dedicated. By Harvey Howes. Fair Haven : D. Lyman Crandall, Printer, Journal Office. 1870. 8vo, pp. 9.
Relates to Woman Suffrage.

COUNCIL OF CENSORS.
—*The Proceedings* of the Council of Censors of the State of Vermont. Windsor. Printed by Hough and Spooner M.DCCC.LXXXVI. 4to, pp. 20.
This was the first Council ; contains the Address only.

—*Proceedings of the Council of Censors* of the State of Vermont, At their Sessions holden at Rutland, in the year 1792. Published by Order of the Council, for the Inspection of the People, in conformity to the XLth Section of the Constitution. And for the Consideration of a Convention of the Freemen of this State, to convene at Windsor, on the First Wednesday of July, 1793. Printed by Anthony Haswell, in Rutland, MDCC.XCII. 12mo, pp. 80.

—*An Address* (and Proceedings) of the Council of Censors, to the People of Vermont. Western District, Vermont. Bennington : Printed by Anthony Haswell. M.DCCC. 8vo, pp. 32,(1).

—*Journal of the Council of Censors*, at their Sessions in June and October, 1813, and January, 1814. Middlebury : Printed by Slade & Ferguson. 1814. 8vo, pp. 56.

—*An Address* of the Council of Censors, to the People of Vermont; together with proposed amendments to the Constitution. Montpelier, Vt.: Printed by Walton & Goss. 1813. 8vo, pp. 16.

—*An Address* (and Proceedings) of the Council of Censors. (Chosen March 26th, 1806.) To the People of Vermont. Bennington : Printed by Anthony Haswell. 1807. 8vo, pp. 12.

·—*The Constitutionalist;* or Amendments of the Constitution proposed by the Council of Censors, supported by the Writings and Opinions of James Wilson, LL. D. Late one of the Associate Justices of the Supreme Court of the United States, and Professor of Law in the College of Philadelphia. Also by the Writings and Opinions of other Eminent Citizens of the United States, with explanatory Notes of modern date. The only skill and knowledge of any value in Politics is that of Governing All by All. Heraclitus, in Sir W. Temple's Miscellany. Montpelier, Vt.: Printed by Walton & Goss. 1814. 8vo, pp. 36.
Supposed by Nathaniel Chipman.

—*Journal of the Council of Censors;* At their Sessions in June & October, 1820 ; and March, 1821. Published by order of the Council. Danville : Ebenezer Eaton, Printer. 1821. 8vo, pp. 64.

—*Articles of Amendment to the Constitution* of the State of Vermont, proposed by the Council of Censors, on the 24th day of March, A. D. 1821. Together with an Address to the People, and an Ordinance, for Calling a Convention. Published by order of the Council of Censors. E. P. Walton, Printer. 1821. 8vo, pp. 28.

—*Journal of the Council of Censors*, at their Sessions at Montpelier and Burlington, in June, October, and November, 1827. Published by order of the Council. Printed by E. P. Walton, Montpelier, Vt. 1828. 8vo, pp. 48.

—*Journal of the Council of Censors*, at their Sessions Holden at Montpelier and Middlebury in June and October, 1834, and January, 1835. Published by order of the Council. Middlebury : Knapp & Jewett, Printers. 1835. 8vo, pp. 68.

—*Journal of the Sessions of the Council of Censors*, of the State of Vermont, Held at Montpelier, in June, and October, A. D. 1841, and at Burlington, in February, A. D. 1842. Burlington : Chauncey Goodrich. 1842. 8vo, pp. 75.

—*Articles of Amendment of the Constitution* of Vermont, proposed by the Council of Censors, in 1842 ; and the Articles proposed to be amended ; with the Address of said Council. Burlington : Chauncey Goodrich. 1842. 8vo, pp. 20.

—*Journal of the Council of Censors* of the State of Vermont, at their several sessions in Montpelier and Burlington, 1848–9. Published by Authority. Burlington : Free Press Office Print. 1849. 8vo, pp. 87.

—*In Council of Censors.* February 14, 1849. Report, by John Pomeroy, for Committee. [n. p. n. d.] 8vo, pp. 7.

—*The Journal of the Council of Censors* of the State of Vermont, at their several sessions in Montpelier and Middlebury, 1855–6. Published by Authority. Middlebury : Printed at the Register Book and Job Office. 1856. 8vo, pp. 108.

—*Address of the Council of Censors* to the General Assembly of the State of Vermont. October, 1855. Montpelier : E. P. Walton, Jr., Printer. 1855. 8vo, pp. 13.

—*Journal of the Council of Censors* of the State of Vermont, at its first session in Montpelier, June, 1862. Published by order of Council. Montpelier : Walton's Steam Printing Establishment. 1862. 8vo, pp. 24.
Also includes the proceedings of the October session.

—*State of Vermont.* Proposed Articles of Amendment to the Constitution, adopted by the Council of Censors; the Articles of the present Constitution to be affected thereby; the Ordinance of Said Council ; and an Address to the People. Council of Censors. 1869. Montpelier, Vt.: Argus and Patriot Printing House. 8vo, pp. 13.

—*State of Vermont.* Proposed Articles of Amendment to the Constitution. Pending in the Council of Censors. Second Session. 1869. Freeman Print. 8vo, pp. 7.

—*State of Vermont.* Report of Special Committee on Woman Suffrage, Council of Censors, Second Session. 1869. Freeman Print. 8vo, pp. 8.

—*Report of Committee* on Taxes and Expenditures. Council of Censors, Second Session, 1869. Freeman Print. 8vo.

—*State of Vermont.* Report of Special Committee on Biennial Sessions and Elections. Council of Censors, Second Session. 1869. Freeman Print. 8vo, pp. 9.

—*Supplemental Report* of Majority of Special Committee on Changing the Mode of Amending the Constitution. Council of Censors, Second Session. 1869. Freeman Print. 8vo, pp. 6.

—*Minority Report* on the Same. Journal Print. 8vo, pp. 11.

—*State of Vermont.* Report of Special Committee on the Resolution of Mr. Lane, Relating to Corporations. Council of Censors. Second Session. 1869. Montpelier : Journal Print. 1869. 8vo, pp. 4.

—*State of Vermont.* Report of Special Committee on the Judiciary. Council of Censors, Second Session. 1869. Freeman Print. 8vo, pp. 23.

—*The Same*, Supplemental Report. Same imprint. 8vo, pp. 4.

—*Report of* Executive Committee. Council of Censors, Second Session. 1869. Journal Print. 8vo, pp. 4.

—*Journal of* the Council of Censors of the State of Vermont, at its several sessions held in Montpelier. 1869. Published by order of the Council. Montpelier: Freeman Steam Printing House and Bindery. 1869. 8vo, pp. 106, (1).

By an amendment to the Constitution in 1870 the Council of Censors was abolished.

ACTS AND LAWS.

The following list of titles to official publications by the State was copied from files in the State Library, and notes as to the condition of the documents relate to those files only, unless otherwise stated. It will be noticed that the file of earlier session laws is incomplete, and that many are imperfect.

—*Acts and Laws* Passed by the General Assembly of the Representatives of the Freemen of the State of Vermont, at their Session, at Bennington, February 11th, A. D. 1779. [Dresden: Judah Paddock & Alden Spooner. 1779]. rl. 8vo, pp. 12, (2), 110.

The Constitution occupies the first 12 pp.
Called the "General Code" of 1779.
The laws of the first three sessions, March, June and October, 1778, are not known to be extant in manuscript or print.
See Brinley catalogue, part 1, 298, for imprint. Brought $20 at Brinley sale.

—*Acts and Laws*, Made and Passed by the General Assembly of the Representatives of the Freemen of the State of Vermont, at their Sessions at Windsor, June 2d, A. D. 1779. rl. 8vo, pp. (4).

Pagination continuous with the above.
Title page wanting.

—*Acts and Laws*, Passed by the General Assembly of the Representatives of the Freemen of the State of Vermont, at their Session at Manchester, October, 1779. Hartford: Printed by Hudson and Goodwin. M.DCC.LXXX. rl. 8vo, pp. (8).

Four acts not published.

—*Acts and Laws*, Passed by the General Assembly of the Representatives of the Freemen of the State of Vermont, at their Session at Westminster, March 8th, A. D. 1780. Hartford: Printed by Hudson & Goodwin. M.DCC. LXXX. rl. 8vo, pp. 5.

One act not printed.
Printed in continuation of the acts of the October Session, at Manchester, and the imprint is at the close for both sessions.

—*Acts and Laws*, Passed by the General Assembly of the Representatives of the State of Vermont, at their Session at Bennington, October, 1780. rl. 8vo, pp. 16.

Imperfect, several leaves, 17 acts, wanting.

—*Acts and Laws*, passed by the General Assembly of the Representatives of the Freemen of the State of Vermont, at their Session at Windsor, February, 1781. Westminster: Printed by Judah P. Spooner and Timothy Green, Printers to the State of Vermont. rl. 8vo, pp. 11.

—*Acts and Laws*, Passed by the General Assembly of the Representatives of the State of Vermont, at their Session at Windsor, April, 1781. rl. 8vo, pp. 4.

Imperfect, several leaves, 15 Acts, wanting.

—*Revised Laws* of the State of Vermont, passed at the Sessions held in Windsor and Manchester, in June and October, 1782. n.p.n.d. pp. 38.

—*Acts and Laws* passed at the Session held at Rutland, in October, 1784. Windsor: Hough & Spooner. 1785. pp. 12.

—*Acts and Laws* Passed at the Session held at Windsor, in October, 1785. [Windsor: Hough & Spooner. 1785.] n. p. n. d. pp. 9.

The three titles above, from Brinley Catalogue, brought $32 at that sale.
The Session Laws of permanent interest of the nineteen sessions from February, 1779, to October, 1786, are reprinted in "Slade's Vermont State Papers," pp. 287-510.

—*Statutes* of the State of Vermont, Passed by the Legislature in February and March, 1787. Windsor: Printed by George Hough and Alden Spooner, Printers to the General Assembly of the State. M.DCC.LXXXVII. 4to, pp. 171.

Sold for $15 at Brinley sale.

—*Acts and Laws*, Passed by the Legislature of the State of Vermont, at their Session at Newbury, the second Thursday of October, 1787. 4to, pp. 16.

Title page wanting.

—*Acts and Laws*, Passed by the Legislature of the State of Vermont, at their session at Manchester, the second Thursday of October, 1788. 4to, pp. 28.

Title page wanting.

—*Acts and Laws*, Passed by the Legislature of the State of Vermont, at their session at Westminster, the second Thursday of October, 1789. Windsor: Hough & Spooner. 4to, pp. 19.

Title page wanting.

—*Acts and Laws*, Passed by the Legislature of the State of Vermont, at their Session at Castleton, the second Thursday of October, 1790. 4to, pp. 11.

Title page wanting.

—*Acts and Laws*, Passed by the Legislature of the State of Vermont, at their Adjourned Session at Bennington, January, 1791. Printed at Bennington by Anthony Haswell, for the Honorable General Assembly. 8vo, pp. 28.

—*Acts and Laws*, Passed by the Legislature of the State of Vermont, at their session at Windsor, October, 1791. Printed at Windsor by Alden Spooner, for the General Assembly. 8vo, pp. 32.

Ten pages wanting.

—*Acts and Laws*, Passed by the Legislature of the State of Vermont, at their Session at Rutland, in October, 1792. Western District. Rutland: Printed by Order of the Legislature, at the Press of Anthony Haswell. 8vo, pp. 95.

—*Acts and Laws*, Passed by the Legislature of the State of Vermont, at their Session at Windsor, October, One Thousand Seven Hundred and Ninety-Three. Windsor: Printed by Alden Spooner. M.DCC.XCIII. 8vo, pp. 70.

—*Acts and Laws*, Passed by the Legislature of the State of Vermont, at their Session Holden at Rutland, on the second Thursday of October, 1794. Western District, Vermont. Bennington: Printed by Order of the Legislature, at the Press of Anthony Haswell. 12mo, pp. 171.

—*Acts and Laws*, Passed by the Legislature of the State of Vermont, at their Session Holden at Windsor, on the second Thursday of October, One Thousand Seven Hundred and Ninety-five. Rutland: Printed by Order of the Legislature. 8vo, pp. 166.

—*Acts and Laws,* Passed by the Legislature of the State of Vermont, at their Session Holden at Rutland, on the second Thursday of October, One Thousand Seven Hundred and Ninety-six. Bennington: Printed by Anthony Haswell. 1796. 8vo, pp. 182.

—*Acts and Laws,* Passed by the Legislature of the State of Vermont, At their Adjourned Session holden at Rutland, February, A. D. One thousand seven hundred and ninety-seven. Bennington: Printed by Anthony Haswell. 1797. 8vo, pp. 100.

—*Acts and Laws* Passed by the Legislature of the State of Vermont, at their Session at Windsor, October, One Thousand Seven Hundred and Ninety-seven. Published by Authority. Printed at Rutland, by Josiah Fay, For the Hon. Legislature. M.DCC.XCVIII. 8vo, pp. 110.

—*Acts and Laws.* Passed by the Legislature of the State of Vermont. At their Session Holden at Vergennes, October One Thousand Seven Hundred and Ninety Eight. Bennington: Printed by Anthony Haswell. 1799. 8vo, pp. 141, (1).

—*Acts and Laws,* Passed by the Legislature of the State of Vermont at their Session Holden at Windsor, In October, A. D. One Thousand Seven Hundred & Ninety Nine. Rutland: Printed by order of the Legislature. 8vo, pp. 183.

—*Acts and Laws* Passed by the Legislature of the State of Vermont, at their Session Holden at Middlebury, In October, M.DCCC. Printed by Order of the Legislature. By Anthony Haswell, Assignee of the Hon. Samuel Williams, esq. deceased. 8vo, pp. 156.

—*Acts and Laws* Passed by the Legislature of the State of Vermont, at their Session at Newbury, In October, 1801. Windsor: Printed by Alden Spooner, Printer to the State of Vermont, for the Eastern District. 1801. 8vo, pp. 171, 12, (1).

—*Acts & Laws* Passed by the Legislature of the State of Vermont, at their Session at Burlington, In October, 1802. Bennington: Printed by Anthony Haswell, & Co. 1802. 8vo, pp. 222.

—*Acts and Laws* Passed by the Legislature of the State of Vermont, at their Session at Westminster, In October, 1803. Windsor: Printed by Alden Spooner, Printer to the State of Vermont, for the Eastern District. 1803. 8vo, pp. 156.

—*Acts and Laws* Passed by the Legislature of the State of Vermont, at their adjourned Session at Windsor, in January, One Thousand Eight Hundred and Four. Windsor: Printed by Alden Spooner, Printer to the State of Vermont, for the Eastern District. 1804. 8vo, pp. 100.

—*Acts and Laws* Passed by the General Assembly of the State of Vermont, at their Session, Begun and Holden at Rutland, In October, 1804. Published by Order of the Legislature. Printed by Haswell and Smead, Bennington. 1805. 8vo, pp. 166, (2), x.

—*Acts and Laws* Passed by the Legislature of the State of Vermont, at their Session at Danville, on the Second Thursday of October, One Thousand Eight Hundred and Five. Windsor: Printed by Alden Spooner, Printer to the State of Vermont. 1805. 8vo, pp. 256.

—*Acts and Laws* Passed by the Legislature of the State of Vermont, at their Session at Middlebury, on the Second Thursday of October, One Thousand Eight Hundred and Six. Bennington: Printed by Anthony Haswell, State Printer. 8vo, pp. 204.

—*Acts and Laws,* passed by the Legislature of the State of Vermont, at their Session at Woodstock, on the Second Thursday of October, One Thousand Eight Hundred and Seven. Randolph: Printed by Sereno Wright, State Printer. 8vo, pp. 214.

—*Acts & Laws* passed by the Legislature of the State of Vermont, at their Session at Montpelier, on the Second Thursday of October One thousand eight hundred and eight. Bennington: Printed by Anthony Haswell, State Printer. 8vo, pp. 192.

—*Acts and Laws* passed by the Legislature of the State of Vermont, at their Session at Montpelier, on the Second Thursday of October, One thousand eight hundred and nine. Published by Order of the Legislature. Randolph: Printed by Sereno Wright, Printer to the State. 1809. 8vo, pp. 140.

—*Acts & Laws* passed by the Legislature of the State of Vermont, at their Session at Montpelier, on the Second Thursday of October, One Thousand Eight Hundred and Ten. Danville: Printed by Ebenezer Eaton, State Printer. 8vo, pp. 183.

—*Acts and Laws,* passed by the Legislature of the State of Vermont, at their Session at Montpelier, on the second Thursday of October, One Thousand Eight Hundred and Eleven. Rutland: Printed by William Fay, Printer to the State. 8vo, pp. 176.

—*Acts and Laws,* passed by the Legislature of the State of Vermont, at their session at Montpelier, on the second Thursday of October, One Thousand Eight Hundred and Twelve. Danville: Printed by Ebenezer Eaton, State Printer. 8vo, pp. 220.

—*Laws,* passed by the Legislature of the State of Vermont, at their session at Montpelier, on the second Thursday of October, One Thousand Eight Hundred and Thirteen. Rutland: Printed by Fay & Davison, For W. Fay, State Printer. 8vo, pp. 208.

—*Laws,* passed by the Legislature of the State of Vermont, at their session at Montpelier, on the second Thursday of October, One Thousand, Eight Hundred and Fourteen. Windsor: Printed by Thomas M. Pomeroy, State Printer. 8vo, pp. 166.

—*Laws,* passed by the Legislature of the State of Vermont, at their session at Montpelier, on the second Thursday of October, One Thousand Eight Hundred and Fifteen. Windsor: Printed by Thomas M. Pomeroy, State Printer. 8vo, pp. 178.

—*Laws*, passed by the Legislature of the State of Vermont, at their session at Montpelier, Commenced on the second Thursday of October, One Thousand Eight Hundred and Sixteen. Windsor: Printed by Jesse Cochran, State Printer. 8vo, pp. 151.

—*Laws* passed by the Legislature of the State of Vermont, at their session at Montpelier, Commenced on the second Thursday of October, One Thousand Eight Hundred and Seventeen. Middlebury: Published by William Slade, Jun. Frederick P. Allen, Printer. 8vo, pp. 144.

—*Laws*, passed by the Legislature of the State of Vermont, at their session at Montpelier, Commenced on the second Thursday of October One Thousand Eight Hundred and Eighteen. Windsor, Vt.: Published for the State By Ide & Aldrich. 8vo, pp. 262.

—*Laws*, passed by the Legislature of the State of Vermont, at their session at Montpelier, commenced on the second Thursday of October, One Thousand Eight Hundred and Nineteen. Rutland, Vt. Published for the State, by Fay & Burt. 8vo, pp. 207.

—*Acts*, passed by the Legislature of the State of Vermont, at their October session, 1820. Published by Authority. Middlebury: Printed by Copeland & Allen. 8vo, pp. 164.

—*Acts*, passed by the Legislature of the State of Vermont, at their October Session, 1821. Published by Authority. Middlebury: Printed by Copeland & Allen. 1821. 8vo, pp. 221.

—*Acts*, passed by the Legislature of the State of Vermont, at their October session, 1822. Published by Authority. Poultney: Printed by Smith & Shute. 1822. 8vo, pp. 102, 4.

—*Acts*, passed by the Legislature of the State of Vermont, at their October session, 1823. Published by Authority. Bennington: Clark & Doolittle, Printers. 8vo, pp. 101.

—*Acts*, passed by the Legislature of the State of Vermont, at their October session, 1824. Published by Authority, by William Haswell. Bennington: Clark & Doolittle, Printers. 8vo, pp. 128.

—*Acts*, passed by the Legislature of the State of Vermont, at their October session, 1825. Published by Authority, by Simeon Ide. 8vo, pp. 152.

—*Acts*, passed by the Legislature of the State of Vermont, at their October session, 1826. Published by Authority. Bennington: D. Clark, printer. 8vo, pp. 112.

—*Acts*, passed by the Legislature of the State of Vermont, at their October session, 1827. Published by Authority. Woodstock Vt.: D. Watson, Printer. 8vo, pp. 102.

—*Acts*, passed by the Legislature of the State of Vermont, at their October session, 1828. Published by Authority. Woodstock: Printed by Rufus Colton. 8vo, pp. 72.

—*The Same*, 1829. Woodstock: D. Watson, Printer. 8vo, pp. 84.

—*The Same*, 1830. Woodstock: R. & A. Colton, Printers. 8vo, pp. 67.

—*The Same*, 1831. Middlebury: Printed for the State by A. Colton. 1831. 8vo, pp. 126.

—*The Same*, 1832. Montpelier: Knapp & Jewett, Printers. 1832. 8vo, pp. 124.

—*The Same*, 1833. Same imprint. 8vo, pp. 110.

—*The Same*, 1834. 8vo, pp. 111.

—*Laws of Vermont.* Acts passed by the Legislature of the State of Vermont, at their October Session, 1835. Published by Authority. Montpelier: E. P. Walton & Son, Printers. 1835. 8vo, pp. 150.

—*The Same*, 1836. Same imprint. 8vo. pp. 181.

—*The Same*, 1837. Same imprint. 8vo, pp. 112.

—*Acts and Resolves* passed by the Legislature of the State of Vermont, at their October Session, 1838. Published by Authority. Montpelier: E. P. Walton & Son, Printers. 1838. 8vo, pp. 115.

—*The Same*, 1839. E. P. Walton & Sons. 8vo, pp. 102.

—*The Same*, 1840. Burlington: Chauncey Goodrich. 1840. 8vo, pp. 68.

—*The Same*, 1841. Montpelier: E. P. Walton & Sons. 1841. 8vo, pp. 69.

—*The Same*, 1842. Same imprint. 8vo, pp. 133.

—*The Same*, 1843. Same imprint. 8vo, pp. 77.

—*The Same*, 1844. Burlington: Chauncey Goodrich. 1844. 8vo, pp. 54, 24.

—*The Same*, 1845. Same imprint. 8vo, pp. 95.

—*The Same*, 1846. Same imprint. 8vo, pp. 96.

—*The Same*, 1847. Same imprint. 8vo, pp. 128.

—*The Same*, 1848. Same imprint. 8vo, pp. 110.

—*The Same*, 1849. Montpelier: E. P. Walton & Son. 1849. 8vo, pp. 172.

—*The Same*, 1850. Same imprint. 8vo, pp. 182.

—*The Same*, 1851. Same imprint. 8vo, pp. 166.

—*The Acts and Resolves Passed* by the General Assembly of the State of Vermont, at their October Session, 1852. Published by Authority. Montpelier: E. P. Walton & Son, Printers. 1852. 8vo, pp. 219.

—*The Same*, 1853. Montpelier: E. P. Walton, Jr., Printer. 1853. 8vo, pp. 220.

—*The Same*, 1854. Same imprint. 8vo, pp. 189.

—*The Same*, 1855. Same imprint. 8vo, pp. 239.

—*The Same*, 1856. Montpelier: E. P. Walton, Printer. 1856. 8vo, pp. 229.

—*The Same*, 1857. Same imprint. 8vo, pp. 199.

—*The Same*, 1858. Bradford: John D. Clark, Printer. 1858. 8vo, pp. 237.

—*The Same*, 1859. Montpelier: E. P. Walton, Printer. 1859. 8vo, pp. 196.

—*The Same*, 1860. Same imprint. 8vo, pp. 200.

—*The Same*, 1861. Same imprint. 8vo, pp. 205.

—*The Same*, 1862. Montpelier: Printed at the Freeman Printing Establishment. 1862. 8vo, pp. 160.

—*The Same*, 1863. Same imprint. 8vo, pp. 140.

—*The Same*, 1864. Same imprint. 8vo, pp. 240.

—*The Same*, 1865. Same imprint. 8vo, pp. 293.

—*The Same*, 1866. Same imprint, 8vo, pp. 348.

—*The Same*, 1867, Same imprint, 8vo, pp. 408.

—*The Same*, 1868. Same imprint. 8vo, pp. 378.

—*The Same*, 1869. Same imprint. 8vo, pp. 344.

—*The Same*, 1870. First Biennial Session. Montpelier: J. & J. M. Poland's Steam Printing Works. 1870. 8vo, pp. 648.

—*The Same*, 1872. Same imprint. 8vo, pp. 747.

—*The Same*, 1874. Montpelier: Freeman Steam Printing House and Bindery. 1874. 8vo, pp. 493, 14.
Includes Laws of Special Session, January, 1875.

—*The Same*, 1876. Rutland: Tuttle & Company, Printers and Publishers. 1876. 8vo, pp. 496.

—*The Same*, 1878. Montpelier: J. & J. M. Poland, Official State Printers. 1878. 8vo, pp. 328.
Continued.

—*Statutes of the State of Vermont;* Revised and Established By Authority, in the year M.DCC.LXXXVII, Including those passed since that period until the session of the assembly of said State, holden at Bennington in January, 1791. Likewise, the several acts respecting sales by the Surveyor General. Printed in Bennington, Vermont, in the year M.DCC.XCI. By Anthony Haswell. 8vo, pp. 315. (5).

—*Laws of the State of Vermont;* Revised and passed by the Legislature, in the year of our Lord, One Thousand Seven Hundred and Ninety-Seven. Together with the Declaration of Independence, the Constitution of the United States, with its Amendments, and the Constitution of the State of Vermont: With an Appendix, Containing The several Laws, which have heretofore been passed by the Legislature, regulating Proprietors' Meetings, granting General Land Taxes, exclusive privileges to Companies for Locks, Toll Bridges, Turnpike Roads, &c. And the Titles of all the Acts which have been repealed, or become obsolete. Published by Authority. State of Vermont. Printed at Rutland, by Jonas Fay. M.DCC, XCVIII. 8vo, pp. 621, 205, (2).

—*The Laws of the State of Vermont*, Digested and Compiled: Including the Declaration of Independence, the Constitution of the United States, and of this State. Volumes first and second, coming down to, and including the year MDCCCXII; With an Appendix, containing titles of Local Acts; and an index of the Laws in Force. Published by Order of the Legislature. Vols. 1 and 2. Randolph: Printed by Sereno Wright, Printer to the State. 1808. 8vo, pp. IV, 503, and IV, 551, (2).

—*Laws of the State of Vermont*, to the close of the Session of the Legislature in the year 1816; with an Appendix, containing the titles of Local Acts, and an Index of the Laws in Force. Vol. III. Rutland: Published by Fay, Davison & Burt. 1817. 8vo, pp. 336.
This is a continuation of the two volume edition of 1808.

—*The Laws of Vermont*, of a Publick and Permanent Nature: Coming down to, and including the year 1824. To which are prefixed the Declaration of Independence, the Articles of Confederation, and the Constitutions of the United States and of Vermont. Compiled by Authority of the Legislature, by Wm. Slade, Jun. Windsor: Published for the State, by Simeon Ide. 1825. 8vo, pp. 756.

—*The Laws of Vermont*, of a Public and Permanent Nature, Coming down to, and including the year 1834. Compiled by Authority of the Legislature, by Daniel P. Thompson. Montpelier: Knapp & Jewett, Printers. 1835. 8vo, pp. 228.
See Kinsman, J. B., for compilation of laws relating to Towns and Town Officers.

—*The Revised Statutes* of the State of Vermont, passed November 19, 1839. To which are added several public Acts now in force; and to which are prefixed the Constitutions of the United States and of the State of Vermont. Published by Order of the Legislature. Burlington: Chauncey Goodrich. 1840. 8vo, pp. xi. 676.
Analysis and Index to Laws. See Parmalee, S. N.

—*The Revised Statutes* of the State of Vermont Reduced to Questions and Answers for the use of Schools and Families. (Vermont Seal and Motto). By William B. Wedgwood, A. M. Revised and corrected By a Member of the Vermont Bar. Brattleboro: Published by Joseph Steen. 1844. 12mo, pp. 96.

—*The Compiled Statutes* of the State of Vermont, being such of the Revised Statutes, and of the Public Acts and Laws Passed since, as are now in force. To which are prefixed the Constitutions of the United States and of the State of Vermont. Compiled, in pursuance of an Act of the Legislature, by Charles L. Williams. Burlington: Chauncey Goodrich. 1851. rl 8vo, pp. 815.

—*The General Statutes* of the State of Vermont: Passed at the Annual Session of the General Assembly, commencing October 9, 1862. Together with certain Public Acts of the year 1862: To which are prefixed the Constitutions of the United States and the State of Vermont: Edited and published in pursuance of an Act of the Legislature. Published by the State of Vermont: 1863. rl 8vo, pp. xi. (1), 1050.

—*The Same*, Second Edition, with an Appendix. Comprising the Public Laws Enacted since the Annual Session of 1862. 1870. rl 8vo, pp. lxii. 1352.

—*The Same*, 1873, also 1877.

—*The Revised Laws of Vermont, 1880:* With the Public Acts of 1880, and the Constitutions of the United States and the State of Vermont. Published by Authority. Rutland: Tuttle & Co., Official Printers and Stationers to the State of Vermont. 1881. rl 8vo, pp. xv 1169.

—*Report upon the Revision of the Laws.* C. W. Willard, W. G. Veazey, Commissioners. Montpelier, Vt.: Freeman Steam Printing House and Bindery. 1880. 8vo, pp. 126.

—*The Statutes* of the State of Vermont relating to the Grand List, In force January 1, 1855.

Published by order of the General Assembly. Montpelier: Printed at the Freeman Office. 1855. 8vo, pp. 38 (1).

—*A Compilation* of the Grand-List Laws of Vermont. Compiled under Authority of the Legislature, and appointment of the Governor. By George Nichols, Secretary of State. Montpelier: J. & J. M. Poland's Steam Printing House. 1875. 8vo, pp. 48.

—*Insurance Laws* of the State of Vermont. 1873. 8vo, pp. 10.
See Vermont, Educational, Compilation of school laws.

—*The Revised Laws* of Vermont, 1880: With the Public Acts of 1880, and the Constitutions of the United States and the State of Vermont. Published by authority. Rutland: Tuttle & Co., official Printers to the State of Vermont. 1881. 8vo, pp. xv, 1169.

—*The Vermont Statutes*. 1894, including the Public Acts of 1894, with the Declaration of Independence, the Articles of Confederation, and the Constitutions of the United States and the State of Vermont. Published by authority. Rutland, Vt.: The Tuttle Company, official Printers and Publishers to the State of Vermont. 1895. 8vo, pp. xvii, 1313.

—*General Laws* of the State of Vermont relating to Fish and Game. Published by Authority. Chapter 189 Vermont Statutes, in force August 1, 1895. Rutland: The Tuttle Co. 1895. 8vo, pp. (21.)

LAW REPORTS.

—*Reports* and Dissertations in two Parts. Part I. Reports of Cases Determined in the Supreme Court of the State of Vermont, in the years 1789, 1790, and 1791. Part II. Dissertations on the Statute adopting the Common Law of England, the Statute of Conveyances, the Statute of Offsets, and on the Negotiability of Notes. With an Appendix, Containing Forms of Special Pleadings in several cases; Forms of Recognizances; of Justices Records: and of Warrants of Commitment. By Nathaniel Chipman, Late Chief Justice. Rutland: Printed by Anthony Haswell, for the Author; M.DCC.XCIII. 16mo, pp. 296.

—*The Same*, Second Edition. Rutland: Published by Tuttle & Co. 1871. 8vo, pp. 146.

—*Reports of Cases* Argued and determined in the Supreme Court of the State of Vermont. Prepared and Published in pursuance of a Statute Law of the State. By Daniel Chipman. Middlebury: Published by D. Chipman & Son. J. W. Copeland, Printer. 1824. (2 vols in one.) 8vo, pp. 504. [1789 to 1797, and 1813 to 1824.]
Vol. 2, Reprinted and Published by George A. Tuttle & Co., 1860. Rutland: 8vo, pp. 145.

—*Reports of Cases* Argued and determined in the Supreme Court of Judicature of the State of Vermont. With Cases of Practice and Rules of Court. Commencing with the Nineteenth Century. By Royall Tyler, Chief Justice of the Supreme Court. Motto. New York: Printed and Published by I. Riley. 1809-10. 2 vols. 8vo, pp. vii. 496; v. 488. [1801 to 1803.]

—*Reports of Cases* Adjudged in the Supreme Court of the State of Vermont, being a collec-

tion of numerous cases decided in the years, commencing in October, 1815, 1816, 1817, 1818, and 1819; Alphabetically Digested under proper Heads. By William Brayton, A Judge of said Supreme Court. Middlebury: Published by Copeland & Allen. 1821. 8vo, pp. 240.

—*Reports of Cases* Argued and Determined in the Supreme Court of the State of Vermont. Prepared and Published in pursuance of a Statute Law of the State. By Asa Aikens. Windsor: Published for the Reporter, by Simeon Ide. 1827-1828. 2 vols. pp. 432, 458. [1826 to 1828.]

—*Reports of Cases* Argued and Determined in the Supreme Court of the State of Vermont. Reported by the Judges of said Court, Agreeably to a Statute Law of the State. St. Albans: J. Spooner, Printer. [1829-1833]. 9 volumes. 8vo. vols. 1, pp. 518; 2, 600; 3, 621; 4, 652. Middlebury: Knapp & Jewett, Printers. [1834-1837]. Vols. 5, 628; 6, 704; 7, 548; 8, 526. Burlington: Chauncey Goodrich. [1838]. Vol. 9, pp. 444.

—*Reports of Cases* Argued and determined in the Supreme Court of the State of Vermont. Vols. X, XI. New Series, Vols. 1-2. By G. B. Shaw. Burlington: Published by Chauncey Goodrich. [1839-40]. 8vo, pp. 621, 728.

—*Reports of Cases* Argued and Determined in the Supreme Court of the State of Vermont. Vols. XII, XIII, XIV. Third Series, Vols. II, III, IV. By William Weston. Burlington: Chauncey Goodrich. [1841-2-3.] 8vo, pp. 733, 684, 589.

—*Reports of Cases*, &c., Volume XV. Fourth Series, Volume I. By William Slade. Burlington: Chauncey Goodrich. 1844. 8vo, pp. 812.

—*Reports of Cases*, &c., Volume XVI, to XXIII, Inclusive. New Series, by Peter T. Washburn, Counsellor at Law. Vols. 1-8, Inclusive. Woodstock: Published by Haskell & Palmer. [1845-1852]. 8vo, pp. 767, 751, 696, 718, 738, 708, 733, 813.

—*Reports of Cases*, &c., Volumes XXIV-XXVI. New Series, by John F. Deane, Counsellor at Law. Volumes I-III. Bellows Falls: Published by O. H. Platt. 1853-1855. 8vo, pp. 720, 760, 821.

—*Reports of Cases*, &c., Volumes 27-29. By Charles L. Williams. Volumes I-III. Rutland: Published by Geo. A. Tuttle & Co. 1856-1858. 8vo, pp. viii. 860; viii. 888; vii. 620.

—*Reports of Cases*, &c. Vols. 30-35. New Series, Vols. 1-6. By William G. Shaw. Rutland: Published by Geo. A. Tuttle & Co. and Tuttle & Gay. 1859-1864. 8vo, pp. vii. 834; vii. 766; vii. 888; vi. (1), 703; vi. (2), 660; vii. 703.

—*Reports of Cases*, &c. By Wheelock G. Veazey. Vols. 36-44. New Series, Vols. 1-9. Rutland: Vols. 1-5. 1865-1868. Published by Tuttle, Gay & Co., and Tuttle & Co. Vols. 6-9. 1869-1872. Montpelier: By J. & J. M. Poland. 8vo, pp. 816, 719, 763, 727, 726, viii, 757, viii, 828, 800, 748.

—*Reports of Cases*, &c. By John W. Rowell. Vols. 45-52. New Series, Vols. 1-8. Montpelier: Published by J. & J. M. Poland. 1873-1880. 8vo, pp. viii. 596; viii. 859; viii. 784; viii.700; viii. 572; viii. 804: viii. 700; viii, 722.

—*Reports of Cases*, &c., by Edwin F. Palmer. 1881-1888. Vols. 53-60. Vol. 53, printed by Jos. Poland, pp. xiv. 774. Vols. 54 and 55, printed at the Watchman and Journal office, pp. xii. 769; xii. 686. Vol. 56, printed by the Tuttle Co., Rutland, pp. xvi. 806. Vols. 57-8, by the Springfield Printing Co., Springfield, Mass.,pp. xvi, 806; xvi. 722. Vols.59-60,by Davenport and Ullery, Brattleboro, pp. xvi, 796; xv, 754.

—*Reports of Cases*, &c., by C. A. Prouty, 1861-96. Vols. 61-68, 1889-1896, Vols. 61-2. Printed by The Tuttle Co., Rutland, pp. xiv, 609; xiii, 548. Vols. 91-2. Printed by The Free Press Association, pp. xvii, 724; xviii. 715. Vols. 66-8, by the Argus and Patriot Printing House, pp. xviii, 748; xv. 762; xv. 770; xvi. 728.

—*A Digest* of all the Cases decided in the Supreme Court of the State of Vermont, as reported in N. Chipman's, Tyler's, Brayton's, D. Chipman's, and Aiken's Reports, and the first fifteen Volumes of the Vermont Reports. Together with many manuscript Cases not hitherto Reported. By Peter T. Washburn, Counsellor at Law. Woodstock: Published by Haskell and Palmer. 1845. 8vo, pp. 823.

—*The Same*, as reported in Volumes Sixteen to twenty-two, inclusive, of the Vermont Reports, &c. Being A Supplement to the Digest of the previous volumes of the Vermont Reports. Same Imprint. 1852. 8vo, pp. 630.

—*A Digest* of all the Reported Decisions of the Supreme Court of the State of Vermont, contained in the Reports of N. Chipman, Tyler, Brayton, D. Chipman, Aikens, and in Forty-eight Volumes of Vermont Reports; also of all the Decisions of the Courts of the United States for the District of Vermont which are found in the Vermont Reports. By Daniel Roberts. Burlington: [Free Press and Times Book print]. 1878. rl 8vo, pp. 866.

JOURNALS OF THE GENERAL ASSEMBLY.

—*A Journal* of the Proceedings of the General Assembly of the State of Vermont, At their adjourned Session, held at Bennington, the third Thursday in February, 1784. Windsor: Printed by Hough and Spooner, Printers to the General Assembly. M.DCC.LXXXIV. 4to, pp. 64.

For Journals 1778, see Slade's State Papers, pp. 257-285.

—*The Same*, Stated Session at Rutland, October, 1784. Same imprint. 4to, pp. 57.

—*The Same*, Adjourned Session held at Norwich, June, 1785. Same imprint. 4to, pp. 52.

—*The Same*, Session at Windsor, October, 1785. Same imprint. 4to, pp. 76, and some leaves wanting at the end.

This copy is in the office of the Secretary of State.

—*The Same*, Session at Bennington, February, 1787. Same imprint. 4to, pp. 63.

—*The Same*, Stated Session at Manchester, October, 1788. Windsor: Printed by Alden Spooner, Printer to the General Assembly of the State of Vermont. 4to, pp. 50.

—*The Same*, Stated Session at Westminster, October, 1789. Same imprint. 4to, pp. 67.

—*The Same*, Stated Session at Castleton, October, 1790. Same imprint. 4to, pp. 54.

—*A Journal* of the Proceedings of the General Assembly of the State of Vermont, at their Session at Bennington, January, 1791. Printed at Bennington by Anthony Haswell, for the Honorable General Assembly, M.DCC.XCI. 8vo, pp. 85.

—*A Journal* of the Proceedings of the General Assembly of the State of Vermont, at their Session at Windsor, October 13th, 1791. Printed at Windsor by Alden Spooner, Printer to the State. 4to, pp. 49.

—*The Same*, at Rutland, Oct. 1792. Western District. Rutland: Printed by Order of the Legislature, at the Press of Anthony Haswell. 4to, pp. 114.

—*The Same*, Session at Windsor, October, 1793. Windsor: Printed by Alden Spooner, For the Honorable General Assembly. M.DCC,XCIV. 12mo, pp. 205.

—*The Same*, Session at Rutland, October, 1794. Western District, Vermont. Bennington: Printed by Order of the Legislature, at the Press of Anthony Haswell. 4to, pp. 229.

—*The Same*, held at Windsor, October 8, 1795. Rutland: Printed by Order of the Legislature. 4to, pp. 170.

—*The Same*, Begun and Held at Rutland, October 13th, 1796. Bennington: Printed by Anthony Haswell. M,DCC,XCVII. 4to, pp. 184.

—*The Same*, at Windsor, Oct. 12, 1797. Published by Order of the General Assembly. Bennington: Printed by A. Haswell, for S. Williams. 1798. 8vo, pp. 287.

The Journal of the February session of 1797 was never printed.

—*The Same*, Begun and Holden at the City of Vergennes, October XIth, M,DCC,XCVIII. Bennington: Printed by Anthony Haswell. 8vo, pp. 300.

—*The Same*, Begun and Held at Windsor, Oct. 10th, 1799. Rutland: Printed by order of the Legislature. 1799. 4to, pp. 157.

—*Journal of the General Assembly* of the State of Vermont, Begun and Held at Middlebury, in the County of Addison, October ninth, one thousand eight hundred. Published by Order of the Legislature. Bennington: Printed at the Press of Anthony Haswell, One thousand eight hundred and one. 8vo, pp. 272.

—*Journals of the General Assembly* of the State of Vermont, At their Session, Begun and Holden at Newbury, in the County of Orange, The Eighth Day of October, A. D. One Thousand Eight Hundred and One. Published by Order of the Legislature. Windsor: Printed by Alden Spooner, Printer to the State of Vermont, for the Eastern District. 1802. 8vo, pp. 272.

—*The Same*, session at Burlington, 14th of October, 1802. Bennington : Printed by Anthony Haswell & Co. 1803. 8vo, pp. 292, VIII.

—*Journals of the General Assembly* of the State of Vermont, at their Session, Begun and Holden at Westminster, in the County of Windham, on Thursday, the thirteenth day of October, A. D. One Thousand Eight Hundred and Three. Published by Order of the Legislature. Windsor : Printed by Alden Spooner, 1804. 8vo, pp. 185, IX.

—*The Same*, Adjourned Session, at Windsor. Jan. 26, 1804. Windsor : Printed by Alden Spooner. 1804. 8vo, pp. 103.

—*The Same*, at Rutland, Oct. 11, 1804. Printed by Haswell & Smead, Bennington. 1805. 8vo, pp. 376, viii.

—*Journals of the General Assembly* of the State of Vermont ; At their Session Begun and Holden at Danville, in the County of Caledonia, on the Second Thursday of October A. D. One Thousand Eight Hundred and Five. Published by Order of the Legislature. Windsor : Printed by Alden Spooner, Printer to the State. 1806. 8vo, pp. 184.

—*The Same*, at Middlebury, October 9th, 1806. Bennington : Printed by Anthony Haswell. 8vo, pp. 255.

—*The Same*, at Woodstock, October 8th, A. D. 1807. Randolph : Printed by Sereno Wright. 8vo, pp. 312.

—*Journals of the General Assembly* of the State of Vermont, at their Session begun and holden at Montpelier, On the second Thursday of October, A. D. 1808. Published according to Law. Printed at Bennington, Anno Domini 1809, per order of the General Assembly, by Anthony Haswell. 8vo, pp. 167, and 8.

—*Journals of the General Assembly* of the State of Vermont, at their Session begun and holden at Montpelier, in the County of Caledonia, on Thursday the Twelfth of October, A. D. 1809. Published According to Law. Randolph : Printed by Sereno Wright, Printer to the State. 1810. 8vo, pp. 186.

—*The Same*, 1810. Danville : Printed by Ebenezer Eaton, Printer to the State. 1811. 8vo, pp. 214.

—*The Same*, 1811. Rutland : Printed by William Fay, Printer to the State. 8vo, pp. 176.

—*The Same*, 1812. Danville : Printed by Ebenezer Eaton, Printer to the State. 1812. 8vo, pp. 322.

—*Journals of the General Assembly* of the State of Vermont, At their Session Begun and Holden at Montpelier, in the County of Jefferson, on Thursday the Fourteenth of October, A. D. 1813. Published according to law. Rutland: Printed by Fay & Davison For W. Fay, State Printer. 8vo, pp. 210.

—*The Same*, 1814. Windsor: Printed by Alden Spooner. 8vo, pp. 196.

—*Journals of the General Assembly* of the State of Vermont, At their Session Begun and held at Montpelier, in the County of Washington, on Thursday the Twelfth of October, A.

D. 1815. Windsor: Printed by A. Spooner. 8vo, pp. 200, and Index (29).

—*Journals of the General Assembly*, of the State of Vermont, at their Session Begun and held at Montpelier, in the County of Washington, on Thursday the Tenth of October, A. D. 1816. Rutland: Printed by Fay & Davison. 8vo, pp. 256.

—*The Same*, 1817. Rutland: Printed by Fay, Davison & Burt. 8vo, pp. 250.

—*The Same*, 1818. Bennington: Printed by William Haswell. 8vo, pp. 216, and grand list tables.

—*The Same*, 1819. Same Imprint. 8vo, pp. 270, and grand list tables.

—*The Same*, 1820. Same Imprint. 8vo, pp. 295.

—*The Same*, 1821. Rutland: Printed by William Fay. 8vo, pp. 248.

—*Journals of the General Assembly* of the State of Vermont, at their Session begun and held at Montpelier, in the County of Washington, on Thursday, 10th October, A. D. 1822. Montpelier: Printed by E. P. Walton, 1823. 8vo, pp. 317, and grand list tables.

—*The Same*, 1823. Bennington: C. Doolittle Printer. 8vo, pp. 229.

—*Journal of the General Assembly*, of the State of Vermont, at their Session begun and held at Montpelier, Washington County, On Thursday, 14th of October, A. D. 1824. Bennington: Printed by Darius Clark. For the Contractor. 8vo. pp. 269.

—*Journal of the General Assembly*, of the State of Vermont, at their Session Begun and Held at Montpelier, Washington County, On Thursday, 13th October, A. D. 1825. Bennington: Printed by Darius Clark. 8vo, pp. 252.

—*Journal of the General Assembly* of the State of Vermont at their session begun and held at Montpelier, Washington County, on Thursday, twelfth Oct. A. D. 1826. Rutland: Printed for the State, by William Fay. 1827. 8vo, pp. 209.

—*The Same*, 1827. Woodstock: Printed by Rufus Colton. 8vo, pp. 259.

—*Journal of the General Assembly* of the State of Vermont, at their Session begun and held at Montpelier, Washington County, on Thursday, 9th October, A. D. 1828. Woodstock: Printed for the State by Rufus Colton. 1829. 8vo, pp. 203.

—*Journal of the General Assembly* of the State of Vermont, at their Session begun and held at Montpelier, Washington County, on Thursday 8th October, A. D. 1829. Woodstock: Printed for the State by R. & A. Colton. 1830. 8vo, pp. 224.

—*The Same*, 1830. Woodstock, Printed by Rufus Colton. 8vo, pp. 231.

—*The Same*, 1831. Same imprint. 8vo, pp. 215.

—*The Same*, 1832. Danville : Printed by Eben'r Eaton. 8vo, pp. 203.

—*Journal of the General Assembly* of the State of Vermont, at their Session begun and holden at Montpelier, in the County of Washington,

on Thursday, 10th October, A. D. 1833. Danville: Printed by Eben'r Eaton. 8vo, pp. 235.
—*The Same*, 1834. Rutland: Printed by William Fay. 1834. 8vo, pp. 272.
—*The Same*, 1835. Middlebury: Knapp & Jewett, Printers, 1835. 8vo, pp. 272.
—*Journal of the House* of Representatives of the State of Vermont, October session 1836. Published by Authority. Middlebury: Printed at the American Office. 1836. 8vo, pp. 316.
—*Journal of the House* of Representatives of the State of Vermont, October Session, 1837. Published by Authority. Montpelier: E. P. Walton & Son, Printers. 1837. 8vo, pp. 293.
—*The Same*, 1838. Montpelier: E. P. Walton & Sons, Printers. 1839. 8vo, pp. 234, and 116.
—*The Same*, 1839, pp. 416; 1840, pp. 296; 1841, pp. 363; 1842, pp. 440; 1843, pp. 304; 1844, pp. 289. All same imprint.
—*The Same*, 1845. Windsor: Printed by Bishop & Tracy. 1846. 8vo, pp. 360.
—*The Same*, 1846. Same imprint. 8vo, pp. 315.
—*The Same*, 1847. Montpelier: E. P. Walton & Sons, Printers. 1848. 8vo, pp. 352.
—*The Same*, 1848. Same imprint. 8vo, pp. 381.
—*The Same*, 1849. Montpelier: E. P. Walton & Sons, Printers. 8vo, pp. 410.
—*The Same*, 1850. Burlington: Chauncey Goodrich. 1851. 8vo, pp. 431.
—*The Same*, 1851, pp. 469, and 1852, pp. 424. Same imprint.
—*The Same*, 1853. Burlington: Printed by Chauncey Goodrich. 1854. 8vo, pp. 654.
—*Journal* of the House of Representatives of the State of Vermont, October Session, 1854. Published by Authority. Montpelier: E. P. Walton, Jr., Printer. 1855. 8vo, pp. 767.
—*Journal* of the House of Representatives of the State of Vermont. October Session, 1855. Published by Authority. Montpelier: E. P. Walton, Printer, 1855. 8vo, pp. 812.
—*Journal* of the House of Representatives of the State of Vermont, October Session, 1856. Published by Authority. Middlebury: Printed at the Register Book and Job Office. 1856. 8vo, pp. 821.
—*The Same*, 1857. Montpelier: E. P. Walton, Printer. 1858. 8vo, pp. 573.
—*Journal* of the House of Representatives of the State of Vermont, October Session, 1858. Published by Authority. Montpelier: E. P. Walton, Printer. 1858. 8vo, pp. 456.
—*Journal* of the House of Representatives of the State of Vermont, October Session, 1859. Published by Authority. Montpelier: E. P. Walton, Printer, 1859. 8vo, pp. 455.
—*Journal* of the House of Representatives of the State of Vermont, October Session, 1860. Published by Authority. Montpelier: E. P. Walton, Printer. 1860. 8vo, pp. 465, and Journal of Extra Session, 1861. pp. 85.
—*Journal* of the House of Representatives of the State of Vermont, October Session, 1861.

Published by Authority. Montpelier: E. P. Walton, Printer. 1861. 8vo, pp. 500.
—*Journal* of the House of Representatives, of the State of Vermont, Annual Session, 1862. Published by Authority. Montpelier: Printed at the Freeman Printing Establishment. 1863. 8vo, pp. 548.
—*Journal* of the House of Representatives, of the State of Vermont, Annual Session, 1863. Published by Authority. Montpelier: Printed at the Freeman Printing Establishment. 1863. 8vo, pp. 368.
—*Journal* of the House of Representatives of the State of Vermont, Annual Session, 1864. Published by Authority. Montpelier: Printed at the Freeman Steam Printing Establishment. 1865. 8vo, pp. 486.
—*The Same*, 1865, pp. 419; 1866, pp. 517; 1867, pp. 492. Same imprint.
—*Journal* of the House of Representatives of the State of Vermont, Annual Session, 1868. Published by Authority. Montpelier: Freeman Steam Printing House and Bindery. 1869. 8vo, pp. 463.
—*The Same*, 1869. Montpelier: Poland's Steam Printing Establishment, Journal Building, State Street. 1870. 8vo, pp. 368.
—*Journal* of the House of Representatives of the State of Vermont. Biennial Session, 1870. Published by Authority. Montpelier: Freeman Steam Printing House and Bindery. 1871. 8vo, pp. 547.
—*The Same*, 1872. Same imprint. 8vo, pp. 647.
—*The Same*, 1874. Same imprint. 8vo, pp. 788.
—*The Same*, 1876. Rutland: Tuttle & Co., Printers and Publishers. 1877. 8vo, pp. 740.
—*The Same*, 1878. Same imprint. 8vo, pp. 562. Continued.
—*Journal* of the Senate of the State of Vermont, October Session, 1836. Published by Authority. Montpelier: E. P. Walton & Son, Printers. 1836. 8vo, pp. 141.
—*The Same*, 1837. Same imprint. 8vo, pp. 131.
—*The Same*, 1838. Montpelier: E. P. Walton & Sons, Printers. 1839. 8vo, pp. 102, xlvii.
—*The Same*, 1839, pp. 213; 1840, pp. 167; 1841, pp. 180; 1842, pp. 239; 1843, pp. 191; 1844, pp. 136. All same imprint.
—*The Same*, 1845. Windsor: Bishop & Tracy. 1846. 8vo, pp. 231.
—*The Same*, 1846. Same imprint. 8vo, pp. 180.
—*The Same*, 1847. Montpelier: E. P. Walton & Sons, Printers. 1848. 8vo, pp. 231.
—*The Same*, 1848. Burlington: Chauncey Goodrich. 1848. 8vo, pp. 226.
—*The Same*, 1849. Burlington: Free Press Office. 1849. 8vo, pp. 206.
—*The Same*, 1850, pp. 329; 1851, pp. 324. Same imprint.
—*The Same*, 1852. Rutland: Tuttle & Co's Steam Job Printing Establishment. 1852. 8vo, pp. 264.

—*The Same*, 1853. Same imprint. 8vo, pp. 269.

—*The Same*, 1854. Middlebury : Printed at the Register Book and Job Office. 1854. 8vo, pp. 263.

—*The Same*, 1855. Same imprint. 8vo, pp. 319.

—*The Same*, 1856. Montpelier : E. P. Walton, Printer. 1857. 8vo, pp. 528.

—*Journal of* the Senate and House of Representatives of the State of Vermont, Special Session. 1857. Published by Authority. Montpelier : E. P. Walton, Printer. 1857. 8vo, pp. 148.

—*Journal of* the Senate of Vermont, October Session. 1857. Published by Authority. Woodstock : Printed by Davis & Greene. 1857. 8vo, pp. 304.

—*The Same*, 1858. Ludlow : Warner's Book and Job Printing Establishment. 1858. 8vo, pp. 435.

—*The Same*, 1859. Montpelier : E. P. Walton, Printer. 1859. 8vo, pp. 444.

—*The Same*, 1860. Same imprint. 8vo, pp. 272, & 66.
Includes Extra Session of 1861.

—*The Same*, 1861. Ludlow : Warner's Book and Job Printing Establishment. 1862. 8vo, pp. 339.

—*The Same*, 1862. Rutland : Printed by Tuttle & Gay. 1863. 8vo, pp. 407.

—*The Same*, 1863. Montpelier : Printed at the Freeman Printing Establishment. 1863. 8vo, pp. 221.

—*The Same*, 1864, pp. 301 ; 1865, pp. 288 ; 1866, pp. 416 ; 1867, pp. 391 ; 1868, pp. 362. All same imprint.

—*The Same*, 1869. Montpelier : Poland's Steam Printing Establishment, Journal Building, State Street. 1870. 8vo, pp. 280.

—*Journal of* the Senate of the State of Vermont. (First) Biennial Session, 1870. Published by Authority. Montpelier : Freeman Steam Printing House and Bindery. 1871. 8vo, pp. 390.

—*The Same*, 1872, pp. 491 ; 1874, pp. 587. Same imprint.

—*The Same*, 1876. Rutland : Tuttle & Co., Printers and Publishers. 1877. 8vo, pp. 642.

—*The Same*, 1878. Same imprint. 8vo, pp. 417.
Continued.
The Messages of the Governors of Vermont are printed in the Assembly Journals, and after 1835 in the House and Senate Journals, and, in addition, printed in pamphlet form separately ; I have not deemed it worth while to give the titles, except as to the war messages of Governor Erastus Fairbanks, which are given under his name.

REPORTS OF STATE OFFICERS.

—*Report of* the Adjutant and Inspector General of the State of Vermont for the year ending November 1, 1862. Montpelier : Walton's Steam Printing Establishment. 1862. 8vo, pp. 110.

—*The Same*, 1863. Same imprint. 8vo, pp. 105.

—*The Same*, 1864. Walton's Steam Press. 8vo, pp. 229, 663, 61, (1).

—*The Same*, 1865, pp. 762; 1866, pp. 368. Same imprint.

After 1866 these reports are included in Legislative Documents, which see.

—*Report of* the Quartermaster General, in compliance with "an act in relation to supplies for Vermont Troops," Approved Oct. 18, 1861. No imprint. 8vo, pp. 4.

—*Report of* the Quartermaster General of the State of Vermont, for the year ending November 1, 1862. Montpelier : Printed at the Freeman Steam Printing Establishment. 1862. 8vo, pp. 37.

—*Report of* the Quartermaster General of the State of Vermont, For the year ending October 1, 1863. Same imprint. 8vo.

—*The Same*, 1864, pp. 38; 1865, pp. 91. Both same imprint.
After 1866 these reports are included in Legislative Documents, which see.

—*State of Vermont*. Annual Report of the Surgeon General of the State of Vermont, to His Excellency the Commander-in-Chief, October 6th, 1865. Burlington : Free Press Print. 1865. 8vo, pp. 40.
In Legislative Documents, after 1865.

—*Comments of* the Officers of the Vermont Asylum for the Insane, on the Report of the Special Commissioners. 1878. Brattleboro : D. Leonard, Steam Printer. 8vo, pp. 17.

—*Auditor's Report* on the Subject of Public Accounts, accompanying the Message of the Governor, Oct. 15, 1842; no imprint. 8vo, pp. 40.
Includes Reports on the State Prison, also State Treasurer, Bank Commissioner, and Bank Inspectors' Reports.

—*Annual Report* of the Auditor of Accounts, of the State of Vermont, made to the Legislature October 12, 1843. Woodstock : Printed by Haskell & Palmer. (Mercury Press.) 1843. 8vo, pp. 100.
Contains in addition to the Report for 1842, Reports on the Asylum for the Insane, and Gov. Paine's Report on the Deaf and Dumb, and Insane Poor.

—*The Same, Oct. 10*, 1844. Same imprint. 8vo, pp. 84.

—*The Same*, 1845. Same imprint. 8vo, pp. 93, (1).

—*The Same*, 1846. Rutland : Printed at the Herald Office. 1846. 8vo. pp. 95, (1).

—*The Same*, 1847, pp. 96; 1848, pp. 64. Same imprint.

—*The Same*, 1849. Montpelier : Printed by E. P. Walton & Sons. 1849. 8vo, pp. 88.

—*The Same*, 1850. Rutland : Union Whig Office. J. K. McLean, Printer. 1850. 8vo, pp. 92.

—*The Same*, 1851. Burlington : Free Press Office. 1851. 8vo, pp. 100.

—*The Same*, 1852. Same imprint. 8vo, pp. 129.

—*The Same*, 1853. Montpelier : E. P. Walton, Jr., Printer. 1853. 8vo, pp. 136.

—*The Same*, 1854, pp. 180 ; 1855, pp. 224. 1856. pp. 208. Same imprint.

—*The Same*, 1857. Montpelier : E. P. Walton, Printer. 1857. 8vo, pp. 212.

—*The Same*, 1858, pp. 240; 1859, pp. 271, (1); 1860, pp. 255. Same imprint.

—*The Same*, 1861. Burlington: Free Press Print. 1861. 8vo, pp. lxx. (3), 204.

—*The Same*, 1862. Burlington: Times Book and Job Printing Establishment. 1862. 8vo, pp. lxxxvii, 161.

—*The Same*, 1863. Montpelier: Printed at the Freeman Printing Establishment. 1863. 8vo, pp. lxxii, 160.

—*The Same*, 1864, Same imprint. 8vo, pp. lxxxvi, (2), 165.

—*The Same*, 1865. Rutland: Tuttle, Gay & Co., Printers. 1865. 8vo, pp. lxxxiii. 144. Included in Legislative Documents after 1865.

—*Report* of the Commissioners To locate and build a Workhouse. Rutland: Tuttle & Co. Stationers and Official Printers to the State of Vermont. 1878. 8vo, pp. 13.

—*Annual Report* of the Inspector of Finance, showing the condition of the Savings Banks and Trust Companies in the State of Vermont, on the first day of July, 1879. Rutland, Vt.: Tuttle & Co., Book and Job Printers, 1879. 8vo, pp. 51. Same for 1378, pp. 34. Hon. William H. DuBois, Inspector. Continued.

VERMONT CAPITOL.

—*Report* of the Superintendent of the Construction of the State House, October 15, 1857. Printed by Order of the General Assembly. (Thomas E. Powers, Superintendent.) Montpelier: E. P. Walton, Printer. 1857. 8vo, pp. 14. Also Report for 1858. pp. 8.

—*The Capitol of Vermont.* Journal of the Proceedings and Debates of the General Assembly of Vermont, at the Special Session, Feb., 1857. Montpelier: E. P. Walton, Printer and Publisher. 1857. 8vo, pp. 300. This work was compiled and edited by the Hon. E. P. Walton, although it does not so appear from the title page.

—*And the Star Chamber.* Testimony and Defence of the Superintendent of Construction. October, 1858. Montpelier: E. P. Walton, Printer, 1858. 8vo, pp. 28, (1.)

—*A Statement of Facts*, concerning the management of affairs, connected with the rebuilding of the Capitol, at Montpelier, Vermont. By Thomas W. Silloway, Architect of the Building. Burlington, Vt.: Daily Times Job Office. 1859. 8vo, pp. 20, (1.)

—*Message and Report* on the State House. Oct. 27, 1859. 8vo, pp. 8.

—*A Description* of the State Houses of Vermont. Published by W. W. Avery and H. B. Davis. Montpelier: E. P. Walton, Printer. 12mo, pp. 24.

—*Memorial of Thomas W. Silloway*, Architect in respect to the Reconstruction of the State House. Printed by Order of the House of Representatives. Montpelier: E. P. Walton, Printer. 1858. 8vo, pp. 6.

—*Report of the Committee* on Public Buildings on the Furniture and Fixtures of the State House. Montpelier: E. P. Walton, Printer. 1859. 8vo, pp. 8.

—*Report of the Minority* of the Joint Committee on Claims, on Senate and House Bills to pay Thomas E. Powers, balance due for services as Superintendent of Construction of the State House, made to the Legislature of Vermont, at their Annual Session, 1861. Montpelier: Printed at the Freeman Printing Establishment. 1861. 8vo, pp. 10.

EDUCATIONAL.

—*Report* of the Board of Commissioners, for Common Schools, submitted to the Legislature of the State of Vermont, October 25, 1828. Ordered to be printed and Circulated to each School District in the State. Woodstock: Printed by Rufus Colton. 1828. 12mo, pp. 12.

—*Circular of the State Superintendent* of Common Schools, to the County Superintendents: And an Address to the Teachers of Common Schools in the State of Vermont. St. Albans: Messenger Print. 1845. 8vo, pp. 23.

—*First Annual Report* of the State Superintendent of Common Schools, made to the Legislature October, 1846. Montpelier, Vt.: Eastman & Danforth, Printers. 8vo, pp. 64.

—*Second Annual Report*, 1847. St. Albans, Vt.: E. B. Whiting, Printer. 8vo, pp. 52.

—*Third Annual Report*, 1848. St. Albans, Vt.: E. B. Whiting, Printer. 8vo, pp. 72.

—*Fourth Annual Report*, 1849. Montpelier: Printed by E. P. Walton & Son. 8vo, pp. 64.

—*Fifth Annual Report*, 1850. Middlebury: Printed by Justus Cobb, Register Office, Main Street. 8vo, pp. 41, (7).

—*Sixth Annual Report*, 1851. Montpelier: Printed by Daniel P. Thompson. 8vo, pp. 46.

—*First Annual Report* of the Secretary of the Vermont Board of Education, made to the Board, September, 1857. Ludlow: Rufus S. Warner, Book and Job Printer. 1857. 8vo, pp. 98, and 2.

—*Second Annual Report*, 1858. Burlington: Free Press Print. pp. 80 and 4.

—*Third Annual Report*, 1859. Burlington: Free Press Print. 8vo, pp. 85, and 37.

—*Fourth Annual Report*, 1860. Same imprint. 8vo, pp. viii, 131, and 37.

—*Fifth Annual Report*, 1861. Burlington: Times Book and Job Printing Establishment. 8vo, pp. xv. 105, and 63.

—*Sixth Annual Report*, 1862. Burlington: Free Press Print. 8vo, pp. iv. 120, and 24.

—*Seventh Annual Report*, 1863. Burlington: Times Book and Job Printing Establishment. 8vo, pp. xiii. 138, and 87.

—*Eighth Annual Report*, 1864. Burlington: Free Press Book and Job Printing Office. 8vo, pp. vii, 165.

—*Ninth Annual Report*, 1865. Burlington: R. S. Styles, Book and Job Printer. 8vo, pp. viii, 142.

—*Tenth Annual Report*, 1866. Burlington: Times Book and Job Office. 8vo, pp. 10, 116.

—*Eleventh Annual Report*, 1867. Burlington: R. S. Styles, Steam Book and Job Printer. 8vo, pp. 12, 190, and 94.

—*Twelfth Annual Report*, 1868. Montpelier: Freeman Steam Printing House and Book Bindery. 8vo, pp. 6, 141.

—*Thirteenth Annual Report*, 1869. Same imprint. 8vo pp. 8, 142, and 79.
See Legislative Documents, 1870–76.

—*The twenty-fifth Vermont School Report*, made by the State Superintendent of Education to the Legislature. October, 1878. Montpelier: J. & J. M. Poland, Official State Printers. 1878. 8vo, pp. 26, 71.

—*Twenty-sixth School Report*. Rutland: Tuttle & Co., Official State Printers. 1880. 8vo, pp. 59, 117.
Continued.

—*Vermont School Laws*, in force at the close of the Session of the General Assembly, 1875, together with a Digest of the Decisions of the Supreme Court of Vermont having reference to the Schools and School Laws of Vermont, and Forms for the use of School District Officers. Compiled under an Act of the Legislature, and Appointment by the Governor, By Gilbert A. Davis, of Reading. Montpelier: J. & J. M. Poland's Steam Printing House, 1875. 8vo, pp. 226.

Vermont Election Sermons.

Year.	Preacher.	Residence.	Graduation.
*1777.	Hutchinson, Aaron,	Pomfret,	Y. C. 1747.
*1778.	Powers, Peter,	Newbury	H. U. 1754.
1778.	Burroughs, Eden,	Hanover, N. H.,	Y. C. 1757.
1779.	Roots, Benajah,	Rutland,	N. J. C. 1754.
1780.	Avery, David,	Bennington,	Y. C. 1769.
1781.	Olcott, Bulkley,	Charlest'n, N. H.,	Y. C. 1758.
*1782.	Lyman, Gershom C.,	Marlboro,	Y. C. 1773.
1783.	Bullen, Joseph,	Westminster,	Y. C. 1772.
1784.	Swift, Job,	Bennington,	Y. C. 1765.
1785.	Burton, Asa,	Thetford,	D. C. 1777.
1786.	Chapin, Pelatiah,	Windsor,	
1787.	Potter, Lyman,	Norwich,	Y. C. 1772.
1788.	Sill, Elijah,	Dorset,	Y. C. 1748.
*1789.	Foster, Dan,	Weathersfield,	
1790.	Cazier, Matthias,	Castleton,	N. J. C. 1785.
*1791.	Shuttlesworth, Samuel,	Windsor,	H. U. 1777.
*1792.	Blood, Caleb,	Shaftsbury,	
1793.	No Sermon preached.		
*1794.	Williams, Samuel,	Rutland,	H. U. 1761.
*1795.	Burton, Asa,	Thetford,	D. C. 1777.
1796.	Kent, Dan,	Dorset.	
*1797.	Whitney, Samuel,	Rockingham,	H. U. 1769.
*1798.	Sanders, Daniel Clarke,	Vergennes,	H. U. 1788.
*1799.	Forsyth, William,		
1800.	Wooster, Benjamin,	Cornwall.	
*1801.	Lambert, Nathaniel,	Newbury,	B. U. 1787.
*1802.	Atwater, Jeremiah,	Middlebury,	Y. C. 1793.
*1803.	Sage, Sylvester,	Westminster,	Y. C. 1787.
*1804.	Hall, Heman,	Rutland,	D. C. 1791.
*1805.	Fitch, John,	Danville,	B. U. 1790.
*1806.	Merrill, Thomas A.,	Middlebury,	D. C. 1801.
*1807.	Gross, Thomas,	Hartford,	D. C. 1784.
*1808.	Eastman, Tilton,	Randolph,	D. C. 1796.
*1809.	Haynes, Sylvanus.	Middletown.	
*1810.	Wright, Chester,	Montpelier,	M. C. 1805.
*1811.	Skeel, Thomas,		
*1812.	Beall, Isaac,	Pawlet.	
*1813.	Marsh, Daniel,	Bennington,	H. U. 1795.
*1814.	Lyman, Elijah,	Brookfield.	D. C. 1787.
*1815.	Davis, Henry,	Middlebury,	Y. C. 1796.
*1816.	Austin, Samuel,	Burlington,	Y. C. 1783.
*1817.	Peck, Phineas,	Lyndon.	
*1818.	Kendrick, Clark,	Poultney.	
*1819.	Converse, James,	Weathersfield,	H. U. 1799.
*1820.	Leonard, George,	Windsor,	D. C. 1805.
*1821.	Bates, Joshua,	Middlebury,	H. U. 1800.
*1822.	Lindsey, John,	Barre.	
*1823.	Sawyer, Joseph W.	Whiting.	
*1824.	Chandler, Amariah,	Waitsfield,	U. V. 1820.
*1825.	Bartlett, Robert,	Hartland.	
*1825.	Morse, William,	Not official.	
*1826.	Fisk, Wilbur,	Lyndon,	B. U. 1815.

Year.	Preacher.	Residence.	Graduation
*1827.	Goodwillie, Thomas,	Barnet.	
*1828.	Woodman, Johnathan,	Sutton.	
*1829.	Walker, Charles,	Rutland.	
*1830.	Ingersoll, George G.,	Burlington,	H. U. 1815.
1831.	Howard, Leland.	Windsor.	
*1832.	Perkins, William S.,	Arlington.	
*1833.	Spicer, Tobias,	Salisbury.	
*1834.	Skinner, Warren,	Cavendish.	
*1856.	Child, Willard,	Castleton,	Y. C. 1817.
*1857.	McKeen, Silas,	Bradford.	
*1858.	Thomas, C. A.,	Brandon.	

Of those with a *, the full titles may be found under the names of the authors.

The sermons in 1790, 1800 and 1831, were not printed. The custom of having Election Sermons was discontinued after 1834, until 1856, but the attempt to renew the practice was again abandoned after three years trial. Although not belonging to the regular series, we place at the head of the list the sermon by the Rev. Aaron Hutchinson, preached at the "Framing" of the State of Vermont, at Windsor, July 2, 1777. The Vermont Historical Society has an original printed copy of this sermon, and the same is reprinted in Vol. 1, of the "Collections of the Society," pp. 67–102.

Vermont Coinage.

See "An Historical Account of American Coinage," by John H. Hickcox; History of "Schoharie County," N. Y., by J. R. Simms, pages 596–598; "Crosby's Early Coins of America," pages 176–202; an excellent authority. Rev. Edmund F. Slafter, "Vermont Coinage," in Vol. 1, pages 291–318, Collections of the Vermont Historical Society; "Hemenway's Vermont Historical Gazetteer," Vol. 1, pp. 227–228; H. Hall's History of Vermont, p. 441, and note; Barber's Historical Collections of Connecticut, under Huel, or Killingworth; Thompson's History of Vermont, p. 227; Vermont laws, edition 1787, p. 105, 161.

LEGISLATIVE DIRECTORIES.

—*1826.* Broadsheet.

—*1832.* Directory and Rules of the House of Representatives, for the Present Session. Montpelier: Knapp & Jewett, Printers. 1832. 16mo, pp. 8.

—*The Same*, for 1833, pp. 15; 1834, pp. 16; and 1835, pp. 16. Same imprint.

—*1837.* Directory and Rules of the Senate and House of Representatives, for October Session, 1837. Montpelier: E. P. Walton & Son, Printers. 16mo, pp. 29, (1).

—*1838.* The Same; same imprint. 16mo, pp. 30.

—*1839.* The Same; E. P. Walton & Sons, Printers. 16mo, pp. 31; same for 1840, pp. 31; 1841, pp. 32; 1842, pp. 32; 1843, pp. 32; 1844, pp. 30, (2); 1845, pp. 30, (2); 1846, pp. 30, (2); 1847, 16mo, pp. 55. All same imprint.
Latter contains diagram of the House of Representatives.

—*The Same*, 1848, pp. 55; and 1849, pp. 55. Same imprint.
A Diagram of the Senate Chamber added to the latter.

—*1850.* The Same. E. P. Walton & Sons, Printers. 16mo, pp. 54.

—*The Same*, for 1851, pp. 54, and 1852, pp. 54. Same imprint.

—*The Same.* 1853. E. P. Walton, Jr., Printer. 16mo, pp. 54.

—*The Same.* 1854 and '55. Same imprint. 16mo, pp. 54.
A map of the State added to latter. See Hicks, G. C.; Deming, P.

—*The Same.* 1856, 16mo, pp. 54; 1857, pp. 48, (2); 1858, pp. 48, (2); 1859, pp. 40; and 1860, 16mo, pp. 40. E. P. Walton, Printer.

—*1861.* The Same. Walton's Steam Printing Establishment. 16mo. pp. 79.

—*The Same.* 1862. 16mo, pp. 79 ; and 1863. Same imprint. 16mo, pp. 40.

—*1864.* Directory, Rules, Constitutions and Manual of Parlimentary Practice. October Session. 1864. Same imprint. 16mo, pp. 104.

—*1865.* Directory, Joint Rules of both Houses, Rules of the Senate and House of Representatives, &c., &c. October Session. 1865. Montpelier: Walton's Steam Press. 16mo, pp. 46, (4).

—*1866. State of Vermont.* Rules, Constitutions and Manual of Parliamentary Practice, including, also, Officers of the State and sundry statistics. Prepared pursuant to a Joint Resolution of the General Assembly. By George Nichols, Secretary of State. Manual of Parliamentary Practice by Henry Clark, Secretary of the Senate. Montpelier: Walton's Steam Printing Establishment. 1866. 16mo, pp. 46, (2).

—*1867. State of Vermont.* Joint Rules, Rules of the Senate, House of Representatives and State Library ; October Session, 1867. Prepared pursuant to a Joint Resolution of the General Assembly, by George Nichols, Secretary of State. Montpelier: Walton's Steam Printing Establishment. 1867. 16mo, pp. 69, (6).

—*1868 and 1869.* The Same. Same imprint. 16mo, pp. 83, (9), each.

—*1870. State of Vermont.* Joint Rules, Rules and orders of the Senate and House of Representatives, and of the State Library, and Legislative Directory: Biennial Session, 1870. Prepared pursuant to an Act of the General Assembly, by George Nichols, Secretary of State. Montpelier: Journal Book and Job Printing Establishment. 1870. 16mo, pp. 116.

—*The Same.* 1872. pp. 116; and 1874, pp. 114. Same imprint.

—*1876.* The same. J. & J. M. Poland, Printers. 16mo, pp. 144.

—*1878.* The Same. Same imprint. 16mo, pp. 156.

—*A Political Manual* for the State of Vermont, for the year 1858. Montpelier: E. P. Walton, Printer. 16mo, pp. 16.

—*The Same.* 1859. pp. 16, (1) and 1860, pp. 16, (1). Same imprint.

—*1861.* Manual of the Legislature of Vermont for the year 1861. Montpelier: Walton's Steam Press. 16mo, pp. 16, (1).

—*1862.* The Same. Walton's Steam Printing Establishment. 16mo, pp. 16, (1).

—*1863.* The same; same imprint. 16mo, pp. 16, (1).

—*1864.* The same; same imprint. 16mo, pp. 28.
Diagrams of the Senate Chamber and Hall of the House of Representatives added.

—*The Same.* 1865. pp. 24, and 1866, pp. 24. Montpelier: Freeman Steam Printing Establishment.

—*1867.* The Same. Rutland: Tuttle & Company, Printers. 1867. 16mo, pp. 24.

—*1868.* The Same. Montpelier: Freeman Steam Printing House and Bindery. 1868. 16mo, pp. 25.

—*1869.* The Same. Montpelier: Journal Book and Job Printing Establishment. 1869. 16mo, pp. 31.

—*The Same.* 1870-71. pp. 56. 1872-73, pp. 48; 1874-75, pp. 48; 1876-77, pp. 40, and 1878-79, pp. 80. same imprint.

—*State of Vermont.* Annual Directory for the use of the General Assembly: Containing the Rules and Orders of the Senate and House, together with the Constitution of the State and that of the United States and a list of the Executive, Legislative and Judicial Departments of the State, State Institutions, their locality and officers, and other Historical and Statistical Information. Prepared pursuant to an Act of the General Assembly by George Nichols, Secretary of State. Manual of Parliamentary Practice by Henry Clark, Secretary of the Senate. Montpelier: Walton's Steam Printing Establishment. 1867. 16mo, pp. 200,(6).

—*1868.* The Same. Montpelier: Poland's Steam Printing Establishment. 1868. 16mo, pp. 214, (4).

—*1869.* The Same. Journal Printing Establishment. Montpelier: 16mo, pp. 251, (7).

—*The Same.* 1870-71. pp. 316; 1872-73, pp. 315; and 1874-75. 16mo, pp. 353, Same imprint.
A new and improved map added to latter.

—*1876-77.* The Same. Same imprint. 16mo, pp. 383.
Continued.

REPORTS OF STATE OFFICERS.

—*Official Reports,* Annual Session of the General Assembly, 1866. Montpelier : 1866. [Bound and indexed by the Secretary of State, in pursuance of the several Acts, Approved Nov. 11, 1863, and Nov. 22, 1864.]
One volume. Contains Governor's Message, Auditor's Report, School Report, Railroad Report, [Adjutant-General's Report omitted, and bound separately], Quartermaster General's Report, Surgeon General's Report, Reform School Report, First Annual Report of the University of Vermont and State Agricultural College, Report on Restoration of Sea Fish, Report of Commissioners on a National Statuary Hall, Oration of W. G. Veazey, Addresses before the Vermont Historical Society.

—*The Same,* one volume. Montpelier : 1867.
Contains in addition to 1866, Report of the Commissioner to attend the Universal Exposition at Paris, Catalogue of Vermont University and State Agricultural College.

—*The Same,* one volume. Montpelier : 1868.
Contains all Legislative Reports.

—*The Same,* 1869. Montpelier : 1869. Published by Authority.
Contains in addition the Sergeant-at-arms' Report, and Insurance Commissioner's Report ; being the first annual report of the latter. One volume.

—*The Same,* made to the Biennial Session of the General Assembly, 1870-71. Montpelier: 1870. Published by Authority.
Contains the same as for 1869. One volume.

—*The Same,* 1872. Same imprint. 3 volumes, 8vo.
Contents : Vol. 1, Governor's Message, 16 pages; Auditor's Report, 339 pp.; Adjutant and Inspector General, 93 pp.; Quartermaster General, 64 pp.; Railroad Commissioner 56 pp.; Asylum for the Insane, 30 pp.; State

Prison, 44 pp.; Reform School, 54 pp.; Sergeant-at-Arms, 12 pp.; University of Vermont, 12 pp.; Insurance Commissioner's Report, 12 pp.; Report of Fish Commissioner, 20 pp.; Address of Dr. Goldsmith on Fish Culture, 16 pp. Vol. 2. Fifteenth Report of the Board of Education, with the Report of the Secretary, made to the Board. 8vo., pp. 410, 167, (*). Vol. 3. First Annual Report of the Vermont State Board of Agriculture, Manufactures and Mining. By Peter Collier, Secretary of the Board. pp. 734.

—*The Same*, 1874. In 4 Volumes. 8vo. same imprint.
Contain in addition to those of 1872, Addresses of C. T. Childs and P. O. Edson, at Re-union of Vermont Officers, pp. 34; Report of Railroad Investigating Committee, appointed in 1872, pp. 470, 56, 4, and 21.

—*The Same*, 1876. 3 volumes. Rutland: 1876. 8vo.
Contain reports of same officers, etc., as in 1872.

—*The Same* for 1878. 1 vol. 8vo. Same imprint.
Contains Reports of Auditor, Adjutant General, Quartermaster General, Commissioner for Insane, Vermont Asylum for Insane, State Prison, Reform School, and Sergeant-at-Arms.
Continued.

—*Report* of the Sergeant-at-Arms, for 1858-59. Montpelier : E. P. Walton, Printer. 1859. 8vo, pp. 15.

—*The Same* for 1861. No imprint. 8vo, pp. 30.

—*The Same* for 1862. Freeman Print. 1862. 8vo, pp. 22.

—*The Same* for 1865. Same imprint. 1865. 8vo, pp.
After 1866, reports included in "Legislative Documents."

—*First Annual Report* of the Railroad Commissioner, of the State of Vermont, to the General Assembly, 1856. Rutland : Geo. A. Tuttle & Co., Printers. 1856. 8vo, pp. 128.

—*The Same*, 1857. Same imprint. 8vo, pp. 163.

—*The Same*, 1858. Burlington : Free Press Print. 1858. 8vo, pp. 131, (1).

—*The Same*, 1859. Same imprint. 8vo, pp. 159, (1.)

—*The Same*, 1860. Rutland : George A. Tuttle & Co., Printers. 1860. 8vo, pp. 127, (1).

—*The Same*, 1861. Same imprint. 8vo, pp. 134, (2).

—*The Same*, 1862. Montpelier : Walton's Steam Printing Establishment. 1862. 8vo, pp. 132, (4).

—*The Same*, 1863. Same imprint. 1863. 8vo, pp. 112.

—*The Same*, 1864. St. Albans : Whiting & Davis, Printers. 1864. 8vo, pp. 107.

—*The Same*, 1865. Same imprint. 8vo, pp. 88.
Included in Legislative Documents after 1865, which see, under Vermont.

—*Biennial Report* of the Officers of the House of Correction, Rutland, for 1893-4. Rutland : The Tuttle Company, Printers. 1894. 8vo, pp. 88

—*Report* of Hon. Justin S. Morrill and Hon. George F. Edmunds, Commissioners for Vermont on the National Statuary Hall, in the Capitol at Washington. Montpelier : Walton's Steam Printing Establishment. 1866. 8vo, pp. 21.

REFORM SCHOOL.

—*Report* of the Commissioners, Under a Resolution of the General Assembly of Vermont, October Session, 1857, Relating to Juvenile Offenders and the establishment of A Reform School. Burlington : Daily Times Job Office. 1858. 12mo, pp. 14.

—*Report* of the Special Committee on the subject of Juvenile Offenders, with a Bill to establish the Vermont Reform School. Montpelier : Printed at the Freeman Steam Printing Establishment. 1865. 8vo, pp. 14.

—*An Act* for the Regulation and Government of the Vermont Reform School, at Waterbury, Approved November 19, 1866. Also the By-Laws, adopted by the Trustees, December 13, 1866. Montpelier : Freeman Steam Printing Establishment. 1866. 12mo, pp. 20.

—*Report* of the Special Committee to visit the Vermont Reform School. Annual Session, 1866. Montpelier : Freeman Steam Printing Establishment. 1866. 8vo, pp. 85.

—*First Annual Report* of the Board of Commissioners of the Vermont Reform School to the Governor of the State of Vermont, for the year 1865-6. Montpelier : Freeman Steam Printing Establishment. 1866. 8vo, pp. 45.
Continued.
This School was removed to Vergennes in 1875, in consequence of the destruction of the buildings at Waterbury, by fire.

REGISTRATION REPORTS.

—*Instructions* relative to the Registry and Return of Births, Marriages and Deaths, in Vermont. Benjamin W. Dean, Secretary of State. Middlebury : Printed at the Register Book and Job Office. 1859. 8vo, pp. 18, (2).

—*First Report* to the Legislature of Vermont, relating to the Registry and Returns of Births, Marriages and Deaths, in this State, for the year ending December 31, 1857. Prepared under the direction of Benj. W. Dean, Secretary of State. Burlington : Daily Times Book and Job Printing Establishment. 1859. 8vo, pp. vi, 118.

—*Second Report*. 1858. Middlebury : Printed at the Register Book and Job Office. 1859. 8vo, pp. vii, 116.

—*Third Report*, 1859. Same imprint, 1860. 8vo, pp. vii, 119.

—*Fourth Report*, 1860. Prepared under the direction of George W. Bailey, Jr., Secretary of State. Same imprint, 1861. 8vo, pp. vii, 116.

—*Fifth Report*, 1861. Montpelier : Printed at the Freeman Printing Establishment. 1863. 8vo, pp. xii, 110.

—*Sixth Report*, 1862. 1865, pp. viii, 112 ; Seventh, 1863, 1866, pp. viii, 104, Same imprint.

—*Eighth Report*, 1864. George Nichols, Secretary of State. Same imprint, 1866. 8vo, pp. viii, 104.

—*Ninth Report*, 1865. Same imprint, 1867. 8vo, pp. viii, 107.

—*Tenth Report*, 1866. Rutland : Tuttle & Co., Printers. 1868. 8vo, pp. vii, 112.

—*Eleventh Report*, 1867, pp. viii, 118 ; Twelfth, 1868, pp. viii, 134 ; Thirteenth, 1869, pp. vii, 144 ; Fourteenth, 1870, pp. vii, 136 ; Fifteenth, 1871, pp. viii, 148 ; Sixteenth, 1872, pp. viii, 158 ; Seventeenth, 1873, pp. viii, 155 ; Eighteenth, 1874, pp. viii, 157 ; and Nineteenth, 1875, pp. viii, 157, all same imprint.

—*Twentieth Report*, 1876. Montpelier : Freeman Print. 1878. 8vo, pp. viii, 145.

—*Twenty-first* and Twenty-Second Reports, 1877-8. In one volume. Same imprint. 8vo, pp. viii, 126 ; viii, 141.
Continued.

VERMONT STATE LIBRARY.

—*Catalogue* of the, 1850. Arranged and prepared by the State Librarian, under the direction of the Governor, agreeably to an Act of the General Assembly. Montpelier: E. P. Walton & Son, Printers. 1850. 8vo, pp. 86.

—*Catalogue* of the, with a list of Duplicates for Exchanges. Montpelier: E. P. Walton Printer. 1858. 8vo, pp. 63.

—*Catalogue of*, September 1, 1872. Montpelier : J. & J. M. Poland, Printers. 1872. 8vo, pp. xiv, 200.

—*Report* of the Commissioner on the condition of the State Library. October 14, 1857. Printed by Order of the Senate. Montpelier : E. P. Walton, Printer. 1857. 8vo, pp. 8.

—*Report* of the Trustees of the Vermont State Library. Submitted Tuesday, October 23, 1860. Montpelier : Freeman Print. 1860. 8vo, pp. 10.

—*Report* of Commissioners to devise a plan for the better Accommodation and Utility of the State Library, State Cabinet, and the Collections of the Vermont Historical Society, &c., &c. Rutland : Tuttle & Co., Stationers and Official Printers to the State of Vt. 1878. 8vo, pp. 12.

VERMONT HISTORICAL SOCIETY.

—*Vermont Historical Society.* Deficiencies in Our History. An Address delivered before the Vermont Historical and Antiquarian Society, at Montpelier, October 16, 1846. By James Davie Butler, Professor in Norwich University. Montpelier : Eastman and Danforth. 1846. 8vo, pp. 36.
Contains in addition the Act of Incorporation, first meeting and organization of the Society in October, 1840; the Constitution and By-Laws; also Vermont Declaration of Independence, January 15, 1777, and Whittier's "Song of the Vermonters."

—*Addresses* on the Battle of Bennington, and The Life and Services of Col. Seth Warner ; delivered before the Legislature of Vermont, in Montpelier, October 20, 1848, By James Davie Butler, (on the Battle of Bennington) and George Frederick Houghton, (on Col. Seth Warner.) Published by Order of the Legislature. Burlington : Free Press Print. 1849. 8vo, pp. 99.
Includes an Appendix which contains Order of Sequestration, 1777; Roll of Captain Robinson's Company in Bennington battle; Receipt for Plunder Money; Report of Council of New Hampshire on lands west of Connecticut river, 1771; Petition to Congress of the Widow of Seth Warner ; and papers in relation to the right of New York to boundary on Connecticut river, etc.

—*An Address* pronounced in the Representative's Hall, Montpelier, 24th October, 1850, before the Vermont Historical Society, in the presence of Both Houses of the General Assembly; By Daniel P. Thompson. Published by Order of the Legislature. Burlington : Free Press Print. 1850. 8vo, pp. 22.

—*Life and Services* of Matthew Lyon. An Address October 29, 1858, before the Society, by Pliny H. White. Burlington : 1858. 8vo, pp. 26.

—*The Marbles of Vermont.* An Address on the same occasion by Albert D. Hager. Burlington: 1858. 8vo, pp. 10.

—*Constitution* and By-Laws of the Vermont Historical Society, with Act of Incorporation and a Catalogue of Officers and Members. Woodstock, Vermont : Davis & Greene, Printers. January, 1860. 8vo, pp. 16.

—*Proceedings* of the Twenty-first Annual Meeting of the Vermont Historical Society, with the Annual Address, by Rev Joseph Torrey, D. D., Montpelier, Oct. 16, 1860. Burlington : Free Press Print. 1860. 8vo, pp. 27.

—*Proceedings* of the Vermont Historical Society, at the Special Meeting, Holden at Burlington, January 23, 1861. Burlington : Free Press Print. 1861. 8vo, pp. 7,-8.
Contains also biographical sketches of Rev. Samuel Austin Worcester, by Pliny H. White ; of Hon. George Tisdale Hodges, by George F. Houghton ; of Governor John S. Robinson, by Hon. Hiland Hall, and of Dr. Noadiah Swift, also by Gov. Hall.

—*Preceedings* of the Vermont Historical Society, at its Twenty-second Annual Meeting, holden at Montpelier, Vermont, Oct. 15 and 16, 1861. St. Albans, Vt.: Printed for the Society. MDCCC,LXI. 8vo, pp. 17.

—*Proceedings* at the Special Meeting held at Burlington, January 22d and 23d, 1862. St. Albans, Vt.: Henry A. Cutler, Printer. MDCCC,-LXII. 8vo, pp. 8, 8.
Includes an Address by Hon. Henry Clark on Town Centennial Celebrations. 8vo, pp. 8.

—*Address* by Mr. Henry B. Dawson, Jan'y 23, 1861, on the "Battle of Bennington," read before the Vt. Hist. Soc. at Burlington.
Printed in the Historical Magazine, May, 1870; reprinted in the Argus and Patriot, Montpelier, Vt., June 27, July 4, 11, 1877.
See Reed, George B, Address, 1862.

—*Gov. Phillip Skene*, Sketch of, read by Henry Hall, Esq., of Rutland, before the Vermont Historical Society, at Windsor, July 2d, 1863.
See (Dawson's) Historical Magazine. Vol. II, 2d series, pp. 280-83.

—*Joseph Bowker*, Sketch of, read by Henry Hall, Esq., before the Vermont Historical Society, at Windsor, Vt., July 1st and 2d, 1863.
See (Dawson's) Historical Magazine. Vol. II, 2d series, pp. 351-54.

—*Evacuation* of Ticonderoga, in 1777 ; an elaborate paper read before the Vermont Historical Society at Brattleboro, July 17, 1862, by Henry Hall.
Printed in (Dawson's) Historical Magazine, August, 1869.

—*Proceedings of the Vermont Historical Society*, October 20 and November 5, 1896. Address : "The Battle of Bennington," Henry D. Hall, Esq.. Address: "Vermont as a Leader in Educational Progress," Rev. A. D. Barber. Presentation of Portrait of the Hon. E. P. Walton, President, 1876-90. Montpelier : Argus and Patriot Press, 1897. 8vo, pp. 108.
Contains Constitution and By-Laws and List of Members.

—*Proceedings* of the Vermont Historical Society, at Meetings held at Brattleboro, July 16

and 17, and at Montpelier, October 14, 1862. St. Albans, Vt.: Printed for the Society. 1863. 8vo, pp. 26.
Contains list of resident, honorary, and corresponding members

—*Secession in Switzerland* and in the United States Compared : being the Annual Address, delivered Oct. 20th. 1863, before the Vermont State Historical Society, in the Hall of Representatives, Capitol, Montpelier, by J. Watts De Peyster. Catskill : Joseph Joesbury, Printer, Journal Office. 1863. 8vo, pp. 72.

—*The Life and Character* of the Hon. Richard Skinner ; A Discourse read before and at the request of the Vermont Historical Society, at Montpelier, October 20, 1863, by Winslow C. Watson. Albany, N. Y.: J. Munsell, 78 State Street. 1863. 8vo, pp. 30.

—*Edward Crafts Hopson.* A Biographical Sketch, read before the Vermont Historical Society, January 25, 1865. By Henry Clark. 8vo, pp. 6.

—*A Sketch of the Life and Character* of Charles Linsley, read before the Vermont Historical Society. By E. J. Phelps. Published by the Society. Albany, N. Y.; J. Munsell, 78 State Street. 1866. 8vo, pp. 20.

—*The Battle of Gettysburgh*, and the part taken by the Vermont Troops. By G. G. Benedict, Lieut. and A. D. C. Burlington : Free Press Print. 1867. 8vo, pp. 24.
Read before the Vermont Historical Society at a special meeting held at Brandon, January 26, 1864. Another edition of 100 copies, with portrait of Gen. George J. Stannard, and 3 engravings of scenes in the battle, was privately printed. 8vo, pp. 27, and Appendix iv.

—*Addresses* delivered before the Vermont Historical Society, in the Representatives' Hall, Montpelier, October 16, 1866. By George F. Edmunds, on the Life, Character and Services of Solomon Foot. By Pliny H. White, on Governor Galusha. By Rev. J. E. Rankin, of Charlestown, Mass., on the Sources of New England Civilization. Published by Order of the General Assembly. Montpelier : Walton's Steam Printing Establishment. 1866. 8vo, pp. 72.

—*Special Meeting at Rutland*, August 20th and 21st. 1868. Programme. 8vo, pp. 6.

—*Theophilus Herrington.* A paper read before the Vermont Historical Society, at a Special Meeting at Rutland, 20th August, 1868. By Rev. Pliny H. White. 8vo, pp. 5.
Cut from a newspaper, and pasted in book form.

—*Memorial Address* on the Life and Character of the Hon. Jacob Collamer. Read before the Vermont Historical Society, in the Representatives' Hall, October 20, 1868. By James Barrett, LL.D., Judge of the Supreme Court. Woodstock, Vt.: 1868. 8vo, pp. 61.

—*Proceedings* of the Vermont Historical Society, October 19 and 20, 1869. Montpelier : Journal Printing Establishment. 8vo, pp. 15

—*Addresses* read before the Vermont Historical Society, October 19 and 20, 1869 : The Capture of Ticonderoga, by Hiland Hall. 8vo, pp. 32.

—*Memorial Address* on the Life and Services of the late Rev. Pliny H. White, by Henry Clark, of Rutland. 8vo, pp. 16.

—*Proceedings* of the Vermont Historical Society, October and November, 1870. Montpelier : Printed for the Society. 1871. 8vo, pp. xxvii, 54.
Includes Memorial Address on the Life and Character of Hon. Charles Marsh, LL.D., by James Barrett, LL.D.

—*Proceedings of the Society*, October 8, 1872. Montpelier : Printed for the Society. 1872. 8vo, pp. xxi, 127.
Includes Address on the Capture of Ticonderoga, by Hon. L. E. Chittenden.

—*Charles Reed.* Memorial Sketch read before the Vermont Historical Society, October 13, 1874. By H. A. Huse. pp. 2.
Cut from a newspaper, and pasted in book form.

—*History of the St. Albans Raid.* Annual Address before the Vermont Historical Society, delivered at Montpelier, Vt., on Tuesday Evening, October 17, 1876. By Hon. Edward A. Sowles. St. Albans : Messenger Printing Works. 1876. 8vo, pp. 48.
Includes Proceedings of the Society.

—*Collections of the Vermont Historical Society*, prepared and published by the Printing and Publishing Committee in pursuance of a vote of the Society. Vol. 1. Montpelier : Printed for the Society. 1870. 8vo, pp. xix, 507.
Contents : General Circular ; Acts relating to the Society ; Constitution ; By Laws ; Rules of Order for the Meetings ; Officers and Resident Members.
Conventions of the Inhabitants of the New Hampshire Grants in opposition to the Claims of New York, 1765 to 1777 : [See Dawson's Historical Magazine, January, 1872, and onward, for a portion of these Conventions.] Committees of Safety ; Regiment of Green Mountain Boys ; The Dorset Conventions, January 16, July 24, and September 25, 1776 ; The Westminster Conventions, October 30, 1776, and January 15, 1777 ; Vermont's Declaration of Independence ; The Windsor Convention, June 4, 1777 ; Name, "Vermont ;" Committee to Repair to Ticonderoga ; Proclamation for a Fast ; The Windsor Convention ; July 2, 1777 ; Adoption of the Constitution ; Mr. Hutchinson's Sermon at Windsor, July 2d, 1777 ; The Vision of Janus the Benningtonite, 1777 ; Miscellaneous Remarks, etc., by Ira Allen, May, 1777 ; Miscellaneous Remarks on the Same Subject, by the same, October, 1777 ; New York Land Grants in Vermont, 1765-1776 ; Documents in Relation to the part taken by Vermont in Resisting the Invasion of Burgoyne in 1777 ; Celebration in 1778 of the Bennington Victory of 1777 ; A speech, by Noah Smith, A. B., and a Poetical Essay by Stephen Jacob ; Petitions to the King, 1766 ; The Vermont Coinage ; The Natural and Political History of the State of Vermont, by Ira Allen ; a reprint of the entire work ; Index to Allen's History. General Index.

—*Vol. II.* Title and imprint the same. 1871. 8vo, pp. xxviii, 530.
Contents : List of Pamphlet Publications, and Officers of the Society. Additions and Corrections to volumes I and II ; Vol. I. Vindicated. The Haldimand Papers, with Contemporaneous History. Opinions of the Haldimand Negotiation ; Completeness of the Haldimand Papers on the Negotiation.
[These papers, etc., give an account of the negotiations between Vermont and the Governor of Canada from January, 1779, to March, 1783 ; the negotiations on the part of Vermont were conducted by half a dozen or so leading men of the State, the general public being kept in entire ignorance of the matter. This period in Vermont history has been a subject of severe criticism, even down to the present time, but one answer alone, to all this is sufficient ; Vermont was a free and independent State or nation, with no alliance whatever with any of the thirteen colonies, and had a right to negotiate with Great Britain or any other nation, as seemed best for the interest of her people.]
Vermont as a Sovereign and Independent State 1783 to 1791 ; The early Eastern Boundary of New York, a Twenty-mile Line from the Hudson. General Index. Portrait.

—*Proceedings of the Vermont Historical Society*, October 15, 1878. Montpelier : J. & J. M. Poland, Official Printers. 1878. 8vo, pp. xvi, 47.

Contains address by Rev. M. H. Buckham on Rev. W. H. Lord, and address by Hon. E. P. Walton, "The First Legislature of Vermont."

—*Proceedings* of the Vermont Historical Society, October 19, 1880. Rutland : Tuttle & Co., Official State Printers, 1880. 8vo, pp. xxviii, (2) 43.

Contain Hon. E. A. Sowles' address on "Fenianism," and By-Laws, etc., of the Society.

—*Address* on the Life and Public Services of the Hon. Samuel Prentiss. Delivered before the Vermont Historical Society, at Montpelier, October 26, 1882, by E. J. Phelps, Esq. With the Proceedings of the Society, October 17, 1882. Montpelier : Watchman and Journal Press. 1883. 8vo, pp. xix, 24.

—*Address on* Early Printing in America. Before the Vermont Historical Society at Montpelier, October 25, 1894, by Henry O. Houghton. With the address of Justin S. Morrill on Presentation of the Senator's Portrait to the Society by Thomas W. Wood. With the proceedings of the Vermont Historical Society, October 16 and 25, 1894. Montpelier ; Press of the Watchman Publishing Co., 1894. 8vo, pp. x, 28.

SOCIETIES AND ASSOCIATIONS.

—*Vermont Academy of Medicine.* Annual Circular of, For the Session of March, 1841. Castleton, Vermont, October, 1840. Castleton : R. E. Huntington & Co., Printers. MDCCCXL. 12mo, pp. 12.

Continued.

—*Vermont Medical College.* Catalogue of the Trustees, Examiners, Faculty and Students, of, for the year 1844 : and of the Alumni and Honorary Graduates, since its foundation in 1830. Woodstock : Printed at the Office of the Vermont Mercury. 1844. 8vo, pp. 16.

Continued.
See Gallup, J. A.; Haddock, C. B., Address, 1842.

—*Vermont Pharmaceutical Association.* Proceedings, Constitution and By-Laws ; Incorporated at the October Session of the Vermont Legislature, 1870. Rutland : Tuttle & Co., Printers. 1871. 8vo, pp. 16.

—*The same*, second and third annual meetings, 1871 and 1872.

Continued.

—*Vermont Medical Society.* The Charter and Bye-Laws of. Also a Sketch of the Proceedings of the Society ; together with A List of Officers for the present year. Compiled by Order of the Society. Montpelier : Printed by E. P. Walton. 1848. 8vo, pp. 23.

Edward Lamb and Calvin Deming, of Jefferson, now Washington county, were the compilers.

—*Vermont Medical Society*, Transactions of the, at the Annual Session, Held at Montpelier, October 19th and 20th, 1864. Woodstock: Vermont Standard Print. 8vo, pp. 66.

Contains the address of Dr. Hiram F. Stevens, giving a history of the Society since its organization in 1814 to 1858.
Continued.

—*Vermont Medical Society*, Constitution and By-Laws of the, Together with the Code of Medical Ethics Adopted by the Society. St. Albans, Vt.: Whiting & Davis, Printers. 1863. 8vo, pp. 16.

—*Vermont Medical Journal.* Issued Bi-Monthly: Jan., Mar., May, July, Sept., Nov., Containing 48 octavo pages. Vol. 1. January, 1874. No. 1. Burlington, Vermont. J. M. Currier, M. D., Editor & Publisher. Terms, $3.00 Per Annum, in advance.

Two numbers only issued. No. 2, pp. 48.

—*Vermont Association* for the Protection and Preservation of Fish and Game. Charter and By-Laws.

See Fish Culture.

—*Vermont Bar Association.* Act of Incorporation. Constitution, Members, and Papers and Addresses read 1878-1881. Montpelier, Vt.: Argus and Patriot Steam Book Press. 1882. 8vo, pp. 98.

—*Vermont Bible Society.* Second Annual Report Communicated to the Society, at their Annual Meeting at Montpelier, October 14, 1814. Montpelier, Vt.: Printed by Walton & Goss. 1814. 8vo, pp. 15.

Continued annually.
This society was organized in 1812, and has continued in vigorous operation ever since. Eighty-third Annual Report published in 1895.

—*Vermont and Boston Telegraph Co.* Report of the Board of Directors of the, submitted to the Stockholders, 1851. Montpelier : E. P. Walton & Sons. 1851. 8vo, pp. 8.

This is the first report of this Company.

—*The Same*, Second Annual Report, with the Act of Incorporation, 1852. Same imprint. pp. 8.

—*The Same*, Third Annual Report, and the By-Laws of the Company. 1853. Same imprint. pp. 16.

—*The Same*, Fourth Annual Report. 1854. Burlington Free Press Office. 1854. pp. 6.

—*The Same*, Fifth Annual Report. 1855. Same imprint. pp. 6.

—*The Same*, Sixth Annual Report. 1856. Same imprint. pp. 6.

—*The Same*, Seventh Annual Report. 1857. Same imprint. pp. 7.

Erroneously numbered as the Sixth.

—*The Same*, Eighth Annual Report. 1858. Same imprint. pp. 6.

Erroneously numbered as the Seventh.

—*The Same*, Ninth Annual Report. 1859. Same imprint. pp. 8.

—*Vermont and Boston Telegraph Co.* Eleventh Annual Report of the Directors at the Annual Meeting of the Stockholders, in Burlington, Vt., January 23, 1861. Burlington : Free Press Print. 1861. 8vo, pp. 8.

—*Vermont Business Directory*, For 1877-78. Briggs & Co., Publishers, 17 Batterymarch Street, Boston, Mass. 8vo, pp. 231, and Advertisements, pp. 48.

—*Business Register* of Manufacturers in the States of Massachusetts, Connecticut, Rhode Island, and New Hampshire, and the Principal Manufacturers in New York, New Jersey, Ohio, Pennsylvania, Maine and Vermont. New York : Freeman, Cleary & Co. 1868-9. 4to, pp. 410.

—*State Directory.* Symonds, Wentworth & Co., Publishers, 10 Central Street, Boston. 1870. 8vo, pp. 214, 104.

Continued annually under various imprints. This was the first State Directory published.

—*Vermont Branch* of the Woman's Board of Missions.
See Woman's Board of Missions.

—*Vermont Canals Proposed.* Letter from the Secretary of War, transmitting a Report of the Surveys of Contemplated Routes for Canals. March 4, 1828. Ordered to be printed. Doc. 173, 20th Congress, 1st Session. Washington: Printed by Gales & Seaton. 1828. 8vo, pp. 58.
Includes reports on the Passumpsic Canal, to connect the waters of the Connecticut with those of Lake Memphremagog, by the valleys of Passumpsic and Barton rivers; Montpelier canal, to connect the waters of Lake Champlain with those of Connecticut river, by the valleys of Onion and White rivers, passing *via* Montpelier, the Capital of the State; and the Rutland canal, to connect by water communication the town of Rutland, Vt., with the northern canal, at Whitehall, N. Y.
See Navigation of Connecticut river; Governor and Council, Vol. 7, pp. 479-82.

—*Vermont Colonization Society.* Ninth Report of, Communicated at the Annual Meeting, at Montpelier, October 17, 1828. Montpelier: Printed by E. P. Walton—Watchman Office. 1828. 8vo, pp. 8.
This Society was organized at Montpelier, October 19, 1819, and reports were made annually, usually accompanied by an address or sermon. The last report we have seen is as follows:

—*The Forty-eighth Annual Report* of the Vermont Colonization Society, Together with the Address of Gen. J. W. Phelps, at the Annual Meeting in Montpelier, October 17th, 1867 Burlington: Free Press Steam Print, 1867. 8vo, pp. 42.
See Yale, Calvin, Sermon, 1827; McKeen, Silas, Sermon, 1828; Mitchell, Wm., discourse, 1843.

—*Vermont Copper Mining Co.* In Chancery. Vermont Copper Mining Co. vs. Henry Barnard. Orange County Court, January Term, 1860. R. Farnham, L. B. Peck, Solicitors. Montpelier: Printed at the Freeman Steam Printing Establishment. 1865. 8vo, pp. 22, (2).

—*In Chancery,* Orange County Court. Joseph I. Bicknell and Thomas Pollard, v. The Vt. Copper Mining Co., *et al.,* and Joseph I. Bicknell, v. The Vt. Copper Mining Co., *et al.* Aug. 1876. no imprint. 8vo, pp. ii, 555.
Contains the testimony for the Orators.

—*The Same.* no imprint. 8vo, pp. 4, 505.
Contains the testimony for the Defendants.

—*State of Vermont.* In Chancery: Orange County: Joseph I. Bicknell and Thomas Pollard, vs. Vermont Copper Mining Company, and others. J. W. Rowell & Asahel Peck, Solicitors for Orators. Roswell Farnham & C. W. Clarke, Solicitors for Defendants New York: Benj. H. Tyrrel, Job Printer, 74 Maiden Lane. 1878. 8vo, pp. 133.

—*Bicknell and Pollard* vs. Vermont Copper Mining Company and others. Chancellor Powers' Opinion and Decretal Order. Bradford: Printed by Orange County Publishing Co. 1879. 8vo, pp. 16.

—*Defendants' Exhibits.* Bicknell and Pollard vs. Vermont Copper Mining Company and others. Supreme Court, General Term. October, 1879. Bradford: Printed by Orange County Publishing Co. 1879. 8vo, pp. 15.

—*In Chancery.* Supreme Court. Orange County. March Term, A. D. 1879. Joseph I. Bicknell and Thomas Pollard, v. Vermont Copper Mining Co. & Ors. and Cross Bill. Vermont Copper Mining Co. v. Bicknell and Pollard, and Joseph I. Bicknell, v. Vermont Copper Mining Co. & Ors., and Cross Bill. Vermont Copper Mining Co. v. Joseph I. Bicknell. Brief for defendants in original bills, and for orators in Cross Bills. By C. W. Clarke, Solicitor. No imprint. 8vo, pp. 86.

—*Supreme Court.* Vermont. Bicknell & Pollard vs. The Copper Mining Company. Defendant's Points. By R. McK. Ormsby, Sol'r for Deft. P. F. McBreen, Law and Job Printer. New York. 8vo, pp. 6.

—*Supreme Court of Vermont,* General Term. Montpelier, October, 1879. Bicknell and Pollard vs. Vermont Copper Mining Company et Alios, and Joseph I. Bicknell vs. Vermont Copper Mining Company, et Alios. Defendant's Brief. Roswell Farnham, Solicitor. Bradford: Printed by Orange County Publishing Co. 1879. 8vo, pp. 99.

—*The Same Case.* Orators' Brief. By J. W. Rowell, of Counsel. 8vo, pp. 82.

—*The Same.* Orators' Brief. By S. M. Gleason, of Counsel. 8vo, pp. 52.

—*Vermont Editors and Publishers Association,* Fourth Annual Meeting, held at Rutland, June 8th, 1872. St. Albans Messenger Print. 1872. 8vo, pp. 24.
Continued. See Publishers.

—*Vermont Missionary Society.*
On the 4th of April, 1804, a circular letter was addressed to the churches in the western district of Vermont, by a committee appointed by the consociations of said district, for the purpose of raising money for missionary purposes in the new settlements. The committee consisted of Benjamin Wooster, Lemuel Haynes, and Jedediah Bushnell. The committee's report, submitted October 10, 1805, has the following title:
Communication of the Vermont Missionary Society. A Circular Letter to the Churches and Congregations in the Western Districts of the State of Vermont.
It is a broadsheet, and contains a "Narrative of Missions, Report of Seth Storrs, Treasurer," by which it appears $327.97 had been raised, $228.96 expended, and $99.01 in the treasury. Also contains an address by the committee to the Consociations.

—*To the Churches* and Congregations of Vermont.
Broadsheet. Contains proceedings and address of the General Convention of Congregational and Presbyterian ministers, assembled at Middlebury, September 1, 1807, relative to the Vermont Missionary Society, which was formally organized at said convention. Martin Tullar, Chairman Thomas A. Merrill, Secretary.

—*A Circular Letter* to the Churches and Congregations of Vermont. 8vo, pp. 10.
This is the second annual report of the Vermont Missionary Society, at Windsor, September 6, 1808.

—*Address* of the Trustees of the Vermont Missionary Society. Broadsheet; Third Report, September 4, 1800.

—*Address* to the Churches and Congregations of Vermont. By the Trustees of the Vermont Missionary Society. To which is prefixed the last Report of the Trustees, and the last Report of the Treasurer, November, 1810. J. D. Huntington, Printer, Middlebury. 8vo, pp. 7.
Reports continued annually to and including the year 1818, when the organization was succeeded by the Vermont Juvenile Missionary S ciety.
See Burton, H. N., Semi-centennial discourse, 1868.
See Bates, Joshua, Sermon, 1818.

—Vermont Juvenile Missionary Society. Constitution of the Vermont Juvenile Missionary Society. A Notice of the Proceedings of the Delegates at their Meeting, held at Castleton, September 16, 1818; together with their Address to the People of the State of Vermont. Middlebury, Vt.: Printed by Francis Burnap. 1818. 8vo, pp. 23.
Continued annually until 1826, when the name was changed to the Vermont Domestic Missionary Society,

—Proceedings of the Vermont Domestic Missionary Society, at their Annual Meeting at Castleton, September 14, 1826. Together with the Reports of the Directors and Treasurer, the Constitution of the Society, etc. Bellows Falls: James I. Cutler & Co., Printers. 1826. 8vo, pp. 24.
Eighth annual report. Continued under the same title, substantially, with various imprints, until 1862, when the reports are included in the "Minutes of the General Convention" of Vermont.
See Proceedings, 1820; Congregational.

—Vermont Sunday School Association.
See Sabbath Schools.

—Vermont State Temperance Society.
See Temperance.

—Vermont Novelty Works Co., 1878. Annual Catalogue of Children's Carriages and Toys, manufactured by the Vermont Novelty Works Co., Springfield, Vermont. Organized 1859. Washed out, 1864. Washed away, 1869. Burned, June 25, 1878. And "We Still Live." No imprint. 8vo, pp. 63.

—Vermont Numismatic Society. Constitution and By-Laws of, Adopted July 3d, 1877. Montpelier, Vt., Argus and Patriot Job Printing House. 1877. 18mo, pp. 12.

—Vermont State Agricultural Society. . Addresses before the Vermont State Agricultural Society, at its Exhibition held at Rutland, September, 1852: Together with the Report of the Committee on Manufactured Goods. Published by the Society. Middlebury: Justus Cobb, Printer, Register Office. 1853. 8vo, pp. 18, 23, 23.
Addresses by W. H. Seward, of New York, and William S. King, of Rhode Island.

—The Thirteenth Annual Fair will be held at Rutland, Sept. 8, 9, 10 and 11, 1863. Windsor: Vermont Journal Office, L. J. McIndoe, Printer. 1863. 8vo, pp. 16.
See Agricultural.

—Premium List of the 27th Annual Fair of the Vermont State Agricultural Society and Wool Growers' Association, to be held at St. Albans, Tuesday, Wednesday and Thursday, September 11, 12 & 13, 1877. Competition open to the world. Rutland: Globe Paper Company, Printers. 1877. 8vo, pp. 24.

—Vermont Stock Journal. Middlebury: 1857-8. Monthly, D. C. Linsley, Editor and Proprietor. 2 volumes, 4to, pp. 192, 192.

—Vermont Merino Sheep Breeder's Association. Spanish Merino Sheep, their importations from Spain. Introduction into Vermont and Improvement Since introduced. A List of Stock Rams with their pedigrees and a Register of pure bred flocks of Improved Spanish Merino Sheep. Volume I. Published by the Vermont Merino Sheep Breeders' Association. 1879. 8vo, pp. 395.

This association was organized in 1876, and in less than two years furnished the above volume containing a vast amount of useful information. Albert Chapman, Esq., of Middlebury, is Secretary.

—Vermont Horse Stock Company. 1874. Catalogue of Blood Horses. Shelburn, Vt. Executive Committee. L. S. Drew, Burlington, James A. Shedd, Burlington, W. A. Weed, Shelburn. Superintendent: C. F. Predmore. Burlington: R. S. Styles & Son, Book and Job Printers. 8vo, pp. 24.

—Vermont State Grange. Proceedings of the Vermont State Grange From its Organization, July 4th, 1872, to and including its Third Annual Session, December 8th and 9th, A. D. 1874 Together with the By-Laws of the State grange, and By-Laws Recommended for Subordinate Granges, As Amended December 9th, 1874. Montpelier, Vt.: Argus and Patriot Steam Printing Establishment. 1875. 12mo, pp. 56.

—Proceedings of the Fourth Annual Meeting of the Vermont State Grange, Held at Burlington, December 14, 15 and 16, 1875. Same imprint. 12mo, pp. 36.

—Fifth Annual Meeting at Windsor, Dec. 12 and 13, 1876. 12mo, pp. 44, and (1).
Continued.

—Rules and Regulations for establishing and governing County Granges. 12mo, pp. 4.

—Proceedings of the Vermont Convention of Fruit-Growers, and the Vermont Horticultural Society, October, 1850. 8vo, pp. 22. No imprint.

—Vermont Dairymen's Association. Transactions of the Vermont Dairymen's Association, 1869-70, with Addresses and Essays. Original and selected. Burlington: Free Press Print. 1870. 8vo, pp. 134.

—The Same. Embracing the Addresses, Essays and Discussions of the Annual and Winter Meetings. St. Albans: Messenger Print. 1872. 8vo, pp. 178.

—Third Annual Report. Transactions of the Vermont Dairymen's Association for the Year Ending October 23, 1872, with Accompanying Papers. St. Albans: Messenger Steam Printing House. 1872. 8vo, pp. 167.

—Fourth Annual Report. Transactions Vermont Dairymen's Association, 1872-74. Published by the Association. St. Albans, Vt.: Albert Clark, Steam Printer. 1873. 8vo, pp. 190.

—Fifth Annual Report. Transactions of the Vermont Dairymen's Association for the Year Ending October 21, 1874. With Accompanying Papers. Montpelier: J. & J. M. Poland's Steam Printing House. 1874. 8vo, pp. 167.

—Sixth Annual Report. Same title and same imprint. 1875. 8vo, pp. 163, (1.)

—Seventh Annual Report. Same title and same imprint. 1876. 8vo, pp. 183, (1.)

—Report of the Twenty-fifth Annual Meeting of the Vermont Dairymen's Association and Third Annual Meeting of the Vermont Maple Sugar Makers' Association, 1895. Brattleboro: Phœnix Office. pp. 240.

—*Report* of the Twenty-sixth Annual Meeting of the Vermont Dairymen's Association. Montpelier: Watchman Pub. Co. 1896. pp. 273.
Continued.

—*The Vermont Agriculturist*, devoted to Agriculture, Horticulture and Floriculture. Vol. 1. May, 1878. No. 8. Brandon, Vt. : Published by Mott Brothers. 8vo, pp. 16.

—*Vermont Agricultural Society.* See Agricultural ; Agricultural Fairs ; Andrew, John A. Address ; Collier, Peter, Addresses.

—*Vermont Agricultural* Experiment Station. Annual Reports from 1887.

—*Fourth Report* of the Vermont Board of Agriculture, for the year 1877. By Henry M. Seeley, Secretary of the Board. Montpelier: J. & J. M. Poland, Official State Printers. 1877. 8vo, pp. 216.

—*Vermont Dairymen's* Association. Report in above volume, being Eighth Annual Report. Same imprint. 8vo, pp. 184.

—*Fifth Annual* Report of Board of Agriculture, 1878. Same imprint. 8vo, pp. 403.
Contains reports of Vermont Dairymen's Association, 9th Report, and of State Geologist; pagination continuous.
Continued.

MISCELLANEOUS VERMONT DOCUMENTS.

—*Vermont Asylum* for the Insane. Its Annals for fifty years. Brattleboro : Printed by Hildreth & Falls. 1887. 8vo, pp. x, 302.

—*A List* of Arrearages of Taxes, due from the several Towns in the State of Vermont, Sept. 15, 1795. Western District, Rutland, Vt. : For the use of Members. 4to.

—*An Act* Establishing Fees. Passed by the Legislature of the State of Vermont, at their Session Holden at Vergennes, October, 1798. Published by Authority. Vergennes : Printed by C. & R. Waite. 1798. 8vo, pp. 15.

—*History* of the Late Ecclesiastical Oppressions in New England and Vermont, &c. Richmond : 1799. 8vo.

—*Observations* on Facts, Vindicating the Rights of Dartmouth College and Moor's Charity School to the Grant made by the Legislature of Vermont in June, 1785. Windsor, Vt. : 1807, 8vo.

—*Official Papers* ; Containing the Governor's (Isaac Tichenor) Speech to the Legislature of Vermont ; Their Answer, with the Proposal of Amendment ; and the Protest of the Minority on the Acceptance of the Answer, by the House. Montpelier : By Samuel Goss. 1808.
Relates chiefly to the Embargo.

—*A Free Enquiry* into the causes both Real and Pretended for laying the Embargo. By a citizen of Vermont. Windsor, Vt. : Printed by Charles Spear. 1808. 8vo, pp. 28.

—*Report* of the Committee, Messrs. Edmond, Olin, G. Robinson, Hoyt, Hotchkiss, and Asa Lyon, appointed to examine the doings of the Canvassing Committee, and to report facts relative to the rejected voters. Published by order of the House. Montpelier, Vt. : Printed by Walton & Goss, November, 1813.
Relates to the election of Governor and the Legislature that year.
See Dunham, Josiah.

—*The Report* of a Committee appointed by a Convention of Republican citizens of the County of Addison, made Feb. 28, 1814, Embracing Facts relative to the Proceedings of the Legislature of Vermont, in October, 1813. Also an Address to the Freemen of Vermont. Middlebury : Slade & Ferguson, Printers. 1814. 8vo, pp. 31.
Relates to the election of Chittenden over Galusha for Governor, in 1813.
See Dunham, Josiah.

—*Proceedings* of the General Assembly of the State of Vermont convened at Montpelier, Oct. 14, 1813. Montpelier: Printed by Wright & Sibley. 1813. 8vo, pp. 52.
Relates to the disputed election of Governor and Council, bribory, etc.

—*Protest* of the Minority [70 Members] of the House of Representatives of the State of Vermont on the Question of Adopting the Reported Answer to His Excellency's [Gov. Martin Chittenden's] Speech, Nov. 10, 1813. Montpelier: Printed by Wright & Sibley. 1813. 8vo, pp. 20.
Relates to the contest between the Federalists and Republicans, as to the prosecution of the war against Great Britain, Gov. Chittenden being of the Federal party.

—*Mr. Niles' Resolution*, calling on the Governor for evidence to substantiate the suggestion, in his Excellency's late Speech, relative to Impressment ; together with His Excellency's Answer. Published by order of the House. Montpelier, Vt.: Printed by Walton & Goss, November, 1813. 8vo, pp. 8.

—*H. C. Denison's Resolutions* calling on the Governor for copies of any Correspondence he may have had with Military Officers, relative to detaching the Militia, etc. Montpelier : Walton and Goss. 1814.
Relates to Governor Martin Chittenden's Proclamation recalling the Vermont Troops from Plattsburgh, etc.

—*Report*, with Sundry Resolutions relative to Appropriations of Public Land for the purposes of Education, to the Senate of Maryland, January 30, 1821. Published by Order of the Legislature. Montpelier, Vt.: Printed by E. P. Walton. 8vo, pp. 22.
A complaint that the Western States were getting too large a portion of the public lands.

—*General List* of the State of Vermont. A. D. 1824. Large broadsheet.

—*Vermont Pension Roll.* As made up under the Act of Congress, passed in 1832. [n. p. n. d.] 8vo, pp. 158.

—*An Appeal* to the Unprejudiced Judgment of the Freemen of Vermont. n. p. n. d. 8vo, pp. 16.
A Jackson pamphlet, as against J. Q. Adams for President of the United States in 1828.

—*Report* and Correspondence on the Subject of a Geological and Topographical Survey of the State of Vermont. 1838.
Includes letters from Prof. G. W. Benedict and Mr. John Johnson, of Burlington, and Col. James Stevens, who made a survey of Massachusetts and Rhode Island. See Geology.

—*Reports* of the Majority, and Minority of the Select Committee of the Senate of Vermont on the Annexation of Texas to the United States. October Session of the Legislature, 1845. Published by Authority. Windsor: Bishop & Tracy. 1845. 8vo, pp. 15.

—*Proceedings* and Instructions Concerning the System of International Literary and Scientific Exchanges, established by Alexandre Vattemare. Published by Order of the Legislature of Vermont. Burlington: Free Press Office. 1848. 8vo, pp. 80.

—*Annual Reports* to the General Assembly in relation to International Exchanges and the Vermont State Library. Published by Order of the Senate. Montpelier, Vt.: E. P. Walton & Son, Printers. 1850. 8vo, pp. 61.

—*Rules* of the Court of Chancery of the State of Vermont; and Rules of Washington County Court. 1850. Montpelier: E. P. Walton & Son, Printers. 16mo, pp. 24.

—*House Document*, No. 1, Report on the Financial Affairs of the State of Vermont, Submitted October 14, 1851, by the Committee appointed by the Governor, under a Resolution of the last Legislature. Published by Authority. Burlington: Free Press Office. 1851. 8vo, pp. 29.

—*The Vermont Letter* on the Nebraska Bill, Respectfully addressed to the House of Representatives of the United States. Collins, Printers. H. Hooker, Phil. 8vo, pp. 16.
  Signed, A Citizen of Vermont.

—*An Address*, to the Freemen of Vermont, by their Delegation to the National Republican Convention, Holden at Baltimore, Md., in December, 1831. Middlebury, Vt.: H. H. Houghton, Printer. 8vo, pp. 16.

—*A Geographical and Historical Poem* on Vermont. By a Citizen of Washington County. Northfield, Vt.: Published by Charles O. Kimball. 1852. 16mo, pp. 12.

—*Report of the Committee* Under the Act Providing for the erection of a Monument over the Grave of Ethan Allen. Printed by order of the Senate. Montpelier: E. P. Walton, Printer. 1858. 8vo, pp. 7.

—*Report of the Commissioners* to settle with the Sureties of the late State Treasurer. 1861. Printed by Order of the House. No imprint. 8vo, pp. 7.

—*Report of Committee* to Examine and Investigate the Accounts and Expenditures of the Governor. Nov. 20, 1861. No imprint. 8vo, pp. 4.

—*Report of the Auditor of Accounts* relative to the Moneys paid by certain officers. Submitted to the Senate, Thursday, October 23, 1862. Montpelier: Freeman Print. 1862. 8vo, pp. 6.

—*Communication from the Governor* to the General Assembly of the State of Vermont. Annual Session, 1863. Montpelier: Printed at the Freeman Printing Establishment. 1863. 8vo, pp. 23.
  Includes the report of John Howe, Jr., relative to State Aid for Soldiers' families in Vermont.

—*General Statutes* as revised by the Commissioners in 1862. rl. 8vo, pp. 980.
  This is a copy of the revision submitted to the Legislature for its action in 1862.

—*Vermont*. Senate Document—No. 36. Report of the Committee on Finance on so much of the Governor's message as relates to the Finances of the State. Montpelier: Freeman Print. 1864. 8vo, pp. 9.

—*Taxation of Income* of United States Bonds. Report of the Committee of Ways and Means of the House of Representatives. 1865. Montpelier: Freeman Print. 1865. 8vo, pp. 8.

—*Documents* communicated to the General Assembly by His Excellency, The Governor, concerning the spread of the Asiatic Cholera. Submitted to the House, October 10, 1865. Burlington: Times Book and Job Printing Establishment. 1865. 8vo, pp. 12.

—*Report of the Committee* on the Judiciary, on State's Attorneys. Senate Doc. Oct. Session, 1865. Montpelier: Walton's Steam Printing Establishment. 1865. 8vo, pp. 7.

—*Report of the Commissioner* to attend the Universal Exposition of 1867, at Paris, France. By Order of the Legislature of Vermont, October Session, 1867. (Albert D. Hager, Commissioner.) Rutland, Vt.: Tuttle & Company, Printers. 1867. 8vo, pp. 49.

—*Tabular Statement* showing the amount due from the State of Vermont to Soldiers in the Late War for the Suppression of the Rebellion. March 20, 1873. "To be kept by Town and County Clerks, to be referred to by any Persons." See Act inside. Montpelier: Freeman Steam Printing House and Bindery. 1873. 8vo, pp. 140.
  Compiled by Hon. John A. Page, State Treasurer.

—*Journal of Proceedings* of the State Equalizing Board for the year 1874. Montpelier: J. & J. M. Poland, Printers. 1874. 8vo, pp. 15.

—*Report of Commission* on Incorporated Villages appointed under Joint Resolution No. 348, Session of 1894. n. p. n. d.. 8vo, pp. 8.

—*A List of Desirable Farms* and Summer Homes in Vermont. Issued by the Board of Agriculture, Victor I. Spear, Statistical Secretary. 1895. Montpelier: 1895. Watchman Pub. Co. 8vo, pp. 109.
  Among other publications of the Vermont Board of Arriculture, are "Resources and Attractions of Vermont," edition of 1891; Same, edition of 1892; and "Vermont, a Glimpse of its Scenery and Industries," 1893.

—*First Biennial Report* of the Board of Library Commissioners of Vermont. Burlington: Free Press Association. 1896. 8vo, pp. 88.

—*Monuments at Gettysburg*. Report of the Vermont Commissioners, 1888. Including illustrations and Recommendations. Rutland: The Tuttle Company. 1888. 8vo, pp. 16.

—*Vermont Day at Gettysburg*. Programme of Dedication of Vermont Monuments at Gettysburg, Pa., Oct. 9, 1889. Burlington: Free Press Asso. 1889. 4to, pp. 19.

—*Vermont Day at San Francisco*, March 3, 1894. Souvenir of California Midwinter Exposition. San Francisco: Published by Geo. W. Hopkins, Gen'l Secretary. 1894. 4to. pp. 63. Portraits and illustrations.

—*Summer Homes* Among the Green Hills of Vermont and along the Shores of Lake Champlain. St. Albans: Messenger Co. Print. 1896. 8vo, pp. 134.
  Published by the Passenger Department of the Central Vermont Railroad.

—*By-Laws* and List of Officers and Members of the Vermont Veterans' Association of Boston and Vicinity. Organized January 17th, 1889. Published May, 1894. 16mo, pp. 19.

—*Vermont Society of Colonial Wars.* Constitution, By-Laws and Officers. Burlington: Free Press Association. 1894.

—*The Vermont Association* of Boston. An Account of the Ninth and Tenth Annual Dinners, January 22, 1895, and January 9, 1896, with Constitution, Officers and Members. Boston; Silver, Burdett & Co., 1896. 8vo, pp. 90.

VERMONT IN THE WAR OF THE REBELLION.

See Adjutant General's Reports, 1861 to 1765. See also:

BENEDICT, G. G. Vermont in the Civil War; Vermont at Gettysburg; Army Life in Virginia.

CARPENTER, GEO. N. History of the Eighth Vermont.

HAYNES, E. M. History of the Tenth Vermont.

HOLBROOK, W. C. History of the Seventh Vermont.

HOSMER, F. C. Glimpses of Andersonville.

PALMER, E. F. The Second Brigade.

PECK, T. S. Revised Roster of Vermont Volunteers.

PETTINGILL, S. B. The College Cavaliers.

RIPLEY, W. Y. W. History of Co. F., First U. S. Sharpshooters.

—*Proceedings* of First and Second Reunions of the Seventh Vermont.

—*Memorial Records* of Essex, Greensboro, Stowe, Waitsfield, Waterford.

SMITH, WM. F. From Chattanooga to Petersburg.

WAITE, O. F. R. Vemont in the Rebellion.

WALKER, ALDACE F. Vermont Brigade in the Shenandoah Valley.

WILLIAMS, J. C. Life in Camp.

—*Proceedings* of Reunion Society of Vermont Officers.

—*Sixteenth Regiment*, Vermont Volunteers, Reunions and Roster, 1878 and 1888.
See also military chapters Hemenway's Vermont Gazetteer.

VERMONT HISTORIES.

See Allen, Ira; Conant; Coolidge; Depuy; Graham; Hall, B. H.; Hall, Hiland; Hoskins; Robinson; Thompson: Williams.

Vermont, The Story of, by John L. Heaton. Boston: D. Lothrop Company. Washington St. opposite Bromfield street. 1889. 12mo, pp. 319.
This is the fourth of the Lothrop Company's series of Stories of the States.

—*A History* of New England, Containing Historical and descriptive Sketches of the Counties, Cities and principal towns of the Six New England States, &c. Edited by Rev. R. H. Howard, A. M., and Prof. Henry E. Crocker. Illustrated. Boston: Crocker & Co., Publishers. 1879. 4to, pp. 805.
Vermont occupies in this volume pp. 677 to 798 inclusive.
The opening chapter by Rev. R. H. Howard occupies 16 pp.

Addison County, by William F. Bascom, Esq., has 9 pp.
Bennington County, by D. K. Simonds, has 10 pp.
Caledonia County, by Hon. Henry Clark, has 11 pp.
Chittenden County, by Rev. R. H. Howard, has 8 pp.
Essex County, by Hiram A. Cutting, M. D., has 10 pp.
Franklin County, by Hon. Henry Clark, has 9 pp.
Grand Isle County, by William E. Graves, has 4 pp.
Lamoille County, by William E. Graves, has 5 pp.
Orange County, by J. T. Child, D. D. S., has 8 pp.
Orleans County, by William E. Graves, has 6 pp.
Rutland County, by Hon. Henry Clark, has 7 pp.
Washington County, by Rev. J. H. Hincks, has 7 pp.
Windham County, by Joseph J. Green, has 8 pp.
Windsor County, by William E. Graves, has 7 pp.
Surely, the above is not much of a history of Vermont.

—*The State of Vermont.* Article by Albert Clarke, in New England Magazine for August, 1891. Illustrated.

—*Centennial Anniversary* of the Independence of Vermont as a State, August 15th, 1877. Formation of the Procession. Head-Quarters Chief Marshal, Bennington, Vt., August 13th, 1887. 8vo, pp. 4.

—*Centennial Anniversary* of the Independence of the State of Vermont and the Battle of Bennington, August 15 and 16, 1877. Westminster, Hubbardton, Windsor. Tuttle & Co., Rutland. Official Printers and Stationers to the State of Vermont. 1879. 8vo, pp. v. (3,) 232.
Five steel Portraits.
See Bennington.

—*Facts for Vermont Voters!* Read and Reflect. [1880.] 8vo, pp. 8.
Relates to the political issues, State and National, in the campaign of 1880.

—*Vermont.* 1781. Yorktown. 1881. The Free Press Association, Printers. [Burlington 1880.] 8vo, pp. 12.
Contains expressions of opinion of nearly the entire newspaper press of Vermont on the proposed Centennial celebration, and the erection of a monument to commemorate the capture of Cornwallis and his army at Yorktown.
See Biographical Sketches.

Vose, John. *A Compendium* of Astronomy, etc., etc. Windsor, Vt.: N. C. Goddard & Co. 1836. 12mo, pp. viii, 184. Plates.

Wait, A. *Speech* made before The Central Association of the National Brotherhood of St. Patrick, Dublin, Ireland, Nov. 24th, 1862. By Augustine Wait. As reported for the Dublin Press, as extracted from The Irishman. Montpelier: Printed by E. P. Walton. 1863. Price 15 cents. 8vo, pp. 20.
Mr. Wait is a native of Stowe, Vt.

Wait, Jenny.
(Pseudonym,) "Minnie Myrtle." A native of Windsor, Vt.; has published many stories in volumes and magazines.

Waite, Otis F. R. *Vermont in the Great Rebellion.* Containing Historical and Biographical Sketches, Etc. By Maj. Otis F. R. Waite. Claremont, N. H.: Tracy, Chase and Company. 1869. 12mo, pp. 288.

Waitsfield. *Manual of the Congregational Church* in Waitsfield, Vt., with a catalogue of Officers and members. Montpelier: Printed at the Freeman Steam Printing Establishment. 1867. 12mo, pp. 24.

—*Memorial Record* of the Town.
See Dascomb, A. B.

—*Annual Reports* of the Officers of the Town of Waitsfield, for the year ending March 7,

1876. Montpelier, Vt.: Argus and Patriot Steam Job Printing House. 1876. 8vo, pp. 8. Continued.

—*Historical Address* by Walter A. Jones, at the centennial of the town of Waitsfield. 8vo, pp. 36.

Waldo, S. Putnam. *A Brief Sketch* of the Indictment, Trial, and Conviction of Stephen and Jesse Boorn, for the Murder of Russel Colvin, at a Term of the Supreme Court of the State of Vermont, Holden at Manchester, October, 1819, Together with Remarks upon that Extraordinary Proceeding. By S. Putnam Waldo, Esq. Hartford: R. Storrs, Printer. 8vo, pp. 12.

Wales, Torrey E. *Banquet* in honor of Torrey E. Wales and Eleazer Ray Hard, at the close of Fifty Years at the Bar, at Burlington, March 29, 1895. 8vo, pp. 32. No imprint.

Walker, Albert H. *Text Book* of the Patent Laws of the United States of America. By Albert H. Walker, of the Hartford Bar. New York: L. K. Strouse & Co., Law Publishers, 95 Nassau St., 1883. 8vo, pp. lvii, 781.
Second edition, 1889.

—*Christ's Christianity.* Being the precepts and doctrines recorded in Matthew, Mark, Luke and John, as taught by Jesus Christ. Analyzed and Arranged according to subjects, by Albert H. Walker, of the Hartford Bar. New York: Henry Holt & Co., 1882. 12mo, pp. xiv, 178.
Mr. Walker was born in Fairfax, Vermont, November 25th, 1844, the son of Sawyer Walker. He graduated from the law department of the Northwestern University: and has had an extensive law practice. In 1888 he was lecturer on patent law in Cornell University. In 1890 he represented the city of Hartford in the Connecticut legislature.

Walker, Rev. Aldace. *A Faithful Life.* Written in commemoration of the Christian Services of Aldace Walker, D. D., Pastor of the Congregational Churches at West Rutland and Wallingford, Vt. By his children. Motto. Rutland: Tuttle & Co., Printers. 1879. 8vo, pp. 86. Portrait.
Prepared by his son, Col. A. F. Walker; and intentionally, or by a strange oversight, the dates of the birth or death of Mr. Walker are not given in the book. Rev. Aldace Walker, brother of Rev. Charles Walker, (post), was born in Strafford, Vt., July 20, 1812; died at Rutland, July 24, 1878. See "Vermont Congregational Minutes," 1879.

Walker, Aldace Freeman. *The Vermont Brigade* in the Shenandoah Valley 1864. By Aldace F. Walker. Burlington, Vt.: Free Press Association. 1869. 12mo, pp. 191.
Col. A. F. Walker, son of Rev. Aldace Walker was born at Rutland, Vt., May 11, 1842; graduated at Middlebury College, 1862; he immediately entered the 11th Vermont Volunteers as 1st Lieutenant, and served until the close of the civil war, having been promoted to the Lieut. Colonelcy of his regiment. After the close of the war Col. Walker read law at Burlington, with Hon. George F. Edmunds, two years, and finished his law studies in New York city, where he was admitted to the Bar, and practiced his profession until August, 1873, when he returned to Rutland, and practiced with the firm of Prout & Walker. State Senator, 1882-4; U. S. Interstate Commerce Commissioner, 1887-9; President Interstate Commerce Railway Association, 1890-4; Receiver Atchison and Topeka Railroad Co., 1895-6.

—*A Legal Mummy,* the present status of the Dartmouth College Case. An Address delivered before the Annual Meeting of the Vermont Bar Association, October 28, 1885, by Aldace F. Walker, President for 1884-5. Montpelier: Argus and Patriot Office. 1886. pp. 27.

Walker, Charles. *A Sermon,* preached at Brandon, (Vt.) on the Sixth Aniversary of the Northwestern Branch of the American Education Society, January 11, 1826. By Charles Walker, A. M., Pastor of the Congregational Church in Rutland. Published by the Society. Middlebury: Printed by J. W. Copeland. 1826. 8vo, pp. 32.
Contains the Annual Report of the Society, with a list of members.

—*A Sermon,* preached at Montpelier, before the Legislature of the State of Vermont, on the day of General Election, October 8, 1829. By Charles Walker, Pastor of the Congregational Church, East Rutland. Published by order of the Legislature. Montpelier: Printed by G. W. Hill, Patriot Office. 1829. 8vo, pp. 27.

—*A Complete List* of the Congregational Ministers and Churches in Windham County, Vt., from its first settlement to the present time. By Rev. Charles Walker of Brattleboro. "Am. Quar. Register," 1840. vol. 13, pp. 29-34.
With historical notes of each town.

—*A Sermon,* preached at the Center Church, Brattleboro, Vt., Dec. 28, 1845. By Charles Walker, Pastor of the Church. Brattleboro, Vt.: 1846. 8vo, pp. 11.

—*Memoir* of Charles Walker, D. D. Boston: [Re-printed from the Congregational Quarterly for July, 1871.] 8vo, pp. 24. Portrait.
By his son, Rev. George L. Walker.
Mr. Walker published in addition: Two sermons in the "National Preacher," Nos. 120 and 172; Tract 494 of the New York Tract Society, entitled "The Spirit of Christ exemplified in Labors for the Conversion of the World"; two small books, entitled respectively, "Faith," and "Repentance, explained to the understanding of the Youth," first published by Richards and Tracy, at the "Chronicle" office, Windsor, Vt., and afterwards issued by the American Tract Society. Both have had a wide circulation, and "Faith" has been translated and published in the Mahratta language, and "Repentance" into the Armenian. A sermon on Temperance, preached at Brattleboro, Vt., in 1845. He also wrote many articles for the "Vermont Chronicle."
Mr. Walker was born at Woodstock, Conn., February 1, 1791; died at Binghampton, N. Y., November 28, 1870. He was of the seventh generation in descent from Richard Walker, who came to this country in 1630; was the son of Leonard and Chloe (Child) Walker, being the eldest born of thirteen children. His grandfather, Phineas Walker, was a man of great energy, and saw service in the old French and the Revolutionary wars; was a pioneer in the settlement of Vermont, purchasing a tract of land in the town of Strafford, some of which is still (1879) occupied by his posterity. In the spring of 1797, when Charles Walker was six years of age, his parents and family of four children, moved to Strafford, and Charles labored with his father until twenty-one years of age. At this time Mr Walker left his father's house, to work his own way in the world, and with a little trunk under his arm he wended his way to his native town, where he found employment in the woolen mill of one of his father's old friends. He remained at Woodstock some four or five years; was converted at a religious revival in the spring of 1815, when he was twenty-four years of age, and during the following year he decided to prepare himself by a course of study to enter the ministry; in September, 1816, he began teaching school at Cherry Valley, N. Y., and reading theology at the same time; after teaching a year he entered the Academy at Plainfield, N. H., finally graduating at Andover Theological Seminary in 1821, at the age of thirty years. After preaching short periods at different places, he was settled as pastor of the Congregational church at Rutland, Vt., 1823-33; at Brattleboro, 1835-46, and then at Pittsford, Vt., until 1865, when at the age of seventy-four he retired from ministerial labors.

Mr. Walker married Lucretia, daughter of Stephen Ambrose, Esq., a prominent citizen of Concord, N. H., September 22, 1823, and their children were : Charles Ambrose, died August 12, 1833, aged nine years ; Anne Ambrose, married Rev. George N. Boardman, D. D., Professor in Chicago Theological Seminary ; George Leon, pastor of the First Congregational church at Hartford, Conn., and one of the most prominent clergymen of his denomination; Lucretia died July 18, 1833, aged 16 months; Stephen Ambrose, a lawyer in New York city, and Henry Freeman, a physician in New York.

Rev. Aldace was a younger brother of the subject of this sketch.

See Memorial of Rev. Charles Walker, by his son, Rev. George L. Walker; Caverly's History of Pittsford, pp. 587-625.

Walker, Edwin Sawyer. *Oak Ridge Cemetery :* Its History and Improvements, Rules and Regulations. National Lincoln Monument, and other monuments. Charter and Ordinances. List of Lot Owners. Springfield, Ill.: H. W. Rokker, Printer and Binder. 1879. 8vo, pp. 100.

—*The Lincoln Monument*, with illustrations. By Edwin S. Walker. Springfield, Ill.: 1879. 12mo, pp. 16.

—*The Story of my Ancestors*, containing histories of the "Walker," "Sawyer," "Gile" and "Gilkey" families, in America. By Rev. Edwin S. Walker, A. M., Chicago. 1895.

—*History* of the Springfield Baptist Association. With Sketches of the Churches of which it is composed, and Biographical Sketches of deceased Ministers. By Edwin S. Walker, A. M. Motto. Springfield, Illinois : H. W. Rokker, Printer and Binder. 1881. 12mo, pp. 140.

Mr. Walker, a brother of Mrs. L. H. Washington, (*post*), was born in Whiting, Vt., August 11, 1828, where he spent his early boyhood. His father removed to Fairfax, Vt., in 1836, from which time the subject of this sketch was occupied, until eighteen years of age, in the ordinary duties of New England farm life, attending school about three months every winter. In September, 1846, he attended for one term the "Bakersfield Academical Institution" at Bakersfield, Vt., of which Professor Jacob S. Spaulding was the distinguished Principal. During the winters of 1848, 1849, and 1850, he taught school in Swanton, Vt. In September, 1850, having decided upon the work of the Christian ministry, he entered " Rochester, N. Y., Collegiate Institute," and in September, 1852, he entered the University of Rochester, from which he was graduated in July, 1856. In September following he entered the Rochester Theological Seminary, and was graduated therefrom in July, 1858. In September, 1858, he was ordained and settled as pastor of the First Baptist Church in Dansville, N. Y. After two years he resigned and accepted the pastoral charge of the First Baptist Church in Ripon, Wis. Here he remained two and a half years, when, in 1863, he resigned, and was settled as pastor of the First Baptist Church in Sparta, Wis. After three and a half years of service in Sparta, his health having become impaired he resigned his pastorate, and removed to Springfield, Ill., where he engaged in real estate and insurance business. In August, 1858, he was married to Miss Emily M. Hunt, of Fairfax, Vt., who died August, 1868, leaving two sons. In December, 1870, he was married to Miss Harriet J. Weeks, of St. Albans, Vt.

Walker, Rev. George Leon. *The Material* and the Spiritual in our National Life, and their present mutual relations. A Sermon preached in State Street Church, Portland, November 24, 1859. By Rev. Geo. Leon Walker, Pastor of the Church. Portland : 1859. 8vo, pp. 30.

—*Seventh Annual Report* of the Portland Y. M. C. Association, and Sermon, Delivered before the Association at the Anniversary Meeting, in State Street Church, Nov. 18, 1860. By Rev. Geo. L. Walker. Published by the Association. Portland : 1860. 8vo, pp. 58.

—*The Offered National Regeneration.* A Sermon, preached in the State Street Church, Portland, on the occasion of the National Fast, September 26, 1861. By Rev. George Leon Walker, Pastor of the Church. Portland : 1861. 8vo, pp. 24.

—*What the Year* has done for us. A Sermon preached in the State Street Church, Portland, on the occasion of the Annual Thanksgiving, November 21, 1861. By George Leon Walker, Pastor of the Church. Portland : 1861. 8vo, pp. 16.

Ministers and Their Households. A Sermon preached before the Maine Congregational Charitable Society, at the Annual Meeting of the Maine State Conference at Searsport, June 21, 1864, By Rev. George Leon Walker. Published by request of the Society. Portland : 1864. 8vo, pp. 12.

—*A Look Back and Before.* National Thanksgiving Sermon, delivered by Rev. George Leon Walker, Pastor of State Street Church, Portland, Maine, December 7th, 1865. Portland : 1865. 8vo, pp. 20.

—*The Sepulchre in the Garden.* Written for the Massachusetts Sabbath School Society, and approved by the Committee of publication. Boston : Congregational Publishing Society, Congregational House, Beacon Street. [1866.] 16mo, pp. 31.

Of this little work several editions have been published, and many thousand copies circulated.

—*Exercises* at the Dedication of the New Congregational Church, Manchester, Vermont, August 23, 1871. Manchester ; D. K. Simonds, Job Printer. 1871. 8vo, pp. 18, (2).

Sermon by Rev. Mr. Walker.

—*Charles Walker, D. D.* Reprinted from the Congregational Quarterly, for July, 1871. Boston : 8vo, pp. 24. Portrait.

—*Sermons* preached in the First Church of Christ, in Hartford, by Rev. Leonard Bacon, D. D., LL. D., and Rev. George Leon Walker, D. D., on the occasion of the Settlement of the latter in the Ministry over that Church. To which is appended some account of the early Meeting-Houses of the First Church. Hartford, Conn.: 1879. 8vo, pp. 45.

—*A Just Balance and a Just Hin.* A Sermon preached in the First Church, Hartford, April 11th, 1880. By Rev. George Leon Walker. Published by Request. Hartford : Mercantile Printing House, 245 Main St. 1880. 8vo, pp. 17.

—*A Sermon* on the death of President Garfield, preached in the First Church of Hartford, by Geo. Leon Walker, Pastor, September 25, 1881. Hartford, Conn.: The Case, Lockwood & Brainard Co. 1881. 8vo, pp. 21.

—*False Ideas of God.* Three Sermons preached in the First Church of Christ in Hartford by Geo. Leon Walker, Pastor of the Church. Published by Request. Hartford, Conn.: Press of The Case, Lockwood & Brainard Company. 1881. 8vo, pp. 54.

—*Discourses* by Rev. Prof. Edwin E. Johnson, D. D., and Rev. George L. Walker, D. D., Delivered in the Center Church, Hartford, at the Seventy-First Anniversary of the Connecticut Bible Society, May 3rd, 1881. Hartford: Reprinted from the Religious Herald. 1881. 8vo, pp. 16.

Mr. Walker preached the sermon at the Vermont Congregational General Convention in 1878, which is printed in the "Minutes," pp. 27-41. Many other sermons by Mr. Walker have been printed in various newspapers.

Rev. George Leon Walker, second son of Rev. Charles Walker, D. D., was born at Rutland, Vt., April 30, 1830. In his later youth he was so much of an invalid as to be compelled to abandon a college course, and his studies therefore were mainly self-directed, and prosecuted alone. At the age of twenty years he began the study of law, which he pursued for about three years, when by renewed illness he was obliged to give it up. Upon recovering his health he turned his attention toward the ministry. He read theology at Andover Theological Seminary for a while, and was settled as a pastor at Portland, Maine, October 13, 1858, where he remained until October, 1867, when he found a suspension of labor necessary, and he retired to Pittsford, Vt., for about one year, when he accepted a call to Centre Church, New Haven, Conn., where he was installed November 18, 1868.

Mr. Walker continued at New Haven until 1875, when continued ill health compelled him to resign; he moved to Brattleboro, Vt., where he acted as pastor of the Congregational church in that place, 1875, until his settlement at Hartford, Conn., February 27, 1879.

Mr. Walker married, 1st, Maria, daughter of N. B. Williston, of Brattleboro; she died August 31, 1865, leaving two children; he married 2d, Amelia Reed, daughter of George Larned, of New Haven, Conn., September 15, 1870. Mr. Walker received the degree of Master of Arts from Middlebury College in 1857, and the degree of D. D., from Yale College, July, 1870.

Dr. Walker occupies a prominent and foremost position in his denomination.

See Caverly's History of Pittsford, pp. 587-8.

—*Walker, Jason F.* The Spiritual Life; A Sermon Preached at the Funeral of Frances Elizabeth Stowe, of Hampton, N. Y., A student of Troy Conference Academy, Who died October 12, 1853. By Rev Jason F. Walker, A. M. (Principal of the Academy.) Rutland: Printed at Tuttle & Co's. Book and Job Office. 1853. 8vo, pp. 16.

—*The Distinction between Salvation and Eternal Life.* A Sermon preached Aug. 24, 1856, before the Independent Congregation in Pawlet and Dorset, Vt., By J. F. Walker, Pastor. n.d. 8vo, pp. 8.

—*Brotherly Kindness.* A Sermon preached before the "Independent Religious Congregation" of Pawlet, Oct. 5, 1856, By J. F. Walker, Pastor. n.d. 8vo. pp. 8.

—*Jesus Our High Priest*: A Sermon preached before the "Independent Religious Congregation" of Pawlet. Vt., August 9, 1857. By Rev. Jason F. Walker, Pastor. New York: Printed for the Author. 1857. 8vo, pp. 16.

Mr. Walker graduated from the University of Vermont, 1842, was Principal of the Methodist Academy at Poultney, Vt., and in 1853 was settled over the Methodist Church in Pawlet, Vt. His views being "progressive," he soon formed an "Independent Religious Society," which flourished under the magnetic and fascinating influence of Mr. Walker. He soon removed to Wisconsin, and the Society died out. He subsequently took orders in the Episcopal Church. He died, 1880.

Walker, Jesse. *Poems*, written during his early professional years, by Hon. Jesse Walker, with a brief notice of the Author by Rev. Montgomery Schuyler. Motto. Buffalo: Phinney &c., Publishers. 1854. 16mo, pp. 196.

Hon. Jesse Walker was the youngest son of Jesse Walker, one of the early emigrants from Rhode Island to Whiting, Vt., where he settled soon after the close of the Revolution.

Mr. Walker was born in Whiting, January 7, 1810, and died of cholera at Buffalo, N. Y., September 6, 1852. He was graduated at Middlebury College, 1833, read law at

Rochester, N. Y., 1833-34, and in Buffalo, 1834-35, where he commenced his professional life in 1836. He was for several years City Clerk of Buffalo, and at the time of his death was Judge of Erie County Court.

For the poem spoken at the opening of the Buffalo Theatre, June 22, 1835, Mr. Walker received the prize, a fifty dollar silver cup.

Mr. Walker was uncle to Rev. E. S. Walker, and Mrs. L. H. Washington.

Walker, John. *Walker's* Critical Pronouncing Dictionary and Expositor of the English Language. Abridged. To which is added an Abridgement of Walker's Key to the Classical Pronunciation of Greek, Latin, and Scripture Proper Names. Stereotyped by A. W. Kingsley, Albany. Bellows Falls, Vt.: Published by James I. Cutler & Co., and sold by them wholesale and Retail at their Book store. S. H. Taylor, Printer. 1834, sm. qto, pp. 423.

Walker, V. J. *In Memoriam*: A Memorial of Versal Jesse Walker, M. A., Professor of the Latin Language and Literature in the University of Minnesota. Motto. Published by the University. 1876. 8vo, pp. 24.

Mr. Walker was born in Brookline, Vt., in 1824. Died in Minnesota, May 17, 1876.

Wallace, John. *An Oration*, delivered before the Washington Benevolent Society in Newbury, Vermont, on the Fourth of July, 1812. By John Wallace. Motto. Windsor: Printed by Thomas M. Pomroy. 1812. 8vo, pp. 14.

—*An Address* delivered at Newbury, Vermont, July 4, 1823. By John Wallace. Haverhill, N. H.: Printed by Sylvester T. Goss. 1823. 8vo, pp. 11.

The author in a note says: "This careless production prepared upon three evenings' notice, was never intended for the public eye," etc.

I quote a few sentences which seem to show that the address is worthy of the public eye for all time; "Since the days of the renowned little republics of Greece, the genius of liberty had been a constant and unrested fugitive," * "Certain it is, that American independence, like the other choicest boons of Heaven, is not unassailed by dangers of the most fearful promise" * * * "They did not escape the prophetic view of Washington, * * * in his last advice and his last benediction; he forewarned them of the hazards to be apprehended from the indulgence of sectional prejudices."

Waller, Mrs. Mary. *A Sermon* written at Bethel, Vermont, in February, 1822, by Mrs. Mary Waller. Now published at the earnest request of her son, David F. Waller. Boston: 1864. 8vo, pp. 16.

Wallingford. *Report* of the Superintendent of Common Schools, Wallingford, Vt. J. P. Farrar, Superintendent. Rutland: Tuttle & Co., Printers. 1872. 12mo, pp. 16. Continued.

—*Report* of the Board of Auditors of the Town of Wallingford for the year ending Feb. 18, 1875. Rutland: Globe Paper Co., Printers. 1875. 8vo, pp. 8. Continued.

—*Catalogue* of the Sabbath School Library of the First Congregational Church of Wallingford. 18mo, pp. 15.

Walter, Rowland. *A Volume of Poems* in the Welch Language. Utica, N. Y.: 1872. 12mo, pp. 320.

The author, a Welchman, and a laborer, is (1889) a resident of Castleton, Vt., working in the marble quarries in that vicinity.

Walton, Eliakim P. *Speech of* Hon. E. P. Walton of Vermont, on the Bill for the Admission of Kansas ; delivered in the House of Representatives, March 31, 1858. Washington : Printed at the Congressional Globe Office. 1858. 8vo, pp. 15.

—*Free Trade* and Protective Tariffs, tested by Official Statistics. Speech of Hon. E. P. Walton of Vermont. Delivered in the House of Representatives, February 7, 1859. Washington, D. C. : Buell & Blanchard, Printers. 1859. 8vo, pp. 14.

—*State of the Union.* Speech of the Hon. E. P. Walton, of Vermont, upon the Report of the Committee of Thirty-Three upon the State of the Union. Delivered in the House of Representatives, February 16, 1861. 8vo, pp. 8.

—*Speech of* Hon. E. P. Walton of Vermont, on the Confiscation of Rebel Property. Delivered in the House of Representatives, May 24, 1862. 8vo, pp. 15.

—*Centennial Address* before the Montpelier Lyceum, Feb. 22, 1832, on George Washington. Manuscript. 4to, pp. 41. In Archives of Vt. Historical Society.

—*Address Delivered* before the Vermont Editors' and Publishers' Association, at Bennington, Aug. 14, 1877. Manuscript. 4to, pp. 13. Archives of Vt. Historical Society.

—*E. P. Walton*, Editor, Publisher, Legislator, Citizen, Born February 17, 1812, Died December 19, 1890. Motto. Burlington : Free Press Association. 1892. 8vo, pp. 18.

Contains Biographical Sketch and Memorial Address by Pres. M. H. Buckham.

Mr. Walton delivered addresses in addition to the above list : "Oration at Northfield, Vt., July 4, 1837, printed in the Watchman and Journal of July 24 ; " "Remarks on the death of Charles Paine, delivered at Northfield, July 29, 1853, and printed in the Watchman and Journal of August 4, and also in pamphlet form ; " "Speech delivered on the Battlefield at Hubbardton, Vt., July 7, 1859, on the inauguration of the battle monument, printed in the Watchman and Journal, and in pamphlet form at Rutland ; " "Address on Hon. Nathaniel Chipman, delivered on the unveiling of his monument at Tinmouth, Vt., Oct. 2, 1873, and printed in Vermont newspapers ; " "Letter to Hon. Geo. F. Edmunds, January, 1872, relating to the apportionment of members of Congress ; printed by order of the U. S. Senate ; " "Address in the House of Representatives, Washington, July 9, 1861, on the death of Hon. Stephen A. Douglas ; " printed in House and Senate proceedings. See Douglas, Stephen Arnold.

Mr. Walton also furnished a large part of the History of Montpelier for Miss Hemenway's Gazetteer of Vt., Vol. IV. printed at Montpelier, 1882. See Montpelier.

See also Vermont, Records of the Council of Safety, and Governor and Council ; Vermont Historical Society Proceedings, 1878, Address on the First Legislature of Vermont.

Eliakim Persons Walton was born in Montpelier, February 17, 1812, and was the first-born son of the late Gen. Ezekiel Parker Walton and Prussia Persons. On the Walton side the genealogy goes back through Ezekiel P.'s father, who was born at New Market, N. H., in 1762, and married Mary Parker, of New Hampshire, to George Walton, a Quaker born in England, in whose house at Newcastle, N. H., in June, 1662, occurred the best authenticated case of witchcraft which has ever been recorded in New England. See Mather's Magnalia Christi Americana, edition of 1820, Vol. 2, p. 393, and Brewster's Rambles about Portsmouth, second series, pp. 343-354. On the Persons side, all that can be asserted is that Eliakim Davis Persons was a native of Long Island, and his wife, Rebecca Dodge, was of Massachusetts, probably Northfield, and had numerous relatives (one of them inter married with a Houghton, uncle of the late Mrs. Samuel Prentiss, of Montpelier,) residing near the southeastern line of Vermont. Her father and two of her brothers, Asa and John, settled in Barre, Vt., and a third, Daniel, in Northern Vermont. They have numerous descendants at this day in Eastern and West-

ern Vermont, and in the Western States. It was and is a race of sterling virtues. The particular subject of this notice was educated first by his mother in letters and reading the notes of music ; second, by an occasional attendance at the district school, in which he was specially noted for his habit of running away on every possible occasion ; third, in Washington County Grammar school, in which he was fitted for College by one of the best Principals that school ever had, the late Jonathan C. Southmayd. But the young E. P. was not permitted to go to college, and thereupon entered the law office of Samuel and Samuel B. Prentiss, when Judge Prentiss was in the United States Senate. Here he obtained the elements of the law, and moreover an insight into national politics, through the books and documents received by Judge Prentiss as Senator. But largely he was educated in his father's printing office, and an excellent school every printing office is to any boy or girl who has obtained the elements of an English education, and will improve the opportunities of the office. From the time the lad was "knee-high to a toad" and had to stand in a chair to get up to the "case," this boy was put into the office and kept there in vacations from school. Another very useful school was the old Montpelier Lyceum, with its written essays and extemporaneous debates. In 1826-7 he spent a year in Essex, N. Y., and there edited and printed his first newspaper, a single issue of the Essex County Republican. The editors and publishers were away, and had suspended publication for a week ; but the young and ardent politician could not have it so. Without any authority from his masters, he got up a paper full of editorial matter—part of it written and part of it composed at the case. The proof-sheets were submitted to the late Gen. Henry H. Ross, of Essex, then a Member of Congress and a zealous Adams man. Bringing them back, the General with his face beaming with smiles, put both hands on the boy's shoulders, and said, "Print it, boy ! print it ! " From that moment, though preferring the law, the business of printer and editor seemed to have been ordained for him. On becoming of age, in 1833, he became a partner with his father in the publication of the Vermont Watchman and State Gazette. Gen. Walton wrote occasionally for that paper, but other branches of a very extensive business demanded his attention, and the newspaper and printing department were in the charge of E. P. Walton, Jr., as his signature commonly was during the life of his father, although not correct except when the initials of it were given. In 1853 the Vermont Watchman and State Journal, came into his possession exclusively, and so continued until the sale to the Messrs. Poland, in 1868.

During all this period the editorship of Walton's Vermont Register was in his charge. The Vermont Capital, 1857, consisted mainly of his reports ; volume two of the collections of the Vermont Historical Society was edited by him ; and also the eight volumes of the Record of the Governor and Council, together with documents touching the early history of the State. Although an active and zealous politician from his youth, and helping many men to high offices, he never sought office for himself. Nevertheless in 1853 he was elected Representative of Montpelier ; and in 1854, greatly to his surprise, he was called upon by the late Senator Foot, and another member of the Vermont delegation still living, to become a candidate for Congress in the first Congressional District, on the grounds that a change was absolutely necessary. Under the very delicate circumstances of the case, Mr. Walton was unwilling to be a candidate, and urged the late Ferrand F. Merrill to stand in his stead. Mr. Merrill refused, and ultimately Mr. Walton was nominated and received three elections, after which he declined further service. In 1870 he was the delegate of Montpelier in the Constitutional Convention ; and he was also Senator for Washington county, 1874 until 1878. The Honorary Degree of Master of Arts was conferred upon Mr. Walton by the University of Vermont, and also by Middlebury College. He was President of the Publishers' and Editors' Association of Vermont for many years, and of the Vermont Historical Society from 1876 until his death. Mr. Walton married June 6, 1836, Sarah Sophia, second daughter of the late Hon. Joseph Howes, of Montpelier. Mrs. Walton died at Montpelier, September 3, 1880. In October, 1882, he married Mrs. Clara P. Field of Columbus. O. He died at Montpelier, Dec. 19, 1890. Walton's Vermont Register and Almanac. See Almanacs.

War of 1812.

A Poem on the Battle of Plattsburg. By an American youth. Montpelier, Vt.: 1819. pp. 46.

See Sketches. etc.; Russell, Jr., J.

Ward, John. *Or the Victimized Assassin.* A Narrative of Facts Connected with the

Crime, Arrest, Trial, Imprisonment, and Execution of the Williston Murderer, who was hung in the State Prison at Windsor, Friday, March 20, 1868 ; Together with his Confession, Intercepted Correspondence, and the Chaplain's Diary of Visits, etc. By the Chaplain, [Rev. Franklin Butler.] Windsor, Vt.: Vermont Journal Print. 1869. 12mo, pp. 138. Portrait.

Wardlaw, G. *The Testimony* of Scripture to the Obligations and Efficacy of Prayer ; more especially of prayer for the Gifts of the Holy Spirit. In three Discourses. By Gilbert Wardlaw, A. M. Minister of the Gospel, Edinburgh. Second American Edition. Windsor : Published by P. Merrifield and J. G. Allen. 1830. 18mo, pp. 8, 101.

Ware, Camilla. *Slavery in Vermont*, and in other parts of the United States. Woodstock, Vt.: Davis & Greene, Printers. n. d. [1858.] 8vo, pp. 16.

The fierce anti-slavery tract with this title was written by Camilla, daughter of Jonathan Ware, mentioned below. She was born in Peacham, Vt., November 28, 1804. Educated in the Ursuline Convent at Three Rivers, Canada, and became her father's close literary companion and co-worker. She had a remarkably bright and active mind, was fond of study, and became a linguist hardly less accomplished than her preceptor himself, mastering no less than six languages besides her own so as to read and teach them—Hebrew, Greek, Latin, French, Spanish and Italian—and gaining some knowledge of German and Russian. Like her father, also, she wanted capacity for affairs, and failed to put her remarkable acquirements to any practicable use beyond the helping of him and some not very successful school teaching. She came to be quite eccentric, and indeed almost crazy; and died in Cabot, August 10, 1871, an old woman before her time.

Ware, Jonathan. *A new introduction* to the English Grammar, composed on the principles of the English language, exclusively. By Jonathan Ware, Esq. Windsor, Vt.: Printed for the author by Jesse Cochran. 1814. sm. 4to, pp. 48.

—*History of Vermont.* (ms.) 4to, pp. 726.

Being a general history of the State brought down to about 1810. It has been stated that this work was presented to the Vermont Historical Society; but it has never been in its possession; the writer traced it to the possession of Ware Butterfield, Esq., of Concord, N. H., a relative of the author; and in 1876 ascertained, through correspondence, that Butterfield had "gone west," but to the present date (1880) his whereabouts have not been discovered.

—*Polyglot Lexicon* of the old Testament. (ms.)

The story of Jonathan Ware's life is that of remarkable ability and learning directed to but little practical purpose, and makes a very curious chapter in the history of Vermont literature. He was born in Wrentham, Mass., April 24, 1767, of parentage, especially on his mother's side, of strongly marked character and no mean literary and scientific culture. He graduated at Harvard in 1790, studied law at Bennington, Vt., married at Pomfret in 1794, and soon after began the practice of his profession at Peacham. Here he was instrumental in starting the *Green Mountain Patriot*, the first newspaper in that part of the State, and was active in public affairs. He was, however, unfortunate in his practice and in money affairs, and so abandoned the profession and moved to Danville. During the war of 1812 he was in the army a short time at Burlington and Plattsburg, and in 1813 moved to Pomfret, where he settled on a rough farm in a secluded part of the town, and there began the literary work and study which only ended with his life. He first wrote and published the little grammar, mentioned above, intending to follow it with a larger work on the same subject; but the book was too eccentric to be useful, and the plan fell to the ground. Becoming pressed for money, he left home and for two or three years taught Greek in schools at Boston and New York, then returned and opened a select school in a log building—which he

called an "Academy," on his own farm. This enterprise was soon abandoned, however, and from about the year 1823 to the time of his death, he lived quietly, working on his farm and preparing the manuscripts named. The most remarkable of these is of course the "Lexicon," which as a monument of persevering toil, is doubtless without a rival in American scholarship, although from its nature it could at most have been useful to but a very few scholars in the end. There seems to have been nothing to lead him to undertake the Herculean task except an enthusiast's love of the subject and of the work involved. The plan under which he began included only four languages, Hebrew, Greek, Latin and English, but finally four others, French, Spanish, Italian and Russian, were added, and Ware toiled on through chapter after chapter, selecting such words as he thought worthy of notice and giving definitions in all the tongues, often very copiously. The manuscript took all his spare time for fully a dozen years, and was within six months of completion, when, in January, 1838, he went to Harvard College to consult some books. He was taken sick on the way back and died at the home of one of his daughters in Andover, N. H., February 1, in the year last named. The manuscript has been bound, and is preserved in the Harvard College Library.

Ware, L. G. *Ten Years* of a Ministry. A Sermon preached in the First Congregational Church in Burlington, Vermont, Sunday, the Ninth of November, 1873. By L. G. Ware. Burlington : Free Press Printing House. 1873. 8vo, pp. 15.

—*Sermon,* 1867.

—*Sermon* in Memory of Henry Loomis, preached Dec. 26, 1886. Free Press Association.

—*In Memoriam.* Jane Haswell Root. Remarks at her Funeral. Burlington : Aug. 9, 1884.

—*In Memoriam.* Samuel White Thayer. Sermon preached Nov. 19, 1882. Free Press Association.

—*In Memory* of Loammi Goodenough Ware. Privately printed. Burlington, Vt. : 1892. 8vo, pp. 53.

Contains portrait; biographical sketch; reports of services in Burlington and Boston ; sonnet by Mrs. Dorr, &c. &c.

Mr. Ware was born in Boston, August 1, 1827; graduated from Harvard College 1850 and from Harvard Divinity School, 1853. Pastor of Christ Church, Augusta, Me., 1854-7; of First Congregational (Unitarian) Society, Burlington, Vt., 1863-91. He received from the University of Vermont, 1889, the honorary degree of Doctor of Letters, being the only person on whom that degree has been conferred by that University.

Died at Burlington, April 10, 1891. "When he died the whole city in its moral, social and patriotic life lost a great friend, benefactor, educator, inspirer and illuminator."

See Burlington, Jubilee.

Waring, Geo. E., Jr. *The Elements* of Agriculture : A Book for Young Farmers, with questions prepared for the use of Schools. By Geo. E. Waring, Jr., Consulting Agriculturist. Montpelier : S. M. Walton. 1855. 12mo, pp. 288.

Warner, William. *Soldier's Suffrage.* Speech of Hon. Wm. Warner of Detroit, in the Legislature of Michigan, January 28, 1864. Detroit: 1864. 8vo, pp. 39.

Mr. Warner was a native of Pittsford.

Warren. *Annual Reports* of the Town of Warren, including the Report of the Superintendent of Schools, for the year ending March 1st, 1881. 8vo, pp. 8.

Continued.

Warren, Amos W. *The Young Man's Companion,* or Mathematical Compendium, Containing a great variety of very useful Rules and examples in Mathematics for the Merchant, Clerk, Accountant and Mechanic, etc.

By Amos W. Warren. Rutland : Tuttle & Co., Printers. 1872. 16mo, pp. vii, 173.

Warren, Charles J. *Carmina Sacra;* or Northern Collection of Sacred Musick. Fairhaven, (Vt.): Published by Colton, Warren & Sprout. Printed by Smith & Shute, Poultney, (Vt.): 1823. oblong 16mo, pp. 308, (4.)

Washburn, A. C. *The Eternal Salvation* of his people the Great Object of a Christian Minister. A Sermon, preached at Stockbridge, Vt., May 27, 1829, at the Ordination of Rev. Gilman Vose. By A. C. Washburn, Pastor of the Congregational Church in Royalton. Published by request of the Committee of the Church and Society. Royalton. Printed by W. Spooner.

Washburn, P. T. *A Supplement* to Aiken's Practical Forms, adapting that work to the present state of the Statutes of Vermont. By Peter T. Washburn, Counsellor at Law. Claremont Manufacturing Company, Simeon Ide, Agent. 1847. 12mo, pp. 110,2.

—*An article* on the law of Copyright.
See Blake's Book Trade list, etc. Claremont: 1847.

—*An Oration* before the Reunion Society of Vermont Officers, in the Representatives' Hall, Montpelier, Vt., October 22d, 1868, By Gen. P. T. Washburn, Woodstock, Vt. Montpelier: J. & J. M. Poland, Printers. 1869. 8vo, pp. 29.

—*Digest of Decisions* of the Supreme Court, &c.
See Vermont, Digest, &c.
Peter Thacher Washburn was born in Lynn, Mass., September 7th, 1814; and died in Woodstock, Vt., February 7, 1870. He removed to Vermont with his father's family in 1817, and was graduated at Dartmouth College in 1835 ; studied law in the office of Hon. William Upham, at Montpelier, and was admitted to the bar in Windsor county, December, 1838. He opened an office in Ludlow, where he continued to practice until 1844, when he removed to Woodstock, where he resided until his death. Was reporter of the decisions of the Supreme Court, 1844 to 1851; a member of the Legislature from Woodstock in 1853-4. On the breaking out of the rebellion he took an active part in raising volunteers, and was Lieut.-Colonel of the First Regiment, Vermont Volunteers, and commanded the battalion of the Regiment at the Battle of Big Bethel, where he distinguished himself; was elected Adjutant General of the State in October, 1861, which office he held until the close of the war. Was elected Governor of the State in 1869, and died before the expiration of his first term.

Washburn, Reubin. *An Address* at the Antimasonic County Convention Holden at Ludlow, Vt., August 17, 1831. Delivered by Reubin Washburn, Esq., Counsellor at Law. Published by order of the Convention. Woodstock : Printed by F. Sherwin. August, 1831. 12mo, pp. 12.
Mr. Washburn resided at Ludlow, and was the father of the late Gov. P. T. Washburn.

Washington. *Report* of the School Superintendent of the Town of Washington, for School year May 1, 1871, to May 1, 1872. Montpelier: Poland's Steam Printing Establishment. 1872. 8vo, pp. 12.
Continued.

Washington County. *County Atlas* of Washington [County,] Vermont. From actual Surveys by and under the direction of F. W. Beers. Published by F. W. Beers & Co., 36 Vesey Street, New York. 1873. Folio, pp. 65.

—*The Bar Docket* of Washington County Court, March Term, Commencing Tuesday, March 12,

1878. Montpelier : Freeman Office. 1878. 12mo, pp. 128.
Continued.

Washington County Teachers' Institute.
See Educational.

Washington, George. *Address* of George Washington, President of the United States, to the People of America, Presented 19th September, 1796, on apprising them that he declined being considered among the number of those out of whom a choice is to be made of one, to administer the executive government of the United States. "Begin with the Infant in his Cradle, Let the first word he lisps be Washington." Bennington : From the Press of A. Haswell, Annoque Domini, 1796. 24mo, pp. 45.

—*George Washington's Resignation* of the Presidency of the United States of America, September 17th, 1796. Windsor : Printed by Alden Spooner. M,DCC,XCVI. 12mo, pp. 23.
Being the Farewell Address.

—*Biographical Memoirs* of the Illustrious Gen. George Washington, Late President of the United States of America, &c., &c. Containing A History of the Principal Events of his Life, with extracts from his Journals, Speeches in Congress, and Public Addresses. Also A Sketch of his private life. Fourth Edition. Brattleborough : Printed by William Fessenden. 1811. 18mo, pp. 211.

—*Washington's Farewell Address*; and the Constitution of the United States. Published for the Washington Benevolent Society. Middlebury : Printed by Timothy C. Strong. 1812. 18mo, pp. 48.

—*Washington's Farewell Address* to the People of the United States. Published for the Washington Benevolent Society. Windsor : Printed and sold by T. M. Pomroy. 1812. 12mo, pp. 40.
Also in same volume is a copy of the United States Constitution, and immediately following the title page of Address is the following: "No. 11. This certifies that . . . Mr. Elihu Emerson . . . has been regularly admitted a Member of the Washington Benevolent Society, of Norwich, in the county of Windsor, Vt., instituted on the 20th day of April, 1812. Elisha Burton, President ; Henry Ingersol, Secretary."

—*Washington's Farewell Address* to the People of the United States. Published for the Washington Benevolent Society. Windsor : Printed and sold by T. M. Pomroy. 1812. 18mo, pp. 23. Portrait.

—*The Valedictory Address* of the Late Illustrious George Washington, to the People of the United States. Motto. Windsor : Published by P. Merrifield & Co. Wright & Sibley, Printers. 1812. 24mo, pp. 61.

—*The Valedictory Address* of the Late Illustrious George Washington, to the People of the United States. Montpelier, Vt.: Published and for Sale by Walton & Goss, Printers. 1812. 24mo, pp. 45.

—*Biographical Memoirs* of the Illustrious General George Washington. Barnard, Vt.: Published by Joseph Dix. J. H. Carpenter, Printer. 12mo, pp. 160.

—*American's Handbook:* Containing the Declaration of Independence, Washington's Farewell Address, and the Constitution of the

United States. Rutland : Published by George A. Tuttle & Co. 1855. 18mo, pp. 72.
See Corry, John; Condie, Thomas; Memoirs of Washington. Brattleborough, 1811.

Washington, Mrs. Lucy H. *Echoes of Song.* By Mrs. Lucy H. Washington. Springfield, Ill.: Edwin S. Walker, Publisher. 1878. 12mo, pp. 200.
Also author of "Memory's Casket." Buffalo, N. Y: 1891. 12mo, pp. 180.
Mrs. Washington, daughter of Sawyer and Melinda Walker, was born in Whiting, Vt., January 4, 1835. When one year of age, her family removed to North Fairfax, where she remained until 17 years of age. A farmer's daughter, she like "Maud Muller," sometimes "raked the meadows sweet with hay," but did not meet the "Judge." This may have been a misfortune to either the "Judge" or herself.
Public sentiment in those days did not allow girls fish-hooks; but Miss Walker caught speckled trout in "Beaver brook" with a bent pin. Public sentiment could not afford girls skates; but with a tight grip at her brother's coat in the rear, she sometimes took a turn and a tangent upon the mill-pond, near the school. Had genius been encouraged, and the medical schools at Castleton been open to girls, she might have made her mark in life, as she was very successful in nursing sick lambs. The only vocation to which ambition might aspire in those days was that of country "schoolmarms;" she climbed to this lofty position in a little brown school house, situated fifty feet above the highway, more or less, in Underhill, Vt. There, at the age of sixteen, she taught the Green Mountain girls and boys 16 weeks for $16, and "boarded round." A little previous to this, her first printed poem appeared in the "Universalist Watchman," published at Montpelier—"Esther," page 18 of "Echoes." She took a course of study in a ladies' seminary in Rochester, N. Y., where she was graduated in 1856. Then, for two years, she was Principal of a collegiate institute at Brockport, N. Y., where she married a Baptist clergyman. She was one of the original temperance crusaders in Iowa, in 1874, and one of the organizers of the Women's Christian Temperance Union. As national organizer of the W. C. T. U. she gave addresses in twenty-four States, which gave her high rank as a platform speaker. Her husband, Rev. S. Washington, is (1895) pastor of the Baptist Church in Port Jervis, N. Y.

Waterbury. *Annual Report* of the Selectmen and other officers of the town of Waterbury at the Annual Meeting, March 7, 1871. Waterbury: H. C. Fay's Book and Job Printing House. 1871. 8vo, pp. (8).
Continued.

—*Report* of the Superintendent of Schools, for the Town of Waterbury, 1876-7. Waterbury, Vt.: Francis G. Hoyt, Printer. 12mo, pp. (10).
Continued.

—*History of,*
See Parker, C. C.

—*Manual* of the First Congregational Church, in Waterbury, Vermont. Waterbury: H. C. Fay, Job Printer. 1868. 8vo, pp. 12.

Waterford. *Soldiers' Record* for the town of Waterford in the War of the Rebellion. By Hon. F. R. Carpenter. St. Johnsbury: C. M. Stone & Co. 1880. 8vo, pp. 31.

Waterman, Rev. Lucius. *Sermon* preached at Bishop Hopkins Hall, at opening of the School, 1890–91, by Rev. Lucius Waterman, M. A., of Littleton, N. H., Sept. 18, 1890. Montpelier: Argus and Patriot Print. 1891. 8vo, pp. 24.

Waters, Reubin D. *A Treatise* by Reubin D. Waters, on the Town of Calais, (Vt.) and vicinity, with some Sketches of Jewish, Pagan, Mahometan, and other Religions ; Character of Bonaparte, Columbus, and Notaries. Published for the Author. 1852. 12mo, pp. 31, (1).
Mr. Waters was a native of Charlton, Mass., and moved to Calais, Vt., about 1807, where he resided until his death, a period of over fifty years.

Watrous, Miss Sophia. *The Gift;* or Miscellaneous Poems. Montpelier: E. P. Walton & Sons, Publishers and Printers. 1841. 12mo, pp. 172.
Miss Watrous was born in Montpelier, and resided there through life, an invalid a large part of the time.

Watrous, Charles.
Son of Erastus Watrous, Esq., who with his family moved from Connecticut to Montpelier in May, 1799. Charles was graduated at Middlebury College, 1817; read theology two years at Montpelier, then learned the printer's trade in the office of E. P. Walton. He went South, taught school and worked at his trade in different States, and died in 1835. "He became deranged, and while perfectly insane wrote and published at Troy, N. Y., a book on the craft and dangers of Masonry."—*Pearson's Middlebury College Graduates.* Question; Was he any more insane that other writers on the same subject? Sophia Watrous was his sister.

Watson, Elkanah. *Men and Times* of the Revolution ; or, Memoirs of Elkanah Watson, including his Journals of Travel in Europe and America from the year 1777 to 1842, and his Correspondence with public Men, and Reminiscences and Incidents of the American Revolution. Edited by his Son, Winslow C. Watson. New York and London : 1857. 12mo, pp. 557.
Relates considerably to Vermont.

Watson, Winslow C. *Eulogium* Commemorative of Gorton T. Thomas, Lieutenant Colonel 22d Regiment, New York Volunteers. Delivered at Keeseville, N. Y., September 10, 1862, by Winslow C. Watson. Burlington : Free Press Print. 1862. 8vo, pp. 20.

—*Pioneer History* of the Champlain Valley ; Being an Account of the Settlement of the Town of Willsborough by William Gilliland, together with His Journal and other Papers, and a Memoir, and Historical and Illustrative notes. By Winslow C. Watson. (Motto.) Albany, N. Y.: J. Munsell, 78 State Street. 1863. 8vo, pp. 231.

—*The Life* and Character of the Hon. Richard Skinner ; A Discourse read before and at the request of the Vermont Historical Society, at Montpelier, October 20, 1863, by Winslow C. Watson. Albany, N. Y.: J. Munsell, 78 State Street. 1863. 8vo, pp. 30.

Watts, Isaac. *Divine Songs,* Together with the Assembly of Divines Catechism. Bennington: Printed by Haswell and Russell. 1790.

—*The Improvement* of the Mind, in two parts. Also, A Discourse on the Education of Youth, and on Remnants of Time employed in prose and verse. By Isaac Watts, D. D. Bennington: Printed by Anthony Haswell. 1807. 12mo, pp. 382.

—*The Psalms of David.* imitated in the Language of the New Testament, and applied to the Christian State of Worship. By I. Watts, D. D. Motto. Montpelier: Published and sold by J. Parks. 1809. 18mo, pp. 340.
Bound with same, Hymns and Spiritual songs, Same imprint, pp. 332.

—*Twelve Sermons,* on various subjects, Divine and Moral: Designed for the use of Pious Families, as well as for the hours of Devout Retirement: with A Hymn, suited to each subject. By Isaac Watts, D. D. Motto. Montpelier: Published by Wright & Sibley. 1811. 12mo, pp. 359.

—*Horæ Lyricæ*. Poems, Chiefly of the Lyric kind, in three Books. Sacred I. To Devotion and Piety. II. To Virtue, Honor and Friendship. III. To the Memory of the Dead. By Isaac Watts, D. D. Motto. Vergennes : Published by Jeptha Shedd & Co. Wright & Sibley, Printers. 1813. 12mo, pp. 216.

—*The Psalms of David*, imitated in the language of the New Testament, and applied to the Christian Worship. By Isaac Watts, D. D. Motto. Montpelier, Vt. : Published by Lucius Q. C. Bowles. Walton & Goss, Printers. 1814. 18mo, pp. 296.
Bound with same, Hymns and Spiritual Songs, same imprint, pp. 259.

—*The Same* : Middlebury, Vt. : Published and Printed by Slade & Ferguson. 1814. 18mo, pp. 346 and 293.

—*Logic, or the Right use of Reason*, in the Inquiry after Truth ; with a variety of rules to guard against Error, etc. By Isaac Watts, D. D. Sixth American Edition. Boston : Published by West, Richardson & Lord. Montpelier, Vt. : E. P. Walton, Printer. 1819. 12mo, pp. 288.

—*Psalms, Hymns and Spiritual Songs*. By the Rev. Isaac Watts, D. D. To which is prefixed a Systematized Index, showing at one view the Contents of all Psalms and Hymns. New and Cheap Edition. Woodstock, Vt. : Printed and Published by D. Watson. 1824. small 16mo, pp. 610.

—*The Psalms of David* imitated in the language of the New Testament, and applied to the Christian State and Worship. By Isaac Watts, D. D. Woodstock, Vt. : Printed and Published by N. Haskell. 24mo.

Weaver, G. S., *Mental Science*. A Series of Lectures delivered before the Anthropological Society of Marietta, Ohio, in the autumn of 1851. New York : Published by S. R. Wells. 1852. 12mo, pp. 225.

—*Hopes and Helps*. For the Young of both sexes. New York : S. R. Wells. 1852. 16mo, pp. 246.

—*Ways of Life*. New York : S. R. Wells. 1855. 16mo, pp. 157.

—*The Christian Household*. Boston : Abel Tompkins. 1855. 16mo, pp. 160.

—*Aims and Aids*. For Girls and Young Women. New York : S. R. Wells. 1856. 16mo, pp. 224.

—*Lectures on the Future Life and State; or the Bible View of Hell*. Madison, Ind. : B. F. Foster & Co. 1852. 12mo, pp. 89.

—*A Sermon on the Rich Man and Lazarus*. St. Louis, Mo. : Chambers & Knapp, Publishers. 1855. 8vo, pp. 28.

—*The Open Way*. Cincinnati, Ohio : Williamson & Cantwell, Publishers. 1871. 16mo, pp. 266.

—*Moses and Modern Science*.

—*A Brief Sketch* of the Life of Rev. G. S. Weaver, D. D., to 1879. Williamson & Cantwell. 1872. 16mo, pp. 232.
On Christmas Eve, December 24, 1818, in Rockingham, Vt., John and Asenath Weaver saw their first child.

Eight other children, four boys and four girls, followed in the succeeding years. This first born was named George Sumner; he, by being the first born, inherited a good deal of the care and work of the family, as well as a close, compact fibrous body, as full of day's works as a nut is of meat. His business, as soon as he could reach the plow handles, became the management and work of a large farm, while his father did jobs of road making, and house, barn and bridge building, in the region round about. The winter district sch ol of ten or twelve weeks a year gave him the key to the mysteries of letters and figures, and quickened in h:m a love of books and information, which by the time he was twenty-one became the absorbing interest of his mind. In the select schools in the villages about him, in special Grammar school, in the Academies at Ludlow, Vt., and Meriden, N. H., in teaching district and select schools, and in reading such books as he could buy and borrow, he spent five years of intense interest and absorbing study. One of these years, spent in Fonda, N. Y., teaching and geologizing among the sands and rocks in the day time, and studying law and holding temperance meetings in the evening, was a year of very profitable study. In the autumn of 1844 a journey to Dayton, Ohio, began to open the world to his mind. Studying law a year and a half in Dayton, and a course of general reading in libraries there gave him fresh opportunities for improvement. In the latter part of 1845 he was admitted to the Bar, and opened an office in Dayton, and for a few weeks spent his time in preparing a course of six lectures on Astronomy, which were delivered before a select audience.

By this time it had become clear to his mind that his strongest inclination was towards the ministry. Though most of the years of his study had been spent in orthodox institutions and associations, and in constant attendance upon orthodox churches, he was a pronounced Universalist. The way opening without his seeking it, and so singularly as to seem to him providential, he preached his first sermon in Springfield, Ohio, in March, 1846, and settled the next month as pastor of the Universalist church in that place. He remained two years, teaching school in the winters in connection with his constant work as a minister.

In June, 1848, he removed to Marietta, Ohio, where in an Academy, built in connection with his church, he labored assiduously, partly as teacher of a class or two, but mostly as a man of all work as gratuitous agent in the vicinity.

In May, 1852, he started for Chicago, Ill., but was detained at St. Louis, Mo., by a new church which had sent him an invitation. He remained in St. Louis till the latter part of 1860, preaching, lecturing, assisting in editing the "Golden Era," a religious paper, and the "Valley Farmer."

In November, 1860, he settled in Lawrence, Mass., where he remained twelve years and a half, when he accepted an invitation to Akron, Ohio, to build up a church in connection with Buchtel College, just then started. Laboring here four years, he accepted an invitation to Galesburg, Ill., to a church in connection with Lombard University, the first College founded by the Universalists of this country. Not being suited with life so far West, he accepted an invitation to settle, January 1, 1879, with a church in Canton, N. Y., in connection with the first theological school of the denomination and the seat of St. Lawrence University.

Without sickness and without interruption, he has labored in the cause of religion, education, morality, temperance, health and patriotism, from 21 to 60, and still has no flagging of energy or zeal. With pen and tongue and hand and book he has had a busy life, which promises well for a continuance for some time to come. (1880.)

Webb, T. S. *The Freemason's Monitor :* Or Illustrations of Masonry. In Two Parts. By Thomas Smith Webb, Past Master of Temple Lodge, Albany, G. II. P. of the Grand R. A. Chapter of Rhode Island, and Grand Master of the Providence Encampment of Knights Templar, etc., etc. Montpelier, Vt. : Published by Lucius Q. C. Bowles, for sale by him and by Cushing & Appleton, Salem, Mass. (Proprietors of the Copyright.) Walton & Goss, Printers. 1816. 12mo, pp. 312.

Webber, G. N. *The Bible* and the Public Schools. A Sermon preached at the Congregational Church, in Middlebury, Vt., Fast Day, April 15, 1870. By G. N. Webber, Acting Pastor. Published by request. Middlebury :

Printed at the Register Office. 1870. 8vo, pp. 18.

Webster, Miss Delia. *A Trial of,*
See Trials, Opinions, etc.

Webster, Noah. *An American Selection* of Lessons in Reading and Speaking. Calculated to Improve the Minds and Refine the Tastes of Youth. To which are Prefixed Rules in Elocution, and Directions for Expressing the Principal Passions of the Mind. By Noah Webster, Esq. [Copied from the Last Revised Edition.] Windsor, (Vt.:) Printed by Nahum Mower. 1805. 12mo, pp. 226.

—*The Elementary Spelling Book*; Being an Improvement on the American Spelling Book. By Noah Webster, LL.D. Montpelier, Vt.: Published by E. P. Walton & Son. 1839. 12mo, pp. 168.

—*Another Edition*, same imprint. 1844. Stereotyped by J. S. Redfield, New York.

—*Another Edition:* Wells River, Vt.: Published by Ira White. Stereotyped by J. S. Redfield, N. Y. 1841. 12mo, pp. 168.

—*The Last Revised Edition.* The American Spelling Book; containing rudiments of the English Language, for the use of Schools in the United States. The Revised Impression, with the latest corrections. Wells River, Vt.: Published by Ira White, Proprietor of the Revised Edition. 1843. 12mo, pp. 168.

—*The Elementary Spelling Book;* being an improvement on the American Spelling Book By Noah Webster, LL.D. Wells River, Vt.: White & Wilcox. 1831. 12mo, pp. 158, and some leaves missing.

—*The Elementary Spelling Book.* By Noah Webster, LL.D. Brattleborough, Vt.: Published by Holbrook & Fessenden. Stereotyped by A. Chandler. n. d. 12mo, pp. 168.

Wedgwood, W. B. *The Revised* Statutes of the State of Vermont, Reduced to Questions and Answers, for the use of Schools and Families. By William B. Wedgwood, A. M. Revised and Corrected by a Member of the Vermont Bar. Brattleboro: Published by Joseph Steen. 1844. 12mo, pp. 98.

Weeks, Rev. Holland. *Election* the Foundation of Obedience. A Sermon Delivered before the General Convention of Congregational and Presbyterian Ministers; At Brookfield, (Vt.) Sept. 5, 1810. By the Rev. Holland Weeks, A. M., Pastor of the Congregational Church in Pittsford. Randolph, Vt.: Printed by Sereno Wright. 1810. 8vo, pp. 16.

—*The Nature* and Influence of Conscience. A Sermon Preached at the Ordination of the Rev. Jonathan Kitchel, at Whitehall, State of New York, March 1, 1810. By Holland Weeks, A. M., Pastor of a Church in Pittsford, Vt. "We feel pleasure or pain, whenever we are approved or condemned by conscience." Dr. Emmons. Middlebury, Vt.: Printed by J. D. Huntington. 1810. 8vo, pp. 32.

—*The Manner* and Object of the Gospel Ministry. A Sermon preached at the Ordination of the Rev. Justin Parsons over the Congrega-

tional Church in Pittsford. He that hath ears to hear let him hear.—Christ. Middlebury: J. Huntington. Feb. 1810. 8vo, pp. 20.

—*Selfish* preachers build up Zion with blood; A Sermon delivered at the Ordination of the Rev. John Truair, over the Church and Congregation at Cambridge, Nov. 21, 1810. By the Rev. Holland Weeks, A. M., Pastor of a Church in Pittsford, Vt. Burlington: Samuel Mills. 1811.

—*The Word of God* a burden to wicked Man; A Sermon preached Nov. 7, 1810, at the Ordination of Rev. Ralph Robinson, A. B., over the Congregational Church at Fairvale, in Granville, and the First Congregational Church at Hartford, in the State of New York. By Rev. Holland Weeks, A. M., Pastor of a Church in Pittsford. Salem, N. Y.: Dodd & Rumsey. 1811.

—*On Prohibited Judging.* A Sermon, preached at Pittsford, Vermont, on the Lord's Day, P. M., February 23, A. D. 1812. By the Rev. Holland Weeks, A. M., Pastor of a Church of Christ in Pittsford. Published at the Request of the Subscribers. Middlebury, Vt.: Printed by T. C. Strong. 1812. 8vo, pp. 11.

—*Jesus* the resort of Christians bereaved of their minister, illustrated in a discourse delivered at Rupert, February 23, 1813, at the interment of the Rev. John B. Preston, A. M., late Pastor of a Church of Christ in Rupert, Vt., by Holland Weeks, A. M., Pastor of a Church of Christ in Pittsford, Vt.: To which is added a brief sketch of the life of the deceased by two of his friends. Published at the request of some of the hearers, for the benefit of the bereaved family. Salem, N. Y.: Dodd & Rumsey. 1813.

Mr. Weeks was born in Brookline, Conn., April 29, 1768, and died at Henderson, N. Y., July 24, 1843. He was graduated at Dartmouth College in 1795, and was settled over the Congregational church at Pittsford, Vt., 1807-1815, which constituted nearly his entire residence in Vermont. He was settled over the Congregational church at Abington, Mass., 1815-1820, when he embraced Swedenborgianism, and removed to Henderson, where he preached the new faith twenty-two years gratuitously.

See History of Pittsford, pp. 614-16; History of Salisbury, pp. 195-200.

Weeks, John M. *A Manual,* or an easy method of Managing Bees, in the most profitable manner to the Owner, with Infallible Rules to Prevent their destruction by the Moth. By John M. Weeks, of Salisbury, Vt. Fourth edition. Brandon: Vermont Telegraph Office. 1839. 18mo, pp. 96.

—*Same* First Edition. 1836. Middlebury, Vt.: Knapp & Jewett, Printers. 16mo, pp. 73.

—*The Beekeepers Guide* to manage Bees in the Vermont Beehive. By John M. Weeks, Salisbury, Vt. Middlebury, Vt.: Argus Office. 1840. 18mo pp. 14.

—*History* of Salisbury, Vt. By John M. Weeks, with a Memoir of the Author. Middlebury, Vt.: Published by A. H. Copeland. 1860. 12mo, pp. 362.

Mr. Weeks was a son of Rev. Holland Weeks, and was born in Litchfield, Conn., May 22, 1788; died in Salisbury, Vt., September 1, 1858. For biographical sketch see History of Salisbury, pp. 352-362.

Weeks, Refine. *The Advantages and Disadvantages* of the Marriage State, as entered into with Religious or Irreligious Persons ; represented under the similitude of a Dream. Versified by Refine Weeks. Stanford: Printed by David Lawrence. 1805. 12mo, pp. 48.

—*The Age of Liberty*. A Poem By Refine Weeks. New York : Printed by John C. Totten, No. 9 Bowery. 1820. 16mo, pp. 24.

—*Poems* on Religious and Historical Subjects. By Refine Weeks. New York : 1820. 12mo, pp. 384.

—*A Second Edition*. New York : 1823. pp. 419.

Mr. Weeks was a resident of Weybridge, Addison county ; we learn from Goodhue's History of Shoreham, page 59, that in 1816 he paid fifteen hundred dollars for a Merino buck ; in 1818 the General Assembly passed an Act to protect the person of Mr. Weeks from arrest and imprisonment on account of debt. He moved to Weybridge about 1800 ; he built the mills at Lower Falls in that town ; he was persecuted by the citizens, and wrote these poems while in the jail limits in Middlebury, as indicated in the preface.

Weeks, William. *Antichrist's Kingdom* Clearly pointed out ; which cannot agree with the Kingdom of Jesus Christ. By William Weeks. Printed for the Author. 1823. 8vo, pp. 27.

—*Catechism of Scripture Doctrine*, embracing copious references to Texts on all the leading Doctrines of Christianity. Middlebury: Printed by Francis Burnap. 1818.

Welch, F. G. *Manual of Gymnastics*, by F. G. Welch, M. D. Published in this Form (by permission of the Author) for her own class, by Mary T. Orcutt, Teacher of Gymnastics in Tilden Ladies' Seminary. Rutland : Tuttle & Co., Printers. 1874. 12mo, pp. 24.

Wells. *History of,*
See Paul, Hiland.

Wells, Ashbel Shipley.
Born in Jericho, Vt., Dec. 3, 1798; died at Fairfield, Iowa, Oct. 30, 1882. He was a Congregational preacher and his field of labor was in Indiana, Michigan, Missouri and Iowa. He published three tracts : "Unfermented Wine," "Anti-Tobacco," and "The King's Highway."
See Congregational Year Book, 1884.

Wells, Horace. *An Essay on the Teeth ;* comprising a Brief Description of their Formation, Diseases, and Proper Treatment. By Horace Wells, Surgeon Dentist. Hartford: Printed for the Author by Case, Tiffany & Co., Pearl Street. 1838. 12mo, pp. 70.
Born in Hartford, Vt., January 21, 1815 ; and died in New York City, January 24, 1848. He read dentistry in Boston, and settled in Hartford, Ct., in 1836 ; he was one of the claimants of the discovery of anæsthesia ; he visited France, from whence he returned in 1847 ; and in March published an account of his discovery. The evidence of his claim was placed before Congress in 1853 by Hon. Truman Smith, and was subsequently published under the title of "An Examination of the Question of Anæsthesia." New York : 1860.
See Allibone ; Drake.

Wells, John C. *Wells' Lawyer*, and United States Form-Book, etc., etc. Seventy-fourth thousand. Burlington, Vt.: Published by John C. Wells. 1850. 12mo, pp. 300.

Wells, Rev. William. *Some observations,* taken in part from an Address delivered in the New Meeting-House in Brattleborough, July 7, 1816, being the first Communion held in that place.

—*Some Communications* first published in the Brattleborough Paper ; with Extracts from

"Candid Reflections on the different Conceptions concerning the Doctrine of the Trinity." By William Wells. Brattleborough : 1816. 8vo, pp. xvi, 40.

Mr. Wells was an Arian-Unitarian, if anybody knows what that is ; he was born in Biggleswade, Bedfordshire, England, in 1744 ; in 1793, with his wife and eight children he immigrated to America, landing at Boston, June 12 of that year. The next year he purchased a farm at Brattleboro, Vt., where he resided until his death, December 27, 1827. It is remarkable that fifty-one years after their arrival in America all his children were alive, and in good health—his youngest son, John Howard, dying in 1844, at the age of sixty. In 1794 Mr. Wells became pastor of the Congregational church at Brattleboro, succeeding the Rev. Abner Reeve, the first pastor, who preached there 26 years. Mr Wells continued as pastor 20 years.

In those days a minister's house was a tavern for all ministers, whether known or unknown. The following anecdote of Rev. Mr. Wells is related by the Rev. Samuel Willard, in "Sprague's Annals": A stranger minister called for rest and refreshment, and the following dialogue ensued:

Stranger—"Are there any heresies among you ?"
Dr. Wells—"I know not whether I understand the drift of your question."
Stranger—"I wish to inquire, sir whether there be any Arminians, Socinians, or Universalists among you."
Dr. Wells—"Oh, sir, there are worse heretics than any of these."
Stranger—"My dear sir, what *can* be worse?"
Dr. Wells—"Why there are some who get drunk, and some who quarrel with their familie, or their neighbors, and some who will not pay their debts, when they might do it, and some are very profane. Such men I think far worse heretics than those for whom you inquire."

At the age of 75, Dr. Wells received the honorary D. D., from Harvard University.

See Sprague's Annals, Vol. viii, pp. 254-61, for an interesting sketch of Dr. Wells.

Wells River. *Manual* of the Congregational Church in Wells River, Vt. Concord, N. H.: 1864. 12mo, pp. 16.

Westfield. *Manual* of the Congregational Church in Westfield, Vt. Compiled by James P. Lane, Acting Pastor. Irasburgh : Printed by A. A. Earle. 1860. 12mo, pp. 12.

Westford. *Historical Addresses* delivered at the Seventy-Fifth Anniversary of the Congregational Church at Westford, Vt., Aug. 8, 1876. Published by the Church. Westford : 1876. 12mo, pp. 60.
Printed by Mr. G. P. Byington, and is the only book ever printed in the town of Westford.

Westminster. *The Confession of Faith,* and Covenant of the Congregational Church in Westminster East Parish, with a Catalogue of Members. May, 1839. Bellows Falls : John W. Moore, Printer, 1839. 12mo, pp. 24.

—*Manual of the Congregational Church* in Westminster, Vermont, with a catalogue of the officers and members from its organization to 1876. Times Steam Job Printing Office, Bellows Falls, 1876.

—*Selectmen's, Overseer's and Auditor's Reports* for the town of Westminster, Vt., for all the years since 1867.

—*Report of the Superintendent* of Common Schools to the town of Westminster for the Year Ending March 1st, 1860. 8vo, pp. 8.
Continued.

—*Westminster Seminary,*
See Educational.

—*Historical Sketch of,*
See White, P. H.

—*Westminster Massacre.* Address by B. H. Hall, Read before the New York Historical

Society, March 1, 1859, in "Historical Magazine," May, 1859, Vol. 3, pp. 133-143.
See Hall's (Hiland) "Early Vermont," pp. 190, 194, 465; Hall's B. H., "Eastern Vermont;" Vermont Governor and Council, Vol. 1, pp. 330-338; a Relation by Reubin Jones, M. D., in "Rural Magazine, or Vermont Repository," 1795, Vol. 1, pp. 200-206; also the same, reprinted in "Slade's State Papers."
For biographical sketch of Dr. Jones, See "Hall's Early Vermont," pp. 465-6.

Weston. Annual Report of the Auditors and Selectmen for the Town of Weston, for the Year ending February 15th, 1868. Rutland, Vt.: Tuttle & Company, Printers, 1868. 8vo, pp. 16.

—*Reunion of the Sons of,*
See Smith, Asa D.

Weston, Thomas. *The Dead Speaking.* A Discourse preached at the funeral of Doct. Elijah W. Carpenter, in the Unitarian Church, in Bernardstown, Nov. 30, 1855. By Thomas Weston, Pastor of the First Church in New Salem, Mass. With an Appendix, Containing Obituary Notices, Etc. Greenfield: Printed by Charles A. Mirick. 1856. 8vo, pp. 18.
Dr. Carpenter was born in Brattleboro, Vt., September 7, 1788; and died in Bernardstown, Mass., November 28, 1855.

West Randolph.
See Randolph.

Wheat, A. F.
—*Before and After* Treatment of Laparotomy, by A. F. Wheat, M. D., Manchester, N. H. Reprinted from *Vermont Medical Monthly.* Burlington: Free Press Print. n. d. 8vo, pp. 14.

Wheeler, Amos D. Jesus and his Disciples in the Jewish Synagogues. By Rev. A. D. Wheeler. Printed for the American Unitarian Association. Boston: James Munroe & Co., 134 Washington Street. September, 1845. 12mo, pp. 14.
Dr. Wheeler was born in Woodstock, Vt., December 13, 1803; was graduated at Williams College in 1827; studied theology at the Divinity School in Cambridge; preached at Standish, Me., 1834-9, and at Topsham, Me., 1839-69; was a missionary of the American Unitarian Association until he died, June 28, 1876.

Wheeler, David Everett.
Mr. Wheeler was born in Grafton, Vt., September 4, 1804; he was graduated at Dartmouth College in 1827, read law and commenced practice in New York city in 1830, where he continued to reside. He was a member of the New York Legislature in 1844, and a member of the Board of Education of the City of New York. His publications are: "A Report on the Quarantine Laws," 1844; "A Discourse before the Order of United Americans." His first wife was Elizabeth, daughter of Hon. William Jarvis, of Weathersfield, Vt. Rev. John Wheeler, D. D., former President of the University of Vermont, was his brother.

Wheeler, Rev. Horace Leslie. Christianity and Life. Sermon by Horace Leslie Wheeler. Preached at Willsborough Point, N. Y., August 23, 1891, during the Twelfth Annual Meeting of the American Canoe Association. Burlington: Privately printed. 1891. 8vo, pp. 8.

Wheeler, John. Difficulties of the Ministry. A Sermon, preached at the Ordination of the Rev. Worthington Smith, in St. Albans, June 4th, 1823. By John Wheeler, Pastor of the First Congregational Church, Windsor, Vt. St. Albans: J. Spooner, Printer. 1823. 8vo, pp. 24.

—*A Sermon,* preached before the Vermont Colonization Society, at Montpelier, October 25, 1825. By John Wheeler, Pastor of the First Congregational Church, Windsor, Vt. Windsor: Printed by W. Spooner. 1825. 8vo, pp. 28.

—*A Sermon,* preached before the Vermont Domestic Missionary Society, at the Annual Meeting, held at Castleton, Sept. 14, 1826. By John Wheeler, Pastor of the First Congregational Church, Windsor. Windsor, Vt.: Printed by Alden Spooner. 1826. 8vo, pp. 39.

—*Address* before the Porter Rhetorical Society of the Theological Seminary, Andover, Mass., Sept. 1834. By John Wheeler, President of the University of Vermont. Andover: Gould and Newman, Publishers. 1836. 8vo, pp. 46.

—*A Discourse,* Occasioned by the Death of Gen. William Henry Harrison, President of the United States, delivered before the Citizens of Burlington and Vicinity, April 23, 1841. By John Wheeler, President of the University of Vermont. Published by Request. Windsor: Chronicle Press. 1841. 8vo, pp. 32.

—*A Discourse,* delivered July 6, 1842, at the Funeral of James Marsh, D. D., Late Professor of Moral and Intellectual Philosophy in the University of Vermont. By John Wheeler, D. D., President of the University. Burlington: Chauncey Goodrich. 1842. 8vo, pp. 22.

—*Historical Discourse,* at the Semi-Centennial of the University of Vermont. 1854. 8vo, pp. 38.
See University of Vermont.

—*A Discourse* at the Funeral of the Hon. John Smith, of St. Albans, Vermont, November 24, 1858. By John Wheeler, D. D. St. Albans: Messenger Office Print. 1859. 8vo, pp. 30.

—*Influence* of the Professions on Civilization. A Valedictory Address, delivered before the Medical Class of the University of Vermont, June 8th, 1859. By John Wheeler, D. D. Burlington: Free Press Print. 1859. 8vo, pp. 29.
President Wheeler was born in Grafton, Vt., March 11, 1798; and died at Burlington, Vt., April 16, 1862. He was graduated at Dartmouth, 1816, and at Andover, 1819; was settled as a pastor at Windsor, Vt., 1821, and continued there until he accepted the Presidency of the University of Vermont, in 1833, which position he held until the health of his family induced him to resign, in 1848. He continued to reside in Burlington until his death. President Wheeler was a liberal benefactor of the University, and its interests were materially advanced during his term of office.

Wheeler, Orville G. *A Discourse* preached at the Funeral of Daniel M. Brown, who was drowned in attempting to cross the Lake from Plattsburg to South Hero, on Monday, May 28th, 1849. By Orville G. Wheeler, Bishop of the Congregational Church in South Hero and Grand Isle. Windsor: Printed at the Chronicle Press. 1849. 8vo, pp. 24.

—*President Taylor.* A Sermon, on the Death of the Late President, preached at South Hero, July 21, 1850; With an Appendix, containing Remarks upon Bishop Hopkins's Address. By Orville G. Wheeler, Bishop of the Congregational Church in South Hero and Grand Isle. Windsor: Printed at the Chronicle Press. 1850. 8vo, pp. 28.

—*Christ the Believer's Everlasting Portion.* A Discourse, delivered at South Hero, Vermont, October, 8, 1855, At the Funeral of Milo Landon. By Orville Gould Wheeler, Pastor of the Congregational Church of South Hero and Grand Isle. Published by Request. Burlington : Printed by Stacy & Jameson. 1855. 8vo, pp. 23.

—*Funeral Discourse.* Mrs. Experience Gordon, at Grand Isle, June 6, 1856. Burlington : Free Press Print. 1856.

—*"He Doeth all Things Well."* A Sermon, delivered on the Occasion of the Death of Mrs. Maria H. Barnes, wife of Melvin Barnes, M. D., of Grand Isle, Vermont, January 19th, 1858. By Orville G. Wheeler. Burlington : Printed by D. A. Danforth. 1858. 8vo, pp. 17.

—*Funeral Discourse.* Helen Kent, at South Hero, July 19, 1858. Burlington : Free Press Print. 1858.

—*A Discourse,* preached at the Funeral of Samuel Boardman, at Milton, Vermont, February 19, 1853. A Discourse, preached at the Funeral of Laura Mott Boardman, at Milton, Vt., Sept. 30, 1859. A Discourse, preached at the Funeral of Homer H. Boardman, at Milton, Vt., October 15th, 1859. By Rev. Orville G. Wheeler. St. Albans : Geo. Church & Co., Printers. 1860. 8vo, pp. 48.

—*A Discourse,* preached at the Funeral of Linda S. Ladd, at North Hero, Vt., June 8, 1860, by Orville G. Wheeler. Burlington : Free Press Print. 1860. 8vo, pp. 17.

—*My Jewsharp;* or Poems, by Orville Gould Wheeler. Windsor, Vt.: Printed by Bishop and Tracy. 1860. 12mo, pp. 312.

—*Two Funeral Discourses.* Lewis Mott, June 25, 1861; Russell R. Mott, March 22, 1863, at South Hero. Burlington : Times Book and Job Office. 1863.

—*Patriotism and its Demands.* A Discourse preached at West Milton, at the Funeral of Major William B. Reynolds, by Orville G. Wheeler. Burlington : Times Steam Printing Establishment. 1864. 8vo, pp. 32.

—*Funeral Discourse.* Myron T. Landon, at South Hero, Oct. 14, 1870. Plattsburgh: J. W. Tuttle. 1870.

—*Funeral Discourse.* James Conro, South Hero, Feby. 14, 1872. Plattsburgh : J. W. Tuttle. 1872.

—*Chastening.* A Discourse delivered in Grand Isle, April 8th, 1872, at the Funeral of William Winfield Brown, by O. G. Wheeler. Plattsburgh: J. W. Tuttle, Book and Job Printer. 1872. 8vo, pp. 16.

—*Woman as a Mother.* A Discourse delivered at the Funeral of Mrs. Jesse Landon, of South Hero, Vt., August 8, 1872, by O. G. Wheeler. Plattsburgh : J. W. Tuttle, Book and Job Printer. 1872. 8vo, pp. 15.

—*Funeral Discourse.* Lyman Martin, at South Hero, Oct. 9, 1873. Plattsburgh : J. W. Tuttle. 1873.

—*Funeral Discourse.* Abel Brown, at Grand Isle, Sept. 12, 1874. Plattsburgh: J. W. Tuttle. 1874.

—*Funeral Discourse.* Mrs. E. P. Herrick, West Mills, Oct. 17, 1876. Burlington: 1876.

—*Light at Evening.* A Discourse, delivered at South Hero, Feb. 18th, 1875, at the Funeral of Eliel Allen, by O. G. Wheeler. Published by Request. Plattsburgh: J. W. Tuttle, Steam Printing House. 1875. 8vo, pp. 11.

—*The Strong Man.* A Discourse, delivered at South Hero, June 16, 1875, at the Funeral of Wallis Mott. By O. G. Wheeler. Published by Request. Winooski, Vt.: Wilson Brothers, Printers. 1875. 12mo, pp. 26.

—*What is Life?* A Sermon, preached at the Funeral of Emogene Mott, at South Hero, May 2, 1869. By O. G. Wheeler. Published by Request. Winooski, Vt.: Wilson Brothers, Printers. 1875. 8vo, pp. 14.

—*The Workman.* A Discourse delivered at the Funeral of David Corbin, at South Hero, Vt., Aug. 13th, 1875, by O. G. Wheeler. Plattsburgh: J. W. Tuttle & Co., Steam Job Printers. 1875. 8vo, pp. 18.

—*The Honorable Counsellor.* A Discourse preached at the Funeral of Hector Adams, Esq., at South Hero, Vt., June 2d, 1875, by O. G. Wheeler. Published by Request. Plattsburg: J. W. Tuttle & Co., Steam Job Printers. 1875. 8vo, pp. 17.

—*A Poem* read at the Semi-Centennial of the University of Vermont. 1854. 8vo, pp. 28.

—*Funeral Discourse,* Proctor B. Adams, at South Hero, January 11, 1877. Burlington: Free Press Print. 1877.

—*Funeral Discourse.* C. G. Mayo, Colchester, Vt., June 16, 1877. Burlington : Free Press Print. 1877.

In addition to the above, Bishop Wheeler writes us that he has published innumerable articles in the newspapers, both religious and political.

We give the Bishop's biographical sketch, as furnished by himself: Born in Charlotte, Vt., August 15, 1817; and was graduated at the University of Vermont in 1837; his father, Sheldon Wheeler, was a tanner and boot and shoe manufacturer, and his grandfather was slain in the massacre of Wyoming.

The Bishop read theology with Rev. James Buckham father of Rev. M. H. Buckham, President of the University of Vermont, and preached his first sermon at Strafford, Vt., then six months at Underhill, Vt., and began his unprofitable ministry in South Hero in April, and was ordained and installed Bishop of the Congregational church of South Hero and Grand Isle, November 5, 1840; and, by the long-suffering of God and wonderful patience of the people, he is Bishop still. He twice represented his county in the Vermont Senate, and served two terms in the lower House ; has been County School Superintendent, Town Clerk and Treasurer, County Grand Juror, and now holds the office of Fence Viewer, with the possibility of sometime being Pound Keeper.

The Bishop was an early abolitionist, and believes in everybody's "being persuaded in his own mind" that he will not tolerate fetters on his own limbs, or put them upon others.

Mr. Wheeler died at his home in South Hero, February 1, 1892.

Wheeler, Rev. S. H. *Remarks* at the Funeral of Mrs. Betsey Carpenter, Waterbury, Vt., Nov. 7, 1875, by Rev. S. H. Wheeler. Montpelier: Press of J. & J. M. Poland. 1876. 8vo, pp. 15.

Wheelock, E. *Historical Sketch* of the Town of Cambridge, July 4th, 1876. By Rev. Edwin Wheelock. Montpelier: Freeman Steam Printing House and Bindery. 1876. 12mo, pp. 15.

Wheelock, James R. *Farewell Sermon,* delivered before the Congregational Church and Society in Newport, (N. H.) March 2, 1823. By

James R. Wheelock, Late Pastor of said Church and Society. Windsor, Vt.: Printed by Simeon Ide. March 12, 1823. 8vo, pp. 18.
For Biographical Sketch, see "Dartmouth Alumni," 1807.

Wheelock, V. G. *Revelation and Science Harmonize.* A Sermon delivered by Rev. V. G. Wheelock, of Wolcott, Vt., at Abercorn, P. Q., Sunday, July 11, 1869. Montpelier: J. & J. M. Poland's Steam Printing House. 1873. 8vo, pp. 12.

—*Growth of the Gospel.* A Sermon delivered by Rev. V. G. Wheelock, of Wolcott, Vt., in Stanbridge, P. Q. Also a Letter to a Methodist Minister at Stanbridge, P. Q., By the same Author. Montpelier: Journal Print. 1871. 8vo, pp. 12.
Mr. Wheelock was a Universalist Clergyman of some note in Vermont, and died at Calais, December 11, 1878, of which town he was a native, born December 16, 1806.

Whelpley, Samuel W., A. M. *A Sermon,* on the Death of Clarissa A. Wainwright, Wife of Alfred Wainwright, Preached at Middlebury, Vt. By Samuel W. Whelpley, A. M., Pastor of the First Presbyterian Church at Plattsburgh: Published by Request. Plattsburgh: Printed by Frederick P. Allen. 1812. 12mo, pp. 22.

Whipple F. P. *Rules* for the pronunciation of the Latin and Greek Languages, etc., to which is added Tables, exhibiting a Systematic order of parsing those Languages. By F. P. Whipple. Middlebury: Published for the Author. O. and J. Miner, Printers. MDCCCXXX. 12mo, pp. 19. (1.)
Mr. Whipple was from Hardwick, Vt., was graduated at Middlebury, 1830; engaged as principal of Granville Academy, N. Y., but died before the close of the year 1830.

Whitcomb, James.
Mr. Whitcomb is a native of Stockbridge, Vt., son of John and Mary (Parmenter) Whitcomb, and was born December 1, 1791; he was graduated at Transylvania University, read law and commenced practice at Bloomington, Indiana, in 1824; was prosecuting attorney for Monroe County in 1826; State Senator 1830-36; was appointed by President Jackson Commissioner of the General Land Office, serving from October 31, 1836 to July 3, 1841, when he returned to Indiana and practiced at Terre Haute; was Governor of the State, 1843-48; United States Senator from Indiana, December 3, 1849 until his death in New York City, October 6, 1852.
In 1841 Mr. Whitcomb prepared a pamphlet on the tariff, which was printed, for popular distribution, under the title of "Facts for the People."

Whitcomb, Lincoln. *Memorials and Memory* of the Events and Associations of Life. By Lincoln Whitcomb, Springfield, Vt. Springfield, Vt.: E. D. Wright, Printer. 1874. 12mo, pp. 10.

Whitcomb, Rev. Luke.
See Tufts, James, for funeral sermon and biographical sketch.

White Bronze Monuments, Statuary, &c. Aaron Bancroft, Agent for Washington County, Montpelier, Vt. New York: 1870. 8vo, pp. 119.

White, Blythe, jr. *Green Mountain Girls;* A story of Vermont. By Blythe White, jr. Illustrations. New York: 1856. 12mo, pp. 406.
Condemned by the New York Criterion, April 12, 1856.

White, Carlos. *Ecce Femina:* An attempt to solve the Woman Question; being An Examination of Arguments in Favor of Female Suffrage, by John Stewart Mill and others, and A Presentation of Arguments against the Proposed Change in the Constitution of Society. By Carlos White. Hanover, N. H.: Boston, Mass.: 1870. 16mo, pp. 258.
Mr. White is a native of Topsham, Vt., where he was born in 1842; studied at Dartmouth College, and subsequently became a book seller.

White, Charles Braman, M. D. *Annual Report* of the Board of Health of the State of Louisiana, to the General Assembly, for the year 1869. 8vo, pp. 48.

—*The Same,* 1870, pp. 83; 1871, pp. 129; 1872 pp. 161; 1873, pp. 203; 1874, pp. 135; 1875, pp. 261.

—*Drainage and Draining Canals.* 1871. 8vo, pp. 10.

—*Disinfection* in Yellow Fever as practiced in New Orleans in the years 1870-1876: A paper submitted to the American Public Health Association, at Boston, October, 1876.
Dr. White has published in addition various small pamphlets on sanitary matters.
Dr. White, son of Rev. Charles White, D.D., and brother of Professor W. C. White, of Crawfordsville, Ind., was born at Thetford, Vt., February 14, 1826; graduated A. B. at Wabash College, 1846; took the degree of M. D. at the University of Louisiana, 1852; Commissioned Assistant Surgeon, U. S. Volunteers, 1862; and as Surgeon 1864; assigned to duty as Medical Director of 13th Army Corps, March, 1865; as Medical Director, District of Texas, with rank of Lieut. Colonel, June, 1865; Made Brevet Lieut. Colonel May, 1866; Honorably mustered out January 27, 1866. President of the Board of Health of Louisiana, 1869-1876; Judge of Group XXIV, Centennial Exposition, 1876; Appointed November, 1878, Sanitary Director of the New Orleans Auxiliary Sanitary Association, and so continued until his death, April 16, 1882.

White, Homer. *The Norwich Cadets;* A Tale of the Rebellion. By Rev. Homer White, Author of "The Captive Boy," &c. St. Albans, Vt.: Published by Albert Clarke. 1873. 8vo, pp. 136.

—*The Vermont Volunteer,* a Poem of the Great Rebellion, by Rev. Homer White. West Randolph: Herald and News Print, 1884. pp. 15.

White, John, Jr. *An Address* to the People of Franklin County. Middlebury, Vermont: Printed by Huntington & Fitch, for the Publisher. March, 1806. 12mo, pp. 10.
Relates to County Officers.

White, Phinehas, Jr. *An Oration* delivered at Dummerston, Vt., July 4, 1815, in Commemoration of the 39th Anniversary of American Independence; By Hon. Phinehas White, Esq. (Published at the request of the Committee of Arrangements.) 8vo, pp. 22.

White, Pliny H. *The Life and Services* of Matthew Lyon. An Address pronounced October 29, 1858, before the Vermont Historical Society, in the Presence of the General Assembly of Vermont; By Pliny H. White. Published by Order of the General Assembly of Vermont. Burlington: Times Job Office Print. 1858. 8vo, pp. 20.

—*Death in the Midst of Life.* A Sermon delivered in the Congregational Church, Coventry, Vt., at the funeral of Henry Hewitt Frost, Esq., November 27, 1859. By Rev. Pliny H. White. Printed by request of the family and friends. Irasburgh: A. A. Earle, Book Printer. 1860. 8vo, pp. 23.

—*Annals* of Salem, Vermont.   By Pliny H. White.   8vo, pp. 4.

—*A History* of Coventry, Orleans County, Vermont.   By Pliny H. White.   "Posterity Delights in Details."   Irasburgh : A. A. Earle, Book Printer.   1859.   8vo, pp. 61, and Appendix VII.

—*A Biographical Sketch* of the Rev. Samuel Austin Worcester, Written for the Vermont Historical Society, and read at a Special Meeting of the Society, at Burlington, January 23, 1861.   8vo, pp. 4.

—*A Sermon* occasioned by the Assassination of Abraham Lincoln, President of the United States, Preached at Coventry, Vt., April 23, 1865, by Rev. Pliny H. White, Acting Pastor of the Congregational Church.   Brattleboro : Printed at the Vermont Record Office.   1865.   8vo, pp. 20.

—*The Ecclesiastical History of Vermont.*   An Essay read before the General Convention of Vermont, at Newbury, 21 June, 1866, by Rev. Pliny H. White.   Published by Order of the Convention.   Montpelier : Walton's Steam Printing Establishment.   1866.   8vo, pp. 7.

—*Jonas Galusha*, the fifth Governor of Vermont, a Memoir read before the Vermont Historical Society, in presence of the General Assembly of Vermont, at Montpelier, 16 October, 1866.   By Rev. Pliny H. White.   Montpelier : E. P. Walton, Printer.   1866.   8vo, pp. 16.

—*A Sermon* preached in Westminster, Vt., 11 June, 1867, by Rev. Pliny H. White, On the One Hundredth Anniversary of the Organization of the Congregational Church.   With a Historical Paper by Rev. Alfred Stevens.   Bellows Falls, Vt. : Printed at the Times Job Office, by A. N. Swain.   1867.   8vo, pp. 48.

—*The Congregational Church* in Westminster, Vt.: its Pastors and the Native Ministers.   By Pliny H. White.   [Reprinted from the Congregational Quarterly for January, 1869.]   Cambridge : Welch, Bigelow and Company, Printers to the University.   1869.   8vo, pp. 20.

—*Manual* of the Congregational Church, Coventry, Vt.   1868.

—*History* of the Congregational Churches in Orleans County, Vt., with Biographical Notices of the Pastors and Native Ministers.   By Pliny H. White, Acting Pastor in Coventry.   Rutland : Tuttle & Co., Printers.   1868.   8vo, pp. 61.

—*History* of Newspapers in Orleans County, Vt.   By Pliny H. White, January 1, 1869.   8vo, pp. 4.   No imprint.

Mr. White was born in Springfield, Vt., October 6, 1822; and died in Coventry, April 24, 1869.   In addition to the works by Mr. White already noticed, he published "Life and Services of Hon. William C. Bradley;" and a "Biographical Sketch of the Hon. Theophilus Herrington."   He was also a profuse contributor to Magazines and Newspapers, among which was "A Bibliography of Vermont," containing about 140 titles, printed in the "Vermont Record."   For a sketch of his life, see Congregational Quarterly," for July, 1869; also Memorial Address before the Vermont Historical Society, by Hon. Henry Clark, at Montpelier, October, 1869.

Whiting, Rev. L.   *Sermon* at the Ordination of the Rev. George E. Sanborne, over the Con-gregational Church, at Georgia Vt., 1857.   With a Historical Sketch of the Church.

Whiting, Samuel.   *A Discourse*, delivered before His Honor, Paul Brigham, Esquire, Lieutenant Governor, The Honorable Council, and House of Representatives, of the State of Vermont, at Windsor, October XII, MDCCXC-VII.   Being the Day of General Election.   By Samuel Whiting, A. M., Pastor of a Church in Rockingham.   Printed at Rutland, by Josiah Fay, for the Hon. Legislature.   MDCCXCVII.   8vo, pp. 23.

Mr. Whiting was born in Franklin, Mass., 1749; graduated at Harvard, 1769; he was pastor of the Congregational church in Rockingham, Vt., 1773–1809; and died May 16, 1819.   "Of the influence and results of Mr. Whiting's long ministry in Rockingham, it is perhaps sufficient to say, that at the close of it there was no visible church in the place."   Rev. Charles Walker, in American Quarterly Register, August 1840, page 33.

Whitingham.   *The Annual Report* of the Auditors for the Town of Whitingham, for the year ending Feb. 22, 1862.   Brattleboro : J. H. Capen, Printer, Masonic Building, High Street.   8vo, pp. 8.

Continued.

—*Green Leaves*, From Whitingham, Vermont.   A History of the town.   By Clark Jillson.   Worcester, Mass.: Printed at the Private Press of the Author.   1894.   8vo, pp. 244.

Whittock, George Clinton.

A Methodist Episcopal Divine and teacher, was born in Hubbardton, Vt., October 4, 1808, and was graduated at Middlebury College, 1834.   He was a teacher in academies at Middleport, N. Y., Medina, N. Y., and Middlebury Academy, New York, 1834–39; Professor in Genesee Wesleyan Seminary, Lima, N. Y., 1838–50; Professor in Genesee College, N. Y., 1850–54, and in Iowa Conference University, Mount Pleasant, 1854, *et seq.*   His publications are : "Elements of Geometry, etc."   "A New System of Surveying."   New York : 8vo; which is commended by Professors B. Pierce, Dodd, Sadler, Allen, DeRug, &c.   He has also contributed to Silliman's Journal.   See "Allibone" and "Pearson's Graduates of Middlebury College."

Whitney, Hiram Rawson.   *Heart Lyrics.*   Poems.   Albany, N. Y.: J. Munsell.   1868.   12mo, pp. 114.

Mr. Whitney was a native of Sheldon, Vt.   See Vermont Historical Gazetteer, Vol. II, p. 382.

Whitney, Rev. S. M.   *The Resurrection of the body.*   A Discourse preached at Braintree, Vt., Sept. 10, 1865, at the funeral of Miss Hattie K. Hodges, daughter of Rev. H. D. Hodges, by Rev. S. M. Whitney.   Printed for private circulation.   Burlington : Free Press Print.   1865.   8vo, pp. 26.

Mr. Whitney was of Colchester, Vt.

Whittier, John G.   *The Song* of the Vermonters.   1779.

Mr. Whittier stated in a letter to the Historical Magazine, and also in a letter to the Hon. Daniel Roberts, of Burlington, the latter under date of July 29, 1877, that this song was written in 1833, and first published by his friend, J. T. Buckingham, Esq., in the New England Magazine, where it may be found, Vol. IV. 1833.   It has been frequently reprinted during the past twenty years, and during the "Vermont Centennial year, 1877," it was printed probably in every newspaper in the State.

Wickham, Joseph D.   *A Discourse* delivered at Dorset, Vt. At the Funeral of Rev. William Jackson, D. D. Pastor of the Congregational Society of Dorset and East Rupert, on Tuesday, Oct. 18, 1842.   By Joseph D. Wickham, Principal of Burr Seminary.   Published by request.   Andover : 1843.   8vo, pp. 24.

Appended is a history of the Church.

—*A Discourse* Commemorative of William A. Burnham, Late Associate Principal of Burr Seminary, who died May 7, 1860, Delivered on the Occasion of his Funeral, May 11, 1860, by Rev. Joseph D. Wickham, Principal of Burr Seminary, Manchester, Vt. Published by Request. Rutland : George A. Tuttle & Co's. Steam Presses. 1860. 8vo, pp. 24.

Wilcox, Rev. Carlos. *Remains of the Rev. Carlos Wilcox,* late Pastor of the North Congregational Church in Hartford. With a Memoir of His Life. Hartford : Published by Edward Hopkins. MDCCCXXVIII. 12mo, pp. 430.

Mr. Wilcox published a poem, "Age of Benevolence"; also "Religion of Taste," a poem delivered before the Phi Beta Kappa Society of Yale College. He was born in Newport, N. H., October 22, 1794, and died at Danbury, Conn., May 29, 1827. His parents removed to Orwell, Vt., when he was about four years of age. He fitted for college at Castleton Academy, and was graduated at Middlebury in 1813, and at Andover Theological Seminary in 1817. He was pastor of various Congregational churches in Connecticut, and at Pittstown, N. Y., from 1819 until his death.

See "Griswold's Poets of America" for a sketch of his life.

Wild, A. W. *A Sermon* preached at Greensboro, Vt., July 10, 1864, on the occasion of the death of Ephraim E. Hartson and Horace Sulham, in the United States Service. By A. W. Wild. Published by request. Montpelier : Printed at the Freeman Office. 1864. 8vo, pp. 18.

—*A Biographical Sketch* of the Rev. B. Wooster, by A. W. Wild. St. Albans : Messenger Steam Printing House. 1874. 12mo, pp. 54.

Mr. Wild has in preparation a history of the Congregational Church in Vermont, with biographical sketches. He has also published "A Sermon at the Funeral of Charles Cook, Esq.," at Greensboro, February 15, 1868, published in the *Orleans Independent Standard;* "Divine Providence," a series of articles in the *Orleans Independent Standard,* from November, 1869, to January, 1870; "History of Caledonia Association," in the *Vermont Chronicle* from May 19 to August 4, 1877; various articles, obituaries, and biographies in the Congregational Quarterly, *Vermont Chronicle,* and the Annual Minutes of the General Convention of Congregational ministers and churches of Vermont.

Rev. Azel W. Wild, son of Rev. Daniel Wild, for forty years pastor of the Congregational church in Brookfield, Vt., was born in Brookfield, June 12, 1836. He graduated from Middlebury College in 1857, and from Andover Theological Seminary in 1862; taught the Craftsbury and Brownington Academies, 1857-59; preached two years at Pittsfield, Vt., 1862-64; pastor of Congregational churches, Greensboro, 1864-73; Peacham, 1874-82; Charlotte, 1882-90; Elizabethtown, N. Y., 1890.

Wild, Edward Payson. *Manuscript History of Brookfield, Vt.*

—*Commemorative Sketch* of Rev. E. P. Wild, D. D., pastor of Congregational churches at Craftsbury, Newport and Manchester, Vt., with selections from his writings. Privately printed. 1892. 12mo, pp. 175.

Mr. Wild, brother of Rev. A. W. Wild, was a native of Brookfield, where he was born June 4, 1839, and was graduated at Middlebury College in 1860, and at Bangor Theological Seminary in 1863. He was pastor of Congregational churches in Craftsbury, 1865; Newport, Vt., 1875-87; Manchester, Vt., 1887-90. He prepared the history of Brookfield, deposited in the office of the Town Clerk at Brookfield. He also prepared the history of Brookfield for Miss Hemenway's Vermont Historical Gazetteer. He published a "Fast Day Sermon," preached at North Craftsbury, April 10, 1868, and "A Sermon upon the Death of Mrs. Laura Hinman Bingham," delivered at Derby, Vt., August 19, 1877. He died Oct. 20, 1890.

Wilkins, W. H. *An original Tragi-Comedy.* In two Acts. Rock Allen, the Orphan ; or Lost and Found. With cast of characters, stage business, costumes, relative positions of the performers, &c. By W. Henri Wilkins. Ludlow : Gazette Job Printing Department. 1871. 12mo, pp. 24.

Willard, Ashton Reed. *A Legislative Handbook* relating to the Preparation of Statutes. With a chapter on the Publication of Statutes. By Ashton R. Willard. Boston : Houghton, Mifflin & Co., 12mo.

—*A Sketch* of the Life and Work of the Painter, Domenico Morelli, by Ashton R. Willard, with eight heliotypes. Boston and New York : Houghton, Mifflin & Co., The Riverside Press, Cambridge. 1895. sq. 8vo, pp. 67.

Mr. Ashton R. Willard is a son of the late Hon. Charles W. Willard.

Willard, C. W. *Proposed Recognition of Cuba.* Speech of the Hon. Charles W. Willard, of Vermont, in the House of Representatives, April 9, 1869. In opposition to the resolution of sympathy with the insurrection in Cuba. Washington. 8vo, pp. 8.

—*Cuban Belligerency* ; Speech of Hon. Charles W. Willard, of Vermont : delivered in the House of Representatives, June 15, 1870. Washington. 1870. 8vo, pp. 15.

—*Interstate Commerce.* Speech of Hon. Charles W. Willard, of Vermont, in the House of Representatives, March 24, 1874. Washington : Government Printing Office. 1874. 8vo, pp. 25.

—*Civil Service.* Speech of Hon. Charles W. Willard, of Vermont, in the House of Representatives, April 17, 1872. 8vo, pp. 8.

— *Vt. and Canada R. Road Co. vs. Vt. Central.* See Railroads—Vermont Central, etc.

Charles Wesley Willard, son of Josiah Cahoon and Abigail (Carpenter) Willard, was born in Lyndon, Vt., June 18, 1827; was graduated at Dartmouth College, 1851; read law and was admitted to the bar at Montpelier in 1853. He married Emily Doane, daughter of the late Hezekiah Hutchins and Martha T. (Barnard) Reed, of Montpelier, October 10, 1855; was Secretary of State for Vermont, 1855-56, declining a re-election ; was a State Senator, 1860-61. He became editor and proprietor of the *Green Mountain Freeman* in 1861, retaining his connection with the paper as editor for about ten years; he was a member of the lower House of Congress, March 4, 1869, to March 4, 1875. In 1878 he accepted an appointment as one of the Commissioners to revise the statutes of Vermont, which labor fell mainly upon Mr. Willard, the other Commissioner, Col. Veazey, having been appointed a judge of the Supreme Court of the State. He died at Montpelier, June 8, 1880.

Willard Emma. *An Address to the Public* ; particularly to the members of the New York Legislature, proposing a plan for improving female education. By Emma Willard. Second Edition. Middlebury : Printed by J. W. Copeland. 1819. 12mo, pp. 66.

—*The Life* of Emma Willard. By John Lord, LL.D. New York : D. Appleton & Company. 1873. 12mo, pp. 351. Two Portraits.

An exceedingly interesting work ; relates considerably to Vermont affairs and persons.

Mrs. Emma (Hart) Willard was from Berlin, Conn., and at the age of twenty she accepted an invitation to take charge of the Female Seminary at Middlebury, Vt., where she continued about two years, until her marriage to Dr. John Willard, August 10, 1809, when she opened a private school for young ladies in Middlebury where she continued with great success until 1819, when she removed her establishment to Waterford, N. Y., for two

years, and thence, in 1821 to Troy, N. Y., where it attained the highest popularity as a young ladies seminary.
See Swift's History of Middlebury.

Willard, John. *Oration at Middlebury, Vt.,* March 4, 1801. By John Willard. Bennington: 1801. pp. 17.

Willard, Samuel.
[Dr. Willard's orthography is after the phonetic system.]

CHICAGO, Ills., 327 Fulton street, }
Februnry 23, 1880.

Dear Sir :— My frend, Prof. A. D. Hager, has urjd me to send yu mi name,—with autobiographic notes, and list of the buks I have ritn. In the Dwight Memoir, "Descendants ov John Dwight of Dedham, Mass.," bi B. W. Dwight, Vol. II, p. 683, yu wil find som account of me, ritn bi Mr. Dwight from notes which I sent; this wil also tel yu ov mi father and grandfather, both Vermonters bi residence, tho' not bi birth.

My grandfather, Rev. John Willard, (1759-1826) was descended from Simon Willard, emigrant in 1634, founder ov Concord, Ms., & from Simon's son Samuel, the Pres't ov Harvard in Mather's tim. He grad. Yale 1782 (I hav his diploma), & was setld in the ministry ov the Congl. Chh. at Meriden, Ct., 1786-1803; then went tu Lunenburg, Vt., az a sort ov home-missionary, and was the first Congl. minister there, 1803; indeed the first minister there. Died there 1826. I have no printed sermons ov his. In 1788 he marid Huldah Langdon ov Berlin, Ct.; born 1762, did 1842. He was in the ministry til his deth.

Mi father, Julius Alphonso Willard, only son that grew up, born 1793, Feb. 2d, now living with me, quite activ for a man ov his aje, 87. He was postmaster at Lunenburg 1821-3; hotel-keeper and postmaster at Franconia, N. H., 1823-25; book-keeper for wholesale houses & banks & RR. offices, etc., in Boston & vicinity 1825-1831 and at various places in Illinois 1831-1871. He marid 1821 Almyra Cady ov Bradford, Vt., 1798-1873.

I was born at Lunenburg, Vt., in the house ov mi grandfather, Dec. 30, 1821. Now nearly 50 yrs I hav bin an Illinoisan; came here Apl. 1831. Grad. A. B. at Illinois College, Jacksonville (oldest college in the State) 1843; A. M., 1846; M. D., at Med. Dep't same Colleg, 1848; was tutor there 1843-4; practiced medisin in Collinsville, Ills. 1850-7; became G. Secy I. O. O. F. for Illinois, 1856, and served 11 yrs, to 1869, omitting 2 years when in army. Prof. Language Ill. State Normal Univy, Bloomington, Ills., one year, 1858-9 & rezind. For 6 yrs (1857-1863) associate or (2 yrs) chief Edr. "Illinois Teacher," ofn riting the most ov ech number, with a variety of signatures. Aug. 26, 1862, entered 97th Reg't Ills. Infy. Vols. (Col. F. S. Rutherford) az surjon; nerly lost mi lif & became helplessly paralyzed in front ov Vicksburg; rezind Feb. 2, 1863. Recovering slowly, became Oct. 1863 chief clerk for Gen. James Oakes at Springfield, who had charg ov recruting servis in Ills. Once there in a press ov work I had 40 clerks under mi orders; generally six in mi own bureau. Never hav rezumd practis ov medisin.

1864 agen G. Secy. I. O. O. F. til 1869. 1865, started & kept up with much labor a Stockholder's Public Library in Springfield, ov 3,000 vols, rising tu 4,000. 1869-70, Supt. Pub. Schools, City of Springfield. 1870-1880 and stil in the place, Prof. History in Chicago Hi Scul.

Marrid 1851 Harriet J. Edgar; hav 8 children, 1852-1871.

(There's 20 tims az much az yu want; but yu can pic for yurself.)

Buks—a short list.

Annual Reports, I. O. O. F., 1856-1862, 1864-1869.

Articles on educational & sientific subjects, Illinois Teacher, & other educational periodicals, 1857-1864. enuf tu make a plump 8vo.

Contributed tu Webster's latest Dictionary, when going thru the pres, from letter P. onward.

For G. L. Ills. I, O. O. F., pamflet Digests of local laws 1852, 1854, 1855.

In book form: "Digests of the Laws of the I. O. O. F. for Illinois." Peoria: 1864. 16mo, pp. viii and 244. The index covers 44 pages, fine print.

"Willard's Fifth Digest. Digest of the Laws of the I. O. O. F. for Illinois, being the fifth under authority of the Grand Lodge of Illinois." Peoria: 1872. 16mo, pp. xvi, 441. Index occupies in fine print 81 pages; and is one ov the few perfect indexes. This is not a new edition of the preceding, but is a new book on the same plan.

"Final Report of the Chicago Relief Committee, I. O. O. F." Chicago: 1873. 8vo, pp. 180. The account of the Chicago Fire, and of the Relief work of the Committee of the Odd Fellows, about half the book, (the rest being tables of details) was by Dr. Willard.

"A Synopsis of History. General History, from B. C.

800 to A. D. 1876, outlined in Diagrams and Tables, with index and Genealogies. For General reference, and for schools and colleges." New York : 1878, D. Appleton & Co. royal 8vo, pp. 116. The full and accurate indexes occupy 28 pages. The book is a set of historical charts on a new plan, the result of the author's experience as a student and teacher. Hily recommended in "The Nation," No. 694, Oct. 17, 1878, and in newspapers.

(Titles in Quotation marks ar taken exactly from titl pages.)

I contributed 83 pp. 8vo. to the Rep't ov the State Sup't Public Instruction ov Ills. for 1873-4, to wit, a pamflet on Scul Libraries, including lists ov bucs ov varius classes recommended, with notes. It much resembled Putnam's littl vol. "Best Reading," but was prepared from mi own researches & nolej.

I hope you believ in Spelling Reform, az Prof. Hager duz. Resp'y Yours Truly,
SAMUEL WILLARD.

Willard, Mrs. S. B. *A Tribute* of Affection to the Memory of Hon. William C. Bradley. By his Grand-daughter, Mrs. S. B. Willard. Boston: Geo. C. Rand & Avery, Printers, 3 Cornhill. 1869. 8vo, pp. 112.

Williams, Avery. *A Sermon,* delivered in Gill, Mass., August 11, 1816. Occasioned by the death of the Rev. Avery Williams, late of Lexington, Mass., who died Feb. 4, 1816. By Josiah W. Cannon, A. M., Pastor of the Church in Gill. Greenfield : Printed by Ansel Phelps. 1816. 8vo, pp. 15.

—*A Century Sermon,* preached at Lexington, Ms., March 31, 1813; being the anniversary of the incorporation of the town.

Mr. Williams was born in Guilford, Vt., January 9, 1782, and died at Spartansburg, S. C., February 4, 1816, whither he had gone for his health. He was graduated at Dartmouth College in 1804. and was pastor of the Congregational church in Lexington, Mass., from 1807 until his death.

Williams, C. H. S. (A Native of Windham County.) *Williams' New System* of healing and educating the Horse, together with diseases and their treatment : Shoeing the Horse, etc. By C. H. S. Williams. Claremont, N. H.: 1877. 12mo, pp. 248.

Williams, Charles K. *Obituary Notices,* and other testimonials of respect, on the occasion of the death of the Hon. Ch's K. Williams, LL.D., formerly Chief Justice of the Supreme Court, and afterwards Governor of the State of Vermont, to which is prefixed a brief biographical notice of the deceased. Prepared for publication in 1852. By the Hon. I. F. Redfield, LL. D., Chief Justice of Vermont. Rutland : Geo. A. Tuttle & Co., Printers. 1854. 8vo, pp. 40.

Mr. Williams, son of Rev. Samuel Williams, Historian of Vermont, was born in Cambridge, Mass., January 24, 1782, and died at Rutland, Vt., March 9, 1853. He came to Rutland with his father and family in 1790; was graduated at Williams College in 1800; he was a tutor there a short time, and was admitted to the Rutland County Bar in 1803. He was connected with the militia of Vermont as Major, 1808-1815; represented the town of Rutland in the General Assembly in 1809, '11, '14, '15, '20, '21, and again in 1849; was State's Attorney for Rutland county 1814, 1815; a Judge of the Supreme Court of Vermont, 1822, '23, 24, and again in 1829, and annually thereafter for sixteen years, the last thirteen of which he was Chief Justice. He was Collector of Customs for Vermont, 1825-29; a member and President of the Council of Censors, 1848, and Governor of the State, 1850-51.

See Williams, Samuel.

Williams, Charles Langdon. *Statistics* of the Rutland County Bar, with Biographical notices of the most distinguished of its deceased members ; also, a list of the county officers from 1781 to 1847. Compiled and prepared by Charles L. Williams, Counselor at Law, of Brandon,

Printed by John F. M'Collam. 1847. 8vo, pp. 32.

See Vermont, Reports of Supreme Court Decisions 1855-7; Compiled Statutes 1851, Reported and compiled by Mr. Williams.

Mr. Williams, son of Hon. Charles K. Williams, was born in Rutland, March 14, 1820, and died there February 10, 1861. He was graduated at Williams' College 1839; he read law, and practiced his profession at Rutland until his death, with the exception of four years, 1844-48 when he resided at Brandon.

Williams, Chauncy Kilborn. *History* of Rutland Newspapers. 8vo, pp. 4.

See Rutland, Centennial Celebration; also Bennington Centennial Celebration.

—*Catalogue* of the valuable private library of the late Chauncy K. Williams, of Rutland, Vermont. Scarce and rare books. 8vo, pp. 4.

A very defective catalogue.

—*The Same.* Second edition, enlarged. 8vo, pp. 32.

Mr. Williams, son of Hon. Charles K. Williams, was born in Rutland, Vt., December 20, 1832; was graduated at Williams' College 1852; read law and established himself at Flint, Michigan, for the practice of his profession; while there he was Circuit Court Commissioner, and held other important trusts. He returned to Rutland in 1861, where he died Jan. 7, 1879. Mr. Williams was for many years editor of the Rutland Herald and subsequently of the Globe, and was well known, in all parts of the State. He was a vigorous and prolific writer, a historical student of no mean repute, and a genial and companionable man.

I cannot refrain from adding a word more as to Mr. Williams. It is well known to Vermont historical students that his library was rich in Vermont material, being the accumulation of three generations; also, that he would seldom allow any one free access to his historical treasures.

Mr. Williams, many years before his death, commenced the preparation of a bibliography of his native State. I was aware of this fact, and one of my first steps in the work which I am now doing was to visit Mr. Williams at his home; I was then but slightly acquainted with him; he received me with a cordiality warm and frank, so differently from my anticipations, inviting me to a free examination of his book treasures, and offering his assistance in every way to facilitate my work, assuring me that he had abandoned the project of a bibliography of Vermont; at the same he was enthusiastic in favor of the scheme. In my subsequent four or five visits Mr. Williams' enthusiasm increased, and he transferred to my possession at a nominal price more than two hundred of his choice Vermont pamphlets; and of Vermont books which he would not part with he copied for me more than three hundred titles, and up to the time of his decease he was, when convenient to himself, at work in his father's library, at the old homestead, in behalf of the "Bibliography of Vermont."

Probably no citizen of Vermont felt more deeply than myself the early death of this friend of his native State, and the descendant of a noble line of ancestors.

Williams College. *Tenth Anniversary* of the Class of 1867, at Williams College, Williamstown, Mass., July 3d, 1877. Rutland, Vt.: Tuttle & Co., Printers. 1877. 8vo, pp. 34, (1).

Williams, Eleazer. *Good News* to the Iroquois Nation. A Tract, on Man's Primitive Rectitude, his Fall, and his Recovery through Jesus Christ. By Eleazer Williams. Burlington, Vt.: Printed by Samuel Mills, January, 1813. 12mo, pp. 12.

Williams, John. *Dr. John Williams'* Last Legacy, or the Useful Family Herbal. MDCCCXXV. Middlebury: Printed at the Argus and Free Press Office. 1837. 8vo, pp. 23.

Williams, J. C. *Life in Camp:* A History of the nine months' service of the Fourteenth Vermont Regiment, from October 21, 1862, when it was mustered into the U. S. Service, to July 21, 1863, including the Battle of Gettysburg. By J. C. Williams, Corp. Co. B, 14th Vt. Regt.

Motto. Claremont, N. H.: Published for the Author, By the Claremont Manufacturing Company. 1864. 16mo, pp. 167, (1).

—*History* and map of Danby, Vermont, By J. C. Williams, Rutland, Vt.: Printed by McLean & Robbins, Independent Office. 1869. 8vo, pp. 393.

Mr. John C. Williams was born in Danby, Vt., June 26, 1843, being a son of Olney Williams, who settled at Danby in 1832, from Rhode Island. He has been publisher and editor of the Otter Creek Valley News, published at Danby. For a full biographical sketch, see History of Danby, pp. 283-4.

WILLIAMS, REV. SAMUEL. *The Natural* and Civil History of Vermont. By Samuel Williams, LL.D., Member of the Meteorological Society in Germany, of the Philosophical Society in Philadelphia, and of the Academy of Arts and Sciences in Massachusetts. Published according to Act of Congress. Printed at Walpole, New Hampshire, By Isaiah Thomas and David Carlisle, Jun. Sold at their Bookstore, in Walpole, and by said Thomas, at his Bookstore, in Worcester. MDCCXCIV. 8vo, pp. 416. Map.

—*The Natural* and Civil History of Vermont. By Samuel Williams, LL.D., Member of the Meteorological Society in Germany, of the Philosophical Society in Philadelphia, and of the Academy of Arts and Sciences in Massachusetts. In two volumes. The Second Edition, corrected and much enlarged. Burlington, Vt.: Printed by Samuel Mills. Sold at his Bookstore in Burlington, by Mills and White, Middlebury, Isaiah Thomas, Jun., Worcester, Thomas and Andrews, Boston, Thomas and Whipple and S. Sawyer and Co., Newburyport. 1809. 8vo, pp. 514, and 487. Map.

—*The Influence* of Christianity on Civil Society, represented in a Discourse Delivered November 10, 1779, at the Ordination of the Rev. John Prince, to the Pastoral Care of the First Church in Salem. By Samuel Williams, A. M., Pastor of the First Church in Bradford. Boston: Printed by John Boyle in Marlborough Street. MDCCLXXX. 8vo, pp. 32.

—*The Love of our Country* Represented and Urged, In a Discourse, delivered October 21st, 1792, at Rutland, in the State of Vermont; By Samuel Williams, LL.D. Printed at the Request of several Members of the Legislature. From the Press of A. Haswell in Rutland. M,DCC,XCII. 8vo, pp. 28.

—*The Evidence of Personal Christianity*, represented in a Discourse delivered June 17th, 1792, at Rutland, in the State of Vermont. By Samuel Williams, LL.D. Printed in Rutland [Vermont] by Anthony Haswell. M,DCC,XCII. 8vo, pp. 32.

—*The Moral principles and blessings of Society.* A Discourse delivered before Centre Lodge, at Rutland, Vt., June 24, 1812: on the Festival of St. John the Baptist. By Samuel Williams, LL.D; Published by Request of the Lodge. Windsor: Printed by Thomas M. Pomroy. 1812. 8vo, pp. 22.

—*A Discourse* delivered before His Excellency Thomas Chittenden, Esq., Governor, the Honorable Council, and House of Representatives of the State of Vermont; At Rutland, October

9th, 1794, Being the Day of General Election, By Samuel Williams, LL.D. Rutland : Printed by James Lyon, By order of Legislature. M,DCC,XCIV. 8vo, pp. 34.

—A History of the American Revolution : Intended as a Reading book for Schools. By Samuel Williams, LL.D. New Haven : Printed and Published by W. Storer, Jun. 1824. 12mo, pp. 204.

This work was first published in the monthly numbers of the *Rural Magazine,* at Rutland, Vt.

See S. Williams & Co.; Sketches of the War.

Mr. Williams was descended from noted ancestors on both sides; on the paternal side from Robert Williams, who emigrated from England to Roxbury, Mass., and was admitted a freeman in 1638, of whom Farmer, in his genealogy, says : "And is the common ancestor of the divines, civilians, and warriors of his name, who have honored the country of their birth." Rev. John Williams, of Indian captivity fame, and the first minister at Deerfield, Mass., was a grandson of Robert, the immigrant. He was also grandfather of our Rev. Samuel Williams, LL.D., through his wife Eunice (Mather). She was descended from Rev. Richard Mather, the immigrant to Roxbury, Mass., who was the ancestor of all the famous Mathers of New England history.

We print the following sketch of Mr. Williams, entire, as printed in the "Williams Genealogy," by Stephen W. Williams, M. D., A. M. It was prepared by Chief Justice and Governor Charles K. Williams, of Rutland, as Dr. S. W. Williams in his preface, makes acknowledgement to the Judge, who greatly assisted him.

I intersperse two brief notes in brackets as explanatory.

Rev. Samuel Williams, LL.D., was son of Rev. Warham Williams, of Waltham, Mass. He was born at Waltham, April 23, 1743; married Miss Jane Kilbourne, May 5, 1768; died January 2, 1817, aged 74. He was graduated at Harvard College in 1761. While there he was selected by Professor Winthrop to go with him to Newfoundland, to observe the transit of Venus, in consequence of which he was not present at the Commencement. He was licensed to preach by the Association of Ministers at Cambridge, October 11, 1763, having spent the intermediate time between his graduation and being licensed, in teaching school at Waltham. He preached some time in Concord, Mass., as a candidate, and afterwards at Bradford, where he was ordained November 20, 1765. [Where he continued until his appointment as a professor in Harvard University.] In the year 1780 he was appointed Hollis Professor of Mathematics and Natural Philosophy at Cambridge. During his residence in Bradford, Benjamin Thomson, afterwards Count Rumford, studied philosophy, etc., under him, and was a member of his family for some time, and with whom he corresponded until 1791. The Rev. Dr. Pierce and the Rev. Dr. Barnard, of Salem, also studied with him, and he preached their ordination sermons. During his continuance at the University, by the request of the American Academy of Arts and Sciences, and at the request of the Corporation of Harvard College, he went to Penobscot Bay to observe a total eclipse of the sun. By order of the General Court of Massachusetts, the Lincoln galley was fitted out for his accommodation. He went on board October 9, 1786, accompanied by Stephen Sewall, Professor of Oriental Languages, James Winthrop, Librarian, Fatisque Vernon, A. B., and Messrs. Dudley Atkins, John Davis, (afterwards Judge of the District of Massachusetts,) George Hall, John Dawson, (afterwards Member of Congress from Virginia,) and Jeremiah Van Rensellaer, student of the University. The eclipse was observed October 20, 1786. During his stay at Penobscot he received every attention and politeness from Captain Henry Mowart, Commander of Her Britannic Majesty's naval force at Penobscot. In the journey he was accompanied by Mr. —— King, a Sophomore, and also by his son Samuel. He kept a regular journal of his proceedings and observations.

He received while at Cambridge as Professor, the honorary degree of Doctor of Laws from Yale College, at New Haven, Conn., and also from the University of Edinburgh, and was an active member of the American Academy of Arts and Sciences, and furnished several papers, which are printed in the first volume of their memoirs. He was elected a member of the Meteorological Society of Manheim, Germany, and of the Philosophical Society in Philadelphia.

In the year 1786, he was appointed one of the agents on the part of Massachusetts, to assist in running and ascertaining the line of jurisdiction between the Commonwealth of Massachusetts and the State of New York.

[Mr. Williams resigned his professorship at Harvard at some period in the year 1788, and immediately removed to Rutland, Vt., though his family did not follow until some time after.]

He afterwards removed to Rutland, Vt., and preached there for about six years. Afterward he preached at Burlington for about two years. He gave a course of lectures at the University, was appointed by His Excellency, Governor Tichenor, under the act of the Legislature in 1805, to ascertain the boundary of the State of Vermont, which service he also performed. His published works are :

Two Sermons on Regeneration, published in 1766.

Sermon on the ordination of the Rev. Mr. Barnard, 1773.

Sermon on the Love of our Country, 1775.

Sermon on the ordination of Mr. Pierce, 1780.

Sermon at General Election in Vermont, 1794.

Sermon on the Evidence of Personal Christianity, 1799.

Sermon on the Love of our Country, 1799.

Sermon delivered before the Centre Lodge.

Natural and Civil History of Vermont, published in one volume, at Walpole, 1794.

Revised Second edition of do. in two vols., 1809.

He left a work, which is yet unpublished, entitled "Philosophical Lectures on the constitution, duty, and religion of man." He also left sermons, manuscripts on Astronomical, Philosophical and Mathematical subjects, and on the variation of the magnetic needle. For the above facts, I am indebted to his son, Gen. Charles Kilbourne Williams, Chief Justice of Vermont.

The following obituary notice of him was published in the *Rutland Herald,* January 8, 1817 :

"Died in this village, after a short illness, Rev. Samuel Williams, LL. D., Edinburgh and New Haven, formerly Hollis Professor of Mathematics and Natural Philosophy, Harvard; Member of the Meteorological Society, and of the Academy of Arts and Sciences in Massachusetts.

In the death of the Reverend and learned gentlemen, his family have sustained an irreparable loss, and his numerous friends and acquaintances will long and deeply lament a dispensation which has thus deprived them of the virtuous, elegant, high and dignified mental entertainments always enjoyed under the beams of this great, philosophic, scientific, and Christian luminary. Nor is it with an ordinary sensibility that every class of society will regard so great a deprivation; for notwithstanding the respectful attention of the good and the great, he would often descend from that eminence to which he was scarcely less entitled by his uncommon literary attainments than by his profession as a Christian minister, to the humble walks of life, when by his frankness, sincerity, and the suavity of his manners, he captivated the affections, and dispensed delight and instruction to all around him."

The funeral sermon was preached by the Rev. Heman Ball, D. D., from a text which he selected in his life time; part of the 43d Psalm, 4 : "Unto God my exceeding joy." His relict, Mrs. Jane Williams, died March 24, 1829. Both were buried in the old burying ground, Rutland, East Parish. Their children were, Jane, born January 22, 1769; Samuel. born October 8, 1771 ; Leonard, born November 6, 1776, died March, 1812 ; Charles Kilbourne, born 1780. died 1780 ; Charles Kilbourne, born January 24, 1782, Judge Charles K. Williams, and Jane, (Mrs. Osgood) are now (1847) the only surviving children in the family.

We print verbatim from the original manuscript, the following important letter from Mr. Williams to his wife; the letter is addressed on the outside : "Mrs. Jane Williams, Cambridge;" it has no postmark, as there were none except local post-routes in Vermont at that time ; it is written in a fine clear hand, the lines close together, and occupied one side of a half sheet of unruled paper, foolscap size; it was double sealed with two of the old fashioned red wafers.

It will be noticed that the letter is dated June 22, 1789, but was held, and a postscript added July 27, 1789; it is probable that no opportunity presented for forwarding it safely, until Mr. Prentiss went below in August, of that year. I insert three explanatory notes in brackets :

RUTLAND, June 22, 1789.

My Dear.—Your letter of May 28th came safe to hand on June 21st. It gave much relief to my mind, but it was extremely painful to find that amidst your other afflictions you had been exercised with sickness. God grant your health and spirits may be preserved ; and that our afflictions may soon be over. I should contrive every way possible to bring you here this summer, but the thing is impossible ; more than fifty miles of the road are impassable but by a slay, and the distress for provisions throughout all Canada and the country round here has been extremely great. Would to God I could afford you some relief ! But there is no money in this country;

only the produce of farms, which will not come in till next fall, and bad off as you must be, I wish I had some of your Cheese, Cyder, Pork, etc.—Having secured what can be done from the Parish, my whole aim now is to influence and persuade the persons of note here to found a college which I hope to get effected next October when the General Assembly come together. N. B. This must not be mentioned at Cambridge by any means. If I can get this effected I think we shall be in a flourishing state once more —I thank you much for the risbands, and for the intelligence respecting Mrs. Emery. With regard to the foreign letters, I wish you to send them. As to the philosophical transactions, I think they had better remain in your hands for the present. Are they directed to me or to the College? *One thing in particular here, look over the contents of each, and see if there is any piece of mine in either, and send me word how this is* as I much wish to know what reception the pieces I sent last fall met with.—The furniture that will be wanted when we move here will be the common and ordinary sort. Large glasses, the best chairs, and everything of that sort will be of no use at present, and there are no buildings here but barns in which they could be housed. Write as much news as you can, as there is but seldom opportunity to send in the summer. With regard to Leonard [his second son, born November 6, 1776.] I shall send for him here if possible. The difficulty is how to get him up. Can he ride on horse back? or could he come in a wagon? If I should send for him give him a charge not to speak of the state of things below; only to say that his father was much injured, and resigned his office; but he does not know the affair, etc.—My tenderest love to Jenny, [Jane, his eldest child, born, 1769.] I have felt everything for her in these times that a father could feel. I have every reason in the world to think it will not be to her disadvantage to remove into this country.—My little dear Charles, [late Chief Justice and Governor of Vermont] God bless him, give my love to him! Do what you can to support all their minds. From your ever affectionate husband. S. WILLIAMS.

P. S.—Mr. Prentiss does not go down till August. S. Walker has been here, and is agoing to study law in this town. I wrote a few lines, by him, which I hope you have received. Anything relative to cloathes that Mr. Prentiss can bring, I wish you to send.

July 27, 1789.

Captain Samuel Prentiss, the probable bearer of the above letter, was a lawyer at Rutland; at a federal celebration there in 1795, "federal toasts were drank, under the discharge of cannon fired by the volunteer corps of artillery, under the direction of Capt. Samuel Prentiss;" he should not be mistaken for Judge Prentiss, of Montpelier. See Vermont, Governor and Council, Vol. 3, pp. 483-4.

I next print an extract from a letter written Sept. 26, 1879, by the present pastor of the church in Bradford, Mass., where Rev. Mr. Williams was pastor for fifteen years, preceding his acceptance of a professorship in Harvard University:

"In regard to the sermons, [one thousand or more in manuscript, which it was thought the church where Mr. Williams was pastor so long might desire to possess] Mr. Williams took a sad mis-step. He went to Harvard, from Bradford, and was for eight years a very brilliant, scholarly man. But he committed some offence, I have heard it called forgery, which led to his instant resignation,—and he went away from the metropolis of culture and refinement, from the society where he had been so honored, to the then new and back-woods town of Rutland. He had great learning and ability, but there was this sad episode in his life, which destroyed the fame of a life which promised so much."

I am not aware that this sad story has ever been referred to in print, in Vermont, except in a single instance; Matthew Lyon, in a letter to his constituents, printed in the "Republican Magazine and Scourge of Aristocracy," for October 1-15, 1798, published by his son, James Lyon, at Fairhaven, Vt., has the following: "In a certain paper, [meaning the "Rutland Herald," then edited by Rev. Samuel Williams] conducted by a man of great learning, the same who some years ago took refuge in this State from a prosecution for forgery."

The "Herald" was an organ of the federal party, and bitterly opposed Col. Lyon's election to Congress.

Col. Lyon's letter was evidently written on the eve of his trial for an alleged violation of the Sedition Law, and with a federal court and federal officers he felt that conviction was certain, and he was right, for after a brief trial of one day at Rutland, he was convicted, and sentenced to four months' imprisonment in close jail, and to pay a fine of one thousand dollars; and on the 8th of October, 1798, he was incarcerated in the jail at Vergennes.

See Lyon, James.

I feel none but the kindest motives, and the vindication of history, in making public in Vermont this sad episode in the life of Mr. Williams. His subsequent upright life and career in Vermont, his services in behalf of the welfare and honor of the State, demand that a momentary act of indiscretion shall be forgotten and remembered no more.

Williams, Samuel. *Memoir of Charles Kilborn Williams.* Reprinted from Vol. 2 of the Memorial Biographies of the New England Historic Genealogical Society. Cambridge: John Wilson and Son. 1882. 8vo, pp. 19.

Mr. Williams is a son of Charles Kilborn, and grandson of Rev. Samuel Williams.

Williams, S. & Co. *The Rural Magazine;* or Vermont Repository. Devoted to Literary, Moral, Historical and Political Improvement. For January, 1795. Volume 1.—Number 1. Rutland; Printed by J. Kirkaldie, for S. Williams & Co. A Few Rods North of the State House. 2 volumes, 8vo, pp. 648, (5), 620, (4).

Williamson, Rev. Isaac Dowd, D. D. *An Argument* for Christianity, in a Series of Discourses. New York: 1836. 18mo, pp. 252.

—*An Exposition* and Defence of Universalism, delivered in the Universalist Church in Baltimore. New York: 1840. 18mo, pp. 227.

—*Address* by the Rev. I. D. Williamson, of Alabama, delivered before the Cadets of Norwich University, at Commencement, 1844. Woodstock: Printed at the Office of the Vermont Mercury. 1844. 8vo, pp. 12.

—*An Examination* of the Doctrine of Endless Punishment. Cincinnati: 1847. 18mo, pp. 225.

—*Sermons for the Times;* and the People. New York: 1849. 18mo, pp. 252.

—*The Universalist Church Companion.* Boston: 1850. 18mo, pp. 216.

—*The Crown of Life:* A series of Discourses. Boston: 1850. 12mo, pp. 407.

—*The Vision of Faith;* A Series of Discourses on the Decalogue and the Lord's Prayer. Madison, Ind.: 1852. 18mo, pp. 203.

—*The Philosophy* of Universalism, or Reasons for our Faith. Cincinnati: 1866. 12mo, pp. 96.

—*Rudiments* of Theological and Moral Science. Cincinnati: 1870. 12mo, pp. 377.

Dr. Williamson also published many sermons and essays in pamphlet form. He was the son of Ransom and Jerusha [Miller] Williamson, and was born in Pomfret, Vt., April 4, 1807; and died in Cincinnati, Ohio, November 26, 1876. He received only a common school education, but his ardent thirst for knowledge, force of character and enthusiasm made amends for lack of external aid. He was a Universalist of the Hosea Ballou school, and adhered to this phase of Christianity all his life. He preached his first sermon October 1, 1827, at Springfield, Vt.; then preached a while in New Hampshire, and was regularly ordained by the Franklin Association, at Townshend, Vt., September 10, 1829. He was settled in many places in various States, and traveled all through the United States, North and South, as an evangelist and missionary, and visited Great Britain in this capacity; but for the last twenty years of his life his home was in Cincinnati. He delivered nearly 4,000 sermons, and for 40 years was editorially connected with periodicals of the Universalist denomination, ten years of which as joint editor and proprietor of the *Star in the West*, at Cincinnati. He was a prominent Odd Fellow, and for many years Grand Chaplain of the Grand Lodge of the United States, and the ritual now in use by that Order was largely from his pen. He received the honorable degree of Doctor of Divinity, from the Norwich, Vt., University, in 1850. He was married September 3, 1826, to Miss Adaline Eliza Guernsey, of Mount Holly, Vt., who survives him (1881) with four children—one son and three daughters—all of whom are married and settled in life.

Williamstown. *Manual* of the Congregational Church in Williamstown, Vt., with a Catalogue of the Officers and Members. Montpelier: Printed at the Freeman Printing Establishment. 1860. 12mo, pp. 20.

—*Annual Report* of the Superintendent of Common Schools, Williamstown, Vt. March 1, 1870. Montpelier: Poland's Steam Printing works. 1870. 8vo, pp. 16.
Continued.

—*Methodism* in Williamstown, Vermont. An Historical Address delivered December 19, 1880, by Rev. J. R. Bartlett, Pastor of the Methodist Episcopal Church, Williamstown, Vt. Montpelier: Messenger Steam Printing House and Bindery. 1880. 12mo, pp. 35.

Willis, Lemuel. *A Semi-Centennial Address* delivered in the Universalist Church, Salem, Mass., Thursday, August 4, 1859, on the occasion of celebrating the Fiftieth Anniversary of the Dedication of the Church, and the Installation of Rev. Edward Turner, both of which took place June 22, 1809. By Rev. Lemuel Willis, of Warner, N. H. With an Appendix. Salem: Register Press. Printed by Charles W. Swazey. 1859. 8vo, pp. 84.
Mr. Willis was born in Windham, Vt., April 24, 1802; studied at Reading, Vt., with Rev. S. C. Loveland; commenced preaching in 1822, and continued in various places in New Hampshire and Massachusetts until he retired to Warner, N. H., more than twenty years ago, where he died July 23, 1878.

Williston. *The Articles of Faith* adopted by the Church of Williston, January 11, 1809. Burlington: Printed by Samuel Mills. April, 1809. 8vo, pp. 7.

—*The Confession of Faith* and Constitution of the First Universalist Church of Williston, Vt. Adopted August, 1867. Montpelier: Printed at the Repository Office. 1868. 12mo pp. 8.

—*Annual Report* of the Auditors & Selectmen of the Town of Williston, Vt., for the year ending February 19, 1876. Burlington: Free Press Book and Job Printing House. 1876. 8vo, pp. 16.
Continued.

Willoughby Association. *Report* to the Willoughby Association, U. S. A. Made by Columbus Smith, A. D. 1864. Containing the Willoughby Constitution and information in his possession relative to the Willoughby Property in England, and the Family Relics brought to America by the Willoughby Family: likewise several Genealogies of different branches of the family in America and England. Published by order of the Willoughby Association. Middlebury: Printed at the Register office. 1864. 8vo, pp. 28.

Wilson Association. *Report* to the Wilson Association, U. S. A., made by H. O. Smith, A. D. 1866. Containing Reports and Information which has been collected from various sources relative to the Wilson property in England, and several pedigrees of different branches of the Wilson Family in America. Published by Order of the Wilson Association. Middlebury: Register Book and Job Printing Establishment. 1866. 8vo, pp. 28.

Wilson, William D. *The Spirit* in the Form. A Sermon preached before the Diocesan Convention of Vermont, in Union Church, St. Albans, Sept. 18, 1844. By Wm. Wilson, A. M., Rector of St. Paul's Church, Windsor, Vt. No imprint. 12mo, pp. 12.

Winchester, E. *The Process and Empire of Christ;* from his Birth to the end of the Mediatorial Kingdom; A Poem, in twelve Books. By Elhanan Winchester. Brattleboro: Printed by William Fessenden. 1805. 12mo, pp. 352.

—*The Universal Restoration.* Exhibited in four Dialogues between a Minister and his Friend. To which is prefixed a Sketch of the Author's Life. Printed at Bellows Falls, Vt.: By Bill Blake & Co. 1819. 12mo, pp. 239.

Windham County. *Atlas* of Windham County, Vt. From actual surveys by and under the direction of F. W. Beers, assisted by Geo. P. Sanford & others. Published by F. W. Beers, A. D. Ellis & G. G. Soule, 95 Maiden Lane, New York: 1869. Folio, pp. 39. (8).

—*Gazetteer and Business Directory* of Windham County, 1724-1884. Compiled and published by Hamilton Child [Author of many county directories named, including Addison, Bennington, Chittenden, Franklin, Grand Isle, Lamoille, Orleans, Rutland and Windsor counties, Vermont.] Permanent Office, Syracuse, N. Y. Syracuse: 1884. 8vo, pp. 624.

—*Windham County*, as represented in the Hartford Convention.
See Hartford Convention.

—*Complete list* of Congregational Churches and Ministers in.
See Walker, Charles.

Windsor. *The Public* papers of the Ascutney Mill-Dam Company. Printed at the Chronicle Press, Windsor, Vt.: 1834. 8vo, pp. 14. (1).

—*A Brief Account* of the Late Revivals of Religion in a Number of Towns in the New England States, and also in Nova Scotia. Extracted chiefly from Letters. Windsor, Vt.: Reprinted by Alden Spooner. 1800. 12mo, pp. 24.

—*Manual* for the use of the First Congregational Church in Windsor, Vt., containing the Confession of Faith and Covenant; some Aids to Candidates; also a Historical Sketch of the Church. Rules, List of Members, &c. Windsor: Printed at the Vermont Chronicle Press. 1855. 12mo, pp. 48.

—*Report* of the Superintendent of Public Schools, for the town of Windsor, for the year ending March 4, 1856. 8vo, pp. 11.
Continued.

—*Manual* of the First Congregational Church, Windsor, Vermont. No. II. June, 1868. Prepared by Direction of the Church. Windsor: Vermont Chronicle and Journal Steam Print. 1868. 12mo, pp. 72.

—*The Centennial* at Windsor, Vermont, July 4, 1876. Being a record of the proceedings of the Celebration; and containing the Address and Poem then delivered; Also a view of Windsor as it now is. Windsor: Printed by the Journal Company. 1876. sm. 4to, pp. 80.

—*Annual Report* of the Town of Windsor, for the year ending February 23, 1876. Windsor: Journal Company. 1877. 8vo, pp. 15.

Windsor County. *A Memorial* to the Congress of the United States, adopted by a Meeting of the Citizens of Windsor County, Vt., Held at Woodstock, Jan. 22, 1833. Published by order of the Convention. Woodstock: Press of the Vermont Courier. 1833. 8vo, pp. 20.

This is a memorial against a reduction of the tariff.

—*Rules* of Windsor County Court; Adopted March Term, 1845. 18mo, pp. 8.

—*Rules* of Windsor County Court, Adopted May Term, 1862. Woodstock: Printed by Luther O. Greene. 16mo, pp. 8.

—*Atlas of Windsor County*, Vermont. From actual Surveys by and under the direction of F. W. Beers, assisted by Geo. P. Sanford & others. Published by F. W. Beers, A. D. Ellis & G. G. Soule, 95 Maiden Lane, New York. 1869. Folio, pp. 47.

—*Manual of the Windsor County Bar;* containing the Rules of Practice in the Supreme Court and Court of Chancery, and of the Windsor County Court. Compiled by George B. French, Clerk of the Courts. Luther O. Greene, Printer. 1873. 12mo, pp. 68.

—*Windsor County Agricultural Society.* Annual Catalogue, containing list of Officers, Premiums, Rules and Regulations, for the year 1876. Thirty-First Fair to be held at Woodstock, Tuesday, Wednesday and Thursday, Sept. 26, 27 and 28. Woodstock, Vt.: David P. Simpson, Printer, Standard Office. 1876. 8vo, pp. 32.

See Kendall, B. F.

Wines, Abijah. *The Criminality of Vain Amusements Exposed.* A Sermon preached at Newport, (N. H.,) 18th December, 1803. By Abijah Wines, A. M., Pastor of the Congregational Church of Christ in Newport. Windsor: Printed by Alden Spooner. MDCCCIV. 8vo, pp. 40.

—*An Inquiry* into the Nature of the Sinner's Inability to Make a New Heart, or to Become Holy. Containing some Remarks on the Hon. Nathaniel Niles' "Letter to a Friend." By Abijah Wines, A. M., Pastor of the Congregational Church of Christ, in Newport, N. H. Motto. Windsor: Published by P. Merrifield & Co. 1812. Thomas M. Pomroy, Printer. 12mo, pp. 169.

Mr. Wines never resided in Vermont.
See Dartmouth Alumni, 1794.

Wing, Joseph A. *"Pluck," and Other Poems.* By Joseph A. Wing. Montpelier, Vt.: Freeman Steam Printing House and Bindery. 1878. 12mo, pp. 252.

Mr. Wing was born in East Montpelier, Vt., October 26, 1810; read law and commenced practice in Plainfield, Vt., in 1835, and in 1858 removed to Montpelier, where he still continues a prominent member of the legal profession. (1880.)

Winkfield, U. E. *The Female American,* or the Extraordinary Adventures of Unca Eliza Winkfield, compiled by herself. Vergennes. 1814. 16mo.

Winnowings from the Mill. U. V. M. Vol. I. Nos. 1–5, Dec. 1875—June, 1876. 4to, bi-monthly.

Winooski. *The By-Laws,* Articles of Faith, Covenant and form of reception of the Congregational Church in Winooski, Vt., with the Roll of Members, September, 1867. Published by order of the Church. Burlington: Free Press Steam Print. 1867. 12mo, pp. 11.

—*The Charter and Ordinances* of the Village of Winooski, adopted January, 1867. Burlington: Free Press Print. 1867. 8vo, pp. 24.

—*Instructors and Course of Study* of the Winooski Graded School. 1896–97. n. p. n. d. 8vo, pp. 12.

Winooski Marble. *Report and Statements* respecting the Winooski Marble at Mallet's Bay, near Burlington, Vermont. Boston: Press of T. R. Marvin & Son, 42 Congress Street. 1866. 8vo, pp. 11.

Winslow, Calvin. *The Experience of Calvin Winslow.* By publishing this sketch of my Experience, I wish to satisfy my friends and glorify God. If my design is answered in this respect, I shall not trouble myself any further. Critics are welcome to the chaff; it will not hurt me to lose it, nor enrich them to have it—hence not worth making a noise about. Printed for the Author. 1807. 12mo, pp. 19, (1).

The Author was born in Massachusetts in 1768, and came to Brandon, Vt., with his father and family in 1776. This book contains his religious experiences, when, after much tribulation, he was born again, and became an exhorter.
Winslow, Gordon M. D., D. D., brother of Rev'ds Hubbard and Miron, and an Episcopal Clergyman, died June 7, 1864.
See Annual Cyclopedia, 1864, pp. 607–8.

Winslow, Hubbard, D. D. *Discourses* on the Nature, Evidence, and Moral Value of the Doctrine of the Trinity. By Hubbard Winslow, Pastor of Bowdoin Street Church, Boston. Boston: Published by Perkins, Marvin & Co. Philadelphia: Henry Perkins. 1834. 16mo, pp. 162.

—*On the Dangerous Tendency to Innovations* and Extremes in Education. Delivered before the American Institute of Instruction, August, 1834. By Hubbard Winslow. Boston: Tuttle & Weeks, Printers. 1835. 8vo, pp. 22.

—*Christianity* applied to our Civil and Social Relations. By Hubbard Winslow, Pastor of Bowdoin Street Church, Boston. Boston: Published by William Peirce, No. 9, Cornhill. Press of Webster and Southard. 1835. 12mo, pp. 184.

—*The Tendency of Religion* to expand and elevate the Mind. A Discourse, preached at the Ordination of Rev. Ray Palmer, over the Third Church and Society in Bath, Maine, July 22, 1835. By Hubbard Winslow, Pastor of Bowdoin Street Church, Boston. Boston: Published by William Peirce, No 9, Cornhill. Press of Webster and Southard. 1835. 8vo, pp. 24.

—*The Young Man's Aid* to Knowledge, Virtue and Happiness. By Rev. Hubbard Winslow, Pastor of Bowdoin Street Church, Boston. Boston: Published by D. K. Hitchcock, Whipple & Damrell, 9 Cornhill. 1837. 12mo, pp. 408.

—*Are you a Christian?* or Aid to Self-Examination for Members of the Church of Christ and those who expect to become Members. Text. By Rev. Hubbard Winslow, Pastor of Bowdoin St. Church. Boston: Published by D. K. Hitchcock, and Whipple & Damrell, 9 Cornhill. 1837. 32mo, pp. 61.

—*The Means of the Perpetuity* and Prosperity of our Republic. An Oration, delivered by request of the Municipal Authorities of the City of Boston, July 4, 1838, in the Old South Church, in Celebration of American Independence. By Hubbard Winslow. Boston: John H. Eastburn, City Printer, No. 18 State Street. 1838. 8vo, pp. 50.

—*Woman as she should be.* I. The Appropriate Sphere of Woman. II. The Influence of Christianity on Woman. III. The Christian Education of Woman. By Rev. Hubbard Winslow. Boston: T. H. Carter, Agent. Philadelphia: Henry Perkins. 1848. 16mo, pp. 81.

—*Rejoice with Trembling.* A Discourse delivered in Bowdoin Street Church, Boston, on the day of Annual Thanksgiving, November 30, 1837. By Hubbard Winslow. Boston: Published by Perkins & Marvin. 1838. 8vo, pp. 32.

—*The Power of Truth*, illustrated in the Life and Happy Death of Caroline Jennison. Boston: Massachusetts Sabbath School Society, Depository, No. 13 Cornhill. 1841. 24mo, pp. 54.

—*The Mode of Baptism.* A Discourse preached in Bowdoin Street Church, on Sunday Morning, April 24, 1842. By Hubbard Winslow, Pastor of the Church. Boston: Henry B. Williams. 1842. 24mo, pp. 60.

—*Elements of Intellectual Philosophy*, designed for a Text-book and for Private Reading. By Hubbard Winslow, A. M. of Boston, Author of Philosophical Tracts, Social and Civil Duties, Young Man's Aid, Christian Doctrines, etc. Boston: Crocker & Brewster, 47 Washington Street. 1850. 12mo, pp. 414.

—*A Sermon* delivered before the Ancient and Hon. Artillery Company, Monday, June 6, 1853, on the 215th Anniversary of the Corps. By Rev. Hubbard Winslow of Boston. Boston: Wright and Hasty, Printers, No. 3 Water Street. 1853. 8vo, pp. 29.

—*Eulogy* on the late Prof. E. A. Andrews, LL.D. delivered at New Britain, Conn., May 19, 1858, by Hubbard Winslow. Boston: Press of Crocker and Brewster, 47 Washington Street. 1858. 8vo, pp. 50.

—*The Former Days.* History of the Presbyterian Church of Geneva, by Hubbard Winslow. Boston: Press of Crocker and Brewster, 47 Washington Street. 1859. 8vo, pp. 40.

—*The Hidden Life;* and the Life of Glory. By Rev. Hubbard Winslow, D. D., Author of "Intellectual Philosophy," "Moral Philosophy," Christian Doctrines," &c. Published by the American Tract Society, 28 Cornhill, Boston. 1863. 16mo, pp. 254.

Hubbard Winslow, brother of Rev. Miron Winslow, was born in Williston, Vt., October 30, 1799; and died there August 13, 1864. He was graduated at Yale College, 1825; read theology, and was pastor of Congregational churches at Dover, 1828-1831; Bowdoin street, Boston, 1832-44; had charge of Mount Vernon or Beacon Hill

Seminary for young ladies in Boston, 1844-53; then visited Europe for a few months; was pastor of Presbyterian churches at Geneva, N. Y., and New York City, 1857-62. Among his other publications are "Sermons on Christian Doctrines;" "Social and Domestic Duties;" "Relation of the Natural Sciences to Revelation," 1839; "Moral Philosophy." 1856. Besides numerous contributions to Journals, Magazines and Reviews. See Drake's Biographical Dictionary, and Allibone's Dictionary of Authors.

Winslow, Rev. Miron, D. D., LL. D. *A Sketch* of Missions, or History of the principal attempts to propagate Christianity among the Heathen. Andover: Flagg and Gould. 1819. 18mo, pp. 432.

—*A Sermon* delivered at the Old South Church, Boston, June 7, 1819, on the evening previous to the sailing of the Rev. Miron Winslow, Levi Spaulding, and Henry Woodward, & Dr. John Scudder, as Missionaries to Ceylon. By Miron Winslow, A. M. Andover: Flagg and Gould, Printers. 1819. 8vo, pp. 22.

—*A Memoir* of Mrs. Harriet Wadsworth Winslow, combining a Sketch of the Ceylon Mission; by Miron Winslow, one of the Missionaries. New York: Published by Leavitt, Lord & Co., 180 Broadway. Boston: Crocker & Brewster. 1835. 12mo, pp. 408.

—*Hints on Missions* to India: with notices of some Proceedings of a Deputation from the American Board, and of Reports to it from the Missions. By Miron Winslow, Missionary at Madras. New York: Published by M. W. Dodd, Brick Church Chapel. 1856. 12mo, pp. 236.

This eminent missionary was born in Williston, Vt., December 11, 1789, and died on his way from India to America, October 22, 1864. He was descended from the English Winslows, of the same stock as the two Governor Winslows of Mayflower and Massachusetts fame; was graduated at Middlebury College, 1815, and at Andover Theological Seminary, 1818; and embarked at Boston, June 8, 1819, as a missionary to India, under the direction of the A. B. C. F. M., where he labored in different places there during the remainder of his life, a period of nearly 46 years. His literary labors were numerous.

His memoir of his first wife, Mrs. Harriet W. Winslow, is one of the standard volumes of the American Tract Society. His "Hints on Missions," was written on his passage from India home, in 1855, as a sort of digest of his labors and observations during a missionary life of 37 years. But his crowning literary labors were the translation of the Bible into Tamil, and the preparation of a Tamil-English Lexicon; the full title of the latter being, "A Comprehensive Tamil and English Dictionary of High and Low Tamil," a work of prodigious labor and great value, occupying a large share of his time for more than 20 years; contains nearly 1,000 4to pages, and more than 67,000 Tamil words. For this work Mr. Winslow received the highest encomiums from the press and literary and official sources of India and England.

He also published several sermons and addresses, and furnished a large amount of correspondence for the "Missionary Herald," "New York Observer," and other periodicals.

Mr. Winslow was five times married, first in 1819, and lastly in 1857; he had by his first wife six children, by the second one, and by the third three; of the ten not more than two or three survived him.

See Vermont Historical Gazetteer, Vol. 1, pp. 929-30; and Allibone's Dictionary of Authors.

Wisdom. *A Poem.* Qui Eam Amat, Vitam Amat. Published by Samuel Wood, No. 362 Pearl Street, New York. Reprinted by Anthony Haswell, Bennington, Vermont, 1806. 12mo, pp. 24.

Withington, Rev. Leonard. *A Review of Sermons*, Addresses and Exhortations, by Rev. Jedediah Burchard: with an appendix, Containing some Account of Proceedings during Protracted Meetings, held under his Direction,

in Burlington, Williston, and Hinesburgh, Vt., December, 1835, and January, 1836., By C. G. Eastman. By Rev. Leonard Withington, (of Newburyport, Mass.) Copied from the Literary and Theological Review for June, 1836. Conducted by Leonard Woods, Jun. Burlington : Chauncey Goodrich. MDCCCXXXVI. 16mo, pp. 23.
See Eastman, C. G.

Withington, Oliver Wendell. *A Poem*, delivered before the Associate Alumni of the University of Vermont; at the Annual Commencement, August, 1849. By Oliver Wendell Withington. Burlington: Free Press Office Print. 1849. 8vo, pp. 21.

Witherspoon, A. *The Hand of God* in our National Conflict, A Discourse delivered before the Citizens of Brandon, on the occasion of the State Fast, April 9, 1863. By A. Witherspoon, D. D. Rutland: Tuttle, Gay & Co., Printers. 1863. 8vo, pp. 15.

Wolcott.
See Hubbell, Seth, Narrative.

Wollage, Elijah. *A Funeral Discourse*, on the Death of Mrs. Catharine Janes, Aged 24 years, Wife of Mr. Horace Janes. Delivered at St. Albans, on the twenty-ninth day of December, A. D. 1808. By the Rev. Elijah Wollage, A. B. (Motto.) Burlington, Vt.: Printed by Samuel Mills. January, 1809. 8vo, pp. 15.
Rev. Mr. Wollage was born in Bernardston, Mass., in 1769; and died at Starkey, Yates county, N. Y., July 18, 1847. He was graduated at Dartmouth College, 1791; and was pastor of Congregational Churches in Guilford, Cambridge, Rockingham, and elsewhere in Vermont, 1793-1821.

Woman's Board of Missions—*Proceedings* of the First Annual Meeting of the Vermont Branch of Woman's Board of Missions, held at Rutland, Vt., October 29th, 1873, with Reports Presented. Rutland, Vt.: Printed by Tuttle & Company. 1873. 12mo, pp. 18, (3).
The same for 1874, 1875, 1876, and continued.

Women's Christian Temperance Union. *Proceedings* of the Fifth Annual Convention of the Women's Christian Temperance Union of Vermont, held in Vergennes, September 24th and 25th, 1879. St. Albans : Messenger Job Print. 1880. 8vo, pp. 40.

Wood, Henry C. *"On Reading."* An address delivered before the Ladies Literary Society of Newbury Seminary, by Henry C. Wood, A. B. Newbury: 1845. 8vo, pp. 12.

Wood, Horace G. *A Treatise* on the Law of Nuisances. By H. G. Wood. Albany : 1875. 8vo.
—*Wood on the* Law of Master and Servant. Covering the Relation, Duties, and Liabilities of Employers and Employés. By H. G. Wood. Albany : 1877. 8vo.
—*A Treatise* on the Law of Fire Insurance, adapted to the present state of the Laws, English and American, with copious Notes and Illustrations. By H. G. Wood. New York: 1878. 8vo.
Mr. Wood is a native of Hartland, Vt., born July 9, 1831; he is a lawyer, and was a member of the Vermont Legislature from Fairhaven, 1867-8-9 and 1870; until recently he resided at Albany, N. Y. Mr. Wood published an additional legal work in 1879, of which we have not the title. Mr. Wood lost his reputation and left Albany under a cloud, 1880.

Wood, Norman Nelson.
Mr. Wood was born in Fairfax, Vt., 1808; and was graduated at Middlebury College, 1835. He was some time a teacher, and was then pastor of Baptist Churches at Lebanon Springs. N. Y., 1838-42; at Vicksburg, Miss., 1842-46; at Zanesville, Ohio, 1846-51; then President of Shurtleff College, Upper Alton, Ill. He has been editor of the *Evangelical Preacher*, and has published several sermons and addresses, and edited a volume of original sermons.

Woodbridge, F. E. *Bread for* our Starving Countrymen. Speech of Hon. F. E. Woodbridge, of Vermont, in the House of Representatives, March 19, 1867. Washington : Printed at the Congressional Globe Office. 1867. 8vo, pp. 8.

—*The Extinction of Slavery.* Speech of Hon. F. E. Woodbridge, of Vermont, in the House of Representatives, January 12, 1865. 8vo, pp. 7, n. p. n. d.
Mr. Woodbridge was born in Vergennes, Vt., August 29, 1818; was graduated at the University of Vermont in 1840; studied law, and came to the bar in 1842; served three years in the State Legislature, two years in the State Senate, three years as State Auditor, and in 1863 was elected to the 38th Congress from Vermont, and re-elected to the 39th and 40th, giving him six years in Congress. He was again a member of the Vermont Legislature from Vergennes for the biennial session of 1876-7.
Mr. Woodbridge died at Vergennes, April 26, 1888.

Woodbury. *Auditors' Report* of the Standing of the Finances of the Town of Woodbury, March 1st, 1877. Montpelier, Vt.: Argus and Patriot Steam Book and Job Printing Establishment, Main Street. 1877. 8vo, pp. 4.
Continued.

Woodbury, U. A. *Message of* Urban A. Woodbury, Governor of the State of Vermont, to the General Assembly, October Session, 1894. Burlington : Free Press Association. 1894. 8vo, pp. 16.

—*Message of* Urban A. Woodbury, Governor of the State of Vermont, to the General Assembly, October Session, 1896. Burlington : Free Press Association. 1896. 8vo, pp. 22.

—*Argument of* Hon. Seneca Haselton, in the Case of Gov. Urban A. Woodbury vs. Herald and Globe Association. Submitted to the Hon. Jonathan Ross, Hon. John W. Rowell, Hon. James M. Tyler, Arbitrators, May, 1896. Burlington : Free Press Asso., Printers. 1897. 8vo, pp. 53.
Urban Adrian Woodbury was born in New Hampshire, July 11, 1838; graduated from the Medical Department of the University of Vermont, 1859; enlisted in Co. H, Second Vt. Vols. in May, 1861; lost his right arm in the first Battle of Bull Run; subsequently Captain of Co. D, Eleventh Vt. Vols.; and later Captain in the Veteran Reserve Corps; established himself in the lumber business in Burlington, 1874; Alderman, 1880-84; Mayor, 1885-6; Lieut.-Governor, 1888-90; Governor, 1894-96.

Woodhouse, Rev. Charles. *The Mission of Odd Fellowship.* Read at Rutland on the Fifty-first Anniversary of Odd Fellowship in America. By Rev. Charles Woodhouse. Rutland, Vt.: 1870. 8vo, pp. 1.

Woodman, Jonathan. *A Discourse* delivered before the Legislature of Vermont, on the day of General Election, at Montpelier, October 9th, 1828. By Rev. Jonathan Woodman. Montpelier : Printed by E. P. Walton, Watchman Office. 1828. 8vo, pp. 23.
Mr. Woodman was pastor of the Baptist Church in Sutton, Vt., nearly thirty years.

Woods, Alva, D. D.

Mr. Woods was born at Shoreham, Vt., son of Elder Abel, a Baptist minister there many years; also a nephew of Leonard Woods, D. D. He was graduated at Harvard College, 1817; read theology, and was ordained in 1821; he was professor of mathematics and natural philosophy in Brown University, 1824-28; and also in Transylvania University, 1828-31, of which he was President; he was President of the University of Alabama, 1831-37; his publications are "Intellectual and Moral Culture; or, Inaugural Discourse; with a Catalogue of Lexington University." Lexington: 1828. 8vo.; "Introductory Lecture before the Alabama Institute." 1834. 8vo. "Baccalaureate Address at the University of Alabama." 1835. Tuscaloosa: 8vo. "Valedictory Address, December 6, 1837, University of the State of Alabama." 8vo, pp. 52. He was residing at Providence, R. I., in 1872. Allibone; Drake.

Wood, Frederick A. *History of Taxation* in Vermont by Frederick A. Wood, Ph. D., Seligman Fellow in Political Science, Columbia, Coll., N. Y. 1894. pp. 128.
No. 3 of Vol. 4 of Studies in History, Economics and Public Law, edited by the Faculty of Columbia College.

Woodstock. *The Annual Reports* of the Selectmen and Auditors and Superintendent of Schools of the Town of Woodstock, March 6, 1861. Woodstock: Printed at the Standard Office. 1861. 8vo, pp. 16.
Continued.

—*Rules and Regulations* for the Public Schools in District No. 8, Woodstock, Vt. Adopted December 1st, 1862. Woodstock: Printed at the Vermont Standard Office. 1862. 8vo, pp. 8.

—*History of Woodstock, Vt.*, by Henry Swan Dana. Boston and New York: Houghton, Mifflin & Co. 1889. 8vo, pp. 15, 641.

—*Rededication*, June 5, 1890, of the Re-constructed Old White Meeting House. 1890. 8vo, pp. 47. Printed by the T. De Vinne Press.

Woodward, James Wheelock. *Sermon* at the funeral of Rev. Eden Burroughs, D. D. Boston: 1814. 8vo.

—*Four Sermons* preached at Norwich, Vt. By James W. Woodward, minister of that town. Published by request. Hanover: Printed by Charles Spear. 1818. 8vo, pp. 62.
Rev. Mr. Woodward, son of Bezaleel and Mary (Wheelock) Woodward, was born in Hanover, N. H., February 6, 1781. His father was a professor at Dartmouth College many years, and prominent in the early history of Vermont, during the union of certain New Hampshire towns with that State. (See "Governor and Council," Vols. 1, 2, 3) Mary Wheelock was a daughter of President Eleazar Wheelock.
Rev. Mr. Woodward was graduated at Dartmouth, 1798, and read theology with Rev. Dr. Burton, of Thetford, Vt., and Rev. Dr. Nathan Smith of Hartford, Conn. In 1801 he went as a missionary to the Black River country in Northern New York, where he traveled 1800 miles and preached 164 times. In 1802-3 he was a missionary to Southwestern New York and Northern Pennsylvania. He was pastor of a Congregational church at Norwich, Vt., 1804-1820; at Brownington, Vt., 1826-8, after which he was a missionary in New York and New Hampshire till he was disabled by paralysis. He died at Waterbury, Vt., July 26, 1847. He married October 4, 1808, Sarah Partridge, a native of Norwich. The late Dr. J. B. Woodward, of Montpelier, was his son.

Woodworth, Samuel, of Montpelier. *The Battle of Plattsburgh.* A poem. Montpelier: 1815. 12mo.

Wooster, Benjamin. *A Sermon* preached at St. Albans, August 8, 1815, before Franklin County Bible Society; By Benjamin Wooster, A. M., Pastor of the Congregational Church in Fairfield, Vt. Published at the request and for the benefit of said Society. T. C. Strong's Print, Middlebury, Vt. 1815. 12mo, pp. 14.

—*Election Sermon.* 1800.
This sermon was never printed.
Rev. Benjamin Wooster was born in Waterbury, Conn., October 29, 1762, and died in Fairfield, Vt., December 18, 1840. He served five years in the Revolutionary war, a part of the time under his great uncle, Gen. Wooster; he also rallied his people in the war of 1812, and led them to the defense of Plattsburgh, and such was his bravery that it elicited from Gov. Tompkins, of New York, a complimentary letter, accompanied by the present of an elegant folio gilt Bible. After the close of the Revolution, Mr. Wooster prepared for and entered Yale College in 1788; after leaving college he studied theology with Dr. Jonathan Edwards, and after itinerating awhile, was ordained over the church in Cornwall, Vt., 1797, where he remained five years, then itinerated three years, and in 1805 he was installed in Fairfield, Vt., where he continued through life, preaching and organizing churches in the various towns in Franklin county, delivering more than 4,000 sermons during his ministry there. See Miss Hemenway's Vermont Historical Gazetteer, Vol. 2, "Fairfield;" See also Wild, A. W., for biographical sketch.

Worcester. *A Record of Births*, Marriages and Deaths in Worcester, Vt., from October 21, 1818, to June 18, 1858. Alphabetically arranged. By Simon C. Abbott. Montpelier: E. P. Walton, Printer. 1858. 18mo, pp. 31.

—*Annual Reports* of the officers of the Town of Worcester for the year ending March 2, 1869. Montpelier: J. & J. M. Poland, Steam Book Printers 1869. 8vo, pp. 4.
Continued.

Worcester & Closson. 1868, 1869. Descriptive Catalogue of the Choicest Varieties of Fruits and Ornamental Trees, Shrubs and Vines, Hardy Herbaceous and Bedding Plants, etc., at Thetford, Vt. Claremont, N. H. 8vo, pp. 22.

Worcester, J. E. *A Comprehensive Pronouncing* and Explanatory Dictionary of the English Language, with Pronouncing Vocabularies of Classical and Scripture Proper Names. By J. E. Worcester. Burlington, Vt.: Published by Chauncey Goodrich. Boston Type and Stereotype Foundry. 1831. pp. 19. (i) 400.

Worcester, Rev. John Hopkins, D. D. *A Sermon*, by Rev. J. H. Worcester, Pastor of the First Calvinistic Congregational Church, Burlington, Vt. Published by request of the Church. Burlington: Tuttle & Stacy. 1850. 8vo, pp. 19.

—*Christian Fellowship.* A Discourse, delivered in the Calvinistic Congregational Church, Burlington, Vt., December 31, 1854. By J. H. Worcester, Pastor. Burlington: Published by Samuel B. Nichols. Stacy & Jameson, Printers. 1855. 8vo, pp 24.
Rev. John Hopkins Worcester was born in Peacham, Vt., May 12, 1812, son of Rev. Leonard Worcester and Elizabeth Hopkins, daughter of Rev. Samuel Hopkins. He graduated from Dartmouth College in 1832; was ordained in 1839; was pastor of the Congregational church in St. Johnsbury, 1839 to 1847, and of the Congregational church in Burlington, 1847-1854. Died at Burlington, January 15, 1897.

Worcester, Rev. J. H., jr., D. D. *Womanhood;* Five Sermons to Young Women, by Rev. J. H. Worcester, jr., preached at the Sixth Presbyterian Church, Chicago, November and December, 1884. Chicago: 1884. pp. 71.

—*Memorial* of Rev. J. H. Worcester, jr., D. D., containing a brief Biography and Selected Sermons. Published by the Sixth Presbyterian Church of Chicago, Illinois, 1893. 12mo. pp. 842.

John H. Worcester, jr., son of Rev. John Hopkins Worcester, D. D., was born in St. Johnsbury, Vt., April 2, 1845; graduated at the University of Vermont, 1865, and at Union Theological Seminary, 1871. Pastor of First Presbyterian church, South Orange, N. J., 1872-83; pastor of Sixth Presbyterian church in Chicago, 1883-91; Professor of Systematic Theology, Union Theological Seminary, 1891, till his death. Died at Lakewood, N. J., February 5, 1893.

Worcester, Rev. Leonard. *Oration Delivered* at Peacham, Vt., on the Death of Washington, Feb. 22, 1800. By Leonard Worcester. Peacham, Vt. : 1800. 8vo.

—*A Sermon*, preached at Peacham, Lord's Day, November 15th, 1801. By Leonard Worcester, Pastor of the Church in Peacham. Published at the earnest desire of a number of the Hearers. Peacham, Vt. : Printed by Samuel Goss. 1801. 8vo, pp. 32.

—*The Doctrine* of Atonement, and Others connected with it, Stated and Vindicated ; in answer to the Rev. Mr. Gibson's Sermon on Isaiah xxxv, 8. By Leonard Worcester, Pastor of the Church in Peacham. Motto. Peacham, Vt. : Printed by Samuel Goss. 1802. 8vo, pp. 47.

—*A Sermon* preached at Peacham, April 28th, 1802 ; being a day of Public Fasting and Prayer, in the State of Vermont. By Leonard Worcester, Pastor of the Church in Peacham. Published at the desire of a number of the Hearers. Peacham, Vt. : Printed by Samuel Goss. 1802. 8vo, pp. 32.

—*A Sermon* preached at Peacham, Lord's Day, November 13th, 1803. By Leonard Worcester, Pastor of the Church in Peacham. Published at the earnest request of some of the hearers. Peacham, Vt. : Printed by Samuel Goss. 1804. 8vo, pp. 32.

—*A Sermon* preached at Montpelier, Lord's Day, October 15, 1809. By Leonard Worcester, Pastor of the Church in Peacham. Second Edition. Peacham, Vt. : From the Press of Samuel Goss. 1809. 8vo, pp. 24.

First Edition printed at Windsor by Farnsworth & Churchill. 1809. 8vo, pp. 16.

—*The Christian* Desirous to be with Christ. A Sermon preached at Hardwick, Vt., August 30th, 1814 ; At the Funeral of Mrs. Lydia French, consort of Samuel French, Esq., who deceased the preceding Lord's Day, August 28th, aged 54. By Leonard Worcester, Minister of the Gospel in Peacham. Montpelier, Vt. : Printed by Walton & Goss. 1814. 8vo, pp. 24.

—*An Appeal* to the Conscience of the Rev. Solomon Aiken, concerning his Appeal to the Churches. By Leonard Worcester. Montpelier, Vt. : Printed by E. P. Walton, October, 1821. 8vo, pp. 16.

See Aiken, Solomon.

—*A Sermon* delivered in Park Street Church, August 25th, 1825. At the ordination of the Rev. Messrs. Elnathan Gridley, and Samuel Austin Worcester As Missionaries to the Heathen. By Leonard Worcester, Pastor of a Church in Peacham, Vt. Boston : Printed by Crocker & Brewster, No. 36 Cornhill. 1825. 8vo, pp. 40.

—*A Discourse* on the Alton Outrage, delivered at Peacham, Vt., December 17, 1837. By Rev. Leonard Worcester. Published by request of the Caledonia Association. Concord, N. H. : Printed by Asa McFarland, State House Square. 1838. 8vo, pp. 16.

Relates to the murder of Elisha P. Lovejoy, in the Alton riots, November 7, 1837.

—*A Memorial* of what God hath Wrought ; A Discourse delivered at Peacham, Vt., March 31, 1839. By Leonard Worcester, Pastor of the Congregational Church. 1839. 8vo, pp. 16.

—*List of* Congregational Churches and Ministers in Caledonia County, Vt., from its first settlement to July 31, 1840. By Rev. Leonard Worcester, A. M., Pastor of the Church in Peacham, Vt. Am. Quar. Register, 1841, Vol. xiii, pp. 280-284.

Rev. Leonard Worcester was born in Hollis, N. H., January 1, 1767; and died in Peacham, Vt., May 28, 1846. He served an apprenticeship at the printer's trade with Isaiah Thomas at Worcester, Mass., and for several years after was associated with him in the printing business, and in the publication of the Massachusetts Spy. He read theology and was licensed to preach March 12, 1799, and in October of the same year became pastor of the Congregational church at Peacham, Vt., where he remained through life. He was the father of 14 children, of whom Samuel A., Evarts, Isaac R., and John H., became Congregational preachers. For a more extended sketch see Vermont Historical Gazetteer, Vol 1. pp. 364-5.

Worcester, Samuel Austin, D. D. *A Translation* of the New Testament into the Cherokee Language. New York : American Bible Society. 1860. 12mo, pp. 408.

—*Opinion* of the Supreme Court of the United States, at January Term, 1832, delivered by Mr. Chief Justice Marshall, in the Case of Samuel A. Worcester, Plaintiff in Error, versus The State of Georgia : With a statement of the case, extracted from the Records of the Supreme Court of the United States. Washington : Printed by Gales and Seaton. 1832. 8vo, pp. 20.

Relates to the imprisonment of Mr. Worcester in the Georgia penitentiary for sixteen months in 1831-2, for refusing to comply with State requirements bearing on the Indians within its borders.

Mr. Worcester was the third son of the Rev. Leonard Worcester, and was born in Worcester, Mass., January 19, 1798 ; was graduated at the University of Vermont in 1819; at Andover Seminary in 1823. In 1825 he went as a Missionary to the Cherokee Indians in Georgia and East Tennessee, where he continued until the removal of the Cherokees to the Indian Territory, whither he accompanied them, and died at Park Hill, Indian Territory, Arkansas, April 20, 1859. His translation of the Testament was revised after his decease with the assistance of a Cherokee preacher, and carried through the Press by the Rev. C. C. Torrey.

Worcester, Thomas, A. M. *Serious Reasons* against Triune Worship, which is Shown to have been an Invention of the Fourth Century. The Substance of an Unanswered Letter, which was respectfully Sent to a Number of Able Ministers. Also, the Author's Confession of Faith. By Thomas Worcester, A. M., Pastor of a Church in Salisbury, N. H. Montpelier, Vt. : Printed by Walton & Goss. 1812.

Wright, Rev. A. H. *Sermon* at the Funeral of Martha Ann Rhea, 1857.

See Rhea, Mrs. Martha Ann.

The Rev. Dr. Austin Hazen Wright was born in Hartford, Vt., November 11, 1811, and died in Persia, where he was a missionary, January 4, 1865. See "Dartmouth Alumni," by Chapman, 1830.

The memory of the widow of Dr. Wright furnishes the following account of his literary labors : "A translation into Syriac of a catechism called the "Theological Class Book," [probably that by Dr. William Cogswell,] Mrs. Wright thinks that he also prepared an arithmetic and geography. He translated, with Dr. Perkins, the Old and New Testaments into Modern Syriac, and revised the ancient Old and New Testaments. After his return to the United States he revised the New Testament, incorporating the notes of the former edition into the text and making it a translation from the Greek, instead of the ancient Peshito version. He assisted in the translation of the Pilgrims Progress, as in all the publications of the mission before 1860. After his return in 1864, he began the translation of the New Testament into Tartar-Turkish. He was for many years the financial agent of the Mission.

Wright, C. *The Federal Compendium:* Being a plain, concise, and easy introduction to Arithmetic ; Designed for the use of Common Schools. By Chester Wright, Preceptor of an English School in Middlebury. First Edition. Middlebury, Vermont : Printed by Huntington & Fitch, for the Author. 1803. 12mo, pp. 108.

—*Ordination* of Rev. Chester Wright, at Montpelier, August 19, 1809 ; Sermon by Rev. Asa Burton. Charge by the Rev. Stephen Fuller, of Vershire, and the Right Hand of Fellowship by the Rev. Calvin Noble, of Chelsea.
　See Burton, Asa.

—*A Sermon*, preached on the day of General Election, at Montpelier, Oct. 11, 1810, before the Honorable Legislature of Vermont, by Chester Wright, A. M. Pastor of the Congregational Church at Montpelier. Randolph, (Vt.) Printed by Sereno Wright. 1810.

—*A Funeral Sermon*, Delivered at Montpelier, Vermont, January 5, 1811, at the interment of Sibyl Brown, aged nine years, Daughter of Amasa Brown. By Chester Wright, Pastor of the Congregational Church in Montpelier. Montpelier, Vermont : Printed at the office of Walton & Goss, January, 1811. 8vo, pp. 12.

—*A Sermon*, delivered at Montpelier, October 28th, 1812, at the First Meeting of the Vermont Bible Society. By Chester Wright, A. M., Pastor of the Congregational Church in Montpelier. Montpelier : Printed by Walton & Goss. 1812. 8vo, pp. 14.

—*Jesus weeping at Lazarus' Grave.* A Sermon preached at Montpelier, Dec. 27, 1813, at the burial of Mrs. Hannah Loomis, wife of Jeduthan Loomis, Esq., by Chester Wright, Minister of the Gospel, Montpelier, Vt. Montpelier : Walton & Goss. 1814.

—*A Sermon*, preached before the Female Foreign Mission Society in Montpelier, 1816. By Chester Wright. Montpelier, Vt.: Printed by E. P. Walton, May, 1817. 8vo, pp. 14.

—*A Sermon*, Preached before the Middlebury College Charitable Society, at Middlebury, Vt. August, 16, 1814. By Chester Wright, A. M. Pastor of the Church in Montpelier. Middlebury : Printed by T. C. Strong. 8vo, pp. 16.

—*The Saints' Resurrection.* A Sermon, at the Funeral of George S. Walton, Montpelier, June 10, 1818. By Chester Wright. "The trumpet shall sound and the dead shall be raised incorruptible." Montpelier : Printed by E. P. Walton, 1818. 8vo, pp. 15.

—*An Address*, on the Death of the Venerable and Illustrious Adams and Jefferson, Ex-Presidents of the United States, delivered before a large Concourse of Citizens, at Montpelier, Vermont, July 25, 1826. By Chester Wright.

Montpelier : Printed by George W. Hill & Co. 1826. 8vo, pp. 19.

—*The Devil* in the Nineteenth Century. Two Discourses, delivered at Hardwick, Vt., May 6, 1838. By Rev. Chester Wright. Published by Request. "For we are not ignorant of his devices." Montpelier, Vt.: E. P. Walton & Son, Printers. 1838. 8vo, pp. 21.

　Rev. Mr. Wright was born in Hanover, N. H., November 6, 1776 ; and died in Montpelier, Vt., April 16, 1840. He was graduated at Middlebury College, 1805, and read theology with the Rev. Dr. Burton, of Thetford, Vt., and the Rev. Dr. Dwight, of New Haven, Ct. He was settled over the Congregational church of 17 members at Montpelier, 1809, and was dismissed in 1830, the church numbering over 400 members ; he was then pastor at Hardwick, Vt., until near the time of his death.
　For a sketch of his life, see "History, Montpelier," pp. 198-203.

Wright, George F. *From the Proceedings* of the Boston Society of Natural History, December 20, 1876, Vol. XIX, pp. 47-63. Some Remarkable Gravel Ridges in the Merrimac Valley. (Abstract.) By George F. Wright.

—*In Memory* of John Dove, Esquire ; A Sermon preached in the Free Church, Andover, Mass., November 26, 1876. By the Pastor, George F. Wright. Andover : Warren F. Draper, Printer, Main Street. 1877. 8vo, pp. 24.

—*The Logic of Christian Evidences.* By Rev. G. Frederick Wright. Andover : Printed by Warren F. Draper. 1880. 16mo, pp. 328.

　Mr. Wright has published in addition: Address, with biography, at the funeral of Josiah F. Brigham, Esq., of Bakersfield, Vt. See Brigham, Josiah F.
　Address at the Exercises of the opening of Brigham Academy, at Bakersfield, August 14, 1879. Andover, 1880. pp. 56, including Appendix.
　The Ground of Confidence in Inductive Reasoning; "New Englander," October, 1871, pp. 601-615.
　The Vermont Farmer's Future. A Paper read at a meeting of the State Board of Agriculture, at St. Albans, March 6th and 7th, 1872. Published in *Vermont Agricultural Reports* for 1872, pp. 510-524.
　The Baptism of Infants, and their Church Membership. Bibliotheca Sacra, (1874) Vol. XXXI, pp. 265-299, 545-575.
　Series of articles in *Bibliotheca Sacra* upon the relation of Science and Religion :
　I. The Nature and Degree of Scientific Proof. Vol. XXXII, (1875) pp. 537-555.
　II. The Divine Method of Producing Living Species. Vol. XXXIII, (1876) pp. 448-493.
　III. Objections to Darwinism, and the Rejoinders of its advocates. pp. 656-694.
　IV. Concerning the true Doctrine of Design or Final Cause in Nature. Vol. XXXIV, (1877) pp. 355-385.
　V. Calvinism and Darwinism. Vol. XXXVII, (1880) pp. 48-76.
　Dr. Hodge's Misrepresentations of President Finney's System of Theology. *Bibliotheca Sacra*, Vol. XXXIII, (1876) pp. 381-392.
　President Finney's System of Theology in its Relation to the so-called New England Theology. *Bibliotheca Sacra*, Vol. XXXIV, (1877) pp. 708-741.
　Max Mueller and his American Critics. *Bibliotheca Sacra*, Vol. XXXIV, (1877) pp. 183-190.
　The Proper Attitude of Religious Teachers toward Scientific Experts. *New Englander* for November, 1878, pp. 776-789.
　The Kames and Moraines of New England. Vol. XX, (1879) pp. 210-220.
　Together with many minor contributions to various periodicals.
　Rev. Mr. Wright was born at Whitehall, N. Y., January 22, 1838; fitted for college in Castleton, Vt., and was graduated from Oberlin College, Ohio, in 1859, and from theology at the same place, 1862.
　He preached for the Congregational church at Bakersfield, Vt., September 1862 to June 1872; since when he has been pastor of the Free Church (Congregational) at Andover, Mass; since 1881 professor in Andover Seminary; and connected with U. S. survey since 1884.

Wright, N. H. *Monody* on the Death of Brigadier General Zebulon Montgomery Pike:

and other poems. By N. Hill Wright. Motto. Middlebury, (Vt.) Printed by Slade & Ferguson. 1814. 8vo, pp. 78.

—*The Fall of Palmyra:* and other Poems. By N. H. Wright. Middlebury, (Vt.) Published by William Slade, Jun. 1817. 24mo, pp. 143.

Wright, Stephen. *History* of the Shaftsbury Baptist Association, from 1781 to 1853; with some Account of the Associations formed from it, and a Tabular view of their Annual Meetings: to which is added an Appendix, embracing Sketches of the most recent Churches in the Body, with Biographic Sketches of some of the Older Ministers, and the Statistics of most of the Churches ever in the Association, and their Direct Branches, to the Present Time. Compiled at the request of the Association, By Stephen Wright. Troy, N. Y.: A. G. Johnson, Steam Press, Printer, Cannon Place, 1853. 12mo, pp. 464.

The Writings of a Pretended Prophet, (In Six Letters,) who assumed the title of a Faithful Servant of Jesus Christ, Officially Commissioned by Almighty God, to Demand and Receive of Abraham Morhouse, Esqr., Two Thousand Pounds, with Terrible Denunciations in case of Refusal. To which is Added, His Recantation; or Four Letters written by him during his confinement. Rutland: Printed for Samuel Williams. Dated, August, 1796.

—*A Second Vermont Edition,* (no imprint.) 1816. 12mo, pp. 12.

Wright, Rev. Worthington. *A Sermon* occasioned by the death of Mrs. Almira Ferris Washburn, wife of Peter T. Washburn, Esq. Woodstock, Vt. Delivered March 19th, 1848. By Rev. Worthington Wright. Woodstock: Printed at the Office of the Vermont Mercury. 1848. 8vo, pp. 11.

—*A Sermon* preached at the Ordination of the Rev. Edwin S. Wright, in Acworth, N. H. January 7, 1846. By Rev. Worthington Wright, Pastor of the Congregational Church in Woodstock, Vt. Woodstock: Printed at the Mercury Office. 1846. 8vo, pp. 16.

Yale, Calvin. *Some Rules* for the investigation of religious truth; and some specimens of argumentation in its support. An Address Delivered before the Society for Religious Inquiry in the University of Vermont, at Burlington August 8, 1826. By Rev. Calvin Yale, of Charlotte, an Honorary Member. Published by request. Montpelier: Printed by E. P. Walton, Watchman Office. 1826. 8vo, pp. 15.

—*A Sermon* delivered before the Vermont Colonization Society, at Montpelier, October 17, 1827. By Calvin Yale, Pastor of the Congregational Church in Charlotte. Published by Request of the Society. Montpelier: Printed by E. P. Walton, Watchman Office. 1827. 8vo, pp. 15.

Yankee Boy from Home, The. Second Edition. New York; 1865. 12mo, pp. 318.
Being sketches of European Travels, by a native of Vermont, Joseph Dattell of Middlebury.

Young, Augustus. *Unity of Purpose:* Being a Treatise designed to elicit Investigation, with the view to eradicate and expel from Science certain popular Errors which now are taught and promulgated as important and fundamental Truths. By Augustus Young. Johnson, Vermont: March 20, 1845. 8vo, pp. 16.
A Circular calling attention to the work to be published.

—*Unity of Purpose,* or Rational Analysis: being A Treatise designed to disclose Physical Truths, and to detect and expose popular errors. By Augustus Young. Motto. Boston: Printed by S. N. Dickenson & Co. 1846. 8vo, pp. 292.

—*Unity of Purpose,* or Rational Analysis: Being A short treatise upon the Quadrature of the Circle, and upon the Theory and Law of Solar attraction. By Augustus Young. Motto. St. Albans, Vt,: Printed at the Messenger Press. 1852. 8vo, pp. 32.
Mr. L. O. Greene, later proprietor of the "Woodstock Standard," worked at the "case," upon the intricate typography of the above work.

—*Unity of Purpose,* or Rational Analysis: Being an Exposition of the Quadrature of the Circle And the Law of Gravity. By Augustus Young. Burlington, Vt.: Printed by Chauncey Goodrich. 1853. 8vo, pp. 35.

—*Preliminary Report* on the Natural History of Vermont.
See Geology of Vermont.
Mr. Young was born in Arlington, Vt., March 20, 1785; and died in St. Albans, June 17, 1857. He commenced the practice of law at Stowe, about 1810; and in about two years removed to Craftsbury, residing there and at Johnson until 1847, when he removed to St. Albans. He was in Congress 1841-43, and held many minor offices in the State; he paid much attention to scientific and literary pursuits.

Young, Brigham.
Mr. Young, "President of the Church of Jesus Christ of Latter Day Saints," is perhaps not strictly entitled to a place here, but he being a native of Vermont, and so intimately connected in his marvellous career with Jo. Smith, another native of this State, it seems proper to notice him. He was born in Whitingham, Vt., June 1, 1801; and died at Salt Lake City, August 29, 1877. His father was a farmer, and had been a soldier in the Revolution. When Brigham was a year old the family moved into New York State, and there he grew up. In 1832 he was converted to Mormonism under the preaching of Elder Samuel H. Smith, a brother of the prophet Joseph; and in September of that year went with the Saints to Kirtland, Ohio, and was rapidly promoted until, upon the death of the Prophet, he became the Head of the Church. That he possessed natural abilities of a high order cannot be questioned; the triumphant march of the Mormon host to Salt Lake, under the direction of Young, was a success perhaps unexampled in history; his iron will was supreme, and successful over all opposition. When Albert Smith, a brother of the prophet, differed from Young, the latter denouncing him in a sermon, said, "Tell Albert Smith to clear out, and that right quick, too; or I will cut his damned throat, and send him to hell across lots."
We suppose Young meant the same pagan hell that Beecher, Bob Ingersoll, and others of various religious sects are so earnestly discussing at the present time. (1879.) "Brother Brigham," as his people called him, was large and portly, with a steel blue eye, a resolute mouth, a ruddy cheek, an imposing carriage and a very impressive manner; plain and simple in his dress, and indeed in all his habits. He had an excessive fondness for tobacco, and his enemies said took too stiff a dram of whiskey; he ate but little, toast, bread and milk being his chief food. He rose early, and attended with great industry to the multitudinous affairs that daily crowded upon him. He established a theocracy, in which lives, property, thought, everything, belonged to the Church, and the Church was Brigham. He exercised unquestioned the power of life and death; he banished, and he re-called; he enriched, and impoverished; he made and unmade; a sovereign absolute, a pontiff infallible as the Pope. He regulated Mormon affairs throughout the world; was Governor, Bishop and Pope of the endowment house, yet women came to him to consult about

their teething babies, and children to complain of their school teachers. He was a "much-married-man," but he gave to the women of Utah the right to vote—a privilege so much clamored for by a few in our own land.

The best account of Brigham Young that we have seen was printed in the New York *World* just after his death, to which we are mainly indebted for the above facts. See Smith, Joseph.

Young against Chipman. *Narrative of the Case*, and a concise statement of the trial at the Circuit Court, before Judges Smith, Thompson, and Elijah Paine, on the fourth of October, 1826, at Rutland. Verdict for the Plaintiff ; Damages $8,927.51. ["The Demand against Davidson, If I recollect, was unliquidated ; at any rate he soon after died a bankrupt." "Middlebury, 3d April, 1821." "Daniel Chipman." "According to Chipman, Mr. Davidson remained in his grave ten years ; but Young declares that the identical Mr. Davidson may be seen and conversed with any day at the house he has lived in for the last forty years, situated about three miles from Burlington."] Vergennes, Vt.: Printed by Gamaliel Small, 1827. 8vo, pp. 176.

A mis-appropriation of funds collected by Daniel Chipman for Alexander Young, a non-resident of the State.

Young, Joshua. *God Greater than Man.* A Sermon preached June 11th, after the rendition of Anthony Burns, by Joshua Young, Minister of the First Congregational Church, Burlington, Vt. * * Burlington : Published by Samuel B. Nichols. Stacy & Jameson, Printers. 1854. 8vo, pp. 26.

—*Come and See!* What it is to be a Unitarian. A Discourse, delivered in Burlington, Vermont, November 26, 1854, with an Appendix, by Joshua Young, Minister of the First Congregational Church. Burlington : Samuel B. Nichols. Printed by Stacy & Jameson. 1855. 8vo, pp. 38.

—*Man better than a sheep.* A Sermon preached Thanksgiving Day, Nov. 24, 1859, By Joshua Young, Minister of the Unitarian Church, Burlington, Vt. Published by Request. Burlington: E. A. Fuller, Bookseller and Stationer. Free Press Print. 8vo, pp. 22.

Rev. Joshua Young was born in Pittston, Me., in 1823, and was graduated at Bowdoin College in 1845; read theology at Cambridge, Mass.; he was settled over the Unitarian church at Burlington, Vt., in 1852, where he continued for ten years.

Young Men's Christian Associations. *Proceedings* of the Fourth Annual Convention of Young Men's Christian Associations in Vermont, Held at St. Johnsbury, Oct. 11th and 12th, 1870. Published by the State Executive Committee. Burlington : R. S. Styles, Steam Book and Job Printer. 1870. 8vo, pp. 36.

Continued.

—*Ninth Annual Convention* of the Young Men's Christian Associations and Churches of Vermont, Held at The Congregational Church, Royalton, September 13th, 14th, 15th, 1875. Burlington : R. S. Styles & Son, Steam Book and Job Printers. 8vo, pp. 26.

—*Constitution* of the Young Men's Christian Association, of Montpelier, Vt. Adopted Feb. 14, 1870. Montpelier : J. & J. M. Poland, Printers. 1870. 12mo, pp. 12.

—*First Annual Joint Convention* of the Young Men's Christian Associations of Vermont and New Hampshire, at Keene, N. H., November 23–25. Burlington : Free Press Association. 1895. 8vo, pp. 57.

Young, Samuel B. *An Oration*, Pronounced at Bennington, August 16, 1819 : In Commemoration of the Battle of Bennington, fought August 16, 1777. By Samuel B. Young.

"Eternal vigilance Is the price we pay for liberty."
"Live free or die; death is better than slavery."

Bennington, Vt.: Printed by Darius Clark, .. August, 1819. 8vo, pp. 13.

Reprinted as below.

—*Oration*, pronounced at Bennington, Vermont, August 16, 1819. In Commemoration of the Battle of Bennington, by Samuel Young, Esq. Montpelier : Argus and Patriot Job Printing House. 1871. 8vo, pp. 4.

Youngs, James. *The substance of a sermon*, delivered in the Methodist Chapel, Middlebury, Vt., January 23, 1820. From Acts xxxi:14. "And when we were all fallen to the earth." By James Youngs, Minister of the Gospel. Published by Request. Motto. Middlebury : Published for Heman Richardson. Copeland and Allen, Printers. 1820. 8vo, pp. 27.

APPENDIX.

Addison County. *Report* of a Meeting in Addison County, relative to Acts of the Legislature of 1813.

Address *to the Freemen of Vermont.* 1814. 8vo, pp. 16.

Agriculture. *Vermont Agricultural Experiment Station,* Bulletin No 54. Burlington: Free Press Association. 1896. 8vo, pp. 78.

—*Report* of the Vermont State Board of Agriculture acting as Cattle Commissioners. Burlington: Free Press Association. 1896. 8vo, pp. 44.

Allen, Joseph William. *Appendix* to the second (American) edition of "Reeves' Domestic Relations." Burlington: Chauncey Goodrich, Publisher. 1857. 16mo, pp. 85.

Almanac. *Walton's Vermont Register* and Business Directory for 1897. Burlington: Walton's Register Company, Publishers of Walton's Vermont and New Hampshire Registers. pp. (86) 386.

American Cooking, *Or the Art of Dressing* Viands, Fish, Poultry, and Vegetables, etc., etc., with cuts. By an Orphan. Second edition, improved. Woodstock, Vt.: Printed and Published for the Author, By A. Colton. 1831. 12mo, pp. 112.

Antisell, Thomas. *Introductory Address,* Vermont Medical College. Woodstock: 1854. 8vo, pp. 24.

Atwill, Rev. E. R. *Sermon* on Woman's Work in St. Paul's Church. Burlington: 1869. 8vo, pp. 19.

Avery, Rev. David. *Sermon,* On Bridling the Tongue. 1791. 8vo, pp. 66.

Bailey, Elijah. *Primitive Trinitarianism* examined. Bennington: 1826. 12mo, pp. 346.

Bailey, Rev. Rufus W. *Treatise* upon English Grammar and Reading. 12mo.

Barre, (Vt.) *Historical Souvenir.* 1894. [Nickerson and Cox, Publishers.] Folio (illustrated), pp. 95.

—*Presbyterian,* Illustrated Supplement, May, 1893, pp. 16.

Benedict, Robert Dewey. *What do we know of the Rhodian Maritime Law?* A Discourse delivered before the Law Department of the Brooklyn Institute, On February 25th, 1897. By Robert D. Benedict, LL. D. No imprint. 8vo, pp. 38. [Printed by the Free Press Association. Burlington: 1897.]

Brief. *United States Supreme Court.* October Term. 1896. Edward Hodgson, plaintiff in error vs. the State of Vermont. Brief for the Plaintiff in Error. W. H. Bliss and E. J.

Phelps, Counsel. Burlington: Free Press Association. n. d. 8vo, pp. 32.

Buckham, James. *The Heart of Life.* By James Buckham. Boston: Copeland and Day. 1897. 16mo, pp. 71.

Burlington. *Burlington Business College.* Burlington: Free Press Print. 1896. 8vo, pp. 24.

—*Constitution* and By-Laws of the Catholic Young Men's Union of Burlington, Vermont. Burlington: Free Press Association. 1896. 24mo, pp. 20.

—*Prospectus* Y. P. S. C. E., Methodist Episcopal Church. Burlington: Free Press Print. 1896. 8vo, pp. 16.

—*Greeting* to Burlington Young Men from the Young Men's Christian Association, Burlington, Vermont. Season of 1896-97. Burlington: Free Press Print. n. d. 12mo, pp. 32.

—*Manual* of the Gospel Tabernacle Church, Burlington, Vermont, Organized October 24th, 1896, Rev. T. Arthur Whitaker, Pastor. Price 10 cents. Burlington: Free Press Association. 1896. 16mo, pp. 32.

Byington, Rev. E. H. *The Puritan in England* and New England. By Ezra Hoyt Byington, D. D., Member of the American Society of Church History. With an introduction by Alexander McKenzie, D. D., Minister of the First Church in Cambridge. Boston: Roberts Brothers. 1896. 12mo, pp. xl, 406.

Congregational. *An Historical Sketch* of Home Missionary Work in Vermont, by the Congregational Churches. By Rev. C. S. Smith. Montpelier: Watchman Publishing Co. 1893. 8vo, pp. 18.

Conley, Stephen. *Four Times round the World,* by Stephen Conley, Isle La Motte. Printed and published by C. W. Ross. 1895. 24mo.

This is supposed to be the only book ever published in Grand Isle County.

Constitution *and By-Laws* of the Battenkill Valley Industrial Society. 1895. 8vo, pp. 80.

Currie, Mrs. Cornelia Walker. *The Key of Eden:* Adam and Eve, or the Garden of Nature. Champlain, N. Y.: H. M. Mott's Counselor Print. 1891. 24mo, pp. 263.

Mrs. Currie is a native of Alburgh, Vt., but has lived for many years at Chazy, Clinton county, N. Y.

Dana, Mrs. Eliza A. *The Broken Fold:* Poems of Memory and Consolation. Private edition. New York: A. D. F. Randolph. 1868. 24mo, pp. 124.

Dorset. "*Dorset Night*" Entertainment. Sketches of Dorset, Vt., from the date of its charter, Aug. 20, 1761, and settlement in the year 1768. A series of Historical, Biographical and Literary Papers pertaining to the development and progress of the town where the corner stone of the Independence of Vermont was laid. Published (by request) by Wm. J. Fuller, Woman's Relief Corps No. 23, Dorset, Vt. Burlington: Free Press Association. 1896. 8vo, pp. 56.

Episcopal. *Diocese of Vermont.* The Bishop's Third Annual Address and Official Journal. 1896. 8vo, pp. 36.

Grout, Josiah. *Message of* Josiah Grout, Governor of the State of Vermont, to the General Assembly, October Session, 1896. Derby, Vt.: L. L. Willey, Printer. 1896. 8vo, pp. 22.

Harrington, Hon. Giles. *Proceedings and Resolutions* of the Grand Isle County Bar, on the death of Hon. Giles Harrington, at North Hero, Vt., Feb. 24, 1874. St. Albans: Advertiser Print. 1874. 18mo, pp. 19.

Hazen, Austin. *Addresses* delivered at Richmond, Vermont, June 28, 1895, in Memory of the Rev. Austin Hazen. Middletown, Conn.: Pelton & King, Printers. 1895. 12mo, pp. 36.

Herbert, Auberon. *The Principles of* Voluntaryism and Free Life, by Mr. Auberon Herbert, author of "Windfall and Waterdrift," Editor of Free Life, &c., &c., With an introductory comment from a New World Point of View by Elijah E. Knott. Burlington: Printed by the Free Press Association. 1897. 8vo, pp. vi,38.

Jericho, *1791-1891. Centennial Anniversary* of the First Congregational Church of Jericho, Vermont, at Jericho Center, June 17, 1891. 8vo, pp. 57.

Lamb, Jonathan. *The Child's Instructor* or Second Book for Primary Schools, By J.Lamb. Burlington: A. & D. Day. 1829. 16mo, pp. 80.
Title not fully given in the body of the Bibliography.

Marvin, Rev. David. *Sermon* preached at the funeral of Capt. Judd M. Mott, of the Michigan Volunteers, at Alburgh, in 1863. St. Albans : Messenger Print.

Masonic. *Grand Imperial Council* of Knights of the Red Cross of Constantine and Attendant Orders for the Jurisdiction of Vermont. Abstract of the Proceedings of its Twenty-Second Annual Assembly held at Burlington, 1896. Burlington: Free Press Association. 1896. 8vo. pp. 25.

—*Proceedings* of the Eighth Annual District Deputy Grand Masters' Meeting F. & A. M., of Vermont, under the Instruction of the Grand Lecturer, Held in Burlington, October 13, A. D. 1896, A. L. 5896. Burlington: Free Press Association. 1896. 8vo, pp. 18.

—*Proceedings* of the Grand Commandery of Knights Templar and the Appendant Orders of the State of Vermont. Fifty-fourth Annual Conclave, Held in the City of Burlington, Tuesday, June 9, A. D. 1896, A. O. 778. Burlington: Free Press Association. 1896. 8vo, pp. 113.

—*Proceedings* of the Fourth Annual Convocation of the District Deputy Grand High Priests Royal Arch Masons, Under the Instruction of the Grand Lecturer, Held in the City of Burl-

ington, Wednesday, Oct. 14th, A. I. 2426, A. D. 1896. n. p. n. d. 8vo, pp. 16.

—*By-Laws* of the Star of Bethlehem Conclave No. 1. Knights of the Red Cross of Constantine and Appendant Orders, Burlington, Vermont, as Revised and Amended to April 6, 1896, by Sir Daniel N. Nicholson, Sir George Otis Tyler and Sir Sayles Nichols, Special Committee. Authorized by a vote of the Conclave at the Regular Assembly, April 1st, 1895. Adopted April 6, 1896. Burlington: Free Press Association. 1896. 24mo, pp. 10.

New Haven. *Manual* of the New Haven [Vermont] Congregational church. n. p. n. d. (1895). 8vo, pp. 19.

Orwell. *History* of the Ladies' Benevolent Society of Orwell, Vermont. 1837-1896. Burlington: Free Press Association. 1896. 12mo, pp. 11.

Pangborn, Zebina K. *The Teacher's Voice*, an educational monthly, published at St. Albans in 1853 and 1854, and perhaps later, with the sanction of the Vermont Teachers' Association. 16mo, pp. 32.

PRINTING.
—*Stowe.*
Rev. Jehiel P. Hendee, father of Gov. George W. Hendee, of Morrisville, printed and published at Stowe in 1832-3, the Christian Luminary, a religious newspaper devoted to the interests of the Christian denomination.
H. M. Mott printed a newspaper called the "Stowe Journal" at Stowe for a year in 1871-2.
—*Ludlow.*
The "Ludlow Tribune" was founded by Mott Brothers in 1876 ; afterward published by E. C. Crane, and now (1897) by Evan Thomas.

Proctor. *By-Laws* and Regulations of the Proctor Hospital, Proctor, Vermont. Together with the Officers, Committees, and hospital Staff. 1897. 12mo, n. p. (pp. 16.)

Rowson, Susanna. *Charlotte Temple;* A Tale of Truth, by Mrs. Rowson, late of the New Theatre, Philadelphia, author of Victoria, the Inquisitor, Fille de Chambre, &c. Brattleborough, (Ver.): Published by William Fessenden. 1813. 48mo, pp. 180.

Rutland. *Annual Statement*, Congregational church, Rutland, Vermont, 1895-6. 12mo, pp. 45.

Sigma Phi. *Sixty-ninth* Sigma Phi Convention and Reunion Reports, Eleventh Annual Meeting, New York City, January 7, 1896. Anniversary Notes, &c. New York: Printed for the Sigma Phi Society [Burlington Free Press Association, Printers and Binders, 1896.] 8vo, pp 66.

—*Seventieth* Sigma Phi Convention and Reunion Reports, Twelfth Annual Meeting, New York City, January 5, 1897. Roll of Chapters, Etc. New York: 1897: Printed for the Sigma Phi Society, [by the Free Press Association] 1897. 8vo, pp. 78.

Titus, Rev. H. R. *Sermon* preached at Alburgh, Vt., March 23, 1889, at the funeral of Mrs. Sarah Mott, wife of Hon. Henry Mott, whose death occurred by drowning at Rouses Point, N. Y., March 21, 1889. Champlain, N. Y.: H. M. Mott's Counselor Print. 1889. 18mo, pp. 7.

Tupper, Rev. J. S. *Sermon* preached at Alburgh, Vt., in 1885, (?) at the funeral of Charles Sowles, who died at sea. Champlain, N. Y.: H. M. Mott's Counselor Print. 1885 (?).

University of Vermont. *Founders Day.* May 1, 1897. Addresses by Perley Orman Ray, 1898; George Maynard Hogan, 1897; and Professor Davis Rich Dewey, Ph. D., 1879, with the Song and Odes written for the Occasion. Burlington: Free Press Association. 1897. 8vo, pp. 34.

Van Ness, Edward. *A Digest* of the Laws of New York and the Six New England States, on Marriage, Dower, Divorce, and Acknowledgement and Attestation of Deeds and Wills. Hartford, Conn.: Case, Lockwood & Brainerd Co. 1877. 16mo, pp. 119.

Walker, William, Rev.
Born in Vershire, Vt., Oct. 3, 1808. Graduated at Amherst College 1838, and Andover Theological Seminary 1841. Missionary of A. B. C. F. M. to Gaboon, West Africa, 1842-71 and 1879-83. He published "Heads of the Mpongwe Language" and a Vocabulary, 1879, pp. 54; a translation of twenty-one books of the Bible into the Mpongwe language, 1885; Mpongwe Hymn book, 1886. pp. 54. Died at Milton, Wis., Dec. 8, 1896.

Whitney, Sybil. *Sybil, the Monomaniac,* or Iniquity Exposed; being a record of five years' experience as a Methodist, in Alburgh, Vt. Burlington: Free Press Print. 1858. 16mo, pp. 114.
Mrs. Sybil (Landon) Whitney was born in South Hero, in the early part of the present century, lived in North Hero from 1826 to 1852, and in Alburgh from 1852 to about 1860.

SUMMARY.

Mr. Gilman commenced the publication of the Bibliography of Vermont in the columns of the Montpelier Argus and Patriot in January, 1879, and the publication was continued in the successive issues of that paper until the 22d of September, 1880, closing with the following remarks and table of Vermont book imprints:

"With the present number, the printing of the Bibliography of Vermont is closed for the present, as all the material on hand has been printed. The work is now being revised and corrected, and additional material gathered will be placed in its proper order.

The Vermont book imprints in the above work are as follows:

Montpelier	767	Wells River	5
Burlington	540	Putney	4
Rutland	380	Westminster	4
Windsor	267	Winooski Falls	4
Middlebury	210	Huntington	3
Brattleboro	130	Newport	3
Bennington	116	Waterbury	3
Woodstock	110	Barton	2
St. Albans	78	Royalton	2
Bellows Falls	40	Arlington	1
Danville	37	Bristol	1
Bradford	36	Chester	1
Randolph	25	Clarendon	1
Brandon	21	Fayetteville	1
Poultney	19	Hinesburgh	1
Vergennes	15	Hyde Park	1
Ludlow	16	Johnson	1
Peacham	14	Sharon	1
Castleton	12	Swanton	1
Newbury	11	Wheelock	2
Manchester	11	Wilmington	1
Irasburgh	8	West Charleston	1
Northfield	8	Westford	1
Barnard	6	Springfield	1
Fairhaven	6		
Weathersfield	6	Total	2,940
Chelsea	5		

The whole number of titles in the work is about 6,000 with references in brief to perhaps an equal number in addition.

In conclusion, it is proper to state that the citizens of Vermont, and natives of the State, scattered throughout the Globe, and Historical people everywhere, as well as myself, are indebted to the proprietor of the Argus and Patriot for his liberality in giving the space required in his great paper for now going on two years, to bring the Bibliography of Vermont to its present standard.

To Mr. Will Sullivan of the editorial staff, who was specially assigned by Mr. Atkins to take charge of the work, read the proof, etc., the thanks of all are due.

With becoming delicacy, I cannot withhold my gratitude to the compositors, ladies as well as gentlemen, who, as I know, have patiently waded through the rough manuscript, and brought the Bibliography of Vermont into its present form.

To individuals, and they are a legion, who have helped us forward, a few of whom are mentioned in the body of the work, the thanks of all are due to all. I cannot however withhold the name of Miss M. E. Stone, a corresponding member of the Vermont Historical Society and Assistant Librarian at the Congregational House, Boston, Mass., for her constant and continued service in behalf of the Bibliography of Vermont ; the compositors especially appreciate her clear and beautiful chirography."

Mr. Gilman, assisted as before by Miss M. E. Stone and others, subsequently added 637 titles to the Bibliography. To these, 563 titles have been added by G. G. Benedict, swelling the number of added titles to 1200, and the grand total to upwards of 7,000.

As thus supplemented and enlarged, the work comprises 3452 Vermont imprints, divided as follows :

Montpelier	857	Putney	5
Burlington	696	Springfield	5
Rutland	431	Wells River	5
Windsor	289	Westminster	5
Middlebury	269	Newport	4
Brattleboro	158	Waterbury	4
Bennington	137	Winooski	4
Woodstock	124	Barton	3
St. Albans	89	Huntington	3
Bellows Falls	44	Royalton	2
Danville	39	Wheelock	2
Bradford	37	Arlington	1
Randolph	30	Barre	1
Brandon	22	Bristol	1
Poultney	19	Chester	1
Ludlow	18	Clarendon	1
Vergennes	18	Derby	1
Castleton	15	Fayetteville	1
Peacham	14	Hinesburgh	1
Newbury	14	Hyde Park	1
Manchester	13	Johnson	1
St. Johnsbury	13	Lyndon	1
Barnard	9	Sharon	1
Irasburgh	9	Swanton	1
Northfield	9	West Charleston	1
Fairhaven	7	Westford	1
Chelsea	6	Wilmington	1
Weathersfield	6		

Among the added titles are 37 of books and pamphlets bearing no imprint but known to have been printed in Vermont. These, if included in the total, would increase the number of Vermont imprints to 3489. Complete lists of book titles issued from the various printing offices in Vermont during the past ten years would unquestionably swell the total by several hundred more Vermont imprints.

www.ingramcontent.com/pod-product-compliance
Lightning Source LLC
Chambersburg PA
CBHW021729110726
47902CB00005B/1399